THE JIMMIE DALE MYSTERY MEGAPACK®

THE JIMMIE
DALE MYSTERY
MEGAPACK®

FRANK L. PACKARD

WILDSIDE PRESS

INTRODUCTION

JOHN BETANCOURT

Frank Lucius Packard (1877–1942) was a Canadian writer best known for his contributions to early pulp fiction, particularly through his creation of Jimmie Dale, one of literature's first gentleman thieves. Born in Montreal, Packard worked as a railroad engineer before turning to writing, a job that adds authentic background texture to much of his adventure fiction. His first major success came with the publication of *The Adventures of Jimmie Dale* in 1917, introducing a character who would influence later masked crime-fighters, including Batman and The Shadow. Jimmie Dale, a wealthy play-boy by day and the mysterious Gray Seal by night, used his wealth—along with skills in burglary and disguise—to fight crime, leaving his signature seal behind at the every scene.

The Jimmie Dale series spanned five books and saw adaptations in other media, including a silent movie serial *(Jimmie Dale, Alias the Gray Seal,* 1917) and a radio series in the 1930s. Though not as widely remembered as some pulp heroes, Jimmie Dale played a crucial role in bridging the gap between the classic gentleman thief of 19th-century fiction and the masked vigilantes of the 20th century.

Packard was a prolific writer, producing dozens of adventure novels, but his legacy remains strongest with Jimmie Dale, whose mix of crime, disguise, and heroism helped shape the modern pulp hero. His influence on later crime and superhero fiction remains undeniable.

This volume collects the first three Jimmie Dale stories:

1. *The Adventures of Jimmie Dale* (1917)
2. *The Further Adventures of Jimmie Dale* (1920)
3. *Jimmie Dale and the Phantom Clue (*1922)

There are two additional novels not included in this MEGAPACK®. They are:

4. *Jimmie Dale and the Blue Envelope Murder* (1930)
5. *Jimmie Dale and the Missing Hour* (1935)

Interested readers can find our edition of *Jimmie Dale and the Blue Envelope Murder* in most ebook stores outside the United States. (It's still in copyright here, so we cannot include it in this volume.)

THE ADVENTURES OF JIMMIE DALE

PART ONE: THE MAN IN THE CASE

CHAPTER 1
THE GRAY SEAL

Among New York's fashionable and ultra-exclusive clubs, the St. James stood an acknowledged leader—more men, perhaps, cast an envious eye at its portals, of modest and unassuming taste, as they passed by on Fifth Avenue, than they did at any other club upon the long list that the city boasts. True, there were more expensive clubs upon whose membership roll scintillated more stars of New York's social set, but the St. James was distinctive. It guaranteed a man, so to speak—that is, it guaranteed a man to be innately a gentleman. It required money, it is true, to keep up one's membership, but there were many members who were not wealthy, as wealth is measured nowadays—there were many, even, who were pressed sometimes to meet their dues and their house accounts, but the accounts were invariably promptly paid. No man, once in, could ever afford, or ever had the desire, to resign from the St. James Club. Its membership was cosmopolitan; men of every walk in life passed in and out of its doors, professional men and business men, physicians, artists, merchants, authors, engineers, each stamped with the "hall mark" of the St. James, an innate gentleman. To receive a two weeks' out-of-town visitor's card to the St. James was something to speak about, and men from Chicago, St. Louis, or San Francisco spoke of it with a sort of holier-than-thou air to fellow members of their own exclusive clubs, at home again.

Is there any doubt that Jimmie Dale was a gentleman—an *innate* gentleman? Jimmie Dale's father had been a member of the St. James Club, and one of the largest safe manufacturers of the United States, a prosperous, wealthy man, and at Jimmie Dale's birth he had proposed his son's name for membership. It took some time to get into the St. James; there was a long waiting list that neither money, influence, nor pull could alter by so much as one iota.

Men proposed their sons' names for membership when they were born as religiously as they entered them upon the city's birth register. At twenty-one Jimmie Dale was elected to membership; and, incidentally, that same year, graduated from Harvard. It was Mr. Dale's desire that his son should enter the business and learn it from the ground up, and Jimmie Dale, for four years thereafter, had followed his father's wishes. Then his father died. Jimmie Dale had leanings toward more artistic pursuits than business. He was credited with sketching a little, writing a little; and he was credited with having received a very snug amount from the combine to which he sold out his safe-manufacturing interests. He lived a bachelor life—his mother had been dead many years—in the house that his father had left him on Riverside Drive, kept a car or two and enough servants to run his menage smoothly, and serve a dinner exquisitely when he felt hospitably inclined.

Could there be any doubt that Jimmie Dale was innately a gentleman?

It was evening, and Jimmie Dale sat at a small table in the corner of the St. James Club dining room. Opposite him sat Herman Carruthers, a young man of his own age, about twenty-six, a leading figure in the newspaper world, whose rise from reporter to managing editor of the *Morning News-Argus* within the short space of a few years had been almost meteoric.

They were at coffee and cigars, and Jimmie Dale was leaning back in his chair, his dark eyes fixed interestedly on his guest.

Carruthers, intently engaged in trimming his cigar ash on the edge of the Limoges china saucer of his coffee set, looked up with an abrupt laugh.

"No; I wouldn't care to go on record as being an advocate of crime," he said whimsically; "that would never do. But I don't mind admitting quite privately that it's been a positive regret to me that he has gone."

"Made too good 'copy' to lose, I suppose?" suggested Jimmie Dale quizzically. "Too bad, too, after working up a theatrical name like that for him—the Gray Seal—rather unique! Who stuck that on him—you?"

Carruthers laughed—then, grown serious, leaned toward Jimmie Dale.

"You don't mean to say, Jimmie, that you don't know about that, do you?" he asked incredulously. "Why, up to a year ago the papers were full of him."

"I never read your beastly agony columns," said Jimmie Dale, with a cheery grin.

"Well," said Carruthers, "you must have skipped everything but the stock reports then."

"Granted," said Jimmie Dale. "So go on, Carruthers, and tell me about him—I dare say I may have heard of him, since you are so distressed about it, but my memory isn't good enough to contradict anything you may have to say about the estimable gentleman, so you're safe."

Carruthers reverted to the Limoges saucer and the tip of his cigar.

"He was the most puzzling, bewildering, delightful crook in the annals of crime," said Carruthers reminiscently, after a moment's silence. "Jimmie, he was the king-pin of them all. Clever isn't the word for him, or dare-devil isn't either. I used to think sometimes his motive was more than half for the pure deviltry of it, to laugh at the police and pull the noses of the rest of us that were after him. I used to dream nights about those confounded gray seals of his—that's where he got his name; he left every job he ever did with a little gray paper affair, fashioned diamond-shaped, stuck somewhere where it would be the first thing your eyes would light upon when you reached the scene, and—"

"Don't go so fast," smiled Jimmie Dale. "I don't quite get the connection. What did you have to do with this—er—Gray Seal fellow? Where do you come in?"

"I? I had a good deal to do with him," said Carruthers grimly. "I was a reporter when he first broke loose, and the ambition of my life, after I began really to appreciate what he was, was to get him—and I nearly did, half a dozen times, only—"

"Only you never quite did, eh?" cut in Jimmie Dale slyly. "How near did you get, old man? Come on, now, no bluffing; did the Gray Seal ever even recognise you as a factor in the hare-and-hound game?"

"You're flicking on the raw, Jimmie," Carruthers answered, with a wry grimace. "He knew me, all right, confound him! He favoured me with several sarcastic notes—I'll show 'em to you some day—explaining how I'd fallen down and how I could have got him if I'd done something else." Carruthers' fist came suddenly down on the table. "And I would have got him, too, if he had lived."

"Lived!" ejaculated Jimmie Dale. "He's dead, then?"

"Yes," averted Carruthers; "he's dead."

"H'm!" said Jimmie Dale facetiously. "I hope the size of the wreath you sent was an adequate tribute of your appreciation."

"I never sent any wreath," returned Carruthers, "for the very simple reason that I didn't know where to send it, or when he died. I said he was dead because for over a year now he hasn't lifted a finger."

"Rotten poor evidence, even for a newspaper," commented Jimmie Dale. "Why not give him credit for having, say—reformed?"

Carruthers shook his head. "You don't get it at all, Jimmie," he said earnestly. "The Gray Seal wasn't an ordinary crook—he was a classic. He was an artist, and the art of the thing was in his blood. A man like that could no more stop than he could stop breathing—and live. He's dead; there's nothing to it but that—he's dead. I'd bet a year's salary on it."

"Another good man gone wrong, then," said Jimmie Dale capriciously. "I suppose, though, that at least you discovered the 'woman in the case'?"

Carruthers looked up quickly, a little startled; then laughed shortly.

"What's the matter?" inquired Jimmie Dale.

"Nothing," said Carruthers. "You kind of got me for a moment, that's all. That's the way those infernal notes from the Gray Seal used to end up: 'Find the lady, old chap; and you'll get me.' He had a damned patronising familiarity that would make you squirm."

"Poor old Carruthers!" grinned Jimmie Dale. "You did take it to heart, didn't you?"

"I'd have sold my soul to get him—and so would you, if you had been in my boots," said Carruthers, biting nervously at the end of his cigar.

"And been sorry for it afterward," supplied Jimmie Dale.

"Yes, by Jove, you're right!" admitted Carruthers, "I suppose I should. I actually got to love the fellow—it was the *game*, really, that I wanted to beat."

"Well, and how about this woman? Keep on the straight and narrow path, old man," prodded Jimmie Dale.

"The woman?" Carruthers smiled. "Nothing doing! I don't believe there was one—he wouldn't have been likely to egg the police and reporters on to finding her if there had been, would he? It was a blind, of course. He worked alone, absolutely alone. That's the secret of his success, according to my way of thinking. There was never so much as an indication that he had had an accomplice in anything he ever did."

Jimmie Dale's eyes travelled around the club's homelike, perfectly appointed room. He nodded to a fellow member here and there, then his eyes rested musingly on his guest again.

Carruthers was staring thoughtfully at his coffee cup.

"He was the prince of crooks and the father of originality," announced Carruthers abruptly, following the pause that had ensued. "Half the time there wasn't any more getting at the motive for the curious things he did, than there was getting at the Gray Seal himself."

"Carruthers," said Jimmy Dale, with a quick little nod of approval, "you're positively interesting tonight. But, so far, you've been kind of scouting around the outside edges without getting into the thick of it. Let's have some of your experiences with the Gray Seal in detail; they ought to make ripping fine yarns."

"Not tonight, Jimmie," said Carruthers; "it would take too long." He pulled out his watch mechanically as he spoke, glanced at it—and pushed back his chair. "Great Scott!" he exclaimed. "It's nearly half-past nine. I'd no idea we had lingered so long over dinner. I'll have to hurry; we're a morning paper, you know, Jimmie."

"What! Really! Is it as late as that." Jimmie Dale rose from his chair as Carruthers stood up. "Well, if you must—"

"I must," said Carruthers, with a laugh.

"All right, O slave." Jimmie Dale laughed back—and slipped his hand, a trick of their old college days together, through Carruthers' arm as they left the room.

He accompanied Carruthers downstairs to the door of the club, and saw his guest into a taxi; then he returned inside, sauntered through the billiard room, and from there into one of the cardrooms, where, pressed into a game, he played several rubbers of bridge before going home.

It was, therefore, well on toward midnight when Jimmie Dale arrived at his house on Riverside Drive, and was admitted by an elderly manservant.

"Hello, Jason," said Jimmie Dale pleasantly. "You still up!"

"Yes, sir," replied Jason, who had been valet to Jimmie Dale's father before him. "I was going to bed, sir, at about ten o'clock, when a messenger came with a letter. Begging your pardon, sir, a young lady, and—"

"Jason"—Jimmie Dale flung out the interruption, sudden, quick, imperative—"what did she look like?"

"Why—why, I don't exactly know as I could describe her, sir," stammered Jason, taken aback. "Very ladylike, sir, in her dress and appearance, and what I would call, sir, a beautiful face."

"Hair and eyes—what color?" demanded Jimmie Dale crisply. "Nose, lips, chin—what shape?"

"Why, sir," gasped Jason, staring at his master, "I—I don't rightly know. I wouldn't call her fair or dark, something between. I didn't take particular notice, and it wasn't overlight outside the door."

"It's too bad you weren't a younger man, Jason," commented Jimmie Dale, with a curious tinge of bitterness in his voice. "I'd have given a year's income for your opportunity tonight, Jason."

"Yes, sir," said Jason helplessly.

"Well, go on," prompted Jimmie Dale. "You told her I wasn't home, and she said she knew it, didn't she? And she left the letter that I was on no account to miss receiving when I got back, though there was no need of telephoning me to the club—when I returned would do, but it was imperative that I should have it then—eh?"

"Good Lord, sir!" ejaculated Jason, his jaw dropped, "that's exactly what she did say."

"Jason," said Jimmie Dale grimly, "listen to me. If ever she comes here again, inveigle her in. If you can't inveigle her, use force; capture her, pull her in, do anything—do anything, do you hear? Only don't let her get away from you until I've come."

Jason gazed at his master as though the other had lost his reason.

"Use force, sir?" he repeated weakly—and shook his head. "You—you can't mean that, sir."

"Can't I?" inquired Jimmie Dale, with a mirthless smile. "I mean every word of it, Jason—and if I thought there was the slightest chance of her giving you the opportunity, I'd be more imperative still. As it is—where's the letter?"

"On the table in your studio, sir," said Jason, mechanically.

Jimmie Dale started toward the stairs—then turned and came back to where Jason, still shaking his head heavily, had been gazing anxiously after his master. Jimmie Dale laid his hand on the old man's shoulder.

"Jason," he said kindly, with a swift change of mood, "you've been a long time in the family—first with father, and now with me. You'd do a good deal for me, wouldn't you?"

"I'd do anything in the world for you, Master Jim," said the old man earnestly.

"Well, then, remember this," said Jimmie Dale slowly, looking into the other's eyes, "remember this—keep your mouth shut and your eyes open. It's my fault. I should have warned you long ago, but I never dreamed that she would ever come here herself. There have been times when it was practically a matter of life and death to me to know who that woman is that you saw tonight. That's all, Jason. Now go to bed."

"Master Jim," said the old man simply, "thank you, sir, thank you for trusting me. I've dandled you on my knee when you were a baby, Master Jim. I don't know what it's about, and it isn't for me to ask. I thought, sir, that maybe you were having a little fun with me. But I know now, and you can trust me, Master Jim, if she ever comes again."

"Thank you, Jason," said Jimmie Dale, his hand closing with an appreciative pressure on the other's shoulder "Good-night, Jason."

Upstairs on the first landing, Jimmie Dale opened a door, closed and locked it behind him—and the electric switch clicked under his fingers. A glow fell softly from a cluster of shaded ceiling lights. It was a large room, a very large room, running the entire depth of the house, and the effect of apparent disorder in the arrangement of its appointments seemed to breathe a sense of charm. There were great cozy, deep, leather-covered lounging chairs, a huge, leather-covered davenport, and an easel or two with half-finished sketches upon them; the walls were panelled, the panels of exquisite grain and matching; in the centre of the room stood a flat-topped rosewood desk; upon the floor was a dark, heavy velvet rug; and, perhaps most inviting of all, there was a great, old-fashioned fireplace at one side of the room.

For an instant Jimmie Dale remained quietly by the door, as though listening. Six feet he stood, muscular in every line of his body, like a well-trained athlete with no single ounce of superfluous fat about him—the grace and ease of power in his poise. His strong, clean-shaven face, as the light fell upon it now, was serious—a mood that became him well—the firm lips closed, the dark, reliant eyes a little narrowed, a frown on the broad forehead, the square jaw clamped.

Then abruptly he walked across the room to the desk, picked up an envelope that lay upon it, and, turning again, dropped into the nearest lounging chair.

There had been no doubt in his mind, none to dispel. It was precisely what he had expected from almost the first word Jason had spoken. It was the same handwriting, the same texture of paper, and there was the same old haunting, rare, indefinable fragrance about it. Jimmie Dale's hands turned the envelope now this way, now that, as he looked at it. Wonderful hands were Jimmie Dale's, with long, slim, tapering fingers whose sensitive tips seemed now as though they were striving to decipher the message within.

He laughed suddenly, a little harshly, and tore open the envelope. Five closely written sheets fell into his hand. He read them slowly, critically, read them over again; and then, his eyes on the rug at his feet, he began to tear the paper into minute pieces between his fingers, depositing the pieces, as he tore them, upon the arm of his chair. The five sheets demolished, his fingers dipped into the heap of shreds on the arm of the chair and tore them over and over again, tore them until they were scarcely larger than bits of confetti, tore at them absently and mechanically, his eyes never shifting from the rug at his feet.

Then with a shrug of his shoulders, as though rousing himself to present reality, a curious smile flickering on his lips, he brushed the pieces of paper into one hand, carried them to the empty fireplace, laid them down in a little pile, and set them afire. Lighting a cigarette, he watched them burn until the last glow had gone from the last charred scrap; then he crunched and scattered them with the brass-handled fender brush, and, retracing his steps across the room, flung back a portiere from where it hung before a little alcove, and dropped on his knees in front of a round, squat, barrel-shaped safe—one of his own design and planning in the years when he had been with his father.

His slim, sensitive fingers played for an instant among the knobs and dials that studded the door, guided, it seemed by the sense of touch alone— and the door swung open. Within was another door, with locks and bolts as intricate and massive as the outer one. This, too, he opened; and then from the interior took out a short, thick, rolled-up leather bundle tied together with thongs. He rose from his knees, closed the safe, and drew the portiere across the alcove again. With the bundle under his arm, he glanced sharply around the room, listened intently, then, unlocking the door that gave on the hall, he switched off the lights and went to his dressing room, that was on the same floor. Here, divesting himself quickly of his dinner clothes, he selected a dark tweed suit with loose-fitting, sack coat from his wardrobe, and began to put it on.

Dressed, all but his coat and vest, he turned to the leather bundle that he had placed on a table, untied the thongs, and carefully opened it out to its full length—and again that curious, cryptic smile tinged his lips. Rolled the opposite away from that in which it had been tied up, the leather strip made a wide belt that went on somewhat after the fashion of a life preserver, the thongs being used for shoulder straps—a belt that, once on, the vest would hide completely, and, fitting close, left no telltale bulge in the outer garments. It was not an ordinary belt; it was full of stout-sewn, up-right little pockets all the way around, and in the pockets grimly lay an array of fine, blued-steel, highly tempered instruments—a compact, powerful burglar's kit.

The slim, sensitive fingers passed with almost a caressing touch over the vicious little implements, and from one of the pockets extracted a thin, flat metal case. This Jimmie Dale opened, and glanced inside—between sheets of oil paper lay little rows of *gray, adhesive, diamond-shaped seals*.

Jimmie Dale snapped the case shut, returned it to its recess, and from another took out a black silk mask. He held it up to the light for examination.

"Pretty good shape after a year," muttered Jimmie Dale, replacing it.

He put on the belt, then his vest and coat. From the drawer of his dresser he took an automatic revolver and an electric flashlight, slipped them into his pocket, and went softly downstairs. From the hat stand he chose a black slouch hat, pulled it well over his eyes—and left the house.

Jimmie Dale walked down a block, then hailed a bus and mounted to the top. It was late, and he found himself the only passenger. He inserted his dime in the conductor's little resonant-belled cash receiver, and then settled back on the uncomfortable, bumping, cushionless seat.

On rattled the bus; it turned across town, passed the Circle, and headed for Fifth Avenue—but Jimmie Dale, to all appearances, was quite oblivious of its movements.

It was a year since she had written him. *She!* Jimmie Dale did not smile, his lips were pressed hard together. Not a very intimate or personal appellation, that—but he knew her by no other. It *was* a woman, surely—the handwriting was feminine, the diction eminently so—and had *she* not come herself that night to Jason! He remembered the last letter, apart from the one tonight, that he had received from her. It was a year ago now—and the letter had been hardly more than a note. The police had worked themselves into a frenzy over the Gray Seal, the papers had grown absolutely maudlin—and she had written, in her characteristic way:

Things are a little too warm, aren't they, Jimmie? Let's let them cool for a year.

Since then until tonight he had heard nothing from her. It was a strange compact that he had entered into—so strange that it could never have known, could never know a parallel—unique, dangerous, bizarre, it was all that and more. It had begun really through his connection with his father's business— the business of manufacturing safes that should defy the cleverest crimi- nals—when his brains, turned into that channel, had been pitted against the underworld, against the methods of a thousand different crooks from Maine to California, the report of whose every operation had reached him in the natural course of business, and every one of which he had studied in minutest detail. It had begun through that—but at the bottom of it was his own restless, adventurous spirit.

He had meant to set the police by the ears, using his gray-seal device both as an added barb and that no innocent bystander of the underworld, innocent for once, might be involved—he had meant to laugh at them and puzzle them to the verge of madness, for in the last analysis they would find only an abortive attempt at crime—and he had succeeded. And then he had gone too far—and he had been caught—by *her*. That string of pearls, which, to study whose effect facetiously, he had so idiotically wrapped around his wrist, and which, so ironically, he had been unable to loosen in time and had been forced to carry with him in his sudden, desperate dash to escape from Marx's the big jeweler's, in Maiden Lane, whose strong room he had toyed with one night, had been the lever which, *at first*, she had held over him.

The bus was on Fifth Avenue now, and speeding rapidly down the deserted thoroughfare. Jimmie Dale looked up at the lighted windows of the St. James Club as they went by, smiled whimsically, and shifted in his seat, seeking a more comfortable position.

She had caught him—how he did not know—he had never seen her—did not know who she was, though time and again he had devoted all his energies for months at a stretch to a solution of the mystery. The morning following the Maiden Lane affair, indeed, before he had breakfasted, Jason had brought him the first letter from her. It had started by detailing his every move of the night before—and it had ended with an ultimatum: "The cleverness, the originality of the Gray Seal as a crook lacked but one thing," she had naively written, "and that one thing was that his crookedness required a leading string to guide it into channels that were worthy of his genius." In a word, *she* would plan the coups, and he would act at her dictation and execute them— or else how did twenty years in Sing Sing for that little Maiden Lane affair appeal to him? He was to answer by the next morning, a simple "yes" or "no" in the personal column of the morning *News-Argus*.

A threat to a man like Jimmie Dale was like flaunting a red rag at a bull, and a rage ungovernable had surged upon him. Then cold reason had come. He was caught—there was no question about that—she had taken pains to show him that he need make no mistake there. Innocent enough in his own conscience, as far as actual theft went, for the pearls would in due course be restored in some way to the possession of their owner, he would have been unable to make even his own father, who was alive then, believe in his innocence, let alone a jury of his peers. Dishonour, shame, ignominy, a long prison sentence, stared him in the face, and there was but one alternative—to link hands with this unseen, mysterious accomplice. Well, he could at least temporise, he could always "queer" a game in some specious manner, if he were pushed too far. And so, in the next morning's *News-Argus*, Jimmie Dale had answered "yes." And then had followed those years in which there had been *no* temporising, in which every plan was carried out to the last detail, those years of curious, unaccountable, bewildering affairs that Carruthers had spoken of, one on top of another, that had shaken the old headquarters on Mulberry Street to its foundations, until the Gray Seal had become a name to conjure with. And, yes, it was quite true, he had entered into it all, gone the limit, with an eagerness that was insatiable.

The bus had reached the lower end of Fifth Avenue, passed through Washington Square, and stopped at the end of its run. Jimmie Dale clambered down from the top, threw a pleasant "good-night" to the conductor, and headed briskly down the street before him. A little later he crossed into West Broadway, and his pace slowed to a leisurely stroll.

Here, at the upper end of the street, was a conglomerate business section of rather inferior class, catering doubtless to the poor, foreign element that congregated west of Broadway proper, and to the south of Washington Square. The street was, at first glance, deserted; it was dark and dreary, with stores and lofts on either side. An elevated train roared by overhead, with a thunderous, deafening clamour. Jimmie Dale, on the right-hand side of the street, glanced interestedly at the dark store windows as he went by. And then, a block ahead, on the other side, his eyes rested on an approaching form. As the other reached the corner and paused, and the light from the street lamp glinted on brass buttons, Jimmie Dale's eyes narrowed a little under his slouch hat. The policeman, although nonchalantly swinging a nightstick, appeared to be watching him.

Jimmie Dale went on half a block farther, stooped to the sidewalk to tie his shoe, glanced back over his shoulder—the policeman was not in sight— and slipped like a shadow into the alleyway beside which he had stopped.

It was another Jimmie Dale now—the professional Jimmie Dale. Quick as a cat, active, lithe, he was over a six foot fence in the rear of a building in a flash, and crouched a black shape, against the back door of an unpretentious, unkempt, dirty, secondhand shop that fronted on West Broadway—the last place certainly in all New York that the managing editor of the *News-Argus*, or anyone else, for that matter, would have picked out as the setting for the second debut of the Gray Seal.

From the belt around his waist, Jimmie Dale took the black silk mask, and slipped it on; and from the belt, too, came a little instrument that his deft fingers manipulated in the lock. A curious snipping sound followed. Jimmie Dale put his weight gradually against the door. The door held fast.

"Bolted," said Jimmie Dale to himself.

The sensitive fingers travelled slowly up and down the side of the door, seeming to press and feel for the position of the bolt through an inch of plank—then from the belt came a tiny saw, thin and pointed at the end, that fitted into the little handle drawn from another receptacle in the leather girdle beneath the unbuttoned vest.

Hardly a sound it made as it bit into the door. Half a minute passed—there was the faint fall of a small piece of wood—into the aperture crept the delicate, tapering fingers—came a slight rasping of metal—then the door swung back, the dark shadow that had been Jimmie Dale vanished and the door closed again.

A round, white beam of light glowed for an instant—and disappeared. A miscellaneous, lumbering collection of junk and odds and ends blocked the entry, leaving no more space than was sufficient for bare passageway. Jimmie Dale moved cautiously—and once more the flashlight in his hand showed the way for an instant—then darkness again.

The cluttered accumulation of secondhand stuff in the rear gave place to a little more orderly arrangement as he advanced toward the front of the store. Like a huge firefly, the flashlight twinkled, went out, twinkled again, and went out. He passed a sort of crude, partitioned-off apartment that did duty for the establishment's office, a sort of little boxed-in place it was, about in the middle of the floor. Jimmie Dale's light played on it for a moment, but he kept on toward the front door without any pause.

Every movement was quick, sure, accurate, with not a wasted second. It had been barely a minute since he had vaulted the back fence. It was hardly a quarter of a minute more before the cumbersome lock of the front door was unfastened, and the door itself pulled imperceptibly ajar.

He went swiftly back to the office now—and found it even more of a shaky, cheap affair than it had at first appeared; more like a box stall with windows around the top than anything else, the windows doubtless to permit the occupant to overlook the store from the vantage point of the high stool that stood before a long, battered, wobbly desk. There was a door to the place, too, but the door was open and the key was in the lock. The ray of Jimmie Dale's flashlight swept once around the interior—and rested on an antique, ponderous safe.

Under the mask Jimmie Dale's lips parted in a smile that seemed almost apologetic, as he viewed the helpless iron monstrosity that was little more than an insult to a trained cracksman. Then from the belt came the thin metal case and a pair of tweezers. He opened the case, and with the tweezers lifted out one of the gray-coloured, diamond-shaped seals. Holding the seal with the tweezers, he moistened the gummed side with his lips, then laid it on a handkerchief which he took from his pocket, and clapped the handkerchief against the front of the safe, sticking the seal conspicuously into place. Jimmie Dale's insignia bore no finger prints. The microscopes and magnifying glasses at headquarters had many a time regretfully assured the police of that fact.

And now his hands and fingers seemed to work like lightning. Into the soft iron bit a drill—bit in and through—bit in and through again. It was dark, pitch black—and silent. Not a sound, save the quick, dull rasp of the ratchet—like the distant gnawing of a mouse! Jimmie Dale worked fast— another hole went through the face of the old-fashioned safe—and then suddenly he straightened up to listen, every faculty tense, alert, and strained, his body thrown a little forward. *What was that!*

From the alleyway leading from the street without, through which he himself had come, sounded the stealthy crunch of feet. Motionless in the utter darkness, Jimmie Dale listened—there was a scraping noise in the rear— someone was climbing the fence that he had climbed!

In an instant the tools in Jimmie Dale's hands disappeared into their respective pockets beneath his vest—and the sensitive fingers shot to the dial on the safe.

"Too bad," muttered Jimmie Dale plaintively to himself. "I could have made such an artistic job of it—I swear I could have cut Carruthers' profile in the hole in less than no time—to open it like this is really taking the poor old thing at a disadvantage."

He was on his knees now, one ear close to the dial, listening as the tumblers fell, while the delicate fingers spun the knob unerringly—the other ear strained toward the rear of the premises.

Came a footstep—a ray of light—a stumble—nearer—the newcomer was inside the place now, and must have found out that the back door had been tampered with. Nearer came the steps—still nearer—and then the safe door swung open under Jimmie Dale's hand, and Jimmie Dale, that he might not be caught like a rat in a trap, darted from the office—but he had delayed a little too long.

From around the cluttered piles of junk and miscellany swept the light— full on Jimmie Dale. Hesitation for the smallest fraction of a second would have been fatal, but hesitation was something that in all his life Jimmie Dale had never known. Quick as a panther in its spring, he leaped full at the light and the man behind it. The rough voice, in surprised exclamation at the sudden discovery of the quarry, died in a gasp.

There was a crash as the two men met—and the other reeled back before the impact. Onto him Jimmie Dale sprang, and his hands flew for the other's throat. It was an officer in uniform! Jimmie Dale had felt the brass buttons as they locked. In the darkness there was a queer smile on Jimmie Dale's tight lips. It was no doubt *the* officer whom he had passed on the other side of the street.

The other was a smaller man than Jimmie Dale, but powerful for his build—and he fought now with all his strength. This way and that the two men reeled, staggered, swayed, panting and gasping; and then—they had lurched back close to the office door—with a sudden swing, every muscle brought into play for a supreme effort, Jimmie Dale hurled the other from him, sending the man sprawling back to the floor of the office, and in the winking of an eye had slammed shut the door and turned the key.

There was a bull-like roar, the shrill *cheep-cheep-cheep* of the patrolman's whistle, and a shattering crash as the officer flung his body against the partition—then the bark of a revolver shot, the tinkle of breaking glass, as the man fired through the office window—and past Jimmie Dale, speeding now for the front door, a bullet hummed viciously.

Out on the street dashed Jimmie Dale, whipping the mask from his face—and glanced like a hawk around him. For all the racket, the neighbourhood had not yet been aroused—no one was in sight. From just overhead came the rattle of a downtown elevated train. In a hundred-yard sprint, Jimmie Dale raced it a half block to the station, tore up the steps—and a moment later dropped nonchalantly into a seat and pulled an evening newspaper from his pocket.

Jimmie Dale got off at the second station down, crossed the street, mounted the steps of the elevated again, and took the next train uptown. His movements appeared to be somewhat erratic—he alighted at the station next above the one by which he had made his escape. Looking down the street it was too dark to see much of anything, but a confused noise as of a gathering crowd reached him from what was about the location of the secondhand store. He listened appreciatively for a moment.

"Isn't it a perfectly lovely night?" said Jimmie Dale amiably to himself. "And to think of that cop running away with the idea that I didn't see him when he hid in a doorway after I passed the corner! Well, well, strange—isn't it?"

With another glance down the street, a whimsical lift of his shoulders, he headed west into the dilapidated tenement quarter that huddled for a handful of blocks near by, just south of Washington Square. It was a little after one o'clock in the morning now and the pedestrians were casual. Jimmie Dale read the street signs on the corners as he went along, turned abruptly into an intersecting street, counted the tenements from the corner as he passed, and—for the eye of anyone who might be watching—opened the street door of one of them quite as though he were accustomed and had a perfect right to do so, and went inside.

It was murky and dark within; hot, unhealthy, with lingering smells of garlic and stale cooking. He groped for the stairs and started up. He climbed one flight, then another—and one more to the top. Here, treading softly, he made an examination of the landing with a view, evidently, to obtaining an idea of the location and the number of doors that opened off from it.

His selection fell on the third door from the head of the stairs—there were four all told, two apartments of two rooms each. He paused for an instant to adjust the black silk mask, tried the door quietly, found it unlocked, opened it with a sudden, quick, brisk movement—and, stepping in side, leaned with his back against it.

"Good-morning," said Jimmie Dale pleasantly.

It was a squalid place, a miserable hole, in which a single flickering, yellow gas jet gave light. It was almost bare of furniture; there was nothing but a couple of cheap chairs, a rickety table—unpawnable. A boy, he was hardly more than that, perhaps twenty-two, from a posture in which he was huddled across the table with head buried in out-flung arms, sprang with a startled cry to his feet.

"Good-morning," said Jimmie Dale again. "Your name's Hagan, Bert Hagan—isn't it? And you work for Isaac Brolsky in the secondhand shop over on West Broadway—don't you?"

The boy's lips quivered, and the gaunt, hollow, half-starved face, white, ashen-white now, was pitiful.

"I—I guess you got me," he faltered "I—I suppose you're a plain-clothes man, though I never knew dicks wore masks."

"They don't generally," said Jimmie Dale coolly. "It's a fad of mine—Bert Hagan."

The lad, hanging to the table, turned his head away for a moment—and there was silence.

Presently Hagan spoke again. "I'll go," he said numbly. "I won't make any trouble. Would—would you mind not speaking loud? I—I wouldn't like her to know."

"Her?" said Jimmie Dale softly.

The boy tiptoed across the room, opened a connecting door a little, peered inside, opened it a little wider—and looked over his shoulder at Jimmie Dale.

Jimmie Dale crossed to the boy, looked inside the other room—and his lip twitched queerly, as the sight sent a quick, hurt throb through his heart. A young woman, younger than the boy, lay on a tumble-down bed, a rag of clothing over her—her face with a deathlike pallor upon it, as she lay in what appeared to be a stupor. She was ill, critically ill; it needed no trained eye to discern a fact all too apparent to the most casual observer. The squalor, the glaring poverty here, was even more pitifully in evidence than in the other room—only here upon a chair beside the bed was a cluster of medicine bottles and a little heap of fruit.

Jimmie Dale drew back silently as the boy closed the door.

Hagan walked to the table and picked up his hat.

"I'm—I'm ready," he said brokenly. "Let's go."

"Just a minute," said Jimmie Dale. "Tell us about it."

"Twon't take long," said Hagan, trying to smile. "She's my wife. The sickness took all we had. I—I kinder got behind in the rent and things. They were going to fire us out of here—tomorrow. And there wasn't any money for the medicine, and—and the things she had to have. Maybe you wouldn't have done it—but I did. I couldn't see her dying there for the want of some-thing a little money'd buy—and—and I couldn't"—he caught his voice in a little sob—"I couldn't see her thrown out on the street like that."

"And so," said Jimmie Dale, "instead of putting old Isaac's cash in the safe this evening when you locked up, you put it in your pocket instead—eh? Didn't you know you'd get caught?"

"What did it matter?" said the boy. He was twirling his misshappen hat between his fingers. "I knew they'd know it was me in the morning when old Isaac found it gone, because there wasn't anybody else to do it. But I paid the rent for four months ahead tonight, and I fixed it so's she'd have medi-cine and things to eat. I was going to beat it before daylight myself—I"—he brushed his hand hurriedly across his cheek—"I didn't want to go—to leave her till I had to."

"Well, say"—there was wonderment in Jimmie Dale's tones, and his English lapsed into ungrammatical, reassuring vernacular—"ain't that queer! Say, I'm no detective. Gee, kid, did you think I was? Say, listen to this! I cracked old Isaac's safe half an hour ago—and I guess there won't be any idea going around that you got the money and I pulled a lemon. Say, I ain't superstitious, but it looks like luck meant you to have another chance, don't it?"

The hat dropped from Hagan's hands to the floor, and he swayed a little.

"You—you ain't a dick!" he stammered. "Then how'd you know about me and my name when you found the safe empty? Who told you?"

A wry grimace spread suddenly over Jimmie Dale's face beneath the mask, and he swallowed hard. Jimmie Dale would have given a good deal to have been able to answer that question himself.

"Oh, that!" said Jimmie Dale. "That's easy—I knew you worked there. Say, it's the limit, ain't it? Talk about your luck being in, why all you've got to do is to sit tight and keep your mouth shut, and you're safe as a church. Only say, what are you going to do about the money, now you've got a four months' start and are kind of landed on your feet?"

"Do?" said the boy. "I'll pay it back, little by little. I meant to. I ain't no—" He stopped abruptly.

"Crook," supplied Jimmie Dale pleasantly. "Spit it right out, kid; you won't hurt my feelings none. Well, I'll tell you—you're talking the way I like to hear you—you pay that back, slide it in without his knowing it, a bit at a time, whenever you can, and you'll never hear a yip out of me; but if you don't, why it kind of looks as though I have a right to come down your street and get my share or know the reason why—eh?"

"Then you never get any share," said Hagan, with a catch in his voice. "I pay it back as fast as I can."

"Sure," said Jimmie Dale. "That's right—that's what I said. Well, so long—Hagan." And Jimmie Dale had opened the door and slipped outside.

An hour later, in his dressing room in his house on Riverside Drive, Jimmie Dale was removing his coat as the telephone, a hand instrument on the table, rang. Jimmie Dale glanced at it—and leisurely proceeded to remove his vest. Again the telephone rang. Jimmie Dale took off his curious, pocketed leather belt—as the telephone repeated its summons. He picked out the little drill he had used a short while before, and inspected it critically—feeling its point with his thumb, as one might feel a razor's blade. Again the telephone rang insistently. He reached languidly for the receiver, took it off its hook, and held it to his ear.

"Hello!" said Jimmie Dale, with a sleepy yawn. "Hello! Hello! Why the deuce don't you yank a man out of bed at two o'clock in the morning and have done with it, and—eh? Oh, that you, Carruthers?"

"Yes," came Carruthers' voice excitedly. "Jimmie, listen—listen! The Gray Seal's come to life! He's just pulled a break on West Broadway!"

"Good Lord!" gasped Jimmie Dale. "You don't say!"

CHAPTER 2
BY PROXY

"The most puzzling bewildering, delightful crook in the annals of crime," Herman Carruthers, the editor of the *Morning News-Argus*, had called the Gray Seal; and Jimmie Dale smiled a little grimly now as he recalled the occasion of a week ago at the St. James Club over their after-dinner coffee. That was before his second debut, with Isaac Brolsky's poverty-stricken premises over on West Broadway as a setting for the break.

She had written: "Things are a little too warm, aren't they, Jimmie? Let's let them cool for a year." Well, they had cooled for a year, and Carruthers as a result had been complacently satisfied in his own mind that the Gray Seal was dead—until that break at Isaac Brolsky's over on West Broadway!

Jimmie Dale's smile was tinged with whimsicality now. The only effect of the year's inaction had been to usher in his renewed activity with a furor compared to which all that had gone before was insignificant. Where the newspapers had been maudlin, they now raved—raved in editorials and raved in headlines. It was an impossible, untenable, unbelievable condition of affairs that this Gray Seal, for all his incomparable cleverness, should flaunt his crimes in the faces of the citizens of New York. One could actually see the editors writhing in their swivel chairs as their fiery denunciations dripped from their pens! What was the matter with the police? Were the police children; or, worse still, imbeciles—or, still worse again, was there someone "higher up" who was profiting by this rogue's work? New York would not stand for it—New York would most decidedly not—and the sooner the police realised that fact the better! If the police were helpless, or tools, the citizens of New York were not, and it was time the citizens were thoroughly aroused.

There was a way, too, to arouse the citizens, that was both good business from the newspaper standpoint, and efficacious as a method. Carruthers, of the *Morning News-Argus*, had initiated it. The *Morning News-Argus* offered twenty-five thousand dollars' reward for the capture of the Gray Seal! Other papers immediately followed suit in varying amounts. The authorities, State and municipal, goaded to desperation, did likewise, and the five million men, women, and children of New York were automatically metamorphosed into embryonic sleuths. New York was aroused.

Jimmie Dale, alias the Gray Seal, member of the ultra-exclusive St. James Club, the latter fact sufficient in itself to guarantee his social standing, graduate of Harvard, inheritor of his deceased father's immense wealth amassed in the manufacture of burglar-proof safes, some of the most ingenious patents on which were due to Jimmie Dale himself, figured with a pencil on the margin of the newspaper he had been reading, using the arm of the big, luxurious, leather-upholstered lounging chair as a support for the paper. The result of his calculations was eighty-five thousand dollars.

He brushed the paper onto the Turkish rug, dove into the pocket of his dinner jacket for his cigarettes, and began to smoke as his eyes strayed around the room, his own particular den in his fashionable Riverside Drive residence.

Eighty-five thousand dollars' reward! Jimmie Dale blew meditative rings of cigarette smoke at the fireplace. What would she say to that? Would she decide it was "too hot" again, and call it off? It added quite a little hazard to the game—*quite* a little! If he only knew who "she" was! It was a strange partnership—the strangest partnership that had ever existed between two human beings.

He turned a little in his chair as a step sounded in the hallway without— that is, Jimmie Dale caught the sound, muffled though it was by the heavy carpet. Came then a knock upon the door.

"Come in," invited Jimmie Dale.

It was old Jason, the butler. The old man was visibly excited, as he extended a silver tray on which lay a letter.

Jimmie Dale's hand reached quickly out, the long, slim tapering fingers closed upon the envelope—but his eyes were on Jason significantly, questioningly.

"Yes, Master Jim," said the old man, "I recognised it on the instant, sir. After what you said, sir, last week, honouring me, I might say, to a certain extent with your confidence, though I'm sure I don't know what it all means, I—"

"Who brought it this time, Jason?" inquired Jimmie Dale quietly.

"Not the young person, begging your pardon, not the young lady, sir. A shuffer in a big automobile. 'Your master at once,' he says, and shoves the letter into my hand, and was off."

"Very good, Jason," said Jimmie Dale. "You may go."

The door closed. Yes, it was from *her*—it was the same texture of paper, there was the same rare, haunting fragrance clinging to it.

He tore the envelope open, and extracted a folded sheet of paper. What was it this time? To call the partnership off again until the present furor should have subsided once more—or the skilfully sketched outline of a new adventure? Which? He glanced at the few lines written on the sheet, and lunged forward from his chair to his feet. It was neither one nor the other. It was—

Jimmie Dale's face was set, and an angry red surge swept his cheeks. His lips moved, muttering audibly fragments of the letter, as he stared at it.

"—incredible that you—a heinous thing—act instantly—this is ruin—"

For an instant—a rare occurrence in Jimmie Dale's life—he stood like a man stricken, still staring at the sheet in his hand. Then mechanically his fingers tore the paper into little pieces, and the little pieces into tiny shreds. Anger fled, and a sickening sense of impotent dismay took its place; the red left his cheeks, and in its stead a grayness came.

"Act instantly!" The words seemed to leap at him, drum at his ears with constant repetition. Act instantly! But how? How? Then his brain—that keen, clear, master brain—sprang from stunned inaction into virility again. Of course—Carruthers! It was in Carruthers' line.

He stepped to the desk—and paused with his hand extended to pick up the telephone. How explain to Carruthers that he, Jimmie Dale, already knew what Carruthers might not yet have heard of, even though Carruthers would naturally be among the first to be in touch with such affairs! No; that would never do. Better get there himself at once and trust to—

The telephone rang.

Jimmie Dale waited until it rang again, then he lifted the receiver from the hook.

"Hello?" he said.

"Hello! Hello! Jimmie!" came a voice. "This is Carruthers. That you, Jimmie?"

"Yes," said Jimmie Dale and sat down limply in the desk chair.

"It's the Gray Seal again. I promised you I'd let you in on the ground floor next time anything happened, so come on down here quick if you want to see some of his work at firsthand."

Jimmie Dale flirted a bead of sweat from his forehead.

"Carruthers," said Jimmie languidly, "you newspaper chaps make me tired with your Gray Seal. I'm just going to bed."

"Bed nothing!" spluttered Carruthers, from the other end of the wire. "Come down, I tell you. It's worth your while—half the population of New

York would give the toes off their feet for the chance. Come down, you blast idiot! The Gray Seal has gone the limit this time—it's *murder*."

Jimmie Dale's face was haggard.

"Oh!" he said peevishly. "Sounds interesting. Where are you? I guess maybe I'll jog along."

"I should think you would!" snapped Carruthers. "You know the Palace on the Bowery? Yes? Well, meet me on the corner there as soon as you can. Hustle! Good——"

"Oh, I say, Carruthers!" interposed Jimmie Dale.

"Yes?" demanded Carruthers.

"Thanks awfully for letting me know, old man."

"Don't mention it!" returned Carruthers sarcastically. "You always were a grateful beast, Jimmie. Hurry up!"

Jimmie Dale hung up the receiver of the city phone, and took down the receiver of another, a private-house installation, and rang twice for the garage.

"The light car at once, Benson," he ordered curtly. "At once!"

Jimmie Dale worked quickly then. In his dressing room, he changed from dinner clothes to tweeds; spent a second or so over the contents of a locked drawer in the dresser, from which he selected a very small but serviceable automatic, and a very small but highly powerful magnifying glass whose combination of little round lenses worked on a pivot, and, closed over one another, were of about the compass of a quarter of a dollar.

In three minutes he was outside the house and stepping into the car, just as it drew up at the curb.

"Benson," he said tersely to his chauffeur, "drop me one block this side of the Palace on the Bowery—and forget there was ever a speed law enacted. Understand?"

"Very good, sir," said Benson, touching his cap. "I'll do my best, sir."

Jimmie Dale, in the tonneau, stretched out his legs under the front seat, and dug his hands into his pockets—and inside the pockets his hands were clenched and knotted fists.

Murder! At times it had occurred to him that there was a possibility that some crook of the underworld would attempt to cover his tracks and take refuge from pursuit by foisting himself on the authorities as the Gray Seal. That was a possibility, a risk always to be run. But that *murder* should be laid to the Gray Seal's door! Anger, merciless and unrestrained, surged over Jimmie Dale.

There was peril here, live and imminent. Suppose that some day he should be caught in some little affair, recognised and identified as the Gray Seal, there would be the charge of murder hanging over him—and the electric chair to face!

But the peril was not the only thing. Even worse to Jimmie Dale's artistic and sensitive temperament was the vilification, the holding up to loathing, contumely, and abhorrence of the name, the stainless name, of the Gray Seal. It *was* stainless! He had guarded it jealously—as a man guards the woman's name he loves.

Affairs that had mystified and driven the police distracted with impotence there had been, many of them; and on the face of them—crimes. But no act ever committed had been in reality a crime—none without the highest of motives, the righting of some outrageous wrong, the protection of some poor stumbling fellow human.

That had been his partnership with her. How, by what amazing means, by what power that smacked almost of the miraculous she came in touch with all these things and supplied him with the data on which to work he did not know—only that, thanks to her, there were happier hearts and happier homes since the Gray Seal had begun to work. "Dear Philanthropic Crook," she often called him in her letters. And now—it was *murder*!

Take Carruthers, for instance. For years, as a reporter before he had risen to the editorial desk, he had been one of the keenest on the scent of the Gray Seal, but always for the sake of the game—always filled with admiration, as he said himself, for the daring, the originality of the most puzzling, bewildering, delightful crook in the annals of crime. Carruthers was but an example. Carruthers now would hunt the Gray Seal like a mad dog. The Gray Seal, to Carruthers and every one else, would be the vilest name in the land—a synonym for murder.

On the car flew—and upon Jimmie Dale's face, as though chiselled in marble, was a look that was not good to see. And a mirthless smile set, frozen, on his lips.

"I'll get the man that did this," gritted Jimmie Dale between his teeth. "I'll *get* him! And, when I get him, I'll wring a confession from him if I have to swing for it!"

The car swept from Broadway into Astor Place, on down the Bowery, and presently stopped.

Jimmie Dale stepped out. "I shall not want you any more, Benson," he said. "You may return home."

Jimmie Dale started down the block—a nonchalant Jimmie Dale now, if anything, bored a little. Near the corner, a figure, back turned, was lounging at the edge of the sidewalk. Jimmie Dale touched the man on the arm.

"Hello, Carruthers!" he drawled.

"Ah, Jimmie!" Carruthers turned with an excited smile. "That's the boy! You've made mighty quick time."

"Well, you told me to hurry," grumbled Jimmie Dale. "I'm doing my best to please you tonight. Came down in my car, and got summoned for three fines tomorrow."

Carruthers laughed. "Come on," he said; and, linking his arm in Jimmie Dale's, turned the corner, and headed west along the cross street. "This is going to make a noise," he continued, a grim note creeping into his voice. "The biggest noise the city has ever heard. I take back all I said about the Gray Seal. I'd always pictured his cleverness as being inseparable with at least a decent sort of man, even if he was a rogue and a criminal, but I'm through with that. He's a rotter and a hound of the rankest sort! I didn't think there was anything more vulgar or brutal than murder, but he's shown me that there is. A guttersnipe's got more decency! To murder a man and then boastfully label the corpse is—"

"Say, Carruthers," said Jimmie Dale plaintively, suddenly hanging back, "I say, you know, it's—it's all right for you to mess up in this sort of thing, it's your beastly business, and I'm awfully damned thankful to you for giving me a look-in, but isn't it—er—rather *infra dig* for me? A bit morbid, you know, and all that sort of thing. I'd never hear the end of it at the club—you know what the St. James is. Couldn't I be Merideth Stanley Annstruther, or something like that, one of your new reporters, or something like that, you know?"

Carruthers chuckled. "Sure, Jimmie," he said. "You're the latest addition to the staff of the *News-Argus*. Don't worry; the incomparable Jimmie Dale won't figure publicly in this."

"It's awfully good of you," said Jimmie gratefully. "I have to have a notebook or something, don't I?"

Carruthers, from his pocket, handed him one. "Thanks," said Jimmie Dale.

A little way ahead, a crowd had collected on the sidewalk before a doorway, and Carruthers pointed with a jerk of his hand.

"It's in Moriarty's place—a gambling hell," he explained. "I haven't got the story myself yet, though I've been inside, and had a look around. Inspector Clayton discovered the crime, and reported it at headquarters. I was at my desk in the office when the news came, and, as you know the interest I've taken in the Gray Seal, I decided to 'cover' it myself. When I got here, Clayton hadn't returned from headquarters, so, as you seemed so keenly interested last week, I telephoned you. If Clayton's back now we'll get the details. Clayton's a good fellow with the 'press,' and he won't hold anything out on us. Now, here we are. Keep close to me, and I'll pass you in."

They shouldered through the crowd and up to an officer at the door. The officer nodded, stepped aside, and Carruthers, with Jimmie Dale following, entered the house.

They climbed one flight, and then another. The card-rooms, the faro, stud, and roulette layouts were deserted, save for policemen here and there on guard. Carruthers led the way to a room at the back of the hall, whose door was open and from which issued a hubbub of voices—one voice rose above the others, heavy and gratingly complacent.

"Clayton's back," observed Carruthers.

They stepped over the threshold, and the heavy voice greeted them.

"Ah, here's Carruthers now! H'are you, Carruthers? They told me you'd been here, and were coming back, so I've been keeping the boys waiting before handing out the dope. You've had a look at that—eh?" He flung out a fat hand toward the bed.

The voices rose again, all directed at Carruthers now.

"Bubble's burst, eh, Carruthers? What about the 'Prince of Crooks'? Artistry in crime, wasn't it, you said?" They were quoting from his editorials of bygone days, a half dozen reporters of rival papers, grinning and joshing him good-naturedly, seemingly quite unaffected by what lay within arm's reach of them upon the bed.

Carruthers smiled a little wryly, shrugged his shoulders—and presented Jimmie Dale to Inspector Clayton.

"Mr. Matthewson, a new man of ours—inspector."

"Glad to know you, Mr. Matthewson," said the inspector.

Jimmie Dale found his hand grasped by another that was flabby and unpleasantly moist; and found himself looking into a face that was red, with heavy rolls of unhealthy fat terminating in a double chin and a thick, apoplectic neck—a huge, round face, with rat's eyes.

Clayton dropped Jimmie Dale's hand, and waved his own in the air. Jimmie Dale remained modestly on the outside of the circle as the reporters gathered around the police inspector.

"Now, then," said Clayton coarsely, "the guy that's croaked there is Metzer, Jake Metzer. Get that?"

Jimmie Dale, scribbling hurriedly in his notebook like all the rest, turned a little toward the bed, and his lower jaw crept out the fraction of an inch. Both gas jets in the room were turned on full, giving ample light. A man fully dressed, a man of perhaps forty, lay upon his back on the bed, one arm outflung across the bedspread, the other dangling, with fingers just touching the floor, the head at an angle and off the pillow. It was as though he had been carried to the bed and flung upon it after the deed had been committed. Jimmie Dale's eyes shifted and swept the room. Yes, everything was in disorder, as though there had been a struggle—a chair upturned, a table canted against the wall, broken pieces of crockery from the washstand on the carpet, and—

"Metzer was a stool pigeon, see?" went on Clayton, "and he lived here. Moriarty wasn't on to him. Metzer stood in thick with a wider circle of crooks than any other snitch in New York."

Jimmie Dale, still scribbling as Clayton talked, stepped to the bed and leaned over the murdered man. The murder had been done with a blackjack evidently—a couple of blows. The left side of the temple was crushed in.

Right in the middle of the forehead, pasted there, a gray-colored, diamond shaped paper seal flaunted itself—the device of the Gray Seal. In Jimmie Dale' hand, hidden as he turned his back, the tiny combination of powerful lenses was focused on the seal.

Clayton guffawed. "That's right!" he called out. "Take a good look. That's a bright young man you've got, Carruthers."

Jimmie Dale looked up a little sheepishly—and got a grin from the assembled reporters, and a scowl from Carruthers.

"Now, then," continued Clayton, "here's the facts—as much of 'em as I can let you boys print at present. You know I'm stretching a point to let you in here—don't forget that when you come to write up the case—honour where's honour's due, you know. Well, me and Metzer there was getting ready to close down on a big piece of game, and I was over here in this room talking to him about it early this afternoon. We had it framed to get our man tonight—see? I left Metzer, say, about three o'clock, and he was to show up over at headquarters with another little bit of evidence we wanted at eight o'clock tonight."

Jimmie Dale was listening—to every word. But he stooped now again over the murdered man's head deliberately, though he felt the inspector's rat's eyes upon him—stooped, and, with his finger nail, lifted back the right-hand point of the diamond-shaped seal where it bordered a faint thread of blood on the man's forehead.

There was a bull-like roar from the inspector, and he burst through the ring of reporters, and grabbed Jimmie Dale by the shoulder.

"Here you, what in hell are you doing!" he spluttered angrily.

Embarrassed and confused, Jimmie Dale drew back, glanced around, and smiled again a little sheepishly as his eyes rested on the red-flushed jowl of the inspector.

"I—I wanted to see how it was stuck on," he explained inanely.

"Stuck on!" bellowed Clayton. "I'll show you how it's stuck on, if you monkey around here! Don't you know any better than that! Where were you dragged up anyway? The coroner hasn't been here yet. You're a hot cub of a reporter, you are!" He turned to Carruthers. "Y'ought to get out printed instructions for 'em before you turn 'em loose!" he snapped.

Carruthers' face was red with mortification. There was a grin, expanded, on the faces of the others.

"Stand away from that bed!" roared Clayton at Jimmie Dale. "And if you go near it again, I'll throw you out of here bodily!"

Jimmie Dale edged away, and, eyes lowered, fumbled nervously with the leaves of his notebook.

Clayton grunted, glared at Jimmie Dale for an instant viciously—and resumed his story.

"I was saying," he said, "that Metzer was to come to headquarters at eight o'clock this evening. Well, he didn't show up. That looked queer. It was mighty important business. We was after one of the biggest hauls we'd ever pulled off. I waited till nine o'clock, an hour ago, and I was getting nervous. Then I started over here to find out what was the matter. When I got here I asked Moriarty if he'd seen Metzer. Moriarty said he hadn't since I was here before. He was a little suspicious that I had something on Metzer—see? Well, by pumping Moriarty, he admitted that Metzer had had a visitor about an hour after I left."

"Who was it? Know what his name is, inspector?" asked one of the reporters quickly.

Inspector Clayton winked heavily. "Don't be greedy boys," he grinned.

"You mean you've got him?" burst out another one of the men excitedly.

"Sure! Sure, I've got him." Inspector Clayton waved his fat hand airily. "Or I will have before morning—but I ain't saying anything more till it's over." He smiled significantly. "Well, that's about all. You've got the details right around you. I left Moriarty downstairs and came up here, and found just what you see—Metzer laying on the bed there, and the gray seal stuck on his forehead—and"—he ended abruptly—"I'll have the Gray Seal himself behind the bars by morning."

A chorus of ejaculations rose from the reporters, while their pencils worked furiously.

Then Jimmie Dale appeared to have an inspiration. Jimmie Dale turned a leaf in his notebook and began to sketch rapidly, cocking his head now on one side now on the other. With a few deft strokes he had outlined the figure of Inspector Clayton. The reporter beside Jimmie Dale leaned over to inspect the work, and another did likewise. Jimmie Dale drew in Clayton's face most excellently, if somewhat flatteringly; and then, with a little flourish of pride, wrote under the drawing: "The Man Who Captured the Gray Seal."

"That's a cracking good sketch!" pronounced the reporter at his side. "Let the inspector see it."

"What is it?" demanded Clayton, scowling.

Jimmie Dale handed him the notebook modestly.

Inspector Clayton took it, looked at it, looked at Jimmie Dale; then his scowl relaxed into a self-sufficient and pleased smile, and he grunted approvingly.

"That's the stuff to put over," he said. "Mabbe you're not much of a reporter, but you can draw. Y're all right, sport—y're all right. Forget what I said to you a while ago."

Jimmie Dale smiled too—deprecatingly. And put the notebook in his pocket.

An officer entered the room hurriedly, and, drawing Clayton aside, spoke in an undertone. A triumphant and malicious grin settled on Clayton's features, and he started with a rush for the door.

"Come around to headquarters in two hours, boys," he called as he went out, "and I'll have something more for you."

The room cleared, the reporters tumbling downstairs to make for the nearest telephones to get their "copy" into their respective offices.

On the street, a few doors up from the house where they were free from the crowd, Carruthers halted Jimmie Dale.

"Jimmie," he said reproachfully, "you certainly made a mark of us both. There wasn't any need to play the 'cub' so egregiously. However, I'll forgive you for the sake of the sketch—hand it over, Jimmie; I'm going to reproduce it in the first edition."

"It wasn't drawn for reproduction, Carruthers—at least not yet," said Jimmie Dale quietly.

Carruthers stared at him. "Eh?" he asked blankly.

"I've taken a dislike to Clayton," said Jimmie Dale whimsically. "He's too patently after free advertising, and I'm not going to help along his boost. You can't have it, old man, so let's think about something else. What'll they do with that bit of paper that's on the poor devil's forehead up there, for instance."

"Say," said Carruthers, "does it strike you that you're acting queer? You haven't been drinking, have you, Jimmie?"

"What'll they do with it?" persisted Jimmie Dale.

"Well," said Carruthers, smiling a little tolerantly, "they'll photograph it and enlarge the photograph, and label it 'Exhibit A' or 'Exhibit B' or something like that—and file it away in the archives with the fifty or more just like it that are already in their collection."

"That's what I thought," observed Jimmie Dale. He took Carruthers by the lapel of the coat. "I'd like a photograph of that. I'd like it so much that I've got to have it. Know the chap that does that work for the police?"

"Yes," admitted Carruthers.

"Very good!" said Jimmie Dale crisply, "Get an extra print of the enlargement from him then—for a consideration—whatever he asks—I'll pay for it."

"But what for?" demanded Carruthers. "I don't understand."

"Because," said Jimmie Dale very seriously, "put it down to imagination or whatever you like, I think I smell something fishy here."

"You *what*!" exclaimed Carruthers in amazement. "You're not joking, are you, Jimmie?"

Jimmie Dale laughed shortly. "It's so far from a joke," he said, in a low tone, "that I want your word you'll get that photograph into my hands by tomorrow afternoon, no matter what transpires in the meantime. And look here, Carruthers, don't think I'm playing the silly thickhead, and trying to mystify you. I'm no detective or anything like that. I've just got an idea that apparently hasn't occurred to anyone else—and, of course, I may be all wrong. If I am, I'm not going to say a word even to you, because it wouldn't be playing fair with someone else; if I'm right the *Morning News-Argus* gets the biggest scoop of the century. Will you go in on that basis?"

Carruthers put out his hand impulsively. "If you're in earnest, Jimmie— you bet!"

"Good!" returned Jimmie Dale. "The photograph by tomorrow afternoon then. And now—"

"And now," said Carruthers, "I've got to hurry over to the office and get a write-up man at work. Will you come along, or meet me at headquarters later? Clayton said in two hours he'd—"

"Neither," said Jimmie Dale. "I'm not interested in headquarters. I'm going home."

"Well, all right then," Carruthers returned. "You can bank on me for to- morrow. Good-night, Jimmie."

"Good-night, old man," said Jimmie Dale, and, turning, walked briskly toward the Bowery.

But Jimmie Dale did not go home. He walked down the Bowery for three blocks, crossed to the east side, and turned down a cross street. Two blocks more he walked in this direction, and halfway down the next. Here he paused an instant—the street was dimly lighted, almost dark, deserted. Jimmie Dale edged close to the houses until his shadow blended with the shadows of the walls—and slipped suddenly into a pitch-black areaway.

He opened a door, stepped into an unlighted hallway where the air was close and evil smelling, mounted a stairway, and halted before another door on the first landing. There was the low clicking of a lock, three times re- peated, and he entered a room, closing and fastening the door behind him.

Jimmie Dale called it his "Sanctuary." In one of the worst neighbour- hoods of New York, where no questions were asked as long as the rent was paid, it had the further advantage of three separate exits—one by the areaway where he had entered; one from the street itself; and another through a back yard with an entry into a saloon that fronted on the next street. It was not often that Jimmie Dale used his Sanctuary, but there had been times when it was no more nor less than exactly what he called it—a sanctuary!

He stepped to the window, assured himself that the shade was down— and lighted the gas, blinking a little as the yellow flame illuminated the room.

It was a rough place, dirty, uninviting; a bedroom, furnished in the most scanty fashion. Neither, apparently, was there anything suspicious about it to reward one curious enough to break in during the owner's absence—some rather disreputable clothes hanging on the wall, and flung untidily across the bed—that was all.

Alone now, Jimmie Dale's face was strained and anxious and, occasionally, as he undressed himself, his hands clenched until his knuckles grew white. The gray seal on the murdered man's forehead was a *genuine gray seal*—one of Jimmie Dale's own. There was no doubt of that—he had satisfied himself on that point.

Where had it come from? How had it been obtained? Jimmie Dale carefully placed the clothes he had taken off under the mattress, pulled a disreputable collarless flannel shirt over his head, and pulled on a disreputable pair of boots. There were only two sources of supply. His own—and the collection that the police had made, which Carruthers had referred to.

Jimmie Dale lifted a corner of the oilcloth in a corner of the room, lifted a piece of the flooring, lifted out a little box which he placed upon the rickety table, and sat down before a cracked mirror. Who was it that would have access to the gray seals in the possession of the police, since, obviously, it was one of those that was on the dead man's forehead? The answer came quick enough—came with the sudden out-thrust of Jimmie Dale's lower jaw. *One of the police themselves*—no one else. Clayton's heavy, cunning face, Clayton's shifty eyes, Clayton's sudden rush when he had touched the dead man's forehead, pictured themselves in a red flash of fury before Jimmie Dale. There was no mask now, no facetiousness, no acted part—only a merciless rage, and the muscles of Jimmie Dale's face quivered and twitched. *Murder*, foisted, shifted upon another, upon the Gray Seal—making of that name a calumny—ruining forever the work that she and he might do!

And then Jimmie Dale smiled mirthlessly, with thinning lips. The box before him was open. His fingers worked quickly—a little wax behind the ears, in the nostrils, under the upper lip, deftly placed-hands, wrists, neck, throat, and face received their quota of stain, applied with an artist's touch— and then the spruce, muscular Jimmie Dale, transformed into a slouching, vicious-featured denizen of the underworld, replaced the box under the flooring, pulled a slouch hat over his eyes, extinguished the gas, and went out.

Jimmie Dale's range of acquaintanceship was wide—from the upper strata of the St. James Club to the elite of New York's gangland. And, adored by the one, he was trusted implicitly by the other—not understood, perhaps, by the latter, for he had never allied himself with any of their nefarious schemes, but trusted implicitly through long years of personal contact. It had stood Jimmie Dale in good stead before, this association, where, in a sort of strange, carefully guarded exchange, the news of the underworld was common property to those without the law. To New York in its millions, the murder of Metzer, the stool pigeon, would be unknown until the city rose in the morning to read the sensational details over the breakfast table; here, it would already be the topic of whispered conversations, here it had probably been known long before the police had discovered the crime. Especially would it be expected to be known to Pete Lazanis, commonly called the

Runt, who was a power below the dead line and, more pertinent still, one in whose confidence Jimmie Dale had rejoiced for years.

Jimmie Dale, as Larry the Bat—a euphonious "monaker" bestowed possibly because this particular world knew him only by night—began a search for the Runt. From one resort to another he hurried, talking in the accepted style through one corner of his mouth to hard-visaged individuals behind dirty, reeking bars that were reared on equally dirty and foul-smelling sawdust-strewn floors; visiting dance halls, secretive back rooms, and certain Chinese pipe joints.

But the Runt was decidedly elusive. There had been no news of him, no one had seen him—and this after fully an hour had passed since Jimmie Dale had left Carruthers in front of Moriarty's. The possibilities however were still legion—numbered only by the numberless dives and dens sheltered by that quarter of the city.

Jimmie Dale turned into Chatham Square, heading for the Pagoda Dance Hall. A man loitering at the curb shot a swift, searching glance at him as he slouched by. Jimmie Dale paused in the doorway of the Pagoda and looked up and down the street. The man he had passed had drawn a little closer; another man in an apparently aimless fashion lounged a few yards away.

"Something up," muttered Jimmie Dale to himself. "Lansing, of headquarters, and the other looks like Milrae."

Jimmie Dale pushed in through the door of the Pagoda. A bedlam of noise surged out at him—a tin-pan piano and a mandolin were going furiously from a little raised platform at the rear; in the centre of the room a dozen couples were in the throes of the tango and the bunny-hug; around the sides, at little tables, men and women laughed and applauded and thumped time on the tabletops with their beer mugs; while waiters, with beer-stained aprons and unshaven faces, juggled marvelous handfuls of glasses and mugs from the bar beside the platform to the patrons at the tables.

Jimmie Dale's eyes swept the room in a swift, comprehensive glance, fixed on a little fellow, loudly dressed, who shared a table halfway down the room with a woman in a picture hat, and a smile of relief touched his lips. The Runt at last!

He walked down the room, caught the Runt's eyes significantly as he passed the table, kept on to a door between the platform and the bar, opened it, and went out into a lighted hallway, at one end of which a door opened onto the street, and at the other a stairway led above.

The Runt joined him. "Wot's de row, Larry?" inquired the Runt.

"Nuthin' much," said Jimmie Dale. "Only I t'ought I'd let youse know. I was passin' Moriarty's an' got de tip. Say, some guy's croaked Jake Metzer dere."

"Aw, ferget it!" observed the Runt airily. "Dat's stale. Was wise to dat hours ago."

Jimmie Dale's face fell. "But I just come from dere," he insisted; "an' de harness bulls only just found it out."

"Mabbe," grunted the Runt. "But Metzer got his early in de afternoon—see?"

Jimmie Dale looked quickly around him—and then leaned toward the Runt.

"Wot's de lay, Runt?" he whispered.

The Runt pulled down one eyelid, and, with his knowing grin, the cigarette, clinging to his upper lip, sagged down in the opposite corner of his mouth.

Jimmie Dale grinned, too—in a flash inspiration had come to Jimmie Dale.

"Say, Runt"—he jerked his head toward the street door—"wot's de fly cops doin' out dere?"

The grin vanished from the Runt's lips. He stared for a second wildly at Jimmie Dale, and then clutched at Jimmie Dale's arm.

"De WOT?" he said hoarsely.

"De fly cops," Jimmie Dale repeated in well-simulated surprise. "Dey was dere when I come in—Lansing an' Milrae, an—"

The Runt shot a hurried glance at the stairway, and licked his lips as though they had gone suddenly dry.

"My Gawd, I—" He gasped, and shrank hastily back against the wall beside Jimmie Dale.

The door from the street had opened noiselessly, instantly. Black forms bulked there—then a rush of feet—and at the head of half a dozen men, the face of Inspector Clayton loomed up before Jimmie Dale. There was a second's pause in the rush; and, in the pause, Clayton's voice, in a vicious undertone:

"You two ginks open your traps, and I'll run you both in!"

And then the rush passed, and swept on up the stairs.

Jimmie Dale looked at the Runt. The cigarette dangled limply; the Runt's eyes were like a hunted beast's.

"Dey got him!" he mumbled. "It's Stace—Stace Morse. He come to me after croakin' Metzer, an' he's been hidin' up dere all afternoon."

Stace Morse—known in gangland as a man with every crime in the calendar to his credit, and prominent because of it! Something seemed to go suddenly queer inside of Jimmie Dale. Stace Morse! Was he wrong, after all? Jimmie Dale drew closer to the Runt.

"Yer givin' me a steer, ain't youse?" He spoke again from the corner of his mouth, almost inaudibly. "Are youse sure it was Stace croaked Metzer? Wot fer? How'd yer know?"

The Runt was listening, his eyes strained toward the stairs. The hall door to the street was closed, but both were quite well aware that there was an officer on guard outside.

"He told me," whispered the Runt. "Metzer was fixin' ter snitch on him ter-night. Dey've got de goods on Stace, too. He made a bum job of it."

"Why didn't he get out of de country den when he had de chanst, instead of hangin' around here all afternoon?" demanded Jimmie Dale.

"He was broke," the Runt answered. "We was gettin' de coin fer him ter fade away wid ter-night, an'—"

A revolver shot from above cut short his words. Came then the sound of a struggle, oaths, the shuffling tread of feet—but in the dance hall the piano still rattled on, the mandolin twanged, voices sang and applauded, and beer mugs thumped time.

They were on the stairs now, the officers, half carrying, half dragging someone between them—and the man they dragged cursed them with utter abandon. As they reached the bottom of the stairs, Jimmie Dale caught sight of the prisoner's face—not a prepossessing one—villainous—low-browed, contorted with a mixture of fear and rage.

"It's a lie! A lie! A lie!" the man shrieked. "I never seen him in me life— blast you!—curse you!—d'ye hear!"

Inspector Clayton caught Jimmie Dale and the Runt by the collars.

"There's nothing to interest you around here!" he snapped maliciously. "Go on, now—beat it!" And he pushed them toward the door.

They had heard the disturbance in the dance hall now and the occupants were swarming to the sidewalk. A patrol wagon came around the corner. In the crowd Jimmie Dale slipped away from the Runt.

Was he wrong, after all? A fierce passion seized him. It was Stace Morse who had murdered Metzer, the Runt had said. In Jimmie Dale's brain the words began to reiterate themselves in a singsong fashion: "It was Stace Morse. It was Stace Morse." Then his lips drew tight together. *Was* it Stace Morse? He would have given a good deal for a chance to talk to the man— even for a minute. But there was no possibility of that now. Later, tomorrow perhaps, if he was wrong, after all!

Jimmie Dale returned to the Sanctuary, removed from his person all evidences of Larry the Bat—and from the Sanctuary went home to Riverside Drive.

In his den there, in the morning after breakfast, Jason, the butler, brought him the papers. Three-inch headlines in red ink screamed, exulted, and shrieked out the news that the Gray Seal, in the person of Stace Morse, fence, yeggman and murderer, had been captured. The public, if it had held any private admiration for the one-time mysterious crook could now once and forever disillusion itself. The Gray Seal was Stace Morse—and Stace Morse was of the dregs of the city's scum, a pariah, an outcast, with no single redeeming trait to lift him from the ruck of mire and slime that had strewn his life from infancy. The face of Inspector Clayton, blandly self-complacent, leaped out from the paper to meet Jimmie Dale's eyes—and with it a column and a half of perfervid eulogy.

Something at first like dismay, the dismay of impotency, filled Jimmie Dale—and then, cold, leaving him unnaturally calm, the old merciless rage took its place. There was nothing to do now but wait—wait until Carruthers should send that photograph. Then if, after all, he were wrong—then he must find some other way. But was he wrong! The notebook that Carruthers had given him, open at the sketch he had made of Clayton, lay upon the desk. Jimmie Dale picked it up—he had already spent quite a little time over it before breakfast—and examined it again minutely, even resorting to his magnifying glass. He put it down as a knock sounded at the door, and Jason entered with a silver card tray. From Carruthers already! Jimmie Dale stepped quickly forward—and then Jimmie Dale met the old man's eyes. It wasn't from Carruthers—it was from *her*!

"The same shuffer brought it, Master Jim," said Jason.

Jimmie Dale snatched the envelope from the tray, and waved the other from the room. As the door closed, he tore open the letter. There was just a single line:

Jimmie—Jimmie, you haven't failed, have you?

Jimmie Dale stared at it. Failed! Failed—*her*! The haggard look was in his face again. It was the bond between them that was at stake—the Gray Seal—the bond that had come, he knew for all time in that instant, to mean his life.

"God knows!" he muttered hoarsely, and flung himself into a lounging chair, still staring at the note.

The hours dragged by. Luncheon time arrived and passed—and then by special messenger the little package from Carruthers came.

Jimmie Dale started to undo the string, then laid the package down, and held out his hands before him for inspection. They were trembling visibly. It was a strange condition for Jimmie Dale either to witness or experience, unlike him, foreign to him.

"This won't do, Jimmie," he said grimly, shaking his head.

He picked up the package again, opened it, and from between two pieces of cardboard took out a large photographic print. A moment, two, Jimmie Dale examined it, used the magnifying glass again; and then a strange gleam came into the dark eyes, and his lips moved.

"I've won," said Jimmie Dale, with ominous softness. "I've *won*!"

He was standing beside the rosewood desk, and he reached for the phone. Carruthers would be at home now—he called Carruthers there. After a moment or two he got the connection.

"This is Jimmie, Carruthers," he said. "Yes, I got it. Thanks.... Yes.... Listen. I want you to get Inspector Clayton, and bring him up here at once.... What? No, no—no!... How?... Why—er—tell him you're going to run a full page of him in the Sunday edition, and you want him to sit for a sketch. He'd go anywhere for that.... Yes.... Half an hour.... *Yes*.... Good-bye."

Jimmie Dale hung up the receiver; and, hastily now, began to write upon a pad that lay before him on the desk. The minutes passed. As he wrote, he scored out words and lines here and there, substituting others. At the end he had covered three large pages with, to anyone but himself, an indecipherable scrawl. These he shoved aside now, and, very carefully, very legibly, made a copy on fresh sheets. As he finished, he heard a car draw up in front of the house. Jimmie Dale folded the copied sheets neatly, tucked them in his pocket, lighted a cigarette, and was lolling lazily in his chair as Jason announced: "Mr. Carruthers, sir, and another gentleman to see you."

"Show them up, Jason," instructed Jimmie Dale.

Jimmie Dale rose from his chair as they came in. Jason, well-trained servant, closed the door behind them.

"Hello, Carruthers; hello, inspector," said Jimmie Dale pleasantly, and waved them to seats. "Take this chair, Carruthers." He motioned to one at his elbow. "Glad to see you, inspector—try that one in front of the desk, you'll find it comfortable."

Carruthers, trying to catch Jimmie Dale's eye for some sort of a cue, and, failing, sat down. Inspector Clayton stared at Jimmie Dale.

"Oh, it's *you*, eh?" His eyes roved around the room, fastened for an instant on some of Jimmie Dale's work on an easel, came back finally to Jimmie Dale—and he plumped himself down in the chair indicated. "Thought you was more'n a cub reporter," he remarked, with a grin. "You were too slick with your pencil. Pretty fine studio you got here. Carruthers says you're going to draw me."

Jimmie Dale smiled—not pleasantly—and leaned suddenly over the desk.

"Yes," he said slowly, a grim intonation in his voice, "going to draw you—*true to life*."

With an exclamation, Clayton slued around in his chair, half rose, and his shifty eyes, small and cunning, bored into Jimmie Dale's face.

"What d'ye mean by that?" he snapped.

"Just exactly what I say," replied Jimmie Dale curtly. "No more, no less. But first, not to be too abrupt, I want to join with the newspapers in congratulating you on the remarkable—shall I call it celerity, or acumen?—with which you solved the mystery of Metzer's death, and placed the murderer behind the bars. It is really remarkable, inspector, so remarkable, in fact, that it's almost—*suspicious*. Don't you think so? No? Well, that's what Mr. Carruthers was good enough to bring you up here to talk over—in an intimate and confidential way, you know."

Inspector Clayton surged up from his chair to his feet, his fists clenched, the red sweeping over his face—and then he shook one fist at Carruthers.

"So that's your game, is it!" he stormed. "Trying to crawl out of that twenty-five thousand reward, eh? And as for you"—he turned on Jimmie Dale—"you've rigged up a nice little plant between you, eh? Well, it won't work—and I'll make you squirm for this, both of you, damn you, before I'm through!" He glared from one to the other for a moment—then swung on his heel. "Good-afternoon, gentlemen," he sneered, as he started for the door.

He was halfway across the room before Jimmie Dale spoke.

"Clayton!"

Clayton turned. Jimmie Dale was still leaning over the desk, but now one elbow was propped upon it, and in the most casual way a revolver covered Inspector Clayton.

"If you attempt to leave this room," said Jimmie Dale, without raising his voice, "I assure you that I shall fire with as little compunction as though I were aiming at a mad dog—and I apologise to all mad dogs for coupling your name with them." His voice rang suddenly cold. "Come back here, and sit down in that chair!"

The colour ebbed slowly from Clayton's face. He hesitated—then sullenly retraced his steps; hesitated again as he reached the chair, and finally sat down.

"What—what d'ye mean by this?" he stammered, trying to bluster.

"Just this," said Jimmie Dale. "That I accuse you of the murder of Jake Metzer—*it was you who murdered Metzer*."

"Good God!" burst suddenly from Carruthers.

"You lie!" yelled Clayton—and again he surged up from his chair.

"That is what Stace Morse said," said Jimmie Dale coolly. "Sit down!"

Then Clayton tried to laugh. "You're—you're having a joke, ain't you? It was Stace—I can prove it. Come down to headquarters, and I can prove it. I got the goods on him all the way. I tell you"—his voice rose shrilly—"it was Stace Morse."

"You are a despicable hound," said Jimmie Dale, through set lips. "Here"—he handed the revolver over to Carruthers—"keep him covered, Carruthers. You're going to the *chair* for this, Clayton," he said, in a fierce monotone. "The chair! You can't send another there in your place—this time. Shall I draw you now—true to life? You've been grafting for years on every disreputable den in your district. Metzer was going to show you up; and so, Metzer being in the road, you removed him. And you seized on the fact of Stace Morse having paid a visit to him this afternoon to fix the crime on— Stace Morse. Proofs? Oh, yes, I know you've manufactured proofs enough to convict him—if there weren't stronger proofs to convict *you*."

"Convict *me*!" Clayton's lower jaw hung loosely; but still he made an effort at bluster. "You haven't a thing on me—not a thing—not a thing."

Jimmie Dale smiled again—unpleasantly.

"You are quite wrong, Clayton. See—here." He took a sheet of paper from the drawer of his desk.

Clayton reached for it quickly. "What is it?" he demanded.

Jimmie Dale drew it back out of reach.

"Just a minute," he said softly. "You remember, don't you, that in the presence of Carruthers here, of myself, and of half a dozen reporters, you stated that you had been alone with Metzer in his room at three o'clock yesterday, and that it was you—alone—who found the body later on at nine o'clock? Yes? I mention this simply to show that from your own lips the evidence is complete that you had an *opportunity* to commit the crime. Now you may look at this, Clayton." He handed over the sheet of paper.

Clayton took it, stared at it, turning it over from first one side to the other. Then a sort of relief seemed to come to him and he gulped.

"Nothing but a damned piece of blank paper!" he mumbled.

Jimmie Dale reached over and took back the sheet.

"You're wrong again, Clayton," he said calmly. "It was quite blank before I handed it to you—but not now. I noticed yesterday that your hands were generally moist. I am sure they are more so now—excitement, you know. Carruthers, see that he doesn't interrupt."

From a drawer, Jimmie Dale took out a little black bottle, the notebook he had used the day before, and the photograph Carruthers had sent him. On the sheet of paper Clayton had just handled, Jimmie Dale sprinkled a little powder from the bottle.

"Lampblack," explained Jimmie Dale. He shook the paper carefully, allowing the loose powder to fall on the desk blotter—and held out the sheet toward Clayton. "Rather neat, isn't it? A very good impression, too. Your thumb print, Clayton. Now don't move. You may look—not touch." He laid the paper down on the desk in front of Clayton. Beside it he placed the notebook, open at the sketch—a black thumb print now upon it. "You recall handling this yesterday, I'm sure, Clayton. I tried the same experiment with the lampblack on it this morning, you see. And this"—beside the notebook he placed the police photograph; that, too, in its enlargement, showed, sharply defined, a thumb print on a diamond-shaped background. "You will no doubt recognise it as an official photograph, enlarged, taken of the gray seal on Metzer's forehead—*and the thumb print of Metzer's murderer*. You have only to glance at the little scar at the edge of the centre loop to satisfy yourself that the three are identical. Of course, there are a dozen other points of similarity equally indisputable, but—"

Jimmie Dale stopped. Clayton was on his feet—rocking on his feet. His face was deathlike in its pallor. Moisture was oozing from his forehead.

"I didn't do it! I didn't do it!" he cried out wildly. "My God, I tell you, I *didn't* do it—and—and—that would send me to the chair."

"Yes," said Jimmie Dale coldly, "and that's precisely where you're going—to the chair."

The man was beside himself now—racked to the soul by a paroxysm of fear.

"I'm innocent—innocent!" he screamed out. "Oh, for God's sake, don't send an innocent man to his death. It was Stace Morse. Listen! Listen! I'll tell the truth." He was clawing with his hands, piteously, over the desk at Jimmie Dale. "When the big rewards came out last week I stole one of the gray seals from the bunch at headquarters to—to use it the first time any crime was committed when I was sure I could lay my hands on the man who did it. Don't you see? Of course he'd deny he was the Gray Seal, just as he'd deny that he was guilty—but I'd have the proof both ways and—and I'd collect the rewards, and—and—" The man collapsed into the chair.

Carruthers was up from his seat, his hands gripping tight on the edge of the desk as he leaned over it.

"Jimmie—Jimmie—what does this mean?" he gasped out.

Jimmie Dale smiled—pleasantly now.

"That he has told the truth," said Jimmie Dale quietly. "It is quite true that Stace Morse committed the murder. Shows up the value of circumstantial evidence though, doesn't it? This would certainly have got him off, and convicted Clayton here before any jury in the land. But the point is, Carruthers, that Stace Morse *isn't* the Gray Seal—and that the Gray Seal is *not* a murderer."

Clayton looked up. "You—you believe me?" he stammered eagerly.

Jimmie Dale whirled on him in a sudden sweep of passion.

"No, you cur!" he flashed. "It's not you I believe. I simply wanted your confession before witnesses." He whipped the three written sheets from his pocket. "Here, substantially, is that confession written out." He passed it to Carruthers. "Read it to him, Carruthers."

Carruthers read it aloud.

"Now," said Jimmie Dale grimly, "this spells ruin for you, Clayton. You don't deserve a chance to escape prison bars, but I'm going to give you one, for you're going to get it pretty stiff, anyhow. If you refuse to sign this, I'll hand you over to the district attorney in half an hour, and Carruthers and I will swear to your confession; on the other hand, if you sign it, Carruthers will not be able to print it until tomorrow morning, and that gives you something like fourteen hours to put distance between yourself and New York. Here is a pen—if you are quick enough to take us by surprise once you have signed, you might succeed in making a dash for that door and effecting your escape—without forcing us to compound a felony—understand?"

Clayton's hand trembled violently as he seized the pen. He scrawled his name—looked from one to the other—wet his lips—and then, taking Jimmie Dale at his word, rushed for the door—and the door slammed behind him.

Carruthers' face was hard. "What did you let him go for, Jimmie?" he said uncompromisingly.

"Selfishness. Pure selfishness," said Jimmie Dale softly. "They'd guy me unmercifully if they ever heard of it at the St. James Club. The honour is all yours, Carruthers. I don't appear on the stage. That's understood? Yes? Well, then"—he handed over the signed confession—"is the 'scoop' big enough?"

Carruthers fingered the sheets, but his eyes in a bewildered way searched Jimmie Dale's face.

"Big enough!" he echoed, as though invoking the universe. "It's the biggest thing the newspaper game has ever known. But how did you come to do it? What started you? Where did you get your lead?"

"Why, from you, I guess, Carruthers," Jimmie Dale answered thoughtfully, with artfully puckered brow. "I remembered that you had said last week that the Gray Seal never left finger marks on his work—and I saw one on the seal on Metzer's forehead. Then, you know, I lifted one corner where the seal overlapped a thread of blood, and, underneath, the thread of blood wasn't in the slightest disturbed; so, of course, I knew the seal had been put on quite a long time after the man was dead—not until the blood had dried thoroughly, to a crust, you know, so that even the damp surface of the sticky side of the seal hadn't affected it. And then, I took a dislike to Clayton somehow—and put two and two together, and took a flyer in getting him to handle the notebook. I guess that's all—no other reason on earth. Jolly lucky, don't you think?"

Carruthers didn't say anything for a moment. When he spoke, it was irrelevantly.

"You saved me twenty-five thousand dollars on that reward, Jimmie."

"That's the only thing I regret," said Jimmie Dale brightly. "It wasn't nice of you, Carruthers, to turn on the Gray Seal that way. And it strikes me you owe the chap, whoever he is, a pretty emphatic exoneration after what you said in this morning's edition."

"Jimmie," said Carruthers earnestly. "You know what I thought of him before. It's like a new lease of life to get back one's faith in him. You leave it to me. I'll put the Gray Seal on a pedestal tomorrow that will be worthy of the immortals—you leave it to me."

And Carruthers kept his word. Also, before the paper had been an hour off the press, Carruthers received a letter. It thanked Carruthers quite genuinely, even if couched in somewhat facetious terms, for his "sweeping vindication," twitted him gently for his "backsliding," begged to remain "his gratefully," and in lieu of signature there was a gray-coloured piece of paper shaped like a diamond.

Only there were no fingerprints on it.

CHAPTER 3

THE MOTHER LODE

It was the following evening, and they had dined together again at the St. James Club—Jimmie Dale, and Carruthers of the *Morning News-Argus*. From Clayton and a discussion of the Metzer murder, the conversation had turned, not illogically, upon the physiognomy of criminals in general. Jimmie Dale, lazily ensconced now in a lounging chair in one of the club's private library rooms, flicked a minute speck of cigar ash from the sleeve of his dinner jacket, and smiled whimsically across the table at his friend.

"Oh, I dare say there's a lot in physiognomy, Carruthers," he drawled. "Never studied the thing, you know—that is, from the standpoint of crime. Personally, I've only got one prejudice: I distrust, on principle, the man who wears a perennial and pompous smirk—which isn't, of course, strictly speaking, physiognomy at all. You see, a man can't help his eyes being beady or his nose pronounced, but pomposity and a smirk, now—" Jimmie Dale shrugged his shoulders.

Carruthers laughed—and then glanced ludicrously at Jimmie Dale, as the door, ajar, was pushed open, and a man entered.

"Speaking of angels," murmured Jimmie Dale—and sat up in his chair. "Hello, Markel!" he observed casually, "You've met Carruthers, of the *News-Argus*, haven't you?"

Markel was fat and important; he had beady black eyes, fastidiously trimmed whiskers—and a pronounced smirk.

Markel blew his nose vigorously, coughed asthmatically, and held out his hand.

"Of course, certainly," said he effusively. "I've met Carruthers several times—used his sheet more than once to advertise a new bond flotation."

The dominant note in Markel's voice was an ingratiating and unpleasant whine, and Carruthers nodded, not very cordially—and shook hands.

Markel went back to the door, closed it carefully, and returned to the table.

"Fact is," he smiled confidentially, "I saw you two come in here a few minutes ago, and I've got something that I thought Carruthers might be glad to have for his society column—say, in the Sunday edition."

He dove into the inside pocket of his coat, produced a large morocco leather jeweller's case, and, holding it out over the table between Carruthers and Jimmie Dale, suddenly snapped the cover open—and then, with a complacent little chuckle that terminated in another fit of coughing, spilled the contents on the table under the electric reading lamp.

Like a thing of living, pulsing fire it rolled before their eyes—a magnificent diamond necklace, of wondrous beauty, gleaming and scintillating as the light rays shot back from a thousand facets.

For a moment, both men gazed at it without a word.

"Little surprise for my wife," volunteered Markel, with a debonair wave of his pudgy hand, and trying to make his voice sound careless.

The case lay open—patently displaying the name of the most famous jewelry house in America. Jimmie Dale's eyes fixed on Markel's whiskers where they were brushed outward in an ornate and fastidious gray-black sweep.

"By Jove!" he commented. "You don't do things by halves, do you, Markel?"

"Two hundred and ten thousand dollars I paid for that little bunch of gewgaws," said Markel, waving his hand again. Then he clapped Carruthers heartily on the shoulder. "What do you think of it, Carruthers—eh? Say, a photograph of it, and one of Mrs. Markel—eh? Please her, you know—she's crazy on this society stunt—all flubdub to me of course. How's it strike you, Carruthers?"

Carruthers, very evidently, liked neither the man nor his manners, but Carruthers, above everything else, was a gentleman.

"To be perfectly frank with you, Mr. Markel," he said a little frigidly, "I don't believe in this sort of thing. It's all right from a newspaper standpoint, and we do it; but it's just in this way that owners of valuable jewelry lay themselves open to theft. It simply amounts to advising every crook in the country that you have a quarter of a million at his disposal, which he can carry away in his vest pocket, once he can get his hands on it—and you invite him to try."

Jimmie Dale laughed. "What Carruthers means, Markel, is that you'll have the Gray Seal down your street. Carruthers talks of crooks generally, but he thinks in terms of only one. He can't help it. He's been trying so long to catch the chap that it's become an obsession. Eh, Carruthers?"

Carruthers smiled seriously. "Perhaps," he admitted. "I hope, though, for Mr. Markel's sake, that the Gray Seal won't take a fancy to it—if he does, Mr. Markel can say good-bye to his necklace."

"Pouf!" coughed Markel arrogantly. "Overrated! His cleverness is all in the newspaper columns. If he knows what's good for him, he'll know enough to leave this alone."

Jimmie Dale was leaning over the table poking gingerly with the tip of his forefinger at the centre stone in the setting, revolving it gently to and fro in the light—a very large stone, whose weight would hardly be less than fifteen carats. Jimmie Dale lowered his head for a closer examination—and to hide a curious, mocking little gleam that crept into his dark eyes.

"Yes, I should say you're right, Markel," he agreed judicially. "He ought to know better than to touch this. It—it would be too hard to dispose of."

"I'm not worrying," declared Markel importantly.

"No," said Jimmie Dale. "Two hundred and ten thousand, you said. Any special—er—significance to the occasion, if the question's not impertinent? Birthday, wedding anniversary—or something like that?"

"No, nothing like that!" Markel grinned, winked secretively, and rubbed his hands together. "I'm feeling good, that's all—I'm going to make the killing of my life tomorrow."

"Oh!" said Jimmie Dale.

Markel turned to Carruthers. "I'll let you in on that, too, Carruthers, in a day or two, if you'll send a reporter around—financial man, you know. It'll be worth your while. And now, how about this? What do you say to a little article and the photos next Sunday?"

There was a slight hint of rising colour in Carruthers' face.

"If you'll send them to the society editor, I've no doubt he'll be able to use them," he said brusquely.

"Right!" said Markel, and coughed, and patted Carruthers' shoulder patronisingly again. "I'll just do that little thing." He picked up the necklace, dangled it till it flashed and flashed again under the light, then restored it very ostentatiously to its case, and the case to his pocket. "Thanks awfully, Carruthers," he said, as he rose from his chair. "See you again, Dale. Goodnight!"

Carruthers glared at the door as it closed behind the man.

"Say it!" prodded Jimmie Dale sweetly. "Don't feel restrained because you are a guest—I absolve you in advance."

"Rotter!" said Carruthers.

"Well," said Jimmie Dale softly. "You see—Carruthers?"

Carruthers' match crackled savagely as he lighted a cigar.

"Yes, I see," he growled. "But I don't see—you'll pardon my saying so—how vulgarity like that ever acquired membership in the St. James Club."

"Carruthers," said Jimmie Dale plaintively, "you ought to know better than that. You know, to begin with, since it seems he has advertised with you, that he runs some sort of brokerage business in Boston. He's taken a summer home up here on Long Island, and some misguided chap put him on the club's visitor's list. His card will *not* be renewed. Sleek customer, isn't he? Trifle familiar—I was only introduced to him last night."

Carruthers grunted, broke his burned match into pieces, and began to toss the pieces into an ash tray.

Jimmie Dale became absorbed in an inspection of his hands—those wonderful hands with long, slim, tapering fingers, whose clean, pink flesh masked a strength and power that was like to a steel vise.

Jimmie Dale looked up. "Going to print a nice little story for him about the 'costliest and most beautiful necklace in America'?" he inquired innocently.

Carruthers scowled. "No," he said bluntly. "I am not. He'll read the *News-Argus* a long time before he reads anything about that, Jimmie."

But therein Carruthers was wrong—the *News-Argus* carried the "story" of Markel's diamond necklace in three-inch "caps" in red ink on the front page in the next morning's edition—and Carruthers gloated over it because the morning *News-Argus* was the *only* paper in New York that did. Carruthers was to hear more of Markel and Markel's necklace than he thought, though for the time being the subject dropped between the two men.

It was still early, barely ten o'clock, when Carruthers left the club, and, preferring to walk to the newspaper offices, refused Jimmie Dale's offer of his limousine. It was but five minutes later when Jimmie Dale, after chatting for a moment or two with those about in the lobby, in turn sought the coat room, where Markel was being assisted into his coat.

"Getting home early, aren't you, Markel?" remarked Jimmie Dale pleasantly.

"Yes," said Markel, and ran his fingers fussily, comb fashion, through his whiskers. "Quite a little run out to my place, you know—and with, you know what, I don't care to be out too late."

"No, of course," concurred Jimmie Dale, getting into his own coat.

They walked out of the club together, and Markel climbed importantly into the tonneau of a big gray touring car.

"Ah—home, Peters," he sniffed at his chauffeur; and then, with a grandiloquent wave of his hand to Jimmie Dale: "'Night, Dale."

Jimmie Dale smiled with his eyes—which were hidden by the brim of his hat.

"Good-night, Markel," he replied, and the smile crept curiously to the corners of his mouth as he watched the gray car disappear down the street.

A limousine drew up, and Benson, Jimmie Dale's chauffeur, opened the door.

"Home, Mr. Dale?" he asked cheerily, touching his cap. "Yes, Benson—home," said Jimmie Dale absently, and stepped into the car.

It was a luxurious car, as everything that belonged to Jimmie Dale was luxurious—and he leaned back luxuriously on the cushions, extended his legs luxuriously to their full length, plunged his hands into his overcoat pockets—and then a change stole strangely, slowly over Jimmie Dale.

The sensitive fingers of his right hand in the pocket had touched, and now played delicately over a sealed envelope that they had found there, played over it as though indeed by the sense of touch alone they could read the contents—and he drew his body gradually erect.

It was another of those mysterious missives from—*her*. The texture of the paper was invariably the same—like this one. How had it come there? Collusion with the coat boy at the club? That was hardly probable. Perhaps it had been there before he had entered the club for dinner—he remembered, now, that there had been several people passing, and that he had been jostled slightly in crossing the sidewalk. What, however, did it matter? It was there mysteriously, as scores of others had come to him mysteriously, with never a clue to her identity, to the identity of his—he smiled a little grimly—accomplice in crime.

He took the envelope from his pocket and stared at it. His fingers had not been at fault—it was one of hers. The faint, elusive, exquisite fragrance of some rare perfume came to him as he held it.

"I'd give," said Jimmie Dale wistfully to himself—"I'd give everything I own to know who you are—and some day, please God, I will know."

Jimmie Dale tore the envelope very gently, as though the tearing almost were an act of desecration—and extracted the letter from within. He began to read aloud hurriedly and in snatches:

Dear Philanthropic Crook:
    Charleton Park Manor—Markel's house is the second one from the gates on the right-hand side—library leads off reception hall on left, door opposite staircase—telephone in reception hall near vestibule entrance, left-hand side—safe is one of your father's make, No. 14,321—clothes closet behind the desk—probably will be kept in cash box—five servants; two men, three maids—quarters on top story—Markel and wife occupy room over library—French windows to dining room on opposite side of the house—opening on the lawn— get it *tonight*, Jimmie—*tomorrow would be too late*—dispose of it— see fit—Henry Wilbur, Marshall Building, Broadway—fifth story—

Through the glass-panelled front of the car, Jimmie Dale could see his chauffeur's back, and the hand that held the letter dropped now to his side, and Jimmie Dale stared—at his chauffeur's back. Then, presently, he read the letter again, as though committing it to memory now; and then, tearing the paper into tiny shreds, as he did with every one of her communications, he reached out of the window and allowed the little pieces to filter gradually from his hand.

The Gray Seal! He smiled in his whimsical way. If it were ever known! He, Jimmie Dale, with his social standing, his wealth, his position—the Gray Seal! Not a police official, not a secret-service bureau probably in the civilised world, but knew the name—not a man, woman, or child certainly in this great city around him but to whom it was as familiar as their own! Danger? Yes. A battle of wits? Yes. His against everybody's—even against Carruthers', his old college chum! For, even as a reporter, before he had risen to the editorial desk, and even now that he had, Carruthers had been one of the keenest on the scent of the Gray Seal.

Danger? Yes. But it was worth it! Worth it a thousand times for the very lure of the danger itself; but worth it most of all for his association with her who, by some amazing means, verging indeed on the miraculous, came into touch with all these things, and supplied him with the data on which to work—that always some wrong might be righted, or gladness come where there had been gloom before, or hope where there had been despair—that into some fellow human's heart should come a gleam of sunshine. Yes, in spite of the howls of the police, the virulent diatribes of the press, an angry public screaming for his arrest, conviction, and punishment, there were those perhaps who even on their bended knees at night asked God's blessing on— the Gray Seal!

Was it strange, then, after all, that the police, seeking a clue through motive, should have been driven to frenzy on every occasion in finding themselves forever confronted with what, from every angle they were able to view it, was quite a purposeless crime! On one point only they were right, the old dogma, the old, old cry, old as the institution of police, older than that, old since time immemorial—*cherchez la femme*! Quite right—but also quite purposeless! Jimmie Dale's eyes grew wistful. He had been "hunting for the woman in the case" himself, now, for months and years indefatigably, using every resource at his command—quite purposelessly.

Jimmie Dale shrugged his shoulders. Why go over all this tonight—there were other things to do. She had come to him again—and this time with a matter that entailed more than ordinary difficulty, more than usual danger, that would tax his wits and his skill to the utmost, not only to succeed, but to get out of it himself with a whole skin. Markel—eh? Jimmie Dale leaned back in his seat, clasped his hands behind his head—and his eyes, half closed now, were studying Benson's back again through the plate-glass front.

He was still sitting in that position as the car approached his residence on Riverside Drive—but, as it came to a stop, and Benson opened the door, it was a very alert Jimmie Dale that stepped to the sidewalk.

"Benson," he said crisply, "I am going downtown again later on, but I shall drive myself. Bring the touring car around and leave it in front of the house. I'll run it into the garage when I get back—you need not wait up."

"Very good, sir," said Benson.

In the hallway, Jason, the butler, who had been butler to Jimmie Dale's father before him, took Jimmie Dale's hat and coat.

"It's a fine evening, Master Jim," said the privileged old man affectionately.

Jimmie Dale took out his silver cigarette case, selected a cigarette, tapped it daintily on the cover of the case—and accepted the match the old man hastily produced.

"Yes, Jason," said Jimmie Dale, pleasantly facetious, "it a fine night, a glorious night, moon and stars and a balmy breeze—quite too fine, indeed, to remain indoors. In fact, you might lay out my gray ulster; I think I will go for a spin presently, when I have changed."

"Yes, sir," said Jason. "Anything else, Master Jim?"

"No; that's all, Jason. Don't sit up for me—you may go to bed now."

"Thank you, sir," said the old man.

Jimmie Dale went upstairs, opened the door of his own particular den on the right of the landing, stepped inside, closed the door, switched on the light—and Jimmie Dale's debonair nonchalance dropped from him as a mask instantly—and it was another Jimmie Dale—the professional Jimmie Dale.

Quick now in every action, he swung aside the portiere that curtained off the squat, barrel-shaped safe in the little alcove, opened the safe, took out that curious leather girdle with its kit of burglar's tools, added to it a flashlight and an automatic revolver, closed the safe—and passed into his dressing room. Here, he proceeded to divest himself rapidly of his evening clothes, selecting in their stead a suit of dark tweed. He heard Jason come up the stairs, pass along the hall, and mount the second flight to his own quarters; and presently came the sound of an automobile without. The dressing room fronted on the Drive—Jimmie Dale looked out. Benson was just getting out of the touring car. Slipping the leather girdle, then, around his waist, Jimmie Dale put on his vest, then his coat—and walked briskly downstairs.

Jason had laid out a gray ulster on the hall stand. Jimmie Dale put it on, selected a leather cap with motor-goggle attachment that pulled down almost to the tip of his nose, tucked a slouch hat into the pocket of the ulster, and, leaving the house, climbed into his car.

He glanced at his watch as he started—it was a quarter of eleven. Jimmie Dale's lips pursed a little.

"I guess it'll make a night of it, and a tight squeeze, at that, to get back under cover before daylight," he muttered. "I'll have to do some tall speeding."

But at first, across the city and through Brooklyn, for all his impatience, it was necessarily slow—after that, Jimmie Dale took chances, and, once on the country roads of Long Island, the big, powerful car tore through the night like a greyhound whose leash is slipped.

A half hour passed—Jimmie Dale's eyes shifting occasionally from the gray thread of road ahead of him under the glare of the dancing lamps, to the road map spread out at his feet, upon which, from time to time, he focused his pocket flashlight. And then, finally, he slowed the car to a snail's pace—he should be very near his destination—that very ultra-exclusive subdivision of Charleton Park Manor.

On either side of the road now was quite a thickly set stretch of wooded land, rising slightly on the right—and this Jimmie Dale scrutinised sharply. In fact, he stopped for an instant as he came opposite to a wagon track—it seemed to be little more than that—that led in through the trees.

"If it's not too far from the seat of war," commented Jimmie Dale to himself, as he went on again, "it will do admirably."

And then, a hundred yards farther on, Jimmie Dale nodded his head in satisfaction—he was passing the rather ornate stone pillars that marked the entrance to Charleton Park Manor, and on which the initial promoters of the subdivision, the real-estate people, had evidently deemed it good advertising policy to expend a small fortune.

Another hundred yards farther on, Jimmie Dale turned his car around and returned past the gates to the wagon track again. The road was deserted—not a car nor a vehicle of any description was in sight. Jimmie Dale made sure of that—and in another instant Jimmie Dale's own car, every light extinguished, had vanished—he had backed it up the wagon track, just far enough in for the trees to screen it thoroughly from the main road.

Nor did Jimmie Dale himself appear again on the main road—until just as he emerged close to the gates of Charleton Park Manor from a short cut through the woods. Also, he was without his ulster now, and the slouch hat had replaced the motor cap.

Jimmie Dale, in the moonlight, took stock of his surroundings, as he passed in at a businesslike walk through the gates. It was a large park, if that name could properly be applied to it at all, and the houses—he caught sight of one set back from the driveway on the right—were quite far apart, each in its own rather spacious grounds among the trees.

"The second house on the right," her letter had said. Jimmie Dale had already passed the first one—the next would be Markel's then—and it loomed ahead of him now, black and shadowy and unlighted.

Jimmie Dale shot a glance around him—there was stillness, quiet everywhere—no sign of life—no sound.

Jimmie Dale's face became tense, his lips tight—and he stepped suddenly from the sidewalk in among the trees. They were not thick here, of course, the trees, and the turf beneath his feet was well kept—and, therefore, soundless. He moved quickly now, but cautiously, from tree to tree, for the moonlight, flooding the lawn and house, threw all objects into bold relief.

A minute, two, three went by—and a shadow flitted here and there across the light-green sward, like the moving of the trees swaying in the breeze—and then Jimmie Dale was standing close up against one side of the house, hidden by the protecting black shadows of the walls.

But here, for a moment, Jimmie Dale seemed little occupied with the house itself—he was staring down past its length to where the woods made a heavy, dark background at the rear. Then he turned his head, to face directly to the main road, then back again slowly, as though measuring an angle. Jimmie Dale had no intention of making his escape by the roundabout way in which he had been forced to come in order to make certain of locating the right house, the second one from the gates—and he was getting the bearings of his car and the wagon track now.

"I guess that'll be about right," Jimmie Dale muttered finally. "And now for—"

He slipped along the side of the house and halted where, almost on a level with the ground, the French windows of the dining room opened on the lawn. Jimmie Dale tried them gently. They were locked.

An indulgent smile crept to Jimmie Dale's lips—and his hand crept in under his vest. It came out again—not empty—and Jimmie Dale leaned close against the window. There was a faint, almost inaudible, scratching sound, then a slight, brittle crack—and Jimmie Dale laid a neat little four-inch square of glass on the ground at his feet. Through the aperture he reached in his hand, turned the key that was in the lock, turned the bolt-rod handle, pushed the doors silently open—wide open—left them open—and stepped into the room.

He could see quite well within, thanks to the moonlight. Jimmie Dale produced a black silk mask from one of the little leather pockets, adjusted it carefully over his face, and crossed the room to the hall door. He opened this—wide open—left it open—and entered the hall.

Here it was dark—a pitch blackness. He stood for a moment, listening—utter silence. And then—alert, strained, tense in an instant, Jimmie Dale crouched against the wall—and then he smiled a little grimly. It was only someone coughing upstairs—Markel—in his sleep, perhaps, or, perhaps—in wakefulness.

"I'm a fool!" confided Jimmie Dale to himself, as he recognised the cough that he had heard at the club. "And yet—I don't know. One's nerves get sort of taut. Pretty stiff business. If I'm ever caught, the penitentiary sentence I get will be the smallest part of what's to pay."

A round button of light played along the wall from the flashlight in his hand—just for an instant—and all was blackness again. But in that instant Jimmie Dale was across the hall, and his fingers were tracing the telephone connection from the instrument to where the wires disappeared in the base-board of the floor. Another instant, and he had severed the wires with a pair of nippers.

Again the quick, firefly gleam of light to locate the stair case and the library door opposite to it—and, moving without the slightest noise, Jimmie Dale's hand was on the door itself. Again he paused to listen. All was silence now.

The door swung under his hand, and, left open behind him, he was in the room. The flashlight winked once—suspiciously. Then he snapped its little switch, keeping the current on, and the ray dodged impudently here and there all over the apartment.

The safe was set in a sort of clothes closet behind the desk, she had said. Yes, there it was—the door, at least. Jimmie Dale moved toward it—and paused as his light swept the top of the intervening desk. A mass of papers, books, and correspondence littered it untidily. The yellow sheet of a telegram caught Jimmie Dale's eye.

He picked it up and glanced at it. It read:

Vein uncovered today. Undoubtedly mother lode. Enormously rich. Put the screws on at once. *Thurl*.

Under the mask, Jimmie Dale's lips twitched.

"I think, Markel, you miserable hound," said he softly, "that God will forgive me for depriving you of a share of the profits. Two hundred and ten thousand, I think it was, you said the sparklers cost." A curious little sound came from Jimmie Dale's lips—like a chuckle.

Jimmie Dale tossed the telegram back on the desk, moved on behind the desk, opened the door of the closet that had been metamorphosed into a vault—and the white light travelled slowly, searchingly, critically over the shining black-enamelled steel, the nickelled knobs, and dials of a safe that confronted him.

Jimmie Dale nodded at it—familiarly, grimly.

"It's number one-four-three-two-one, all right," he murmured. "And one of the best we ever made. Pretty tough. But I've done it before. Say, half an hour of gentle persuasion. It would be too bad to crack it with 'soup'—besides, that's crude—Carruthers would never forgive the Gray Seal for that!"

The light went out—blackness fell. Jimmie Dale's slim, sensitive fingers closed on the dial's knob, his head touched the steel front of the safe as he pressed his ear against it for the tumblers' fall.

And then silence. It seemed to grow heavier, that silence, with each second—to palpitate through the quiet house—to grow pregnant, premonitory of dread, of fear—it seemed to throb in long undulations, and the stillness grew *loud*. A moonbeam filtered in between the edge of the drawn shade and the edge of the window. It struggled across the floor in a wavering path, strayed over the desk, and died away, shadowy and formless, against the blackness of the opened recess door, against the blackness of the great steel safe, the blackness of a huddled form crouched against it. Only now and then, in a strange, projected, wraithlike effect, the moon ray glinted timidly on the tip of a nickel dial, and, ghostlike, disclosed a human hand.

Upstairs, Markel coughed again. Then from the safe a whisper, heavy-breathed as from great exertion:

"Missed it!"

The dial whirled with faint, musical, little metallic clicks; then began to move slowly again, very, very slowly. The moonbeam, as though petulant at its own abortive attempt to satisfy its curiosity, retreated back across the floor, and faded away.

Blackness!

Time passed. Then from the safe again, but now in a low gasp, a pant of relief:

"Ah!"

The ear might barely catch the sound—it was as of metal sliding in well-oiled grooves, of metal meeting metal in a padded thud. The massive door swung outward. Jimmie Dale stood up, easing his cramped muscles, and flirted the sweat beads from his forehead.

After a moment, he knelt again. There was still the inner door—but that was a minor matter to Jimmie Dale compared with what had gone before.

Stillness once more—a long period of it. And then again that cough from above—a prolonged paroxysm of it this time that went racketing through the house.

Jimmie Dale, in the act of swinging back the inner door of the safe, paused to listen, and little furrows under his mask gathered on his forehead. The coughing stopped. Jimmie Dale waited a moment, still listening—then his flashlight bored into the interior of the safe.

"The cash box, probably," quoted Jimmie Dale, beneath his breath—and picked it up from where it lay in the bottom compartment of the safe.

The lock snipped under the insistent probe of a delicate little blued-steel instrument, and Jimmie Dale lifted the cover. There was a package of papers and documents on top, held together with elastic bands. Jimmie Dale spent a moment or two examining these, then his fingers dived down underneath, and the next minute, under the flashlight, the morocco leather case open, the diamond necklace was sparkling and flashing on its white satin bed.

"A tempting little thing, isn't it?" said Jimmie Dale gently. "It was really thoughtful of you, Markel, to buy that this afternoon!"

Jimmie Dale replaced the necklace in the cash box, set the cash box on the floor, closed the inner door of the safe, and swung the outer door a little inward—but left it flauntingly ajar. Then from a pocket of the leather girdle beneath his vest he produced his small, thin, flat, metal case. From this, from between sheets of oil paper, with the aid of a pair of tweezers, he lifted out a gray, diamond-shaped seal. Jimmie Dale was apparently fastidious. He held the seal with the tweezers as he moistened the adhesive side with his tongue, laid the seal on his handkerchief, and pressed the handkerchief firmly against the safe—as usual, Jimmie Dale's insignia bore no finger prints as it lay neatly capping the knob of the dial.

He reached down, picked up the cash box—and then, for the second time that night, held suddenly tense, alert, listening, his every muscle taut. A door opened upstairs. There came a murmur of voices. Then a momentary lull.

Jimmie Dale listened. Like a statue he stood there in the black, absolutely motionless—his head a little forward and to one side. Nothing—not a sound. Then a very low, curious, swishing noise, and a faint creak. *Somebody was coming down the stairs!*

Jimmie Dale moved stealthily from the recess, and noiselessly to the desk. Very faintly, but distinctly now, came a pad of either slippered or bare feet on the stairway carpet. Like a cat, soundless in his movements, Jimmie Dale crept toward the door of the room. Down the stairs came that pad of feet; occasionally came that swishing sound. Nearer the door crept Jimmie Dale, and his lips were thinned now, his jaws clamped. How near were they together, he and this night prowler? At times he could not hear the other at all, and, besides, the heavy carpet made the judgment of distance an impossibility. If he could gain the hall, and, in the darkness, elude the other, the way of escape through the dining room was open. And then, within a few feet of the door, Jimmie Dale halted abruptly, as a woman's voice rose querulously from the hallway above:

"You are making a perfect fool of yourself, Theodore Markel! Come back here to bed!"

Jimmie Dale's face hardened like stone—the answer came almost from the very threshold in front of him:

"I can't sleep, I tell you"—it was Markel's voice, in a disgruntled snarl. "I was a fool to bring the confounded thing home. I'm going to take the library couch for the rest of the night."

It happened quick, then—quick as the winking of an eye. Two sharp, almost simultaneous, clicks of the electric-light buttons pressed by Markel, and the hall and library were a flood of light—and Jimmie Dale leaped forward to where, in dressing gown and pajamas, blankets and bedding over one arm, a revolver dangling in the other hand, Markel stood full before the door in the hallway without.

There was a wild yell of terror and surprise from Markel, then a deafening roar and a spit of flame from his revolver—a bitter, smothered exclamation from Jimmie Dale as the cash box crashed to the floor from his left hand, and he was upon the other like a tiger.

With the impact, both men went to the floor, grappled, and rolled over and over. Half mad with fear, shock, and surprise, Markel fought like a maniac, and his voice, in gasping shouts, rang through the house.

A minute, two passed—and the men rolled about the hall floor. Markel, over middle age and unheathily fat, against Jimmie Dale's six feet of muscle—only Jimmie Dale's left hand, dripping a red stream now, was almost useless.

From above came wild confusion—women's voices in little shrieks; men's voices shouting in excitement; doors opening, running feet. And then Jimmie Dale had snatched the revolver from the floor where Markel had dropped it in the scuffle, and was pressing it against Markel's forehead—and Markel, terror-stricken, had collapsed in a flabby, pliant heap.

Jimmie Dale, still covering Markel with the weapon, stood up. The frightened faces of women protruded over the banisters above. The two men-servants, at best none too enthusiastically on the way down, stopped as though stunned as Jimmie Dale swung the revolver upon them.

Then Jimmie Dale spoke—to Markel—pointing the weapon at Markel again.

"I don't like you, Markel," he said, with cold impudence. "The only decent thing you'll ever do will be to die—and if those men of yours on the stairs move another step it will be your death warrant. Do you understand? I would suggest that you request them to stay where they are."

Cold sweat was on Markel's face as he stared into the muzzle of the revolver, and his teeth chattered.

"Go back!" he screamed hysterically at the servants. "Go back! Sit down! Don't move! Do what he tells you!"

"Thank you!" said Jimmie Dale grimly. "Now, get up yourself!"

Markel got up.

Jimmie Dale backed to the library door, picked up the cash box, tucked it under his left armpit, and faced those on the stairs.

"Mr. Markel and I are going out for a little walk," he announced coolly. "If one of you make a move or raise an alarm before your master comes back, I shall be obliged, in self-defence, to shoot—Mr. Markel. Mr. Markel quite understands that—I am sure. Do you not, Mr. Markel?"

"Helen," screamed Markel to his wife, "don't let 'em move! For God's sake, do as he says!"

Jimmie Dale's lips, just showing beneath the edge of his mask, broadened in a pleasant little smile.

"Will you lead the way, Mr. Markel?" he requested, with ironic deference. "Through the dining room, please. Yes, that's right!"

Markel walked weakly into the dining room, and Jimmie Dale followed. A prod in the back from the revolver muzzle, and Markel stepped through the

French windows and out on the lawn. Jimmie Dale faced the other toward the woods at the rear of the house.

"Go on!" Jimmie Dale's voice was curt now, uncompromising. "And step lively!"

They passed on along the side of the house and in among the trees. Fifty yards or so more, and Jimmie Dale halted. He backed Markel up against a large tree—not over gently.

"I—I say"—Markel's teeth were going like castanets. "I—"

"You'll oblige me by keeping your mouth shut," observed Jimmie Dale politely—and he whipped the cord of Markel's dressing gown loose and began to tie the man to the tree. "You have many unpleasant characteristics, Markel—your voice is one of them. Shall I repeat that I do not like you?" He stepped to the back of the tree. "Pardon me if I draw this uncomfortably tight. I don't think you can reach around to the knot. No? The trunk is too large? Quite so!" He stepped around to face Markel again—the man was thoroughly frightened, his face was livid, his jaw sagged weakly, and his eyes followed every movement of the revolver in Jimmie Dale's hand in a sort of miserable fascination. Jimmie Dale smiled unhappily. "I am going to do something, Markel, that I should advise no other man to do—I am going to put you on your honour! For the next fifteen minutes you are not to utter a sound. Do you understand?"

"Y-yes," said Markel hoarsely.

"No," said Jimmie Dale sadly, "I don' think you do. Let me be painfully explicit. If you break your vow of silence by so much as a second, then to-morrow, or the next day, or the day after, at my convenience, Markel, you and I will meet again—for the last time. There can be no possible misapprehension on your part now—Markel?"

"N-no,"—Markel could scarcely chatter out the word.

"Quite so," said Jimmie Dale, in velvet tones. He stood for an instant looking at the other with cool insolence; then: "Good-night, Markel"—and five minutes later a great touring car was tearing New Yorkward over the Long Island roads at express speed.

It was one o'clock in the morning as Jimmie Dale swung the car into a cross street off lower Broadway, and drew up at the curb beside a large office building. He got out, snuggled the cash box under his ulster, went around to the Broadway entrance, glanced up to note that a light burned in a fifth-story window, and entered the building.

The hallway was practically in darkness, one or two incandescents only threw a dim light about. Jimmie Dale stopped for a moment at the foot of the stairs, beside the elevator well, to listen—if the watchman was making rounds, it was in another part of the building Jimmie Dale began to climb.

He reached the fifth floor, turned down the corridor, and halted in front of a door, through the ground-glass panel of which a light glowed faintly—as though coming from an inner office beyond. Jimmie Dale drew the black silk mask from his pocket, adjusted it, tried the door, found it unlocked, opened it noiselessly, and stepped inside. Across the room, through another door, half open, the light streamed into the outer office, where Jimmie Dale stood.

Jimmie Dale stole across the room, crouched by the door to look into the inner office—and his face went suddenly rigid.

"Good God!" he whispered. "As bad as that!"—but it was a nonchalant Jimmie Dale to all outward appearances that, on the instant, stepped unconcernedly over the threshold.

An elderly man, white-haired, kindly-faced, kindly-eyed, save now that the face was drawn and haggard, the eyes full of weariness, was standing behind a flat-topped desk, his fingers twitching nervously on a revolver in his hand. He whirled, with a startled cry, at Jimmie Dale's entrance, and the revolver clattered from his fingers to the floor.

"I am afraid," said Jimmie Dale, smiling pleasantly, "that you were going to shoot yourself. Your name is Wilbur, Henry Wilbur, isn't it?"

Unmanned, trembling, the other stood—and nodded mechanically.

"It's really not a nice thing to do," said Jimmie Dale confidentially. "Makes a mess, you see, too"—he was pulling off his motor gauntlet, his ulster, his jacket, and, having set the cash box on the desk, was rolling back his sleeve as he spoke. "Had a little experience myself this evening." He held out his hand that, with the forearm, was covered with blood. "A little above the wrist—fortunately only a flesh wound—a little memento from a chap named Markel, and—"

"Markel!" The word burst, quivering, from the other's lips.

"Yes," said Jimmie Dale imperturbably. "Do you mind if I wash a bit— and could you oblige me with a towel, or something that would do for a bandage?"

The man seemed dazed. In a subconscious way, he walked from the desk to a little cupboard, and took out two towels.

Jimmie Dale stooped, while the other's back was turned, picked up the revolver from the floor, and slipped it into his trousers pocket.

"Markel?" said Wilbur again, the same trembling anxiety in his voice, as he handed Jimmie Dale the towels and motioned toward a washstand in the corner of the room. "Did you say Markel—Theodore Markel?"

"Yes," said Jimmie Dale, examining his wound critically.

"You had trouble—a fight with him? Is he—he—dead?"

"No," said Jimmie Dale, smiling a little grimly. "He's pretty badly hurt, though, I imagine—but not in a physical way."

"Strange!" whispered Wilbur, in a numbed tone to himself; and he went back and sank down in his desk chair. "Strange that you should speak of Markel—strange that you should have come here tonight!"

Jimmie Dale did not answer. He glanced now and then at the other, as he deftly dressed his wrist—the man seemed on the verge of collapse, on the verge of a nervous breakdown. Jimmie Dale swore softly to himself. Wilbur was too old a man to be called upon to stand against the trouble and anxiety that was mirrored in the misery in his face, that had brought him to the point of taking his own life.

Jimmie Dale put on his coat again, walked over to the desk, and picked up the phone.

"If I may?" he inquired courteously—and confided a number to the mouthpiece of the instrument.

There was a moment's wait, during which Wilbur, in a desperate sort of way, seemed to be trying to rally himself, to piece together a puzzle, as it were; and for the first time he appeared to take a personal interest in the masked figure that leaned against his desk. He kept passing his hands across his eyes, staring at Jimmie Dale.

Then Jimmie Dale spoke—into the phone.

"*Morning News-Argus* office? Mr. Carruthers, please. Thank you."

Another wait—then Jimmie Dale's voice changed its pitch and register to a pleasant and natural, though quite unrecognisable bass.

"Mr. Carruthers? Yes. I thought it might interest you to know that Mr. Theodore Markel purchased a very valuable diamond necklace this afternoon.... Oh, you knew that, did you? Well, so much the better; you'll be all the more keenly interested to know that it is no longer in his possession.... I beg pardon? Oh, yes, I quite forgot—this is the Gray Seal speaking.... Yes.... The Gray Seal.... I have just come from Mr. Markel's country house, and if you hurry a man out there you ought to be able to give the public an exclusive bit of news, a scoop, I believe you call it—you see, Mr. Carruthers, I am not ungrateful for, I might say, the eulogistic manner in which the *Morning News-Argus* treated me in that last affair, and I trust I shall be able to do you many more favours—I am deeply in your debt. And, oh, yes, tell your reporter not to overlook the detail of Mr. Markel in his pajamas and dressing gown tied to a tree in his park—Mr. Markel might be inclined to be reticent on that point, and it would be a pity to deprive the public of any—er—'atmosphere' in the story, you know.... What?... No; I am afraid Mr. Markel's phone is—er—out of order.... Yes.... And, by the way, speaking of phones, Mr. Carruthers, between gentlemen, I know you will make no effort under the circumstances to discover the number I am calling from. Good-night, Mr. Carruthers." Jimmie Dale hung the receiver abruptly on the hook.

"You see," said Jimmie Dale, turning to Wilbur—and then he stopped. The man was on his feet, swaying there, his face positively gray.

"My God!" Wilbur burst out. "What have you done? A thousand times better if I had shot myself, as I would have done in another moment if you had not come in. I was only ruined then—I am disgraced now. You have robbed Markel's safe—I am the one man in the world who would have a reason above all others for doing that—and Markel knows it. He will accuse me of it. He can prove I had a motive. I have not been home tonight. Nobody knows I am here. I cannot prove an alibi. What have you done!"

"Really," said Jimmie Dale, almost plaintively, swinging himself up on the corner of the desk and taking the cash box on his knee, "really, you are alarming yourself unnecessarily. I—"

But Wilbur stopped him. "You don't know what you are talking about!" Wilbur cried out, in a choked way; then, his voice steadying, he rushed on: "Listen! I am a ruined man, absolutely ruined. And Markel has ruined me—I did not see through his trick until too late. Listen! For years, as a mining engineer, I made a good salary—and I saved it. Two years ago I had nearly seventy thousand dollars—it represented my life work. I bought an abandoned mine in Alaska for next to nothing—I was certain it was rich. A man by the name of Thurl, Jason T. Thurl, another mining engineer, a steamer acquaintance, was out there at the time—he was a partner of Markel's, though I didn't know it then. I started to work the mine. It didn't pan out. I dropped nearly every cent. Then I struck a small vein that temporarily recouped me, and supplied the necessary funds with which to go ahead for a while. Thurl, who had tried to buy the mine out from under my option in the first place, repeatedly then tried to buy it from me at a ridiculous figure. I refused. He persisted. I refused—I was confident, I *knew* I had one of the richest properties in Alaska."

Wilbur paused. A little row of glistening drops had gathered on his forehead. Jimmie Dale, balancing Markel's cash box on one knee, drummed softly with his finger tips on the cover.

"The vein petered out," Wilbur went on. "But I was still confident. I sank all the proceeds of the first strike—and sank them fast, for unaccountable accidents that crippled me both financially and in the progress of the work began to happen." Wilbur flung out his hands impotently. "Oh, it's a long story—too long to tell. Thurl was at the bottom of those accidents. He knew as well as I did that the mine was rich—better than I did, for that matter, for we discovered before we ran him out of Alaska that he had made secret borings on the property. But what I did not know until a few hours ago was that he had actually uncovered what we uncovered only yesterday—the mother lode. He was driving me as fast as he could into the last ditch—for Markel. I didn't know until yesterday that Markel had any thing to do with it. I struggled on out there, hoping every day to open a new vein. I raised money on everything I had, except my insurance and the mine—and sank it in the mine. No one out there would advance me anything on a property that looked like a failure, that had once already been abandoned. I have always kept an office here, and I came back East with the idea of raising something on my insurance. Markel, quite by haphazard as I then thought, was introduced to me just before we left San Francisco on our way to New York. On the run across the continent we became very friendly. Naturally, I told him my story. He played sympathetic good fellow, and offered to lend me fifty thousand dollars on a demand note. I did not want to be involved for a cent more than was necessary, and, as I said, I hoped from day to day to make another strike. I refused to take more than ten thousand. I remember now that he seemed strangely disappointed."

Again Wilbur stopped. He swept the moisture from his forehead—and his fist, clenched, came down upon the desk.

"You see the game!"—there was bitter anger in his voice now. "You see the game! He wanted to get me in deep enough so that I couldn't wriggle out, deeper than ten thousand that I could get at any time on my insurance, he wanted me where I couldn't get away—and he got me. The first ten thousand wasn't enough. I went to him for a second, a third, a fourth, a fifth—hoping always that each would be the last. Each time a new note, a demand note for the total amount, was made, cancelling the former one. I didn't know his game, didn't suspect it—I blessed God for giving me such a friend—until this, or, rather, yesterday afternoon, when I received a telegram from my manager at the mine saying that he had struck what looked like a very rich vein—the mother lode. And"—Wilbur's fist curled until the knuckles were like ivory in their whiteness—"he added in the telegram that Thurl had wired the news of the strike to a man in New York by the name of Markel. Do you see? I hadn't had the telegram five minutes, when a messenger brought me a letter from Markel curtly informing me that I would have to meet my note tomorrow morning. I can't meet it. He knew I couldn't. With wealth in sight—I'm wiped out. A *demand* note, a call loan, do you understand—and with a few months in which to develop the new vein I could pay it readily. As it is—I default the note—Markel attaches all I have left, which is the mine. The mine is sold to satisfy my indebtedness. Markel buys it in legally, upheld by the law—and acquires, *robs* me of it, and—"

"And so," said Jimmie Dale musingly, "you were going to shoot yourself?"

Wilbur straightened up, and there was something akin to pathetic grandeur in the set of the old shoulders as they squared back.

"Yes!" he said, in a low voice. "And shall I tell you why? Even if, which is not likely, there was something reverting to me over the purchase price, it would be a paltry thing compared with the mine. I have a wife and children. If I have worked for them all my life, could I stand back now at the last and see them robbed of their inheritance by a black-hearted scoundrel when I could still lift a hand to prevent it! I had one way left. What is my life? I am too old a man to cling to it where they are concerned. I have referred to my insurance several times. I have always carried heavy insurance"—he smiled a little curious, mirthless smile—"*that has no suicide clause.*" He swept his hand over the desk, indicating the papers scattered there. "I have worked late tonight getting my affairs in order. My total insurance is fifty-two thousand dollars, though I couldn't *borrow* anywhere near the full amount on it—but at my death, paid in full, it would satisfy the note. My executors, by instruction would pay the note—and no dollar from the mine, no single grain of gold, not an ounce of quartz, would Markel ever get his hands on, and my wife and children would be saved. That is—"

His words ended abruptly—with a little gasp. Jimmie Dale had opened the cash box and was dangling the necklace under the light—a stream of fiery, flashing, sparkling gems.

Then Wilbur spoke again, a hard, bitter note in his voice, pointing his hand at the necklace.

"But now, on top of everything, you have brought me disgrace—because you broke into his safe tonight for *that*? He would and will accuse me. I have heard of you—the Gray Seal—you have done a pitiful night's work in your greed for that thing there."

"For this?" Jimmie Dale smiled ironically, holding the necklace up. Then he shook his head. "I didn't break into Markel's safe for this—it wouldn't have been worth while. It's only paste."

"Paste!" exclaimed Wilbur, in a slow way.

"Paste," said Jimmie Dale placidly, dropping the necklace back into its case. "Quite in keeping with Markel, isn't it—to make a sensation on the cheap?"

"But that doesn't change matters!" Wilbur cried out sharply, after a numbed instant's pause. "You still broke into the safe, even if you didn't know then that the necklace was paste."

"Ah, but, you see—I did know then," said Jimmie Dale softly. "I am really—you must take my word for it—a very good judge of stones, and I had—er—seen these before."

Wilbur stared—bewildered, confused.

"Then why—what was it that—"

"A paper," said Jimmie Dale, with a little chuckle—and produced it from the cash box. "It reads like this: 'On demand, I promise to pay—'"

"My note!" It came in a great, surging cry from Wilbur; and he strained forward to read it.

"Of course," said Jimmie Dale. "Of course—your note. Did you think that I had just happened to drop in on you? Now, then, see here, you just buck up, and—er—smile. There isn't even a possibility of you being accused of the theft. In the first place, Markel saw quite enough of me to know that it wasn't you. Secondly, neither Markel nor anyone else would ever dream that the break was made for anything else but the necklace, with which you have no connection—the papers were in the cash box and were just taken along with it. Don't you see? And, besides, the police, with my very good friend,

Carruthers at their elbows, will see very thoroughly to it that the Gray Seal gets full and ample credit for the crime. But"—Jimmie Dale pulled out his watch, and yawned under his mask—"it's getting to be an unconscionable hour—and you've still a letter to write."

"A letter?" Wilbur's voice was broken, his lips quivering.

"To Markel," said Jimmie Dale pleasantly. "Write him in reply to his letter of the afternoon, and post it before you leave here—just as though you had written it at once, promptly, on receipt of his. He will still get it on the morning delivery. State that you will take up the note immediately on presentation at whatever bank he chooses to name. That's all. Seeing that he hasn't got it, he can't very well present it—can he? Eventually, having—er—no use for fake diamonds, I shall return the necklace, together with the papers in his cash box here—including your note."

"Eventually?" Uncomprehendingly, stumblingly, Wilbur repeated the word.

"In a month or two or three, as the case may be," explained Jimmie Dale brightly. "Whenever you insert a personal in the *News-Argus* to the effect that the mother lode has given you the cash to meet it." He replaced the note in the cash box, slipped down to his feet from the desk—and then he choked a little. Wilbur, the tears streaming down his face, unable to speak, was holding out his hands to Jimmie Dale. "I—er—good-night!" said Jimmie Dale hurriedly—and stepped quickly from the room.

Halfway down the first flight of stairs he paused. Steps, running after him, sounded along the corridor above; and then Wilbur's voice.

"Don't go—not yet," cried the old man. "I don't understand. How did you know—who told you about the note?"

Jimmie Dale did not answer—he went on noiselessly down the stairs. His mask was off now, and his lips curved into a strange little smile.

"I wish I knew," said Jimmie Dale wistfully to himself.

CHAPTER 4

THE COUNTERFEIT FIVE

It was still early in the evening, but a little after nine o'clock. The Fifth Avenue bus wended its way, jouncing its patrons, particularly those on the top seats, across town, and turned into Riverside Drive. A short distance behind the bus, a limousine rolled down the cross street leisurely, silently.

As the lights of passing craft on the Hudson and a myriad scintillating, luminous points dotting the west shore came into view, Jimmie Dale rose impulsively from his seat on the top of the bus, descended the little circular iron ladder at the rear, and dropped off into the street. It was only a few blocks farther to his residence on the Drive, and the night was well worth the walk; besides, restless, disturbed, and perplexed in mind, the walk appealed to him.

He stepped across to the sidewalk and proceeded slowly along. A month had gone by and he had not heard a word from—*her*. The break on West Broadway, the murder of Metzer in Moriarty's gambling hell, the theft of Markel's diamond necklace had followed each other in quick succession— and then this month of utter silence, with no sign of her, as though indeed she had never existed.

But it was not this temporary silence on her part that troubled Jimmie Dale now. In the years that he had worked with this unknown, mysterious accomplice of his whom he had never seen, there had been longer intervals than a bare month in which he had heard nothing from her—it was not that. It was the failure, total, absolute, and complete, that was the only result for the month of ceaseless, unremitting, doggedly-expended effort, even as it had been the result many times before, in an attempt to solve the enigma that was so intimate and vital a factor in his own life.

If he might lay any claims to cleverness, his resourcefulness, at least, he was forced to admit, was no match for hers. She came, she went without being seen—and behind her remained, instead of clues to her identity, only an amazing, intangible mystery, that left him at times appalled and dismayed. How did she know about those conditions in West Broadway, how did she know about Metzer's murder, how did she know about Markel and Wilbur— how did she know about a hundred other affairs of the same sort that had happened since that night, years ago now, when out of pure adventure he had tampered with Marx's, the jeweller's strong room in Maiden Lane, and she had, mysteriously then, too, solved *his* identity, discovered him to be the Gray Seal?

Jimmie Dale, wrapped up in his own thoughts, entirely oblivious to his surroundings, traversed another block. There had never been since the world began, and there would never be again, so singular and bizarre a partner- ship as this—of hers and his. He, Jimmie Dale, with his strange double life, one of New York's young bachelor millionaires, one whose social status was unquestioned; and she, who—who *what*? That was just it! Who what? What was she? What was her name? What one personal, intimate thing did he know about her? And what was to be the end? Not that he would have severed his association with her—not for worlds!—though every time, that, by some new and curious method, one of her letters found its way into his hands, out- lining some fresh coup for him to execute, his peril and danger of discovery was increased in staggering ratio. Today, the police hunted the Gray Seal as they hunted a mad dog; the papers stormed and raved against him: in every detective bureau of two continents he was catalogued as the most notorious criminal of the age—and yet, strange paradox, no single crime had ever been committed!

Jimmie Dale's strong, fine-featured face lighted up. Crime! Thanks to her, there were those who blessed the name of the Gray Seal, those into whose lives had come joy, relief from misery, escape from death even—and their blessings were worth a thousandfold the risk and peril of disaster that threatened him at every minute of the day.

"Thank God for her!" murmured Jimmie Dale softly. "But—but if I could only find her, see her, know who she is, talk to her, and hear her voice!" Then he smiled a little wanly. "It's been a pretty tough month—and nothing to show for it!"

It had! It had been one of the hardest months through which Jimmie Dale had ever lived. The St. James, that most exclusive club, his favourite haunt, had seen nothing of him; the easel in his den, that was his hobby, had been untouched; there had been days even when he had not crossed the threshold of his home. Every resource at his command he had called into play in an effort to solve the mystery. For nearly the entire month, following first this lead and then that, he had lived in the one disguise that he felt confident she knew nothing of—that was, or, rather, had become, almost a dual personality with him. From the Sanctuary, that miserable and disreputable room in a tenement on the East Side, a tenement that had three separate means of entrance and exit, he had emerged day after day as Larry the Bat, a character as well known and as well liked in the exclusive circles of the underworld as was Jimmie Dale in the most exclusive strata of New York's society and fashion. And it had been useless—all useless. Through his own endeavours, through the help of his friends of the underworld, the lives of half a dozen men, Bert Hagan's on West Broadway, for instance, Markel's, and others', had been laid bare to the last shred, but nowhere could be found the one vital point that linked their lives with hers, that would account for her intimate knowledge of them, and so furnish him with the clue that would then with certainty lead him to a solution of her identity.

It was baffling, puzzling, unbelievable, bordering, indeed, on the miraculous—herself, everything about her, her acts, her methods, her cleverness, intangible in one sense, were terrifically real in another. Jimmie Dale shook his head. The miraculous and this practical, everyday life were wide and far apart. There was nothing miraculous about it—it was only that the key to it was, so far, beyond his reach.

And then suddenly Jimmie Dale shrugged his shoulders in consonance with a whimsical change in both mood and thought.

"Larry the Bat, is a hard taskmaster!" he muttered facetiously. "I'm afraid I'm not very presentable this evening—no bath this morning, and no shave, and, after nearly a month of make-up, that beastly grease paint gets into the skin creases in a most intimate way." He chuckled as the thought of old Jason, his butler, came to him. "I saw Jason, torn between two conflicting emotions, shaking his head over the black circles under my eyes last night—

he didn't know whether to worry over the first signs of a galloping decline, or break his heart at witnessing the young master he had dandled on his knees going to the damnation bowwows and turning into a confirmed roue! I guess I'll have to mind myself, though. Even Carruthers detached his mind far enough from his editorial desk and the hope of exclusively publishing the news of the Gray Seal's capture in the *Morning News-Argus,* to tell me I was looking seedy. It's wonderful the way a little paint will metamorphose a man! Well, anyway, here's for a good hot tub tonight, and a fresh start!"

He quickened his pace. There were still three blocks to go, and here was no hurrying, jostling crowd to impede his progress; indeed, as far as he could see up the Drive, there was not a pedestrian in sight. And then, as he walked, involuntarily, insistently, his mind harked back into the old groove again.

"I've tried to picture her," said Jimmie Dale softly to himself. "I've tried to picture her a hundred, yes, a thousand times, and—"

A bus, rumbling cityward, went by him, squeaking, creaking, and rattling in its uneasy joints—and out of the noise, almost at his elbow it seemed, a voice spoke his name—and in that instant intuitively he *knew*, and it thrilled him, stopped the beat of his heart, as, dulcet, soft, clear as the note of a silver bell it fell—and only one word:

"Jimmie!"

He whirled around. A limousine, wheels just grazing the curb, was gliding slowly and silently past him, and from the window a woman's arm, white-gloved and dainty, was extended, and from the fingers to the pavement fluttered an envelope—and the car leaped forward.

For the fraction of a second, Jimmie Dale stood dazed, immovable, a gamut of emotions, surprise, fierce exultation, amazement, a strange joy, a mighty uplift, swirling upon him—and then, snatching up the envelope from the ground, he sprang out into the road after the car. It was the one chance he had ever had, the one chance she had ever given him, and he had seen—a white-gloved arm! He could not reach the car, it was speeding away from him like an arrow now, but there was something else that would do just as well, something that with all her cleverness she had overlooked—the car's number dangling on the rear axle, the rays of the little lamp playing on the enamelled surface of the plate! Gasping, panting, he held his own for a yard or more, and there floated back to him a little silvery laugh from the body of the limousine, and then Jimmie Dale laughed, too, and stopped—it was No. 15,836!

He stood and watched the car disappear up the Drive. What delicious irony! A month of gruelling, ceaseless toil that had been vain, futile, useless—and the key, when he was not looking for it, unexpectedly, through no effort of his, was thrust into his hand—No. 15,836!

Jimmie Dale, the gently ironic smile still on his lips, those slim, super-sensitive fingers of his subconsciously noting that the texture of the envelope was the same as she always used, retraced his steps to the sidewalk.

"Number fifteen thousand eight hundred and thirty-six," said Jimmie Dale aloud—and halted at the curb as though rooted to the spot. It sounded strangely familiar, that number! He repeated it over again slowly: "One-five-eight-three-six." And the smile left his lips, and upon his face came the look of a chastened child. She had used a duplicate plate! Fifteen thousand eight hundred and thirty-six was the number of one of his own cars—his own particular runabout!

For a moment longer he stood there, undecided whether to laugh or swear, and then his eyes fastened mechanically on the envelope he was twirling in his fingers. Here, at least, was something that was not elusive; that, on the contrary, as a hundred others in the past had done, outlined probably a grim night's work ahead for the Gray Seal! And, if it were as those others had been, every minute from the moment of its receipt was precious time. He stepped under the nearest street light, and tore the envelope open.

"Dear Philanthropic Crook," it began—and then followed two closely written pages. Jimmie Dale read them, his lips growing gradually tighter, a smouldering light creeping into his dark eyes, and once he emitted a short, low whistle of consternation—that was at the end, as he read the post-script that was heavily underscored: "Work quickly. They will raid tonight. Be careful. Look out for Kline, he is the sharpest man in the United States secret service."

For a brief instant longer, Jimmie Dale stood under the street lamp, his mind in a lightning-quick way cataloguing every point in her letter, viewing every point from a myriad angles, constructing, devising, mapping out a plan to dove-tail into them—and then Jimmie Dale swung on a downtown bus. There was neither time nor occasion to go home now—that marvellous little kit of burglar's tools that peeped from their tiny pockets in that curious leather undervest, and that reposed now in the safe in his den, would be useless to him tonight; besides, in the breast pocket of his coat, neatly folded, was a black silk mask, and, relics of his role of Larry the Bat, an automatic revolver, an electric flashlight, a steel jimmy, and a bunch of skeleton keys, were distributed among the other pockets of his smart tweed suit.

Jimmie Dale changed from the bus to the subway, leaving behind him, strewn over many blocks, the tiny and minute fragments into which he had torn her letter; at Astor Place he left the subway, walked to Broadway, turned uptown for a block to Eighth Street, then along Eighth Street almost to Sixth Avenue—and stopped.

A rather shabby shop, a pitiful sort of a place, displaying in its window a heterogeneous conglomeration of cheap odds and ends, ink bottles, candy, pencils, cigarettes, pens, toys, writing pads, marbles, and a multitude of other small wares, confronted him. Within, a little, old, sweet-faced, gray-haired woman stood behind the counter, pottering over the rearrangement of some articles on the shelves.

"My word!" said Jimmie Dale softly to himself. "You wouldn't believe it, would you! And I've always wondered how these little stores managed to make both ends meet. Think of that old soul making fifteen or twenty thousand dollars from a layout like this—even if it has taken her a lifetime!"

Jimmie Dale had halted nonchalantly and unconcernedly by the curb, not too near the window, busied apparently in an effort to light a refractory cigarette; and then, about to enter the store, he gazed aimlessly across the street for a moment instead. A man came briskly around the corner from Sixth Avenue, opened the store door, and went in.

Jimmie Dale drew back a little, and turned his head again as the door closed—and a sudden, quick, alert, and startled look spread over his face.

The man who had entered bent over the counter and spoke to the old lady. She seemed to listen with a dawning terror creeping over her features, and then her hands went piteously to the thin hair behind her ears. The man motioned toward a door at the rear of the store. She hesitated, then came out from behind the counter, and swayed a little as though her limbs would not support her weight.

Jimmie Dale's lips thinned.

"I'm afraid," he muttered slowly, "I'm afraid that I'm too late even now." And then, as she came to the door and turned the key on the inside: "Pray Heaven she doesn't turn the light out—or somebody might think I was trying to break in!"

But in that respect Jimmie Dale's fears were groundless. She did not turn out either of the gas jets that lighted the little shop; instead, in a faltering, reluctant sort of manner, she led the way directly through the door in the rear, and the man followed her.

The shop was empty—and Jimmie Dale was standing against the door on the outside. His position was perfectly natural—a hundred passers-by would have noted nothing but a most commonplace occurrence—a man in the act of entering a store. And, if he appeared to fumble and have trouble with the latch, what of it! Jimmie Dale, however, was not fumbling—hidden by his back that was turned to the street, those wonderful fingers of his, in whose tips seemed embodied and concentrated every one of the human senses, were working quickly, surely, accurately, without so much as the wasted movement of a single muscle.

A faint tinkle—and the key within fell from the lock to the floor. A faint click—and the bolt of the lock slipped back. Jimmie Dale restored the skeleton keys and a little steel instrument that accompanied them to his pocket— and quietly opened the door. He stepped inside, picked up the key from the floor, inserted it in the lock, closed the door behind him, and locked it again.

"To guard against interruption," observed Jimmie Dale, a little quizzically.

He was, perhaps, thirty seconds behind the others. He crossed the shop noiselessly, cautiously, and passed through the door at the rear. It opened into a short passage that, after a few feet, gave on a sort of corridor at right angles—and down this latter, facing him, at the end, the door of a lighted room was open, and he could see the figure of the man who had entered the shop, back turned, standing on the threshold. Voices, indistinct, came to him.

The corridor itself was dark; and Jimmie Dale, satisfied that he was fairly safe from observation, stole softly forward. He passed two doors on his left—and the curious arrangement of the building that had puzzled him for a moment became clear. The store made the front of an old tenement building, with apartments above, and the rear of the store was a sort of apartment, too—the old lady's living quarters.

Step by step, testing each one against a possible creaking of the floor, Jimmie Dale moved forward, keeping close up against one wall. The man passed on into the room—and now Jimmie Dale could distinguish every word that was being spoken; and, crouched up, in the dark corridor, in the angle of the wall and the door jamb itself, could see plainly enough into the room beyond. Jimmie Dale's jaw crept out a little.

A young man, gaunt, pale, wrapped in blankets, half sat, half reclined in an invalid's chair; the old lady, on her knees, the tears streaming down her face, had her arms around the sick man's neck; while the other man, apparently upset at the scene, tugged vigorously at long, gray mustaches.

"Sammy! Sammy!" sobbed the woman piteously. "Say you didn't do it, Sammy—say you didn't do it!"

"Look here, Mrs. Matthews," said the man with the gray mustaches gently, "now don't you go to making things any harder. I've got to do my duty just the same, and take your son."

The young man, a hectic flush beginning to burn on his cheeks, gazed wildly from one to the other.

"What—what is it?" he cried out.

The man threw back his coat and displayed a badge on his vest.

"I'm Kline of the secret service," he said gravely. "I'm sorry, Sammy, but I want you for that little job in Washington at the bureau—before you left on sick leave!"

Sammy Matthews struggled away from his mother's arms, pulled himself forward in his chair—and his tongue licked dry lips.

"What—what job?" he whispered thickly.

"You know, don't you?" the other answered steadily. He took a large, flat pocketbook from his pocket, opened it, and took out a five-dollar bill. He held this before the sick man's eyes, but just out of reach, one finger silently indicating the lower left-hand corner.

Matthews stared at it for a moment, and the hectic flush faded to a grayish pallor, and a strange, impotent sound gurgled in his throat.

"I see you recognise it," said the other quietly. "It's open and shut, Sammy. That little imperfection in the plate's got you, my boy."

"Sammy! Sammy!" sobbed the woman again. "Sammy, say you didn't do it!"

"It's a lie!" said Matthews hoarsely. "It's a lie! That plate was condemned in the bureau for that imperfection—condemned and destroyed."

"Condemned *to be* destroyed," corrected the other, without raising his voice. "There's a little difference there, Sammy—about twenty years' difference—in the Federal pen. But it wasn't destroyed; this note was printed from it by one of the slickest gangs of counterfeiters in the United States—but I don't need to tell you that, I guess you know who they are. I've been after them a long time, and I've got them now, just as tight as I've got you. Instead of destroying that plate, you stole it, and disposed of it to the gang. How much did they give you?"

Matthews' face seemed to hold a dumb horror, and his fingers picked at the arms of the chair. His mother had moved from beside him now, and both her hands were patting at the man's sleeve in a pitiful way, while again and again she tried to speak, but no words would come.

"It's a lie!" said Matthews again, in a colourless, mechanical way.

The man glanced at Mrs. Matthews as he put the five-dollar note back into his pocket, seemed to choke a little, shook his head, and all trace of the official sternness that had crept into his voice disappeared.

"It's no good," he said in a low tone. "Don't do that, Mrs. Matthews, I've got to do my duty." He leaned a little toward the chair. "It's dead to rights, Sammy. You might as well make a clean breast of it. It was up to you and Al Gregor to see that the plate was destroyed. It *wasn't* destroyed; instead, it shows up in the hands of a gang of counterfeiters that I've been watching for months. Furthermore, I've got the plate itself. And finally, though I haven't placed him under arrest yet for fear you might hear of it before I wanted you to and make a get-away, I've got Al Gregor where I can put my hands on him, and I've got his confession that you and he worked the game between you to get that plate out of the bureau and dispose of it to the gang."

"Oh, my God!"—it came in a wild cry from the sick man, and in a desperate, lurching way he struggled up to his feet. "Al Gregor said that? Then— then I'm done!" He clutched at his temples. "But it's not true—it's not true! If the plate was stolen, and it must have been stolen, or that note wouldn't have been found, it was Al Gregor who stole it—I didn't, I tell you! I knew nothing of it, except that he and I were responsible for it and—and I left it to him—that's the only way I'm to blame. He's caught, and he's trying to get out of it with a light sentence by pretending to turn State's evidence, but— but I'll fight him—he can't prove it—it's only his word against mine, and—"

The other shook his head again.

"It's no good, Sammy," he said, a touch of sternness back in his tones again. "I told you it was open and shut. It's not only Al Gregor. One of the gang got weak knees when I got him where I wanted him the other night, and he swears that you are the one who delivered the plate to them. Between him and Gregor and what I know myself, I've got evidence enough for any jury against every one of the rest of you."

Horror, fear, helplessness seemed to mingle in the sick man's staring eyes, and he swayed unsteadily upon his feet.

"I'm innocent!" he screamed out. "But I'm caught, I'm caught in a net, and I can't get out—they lied to you—but no one will believe it any more than you do and—and it means twenty years for me—oh, God!—twenty years, and—" His hands went wriggling to his temples again, and he toppled back in a faint into the chair.

"You've killed him! You've killed my boy!" the old lady shrieked out piteously, and flung herself toward the senseless figure.

The man jumped for the table across the room, on which was a row of bottles, snatched one up, drew the cork, smelled it, and ran back with the bottle. He poured a little of the contents into his cupped hand, held it under young Matthews' nostrils, and pushed the bottle into Mrs. Matthews' hands.

"Bathe his forehead with this, Mrs. Matthews," he directed reassuringly. "He'll be all right again in a moment. There, see—he's coming around now."

There was a long, fluttering sigh, and Matthews opened his eyes; then a moment's silence; and then he spoke, with an effort, with long pauses between the words:

"Am—I—to—go—now?"

The words seemed to ring absolute terror in the old lady's ears. She turned, and dropped to her knees on the floor.

"Mr. Kline, Mr. Kline," she sobbed out, "oh, for God's love, don't take him! Let him off, let him go! He's my boy—all I've got! You've got a mother, haven't you? You know—" The tears were streaming down the sweet, old face again. "Oh, won't you, for God's dear name, won't you let him go? Won't—"

"Stop!" the man cried huskily. He was mopping at his face with his handkerchief. "I thought I was case-hardened, I ought to be—but I guess I'm not. But I've got to do my duty. You're only making it worse for Sammy there, as well as me."

Her arms were around his knees now, clinging there.

"Why can't you let him off!" she pleaded hysterically. "Why can't you! Why can't you! Nobody would know, and I'd do anything—I'd pay anything—anything—I'll give you ten—fifteen thousand dollars!"

"My poor woman," he said kindly, placing his hand on her head, "you are talking wildly. Apart altogether from the question of duty, even if I succeeded in hushing the matter up, I would probably at least be suspected and certainly discharged, and I have a family to support—and if I were caught I'd get ten years in the Federal prison for it. I'm sorry for this; I believe it's your boy's first offence, and if I could let him off I would."

"But you can—you can!" she burst out, rocking on her knees, clinging tighter still to him, as though in a paroxysm of fear that he might somehow elude her. "It will kill him—it will kill my boy. And you can save him! And even if they discharged you, what would that mean against my boy's life! You wouldn't suffer, your family wouldn't suffer, I'll—I'll take care of that—perhaps I could raise a little more than fifteen thousand—but, oh, have pity, have mercy—don't take him away!"

The man stared at her a moment, stared at the white face on the reclining chair—and passed his hand heavily across his eyes.

"You will! You will!" It came in a great surging cry of joy from the old lady. "You will—oh, thank God, thank God!—I can see it in your face!"

"I—I guess I'm soft," he said huskily, and stooped and raised Mrs. Matthews to her feet. "Don't cry any more. It'll be all right—it'll be all right. I'll—I'll fix it up somehow. I haven't made any arrests yet, and—well, I'll take my chances. I'll get the plate and turn it over to you tomorrow, only—only it's got to be destroyed in my presence."

"Yes, yes!" she cried, trying to smile through her tears—and then she flung her arms around her son's neck again. "And when you come tomorrow, I'll be ready with the money to do my share, too, and—"

But Sammy Matthews shook his head.

"You're wrong, both of you," he said weakly. "You're a white man, Kline. But destroying that plate won't save me. The minute a single note printed from it shows up, they'll know back there in Washington that the plate was stolen, and—"

"No; you're safe enough there," the other interposed heavily. "Knowing what was up, you don't think I'd give the gang a chance to get them into circulation, do you? I got them all when I got the plate. And"—he smiled a little anxiously—"I'll bring them here to be destroyed with the plate. It would finish me now, as well as you, if one of them ever showed up. Say," he said suddenly, with a catch in his breath, "I—I don't think I know what I'm doing."

Mrs. Matthews reached out her hands to him.

"What can I say to you!" she said brokenly, "What—"

Jimmie Dale drew back along the wall. A little way from the door he quickened his pace, still moving, however, with extreme caution. They were still talking behind him as he turned from the corridor into the passageway leading to the store, and from there into the store itself. And then suddenly, in spite of caution, his foot slipped on the bare floor. It was not much—just enough to cause his other foot, poised tentatively in air, to come heavily down, and a loud and complaining creak echoed from the floor.

Jimmie Dale's jaws snapped like a steel trap. From down the corridor came a sudden, excited exclamation in the little old lady's voice, and then her steps sounded running toward the store. In the fraction of a second Jimmie Dale was at the front door.

"Clumsy, blundering fool!" he whispered fiercely to himself as he turned the key, opened the door noiselessly until it was just ajar, and turned the key in the lock again, leaving the bolt protruding out. One step backward, and he was rapping on the counter with his knuckles. "Isn't anybody here?" he called out loudly. "Isn't any—oh!"—as Mrs. Matthews appeared in the back doorway. "A package of cigarettes, please."

She stared at him, a little frightened, her eyes red and swollen with recent crying.

"How—how did you get in here?" she asked tremendously.

"I beg your pardon?" inquired Jimmie Dale, in polite surprise.

"I—I locked the door—I'm sure I did," she said, more to herself than to Jimmie Dale, and hurried across the floor to the door as she spoke.

Jimmie Dale, still politely curious, turned to watch her. For a moment bewilderment and a puzzled look were in her face—and then a sort of surprised relief.

"I must have turned the key in the lock without shutting the door tight," she explained, "for I knew I turned the key."

Jimmie Dale bent forward to examine the lock—and nodded.

"Yes," he agreed, with a smile. "I should say so." Then, gravely courteous: "I'm sorry to have intruded."

"It is nothing," she answered; and, evidently anxious to be rid of him, moved quickly around behind the counter. "What kind of cigarettes do you want?"

"Egyptians—any kind," said Jimmie Dale, laying a bill on the counter.

He pocketed the cigarettes and his change, and turned to the door.

"Good-evening," he said pleasantly—and went out.

Jimmie Dale smiled a little curiously, a little tolerantly. As he started along the street, he heard the door of the little shop close with a sort of super-careful bang, the key turned, and the latch rattle to try the door—the little old lady was bent on making no mistake a second time!

And then the smile left Jimmie Dale's lips, his face grew strained and serious, and he broke into a run down the block to Sixth Avenue. Here he paused for an instant—there was the elevated, the surface cars—which would be the quicker? He looked up the avenue. There was no train coming; the nearest surface car was blocks away. He bit his lips in vexation—and then with a jump he was across the street and hailing a passing taxicab that his eyes had just lighted on.

"Got a fare?" called Jimmie Dale.

"No, sir," answered the chauffeur, bumping his car to an abrupt halt.

"Good!" Jimmie Dale ran alongside, and yanked the door open. "Do you know where the Palace Saloon on the Bowery is?"

"Yes, sir," replied the man.

Jimmie Dale held a ten-dollar bank note up before the chauffeur's eyes.

"Earn that in four minutes, then," he snapped—and sprang into the cab.

The taxicab swerved around on little better than two wheels, started on a mad dash down the Avenue—and Jimmie Dale braced himself grimly in his seat. The cab swerved again, tore across Waverly Place, circuited Washington Square, crossed Broadway, and whirled finally into the upper end of the Bowery.

Jimmie Dale spoke once—to himself—plaintively.

"It's too bad I can't let old Carruthers in on this for a scoop with his precious *Morning News-Argus*—but if I get out of it alive myself, I'll do well! Wonder if the day'll ever come when he finds out that his very dear friend and old college pal, Jimmie Dale, is the Gray Seal that he's turned himself inside out for about four years now to catch, and that he'd trade his soul with the devil any time to lay hands on! Good old Carruthers! 'The most puzzling, bewildering, delightful crook in the annals of crime'—am I?"

The cab drew up at the curb. Jimmie Dale sprang out, shoved the bill into the chauffeur's hand, stepped quickly across the sidewalk, and pushed his way through the swinging doors of the Palace Saloon. Inside leisurely and nonchalantly, he walked down past the length of the bar to a door at the rear. This opened into a passageway that led to the side entrance of the saloon on the cross street. Jimmie Dale emerged from the side entrance, crossed the street, retraced his steps to the Bowery, crossed over, and walked rapidly down that thoroughfare for two blocks. Here he turned east into the cross street; and here, once more, his pace became leisurely and unhurried.

"It's a strange coincidence, though possibly a very happy one," said Jimmie Dale, as he walked along, "that it should be on the same street as the Sanctuary—ah, this ought to be the place!"

An alleyway, corresponding to the one that flanked the tenement where, as Larry the Bat, he had paid room rent as a tenant for several years, in fact, the alleyway next above it, and but a short block away, intersected the street, narrow, black, and uninviting. Jimmie Dale, as he passed, peered down its length.

"No light—that's good!" commented Jimmie Dale to himself. Then: "Window opens on alleyway ten feet from ground—shoe store, Russian Jew, in basement—go in front door—straight hallway—room at end—Russian Jew probably accomplice—be careful that he does not hear you moving overhead"—Jimmie Dale's mind, with that curious faculty of his, was subconsciously repeating snatches from her letter word for word, even as he noted the dimly lighted, untidy, and disorderly interior of what, from strings of leather slippers that decorated the cellarlike entrance, was evidently a cheap and shoddy shoe store in the basement of the building.

The building itself was rickety and tumble-down, three stories high, and given over undoubtedly to gregarious foreigners of the poorer class, a rabbit burrow, as it were, having a multitude of roomers and lodgers. There was nothing ominous or even secretive about it—up the short flight of steps to the entrance, even the door hung carelessly half open.

Jimmie Dale's slouch hat was pulled a little farther down over his eyes as he mounted the steps and entered the hallway. He listened a moment. A sort of subdued, querulous hubbub seemed to hum through the place, as voices, men's, women's, and children's, echoing out from their various rooms above, mingled together, and floated down the stairways in a discordant medley. Jimmie Dale stepped lightly down the length of the hall—and listened again; this time intently, with his ear to the keyhole of the door that made the end of the passage. There was not a sound from within. He tried the door, smiled a little as he reached for his keys, worked over the lock—and straightened up suddenly as his ear caught a descending step on the stairs. It was two flights up, however—and the door was unlocked now. Jimmie Dale opened it, and, like a shadow, slipped inside; and, as he locked the door behind him, smiled once more—the door lock was but a paltry makeshift at best, but *inside* his fingers had touched a massive steel bolt that, when shot home, would yield when the door itself yielded—and not before. Without moving the bolt, he turned—and his flashlight for a moment swept the room.

"Not much like the way they describe this sort of place in storybooks!" murmured Jimmie Dale capriciously. "But I get the idea. Mr. Russian Jew downstairs makes a bluff at using it for a storeroom."

Again the flashlight made a circuit. Here, there, and everywhere, seemingly without any attempt at order, were piles of wooden shipping cases. Only the centre of the room was clear and empty; that, and a vacant space against the wall by the window.

Jimmie Dale, moving without sound, went to the window. There was a shade on it, and it was pulled down. He reached up underneath it, felt for the window fastening, and unlocked it; then cautiously tested the window itself by lifting it an inch or two—it slid easily in its grooves.

He stood then for a moment, hardfaced, a frown gathering his forehead into heavy furrows, as the flashlight's ray again and again darted hither and thither. There was nothing, absolutely nothing in the room but wooden packing cases. He lifted the cover of the one nearest to him and looked inside. It was quite empty, except for some pieces of heavy cord, and a few cardboard shoe boxes that, in turn, were empty, too.

"It's here, of course," said Jimmie Dale thoughtfully to himself. "Clever work, too! But I can't move half a hundred packing cases without that chap below hearing me; and I can't do it in ten minutes, either, which, I imagine is the outside limit of time. Fortunately, though, these cases are not without their compensation—a dozen men could hide here."

He began to move about the room. And now he stooped before one pile of boxes and then another, curiously attempting to lift up the entire pile from the bottom. Some he could not move; others, by exerting all his strength, gave a little; and then, finally, over in one corner, he found a pile that appeared to answer his purpose.

"These are certainly empty," he muttered.

There was just room to squeeze through between them and the next stack of cases alongside; but, once through, by the simple expedient of moving the cases out a little to take advantage of the angle made by the corner of the room, he obtained ample space to stand comfortably upright against the wall. But Jimmie Dale was not satisfied yet. Could he see out into the room? He experimented with his flashlight—and carefully shifted the screen of cases before him a little to one side. And yet still he was not satisfied. With a sort of ironical droop at the corners of his lips, as though suddenly there had flashed upon him the inspiration that fathered one of those whimsical ideas and fancies that were so essentially a characteristic of Jimmie Dale, he came out from behind the cases, went across the room to the case he had opened when he first entered, took out the cord and the cover of one of the cardboard shoe boxes, and with these returned to his hiding place once more.

The sounds from the upper stories of the tenement now reached him hardly at all; but from below, directly under his feet almost, he could hear someone, the proprietor of the shoe store probably, walking about.

Tense, every faculty now on the alert, his head turned in a strained, attentive attitude, Jimmie Dale threw on the flashlight's tiny switch, took that intimate and thin metal case from his pocket, extracted a diamond-shaped, gray paper seal with the little tweezers, moistened the adhesive side, and stuck it in the centre of the white cardboard-box cover, then tore the edges of the cardboard down until the whole was just small enough to slip into his pocket. Through the cardboard he looped a piece of cord, placard fashion, and with his pencil printed the four words—"with the compliments of"—above the gray seal. He surveyed the result with a grim, mirthless chuckle—and put the piece of cardboard in his pocket.

"I'm taking the longest chances I ever took in my life," said Jimmie Dale very seriously to himself, as his fingers twisted, and doubled, and tied the remaining pieces of cord together, and finally fashioned a running noose in one end. "I don't—" The cord and the flashlight went into his pocket, the room was in darkness, the black mask was whipped from his breast pocket and adjusted to his face, and his automatic was in his hand.

Came the creak of a footstep, as though on a ladder exactly below him, another, and another, receding curiously in its direction, yet at the same time growing louder in sound as if nearer the floor—then a crack of light showed in the floor in the centre of the room. This held for an instant, then expanded suddenly into a great luminous square—and through a trapdoor, opened wide now, a man's head appeared.

Jimmie Dale's eyes, fixed through the space between the piles of cases, narrowed—there was, indeed, little doubt but that the shoe-store proprietor below was an accomplice! The store served a most convenient purpose in every respect—as a secret means of entry into the room, as a sort of guarantee of innocence for the room itself. Why not! To the superficial observer, to the man who might by some chance blunder into the room—it was but an adjunct of the store itself!

The man in the trap-doorway paused with his shoulders above the floor, looked around, listened, then drew himself up, walked across the floor, and shot the heavy bolt on the door that led into the hallway of the house. He returned then to the trapdoor, bent over it, and whistled softly. Two more men, in answer to the summons, came up into the room.

"The Cap'll be along in a minute," one of them said. "Turn on the light."

A switch clicked, flooding the room with sudden brilliancy from half a dozen electric bulbs.

"Too many!" grunted the same voice again. "We ain't working tonight—turn out half of 'em."

The sudden transition from the darkness for a moment dazzled Jimmie Dale's eyes—but the next moment he was searching the faces of the three men. There were few crooks, few denizens of the crime world below the now obsolete but still famous dead line that, as Larry the Bat, he did not know at least by sight.

"Moulton, Whitie Burns, and Marty Dean," confided Jimmie Dale softly to himself. "And I don't know of any worse, except—the Cap. And gun fighters, every one of them, too—nice odds, to say nothing of—"

"Here's the Cap now!" announced one of the three. "Hello, Cap, where'd you raise the mustache?"

Jimmie Dale's eyes shifted to the trapdoor, and into them crept a contemptuous and sardonic smile—the man who was coming up now and hoisting himself to the floor was the man who, half an hour before, had threatened young Sammy Matthews with arrest.

The Cap, alias Bert Malone, alias a score of other names, closed the trapdoor after him, pulled off his mustache and gray wig, tucked them in his pocket, and faced his companions brusquely.

"Never mind about the mustache," he said curtly. "Get busy, the lot of you. Stir around and get the works out!"

"What for?" inquired Whitie Burns, a sharp, ferret-faced little man. "We got enough of the old stuff on hand now, and that bum break Gregor made when he pinched the cracked plate put the finish on that. Say, Cap—"

"Close your face, Whitie, and get the works out!" Malone cut in shortly. "We've only got the whole night ahead of us—but we'll need it all. We're going to run the queer off that cracked plate."

One of the others, Marty Dean this time, a certain brutal aggressiveness in both features and physique, edged forward.

"Say, what's the lay?" he demanded. "A joke? We printed one fiver off that plate—and then we knew enough to quit. With that crack along the corner, you couldn't pass 'em on a blind man! And Gregor saying he thought we could patch the plate up enough to get by with gives me a pain—he's got jingles in his dome factory! Run them fivers eh—say, are you cracked, too?"

"Aw, forget it!" observed Malone caustically. "Who's running this gang?" Then, with a malicious grin: "I got a customer for those fivers—fifteen thousand dollars for all we can turn out tonight. See?"

The others stared at him for a moment, incredulity and greed mingling in a curious half-hesitant, half-expectant look on their faces.

Then Whitie Burns spoke, circling his lips with the tip of his tongue:

"D'ye mean it, Cap—honest? What's the lay? How'd you work it?"

Malone, unbending with the sensation he had created, grinned again.

"Easy enough," he said offhandedly. "It was like falling off a log. Gregor said, didn't he, that the only way he had been able to get his claws on that plate was on account of young Matthews going away sick—eh? Well, the old Matthews woman, his mother, has got money—about fifteen thousand. I guess she ain't got any more than that, or I'd have raised the ante. Aw, it was easy. She threw it at me. I framed one up on them, that's all. I'm Kline, of the secret service—see? I don't suppose they'd ever seen him, though they'd know his name fast enough, but I made up something like him. I showed them where I had a case against Sammy for pinching the plate that was strong enough to put a hundred innocent men behind the bars. Of course, he knew well enough he was innocent, but he could see the twenty years I showed him with both eyes. Say, he mussed all over the place, and went and fainted like a girl. And then the old woman came across with an offer of fifteen thousand for the plate, and corrupted me." Malone's cunning, vicious face, now that the softening effects of the gray hair and mustache were gone, seemed accentuated diabolically by the grin broadening into a laugh, as he guffawed.

Marty Dean's hand swung with a bang to Malone's shoulder.

"Say, Cap—say, you're all right!" he exclaimed excitedly. "You're the boy! But what's the good of running anything off the plate before turning it over to 'em. The stuff's no good to us."

"You got a wooden nut, with sawdust for brains," said Malone sarcastically. "If he'd thought the gang of counterfeiters that was supposed to have bought the plate from him had run off only one fiver and then stopped because they say it wouldn't get by, and weren't going to run any more, and just destroy the plate like it was supposed to have been destroyed to begin with, and it all end up with no one the wiser, where d'ye think we'd have banked that fifteen thousand! I told him I had the whole run confiscated, and that the queer went with the plate, so we'll just make that little run tonight—that's why I sent word around to you this morning."

"By the jumping!" ejaculated Whitie Burns, heavy with admiration. "You got a head on you, Cap!"

"It's a good thing for some of you that I have," returned Malone complacently. "But don't stand jawing all night. Go on, now—get busy!"

There was no surprise in Jimmie Dale's face—he had chosen his position behind a pile of cases that he had been extremely careful, as a man is careful when his life hangs in the balance, to assure himself were empty. None of the four came near or touched the pile behind which he stood; but, here and there about the room, they pulled this one and that one out from various stacks. In scarcely more than a moment, the room was completely transformed. It was no longer a storeroom for surplus stock, for the storage of bulky and empty packing cases! From the cases the men had picked out, like a touch of magic, appeared a veritable printing plant, an elaborate engraver's outfit—a highly efficient foot-power press, rapidly being assembled by Whitie Burns; an electric dryer, inks, a pile of white, silk-threaded bank-note paper, a cutter, and a score of other appurtenances.

"Yes," said Jimmie Dale very gently to himself. "Yes, quite so—but the plate? Ah!" Malone was taking it out from the middle of a bundle of old newspapers, loosely tied together, that he had lifted from one of the cases.

Jimmie Dale's eyes fastened on it—and from that instant never left it. A minute passed, two, three of them—the four men were silently busy about the room—Malone was carefully cleaning the plate.

"They will raid tonight. Look out for Kline, he is the sharpest man in the United State secret service"—the warning in her letter was running through Jimmie Dale's mind. Kline—the real Kline—was going to raid the place tonight. When? At what time? It must be nearly eleven o'clock already, and—

It came sudden, quick as the crack of doom—a terrific crash against the bolted door—but the door, undoubtedly to the surprise of those without, held fast, thanks to the bolt. The four men, white-faced, seemed for an instant turned to statues. Came another crash against the door—and a sharp, imperative order to those within to open it and surrender.

"We're pinched! Beat it!" whispered Whitie Burns wildly—and dashed for the trapdoor.

Like a rat for its hole, Marty Dean followed. Malone, farther away, dropped the plate on the floor, and rushed, with Moulton beside him, after the others—but he never reached the trapdoor.

Over the crashing blows, raining now in quick succession on the door of the room, over a startled commotion as lodgers, roomers, and tenants on the floor above awoke into frightened activity with shouts and cries, came the louder crash of a pile of packing boxes hurled to the floor. And over them, vaulting those scattered in his way, Jimmie Dale sprang at Malone. The man reeled back, with a cry. Moulton dashed through the trapdoor and disappeared. The short, ugly barrel of Jimmie Dale's automatic was between Malone's eyes.

"You make a move," said Jimmie Dale, in a low sibilant way, "and I'll drop you where you stand! Put your hands behind your back—palms together!"

Malone, dazed, cowed, obeyed. A panel of the door split and rent down its length—the hinges were sagging. Jimmie Dale worked like lightning. The cord with the slip noose from his pocket went around Malone's wrists, jerked tight, and knotted; the placard, his lips grim, with no sign of humour, Jimmie Dale dangled around the man's neck.

"An introduction for you to Mr. Kline out there—that you seem so fond of!" gritted Jimmie Dale. Then, working as he talked: "I've got no time to tell you what I think of you, you pitiful hound"—he snatched up the plate from the floor and put it in his pocket—"Twenty years, I think you said, didn't you?"—his hand shot into Malone's pocket-book, and extracted the five-dollar note—"If you can open this with your toes maybe you can get a way"—he wrenched the trapdoor over and slammed it shut—"good-night, Malone"—and he leaped for the window.

The door tottered inward from the top, ripping, tearing, smashing hinges, panels, and jamb. Jimmie Dale got a blurred vision of brass buttons, blue coats, and helmets, and, in the forefront, of a stocky, gray-mustached, gray-haired man in plain clothes.

Jimmie Dale threw up the window, swung out, as with a rush the officers burst through into the room and a revolver bullet hummed viciously past his ear, and dropped to the ground—into encircling arms!

"Ah, no, you don't, my bucko!" snapped a hoarse voice in his ear. "Keep quiet now, or I'll crack your bean—understand!"

But the officer, too heavy to be muscular, was no match for Jimmie Dale, who, even as he had dropped from the sill, had caught sight of the lurking form below; and now, with a quick, sudden, lithe movement he wriggled loose, his fist from a short-arm jab smashed upon the point of the other's jaw, sending the man staggering backward—and Jimmie Dale ran.

A crowd was already collecting at the mouth of the alleyway, mostly occupants of the house itself, and into these, scattering them in all directions, eluding dexterously another officer who made a grab for him, Jimmie Dale charged at top speed, burst through, and headed down the street, running like a deer.

Yells went up, a revolver spat venomously behind him, came the shrill *cheep-cheep!* of the police whistle, and heavy boots pounding the pavement in pursuit.

Down the block Jimmie Dale raced. The yells augmented in his rear. Another shot—and this time he heard the bullet buzz. And then he swerved—into the next alleyway—that flanked the Sanctuary.

He had perhaps a ten yards' lead, just a little more than the distance from the street to the side door of the Sanctuary that opened on the alleyway. And, as he ran now, his fingers tore at his clothing, loosening his tie, unbuttoning coat, vest, collar, shirt, and undershirt. He leaped at the door, swung it open, flung himself inside—and then sacrificing speed to silence, went up the stairs like a cat, cramming his mask now into his pocket.

His room was on the first landing. In an instant he had unlocked the door, entered, and locked it again behind him. From outside, an excited street urchin's voice shrilled up to him:

"He went in that door! I seen him!"

The police whistle chirped again; and then an authoritative voice:

"Get around and watch the saloon back of this, Heeney—there's a way out through there from this joint."

Jimmie Dale, divested of every stitch of clothing that he had worn, pulled a disreputable collarless flannel shirt over his head, pulled on a dirty and patched pair of trousers, and slipped into a threadbare and filthy coat. Jimmie Dale was working against seconds. They were at the lower door now. He lifted the oilcloth in the corner of the room, lifted up the loose piece of the flooring, shoved his discarded garments inside, and from a little box that was there smeared the hollow of his hand with some black substance, possessed himself of two little articles, replaced the flooring, replaced the oilcloth, and, in bare feet, stole across the room to the door. Against the door, without a sound, Jimmie Dale placed a chair, and on the chair seat he laid the two little articles he had been carrying in his hand. It was intensely black in the room, but Jimmie Dale needed no light here. From under the bed he pulled out a pair of woolen socks and a pair of congress boots, both as disreputable as the rest of his attire, put them on—and very quietly, softly, cautiously, stretched himself out on the bed.

The officers were at the top of the stairs. A voice barked out:

"Stand guard on this landing, Peters. Higgins, you take the one above. We'll start from the top of the house and work down. Allow no one to pass you."

"Yes, sir! Very good, Mr. Kline," was the response.

Kline!—the sharpest man in the United States secret service, she had said. Jimmie Dale's lips set.

"I'm glad I had no shave this morning," said Jimmie Dale grimly to himself.

His fingers were working with the black substance in the hollow of his hand—and the long, slim, tapering fingers, the shapely, well-cared-for hands grew unkempt and grimy, black beneath the finger nails—and a little, too, played its part on the day's growth of beard, a little around the throat and at the nape of the neck, a little across the forehead to meet the locks of straggling and disordered hair. Jimmie Dale wiped the residue from the hollow of his hand on the knee of his trousers—and lay still.

An officer paced outside. Upstairs doors opened and closed. Gruff, harsh tones in commands echoed through the house. The search party descended to the second floor—and again the same sounds were repeated. And then, thumping down the creaking stairs, they stopped before Jimmie Dale's room. someone tried the door, and, finding it locked, rattled it violently.

"Open the door!" It was Kline's voice.

Jimmie Dale's eyes were closed, and he was breathing regularly, though just a little slower than in natural respiration.

"Break it down!" ordered Kline tersely.

There was a rush at it—and it gave. It surged inward, knocked against the chair, upset the latter, something tinkled to the floor—and four officers, with Kline at their head, jumped into the room.

Jimmie Dale never moved. A flashlight played around the room and focused upon him—and then he was shaken roughly—only to fall inertly back on the bed again.

"I guess this is all right, Mr. Kline," said one of the officers. "It's Larry the Bat, and he's doped to the eyes. There's the stuff on the floor we knocked off the chair."

"Light the gas!" directed Kline curtly; and, being obeyed, stooped to the floor and picked up a hypodermic syringe and a small bottle. He held the bottle to the light, and read the label: *liquor morphinae*. "Shake him again!" he commanded.

None too gently, a policeman caught Jimmie Dale by the shoulder and shook him vigorously—again Jimmie Dale, once the other let go his hold, fell back limply on the bed, breathing in that same, slightly slowed way.

"Larry the Bat, eh?" grunted Kline; then, to the officer who had volunteered the information: "Who's Larry the Bat? What is he? And how long have you known him?"

"I don't know who he is any more than what you can see there for yourself," replied the officer. "He's a dope fiend, and I guess a pretty tough case, though we've never had him up for anything. He's lived here ever since I've been on the beat, and that's three years or—"

"All right!" interrupted Kline crisply. "He's no good to us! You say there's an exit from this house into that saloon at the back?"

"Yes, sir but the fellow, whoever he is, couldn't get away from there. Heeney's been over on guard from the start."

"Then he's still inside there," said Kline, clipping off his words. "We'll search the saloon. Nice night's work this is! One out of the whole gang—and that one with the compliments of the Gray Seal!"

The men went out and began to descend the stairs.

"One," said Jimmie Dale to himself, still motionless, still breathing in that slow way so characteristic of the drug. "Two. Three. Four."

The minutes went by—a quarter of an hour—a half hour. Still Jimmie Dale lay there—still motionless—still breathing with slow regularity. His muscles began to cramp, to give him exquisite torture. Around him all was silence—only distant sounds from the street reached him, muffled, and at intervals. Another quarter of an hour passed—an eternity of torment. It seemed to Jimmie Dale, for all his will power, that he could not hold himself in check, that he must move, scream out even in the torture that was passing all endurance. It was silent now, utterly silent—and then out of the silence, just outside his door, a footstep creaked—and a man walked to the stairs and went down.

"Five," said Jimmie Dale to himself. "The sharpest man in the United States secret service."

And then for the first time Jimmie Dale moved—to wipe away the beads of sweat that had sprung out upon his forehead.

CHAPTER 5
THE AFFAIR OF THE PUSHCART MAN

Larry the Bat shambled out of the side door of the tenement into the back alleyway; shambled along the black alleyway to the street—and smiled a little grimly as a shadow across the roadway suddenly shifted its position. The game was growing acute, critical, desperate even—and it was his move.

Larry the Bat, disreputable denizen of the underworld, alias Jimmie Dale, millionaires' clubman, alias the Gray Seal, whom Carruthers of the *Morning News-Argus* called the master criminal of the age, shuffled along in the direction of the Bowery, his hands plunged deep in the pockets of his frayed and tattered trousers, where his fingers, in a curious, wistful way, fondled the keys of his own magnificent residence on Riverside Drive. It was his move—and it was an impasse, ironical, sardonic, and it was worse—it was full of peril.

True, he had outwitted Kline of the secret service two nights before, when Kline had raided the counterfeiters' den; true, he had no reason to believe that Kline suspected *him* specifically, but the man Kline wanted *had* entered the tenement that night, and since then the house had been shadowed day and night. The result was both simple and disastrous—to Jimmie Dale. Larry the Bat, a known inmate of the house, might come and go as he pleased—but to emerge from the Sanctuary in the person of Jimmie Dale would be fatal. Kline had been outwitted, but Kline had not acknowledged final defeat. The tenement had been searched from top to bottom—unostentatiously. His own room on the first landing had been searched the previous afternoon, when he was out, but they had failed to find the cunningly contrived opening in the floor under the oilcloth in the corner, an impromptu wardrobe, that would proclaim Larry the Bat and Jimmie Dale to be one and the same person—that would inevitably lead further to the establishment of his identity as the Gray Seal. In time, of course, the surveillance would cease—but he could not wait. That was the monumental irony of it—the factor that, all unknown to Kline, was forcing the issue hard now. It was his move.

Since, years ago now, as the Gray Seal, he had begun to work with *her*, that unknown, mysterious accomplice of his, and the police, stung to madness both by the virulent and constant attacks of the press and by the humiliating prod of their own failures, sought daily, high and low, with every resource at their command, for the Gray Seal, he had never been in quite so strange and perilous a plight as he found himself at that moment. To preserve inviolate the identity of Larry the Bat was absolutely vital to his safety. It was the one secret that even she, who so strangely appeared to know all else about him, he was sure, had not discovered—and it was just that, in a way, that had brought the present impossible situation to pass.

In the month previous, in a lull between those letters of hers, he had set himself doggedly and determinedly to the renewed task of what had become so dominantly now a part of his very existence—the solving of *her* identity. And for that month, as the best means to the end—means, however, that only resulted as futilely as the attempts that had gone before—he had lived mostly as Larry the Bat, returning to his home in his proper person only when occasion and necessity demanded it. He had been going home that evening, two nights before, walking along Riverside Drive, when from the window of the limousine she had dropped the letter at his feet that had plunged him into the affair of the Counterfeit Five—and he had not gone home! Eventually, to save himself, he had, in the Sanctuary, performing the transformation in desperate haste, again been forced to assume the role of Larry the Bat.

That was really the gist of it. And yesterday morning he had remembered, to his dismay, that he had had little or no money left the night before. He had intended, of course, to replenish his supply—when he got home. Only he hadn't gone home! And now he needed money—needed it badly, desperately. With thousands in the bank, with abundance even in his safe, in his own den at home, a supply kept there always for an emergency, he was facing actual want—he rattled two dimes, a nickel, and a few odd pennies thoughtfully against the keys in his pocket.

To a certain extent, old Jason, his butler, could be trusted. Jason even knew that mysterious letters of tremendous secretive importance came to the house, and the old man always meant well—but he dared not trust even Jason with the secret of his dual personality. What was he to do? He needed money imperatively—at once. Thanks to Kline, for the time being, at least, he could not rid himself of the personality of Larry the Bat by the simple expedient or slipping into the clothes of Jimmie Dale—he must live, act, and remain Larry the Bat until the secret service officer gave up the hunt. How bridge the gulf between Jimmie Dale and Larry the Bat in old Jason's eyes!

Nor was that all. There was still another matter, and one that, in order to counteract it, demanded at once a serious inroad—to the extent of a telephone call—upon his slender capital. A too prolonged and unaccounted-for absence from home, and old Jason, in his anxious, blundering solicitude, would have the fat in the fire at that end—and the city, and the social firmament thereof, would be humming with the startling news of the disappearance of a well-known millionaire. The complications that would then ensue, with himself powerless to lift a finger, Jimmie Dale did not care to think about—such a contretemps must at all hazards be prevented.

Jimmie Dale reached the corner of the street, where it intersected the Bowery, and paused languidly by the curb. No one appeared to be following. He had not expected that there would be—but it was as well to be sure. He walked then a few steps along the Bowery—and slipped suddenly into a doorway, from where he could command a view of the street corner that he had just left. At the end of ten minutes, satisfied that no one had any concern in his immediate movements, he shambled on again down the Bowery.

There was a saloon two blocks away that boasted a private telephone booth. Jimmie Dale made that his destination.

Larry the Bat was a very well-known character in that resort, and the bullet-headed dispenser of drinks behind the bar nodded unctuously to him over the heads of those clustered at the rail as he entered; Larry the Bat, as befitted one of the elite of the underworld, was graciously pleased to acknowledge the proletariat salutation with a curt nod. He walked down to the end of the room, entered the telephone booth—and was carelessly careful to close the door tightly behind him.

He gave the number of his residence on Riverside Drive, and waited for the connection. After some delay, Jason's voice answered him.

"Jason," said Jimmie Dale, in matter-of-fact tones, "I shall be out of the city for another three or four days, possibly a week, and—" he stopped abruptly, as a sort of gasp came to him over the wire.

"Thank God that's you, sir!" exclaimed the old butler wildly. "I've been near mad, sir, all day!"

"Don't get excited, Jason!" said Jimmie Dale a little sharply. "The mere matter of my absence for the last two days is nothing to cause you any concern. And while I am on the subject, Jason, let me say now that I shall be glad if you will bear that fact in mind in future."

"Yes, sir," stammered Jason. "But, sir, it ain't that—good Lord, Master Jim, it ain't that, sir! It's—it's one of them letters."

Something like a galvanic shock seemed to jerk the disreputable, loose-jointed frame of Larry the Bat suddenly erect—and a strained whiteness crept over the dirty, unwashed face.

"Go on, Jason," said Jimmie Dale, without a quiver in his voice.

"It came this morning, sir—that shuffer with his automobile left it. I had just time to say you weren't at home, sir, and he was gone. And then, sir, there ain't been an hour gone by all through the day that a woman, sir—a lady, begging your pardon, Master Jim—hasn't rung up on the telephone, asking if you were back, and if I could get you, and where you were, and half frantic, sir, half sobbing, sometimes, sir, and saying there was a life hanging on it, Master Jim."

Larry the Bat, staring into the mouthpiece of the instrument, subconsciously passed his hand across his forehead, and subconsciously noted that his fingers, as he drew them away, were damp.

"Where is the letter now, Jason?" inquired Jimmie Dale coolly.

"Here on your desk, Master Jim. Shall I bring it to you?"

Bring it to him! How? When? Where? Bring it to him! The ghastly irony of it! Jimmie Dale tried to think—prodding, spurring desperately that keen, lightning brain of his that had never failed him yet. How bridge the gulf between Larry the Bat and Jimmie Dale in Jason's eyes—not just for the replenishing of funds now, but with a life at stake!

"No—I think not, Jason," said Jimmie Dale calmly. "Just leave it where it is. And if she telephones again, say that you have told me—that will be sufficient to satisfy any further inquiries. And Jason—"

"Yes, sir?"

"If she telephones again, try and find out where the call comes from."

"I haven't forgotten what you said once, Master Jim, sir," said the old man eagerly. "And I've been trying that sir, all day. They've all come from different pay stations, sir."

A mirthless little smile tinged Jimmie Dale's lips. Of course! He might have known! It was always that way, always the same. He was as near to the solution of her identity at that moment as he had been years ago, when she, in some mysterious way, alone of all the world, had identified him as the Gray Seal!

"Very good, Jason," he said quietly. "Don't bother about it any more. It will be all right. You can expect me when you see me. Good-night." He hung the receiver on the hook, walked out of the booth, and mechanically reached the street.

All right! It was far from "all right"—very far from it. It was no trivial thing, that letter; they never had been trivial things, those letters of hers, that involved so often a matter of life and death—as this one now, perhaps, as her actions would seem to indicate, involved life and death more urgently than any that had gone before. It was far from all right—at a moment when his own position, his own safety, was at best but a desperate chance; when his every energy, brain, wit, and cunning were taxed to the utmost to save himself! And yet, somehow, some way, at any cost, he must get that letter—and at any cost he must act upon it! To fail her was to fail utterly in everything that failure in its most miserable, its widest sense, implied—failure in that which rose paramount to every other consideration in life!

Fail her! Jimmie Dale's lips thinned into a hard, drawn line—and then parted slowly in a curiously whimsical smile. It would be a strange burglary that he had decided upon, in order that he might not fail her—stranger than any the Gray Seal had ever committed, and, in some respects, even more perilous!

He started along the Bowery, walking briskly now, toward the nearest subway station, at Astor Place, his mind for the moment electing to face the situation in a humour as whimsical as his smile. Supposing that, as Larry the Bat, he were caught and arrested during the next hour, in Jimmie's Dale's residence on Riverside Drive! With his arrest as Larry the Bat, Jimmie's Dale would automatically disappear. Would follow then the suspicion that Jimmie Dale, the millionaire, had met with foul play, and as time went on, and Jimmie Dale, being then in prison as Larry the Bat, did not reappear, the assurance of it; then the certainty that suspicion would focus on Larry the Bat as being connected with the millionaire's death, since Larry the Bat had been caught in Jimmie Dale's home—and he would be accused of his own murder! It was quite humourous, of course, quite grotesquely bizarre—but it was equally an exceedingly grim possibility! There were drawbacks to a dual personality!

"In a word," confided Jimmie Dale softly to himself, and a serious light crept into the dark, steady eyes, "I'm in a bit of a nasty mess!"

At Astor Place he entered the subway; at Fourteenth Street he changed to an express, and at Ninety-sixth Street he got out. It was but a short walk west to Riverside Drive, and from there his house was only a few blocks farther on.

Jimmie Dale did not slouch now. And for all his disreputable attire, incongruous as it was in that neighbourhood, few people that he passed paid any attention to him, none gave him more than a casual glance—Jimmie Dale swung along, upright, with no attempt to make himself inconspicuous, hurrying a little, as one intent upon a definite errand. As he neared his house he slowed his pace a little until a couple, who were passing in front of it, had gone on; then he went up the steps, but noiselessly as a shadow now, to the front door, opened it softly, closed it softly behind him, and crouched for a moment in the vestibule.

Through the monogrammed lace on the plate glass of the inner doors he could see, a little indistinctly, into the reception hall beyond. The hall was empty. Jason, for that matter, would be the only one likely to be about; the other servants would have no business there in any case, and whether in their quarters above or below, they had their own stairs at the rear.

Jimmie Dale inserted the key in the spring lock, and opened the door a cautious fraction of an inch—to listen. There was no sound—yes, a subdued murmured—the servants were downstairs in the basement. He slipped inside, slipped, in a flash, across the hall, and, treading like a cat, went up the stairs. He scarcely seemed to breathe until, with a little sigh of relief, he stood inside his den on the first floor, with the door shut behind him.

"I must speak to Jason about being a little more watchful," muttered Jimmie Dale facetiously. "Here's all my property at the mercy of—Larry the Bat!"

An instant he stood by the door, looking about him—in the bright moonlight streaming in through the side windows the room's appointments stood out in soft shadows, the huge davenport, the great, luxurious easy-chairs, an easel with a half-finished canvas, as he had left it; the big, flat-topped, rosewood desk, the open fireplace—and then, his steps silent on the thick velvet rug under foot, he walked quickly to the desk.

Yes, there it was—the letter. He placed it hurriedly in his pocket—the moonlight was not strong enough to read by, and he dared not turn on the lights.

And now money—funds. In the alcove behind the portiere, Jimmie Dale dropped on his knees before the squat, barrel-shaped safe, and opened it. He reached inside, took out a package of banknotes, placed the bills in his pocket—and hesitated a moment. What else would he require? What act did that letter call upon the Gray Seal to perform in the next few hours? Jimmie Dale stared thoughtfully into the interior of the safe. Whatever it was, it must be performed in the role of Larry the Bat, for though he could get into his dressing room now, and become Jimmie Dale again, there were still those watchers outside the Sanctuary—*they* must not become suspicious—and if Larry the Bat disappeared mysteriously, Larry the Bat would be the man that Kline and the secret service of the United States would never cease hunting for, and that would mean that he could never reassume a character that was as necessary for his protection as breath was to life, so long as the Gray Seal worked. True, he could change now to Jimmie Dale, but he would have to change back again and return to the Sanctuary before morning, as Larry the Bat—and remain there until Kline, beaten, called off his human bloodhounds. No, a change was not to be thought of.

What, then, would he require—that compact little kit of burglar tools, rolled in its leather jacket, that, unrolled slipped about his body like a close-fitting undervest? As well to take it anyway. He removed his coat and vest, took out the leather bundle from the safe, untied the thongs that bound it together, unrolled it, passed it around his body, life belt fashion, secured the thongs over his shoulders, and put on his coat and vest again. A revolver, a flashlight? He had both—at the Sanctuary, under the flooring—but there were duplicates here! He slipped them into his pockets. Anything else—to forestall and provide for any possible contingency? He hesitated again for a moment, thinking, then slowly closed the inner door of the safe, locked it, swung the outer door shut—and, in the act of twirling the knobs, sprang suddenly to his feet. Sharp, shrill in the stillness of the room, the telephone bell on the desk rang out clamourously.

Jimmie Dale's face set hard, as he leaped out from behind the curtain—had Jason heard it! It rang again before he could reach the desk—was ringing as he snatched the receiver from the hook.

"Yes, yes!" he called, in a low, guarded, hasty way, into the mouthpiece. "Hello! What is it?" And then one hand, resting on the desk, closed around the edge, and tightened until the skin over the knuckles grew ivory white. It was—*she*! She! It was *her* voice—he had only heard it once in all his life—that night, two nights before, in a silvery laugh from the limousine as it had sped away from him down the road—but he knew! It thrilled him now with a mad rhapsody, robbing him for the moment of every thought save that she was living, real, existent—that it was *her* voice. "It's you—*you*!" he said hoarsely.

"Oh, Jimmie—you at last!"—it came in a little gasping cry of relief. "The letter—"

"Yes, I've got it—it's all right—it's all right"—the words would not seem to come fast enough in his desperate haste. "But it's you now. Listen! Listen!" he pleaded. "Tell me who you are! My God! How I've tried to find you, and—"

That rippling, silvery laugh again, but now, too, it seemed to his eager ear, with just the faintest note of wistfulness in it.

"Some day, Jimmie. That letter now. It—"

Jimmie Dale straightened up suddenly—Jason's steps, running, sounded outside the room along the corridor—there was not an instant to lose.

"Hang up! Good-bye! Danger! Don't ring again!" he whispered hurriedly, and, with a miserable smile, replacing the receiver bitterly on the hook, he jumped for the curtain.

He reached it none too soon. The door opened, an electric-light switch clicked, and the room was flooded with light. Jason, still running, headed for the desk.

"It'll be her again!" Jimmie Dale heard the old man mutter, as from the edge of the portiere he watched the other's actions.

Jason picked up the telephone.

"Hello! Hello!" he called—then began to click impatiently with the receiver hook. "Hello!... Who?... Central?... I don't want any number—somebody was calling here.... What?... Nobody on the wire!"

He set the telephone back on the desk with a bewildered air.

"That's odd!" he exclaimed. "I could have sworn I heard it ring twice, and—" He stopped abruptly, and, leaning across the desk, hung there, wide-eyed, staring, while a sickly pallor began to steal into his face. "The letter!" he mumbled wildly. "The letter—Master Jim's letter—the letter—it's *gone*!"

Trembling, excited, the old man began to search the desk, then down on his knees on the floor under it; and then, growing more frantic with every instant, rose and began to hunt around the room in an agitated, aimless fashion.

Jason's distress was very real—he was almost beside himself now with fear and anxiety. A whimsical, affectionate smile played over Jimmie Dale's lips at the old man's antics—and changed suddenly into one of consternation. Jason was making directly now for the curtain behind which he stood! Perhaps, though, he would pass it by, and—Jason's hand reached out and grasped the portiere.

"Jason!" said Jimmie Dale sharply.

The old man staggered back as though he had been struck, tried to speak, choked, and gazed at the curtain with distended eyes.

"Is—is that you, sir—Master Jim—behind the curtain there?" he finally blurted out. "I—sir—you gave me a start—and the letter, Master Jim—"

"Don't lose your head, Jason," said Jimmie Dale coolly. "I've got the letter. Now do as I bid you."

"Yes—Master Jim," faltered the old man.

"Pull down the window shades and draw the portiere together," directed Jimmie Dale.

Jason, still overwrought and excited, obeyed a little awkwardly.

"Now the lights, Jason," instructed Jimmie Dale. "Turn them off, and go and sit down in that chair at the desk."

Again Jason obeyed, stumbling in the darkness as he returned from the electric-light switch at the farther end of the room. He sat down in the chair.

Larry the Bat stepped out from behind the curtain. "I came for that letter, Jason," he explained quietly. "I am going out again now. I may be back tomorrow; I may not be back for a week. You will say nothing, not a word, of my having been here tonight. Do you understand, Jason?"

"Yes, sir," said Jason; then hesitantly: "Would you mind saying, sir, when you came in?"

"It's of no consequence, Jason—is it?"

"No, sir," said Jason.

Jimmie Dale smiled in the darkness.

"Jason!"

"Yes, sir."

"I wish you to remain where you are, without leaving that chair, for the next ten minutes." He moved across the room to the door. "Good-night, Jason," he said.

"Good-night, Master Jim—good-night, sir—oh, Lord!"

Jimmie Dale did not require that ten minutes; it was a very wide margin of safety to obviate the possibility of Jason, from a window, detecting the exit of a disreputable character from the house—in three minutes he was turning the corner of the first cross street and walking rapidly away from Riverside Drive.

In the subway station Jimmie Dale read the letter—read it twice over, as he always read those strange epistles of hers that opened the door to new peril, new danger to the Gray Seal, but too, that seemed somehow to draw tighter, in a glad, big way, the unseen bond between them; read it, as he always read those letters, almost subconsciously committing the very words to memory with that keen faculty of brain of his. But now as he began to tear the sheet and envelope into minute particles, a strained, hard look was on his face and in his eyes, and his lips, half parted, moved a little.

"It's a death warrant," muttered Jimmie Dale. "I—I guess tonight will see the end of the Gray Seal. She says I needn't do it, but I guess it's worth the risk—a human life!"

A downtown express roared into the station.

"What time is it?" Jimmie Dale asked the guard, as he stepped aboard.

"'Bout midnight," the man answered tersely.

The forward car was almost empty, and Jimmie Dale chose a seat by himself. How did she know? How did she know not only this, but the hundred other affairs that she had outlined in those letters of hers? By what means, superhuman, indeed, it seemed, did she—Jimmie Dale jerked himself erect suddenly. What good did it do to speculate on that now, when every minute was priceless? What was *he* to do, how was he to act, what plan could he formulate and carry out, and *win* against odds that, at the outset, were desperate enough even to forecast almost certain failure—and death!

Who would ever have suspected old Tom Ludgate, known for years throughout the squalour of the East Side as old Luddy, the pushcart man, of having a bag of unset diamonds under his pillow—or under the sack, rather, that he probably used for a pillow! What a strange thing to do! But then, old Luddy was a character—apparently always in the most poverty-stricken condition, apparently hardly more than keeping body and soul together, trusting no one, and obsessed by the dread that by depositing in a bank someone would discover that he had money, and attempt to force it from him, he had put his savings, year after year, for twenty years, twenty-five years, perhaps, into unset stone—diamonds. How had she found that out?

Jimmie Dale sank into a deeper reverie. He could steal them all right, and they would be well worth the stealing—old Luddy had done well, and lived and existed on next to nothing—the stones, she said, were worth about fifteen thousand dollars. Not so bad, even for twenty-five years of vegetable selling from a pushcart! He could steal them all right; it would tax the Gray Seal's ingenuity little to do so simple a thing as that, but that was not all, nor, indeed, hardly a factor in it—it was vital that if he were to succeed at all he must steal them *publicly*, as it were.

And after that—*what*? His own chances were pretty slim at best. Jimmie Dale, staring at the grayness of the subway wall through the window, shook his head slowly—then, with a little philosophical shrug of his shoulders, he smiled gravely, seriously. It was all a part of the game, all a part of the life—of the Gray Seal!

It was half-past twelve, or a little later, as nearly as he could judge, for Larry the Bat carried no such ornate thing in evidence as a watch, as he halted at the corner of a dark, squalid street in the lower East Side. It was a miserable locality—in daylight humming with a cosmopolitan hive of pitiful humans dragging out as best they could an intolerable existence, a locality peopled with every nationality on earth, their community of interest the struggle to maintain life at the lowest possible expenditure, where necessity even was pared and shaved down to a minimum; but now, at night time, or rather in the early-morning hours, the darkness, in very mercy, it seemed, covered it with a veil, as it were, and in the quiet that hung over it now hid the bald, the hideous, aye, and the piteous, too, from view.

It was a narrow street, and the row of tenement houses, each house almost identical with its neighbour, that flanked the pavement on either side, seemed, from where Jimmie Dale stood looking down its length, from the corner, to converge together at a point a little way beyond, giving it an unreal, ominous, cavernlike effect. And, too, there seemed something ominous even in its quiet. It was as though one sensed acutely the crouching of some Thing in its lair—waiting silently, viciously, with sullen patience.

A footstep sounded—another. Jimmie Dale drew quickly back around the corner into an areaway. Two men passed—in helmets—swinging their nightsticks—that beat was always policed in pairs!

They passed on, turned the corner, and went down the narrow cross street that Jimmie Dale had just been inspecting. He started to follow—and drew back again abruptly. A form flitted suddenly across the road and disappeared in the darkness in the officers' wake—ten yards behind the first another followed—at the same interval of distance still another—and yet still one more—four in all.

The darkness hid all six, the two policemen, the four men behind them—the only sounds were the officers' footsteps dying away in the distance.

Jimmie Dale's fingers were mechanically testing the mechanism of the automatic in his pocket.

"The Skeeter's gang!" he muttered to himself. "Red Mose, the Midget, Harve Thoms—and the Skeeter! The Worst apaches in the city of New York; death contractors—the lowest bidders! Professional assassins, and a man's life any time for twenty-five dollars! I wonder—I've never done it yet—but I wonder if it would be a crime in God's sight if one shot—to *kill*!"

Jimmie Dale was at the corner again—again the street before him was black, deserted, empty. He chose the right hand side, and, well in the shadow of the houses, as an extra precaution, stole along silently. He stopped finally before one where, in the doorway, hung a little sign. Jimmie Dale mounted the porch, and with his eyes close to the sign could just make out the larger words in the big printed type:

ROOM TO RENT—TOP FLOOR

Jimmie Dale nodded. That was right. The first house on the right-hand side, with the room-to-rent sign, her letter had said. His fingers were testing the doorknob. The door was not locked.

"Naturally, it wouldn't be locked," Jimmie Dale told himself grimly—and stepped inside.

He stood for an instant without movement, every faculty on the alert. Far up above him a step, guarded though his trained ear made it out to be, creaked faintly upon the stairs—there was no other sound. The creaking, almost inaudible at its loudest, receded farther up—and silence fell.

In the darkness, noiselessly, Jimmie Dale groped for the stairway, found it, and began to ascend. The minutes passed—it seemed a minute even from step to step, and there were three flights to the top! There must be no creaking this time—the slightest sound, he knew well enough, would be not only fatal to the work he had to do, but probably fatal to himself as well. He had been near death many times—the consciousness that he was nearer to it now, possibly, than he had ever been before, seemed to stimulate his senses into acute and abnormal energy. And, too, the physical effort, as, step by step, the flexed muscles relaxing so slowly, little by little, gradually, each time as he found foothold on the step higher up, was a terrific strain. At the top his face was bathed in perspiration, and he wiped it off with his coat sleeve.

It was still dark here, intensely dark, and his eyes, though grown accustomed to it, could make out nothing but the deeper shadow of the walls. But thanks to her, always a mistress of accurate and minute detail, he possessed a mental plan of his surroundings. The head of the stairs gave on the middle of the hallway—the hallway ran to his right and left. To his right, on the opposite side of the hall, was the door of old Luddy's squalid two-room apartment.

For a moment Jimmie Dale stood hesitant—a sudden perplexity and anxiety growing upon him. It was strange! What did it mean? He had nerved himself to a quick, desperate attempt, trusting to surprise and his own wit and agility for victory—there had seemed no other way than that, since he had seen those four men at the corner—since they were ahead of him. True, they were not much ahead of him, not enough to have accomplished their purpose—and, furthermore, they were not in that room. He knew that absolutely, beyond question of doubt. He had listened for just that all the nerve-racking way up the stairs. But where were they? There was no sound—not a sound—just blackness, dark, impenetrable, utter, that began to palpitate now.

It came in a whisper, wavering, sibilant—from his left. A sort of relief, fierce in the breaking of the tense expectancy, premonitory in the possibilities that it held, swept Jimmie Dale. He crept along the hall. The whisper had come from that room, presumably empty—that was for rent!

By the door he crouched—his sensitive fingers, eyes to Jimmie Dale so often—feeling over jamb and panels with a delicate, soundless touch. The door was just ajar. The fingers crept inside and touched the knob and lock—there was no key within.

The whispering still went on—but it seemed like a screaming of vultures now in Jimmie Dale's ears, as the words came to him.

"Aw, say, Skeeter, dis high-brow stunt gives me de pip! Me fer goin' in dere an' croakin' de geezer reg'lar, widout de frills. Who's to know? Say, just about two minutes, an' we're beatin' it wid de sparklers."

An inch, a half inch at a time, the knob slowly, very, very slowly turning, the door was being closed by the crouched form on the threshold.

"Close yer trap, Mose!" came a fierce response. "We ain't fixed the lay all day for nothin'. There ain't a soul on earth knows he's got any sparklers, 'cept us. If there was, it would be different—then they'd know that was what whoever did it was after, see?"

The door was closed—the knob slowly, very, very slowly being released again. From one of the leather pockets under Jimmie Dale's vest came a tiny steel instrument that he inserted in the key-hole.

The same voice spoke on:

"That's what we're croaking him for, 'cause nobody knows about them diamonds, and so's he can't *tell* anybody afterward that any were pinched. An' that's why it's got to look like he just got tired of living and did it himself. I guess that'll hold the police when they find the poor old duck hanging from the ceiling, with a bit of cord around his neck, and a chair kicked out from under his feet on the floor. Ain't you got the brains of a louse to see that?"

"Sure"—the whisper came dully, in grudging intonation through the panels—the door was locked. "Sure, but it's de hangin' 'round waitin' to get busy that's gettin' me goat, an'—"

Jimmie Dale straightened up and began to retreat along the corridor. A merciless rage was upon him now, every fiber of his being seemed to tingle and quiver with it—the damnable, hellish ingenuity of it all seemed to choke and suffocate him.

"Luck!" muttered Jimmie Dale between his clenched teeth. "Oh, the blessed luck to get that door locked! I've got time now to set the stage for my own get-away before the showdown!"

He stole on along the corridor. Excerpts from her letter were running through his brain: "It would do no good to warn him, Jimmie—the Skeeter and his gang would never let up on him until they got the stones.... It would do no good for you to steal them first, for they would only take that as a ruse of old Luddy's, and murder the man first and hunt afterward.... In some way you must let the Skeeter see you steal them, make them think, make them certain that it is a bona-fide theft, so that they will no longer have any interest or any desire to do old Luddy harm.... And for it to appear real to them, it must appear real to old Luddy himself—do not take any chances there."

Jimmie Dale's eyes narrowed. Yes, it was simple enough now with that pack of hell's wolves guarded for the moment by a locked door, forced to give him warning by breaking the door before they could get out. It was simple enough now to enter old Luddy's room, steal the stones at the revolver point, then make enough disturbance—when he was ready—to set the gang in motion, and, as they rushed in open him, to make his escape with the stones to the roof through Luddy's room. That was simple enough—there was an opening to the roof in Luddy's room, she had said, and there was a ladder kept there in place. On hot nights, it seemed, the old man used to go up there and sleep on the roof—not now, of course. It was too late in the year for that—but the opening in the roof was there, and the ladder remained there, too.

Yes, it was simple enough now. And the next morning the papers would rave with execrations against the Gray Seal—for the robbery of the life savings of a poor, defenseless old man, for committing as vile and pitiful a crime as had ever stirred New York! Even Carruthers, of the *Morning News-Argus*, would be moved to bitter attack. Good old Carruthers—who little thought that the Gray Seal was his old college pal, his present most intimate friend, Jimmie Dale! And afterward—after the next morning? Well, that, at least, had never been in doubt. Old Luddy could be made to leave New York, and, once away, with the Skeeter and his gang robbed of incentive to pay any further attention to him, the stones could be secretly returned to the old man. And it would to the public, to the police, be just another of the Gray Seal's crimes—that was all!

Jimmie Dale had reached old Luddy's door. The Gray Seal? Oh, yes, they would know it was the Gray Seal—the insignia was familiar enough; familiar to the crooks of the underworld, who held it in awe; familiar to the police, to whom it was an added barb of ridicule. He was placing it now, that insignia, a diamond-shaped, gray paper seal, on the panel of the door; and now, a black silk mask adjusted over his face, Jimmie Dale bent to insert the little steel instrument in the lock—a pitiful, paltry thing, a cheap lock, to fingers that could play so intimately with twirling knobs and dials, masters of the intricate mechanism of vaults and safes!

And then, about to open the door, a sort of sudden dismay fell upon him. He had not thought of that—somehow, it had not occurred to him! *What was it they were waiting for?* Why had they not struck at once, as, when he had first entered the house, he had supposed they would do? What was it? Why was it? Was old Luddy out? Were they waiting for his return—or what?

The door, without sound, moved gradually under his hand. A faint odor assailed his nostrils! It was dark, very dark. Across the room, in a direct line, was the doorway of the inner room—she had explained that in her letter. It was slow progress to cross that room without sound, in silence—it was a snail's movement—for fear that even a muscle might crack.

And now he stood in the inner doorway. It was dark here, to—and yet, how bizarre, a star seemed to twinkle through the very roof of the room itself! The odour was pungent now. There was a long-drawn sigh—then a low, indescribable sound of movement. *Somebody, apart from old luddy, was in the room!*

It swept, the full consciousness of it, upon Jimmie Dale in an instantaneous flash. Chloroform; the open scuttle in the roof; the waiting of those others—all fused into a compact logical whole. They had loosened the scuttle during the day, probably when old Luddy was away—one of them had crept down there now to chloroform the old man into insensibility—the others would complete the ghastly work presently by stringing their victim up to the ceiling—and it would be suicide, for, long before morning came, long before the old man would be discovered, the fumes of the chloroform would be gone.

It seemed like a cold hand, deathlike, clutching at his heart. Was he too late, after all! Chloroform alone could—kill! To the right, just a little to the right—he must make no mistake—his ear placed the sound! He whipped his hands from the side pockets of his coat—the ray of his flashlight cut across the room and fell upon an aged face upon a bed, upon a hand clutching a wad of cloth, the cloth pressed horribly against the nose and mouth of the upturned face—and then, roaring in the stillness, spitting a vicious lane of fire that paralleled the flashlight's ray, came the tongue flame of his automatic.

There was a yell, a scream, that echoed out, reverberated, and went racketing through the house, and Jimmie Dale leaped forward—over a table, sending it crashing to the floor. The man had reeled back against the wall, clutching at a shattered wrist, staring into the flashlight's eye, white-faced, jaw dropped, lips working in mingled pain and fear.

"Harve Thoms—you, eh?" gritted Jimmie Dale.

A cunning look swept the distorted face. Here, apparently, was only one man—there were pals, three of them, only a few yards away.

"You ain't got nothing on me!" he snarled, sparring for time. "You police are too damned fresh with your guns!"

"I'll take yours!" snapped Jimmie Dale, and snatched it deftly from the other's pocket. "This ain't any police job, my bucko, and you make a move and I'll drop you for keeps, if what you've got already ain't enough to teach you to keep your hands off jobs that belong to your betters!"

He was working with mad haste as he spoke. One minute at the outside was, perhaps, all he could count upon. Already he had caught the rattle of the locked door down the hall. He lit a match and turned on the gas over the bed—it was the most dangerous thing he could do—he knew that well enough, none knew it better—it was offering himself as a fair mark when the others rushed in, as they would in a moment now—but the Skeeter and his gang and this man here must have no misconception of his purpose, his reason for being there, the same as their own, the theft of the stones—and no misconception as to his *success*.

"Y'ain't the police!"—it came in a choked gasp from the other, as he blinked in the sudden light "Say then—"

"Shut up!" ordered Jimmie Dale curtly. "And mind what I told you about moving!" He leaned over the bed. Old Luddy, though under the influence of the chloroform, was moving restlessly. Thoms had evidently only begun to apply the chloroform—old Luddy was safe! Jimmie Dale ran his hand in under the pillow. "If you ain't swiped them already they ought to be here!" he growled; "and if you have I'll—ah!" A little chamois bag was in his hand. He laughed sneeringly at Thoms, opened the bag, allowed a few stones to trickle into his hand—and then, without stopping to replace them, dashed stones and bag into his pocket. The door along the corridor crashed open.

"What's that?" he gasped out, in well-simulated fright—and sprang for the ladder that led up to the roof.

It had all taken, perhaps, the minute that he had counted on—no more. Noises came from the floors below now, a confusion of them—the shot, the scream had been heard by others, save those who had been in the locked room. And the latter were outside now in the corridor, running to their accomplice's aid.

There was a pause at the outer door—then an oath—and coupled with the oath an exclamation:

"The Gray Seal!"

They had swept a flashlight over the door panel—Jimmie Dale, halfway up the ladder, smiled grimly.

The door opened—there was a rush of feet. The man with the shattered wrist yelled, cursing wildly:

"Here he is—on the ladder! Let him have it! Fill him full of holes!"

Jimmie Dale was in the light—they were in the dark of the outer room. He fired at the threshold, checking their rush—as a hail of bullets chipped and tore at the ladder and spat wickedly against the wall. He swung through to the roof, trying, as he did so, to kick the ladder loose behind him. It was fastened!

The three gunmen jumped into the room—from the roof Jimmie Dale got a glimpse of them below, as he flung himself clear of the opening. Bullets whistled through the aperture—a voice roared up as he gained his feet:

"Come on! After him! The whole place is alive, but this lets us out. We can frame up how we came to be here easy enough. Never mind the old geezer there any more! Get the Gray Seal—the reward that's out for him is worth twice the sparklers, and—"

Jimmie Dale hurled the cover over the scuttle. He could have stood them off from above and kept the ladder clear with his revolver, but the alarm seemed general now—windows were opening, voices were calling to one another—from the windows across the street he must stand out in sharp outline against the sky. Yes—he was seen now.

A woman's voice, from a top-story window across the street, screamed out, high-pitched in excitement:

"There he is! There he is! On the roof there!"

Jimmie Dale started on the run along the roof. The houses, built wall to wall, flat-roofed, seemed to offer an open course ahead of him—until a lane or an intersecting street should bar his way! But they were not quite all on the same level, though—the wall of the next house rose suddenly breast high in front of him. He flung himself up, regained his feet—and ducked instantly behind a chimney.

The crack of a revolver echoed through the night—a bullet drummed through the air—the Skeeter and his gang were on the roof now, dashing forward, firing as they ran. Two shots from Jimmie Dale's automatic, in quick succession cooled the ardour of their rush—and they broke, black, flitting forms, for the shelter of chimneys, too.

And now the whole neighbourhood seemed awakened. A dull-toned roar, as from some great gulf below, rolled up from the street, a medley of slamming windows, the rush of feet as people poured from the houses, cries, shouts, and yells—and high over all the shrill call of the police-patrol whistle—and the *crack, crack, crack* of the Skeeter's revolver shots—the Skeeter and his hellhounds for once self-appointed allies of the law!

Twice again Jimmie Dale fired—then crouching, running low, he zigzagged his way across the next roof. The bullets followed him—once more his pursuers dashed forward. And again Jimmie Dale, his face set like stone now, his breath coming in hard gasps, dodged behind a chimney, and with his gun checked their rush for the third time.

He glanced about him—and with a growing sense of disaster saw that two houses farther on the stretch of roof appeared to end. There would be a lane or a street there! And in another minute or two, if it were not already the case, others would be following the gunmen to the roof, and then he would be—he caught his breath suddenly in a little strangled cry of relief. Just back of him, a few yards away, his eyes made out what, in the darkness, seemed to be a glass skylight.

A dark form sped like a deeper shadow across the black in front of him, making for a chimney nearer by, closing in the range. Jimmie Dale fired— wide. Tight as was the corner he was in, little as was the mercy deserved at his hands, he could not, after all, bring himself to shoot—to kill.

A voice, the Skeeter's, bawled out raucously:

"Rush him all together—from different sides at once!"

A backward leap! Jimmie Dale's boot was crashing glass and frame, stamping at it desperately, making a hole for his body through the skylight. A yell, a chorus of them, answered this—then the crunch of racing feet on the gravel roof. He emptied his revolver, sweeping the darkness with a semi-circle of vicious flashes.

It seemed an hour—it was barely the fraction of a second, as he hung by his hands from the side of the skylight frame, his body swinging back and forth in the unknown blackness below. The skylight might be, probably was, directly over the stair well, and open clear to the basement of the house—but it was his only chance. He swung his body well out, let go—and dropped. With the impetus he smashed against a wall, was flung back from it in a sort of rebound, and his hands closed, gripping fiercely, on banisters. It had been the stair well beyond any question of doubt, but his swing had sent him clear of it.

Above, they had not yet reached the skylight. Jimmie Dale snatched a precious moment to listen, as he rose, and found himself, apart from bruises, perhaps unhurt. There was commotion, too, in this house below, the alarm had extended and spread along the block—but the commotion was all in the *front* of the house—the street was the lure.

Jimmie Dale started down the stairs, and in an instant he had gained the landing. In another he had slipped to the rear of the hall—somewhere there, from the hall itself, from one of the rear rooms, there must be an exit to the fire escape. To attempt to leave by the front way was certain capture.

They were yelling, shouting down now through the sky-light above, as Jimmie Dale softly raised the window sash at the rear of the hall. The fire escape was there. Shouts from along the corridor, from the tenement dwellers who had been crowding their neighbours' rooms, craning their necks probably from the front windows, answered the shouts now from the roof and the skylight; doors opened; forms rushed out—but it was dark in the corridor, only a murky yellow at the upper end from the opened doors.

Jimmie Dale slipped through the window to the fire escape, and, working cautiously, silently, but with the speed of a trained athlete, made his way down. At the bottom he dropped from the iron platform into the back yard, ran for the fence and climbed over into a lane on the other side.

And then, as he ran, Jimmie Dale snatched the mask from his face and put it in his pocket. He was safe now. He swept the sweat drops from his forehead with the back of his hand—noticing them for the first time. It had been close—almost as close for him as it had been for old Luddy. And tomorrow the papers would execrate the Gray Seal! He smiled a little wanly. His breath was still coming hard. Presently they would scour the lane—when they found that their quarry was not in the house. What a racket they were making! The whole district seemed roused like a swarm of angry bees.

He kept on along the lane—and dodged suddenly into a cross street where the two intersected. The clang of a bell dinned discordantly in his ears—a patrol wagon swept by him, racing for the scene of the disturbance—the riot call was out!

Again Jimmie Dale smiled wearily, passing his hand across his eyes.

"I guess," said Jimmie Dale, "I'm pretty near all in. And I guess it's time that Larry the Bat went—home."

And a little later a figure turned from the Bowery and shambled down the cross street, a disreputable figure, with hands plunged deep in his pockets—and a shadow across the roadway suddenly shifted its position as the shambling figure slouched into the black alleyway and entered the tenement's side door.

And Larry the Bat smiled softly to himself—Kline's men were still on guard!

CHAPTER 6

DEVIL'S WORK

A white-gloved arm, a voice, and a silvery laugh! Just that—no more! Jimmie Dale, in his favourite seat, an aisle seat some seven or eight rows back from the orchestra, stared at the stage, to all outward appearances absorbed in the last act of the play; inwardly, quite oblivious to the fact that even a play was going on.

A white-gloved arm, a voice, and a silvery laugh! The words had formed themselves into a sort of singsong refrain that, for the last few days, had been running through his head. A strange enough guiding star to mould and dictate every action in his life! And that was all he had ever seen of her, all that he had ever heard of her—except those letters, of course, each of which had outlined the details of some affair for the Gray Seal to execute.

Indeed, it seemed a great length of time now since he had heard from her even in that way, though it was not so many days ago, after all. Perhaps it was the calm, as it were, that, by contrast, had given place to the strenuous months and weeks just past. The storm raised by the newspapers at the theft of Old Luddy's diamonds had subsided into sporadic diatribes aimed at the police; Kline, of the secret service, had finally admitted defeat, and a shadow no longer skulked day and night at the entrance to the Sanctuary—and Larry the Bat bore the government indorsement, so to speak, of being no more suspicious a character than that of a disreputable, but harmless, dope fiend of the underworld.

Larry the Bat! The Gray Seal! Jimmie Dale the millionaire! What if it were ever known that that strange three were one! What if—Jimmie Dale smiled whimsically. A burst of applause echoed through the house, the orchestra was playing, the lights were on, seats banged, there was the bustle of the rising audience, the play was at an end—and for the life of him he could not have remembered a single line of the last act!

The aisle at his elbow was already crowded with people on their way out. Jimmie Dale stooped down mechanically to reach for his hat beneath his seat—and the next instant he was standing up, staring wildly into the faces around him.

It had fallen at his feet—a white envelope. Hers! It was in his hand now, those slim, tapering, wonderfully sensitive fingers of Jimmie Dale, that were an "open sesame" to locks and safes, subconsciously telegraphing to his mind the fact that the texture of the paper—was hers. Hers! And she must be one of those around him—one of those crowding either the row of seats in front or behind, or one of those just passing in the aisle. It had fallen at his feet as he had stooped over for his hat—but from just exactly what direction he could not tell. His eyes, eagerly, hungrily, critically, swept face after face. Which one was hers? What irony! She, whom he would have given his life to know, for whom indeed he risked his life every hour of the twenty-four, was close to him now, within reach—and as far removed as though a thousand miles separated them. She was there—but he could not recognise a face that he had never seen!

With an effort, he choked back the bitter, impotent laugh that rose to his lips. They were talking, laughing around him. Her *voice*—yes, he had once heard that, and that he would recognise again. He strained to catch, to individualise the tone sounds that floated in a medley about him. It was useless—of course—every effort that he had ever made to find her had been useless. She was too clever, far too clever for that—she, too, would know that he could and would recognise her voice where he could recognise nothing else.

And then, suddenly, he realised that he was attracting attention. Level stares from the women returned his gaze, and they edged away a little from his vicinity as they passed, their escorts crowding somewhat belligerently into their places. Others, in the same row of seats as his own, were impatiently waiting to get by him. With a muttered apology, Jimmie Dale raised the seat of his chair, allowing these latter to pass him—and then, slipping the letter into his pocketbook, he snatched up his hat from the seat rack.

There was still a chance. Knowing he was there, she would be on her guard; but in the lobby, among the crowd and unaware of his presence, there was the possibility that, if he could reach the entrance ahead of her, she, too, might be talking and laughing as she left the theatre. Just a single word, just a tone—that was all he asked.

The row of seats at whose end he stood was empty now, and, instead of stepping into the thronged aisle, he made his way across to the opposite side of the theatre. Here, the far aisle was less crowded, and in a minute he had gained the foyer, confident that he was now in advance of her. The next moment he was lost in a jam of people in the lobby.

He moved slowly now, very slowly—allowing those behind to press by him on the way to the entrance. A babel of voices rose about him, as, tight-packed, the mass of people jostled, elbowed, and pushed good-naturedly. It was a voice now, her voice, that he was listening for; but, though it seemed that every faculty was strained and intent upon that one effort, his eyes, too, had in no degree relaxed their vigilance—and once, half grimly, half sardonically, he smiled to himself. There would be an unexpected aftermath to this exodus of expensively gowned and bejewelled women with their prosperous, well-groomed escorts! There was the Wowzer over there—sleek, dapper, squirming in and out of the throng with the agility and stealth of a cat. As Larry the Bat he had met the Wowzer many times, as indeed he had met and was acquainted with most of the elite of the underworld. The Wowzer, beyond a shadow of doubt, in his own profession stood upon a plane entirely by himself—among those qualified to speak, no one yet had ever questioned the Wowzer's claim to the distinction of being the most dexterous and finished "poke getter" in the United States!

The crowd thinned in the lobby, thinned down to the last few belated stragglers, who passed him as he still loitered in the entrance; and then Jimmie Dale, with a shrug of his shoulders that was a great deal more philosophical than the maddening sense of chagrin and disappointment that burned within him, stepped out to the pavement and headed down Broadway. After all, he had known it in his heart of hearts all the time—it had always been the same—it was only one more occasion added to the innumerable ones that had gone before in which she had eluded him!

And now—there was the letter! Automatically he quickened his steps a little. It was useless, futile, profitless, for the moment, at least, to disturb himself over his failure—there was the letter! His lips parted in a strange, half-serious, half-speculative smile. The letter—that was paramount now. What new venture did the night hold in store for him? What sudden emergency was the Gray Seal called upon to face this time—what role, unrehearsed, without warning, must he play? What story of grim, desperate rascality would the papers credit him with when daylight came? Or would they carry in screaming headlines the announcement that the Gray Seal was caged and caught at last, and in three-inch type tell the world that the Gray Seal was—Jimmie Dale!

A block down, he turned from Broadway out of the theatre crowds that streamed in both directions past him. The letter! Almost feverishly now he was seeking an opportunity to open and read it unobserved; an eagerness upon him that mingled exhilaration at the lure of danger with a sense of premonition that, irritably, inevitably was with him at moments such as these. It seemed, it always seemed, that, with an unopened letter of hers in his possession, it was as though he were about to open a page in the Book of Fate and read, as it were, a pronouncement upon himself that might mean life or death.

He hurried on. People still passed by him—too many. And then a cafe, just ahead, making a corner, gave him the opportunity that he sought. Away from the entrance, on the side street, the brilliant lights from the windows shone out on a comparatively deserted pavement. There was ample light to read by, even as far away from the window as the curb, and Jimmie Dale, with an approving nod, turned the corner and walked along a few steps until opposite the farthest window—but, as he halted here at the edge of the street, he glanced quickly behind him at a man whom he had just passed. The other had paused at the corner and was staring down the street. Jimmie Dale instantly and nonchalantly produced his cigarette case, selected a cigarette, and fastidiously tapped its end on his thumb nail.

"Inspector Burton in plain clothes," he observed musingly to himself. "I wonder if it's just a fluke—or something else? We'll see."

Jimmie Dale took a box of matches from his pocket. The first would not light. The second broke, and, with an exclamation of annoyance, he flung it away. The third was making a fitful effort at life, as another man emerged hastily from the cafe's side door, hurried to the corner, joined the man who was still loitering there, and both together disappeared at a rapid pace down the street.

Jimmie Dale whistled softly to himself. The second man was even better known than the first; there was not a crook in New York but would side-step Lannigan of headquarters, and do it with amazing celerity—if he could!

"Something up! But it's not my hunt!" muttered Jimmie Dale; then, with a shrug of his shoulders: "Queer the way those headquarters chaps fascinate and give me a thrill every time I see them, even if I haven't a ghost of a reason for imagining that—"

The sentence was never finished. Jimmie Dale's face was gray. The street seemed to rock about him—and he stared, like a man stricken, white to the lips, ahead of him. *The letter was gone!* His hand, wriggling from his empty pocket, swept away the sweat beads that were bursting from his forehead. It had come at last—the pitcher had gone once too often to the well!

Numbed for an instant, his brain cleared now, working with lightning speed, leaping from premise to conclusion. The crush in the theatre lobby—the pushing, the jostling, the close contact—the Wowzer, the slickest, cleverest pickpocket in the United States! For a moment he could have laughed aloud in a sort of ghastly, defiant mockery—he himself had predicted an unexpected aftermath, had he not!

Aftermath! It was—the *end*! An hour, two hours, and New York would be metamorphosed into a seething caldron of humanity bubbling with the news. It seemed that he could hear the screams of the newsboys now shouting their extras; it seemed that he could see the people, roused to frenzy, swarming in excited crowds, snatching at the papers; he seemed to hear the mob's shouts swell in execration, in exultation—it seemed as though all around him had gone mad. The mystery of the Gray Seal was solved! It was Jimmie Dale, Jimmie Dale, Jimmie, Dale, the millionaire, the lion of society—and there was ignominy for an honoured name, and shame and disaster and convict stripes and sullen penitentiary walls—or death! A felon's death—the chair!

He was running now, his hands clenched at his sides; his mind, working subconsciously, urging him onward in a blind, as yet unrealised, objectless way. And then gradually impulse gave way to calmer reason, and he slowed his pace to a quick, less noticeable walk. The Wowzer! That was it! There was yet a chance—the Wowzer! A merciless rage, cold, deadly, settled upon him. It was the Wowzer who had stolen his pocketbook, and with it the letter. There could be no doubt of that. Well, there would be a reckoning at least before the end!

He was in a downtown subway train now—the roar in his ears in consonance, it seemed, with the turmoil in his brain. But now, too, he was Jimmie Dale again; and, apart from the slightly outthrust jaw, the tight-closed lips, impassive, debonair, composed.

There was yet a chance. As Larry the Bat he knew every den and lair below the dead line, and he knew, too, the Wowzer's favourite haunts. There was yet a chance, only one in a thousand, it was true, almost too pitiful to be depended upon—but yet a chance. The Wowzer had probably not worked alone, and he and his pal, or pals, would certainly not remain uptown either to examine or divide their spoils—they would wait until they were safe somewhere in one of their hell holes on the East Side. If he could find the Wowzer, reach the man *before the letter was opened*—Jimmie Dale's lips grew tighter. *That* was the chance! It he failed in that—Jimmie Dale's lips drooped downward in grim curves at the corners. A chance! Already the Wowzer had at least a half hour's lead, and, worse still, there was no telling which one of a dozen places the man might have chosen to retreat to with his loot.

Time passed. His mind obsessed, Jimmie Dale's physical acts were almost wholly mechanical. It was perhaps fifteen minutes since he had discovered the loss of the letter, and he was walking now through the heart of the Bowery. Exactly how he had got there he could not have told; he had only a vague realisation that, following an intuitive sense of direction, he had lost not a second of time in making his way downtown.

And now he found himself hesitating at the corner of a cross street. Two blocks east was that dark, narrow alleyway, that side door that made the entrance to the Sanctuary. It would be safer, a hundred times safer, to go there, change his clothes and his personality, and emerge again as Larry the Bat—infinitely safer in that role to explore the dens of the underworld, many of them indeed unknown and undreamed of by the police themselves, than to trust himself there in well-cut, fashionable tweeds—but that would take time. Time! When, with every second, the one chance he had, desperate as that already was, was slipping away from him. No; what was apparently the greater risk at least held out the only hope.

He went on again—his brain incessantly at work. At the worst, there was one mitigating factor in it all. He had no need to think of her. Whatever the ruin and disaster that faced him in the next few hours, she in any case was safe. There was no clue to *her* identity in the letter; and where he, for months on end, with even more to work upon, had failed at every turn to trace her, there was little fear that anyone else would have any better success. She was safe. As for himself—that was different. The Gray Seal would be referred to in the letter, there would be the outline, the data for the "crime" she had planned for that night; and the letter, though unaddressed, being found in his pocketbook, where cards and notes and a dozen different things among its contents proclaimed him Jimmie Dale, needed no further evidence as to its ownership nor the identity of the Gray Seal.

Jimmie Dale's fingers crept inside his vest and fumbled there for a moment—and a diamond stud, extracted from his shirt front, glistened sportively in the necktie that was now tucked jauntily in at one side of his shirt bosom. He had reached the Blue Dragon, one of Wowzer's usual hang outs, and, swerving from the sidewalk, entered the place. There was wild tumult within—a constant storm of applause, derision, and hilarity that was hurled from the tables around the room at the turkey-trotting, tango-writhing couples on the somewhat restricted space of polished hardwood flooring in the centre. Jimmie Dale swaggered down the room, a cigar tilted up at an angle between his teeth, his soft felt hat a little rakishly on one side of his head and well over his nose.

At the end of the room, at the bar, Jimmie Dale leaned toward the barkeeper and talked out of the corner of his mouth. There were private rooms upstairs, and he jerked his head surreptitiously ceilingward.

"Say, is de Wowzer up dere?" he inquired in a cautious whisper.

The man behind the bar, well known to Jimmie Dale as one of the Wowzer's particular pals, favoured him with a blank stare.

"Never heard of de guy!" he announced brusquely. "Wot's yours?"

"Gimme a mug of suds," said Jimmie Dale, reaching for a match. He puffed at his cigar, blew out the match, and, after a moment, flung the charred end away—but on his hand, as, palm outward, he raised it to take his glass, the match had traced a small black cross.

The barkeeper put down the beer he had just drawn, wiped his hand hurriedly, and with sudden enthusiasm thrust it across the bar.

"Glad to know youse, cull!" he exclaimed. "Wot's de lay?"

Jimmie Dale smiled.

"Nix!" said Jimmie Dale. "I just blew in from Chicago. Used to know de Wowzer dere. He said dis place was on de level, an' I could always find him here, dat's all."

"Sure, youse can!" returned the barkeeper heartily. "Only he ain't here now. He beat it about fifteen minutes ago, him an' Dago Jim. I guess youse'll find him at Chang's, I heard him an' Dago say dey was goin' dere. Know de place?"

Jimmie Dale shook his head.

"I ain't much wise to New York," he explained.

"Aw, dat's easy," whispered the barkeeper. "Go down to Chatham Square, an' den any guy'll show youse Chang Foo's." He winked confidentially. "I guess youse won't bump yer head none gettin' around inside."

Jimmie Dale nodded, grinned back, emptied his glass, and dug for a coin.

"Forget it!" observed the barkeeper cordially. "Dis is on me. Any friend of de Wowzer's gets de glad hand here any time."

"T'anks!" said Jimmie Dale gratefully, as he turned away. "So long, then—see youse later."

Chang Foo's! Jimmie Dale's face set even a little harder than it had before, as he swung on again down the Bowery. Yes; he knew Chang Foo's—too well. Underground Chinatown—where a man's life was worth the price of an opium pill—or less! Mechanically his hand slipped into his pocket and closed over the automatic that nestled there. Once in—where he had to go—and the chances were even, just even, that was all, that he would ever get out. Again he was tempted to return to the Sanctuary and make the attempt as Larry the Bat. Larry the Bat was well enough known to enter Chang Foo's unquestioned, and—but again he shook his head and went on. There was not time. The Wowzer and his pal—it was Dago Jim it seemed—had evidently been drinking and loitering their way downtown from the theatre, and he had gained that much on them; but by now they would be smugly tucked away somewhere in that maze of dens below the ground, and at that moment probably were gloating over the biggest night's haul they had ever made in their lives!

And if they were! What then? Once they knew the contents of that letter—what then? Buy them off for a larger amount than the many thousands offered for the capture of the Gray Seal? Jimmie Dale gritted his teeth. That meant blackmail from them all his life, an intolerable existence, impossible, a hell on earth—the slave, at the beck and call of two of the worst criminals in New York! The moisture oozed again to Jimmie Dale's forehead. God, if he could get that letter before it was opened—before they KNEW! If he could only get the chance to fight for it—against *any* odds! Life! Life was a pitiful consideration against the alternative that faced him now!

From the Blue Dragon to Chang Foo's was not far; and Jimmie Dale covered the distance in well under five minutes. Chang Foo's was just a tea merchant's shop, innocuous and innocent enough in its appearance, blandly so indeed, and that was all—outwardly; but Jimmie Dale, as he reached his destination, experienced the first sensation of uplift he had known that night, and this from what, apparently, did not in the least seem like a contributing cause.

"Luck! The blessed luck of it!" he muttered grimly, as he surveyed the sight-seeing car drawn up at the curb, and watched the passengers crowding out of it to the ground. "It wouldn't have been as easy to fool old Chang as it was that fellow back at the Dragon—and, besides, if I can work it, there's a better chance this way of getting out alive."

The guide was marshalling his "gapers"—some two dozen in all, men and women. Jimmie Dale unostentatiously fell in at the rear; and, the guide leading, the little crowd passed into the tea merchant's shop. Chang Foo, a wizened, wrinkled-faced little Celestial, oily, suave, greeted them with profuse bows, chattering the while volubly in Chinese.

The guide made the introduction with an all-embracing sweep of his hand.

"Chang Foo—ladies and gentlemen," he announced; then held up his hand for silence. "Ladies and gentlemen," he said impressively, "this is one of the most notorious, if not *the* most notorious dive in Chinatown, and it is only through special arrangement with the authorities and at great expense that the company is able exclusively to gain an entree here for its patrons. You will see here the real life of the Chinese, and in half an hour you will get what few would get in a lifetime spent in China itself. You will see the Chinese children dance and perform; the Chinese women at their household tasks; the joss, the shrine of his hallowed ancestors, at which Chang Foo here worships; and you will enter the most famous opium den in the United States. Now, if you will all keep close together, we will make a start."

In spite of his desperate situation, Jimmie Dale smiled a little whimsically. Yes; they would see it all—*upstairs!* The same old bunk dished out night after night at so much a head—and the nervous little schoolma'am of uncertain age, who fidgeted now beside him, would go back somewhere down in Maine and shiver while she related her "wider experiences" in tremulous whispers into the shocked ears of envious other maiden ladies of equally uncertain age. The same old bunk—and a profitable one for Chang Foo for more reasons than one. It was dust in the eyes of the police. The police smiled knowingly at mention of Chang Foo. Who should know, if they didn't, that it was all harmless fake, all bunk! And so it was—*upstairs!*

They were passing out of the shop now, bowed out through a side door by the obsequious and oily Chang Foo. And now they massed again in a sort of little hallway—and Chang Foo, closing the door upon Jimmie Dale, who was the last in the line, shuffled back behind the counter in his shop to resume his guard duty over customers of quite another ilk. With the door closed, it was dark, pitch dark. And this, too, like everything else connected with Chang Foo's establishment, for more reasons than one—for effect—and for security. Nervous little twitters began to emanate from the women—the guide's voice rose reassuringly:

"Keep close together, ladies and gentlemen. We are going upstairs now to—"

Jimmie Dale hugged back against the wall, sidled along it, and like a shadow slipped down to the end of the hall. The scuffling of two dozen pairs of feet mounting the creaky staircase drowned the slight sound as he cautiously opened a door; the darkness lay black, impenetrable, along the hall. And then, as cautiously as he had opened it, he closed the door behind him, and stood for an instant listening at the head of a ladder-like stairway, his automatic in his hand now. It was familiar ground to Larry the Bat. The steps led down to a cellar; and diagonally across from the foot of the steps was an opening, ingeniously hidden by a heterogeneous collection of odds and ends, boxes, cases, and rubbish from the pseudo tea shop above; a low opening in the wall to a passage that led on through the cellars of perhaps half a dozen adjoining houses, each of which latter was leased, in one name or another— by Chang Foo.

Jimmie Dale crept down the steps, and in another moment had gained the farther side of the cellar; then, skirting around the ruck of cases, he stooped suddenly and passed in through the opening in the wall. And now he halted once more. He was straining his eyes down a long, narrow passage, whose blackness was accentuated rather than relieved by curious wavering, gossamer threads of yellow light that showed here and there from under makeshift thresholds, from doors slightly ajar. Faint noises came to him, a muffled, intermittent clink of coin, a low, continuous, droning hum of voices; the sickly sweet smell of opium pricked at his nostrils.

Jimmie Dale's face set rigidly. It was the resort, not only of the most depraved Chinese element, but of the worst "white" thugs that made New York their headquarters—here, in the succession of cellars, roughly partitioned off to make a dozen rooms on either side of the passage, dope fiends sucked at the drug, and Chinese gamblers spent the greater part of their lives; here, murder was hatched and played too often to its hellish end; here, the scum of the underworld sought refuge from the police to the profit of Chang Foo; and here, somewhere, in one of these rooms, was—the Wowzer.

The Wowzer! Jimmie Dale stole forward silently, without a sound, swiftly—pausing only to listen for a second's space at the doors as he passed. From this one came that clink of coin; from another that jabber of Chinese; from still another that overpowering stench of opium—and once, iron-nerved as he was, a cold thrill passed over him. Let this lair of hell's wolves, so intent now on their own affairs, be once roused, as they certainly must be roused before he could hope to finish the Wowzer, and his chances of escape were—

He straightened suddenly, alert, tense, strained. Voices, raised in a furious quarrel, came from a door just beyond him on the other side of the passage, where a film of light streamed out through a cracked panel—it was the Wowzer and Dago Jim! And drunk, both of them—and both in a blind fury!

It happened quick then, almost instantaneously it seemed to Jimmie Dale. He was crouched now close against the door, his eye to the crack in the panel. There was only one figure in sight—Dago Jim—standing beside a table on which burned a lamp, the table top littered with watches, purses, and small chatelaine bags. The man was lurching unsteadily on his feet, a vicious sneer of triumph on his face, waving tauntingly an open letter and Jimmie Dale's pocket-book in his hands—waving them presumably in the face of the Wowzer, whom, from the restrictions of the crack, Jimmie Dale could not see. He was conscious of a sickening sense of disaster. His hope against hope had been in vain—the letter had been opened and read—*the identity of the Gray Seal was solved.*

Dago Jim's voice roared out, hoarse, blasphemous, in drunken rage:

"De Gray Seal—see! Youse betcher life I knows! I been waitin' fer somet'ing like dis, damn youse! Youse been stallin' on me fer a year every time it came to a divvy. Youse've got a pocketful now youse snitched tonight dat youse are tryin' to do me out of. Well, keep 'em.—he shoved his face forward. "I keeps dis—see! Keep 'em Wowzer, youse cross-eyed—"

"Everyt'ing I pinched tonight's on de table dere wid wot youse pinched yerself," cut in the Wowzer, in a sullen, threatening growl.

"Youse lie, an' youse knows it!" retorted Dago Jim. "Youse have given me de short end every time we've pulled a deal!"

"Dat letter's mine, youse—" bawled the Wowzer furiously.

"Why didn't youse open it an' read it, den, instead of lettin' me do it to keep me busy while youse short-changed me?" sneered Dago Jim. "Youse t'ought it was some sweet billy-doo, eh? Well, t'anks, Wowzer—dat's wot it is! Say," he mocked, "dere's a guy'll cash a t'ousand century notes fer dis, an' if he don't—say, dere's *some* reward out fer the Gray Seal! Wouldn't youse like to know who it is? Well, when I'm ridin' in me private buzz wagon, Wowzer, youse stick around an' mabbe I'll tell youse—an' mabbe I won't!"

"By God"—the Wowzer's voice rose in a scream—"youse hand over dat letter!"

"Youse go to—"

Red, lurid red, a stream of flame seemed to cut across Jimmie Dale's line of vision, came the roar of a revolver shot—and like a madman Jimmie Dale flung his body at the door. Rickety at best, it crashed inward, half wrenched from its hinges, precipitating him inside. He recovered himself and leaped forward. The room was swirling with blue eddies of smoke; Dago Jim, hands flung up, still grasping letter and pocketbook, pawed at the air—and plunged with a sagging lurch face downward to the floor. There was a yell and an oath from the Wowzer—the crack of another revolver shot, the hum of the bullet past Jimmie Dale's ear, the scorch of the tongue flame in his face, and he was upon the other.

Screeching profanity, the Wowzer grappled; and, for an instant, the two men rocked, reeled, and swayed in each other's embrace; then, both men losing their balance, they shot suddenly backward, the Wowzer, undermost, striking his head against the table's edge—and men, table, and lamp crashed downward in a heap to the floor.

It had been no more, at most, than a matter of seconds since Jimmie Dale had hurled himself into the room; and now, with a gurgling sigh, the Wowzer's arms, that had been wound around Jimmie Dale's back and shoulders, relaxed, and, from the blow on his head the man, lay back inert and stunned. And then it seemed to Jimmie Dale as though pandemonium, unreality, and chaos at the touch of some devil's hand reigned around him. It was dark—no, not dark—a spurt of flame was leaping along the line of trickling oil from the broken lamp on the floor. It threw into ghastly relief the sprawled form of Dago Jim. Outside, from along the passageway, came a confused jangle of commotion—whispering voices, shuffling feet, the swish of Chinese garments. And the room itself began to spring into weird, flickering shadows, that mounted and crept up the walls with the spreading fire.

There was not a second to lose before the room would be swarming with that rush from the passageway—and there was still the letter, the pocketbook! The table had fallen half over Dago Jim—Jimmie Dale pushed it aside, tore the crushed letter and the pocketbook from the man's hands—and felt, with a grim, horrible sort of anxiety, for the other's heartbeat, for the verdict that meant life or death to himself. There was no sign of life—the man was dead.

Jimmie Dale was on his feet now. A face, another, and another showed in the doorway—the Wowzer was regaining his senses, stumbling to his knees. There was one chance—just one—to take those crowding figures by surprise. And with a yell of "Fire!" Jimmie Dale sprang for the doorway.

They gave way before his rush, tumbling back in their surprise against the opposite wall; and, turning, Jimmie Dale raced down the passageway. Doors were opening everywhere now, forms were pushing out into the semidarkness—only to duck hastily back again, as Jimmie Dale's automatic barked and spat a running fire of warning ahead of him. And then, behind, the Wowzer's voice shrieked out:

"Soak him! Kill de guy! He's croaked Dago Jim! Put a hole in him, de—"

Yells, a chorus of them, took up the refrain—then the rush of following feet—and the passageway seemed to racket as though a Gatling gun were in play with the fusillade of revolver shots. But Jimmie Dale was at the opening now—and, like a base runner plunging for the bag, he flung himself in a low dive through and into the open cellar beyond. He was on his feet, over the boxes, and dashing up the stairs in a second. The door above opened as he reached the top—Jimmie Dale's right hand shot out with clubbed revolver— and with a grunt Chang Foo went down before the blow and the headlong rush. The next instant Jimmie Dale had sprung through the tea shop and was out on the street.

A minute, two minutes more, and Chinatown would be in an uproar— Chang Foo would see to that—and the Wowzer would prod him on. The danger was far from over yet. And then, as he ran, Jimmie Dale gave a little gasp of relief. Just ahead, drawn up at the curb, stood a taxicab—waiting, probably, for a private slumming party. Jimmie Dale put on a spurt, reached it, and wrenched the door open.

"Quick!" he flung at the startled chauffeur. "The nearest subway station—there's a ten-spot in it for you! Quick man—*quick!* Here they come!"

A crowd of Chinese, pouring like angry hornets from Chang Foo's shop, came yelling down the street—and the taxi took the corner on two wheels— and Jimmie Dale, panting, choking for his breath like a man spent, sank back against the cushions.

But five minutes later it was quite another Jimmie Dale, composed, nonchalant, imperturbable, who entered an uptown subway train, and, choosing a seat alone near the centre of the car, which at that hour of night in the downtown district was almost deserted, took the crushed letter from his pocket. For a moment he made no attempt to read it, his dark eyes, now that he was free from observation, full of troubled retrospect, fixed on the window at his side. It was not a pleasant thought that it had cost a man his life, nor yet that that life was also the price of his own freedom. True, if there were two men in the city of New York whose crimes merited neither sympathy nor mercy, those two men were the Wowzer and Dago Jim—but yet, after all, it was a human life, and, even if his own had been in the balance, thank God it had been through no act of his that Dago Jim had gone out! The Wowzer, cute and cunning, had been quick enough to say so to clear himself, but—Jimmie

Dale smiled a little now—neither the Wowzer, nor Chang Foo, nor China-town would ever be in a position to recognise their uninvited guest!

Jimmie Dale's eyes shifted to the letter speculatively, gravely. It seemed as though the night had already held a year of happenings, and the night was not over yet—there was the letter! It had already cost one life; was it to cost another—or what?

It began as it always did. He read it through once, in amazement; a second time, with a flush of bitter anger creeping to his cheeks; and a third time, curiously memorising, as it were, snatches of it here and there.

Dear Philanthropic Crook:

Robbery of Hudson-Mercantile National Bank—trusted employee is ex-convict, bad police record, served term in Sing Sing three years ago—known to police as Bookkeeper Bob, real name is Robert Moyne, lives at —— Street, Harlem—Inspector Burton and Lannigan of headquarters trailing him now—robbery not yet made public—

There was a great deal more—four sheets of closely written data. With an exclamation almost of dismay, Jimmie Dale pulled out his watch. So that was what Burton and Lannigan were up to! And he had actually run into them! Lord, the irony of it! The—And then Jimmie Dale stared at the dial of his watch incredulously. It was still but barely midnight! It seemed impossible that since leaving the theatre at a few minutes before eleven, he had lived through but a single hour!

Jimmie Dale's fingers began to pluck at the letter, tearing it into pieces, tearing the pieces over and over again into tiny shreds. The train stopped at station after station, people got on and off—Jimmie Dale's hat was over his eyes, and his eyes were glued again to the window. Had Bookkeeper Bob returned to his flat in Harlem with the detectives at his heels—or were Burton and Lannigan still trailing the man downtown somewhere around the cafe's? If the former, the theft of the letter and its incident loss of time had been an irreparable disaster; if the latter—well, who knew! The risk was the Gray Seal's!

At One Hundred and Twenty-Fifth Street Jimmie Dale left the train; and, at the end of a sharp four minutes' walk, during which he had dodged in and out from street to street, stopped on a corner to survey the block ahead of him. It was a block devoted exclusively to flats and apartment houses, and, apart from a few belated pedestrians, was deserted. Jimmie Dale strolled leisurely down one side, crossed the street at the end of the block, and strolled leisurely back on the other side—there was no sign of either Burton or Lannigan. It was a fairly safe presumption then that Bookkeeper Bob had not returned yet, or one of the detectives at least would have been shadowing the house.

Jimmie Dale, smiling a little grimly, retraced his steps again, and turned deliberately into a doorway—whose number he had noted as he had passed a moment or so before. So, after all, there was time yet! This was the house. "Number eighteen," she had said in her letter. "A flat—three stories—Moyne lives on ground floor."

Jimmie Dale leaned against the vestibule door—there was a faint click—a little steel instrument was withdrawn from the lock—and Jimmie Dale stepped into the hall, where a gas jet, turned down, burned dimly.

The door of the ground-floor apartment was at his right, Jimmie Dale reached up and turned off the light. Again those slim, tapering, wonderfully sensitive fingers worked with the little steel instrument, this time in the lock of the apartment door—again there was that almost inaudible click—and then cautiously, inch by inch, the door opened under his hand. He peered inside—down a hallway lighted, if it could be called lighted at all, by a sub-dued glow from two open doors that gave upon it—peered intently, listening intently, as he drew a black silk mask from his pocket and slipped it over his face. And then, silent as a shadow in his movements, the door left just ajar behind him, he stole down the carpeted hallway.

Opposite the first of the open doorways Jimmie Dale paused—a curi-ously hard expression creeping over his face, his lips beginning to droop ominously downward at the corners. It was a little sitting room, cheaply but tastefully furnished, and a young woman, Bookkeeper Bob's wife evidently, and evidently sitting up for her husband, had fallen sound asleep in a chair, her head pillowed on her arms that were outstretched across the table. For a moment Jimmie Dale held there, his eyes on the scene—and the next mo-ment, his hand curved into a clenched fist, he had passed on and entered the adjoining room.

It was a child's bedroom. A night lamp burned on a table beside the bed, and the soft rays seemed to play and linger in caress on the tousled golden hair of a little girl of perhaps two years of age—and something seemed to choke suddenly in Jimmie Dale's throat—the sweet, innocent little face, up-turned to his, was smiling at him as she slept.

Jimmie Dale turned away his head—his eyelashes wet under his mask. *"Beneath the mattress of the child's bed,"* the letter had said. His face like stone, his lips a thin line now, Jimmie Dale's hand reached deftly in without disturbing the child and took out a package—and then another. He straight-ened up, a bundle of crisp new hundred-dollar notes in each hand—and on the top of one, slipped under the elastic band that held the bills together, an un-sealed envelope. He drew out the latter, and opened it—it was a second-class steamship passage to Vera Cruz, made out in a fictitious name, of course, to John Davies, the booking for next day's sailing. From the ticket, from the stolen money, Jimmie Dale's eyes lifted to rest again on the little golden head, the smiling lips—and then, dropping the packages into his pockets, his own lips moving oddly, he turned abruptly to the door.

"My God, the shame of it!" he whispered to himself.

He crept down the corridor, past the open door of the room where the young woman still sat fast asleep, and, his mask in his pocket again, stepped softly into the vestibule, and from there to the street.

Jimmie Dale hurried now, spurred on it seemed by a hot, insensate fury that raged within him—there was still one other call to make that night—still those remaining and minute details in the latter part of her letter, grim and ugly in their portent!

It was close upon one o'clock in the morning when Jimmie Dale stopped again—this time before a fashionable dwelling just off Central Park. And here, for perhaps the space of a minute, he surveyed the house from the sidewalk—watching, with a sort of speculative satisfaction, a man's shadow that passed constantly to and fro across the drawn blinds of one of the lower windows. The rest of the house was in darkness.

"Yes," said Jimmie Dale, nodding his head, "I rather thought so. The servants will have retired hours ago. It's safe enough."

He ran quickly up the steps and rang the bell. A door opened almost instantly, sending a faint glow into the hall from the lighted room; a hurried step crossed the hall—and the outer door was thrown back.

"Well, what is it?" demanded a voice brusquely.

It was quite dark, too dark for either to distinguish the other's features—and Jimmie Dale's hat was drawn far down over his eyes.

"I want to see Mr. Thomas H. Carling, cashier of the Hudson-Mercantile National Bank—it's very important," said Jimmie Dale earnestly.

"I am Mr. Carling," replied the other. "What is it?"

Jimmie Dale leaned forward.

"From headquarters—with a report," he said, in a low tone.

"Ah!" exclaimed the bank official sharply. "Well, it's about time! I've been waiting up for it—though I expected you would telephone rather than this. Come in!"

"Thank you," said Jimmie Dale courteously—and stepped into the hall.

The other closed the front door. "The servants are in bed, of course," he explained, as he led the way toward the lighted room. "This way, please."

Behind the other, across the hall, Jimmie Dale followed and close at Carling's heels entered the room, which was fitted up, quite evidently regardless of cost, as a combination library and study. Carling, in a somewhat pompous fashion, walked straight ahead toward the carved-mahogany flat-topped desk, and, as he reached it, waved his hand.

"Take a chair," he said, over his shoulder—and then, turning in the act of dropping into his own chair, grasped suddenly at the edge of the desk instead, and, with a low, startled cry, stared across the room.

Jimmie Dale was leaning back against the door that was closed now behind him—and on Jimmie Dale's face was a black silk mask.

For an instant neither man spoke nor moved; then Carling, spare-built, dapper in evening clothes, edged back from the desk and laughed a little uncertainly.

"Quite neat! I compliment you! From headquarters with a report, I think you said?"

"Which I neglected to add," said Jimmie Dale, "was to be made in private."

Carling, as though to put as much distance between them as possible, continued to edge back across the room—but his small black eyes, black now to the pupils themselves, never left Jimmie Dale's face.

"In private, eh?"—he seemed to be sparring for time, as he smiled. "In private! You've a strange method of securing privacy, haven't you? A bit melodramatic, isn't it? Perhaps you'll be good enough to tell me who you are?"

Jimmie Dale smiled indulgently.

"My mask is only for effect," he said. "My name is—Smith."

"Yes," said Carling. "I am very stupid. Thank you. I—" he had reached the other side of the room now—and with a quick, sudden movement jerked his hand to the dial of the safe that stood against the wall.

But Jimmie Dale was quicker—without shifting his position, his automatic, whipped from his pocket, held a disconcerting bead on Carling's forehead.

"Please don't do that," said Jimmie Dale softly. "It's rather a good make, that safe. I dare say it would take me half an hour to open it. I was rather curious to know whether it was locked or not."

Carling's hand dropped to his side.

"So!" he sneered. "That's it, is it! The ordinary variety of sneak thief!" His voice was rising gradually. "Well, sir, let me tell you that—"

"Mr. Carling," said Jimmie Dale, in a low, even tone, "unless you moderate your voice someone in the house might hear you—I am quite well aware of that. But if that happens, if anyone enters this room, if you make a move to touch a button, or in any other way attempt to attract attention, I'll drop you where you stand!" His hand, behind his back, extracted the key from the door lock, held it up for the other to see, then dropped it into his pocket—and his voice, cold before, rang peremptorily now. "Come back to the desk and sit down in that chair!" he ordered.

For a moment Carling hesitated; then, with a half-muttered oath, obeyed.

Jimmie Dale moved over, and stood in front of Carling on the other side of the desk—and stared silently at the immaculate, fashionably groomed figure before him.

Under the prolonged gaze, Carling's composure, in a measure at least, seemed to forsake him. He began to drum nervously with his fingers on the desk, and shift uneasily in his chair.

And then, from first one pocket and then the other, Jimmie Dale took the two packages of banknotes, and, still with out a word, pushed them across the desk until they lay under the other's eyes.

Carling's fingers stopped their drumming, slid to the desk edge, tightened there, and a whiteness crept into his face. Then, with an effort, he jerked himself erect in his chair.

"What's this?" he demanded hoarsely.

"About ten thousand dollars, I should say," said Jimmie Dale slowly. "I haven't counted it. Your bank was robbed this evening at closing time, I understand?"

"Yes!" Carling's voice was excited now, the colour back in his face. "But you—how—do you mean that you are returning the money to the bank?"

"Exactly," said Jimmie Dale.

Carling was once more the pompous bank official. He leaned back and surveyed Jimmie Dale critically with his little black eyes.

"Ah, quite so!" he observed. "That accounts for the mask. But I am still a little in the dark. Under the circumstances, it is quite impossible that you should have stolen the money yourself, and—"

"I didn't," said Jimmie Dale. "I found it hidden in the home of one of your employees."

"You found it—*where*?"

"In Moyne's home—up in Harlem."

"Moyne, eh?" Carling was alert, quick now, jerking out his words. "How did you come to get into this, then? His pal? Double-crossing him, eh? I suppose you want a reward—we'll attend to that, of course. You're wiser than you know, my man. That's what we suspected. We've had the detectives trailing Moyne all evening." He reached forward over the desk for the telephone. "I'll telephone headquarters to make the arrest at once."

"Just a minute," interposed Jimmie Dale gravely. "I want you to listen to a little story first."

"A story! What has a story got to do with this?" snapped Carling.

"The man has got a home," said Jimmie Dale softly. "A home, and a wife—and a little baby girl."

"Oh, that's the game then, eh? You want to plead for him?" Carling flung out gruffly. "Well, he should have thought of all that before! It's quite useless for you to bring it up. The man has had his chance already—a better chance than anyone with his record ever had before. We took him into the bank knowing that he was an ex-convict, but believing that we could make an honest man of him—and this is the result."

"And yet—"

"No!" said Carling icily.

"You refuse—absolutely?" Jimmie Dale's voice had a lingering, wistful note in it.

"I refuse!" said Carling bluntly. "I won't have anything to do with it."

There was just an instant's silence; and then, with a strange, slow, creeping motion, as a panther creeps when about to spring, Jimmie Dale projected his body across the desk—far across it toward the other. And the muscles of his jaw were quivering, his words rasping, choked with the sweep of fury that, held back so long, broke now in a passionate surge.

"And shall I tell you why you won't? Your bank was robbed tonight of one hundred thousand dollars. There are ten thousand here. *The other ninety thousand are in your safe!*"

"You lie!" Ashen to the lips, Carling had risen in his chair. "You lie!" he cried. "Do you hear! You lie! I tell you, you lie!"

Jimmie Dale's lips parted ominously.

"Sit down!" he gritted between his teeth.

The white in Carling's face had turned to gray, his lips were working—mechanically he sank down again in his chair.

Jimmie Dale still leaned over the desk, resting his weight on his right elbow, the automatic in his right hand covering Carling.

"You cur!" whispered Jimmie Dale. "There's just one reason, only one, that keeps me from putting a bullet through you while you sit there. We'll get to that in a moment. There is that little story first—shall I tell it to you now? For the past four years, and God knows how many before that, you've gone the pace. The lavishness of this bachelor establishment of yours is common talk in New York—far in excess of a bank cashier's salary. But you were supposed to be a wealthy man in your own right; and so, in reality you were—once. But you went through your fortune two years ago. Counted a model citizen, an upright man, an honour to the community—what were you, Carling? What *are* you? Shall I tell you? Roue, gambler, leading a double life of the fastest kind. You did it cleverly, Carling; hid it well—but your game is up. Tonight, for instance, you are at the end of your tether, swamped with debts, exposure threatening you at any moment. Why don't you tell me again that I lie—Carling?"

But now the man made no answer. He had sunk a little deeper in his chair—a dawning look of terror in the eyes that held, fascinated, on Jimmie Dale.

"You cur!" said Jimmie Dale again. "You cur, with your devil's work! A year ago you saw this night coming—when you must have money, or face ruin and exposure. You saw it then, a year ago, the day that Moyne, concealing nothing of his prison record, applied through friends for a position in the bank. Your co-officials were opposed to his appointment, but you, do you remember how you pleaded to give the man his chance—and in your hellish ingenuity saw your way then out of the trap! An ex-convict from Sing Sing! It was enough, wasn't it? What chance had he!" Jimmie Dale paused, his left hand clenched until the skin formed whitish knobs over the knuckles.

Carling's tongue sought his lips, made a circuit of them—and he tried to speak, but his voice was an incoherent muttering.

"I'll not waste words," said Jimmie Dale, in his grim monotone. "I'm not sure enough myself—that I could keep my hands off you much longer. The actual details of how you stole the money today do not matter—*now*. A little later perhaps in court—but not now. You were the last to leave the bank, but before leaving you pretended to discover the theft of a hundred thousand dollars—that, done up in a paper parcel, was even then reposing in your desk. You brought the parcel home, put it in that safe there—and notified the president of the bank by telephone from here of the robbery, suggesting that police headquarters be advised at once. He told you to go ahead and act as you saw best. You notified the police, speciously directing suspicion to—the ex-convict in the bank's employ. You knew Moyne was dining out tonight, you knew where—and at a hint from you the police took up the trail. A little later in the evening, you took these two packages of banknotes from the rest, and with this steamship ticket—which you obtained yesterday while out at lunch by sending a district messenger boy with the money and instructions in a sealed envelope to purchase for you—you went up to the Moynes' flat in Harlem for the purpose of secreting them somewhere there. You pretended to be much disappointed at finding Moyne out—you had just come for a little social visit, to get better acquainted with the home life of your employees! Mrs. Moyne was genuinely pleased and grateful. She took you in to see their little girl, who was already asleep in bed. She left you there for a moment to answer the door—and you—you"—Jimmie Dale's voice choked again—"you blot on God's earth, you slipped the money and ticket under the child's mattress!"

Carling came forward with a lurch in his chair—and his hands went out, pawing in a wild, pleading fashion over Jimmie Dale's arm.

Jimmie Dale flung him away.

"You were safe enough," he rasped on. "The police could only construe your visit to Moyne's flat as zeal on behalf of the bank. And it was safer, much more circumspect on your part, not to order the flat searched at once, but only as a last resort, as it were, after you had led the police to trail him all evening and still remain without a clue—and besides, of course, not until you had planted the evidence that was to damn him and wreck his life and home! You were even generous in the amount you deprived yourself of out of the hundred thousand dollars—for less would have been enough. Caught with ten thousand dollars of the bank's money and a steamship ticket made out in a fictitious name, it was prima-facie evidence that he had done the job and had the balance somewhere. What would his denials, his protestations of innocence count for? He was an ex-convict, a hardened criminal caught red-handed with a portion of the proceeds of robbery—he had succeeded in hiding the remainder of it too cleverly, that was all."

Carling's face was ghastly. His hands went out again—again his tongue moistened his dry lips. He whispered:

"Isn't—isn't there some—some way we can fix this?"

And then Jimmie Dale laughed—not pleasantly.

"Yes, there's a way, Carling," he said grimly. "That's why I'm here." He picked up a sheet of writing paper and pushed it across the desk—then a pen, which he dipped into the inkstand, and extended to the other. "The way you'll fix it will be to write out a confession exonerating Moyne."

Carling shrank back into his chair, his head huddling into his shoulders.

"No!" he cried. "I won't—I can't—my God!—I—I—won't!"

The automatic in Jimmie Dale's hand edged forward the fraction of an inch.

"I have not used this—yet. You understand now why—don't you?" he said under his breath.

"No, no!" Carling pushed away the pen. "I'm ruined—ruined as it is. But this would mean the penitentiary, too—"

"Where you tried to send an innocent man in your place, you hound; where you—"

"Some other way—some other way!" Carling was babbling. "Let me out of this—for God's sake, let me out of this!"

"Carling," said Jimmie Dale hoarsely, "I stood beside a little bed tonight and looked at a baby girl—a little baby girl with golden hair, who smiled as she slept."

Carling shivered, and passed a shaking hand across his face.

"Take this pen," said Jimmie Dale monotonously; "or—*this*!" The automatic lifted until the muzzle was on a line with Carling's eyes.

Carling's hand reached out, still shaking, and took the pen; and his body, dragged limply forward, hung over the desk. The pen spluttered on the paper—a bead of sweat spurting from the man's forehead dropped to the sheet.

There was silence in the room. A minute passed—another. Carling's pen travelled haltingly across the paper then, with a low cry as he signed his name, he dropped the pen from his fingers, and, rising unsteadily from his chair, stumbled away from the desk toward a couch across the room.

An instant Jimmie Dale watched the other, then he picked up the sheet of paper. It was a miserable document, miserably scrawled:

I guess it's all up. I guess I knew it would be some day. Moyne hadn't anything to do with it. I stole the money myself from the bank tonight. I guess it's all up.

Thomas H. Carling.

From the paper, Jimmie Dale's eyes shifted to the figure by the couch—and the paper fluttered suddenly from his fingers to the desk. Carling was reeling, clutching at his throat—a small glass vial rolled upon the carpet. And then, even as Jimmie Dale sprang forward, the other pitched head long over the couch—and in a moment it was over.

Presently Jimmie Dale picked up the vial—and dropped it back on the floor again. There was no label on it, but it needed none—the strong, penetrating odor of bitter almonds was telltale evidence enough. It was prussic, or hydrocyanic acid, probably the most deadly poison and the swiftest in its action that was known to science—Carling had provided against that "some day" in his confession!

For a little space, motionless, Jimmie Dale stood looking down at the silent, outstretched form—then he walked slowly back to the desk, and slowly, deliberately picked up the signed confession and the steamship ticket. He held them an instant, staring at them, then methodically began to tear them into little pieces, a strange, tired smile hovering on his lips. The man was dead now—there would be disgrace enough for someone to bear, a mother perhaps—who knew! And there was another way now—since the man was dead.

Jimmie Dale put the pieces in his pocket, went to the safe, opened it, and took out a parcel, locked the safe carefully, and carried the parcel to the desk. He opened it there. Inside were nearly two dozen little packages of hundred-dollar bills. The other two packages that he had brought with him he added to the rest. From his pocket he took out the thin metal insignia case, and with the tiny tweezers lifted up one of the gray-coloured, diamond-shaped paper seals. He moistened the adhesive side, and, still holding it by the tweezers, dropped it on his handkerchief and pressed the seal down on the face of the topmost package of banknotes. He tied the parcel up then, and, picking up the pen, addressed it in printed characters:

HUDSON-MERCANTILE NATIONAL BANK,

NEW YORK CITY.

"District messenger—some way—in the morning," he murmured.

Jimmie Dale slipped his mask into his pocket, and, with the parcel under his arm, stepped to the door and unlocked it. He paused for an instant on the threshold for a single, quick, comprehensive glance around the room—then passed on out into the street.

At the corner he stopped to light a cigarette—and the flame of the match spurting up disclosed a face that was worn and haggard. He threw the match away, smiled a little wearily—and went on.

The Gray Seal had committed another "crime."

CHAPTER 7
THE THIEF

Choosing between the snowy napery, the sparkling glass and silver, the cozy, shaded table-lamps, the famous French chef of the ultra-exclusive St. James Club, his own home on Riverside Drive where a dinner fit for an epicure and served by Jason, that most perfect of butlers, awaited him, and Marlianne's, Jimmie Dale, driving in alone in his touring car from an afternoon's golf, had chosen—Marlianne's.

Marlianne's, if such a thing as Bohemianism, or, rather, a concrete expression of it exists, was Bohemian. A two-piece string orchestra played valiantly to the accompaniment of a hoarse-throated piano; and between courses the diners took up the refrain—and, as it was always between courses with someone, the place was a bedlam of noisy riot. Nevertheless, it was Marlianne's—and Jimmie Dale liked Marlianne's. He had dined there many times before, as he had just dined in the person of Jimmie Dale, the millionaire, his high-priced imported car at the curb of the shabby street outside—and he had dined there, disreputable in attire, seedy in appearance, with the police yelping at his heels, as Larry the Bat. In either character Marlianne's had welcomed him with equal courtesy to its spotted linen and most excellent table-d'hote with *vin ordinaire*—for fifty cents.

And now, in the act of reaching into his pocket for the change to pay his bill, Jimmie Dale seemed suddenly to experience some difficulty in finding what he sought, and his fingers went fumbling from one pocket to another. Two men at the table in front of him were talking—their voices, over a momentary lull in violin squeaks, talk, laughter, singing, and the clatter of dishes, reached him:

"Carling commit suicide! Not on your life! No; of course he didn't! It was that cursed Gray Seal croaked him, just as sure as you sit in that chair!"

The other grunted. "Yes; but what'd the Gray Seal want to pinch a hundred thousand out of the bank for, and then give it back again the next morning?"

"What's he done a hundred other things for to cover up the real object of what he's after?" retorted the first speaker, with a short, vicious laugh; then, with a thump of his fist on the table: "The man's a devil, a fiend, and anywhere else but New York he'd have been caught and sent to the chair where he belongs long ago, and—"

A burst of ragtime drowned out the man's words. Jimmie Dale placed a fifty-cent piece and a tip beside it on his dinner check, pushed back his chair, and rose from the table. There was a half-tolerantly satirical, half-angry glint in his dark, steady eyes. It was not only the police who yelped at his heels, but every man, woman, and child in the city. The man had not voiced his own sentiments—he had voiced the sentiments of New York! And it was quite on the cards that if he, Jimmie Dale, were ever caught his destination would not even be the death cell and the chair at Sing Sing—his fellow citizens had reached a pitch where they would be quite capable of literally tearing him to pieces if they ever got their hands on him!

And yet there were a few, a very few, a handful out of five millions, who sometimes remembered perhaps to thank God that the Gray Seal lived—that was his reward. That—and *she*, whose mysterious letters prompted and impelled his, the Gray Seal's, acts! She—nameless, fascinating in her brilliant resourcefulness, amazing in her power, a woman whose life was bound up with his and yet held apart from him in the most inexplicable, absorbing way; a woman he had never seen, save for her gloved arm in the limousine that night, who at one unexpected moment projected a dazzling, impersonal existence across his path, and the next, leaving him battling for his life where greed and passion and crime swirled about him, was gone!

Jimmie Dale threaded the small, crowded rooms—the interior of Marlianne's had never been altered from the days when the place had been a family residence of some pretension—and, reaching the hall, received his hat from the frowsy-looking boy in attendance. He passed outside, and, at the top of the steps, paused as he took his cigarette case from his pocket. It was nearly a week since Carling, the cashier of the Hudson-Mercantile National Bank, had been found dead in his home, a bottle that had contained hydrocyanic acid on the floor beside him; nearly a week since Bookkeeper Bob, unaware that he had ever been under temporary suspicion for the robbery of the bank, had, equally unknown to himself, been cleared of any complicity in that affair—and yet, as witness the conversation of a moment ago, it was still the topic of New York, still the vital issue that filled the maw of the newspapers with ravings, threats, and execrations against the Gray Seal, snarling virulently the while at the police for the latter's ineptitude, inefficiency, and impotence!

Jimmie Dale closed his cigarette case with a snap that was almost human in its irony, dropped it back into his pocket, and lighted a match—but the flame was arrested halfway to the tip of his cigarette, as his eyes fixed suddenly and curiously on a woman's form hurrying down the street. She had turned the corner before he took his eyes from her, and the match between his fingers had gone out. Not that there was anything very strange in a woman walking, or even half running, along the street; nor that there was anything particularly attractive or unusual about her, and if there had been the street was too dark for him to have distinguished it. It was not that—it was the fact that she had neither passed by the house on whose steps he stood, nor come out of any of the adjoining houses. It was as though she had suddenly and miraculously appeared out of thin air, and taken form on a sidewalk a little way down from Marlianne's.

"That's strange!" commented Jimmie Dale to himself. "However—" He took out another match, lighted his cigarette, jerked the match stub away from him, and, with a lift of his shoulders, went down the steps.

He crossed the pavement, walked around the front of his machine, since the steering wheel was on the side next to the curb, and, with his hand out to open the car door—stopped. Someone had been tampering with it—it was not quite closed. There was no mistake. Jimmie Dale made no mistakes of that kind, a man whose life hung a dozen times a day on little things could not afford to make them. He had closed it firmly, even with a bang, when he had got out.

Instantly suspicious, he wrenched the door wide open, switched on the light under the hood, and, with a sharp exclamation, bent quickly forward. A glove, a woman's glove, a white glove lay on the floor of the car. Jimmie Dale's pulse leaped suddenly into fierce, pounding beats. It was *hers*! He *knew* that intuitively—knew it as he knew that he breathed. And that woman he had so leisurely watched as she had disappeared from sight was, must have been—she!

He sprang from the car with a jump, his first impulse to dash after her—and checked himself, laughing a little bitterly. It was too late for that now—he had already let his chance slip through his fingers. Around the corner was Sixth Avenue, surface cars, the elevated, taxicabs, a multitude of people, any one of a hundred ways in which she could, and would, already have discounted pursuit from him—and, besides, he would not even have been able to recognise her if he saw her!

Jimmie Dale's smile was mirthless as he turned back to the car, and picked up the glove. Why had she dropped it there? It could not have been intentional. Why had—he began to tear suddenly at the glove's little finger, and in another second, kneeling on the car's step, his shoulders inside, he was holding a ring close under the little electric bulb.

It was a gold seal ring, a small, dainty thing that bore a crest: a bell, surmounted by a bishop's mitre—the bell, quaint in design, harking the imagination back to some old-time belfry tower. And underneath, in the scroll—a motto. It was a full minute before Jimmie Dale could decipher it, for the lettering was minute and the words, of course, reversed. It was in French: *sonnez le Tocsin*.

He straightened up, the glove and ring in his hand, a puzzled expression on his face. It was strange! Had she, after all, dropped the glove there intentionally; had she at last let down the barriers just a little between them, and given him this little intimate sign that she——

And then Jimmie Dale laughed abruptly, self-mockingly. He was only trying to deceive himself, to argue himself into believing what, with heart and soul, he wanted to believe. It was not like her—and neither was it so! His eyes had fixed on the seat beside the wheel. He had not used the lap rug all that day, he couldn't use a rug and drive, he had left it folded and hanging on the rack in the tonneau—it was now neatly folded and reposing on the front seat!

"Yes," said Jimmie Dale, a sort of self-pity in his tones, "I might have known."

He lifted the rug. Beneath it on the leather seat lay a white envelope. Her letter! The letter that never came save with the plan of some grim, desperate work outlined ahead—the call to arms for the Gray Seal. *Sonnez le Tocsin!* Ring the Tocsin! Sound the alarm! The Tocsin! The words were running through his brain. A strange motto on that crest—that seemed so strangely apt! The Tocsin! Never once in all the times that he had heard from her, never once in the years that had gone since that initial letter of hers had struck its first warning note, had any communication from her been but to sound again a new alarm—the Toscin! The Tocsin—the word seemed to visualise her, to give her a concrete form and being, to breathe her very personality.

"The Tocsin!"—Jimmie Dale whispered the word softly, a little wistfully. "Yes; I shall call you that—the Tocsin!"

He folded the glove very carefully, placed it with the ring in his pocketbook, picked up the letter—and, with a sharp exclamation, turned it quickly over in his fingers, then bent hurriedly with it to the light.

Strange things were happening that night! For the first time, the letter was not even sealed! That was not like her, either! What did it mean? Quick, alert now, anxious even, he pulled the double, folded sheets from the envelope, glanced rapidly through them—and, after a moment, a smile, whimsical, came slowly to his lips.

It was quite plain now—all of it. The glove, the ring, and the unsealed letter—and the postscript held the secret; or, rather, what had been intended for a postscript did, for it comprised only a few words, ending abruptly, unfinished: "Look in the cupboard at the rear of the room. The man with the red wig is——" That was all, and the words, written in ink, were badly blurred, as though the paper had been hastily folded before the ink was dry.

It was quite plain; and, in view of the real explanation of it all, eminently characteristic of her. With the letter already written, she had come there, meaning to place it on the seat and cover it with the rug, as, indeed, she had done; then, deciding to add the postscript, and because she would attract less attention that way than in any other, she had climbed into the car as though it belonged to her, and had seated herself there to write it. She would have been hurried in her movements, of course, and in pulling off her glove to use the fountain pen the ring had come with it. The rest was obvious. She had but just begun to write when he had appeared on the steps. She had slipped instantly down to the floor of the car, probably dropping the glove from her lap, hastily inclosed the letter in the envelope which she had no time to seal, thrust envelope under the rug, and, forgetting her glove and fearful of risking his attention by attempting to close the door firmly, had stolen along the body of the car, only to be noticed by him too late—when she was well down the street!

And at that latter thought, once more chagrin seized Jimmie Dale—then he turned impulsively to the letter. All this was extraneous, apart—for another time, when every moment was not a priceless asset as it very probably was now.

"Dear Philanthropic Crook"—it always began that way, never any other way. He read on more and more intently, crouched there close to the light on the floor of his car, lips thinning as he proceeded—read it to the end, absorbing, memorising it—and then the abortive postscript:

"Look in the cupboard at the rear of the room. The man with the red wig is—"

For an instant, as mechanically he tore the letter into little shreds, he held there hesitant—and the next, slamming the door tight, he flung himself into the seat behind the wheel, and the big, sixty-horse-power, self-starting machine was roaring down the street.

The Tocsin! There was a grim smile on Jimmie Dale's lips now. The alarm! Yes, it was always an alarm, quick, sudden, an emergency to face on the instant—plans, decisions to be made with no time to ponder them, with only that one fact to consider, staggering enough in itself, that a mistake meant disaster and ruin to someone else, and to himself, if the courts were merciful where he had little hope for mercy, the penitentiary for life!

And now tonight again, as it almost always was when these mysterious letters came, every moment of inaction was piling up the odds against him. And, too, the same problem confronted him. How, in what way, in what role, must he play the night's game to its end? As Larry the Bat?

The car was speeding forward. He was heading down Broadway now, lower Broadway, that stretched before him, deserted like some dark, narrow canyon where, far below, like towering walls, the buildings closed together and seemed to converge into some black, impassable barrier. The street lights flashed by him; a patrolman stopped the swinging of his night-stick, and turned to gaze at the car that rushed by at a rate perilously near to contempt of speed laws; street cars passed at indifferent intervals; pedestrians were few and far between—it was the lower Broadway of night.

Larry the Bat? Jimmie Dale shook his head impatiently over the steering wheel. No; that would not do. It would be well enough for this young Burton, perhaps, but not for old Isaac, the East Side fence—for Isaac knew him in the character of Larry the Bat. His quick, keen brain, weaving, eliminating, devising, scheming, discarded that idea. The final coup of the night, as yet but sensed in an indefinite, unshaped way, if enacted in the person of Larry the Bat would therefore stamp Larry the Bat and the Gray Seal as one—a contretemps but little less fatal, in view of old Issac, than to bracket the Gray Seal and Jimmie Dale! Larry the Bat was not a character to be assumed with impunity, nor one to jeopardize—it was a bulwark of safety, at it were, to which more than once he owed escape from capture and discovery.

He lifted his shoulders with a sudden jerk of decision as the car swerved to the left and headed for the East Side. There was only one alternative then—the black silk mask that folded into such tiny compass, and that, together with an automatic and the curious, thin metal case that looked so like a cigarette case, was always in his pocket for an emergency!

The car turned again, and, approaching its destination, Jimmie Dale slowed down the speed perceptibly. It was a strange case, not a pleasant one—and the raw edges where they showed were ugly in their nakedness. Old Isaac Pelina, young Burton, and Maddon—K. Wilmington Maddon, the wall-paper magnate! Curious, that of the three he should already know two—old Isaac and Maddon! Everybody in the East Side, every denizen of the underworld, and many who posed on a far higher plane knew old Isaac—fence to the most select clientele of thieves in New York, unscrupulous, hand in glove with any rascality or crime that promised profit, a money lender, a Shylock without even a Shylock's humanity as a saving grace! Yes; as Larry the Bat he knew old Isaac, and he knew him not only personally but by firsthand reputation—he had heard the man cursed in blasphemous, whole-souled abandon by more than one crook who was in the old fence's toils. They dealt with him, the crooks, while they swore to "get" him because he was "safe," but—Jimmie Dale's lips parted in a mirthless smile—some day old Isaac would be found in that spiders' den of his back of the dingy loan office with a knife in his heart or a bullet through his head! And K. Wilmington Maddon—Jimmie Dale's smile grew whimsical—he had known Maddon quite intimately for years, had even dined with him at the St. James Club only a few nights before. Maddon was a man in his own "set"—and Maddon, interfered with, was likely to prove none too tractable a customer to handle. And young Burton, the letter had said, was Maddon's private and confidential secretary. Jimmie Dale's lips thinned again. Well, Burton's acquaintance was still to be made! It was a curious trio—and it was dirty work, more raw than cunning, more devilish than ingenious; blackmail in its most hellish form; the stake, at the least calculation, a cool half million. A heavy price for a single slip in a man's life!

He brought the car abruptly to a halt at the edge of the curb, and sprang out to the ground. He was in front of "The Budapest" restaurant, a garish establishment, most popular of all resorts for the moment on the East Side, where Fifth Avenue, in the fond belief that it was seeing the real thing in "seamy" life, engaged its table a week in advance. Jimmie Dale pushed a bill into the door attendant's hand, accompanied by an injunction to keep an eye on the machine, and entered the cafe.

But for a sort of tinselled ostentation the place might well have been the Marlianne's that he had just left—it was crowded and riot was at its height; a stringed orchestra in Hungarian costume played what purported to be Hungarian airs; shouts, laughter, clatter of dishes, and thump of steins added to the din. He made his way between the close-packed tables to the stairs, and descended to the lower floor. Here, if anything, the confusion was greater than above; but here, too, was an exit through to the rear street—and a moment later he was sauntering past the front of an unkempt little pawnshop, closed for the night, over whose door, in the murk of a distant street lamp, three balls hung in sagging disarray, tawny with age, and across whose dirty, unwashed windows, letters missing, ran the legend:

IS AC PELINA
Pawn brok r

The pawnshop made the corner of a very dark and narrow lane—and, with a quick glance around him to assure himself that he was unobserved, Jimmie Dale stepped into the alleyway, and, lost instantly in the blacker shadows, stole along by the wall of the pawnshop. Old Isaac's business was not all done through the front door.

And then suddenly Jimmie Dale shrank still closer against the wall. Was it intuition, premonition—or reality? There seemed an uncanny feeling of presence around him, as though perhaps he were watched, as though others beside himself were in the lane. Yes; ahead of him a shadow moved—he could just barely distinguish it now that his eyes had grown accustomed to the darkness. It, like himself, was close against the wall, and now it slunk noiselessly down the length of the lane until he lost sight of it. *And what was that?* He strained his ears to listen. It seemed like a window being opened or closed, cautiously, stealthily, the fraction of an inch at a time. And then he located the sound—it came from the other side of the lane and very nearly opposite to where, on the second floor, a dull, yellow glow shone out from old Isaac's private den in the rear of the pawnshop's office.

Jimmie Dale's brows were gathered in sharp furrows. There was evidently something afoot tonight of which the Tocsin had *not* sounded the alarm. And then the frown relaxed, and he smiled a little. Miraculous as was the means through which she obtained the knowledge that was the basis of their strange partnership, it was no more miraculous than her unerring accuracy in the minutest details. The Tocsin had never failed him yet. It was possible that something was afoot around him, quite probable, indeed, since he was in the most vicious part of the city, in the heart of gangland; but whatever it might be, it was certainly extraneous to his mission or she would have mentioned it.

The lane was empty now, he was quite sure of that—and there was no further sound from the window opposite. He started forward once more—only to halt again for the second time as abruptly as before, squeezing if possible even more closely against the wall. Someone had turned into the lane from the sidewalk, and, walking hurriedly, choosing with evident precaution the exact centre of the alleyway, came toward him.

The man passed, his hurried stride a half run; and, a few feet beyond, halted at old Isaac's side door. From somewhere inside the old building Jimmie Dale's ears caught the faint ringing of an electric bell; a long ring, followed in quick succession by three short ones—then the repeated clicking of a latch, as though pulled by a cord from above, and the man passed in through the door, closing it behind him.

Jimmie Dale nodded to himself in the darkness. It was a spring lock; the signal was one long ring and three short ones—the Tocsin had not missed even those small details. Also, Burton was late for his appointment, for that must have been Burton—business such as old Isaac had in hand that night would have permitted the entrance of no other visitor but K. Wilmington Maddon's private secretary.

He moved down the lane to the door, and tried it softly. It was locked, of course. The slim, tapering, sensitive fingers, whose tips were eyes and ears to Jimmie Dale, felt over the lock—and a slender little steel instrument slipped into the keyhole. A moment more and the catch was released, and the door, under his hand, began to open. With it ajar, he paused, his eyes searching intently up and down the lane. There was nothing, no sign of anyone, no moving shadows now. His gaze shifted to the window opposite. Directly facing it now, with the dull reflection upon it from the lighted window of old Isaac's den above his head, he could make out that it was open—but that was all.

Once more he smiled—a little tolerantly at himself this time. Someone had been in the lane; someone had opened the window of his or her room in that tenement house across from him—surely there was nothing surprising, unnatural, or even out of the commonplace in that. He had been a little bit on edge himself, perhaps, and the sudden movement of that shadow, unexpected, had startled him for the moment, as, in all probability, the opening of the window had startled the skulking figure itself into action.

The door was open now. He stepped noiselessly inside, and closed it noiselessly behind him. He was in a narrow hall, where a few yards away, a light shone down a stairway at right angles to the hall itself.

"Rear door of pawnshop opens into hall, and exactly opposite very short flight of stairs leading directly to doorway of Isaac's den above. Ramshackle old place, low ceilings. Isaac, when sitting in his den, can look down, and, by means of a transom over the rear door of the shop, see the customers as they enter from the street, while he also keeps an eye on his assistant. Latter always locks up and leaves promptly at six o'clock—" Jimmie Dale was subconsciously repeating to himself snatches from the Tocsin's letter, which, as subconsciously in reading, he had memorised almost word for word.

And now voices reached him—one, excited, nervous, as though the speaker were labouring under mental strain that bordered closely on the hysterical; the other, curiously mingling a querulousness with an attempt to pacify, but dominantly contemptuous, sneering, cold.

Jimmie Dale moved along the hall—very slowly—without a sound—testing each step before he threw his body weight from one leg to the other. He reached the foot of the stairs. The Tocsin had been right; it was a very short flight. He counted the steps—there were eight. Above, facing him, a door was open. The voices were louder now. It was a sordid-looking room, what he could see of it, poverty-stricken in its appearance, intentionally so probably for effect, with no attempt whatever at furnishing. He could see through the doorway to the window that opened on the alleyway, or, rather, just glimpse the top of the window at an angle across the room—that and a bare stretch of floor. The two men were not in the line of vision.

Burton's voice—it was unquestionably Burton speaking—came to Jimmie Dale now distinctly.

"No, I didn't! I tell you, I didn't! I—I hadn't the nerve."

Jimmie Dale slipped his black silk mask over his face; and with extreme caution, on hands and knees, began to climb the stairs.

"So!" It was old Isaac now, in a half purr, half sneer. "And I was so sure, my young friend, that you had. I was so sure that you were not such a fool. Yes; I could even have sworn that they were in your pocket now—what? It is too bad—too bad! It is not a pleasant thing to think of, that little chair up the river in its horrible little room where—"

"For God's sake, Isaac—not that! Do you hear—not that! My God, I didn't mean to—I didn't know what I was doing!"

Jimmie Dale crept up another step, another, and another. There was silence for a moment in the room; then Burton again, hoarse-voiced:

"Isaac, I'll make good to you some other way. I swear I will—I swear it! If I'm caught at this I'll—I'll get fifteen years for it."

"And which would you rather have?" Jimmie Dale could picture the oily smirk, the shrug of his shoulders, the outthrust hands, palms upward, elbows in at the hips, the fingers curved and wide apart—"fifteen years, or what you get—for murder? Eh, my friend, you have thought of that—eh? It is a very little price I ask—yes?"

"Damn you!" Burton's voice was shrill, then dropped to a half sob. "No, no, Isaac, I didn't mean that. Only, for God's sake be merciful! It is not only the risk of the penitentiary; it's more than that. I—I tried to play white all my life, and until that cursed night there's no man living could say I haven't. You know that—you know that, Isaac. I tell you I couldn't do it this afternoon—I tell you I couldn't. I tried to and—and I couldn't."

Jimmie Dale was lying flat on the little landing now, peering into the room. Back a short distance from the doorway, a repulsive-looking little man in unkempt clothes and soiled linen, with yellowish-skinned, parchment face, out of which small black eyes shone cunningly and shrewdly, sat at a bare deal table in a rickety chair; facing him across the table stood a young man of not more than twenty-five, clean cut, well dressed, but whose face was unnaturally white now, and whose hand, as he extended it in a pleading gesture toward the other, trembled visibly. Jimmie Dale's hand made its way quietly to his side pocket and extracted his automatic.

Old Isaac humped his shoulders, and leered at his visitor.

"We talk a great deal, my young friend. What is the use? A bargain is a bargain. A few rubies in exchange for your life. A few rubies and my mouth is shut. Otherwise"—he humped his shoulders again. "Well?"

Burton drew back, swept his hand in a dazed way across his eyes—and laughed out suddenly in bitter mirth.

"A few rubies!" he cried. "The most magnificent stones on this side of the water—a *few* rubies! It's been Maddon's life hobby. Every child in New York knows that! A few—yes, there's only a few—but those few are worth a fortune. He trusts me, the man has been like a father to me, and—"

"So you are the very last to be suspected," observed old Isaac suavely. "Have I not told you that? There is nothing to fear. Did we not arrange everything so nicely—eh, my young friend? See, it was tonight that Maddon gives a little reception to his friends, and did you not say that the rubies would be taken from the safe-deposit vault this afternoon since his friends always clamoured to see them as a very fitting conclusion to an evening's entertainment? And did you not say that you very naturally had access to the safe in the library where you worked, and that he would not notice they were gone until he came to look for them some time this evening? I think you said all that. And what suspicion let alone proof, would attach itself to you? You were out of the room once when he, too, was absent for perhaps half an hour. It is very simple. In that half hour, someone, somehow, abstracted them. Certainly it was not you. You see how little I ask—and I pay well, do I not? And so I gave you until tonight. Three days have gone, and I have said nothing, and the body has not been found—eh? But tonight—eh—it was understood! The rubies—or the chair."

Burton's lips moved, but it was a moment before he could speak.

"You wouldn't dare!" he whispered thickly. "You wouldn't dare! I'd tell the story of—of what you tried to make me do, and they'd send you up for it."

Old Isaac shrugged with pitying contempt.

"Is it, after all, a fool I am dealing with!" he sneered. "And I—what should I say? That you had stolen the stones from your employer and offered them as a bribe to silence me, and that I had refused. The very act of handing you over to the police would prove the truth of what I said and rob you of even a chance of leniency—*for that other thing*. Is it not so—eh? And why did I not hand you over at once three nights ago? Believe me, my young friend, I should have a very good reason ready, a dozen, if necessary, if it came to that. But we are borrowing trouble, are we not? We shall not come to that—eh?"

For a moment it seemed to Jimmie Dale, as he watched, that Burton would hurl himself upon the other. White to the lips, the muscles of his face twitching, Burton clenched his fists and leaned over the table—and then, with sudden revulsion of emotion, he drew back once more, and once more came that choked sob:

"You'll pay for this, Isaac—your turn will come for this!"

"I have been threatened very often," snapped the other contemptuously. "Bah, what are threats! I laugh at them—as I always will." Then, with a quick change of front, his voice a sudden snarl: "Well, we have talked enough. You have your choice. The stones or—eh? And it is tonight—*now*!"

The old pawnbroker sprawled back in his chair, a cunning leer on his vicious face, a gleam of triumph, greed, in the beady, ratlike eyes that never wavered from the other. Burton, moisture oozing from his forehead, stood there, hesitant, staring back at old Isaac, half in a fascinated gaze, half as though trying to read some sign of weakness in the bestial countenance that confronted him. And then, very slowly, in an automatic, machine-like way, his hand groped into the inside pocket of his vest—and old Isaac cackled out in derision.

"So! You thought you could bluff me, eh—you thought you could fool old Isaac! Bah! I read you like a book! Did I not tell you a while back that you had them in your pocket? I know your kind, my young friend; I know your kind very well indeed—it is my business. You would not have dared to come here tonight without the price. So! You took them this afternoon as we agreed. Yes, yes; you did well. You will not regret it. And now let me see them"—his voice rose eagerly—"let me see them now, my young friend."

"Yes, I took them." Burton spoke listlessly. "God help me!"

Old Isaac, quivering, excited, like a different creature now, sprang from his chair, and, as Burton drew a long, flat, leather case from his pocket, snatched it from the other's hand. His fingers in their rapacious haste could not at first manipulate the catch, and then finally, with the case open, he bent over the table feverishly. The light reflected back as from some living mass of crimson fire, now shading darkly, now glowing into wondrous, colourful transparency as he moved the case to and fro with jerky motions of his hands—and he was babbling, crooning to himself like one possessed.

"Ah, the little beauties! Ah, the pretty little things! Yes, yes; these are the ones! This is the great Aracon—see, see, the six-sided prism terminated by the six-sided pyramid. But it must be cut—it must be cut to sell it, eh? Ah, it is too bad—too bad! And this, this one here, I know them all, this is—"

But his sentence was never finished—it was Jimmie Dale, on his feet now, leaning against the jamb of the door, his automatic covering the two men at the table, who spoke.

"Quite so, Isaac," he said coolly; "you know them all! Quite so, Isaac—but be good enough to *drop* them!"

The case fell from Isaac's hand, the flush on his cheeks died to a sickly pallor, and, his mouth half open, he stood like a man turned to stone, his hands with curved fingers still outstretched over the table, over the crimson gems that, spilled from the case, lay scattered now on the tabletop. Burton neither spoke nor moved—a little whiter, the misery in his face almost apathetic, he moistened his lips with the tip of his tongue.

Jimmie Dale walked across the room, halted at the end of the table, and surveyed the two men grimly. And then, while one hand with revolver extended rested easily on the table, the other gathered up the stones, placed them in the case, and, the case in his pocket, Jimmie Dale's lips parted in an uninviting smile.

"I guess I'm in luck tonight, eh, Isaac?" he drawled. "Between you and your young friend, as I believe you call him, it would appear as though I had fallen on my feet. That Aracon's worth—what would you say?—a hundred, two hundred thousand alone, eh? A very famous stone, that—had your eye on it for quite a time, Isaac, you miserable blood leech, eh?"

Isaac did not answer; but, while he still held back from the table, he seemed to be regaining a little of his composure—burglars of whatever sort were no novelty to him—and was staring fixedly at Jimmie Dale.

"Can't place me—though there's not many in the profession you don't know? Is that it?" inquired Jimmie Dale softly. "Well, don't try, Isaac; it's hardly worth your while. *I've* got the stones now, and—"

"Wait! Wait! Listen!" It was Burton, speaking for the first time, his words coming in a quick, nervous rush. "Listen! You don't—"

"Hold your tongue!" cried old Isaac, with sudden fierceness. "You are a fool!" He leaned toward Jimmie Dale, a crafty smile on his face, quite in control of himself once more. "Don't listen to him—listen to me. You're right. I can't place you, and it doesn't make any difference"—he took a step forward—"but—"

"Not too close, Isaac!" snapped Jimmie Dale sharply. "I know *you*!"

"So!" ejaculated old Isaac, rubbing his hands together. "So! That is good! That is what I want. Listen, we will make a bargain. We are birds of a feather, eh? All thieves, eh? You've got the drop on us who did all the work, but you'll give us our share—eh? Listen! You couldn't get rid of those stones alone. You know that; you're not so green at the game, eh? You'd have to go to someone. You know me; you know old Isaac, you say. Well, then, you know there isn't another man in New York could dispose of those rubies and play *safe* doing it except me. I'll make a good bargain with you."

"Isaac," said Jimmie Dale pensively, "you've made a good many 'good' bargains. I wonder when you'll make your last! There's more than one looking for 'interest' on those bargains in a pretty grim sort of way."

"Bah!" ejaculated old Isaac. "It is an old story. They are all alike. I am afraid of none of them. I hold them all like—*that*!" His hand opened and closed like a taloned claw.

"And you'd add me to the lot, eh?" said Jimmie Dale. He lifted the revolver, its muzzle on old Isaac, examined the mechanism thoughtfully, and lowered it again. "Very well, I'll make a bargain with you—providing it is agreeable to your young friend here."

"Ah!" exclaimed old Isaac shrilly. "So! That is good! It is done then." He chuckled hoarsely. "Any bargain I make he will agree to. Is it not so?" He fixed his eyes on Burton. "Well, is it not so? Speak up! Say—"

He stopped—the words cut short off on his lips. It came without warning—a crash, a pound on the door below—another.

Burton shrank back against the wall.

"My God! The police!" he gasped. "Maddon's found out! We're—we're caught!"

Jimmie Dale's eyes, on old Isaac, narrowed. The pounding in the alleyway grew louder, more insistent. And then his first suspicion passed—it was no "game" of Isaac's. Crafty though the old fox was, the other's surprise and agitation was too genuine to be questioned.

Still the pounding continued—someone was kicking viciously at the door, and banging a tattoo on the panels with his fists.

Old Isaac's clawlike hands doubled suddenly.

"It is some drunken sot," he snarled out, "that knows no better than to come here and rouse the whole neighbourhood! It is true, in a moment we will have the police running in from the street. But wait—wait—I'll teach the fool a lesson!" He dashed around the table, ran for the window, wrenched the catch up, flung the window open, and, snarling again, leaned out—and instantly the knocking ceased.

And instantly then, with a sharp cry, as the whole ghastly meaning of it swept upon him, Jimmie sprang after the other—too late! Came the roar of a revolver shot, a stream of flame cutting the darkness of the alleyway from the window in the house opposite—and, without a sound, old Isaac crumpled up, hung limply for a moment over the sill, and slid in a heap to the floor.

On his hands and knees, protected from the possibility of another bullet by the height of the sill, Jimmie Dale, quick in every movement now, dragged the inert form toward the table away from the window, and bent hurriedly over the other. A minute perhaps he stayed there—and then rose slowly.

Burton, horror-stricken, unmanned, beside himself, was hanging, clutching with both hands at the table edge.

"He's dead," said Jimmie Dale laconically.

Burton flung out his hands.

"Dead!" he whispered hoarsely. "I—I think I'm going mad. Three days of hell—and now this. We'd—we'd better get out of here quick—they'll get us if—"

Jimmie Dale's hand fell with a tight grip on Burton's shoulder.

"There won't be any more shots fired—pull yourself together!"

Burton stared at him in a demented way.

"What's—what's it mean?" he stammered.

"It means that I didn't put two and two together," said Jimmie Dale a little bitterly. "It means that there's a dozen crooks been dancing old Isaac's tune for a long time—and that some of them have got him at last."

Burton reached out suddenly and clutched Jimmie Dale's arm.

"Then I'm safe!" He mumbled the words, but there was dawning hope, relief in his white face. "Safe! I'm safe—if you'll only give me back those stones. Give them back to me, for God's sake give them back to me! You don't know—you don't understand. I stole them because—because he made me—because I—it was the only chance I had. Oh, my God, you don't know what the last three days have been! Give them back to me, won't you—won't you? You—you don't know!"

"Don't lose your nerve!" said Jimmie Dale sharply. "Sit down!" He pushed the other into the chair. "There's no one will disturb us here for some time at least. What is it that I don't know? That three nights ago you were in a gambling hell, Sagosto's, to be exact, one of the most disreputable in New York—and you went there on the invitation of a stray acquaintance, a man named Perley—shall I describe him for you? A short, slim-built man, black eyes, red hair, beard, and—"

"*You* know that!" The misery, the hopelessness was back in Burton's face again—and suddenly he bent over the table and buried his head in his outflung arms.

There was silence for a moment. Tight-lipped, Jimmie Dale's eyes travelled from Burton's shaking shoulders to the motionless form on the floor. Then he spoke again:

"You're a bit of a rounder, Burton, but I think you've had a lesson that will last you all your life. You were half-drunk when you and Perley began to hobnob over a downtown bar. He said he'd show you some real life, and you went with him to Sagosto's. He gave you a revolver before you went in, and told you the place wasn't safe for an unarmed man. He introduced you to Sagosto, the proprietor, and you were shown to a back room. You drank quite a little there. You and Perley were alone, throwing dice. You got into a quarrel. Perley tried to draw his revolver. You were quicker. You drew the one he had given you—and fired. He fell to the floor—you saw the blood gush from his breast just above the heart—he was dead. In a panic you rushed from the place and out into the street. I don't think you went home that night."

Burton raised his head, showing his haggard face.

"I guess it's no use," he said dully. "If you know, others must. I thought only Isaac and Sagosto knew. Why haven't I been arrested? I wish to God I had—I wouldn't have had today to answer for."

"I am not through yet," said Jimmie Dale gravely. "The next day old Isaac here sent for you. He said Sagosto had told him of the murder, and had offered to dispose of the corpse and keep his mouth shut for fifty thousand dollars—that no one in his place knew of it except himself. Isaac, for his share, wanted considerably more. You told him you had no such sums, that you had no money. He told you how you could get it—you had access to Maddon's safe, you were Maddon's confidential secretary, fully in your employer's trust, the last man on earth to be suspected—and there were Maddon's famous, priceless rubies."

Jimmie Dale paused. Burton made no answer.

"And so," said Jimmie Dale presently, "to save yourself from the death penalty you took them."

"Yes," said Burton, scarcely above his breath. "Are you an officer? If you are, take me, have done with it! Only for Heaven's sake end it! If you're not—"

Jimmie Dale was not listening. "The cupboard at the rear of the room," she had said. He walked across to it now, opened it, and, after a little search, found a small bundle. He returned with it in his hand, and, kneeling beside the dead man on the floor, his back to Burton, untied it, took out a red wig and beard, and slipped them on to old Isaac's head and face.

"I wonder," he said grimly, as he stood up, "if you ever saw this man before?"

"My God—*Perley*!" With a wild cry, Burton was on his feet, straining forward like a man crazed.

"Yes," said Jimmie Dale, "Perley! Sort of an ironic justice in his end as far as you are concerned, isn't there? I think we'll leave him like that—as Perley. It will provide the police with an interesting little problem—which they will never solve, and—*steady*!"

Burton was rocking on his feet, the tears were streaming down his face. He lurched heavily—and Jimmie Dale caught him, and pushed him back into the chair again.

"I thought—I thought there was blood on my hands," said Burton brokenly; "that—that I had taken a man's life. It was horrible, horrible! I've lived through three days that I thought would drive me mad, while I—I tried to do my work, and—and talk to people, just as if nothing had happened. And every one that spoke to me seemed so carefree and happy, and I would have sold my soul to have changed places with them." He stared at the form on the floor, and shivered suddenly. "It—it was like that I saw him last!" he whispered. "But—but I do not understand."

Jimmie Dale smiled a little wearily.

"It was simple enough," he said. "Old Isaac had had his eyes on those rubies for a long time. The easiest way of getting them was through you. The revolver he gave you before you entered Sagosto's was loaded with blank cartridges, the blood you saw was the old, old trick—a punctured bladder of red pigment concealed under the vest."

"Let us get out of here!" Burton shuddered again. "Let us get out of here—at once—now. If we're found here, we'll be accused of—*that*!"

"There is no hurry," Jimmie Dale answered quietly. "I have told you that no one is liable to come here tonight—and whoever did this certainly will not raise an alarm. And besides, there is still the matter of the rubies—Burton."

"Yes," said Burton, with a quick intake of his breath.

"Yes—the rubies—what are you going to do with them? I—I had forgotten them. You'll—" He stopped, stared at Jimmie Dale, and burst into a miserable laugh. "I'm a fool, a blind fool!" he moaned. "It does not matter what you do with them. I forgot Sagosto. When they find Isaac here, Sagosto will either tell his story, which will be enough to convict me of this night's work, the *real* murder, even though I'm innocent; or else he'll blackmail me just as Isaac did."

Jimmie Dale shook his head.

"You are doing Isaac's cunning an injustice," he said grimly. "Sagosto was only a tool, one of many that old Isaac had in his power—and, for that matter, as likely as anyone else to have had a hand in Isaac's murder tonight. Sagosto saw you once when Isaac brought you into his place—not because Isaac wanted Sagosto to see you, but because he wanted *you* to see Sagosto. Do you understand? It would make the story that Sagosto came to him with the tale of the murder the next day ring true. Sagosto, however, did not go to old Isaac the next day to tell about any fake murder—naturally. Sagosto would not know you again from Adam—neither does he know anything about the rubies, nor what old Isaac's ulterior motives were. He was paid for his share in the game in old Isaac's usual manner of payment probably—by a threat of exposure for some old-time offence, that Isaac held over him, if he didn't keep his mouth shut."

Burton's hand brushed his eyes.

"Yes," he muttered. "Yes—I see it now."

Jimmie Dale stooped down, picked up the paper from the floor in which the wig and beard had been wrapped, walked back with it, and replaced it in the cupboard. And then, with his back to Burton again, he took the case of gems from his pocket, opened it, and laid it on the cupboard shelf. Also from his pocket came that thin metal case, and from the case, with a pair of tweezers that obviated the possibility of telltale finger prints, a gray, diamond-shaped piece of paper, adhesive on one side that, cursed by the distracted authorities in every police headquarters on both sides of the Atlantic, and raved at by a virulent press whose printed reproductions had made it familiar in every household in the land—was the insignia of the Gray Seal. He moistened the adhesive side, dropped it from the tweezers to his handkerchief, and pressed it down firmly on the inside of the cover of the jewel case. He put both cases back in his pockets, and returned to Burton.

"Burton," he said a little sharply, "while I was outside that doorway there, I heard you beg old Isaac to let you keep the rubies, and three times already you have asked the same of me. What would you do with them if I gave them back to you?"

Burton did not reply for a moment—he was gazing at the masked face in a half-eager, half-doubtful way.

"You—you mean you will give them back!" he burst out finally.

"Answer my question," prompted Jimmie Dale.

"Do with them?" Burton repeated slowly. "Why, I've told you. They'd go back to Mr. Maddon—I'd take them back."

"Would you?" Jimmie Dale's voice was quizzical.

A puzzled expression came to Burton's face.

"I don't know what you mean by that," he said. "Of course, I would!"

"How?" asked Jimmie Dale. "Do you know the combination of Mr. Maddon's safe?"

"No," said Burton.

"And the safe would be locked, wouldn't it?"

"Yes."

"Quite so," said Jimmie Dale musingly. "Then, granted that Mr. Maddon has not already discovered the theft, how would you replace the stones before he does discover it? And if he already knows that they are gone, how would you get them back into his hands?"

"Yes, I know," Burton answered a little listlessly. "I've thought of that. There's only one way—to take them back to him myself, and make a clean breast of it, and—" He hesitated.

"And tell him you stole them," supplied Jimmie Dale.

Burton nodded his head. "Yes," he said.

"And then?" prodded Jimmie Dale. "What will Maddon do? From what I've heard of him, he's not a man to trifle with, nor a man to take an overly complacent view of things—not the man whose philosophy is 'all's well that ends well.'"

"What does it matter?" Burton's voice was low. "It isn't that so much. I'm ready for that. It's the fact that he trusted me implicitly, and I—well, I played the fool, or I'd never have got into a mess like this."

For an instant Jimmie Dale looked at the other searchingly, and then, smiling strangely, he shook his head.

"There's a better way than that, Burton," he said quietly.

"I think, as I said before, you've had a lesson tonight that will last you all your life. I'm going to give you another chance—with Maddon. Here are the stones." He reached into his pocket and laid the case on the table.

But now Burton made no effort to take the case—his eyes, in that puzzled way again, were on Jimmie Dale.

"A better way?" he repeated tensely. "What do you mean? What way?"

"Well, say at the expense of another man's reputation—of mine," suggested Jimmie Dale, with his whimsical smile. "You need only say that a man came to you this evening, told you that he stole these rubies from Mr. Maddon during the afternoon, and asked you, as Mr. Maddon's private secretary, to restore them with his compliments to their owner."

A slow flush of disappointment, deepening to one of anger dyed Burton's cheeks.

"Are you trying to make a fool of me?" he cried out. "Go to Maddon with a childish tale like that! There's no man living would believe such a cock-and-bull story!"

"No?" inquired Jimmie Dale softly. "And yet I am inclined to think there are a good many—that even Maddon would, hard-headed as he is. You might say that when the man handed you the case you thought it was some practical joke being foisted on you, until you opened the case"—Jimmie Dale pushed it a little farther across the table, and Burton, mechanically, his eyes still on Jimme Dale, loosened the catch with his thumb nail—"until you opened the case, saw the rubies, and—"

"The Gray Seal!" Burton had snatched the case toward him, and was straining his eyes at the inside cover. "You—the Gray Seal!"

"Well?" said Jimmie Dale whimsically.

Motionless, the case held open in his hands, Burton stood there.

"The Gray Seal!" he whispered. Then, with a catch in his voice: "You mean this? You mean to let me have these back—you mean—you mean all you've said? For God's sake, don't play with me—the Gray Seal, the most notorious criminal in the country, to give back a fortune like this! You—you—"

"Dog with a bad name," said Jimmie Dale, with a wry smile; then, a little gruffly: "Put it in your pocket!"

Slowly, almost as though he expected the case to be snatched back from him the next instant, Burton obeyed.

"I don't understand—I *can't* understand!" he murmured. "They say that you—and yet I believe you now—you've saved me from a ruined life to-night. The Gray Seal! If—if every one knew what you had done, they—"

"But every one won't," Jimmie Dale broke in bluntly, "Who is to tell them? You? You couldn't very well, when you come to think of it—could you? Well, who knows, perhaps there have been others like you!"

"You mean," said Burton excitedly, "you mean that all these crimes of yours that have seemed without motive, that have been so inexplicable, have really been like tonight to—"

"I don't mean anything at all," interposed Jimmie Dale a little hurriedly. "Nothing, Burton—except that there is still one little thing more to do to bolster up that 'childish' story of mine—and then get out of here." He glanced sharply, critically around the room, his eyes resting for a moment at the last on the form on the floor. Then tersely: "I am going to turn out the light—we will have to pass the window to get to the door, and we will invite no chances. Are you ready?"

"No; not yet," said Burton eagerly. "I haven't said what I'd like to say to you, what I—"

"Walk straight to the door," said Jimmie Dale curtly. There was the click of an electric-light switch, and the room was in darkness. "Now, no noise!" he instructed.

And Burton, perforce, made his way across the room—and at the door Jimmie Dale joined him and led him down the short flight of stairs. At the bottom, he opened the door leading into the rear of the pawnshop itself, and, bidding Burton follow, entered.

"We can't risk even a match; it could be seen from the street," he said brusquely, as he fumbled around for a moment in the darkness. "Ah—here it is!" He lifted a telephone receiver from its hook, and gave a number.

Burton caught him quickly by the arm.

"Good Lord, man, what are you doing?" he protested anxiously. "That's Mr. Maddon's house!"

"So I believe," said Jimmie Dale complacently. "Hello! Is Mr. Maddon there?… I beg pardon?… Personally, yes, if you please."

There was a moment's wait. Burton's hand was still nervously clutching at Jimmie Dale's sleeve. Then:

"Mr. Maddon?" asked Jimmie Dale pleasantly. "Yes?… I am very sorry to trouble you, but I called you up to inquire if you were aware that your rubies, and among them your Aracon, had been stolen?… I beg pardon!… Rubies—yes…. You weren't…. Oh, no, I am quite in my right mind; if you will take the trouble to open your safe you will find they are gone—shall I hold the line while you investigate?… What?… Don't shout, please—and stand a little farther away from the mouthpiece." Jimmie Dale's tone was one of insolent composure now. "There is really no use in getting excited….

I beg pardon?... Certainly, this is the Gray Seal speaking.... What?" Jimmie Dale's voice grew plaintive, "I really can't make out a word when you yell like that.... Yes.... I had occasion to use them this afternoon, and I took the liberty of borrowing them temporarily—are you still there, Mr. Maddon?... Oh, quite so! Yes, I hear you *now*.... No, that is all, only I am returning them through your private secretary, a very estimable young man, though I fear somewhat excitable and shaky, who is on his way to you with them now.... *What's that you say?* You repeat that," snapped Jimmie Dale suddenly, icily, "and I'll take them from under your nose again before morning!... Ah! That is better! Good-night—Mr. Maddon."

Jimmie Dale hung up the receiver and shoved Burton toward the door.

"Now then, Burton, we'll get out of her—and the sooner you reach Fifth Avenue and Mr. Maddon's house the better. No; not that way!" They had reached the hall, and Burton had turned toward the side door that opened on the alleyway. "Whoever they were who settled their last account with Isaac may still be watching. They've nothing against anyone else, but they know someone was in here at the time, and, if the police are clever enough ever to get on their track, they might find it very convenient to be able to say *who* was in the room when Isaac was murdered—there's nothing to show, since Isaac so obligingly opened the window for them, that the shot was fired *through* the window and not from the inside of the room. And even if they have already taken to their heels"—Jimmie Dale was leading Burton up the stairs again as he talked—"it might prove exceedingly inconvenient for us if some passer-by should happen to recollect that he saw two men of our general appearance leaving the premises. Now keep close—and follow me."

They passed the door of Isaac's den, turned down a narrow corridor that led to the rear of the house—Jimmie Dale guiding unerringly, working from the mental map of the house that the Tocsin had drawn for him—descended another short flight of stairs that gave on the kitchen, crossed the kitchen, and Jimmie Dale opened a back door. He paused here for a moment to listen; then, cautioning Burton to be silent, moved on again across a small back yard and through a gate into a lane that ran at right angles to the alleyway by which both had entered the house—and, a minute later, they were crouched against a building, a half block away, where the lane intersected the cross street.

Here Jimmie Dale peered out cautiously. There was no one in sight. He touched Burton's shoulder, and pointed down the street.

"That's your way, Burton—mine's the other. Hurry while you've got the chance. Good-night."

Burton's hand reached out, caught Jimmie Dale's, and wrung it.

"God bless you!" he said huskily. "I—"

And Jimmie Dale pushed him out on to the street.

Burton's steps receded down the sidewalk. Jimmie Dale still crouched against the wall. The steps grew fainter in the distance and died finally away. Jimmie Dale straightened up, slipped the mask from his face to his pocket, stepped out on the street—and five minutes later was passing through the noisy bedlam of the Hungarian restaurant on his way to the front door and his car.

"*Sonnez le Tocsin*," Jimmie Dale was saying softly to himself. "I wonder what she'll do when she finds I've got the ring?"

CHAPTER 8
THE MAN HIGHER UP

The Tocsin! By neither act, sign, nor word had she evidenced the slightest interest in that ring—and yet she must know, she certainly must know that it was now in his possession. Jimmie Dale was disappointed. Somehow, he had counted more than he had cared to admit on developments from that ring.

He pulled a little viciously at his cigarette, as he stared out of the St. James Club window. That was how long ago? Ten days? Yes; this would be the eleventh. Eleven days now and no word from her—eleven days since that night at old Isaac's, since she had last called him, the Gray Seal, to arms. It was a long while—so long a while even that what had come to be his prerogative in the newspapers, the front page with three-inch type recounting some new exploit of that mysterious criminal the Gray Seal, was being usurped. The papers were howling now about what they, for the lack of a better term, were pleased to call a wave of crime that had inundated New York, and of which, for once, the Gray Seal was not the storm centre, but rather, for the moment, forgotten.

He drew back from the window, and, settling himself again in the big leather lounging chair, resumed the perusal of the evening paper. His eye fell on what was common to every edition now, a crime editorial—and the paper crackled suddenly under the long, slim, tapering fingers, so carefully nurtured, whose sensitive tips a hundred times had made mockery of the human ingenuity squandered on the intricate mechanism of safes and vaults. No; he was wrong—the Gray Seal had not been forgotten.

"We should not be surprised," wrote the editor virulently, "to discover at the bottom of these abominable atrocities that the guiding spirit, in fact, was the Gray Seal—they are quite worthy even of his diabolical disregard for the laws of God and man."

Jimmie Dale's lips straightened ominously, and an angry glint crept into his dark, steady eyes. There was nothing then, nothing too vile that, in the public's eyes, could not logically be associated with the Gray Seal—even this! A series of the most cold-blooded, callous murders and robberies, the work, on the face of it, of a well-organized band of thugs, brutal, insensate, little better than fiends, though clever enough so far to have evaded capture, clever enough, indeed, to have kept the police still staggering and gasping after a clue for one murder—while another was in the very act of being committed! The Gray Seal! What exquisite irony! And yet, after all, the papers were not wholly to blame for what they said; he had invited much of it. Seeming crimes of the Gray Seal had apparently been genuine beyond any question of doubt, as he had intended them to appear, as in the very essence of their purpose they had to be.

Yes; he had invited much—he and she together—the Tocsin and himself. He, Jimmie Dale, millionaire, clubman, whose name for generations in New York had been the family pride, was "wanted" as the Gray Seal for so many "crimes" that he had lost track of them himself—but from any one of which, let the identity of the Gray Seal be once solved, there was and could be no escape! What exquisite irony—yet full, too, of the most deadly consequences!

Once more Jimmie Dale's eyes sought the paper, and this time scanned the headlines of the first page:

BRUTAL MURDER OF MILL PAYMASTER.

THE CRIME WAVE STILL AT ITS HEIGHT.

HERMAN ROESSLE FOUND DEAD NEAR HIS CAR.

ASSASSINS ESCAPE WITH $20,000.

Jimmie Dale read on—and as he read there came again that angry set to his lips. The details were not pleasant. Herman Roessle, the paymaster of the Martindale-Kensington Mills, whose plant was on the Hudson, had gone that morning in his runabout to the nearest town, three miles away, for the monthly pay roll; had secured the money from the bank, a sum of twenty-odd thousand dollars; and had started back with it for the mill. At first, it being broad daylight and a well-frequented road, his nonappearance caused no apprehension; but as early afternoon came and there was still no sign of Roessle the mill management took alarm. Discovering that he had left the bank for the return journey at a few minutes before eleven, and that nothing had been seen of him at his home, the police were notified. Followed then several hours of fruitless search, until finally, with the whole countryside aroused and the efforts of the police augmented by private search parties, the car was found in a thicket at the edge of a crossroad some four miles back from the river, and, a little way from the car, the body of Roessle, dead, the man's head crushed in where it had been fiendishly battered by some blunt, heavy object. There was no clue—no one could be found who had seen the car on the crossroad—the murderer, or murderers, and the twenty-odd thousand dollars in cash had disappeared leaving no trace behind.

There were several columns of this, which Jimmie Dale skimmed through quickly; but at the end he stared for a long time at the last paragraph. Somehow, strange, to relate, the paper had neglected to turn its "sob" artist loose, and the few words, added almost as though they were an afterthought, for once rang true and full of pathos in their very simplicity—at the Roessle home, where Mrs. Roessle was prostrated, two little tots of five and seven, too young to understand, had gravely received the reporter and told him that some bad man had hurt their daddy.

"Mr. Dale, sir!"

Jimmie Dale lowered his paper. A club attendant was standing before him, respectfully extending a silver card tray. From the man, Jimmie Dale's eyes fixed on a white envelope on the tray. One glance was enough—it was *hers*, that letter. The Tocsin again! His brain seemed suddenly to be afire, and he could feel his pulse quicken, the blood begin to pound in fierce throbs at his heart. Life and death lay in that white, innocent-looking, unaddressed envelope, danger, peril—it was always life and death, for those were the stakes for which the Tocsin played. But, master of many things, Jimmie Dale was most of all master of himself. Not a muscle of his face moved. He reached nonchalantly for the letter.

"Thank you," said Jimmie Dale.

The man bowed and started away. Jimmie Dale laid the envelope on the arm of the lounging chair. The man had reached the door when Jimmie Dale stopped him.

"Oh, by the way," said Jimmie Dale languidly, "where did this come from?"

"Your chauffeur, sir," replied the other. "Your chauffeur gave it to the hall porter a moment ago, sir."

"Thank you," said Jimmie Dale again.

The door closed.

Jimmie Dale glanced around the room. It was the caution of habit, that glance; the habit of years in which his life had hung on little things. He was alone in one of the club's private library rooms. He picked up the envelope, tore it open, took out the folded sheets inside, and began to read. At the first words he leaned forward, suddenly tense in his chair. He read on, turning the pages hurriedly, incredulity, amazement, and, finally, a strange menace mirroring itself in turn upon his face.

He stood up—the letter in his hand.

"My God!" whispered Jimmie Dale.

It was a call to arms such as the Gray Seal had never received before—such as the Tocsin had never made before. And if it were true it—True! He laughed aloud a little gratingly. True! Had the Tocsin, astounding, unbelievable, mystifying as were the means by which she acquired her knowledge not only of this, but of countless other affairs, ever by so much as the smallest detail been astray. If it were true!

He pulled out his watch. It was half-past nine. Benson, his chauffeur, had sent the letter into the club. Benson had been waiting outside there ever since dinner. Jimmie Dale, for the first time since the first communication that he had ever received from the Tocsin, did not immediately destroy her letter now. He slipped it into his pocket—and stepped quickly from the room.

In the cloakroom downstairs he secured his hat and overcoat, and, though it was a warm evening, put on the latter since he was in evening clothes, then walked leisurely out of the club.

At the curb, Benson, the chauffeur, sprang from his seat, and, touching his cap, opened the door of a luxurious limousine.

Jimmie Dale shook his head.

"I shall not keep you waiting any longer, Benson," he said. "You may take the car home, and put it up. I shall probably be late tonight."

"Very good, sir," replied the chauffeur.

"You sent in a letter a moment or so ago, Benson?" observed Jimmie Dale casually, opening his cigarette case.

"Yes, sir," said Benson. "I hope I didn't do wrong, sir. He said it was important, and that you were to have it at once."

"He?" Jimmie Dale was lighting his cigarette now.

"A boy, sir," Benson amplified. "I couldn't get anything out of him. He just said he'd been told to give it to me, and tell me to see that you got it at once. I hope, sir, I haven't—"

"Not at all, Benson," said Jimmie Dale pleasantly. "It's quite all right. Good-night, Benson."

"Good-night, sir," Benson answered, climbing back to his seat.

There was a little smile on Jimmie Dale's lips, as he watched the great car swing around in the street and glide noiselessly away—a little smile that still held there even after he himself had started briskly along the avenue in a downtown direction. It was invariably the same, always the same—the letters came unexpectedly, when least looked for, now by this means, now by that, but always in a manner that precluded the slightest possibility of tracing them to their source. Was there anything, in his intimate surroundings, in his intimate life, that she did not know about him—who knew absolutely nothing about her! Benson, for instance—that the man was absolutely trustworthy—or else she would never for an instant have risked the letter in his possession. Was there anything that she did not—yes, one thing—she did not know him in the role he was going to play tonight. That at least was one thing that surely she did not know about him; the role in which, many times, for weeks on end, he had devoted himself body and soul in an attempt to solve the mystery with which she surrounded herself; the role, too, that often enough had been a bulwark of safety to him when hard pressed by the police; the role out of which he had so carefully, so painstakingly created a now recognised and well-known character of the underworld—the role of Larry the Bat.

Jimmie Dale turned from Fifth Avenue into Broadway, continued on down Broadway, across to the Bowery, kept along the Bowery for several more blocks—and finally headed east into the dimly lighted cross street on which the Sanctuary was located.

And now Jimmie Dale became cautious in his movements. As he approached the black alleyway that flanked the miserable tenement, he glanced sharply behind and about him; and, at the alleyway itself, without pause, but with a curious lightning-like side step, no longer Jimmie Dale now, but the Gray Seal, he disappeared from the street, and was lost in the deep shadows of the building.

In a moment he was at the side door, listening for any sound from within—none had ever seen or met the lodger or the first floor either ascending or descending, except in the familiar character of Larry the Bat. He opened the door, closed it behind him, and in the utter blackness went noiselessly up the stairs—stairs so rickety that it seemed a mouse's tread alone would have set them creaking. There seemed an art in the play of Jimmie Dale's every muscle; in the movements, lithe, balanced, quick, absolutely silent. On the first landing he stopped before another door, there was the faint click of a key turning in the lock; and then this door, too, closed behind him. Sounded the faint click of the key as it turned again, and Jimmie Dale drew a long breath, stepped across the room to assure himself that the window blind was down, and lighted the gas jet.

A yellow, murky flame spurted up, pitifully weak, almost as though it were ashamed of its disreputable surroundings. Dirt, disorder, squalour, the evidence of low living testified eloquently enough to anyone, the police, for instance, in times past inquisitive until they were fatuously content with the belief that they knew the occupant for what he was, that the place was quite in keeping with its tenant, a mute prototype, as it were, of Larry the Bat, the dope fiend.

For a little space, Jimmie Dale, immaculate in his evening clothes, stood in the centre of the miserable room, his dark eyes, keen, alert, critical, sweeping comprehensively over every object about him—the position of a chair, of a cracked drinking glass on the broken-legged table, of an old coat thrown with apparent carelessness on the floor at the foot of the bed, of a broken bottle that had innocently strewn some sort of white powder close to the threshold, inviting unwary foot tracks across the floor. And then, taking out the Tocsin's letter, he laid it upon the table, placed what money he had in his pockets beside it, and began rapidly to remove his clothes. The Sanctuary had not been invaded since his last visit there.

He turned back the oilcloth in the far corner of the room, took up the piece of loose flooring, which, however, strangely enough, fitted so closely as to give no sign of its existence even should it inadvertently, by some curious visitor again be trod upon; and from the aperture beneath lifted out a bundle of clothes and a small box.

Undressed now, he carefully folded the clothes he had taken off, laid them under the flooring, and began to dress again, his wardrobe supplied by the bundle he had taken out in exchange—an old pair of shoes, the laces broken; mismated socks; patched trousers, frayed at the bottoms; a soiled shirt, collarless, open at the neck. Attired to his satisfaction, he placed the box upon the table, propped up a cracked mirror, sat down in front of it, and, with a deft, artist's touch, began to apply stain to his hands, wrists, neck, throat, and face—but the hardness, the grim menace that now grew into the dominant characteristic of his features was not due to the stain alone.

"Dear Philanthropic Crook"—his eyes were on the Tocsin's letter that lay before him. He read on—for once, even to Jimmie Dale's keen, facile mind, a first reading had failed to convey the full significance of what she had written. It was too amazing, almost beyond belief—the series of crimes, rampant for the past few weeks, at which the community had stood aghast, the brutal murder of Roessle but a few hours old, lay bare before his eyes. It was all there, all of it, the details, the hellish cleverness, the personnel even of the thugs, all, everything—except the proof.

"Get him, Jimmie—the man higher up. Get him, Jimmie—before another pays forfeit with his life"—the words seemed to leap out at him from the white page in red, dancing lines—"Get him—Jimmie—the man higher up."

Jimmie Dale finished the second reading of the letter, read it again for the third time, then tore it into tiny fragments. His fingers delved into the box again, and the transformation of Jimmie Dale, member of New York's most exclusive social set, into a low, vicious-featured denizen of the underworld went on—a little wax applied skilfully behind the ears, in the nostrils and under the upper lip.

It was all there—all except the proof. And the proof—he laughed aloud suddenly, unpleasantly. There seemed something sardonic in it; ay, more than that, all that was grim in irony. The proof, in Stangeist's own writing, sworn to before witnesses in the presence of a notary, the text of the document, of course, unknown to both witnesses and notary, evidence, absolute and final, that would be admitted in any court, for Stangeist was a lawyer, and would see to that, was in Stangeist's own safe, for Stangeist's own protection—Stangeist, who was himself the head and brains of this murder gang—Stangeist, who was the man higher up!

It was amazing, without parallel in the history of crime—and yet ingenious, clever, full of the craft and cunning that had built up the shyster lawyer's reputation below the dead line.

Jimmie Dale's lips were curiously thin now. So it was Stangeist! A Doctor Jekyll and Mr. Hyde with a vengeance! He knew Stangeist—not personally; not by the reputation Stangeist held, low even as that was, among his brother members of the profession; but as the man was known for what he really was among the crooks and criminals of the underworld, where, in that strange underground exchange, whispered confidences passed between those whose common enemy was the law, where Larry the Bat himself was trusted in the innermost circles.

Stangeist was a power in the Bad Lands. There were few among that unholy community that Stangeist, at one time or another, in one way or another, had not rescued from the clutches of the law, resorting to any trick or cunning, but with perjury, that he could handle like the master of it that he was, employed as the most common weapon of defence for his clients—provided he were paid well enough for it. The man had become more than the attorney for the crime world—he had become part of it. Cunning, shrewd, crafty, conscienceless, cold-blooded—that was Stangeist.

The form and features of the man pictured themselves in Jimmie Dale's mind—the six-foot muscular frame, that was invariably clothed in attire of the most fashionable cut; the thin lips with their oily, plausible smile, the straight black hair that straggled into pin point, little black eyes, the dark face with its high cheek bones, which, with the pronounced aquiline nose and the persistent rumour that he was a quarter caste, had led the underworld, prejudiced always in favour of a "monaker," to dub the man the "Indian Chief."

Jimmie Dale laughed again—still unpleasantly. So Stangeist had taken the plunge at last and branched out into a wider field, had he? Well, there was nothing surprising in that—except that he had not done it before! The irony of it lay in the fact that at last he had been *too* clever, overstepped himself in his own cleverness, that was all. It was Australian Ike, The Mope, and Clarie Deane that Stangeist had gathered around him, the Tocsin had said—and there were none worse in Larry the Bat's wide range of acquaintanceship than those three. Stangeist had made himself master of Australian Ike, The Mope, and Clarie Deane—and he had driven them a little too hard on the division of the spoils—and laughed at them, and cracked the whip much after the fashion that the trainer in the cage handles the growling beasts around him.

A dozen of the crimes that had appalled and staggered New York they had committed under his leadership; and then, it seemed, they had quarrelled furiously, the three pitted against Stangeist, threatening him, demanding a more equitable share of the proceeds. None was better aware than Stangeist that threats from men of their calibre were likely to result in a grim aftermath—and Stangeist, yesterday, the Tocsin said, had answered them as no other man than Stangeist would either have thought of or have dared to do. One by one, at separate times, covering the other with a revolver, Stangeist had permitted them to read a document that was addressed to the district attorney. It was a confession, complete in every detail, of every crime the four together had committed, implicating Stangeist as fully and unreservedly as it did the other three. It required no commentary! If anything happened to Stangeist, a stab in the dark, for instance, a bullet from some dark alleyway, a blackjack deftly wielded, as only Australian Ike, The Mope or Clarie Deane knew how to wield it—the document automatically became a *death sentence* for Australian Ike, The Mope, and Clarie Deane!

It was very simple—and, evidently, it had been effective, as witness the renewal of their operations in the murder of Roessle that afternoon. Fear and avarice had both probably played their part; fear of the man who would with such consummate nerve fling his life into the balance to turn the tables upon them, while he jeered at them; avarice that prompted them to get what they could out of Stangeist's brains and leadership, and to be satisfied with what they *could* get—since they could get no more!

Satisfied? Jimmie Dale shook his head. No; that was hardly the word—cowed, perhaps, for the moment, would be better. But afterward, with a document like that in existence, when they would never be safe for an instant—well, beasts in the cages had been known to get the better of the man with the whip, and beasts were gentle things compared with Australian Ike, The Mope, and Clarie Deane! Some day they would reverse the tables on the Indian Chief—if they could. And if they couldn't it would not be for the lack of trying.

There would be another act in that drama of the House Divided before the curtain fell! And there would be a sort of grim, poetic justice in it, a temptation almost to let the play work itself out to its own inevitable conclusion, only—Jimmie Dale, the final touches given to his features, stood up, and his hands clenched suddenly, fiercely—it was not just the man higher up alone, there were the other three as well, the whole four of them, all of them, crimes without number at their door, brutal, fiendish acts, damnable outrages, murder to answer for, with which the public now was beginning to connect the name of the Gray Seal! The Gray Seal!

Jimmie Dale's hands, whose delicate fingers were artfully grimed and blackened now beneath the nails, clenched still tighter—and then, with a quick shrug of his shoulders, a thinning of the firmly compressed lips, he picked up the coat from where it lay upon the floor, put it on, put the money that was on the table in his pocket, and replaced the box under the flooring.

In quick succession, from the same hiding place, an automatic, a black silk mask, an electric flashlight, that thin metal box like a cigarette case, and a half dozen vicious-looking little blued-steel burglar's tools were stowed away in his pockets, the flooring carefully replaced, the oilcloth spread back again; and then, pulling a slouch hat well down over his eyes, he reached up to turn off the gas.

For an instant his hand held there, while his eyes, sweeping around the apartment, took in every single detail about him in that same alert, comprehensive way as when he had entered—then the room was in darkness, and the Gray Seal, as Larry the Bat, a shuffling, unkempt creature of the underworld, alias Jimmie Dale, the lionised of clubs, the matrimonial target of exclusive drawing-rooms, closed the door of the Sanctuary behind him, shuffled down the stairs, shuffled out into the lane, and shuffled along the street toward the Bowery.

A policeman on the corner accosted him familiarly.

"Hello, Larry!" grinned the officer.

"'Ello!" returned Jimmie Dale affably through the side of his mouth. "Fine night, ain't it?"—and shuffled on along the street.

And now Jimmie Dale began to hurry—still with that shuffling tread, but covering the ground nevertheless with amazing celerity. He had lost no time since receiving the Tocsin's letter, it was true, but, for all that, it was now after ten o'clock. Stangeist's house was "dark" that evening, she had said, meaning that the occupants, Stangeist as well as whatever servants there might be, for Stangeist had no family, were out—the servants in town for a theatre or picture show probably—and Stangeist himself as yet not back, presumably from that Roessle affair. The stub of an old cigar, unlighted, shifted with a sudden, savage twist of the lips from one side of Jimmie Dale's mouth to the other. There was need for haste. There was no telling when Stangeist might get back—as for the servants, that did not matter so much; servants in suburban homes had a marked affinity for "last trains!"

Jimmie Dale boarded a cross-town car, effected a transfer, and in a quarter of an hour after leaving the Sanctuary was huddled, an inoffensive heap, like a tired-out workingman, in a corner seat of a Long Island train. From here, there was only a short run ahead of him, and, twenty minutes later, descending from the train at Forest Hills, he had passed through the more thickly settled portion of the little place, and was walking briskly out along the country road.

Stangeist's house lay, approximately, a mile and a half from the station, quite by itself, and set well back from the road. Jimmie Dale could have found it with his eyes blindfolded—the Tocsin's directions had lacked none of their usual explicit minuteness. The road was quite deserted. Jimmie Dale met no one. Even in the houses that he passed the lights were in nearly every instance already out.

Something, merciless in its rage, swept suddenly over Jimmie Dale, as, unbidden, of its own volition, the last paragraph he had read in that evening's paper began to repeat itself over and over again in his mind. The two little kiddies—it seemed as though he could see them standing there—and from Jimmie Dale's lips, not given to profanity, there came a bitter oath. It might possibly be that, even if he were successful in what was before him tonight, the authors of the Roessle murder would never be known. That confession of Stangeist's was written prior to what had happened that afternoon, and there would be no mention, naturally, of Roessle. And, for a moment, that seemed to Jimmie Dale the one thing paramount to all others, the one thing that was vital; then he shook his head, and laughed out shortly. After all, it did not matter—whether Stangeist and the blood wolves he had gathered around him paid the penalty specifically for one particular crime or for another could make little difference—they would *pay*, just as surely, just as certainly, once that paper was in his possession!

Jimmie Dale was counting the houses as he passed—they were more infrequent now, farther apart. Stangeist was no fool—not the fool that he would appear to be for keeping a document like that, once he had had the temerity to execute it, in his own safe; for, in a day or two, the Tocsin had hinted at this, after holding it over the heads of Australian Ike, The Mope, and Clarie Deane again to drive the force of it a little deeper home, he would undoubtedly destroy it—and the *supposition* that it was still in existence would have equally the same effect on the minds of the other three! Stangeist was certainly alive to the peril that he ran with such a thing in his possession, only the peril had not appealed to him as imminent either from the three thugs with whom he had allied himself, or, much less, from anyone else, that was all.

Jimmie Dale halted by a low, ornamental stone fence, some three feet high, and stood there for a moment, glancing about him. This was Stangeist's house—he could just make out the building as it loomed up a shadowy, irregular shape, perhaps two hundred yards back from the fence. The house was quite dark, not a light showed in any window. Jimmie Dale sat down casually on the fence, looked carefully again up and down the road—then, swinging his legs over, quick now in every action, he dropped to the other side, and stole silently across the grass to the rear of the house.

Here he stopped again, reached up to a window that was about on a level with his shoulders, and tested its fastenings. The window—it was the window of Stangeist's private sanctum, according to the plan in her letter—was securely locked. Jimmie Dale's hands went into his pocket—and the black silk mask was slipped over his face. He listened intently—then a little steel instrument began to gnaw like a rat.

A minute passed—two of them. Again Jimmie Dale listened. There was not a sound save the night sounds—the light breeze whispering through the branches of the trees; the far-off rumble of a train; the whir of insects; the hoarse croaking of a frog from some near-by creek or pond. The window sash was raised an inch, another, and gradually to the top. Like a shadow, Jimmie Dale pulled himself up to the sill, and, poised there, his hand parted the heavy portieres that hung within. It was too dark to distinguish even a single object in the room. He lowered himself to the floor, and slipped cautiously between the portieres.

From somewhere in the house, a clock began to strike. Jimmie Dale counted the strokes. Eleven o'clock. It was getting late—too late! Stangeist was likely to be back at any moment. The flashlight, in Jimmie Dale's hand now, circled the room with its little round white ray, lingering an instant in an inquisitive sort of way here and there on this object and that—and went out. Jimmie Dale nodded—the flat desk in the centre of the floor, the safe in the corner by the rear wall, the position of everything in the room, even to the chairs, was photographed on his mind.

He stepped from the portieres to the safe, and the flashlight played again—this time reflecting back from the glistening nickelled knobs. Jimmie Dale's lips tightened. It was a small safe, almost ludicrously small; but to such height as the art of safe design had been carried, that design was embodied in the one before him.

"Type K-four-two-eight-Colby," muttered Jimmie Dale. "A nasty little beggar—and it's eleven o'clock now! I'd use 'soup' for once, if it weren't that it would put Stangeist wise, and give him a chance to make his get-away before the district attorney got the nippers on the four of them."

The light went out. Jimmie Dale dropped to his knees; and, while his left hand passed swiftly, tentatively over dials and handle, he rubbed the fingers of his right hand rapidly to and fro over the carpet. Wonderful finger tips were those of Jimmie Dale, sensitive to an abnormal degree; and now, tingling with the friction, the nerves throbbing at the skin surface, they closed in a light, delicate touch upon the knob of the dial—and Jimmie Dale's ear pressed close against the face of the safe.

Time passed. The silence grew heavy—seemed to palpitate through the room. Then a deep breath, half like a sigh, half like a fluttering sob as of a strong man taxed to the uttermost of his endurance, came from Jimmie Dale, and his left hand swept away the sweat beads that had spurted to his forehead.

"Eight—thirteen—twenty-two," whispered Jimmie Dale.

There was a click, a low metallic thud as the bolts slid back, and the door swung open.

And now the flashlight again, searching the mechanism of the inner door—then darkness once more.

Five minutes, ten minutes went by. The clock struck again—and the single stroke seemed to boom out through the house in a weird, raucous, threatening note, and seemed to linger, throbbing in the air.

The inner door was open—the flashlight's ray was flooding a nest of pigeonholes and little drawers. The pigeonholes were crammed with papers, as, presumably, too, were the drawers. Jimmie Dale sucked in his breath. He had already been there well over half an hour—every minute now, every second was counting against him, and to search that mass of papers before Stangeist returned was—

"Ah!"—it came in a fierce little ejaculation from Jimmie Dale. From the centre pigeonhole, almost the first paper he had touched, he drew a long, sealed envelope and at a single swift glance had read the inscription upon it, written in longhand:

To the District Attorney, New York City. Important. Urgent.

The words in the corners were underscored three times.

Swiftly, deftly, Jimmie Dale's hands rolled the rounded end of one of his collection of the legal instruments under the flap of the envelope, turned the sheets over and drew out the folded document inside. There were eight sheets of legal foolscap, neatly fastened together at the top left-hand corner with green tape. He opened them out, read a few words here and there, and turned the pages hurriedly over to scrutinise the last one—and nodded grimly. Three witnesses had testified to the signature of Stangeist, and a notary's seal, accompanied by the usual legal formula, was duly affixed.

Jimmie Dale slipped the document into his pocket, and, with the envelope in his hand, moved to the desk. He opened first one drawer and then another, and finally discovering a pile of blank foolscap, took out four sheets, folded them, and placed them in the envelope, sealing the flap of the latter again. That it did not seal very well now brought a quizzical twitch to Jimmie Dale's lips. Sealed or unsealed, perhaps, it made little difference; but, for all that, he was not through with it yet. Apart from bringing the four to justice, there was, after all, a chance to vindicate the Gray Seal in this matter at least, and repudiate the newspaper theory which the public, to whom the Gray Seal was already a monster of iniquity, would seize upon with avidity.

There was no further need of light now. Jimmie Dale replaced the flashlight in his pocket, took out the thin, metal case, opened it, and with the tiny pair of tweezers that likewise nestled there, lifted out one of the gray, diamond-shaped paper seals. There was no question but that, once under arrest, Stangeist's effects would be immediately and thoroughly searched by the authorities! Jimmie Dale's smile from quizzical became ironic. It would afford the police another little, bewildering reminder of the Gray Seal, and give Carruthers, good old Carruthers of the *Morning News-Argus*, so innocently ignorant that the Gray Seal was his old college pal, yet the one editor of them all who was not forever barking and yelping at the Gray Seal's heels, a chance to vindicate himself a little, too! Jimmie Dale moistened the adhesive side of the gray seal, and, still mindful of tell-tale finger prints, laid it with the tweezers on the flap of the envelope, and pressed it firmly into place with his elbow.

And then, suddenly, every faculty instantly on the alert, he snatched up the envelope from the desk, and listened. Was it imagination, a trick of nerves, or—no, there it was again!—a footfall on the gravel walk at the front of the house. The sound became louder, clearer—two footfalls instead of one. It was Stangeist, and somebody was with him.

In an instant Jimmie Dale was across the room and kneeling again before the safe. His fingers were flying now. The envelope shot back into the pigeonhole from which he had taken it—the inner door of the safe closed silently and swiftly.

A dry chuckle came from Jimmie Dale's lips. It was just like fiction, just precisely time enough to have accomplished what he had come for before he was interrupted, not a second more or less, the villain foiled at the psychological moment! The key was rattling in the front door now—they were in the hall—he could hear Stangeist's voice—there came a dull glow from the hallway, following the click of an electric-light switch. The outer door of the safe swung shut, the bolts slid into place, the dial whirled under Jimmie Dale's fingers. It was only a step to the portieres, the open window—and escape. He straightened up, stepped back, the portieres closed behind him—and the chuckle died on Jimmie Dale's lips.

He was trapped—caught without so much as a corner in which to turn! Stangeist was even then coming into the room—and *outside*, darkly outlined, two forms stood just beneath the window. Instinctively, quick as a flash, Jimmie Dale crouched below the sill. Who were they? What did it mean? Questions swept in swift sequence through his brain. Had they seen him? It would be very dark against the background of the portieres, but yet if they were watching—he drew a breath of relief. He had not been seen. Their voices reached him in low, guarded whispers.

"Say, youse, Ike, pipe it! Dere's a window open in the snitch's room. Come on, we'll get in dere. It'll make the hair stand up on the back of his neck fer a starter."

"Aw, ferget it!" replied another voice. "Can the tee-ayter stunt! Clarie leaves the front door unfastened, don't he? An' dey'll be in dere in a minute now. Wotcher want ter do? Crab the game? He might hear us an' fix Clarie before we had a chanst, the skinny old fox! An' dere's the light now—see! Beat it on yer toes fer the front of the house!"

The room was flooded with light. Through the portieres, that Jimmie Dale parted by the barest fraction of an inch, he could see Stangeist and another man, a thick-set, ugly-faced-looking customer—Clarie Deane, according to that brief, whispered colloquy that he had heard outside. He looked again through the window. The two dark forms had disappeared now, but they had disappeared just a few seconds too late—with the two other men now in the room, and one of them so close that Jimmie Dale could almost have reached out and touched him, it was impossible to get through the window without being detected, when the slightest sound would attract instant attention and equally instant suspicion. It was a chance to be taken only as a last resort.

Jimmie Dale's face grew hard, as his fingers closed around his automatic and drew the weapon from his pocket. It was all plain enough. That last act in the drama which he had speculatively anticipated was being staged with little loss of time—and in a grim sort of way the thought flashed across his mind that, perilous as his own position was, Stangeist at that moment was in even greater peril than himself. Australian Ike, The Mope, and Clarie Deane, given the chance, and they seemed to have made that chance now, were not likely to deal in half measures—Clarie Deane had dropped into a chair beside the desk; and The Mope and Australian Ike were creeping around to the front door!

The parting in the portieres widened a little more, a very little more, slowly, imperceptibly, until Jimmie Dale, by the simple expedient of moving his head, could obtain an unobstructed view of the entire room.

Stangeist tossed a bag he had been carrying on the desk, pulled up a chair opposite to Clarie Deane, and sat down. Both men were side face to Jimmie Dale.

"You tell the boys," said Stangeist abruptly, "to fade away after this for a while. Things are getting too hot. And you tell The Mope I dock him five hundred for that extra crunch on Roessle's skull. That sort of thing isn't necessary. That's the kind of stunt that gets the public sore—the man was dead enough as it was. See?"

"Sure!" Clarie Deane's ejaculation was a grunt.

Stangeist opened the bag, and dumped the contents on the desk—pile after pile of banknotes, the pay roll of the Martindale-Kensington Mills.

"Some haul!" observed Clarie Deane, with a hoarse chuckle. "The papers said over twenty thousand."

"You can't always believe what the papers say," returned Stangeist curtly; and, taking a scribbling pad from the desk, began to check up the packages.

Clarie Deane's cigar had gone out. He rolled the short stub in his mouth, and leaned forward.

The bills were evidently just as they had been delivered to the murdered paymaster at the bank, done up with little narrow paper bands in packages of one hundred notes each, save for a small bundle of loose bills which latter, with the rolls of silver, Stangeist swept to one side of the desk.

Package by package, Stangeist went on jotting the amounts down on the pad.

"Nix!" growled Clarie Deane suddenly. "Cut that out! Them's fivers in that wad. Make that five hundred instead of one—I'm onter yer!"

"Mistake," said Stangeist suavely, changing the figures with his pencil. "You're pretty wide awake for this time of night, aren't you, Clarie?"

"Oh, I dunno!" responded Clarie Deane gruffly. "Not so very!"

Stangeist, finished with the packages, picked up the loose bills, and, with a short laugh, tossed them into the bag and followed them with the rolls of silver. He pushed the bag toward Clarie Deane.

"That's a little extra for you," he said. "The trouble with you fellows is that you don't know when you're well off—but the sooner you find it out the better, unless you want another lesson like yesterday." He made the addition on the pad. "Fifteen thousand, eight hundred dollars," he announced softly. "That's seven thousand, nine hundred for the three of you to divide, less five hundred from The Mope."

Clarie Deane's eyes narrowed. His hands were on his knees, hidden by the desk.

"There's more'n twenty there," he said sullenly—and drew a match across the under edge of the desk with a long, crackling noise.

Stangeist's face lost its suavity, a snarl curled his lips; but, about to reply, he sprang suddenly to his feet instead, his head turned sharply toward the door.

"What's that!" he said hoarsely. "It's not the servants, they wouldn't dare to—"

Stangeist's words ended in a gulp. He was staring into the muzzle of a heavy-calibered revolver that Clarie Deane had jerked up from under the desk.

"You sit down, or I'll blow your block off!" said Clarie Deane, with a sudden leer.

It happened then almost before Jimmie Dale could grasp the details; before even Clarie Deane himself could interfere. The door burst open, two men rushed in—and one, with a bound, flung himself at Stangeist. The man's hand, grasping a clubbed revolver, rose in the air, descended on Stangeist's head—and Stangeist went down in a limp heap, crashed into the chair, and slid from the chair with a thud to the floor.

There was an oath from Clarie Deane. He jumped from his seat, and with a violent shove sent the man reeling half across the room.

"Blast you, Mope!" he snarled. "You're too blamed fly! D'ye wanter queer the whole biz?"

"Aw, wot's the matter wid youse!" The Mope, purple-faced with rage, little black eyes glittering, mouth working under a flattened nose that some previous encounter had broken and bent over the side of his face, advanced belligerently.

Australian Ike, who had entered the room with him, pulled him back.

"Ferget it!" he flung out. "Clarie's dealin' the deck. Ferget it!"

The Mope glared from one to the other; then shook his fist at Stangeist on the floor.

"Youse two make me sick!" he sneered. "Wot's the use of waitin' all night? We was to bump him off, anyway, wasn't we? Dat's wot youse said yerselves, 'cause wot was ter stop him writin' out another paper if we didn't fix him fer keeps?"

"That's all right," rejoined Clarie Deane; "but that's the second act, you bonehead, see! We ain't got the paper yet, have we? Say, take a look at that safe! It's easier ter scare him inter openin' it than ter crack it, ain't it?"

Jimmie Dale, from his crouched position, began to rise to his feet slowly, making but the slightest movement at a time, cautious of the least sound. His lips were like a thin line, his fingers tightly pressed over the automatic in his hand. There was not room for him between the portieres and the window; and, do what he could, the hangings bulged a little. Let one of the three notice that, or inadvertently brush against the portieres, and his life would not be worth an instant's purchase.

They were lifting Stangeist up now, propping him up in the chair. Stangeist moaned, opened his eyes, stared in a dazed way at the three faces that leered into his, then dawning intelligence came, and his face, that had been white before, took on a pasty, grayish pallor.

"You—the three of you!" he mumbled. "What's this mean?"

And then Clarie Deane laughed in a low, brutal way.

"Wot d'ye think it means? We want that paper, an' we want it damn quick—see! D'ye think we was goin' ter stand fer havin' a trip ter Sing Sing an' the wire chair danglin' over our heads!"

Stangeist closed his eyes. When he opened them again, something of the old-time craftiness was in his face.

"Well, what are you going to do about it?" he inquired, almost sharply. "You know what will happen to you, if anything happens to me."

"Don't youse kid yerself!" retorted Clarie Deane. "D'ye think we're fools? This ain't like it was yesterday—see! We gets the paper this time— so there won't nothin' happen to us. You come across with it blasted quick now, or The Mope'll give you another on the bean that'll put you to sleep fer keeps!"

The blood was running down Stangeist's face. He wiped it away from his eyes.

"It's not here," he said innocently. "It's in my box in the safety-deposit vaults."

"Aw," blurted out Australian Ike, pushing suddenly forward, "youse can't work dat crawl on—"

"Cut it out, Ike!" snapped Clarie Dane. "I'm runnin' this! So it's in the vaults, eh?" He shoved his face toward Stangeist's.

"Yes," said Stangeist easily. "You see—I was looking for something like this."

Clarie Deane's fist clenched.

"You lie!" he choked. "The Mope, here, was the last of us you showed the paper to yesterday afternoon, an' the vaults was closed then—an' you ain't been there today, 'cause you've been watched. That's why we fixed it fer tonight after the divvy that you've just tried ter do us on again, 'cause we knew you had it here."

"I tell you, it's not here," said Stangeist evenly.

"You lie!" said Clarie Deane again. "It's in that safe. The Mope heard you tell the girl in yer office that if anything happened to you she was ter wise up the district attorney that there was a paper in your safe at home fer him that was important. Now then, you beat it over ter that safe, an' open it up—we'll give you a minute ter do it in."

"The paper's not there, I tell you," said Stangeist once more.

"That's all right," submitted Clarle Deane grimly. "There's a quarter of that minute gone."

"I won't!" Stangeist flashed out violently.

"That's all right," repeated Clarie Deane. "There's half of that minute gone."

Jimmie Dale's eyes, in a fascinated sort of way, were on Stangeist. The man's face was twitching now, moisture began to ooze from his forehead, as the callous brutality of the scowling faces seemed to get him—and then he lurched suddenly forward in his chair.

"My God!" he cried out, a ring of terror in his voice "What do you mean to do? You'll pay for it! They'll get you! The servants will be back in a minute."

"Two skirts!" jeered Clarie Deane. "We ain't goin' ter run away from them. If they comes before we goes, we'll fix 'em. That minute's up!"

Stangeist licked his lips with his tongue.

"Suppose—suppose I refuse?" he said hoarsely.

"You can suit yerself," said Clarie Deane, with a vicious grin. "We know the paper's there, an' we gets it before we leaves here—see? You can take yer choice. Either you goes over ter the safe an' opens it yerself, or else"—he paused and produced a small bottle from his pocket—"this is nitro-glycerin', an' we opens it fer you with this. Only if we does the job we does it proper. We ties you up and sets you against the door of the safe before we touches off the 'soup,' an' mabbe if yer a good guesser you can guess the rest."

There was a short, raucous guffaw from The Mope.

Stangeist turned a drawn face toward the man, stared at him, and stared in a miserable way at the other two in turn. He licked his lips again—none was in a better position than himself to know that there would be neither scruples nor hesitancy to interfere with carrying out the threat.

"Suppose," he said, trying to keep his voice steady, "suppose I open the safe—what then—afterward?"

"We ain't got the safe open yet," countered Clarie Deane uncompromisingly. "An' we ain't got no more time ter fool over it, either. You get a move on before I counts five, or The Mope an' Ike ties you up! One—"

Stangeist staggered to his feet, wiped the blood out of his eyes for the second time, and, with lips working, went unsteadily across the room to the safe.

He knelt before it, and began to manipulate the dial; while the others crowded around behind him. The Mope was fingering his revolver again club fashion. Australian Ike's elbow just grazed the portieres, and Jimmie Dale flattened himself against the window, holding his breath—a smile on his lips that was mirthless, deadly, cold. The end was not far off now; and then—*what*?

Stangeist had the outer door of the safe open now—and now the inner door swung back. He reached in his hand to the pigeonhole, drew out the envelope—and with a sudden, wild cry, reeled to his feet.

"My God!" he screamed out. "What's—what's this!"

Clarie Deane snatched the envelope from him.

"The Gray Seal!"—the words came with a jerk from his lips. He ripped the envelope open frantically—and like a man stunned gazed at the four blank sheets, while the colour left his face. "It's gone!" he cried out hoarsely.

"Gone!" There was a burst of oaths from Australian Ike. "Gone! Den we're nipped—de lot of us!"

The Mope's face was like a maniac's as he whirled on Stangeist.

"Sure!" he croaked. "But youse gets yers first, youse—"

With a cry, Stangeist, to elude the blow, ducked blindly backward—into the portieres—and with a rip and tear the hangings were wrenched apart.

It came instantaneously—a yell of mingled surprise and fury from the three—the crash and spit of Jimmie Dale's revolver as he fired one shot at the floor to stop their rush—then he flung himself at the window, through it, and dropped sprawling to the ground.

A stream of flame cut the darkness above him, a bullet whistled by his head—another—and another. He was on his feet, quick as a cat, and running close alongside of the wall of the house. He heard a thud behind him, still another, and yet a third—they were dropping through the window after him. Came another shot, an angry hum of the bullet closer than before—then the pound of racing feet.

Jimmie Dale swung around the corner of the house, running at top speed. Something that was like a hot iron suddenly burned and seared along the side of his head just above the ear. He reeled, staggered, recovered himself, and dashed on. It nauseated him, that stinging in his head, and all at once seemed to be draining his strength away. The shouts, the shots, the running feet became like a curious buzzing in his ears. It seemed strange that they should have hit him, that he should be wounded! If he could only reach the low stone wall by the road, he could at least make a fight for his life on the other side!

Red streaks swam before Jimmie Dale's eyes. The wall was such a long way off—a yard or two was a very long way more to go—the weakness seemed to be creeping up now even to numb his brain. No, here was the wall—they hadn't hit him again—he laughed in a demented way—and rolled his body over, and fell to the other side.

"Jimmie!"

The cry seemed to reach some inner consciousness, revive him, send the blood whipping through his veins. That voice! It was her—*hers*! The Tocsin! There was an automobile, engine racing, standing there in the road. He won to his feet—dark, rushing forms were almost at the wall. He fired—once—twice—fired again—and turned, staggering for the car.

"Jimmie! Jimmie—*quick*!"

Panting, gasping, he half fell into the tonneau. The car leaped forward, yells filled the air—but only one thing was dominant in Jimmie Dale's reeling brain now. He pulled himself up to his feet, and leaned over the back of the seat, reaching for the slim figure that was bent over the wheel.

"It's you—you at last!" he cried. "Your face—let me lee your face!"

A bullet split the back panel of the car—little spurting flames were dancing out from the roadway behind.

"Are you mad!" she shouted back at him. "Let me steer—do you want them to hit me!"

"No-o," said Jimmie Dale, in a singsong sort of way, and his head seemed to spin dizzily around. "No—I guess—" He choked. "The paper—it's in—my pocket"—and he went down unconscious on the floor of the car.

When he recovered his senses he was lying on a couch in a plainly furnished room, and a man, a stranger, red, jovial-faced, farmerish looking, was bending over him.

"Where am I?" he demanded finally, propping himself up on his elbow.

"You're all right," replied the man. "She said you'd come around in a little while."

"Who said so?" inquired Jimmie Dale.

"She did. The woman who brought you here about five minutes ago. She said she ran you down with her car."

"Oh!" said Jimmie Dale. He felt his head—it was bandaged, and it was bandaged, he was quite sure, with a piece of torn underskirt. He looked at the man again. "You haven't told me yet where I am."

"Long Island," the other answered. "My name's Hanson. I keep a bit of a truck garden here."

"Oh," said Jimmie Dale again.

The man crossed the room, picked up an envelope from the table, and came back to Jimmie Dale.

"She said to give you this as soon as you got your senses, and asked us to put you up for a while, as long as you wanted to stay, and paid us for it, too. She's all right, she is. You don't want to hold the accident up against her, she was mighty sorry about it. And now I'll go and see if the old lady's got your room ready while you're readin' your letter."

The man left the room.

Jimmie Dale sat up on the couch, and tore the envelope open. The note, scrawled in pencil, began abruptly:

"You were quite a problem. I couldn't take you *home*—could I? I couldn't take you to what you call the Sanctuary could I? I couldn't take you to a hospital, nor call in a doctor—the stain you use wouldn't stand it. But, thank God! I know it's only a flesh wound, and you are all right where you are for the day or two that you must keep quiet and take care of yourself. By the time you read this the paper will be on the way to the proper hands, and by morning the four where they should be. There were a few articles in your clothes I thought it better to take charge of in case—well, in case of *accident*."

Jimmie Dale tore the note up, and smiled wryly at the door. He felt in his pockets. Mask, revolver, burglar's tools, and the thin metal insignia case were gone.

"And I had the sublime optimism," murmured Jimmie Dale, "to spend months trying to find her as Larry the Bat!"

CHAPTER 9
TWO CROOKS AND A KNAVE

The bullet wound along the side of his head and just above his ear would have been a very awkward thing indeed, in more ways than one, for Jimmie Dale, the millionaire, to have explained at his club, in his social set, or even to his servants, and of these latter to Jason the Solicitous in particular; but for Jimmie Dale as Larry the Bat it was a matter of little moment. There was none to question Larry the Bat, save in a most casual and indifferent way; and a bandage of any description, primarily and above all one that he could arrange himself, with only himself to take note of the incongruous hues of skin where the stain, the grease paint, and the make-up was washed off, would excite little attention in that world where daily affrays were common-place happenings, and a wound, for whatever reason, had long since lost the tang of novelty. Why then should it arouse even a passing interest if Larry the Bat, credited as the most confirmed of dope fiends, should have fallen down the dark, rickety stairs of the tenement in one of his orgies, and, in the expressive language of the Bad Lands, cracked his bean!

And so Jimmie Dale had been forced to maintain the role of Larry the Bat for a far longer period than he had anticipated when, ten days before, he had assumed it for the night's work that had so nearly resulted fatally for himself, though it had placed Roessle's murderers behind the bars. For, the next day, unwilling to court the risk of remaining in that neighbourhood, he had left Hanson's, the farmer's, house on Long Island where the Tocsin had carried him in an unconscious state, telephoned Jason that he had been unexpectedly called out of town for a few days, and returned to the Sanctuary in New York. And here, to his grim dismay, he had found the underworld in a state of furious, angry unrest, like a nest of hornets, stirred up, seeking to wreak vengeance on an unseen assailant.

For years, as the Gray Seal, Jimmie Dale had lived with the slogan of the police, "The Gray Seal dead or alive—but the Gray Seal!" sounding in his ears; with the newspapers screaming their diatribes, arousing the people against him, nagging the authorities into sleepless, frenzied efforts to trap him; with a price upon his head that was large enough to make a man, not too pretentious, rich for life—but in the underworld, until then, the name of the Gray Seal had been one to conjure with, for the underworld had sworn by the unknown master criminal, and had spoken his name with a reverence that was none the less genuine even if pungently tainted with unholiness. But now it was different. Up and down through the Bad Lands, in gambling hells, in vicious resorts, in the hiding places where thugs and crooks burrowed themselves away from the daylight, through the heart and the outskirts of the underworld travelled the fiat, whispered out of mouths crooked to one side—*Death to the Gray Seal!*

Gangland differences were forgotten in the larger issue of the common weal. The gang spirit became the spirit of a united whole, and the crime fraternity buzzed and hummed poisonously, spurred on by hatred, thirst for revenge, fear, and, perhaps most potent of all, a hideous suspicion now of each other.

The underworld had received a shock at which it stood aghast, and which, with its terrifying possibilities, struck consternation into the soul of every individual of that brotherhood whose bond was crime, who was already "wanted" for some offence or other, whether it ranged from murder in the first degree to some petty piece of sneak thievery. Stangeist, the Indian chief, the lawyer whose cunning brain had stood as a rampart between the underworld and a prison cell, was himself now in the Tombs with the certainty of the electric chair before him; and with him, the same fate equally assured, were Australian Ike, The Mope, and Clarie Deane! Aristocrats of the Bad Lands, peers of that inglorious realm were those four—and the blow had fallen with stunning force, a blow that in itself would have been enough to have stirred the underworld to its depths. But that was not all—from the cells in the Tombs, from the four came the word, and passed from mouth to mouth in that strange underground exchange until all had heard it, that the Gray Seal had "squealed." The Gray Seal who, though unknown, they had counted the most eminent among themselves, had squealed! Who was the Gray Seal? It he had held the secrets of Stangeist and his band, what else might he not know? Who else might not fall next? The Gray Seal had become a snitch, a menace, a source of danger that stalked among them like a ghastly spectre. Who was the Gray Seal? None knew.

"Death to the Gray Seal! Run him to earth!" went the whisper from lip to lip; and with the whisper men stared uncertainly into each other's faces, fearful that the one to whom they spoke might even be—the Gray Seal!

Jimmie Dale's lips twisted as he looked around him at the squalid appointments of the Sanctuary. The police were bad enough, the papers were worse; but this was a still graver peril. With every denizen of the underworld below the dead line suspicious of each other, their lives, the penitentiary, or a prison sentence the stakes against which each one played, the role of Larry the Bat, clever as was the make-up and disguise, was fraught now more than ever before with danger and peril. It seemed as though slowly the net was beginning at last to tighten around him.

The murky, yellow flame of the gas jet flickered suddenly, as though in acquiescence with the quick, impulsive shrug of Jimmie Dale's shoulders—and Jimmie Dale, bending to peer into the cracked mirror that was propped up on the broken-legged table, knotted his dress tie almost fastidiously. The hair, if just a trifle too long, covered the scar on his head now, the wound no longer required a bandage, and Larry the Bat, for the time being at least, had disappeared. Across the foot of the bed, neatly folded, lay his dress coat and overcoat, but little creased for all that they had lain in that hiding-place under the flooring since the night when, hurrying from the club, he had placed them there to assume instead the tatters of Larry the Bat. It was Jimmie Dale in his own person again who stood there now in Larry the Bat's disreputable den, an incongruous figure enough against the background of his miserable surroundings, in perfect-fitting shoes and trousers, the broad expanse of spotless white shirt bosom glistening even in the poverty-stricken flare from the single, sputtering gas jet.

Jimmie Dale took the watch from his pocket that had not been wound for many days, wound it mechanically, set it by guesswork—it was not far from eight o'clock—and replaced it in his pocket. Carefully then, one at a time, he examined his fingers, long, slim, sensitive, tapering fingers, magical masters of safes and locks and vaults of the most intricate and modern mechanism— no single trace of grime remained, they were metamorphosed hands from the filthy paws of Larry the Bat. He nodded in satisfaction; and picked up the mirror for a final inspection of himself, that, this time, did not miss a single line in his face or neck. Again Jimmie Dale nodded. As though he had vanished into thin air, as though he had never existed, not a trace of Larry the Bat remained—except the heap of rags upon the floor, the battered slouch hat, the frayed trousers, the patched boots with their broken laces, the mismated socks, the grimy flannel shirt, and the old coat that he had just discarded.

The mirror was replaced on the table; and, pushing the heap of clothes before him with his foot, Jimmie Dale knelt down in the corner of the room where the oilcloth had been turned up and the loose planking of the floor removed, and began to pack the articles away in the hole. Jimmie Dale rolled the trousers of Larry the Bat into a compact little bundle, and stuffed them under the flooring. The gas jet seemed to blink again in a sort of confidential approval, as though the secret lay inviolate between itself and Jimmie Dale. Through the closed window, shade tightly drawn, came, low and muffled, the sound of distant life from the Bowery, a few blocks away. The gas jet, suffering from air somewhere within the pipes, hissed angrily, the yellow flame died to a little blue, forked spurt—and Jimmie Dale was on his feet, his face suddenly hard and white as marble.

Someone was knocking at the door!

For the fraction of a second Jimmie Dale stood motionless. Found as Jimmie Dale in the den of Larry the Bat, and the consequences required no effort of the imagination to picture them; police or denizen of the underworld who was knocking there, it was all the same, the method of death would be a little different, that was all—one legalised, the other not. Jimmie Dale, Larry the Bat, the Gray Seal, once uncovered, could expect as much quarter as would be given to a cornered rat. His eyes swept the room with a swift, critical glance—evidences of Larry the Bat, the clothes, were still about, even if he in the person of Jimmie Dale, alone damning enough, were not standing there himself. And he was even weaponless—the Tocsin had taken the revolver from his pocket, together with those other telltale articles, the mask, the flashlight, the little blued-steel tools, before she had intrusted him that night, wounded and unconscious, to Hanson's care.

Jimmie Dale slipped his feet out of his low evening pumps, snatched up the old coat and hat from the pile, put them on, and, without a sound, reached the gas jet and turned it off. A second had gone by—no more—the knocking still sounded insistently on the door. It was dark now, perfectly black. He started across the room, his tread absolutely silent as the trained muscles, relaxing, threw the body weight gradually upon one foot before the next step was taken. It was like a shadow, a little blacker in outline than the surrounding blackness, stealing across the floor.

Halfway to the door he paused. The knocking had ceased. He listened intently. It was not repeated. Instead, his ear caught a guarded step retreating outside in the hall. Jimmie Dale drew a breath of relief. He went on again to the door, still listening. Was it a trap—that step outside?

At the door now, tense, alert, he lowered his ear to the keyhole. There came the faintest creak from the stairs. Jimmie Dale's brows gathered. It was strange! The knocking had not lasted long. Whoever it was was going away—but it required the utmost caution to descend those stairs, rickety and tumble-down as they were, with no more sound than that! Why such caution? Why not a more determined and prolonged effort at his door—the visitor had been easily satisfied that Larry the Bat was not within. *Too* easily satisfied!

Jimmie Dale turned the key noiselessly in the lock. He opened the door cautiously—half inch—an inch, there was no sound of footsteps now. Occasionally a lodger moved about on the floor above; occasionally from somewhere in the tenement came the murmur of voices as from behind closed door—that was all. All else was silence and darkness now.

The door, on its well-oiled hinges, swung wide open. Jimmie Dale thrust out his head into the hall—and something fell upon the threshold with a little thud—but for a moment Jimmie Dale did not move. Listening, trying to pierce the darkness, he was as still as the silence around him; then he stooped and groped along the threshold. His hand closed upon what seemed like a small box wrapped in paper. He picked it up, closed and locked the door again, and retreated back across the room. It was strange—unpleasantly strange—a box propped stealthily against the door so that it would fall to the threshold when the door was opened! And why the stealth? What did it mean? Had the underworld with its thousand eyes and ears already succeeded in a few days where the police had failed signally for years—had they sent him this, whatever it was, as some grim token that they had run Larry the Bat to earth? He shook his head. No; gangland struck more swiftly, with less finesse than that—the "cat-and-mouse" act was never one it favoured, for the mouse had been known to get away.

Jimmie Dale lighted the gas again, and turned the package over in his hands. It was, as he had surmised, a small cardboard box; and it was wrapped in plain paper and tied with a string. He untied the string, and still suspicious, as a man is suspicious in the knowledge that he is stalked by peril at every turn, removed the wrapper a little gingerly. It was still without sign or marking upon it, just an ordinary cardboard box. He lifted off the cover, and, with a short, sudden laugh, stared, a little out of countenance, at the contents.

On the top lay a white, unaddressed envelope. *Hers!* Beneath—he emptied the box on the table—his black silk mask, his automatic revolver, the kit of fine, small blued-steel burglar's tools, his pocket flashlight, and the thin metal insignia case. The Tocsin! Impulsively Jimmie Dale turned toward the door—and stopped. His shoulders lifted in a shrug that, meant to be philosophical, was far from philosophical. He could not, dared not venture far through the tenement dressed as he was; and even if he could there were three exits to the Sanctuary, a fact that now for the first time was not wholly a source of unmixed satisfaction to him; and besides—she was gone!

Jimmie Dale opened the letter, a grim smile playing on his lips. He had forgotten for the moment that the illusion he had cherished for years in the belief that she did not know Larry the Bat as an alias of Jimmie Dale was no more than—an illusion. Well, it had been a piece of consummate egotism on his part, that was all. But, after all, what did it matter? He had had his innings, tried in the role of Larry the Bat to solve her identity, devoted weeks on end to the attempt—and failed. Some day, perhaps, his turn would come;

some day, perhaps, she would no longer be able to elude him, unless—the letter crackled suddenly in his fingers—unless the house that they had built on such strange and perilous foundations crashed at some moment, without an instant's warning, in disaster and ruin to the ground. Who knew but that this letter now, another call to the Gray Seal to act, another peril invited, would be the *last*? There must be an end some day; luck and nerve had their limitations—it had almost ended last week!

"Dear Philanthropic Crook"—it was the same inevitable beginning. "You are well enough again, aren't you, Jimmie?—I am sending these little things back to you, for you will need them tonight."—Jimmie Dale read on, muttering snatches of the letter aloud: "Michael Breen prospecting in Alaska—map of location of rich mining claim—Hamvert, his former partner, had previously fleeced him of fifteen thousand dollars—his share of a deal together—Breen was always a very poor man—Breen later struck a claim alone; but, taking sick, came back home—died on arrival in New York after giving map to his wife—wife in very needy circumstances—lives with little daughter of seven in New Rochelle—works out by the day at Henry Mittel's house on the Sound near-by—wife intrusted map for safe-keeping and advice to Mittel—Hamvert after map—telephone wires cut—room one hundred and forty-eight, corner, right, first floor, Palais-Metropole Hotel, unoccupied—connecting doors—quarter past nine tonight—the Weasel—Mittel's house later—the police—look out for both the Weasel and the police, Jimmie—"

There was more, several pages of it, explanations, specific details down to a minute description of the locality and plan of the house on the Sound. Jimmie Dale, too intent now to mutter, read on silently. At the end he shuffled the sheets a little abstractedly, as his face hardened. Then his fingers began to tear the letter into little shreds, tearing it over and over again, tearing the shreds into tiny particles. He had not been far wrong. From what the night promised now, this might well be the last letter. Who knew? There would be need of all the wit and luck and nerve tonight that the Gray Seal had ever had before.

With a jerk, Jimmie Dale roused himself from the momentary reverie into which he had fallen; and, all action now, stuffed the torn pieces of the letter into his trousers pocket to be disposed of later in the street; took off the old coat and slouch hat again, and resumed the disposal of Larry the Bat's effects under the flooring.

This accomplished, he replaced the planking and oilcloth, stood up, put on his dress coat and light overcoat, and, from the table, stowed the black silk mask, the automatic, the little kit of tools, the flashlight, and the thin metal case away in his pockets.

Jimmie Dale raised his hand to the gas fixture, circled the room with a glance that missed no single detail—then the light went out, the door closed behind him, locked, a dark shadow crept silently down the stairs, out through the side door into the alleyway, along the alleyway close to the wall of the tenement where it was blackest, and, satisfied that for the moment there were no passers-by, emerged on the street, walking leisurely toward the Bowery.

Once well away from the Sanctuary, however, Jimmie Dale quickened his steps; and twenty minutes later, having stopped but once to telephone to his home on Riverside Drive for his touring car, he was briskly mounting the steps of the St. James Club on Fifth Avenue. Another twenty minutes after that, and he had dismissed Benson, his chauffeur, and, at the wheel of his big, powerful machine, was speeding uptown for the Palais-Metropole Hotel.

It was twelve minutes after nine when he drew up at the curb in front of the side entrance of the hotel—his watch, set by guesswork, had been a little slow, and he had corrected it at the club. He was replacing the watch in his pocket as he sauntered around the corner, and passed in through the main entrance to the big lobby.

Jimmie Dale avoided the elevators—it was only one flight up, and elevator boys on occasions had been known to be observant. At the top of the first landing, a long, wide, heavily carpeted corridor was before him. "Number one hundred and forty-eight, the corner room on the right," the Tocsin had said. Jimmie Dale walked nonchalantly along—past No. 148. At the lower end of the hall a group of people were gathered around the elevator doors; halfway down the corridor a bell boy came out of a room and went ahead of Jimmie Dale.

And then Jimmie Dale stopped suddenly, and began to retrace his steps. The group had entered the elevator, the bell boy had disappeared around the farther end of the hall into the wing of the hotel—the corridor was empty. In a moment he was standing before the door of No. 148; in another, under the persuasion of a little steel instrument, deftly manipulated by Jimmie Dale's slim, tapering fingers, the lock clicked back, the door opened, and he stepped inside, closing and locking the door again behind him.

It was already a quarter past nine, but no one was as yet in the connecting room—the fanlight next door had been dark as he passed. His flashlight swept about him, located the connecting door—and went out. He moved to the door, tried it, and found it locked. Again the little steel instrument came into play, released the lock, and Jimmie Dale opened the door. Again the flashlight winked. The door opened into a bathroom that, obviously, at will, was either common to the two rooms or could, by the simple expedient of locking one door or the other, be used by one of the rooms alone. In the present instance, the occupant of the adjoining apartment had taken "a room with a bath."

Jimmie Dale passed through the bathroom to the opposite door. This was already three-quarters open, and swung outward into the bedroom, near the lower end of the room by the window. Through the crack of the door by the hinges, Jimmie Dale flashed his light, testing the radius of vision, pushed the door a few inches wider open, tested it again with the flashlight—and retreated back into No. 148, closing the door on his side until it was just ajar.

He stood there then silently waiting. It was Hamvert's room next door, and Hamvert and the Weasel were already late. A step sounded outside in the corridor. Jimmie Dale straightened intently. The step passed on down the hallway and died away. A false alarm! Jimmie Dale smiled whimsically. It was a strange adventure this that confronted him, quite the strangest in a way that the Tocsin had ever planned—and the night lay before him full of peril in its extraordinary complications. To win the hand he must block Hamvert and the Weasel without allowing them an inkling that his interference was anything more than, say, the luck of a hotel sneak thief at most. The Weasel was a dangerous man, one of the slickest second-story workers in the country, with safe cracking as one of his favourite pursuits, a man most earnestly desired by the police, provided the latter could catch him "with the goods." As for Hamvert, he did not know Hamvert, who was a stranger in New York, except that Hamvert had fleeced a man named Michael Breen out of his share in a claim they had had together when Breen had first gone to Alaska to try his luck, and now, having discovered that Breen, when prospecting alone somewhere in the interior a month or so ago, had found a rich vein and had made a map or diagram of its location, he, Hamvert, had followed the other to New York for the purpose of getting it by hook or crook. Breen's "find" had been too late; taken sick, he had never worked his claim, had barely got back home before he died, and only in time to hand his wife the strange legacy of a roughly scrawled little piece of paper, and—Jimmie Dale straightened up alertly once more. Steps again—and this time coming from the direction of the elevator; then voices; then the opening of the door of the next room; then a voice, distinctly audible:

"Pull up a chair, and we'll get down to business. You're late, as it is. We haven't any time to waste, if we're going to wash pay-dirt tonight."

"Aw, dat's all right!" responded another voice—quite evidently the Weasel's. "Don't youse worry—de game's cinched to a fadeaway."

There was the sound of chairs being moved across the floor. Jimmie Dale slipped the black silk mask over his face, opened the door on his side of the bathroom cautiously, and, without a sound, stepped into the bathroom that was lighted now, of course, by the light streaming in through the partially opened door of Hamvert's room. The two were talking earnestly now in lower tones. Jimmie Dale only caught a word here and there—his faculties for the moment were concentrated on traversing the bathroom silently. He reached the farther door, crouched there, peered through the crack—and the old whimsical smile flickered across his lips again.

The Palais-Metropole was high class and exclusive, and the Weasel for once looked quite the gentleman, and, for all his sharp, ferret face, not entirely out of keeping with his surroundings—else he would never have got farther than the lobby. The other was a short, thickset, heavy-jowled man, with a great shock of sandy hair, and small black eyes that looked furtively out from overhanging, bushy eyebrows.

"Well," Hamvert was saying, "the details are your concern. What I want is results. We won't waste time. You're to be back here by daylight—only see that there's no come-back."

"Leave it to me!" returned the Weasel, with assurance. "How's dere goin' ter be any come-back? Mittel keeps it in his safe, don't he? Well, gentlemen's houses has been robbed before—an' dis job'll be a good one. De geographfy stunt youse wants gets pinched wid de rest, dat's all. It disappears—see? Who's ter know youse gets yer claws on it? It's just lost in de shuffle."

"Right!" agreed Hamvert briskly—and from his inside pocket produced a package of crisp new bills, yellow-backs, and evidently of large denominations. "Half down and half on delivery—that's our deal."

"Dat's wot!" assented the Weasel curtly.

Hamvert began to count the bills.

Jimmie Dale's hand stole into his pocket, and came out with his handkerchief and the thin metal insignia case. From the latter, with its little pair of tweezers, he took out one of the adhesive gray seals. His eyes warily on the two men, he dropped the seal on his handkerchief, restored the thin metal case to his pocket—and in its stead the blue-black ugly muzzle of his automatic peeped from between his fingers.

"Five thousand down," said Hamvert, pushing a pile of notes across the table, and tucking the remainder back into his pocket; "and the other five's here for you when you get back with the map. Ordinarily, I wouldn't pay a penny in advance, but since you want it that way and the map's no good to you while the rest of the long green is, I—" He swallowed his words with a startled gulp, clutched hastily at the money on the table, and began to struggle up from his chair to his feet.

With a swift, noiseless side-step through the open door, Jimmie Dale was standing in the room.

Jimmie Dale's tones were conversational. "Don't get up," said Jimmie Dale coolly. "And take your hand off that money!"

The Weasel, whose back had been to the door, squirmed around in his chair—and in his turn stared into the muzzle of Jimmie Dale's revolver, while his jaw dropped and sagged.

"Good-evening, Weasel," observed Jimmie Dale casually. "I seem to be in luck tonight. I got into that room next door, but an empty room is slim picking. And then it seemed to me I heard someone in here mention five thousand dollars twice, which makes ten thousand, and which happens to be just exactly the sum I need at the present moment—if I can't get any more! I haven't the honour of your wealthy friend's acquaintance, but I am really charmed to meet him. You—er—understand, both of you, that the slightest sound might prove extremely embarrassing."

Hamvert's face was white, and he stirred uneasily in his chair; but into the Weasel's face, the first shock of surprised dismay past, came a dull, angry red, and into the eyes a vicious gleam—and suddenly he laughed shortly.

"Why, youse damned fool," jeered the Weasel, "d'youse t'ink youse can get away wid dat! Say, take it from me, youse are a piker! Say, youse make me tired. Wot d'youse t'ink youse are? D'youse t'ink dis is a tee-ayter, an' dat youse are a cheap-skate actor strollin' acrost de stage? Aw, beat it, youse make me sick! Why, say, youse pinch dat money, an' youse have got de same chanst of gettin' outer dis hotel as a guy has of breakin' outer Sing Sing! By de time youse gets five feet from de door of dis room we has de whole works on yer neck."

"Do you think so, Weasel?" inquired Jimmie Dale politely. He carried his handkerchief to his mouth to cloak a cough—and his tongue touched the adhesive side of the little diamond-shaped gray seal. Hand and handkerchief came back to the table, and Jimmie Dale leaned his weight carelessly upon it, while the automatic in his right hand still covered the two men. "Do you think so, Weasel?" he repeated softly. "Well, perhaps you are right; and yet; somehow, I am inclined to disagree with you. Let me see, Weasel—it was Tuesday night, two nights ago; wasn't it, that a trifling break in Maiden Lane at Thorold and Sons disturbed the police? It was a three-year job for even a first offender, ten for one already on nodding terms with the police and fifteen to twenty for—well, say, for a man like you, Weasel—*if he were caught!* Am I making myself quite plain?"

The colour in the Weasel's cheeks faded a little—his eyes were holding in sudden fascination upon Jimmie Dale.

"I see that I am," observed Jimmie Dale pleasantly. "I said, 'if he were caught,' you will remember. I am going to leave this room in a moment, Weasel, and leave it entirely to your discretion as to whether you will think it wise or not to stir from that chair for ten minutes after I shut the door. And now"—Jimmie Dale nonchalantly replaced his handkerchief in his pocket, nonchalantly followed it with the banknotes which he picked up from the table—and smiled.

With a gasp, both men had strained forward, and were staring, wild-eyed, at the gray seal stuck between them on the tabletop.

"The Gray Seal!" whispered the Weasel, and his tongue circled his lips.

Jimmie Dale shrugged his shoulders.

"That *was* a bit theatrical, Weasel," he said apologetically; "and yet not wholly unnecessary. You will recall Stangeist, The Mope, Australian Ike, and Clarie Deane, and can draw your own inference as to what might happen in the Thorold affair if you should be so ill-advised as to force my hand. Permit me"—the slim, deft fingers, like a streak of lightning, were inside Hamvert's coat pocket and out again with the remainder of the banknotes—and Jimmie Dale was backing for the door—not the door of the bathroom by which he had entered, but the door of the room itself that opened on the corridor. There he stopped, and his hand swept around behind his back and turned the key in the locked door. He nodded at the two men, whose faces were working with incongruously mingled expressions of impotent rage, bewilderment, fear, and fury—and opened the door a little. "Ten minutes, Weasel," he said gently. "I trust you will not have to use heroic measures to restrain your friend for that length of time, though if it is necessary I should advise you for your own sake to resort almost—to murder. I wish you good evening, gentlemen."

The door opened farther; Jimmie Dale, still facing inward, slipped between it and the jamb, whipped the mask from his face, closed the door softly, stepped briskly but without any appearance of haste along the corridor to the stairs, descended the stairs, mingled with a crowd in the lobby for an instant, walked, seemingly a part of it, with a group of ladies and gentlemen down the hall to the side entrance, passed out—and a moment later, after drawing on a linen dust coat which he took from under the seat, and exchanging his hat for a tweed cap, the car glided from the curb and was lost in a press of traffic around the corner.

Jimmie Dale laughed a little harshly to himself. So far, so good—but the game was not ended yet for all the crackle of the crisp notes in his pocket. There was still the map, still the robbery at Mittel's house—the ten-thousand-dollar "theft" would not in any way change that, and it was a question of time now to forestall any move the Weasel might make.

Through the city Jimmie Dale alternately dodged, spurted, and dragged his way, fuming with impatience; but once out on the country roads and headed toward New Rochelle, the big machine, speed limits thrown to the winds, roared through the night—a gray streak of road jumping under the powerful lamps; a village, a town, a cluster of lights flashing by him, the steady purr of his sixty-horse-power engines; the gray thread of open road again.

It was just eleven o'clock when Jimmie Dale, the road to himself for the moment at a spot a little beyond New Rochelle, extinguished his lights, and very carefully ran his car off the road, backing it in behind a small clump of trees. He tossed the linen dust coat back into the car, and set off toward where, a little distance away, the slap of waves from the stiff breeze that was blowing indicated the shore line of the Sound. There was no moon, and, while it was not particularly dark, objects and surroundings at best were blurred and indistinct; but that, after all, was a matter of little concern to Jimmie Dale—the first house beyond was Mittel's. He reached the water's edge and kept along the shore. There should be a little wharf, she had said. Yes; there it was—and there, too, was a gleam of light from the house itself.

Jimmie Dale began to make an accurate mental note of his surroundings. From the little wharf on which he now stood, a path led straight to the house, bisecting what appeared to be a lawn, trees to the right, the house to the left. At the wharf, beside him, two motor boats were moored, one on each side. Jimmie Dale glanced at them, and, suddenly attracted by the familiar appearance of one, inspected it a little more closely. His momentarily awakened interest passed as he nodded his head. It had caught his attention, that was all—it was the same type and design, quite a popular make, of which there were hundreds around New York, as the one he had bought that year as a tender for his yacht.

He moved forward now toward the house, the rear of which faced him— the light that flooded the lawn came from a side window. Jimmie Dale was figuring the time and distance from New York as he crept cautiously along. How quickly could the Weasel make the journey? The Weasel would undoubtedly come, and if there was a convenient train it might prove a close race—but in his own favour was the fact that it would probably take the Weasel quite some little time to recover his equilibrium from his encounter with the Gray Seal in the Palais-Metropole, also the further fact that, from the Weasel's viewpoint, there was no desperate need of haste. Jimmie Dale crossed the lawn, and edged along in the shadows of the house to where the light streamed out from what now proved to be open French windows. It was a fair presumption that he would have an hour to the good on the Weasel.

The sill was little more than a couple of feet from the ground, and, from a crouched position on his knees below the window, Jimmie Dale raised himself slowly and peered guardedly inside. The room was empty. He listened a moment—the black silk mask was on his face again—and with a quick, agile, silent spring he was in the room.

And then, in the centre of the room, Jimmie Dale stood motionless, staring around him, an expression, ironical, sardonic, creeping into his face. *The robbery had already been committed!* At the lower end of the room everything was in confusion; the door of a safe swung wide, the drawers of a desk had been wrenched out, even a liqueur stand, on which were well-filled decanters, had been broken open, and the contents of safe and desk, the thief's discards as it were, littered the floor in all directions.

For an instant Jimmie Dale, his eyes narrowed ominously, surveyed the scene; then, with a sort of professional instinct aroused, he stepped forward to examine the safe—and suddenly darted behind the desk instead. Steps sounded in the hall. The door opened—a voice reached him:

"The master said I was to shut the windows, and I haven't dast to go in. And he'll be back with the police in a minute now. Come on in with me, Minnie."

"Lord!" exclaimed another voice. "Ain't it a good thing the missus is away. She'd have highsteericks!"

Steps came somewhat hesitantly across the floor—from behind the desk, Jimmie Dale could see that it was a maid, accompanied by a big, rawboned woman, sleeves rolled to the elbows over brawny arms, presumably the Mittels' cook.

The maid closed the French windows, there were no others in the room, and bolted them; and, having gained a little confidence, gazed about her.

"My, but wasn't he cute!" she ejaculated. "Cut the telephone wires, he did. And ain't he made an awful mess! But the master said we wasn't to touch nothing till the police saw it."

"And to think of it happening in *our* house!" observed the cook heavily, her hands on her hips, her arms akimbo. "It'll all be in the papers, and mabbe they'll put our pictures in, too."

"I won't get over it as long as I live!" declared the maid. "The yell Mr. Mittel gave when he came downstairs and put his head in here, and then him shouting and using the most terrible language into the telephone, and then finding the wires cut. And me following him downstairs half dead with fright. And he shouts at me. 'Bella,' he shouts, 'shut those windows, but don't you touch a thing in that room. I'm going for the police.' And then he rushes out of the house."

"I was going to bed," said the cook, picking up her cue for what was probably the twentieth rehearsal of the scene, "when I heard Mr. Mittel yell, and—Lord, Bella, there he is now!"

Jimmie Dale's hands clenched. He, too, had caught the scuffle of footsteps, those of three or four men at least, on the front porch. There was one way, only one, of escape—through the French windows! It was a matter of seconds only before Mittel, with the police at his heels, would be in the room—and Jimmie Dale sprang to his feet. There was a wild scream of terror from the maid, echoed by another from the cook—and, still screaming, both women fled for the door.

"Mr. Mittel! Mr. Mittel!" shrieked the maid—she had flung herself out into the hall. "He's—he's back again!"

Jimmie Dale was at the French windows, tearing at the bolts. They stuck. Shouts came from the front entryway. He wrenched viciously at the fastenings. They gave now. The windows flew open. He glanced over his shoulder. A man, Mittel presumably, since he was the only one not in uniform, was springing into the room. There was a blur of forms and brass buttons behind Mittel—and Jimmie Dale leaped to the lawn, speeding across it like a deer.

But quick as he ran, Jimmie Dale's brain was quicker, pointing the single chance that seemed open to him. The motor boat! It seemed like a God-given piece of luck that he had noticed it was like his own; there would be no blind, and that meant fatal, blunders in the dark over its mechanism, and he could start it up in a moment—just the time to cast her off, that was all he needed.

The shouts swelled behind him. Jimmie Dale was running for his life. He flung a glance backward. One form—Mittel, he was certain—was perhaps a hundred yards in the rear. The others were just emerging from the French windows—grotesque, leaping things they looked, in the light that streamed out behind them from the room.

Jimmie Dale's feet pounded the planking of the wharf. He stooped and snatched at the mooring line. Mittel was almost at the wharf. It seemed an age, a year to Jimmie Dale before the line was clear. Shouts rang still louder across the lawn—the police, racing in a pack, were more than halfway from the house. He flung the line into the boat, sprang in after it—and Mittel, looming over him, grasped at the boat's gunwhale.

Both men were panting from their exertions.

"Let go!" snarled Jimmie Dale between clenched teeth.

Mittel's answer was a hoarse, gasping shout to the police to hurry—and then Mittel reeled back, measuring his length upon the wharf from a blow with a boat hook full across the face, driven with a sudden, untamed savagery that seemed for the moment to have mastered Jimmie Dale.

There was no time—not a second—not the fraction of a second. Desperately, frantically he shoved the boat clear of the wharf. Once—twice—three times he turned the engine over without success—and then the boat leaped forward. Jimmie Dale snatched the mask from his face, and jumped for the steering wheel. The police were rushing out along the wharf. He could just faintly discern Mittel now—the man was staggering about, his hands clapped to his face. A peremptory order to halt, coupled with a threat to fire, rang out sharply—and Jimmie Dale flung himself flat in the bottom of the boat. The wharf edge seemed to open in little, crackling jets of flame, came the roar of reports like a miniature battery in action, then the *flop, flop, flop,* as the lead tore up the water around him, the duller thud as a bullet buried its nose in the boat's side, and the curious rip and squeak as a splinter flew. Then Mittel's voice, high-pitched, as though in pain:

"Can't any of you run a motor boat? He's got me bad, I'm afraid. That other one there is twice as fast."

"Sure!" another voice responded promptly. "And if that's right, he's run his head into a trap. Cast loose, there, MacVeay, and pile in, all of you! You go back to the house, Mr. Mittel, and fix yourself up. We'll get him!"

Jimmie Dale's lips thinned. It was true! If the other boat had any speed at all, it was only a question of time before he would be overtaken. The only point at issue was how much time. It was dark—that was in his favour—but it was not so dark but that a boat could be distinguished on the water for quite a distance, for a longer distance than he could hope to put between them. There was no chance of eluding the police that way! The keen, facile brain that had saved the Gray Seal a hundred times before was weaving, planning, discarding, eliminating, scheming a way out—with death, ruin, disaster the price of failure. His eyes swept the dim, irregular outline of the shore. To his right, in the opposite direction from where he had left his car, and perhaps a mile ahead, as well as he could judge, the land seemed to run out into a point. Jimmie Dale headed for it instantly. If he could reach it with a little lead to the good, there was a chance! It would take, say, six minutes, granting the boat a speed of ten miles an hour—and she could do that. The others could hardly overtake him in that time—they hadn't got started yet. He could hear them still shouting and talking at the wharf. And Mittel's "twice as fast" was undoubtedly an exaggeration, anyhow.

A minute more passed, another—and then, astern, Jimmie Dale caught the racket from the exhaust of a high-powered engine, and a white streak seemed to shoot out upon the surface of the water from where, obscured now, he placed the wharf. A quarter-mile lead, roughly four hundred yards; yes, he had as much as that—but that, too, was very little.

He bent over his engine, coaxing it, nursing it to its highest efficiency; his eyes strained now upon the point ahead, now upon his pursuers behind. He was running with the wind, thank Heaven! or the small boat would have had a further handicap—it was rolling up quite a sea.

The steering gear, he found, was corded along the side of the boat, permitting its manipulation from almost any position, and, abruptly now, Jimmie Dale left the engine to rummage through the little locker in the stern of the boat. But as he rummaged, his eyes held speculatively on the boat astern. She was gaining unquestionably, steadily, but not as fast as he had feared. He would still have a hundred yards' lead, at least, abreast the point—and, he was smiling grimly now, a hundred yards there meant life to the Gray Seal! The locker was full of a heterogeneous collection of odds and ends—a suit of oilskins, tools, tins, and cans of various sizes and descriptions. Jimmie Dale emptied the contents, some sort of powder, of a small, round tin box overboard, and from his pocket took out the banknotes, crammed them into the box, crammed his watch in on top of them, and screwed the cover on tightly. His fingers were flying now. A long strip torn from the trousers' leg of the oilskins was wrapped again and again around the box—and the box was stuffed into his pocket.

The flash of a revolver shot cut the blackness behind him, then another, and another. They were firing in a continuous stream again. It was fairly long range, but there was always the chance of a stray bullet finding its mark. Jimmie Dale, crouching low, made his way to the bow of the boat again.

The point was looming almost abreast now. He edged in nearer, to hug it as closely as he dared risk the depth of the water. Behind, remorselessly, the other boat was steadily closing the gap; and the shots were not all wild—one struck, with a curious singing sound, on some piece of metal a foot from his elbow. Closer to the shore, running now parallel with the head of the point,

Jimmie Dale again edged in the boat, his jaws, clamped, working in little twitches.

And then suddenly, with a swift, appraising glance behind him, he swerved the boat from her course and headed for the shore—not directly, but diagonally across the little bay that, on the farther side of the point, had now opened out before him. He was close in with the edge of the point, ten yards from it, sweeping past it—the point itself came between the two boats, hiding them from each other—and Jimmie Dale, with a long spring, dove from the boat's side to the water.

The momentum from the boat as he sank robbed him for an instant of all control over himself, and he twisted, doubled up, and rolled over and over beneath the water—but the next moment his head was above the surface again, and he was striking out swiftly for the shore. It was only a few yards—but in a few *seconds* the pursuing boat, too, would have rounded the point. His feet touched bottom. It was haste now, nothing else, that counted. The drum of the racing engines, the crackling roar of the exhaust from the oncoming boat was in his ears. He flung himself upon the shore and down behind a rock. Around the point, past him, tore the police boat, dark forms standing clustered in the bow—and then a sudden shout:

"There she is! See her? She's heading into the bay for the shore!"

Jimmie Dale's lips relaxed. There was no doubt that they had sighted their quarry again—a perfect fusillade of revolver shots directed at the now empty boat was quite sufficient proof of that! With something that was almost a chuckle, Jimmie Dale straightened up from behind the rock and began to run back along the shore. The little motor boat would have grounded long before they overtook her, and, thinking naturally enough, that he had leaped ashore from her, they would go thrashing through the woods and fields searching for him!

It was a longer way back by the shore, a good deal longer; now over rough, rocky stretches where he stumbled in the darkness, now through marshy, sodden ground where he sank as in a quagmire time and again over his ankles. It was even longer than he had counted on, and time, with the Weasel on one hand and the return of the police on the other, was a factor to be reckoned with again, as, a half hour later, Jimmie Dale stole across the lawn of Mittel's house for the second time that night, and for the second time crouched beneath the open French windows.

Masked again, the water still dripping from what were once immaculate evening clothes but which now sagged limply about him, his collar a pasty string around his neck, the mud and dirt splashed to his knees, Jimmie Dale was a disreputable and incongruous-looking object as he crouched there, shivering uncomfortably from his immersion in spite of his exertions. Inside the room, Mittel passed the windows, pacing the floor, one side of his face badly cut and bruised from the blow with the boat hook—and as he passed, his back turned for an instant, Jimmie Dale stepped into the room.

Mittel whirled at the sound, and, with a suppressed cry, instinctively drew back—Jimmie Dale's automatic was dangling carelessly in his right hand.

"I am afraid I am a trifle melodramatic," observed Jimmie Dale apologetically, surveying his own bedraggled person; "but I assure you it is neither intentional nor for effect. As it is, I was afraid I would be late. Pardon me if I take the liberty of helping myself; one gets a chill in wet clothes so easily"— he passed to the liqueur stand, poured out a generous portion from one of the decanters, and tossed it off.

Mittel neither spoke nor moved. Stupefaction, surprise, and a very obvious regard for Jimmie Dale's revolver mingled themselves in a helpless expression on his face.

Jimmie Dale set down his glass and pointed to a chair in front of the desk.

"Sit down, Mr. Mittel," he invited pleasantly. "It will be quite apparent to you that I have not time to prolong our interview unnecessarily, in view of the possible return of the police at any moment, but you might as well be comfortable. You will pardon me again if I take another liberty"—he crossed the room, turned the key in the lock of the door leading into the hall, and returned to the desk. "Sit down, Mr. Mittel!" he repeated, a sudden rasp in his voice.

Mittel, none too graciously, now seated himself.

"Look here, my fine fellow," he burst out, "you're carrying things with a pretty high hand, aren't you? You seem to have eluded the police for the moment, somehow, but let me tell you I—"

"No," interrupted Jimmie Dale softly, "let *me* tell you—all there is to be told." He leaned over the desk and stared rudely at the bruise on Mittel's face. "Rather a nasty crack, that," he remarked.

Mittel's fists clenched, and an angry flush swept his cheeks.

"I'd have made it a good deal harder," said Jimmie Dale, with sudden insolence, "if I hadn't been afraid of putting you out of business and so precluding the possibility of this little meeting. Now then"—the revolver swung upward and held steadily on a line with Mittel's eyes— "I'll trouble you for the diagram of that Alaskan claim that belongs to Mrs. Michael Breen!"

Mittel, staring fascinated into the little, round, black muzzle of the automatic, edged back in his chair.

"So—so that's what you're after, is it?" he jerked out. "Well"—he laughed unnaturally and waved his hand at the disarray of the room—"it's been stolen already."

"I know that," said Jimmie Dale grimly. "By—*you!*"

"Me!" Mittel started up in his chair, a whiteness creeping into his face. "Me! I—I—"

"Sit down!" Jimmie Dale's voice rang out ominously cold. "I haven't any time to spare. You can appreciate that. But even if the police return before that map is in my possession, they will still be *too late* as far as you are concerned. Do you understand? Furthermore, if I am caught—you are ruined. Let me make it quite plain that I know the details of your little game. You are a curb broker, Mr. Mittel—ostensibly. In reality, you run what is nothing better than an exceedingly profitable bucket shop. The Weasel has been a customer and also a stool for you for years. How Hamvert met the Weasel is unimportant—he came East with the intention of getting in touch with a slick crook to help him—the Weasel is the coincidence, that is all. I quite understand that you have never met Hamvert, nor Hamvert you, nor that Hamvert was aware that you and the Weasel had anything to do with one another and were playing in together—but that equally is unimportant. When Hamvert engaged the Weasel for ten thousand dollars to get the map from you for him, the Weasel chose the line of least resistance. He *knew* you, and approached you with an offer to split the money in return for the map. It was not a question of your accepting his offer—it was simply a matter of how you could do it and still protect yourself. The Weasel was well qualified to point the way—a fake robbery of your house would answer the purpose admirably—you could not be held either legally or morally responsible for a document that was placed, unsolicited by you, in your possession, if it were stolen from you."

Mittel's face was ashen, colourless. His hands were opening and shutting with nervous twitches on the top of the desk.

Jimmie Dale's lips curled.

"But"—Jimmie Dale was clipping off his words now viciously—"neither you nor the Weasel were willing to trust the other implicitly—perhaps you know each other too well. You were unwilling to turn over the map until you had received your share of the money, and you were equally unwilling to turn it over until you were *safe*; that is, until you had engineered your fake robbery even to the point of notifying the police that it had been committed; the Weasel, on the other hand, had some scruples about parting with any of the money without getting the map in one hand before he let go of the banknotes with the other. It was very simply arranged, however, and to your mutual satisfaction. While you robbed your own house this evening, he was to get half the money in advance from Hamvert, giving Hamvert to understand that *he* had planned to commit the robbery himself tonight. He was to come out here then, receive the map from you in exchange for your share of the money, return to Hamvert with the map, and receive in turn his own share. I might say that Hamvert actually paid down the advance—and it was perhaps unfortunate for you that you paid such scrupulous attention to details as to cut your own telephone wires! I had not, of course, an exact knowledge of the hour or minute in which you proposed to stage your little play here. The object of my first visit a little while ago was to forestall your turning the diagram over to the Weasel. Circumstances favoured you for the moment. I am back again, however, for the same purpose—the map!"

Mittel, in a cowed way, was huddled back in his chair. He smiled miserably at Jimmie Dale.

"Quick!" Jimmie Dale flung out the word in a sharp, peremptory bark. "Do you need to be told that the *cartridges* are dry?"

Mittel's hand, trembling, went into his pocket and produced an envelope.

"Open it!" commanded Jimmie Dale. "And lay it on the desk, so that I can read it—I am too wet to touch it."

Mittel obeyed—like a dog that has been whipped.

A glance at the paper, and Jimmie Dale's eyes lifted again—to sweep the floor of the room. He pointed to a pile of books and documents in one corner that had been thrown out of the safe.

"Go over there and pick up that check book!" he ordered tersely.

"What for?" Mittel made feeble protest.

"Never mind what for!" snapped Jimmie Dale. "Go and get it—and HURRY!"

Once more Mittel obeyed—and dropped the book hesitantly on the desk.

Jimmie Dale stared silently, insolently, contemptuously at the other.

Mittel stirred uneasily, sat down, shifted his feet, and his fingers fumbled aimlessly over the top of the desk.

"Compared with you," said Jimmie Dale, in a low voice, "the Weasel, ay, and Hamvert, too, crooks though they are, are gentlemen! Michael Breen, as he died, told his wife to take that paper to someone she could trust, who would help her and tell her what to do; and, knowing no one to go to, but because she scrubbed your floors and therefore thought you were a fine gentleman, she came timidly to you, and trusted you—you cur!"

Jimmie Dale laughed suddenly—not pleasantly. Mittel shivered.

"Hamvert and Breen were partners out there in Alaska when Breen first went out," said Jimmie Dale slowly, pulling the tin can wrapped in oilskin from his pocket. "Hamvert swindled Breen out of the one strike he made, and Mrs. Breen and her little girl back here were reduced to poverty. The amount of that swindle was, I understand, fifteen thousand dollars. I have ten of it here, contributed by the Weasel and Hamvert; and you will, I think, recognise therein a certain element of poetic justice—but I am still short five thousand dollars."

Jimmie Dale removed the cover from the tin can. Mittel gazed at the contents numbly.

"You perhaps did not hear me?" prompted Jimmie Dale coldly. "I am still short five thousand dollars."

Mittel circled his lips with the tip of his tongue.

"What do you want?" he whispered hoarsely.

"The balance of the amount." There was an ominous quiet in Jimmie Dale's voice. "A check payable to Mrs. Michael Breen for five thousand dollars."

"I—I haven't got that much in the bank," Mittel fenced, stammering.

"No? Then I should advise you to see that you have by ten o'clock tomorrow morning!" returned Jimmie Dale curtly. "Make out that check!"

Mittel hesitated. The revolver edged insistently a little farther across the desk—and Mittel, picking up a pen, wrote feverishly. He tore the check from its stub, and, with a snarl, pushed it toward Jimmie Dale.

"Fold it!" instructed Jimmie Dale, in the same curt tones. "And fold that diagram with it. Put them both in this box. Thank you!" He wrapped the oilskin around the box again, and returned the box to his pocket. And again with that insolent, contemptuous stare, he surveyed the man at the desk—then he backed to the French windows. "It might be as well to remind you, Mittel," he cautioned sternly, "that if for any reason this check is not honoured, whether through lack of funds or an attempt by you to stop payment, you'll be in a cell in the Tombs tomorrow for this night's work—that is quite understood, isn't it?"

Mittel was on his feet—sweat glistened on his forehead.

"My God!" he cried out shrilly. "Who are you?"

And Jimmie Dale smiled and stepped out on the lawn.

"Ask the Weasel," said Jimmie Dale—and the next instant, lost in the shadows of the house, was running for his car.

CHAPTER 10

THE ALIBI

"Death to the gray seal!"—through the underworld, in dens and dives that sheltered from the law the vultures that preyed upon society, prompted by self-fear, by secret dread, by reason of their very inability to carry out their purpose, the whispered sentence grew daily more venomous, more insistent. *The Gray Seal, dead or alive—but the Gray Seal!"* It was the "standing orders" of the police. Railed at by a populace who angrily demanded at its hands this criminal of criminals, mocked at and threatened by a virulent press, stung to madness by the knowledge of its own impotence, flaunted impudently to its face by this mysterious Gray Seal to whose door the law laid a hundred crimes, for whom the bars of a death cell in Sing Sing was the certain goal could he but be caught, the police, to a man, was like an uncaged beast that, flicked to the raw by some unseen assailant and murderous in its

fury, was crouched to strike. Grim paradox—a common bond that linked the hands of the law with those that outraged it!

Death to the Gray Seal! Was it, at last, the beginning of the end? Jimmie Dale, as Larry the Bat, unkempt, disreputable in appearance, supposed dope fiend, a figure familiar to every denizen below the dead line, skulked along the narrow, ill-lighted street of the East Side that, on the corner ahead, boasted the notorious resort to which Bristol Bob had paid the doubtful, if appropriate, compliment of giving his name. From under the rim of his battered hat, Jimmie Dale's eyes, veiled by half-closed, well-simulated drug-laden lids, missed no detail either of his surroundings or pertaining to the passers-by. Though already late in the evening, half-naked children played in the gutters; hawkers of multitudinous commodities cried their wares under gasoline banjo torches affixed to their pushcarts; shawled women of half a dozen races, and men equally cosmopolitan, loitered at the curb, or blocked the pavement, or brushed by him. Now a man passed him, flinging a greeting from the corner of his mouth; now another, always without movement of the lips—and Jimmie Dale answered them—from the corner of his mouth.

But while his eyes were alert, his mind was only subconsciously attune to his surroundings. Was it indeed the beginning of the end? Some day, he had told himself often enough, the end must come. Was it coming now, surely, with a sort of grim implacability—when it was too late to escape! Slowly, but inexorably, even his personal freedom of action was narrowing, being limited, and, ironically enough, through the very conditions he had himself created as an avenue of escape.

It was not only the police now; it was, far more to be feared, the underworld as well. In the old days, the role of Larry the Bat had been assumed at intervals, at his own discretion, when, in a corner, he had no other way of escape; now it was forced upon him almost daily. The character of Larry the Bat could no longer be discarded at will. He had flung down the gauntlet to the underworld when, as the Gray Seal, he had closed the prison doors behind Stangeist, The Mope, Australian Ike, and Clarie Deane, and the underworld had picked the gauntlet up. Betrayed, as they believed, by the one who, though unknown to them; they had counted the greatest among themselves, and each one fearful that his own betrayal might come next, every crook, every thug in the Bad Lands now eyed his oldest pal with suspicion and distrust, and each was a self-constituted sleuth, with the prod of self-preservation behind him, sworn to the accomplishment of that unhallowed slogan—death to the Gray Seal. Almost daily now he must show himself as Larry the Bat in some gathering of the underworld—a prolonged absence from his haunts was not merely to invite certain suspicion, where all were suspicious of each other, it was to invite certain disaster. He had now either to carry the role like a little old man of the sea upon his back, or renounce it forever. And the latter course he dared not even consider—the Sanctuary was still the Sanctuary, and the role of Larry the Bat was still a refuge, the trump card in the lone hand he played.

He reached the corner, pushed open the door of Bristol Bob's, and shuffled in. The place was a glare of light, a hideous riot of noise. On a polished section of the floor in the centre, a turkey trot was in full swing; laughter and shouting vied raucously with an impossible orchestra.

Jimmie Dale slowly made the circuit of the room past the tables, that, ranged around the sides, were packed with occupants who thumped their glasses in tempo with the music and clamoured at the rushing waiters for replenishment. A dozen, two dozen, men and women greeted him. Jimmie Dale indifferently returned their salutes. What a galaxy of crooks—the cream of the underworld! His eyes, under half-closed lids, swept the faces—lags, dips, gatmen, yeggs, mob stormers, murderers, petty sneak thieves, stalls, hangers-on—they were all there. He knew them all; he was known to all.

He shuffled on to the far end of the room, his leer a little arrogant, a certain arrogance, too, in the tilt of his battered hat. He also was quite a celebrity in that gathering—Larry the Bat was of the aristocracy and the elite of gangland. Well, the show was over; he had stalked across the stage, performed for his audience—and in another hour now, free until he must repeat the same performance the next day in some other equally notorious dive, he would be sitting in for a rubber of bridge at that most exclusive of all clubs, the St. James, where none might enter save only those whose names were vouched for in the highest and most select circles, and where for partners he would possibly have a justice of the supreme court, or mayhap an eminent divine! He looked suddenly around him, as though startled. It always startled him, that comparison. There was something too stupendous to be simply ironical in the incongruity of it. If—if he were ever run to earth!

His eyes met those of a heavy-built, coarse-featured man, the chewed end of a cigar in his mouth, who stepped from behind the bar, carrying a tin tray with two full glasses upon it. It was Bristol Bob, ex-pugilist, the proprietor.

"How're you, Larry?" grunted the man, with what he meant to be a smile.

Jimmie Dale was standing in the doorway of a passage that prefaced a rear exit to the lane. He moved aside to allow the other to pass.

"'Ello, Bristol," he returned dispassionately.

Bristol Bob went on along down the passage, and Jimmie Dale shuffled slowly after him. He had intended to leave the place by the rear door—it obviated the possibility of an undesirable acquaintance joining company with him if he went out by the main entrance. But now his eyes were fixed on the proprietor's back with a sort of speculative curiosity. There was a private room off the passage, with a window on the lane; but they must be favoured customers indeed that Bristol Bob would condescend to serve personally— anyone who knew Bristol Bob knew that.

Jimmie Dale slowed his shuffling gait, then quickened it again. Bristol Bob opened the door and passed into the private room—the door was just closing as Jimmie Dale shuffled by. He had had only a glance inside—but it was enough. They were favoured customers indeed! It was no wonder that Bristol Bob himself was on the job! Two men were in the room: Lannigan of headquarters, rated the smartest plain-clothes man in the country—and, across the table from Lannigan, Whitey Mack, as clever, finished and daring a crook as was to be found in the Bad Lands, whose particular "line" was diamonds, or, in the vernacular of his ilk, "white stones," that had earned him the sobriquet of "Whitey." Lannigan of headquarters, Whitey Mack of the underworld, sworn enemies those two—in secret session! Bristol Bob might well play the part of outer guard. If a choice few of those outside in the dance hall could get a glimpse into that private room it would be "good-night" to Whitey Mack.

Jimmie Dale's eyes were narrowed a little as he shuffled on down the passage. Lannigan and Whitey Mack with their heads together! What was the game? There was nothing in common between the two men. Lannigan, it was well known, could not be "reached." Whitey Mack, with his ingenious cleverness, coupled with a cold-blooded fearlessness that had made him an object of unholy awe and respect in the eyes of the underworld, was a thorn that was sore beyond measure in the side of the police. Certainly, it was no ordinary thing that had brought these two together; especially, since, with the unrest and suspicion that was bubbling and seething below the dead line, and with which there was none more intimate than Whitey Mack, Whitey Mack was inviting a risk in "making up" with the police that could only be accounted for by some urgent and vital incentive.

Jimmie Dale pushed open the door that gave on the lane. Behind him, Bristol Bob closed the door of the private room and retreated back along the passage. Jimmie Dale stepped out into the lane—and instinctively his eyes sought the window of the private room. The shade was drawn, only a yellow murk filtered out into the black, unlighted lane, but suddenly he started noiselessly toward it. The window was open a bare inch or so at the bottom!

The sill was just shoulder high, and, placing his ear to the opening, he flattened himself against the wall. He could not see inside, for the shade was drawn well to the bottom; but he could hear as distinctly as though he were at the table beside the two men—and at the first words, the loose, disjointed frame of Larry the Bat seemed to tauten curiously and strain forward lithe and tense.

"This Gray Seal dope listens good, Whitey; but, coming from you, I'm leery. You've got to show me."

"Don't you want him?" There was a nasty laugh from Whitey Mack.

"You *bet* I want him!" returned the headquarters man with a suppressed savagery that left no doubt as to his earnestness. "I want him fast enough, but—"

"Then, blast him, so do I!" Whitey Mack rapped out with a vicious snarl. "So does every guy in the fleet down here. We got it in for him. You get that, don't you? He's got Stangeist and his gang steered for the electric chair now; he put a crimp in the Weasel the other night—get that? He's like a blasted wizard with what he knows. And who'll he deal the icy mitt to next? Me—damn him—me, for all I know!"

"That's all right," observed Lannigan coolly. "I'm not questioning your sincerity for a minute; I know all about that; but that doesn't land the Gray Seal. I'll work with you if you've anything to offer, but we've had enough 'tips' and 'information' handed us at headquarters in the last few years to make us a trifle skeptical. Show me what you've got, Whitey?"

"Show you!" echoed Whitey Mack passionately. "Sure, I'll show you! That's what I'm going to do—show you. I'll show you the Gray Seal! I ain't handing you any tips. *I've found out who the Gray Seal is!*"

There was a tense silence. It seemed to Jimmie Dale as though cold fingers were clutching at his heart, stifling its beat—then the blood came bursting to his forehead. He could not see into the room, but that silence was eloquent. It seemed as though he could picture the two men—Lannigan leaning suddenly forward—Lannigan and Whitey Mack staring tensely into each other's eyes.

"You—*what*!" It came low and grim from Lannigan.

"That's what!" asserted Whitey Mack bluntly. "You heard me! That's what I said! I know who the Gray Seal is—and I'm the only guy that's wise to him. Am I letting you in right?"

"You're sure?" demanded Lannigan hoarsely. "You're sure? Who is he, then?"

There was a half laugh, half snarl from Whitey Mack.

"Oh, no, you don't!" he growled. "Nix on that! What do you take me for—a fool? You beat it out of here and round him up—eh—while I suck my thumbs? Say, forget it! Do you think I'm doing this because I love you? Why, blame you, you've been aching for a year to put the bracelets on me yourself! Say, wake up! I'm in on this myself."

Again that silence. Then Lannigan spoke slowly, in a puzzled way.

"I don't get you, Whitey," he said. "What do you mean?" Then, a little sharply: "You're quite right; you've got some reputation yourself, and you're badly 'wanted' if we could get the 'goods' on you. If you're trying to plant something, look out for yourself, or—"

"Can that!" snapped Whitey Mack threateningly. "Can that sort of spiel right now—or quit! I ain't telling you his name—yet. *But I'll take you to him tonight*—and you and me nabs him together. Is that straight enough goods for you?"

"Don't get sore," said Lannigan, more pacifically. "Yes, if you'll do that it's good enough for any man. But lay your cards on the table face up, Whitey—I want to see what you opened the pot on."

"You've seen 'em." Whitey Mack answered ungraciously. "I've told you already. The Gray Seal goes out for keeps—curse him for a snitch! If I bumped him off, or wised up any of the guys to it, and we was caught, we'd get the juice for it even if it was the Gray Seal, wouldn't we? Well, what's the use! If one of you dicks get him, he gets bumped off just the same, only regular, up in the wire parlour at Sing Sing. I ain't looking for that kind of trouble when I can duck it. See?"

"Sure," said Lannigan.

"Besides, and moreover," continued Whitey Mack, "there's *some* reward hung out for him that I'm figuring to born in on. I'd swipe it all myself, don't you make any mistake about that, and you'd never get a look-in, only, sore as the mob is on the Gray Seal, it ain't healthy for any guy around these parts to get the reputation of being a snitch, no matter who he snitches on. Bump him off—sure! Snitching—well, you get the idea, eh? I'm ducking that too. Get me?"

"I get you," said Lannigan, with a short, pleased laugh.

"Well, then," announced Whitey Mack, "here's my proposition, and it's my turn to hand out the 'look-out-for-your-self' dope. I'm busting the game wide open for you to play, but you throw me down, and"—his voice sank into a sullen snarl again—"you can take it from me, I'll get you for it!"

"All right," responded Lannigan soberly. "Let's hear it. If I agree to it, I'll stick to it."

"I believe you," said Whitey Mack curtly. "That's why I picked you out for the medal they'll pin on you for this. And here's getting down to tacks! I'll lead you to the Gray Seal tonight and help you nab him and stay with you to the finish, but there's to be nobody but you and me on the job. When it's done I fade away, and nobody's to know I snitched, and no questions asked as to how I found out about the Gray Seal. I ain't looking for any of the glory—you can fix that up to suit yourself. The cash is different—you come across with half the reward the day they pay it."

"You'll get it!" There was savage elation in Lannigan's voice, the emphatic smash of a fist on the table. "You're on, Whitey. And if we get the Gray Seal tonight, I'll do better by you than that."

"We'll get him!" said Whitey Mack, with a vicious oath. "And—"

Jimmie Dale crouched suddenly low down, close against the wall. The crunch of a footstep sounded from the end of the lane. Someone had turned in from the cross street, some fifty yards away, and was heading evidently for the back entrance to Bristol Bob's. Jimmie Dale edged noiselessly, cautiously back past the doorway, kept on, pressed close against the wall, and finally paused. He had not been seen. The back door of Bristol Bob's opened and closed. The man had gone in.

For a moment Jimmie Dale stood hesitant. There was a wild surging in his brain, something like a myriad batteries of trip hammers seemed to be pounding at his temples. Then, almost blindly, he kept on down the lane in the same direction in which he had started to retreat—as well one cross street as another.

He turned into the cross street, went along it—and presently emerged into the full tide of the Bowery. It was garishly lighted; people swarmed about him. Subconsciously, there were crowded sidewalks; subconsciously, he was on the Bowery—that was all.

Ruin, disaster, peril faced him—faced him, and staggered him with the suddenness of the shock. Was it true? No; it could not be true! It was a bluff—Whitey Mack was bluffing. Jimmie Dale's lips grew thin in a mirthless smile as he shook his head. Neither Whitey Mack nor any other man would dare to bluff like that. It was too straight, too open-handed, Whitey Mack had laid his cards too plainly on the table. Whitey Mack's words rang in his ears: "I'll lead you to the Gray Seal tonight and help you nab him and stay with you to the finish." The man meant what he said, meant what he said, too, about the "finish" of the Gray Seal; not a man in the Bad Lands but meant—death to the Gray Seal! But how, by what means, when, where had Whitey Mack got his information? "I'm the only one that's wise," Whitey Mack had said. It seemed impossible. It *was* impossible! Whitey Mack was sincere enough probably in what he had said, but the man simply could not know. Whitey Mack could only have spotted someone that, for some reason or other, he *imagined* was the Gray Seal. That was it—must be it! Whitey Mack had made a mistake. What clue could he have obtained to—

Over the unwashed face of Larry the Bat a gray pallor spread slowly. His fingers were plucking at the frayed edge of his inside vest pocket. The dark eyes seemed to turn coal-black. A laugh, like the laugh of one damned, rose to his lips, and was choked back. It was gone! Gone! That thin metal case, like a cigarette case, that, between the little sheets of oil paper, held those diamond-shaped, gray-coloured, adhesive seals, the insignia of the Gray Seal—was gone! Clue! It seemed as though there were an overpowering nausea upon him. *Clue!* That little case was not a clue—it was a death warrant!

His hands clenched fiercely. If he could only think for a moment! The lining of his pocket had given away. The case had dropped out. But there was nothing about the case to identify anyone as the Gray Seal unless it were found in one's actual possession. Therefore Whitey Mack, to have solved his identity, must have seen him drop the case. There could be no question about that. It was equally obvious then that Whitey Mack would know the Gray

Seal as Larry the Bat. Did he also know him as Jimmie Dale? Yes, or no? It was a vital question. His life hung on it.

That keen, facile brain, numbed for the moment, was beginning to work with lightning speed. It was four o'clock that afternoon when he had assumed the character of Larry the Bat—some time between four o'clock and the present, it was now well after eleven, the case had dropped from his pocket. There had been ample time then for Whitey Mack to have made that appointment with Lannigan—and ample time to have made a surreptitious visit to the Sanctuary. Had Whitey Mack gone there? Had Whitey Mack found that hiding place in the flooring under the oilcloth? Had Whitey Mack discovered that the Gray Seal was not only Larry the Bat—but Jimmie Dale?

Jimmie Dale swept his hand across his forehead. It was damp from little clinging beads of moisture. Should he go to the Sanctuary and change—become Jimmie Dale again? Was it the safest thing to do—or the most dangerous? Even if Whitey Mack had been there and discovered the dual personality of Larry the Bat, how would he, Jimmie Dale, know it? The man would have been crafty enough to have left no sign behind him. Was it to the Sanctuary that Whitey Mack meant to lead Lannigan that evening—or did Whitey Mack know him as Jimmie Dale, and to make it the more sensational, plan to carry out the coup, say, at the St. James Club? Whitey Mack and Lannigan were still at Bristol Bob's; he had probably time, if he so elected, to reach the Sanctuary, change, and get away again. But every minute was priceless now. What should he do? Run from the city as he was for cover—or take the gambler's chance? Whitey Mack knew him as Larry the Bat—it was not certain that Whitey Mack knew him as Jimmie Dale.

He had halted, absorbed, in front of a moving-picture theatre. Great placards, at first but a blur of colour, suddenly forced themselves in concrete form upon his consciousness. Letters a foot high leaped out at him: *"The double life."* There was the picture of a banker in his private office hastily secreting a forged paper as the hero in the guise of a clerk entered; the companion picture was the banker in convict stripes staring out from behind the barred doors of a cell. There seemed a ghastly augury in the coincidence. Why should a thing like that be thrust upon him to shake his nerve when he needed nerve now more than he had ever needed it in his life before?

He raised his hand to jerk aimlessly at the brim of his hat, dropped his hand abruptly to his side again, and started quickly, hurriedly away through the throng around him. A sort of savagery had swept upon him. In a flash he had made his decision. He would take the gambler's chance! And afterward—Jimmie Dale's lips were like a thin, straight line—it was Whitey Mack's life or his own! Whitey Mack had said he was the only one that was wise—and Whitey Mack had not told Lannigan yet, wouldn't tell Lannigan until the show-down. If he, Jimmie Dale, got to the Sanctuary, became Jimmie Dale and got away again, even if Whitey Mack knew him as Jimmie

Dale, there was still a chance. It was his life or Whitey Mack's—Whitey Mack, with his lean-jawed, clean-shaven wolf's face! If he could get Whitey Mack before the other was ready to tell Lannigan! Surely he had the right of self-preservation! Surely his life was as valuable as Whitey Mack's, as valuable as a man's who, as those in the secrets of the underworld knew well enough, had blood upon his hands, who lived by crime, who was a menace to the community! Had he not the right to preserve his own life at the expense of one such as that? He had never taken life—the thought was abhorrent! But was there any other way in event of Whitey Mack knowing him as Jimmie Dale? His back was against the wall; he was trapped; certain death, and, worse, dishonour stared him in the face. Lannigan and Whitey Mack would be together—the odds would be two to one against him—and he had no quarrel with Lannigan—somehow he must let Lannigan out of it.

The other side of the street was less crowded. He crossed over, and, still with the shuffling tread that dozens around him knew as the characteristic gait of Larry the Bat, but covering the ground with amazing celerity, he hurried along. It was only at the end of the block, that cross street from the Bowery that led to the Sanctuary. How much time had he? He turned the corner into the darker cross street. Whitey Mack would have learned from Bristol Bob that Larry the Bat had just been there; that is, that Larry the Bat was not at the Sanctuary. Whitey Mack would probably be in no hurry—he and Lannigan might wait until later, until Whitey Mack should be satisfied that Larry the Bat had gone home. It was the line of least resistance; they would not attempt to scour the city for him. They might even wait in that private room at Bristol Bob's until they decided that it was time to sally out. He might perhaps still find them there when he got back; at any rate, from there he must pick up their trail again. On the other hand—all this was but supposition—they might make at once for the Sanctuary to lie in wait for him. In any case there was need, desperate need, for haste.

He glanced sharply around him; and, by the side of the tenement house now that bordered on the alleyway, with a curious, swift, gliding motion, he seemed to blend into the shadow and darkness. It was the Sanctuary, that room on the first floor of the tenement, the tenement that had three entrances, three exits—a passageway through to the saloon on the next street that abutted on the rear, the usual front door, and the side door in the alleyway. Gone was the shuffling gait. Quick, alert, he ran, crouching, bent down, along the alleyway, reached the side door, opened it stealthily, closed it behind him with equal caution, and, in the dark entry, stood motionless, listening intently.

There was no sound. He began to mount the rickety, dilapidated stairs; and, where it seemed that the lightest tread must make them creak out in blatant protest, his trained muscles, delicately compensating his body weight, carried him upward with a silence that was almost uncanny. There was need of silence, as there was need of haste. He was not so sure now of the time at his disposal—that he had even reached the Sanctuary *first*. How long had he loitered in that half-dazed way on the Bowery? He did not know—perhaps longer than he had imagined. There was the possibility that Whitey Mack and Lannigan were already above, waiting for him; but, even if they were not already there and he got away before they came, it was imperative that no one should know that Larry the Bat had come and gone.

He reached the landing, and paused again, his right hand, with a vicious muzzle of his automatic peeping now from between his fingers, thrown a little forward. It was black, utterly black, around him. Again that stealthy, catlike tread—and his ear was at the keyhole of the Sanctuary door. A full minute, priceless though it was, passed; then, satisfied that the room was empty, he drew his head back from the keyhole, and those slim, tapering fingers, that in their tips seemed to embody all the human senses, felt over the lock. Apparently it had been undisturbed; but that was no proof that Whitey Mack had not been there after finding the metal case. Whitey Mack was known to be clever with a lock—clever enough for that, anyhow.

He slipped in the key, turned it, and, on hinges that were always oiled, silently pushed the door open and stepped across the threshold. He closed the door until it was just ajar, that any sound might reach him from without—and, whipping off his coat, began to undress swiftly.

There was no light. He dared not use the gas; it might be seen from the alleyway. He was moving now quickly, surely, silently here and there. It was like some weird spectre figure, a little blacker than the surrounding darkness, flitting about the room. The oilcloth in the corner was turned back, the loose flooring lifted, the clothes of Jimmie Dale taken out, the rags of Larry the Bat put in. The minutes flew by. It was not the change of clothing that took long—it was the eradication of Larry the Bat's make-up from his face, throat, neck, wrists, and hands. Occasionally his head was turned in a tense, listening attitude; but always the fingers were busy, working with swift deftness.

It was done at last. Larry the Bat had vanished, and in his place stood Jimmie Dale, the young millionaire, the social lion of New York, immaculate in well-tailored tweeds. He stooped to the hole in the flooring, and, his fingers going unerringly to their hiding place, took out a black silk mask and an electric flashlight—his automatic was already in his possession. His lips parted grimly. Who knew what part a flashlight might not play—and he would need the mask for Lannigan's benefit, even if it did not disguise him from Whitey Mack. Had he left any telltale evidence of his visit? It was almost worth the risk of a light to make sure. He hesitated, then shook his head, and, stooping again, carefully replaced the flooring and laid the oilcloth over it—he dared not show a light at any cost.

But now even more caution than before was necessary. At times, the lodgers had naturally enough seen their fellow lodger, Larry the Bat, enter and leave the tenement—none had ever seen Jimmie Dale either leave or enter. He stole across the room to the door, halted to assure himself that the hall was empty, slipped out into the hall, and locked the door behind him. Again that trained, long-practiced, silent tread upon the stairs. It seemed as though an hour passed before he reached the bottom, and his brain was shrieking at him to hurry, hurry, *hurry*! The entryway at last, the door, the alleyway, a long breath of relief—and he was on the cross street.

A step, two, he took in the direction of the Bowery—and he was bending down as though to tie his shoe, his automatic, from his side pocket, concealed in his hand. *Was that someone there?* He could have sworn he saw a shadow-like form start out from behind the steps of the house on the opposite side of the street as he had emerged from the alleyway. In his bent posture, without seemingly turning his head, his eyes swept sharply up and down the other side of the ill-lighted street. Nothing! There was not even a pedestrian in sight on the block from there to the Bowery.

Jimmie Dale straightened up nonchalantly, and stooped almost instantly again, as though the lace were still proving refractory. Again that sharp, searching glance. Again—nothing! He went forward now in apparent unconcern; but his right hand, instead of being buried in his coat pocket, swung easily at his side.

It was strange! His ineffective ruse to the contrary, he was certain that he had not been mistaken. Was it Whitey Mack? Was the question answered? Was the Gray Seal known, too, as Jimmie Dale? Were they trailing him now, with the climax to come at the club, at his own palatial home, wherever the surroundings would best lend themselves to assuaging that inordinate thirst for the sensational that was so essentially a characteristic of the confirmed criminal? What a headline in the morning's papers it would make!

At the corner he loitered by the curb to light a cigarette—still not a soul in sight on either side of the street behind him, except a couple of Italians who had just passed by. Strange again! The intuition, if it were only intuition, was still strong. He swung abruptly on his heel, mingled with the passersby on the Bowery, walked a rapid half dozen steps until the building hid the cross street, then ran across the road to the opposite side of the Bowery, and, in a crowd now, came back to the corner. He crossed from curb to curb slowly, sheltered by a fringe of people that, however, in no way obstructed his view down the side street. And then Jimmie Dale shrugged his shoulders. He had evidently been mistaken, after all. He was overexcited; his nerves were raw—that, perhaps, was the solution. Meanwhile, every minute was counting, if Whitey Mack and Lannigan should still be at Bristol Bob's.

He kept on down the Bowery, hurrying with growing impatience through the crowds that massed in front of various places of amusement. He had not intended to come along the Bowery, and, except for what had occurred, would have taken a less frequented street. He would turn off at the next block.

He was in front of that moving-picture theatre again. *"The double life"*—his eyes were attracted involuntarily to the lurid, overdone display. It seemed to threaten him; it seemed to dangle before him a premonition as it were, of what the morning held in store; but now, too, it seemed to feed into flame that smouldering fury that possessed him. His life—or Whitey Mack's! Men, women, and the children who turned night into day in that quarter of the city were clustered thick around the signs, hiving like bees to the bald sensationalism. Almost savagely he began to force his way through the crowd—and the next instant, like a man stunned, had stopped in his tracks. His fingers had closed in a fierce, spasmodic clutch over an envelope that had been thrust suddenly into his hand.

"Jimmie!" from somewhere came a low, quick voice. "Jimmie, it is half-past eleven now—hurry."

He whirled, scanning wildly this face, then that. It was her voice—*her* voice! The Tocsin! The sensitive fingers were telegraphing to his brain, as they always did, that the texture of the envelope, too, was hers. Her voice; yes, anywhere, out of a thousand voices, he would distinguish hers—but her face, he had never seen that. Which, out of all the crowd around him, was hers? Surely he could tell her by her dress; she would be different; her personality alone must single her out. She—

"Say, have youse got de pip, or do youse t'ink youse owns de earth!" a man flung at him, heaving and pushing to get by.

With a start, though he scarcely heard the man, Jimmie Dale moved on. His brain was afire. All the irony of the world seemed massed in a sudden, overwhelming attack upon him. It was useless—intuitively he had known it was useless from the instant he had heard her voice. It was always the same—always! For years she had eluded him like that, come upon him without warning and disappeared, but leaving always that tangible proof of her existence—a letter, the call of the Gray Seal to arms. But tonight it was as it had never been before. It was not alone baffled chagrin now, not alone the longing, the wild desire to see her face, to look into her eyes—it was life and death. She had come at the very moment when she, perhaps alone of all the world, could have pointed the way out, when life, liberty, everything that was common to them both was at stake, in deadly peril—and she had gone, ignorant of it all, leaving him staggered by the very possibility of the succour that was held up before his eyes only to be snatched away without power of his to grasp it. His intuition had not been at fault—he had made no mistake in that shadow across the street from the Sanctuary. It had been the Tocsin. He had been followed; and it was she who had followed him, until, in a crowd, she had seized the opportunity of a moment ago. Though ultimately, perhaps, it changed nothing, it was a relief in a way to know that it was she, not Whitey Mack, who had been lurking there; but her persistent, incomprehensible determination to preserve the mystery with which she surrounded herself was like now to cost them both a ghastly price. If he could only have had one word with her—just one word!

The letter in his hand crackled under his clenched fist. He stared at it in a half-blind, half-bitter way. The call of the Gray Seal to arms! Another coup, with its incident danger and peril, that she had planned for him to execute! He could have laughed aloud at the inhuman mockery of it. The call of the Gray Seal to arms—*now!* When with every faculty drained to its last resource, cornered, trapped, he was fighting for his very existence!

"Jimmie, it is half-past eleven now—*hurry!*" The words were jangling discordantly in his brain.

And now he laughed outright, mirthlessly. A young girl hanging on her escort's arm, passing, glanced at him and giggled. It was a different Jimmie Dale for the moment. For once his immobility had forsaken him. He laughed again—a sort of unnatural, desperate indifference to everything falling upon him. What did it matter, the moment or two it would take to read the letter? He looked around him. He was on the corner in front of the Palace Saloon, and, turning abruptly, he stepped in through the swinging doors. As Larry the Bat, he knew the place well. At the rear of the barroom and along the side of the wall were some half dozen little stalls, partitioned off from each other. Several of these were unoccupied, and he chose the one farthest from the entrance. It was private enough; no one would disturb him.

From the aproned individual who presented himself he ordered a drink. The man returned in a moment, and Jimmie Dale tossed a coin on the table, bidding the other keep the change. He wanted no drink; the transaction was wholly perfunctory. The waiter was gone; he pushed the glass away from him, and tore the envelope open.

A single sheet, closely written on both sides of the paper, was in his hand. It was her writing; there was no mistaking that, but every word, every line bore evidence of frantic haste. Even that customary formula, "dear philanthropic crook," that had prefaced every line she had ever written him before, had been omitted. His eyes traversed the first few lines with that strange indifference that had settled upon him. What, after all, did it matter what it was; he could do nothing—not even save himself probably. And then, with a little start, he read the lines over again, muttering snatches from them.

"...Max Diestricht—diamonds—the Ross-Logan stones—wedding— sliding panel in wall of workshop—end of the room near window—ten boards to the right from side wall—press small knot in the wood in the centre of the tenth board—tonight..."

It brought a sudden thrill of excitement to Jimmie Dale that, impossible as he would have believed it an instant ago, for the moment overshadowed the realisation of his own peril. A robbery such as that, if it were ever accomplished, would stir the country from end to end; it would set New York by the ears; it would loose the police in full cry like a pack of bloodhounds with their leashes slipped. The society columns of the newspapers had been busy for months featuring the coming marriage of the Ross-Logans' daughter to one of the country's young merchant princes. The combined fortunes of the two families would make the young couple the richest in America. The prospective groom's wedding gift was to be a diamond necklace of perfectly matched, large stones that would eclipse anything of the kind in the country. Europe, the foreign markets, had been literally combed and ransacked to supply the gems. The stones had arrived in New York the day before, the duty on them alone amounting to over fifty thousand dollars. All this had appeared in the papers.

Jimmie Dale's brows drew together in a frown. On just exactly what percentage the duty was figured he did not know; but it was high enough on the basis of fifty thousand dollars to assume safely that the assessed value of the stones was not less than four times that amount. Two hundred thousand dollars—laid down, a quarter of a million! Well, why not? In more than one quarter diamonds were ranked as the soundest kind of an investment. Furthermore, through personal acquaintance with the "high contracting parties," who were in his own set, he knew it to be true.

He shrugged his shoulders. The papers, too, had thrown the limelight on Max Diestricht, who, though for quite a time the fashion in the social world, had, up to the present, been comparatively unknown to the average New Yorker. His own knowledge of Max Diestricht went deeper than the superficial biography furnished by the newspapers—the old Hollander had done more than one piece of exquisite jewelry work for him. The old fellow was a character that beggared description, eccentric to the point of extravagance, and deaf as a post; but, in craftmanship, a modern Cellini. He employed no workmen, lived alone over his shop on one of the lower streets between Fifth and Sixth Avenues near Washington Square—and possessed a splendid contempt for such protective contrivances as safes and vaults. If his prospective patrons expostulated on this score before intrusting him with their valuables, they were at liberty to take their work elsewhere. It was Max Diestricht who honoured you by accepting the commission; not you who honoured Max Diestricht by intrusting him with it. "Of what use is it to me, a safe!" he would exclaim. "It hides nothing; it only says, 'I am inside; do not look farther; come and get me!' Yes? It is to explode with the nitro-glycerin—*pouf!*—and I am deaf and I hear nothing. It is a foolishness, that"—he had a habit of prodding at one with a levelled fore-finger—"every night somewhere they are robbed, and have I been robbed? *Hein*, tell me that; have I been robbed?"

It was true. In ten years, though at times having stones and precious metal aggregating large amounts deposited with him by his customers, Max Diestricht had never lost so much as the gold filings. There was a smile on Jimmie Dale's lips now. The knot in the tenth board was significant! Max Diestricht was scrupulously honest, a genius in originality and conception of design, a master in the perfection and delicacy of his finished work—he had been commissioned to design and set the Ross-Logan necklace.

The brain works quickly. All this and more had flashed almost instantaneously through Jimmie Dale's mind. His eyes fell to the letter again, and he read on. Halfway through, a sudden whiteness blanched his face, and, following it, a surging tide of red that mounted to his temples. It dazed him; it seemed to rob him for the moment of the power of coherent thought. He was wrong; he had not read aright. It was incredible, dare-devil beyond belief—and yet in its very audacity lay success. He finished the letter, read it once more—and his fingers mechanically began to tear it into little shreds. His brain was in a whirl, a vortex of conflicting emotions. Had Whitey Mack and Lannigan left Bristol Bob's yet? Where were they now? Was there time for—this? He was staring at the little torn scraps of paper in his hand. He thrust them suddenly into his pocket, and jerked out his watch. It was nearly midnight. The broad, muscular shoulders seemed to square back curiously, the jaws to clamp a little, the face to harden and grow cold until it was like stone. With a swift movement he emptied his glass into the cuspidor, set the glass back on the table, and stepped out from the stall. His destination was Max Diestricht's.

The Palace Saloon was near the upper end of the Bowery, and, failing a taxicab, of which none was in sight, his quickest method was to walk, and he started briskly forward. It was not far; and it was barely ten minutes from the time he had left the Palace Saloon when he swung through Washington Square to Fifth Avenue, and, a moment later, turned from that thoroughfare, heading west toward Sixth Avenue, along one of those streets which, with the city's northward trend, had quite lost any distinctive identity, and from being once a modestly fashionable residential section had now become a conglomerate potpourri of small tradesmen's stores, shops and apartments of the poorer class. He knew Max Diestricht's—he could well have done without the aid of the arc lamp which, even if dimly, indicated that low, almost tumble-down, two-story structure tucked away between the taller buildings on either side that almost engulfed it. It was late. The street was quiet. The shops and stores had long since been closed, Max Diestricht's among them—the old Hollanders' name in painted white letters stood out against the background of a darkened workshop window. In the story above, the lights, too, were out; Max Diestricht was probably fast asleep—and he was stone deaf!

A glance up and down the street, and Jimmie Dale was standing, or, rather, leaning against Max Diestricht's door. There was no one to see, and if there were, what was there to attract attention to a man standing nonchalantly for a moment in a doorway? It was only for a moment. Those master fingers of Jimmie Dale were working surely, swiftly, silently. A little steel instrument that was never out of his possession was in the lock and out again. The door opened, closed; he drew the black silk mask from his pocket and slipped it over his face. Immediately in front of him the stairs led upward; immediately to his right was the door into the shop—the modest street entrance was common to both.

The door into the workshop was not locked. He opened it, stepped inside, and closed it quietly behind him. The place was in blackness. He stood for a moment silent, straining his ears to catch the slightest sound, reconstructing the plan of his surroundings in his mind as he remembered it. It was a narrow, oblong room, running the entire depth of the building, a very long room, blank walls on either side, a window in the middle of the rear wall that gave on a back yard, and from the back yard there was access to the lane; also, as he remembered the place, it was a riot of disorder, with workbenches and odds and ends strewn without system or reason in every direction—one had need of care to negotiate it in the dark. He took his flashlight from his pocket, and, preliminary to a more intimate acquaintance with the interior, glanced out through the front window near which he stood—and, with a suppressed cry, shrank back instinctively against the wall.

Two men were crossing the street, heading directly for the shop door. The arc lamp lighted up their faces. *It was Inspector Lannigan of Headquarters and Whitey Mack!* The quick intake of Jimmie Dale breath was sucked through clenched teeth. They were close on his heels then—far closer than he had imagined. It would take Whitey Mack scarcely any longer to open that front door than it had taken him. Close on his heels! His face was rigid. He could hear them now at the door. The flashlight in his hand winked down the length of the room. If was a dangerous thing to do, but it was still more dangerous to stumble into some object and make a noise. He darted forward, circuiting a workbench, a stool, a small hand forge. Again the flashlight gleamed. Against the side wall, near the rear, was another workbench, with a sort of coarse canvas curtain hanging part way down in front of it, evidently to protect such things as might be stored away beneath it from dust, and Jimmie Dale sprang for it, whipped back the canvas, and crawled underneath. He was not an instant too soon. As the canvas fell back into place, the shop door opened, closed, and the two men had stepped inside.

Whitey Mack's voice, in a low whisper though it was, seemed to echo raucously through the shop.

"Mabbe we'll have a sweet wait, but I got the straight dope on this. He's going to make a try for Dutchy's sparklers tonight. We'll let him go the limit, and we don't either of us make a move till he's pinched them, and then we get him with the goods on him. He can't get away; he hasn't a hope! There's only two ways of getting in here or getting out—this door and window here, and a window that's down there at the back. You guard this, and I'll take care of the other end. Savvy?"

"Right!" Lannigan answered grimly. "Go ahead!"

There was the sound of footsteps moving forward, then a vicious bump, the scraping of some object along the floor, and a muffled curse from Whitey Mack.

"Use your flashlight!" advised the inspector, in a guarded voice.

"I haven't got one, damn it!" growled Whitey Mack. "It's all right. I'll get along."

Again the steps, but more warily now, as though the man were cautiously feeling ahead of him for possible obstacles. Jimmie Dale for a moment held his breath. He could have reached out and touched the man as the other passed. Whitey Mack went on until he had taken up a position against the rear wall. Jimmie Dale heard him as he brushed against it.

Then silence fell. He was between them now. Stretched full length on the floor, Jimmie Dale raised the lower portion of the canvas away from in front of his face. He could see nothing; the place was in Stygian blackness; but it had been close and stifling, and, at least, it gave him more air.

The minutes dragged by—each more interminable than the one that had gone before. Not a movement, not a sound, and then, through the stillness, very faint at first, came the regular, repressed breathing of Whitey Mack, who was much the nearer of the two men. And, once noticeable, almost imperceptible as it was it seemed to pervade the room and fill it with a strange, ominous resonance that rose and fell until the blackness palpitated with it.

Slowly, very slowly, Jimmie Dale's hand crept into his pocket—and crept out again with his automatic. He lay motionless once more. Time in any concrete sense ceased to exist. Fancied shapes began to assume form in the darkness. By the door, Lannigan stirred uneasily, shifting his position slightly.

Was it hours—was it only minutes? It seemed to ring through the nerve-racking stillness like the shriek of a hurtling shell—and it was only a whisper.

"Watch yourself, Lannigan," whispered Whitey Mack. "He's coming now through the yard! Don't move till I start something. Let him get his paws on the sparklers."

Silence again. And then a low rasping at the window, like the gnawing of a rat; then, inch by inch, the sash was lifted. There was the sound as of a body forcing its way over the sill cautiously, then a step upon the floor inside, another, and still another. The figure of a man loomed up suddenly against the glow of a flashlight as he threw the round, white ray inquisitively here and there over the rear wall. And now he appeared to be counting the boards. One, two, three—ten. His hand ran up and down the tenth board. Again and again he repeated the operation, and something like the snarl of a baited beast echoed through the room. He half turned to snatch at something in his pocket, and the light for a moment showed a black-bearded, lowering face, partially hidden by a peaked cap that was pulled far down over his eyes.

There was the rip and tear of rending wood, as a steel jimmy, in lieu of the spring the man evidently could not find, bit in between the boards, a muttered oath of satisfaction, and a portion of the wall slid back, disclosing what looked like a metal-lined cupboard. He reached in, seized one of a dozen little boxes, and wrenched off the cover. A blue, scintillating gleam seemed to leap out to meet the white ray of the flashlight. The man chuckled hoarsely, and began to cram the rest of the boxes into his pockets.

Jimmie Dale stirred. On hands and knees he was creeping now from beneath the workbench. Something caught and tore behind him—the canvas curtain. And at the sound, with a sharp cry, the man at the wall whirled, the light went out, and he sprang toward the window. Jimmie Dale gained his feet and leaped forward. A revolver shot cut a lane of fire through the blackness; and, above the roar of the report, Whitey Mack's voice in a fierce yell:

"It's all right, Lannigan! I got him! No—*hell*!" There was a terrific crash of breaking glass. "He's got away!"

"Not yet, he hasn't!" gritted Jimmie Dale between his teeth, and his clubbed revolver swung crashing to the head of a dark form in front of him.

There was a half sigh, half moan. The form slid limply to the floor. Lannigan was floundering down the shop, leaping obstacles in a mad rush, his flashlight picking out the way.

Jimmie Dale stepped swiftly backward, and his hand groped out for the droplight, over the end of the bench, that he had knocked against in his own rush. His fingers clutched it—and the lower end of the shop was flooded with light. Except for his felt hat that lay a little distance away, there was no sign of Whitey Mack; the huddled form of the man, who but a moment since had chuckled as he pocketed old Max Diestricht's gems, lay sprawled, inert, upon the floor, and Lannigan was staring into the muzzle of Jimmie Dale's automatic.

"Drop that gun, Lannigan!" said Jimmie Dale coolly. "And I'll trouble you not to make a noise; it might attract attention from the street; there's been too much already. *Drop that gun!*"

The revolver clattered from Lannigan's hand to the floor. A step forward, and Jimmie Dale's toe sent it spinning under a bench. Another step, and, his revolver still covering the other, he had whipped a pair of handcuffs from the officer's side pocket.

Lannigan, as though the thought had never occurred to him, offered no resistance. He was staring in a dazed sort of way back and forth from Jimmie Dale to the man on the floor.

"What's this mean?" he burst out suddenly, "Where's—"

"Your wrist, please!" requested Jimmie Dale pleasantly. "No—the left one. Thank you"—as the handcuff snapped shut. "Now go over there and sit down on the floor beside that fellow. *Quick!*" Jimmie Dale's voice rasped suddenly, imperatively.

Still bewildered, but a little sullen now, Lannigan obeyed. Jimmie Dale stooped quickly, and snapped the other link of the handcuff over the unconscious man's right wrist.

Jimmie Dale smiled.

"That's the approved way of taking your man, isn't it? Left wrist to the prisoner's right. He's only stunned; he'll be around in a moment. Know him?"

Lannigan shook his head.

"Take a good look at him," invited Jimmie Dale. "You ought to know most of them in the business."

Lannigan bent over a little closer, and then, with an amazed cry, his free hand shot forward and tore away the other's beard.

It was Whitey Mack!

"My God!" gasped Lannigan.

"Quite so!" said Jimmie Dale evenly. "You'll find the diamonds in his pockets, and, excuse me"—his fingers were running through Whitey Mack's clothes—"ah, here it is"—the thin metal case was in his hand—"a little article that belongs to me, and whose loss, I am free to admit, caused me considerable concern until I was informed that he had only found it without having the slightest idea as to whom it belonged. It made quite a difference!" He had opened the case carelessly before Lannigan's eyes. "'The Gray Seal!' I'll say it for you," said Jimmie Dale whimsically. "This is what probably put the idea into his head, after first, in some way, having discovered old Max Diestricht's hiding place; and, if I had given him time enough, he would probably have stuck one of these seals, in clumsy imitation of that little eccentricity of mine, on the wall over there to stamp the job as genuine. You begin to get it, don't you Lannigan? Pretty sure-fire as an alibi, eh? And he'd have got away with it, too, as far as you were concerned. He had only to fire that shot, smash the window, tuck his false beard, mustache, and peaked cap into his pocket, put on his own hat that you see there on the floor—and yell that the man had escaped. He'd help you chase the thief, too! Rather neat, don't you think, Lannigan? And worth the risk, too, considering the howl that would go up at the theft of those stones, and that, known as the slickest diamond thief in the country, he would be the first to be suspected—except that the police themselves, in the person of Inspector Lannigan of headquarters, would be prepared to prove a perfectly good alibi for him."

Lannigan's head was thrust forward; his eyes, hard, were riveted on Whitey Mack.

"My God!" he said again under his breath. Then fiercely: "He'll get his for this!"

It was a moment before Jimmie Dale spoke; he was musingly examining the automatic in his hand.

"I am going now, Lannigan," he observed quietly. "I require, say, fifteen minutes in which to effect my escape. It is, of course, obvious that an alarm raised by you might prove extremely awkward, but a piece of canvas from that bench there, together with a bit of string, would make a most effective gag. I prefer, however, not to submit you to that indignity. Instead, I offer you the alternative of giving me your word to remain quietly where you are for—fifteen minutes."

Lannigan hesitated.

Jimmie Dale smiled.

"I agree," said Lannigan shortly.

Jimmie Dale stepped back. The electric-light switch clicked. The place was in darkness. There was a moment, two, of utter stillness; then softly, from the front end of the shop, a whisper:

"If I were you, Lannigan, I'd take that gun from Whitey's pocket before he comes round and beats you to it."

And the door had closed silently behind Jimmie Dale.

CHAPTER 11

THE STOOL-PIGEON

In the subway, ten minutes before, a freckled-faced messenger boy had squeezed himself into a seat beside Jimmie Dale, yanked a dime novel from a refractory pocket, and, blissfully lost to all the world, had buried his head in its pages. Jimmie Dale's glance at the youngster had equally, perforce, embraced the lurid title of the thriller, "Dicing with Death," so imperturbably thrust under his nose. At the time, he had smiled indulgently; but now, as he left the subway and headed for his home on Riverside Drive, the words not only refused to be ignored, but had resolved themselves into a curiously persistent refrain in his mind. They were exactly what they purported to be, dime-novelish, of the deepest hue of yellow, melodramatic in the extreme; but also, to him now, they were grimly apt and premonitorily appropriate. "Dicing with Death"—there was not an hour, not a moment in the day, when he was not literally dicing with death; when, with the underworld and the police allied against him, a single false move would lose him the throw that left death the winner!

The risk of the dual life enforced upon him grew daily greater, and in the end there must be the reckoning. He would have been a madman to have shut his eyes in the face of what was obvious—but it was worth it all, and in his soul he knew that he would not have had it otherwise even now. Tonight, tomorrow, the day after, would come another letter from the Tocsin, and there would be another "crime" of the Gray Seal's blazoned in the press—would that be the last affair, or would there be another—or tonight, tomorrow, the day after, would he be trapped before even one more letter came!

He shrugged his shoulders, as he ran up the steps of his house. Those were the stakes that he himself had laid on the table to wager upon the game, he had no quarrel there; but if only, before the end came, or even with the end itself, he could find—*her*!

With his latchkey he let himself into the spacious, richly furnished, well-lighted reception hall, and, crossing this, went up the broad staircase, his steps noiseless on the heavy carpet. Below, faintly, he could hear some of the servants—they evidently had not heard him close the door behind him. Discipline was relaxed somewhat, it was quite apparent, with Jason, that peer of butlers, away. Jason, poor chap, was in the hospital. Typhoid, they had thought it at first, though it had turned out to be some milder form of infection. He would be back in a few days now; but meanwhile he missed the old man sorely from the house.

He reached the landing, and, turning, went along the hall to the door of his own particular den, opened the door, closed it behind him—and in an instant the keen, agile brain, trained to the little things that never escaped it, that daily held his life in the balance, was alert. The room was unusually dark, even for night-time. It was as though the window shades had been closely drawn—a thing Jason never did. But then Jason wasn't there! Jimmie Dale, smiling then a little quizzically at himself, reached up for the electric-light switch beside the door, pressed it—and, his finger still on the button, whipped his automatic from his pocket with his other hand. *The room was still in darkness.*

The smile on Jimmie Dale's lips was gone, for his lips now had closed together in a tight, drawn line. The lights in the rest of the house, as witness the reception hall, were in order. This was no *accident*! Silent, motionless, he stood there, listening. Was he trapped at last—in his own house! By whom? The police? The thugs of the underworld? It made little difference—the end would differ only in the method by which it was attained! What was that! Was there a slight stir, a movement at the lower end of the room—or was it his imagination? His hand fell from the electric-light switch to the doorknob behind his back. Slowly, without a sound, it began to turn under his slim, tapering fingers, whose deft, sensitive touch had made him known and feared as the master cracksman of them all; and, as noiselessly, the door began to open.

It was like a duel—a duel of silence. What was the intruder, whoever he might be, waiting for? The abortive click of the electric-light switch, to say nothing of the opening of the door when he had entered, was evidence enough that he was there. Was the other trying to place him exactly through the darkness to make sure of his attack! The door was open now. And suddenly Jimmie Dale laughed easily aloud—and on the instant shifted his position.

"Well?" inquired Jimmie Dale coolly from the other side of the threshold.

It seemed like a long-drawn sigh fluttering through the room, a gasp of relief—and then the blood was pounding madly at his temples, and he was back in the room again, the door closed once more behind him.

"Oh, Jimmie—why didn't you speak? I had to be sure that it was you."

It was her voice! *Hers!* The Tocsin! *Here!* She was here—here in his house!

"You!" he cried. "You—here!" He was pressing the electric-light switch frantically, again and again.

Her voice came out of the darkness from across the room:

"Why are you doing that, Jimmie? You know already that I have turned off the lights."

"At the sockets—of course!" He laughed out the words almost hysterically. "Your face—I have never seen your face, you know." He was moving quickly toward the reading lamp on his desk.

There was a quick, hurried swish of garments, and she was blocking his way.

"No," she said, in a low voice; "you must not light that lamp."

He laughed again, shortly, fiercely now. She was close to him, his hands reached out for her, touched her, and thrilling at the touch, swept her toward him.

"Jimmie—Jimmie—are you mad!" she breathed.

Mad! Yes—he was mad with the wildest, most passionate exhilaration he had ever known. He found his voice with an effort.

"These months and years that I have tried until my soul was sick to find you!" he cried out. "And you are here now! Your face—I must see your face!"

She had wrenched herself away from him. He could hear her breath coming sharply in little gasps. He groped his way onward toward the desk.

"WAIT!"—her tones seemed to ring suddenly vibrant through the room. "Wait, before you touch that lamp! I—I put you on your honour not to light it."

He stopped abruptly.

"My—honour?" he repeated mechanically.

"Yes! I came here tonight because there was no other way. No other way—do you understand? I came, trusting to your honour not to take advantage of the conditions that forced me to do this. I had no fear that I was wrong—I have no fear now. You will not light that lamp, and you will not make any attempt to prevent my going away as I came—unknown. Is there any question about it, Jimmie? I am in *your* house."

"You don't know what you are saying!" he burst out wildly. "I've risked my life for a chance like this again and again; I've gone through hell, living in squalour for a month on end as Larry the Bat in the hope that I might discover who you are—and do you think I'll let anything stop me now! I tell you, no—a thousand times no!"

She made no answer. There was only her low, quick breathing coming from somewhere near him. He made another step toward the lamp—and stopped.

"I tell you, no!" he said again, and took another step forward—and stopped once more.

Still she made no answer. A minute passed—another. His hand lifted and swept across his forehead in an agitated way. Still silence. She neither moved nor spoke. His hand dropped slowly to his side. There was a twisted smile upon his lips.

"You win!" he said hoarsely.

"Thank you, Jimmie," she said simply.

"And your name, who you are"—he was speaking, but he did not seem to recognise his own voice—"the hundred other things I've sworn I'd make you explain when I found you, are all taboo as well, I suppose!"

"Yes," she said.

He laughed bitterly.

"Don't you know," he cried out, "that between the police and the underworld, our house of cards is likely to collapse at any minute—that they are hunting the Gray Seal day and night! Is it to be always like this—that I am never to know—until it is too late!"

She came toward him out of the darkness impulsively.

"They will never get you, Jimmie," she said, in a suppressed voice. "And some day, I promise you now, you shall have your reward for tonight. You shall know—everything."

"When?" The word came from him with fierce eagerness.

"I do not know," she answered gently. "Soon, perhaps—perhaps sooner than either of us imagine."

"And by that you mean—what?" he asked, and his hand reached out for her again through the blackness.

This time she did not draw away. There was an instant's hesitation; then she spoke again hurriedly, a note of anxiety in her voice.

"You are beginning all over again, aren't you, Jimmie? And I have told you that tonight I can explain nothing. And, besides, it is what has brought me here that counts now, and every moment is of—"

"Yes. I know," he interposed; "but, then, at least you will tell me one thing: Why did you come tonight, instead of sending me a letter as you always have before?"

"Because it is different tonight than it ever was before," she replied earnestly. "Because there is something in what has happened that I cannot explain myself; because there is danger, and where I could not see clearly I feared a trap, and so I dared not send what, in a letter, could at best be only vague and incomplete details. Do you see?"

"Yes," said Jimmie Dale—but he was only listening in an abstracted way. If he could only see that face, so close to his! He had yearned for that with all his soul for years now! And she was here, standing beside him, and his hand was upon her arm; and here, in his own den, in his own house, he was listening to another call to arms for the Gray Seal from her own lips! Honour! Was he but a poor, quixotic fool! He had only to step to the desk and switch on the light! Why should—he steadied himself with a jerk, and drew away his hand. She was in *his* house. "Go on," he said tersely.

"Do you know, or did you ever hear of old Luther Doyle?" she asked.

"No," said Jimmie Dale.

"Do you know a man, then, named Connie Myers?"

Connie Myers! Who in the Bad Lands did not know Connie Myers, who boasted of the half dozen prison sentences already to his credit? Yes; he knew Connie Myers! But, strangely enough, it was not in the Bad Lands or as Larry the Bat that he knew the man, or that the other knew him—it was as Jimmie Dale. Connie Myers had introduced himself one night several years ago with a blackjack that had just missed its mark as the man had jumped out from a dark alleyway on the East Side, and he, Jimmie Dale, had thrashed the other to within an inch of his life. He had reason to know Connie Myers—and Connie Myers had reason to remember him!

"Yes," he said, with a grim smile; "I know Connie Myers."

"And the tenement across the street from where you live as Larry the Bat—that, of course, you know." He leaned toward her wonderingly now.

"Of course!" he ejaculated. "Naturally!"

"Listen, then, Jimmie!" She was speaking quickly now. "It is a strange story. This Luther Doyle was already over fifty, when, some eight or nine years ago, his parents died within a few months of each other, and he inherited somewhere in the neighbourhood of a hundred thousand dollars; but the man, though harmless enough, was mildly insane, half-witted, and the old couple, on account of their son's mental defects, took care to leave the money securely invested, and so that he could only touch the interest. During these eight or nine years he has lived by himself in the same old family house where he had lived with his parents, in a lonely spot near Pelham. And he has lived in a most frugal, even miserly, manner. His income could not have been less than six thousand dollars a year, and his expenditures could not have been more than six hundred. His dementia, ironically enough from the day that he came into his fortune, took the form of a most pitiable and abject fear that he would die in poverty, misery, and want; and so, year after year, cashing his checks as fast as he got them, never trusting the bank with a penny, he kept hiding away somewhere in his house every cent he could scrape and save from his income—which today must amount, at a minimum calculation, to fifty thousand dollars."

"And," observed Jimmie Dale quietly. "Connie Myers robbed him of it, and—"

"No!" Her voice was quivering with passion, as she caught up his words. "Twice in the last month Connie Myers *tried* to rob him, but the money was too securely hidden. Twice he broke into Doyle's house when the old man was out, but on both occasions was unsuccessful in his search, and was interrupted and forced to make his escape on account of Doyle's return. Tonight, an hour ago, in an empty room on the second floor of that tenement, in the room facing the landing, old Luther Doyle was *murdered*!"

There was silence for an instant. Her hand had closed in a tight pressure on his arm. The darkness seemed to add a sort of ghastly significance to her words.

"In God's name, how do you know all this?" he demanded wildly. "How do you know all these things?"

"Does that matter now?" she answered tensely. "You will know that when you know the rest. Oh, don't you understand, Jimmie, there is not a moment to lose now? It was easy to lure a half-witted creature like that anywhere; it was Connie Myers who lured him to the tenement and murdered him there—but from that point, Jimmie, I am not sure of our ground. I do not know whether Connie Myers is alone in this or not; but I do know that he is going to Doyle's house again tonight to make another search for the money. There is no question but that old Doyle was murdered to give Connie Myers and his accomplices, if there are any, a chance to tear the house inside out to find the money, to give them the whole night to work in without interruption if necessary—but Doyle dead in his own house could have interfered no more with them than Doyle dead in that tenement! Why was he lured to the tenement by Connie Myers when he could much more easily have been put out of the way in his own house? Jimmie, there is something behind this, something more that you must find out. There may be others in this besides Connie Myers, I do not know; but there is something here that I am afraid of. Jimmie, you must get that man, you must get the others if there are others, and you must stop them from getting the money in that house tonight! Do you understand now why I have come here? I could not explain in a letter; I do not quite seem to be explaining now. It would seem as though there were no need for the Gray Seal—that simply the police should be notified. But I *know*, Jimmie, call it intuition, what you will, I know that there is need for us, for you tonight—that behind all this is a tragedy, deeper, blacker, than even the brutal, cold-blooded murder that is already done."

Her voice, in its passionate earnestness, died away; and an anger, cold, grim, remorseless, settled upon Jimmie Dale—settled as it always settled upon him at her call to arms. His brain was already at work in its quick, instant way, probing, sifting, planning. She was right! It was strange, it was more than strange that, with the added risk, the danger, the difficulty, the man should have been brought miles to be done away with in that tenement! Why? Connie Myers took form before him—the coarse features, the tawny hair that straggled across the low forehead, the shifty eyes that were an indeterminate colour between brown and gray, the thin lips that seemed to draw in and give the jaw a protruding, belligerent effect. And Connie Myers knew him as Jimmie Dale—it would have to be then as Larry the Bat that the Gray Seal must work. That meant time—to go to the Sanctuary and change.

"The police," he asked suddenly, aloud, "they have not yet discovered the body?"

"Not yet," she replied hurriedly. "And that is still another reason for haste—there is no telling when they will. See—here!" She thrust a paper into his hand. "Here is a plan of old Doyle's house, and directions for finding it. You must get Connie Myers red-handed, you must make him convict himself, for the evidence through which I know him to be guilty can never be used against him. And, Jimmie, be careful—I know I am not wrong, that there is still something more behind all this. And now go, Jimmie, go! There is no time to lose!" She was pushing him across the room toward the door.

Go! The word seemed suddenly to bring dismay. It was she again who was dominant now in his mind. Who knew if tonight, when he was taking his life in his hands again, would not be the last! And she was here now, here beside him—where she might never be again!

She seemed to divine his thoughts, for she spoke again, a strange new note of tenderness in her voice that thrilled him.

"You must never let them get you, Jimmie—for my sake. It will not last much longer—it is near the end—and I shall keep my promise. But go, now, Jimmie—go!"

"Go?" he repeated numbly. "Go? But—but you?"

"I?" She slipped suddenly away from him, retreating back down the room. "I will go—as I came."

"Wait! Listen!" he pleaded.

There was no answer.

She was there—somewhere back there in the darkness still. He stood hesitant at the door. It seemed that every faculty he possessed urged him back there again—to her. Could he let her escape him now when she was so utterly in his power, she who meant everything in his life! And then, like a cold shock, came that other thought—she who had trusted to his honour! With a jerk, his hand swept out, felt for the doorknob, and closed upon it.

"Good-night!" he said heavily, and stepped out into the hall.

It seemed for a while, even after he had gained the street and made his way again to the subway, that nothing was concrete around him, that he was living through some fantastical dream. His head whirled, and he could not think rationally—and then slowly, little by little, his grip upon himself came back. She had come—and gone! With the roar of the subway in his ears, its raucous note seeming to strike so perfectly in consonance with the turmoil within him, he smiled mirthlessly. After all, it was as it always was! She was gone—and ahead of him lay the chances of the night!

"Dicing with death!" The words, unbidden, came back once more. If they were true before, they were doubly applicable now. It was different tonight from what it had ever been before, as she had said. Usually, to the smallest detail, everything was laid open, clear before him in those astounding letters. Tonight, it was vague at best. A man had been murdered. Connie Myers had committed the murder under circumstances that pointed strongly to some hidden motive behind and beyond the mere chance it afforded him to search his victim's house for the hidden cash. What was it?

Jimmie Dale stared out at the black subway walls. The answer would not come. Station after station passed. At Fourteenth Street he changed from the express to a local, got out at Astor Place, and a few minutes later was walking rapidly down the upper end of the Bowery.

The answer would not come—only the fact itself grew more and more deeply significant. The ghastly, callous fiendishness that lured an old, half-witted man to his death had Jimmie Dale in that grip of cold, merciless anger again, and there was a dull flush now upon his cheeks. Whatever it meant, whatever was behind it, one thing at least was certain—*he would get Connie Myers!*

He was close to the Sanctuary now—it was down the next cross street. He reached the corner and turned it, heading east; but his brisk walk had changed to a nonchalant saunter—there were some people coming toward him. It was the Gray Seal now, alert and cautious. The little group passed by. Ahead, the tenement bordering on the black alleyway loomed up—the Sanctuary, with its three entrances and exits; the home of Larry the Bat. And across from it was that other tenement, that held a new interest for him now, where, in an empty room on the second floor, she had said, old Doyle still lay. Should he go there? He was thinking quickly now, and shook his head. It would take what he did not have to spare—time. It was already ten o'clock; and, granted that Connie Myers had committed the crime only a little over an hour ago, the man by this time would certainly be on his way to Doyle's house near Pelham, if, indeed, he were not already there. No, there was no time to spare—the question resolved itself simply into how long, since he had already searched twice and failed on both occasions, it would take Connie Myers to unearth old Doyle's hiding place for the money.

Jimmie Dale glanced sharply around him, slipped into the alleyway, and, crouching against the tenement wall, moved noiselessly along to the side entrance. A moment more, and he had negotiated the rickety stairs with practiced, soundless tread, was inside the squalid quarters of Larry the Bat, and the door of the Sanctuary was locked and bolted behind him.

Perhaps five minutes passed—and then, where Jimmie Dale, the millionaire, had entered, there emerged Larry the Bat, of the aristocracy and the elite of the Bad Lands. But instead of leaving by the side door and the alleyway, as he had entered, he went along the lower hallway to the front entrance. And here, instinctively, he paused a moment at the top of the steps, as his eyes rested upon the tenement on the opposite side of the street.

It was strange that the crime should have been committed there! Something again seemed to draw him toward that empty room on the second story. He had decided once that he would not go, that there was not time; but, after all, it would not take long, and there was at least the possibility of gaining something more valuable even than time from the scene of the crime itself—there might even be the evidence he wanted there that would disclose the whole of Connie Myers' game.

He went down the steps, and started across the street; but halfway over, he hesitated uncertainly, as a child's cry came petulantly from the doorway. It was dark in the street; and, likewise, it was one of those hot, suffocating evenings when, in the crowded tenements of the poorer class, miserable enough in any case, misery was added to a hundredfold for lack of a single God-given breath of air. These two facts, apparently irrelevant, caused Jimmie Dale to change his mind again. He had not noticed the woman with the baby in her arms, sitting on the doorstep; but now, as he reached the curb, he not only saw, but recognised her—and he swung on down the street toward the Bowery. He could not very well go in without passing her, without being recognised himself—and that was a needless risk.

He smiled a little wanly. Once the crime was discovered, she would not have hesitated long before informing the police that she had seen him enter there! Mrs. Hagan was no friend of his! One could not live as he had lived, as Larry the Bat, and not see something in an intimate way of the pitiful little tragedies of the poor around him; for, bad, tough, and dissolute as the quarter was, all were not degraded there, some were simply—poor. Mrs. Hagan was poor. Her husband was a day labourer, often out of a job—and sometimes he drank. That was how he, Jimmie Dale, or rather, Larry the Bat, had come to earn Mrs. Hagan's enmity. He had found Mike Hagan drunk one night, and in the act of being arrested, and had wheedled the man away from the officer on the promise that he would take Hagan home. And he was Larry the Bat, a dope fiend, a character known to all the neighbourhood, and Mrs. Hagan had laid her husband's condition to *his* influence and companionship! He had taken Mike Hagan home—and Mrs. Hagan had driven Larry the Bat from the door of her miserable one-room lodging in that tenement with the bitter words on her tongue that only a woman can use when shame and grief and anger are breaking her heart.

He shrugged his shoulders, as, back along the Bowery, he retraced his steps, but now, with the hurried shuffle of Larry the Bat where before had been the brisk, athletic stride of Jimmie Dale.

At Astor Place again, he took the subway, this time to the Grand Central Station—and, well within an hour from the time he had left the Sanctuary, including the train journey to Pelham, he was standing in a clump of trees that fringed a deserted roadway. He had passed but few houses, once he was away from Pelham, and, as well as he could judge, there was none now within a quarter of a mile of him—except this one of old Luther Doyle's that showed up black and shadowy just beyond the trees.

Jimmie Dale's eyes narrowed as he surveyed the place. It was little wonder that, known to have money, an attempt to rob old Doyle should have been made in a place like this! It was even more grimly significant than ever of some deeper meaning that, in its loneliness an ideal place for a murder, the man should have been lured from there for that purpose to a crowded tenement in the city instead! What did it mean? Why had it been done? He shook his head. The answer would not come now any more than it had come before in the subway, or in the train on the way out, when he had set his brain so futilely to solve the problem.

From a survey of the house, Jimmie Dale gave attention to the details of his surroundings: the trees on either side; the open space in front, a distance of fifty yards to the road; the absence of any fence. And then, abruptly, he stole forward. There was no light to be seen anywhere about the house. Was it possible that Connie Myers was not yet there? He shook his head again impatiently. Connie Myers would not have wasted any time—as the Tocsin had said, there was always present the possibility that the crime in that tenement might be discovered at *any* moment. Connie Myers would have lost no time; for, let the discovery be made, let the police identify the body, as they most certainly would, and they would be out here hotfoot. Jimmie Dale stood suddenly still. What did it mean! He had not thought of that before! If old Doyle had been murdered *here*, there would not have been even the possibility of discovery until the morning at the earliest, and Connie Myers would have had all the time he wanted!

What was that sound! A low, muffled tapping, like a succession of hammer blows, came from within the house. Jimmie Dale darted forward, reached the side of the house, and dropped on hands and knees. One question at least was answered—Connie Myers was inside.

The plan that she had given him showed an old-fashioned cellarway, closed by folding trapdoors, that was located a little toward the rear and, in a moment, creeping along, he came upon it. His hands felt over it. It was shut, fastened by a padlock on the outside. Jimmie Dale's lips thinned a little, as he took a small steel instrument from his pocket. Either through inadvertence or by intention, Connie Myers had passed up an almost childishly simple means of entrance into the house! One side of the trapdoor was lifted up silently—and silently closed. Jimmie Dale was in the cellar. The hammering, much more distinct now, heavy, thudding blows, came from a room in the front—the connection between the cellar and the house, as shown on the Tocsin's plan, was through another trapdoor in the floor of the kitchen.

Jimmie Dale's flashlight played on a short, ladderlike stairway, and in an instant he was climbing upward. The sounds from the front of the house continued now without interruption; there was little fear that Connie Myers would hear anything else—even the protesting squeak of the hinges as Jimmie Dale cautiously pushed back the trapdoor in the flooring above his head. An inch, two inches he lifted it; and, his eyes on a level with the opening now, he peered into the room. The kitchen itself was intensely dark; but through an open doorway, well to one side so that he could not see into the room beyond, there struggled a curiously faint, dim glimmer of light. And then Jimmie Dale's form straightened rigidly on the stairs. The blows stopped, and a voice, in a low growl, presumably Connie Myers', reached him.

"Here, take a drive at it from the lower edge!"

There was no answer—save that the blows were resumed again. Jimmie Dale's face had set hard. Connie Myers was not alone in this, then! Well, the odds were a little heavier, *doubled*—that was all! He pushed the trapdoor wide open, swung himself up through the opening to the floor; and the next instant, back a little from the connecting doorway, his body pressed closely against the kitchen wall, he was staring, bewildered and amazed, into the next room.

On the floor, presumably to lessen the chance of any light rays stealing through the tightly drawn window shades, burned a small oil lamp. The place was in utter confusion. The right-hand side of a large fireplace, made of rough, untrimmed stone and cement, and which occupied almost the entire end of the room, was already practically demolished, and the wreckage was littered everywhere; part of the furniture was piled unceremoniously into one corner out of the way; and at the fireplace itself, working with sledge and bar, were two men. One was Connie Myers. An ironical glint crept into Jimmie Dale's eyes. The false beard and mustache the man wore would deceive no one who knew Connie Myers! And that he should be wearing them now, as he knelt holding the bar while the other struck at it, seemed both uncalled for and absurd. The other man, heavily built, roughly dressed, had his back turned, and Jimmie Dale could not see his face.

The puzzled frown on Jimmie Dale's forehead deepened. Somewhere in the masonry of the fireplace, of course, was where old Luther Doyle had hidden his money. That was quite plain enough; and that Connie Myers, in some way or other, had made sure of that fact was equally obvious. But how did old Luther Doyle get his money *in* there from time to time, as he received the interest and dividends whose accumulation, according to the Tocsin, comprised his hoard! And how did he get it *out* again?

"All right, that'll do!" grunted Connie Myers suddenly. "We can pry this one out now. Lend a hand on the bar!"

The other dropped his sledge, turned sideways as he stooped to help Connie Myers, his face came into view—and, with an involuntary start, Jimmie Dale crouched farther back against the wall, as he stared at the other. It was Hagan! Mrs. Hagan's husband! Mike Hagan!

"My God!" whispered Jimmie Dale, under his breath.

So that was it! That the murder had been committed in the tenement was not so strange now! A surge of anger swept Jimmie Dale—and was engulfed in a wave of pity. Somehow, the thin, tired face of Mrs. Hagan had risen before him, and she seemed to be pleading with him to go away, to leave the house, to forget that he had ever been there, to forget what he had seen, what he was seeing now. His hands clenched fiercely. How realistically, how importunately, how pitifully she took form before him! She was on her knees, clasping his knees, imploring him, terrified.

From Jimmie Dale's pocket came the black silk mask. Slowly, almost hesitantly, he fitted it over his face—Mike Hagan knew Larry the Bat. Why should he have pity for Mike Hagan? Had he any for Connie Myers? What right had he to let pity sway him! The man had gone the limit; he was Connie Myers' accomplice—a murderer! But the man was not a hardened, confirmed criminal like Connie Myers. Mike Hagan—a murderer! It would have been unbelievable but for the evidence before his own eyes now. The man had faults, brawled enough, and drank enough to have brought him several times to the notice of the police—but this!

Jimmie Dale's eyes had never left the scene before him. Both men were throwing their weight upon the bar, and the stone that they were trying to dislodge—they were into the heart of the masonry now—seemed to move a little. Connie Myers stood up, and, leaning forward, examined the stone critically at top and bottom, prodding it with the bar. He turned from his examination abruptly, and thrust the bar into Hagan's hands.

"Hold it!" he said tersely. "I'll strike for a turn."

Crouched, on his hands and knees, Hagan inserted the point of the bar into the crevice. Connie Myers picked up the sledge.

"Lower! Bend lower!" he snapped—and swung the sledge.

It seemed to go black for a moment before Jimmie Dale's eyes, seemed to paralyse all action of mind and body. There was a low cry that was more a moan, the clang of the iron bar clattering on the floor, and Mike Hagan had pitched forward on his face, an inert and huddled heap. A half laugh, half snarl purled from Connie Myers' lips, as he snatched a stout piece of cord from his pocket and swiftly knotted the unconscious man's wrists together. Another instant, and, picking up the bar, prying with it again, the loosened stone toppled with a crash into the grate.

It had come sudden as the crack of doom, that blow—too quick, too unexpected for Jimmie Dale to have lifted a finger to prevent it. And now that the first numbed shock of mingled horror and amazement was past, he fought back the quick, fierce impulse to spring out on Connie Myers. Whether the man was killed or only stunned, he could do no good to Mike Hagan now, and there was Connie Myers—he was staring in a fascinated way at Connie Myers. Behind the stone that the other had just dislodged was a large hollow space that had been left in the masonry, and from this now Connie Myers was eagerly collecting handfuls of banknotes that were rolled up into the shape of little cylinders, each one grotesquely tied with a string. The man was feverishly excited, muttering to himself, running from the fireplace to where the table had been pushed aside with the rest of the furniture, dropping the curious little rolls of money on the table, and running back for more. And then, having apparently emptied the receptacle, he wriggled his body over the dismantled fireplace, stuck his head into the opening, and peered upward.

"Kinks in his nut, kinks in his nut!" Connie Myers was muttering. "I'll drop the bar through from the top, mabbe there's some got stuck in the pipe."

He regained his feet, picked up the bar, and ran with it into what was evidently the front hall—then his steps sounded running upstairs.

Like a flash, Jimmie Dale was across the room and at the fireplace. Like Connie Myers, he, too, put his head into the opening; and then, an unpleasant smile on his lips, he bent quickly over the man on the floor. Hagan was no more than stunned, and was even then beginning to show signs of returning consciousness. There was a rattle, a clang, a thud—and the bar, too long to come all the way through, dropped into the opening and stood upright. Connie Myers' footsteps sounded again, returning on the run—and Jimmie Dale was back once more on the other side of the kitchen doorway.

It was all simple enough—once one understood! The same odd smile was still flickering on Jimmie Dale's lips. There was no way to get the money out, except the way Connie Myers had got it out—by digging it out! With the irrational cunning of his mad brain, that had put the money even beyond his own reach, old Doyle had built his fireplace with a hollow some eighteen inches square in a great wall of solid stonework, and from it had run a two-inch pipe up somewhere to the story above; and down this pipe he had dropped his little string-tied cylinders of banknotes, satisfied that his hoard was safe! There seemed something pitifully ironic in the elaborate, insane craftiness of the old man's fear-twisted, demented mind.

And now Connie Myers was back in the room again—and again a puzzled expression settled upon Jimmie Dale's face as he watched the other. For perhaps a minute the man stood by the table sifting the little rolls of money through his fingers gloatingly—then, impulsively, he pushed these to one side, produced a revolver, laid it on the table, and from another pocket took out a little case which, as he opened it, Jimmie Dale could see contained a hypodermic syringe. One more article followed the other two—a letter, which Connie Myers took out of an unsealed envelope. He dropped this suddenly on the table, as Mike Hagan, three feet away on the floor, groaned and sat up.

Hagan's eyes swept, bewildered, confused, around him, questioningly at Connie Myers—and then, resting suddenly on his bound wrists, they narrowed menacingly.

"Damn you, you smashed me with that sledge on *purpose!*" he burst out—and began to struggle to his feet.

With a brutal chuckle, Connie Myers pushed Hagan back and shoved his revolver under the other's nose.

"Sure!" he admitted evenly. "And you keep quiet, or I'll finish you now—instead of letting the police do it!" He laughed out jarringly. "You're under arrest, you know, for the murder of Luther Doyle, and for robbing the poor old nut of his savings in his house here."

Hagan wrenched himself up on his elbow.

"What—what do you mean?" he stammered.

"Oh, don't worry!" said Connie Myers maliciously. "*I'm* not making the arrest, I'd rather the police did that. I'm not mixing up in it, and by and by"— he lifted up the hypodermic for Hagan to see—"I'm going to shoot a little dope into you that'll keep you quiet while I get away myself."

Hagan's face had gone a grayish white—he had caught sight of the money on the table, and his eyes kept shifting back and forth from it to Myers' face.

"Murder!" he said huskily. "There is no murder. I don't know who Doyle is. You said this house was yours—you hired me to come here. You said you were going to tear down the fireplace and build another. You said I could work evenings and earn some extra money."

"Sure, I did!" There was a vicious leer now on Connie Myers' lips. "But you don't think I picked you out by *accident*, do you? Your reputation, my bucko, was just shady enough to satisfy anybody that it wouldn't be beyond you to go the limit. Sure, you murdered Doyle! Listen to this." He took up the letter:

To the police:

Luther Doyle was murdered this evening in the tenement at 67 —— Street. You'll find his body in a room on the second floor. If you want to know who did it, look in Mike Hagan's room on the floor above. There's a paper stuck under the edge of Hagan's table with a piece of chewing gum, where he hid it. You'll know what it is when you go out and take a look at Doyle's house in Pelham.

Mike Hagan did not speak—his lips were twitching, and there was horror creeping into his eyes.

"D'ye get me!" sneered Connie Myers. "Tell your story—who'd believe it! I got you cinched. Twice I tried to get this old dub's coin out here, and couldn't find it. But the second time I found something else—a piece of paper with a drawing of the fireplace on it, and a place in the drawing marked with an X. That was good enough, wasn't it? That's the paper I stuck under your table this afternoon when your wife was out—see? Somebody's got to stand for the job, and if it's somebody else it won't be me—get me! When I had a look at that fireplace I knew I couldn't do the job alone in a week, and I didn't dare blast it with 'soup' for fear of spoiling what was inside. And since I had to have somebody to help me, I thought I might as well let him help me all the way through—and stand for it. I picked you, Mike—that's why I croaked old Doyle in your tenement tonight. I wrote this letter while I was waiting for you to show up at the station to come out here with me, and I'm going to see that the police get it in the next hour. When they find Doyle in the room below yours, and that paper in your room, and the busted fireplace here—I guess they won't look any farther for who did it. And say"—he leaned forward with an ugly grin—"mabbe you think I'm soft to be telling you all this? But don't you fool yourself. You don't know me—you don't know who I am. So tell 'em the *truth*! They won't believe you anyway with evidence like that against you—and the neater the story the more they'll think it shows brains enough on your part to have pulled a job like this!"

"My God!" Hagan was rocking on his knees, beads of sweat were starting out on his forehead. "You wouldn't plant a man like that!" he cried brokenly. "You wouldn't do it, would you? My God—you wouldn't do that!"

Jimmie Dale's face under his mask was white and rigid. There was something primal, elemental in the savagery that was sweeping upon him. He had it all now—*all*! She had been right—there was need tonight for the Gray Seal. So that was the game, inhuman, hellish, the whole of it, to the last filthy dregs—Connie Myers, to protect himself, was railroading an innocent man to death for the crime that he himself had committed! There was a cold smile on Jimmie Dale's lips now, as he took his automatic from his pocket. No, it wasn't quite all the game—there was still *his* hand to play! He edged forward a little nearer to the door—and halted abruptly, listening. An automobile had stopped outside on the road. Hagan was still pleading in a frenzied way; Connie Myers was callously folding his letter, while he watched the other warily—neither of the men had heard the sound.

And then, quick, almost on the instant, came a rush of feet, a crash upon the front door—an imperative command to open in the name of the law. *The police!* Jimmie Dale's brain was working now with lightning speed. Somehow the police had stumbled upon the crime in that tenement; and, as he had foreseen in such an event, had identified Doyle. But they could not be sure that anyone was present here in the house now—they could not see a light any more than he had. He must get Mike Hagan away—must see that Connie Myers did *not* get away. Myers was on his feet now, fear struck in his turn, the letter clutched in a tight-closed fist, his revolver swung out, poised, in the other hand. Hagan, too, was on his feet, and, unheeded now by Connie Myers, was wrenching his wrists apart.

Another crash upon the door—another. Another demand in a harsh voice to open it. Then someone running around to the window at the side of the house—and Jimmie Dale sprang forward.

There was the roar of a report, a blinding flash almost in Jimmie Dale's eyes, as Connie Myers, whirling instantly at his entrance, fired—and missed. It happened quick then, in the space of the ticking of a watch—before Jimmie Dale, flinging himself forward, had reached the man. Like a defiant challenge to their demand it must have seemed to the officers outside, that shot of Connie Myers at Jimmie Dale, for it was answered on the instant by another through the side window. And the shot, fired at random, the interior of the room hidden from the officers outside by the drawn shades, found its mark—and Connie Myers, a bullet in his brain, pitched forward, dead, upon the floor.

"Quick!" Jimmie Dale flung at Hagan. "Get that letter out of his hand!" He jumped for the lamp on the floor, extinguished it, and turned again toward Hagan. "Have you got it?" he whispered tensely.

"Yes," said Hagan, in a numbed way.

"This way, then!" Jimmie Dale caught Hagan's arm, and pulled the other across the room and into the kitchen to the trapdoor. "Quick!" he breathed again. "Get down there—quick! And no noise! They don't know how many are in the house. When they find *him* they'll probably be satisfied."

Hagan, stupefied, dazed, obeyed mechanically—and, in an instant, the trapdoor closed behind them, Jimmie Dale was standing beside the other in the cellar.

"Not a sound now!" he cautioned once more.

His flashlight winked, went out, winked again; then held steadily, in curious fascination it seemed, as, in its circuit, the ray fell upon Hagan—*fell upon the torn, ragged edge of a paper in Hagan's hand!* With a suppressed cry, Jimmie Dale snatched it away from the other. It was but a torn *half* of the letter! "The other half! The other half, Hagan—where is it?" he demanded hoarsely.

Hagan, almost in a state of collapse, muttered inaudibly. The crash of a toppling door sounded from above. Jimmie Dale shook the man desperately.

"Where is it?" he repeated fiercely.

"He—he was holding it tight, it—it tore in his hand," Hagan stammered. "Does it make any difference? Oh, let's get out of here, whoever you are—for God's sake let's get out of here!"

Any difference! Jimmie Dale's jaws were clamped like a steel vise. Any difference! The difference between life and death for the man beside him—that was all! He was reading the portion in his hand. It was the last part of the letter, beginning with: "There's a paper stuck under the edge of Hagan's table—" From above, from the floor of the front room now, came the rush and trample of feet. He could not go back for the other half. And any attempt to conceal the fact that Connie Myers had been alone in the house was futile now. They would find the torn letter in the dead man's hand, proof enough that someone else had been there. What was in that part of the letter that was still clutched in that death grip upstairs? A sentence from it, that he had heard Connie Myers read, seemed to burn itself into his brain. *"If you want to know who did it, look in Mike Hagan's room on the floor above."* And then, suddenly, like light through the darkness, came a ray of hope. He pulled Hagan to the cellarway, and stealthily lifted one side of the double trapdoor. There was a chance, desperate enough, one in a thousand—but still a chance!

Voices from the house came plainly now, but there was no one in sight. The police, to a man, were evidently all inside. From the road in front showed the lamp glare of their automobile.

"Run for the car!" Jimmie Dale jerked out from between set teeth—and with Hagan beside him, steadying the man by the arm, dashed across the intervening fifty yards.

They had not been seen. A minute more, and the car, evidently belonging to the local police, for it was headed in the direction of New York, and as though it had come from Pelham, swept down the road, swept around a turn, and Jimmie Dale, with a gasp of relief, straightened up a little from the wheel.

How much time had he? The police must have heard the car; but, equally, occupied as they were, they might well give it no thought other than that it was but another car passing by. There was no telephone in the house; the nearest house was a quarter of a mile away, and that might or might not have a telephone. Could he count on half an hour? He glanced anxiously at the crouched figure beside him. He would have to! It was the only chance. They would telephone the contents of the dead man's half of the letter to the New York police. Could he get to Hagan's room *first*! "Look in Hagan's room," their part of the letter read—but it did not say for *what*, or exactly *Where!* If they found nothing, Hagan was safe. Connie Myers' reputation, the fact that he was found in disguise at Doyle's house, was, barring any incriminating evidence, quite enough to let Hagan out. There would only remain in the minds of the police the question of who, beside Connie Myers, had been in old Doyle's house that night? And now Jimmie Dale smiled a little whimsically. Well, perhaps he could answer that—and, if not quite to the satisfaction of the police, at least to the complete vindication of Mike Hagan.

But he could not drive through towns and villages with a mask on his face; and there, ahead now, lights were beginning to show. And more than ever now, with what was before him, it was imperative that Mike Hagan should not recognise Larry the Bat. Jimmie Dale glanced again at Hagan—and slowed down the car. They were on the outskirts of a town, and off to the right he caught the twinkling lights of a street car.

"Hagan," he said sharply, "pull yourself together, and listen to me! If you keep your mouth shut, you've nothing to fear; if you let out a word of what's happened tonight, you'll probably go to the chair for a crime you know nothing about. Do you understand?—keep your mouth shut!"

The car had stopped. Hagan nodded his head.

"All right, then. You get out here, and take a street car into New York," continued Jimmie Dale crisply. "But when you get there, keep away from your home for the next two or three hours. Hang around with some of the boys you know, and if you're asked anything afterward, say you were batting around town all evening. Don't worry—you'll find you're out of this when you read the morning papers. Now get out—hurry!" He pushed Hagan from the car. "I've got to make my own get-away."

Hagan, standing in the road, brushed his hand bewilderingly across his eyes.

"Yes—but you—I—"

"Never mind about that!" Jimmie Dale leaned out, and gripped Hagan's arm impressively. "There's only one thing you've got to think of, or remember. Keep your mouth shut! No matter what happens, keep your mouth shut—if you want to save your neck! Good-night, Hagan!"

The car was racing forward again. It shot streaking through the streets of the town ahead, and, dully, over its own inferno, echoed shouts, cries, and execrations of an outraged populace—then out into the night again, roaring its way toward New York.

He had half an hour—perhaps! It was a good thing Hagan did not know, or had not grasped the significance of that torn letter—the man would have been unmanageable with fear and excitement. It would puzzle Hagan to find no paper stuck under his table when he came to look for it! But that was a minor consideration, that mattered not at all.

Half an hour! On roared the car—towns, black roads, villages, wooded lands were kaleidoscopic in their passing. Half an hour! Had he done it? Had he come anywhere near doing it? He did not know. He was in the city at last—and now he had to moderate his speed; but, by keeping to the less frequented streets, he could still drive at a fast pace. One piece of good fortune had been his—the long motor coat he had found in the car with which to cover the rags of Larry the Bat, and without which he would have been obliged to leave the car somewhere on the outskirts of the city, and to trust, like Mike Hagan, to other and slower means of transportation.

Blocks away from Hagan's tenement, he ran the car into a lane, slipped off the motor coat, and from his pocket whipped out the little metal insignia case—and in another moment a diamond-shaped gray seal was neatly affixed to the black ebony rim of the steering wheel. He smiled ironically. It was necessary, quite necessary that the police should have no doubt as to who had been in Doyle's house with Connie Myers that night, or to whom they had so considerately loaned their automobile!

He was running now—through lanes, dodging down side streets, taking every short cut he knew. Had he beaten the police to Mike Hagan's room? It would be easy then. If they were ahead of him, then, by some means or other, he must still get that paper first.

He was at the tenement now—shuffling leisurely up the steps. The front door was open. He entered, and went up the first flight of stairs, then along the hall, and up the next flight. He had half expected the place to be bustling with excitement over the crime; but the police evidently had kept the affair quiet, for he had seen no one since he had entered. But now, as he began to mount the third flight, he went more slowly—someone was ahead of him. It was very dark—he could not see. The steps above died away. He reached the landing, started along for Hagan's room—and a light blazed suddenly in his face, and a hard, quick grip on his shoulder forced him back against the wall. Then the flashlight wavered, glistened on brass buttons went out, and a voice laughed roughly:

"It's only Larry the Bat!"

"Larry the Bat, eh?" It was another voice, harsh and curt. "What are you doing here?"

He was not first, after all! The telephone message from Pelham—it was almost certainly that—had beaten him! They were ahead of him, just ahead of him, they had only been a few steps ahead of him going up the stairs, just a second ahead of him on their way to Hagan's room! Jimmie Dale was thinking fast now. He must go, too—to Hagan's room with them—somehow—there was no other way—there was Hagan's life at stake.

"Aw, I ain't done nothin'!" he whined. "I was just goin' ter borrow the price of a feed from Mike Hagan—lemme go!"

"Hagan, eh!" snapped the questioner. "Are you a friend of his?"

"Sure, I am!"

The officers whispered for a moment together.

"We'll try it," decided the one who appeared to be in command. "We're in the dark, anyhow, and the thing may be only a steer. Mabbe it'll work—anyway, it won't do any harm." His hand fell heavily on Jimmie Dale's shoulder. "Mrs. Hagan know you?" brusquely.

"Sure she does!" sniffled Larry the Bat.

"Good!" rasped the officer. "Well, we'll make the visit with you. And you do what you're told, or we'll put the screws on you—see? We're after something here, and you've blown the whole game—savvy? You've spilled the gravy—understand?"

In the darkness, Jimmie Dale smiled grimly. It was far more than he had dared to hope for—they were playing into his hands!

"But I don't know 'bout any game," grovelled Larry the Bat piteously.

"Who in hell said you did!" growled the officer. "You're supposed to have snitched the lay to us, that's all—and mind you play your part! Come on!"

It was two doors down the hall to Mike Hagan's room, and there one of the officers, putting his shoulder to the door, burst it open and sprang in. The other shoved Jimmie Dale forward. It was quickly done. The three were in the room. The door was closed again.

Came a cry of terror out of the darkness, a movement as of someone rising up hurriedly in bed; and then Mrs. Hagan's voice:

"What is it! Who is it! Mike!"

The table—it was against the right-hand wall, Jimmie Date remembered. He sidled quickly toward it.

"Strike a light!" ordered the officer in charge.

Jimmie Dale's fingers were feeling under the edge of the table—a quick sweep along it—*nothing*! He stooped, reaching farther in—another sweep of his arm—and his fingers closed on a sheet of paper and a piece of hard gum. In an instant they were in his pocket.

A match crackled and flared up. A lamp was lighted. Larry the Bat sulked sullenly against the wall.

Terror-stricken, wide-eyed, Mrs. Hagan had clutched the child lying beside her to her arms, and was sitting bolt upright in bed.

"Now then, no fuss about it!" said the officer in charge, with brutal directness. "You might as well make a clean breast of Mike's share in that murder downstairs—Larry the Bat, here, has already told us the whole story. Come on, now—out with it!"

"Murder!"—her face went white. "My Mike—*murder*!" She seemed for an instant stunned—and then down the worn, thin, haggard face gushed the tears. "I don't believe it!" she cried. "I don't believe it!"

"Come on now, cut that out!" prodded the officer roughly. "I tell you Larry the Bat, here, has opened everything up wide. You're only making it worse for yourself."

"Him!" She was staring now at Jimmie Dale. "Oh, God!" she cried. "So that's what you are, are you—a stool-pigeon for the cops? Well, whatever you told them, you lie! You're the curse of this neighbourhood, you are, and if my Mike is bad at all, it's you that's helped to make him bad. But murder—you *lie*!"

She had risen slowly from the bed—a gaunt, pitiful figure, pitifully clothed, the black hair, gray-streaked, streaming thinly over her shoulders, still clutching the baby that, too, was crying now.

The officers looked at one another and nodded.

"Guess she's handing it straight—we'll have a look on our own hook," the leader muttered.

She paid no attention to them—she was walking straight to Jimmie Dale.

"It's you, is it," she whispered fiercely through her sobs "that would bring more shame and ruin here—you that's selling my man's life away with your filthy lies for what they're paying you—it's you, is it, that—" Her voice broke.

There was a frightened, uneasy look in Larry the Bat's eyes, his lips were twitching weakly, he drew far back against the wall—and then, glancing miserably at the officers, as though entreating their permission, began to edge toward the door.

For a moment she watched him, her face white with outrage, her hand clenched at her side—and then she found her voice again.

"Get out of here!" she said, in a choked, strained way pointing to the door. "Get out of here—you dirty skate!"

"Sure!" mumbled Larry the Bat, his eyes on the floor. "Sure!" he mumbled—and the door closed behind him.

PART TWO: THE WOMAN IN THE CASE

CHAPTER 1

BELOW THE DEAD LINE

Whisperings! Always whisperings, low, sibilant, floating errantly from all sides, until they seemed a component part of the drug-laden atmosphere itself. And occasionally another sound: the soft *slap-slap* of loose-slippered feet, the faint rustle of equally loose-fitting garments. And everywhere the sweet, sickish smell of opium. It was Chang Foo's, simply a cellar or two deeper in Chang Foo's than that in which Dago Jim had quarrelled once—and died!

Larry the Bat, vicious-faced, unkempt, disreputable, lay sprawled out on one of the dive's bunks, an opium pipe beside him. But Larry the Bat was not smoking; instead, his ear was pressed closely against the boarding that formed the rather flimsy partition at the side of the bunk. One heard many things in Chang Foo's if one cared to listen—if one could first win one's way through the carefully guarded gateway, that to the uninitiated offered nothing more interesting than the entrance to a Chinese tea-shop, and an uninviting one at that!

Had he been followed in here? He had been shadowed for the last hour; of that, at least, he was certain. Why? By whom? For an hour he had dodged in and out through the dens of the underworld, as only one who was at home there and known to all could do—and at last he had taken refuge in Chang Foo's like a fox burrowing deep into its hole.

Few could find their way into the most infamous opium den in all New York, where not only the poppy ruled as master, but where crime was hatched, ay, and carried to its ghastly consummation, sometimes, as well; and of those few, not one but was of the underworld itself. And it was that fact which held his muscles strained and rigid now under the miserable rags that covered them, and it was that which kept the keen, quick brain alert and active, every faculty keyed up and tense. If it were the police, he had little to fear, for they could not force their way in without warning; but if it were the underworld, he was in imminent peril, and had done little better than run himself into a trap from which there was no escape.

"Death to the Gray Seal!"—he had heard that whispered more than once in this very place. Who knew at what moment the role of Larry the Bat would be uncovered, and the underworld, where now he held so high a place, would be at his throat like a pack of snarling wolves! Who had been shadowing him during the last hour?

Whisperings! Nothing tangible! He could catch no words. Only the never-ending whisperings of gathered groups here and there—and sometimes the clink of coin where some game was in progress.

The curtain before his bunk was drawn suddenly aside—and Larry the Bat's fingers, where his hand was carelessly hidden by his body tightened upon his automatic.

"Smokee some more?"

The fingers relaxed. It was only Sam Wah, one of the attendants.

"Nix!" said Larry the Bat, in a slightly muddled tone. "Got enough."

The curtain fell into place again. Larry the Bat's lips set in a thin smile. Ultimately it made little difference whether it was the police or the underworld! The smile grew thinner. It was the flip of a coin, that was all! With one there was the death house at Sing Sing for the Gray Seal; with the other— well, there were many ways, from a shot or a knife thrust in the open street, to his murder in some hidden dive like this of Chang Foo's, for instance, where he now was—the Gray Seal was responsible for the occupancy of too many penitentiary cells by those of the underworld to look for any other fate!

He raised himself up sharply on his elbow. A shrill, high note, like the scream of a parrakeet, rang out a second time. He tore the curtain aside, and jumped to his feet. All around him, in the twinkling of an eye, Chinamen in fluttering blouses, chattering like magpies, mingled with snarling, cursing

"Nuthin' doin'!" the other answered. "I was in dere meself. De whole mob beat it clean, an' de bulls never batted an eye. Didn't youse pipe me make me get-away outer Shanghai's a minute ago? De bulls never went nowhere except into Chang's. Dere's a new lootenant in de precinct inaugeratin' himself, dat's all. S'long, Larry—I gotta date."

"S'long, Chick!" responded Jimmie Dale—and started slowly back along the cross street.

It was not the police, then, who were interested in his movements! Then who? He shook his head with a little, savage, impotent gesture. One thing was clear: it was too early to risk a return to the Sanctuary and attempt the rehabilitation of Jimmie Dale. If anyone was on the hunt for Larry the Bat, the Sanctuary would be the last place to be overlooked.

He turned the next corner, hesitated a moment in front of a garishly lighted dance hall, and finally shuffled in through the door, made his way across the floor, nodding here and there to the elite of gangland, and, with a somewhat arrogant air of proprietorship, sat down at a table in the corner. Little better than a tramp in appearance, certainly the most disreputable-looking object in the place, even the waiter who approached him accorded him a certain curious deference—was not Larry the Bat the most celebrated dope fiend below the dead line?

"Gimme a mug o' suds!" ordered Jimmie Dale, and sprawled royally back in his chair.

Under the rim of his slouch hat, pulled now far over his eyes, he searched the faces around him. If he had been asked to pick the actors for a revel from the scum of the underworld, he could not have improved upon the gathering. There were perhaps a hundred men and women in the room, the majority dancing, and, with the exception of a few sight-seeing slummers, they were men and women whose acquaintance with the police was intimate but not cordial—far from cordial.

Jimmie Dale shrugged his shoulders, and sipped at the glass that had been set before him. It was grimly ironic that he should be, not only there, but actually a factor and a part of the underworld's intimate life! He, Jimmie Dale, a wealthy man, a member of New York's exclusive clubs, a member of New York's most exclusive society! It was inconceivable. He smiled sardonically. Was it? Well, then, it was none the less true. His life unquestionably was one unique, apart from any other man's, but it was, for all that, actual and real.

There had been three years of it now—since *she* had come into his life. Jimmie Dale slouched down a little in his chair. The ice was thin, perilously thin, that he was skating on now. Each letter, with its demand upon him to match his wits against police or underworld, or against both combined, perhaps, made that peril a little greater, a little more imminent—if that were possible, when already his life was almost literally carried, daily, hourly, in his hand. Not that he rebelled against it; it was worth the price that some day he expected he must pay—the price of honour, wealth, a name disgraced, ruin, death. Was he quixotic? Immoderately so? He smiled gravely. Perhaps. But he would do it all over again if the choice were his. There were those who blessed the name of the Gray Seal, as well as those who cursed it. And there was the Tocsin!

Who was she? He did not know, but he knew that he had come to love her, come to care for her, and that she had come to mean everything in life to him. He had never seen her, to know her face. He had never seen her face, but he knew her voice—ay, he had even held her for a moment, the moment of wildest happiness he had ever known, in his arms. That night when he had entered his library, his own particular den in his own house, and in the darkness had found her there—found her finally through no effort of his own, when he had searched so fruitlessly for years to find her, using every resource at his command to find her! And she, because she had come of her own volition, relying upon him, had held him in honour to let her go as she had come—without looking upon her face! Exquisite irony! But she had made him a promise then—that the work of the Gray Seal was nearly over— that soon there would be an end to the mystery that surrounded her—that he should know all—that he should know *her*.

He smiled again, but it was a twisted smile on the mechanically mis- shapen lips of Larry the Bat. *nearly* over! Who knew? That "nearly" might be too late! Even tonight he had been shadowed, was skulking even now in this place as a refuge. Who knew? Another hour, and the newsboys might be shrieking their "Uxtra! Uxtra! De Gray Seal caught! De millionaire Jimmie Dale de Jekyll an' Hyde of real life!"

Jimmie Dale straightened up suddenly in his seat. There was a shout, an oath bawled out high above the riot of noise, a chorus of feminine shrieks from across the room. What was the matter with the underworld tonight? He seemed fated to find nothing but centres of disturbance—first a raid at Chang Foo's, and now this. What was the matter here? They were stampeding to- ward him from the other side of the room. There was the roar of a revolver shot—another. Black Ike! He caught an instant's glimpse of the gunman's distorted face through the crowd. That was it probably—a row over some moll.

And then, as Jimmie Dale lunged up from his chair to his feet to escape the rush, pandemonium itself seemed to break loose. Yells, shots, screams, and oaths filled the air. The crowd surged this way and that. Tables were overturned and sent crashing to the floor. And then came sudden darkness, as someone of the attendants in misguided excitability switched off the lights.

The darkness but served to increase the panic, not allay it. With a savage snap of his jaws, Jimmie Dale swung from his table in the corner with the intention of making his way out by a side door behind him—it was a case of the police again, and the patrolman outside would probably be pulling a riot call by now. And the police—He stopped suddenly, as though he had been struck. An envelope, thrust there out of the darkness, was in his hand; and her voice, *hers*, the Tocsin's, was sounding in his ears:

"Jimmie! Jimmie! I've been trying all evening to catch you! Quick! Get to the Sanctuary and change your clothes. There's not an instant to lose! It's for my sake tonight!"

And then a surging mob was around him on every side, and, pushing, jostling, half lifting him at times from his feet, carried him forward with its rush, and with him in its midst burst through the door and out into the street.

CHAPTER 2

THE CALL TO ARMS

Not a sound as the key turned in the lock; not a sound as the door swung back on its carefully oiled hinges; not a sound as Larry the Bat slipped like a shadow into the blackness of the room, closing the door behind him again. With a tread as noiseless as a cat's, he was across the room to satisfy himself that the shutters were tightly closed; and then the single gas jet flared up, murky, yellow, illuminating the miserable, squalid room—the Sanctuary—the home of Larry the Bat. There was need for silence, need for caution. In five minutes, ten at the outside, he must emerge again—as Jimmie Dale.

With a smile on his lips that mingled curiously chagrin and self-commiseration, he took the letter from his pocket and tore it open. It was she, then, who had been following him all evening, and, like a blundering idiot, he had wasted precious, perhaps irreparable, hours! What had she meant by "It's for my sake tonight"? The words had been ringing in his ears since the moment she had whispered them in that panic-stricken crowd. Was it not always for her sake that he answered these calls to arms? Was it not always for her sake that he, as the Gray Seal, was—The mental soliloquy came to an abrupt end. He had subconsciously read the first sentence of the letter, and now, with sudden feverish eagerness and excitement, he was reading it to the last word.

Dear Philanthropic Crook:

In an hour after you receive this, if all goes well, you shall know everything—everything. Who I am—yes, and my name. It has been more than three years now, hasn't it? It has been incomprehensible to you, but there has been no other way. I dared not take the chance of discovery by anyone; I dared not expose you to the risk of being known by me. Your life would not have been worth a moment's purchase. Oh, Jimmie, am I only making the mystery more mystifying? But tonight, I think, I hope, I pray that it is all at an end: though against me, and against you tonight when you go to help me, is the most powerful and pitiless organisation of criminals that the world has ever known; and the stake we are playing for is a fortune of millions—and my life. And yet somehow I am afraid now, just because the end is so near, and the victory seems so surely won. And so, Jimmie, be careful; use all that wonderful cleverness of yours as you have never used it before, and—But there should be no need for that, it is so simple a thing that I am going to ask you to do. Why am I writing so illogically! Nothing, surely, can possibly happen. This is not like one of my usual letters, is it? I am beside myself tonight with hope, anxiety, fear, and excitement.

Listen, then, Jimmie: Be at the northeast corner of Sixth Avenue and Waverly Place at exactly half-past ten. A taxicab will drive up, as though you had signalled it in passing, and the chauffeur will say: 'I've another fare, in half an hour, sir, but I can get you most anywhere in that time.' You will be smoking a cigarette. Toss it out into the street, make any reply you like, and get into the cab. Give the chauffeur that little ring of mine with the crest of the bell and belfry and the motto, 'Sonnez le Tocsin,' that you found the night old Isaac Pelina was murdered, and the chauffeur will give you in exchange a sealed packet of papers. He will drive you to your home, and I will telephone to you there.

I need not tell you to destroy this. Keep the appointment in your proper person—as Jimmie Dale. Carry nothing that might identify you as the Gray Seal if any accident should happen. And, lastly, trust the pseudo chauffeur absolutely.

There was no signature. Her letters were never signed. He stood for a moment staring at the closely written sheets in his hand, a heightened colour in his cheeks, his lips pressed tightly together—and then his fingers automatically began to tear the letter into pieces, and the pieces again into little shreds. Tonight! It was to be tonight, the end of all this mystery. Tonight was to see the end of this dual life of his, with its constant peril! Tonight the Gray Seal was to exit from the stage forever! Tonight, a wonderful climax of the years, he was to see *her*!

His blood was quickened now, his heart pounding in a faster beat; a mad elation, a fierce uplift was upon him. He thrust the torn bits of paper into his pocket hurriedly, stepped across the room to the corner, rolled back the oilcloth, and lifted up the loose plank in the flooring, so innocently dustladen, as, more than once, to have eluded the eyes of inquisitive visitors in the shape of police and plain clothes men from headquarters.

From the space beneath he removed a neatly folded pile of clothes, laid these on the bed, and began to undress. He was working rapidly now. Tiny pieces of wax were removed from his nostrils, from under his lips, from behind his ears; water from a cracked pitcher poured into a battered tin basin, and mixed with a few drops of some liquid from a bottle which he procured from its hiding place under the flooring, banished the make-up stain from his face, his neck, his wrists, and hands as if by magic. It was a strange metamorphosis that had taken place—the coarse, brutal-featured, blear-eyed, leering countenance of Larry the Bat was gone, and in its place, clean-cut, square-jawed, clear-eyed, was the face of Jimmie Dale. And where before had slouched a slope-shouldered, misshapen, flabby creature, a broad-shouldered form well over six feet in height now stood erect, and under the clean white skin the muscles of an athlete, like knobs of steel played back and forth with every movement of his body.

In the streaked and broken mirror Jimmie Dale surveyed himself critically, methodically, and, with a nod of satisfaction, hastily donned the fashionably cut suit of tweeds upon the bed. He rummaged then through the ragged garments he had just discarded, transferred to his pockets a roll of bills and his automatic, and paused hesitantly, staring at the thin metal case, like a cigarette case, that he held in the palm of his hand. He shrugged his shoulders a little whimsically; it seemed strange indeed that he was through with that! He snapped it open. Within, between sheets of oil paper, lay the scores of little diamond-shaped, gray-coloured, adhesive paper seals—the insignia of the Gray Seal. Yes, it seemed strange that he was never to use another! He closed the case, gathered up the clothes of Larry the Bat, tucked the case in among them, and shoved the bundle into the hole under the flooring. All these things would have to be destroyed, but there was not time tonight; tomorrow, or the next day, would do for that. What would it be like to live a normal life again, without the menace of danger lurking on every hand, without that grim slogan of the underworld, "Death to the Gray Seal!" or that savage fiat of the police, "The Gray Seal, dead or alive—but the Gray Seal!" forever ringing in his ears? What would it be like, this new life—with her?

The thought was thrilling him again, bringing again that eager, exultant uplift. In an hour, *one* hour, and the barriers of years would be swept away, and she would be in his arms!

"It's for my sake tonight!" His face grew suddenly tense, as the words came back to him. That "hour" wasn't over yet! It was no hysterical exaggeration that had prompted her to call her enemies the most powerful and pitiless organisation of criminals that the world had ever known. It was not the Tocsin's way to exaggerate. The words would be literally true. The very life she had led for the three years that had gone stood out now as a grim proof of her assertion.

Jimmie Dale replaced the flooring, carefully brushed the dust back into the cracks, spread the oilcloth into place, and stood up. Who and what was this organisation? What was between it and the Tocsin? What was this immense fortune that was at stake? And what was this priceless packet that was so crucial, that meant victory now, ay, and her life, too, she had said?

The questions swept upon him in a sort of breathless succession. Why had she not let him play a part in this? True, she had told him why—that she dared not expose him to the risk. Risk! Was there any risk that the Gray Seal had not taken, and at her instance! He did not understand, he smiled a little uncertainly, as he reached up to turn out the gas. There were a good many things that he did not understand about the Tocsin!

The room was in darkness, and with the darkness Jimmie Dale's mind centred on the work immediately before him. To enter the tenement where he was known and had an acknowledged right as Larry the Bat was one thing; for Jimmie Dale to be discovered there was quite another.

He crossed the room, opened the door silently, stood for a moment listening, then stepped out into the black, musty, ill-smelling hallway, closing the door behind him. He stooped and locked it. The querulous cry of a child reached him from somewhere above—a murmur of voices, muffled by closed doors, from everywhere. How many families were housed beneath that sordid roof he had never known, only that there was miserable poverty there as well as vice and crime, only that Larry the Bat, who possessed a room all to himself, was as some lordly and super-being to these fellow tenants who shared theirs with so many that there was not air enough for all to breathe.

He had no doors to pass—his was next to the staircase. He began to descend. They could scream and shriek, those stairs, like aged humans, twisted and rheumatic, at the least ungentle touch. But there was no sound from them now. There seemed something almost uncanny in the silent tread. Stair after stair he descended, his entire weight thrown gradually upon one foot before the other was lifted. The strain upon the muscles, trained and hardened as they were, told. As he moved from the bottom step, he wiped little beads of perspiration from his forehead.

The door, now, that gave on the alleyway! He opened it, slipped outside, darted across the narrow lane, stole along where the shadows of the fence were blackest, paused, listening, as he reached the end of the alleyway, to assure himself that there was no near-by pedestrian—and stepped out into the street.

He kept on along the block, turned into the Bowery, and, under the first lamp, consulted his watch. It was a quarter past ten. He could make it easily in a leisurely walk. He continued on up the Bowery, finally crossed to Broadway, and shortly afterward turned into Waverly Place. At the corner of Fifth Avenue he consulted his watch again—and now he lighted a cigarette. Sixth Avenue was only a block away. At precisely half-past ten, to the second, he halted on the designated corner, smoking nonchalantly.

A taxicab, coincidentally coming from an uptown direction, swung in to the curb.

"Taxi, sir? Yes, sir?" Then, with an admirable mingling of eagerness to secure the fare and a fear that his confession might cause him the loss of it: "I've another fare in half an hour, sir, but I can get you most anywhere in that time."

Jimmie Dale's cigarette was tossed carelessly into the street.

"St. James Club!" he said curtly, and stepped into the cab.

The cab started forward, turned the corner, and headed along Waverly Place toward Broadway. The chauffeur twisted around in his seat in a matter-of-fact way, as though to ask further directions.

"Have you anything for me?" he inquired casually.

It lay where it always lay, that ring, between the folds of that little white glove in his pocketbook. Jimmie Dale took it out now, and handed it silently to the chauffeur.

The other's face changed instantly—composure was gone, and a quick, strained look was in its place.

"I'm afraid I've been watched," he said tersely. "Look behind you, will you, and tell me if you see anything?"

Jimmie Dale glanced backward through the little window in the hood.

"There's another taxi just turned in from Sixth Avenue," he reported the next instant.

"Keep your eye on it!" instructed the chauffeur shortly.

The speed of the cab increased sensibly.

With a curious tightening of his lips, Jimmie Dale settled himself in his seat so that he could watch the cab behind. There was trouble coming, intuitively he sensed that; and, he reflected bitterly, he might have known! It was too marvellous, too wonderful ever to come to pass that this one hour, the thought of which had fired his blood and made him glad beyond any gladness life had ever held for him before, should bring its promised happiness.

"Where's the cab now?" the chauffeur flung back over his shoulder.

They had passed Fifth Avenue, and were nearing Broadway.

"About the same distance behind," Jimmie Dale answered.

"That looks bad!" the chauffeur gritted between his teeth. "We'll have to make sure. I'll run down Lower Broadway."

"If you think we're followed," suggested Jimmie Dale quietly, "why not run uptown and give them the slip somewhere where the traffic is thick? Lower Broadway at this time of night is as empty and deserted as a country road."

The chauffeur's sudden laugh was mirthless.

"My God, you don't know what you are talking about!" he burst out. "If they're following, all hell couldn't throw them off the track. And I've got to know, I've got to be *sure* before I dare make a move tonight. I couldn't tell up in the crowded districts if I was followed, could I? They won't come out into the open until their hands are forced."

The car swerved sharply, rounded the corner, and, speeding up faster and faster, began to tear down Lower Broadway.

"Watch! *Watch*!" cried the chauffeur.

There was no word between them for a moment; then Jimmie Dale spoke crisply:

"It's turned the corner! It's coming this way!"

The taxicab was rocking violently with the speed; silent, empty, Lower Broadway stretched away ahead. Apart from an occasional street car, probably there would be nothing between them and the Battery. Jimmie Dale glanced at his companion's face as a light, flashing by, threw it into relief. It was set and stern, even a little haggard; but, too, there was something else there, something that appealed instantly to Jimmie Dale—a sort of bulldog grit that dominated it.

"If he holds our speed, we'll know!" the chauffeur was shouting now to make himself heard over the roar of the car. "Look again! Where is it now?"

Once more Jimmie Dale looked through the little rear window. The cab had been a block behind them when it had turned the corner, and he watched it now in a sort of grim fascination. There was no possible doubt of it! The two bobbing, bouncing headlights were creeping steadily nearer. And then a sort of unnatural calm settled upon Jimmie Dale, and his hand went mechanically to his pocket to feel his automatic there, as he turned again to the chauffeur.

"If you've got any more speed, you'd better use it!" he said significantly.

The man shot a quick look at him.

"They are following us? You are *sure*?"

"Yes," said Jimmie Dale.

The chauffeur laughed again in that mirthless, savage way.

"Lean over here, where I can talk to you!" he rasped out. "The game's up, as far as I am concerned, I guess! But there's a chance for you. They don't know you in this."

"Give her more speed—or dodge into a cross street!" suggested Jimmie Dale coolly. "They haven't got us yet, by a long way!"

The other shook his head.

"It's not only that cab behind," he answered, through set lips. "You don't know what we're up against. If they're really after us, there's a trap laid in every section of this city—the devils! It's the package they want. Thank God for the presentiment that made me leave it behind! I was going back for it, you understand, if I was satisfied that we weren't followed. Listen! There's a chance for you—there's none for me. That package—remember this!—no one else knows where it is, and it's life and death to the one who sent you here. It's in Box 428 at—My God, *look*! Look there!" he yelled, and, with a wrench at the wheel, sent the taxi lurching and staggering for the car tracks in the centre of the street.

The scene, fast as thought itself, was photographing itself in every detail upon Jimmie Dale's brain. From the cross street ahead, one from each corner, two motor cars had nosed out into Broadway, blocking the road on both sides. And now the car on the left-hand side was moving forward across the tracks to counteract the chauffeur's move, deliberately insuring a collision. There was no chance, no further room to turn, no time to stop—the man driving the other car jumped for safety—they would be into it in an instant.

"Box 428!" Jimmie pleaded fiercely. "Go on, man! Go on! *Finish!*"

"Yes!" cried the chauffeur. "John Johansson, at—"

But Jimmie Dale heard no more. There was the crash of impact as the taxicab plowed into the car that had been so craftily manoeuvered in front of it, and Jimmie Dale, lifted from his feet, was hurled violently forward with the shock, and all went black before his eyes.

CHAPTER 3

THE CRIME CLUB

For what length of time he had remained unconscious, Jimmie Dale had not the slightest idea. He regained his senses to find himself lying on a couch in a strange room that had a most exquisitely brass-wrought dome light in the ceiling. That was what attracted his attention, because the light hurt his eyes, and his head was already throbbing as though a thousand devils were beating a diabolical tattoo upon it.

He closed his eyes against the light. Where was he? What had happened? Oh, yes, he remembered now! That smash on Lower Broadway! He had been hurt. He moved first one limb and then another tentatively, and was relieved to find that, though his body ached as if it had been severely shaken, and his head was bad, he had apparently escaped without serious injury.

Where was he? In a hospital? His fingers, resting at his side upon the couch, supplied him with the information that it was a very expensive couch, upholstered in finest leather. If he were in a hospital, he would be in a cot.

He opened his eyes again to glance curiously around him. The room was quite in keeping with the artistic lighting fixture and the refined, if expensive, taste that was responsible for the couch. A heavy velvet rug of rich, dark green was bordered by a polished hardwood floor; panellings of dark-green frieze and beautifully grained woodwork made the lower walls; while above, on a background of some soft-toned paper, hung a few, and evidently choice, oil paintings. There was a big, inviting lounging chair; a massive writing table, or more properly, a desk of walnut; and behind the desk, his back half turned, apparently intent upon a book, sat a man in immaculate evening dress.

Jimmie Dale closed his eyes again. There was something reassuring about it all, comfortably reassuring. Though why there should be any occasion for a feeling of reassurance at all, he could not for the moment make out. And then, in a sudden flash, the details of the night came back to him. The Tocsin's letter—the package he was to get—the taxicab—the chauffeur, who was not a chauffeur—the chase—the trap. He lay perfectly still. It was the professional Jimmie Dale now whose brain, in spite of the throbbing, brutally aching head, was at work, keen, alert.

The chauffeur! What had happened to him? Had the man been killed in the auto smash; or, less fortunate than himself, fallen into the hands of those whose power he seemed both to fear and rate so highly? And that package! Box—what was the number?—yes, 428. What did that mean? What box? Where was it? Who was John Johansson? He hadn't heard any more than that; the smash had come then. And lastly, he was back again to the same question he had begun with: Where was he now himself? It looked as though some good Samaritan had picked him up. Who was this gentleman so quietly reading there at the desk?

Jimmie Dale opened his eyes for the third time. How still, how absolutely silent the room was! He studied the man's back speculatively for a moment, then his gaze travelled on past the man to the wall, riveted there, and his fingers, without movement of his arm, pressed against the outside of his coat pocket. He thought as much! His automatic was gone!

Not a muscle of Jimmie Dale's face moved. His eyes shifted to a picture on the wall. *The man was watching him—not reading!* Just above the level of the desk, a small mirror held the couch in focus—but, equally, it held the man in focus, and Jimmie Dale had seen the other's eyes, through a black mask that covered the face to the top of the upper lip, fixed intently upon him.

There was a chill now where before there had been reassurance, something ominous in the very quiet and refinement of the room; and Jimmie Dale smiled inwardly in bitter irony—his good Samaritan wore a mask! His self-congratulations had come too soon. Whatever had happened to the chauffeur, it was evident enough that he himself was caught! What was it the chauffeur had said? Something about a chance through being unknown. Was it to be a battle of wits, then? God, if his head did not ache so frightfully! It was hard to think with the brain half sick with pain.

Those two eyes shining in that mirror! There seemed something horribly spectre-like about it. He did not look again, but he knew they were there. It was like a cat watching a mouse. Why did not the man speak, or move, or do something, and—He turned his head slowly; the man was laughing in a low, amused way.

"You appear to be taken with that picture," observed a pleasant voice. "Perhaps you recognise it from there? It is a Corot."

Jimmie Dale, with a well-simulated start, sat up—and, with another quite as well simulated, stared at the masked man. The other had laid down his book, and swung around in his chair to face the couch. Jimmie Dale stood up a little shakily.

"Look here!" he said awkwardly. "I—I don't quite understand. I remember that my taxi got into a smash-up, and I suppose I have to thank you for the assistance you must have rendered me; only, as I say"—he looked in a puzzled way around the room, and in an even more perplexed way at the mask on the other's face—"I must confess I am at a loss to understand quite the meaning of this."

"Suppose that instead of trying to understand you simply accept things as you find them." The voice was soft, but there was a finality in it that its blandness only served to make the more suggestive.

Jimmie Dale drew himself up, and bowed coldly.

"I beg your pardon," he said. "I did not mean to intrude. I have only to thank you again, then, and bid you good-night."

The lips beneath the mask parted slightly in a politely deprecating smile.

"There is no hurry," said the man, a sudden sharpness creeping into his tones. "I am sorry that the rule I apply to you does not work both ways. For instance, I might be quite at a loss to account for your presence in that taxi-cab."

Jimmie Dale's smile was equally polite, equally deprecating.

"I fail to see how it could be of the slightest possible interest to you," he replied. "However, I have no objection to telling you. I hailed the taxi at the corner of Sixth Avenue and Waverly Place, told the chauffeur to drive me to the St. James Club, and—"

"The St. James Club," broke in the other coldly, "is, I believe, north, not south of Waverly Place—and on Broadway not at all."

Jimmie Dale stared at the other for an instant in patient annoyance.

"I am quite well aware of that," he said stiffly. "Nevertheless I told the man to drive me to the St. James Club. We came across Waverly Place, but on reaching Broadway, instead of turning uptown, he suddenly whirled in the other direction and sent the car flying at full speed down Lower Broadway. I shouted at the man. I don't know yet whether he was drunk or crazy or"—Jimmie Dale's eyes fixed disdainfully on the other's mask—"whether there might not, after all, have been method in his madness. I can only say that before we had gone more than two or three blocks, a wild effort on his part to avoid a collision with an auto swinging out from a side street resulted in an even more disastrous smash with another on the other side, and I was knocked senseless."

"'Victim,' I presume, is the idea you desire to convey," observed the other evenly. "You were quite the victim of circumstances, as it were!"

Jimmie Dale's eyebrows lifted slightly.

"It would appear to be fairly obvious, I should say."

"Very clever!" commented the man. "But now suppose we remove the buttons from the foils!" His voice rasped suddenly. "You are quite as well aware as I am that what has happened tonight was not an accident. Nor—in case the possibility may have occurred to you—are the police any the wiser, save for the existence of two wrecked cars on Lower Broadway, and another which escaped, and for which doubtless they are still searching assiduously. The ownership of the taxicab you so inadvertently entered they will have no difficulty in establishing—you, perhaps, however, are in a better position than I am to appreciate the fact that the establishment of its ownership will lead them nowhere. As I understand it, the man who drove you tonight obtained the loan of the cab from one of the company's chauffeur's in return for a hundred-dollar bill. Am I right?"

"In view of what has happened," admitted Jimmie Dale simply, "I should not be surprised."

There was a sort of sardonic admiration in the other's laugh.

"As for the other car," he went on, "I can assure you that its ownership will never be known. When the nearest patrolman rushed up, there were no survivors of the disaster, save those in the third car which he was powerless to stop—which accounts for your presence here. You will admit that I have been quite frank."

"Oh, quite!" said Jimmie Dale, a little wearily. "But would you mind telling me what all this is leading to?"

The man had been leaning forward in his chair, one hand, palm downward, resting lightly on the desk. He shifted his hand now suddenly to the arm of his chair.

"This!" he said, and on the desk where his hand had been lay the Tocsin's gold signet ring.

Jimmie Dale's face expressed mild curiosity. He could feel the other's eyes boring into him.

"We were speaking of ownership," said the man, in a low, menacing tone. "I want to know where the woman who owns this ring can be found tonight."

There was no play, no trifling here; the man was in deadly earnest. But it seemed to Jimmie Dale, even with the sense of peril more imminent with every instant, that he could have laughed outright in savage mockery at the irony of the question. Where was she? Even *who* was she? And this was the hour in which he was to have known!

"May I look at it?" he requested calmly.

The other nodded, but his eyes never left Jimmie Dale.

"It will give you an extra moment or so to frame your answer," he said sarcastically.

Jimmie Dale ignored the thrust, picked up the ring, examined it deliberately, and set it back again on the table.

"Since I do not know who owns it," he said, "I cannot answer your question."

"No! Well, then, there is still another matter—a little package that was in the taxicab with you. Where is that?"

"See here!" said Jimmie Dale irritably. "This has gone far enough! I have seen no package, large or small, or of any description whatever. You are evidently mistaking me for someone else. You have only to telephone to the St. James Club." He reached toward his pocket for his cardcase. "My name is—"

"Dale," supplied the other curtly. "Don't bother about the card, Mr. Dale. We have already taken the liberty of searching you." He rose abruptly from his chair. "I am afraid you do not quite realise your position, Mr. Dale," he said, with an ominous smile. "Let me make it clear. I do not wish to be theatrical about this, but we do not temporise here. You will either answer both of those questions to my satisfaction, *or you will never leave this place alive.*"

Jimmie Dale's face hardened. His eyes met the other's steadily.

"Ah, I think I begin to see!" he said caustically. "When I have been thoroughly frightened I shall be offered my freedom at a price. A sort of up-to-date game of holdup! The penalty of being a wealthy man! If you had named your figure to begin with, we would have saved a lot of idle talk, and you would have had my answer the sooner: *nothing*!"

"Do you know," said the other, in a grimly musing way, "there has always been one man, but only one until now, that I have wished I might add to my present associates. I refer to the so-called Gray Seal. Tonight there are two. I pay you the compliment of being the other. But"—he was smiling ominously again—"we are wasting time, Mr. Dale. I am willing to expose my hand to the extent of admitting that the information you are withholding is infinitely more valuable to me than the mere wreaking of reprisal upon you for a refusal to talk. Therefore, if you will answer, I pledge you my word you will be free to leave here within five minutes. If you refuse, you are already aware of the alternative. Well, Mr. Dale?"

Who was this man? Jimmie Dale was studying the other's chin, the lips, the white, even teeth, the jet-black hair. Some day the tables might be turned. Could he recognise again this cool, imperturbable ruffian who so callously threatened him with murder?

"Well, Mr. Dale? I am waiting!"

"I am not a magician," said Jimmie Dale contemptuously. "I could not answer your questions if I wanted to."

The other's hand slid instantly to a row of electric buttons on the desk.

"Very well, Mr. Dale!" he said quietly. "You do not believe, I see, that I would dare to carry my threat into execution; you perhaps even doubt my power. I shall take the trouble to convince you—I imagine it will stimulate your memory."

The door opened. Two men were standing on the threshold, both in evening dress, both masked. The man behind the desk came forward, took Jimmie Dale's arm almost courteously, and led him from the room out into a corridor, where he halted abruptly.

"I want to call your attention first, Mr. Dale, to the fact that as far as you are concerned you neither have now, nor ever will have, any idea whether you are in the heart of New York or fifty miles away from it. Now, listen! Do you hear anything?"

There was nothing. Only the strange silence of that other room was intensified now. There was not a sound; stillness such as it seemed to Jimmie Dale he had never experienced before was around him.

"You may possibly infer from the silence that you are *not* in the city," suggested the other, after a moment's pause. "I leave you to your own conclusions in that respect. The cause, however, of the silence is internal, not external; we had sound-proof principles in mind to a perhaps exaggerated degree when this building was constructed. If you care to do so, you have my permission to shout, say, for help, to your heart's content. We shall make no effort to stop you."

Jimmie Dale shrugged his shoulders. He was staring down a brilliantly lighted, richly carpeted corridor. There were doors on one side, windows on the other, the windows all hung with heavy, closely drawn portieres. The corridor was certainly not on the ground floor, but whether it was on the second or third, or even above that again, he had no means of knowing. From appearances, though, the place seemed more like a large, private mansion than anything else.

"Just one word more before we proceed," continued the other. "I do not wish you to labour under any illusion. Here we are frankly criminals. This is our home. It should have some effect in impressing you with the power and resource at our command, and also with the class of men with whom you are dealing. There is not one among us whose education is not fully equal to your own; not one, indeed, but who is chosen, granting first his criminal tendencies, because he is a specialist in his own particular field—in commerce, in the government diplomatic service, in the professions of law and medicine, in the ranks of pure science. We are bordering on the fantastical, are we not? Dreaming, you will probably say, of the Utopian in crime organisation. Quite so, Mr. Dale. I only ask you to consider the *possibilities* if what I say is true. Now let us proceed. I am going to take you into three rooms—the three whose doors you see ahead of you. You will notice that, including the one you have just left, there are four on this corridor. I do not wish to strain your credulity, or play tricks upon you; so I am going to ask you to fix an approximate idea of the length of the corridor in your mind, as it will perhaps enable you to account more readily for what may appear to be a discrepancy in the corresponding size of the rooms."

One of the men opened the door ahead. Jimmie Dale, at a sign from his conductor, moved forward and entered. Just what he had expected to find he could not have told; his brain was whirling, partly from his aching head, partly from his desperate effort to conceive some way of escape from the peril which, for all his nonchalance, he knew only too well was the gravest he had ever faced; but what he saw was simply a cozily furnished bedroom. There was nothing peculiar about it; nothing out of the way, except perhaps that it was rather narrow.

And then suddenly, rubbing his eyes involuntarily, he was staring in a dazed way before him. The whole right-hand side of the wall was sinking without a sound into the floor, increasing the width of the room by some five or six feet—and in this space was disclosed what appeared to be a sort of chemical laboratory, elaborately equipped, extending the entire length of the room.

"The wall is purely a matter of mechanical construction, operated hydraulically." The man was speaking softly at Jimmie Dale's side. "The room beneath is built to correspond; the base, ceiling, and wall mouldings here do not have to be very ingenious to effect a disguise. I might say, however, that few visitors, other than yourself, have ever seen anything here but a bedroom." He waved his hand toward the retorts, the racks of test tubes, the hundred and one articles that strewed the laboratory bench. "As for this, its purpose is twofold. We, as well, as the police, have often need of analysis. We make it. If we require a drug, a poison, say, we compound it from its various ingredients, or, as the case may be, distil it, perhaps—it is, you will agree, somewhat more difficult to trace to its source if procured that way. And speaking of poisons"—he stepped forward, and lifted a glass-stoppered bottle containing a colourless liquid from a shelf—"in a modest way we have even done some original research work here. This, for instance, is as Utopian from our standpoint as the formation, and personnel of the organisation I have briefly outlined to you. It possesses very essential qualities. It is almost instantaneous in its action, requires a very small quantity, and defies detection even by autopsy." He uncorked the bottle, and dipped in a long glass rod. "Will you watch the experiment?" he invited, with a sort of ghastly pleasantry. "I do not want you to accept anything on trust."

With a start, Jimmie Dale swung around. He had heard no sound, but another man was at his elbow now—and, struggling in the man's hand, was a little white rabbit.

It was over in an instant. A single drop in the rabbit's mouth, and the animal had stiffened out, a lifeless thing.

"It is quite as effective on the human organism," continued the other, "only, instead of one drop, three are required. If I make it ten"—he was carefully measuring the liquid into two wineglasses—"it is only that even you may be satisfied that the quantity is fatal." He filled up the glasses with what was apparently wine of some description, which he poured from a decanter, and held out the glasses in front of him.

And again Jimmie Dale started, again he had heard no one enter, and yet two men had stepped forward from behind him and had taken the glasses from their leader's hands. He glanced around him, counting quickly—they were surely the two who had entered with him from the corridor. No! Including the leader, there were now six men, all in evening dress, all masked, in the room with him.

A wave of the leader's hand, and the two men holding the glasses left the room. The man turned to Jimmie Dale again.

"Shall we proceed to the second room, Mr. Dale?" he asked politely. "I think it is now prepared for us—I do not wish to bore you with a repetition of magical sliding walls."

There was something now that numbed the ache in Jimmie Dale's brain—a sense of some deadly, remorseless thing that seemed to be constantly creeping closer to him, clutching at him—to smother him, to choke him. There was something absolutely fiendish, terrifying, in the veneer of culture around him.

They had entered the second room. This, like the other, was a pseudo-bedroom; but here the movable wall was already down. Ranged along the right-hand side were a great number of cabinets that slid in and out, much after the style and fashion used by clothing dealers to stock and display their wares. These cabinets were now all open, displaying hundreds of costumes of all kinds and descriptions, and evidently complete to the minutest detail. The cabinets were flanked by full-length mirrors at each end of the room, and on little tables before the mirrors was an assortment, that none better than Jimmie Dale himself could appreciate, of make-up accessories.

The man smiled apologetically.

"I am afraid this is rather uninteresting," he said. "I have shown it to you simply that you may understand that we are alive to the importance of detail. Disguise, that is daily vital to us, is an art that depends essentially on detail. I venture to say we could impersonate any character or type or nationality or class in the United States at a moment's notice. But"—he took Jimmie Dale's arm again and conducted him out into the corridor, while the two men who were evidently acting the role of guards followed closely behind—"there is still the third room—here." He halted Jimmie Dale before the door. "I have asked you to answer two questions, Mr. Dale," he said softly. "I ask you now to remember the alternative."

They still stood before the door. There was that uncanny silence again—it seemed to Jimmie Dale to last interminably. Neither of the three men surrounding him moved nor spoke. Then the door before him was opened on an unlighted room, and he was led across the threshold. He heard the door close behind him. The lights came on. And then it seemed as though he could not move, as though he were rooted to the spot—and the colour ebbed from his face. Three figures were before him: the two men who had carried the glasses from the first room, and the chauffeur who had driven him in the taxicab. The two men still held the glasses—the chauffeur was bound hand and foot in a chair. One of the glasses was empty; the other was still significantly full.

Jimmie Dale, with a violent effort at self-control, leaned forward.

The man in the chair was dead.

CHAPTER 4

THE INNOCENT BYSTANDER

There was not a sound. That stillness, weird, unnerving, that permeated, as it were, everywhere through that mysterious house, was, if that were possible, accentuated now. The four masked men in evening dress, five including their leader, for the man who had appeared in that other room with the rabbit was not here, were as silent, as motionless, as the dead man who was lashed there in the chair. And to Jimmie Dale it seemed at first as though his brain, stunned and stupefied at the shock, refused its functions, and left him groping blindly, vaguely, with only a sort of dull, subconscious realisation of menace and a deadly peril, imminent, hanging over him.

He tried to rouse himself mentally, to prod his brain to action, to pit it in a fight for life against these self-confessed criminals and murderers with their mask of culture, who surrounded him now. Was there a way out? What was it the Tocsin had said—"the most powerful and pitiless organisation of criminals the world has ever known—the stake a fortune of millions—her life!" There had, indeed, been no overemphasis in the words she had used! They had taken pains themselves to make that ominously clear, these men! Every detail of the strange house, with its luxurious furnishings, its cleverly contrived appointments, breathed a horribly suggestive degree of power, a deadly purpose, and an organisation swayed by a master mind; and, grim evidence of the merciless, inexorable length to which they would go, was the ghastly white face of the dead chauffeur, bound hand and foot, in the chair before him!

That *empty* glass in the hand of one of the men! He could not take his eyes from it—except as his eyes were drawn magnetically to that *full* glass in the hand of one of the others. What height of sardonic irony! He was to drink that other glass, to die because he refused to answer questions that for years, with every resource at his command, risking his liberty, his wealth, his name, his life, with everything that he cared for thrown into the scales, he had struggled to solve—and failed!

And then the leader spoke.

"Mr. Dale," he said, with cold significance, "I regret to admit that your pseudo taxicab driver was so ill-advised as to refuse to answer the *same* questions that I have put to you."

Five to one! That was the only way out—and it was hopeless. It was the only way out, because, convinced that he could answer those questions if he wanted to, these men were in deadly earnest; it was hopeless, because they were—five to one! And probably there were as many more, twice or three times as many more within call. But what did it matter how many more there were! He could fight until he was overpowered, that was all he could do, and the five could accomplish that. Still, if he could knock the full glass out of that man's hand, and gain the door, then perhaps—he turned quickly, as the door opened. It was as though they had read his thoughts. A number of men were grouped outside in the corridor, then the door closed again with a cordon ranged against it inside the room; and at the same instant his arms and wrists were caught in a powerful grasp by the two men immediately behind him, who all along had enacted the role of guards.

Again the leader spoke.

"I will repeat the questions," he said sharply. "Where is the woman whose ring was found on that man there in the chair? And where is the package that you two men had with you in the taxicab tonight?"

Jimmie Dale glanced from the tall, straight, immaculately clothed figure of the speaker, from the threatening smile on the set lips that just showed under the edge of the mask, to the dead man in the chair. He had faced the prospect of death before many times, but it had come with the heat of passion accompanying it, it had come quickly, abruptly, with every faculty called into action to combat it, without time to dwell upon it, to sift, weigh, or measure its meaning, and if there had been fear it had been subordinate to other emotions. But it was different now. He could not, of course, answer those questions; nor, he was doggedly conscious, would he have answered them if he could—and there was no middle course.

Death, within the next few moments, stared him in the face; and it seemed curiously irrelevant that, in a sort of unnatural calmness, he should be attempting to analyse his feelings and emotions concerning it. All his life it had seemed to him that the acme of human mental torture was the cell of a condemned criminal, with the horror of its hopelessness, with the time to dwell upon it; and that the acme of that torture itself must be that awful moment immediately preceding execution, when anticipation at last was to merge into soul-sickening reality.

Strange that thought should come! Strange that he should be framing a brain picture of such a scene, vivid, minute in detail! No—not strange. He was picturing himself. The analogy was not perfect, it was true, he had not had the months, weeks, days and hours of suspense; but it was perfect enough to bring home to him with appalling force the realisation of his position. He was standing as a condemned man might stand in those last, final moments, those moments which he had imagined must be the most terrible that could exist in life; but that dismay of soul, the horror, the terror were not his—there was, instead, a smouldering fury, a passionate amazement that it was his own life that was threatened. It seemed impossible that it could be his voice that was speaking now in such quiet, measured tones.

"Is it worth while, will it convince you now, any more than before, to repeat that there is some mistake here? I am no more able to answer your questions than you are yourselves. I never saw that man in the chair there in my life until the moment that I hailed him in his cab tonight. I do not know who the woman is to whom that ring belongs, much less do I know where she is. And if there was a package of any sort in the taxicab, as you state, I never saw it."

The lips under the mask curved into a lupine smile.

"Think well, Mr. Dale!" The man's voice was low, menacing. "Ethically, if you so choose to consider it, your refusal may be the act of a brave man; practically, it is the act of—a fool. Now—your answer!"

"I have answered you," said Jimmie Dale—and, relaxing the muscles in his arms, let them hang limply for an instant in the grip of the two men behind him. "I have no other answer."

It was only a sign, a motion of the leader's hand—but with it, quick as a lightning flash, Jimmie Dale was in action. The limp arms tautened into steel as he wrenched them loose, and, whirling around, he whipped his fist to the chin of one of the two guards.

In an instant, with the blow, as the man staggered backward, the room was in pandemonium. There was a rush from the door, and two, three, four leaping forms hurled themselves upon Jimmie Dale. He shook them off—and they came again. There was no chance ultimately, he knew that; it was only the elemental within him that rose in fierce revolt at the thought of tame submission, that bade him sell his life as dearly as he could. Panting, gasping for breath, dragging them by sheer strength as they clung to him, he got his back to the wall, fighting with the savage fury and abandon of a wild cat.

But it could not last. Where one man went down before him, two remorselessly appeared—the room seemed filled with men—they poured in through the door—he laughed at them in a half-demented way—more and more of them came—there was no play for his arms, no room to fight—they seemed so close around him, so many of them upon him, that he could not breathe—and he was bending, being crushed down as by an intolerable weight. And then his feet were jerked from beneath him, he crashed to the floor, and, in another moment, bound hand and foot, he was tied into a chair beside that other chair whose grim occupant sat in such ghastly apathy of the scene.

The room cleared instantly of all but the original five. His head was drawn suddenly, violently backward, and clamped in that position; and a metal instrument, forced into his mouth, while his lips bled in their resistance, pried jaws apart and held them open.

"One drop!" the leader ordered curtly.

The man with the full glass bent over him, and dipped a glass rod into the liquid. The drop glistened a ruby red on the end of the rod—and fell with a sharp, acrid, burning sensation upon Jimmie Dale's tongue.

For a moment Jimmie Dale's animation, mental and physical, seemed swept away from him in, as it were, a hiatus of hideous suspense. What was it to be like this passing? Why did it not act at once, as it had acted on the rabbit they had showed him in the other room? Yes, he remembered! It took more than one drop for a man; and besides, this was diluted. One drop had no effect on a man; it required—Good God, *one drop even of this was enough?* He strained forward in the chair until the sweat in great beads sprang from his forehead, strained and fought and tore at his bonds in a paroxysm of madness to free himself while there still remained a little strength. There was something filming before his eyes, a numbed feeling was creeping through his limbs, robbing them, sapping them of their vitality and power. He felt himself slipping away into a state of utter weakness, and his brain began to grow confused.

A voice seemed to float in the air near him: "For the last time—will you answer?"

With a supreme effort, Jimmie Dale strove to rally his tottering senses. Did they not understand the stupendous mockery of their questions? Did they not understand that he did not know? He had told them so—perhaps he had better tell them so again.

"I—" He tried to speak, and found the words thick upon his tongue. "I—do not—know."

The glass itself was thrust abruptly between his lips. Some of the contents spilled and trickled upon his chin, and then a flood of it, burning, fiery, poured down his throat. A flood of it—and it needed but *three* drops and there had been *ten* in the glass!

So this was death—a hazy, nebulous thing! There was no pain. It was like—like—nothingness. And out of the nothingness *she* came. Strange that she should come! Alone she had fought these fiends and outwitted them for—how long was it? Three years! She would be more than ever alone now. Pray God she did not finally fall into their clutches!

How it burned now, that fatal draught they had forced down his throat, and how it gripped at him and seemed to eat and bore its way into the very tissues! It was the end, and—no! It was *stimulating* him! Strength seemed to be returning to his limbs; it seemed as though he were being carried, as though the bonds about him were being loosened; and now his brain seemed to be growing clearer.

He roused up with a startled exclamation. He was back in the same room in which he had first returned to consciousness after the accident. He was on the same couch. The same masked figure was at the same desk. Had he been dreaming? Was this then only some horrible, ghastly nightmare through which he had passed?

No, it had been real enough; his clothes, rent and torn, and the blood upon his hands, where the skin had been scraped from his knuckles in the fight, bore evidence to that. He must then have lost consciousness for a while, though it seemed to him that at no moment, hazy, irrational though his brain might have been, had he become entirely oblivious to what was taking place around him. And yet it must have been so!

The eyes from behind the mask were fixed steadily upon him, and below the mask there was the hard, unpleasant set to the lips that Jimmie Dale had grown accustomed to expect.

The man spoke abruptly.

"That you find yourself alive, Mr. Dale," he said grimly, "is no confession of weakness upon the part of those with whom you have had to deal here. To bear witness to that there is one who is not alive, as you have seen. That man we knew. With you it was somewhat different. Your presence in the taxicab was only suspicious. There was always the possibility that you might be one of those ubiquitous 'innocent bystanders.' Your name, your position, the improbability that you could have anything in common with—shall we say, the matter that so deeply interests us?—was all in your favour. However, presumption and probability are the tools of fools. We do not depend upon them—we apply the test. And having applied the test, we are convinced that you have told the truth—that is all."

He rose from his chair brusquely. "I shall not apologise to you for what has happened. I doubt very much if you are in a frame of mind to accept anything of the sort. I imagine, rather, that you are promising yourself that we shall pay, and pay dearly, for this—that, among other things, we shall answer for the murder of that man in the other room. All this will be quite within your province, Mr. Dale—and quite fruitless. Tomorrow morning the story that you are preparing to tell now would sound incredible even in your own ears; furthermore, as we shall take pains to see that you leave this place with as little knowledge of its location as you obtained when you arrived, your story, even if believed, would do little service to you and less harm to us. I think of nothing more, Mr. Dale, except—" There was a whimsical smile on the lips now. "Ah, yes, the matter of your clothes. We can, and shall be glad to make reparation to you to the slight extent of offering you a new suit before you go."

Jimmie Dale scowled. Sick, shaken, and weak as he was, the cool, imperturbable impudence of the man was fast growing unbearable.

The man laughed. "I am sure you will not refuse, Mr. Dale—since we insist. The condition of the clothes you have on at present might—I say 'might'—in a measure support your story with some degree of tangible evidence. It is not at all likely, of course; but we prefer to discount even so remote a possibility. When you have changed, you will be motored back to your home. I bid you good-night, Mr. Dale."

Jimmie Dale rubbed his eyes. The man was gone—through a door at the rear of the desk, a door that he had not noticed before, that was not even in evidence now, that was simply a movable section of the wall panelling—and for an instant Jimmie Dale experienced a sense of sickening impotence. It was as though he stood defenceless, unarmed, and utterly at the mercy of some venomous power that could crush what it would remorselessly and at will in its might.

The place was a veritable maze, a lair of hellish cleverness. He had no illusions now, he laboured under no false estimate of either the ingenuity or the resources of this inhuman nest of vultures to whom murder was no more than a matter of detail. And it was against these men that henceforth he was to match his wits! There could be no truce, no armistice. It was their lives, or hers, or his! Well, he was alive now, the first round was over, and so far he had won. His brows furrowed suddenly. Had he? He was not so sure, after all. He was conscious of a disquieting, premonitory intuition that, in some way which he could not explain, the honours were not entirely his.

He was apparently—the "apparently" was a mental reservation—quite alone in the room. He got up from the couch and walked shakily across the floor to the desk. A revolver lay invitingly upon the blotting pad. It was his own, the one they had taken from him after the accident. Jimmie Dale picked it up, examined it—and smiled a little sarcastically at himself for his trouble. It was unloaded, of course. He was twirling it in his hand, as a man, masked as every one in the house was masked, and carrying a neatly folded suit over his arm, entered from the corridor.

"The car is ready as soon as you are dressed," announced the other briefly. He laid the clothes upon the couch—and settled himself significantly in a chair.

Jimmie Dale hesitated. Then, with a shrug of his shoulders, recrossed the room, and began to remove his torn garments. What was the use! They would certainly have their own way in the end. It wasn't worth another fight, and there was nothing to be gained by a refusal except to offer a sop to his own exasperation.

He dressed quickly, in what proved to be an exceedingly well-fitting suit; and finally turned tentatively to the man in the chair.

The other stood up, and produced a heavy black silk scarf.

"If you have no objections," he said curtly, "I'll tie this over your eyes."
Again Jimmie Dale shrugged his shoulders.

"I am glad enough to get out on any conditions," he answered caustically.

"'Fortunate' would be the better word," rejoined the other meaning-fuly—and, deftly knotting the scarf, led Jimmie Dale blindfolded from the room.

CHAPTER 5
ON GUARD

Was he in the city? In a suburban town? On a country road? It seemed child-ishly absurd that he could not at least differentiate to that extent; and yet, from the moment he had been placed in the automobile in which he now found himself, he was forced to admit that he could not tell. He had started out with the belief that, knowing New York and its surroundings as minutely as he knew them, it would be impossible, do what they would to prevent it, that at the end of the journey he should be without a clue, and a very good clue at that, to the location of what he now called, appropriately enough it seemed, the Crime Club.

But he had never ridden blindfolded in a car before! He could see ab-solutely nothing. And if that increased or accentuated his sense of hearing, it helped little—the roar of the racing car beat upon his eardrums the more heavily, that was all. He could tell, of course, the nature of the roadbed. They were running on an asphalt road, that was obvious enough; but city streets and suburban streets and hundreds of miles of country road around New York were of asphalt!

Traffic? He was quite sure, for he had strained his ears in an effort to detect it, that there was little or no traffic; but then, it must be one or two o'clock in the morning, and at that hour the city streets, certainly those that would be chosen by these men, would be quite as deserted as any country road! And as for a sense of direction, he had none whatever—even if the car had not been persistently swerving and changing its course every little while. If he had been able to form even an approximate idea of the compass direc-tion in which they had started, he might possibly have been able in a general way to counteract this further effort of theirs to confuse him; but without the initial direction he was essentially befogged.

With these conclusions finally thrust home upon him, Jimmie Dale phil-osophically subordinated the matter in his mind, and, leaning back, com-posed himself as comfortably as he could upon his seat. There was a man beside him, and he could feel the legs of two men on the seat facing him. These, with the driver, would make four. He was still well guarded! The car itself was a closed car—not hooded, the sense of touch told him—therefore a limousine of some description. These facts, in a sense inconsequential, were absorbed subconsciously; and then Jimmie Dale's brain, remorselessly active, in spite of the pain from his throbbing head, was at work again.

It seemed as though a year had passed since, in the early evening, as Larry the Bat, he had burrowed so ironically for refuge in Chang Foo's den—from her! It seemed like some mocking unreality, some visionary dream that, so short a while before, he had read those words of hers that had sent the blood coursing and leaping through his veins in mad exultation at the thought that the culmination of the years had come, that all he longed for, hoped for, that all his soul cried out for was to be his—"in an hour." An hour—and he was to have seen her, the woman whose face he had never seen, the woman whom he loved! And the hour instead, the hours since then, had brought a nightmare of events so incredible as to seem but phantoms of the imagination.

Phantoms! He sat up suddenly with a jerk. The face of the dead chauffeur, the limp form lashed in that chair, the horrible picture in its entirety, every detail standing out in ghastly relief, took form before him. God knew there was no phantom there!

The man beside him, at the sudden start, lifted a hand and felt hurriedly over the bandage across Jimmie Dale's eyes.

Jimmie Dale was scarcely conscious of the act. With that face before him, with the scene re-enacting itself in his mind again, had come another thought, staggering him for a moment with the new menace that it brought. He had had neither time nor opportunity to think before; it had been all horror, all shock when he had entered that room. But now, like an inspiration, he saw it all from another angle. There was a glaring fallacy in the game these men had played for his benefit tonight—a fallacy which they had counted on glossing over, as it had, indeed, been glossed over, by the sudden shock with which they had forced that scene upon him; or, failing in that, they had counted on the fact that his, or any other man's nerve would have failed when it came to open defiance based on a supposition which might, after all, be wrong, and, being wrong, meant death.

But it was not supposition. Either he was right now, or these men were childish, immature fools—and, whatever else they might be, they were not that! *Not a single drop of poison had passed the chauffeur's lips.* The man had not been murdered in that room. He had not, in a sense, been murdered at all. The man, absolutely, unquestionably, without a loophole for doubt, had either been killed outright in the automobile accident, or had died immediately afterward, probably without regaining consciousness, certainly without supplying any of the information that was so determinedly sought.

Yes, he saw it now! Their backs were against the wall, they were at their wits' end, these men! The knowledge that the chauffeur possessed, that they *knew* he possessed, was evidently life and death to them. To kill the man before they had wormed out of him what they wanted to know, or, at least, until, by holding him a prisoner, they had exhausted every means at their command to make him speak, was the last thing they would do!

Jimmie Dale sat for a long time quite motionless. The car was speeding at a terrific rate along a straight stretch of road. He could almost have sworn, guided by some intuitive sense, that they were in the country. Well, even if it were so, what did that prove! They might have started *from* New York itself—only to return to it when they had satisfied themselves that he was sufficiently duped. Or they might have started legitimately from outside New York, and be going toward the city now. Since the ultimate destination was New York, and they had made no attempt to hide that from him, it was useless to speculate—for at best it could be only speculation. He had decided that once before! The man at his side felt again over the scarf to see that it was in place.

Curiously now Jimmie Dale recalled the inward monitor that had warned him the honours had not all been his in this first round with the Crime Club tonight. If they had deliberately murdered the chauffeur because of a refusal to answer, they would equally have done the same to him. Fool that he had been not to have seen that before! And yet would it have made any difference? He shook his head. He could not have acted to any better advantage than he had done. He could not—his lips curled in grim derision—have been any more convincing.

Convincing! It was all clear enough now! If the chauffeur had suffered death rather than talk, even admitting the fact that they had more grounds for suspecting the chauffeur's complicity, would his, Jimmie Dale's, mere denial, his choice, too, of death, have been any the more convincing, or have saved his life where it had not saved the other's? A certain added respect for these men, against whom, until the end now, his victory or theirs, he realised he was fighting for his life, came over him as he recognised the touch of a master hand. They did not know where to find the Tocsin; the package that she had said was vital to them was still beyond their reach; the chauffeur was dead; and he, Jimmie Dale, alone remained—a clue that they had still to prove valid or invalid it was true, but the only clue in their possession. And, gaining nothing from him by a show of force, to throw him off his guard, they had let him go—meaning him to believe they were convinced he knew nothing, and that the episode, the adventure of the night, was, as far as they were concerned, ended, finished, and done with!

Time passed, a very long time, as he sat there. It might have been an hour—he could only hazard a guess. Not one of the men in the car had spoken a word. But to Jimmie Dale, the car itself, the ride, its duration, these three strange companions, were for the time being extraneous. Even that sick giddiness in his head had, at least temporarily, gone from him.

And so, all unsuspectingly, he was to lead them to the Tocsin and fall into the trap himself! His hands, thrust deep in his pockets, were tightly clenched. They were clever enough, ingenious enough, powerful enough to watch him henceforth at every turn—and from now on, day and night, they were to be reckoned with. Suppose that in some way, as it might well have happened, for it was now vitally necessary that she should communicate with him and he with her, he had played blindly into their hands, and through him she should have fallen into their power! It brought a sickening chill, a sort of hideous panic to Jimmie Dale—and then fury, anger, in a torrent, surged upon him, and there came a merciless desire to crush, to strangle, to stamp out this inhuman band of criminals that, with intolerable effrontery to the laws of God and man, were so elaborately and scientifically equipped for their monstrous purposes!

And then Jimmie Dale, in the darkness, smiled again grimly as the leader's reference to the Gray Seal recurred to him. Well, perhaps, who knew, they would have reason more than they dreamed of to wish the Gray Seal enrolled in their own ranks! It was strange, curious! He had thought all that was ended. Only a few short hours before he had hidden away all, everything that was incident to the life of the Gray Seal, the clothes of Larry the Bat, that little metal case with the gray-coloured, adhesive seals, a dozen other things, believing that it only remained for him to return and destroy them at his leisure as a finishing touch to the Gray Seal's career—and now, instead, he was face to face with the gravest and most dangerous problem that she had ever called upon him to undertake!

Well, at least, the odds were not all in the Crime Club's favour. Where they now certainly believed him to be entirely off his guard, he was thoroughly on his guard; and where they might suspect him, watch him, they would suspect and watch only the character, the person of Jimmie Dale, and count not at all upon either Larry the Bat or—the Gray Seal.

A sort of savage elation fell upon Jimmie Dale. His brain, that had been stagnant, confused, physically sick with pain and suffering, was working now with its old-time vigour and ease, mapping, planning, scheming the way ahead. To strike, and strike quickly—to strike *first*! It must be his move next—not theirs! And he must act tonight at once, the moment he was given this pretence to liberty that they had in store for him, before they had an opportunity of closing down around him with a network of spies that he could not elude. By morning, Jimmie Dale would be Larry the Bat, and inhabiting the Sanctuary again. And a tip to Jason, his old butler, to the effect, say, that he had gone away for a trip, would account for his disappearance satisfactorily enough; it would not necessarily arouse their suspicions when they eventually discovered he was gone, for against that was always the possible, and quite likely presumption that, where they had succeeded in nothing else, they had at least succeeded in frightening him thoroughly and to the extent of imbuing him with a hasty desire to put a safe distance between himself and them.

And now, with his mind made up to his course of action, an intense impatience to put his plan into effect, an irritation at the useless twistings and turnings of the car that had latterly become more frequent, took hold upon him. How much longer was this to last! They must have been fully an hour and a half on the road already, and—ah, the car was stopping now!

He straightened up in his seat as the machine came to a halt—but the man at his side laid a restraining hand upon him. The car door opened, and one of the men got out. Jimmie Dale caught an indistinct murmur of voices from without, then the man returned to his seat, and the car went on again.

Another half hour passed, that, curbing his irritation and impatience, was filled with the conjectures and questions that anew came crowding in upon his mind. Why had the car made that stop? It was rather curious. It was certainly a prearranged meeting place. Why? And these clothes that he now wore—why had they made him change? His own had not been very badly torn. The reason given him was, on the face of it now, in view of what he now knew, mere pretence. What was the ulterior motive behind that pretence? What did this package, that had already cost a man his life tonight, contain? Who was the chauffeur? What was this death feud between the Tocsin and these men? Did she know where the Crime Club was? Who and where was John Johansson? What was this box that was numbered 428? Could she supply the links that would forge the chain into an unbroken whole?

And then for the second time the car slowed down—and this time the man on the seat beside Jimmie Dale reached up and untied the scarf.

"You get out here," said the man tersely.

CHAPTER 6

THE TRAP

Had it not been for the stop the car had previously made, for the possibility that he might have obtained a glimpse outside when the door had been opened, the scarf over his eyes would have been superfluous; for now, with it removed, he could scarcely distinguish the forms of the three men around him, since the window curtains of the car were tightly drawn. Nor was he given the opportunity to do more, even had it been possible. The car stopped, the door was opened, he was pushed toward it—and even as he reached the ground, the door was closed behind him, and the car was speeding on again. But where he could not see before, it took now but a glance to obtain his bearings—he was standing on a corner on Riverside Drive, within a few doors of his own house.

Jimmie Dale stood still for a moment, watching the car as it disappeared rapidly up the Drive. And with a sort of grim facetiousness his brain began to correlate time and distance. Where had he come from? Where was this Crime Club? They had been, as nearly as he could estimate, two hours in making the journey; and, as nearly as he could estimate, in their turnings and twistings had covered at least twice the distance that would be represented by a direct route. Granting, then, an average speed of forty miles an hour, which was overgenerous to be on the safe side, and the fact that they certainly had not crossed the Hudson, which now lay before him, flanking the Drive, the Crime Club was somewhere within the area of a semicircle, whose centre was the corner on which he now stood, and whose radius was forty miles— *or forty yards!* He forced a laugh. It was just that, no more, no less—he was as likely to have started on his ride from within a biscuit throw of where he now stood, as to have started on it from miles away!

But—he aroused himself with a start—he was wasting time! It must be very late, near morning, and he would have need for every moment that was left between now and daylight. He turned, walked quickly to his house, mounted the steps, and with his latch-key—they had at least permitted him to retain the contents of his pockets when they had forced him to change his clothes—opened the front door softly, and, stepping inside, closed the door as silently as he had opened it.

He paused for an instant to listen. There was not a sound. The servants, naturally, would have been in bed hours ago. Even old Jason—Jimmie Dale smiled, half whimsically, half affectionately—whose paternal custom it was to sit up for his Master Jim, who, as he was fond of saying, he had dandled as a baby on his knee, had evidently given it up as a bad job on this occasion and had turned in himself. Jason, however, had left the light burning here in the big reception hall.

Jimmie Dale stepped to the switch and turned off the light; then stood hesitant in the darkness. Was there anything to be gained by rousing Jason now and telling him what he intended to do—to instruct him to answer any inquiries by the statement that "Mr. Dale had gone away for a trip"? He could trust Jason; Jason already knew much—more than one of those mysterious letters of the Tocsin's had passed through Jason's hands.

Jimmie Dale shook his head. No; he could communicate with Jason from downtown in the morning. He had half expected to find Jason up, and, in that case, would have taken the other, as far as necessary, into his confidence; but it was not a matter that pressed for the moment. He could get into touch with Jason at any time readily enough. Was there anything else before he went? He would not be able to get back as easily as he got out! Money! He shook his head again—a little grimly this time. He had been caught once before as Larry the Bat without funds! There was plenty of money now hidden in the Sanctuary, enough for any emergency, enough to last him indefinitely.

He stepped forward along the hall, his tread noiseless on the rich, heavy rug, passed into the rear of the house, descended the back stairs, and reached the cellar. It was below the level of the ground, of course; but a narrow window here, though quite large enough to permit of egress, gave on the driveway at the side of the house that led to the garage in the rear.

Cautiously now, for the cement flooring was, in the stillness, little less than a sounding board, Jimmie Dale reached the wall and felt along it to the window, the lower edge of whose sill was just slightly below the level of his shoulder. It opened inward, if he remembered correctly. His fingers were feeling for the fastenings. It was too dark to see a thing. He muttered in annoyance. Where were the fastenings! At the sides, or at the bottom? His hand began to make a circuit of the sill—and then suddenly, with a low, sharp cry, he leaned forward!

What did this mean? Wires! No wires had ever been there before! His fingers were working now with feverish haste, telegraphing their message to his brain. The wires ran through the sill close to the corner of the wall—tiny fragments of wood, as from an auger, were still on the sill—and here was a small particle of wire insulation that, those sensitive finger tips proclaimed, was *fresh.*

A cold thrill ran through Jimmie Dale; and there came again that sickening sense of impotency in the face of the malignant, devilish cunning arrayed against him, that once before he had experienced, that night. He had thought to forestall them—and he had been forestalled himself! This could only have been done—they had had no interest in him before then—while they held him at the Crime Club, while he was spending that two hours in the car! Was that why they had taken so long in coming? Was that why the car had stopped that time—that those with him might be told that the work here had been completed, and he need no longer be kept away?

He edged away from the window, and, as cautiously as he had come, retraced his steps across the cellar and up the stairs—and then, the possibility of being heard from without gone, he broke into a run. There was no need to wonder long what those wires meant. They could mean only one of two things—and the Crime Club would have little concern in his electric light! *They had tapped his telephone.* The mains, he knew, ran into the cellar from the underground service in the street. He was racing like a madman now. How long ago, how many hours ago, had they done that! Great Scott, *she* was to have telephoned! Had she done so? Was the game, all, everything, she herself, at their mercy already? If she had telephoned, Jason would have left a message on his desk—he would look there first—afterward he would waken Jason.

He gained the door of his den on the first landing, a room that ran the entire length of one side of the house from front to rear, burst in, switched on the light—and stood stock-still in amazement.

"Jason!" he cried out.

The old butler, fully dressed, rubbing and blinking his eyes at the light, and with a startled cry, rose up from the depths of a lounging chair.

"Jason!" exclaimed Jimmie Dale again.

"I beg pardon, sir, Master Jim," stammered the man. "I—I must have fallen asleep, sir."

"Jason, what are you doing here?" Jimmie Dale demanded sharply.

"Well, sir," said Jason, still fumbling for his words, "it—it was the telephone, sir."

"The—*telephone*!"

"Yes, sir. A woman, begging your pardon, Master Jim, a lady, sir, has been telephoning every hour or so, and she—"

"*Yes*!" Jimmie Dale had jumped across the room and had caught the other fiercely by the shoulder. "Yes—yes! What did she say? *Quick*, man!"

"Good Lord, Master Jim!" faltered Jason. "I—she—"

"Jason," said Jimmie Dale, suddenly as cold as ice, "what did she say? Think, man! Every word!"

"She didn't say anything, Master Jim. Nothing at all, sir—except to keep asking each time if she could speak to you."

"Nothing else, Jason?"

"No, sir."

"You are *sure*?"

"I'm sure, Master Jim. Not another thing but that, sir, just as I've told you."

"Thank God!" said Jimmie Dale, in a low voice.

"Yes, sir," said Jason mechanically.

"How long ago was it since she telephoned last?" asked Jimmie Dale quickly.

"Well, sir, I couldn't rightly say. You see, as I said, Master Jim, I must have gone to sleep, but—"

They were staring tensely into each other's face. The telephone on the desk was ringing vibrantly, clamourously, through the stillness of the room.

Jason, white, frightened, bewildered, touched his lips with the tip of his tongue.

"That'll be her again, sir," he said hoarsely.

"Wait!" said Jimmie Dale tersely.

He was trying to think, to think faster than he had ever thought before. He could not tell Jason to say that he had not yet come in—*they* knew he was in, it would be but showing his hand to that "someone" who would be listening now on the wire. He dared not speak to her, or, above all, allow her to expose herself by a single inadvertent word. He dared not speak to her—and she was here now, calling him! He could not speak to her—and it was life and death almost that she should know what had happened; life and death almost for both of them that he should know all and everything she could tell him. True, it would take but a minute to run to the cellar and cut those wires, while Jason held her on the pretence of calling him, Jimmie Dale, to the phone; only a minute to cut those wires—and in so doing advertise to these fiends the fact that he had discovered their trick; admit, as though in so many words, that their suspicions of him were justified; lay himself open to some new move that he could not hope to foresee; and, paramount to all else, rob her and himself of this master trump the Crime Club had placed in his hands, by means of which there was a chance that he could hoist them with their own petard!

The telephone rang again—imperatively, persistently.

"Listen, Jason." Jimmie Dale was speaking rapidly, earnestly. "Say that I've come in and have gone to bed—in a vile humour. That you told me a lady had been calling, but that I said if she called again I wasn't to be disturbed if it was the Queen of Sheba herself—that I wouldn't answer any phone tonight for anybody. Do you understand? No argument with her—just that. Now, answer!"

Jason lifted the receiver from the hook.

"Yes—hello!" he said. "Yes, ma'am, Mr. Dale has come in, but he has retired.… Yes, I told him; but, begging your pardon, ma'am, he was in what I might say was a bit of a temper, and said he wasn't to be disturbed by any-one."

Jimmie Dale snatched the receiver from Jason, and put it to his own ear.

"Kindly tell Mr. Dale that unless he comes to the phone now," a feminine voice, her voice, in well-simulated indignation, was saying, "it will be a very long day before I shall trouble myself to—"

Jimmie Dale clapped his hand firmly over the mouthpiece of the instrument. Thank God for that clever brain of hers! She understood!

"Repeat what you said before, Jason," he instructed hurriedly. "Then say 'Good-night.'"

He removed his hand from the mouthpiece.

"It's quite useless, ma'am," said Jason apologetically. "In the rare temper he was in, he wouldn't come, to use his own words, ma'am, not for the Queen of Sheba herself, ma'am. Good-night, ma'am."

Jimmie Dale hung the receiver back on the hook—and with his hand flirted away a bead of moisture that had sprung to his forehead.

"Good Lord, Master Jim, what's wrong, sir? What's happened, sir? And—and those clothes, Master Jim, sir! They aren't the ones you went out in, sir—they aren't yours at all, sir!" Jason ventured anxiously.

"Jason," said Jimmie Dale, "switch off the light, and go to the front window and look out. Keep well behind the curtains. Don't show yourself. Tell me if you see anything."

"Yes, sir," said Jason obediently.

The light went out. Jimmie Dale moved to the rear of the room—to the window overlooking the garage and yard.

"I don't see anything, sir," Jason called.

"Watch!" Jimmie Dale answered.

A minute passed—two—three. Jimmie Dale was staring down into the black of the yard. She understood! She knew, of course, before she phoned that something had gone wrong tonight. She knew that only peril of the gravest moment would have kept him from the phone—and her. She knew now, as a logical conclusion, that it was dangerous to attempt to communicate with him at his home. Those wires! Where did they lead to? Not far away—that would be almost a mechanical impossibility. Was it into the Crime Club itself—near at hand? Or the basement, say, of that apartment house across the driveway? Or—where?

And then Jimmie Dale spoke again:

"Do you see anything, Jason?"

"I'm not sure, sir," Jason answered hesitantly. "I thought I saw a man move behind a tree out there across the road a minute ago, sir. Yes, sir—there he is again!"

There was a thin, mirthless smile on Jimmie Dale's lips.

Below, in the shadow of the garage, a dark form, like a deeper shadow, stirred—and was still again.

"What time is it, Jason?" Jimmie Dale asked presently.

"It'll be about half-past four, sir."

"Go to bed, Jason."

"Yes, sir; but"—Jason's voice, low, troubled, came through the darkness from the upper end of the room—"Master Jim, sir, I—"

"Go to bed, Jason—and not a word of this."

"Yes, sir. Good-night, Master Jim."

"Good-night, Jason."

Jimmie Dale groped his way to the big lounging chair in which he had found Jason asleep, and flung himself into it. They had struck quickly, these ingenious, dress-suited murderers of the Crime Club! The house was already watched, would be watched now untiringly, unceasingly; not a movement of his henceforth but would be under their eyes!

His hands, resting on the arms of the chair, closed slowly until they became tight-clenched, knotted fists. What was he to do? It was not only the Crime Club, it was not only the Tocsin and her peril—there was the underworld snapping and snarling at his heels, there was the police, dogged and sullen, ever on the trail of the Gray Seal! His life, even before this, in his fight against the underworld and the police, had depended upon his freedom of action—and now, at one and the same time, that freedom was cut away from beneath his feet, as it were, and a third foe, equally as deadly as the others, was added to the list!

For months, to preserve and sustain the character of Larry the Bat, he had been forced to assume the role almost daily; for, in that sordid empire below the dead line, whose one common bond and aim was the Gray Seal's death, where suspicion, one of the other, was rampant and extravagant, where each might be the one against whom all swore their vengeance, Larry the Bat could not mysteriously disappear from his accustomed haunts without inviting suspicion in an active and practical form—an inquisitorial visit to his squalid lodgings, the Sanctuary—and the end of Larry the Bat!

If, as he had thought only a few hours before, he was through forever with his dual life, that would not have mattered, the underworld would have been welcome to make what it chose of it—but now the preservation of the character of Larry the Bat was more vital and necessary to him than it had ever been before. It was a means of defense and offense against these men who lurked now outside his doors. It was the sole means now of communication with her; for, warned both by Jason's words, and what must be an obvious fact to her, that their plans had miscarried, that it was dangerous to communicate with him as Jimmie Dale, she would expect him, count on him to make that move. There would be no longer either reason or attempt on her part to maintain the mystery with which she had heretofore surrounded herself, the crisis had come, she would be watching, waiting, hoping, seeking for him more anxiously and with far more at stake than he had ever sought for her—until now!

He got up impulsively from his chair, and, in the blackness, began to pace the room. The next move was clear, pitifully clear; it had been clear from the first, it had been clear even in that ride in the car—it was so clear that it seemed veritably to mock him as he prodded his brains for some means of putting it into execution. He must get to the Sanctuary, become Larry the Bat—but how? *How!* The question seemed at last to become resonant, to ring through the room with the weight of doom upon it.

Schemes, plans, ideas came, bringing a momentary uplift—only to be discarded the next instant with a sort of bitter, desperate regret. These men were not men of mere ordinary intelligence; their cleverness, their power, the amazing scope of their organisation, all bore grim witness to the fact that they would be blinded not at all by any paltry ruse.

He could walk out of the house in the morning as Jimmie Dale without apparent hindrance—that was obvious enough. And so long as he pursued the usual avocations of Jimmie Dale, he would not be interfered with—only *watched*. It was useless to consider that plan for a moment. It would not help him to reach the Sanctuary—without leading them there behind him! True, there was always the chance that he might shake them off his trail, but he could hardly hope to accomplish anything like that without their knowing that it was done *deliberately*—and that he dared not risk. The strongest weapon in his hands now was his secret knowledge that he was being watched.

That telephone there, for instance, that most curiously kept on insisting in his mind that it, and it alone was the way out, was the last thing he could place in jeopardy. Besides, there was another reason why such a plan would not do; for, granting even that he succeeded in eluding them on the way, and managed to reach the Sanctuary, his freedom of action would be so restricted and limited as to be practically worthless—he would have to return to his home here again within a reasonable time as Jimmie Dale, within a few hours at most—or again they would be in possession of the fact that he had discovered their surveillance.

That, it was true, had been his original plan when he had entered the house half an hour previously, but it was an entirely different matter now. Then, he had counted on *getting away* without their knowing it, before they, as he had fondly thought, would have had a chance to establish their espionage, and when they would have had no reason to suspect, for a time at least, that he was not still within the house, when they would have been watching, as it were, an empty cage.

He stopped in his walk, and, after a moment, dropped down into the lounging chair again. That was it, of course. An empty cage! If he could escape from the house! Not so much without their seeing him; that was more or less a mechanical detail. But escape—and leave them in possession of a sort of guarantee or assurance that he was still there! That would give him the freedom of action that he must have. He smiled with bitter irony. That solved the problem! That was all there was to it—just that! It was very simple, exceedingly simple; it was only—impossible!

The smile left his lips, and once more his hands, clenched fiercely. No; it was not impossible! It *must* be done—if he was to win through, if he was even to save himself! It must be done—or fail her! It *could* be done; there was a way—if he could only see it!

CHAPTER 7
THE "HOUR"

As the minutes passed, many of them, Jimmie Dale sat there motionless, staring before him at the desk that was faintly outlined in the unlighted room. Then somewhere in the house a clock struck the hour. Five o'clock! He raised his head. *Yes!* It could be done! There was a way! He had the germ of it now. And now the plan began to grow, to take form and shape in his mind, to dovetail, to knit the integral parts into a comprehensive whole. There was a way—but he must have assistance. Jason—yes, assuredly. Benson, his chauffeur—yes, equally as trustworthy as Jason. Benson was devoted to him; and moreover Benson was young, alert, daring, cool. He had had more than one occasion to test Benson's resourcefulness and nerve!

Jimmie Dale rose abruptly, went to the rear window, and, parting the curtains cautiously, stood peering down into the courtyard. Yes, it was feasible; even a little more than feasible. The garage fronted the driveway, of course, to give free entrance and egress to the cars, but where the wall of the garage and the rear wall of the house overlapped, as it were, the space between them was not much more than ten yards; and here the shadows of the two walls, mingling, lay like a black, impenetrable pathway—not like that other shadow he had seen moving at the side of the garage, and that, if not for the moment discernible, was none the less surely still lurking there!

Satisfied, Jimmie Dale swung briskly from the window, and, going now to his bedroom across the hall, undressed and went to bed—but not to sleep. There would be time enough to sleep, all day, if he wished; now, there were still the little details to be thought out that, more than anything else, could make or wreck his plans. A point overdone, the faintest suggestion of a false note where men of the calibre of those against whom he was now fighting for his life were concerned, would not only make his scheme abortive, but would place him utterly at their mercy.

It was nine o'clock when he rang for Jason.

"Jason," he said abruptly, as the other entered, "I want you to telephone for Doctor Merlin."

"The doctor, sir!" exclaimed the old man anxiously. "You're—you're not ill, Master Jim, sir?"

"Do I look ill, Jason?" inquired Jimmie Dale gravely.

"Well, sir," admitted Jason, in concern; "a bit done up, sir, perhaps. A little pale, sir; though I'm sure—"

"I'm glad to hear it," said Jimmie Dale, sitting up in bed. "The worse I look, the better!"

"I—I beg pardon, sir?" stammered Jason.

"Jason," said Jimmie Dale, gravely again, "you have had reason to know that on several occasions my life has been threatened. It is threatened now. You know from last night that this house is now watched. You may, or you may not have surmised—that our telephone wires have been tapped."

"Tapped, sir!"—Jason's face had gone a little gray.

"Yes; a party line, so to speak," said Jimmie Dale grimly. "Do you understand? You must be careful to say no more, no less than exactly what I tell you to say. Now go and telephone! Ask the doctor to come over and see me this morning. Simply say that I am not feeling well; but that, apart from being apparently in a very nervous condition, you do not know what is the matter."

"Yes, sir—good Lord, sir!" gasped Jason—and left the room to carry out his orders.

An hour later, Doctor Merlin had been and gone—and had left two prescriptions; one written, the other verbal. With the written one, Benson, in his chauffeur's livery, was dispatched to the drug store; the verbal one was precisely what Jimmie Dale had expected from the fussy old family physician: "Two or three days of quiet in the house James; and if you need me again, let me know."

"Now, Jason," said Jimmie Dale, when the old man had returned from ushering Doctor Merlin from the house, "our friends out there will be anxious to learn the verdict. I was to dine with the Ross-Hendersons tomorrow night, was I not?"

"Yes, sir; I think so, sir."

"Make sure!" said Jimmie Dale. "Look in my engagement book there on the table."

Jason looked.

"Yes, sir, that's right," he announced.

"Very good," said Jimmie Dale softly. "Now go and telephone again, Jason. Present my regrets and excuses to the Ross-Hendersons, and say that under the doctor's orders I am confined to the house for the next few days— and, Jason!"

"Yes, sir?"

"When Benson returns with the medicine let him bring it here himself— and I shall want you as well."

Jimmie Dale propped himself up a little wearily on the pillows, as Jason went out of the room. After all, his condition was not entirely feigned. He was, as a matter of fact, pretty well played out, both mentally and physically. Certainly, that he should require a doctor and be confined to the house could not arouse suspicion even in the minds of those alert, aristocratic thugs of the Crime Club, prone as they would be to suspect anything—a man who had been knocked unconscious in an automobile smash the night before, had been in a fight, had been subjected to a terrific mental shock, to say nothing of the infernal drug that had been administered to him, might well be expected to be indisposed the next morning, and for several mornings following that! It might, indeed, even cause them to relax their vigilance for the time being—though he dared build nothing on that. Well, he had only to coach Benson and Jason in the parts they were to play, and the balance of the morning and all the afternoon was his in which to rest.

He reached over to the table, picked up a pencil and paper, and began to jot down memoranda. He had just tossed the pencil back on the table as the two men entered.

Jason, at a sign, closed the door quietly.

Jimmie Dale looked at Benson half musingly, half whimsically, for a moment before he spoke.

"Benson," he said, "the back seat of the large touring car is hinged and lifts up, once the cushion is removed, doesn't it?"

"Yes, sir," Benson answered promptly.

"And there's space enough for, say, a man inside, isn't there?"

"Why, yes, sir; I suppose so—at a squeeze"—Benson stared blankly.

"Quite so!" said Jimmie Dale calmly. "Now, another matter, Benson: I believe some chauffeurs have a habit, when occasion lends itself, of taking, shall we say, their 'best girl' out riding in their masters' machines?"

"*Some* might," Benson replied, a little stiffly. "I hope you don't think, sir, that—"

"One moment, Benson. The point is, it's done—quite generally?"

"Yes, sir."

"And you have a 'best girl,' or at least could find one for such a purpose, if you were so inclined?"

"Yes, sir," said Benson; "but—"

"Very good!" Jimmie Dale interrupted. "Then tonight, Benson, taking advantage of my illness, and tomorrow night, and the nights after that until further notice, you will acquire and put into practice that reprehensible habit."

"I—I don't understand, Mr. Dale."

"No; I dare say not," said Jimmie Dale—and then the whimsicality dropped from him. "Benson," he said slowly, "do you remember a night, nearly four years ago, the first night you ever saw me? You had, indiscreetly, I think, displayed more money than was wise in that East Side neighbourhood."

"I remember," said Benson, with a sudden start; then simply: "I wouldn't be here now, sir, if it hadn't been for you."

"Well," said Jimmie Dale quietly, "the tables are turned today, Benson. As Jason already knows, this house is watched. For reasons that I cannot explain, I am in great danger. Bluntly, I am putting my life in your hands—and Jason's."

Benson looked for an instant from Jimmie Dale to Jason, caught the strained, troubled expression on the old man's face, then back again at Jimmie Dale.

"D'ye mean that, sir!" he cried. "Then you can count on me, Mr. Dale, to the last ditch!"

"I know that, Benson," Jimmie Dale said softly. "And now, both of you, listen! It is imperative that I should get away from the house; and equally imperative that those watching should believe that I am still here. Not even the servants are to be permitted a suspicion that I am not here in my bed, ill. That, Jason, is your task. You will allow no one to wait on me but yourself; you will bring the meal trays up regularly—and eat the food yourself. You will answer all inquiries, telephone and otherwise, in person—I am not seeing anyone. You understand perfectly, Jason?"

"I understand, Master Jim. You need have no fear, sir, on that score."

"Now, you, Benson," Jimmie Dale went on. "A few minutes ago I sent you out in your chauffeur's togs with that prescription. You were undoubtedly observed. I wanted you to be. It was quite necessary that they should know and be able to recognise you again—to disabuse their minds later on of the possibility that I might be masquerading in your clothes; and also, of course, that they should know who you were, and what your position was in the household. Very well! Tonight, at eight o'clock exactly, you are to go out from the back door of the house to the garage. On the way out—it will be quite dark then—I want you to drop something, say, a bunch of keys that you had been jingling in your hand. You are to experience some difficulty in finding it again, move about a little to force anyone that may be lurking by the garage to retreat around the corner. Grumble a bit and make a little noise; but you are not to overdo it—a couple of minutes at the outside is enough, by that time I shall be under the car seat. You will then run the machine out to the street and stop at the curb, jump out, and, as though you had forgotten something, hurry back to the garage. You must not be away long—enough only to permit, say, a passer-by to glance into the car and satisfy himself that it is empty. You understand, of course, Benson, that the hood must be down—no closed car to invite even the suggestion of concealment—that would be a fatal blunder. Drive then to the young lady's home by as direct a route as you can—give no appearance of being aware that you are followed, as you will be, and much less the appearance of attempting to elude pursuit. Act naturally. Between here and your destination I will manage readily enough to leave the car. You will then take the young lady for her drive—that is what they will be interested in—your motive for going out tonight. And, as I said, take her driving again on each succeeding night—establish the *habit* to their satisfaction."

Jimmie Dale paused, glanced at the paper which he still held in his hand, then handed it to Benson.

"Just one thing more, Benson," he said: "Listed on that paper you will find a different rendezvous for each night for the next five nights, excluding tonight, which, after you have returned the young lady to her home, you are to pass by on your way back here. See that your drive is always over in time for you to pass each night's rendezvous at half past eleven sharp. Don't stop unless I signal you. If I am not there, go right on home, and be at the next place on the following night. I am fairly well satisfied they will not bother about you after tonight, or tomorrow night at the most; but, for all that, you must take no chances, so, except in the route you take in going to the young lady's, always avoid covering the same ground twice, which might give the appearance of having some ulterior purpose in view—even in your drives, vary your runs. Is this clear, Benson?"

"Yes, sir," said Benson earnestly.

"Very well, then," said Jimmie Dale. "Eight o'clock to the dot, Benson—compare your time with Jason's. And now, Jason, see that I get a chance to sleep until dinner time tonight."

The hours that followed were hours of sound and much-needed sleep for Jimmie Dale, and from which he awoke only on Jason's entrance that evening with the dinner tray.

"I've slept like a log, Jason!" he cried briskly, as he leaped out of bed. "Anything new—anything happened?"

"No, sir; not a thing," Jason answered. "Only, Master Jim, sir"—the old man twisted his hands nervously—"I—you'll excuse my saying so, sir—I do hope you'll be careful tonight, sir. I can't help being afraid that something'll happen to you, Master Jim."

"Nonsense, Jason!" Jimmie Dale laughed cheerfully. "There's nothing going to happen—to me! You go ahead now and stay with the servants, and get them out of the road at the proper time."

He bathed, dressed, ate his dinner, and was slipping cartridges into the magazine of his automatic when, within a minute or two of eight o'clock, Jason's whisper came from the doorway.

"It's all clear now, Master Jim, sir."

"Right!" Jimmie Dale responded—and followed Jason down the stairway, and to the head of the cellar stairs.

Here Jason halted.

"God keep you, Master Jim!" said the old man huskily. "Good-night, Jason," Jimmie Dale answered softly; and, with a reassuring squeeze on the other's arm, went on down to the cellar.

Here he moved quickly, noiselessly across to the window—not the window of the night before, but another of the same description, almost directly beneath the one in his den above, that faced the garage and lay in the line of that black shadow path between the two buildings. Deftly, cautiously without sound, a half inch, an inch at a time he opened it. He stood listening, then. A minute passed. Then he heard Benson open and shut the back door; then Benson in the yard; and then Benson's voice in a muttered and irritable growl, talking to himself, as he stamped around on the ground.

With a lithe, agile movement, Jimmie Dale pulled himself up and through the window—and began to creep rapidly on hands and knees toward the garage. It was dark, intensely dark. He could barely distinguish Benson's form, though, as he passed the other, the slight sounds he made drowned out by the chauffeur's angry mumblings, he could have reached out and touched Benson easily.

He gained the interior of the garage, and, as Benson, came on again, stepped lightly into the car, lifted the seat, and wriggled his way inside.

It was close, stuffy, abominably cramped, but Jimmie Dale was smiling grimly now. Thanks to Benson, there wasn't a possibility that he had been seen. He both felt and heard Benson start the car. Then the car moved forward, ran the length of the driveway, bumped slightly as it made the street—and stopped. He heard Benson jump out and run back—and then he listened intently, and the grim smile flickered on his lips again. Came the sound of a footstep on the sidewalk close beside the car—then silence—the car shook a little as though someone's weight was on the step—then the footsteps receded—Benson returned on the run—and the car started forward once more.

Perhaps ten minutes passed. Three times the car had swerved sharply, making a corner turn. Then Jimmie Dale pushed up the seat, and, protected from observation from behind by the back of the car itself, crawled out and crouched down on the floor of the tonneau.

"Don't look around, Benson," he said calmly. "Are we followed?"

"Yes, sir." Benson answered. "At least, there's always been a car behind us, though not the same one. They're pretty clever. There must be three or four, each following the other. Every time I turn a corner it's a different car that turns it behind me."

"How far behind?" Jimmie Dale asked.

"Half a block."

"Slow down a little," instructed Jimmie Dale; "and don't turn another corner until they've had a chance to accommodate themselves to your new speed. You are going too fast for me to jump, and I don't want them to notice any change in speed, except what is made in plain sight. Yes; that's better. Where are we, Benson?"

"That's Amsterdam Avenue ahead," replied Benson.

"All right," said Jimmie Dale quietly. "Turn into it. The more people the better. Tell me just as you are about to turn."

"Yes, sir," said Benson; then, almost on the instant, "All ready, sir!"

Jimmie Dale's hand reached out for the door catch, edged the door ajar, the car swerved, took the corner—and Jimmie Dale stepped out on the running board, hung there negligently for a moment as though chatting with Benson, and then with an airy "good-night" dropped nonchalantly to the ground, and the next instant had mingled with the throng of pedestrians on the sidewalk.

A half minute later, a large gray automobile turned the corner and followed Benson—and Jimmie Dale, stepping out into the street again, swung on a downtown car. The road to the Sanctuary was open!

In his impatience, now, the street car seemed to drag along every foot of the way; but a glance at his watch, as he finally reached the Bowery, and, walking then, rapidly approached the cross street a few steps ahead that led to the Sanctuary, told him that it was still but a quarter to nine. But even at that he quickened his steps a little. He was free now! There was a sort of savage, elemental uplift upon him. He was free! He could strike now in his own defense—and hers! In a few moments he would be at the Sanctuary; in a few more he would be Larry the Bat, and by tomorrow at the latest he would see—The Tocsin. After all, that "hour" was not to be taken from him! It was not, perhaps, the hour that she had meant it should be, thought and prayed, perhaps, that it might be! It was not the hour of victory. But it was the hour that meant to him the realisation of the years of longing, the hour when he should see her, see her for the first time face to face, when there should be no more barriers between them, when—

"Fer Gawd's sake, mister, buy a pencil!"

A hand was plucking at his sleeve, the thin voice was whining in his ear. He halted mechanically. A woman, old, bedraggled, ragged, was thrusting a bunch of cheap pencils imploringly toward him—and then, with a stifled cry, Jimmie Dale leaned forward. The eyes that lifted to his for an instant were bright and clear with the vigor of youth, great eyes of brown they were, and trouble, hope, fear, wistfulness, ay, and a glorious shyness were in their depths. And then the voice he knew so well, the Tocsin's was whispering hurriedly:

"I will be waiting here, Jimmie—for Larry the Bat."

CHAPTER 8
THE TOCSIN

It was only a little way back along the street from the Sanctuary to the corner on the Bowery where as Jimmie Dale he had left her, where as Larry the Bat now he was going to meet her again; it would take only a moment or so, even at Larry the Bat's habitual, characteristic, slouching, gait—but it seemed that was all too slow, that he must throw discretion to the winds and run the distance. His blood was tingling; there was elation upon him, coupled with an almost childlike dread that she might be gone.

"The Tocsin! The Tocsin!" he kept saying to himself.

Yes; she was still there, still whiningly imploring those who passed to buy her miserable pencils—and then, with a quick-flung whisper to him to follow as he slouched up close to her, she had started slowly down the street.

"The Tocsin! The Tocsin! The Tocsin!"—his brain seemed to be ringing with the words, ringing with them in a note clear as a silver bell. The Tocsin—at last! The woman who so strangely, so wonderfully, so mysteriously had entered into his life, and possessed it, and filled it with a love and yearning that had come to mold and sway and actuate his very existence—the woman for whom he had fought; for whom he had risked, and gladly risked, his wealth, his name, his honour—everything; the woman for whose sake he, the Gray Seal, was sought and hounded as the most notorious criminal of the age; she whose cleverness, whose resourcefulness, whose amazing intimacy with the hidden things of the underworld had seemed, indeed, to border on the supernatural; she, the Tocsin—the woman whose face he had never seen before! The woman whose face he had never seen before—and who now was that wretched hag that hobbled along the street before him, begging, whining, and importuning the passers-by to purchase of her pitiful wares!

He laughed a little—buoyantly. He had never pictured a first meeting such as this! A hag? Yes! And one as disreputable in appearance as he himself, as Larry the Bat, was disreputable! But he had seen her eyes! Inimitable as was her disguise, she could not hide her eyes, or hide the pledge they held of the beauty of form and feature beneath the tattered rags and the touch of a master in the make-up that brought haggard want and age into the face—and dimly he began to divine the source, the means by which she had acquired the information that for years had enabled her to plan their coups, that had enabled him to execute them under the guise of crime, that for years had seemed beyond all human reach.

Where was she going? Where was she taking him? But what did it matter! The years of waiting were at an end—the years of mystery in a few moments now would be mystery no more!

Ah! She had turned from the Bowery, and was heading east. He shuffled on after her, guardedly, a half block behind. It was well that Jimmie Dale had disappeared, that he was Larry the Bat again—the neighbourhood was growing more and more one that Jimmie Dale could not long linger in without attracting attention; while, on the other hand, it was the natural environment of such as Larry the Bat and such as she, who was leading him now to the supreme moment of his life. Yes, it was that—the fulfillment of the years! The thought of it alone filled his mind, his soul; it brushed aside, it blotted out for the time being the danger, the peril, the deadly menace that hung over them both. It was only that she, the Tocsin, was here—only that at last they would be together.

On she went, traversing street after street, the direction always trending toward the river—until finally she halted before what appeared to be, as nearly as he could make out in the almost total darkness of the ill-lighted street, a small and tumble-down, self-contained dwelling that bordered on what seemed to be an unfenced store yard of some description. He drew his breath in sharply. She had halted—waiting for him to come up with her. She was waiting for him—*waiting* for him! It seemed as though he drank of some strange, exhilarating elixir—he reached her side eagerly—and then— and then—her hand had caught his, and she was leading him into the house, into a black passage where he could see nothing, into a room equally black over whose threshold he stumbled, and her voice in a low, conscious way, with a little tremour, a half sob in it that thrilled him with its promise, was in his ears:

"We are safe here, Jimmie, for a little while—but, oh, Jimmie, what have I done! What have I done to bring you into this—only—only—I was so sure, so sure, Jimmie, that there was nothing more to fear!"

The blood was beating in hammer blows at his temples. It seemed all unreal, untrue that this moment could be his, that it was not a dream—a dream which was presently to be snatched from him in a bitter awakening. And then he laughed out wildly, passionately. No—it was true, it was real! Her breath was on his cheek, it was a living, pulsing hand that was still in his—and then soul and mind and body seemed engulfed and lost in a mad ecstasy—and she was in his arms, crushed to him, and he was raining kisses upon her face.

"I love you! I love you!" he was crying hoarsely; and over and over again: "I love you! I love you!"

She did not struggle. The warm, rich lips were yielding to his; he could feel the throb, the life in the young, lithe form against his own. She was his—his! The years, the past, all were swept away—and she was his at last—his for always. And there came a mighty sense of kingship upon him, as though all the world were at his feet, and virility, and a great, glad strength above all other men's, and a song was in his soul, a song triumphant—for she was his!

"You!" he cried out—and strained her to him. "You!" he cried again—and kissed her lips and her eyelids and her lips again.

And then her head was buried on his shoulder, and she was crying softly; but after a moment she raised her hands and laid them upon his face, and held them there, and because it was dark, dared to raise her head as well, and her eyes to look into his.

Then for a long time they stood there so, and for a long time neither spoke—and then with a little startled, broken cry, as though the peril and the menace hanging over them, forgotten for the moment, were thrust like a knife stab suddenly upon her, she drew herself away, and ran from him, and went and got a lamp, and lighted it, and set it upon the table.

And Jimmie Dale, still standing there, watched her. How gloriously her eyes shone, dimmed and misty with the tears that filled them though they were! And there was nothing incongruous in the rags that clothed her, in the squalour and poverty of the bare room, in the white furrows that the tears had plowed through the grime and make-up on her cheeks.

"You wonderful, wonderful woman!" Jimmie Dale whispered.

She shook her head as though almost in self-reproach.

"I am not wonderful, Jimmie," she said, in a low voice. "I"—and then she caught his arm, and her voice broke a little—"I've brought you into this—probably to your death. Jimmie, tell me what happened last night, and since then. I—I've thought at times today I should go mad. Oh, Jimmie, there is so much to say tonight, so much to do if—if we are ever to be together for—for always. Last night, Jimmie—the telephone—I knew there was danger—that all had gone wrong—what was it?"

His arms were around her shoulders, drawing her close to him again.

"I found the wires tapped," he said slowly.

"Yes, and—and the man you met—the chauffeur?"

"He is dead," Jimmie Dale answered gently.

He felt her hand close with a quick, spasmodic clutch upon his arm; her face grew white—and for a moment she turned away her head.

"And—and the package?" she asked presently.

"I do not know," replied Jimmie Dale. "He did not have it with him; he—"

"Wait!" she interrupted quickly. "We are only wasting time like this! Tell me everything, everything just as it happened, everything from the moment you received my letter."

And, holding her there in his arms, softening as best he could the more brutal details, he told her. And, at the end, for a little while she was silent; then in a strained, impulsive way she asked again:

"The chauffeur—you are sure—you are positive that he is dead?"

"Yes," said Jimmie Dale grimly; "I am sure." And then the pent-up flood of questions burst from his lips. Who was the chauffeur? The package, the box numbered 428, and John Johansson? And the Crime Club? And the issue at stake? The danger, the peril that surrounded her? And she—above all—more than anything else—about herself—her strange life, its mystery?

She checked him with a strangely wistful touch of her finger upon his lips, with a shake of her head.

"No, Jimmie; not that way. You would never understand. I cannot—"

"But I am to know—now! Surely I am to know *now*!" he cried, a sudden sense of dismay upon him. Three years! Three years—and always the "next" time! "I must know now, if I am to help you!"

She smiled a little wanly at him, as she drew herself away, and, dropping into a chair, placed her elbows on the rickety table, cupping her chin in her hands.

"Yes; you are to know now," she said, almost as though she were talking to herself; then, with a swift intake of her breath, impulsively: "Jimmie! Jimmie! I had thought that it would be all so different when—when you came. That—that I would have nothing to fear—for you—for me—because—it would be all over. And now you are here, Jimmie—and, oh, thank God for you!—but I feel tonight almost—almost as though it were hopeless, that—that we were beaten."

"Beaten!" He stepped quickly to the table, and sat down, and took one of her hands away from her face to hold it in both his own. "Beaten!" he laughed out defiantly; then, playfully, soothingly, to reassure her: "Jimmie Dale and Larry the Bat and the Gray Seal and the Tocsin—*beaten!* And after we have just scored the last trick!"

"But we do not hold many trumps, Jimmie," she answered gravely. "You have seen something of this Crime Club's power, its methods, its merciless, cruel, inhuman cunning, and you, perhaps, think that you understand—but you have not begun to grasp the extent of either that power or cunning. This horrible organisation has been in existence for many years. I do not know how many. I only know that the men of whom it is composed are not ordinary criminals, that they do not work in the ordinary way—today, they set the machinery of fraud, deception, robbery, and murder in motion that ten years from now, and, perhaps, only then, will culminate in the final success of their schemes—and they play only for enormous stakes. But"—her lips grew set—"you will see for yourself. I must not talk any longer than is necessary; we must not take too much time. You count on three days before they begin to suspect that all is not right with Jimmie Dale—I know them better than you, and I give you two days, forty-eight hours at the outside, and possibly far less. Jimmie"—abruptly—"did you ever hear of Peter LaSalle?"

"The capitalist? Yes!" said Jimmie Dale. "He died a few years ago. I know his brother Henry well—at the club, and all that."

"Do you!" she said evenly. "Well, the man you know is not Peter LaSalle's brother; he is an impostor—and one of the Crime Club."

"Not—Peter LaSalle's brother!"—Jimmie Dale repeated the words mechanically. And suddenly his brain was whirling. Vaguely, dimly, in little memory snatches, events, not pertinent then, vitally significant now, came crowding upon him. Peter LaSalle had come from somewhere in the West to live in New York; and very shortly afterward had died. The estate had been worth something over eleven millions. And there had been—he leaned quickly, tensely forward over the table, staring at her. "My God!" he whispered hoarsely. "You are not, you cannot be—the—the daughter—Peter LaSalle's daughter, who disappeared strangely!"

"Yes," she said quietly. "I am Marie LaSalle."

CHAPTER 9
THE TOCSIN'S STORY

LaSalle! The old French name! That old French inscription on the ring: *"Sonnez le Tocsin!"* Yes; he began to understand now. She was Marie LaSalle! He began to remember more clearly.

Marie LaSalle! They had said she was one of the most beautiful girls who had ever made her entree into New York society. But he had never met her—as Marie LaSalle; never met her—until now, as the Tocsin, in this bare, destitute, squalid hovel, here at bay, both of them, for their lives.

He had been away when she had come with her father to New York; and on his return there had only been the father's brother in the father's place—and she was gone. He remembered the furor her disappearance had caused; the enormous rewards her uncle had offered in an effort to trace her; the thousand and one speculations as to what had become of her; and that then, gradually, as even the most startling and mystifying of events and happenings always do, the affair had dropped into oblivion and had been forgotten by the public at least. He began to count back. Yes, it must have been nearly five years ago; two years before she, as the Tocsin, and he, as the Gray Seal, had formed their amazing and singular partnership, that—he started suddenly, as she spoke.

"I want to tell you in as few words as I can," she said abruptly, breaking the silence. "Listen, then, Jimmie. My mother died ten years ago. I was little more than a child then. Shortly after her death, father made a business trip to New York, and, on the advice of some supposed friends, he had a new will drawn up by a lawyer whom they recommended, and to whom they introduced him. I do not know who those men were. The lawyer's name was Travers, Hilton Travers." She glanced curiously at Jimmie Dale, and added quickly: "He was the chauffeur—the man who was killed last night."

"You mean," Jimmie Dale burst out, "you mean that he was—but, first, the will! What was in the will?"

"It was a very simple will," she answered. "And from the nature of it, it was not at all strange that my father should have been willing to have had it drawn by a comparative stranger, if that is what you are thinking. Summarised in a few words, the will left everything to me, and appointed my Uncle Henry as my guardian and the sole executor of the estate until I should have reached my twenty-fifth birthday. It provided for a certain sum each year to be paid to my uncle for his services as executor; and at the expiration of the trust period—that is, when I was twenty-five—bequeathed to him the sum of one hundred thousand dollars."

Jimmie Dale nodded. "Go on!" he prompted.

"It is hard to tell it in logical sequence," she said, hesitating a moment. "So many things seem to overlap each other. You must understand a little more about Hilton Travers. During the five years following the signing of the will father came frequently to New York, and became, not only intimate with Travers, but so much impressed with the other's cleverness and ability that he kept putting more and more of his business into Travers' hands. At the end of that five years, we moved to New York, and father, who was then quite an old man, retired from all active business, and turned over a great many of his personal affairs to Travers to look after for him, giving Travers power of attorney in a number of instances. So much for Travers. Now about my uncle. He was my father's only brother; in fact, they were the only surviving members of their family, apart from very distant connections in France, from where, generations back, the family originally came." Her hand touched Jimmie Dale's for an instant. "That ring, Jimmie, with its crest and inscription, is the old family coat of arms."

"Yes," he said briefly; "I surmised as much."

"Strange as it may seem, in view of the fact that they had not seen each other for twenty years," she went on hurriedly "my father and my uncle were more than ordinarily attached to each other. Letters passed regularly between them, and there was constant talk of one paying the other a visit—but the visit never materialised. My uncle was somewhere in Australia, my father was here, and consequently I never saw my uncle. He was quite a different type of man from father—more restless, less settled, more rough and ready, preferring the outdoor life of the Australian bush to the restrictions of any so-called civilisation, I imagine. Financially, I do not think he ever succeeded very well, for twice, in one way or another, he lost every sheep on his ranch and father set him up again; and I do not think he could ever have had much of a ranch, for I remember once, in one of the letters he wrote, that he said he had not seen a white man in weeks, so he must have lived a very lonely life. Indeed, at about the time father drew the new will, my uncle wrote, saying that he had decided to give up sheep running on his own account as it did not pay, and to accept a very favourable offer that had been made to him to man-age a ranch in New Zealand; and his next letter was from the latter country, stating that he had carried out his intentions, and was well satisfied with the change he had made. The long-proposed visit still continued to occupy my father's thoughts, and on his retirement from business he definitely made up his mind to go out to New Zealand, taking me with him. In fact, the plans were all arranged, my uncle expressed unbounded delight in his letters, and we were practically on the eve of sailing, when a cable came from my uncle, telling us to postpone the visit for a few months, as he was obliged to make a buying trip for his new employer that would keep him away that length of time—and then"—her fingers, that had been abstractedly picking out the lines formed by the grain of the wood in the table top, closed suddenly into tight-clenched fists—"and then—my father died."

Jimmie Dale turned away his head. There were tears in her eyes. The old sense of unreality was strong upon him again. He was listening to the Tocsin's story. It was strange that he should be doing that—that it could be really so! It seemed as though magically he had been transported out of the world where for years past he had lived with danger lurking at every turn, where men set watch about his house to trap him, where the denizens of the underworld yowled like starving beasts to sink their fangs in him, where the police were ceaselessly upon his trail to wreak an insensate vengeance upon him; it seemed as though he had been transported away from all that to something that he had dreamed might, perhaps, sometime happen, that he had hoped might happen, that he had longed for always, but now that it was his, that it also was full of the sense of the unreal. And yet as his mind fol-lowed the thread of her story, and leaped ahead and vaguely glimpsed what was to come, he was conscious in a sort of premonitory way of a vaster peril than any he had ever known, as though forces, for the moment masked, were arrayed against him whose strength and whose malignity were beyond hu-man parallel. In what a strange, almost incoherent way his brain was working! He roused himself a little and looked around him—and, with a shock, the starkness of the room, the abject, pitiful air of destitution brought home to him with terrific, startling force the significance of the scene in which he was playing a part. His face set suddenly in hard lines. That she should have been brought to assume such a life as this—forced out of her environment of wealth and refinement, forced in her purity to rub shoulders with the vile, the dissolute, forced to exist as such a creature amid the crime and vice, the wretched horror of the underworld that swirled around her! There was anger now upon him, burning, hot—a merciless craving that was a savage, hungry lust for vengeance.

And then she was speaking again:

"Father's death occurred very shortly after my uncle's message advising us to postpone our trip was received. On his death, Travers, very naturally, as father's lawyer, cabled my uncle to come to New York at once; and my uncle replied, saying that he was coming by the first steamer."

She paused again—but only for an instant, as though to frame her thoughts in words.

"I have told you that I had never seen my uncle, that even my father had not seen him for twenty years; and I have told you that the man you know as Henry LaSalle is an impostor—I am using the word 'uncle' now when I refer to him simply to avoid confusion. You are, perhaps, expecting me to say that I took a distinctive dislike to him from the moment he arrived? On the contrary, I had every reason to be predisposed toward him; and, indeed, was rather agreeably surprised than otherwise—he was not nearly so uncouth and unpolished as, somehow, I had pictured his life would have made him. Do you understand, Jimmie? He was kind, sympathetic; and, in an apathetic way, I liked him. I say 'apathetic' because I think that best describes my own attitude toward every one and everything following father's death until—that night."

She rose abruptly from her chair, as though a passive position of any kind had suddenly become intolerable.

"Why tell you what my father and I were to each other!" she cried out in a low, passionate voice. "It seemed as though everything that meant anything had gone out of my life. I became worn out, nervous; and though the days were bad enough, the nights were a source of dread. I began to suffer from insomnia—I could not sleep. This was even before my supposed uncle came. I used to read for hours and hours in my room after I had gone to bed. But"— she flung out her hand with an impatient gesture—"there is no need to dwell on that. One night, about a week after that man had arrived, and a little over a month after father had died, I was in my room and had finished a book I was reading. I remember that it was well after midnight. I had not the slight- est inclination to sleep. I picked up another book—and after that another. There were plenty in my room; but, irrationally, of course, none pleased me.

I decided to go down to the library—not that I think I really expected to find anything that I actually wanted, but more because it was an impulse, and furnished me for the moment with some definite objective, something to do. I got up, slipped on a dressing gown, and went downstairs. The lights were all out. I was just on the point of switching on those in the reception hall, when suddenly it seemed as though I had not strength to lift my hand, and I remember that for an instant I grew terribly cold with dread and fear. From the room on my right a voice had reached me. The door was closed, but the voice was raised in an outburst of profanity. I—I could hear every word.

"'If she's out of the way, there's no come-back,' the voice snarled. 'I won't listen to anything else! Do you hear! Why, you fool, what are you trying to do—hand me one! Turn everything into cash, and divvy, and beat it— eh? And I'm the goat, and I get caught and get twenty years for stealing trust funds—and the rest of you get the coin!' He swore terribly again. 'Who's taken the risk in this for the last five years! There'll be no smart Aleck lawyer tricks—there'll be no halfway measures! And who are you to dictate! She goes out—that's safe—I inherit as next of kin, with no one to dispute it, and that's all there is to it!'

"I stood there and could not move. It was the voice of the man I knew as my uncle! My heart seemed to have stopped beating. I tried to tell myself that I was dreaming, that it was too horrible, too incredible to be real; that they could not really mean to—to *murder* me. And then I recognised Hilton Travers' voice.

"'I am not dictating, and you are not serious, of course,' he said, with what seemed an uneasy laugh. 'I am only warning you that you are forgetting to take the real Henry LaSalle into account. He is bound to hear of this eventually, and then—'

"Another voice broke in—one I did not recognise.

"'You're talking too loud, both of you! Travers doesn't understand, but he's to be wised up tonight, according to orders, and—'

"The voice became inaudible, muffled—I could not hear any more. I suppose I remained there another three or four minutes, too stunned to know what to do; and then I ran softly along the hall to the library door. The library, you understand, was at the rear of the room they were in, and the two rooms were really one; that is, there was only an archway between them. I cannot tell you what my emotions were—I do not know. I only know that I kept repeating to myself, 'they are going to kill me, they are going to kill me!' and that it seemed I must try and find out everything, everything I could."

She turned away from the table, and began to pace nervously up and down the miserable room.

Jimmie Dale rose impulsively from his chair—but she waved him back again.

"No; wait!" she said. "Let me finish. I crept into the library. It took me a long time, because I had to be so careful not to make the slightest noise. I suppose it was fully six or seven minutes from the time I had first heard my supposed uncle's voice until I had crept far enough forward to be able to see into the room beyond. There were three men there. The man I knew as my uncle was sitting at one end of the table; another had his back toward me; and Travers was facing in my direction—and I think I never saw so ghastly a face as was Hilton Travers' then. He was standing up, sort of swaying, as he leaned with both hands on the table.

"'Now then, Travers,' the man whose back was turned to me was saying threateningly, 'you've got the story now—sign those papers!'

"It seemed as though Travers could not speak for a moment. He kept looking wildly from one to the other. He was white to the lips.

"'You've let me in for—*this*!' he said hoarsely, at last, 'You devils—you devils—you devils! You've let me in for—murder! Both of them! Both Peter and his brother—*murdered*!'"

She stopped abruptly before Jimmie Dale, and clutched his arm tightly.

"Jimmie, I don't know why I did not scream out. Everything went black for a moment before my eyes. It was the first suspicion I had had that my father had met with foul play, and I—"

But now Jimmie Dale swayed up from his chair.

"Murdered!" he exclaimed tensely. "Your father! But—but I remember perfectly, there was no hint of any such thing at the time, and never has been since. He died from quite natural causes."

She looked at him strangely.

"He died from—inoculation," she said. "Did—did you not see something of that laboratory in the Crime Club yourself the night before last—enough to understand?"

"Good God!" muttered Jimmie Dale, in a startled way then: "Go on! Go on! What happened then?"

She passed her hand a little wearily across her eyes—and sank down into her chair again.

"Travers," she continued, picking up the thread of her story, "had raised his voice, and the third man at the table leaned suddenly, aggressively toward him.

"'Hold your tongue!' he growled furiously. 'All you're asked to do is sign the papers—not talk!'

"Travers shook his head.

"'I won't!' he cried out. 'I won't have any hand in another murder—in hers! My God, I won't—I won't, I tell you! It's horrible!'

"'Look here, you fool!' the man who was posing as my uncle broke in then. 'You're in this too deep to get out now. If you know what's good for you, you'll do as you're told!'

"Jimmie, I shall never forget Travers' face. It seemed to have changed from white to gray, and there was horror in his eyes: and then he seemed to lose all control of himself, shaking his fists in their faces, cursing them in utter abandon.

"'I'm bad!' he cried. 'I've gone everything, everything but the limit—everything but murder. I stop there! I'll have no more to do with this. I'm through! You—you pulled me into this, and—and I didn't know!'

"'Well, you know now!' the third man sneered. 'What are you going to do about it?'

"'I'm going to see that no harm comes to Marie LaSalle,' Travers answered in a dull way.

"The other man now was on his feet—and, I do not know quite how to express it, Jimmie, he seemed ominously quiet in both his voice and his movements.

"'You'd better think that over again, Travers!' he said. 'Do you mean it?'

"'I mean it,' Travers said. 'I mean it—God help me!'

"'You may well add that!' returned the other, with an ugly laugh. He reached out his hand toward the telephone on the table. 'Do you know what will happen to you if I telephone a certain number and say that you have turned—traitor?'

"'I'll have to take my chances,' Travers replied doggedly. 'I'm through!'

"'Take them, then!' flung out the other. 'You'll have little time given you to do us any harm!'

"Travers did not answer. I think he almost expected an attack upon him then from the two men. He hesitated a moment, then backed slowly toward the door. What happened in the next few moments in that room, I do not know. I stole out of the library. I was obsessed with the thought that I must see Travers, see him at all costs, before he got away from the house. I reached the end of the hall as the room door opened, and he came out. It was dark, as I said, and I could not see distinctly, but I could make out his form. He closed the door behind him—and then I called his name in a whisper. He took a quick step toward me, then turned and hurried toward the front door, and I thought he was going away—but the next instant I understood his ruse. He opened the front door, shut it again quite loudly, and crept back to me.

"'Take me somewhere where we will be safe—quick!' he whispered.

"There was only one place where I was sure we would be safe. I led him to the rear of the house and up the servants' stairs, and to my boudoir."

She broke off abruptly, and once more rose from her chair, and once more began to pace the room. Back in his chair, Jimmie Dale, tense and motionless now, watched her without a word.

"It would take too long to tell you all that passed between us," she went on hurriedly. "The man was frankly a criminal—but not to the extent of murder. And in that respect, at least, he was honest with himself. Almost the first words he said to me were: 'Miss LaSalle, I am as good as a dead man if I am caught by the devils behind those two men downstairs.' And then he began to plead with me to make my own escape. He did not know who the man was that was posing as my uncle, had never seen him before until he presented himself as Henry LaSalle; the other man he knew as Clarke, but knew also that 'Clarke' was merely an assumed name. He had fallen in with Clarke almost from the time that he had begun to practise his profession, and at Clarke's instigation had gone from one crooked deal to another, and had made a great deal of money. He knew that behind Clarke was a powerful, daring, and unscrupulous band of criminals, organised on a gigantic scale, of which he himself was, in a sense—a probationary sense, as he put it—a member; but he had never come into direct contact with them—he had received all his orders and instructions through Clarke. He had been told by Clarke that he was to cultivate father following the introduction, to win father's confidence, to get as many of father's affairs into his hands as possible, to reach the position, in fact, of becoming father's recognised attorney—and all this with the object, as he supposed of embezzling from father on a large scale. Then father died, and Travers was instructed to cable my uncle. He knew that the man who answered that summons was an impostor; but he did not know, until they had admitted it to him that night, that both my father and my uncle had been murdered, and that I, too, was to be made away with."

She looked at Jimmie Dale, and suddenly laughed out bitterly.

"No; you don't understand, even yet, the patient, ingenious deviltry of those fiends. It was they, at the time the new will was drawn, who offered to buy out my real uncle's sheep ranch in that lonely, unsettled district in Australia, and offered him that new position in New Zealand. My uncle never reached New Zealand. He was murdered on his way there. And in his place, assuming his name, appeared the man who has been posing as my uncle ever since. Do you begin to see! For five years they were patiently working out their plans, for five years before my father's death that man lived and became known and accepted, and *established* himself as Henry LaSalle. Do you see now why he cabled us to postpone our visit? He ran very little risk. The chances were one in a thousand that any of his few acquaintances in Australia would ever run across him in New Zealand; and besides, he was chosen because it seems there was a slight resemblance between him and the real Henry LaSalle—enough, with his changed mode of living and more elaborate and pretentious surroundings, to have enabled him to carry through a bluff had it become necessary. He had all of my uncle's papers; and the Crime Club furnished him with every detail of our lives here. I forgot to say, too, that from the moment my uncle was supposed to have reached New Zealand all his letters were typewritten—an evidence in father's eyes that his brother had secured a position of some importance; as, indeed, from apparently unprejudiced sources, they took pains to assure father was a fact.

This left them with only my uncle's signature to forge to the letters—not a difficult matter for them!

"Believing that they had Travers so deeply implicated that he could do nothing, even if he had the inclination, which they had not for a moment imagined, and arrogant in the belief in their own power to put him out of the way in any case if he proved refractory, they admitted all this to him that night when he brought up the issue of the real Henry LaSalle putting in an appearance sooner or later, and when they wanted him to smooth their path by releasing all documents where his power of attorney was involved. Do you see now the part they gave Travers to play? It was to put the stamp of genuineness upon the false Henry LaSalle. Not but that they were prepared with what would appear to be overwhelmingly convincing evidence to prove it if it were necessary; but if the man were accepted by the estate's lawyer there was little chance of anyone else questioning his identity."

She halted again by the table—and forced a smile, as her eyes met Jimmie Dale's.

"I am almost through, Jimmie. That night was a terrible one for both of us. Travers' life was not worth a moment's purchase once they found him—and mine was only under reprieve until sufficient time to obviate suspicion should have elapsed after father's death. We had no proof that would stand in any court—even if we should have been given the chance to adopt that course. And without absolute, irrefutable proof, it was all so cleverly woven, stretched over so many years, that our charge must have been held to be too visionary and fantastic to have any basis in fact.

"All Travers would have been able to advance was the statement that the supposed Henry LaSalle had admitted being an impostor and a murderer to him! Who would believe it! On the face of it, it appeared to be an absurdity. And even granted that we were given an opportunity to bring the charge, they would be able to prove by a hundred influential and well-known men in New Zealand that the impostor was really Henry LaSalle; and were we able to find any of my uncle's old acquaintances in Australia, it would be necessary to get them here—and not one of them would have reached America alive.

"But there was not a chance, not a chance, Jimmie, of doing that—they would have killed Travers the moment he showed himself in the open. The only thing we could do that night was to try and save our own lives; the only thing we could look forward to was acquiring in some way, unknown to them, the proof, fully established, with which we could crush them in a single stroke, and before they would have time to strike back.

"The vital thing was proof of my uncle's death. That, if it could be obtained at all, could only be obtained in Australia. Travers was obliged to go somewhere, to disappear from that moment if he wanted to save his life, and he volunteered to go out there. He left the house that night by the back entrance in an old servant's suit, which I found for him—and I never heard from him again until a month ago in the 'personal' column of the *Morning News-Argus*, through which we had agreed to communicate.

"As for myself, I left the house the next morning, telling my pseudo uncle that I was going to spend a few days with a friend. And this I actually did; but in those few days I managed to turn all my own securities, that had been left me by my mother and which amounted to a considerable sum, into cash. And then, Jimmie, I came to—this, I have lived like this and in different disguises, as a settlement worker, as a widow of means in a fashionable uptown apartment, but mostly as you see me now—for five years. For five years I have watched my supposed uncle, hoping, praying that through him I could get to know the others associated with him; hoping, praying that Travers would succeed; hoping, praying that we would get them all—and watching day after day, and year after year the 'personal' column of the paper, until at last I began to be afraid that it was all useless. And there was nothing, Jimmie, nothing anywhere, and I had no success"—her voice choked a little. "Nothing! Even Clarke never went again to the house. You can understand now how I came to know the strange things that I wrote to the Gray Seal, how the life that I have led, how this life here in the underworld, how the constant search for some clue on my own account brought them to my knowledge; and you can understand now, too, why I never dared to let you meet me, for I knew well enough that, while I worked to undermine my father's and my uncle's murderers, they were moving heaven and earth to find me.

"That is all, Jimmie. The day before yesterday, a month after Travers' first message to let me know that he was coming, there was another 'personal' giving me an hour and a telephone number. He was back! He had everything—everything! We dared not meet; he was afraid, suspicious that they had got track of him again. You know the rest. That package contained the proof that, with Travers' death, can probably never be obtained again. Do you understand why *they* want it—why it is life and death to me? Do you understand why my supposed uncle offered huge rewards for me, why secretly every resource of that hideous organisation has been employed to find me—that it is only by my *death* the estate can pass into their hands, and now—"

She flung out her hands suddenly toward Jimmie Dale. "Oh, Jimmie, Jimmie, I've—I've fought so long alone! Jimmie, what are we to do?"

He came slowly to his feet. She had fought so long—alone. But now—now it was his turn to fight—for her. But how? She had not told him all—surely she had not told him all, for everything depended upon that package. There had been so much to tell that she had not thought of all, and she had not told him the details about that.

"That box—No. 428!" he cried quickly. "What is that? What does it mean?"

She shook her head.

"I do not know," she answered.

"Then who is this John Johansson?"

"I do not know," she said again.

"Nor where the Crime Club is?"

"No"—dully.

He stared at her for a moment in a dazed way.

"My God!" Jimmie Dale murmured.

And then she turned away her head.

"It's—it's pretty bad, isn't it, Jimmie? I—I told you that we did not hold many trumps."

CHAPTER 10

SILVER MAG

There was silence between them. Minute after minute passed. Neither spoke.

Jimmie Dale dropped back into his chair again, and stared abstractedly before him. "We do not hold many trumps, Jimmie—we do not hold many trumps"—her words were repeating themselves over and over in his mind. They seemed to challenge him mockingly to deny what was so obviously a fact, and because he could not deny it to taunt and jeer at him—to jeer at him, when all that was held at stake hung literally upon his next move!

He looked up mechanically as the Tocsin walked to a broken mirror at the rear of the miserable room; nodded mechanically in approval as she began deftly to retouch the make-up on her face where the tears had left their traces—and resumed his abstracted gaze before him.

Box number four-two-eight—John Johansson—the Crime Club—the identity of the man who was posing as Henry LaSalle! If only he could hit upon a clue to the solution of a single one of those things, or a single phase of one of them—if only he could glimpse a ray of light that would at least prompt action, when every moment of inaction was multiplying the odds against them!

There were the men who were watching his house at that moment on Riverside Drive—he, as Larry the Bat, might in turn keep watch on them. He had though of that. In time, perhaps, he might, by so doing, discover the whereabouts of the Crime Club. In time! It was just that—he had no time! Forty-eight hours, the Tocsin insisted, was all the time that he could count upon before they would become suspicious of Jimmie Dale's "illness," before they would discover that they were watching an empty house!

He might—though this was even more hazardous—make an attempt to trace the wires that tapped those of his telephone through the basement window that gave on the garage driveway. And what then? True, they could not lead very far away; but, even if successful, what then? They would not lead him to the Crime Club, but simply to some confederate, to some man or woman playing the part of a servant, perhaps, in the house next door, who, in turn, would have to be shadowed and watched.

Jimmie Dale shook his head. Better, of the two, to start in at once and shadow those who were shadowing his house. But that was not the way! He knew that intuitively. He hated to eliminate it from consideration, for he had no other move to take its place—but such a move was almost suicide in itself. Time, and time alone, was the vital factor. They, the Tocsin and he, must act quickly—and strike that night if they were to win. His fingers, the grimy fingers, dirty-nailed, of Larry the Bat, that none now would recognise as the slim tapering, wonderfully sensitive fingers of Jimmie Dale, the fingers that had made the name of the Gray Seal famous, whose tips mocked at bars and safes and locks, and seemed to embody in themselves all the human senses, tightened spasmodically on the edge of the table. Time! Time! Time! It seemed to din in his ears. And while he sat there powerless, impotent, the Crime Club was moving heaven and earth to find what *he* must find—that package—if he was to save this woman here, the woman whom he loved, she who had been forced, through the machinations of these hell fiends, to adopt the life of a wretched hag, to exist among the dregs of the underworld, whose squalour and vice and wantonness none knew better than he!

Jimmie Dale's face set grimly. Somewhere—somewhere in the past five years of this life of hers in which she had been fighting the Crime Club, pitting that clever brain of hers against it, *must* lie a clue. She had told him her story only in baldest outline, with scarcely a reference to her own personal acts, with barely a single detail. There must be something, something that perhaps she had overlooked, something, just the merest hint of something that would supply a starting point, give him a glimmer of light.

She came back from across the room, and sank down in her chair again. She did not speak—the question, that meant life and death to them both, was in her eyes.

Jimmie answered the mute interrogation tersely.

"Not yet!" he said. Then, almost curtly, in a quick, incisive way, as the keen, alert brain began to delve and probe: "You say this man Clarke never returned to the house after that night?"

She nodded her head quietly.

"You are sure of that?" he insisted.

"Yes," she said. "I am sure."

"And you say that all these years you have kept a watch on the man who is posing as your uncle, and that he never went anywhere, or associated with anyone, that would afford you a clue to this Crime Club?"

"Yes," she said again.

It was a moment before Jimmie Dale spoke.

"It's very strange!" he said musingly, at last. "So strange, in fact, that it's impossible. He must have communicated with the others, and communicated with them often. The game they were playing was too big, too full of details, to admit of any other possibility. And the telephone as an explanation isn't good enough."

"And yet," she said earnestly, "possible or impossible, it is nevertheless true. That he might have succeeded in eluding me on occasions was perhaps to be expected; but that in all those years I should not catch him once in what, if you are correct, must have been many and repeated conferences with the same men is too improbable to be thought of seriously."

Jimmie Dale shook his head again.

"If you had been able to watch him night and day, that might be so," he said crisply. "But, at best, you could only watch him a very small portion of the time."

She smiled at him a little wanly.

"Do you think, Jimmie, from what you, as the Gray Seal, know of me, that I would have watched in any haphazard way like that?"

He glanced at her with a sudden start.

"What do you mean?" he asked quickly.

"Look at me!" she said quietly. "Have you ever seen me before? I mean as I am now."

"No," he answered, after an instant. "Not that I know of."

"And yet"—she smiled wanly again—"you have not lived, or made the place you hold in the underworld, without having heard of Silver Mag."

"You!" exclaimed Jimmie Dale. "You—Silver Mag!" He stared at her wonderingly, as, crouch-shouldered now, the hair, gray-threaded, straggling out from under the hood of a faded, dark-blue, seam-worn cloak, she sat before him, a typical creature of the underworld, her role an art in its conception, perfect in its execution. Silver Mag! Yes, he had heard of Silver Mag—as every one in the Bad Lands had heard of her. Silver Mag and her pocketful of coin! Always a pocketful of silver, so they said, that was dispensed prodigally to the wives and children temporarily deprived of support by husbands and fathers unfortunate enough in their clashes with the law to be doing "spaces" up the river—and therefore the underworld swore by Silver Mag. Always silver, never a bill; Silver Mag had never been seen with a banknote—that was her eccentricity. Much or little, she gave or paid out of her pocketful of jangling silver. She was credited with being a sworn enemy of the police, and—yes, he remembered, too—with having done "time" herself. "I don't quite understand," he said, in a puzzled way. "I haven't run across you personally because you probably took care to see that I shouldn't; but—it's no secret—every one says you've served a jail sentence yourself."

"That is simply enough explained," she answered gravely. "The story is of my own making. When I decided to adopt this life, both for my own safety and as the best means of keeping a watch on that man, I knew that I must win the confidence of the underworld, that I must have help, and that in order to obtain that help I must have some excuse for my enmity against the man known as Henry LaSalle. To be widely known in the underworld was of inestimable value—nothing, I knew, could accomplish that as quickly as eccentricity. You see now how and why I became known as Silver Mag. I gained the confidence of every crook in New York through their wives and children. I told them the story of my jail sentence—while I swore vengeance on Henry LaSalle. I told them that he had had me arrested for something I never stole while I was working for him as a charwoman, and that he had had me railroaded to jail. There wasn't one but gave me credit for the theft, perhaps; but equally, there wasn't one but understood, and my eccentricity helped this out, my wanting to 'get' Henry LaSalle. Well—do you see now, Jimmie? I had money, I had the confidence of the underworld, I had an excuse for my hatred of Henry LaSalle, and so I had all the help I wanted. Day and night that man has been watched. He receives no visitors—what social life he has is, as you know, at the club. There is not a house that he has ever entered that, sooner or later, I have not entered after him in the hope of finding the headquarters of the clique. Even the men and women, as far as human possibility could accomplish it, that he has talked to on the streets have been shadowed, and their identity satisfactorily established—and the net result has been failure; utter, absolute, complete failure!"

Jimmie Dale's eyes, that had held steadily on her face, shifted, troubled and perplexed, to the table top.

"You are wonderful!" he said, under his breath. "Wonderful! And—and that makes it all the more amazing, all the more incomprehensible. It is still impossible that he has not been in close and constant touch with his accomplices. He *must* have been! We would be blind fools to argue against it! It could not, on the face of it, have been otherwise!"

"Then how, when, where has he done it?" she asked wearily.

"God knows!" he said bitterly. "And if they have been clever enough to escape you all these years, I'm almost inclined to say what you said a little while ago—that we're beaten."

She watched him miserably, as he pushed back his chair impulsively and, standing up, stared down at her.

"We're against it—*hard*!" he said, with a mirthless laugh. Then, his lips tightening: "But we'll try another tack—the chauffeur—Travers. Though even here the Crime Club has a day's start of us, even if last night they knew no more about the whereabouts of that package than we know now. I'm afraid of it! The chances are more than even that they've already got it. If they were able to catch Travers as the chauffeur, they would have had something tangible to work back from"—Jimmie Dale was talking more to himself than to the Tocsin now, as though he were muttering his thoughts aloud. "How did they get track of him? When? Where? What has it led to?

And what in Heaven's name," he burst out suddenly, "is this box number four-two-eight!"

"A safety-deposit vault, perhaps, that he has taken somewhere," she hazarded.

Jimmie Dale laughed mirthlessly again.

"That is the one definite thing I do know—that it isn't!" he said positively. "It is nothing of that kind. It was half-past ten o'clock at night when I met him, and he said that he had intended going back for the package if it had been safe to do so. Deposit vaults are not open at that hour. The package is, or was, if they have not already got it, readily accessible—and at any hour. Now go over everything again, every detail that passed between you and Travers. He let you know that he was back in New York by means of a 'personal,' you said. What else was in that 'personal' besides the telephone number and the hour you were to call him? Anything?"

"Nothing that will help us any," she replied colourlessly. "There were simply the words 'northeast corner of Sixth Avenue and Waverly Place,' and the signature that we had agreed upon, the two first and two last letters of the alphabet transposed—B-A-Z-Y."

"I see," said Jimmie Dale quickly. "And over the phone he completed his message. Clever enough!"

"Yes," she said. "In that way, if anyone were listening, or overhead the plan, there could be little harm come of it, for the essential feature of all, the place of rendezvous, was not mentioned. It has not been Travers' fault that this happened—and in spite of every precaution it has cost him his life. He wanted nothing to give them a clue to my whereabouts; he was trying to guard against the slightest evidence that would associate us one with the other. He even warned me over the phone not to tell him how, where, or the mode of life I was living. And naturally, he dared give me no particulars about himself. I was simply to select a third party whom I could trust, and to follow out his instructions, which were those that I sent to you in my letter."

Jimmie Dale began to pace nervously up and down the room.

"Nothing else?" he queried, a little blankly.

"Nothing else," she said monotonously.

"But since last night, since you knew that things had gone wrong," he persisted, "surely you traced that telephone number—the one you called up?"

"Yes," she said, and shrugged her shoulders in a tired way. "Naturally I did that—but, like everything else, it amounted to nothing. He telephoned from Makoff's pawnshop on that alley off Thompson Street, and—"

"*Where!*" Jimmie Dale, suddenly stock-still, almost shouted the word. "He telephoned from—where! Say that again!"

She looked at him in amazement, half rising from her chair.

"Jimmie, what is it?" she cried. "You don't mean that—"

He was beside her now, his hands pressed upon her shoulders, his face flushed.

"Box number four-two-eight!" He laughed out hysterically in his excitement. "John Johansson—box number four-two-eight! And like a fool I never thought of it! Don't you see? Don't you know now yourself? *The underground post office!"*

She stood up, clinging to him; a wild relief, that was based on her confidence in him, in her eyes and face, even while she shook her head.

"No," she said frantically. "No—I do not know. Tell me, Jimmie! Tell me quickly! You mean at Makoff's?"

"No! Not Makoff's—at Spider Jack's, on Thompson Street!"—he was clipping off his words, still holding her tightly by the shoulders, still staring into her eyes. "You know Spider Jack! Jack's little novelty store! Ah, you have not learned all of the underworld yet! Spider Jack is the craftiest 'fence' in the Bad Lands—and Makoff is his partner. Spider buys the crooks' stuff, and Makoff disposes of it through the pawnshop—it's only a step through the connecting back yard from one to the other, and—"

"Yes—but," she interrupted feverishly, "the package—you said—"

"Wait!" Jimmie Dale cried. "I'm coming to that! If Travers stood in with Makoff, he stood in with Spider Jack. For years Spider has been a sort of clearing house for the underworld—for years he has conducted, and profitably, too, his underground post office. Crooks from all over the country, let alone those in New York, communicate with each other through Spider Jack. These, for a fee, are registered at Spider's, and given a number—a box number he calls it, though, of course, there are no actual boxes. Letters come by mail addressed to him—the sealed envelope within containing the actually intended recipient's name. These Spider either forwards, or delivers in person when they are called for. Dozens of crooks, too, unwilling, perhaps, to dispose of small ill-gotten articles at ruinous 'fence' prices, and finding it unhealthy for the moment to keep them in their possession, use this means of depositing them temporarily for safe-keeping. You see now, don't you? It's certain that's where Travers left the package. He used the name of John Johansson, not to hoodwink Spider Jack, I should say, but as an added safeguard against the Crime Club. Travers must have known both Makoff and Spider Jack in the old days, and probably had reason, and good reason, to trust them both—possibly, a crook then himself, as he confessed, he may have acted in a legal capacity for them in their frequent tangles with the police."

"Then," she said—and there was a glad, new note in her voice, "then, Jimmie—Jimmie, we are safe! You can get it, Jimmie! It is only a little thing for the Gray Seal to do—to get it now that we know where it is."

"Yes," he said tersely. "Yes—if it is still there."

"Still there!"—she repeated the words quickly, nervously. "Still there! What do you mean?"

"I mean if they, too, have not discovered that he was at Makoff's—if they have not got there first!" he said grimly. "There seems to be no limit to their cleverness, or their power. They penetrated his disguise as a chauffeur, and who knows what more they have learned since last night? We are fighting them in the dark, and—*what's that*!" he whispered tensely, suddenly—and leaning forward like a flash, as he whipped his automatic from his pocket, he blew out the lamp.

The room was in darkness. They stood there rigid, silent, listening. Her hand found and caught his arm.

And then it came again—a low sound, the sound of a stealthy footstep just outside the window that faced on the storage yard.

CHAPTER 11

THE MAGPIE

A minute passed—another. The automatic at Jimmie Dale's hip, the muzzle just peeping over the table top, held a steady bead on the window. Came the footstep again—and then suddenly, a series of low, quick tappings upon the windowpane. The Tocsin's hand slipped away from his arm. Jimmie Dale's set face relaxed as he read the underground Morse, and he replaced his revolver slowly in his pocket.

"The Magpie!" said Jimmie Dale, in an undertone. "What's he want?"

"I don't know," she answered, in a whisper. "He never came here before. There's a back way out, Jimmie, if you—"

"No," he said quickly. "We've enemies enough, with out making one of the Magpie. He knows someone is here with you—our shadows were on the blind. Don't queer yourself. Let him in. I'll light the lamp."

He struck a match, as she ran from the room, and, lifting the hot lamp chimney with the edge of his ragged coat, lighted the lamp. He turned the wick down a little, shading and dimming the room—and then, as he flirted a bead of moisture from his forehead, whimsically stretched out his hand to watch it in the lamplight.

"That's bad, Jimmie," he muttered gravely to himself, as he noted an almost imperceptible tremour. "Got a start, didn't you! Under a bit of a strain, eh? Well"—grimly—"never mind! It looks as though the luck had turned Makoff and Spider Jack!"

His hand reached up to his hat, jerked the brim at a rakish angle over his eyes—and he sprawled himself out on a chair. He heard the Tocsin's voice at the front door, and a man's voice, low and guarded, answer her. Then the door closed, and their steps approached the room. It was rather curious, that—a visit from the Magpie! What could the Magpie want? What could there be in common between the Magpie and Silver Mag? The Magpie, alias Slimmy Joe, was counted the cleverest safe worker in the United States, barring only and always one—a smile flickered across the lips of Larry the Bat—one whose pre-eminence the Magpie, much to his own chagrin, admitted himself—the Gray Seal!

He looked up, twisting the stub of a cigarette between his grimy fingers and fumbling for a match, as the Tocsin and, behind her, the Magpie, short, slim, and wiry, shrewd-faced, with sharp, quick-glancing little black eyes, entered the room.

"'Ello, Larry!" grinned the Magpie. "Got yer breath back yet? I felt it through de windowpane when youse let go at de lamp!"

"'Ello, Slimmy!" returned Jimmie Dale ungraciously, speaking through the corner of his mouth. "Ferget it!"

"Sure!" said the Magpie unconcernedly. He stared about him, and finally, drawing a chair up to the table, sat down, motioned the Tocsin to do the same, and leaned forward amiably. "I didn't mean to throw no scare into youse," he said, in a conciliating tone. "But I had a little business wid Mag, an' I was kind of interested in whether she was entertainin' company or not—see? I didn't know youse an' Mag was workin' together."

"Mabbe," observed Jimmie Dale, as ungraciously as before, "mabbe dere's some more t'ings youse don't know!"

"Aw, cough up de grouch!" advised the Magpie, with a hint of impatience creeping into his voice. "Youse don't need to be sore all night! I told youse I wasn't tryin' to hand youse one, didn't I?"

"Never mind Larry, Slimmy," put in the Tocsin petulantly. "He's down on his luck, dat's all. He ain't had de price of a pinch of coke fer two days."

"Oho!" exclaimed the Magpie, grinning again. "So dat's wot's givin' youse de pip, eh, Larry? Well, den, say, youse can take it from me dat mabbe youse'll be glad I blew around. I was lookin' fer a guy about yer size fer a little job tonight, an' I was t'inkin' of lettin' Young Dutchy in on it, but seem' youse are here an' in wid Mag, an' dat I got to get Mag in, too, youse are on if youse say de word."

"Wot's de lay?" inquired Larry the Bat, unbending a little.

The Magpie cocked his eye, and stuck his tongue in his cheek.

"GOOD-night!" he said tersely. "Nothin' like dat! Are youse on, or ain't youse?"

"Well, den, wot's in it fer me?" persisted Larrry the Bat.

"More'n de price of a coke sneeze!" returned the Magpie pertinently. "Dere's a century note fer youse, an' mabbe two or t'ree of dem fer Mag."

Larry the Bat's eyes gleamed avariciously.

"Aw, quit yer kiddin'!" he said gruffly. "A century note—fer me!"

"Dat's wot I said! Youse heard me!" rejoined the Magpie shortly. "Only if it listens good to youse now, I don't want no squealin' after the divvy. I'm takin' de chances, youse has de soft end of it. One century note fer youse—an' de rest is none of yer business! Dat's puttin' it straight, ain't it? Well, wot do youse say, an' say it quick—'cause if youse ain't comin' in, youse can beat it out of here so's I can talk to Mag."

"Dere ain't nothin' I wouldn't take a chance on fer a hundred plunks!" declared Larry the Bat, with sudden fervency—and stared, anxiously expectant, at the Magpie. "Sure, I'm on Slimmy! Sure, I am! Cut it loose! Spill de story!"

"Well, den," said the Magpie, "I wants—"

"Youse ain't through yet!" interrupted the Tocsin tartly. "I ain't heard youse askin' me nothin'! I ain't on me uppers like Larry, an' mabbe de price don't cut so much ice—see?"

"Aw," said the Magpie, with a smirk, "I don't have to ask youse on dis lay. Dis is where youse'd come in on it fer marbles. Say, dis is where we gets de hook into a guy by de name of Henry LaSalle! Get me?"

Henry Lasalle! Under the table, Jimmie Dale's hand clenched suddenly; but not a muscle of his face moved, save, as with the tip of his tongue, he shifted the butt of the cigarette that was hanging royally from his lower lip to the other corner of his mouth.

"Sure! She's 'got' youse, Slimmy!" he flung out, with a grin, as the Tocsin wrinkled up her face menacingly and began to mumble to herself. "He's de guy dat handed her one when she was young, an' she's been layin' fer him ever since! Sure! I know! Ain't I worked him fer her till I wears me shoes out tryin' to get somet'ing on him! Sure, she's in on it! Go on, Slimmy, wot's de lay? Wot do I do fer dat century?"

The Magpie hitched his chair closer to the table and, as his sharp, little, ferret eyes glanced around the room, motioned the two to brings their heads nearer.

"One of me influential broker friends down on Wall Street put me wise," he said, with a wink. "Dat's good enough fer youse two, as far as dat goes. But take it from me, I got it dead straight." He lowered his voice "Say, he's one of de richest mugs in New York, ain't he? Well, he's been sellin' stocks an' bonds all day, t'ousands an' t'ousands of dollars' worth—fer cash."

"All dem t'ings is always sold fer cash," remarked Larry the Bat fatuously.

"Aw, ferget it!" said the Magpie earnestly. "Fer *cash*, I said—de coin, de long green—understand? He wasn't shovin' no checks fer what he sold into de bank except to get dem cashed. Dat's wot he's been doin' all day—gettin' de checks cashed, an' gettin' de money in big bills—see! I know of one bunch of eighty t'ousand—an' dat's only one!"

"Wot fer?" inquired Larry the Bat. It was the question that was pounding at his brain, as he stared innocently at the Magpie. What did it mean? Why was Henry LaSalle turning, and, if the Magpie was right, feverishly turning every security he could lay his hands on into cash? And then, in a flash, the answer came. *They had not found the package!* Equally to them, as to the Tocsin, sitting there before him, it meant life and death. If the package were found by the Tocsin instead of themselves, the game was up! They were preparing for eventualities. If they were forced to run at a moment's notice, they at least were not going to run empty-handed! Far from empty-handed, it seemed! It would not be difficult for the estate's executor to realise a vast sum in short order on instantly marketable, gilt-edged securities—say, half a million dollars. Not very bulky, either—in large bills! Five thousand hundred-dollar bills would make half a million. It was astonishing how small a hand bag, say, might hold a fortune! "Wot fer, Slimmy?" he inquired again, wiggling his cigarette butt on his tongue tip. "Wot'd he do dat fer?"

"How de hell do youse suppose I knows!" demanded the Magpie, politely scornful. "Dat's his business—dat ain't wot's worryin' me!"

"No—sure, it ain't!" admitted Larry the Bat ingratiatingly. "But go on, keep movin', Slimmy! Wot's he done wid de stuff?"

"Done wid it!" echoed the Magpie, with a short laugh. "Wot do youse t'ink! He's been luggin' it home to his swell joint up dere on de avenoo, an' crammin' his safe full of it."

Larry the Bat sucked in his breath.

"Gee, dat's soft!" he murmured, and then suddenly, as though with painful inspiration: "Say, Slimmy—say, are youse sure youse ain't been handed a steer?"

The Magpie grinned wickedly.

"I ain't fallin' fer steers!" he said shortly. "Dis is on de level."

Jimmie Dale lurched up from his chair, and, leaning over the lamp chimney, drew wheezily on his cigarette to get a light. His eyes sought the Tocsin's face. To all intents and purposes she was entirely absorbed in the Magpie. He sat down again to gape, with well-stimulated, doglike admiration, at Slimmy Joe. *Was this, too, a plant?* Why had the Magpie come to *them* with this story of Henry LaSalle? And then, the next instant, as the Magpie spoke, his suspicions were allayed.

"Let's get down to cases!" the Magpie invited crisply. "I didn't blow in here just by luck. Dis Henry LaSalle is de guy youse worked fer once, ain't he, Mag? Dat's de spiel, ain't it?—he sent youse up fer pinchin' de tacks out of his carpets!"

"I never pinched nothin'!" snarled Silver Mag truculently. "He's a dirty liar! I never did!"

"Cut it out! Cut it out! Can dat!" complained the Magpie patiently. "De point is, youse worked in his house, didn't youse?"

"Sure I did!" snapped the Tocsin, sullenly aggressive; "but—"

"Well, den, dat's wot I want, dat's wot I come fer, Mag—a plan of de house. See?"

Jimmie Dale could feel the Tocsin's eyes upon him, questioning, searching, seeking a cue. A plan of the house—yes or no? And a decision on the instant!

"Sure!" said Larry the Bat brightly. "Dat's wot I was t'inkin' youse were after all de time. Say, youse are all right, Slimmy! Youse are de kind to work wid! Go on, Mag, draw de dope fer Slimmy. Dat's better dan tryin' to put one over on de swell guy. Dis'll make him squeal fer fair!"

The Magpie produced a pencil and a piece of paper from his pocket, and laid them on the table in front of the Tocsin.

"Dere youse are," he announced. "Help yerself, an' go to it, Mag!"

The Tocsin, evidently not quite certain of her part, wet the pencil doubtfully on the end of her tongue.

"I ain't never drawed plans," she said anxiously. "Mabbe"—she glanced at Jimmie Dale—"mabbe I dunno how to do it right."

"Aw, go ahead!" nodded Larry the Bat. "Youse can do it right, Mag. Youse don't have to make no oil paintin'! All de Magpie wants is de doors an' windows, eh, Slimmy?"

"Sure," agreed the Magpie encouragingly. "Dat's all, Mag. Just mark de rooms out on de first floor, an' de basement. Youse can explain wot youse 're doin' as youse goes along. I'll get youse."

The Tocsin cackled maliciously in assent; and then, while the Magpie got up from his chair and stood peering over her shoulder, she began to draw labouriously, her brows knitted, the pencil hooked awkwardly between cramped-up forefinger and thumb.

Larry the Bat, slouched forward over the table, his chin in his hands, appeared to watch the proceedings with mild interest—but his eyes, like a hawk's, were following every line on the paper, transferring them to his brain, photographing every detail of the plan in his mind. And as he watched, there seemed something that was near to the acme of all that was ironical in the Magpie standing there, his sharp, little, black eyes drinking in greedily the Tocsin's work, in the Tocsin herself aiding and abetting in the projected theft—of *her own money!* How far would he let the Magpie go? He did not know. Perhaps—who could tell!—all the way. Between now and then there lay that package! If it were at Makoff's, at Spider Jack's, if he could find it, get it—the Magpie as a temporary custodian of the estate's money would at least preclude its loss by flight if the Crime Club took alarm too quickly. Larry the Bat's eyes, under half-closed lids, rested musingly on the Magpie's face. The Magpie would not get very far away with it! On the other hand, if he failed at Spider Jack's, if, after all, he was wrong, and the package had never been there, or if they had forestalled him, turned the trick upon him, already secured it, then—Larry the Bat's lips, working on his cigarette, formed in a twisted smile—then, well then, that was quite another matter! Perhaps he and the Magpie might not agree so far! A half million dollars was perhaps not much out of eleven millions, but it was a salvage not to be despised! Why did he say half a million! Well, why not? If the Magpie knew of a single transaction of eighty thousand, and there had been many transactions during the day, a half million was little likely to prove an exaggeration—and the less likely in view of the fact that, if those in the Crime Club were preparing for an emergency, they would not stint themselves in the disposal of securities.

The Magpie was keeping up a running fire of questions, as the Tocsin toiled on with her pencil. Where did the hall lead to? How many windows in the library? Did she remember the kind of fastenings? Did the servants sleep in the basement, or above? And finally, twice over, as she finished the clumsy drawing and pushed it toward him, he demanded minute details of the position of the safe.

"Aw, dat's all right, Slimmy!" Larry the Bat cut in airily. "If youse ferget anyt'ing when youse get in dere, youse can ask me. I got it cinched!"

The Magpie folded the paper and stowed it carefully away in his pocket.

"Ask youse, eh!" he grunted sarcastically. "An' where do youse t'ink youse'll be about dat time?"

"In dere wid youse, of course," replied Larry the Bat promptly. "Dat's wot youse said."

"Yes, youse will—*not*!" announced the Magpie, with cold finality. "Do youse t'ink I want to queer myself! A hot one youse'd be on an inside job! Youse'll be *outside*, wid yer peepers skinned for de bulls—youse an' Mag here, too. See! Get dat straight. While I'm on de job youse two plays de game. Now youse listen to me, both of youse. Don't start nothin' unless youse has to. If it's a cinch I got to make a get-away, youse two start a drunk fight. Get me? Youse know de lay. T'row de talk loud—an' I'll fade. Dat's all! We'll crack de crib early—it'll be quiet enough up dere by one o'clock."

One o'clock! Larry the Bat shook his head. What time was it now? It was about nine when he had first met the Tocsin, then the Sanctuary, then the long walk as he had followed her—say a quarter of ten for that. And he had certainly been here with her not less than an hour and a half. It must be after eleven, then. One o'clock! And before that must come Makoff and Spider Jack! The night that half an hour ago had seemed so sterile, was crowding a program of events upon him now—too fast!

"Nothin' doin'!" he said thoughtfully. "Youse are in wrong dere, Slimmy. One o'clock don't go! Say, take it from me, I've watched dat guy too many nights fer Mag. 'Tain't often he leaves de club before one o'clock—an' he ain't never in bed before two."

"All right," agreed the Magpie, after a moment's reflection. "Youse ought to know. Make it three o'clock." He pulled a cigar from his pocket, lighted it, and, leaning back in his chair, stuck his feet up on the table. "If youse don't mind, Mag, I'll stick around a while," he decided calmly. "Mabbe de less I'm seen tonight de better—an' I guess dere won't be nobody lookin' fer me here."

Larry the Bat coughed suddenly, and rose up a little heavily from his chair. He had not counted on that! If the Magpie was settling down for a prolonged stay, it devolved upon him, Jimmie Dale, to get away, and at once—and without exciting the Magpie's suspicions. He coughed again, looked nervously from the Tocsin to the Magpie—stammered—swallowed hard—and coughed once more.

"Well, wot's bitin' youse?" inquired the Magpie ironically.

"Nothin'," said Larry the Bat—and hesitated. "Nothin', only—" He hesitated again; and then, the words in a rush:

"Say, Slimmy, couldn't youse come across wid a piece of dat century now?"

"Wot fer?" demanded the Magpie, a little aggressively.

Larry the Bat cleared his throat with a desperate effort.

"Youse knows," he admitted sheepishly. "Just gimme de price of one, Slimmy—just one."

"Coke!" exploded the Magpie. "An' get soaked to de eyes—not by a damn sight!"

"No! Honest to Gawd, no, Slimmy—just one!" pleaded Larry the Bat.

"Nix!" said the Magpie shortly.

Larry the Bat thrust out a hand before the Magpie's eyes that shook tremulously.

"I got to have it!" he declared, with sudden fierceness. "I *got* to—see! Look at me! I ain't goin' to be no good tonight if I don't. I tell youse, I got to! I ain't goin' to t'row youse down, Slimmy—honest, I ain't! Just one—an' it'll set me up. If I don't get none I'll be on de rocks before mornin'! Dat's straight, Slimmy—ask Mag, she knows."

"Aw, let him go get it!" broke in the Tocsin wearily. "Dat's de best t'ing youse can do, Slimmy—dey're all alike when dey gets in his class."

"Youse cocaine sniffers gives me de pip!" snorted the Magpie, in disgust. He dug down into his pocket, produced a bill, and flung it across the table to Larry the Bat. "Well, dere youse are; but youse can take it from me, Larry, dat if youse gets whiffed"—he swore threateningly—"I'll crack every bone in yer face! Get me?"

"Slimmy," said Larry the Bat fervently, grabbing at the bill with a hungry hand, "youse can count on me. I'll be up dere on de job before youse are. Three o'clock, eh? Well, so long, Slimmy"—he slouched eagerly to the door. "So long, Mag"—he paused on the threshold for a single, quick-flung, significant glance. "See youse on de avenoo, Mag—I'll be up dere before youse are. So long!"

"Oh, so long!" said the Tocsin contemptuously.

And, an instant later, Jimmie Dale closed the outer door behind him.

CHAPTER 12
JOHN JOHANSSON—FOUR-TWO-EIGHT

Nearly midnight already! It was even later than he had thought. Larry the Bat pressed his face against a shop's windowpane on the Bowery for a glance at a clock that had caught his eye on the wall within. Nearly midnight!

He slouched on again hurriedly, still debating in his mind, as he had been debating it all the way from the Tocsin's, the question of returning again to the Sanctuary. So far, the way both to Spider Jack's and the Sanctuary had been in the same direction—but the Sanctuary was on the next street.

Jimmie Dale reached the corner—and hesitated. It was strange how strong was the intuition upon him tonight that bade him go on and make all speed to Spider Jack's—while equally strong was the cold, stubborn logic that bade him go first to the Sanctuary. There were things that he needed there that would probably be absolutely essential to him before the night was out, things without which he might be so badly handicapped as to invite failure from the start; and yet—it was already midnight!

Ostensibly both Makoff and Spider Jack closed their places at eleven. But that might mean anything—depending upon their own respective inclinations, or on what of their own peculiar brand of deviltry might be afoot. If they were still about, still in evidence, he was still too early, midnight though it was; though, on the other hand, if the coast was clear, he could ill afford to lose a moment of the time between now and the hour that the Magpie had planned for the robbery of Henry LaSalle, for it would not be an easy matter, even once inside Spider Jack's, to find that package—since it was Spider's open boast that things committed to his care were where the police, or anyone else, might as well whistle and suck their thumbs as try to find them!

And then, with sudden decision, taking his hesitation, as it were, by the throat, Jimmie Dale hurried on again—to the Sanctuary. At most, it could delay him but another fifteen minutes, and by half-past twelve, or a quarter to one at the latest, he would be at Spider Jack's.

Disdaining the secrecy of the side door on the alley, for who had a better right or was better known there than Larry the Bat, a tenant of years, he entered the tenement by the front door, scuffled up the stairs to the first landing, and let himself into his disreputable room. He locked the door behind him, lighted the choked and wheezy gas jet, in a single, sharp-flung glance assured himself that the blinds were tightly shut, and, kneeling in the far corner, threw back the oilcloth and lifted up the loose section of the flooring beneath. He reached inside, fumbling under the neatly folded clothes of

Jimmie Dale, and in a moment laid his leather girdle with its kit of burglar's tools on the floor beside him; and beside that again an electric flashlight, a black silk mask, and—what he had never expected to use again when, early the night before, he had, as he had believed, put it away forever—the thin, metal insignia case of the Gray Seal. Another moment, and, with the flooring replaced, the oilcloth rolled back into position, he had stripped off his coat and was pulling his spotted, greasy shirt off over his head; then, stooping quickly, he picked up the girdle, put it on, put on his shirt again over it, put on his coat, put the metal case, the flashlight, and the mask in his pockets—and once more the Sanctuary was in darkness.

It was perhaps fifteen minutes later that Jimmie Dale turned into the upper section of Thompson Street. Here he slowed his pace, that had been almost a run since he had left the Sanctuary, and began to shuffle leisurely along; for the street, that a few hours before would have been choked with its pushcarts and venders, its half naked children playing where they could find room in the gutters, its sidewalks thronged with shawled women and pictur-esquely dressed, earringed, dark-visaged men, a scene, as it were, transport-ed from some foreign land, was still far from deserted; the quiet, if quiet it could be called, was but comparative, there were many yet about, and he had no desire to attract attention by any evidence of undue haste. And, besides, Spider Jack's was just ahead, making the corner of the alleyway a few hun-dred feet farther on, and he had very good reasons for desiring to approach Spider's little novelty store at a pace that would afford him every opportunity for observation.

On he shuffled along the street, until, reaching Spider Jack's, a little two-storied, tumble-down brick structure, a muttered exclamation of satisfaction escaped him. The shop was closed and dark; and, though Spider Jack lived above the store, there were no lights even in the upper windows. Spider Jack presumably was either out, or in bed! So far, then, he could have asked for nothing more.

Jimmie Dale edged in close to the building as he slouched by, so close that his hat brim seemed to touch the windowpane. It was possible that from a room at the rear of the store there might be a light with a telltale ray perhaps filtering through, say, a door crack. But there was nothing—only blackness within.

He paused at the corner of the building by the alleyway. Down here, adjoining the high board fence of Spider Jack's back yard, Makoff made pre-tense at pawnbrokering in a small and dingy wooden building, that was little more pretentious than a shed—and in Makoff's place, so far as he could see, there was no light, either.

Jimmie Dale's fingers were industriously rolling a cigarette, as, under the brim of his slouch hat, his eyes were noting every detail around him. A yard in against the wall of Spider Jack's, the wall cutting off the rays of the street lamp at a sharp angle, it was shadowy and black—and beyond that, farther in, the alleyway was like a pit. It would take less, far less, than the fraction of a second to gain that yard, but someone was approaching behind him, and a little group of people loitered, with annoying persistency, directly across the way on the other side of the street. Jimmie Dale stuck the cigarette between his lips, fumbled in his pockets, and finally produced a box of matches. The group opposite was moving on now; the footsteps he had heard behind him, those of a man, drew nearer, the man passed by—and the box of matches in Jimmie Dale's hand dropped to the ground. He reached to pick them up, and in his stooping posture, without seeming to turn his head, flung a quick glance behind him up the street. No one, for that fraction of a second that he needed, was near enough to see—and in that fraction of a second Jimmie Dale disappeared.

A dozen yards down the lane, he sprang for the top of the high fence, gripped it, and, lithe and active as a cat, swung himself up and over, and dropped noiselessly to the ground on the other side. Here he stood motionless for a moment, close against the fence, to get his bearings. The rear of Spider Jack's building loomed up before him—the back windows as unlighted as those in front. Luck so far, at least, was with him! He turned and looked about him, and, his eyes growing accustomed to the darkness, he could just make out Makoff's place, bordering the end of the yard—nor, from this new vantage point, could he discover, any more than before, a single sign of life about the pawnbroker's establishment.

Jimmie Dale stole forward across the yard, mounted the three steps of the low stoop at Spider Jack's back door, and tried the door cautiously. It was locked. From his pocket came the small steel instrument that had stood Larry the Bat in good stead a hundred times before in similar circumstances. He inserted it in the keyhole, worked deftly with it for an instant—and tried the door again. It was still locked. And then Jimmie Dale smiled almost apologetically. Spider Jack did not use ordinary locks on his back door!

The discountenanced instrument went back into his pocket, and now Jimmie Dale's hand slipped inside his shirt, and from one of the little, upright pockets of the leather belt, and from still another, and from after that a third, came the vicious little blued-steel tools. The sensitive fingers travelled slowly up and down the side of the door—and then he was at work in earnest. A minute passed—another—there was a dull, low, grating sound, a snick as of metal yielding suddenly—and Jimmie Dale was coolly stowing away his tools again inside his shirt.

He pushed the door open an inch, listened, then swung it wide, stepped inside, and closed it behind him. A round, white beam of light flashed in a quick circle—and went out. It was a sort of storeroom, innocent enough and orderly enough in appearance, bare-floored, with boxes and packing cases piled neatly against the walls. In one corner a staircase led to the story above—and from above, quite audibly now, he caught the sound of snoring. Spider Jack was in bed, then!

Directly facing him was the open door of another room, and Jimmie Dale, moving softly forward, entered it. He had never been in Spider Jack's before, and his first concern was to form an intimate acquaintanceship with his surroundings. Again the flashlight circled, and again went out.

"No windows!" muttered Jimmie Dale under his breath. "Nothing very fancy about the architecture! Three rooms in a row! Store in front of this room through that door of course. Wonder if the door's locked, though it's a foregone conclusion the package wouldn't be in there."

Not a sound, his tread silent, he crossed to the closed door that he had noticed. It was unlocked, and he opened it tentatively a little way. A faint glow of light diffused itself through the opening. Jimmie Dale nodded his head and closed the door again. The street lamp, shining through the shop windows, accounted for the light.

And now the flashlight played with steady inquisitiveness about him. The room in which he stood seemed to combine a sort of office, with a lounging room, in which Spider Jack, no doubt, entertained his particular cronies. There was table in the centre, cards still upon it, chairs about it. Against the wall farthest away from the shop stood a huge, old-fashioned cabinet; and a little farther along, anglewise, partitioning off the corner, as it were, hung, for some purpose or other, a cretonne curtain. Also, against the wall next to the lane, bringing a commiserating smile to Jimmie Dale's lips as his eyes fell upon it, was a clumsy, lumbering, antique safe.

Jimmie Dale's eyes returned to the curtain. What was it doing there? What was it for? Instinctively he stepped over to examine it. A single glance, however, as he lifted it aside, sufficed. It was nothing but a make-shift clothes closet. He turned from it, switched off the flashlight, and stood staring meditatively into the darkness. In a strange house, with the knowledge to begin with that what he sought was carefully hidden, it was no sinecure to find that package. He had never for a moment imagined that it would be. But of one thing, however, there was no uncertainty in his mind—he would get the package!—by search if possible, by other means if search failed. It was now close to one o'clock. If by two o'clock his efforts had been fruitless, Spider Jack would hand over the package—at the revolver point! It was quite simple! Meanwhile—Jimmie Dale shrugged his shoulders, and, going over to the safe, knelt down in front of it—meanwhile, as well begin here as anywhere else.

The trained fingers closed on the handle—and on the instant, as though in startled amazement, shifted to the dial. They came back to the handle—a wrench—then a low, amused chuckle—and the door swung open. The great, unwieldy thing was only a monumental bluff! It not only had not been locked, but it *could not* be locked—the mechanism was out of order, the bolts could not be moved by so much as a hair's breadth!

Still chuckling, Jimmie Dale shot the flashlight's ray into the interior of the safe—and the chuckle died on his lips, and into his face came a look of strained bewilderment. Inside, everything was in chaos, books, papers, a miscellany of articles, as though they had first been ruthlessly pulled out on the floor, then gathered up in an armful and crammed back inside again. For an instant he did not move, and then a hard, mirthless smile drew down the corners of his mouth. With a sort of bitter, expectant nod of his head, he turned the light upon the door of the safe. Yes, there were the scratches that the tools had left; and, as though in sardonic jest, the holes, where the steel bit had bored, were plugged with putty and rubbed over with some black substance that was still wet and came off, smearing his finger, as he touched it. It could not have been done long ago, then! How long? A half hour—an hour? Not more than that!

Mechanically he closed the door of the safe, rose to his feet and, almost heedless of noise now, the flashlight ray dancing before him, he jumped across to the old-fashioned cabinet and pulled the door open. Here, as within the safe, all inside, plain evidence of thorough, if hasty, search, was scattered and tossed about in hopeless confusion.

He shut the cabinet door; the flashlight went out; and he stood like a man stunned, the sense of some abysmal disaster upon him. He was too late! The game was up! If it had ever been here, the package was gone now—*gone*! The Crime Club had been here before him!

"The game was up! The game was up!"—his mind seemed to keep on repeating that. The Crime Club had beaten him by an hour, at most, and had been here, and had searched. It was strange, though, that they should have been at such curious pains to cover their tracks by leaving the room in order, by such paltry efforts to make the safe appear untouched when the first glance that was at all critical would disclose immediately what had been done! Why should they need to cover their tracks at all; or, if it was necessary, why, above all, in such a pitifully inadequate way! His mind barked back to the same ghastly refrain—"the game was up!"

No! Not yet! There was still a chance! There was still Spider Jack! Suppose, in spite of their search, they had failed to find the package! Jimmie Dale's lips set in a thin line, as he started abruptly toward the door. There was still that chance, and one thing was grimly certain—Spider Jack would, at least, show him where the package *had been*!

And then, halfway to the door, he halted suddenly, and stood still—listening. An electric bell was ringing loudly, imperiously, somewhere upstairs. Followed almost immediately the sound of someone, Spider Jack presumably, moving hurriedly about overhead; and then, a moment later, steps coming down the staircase in the adjoining room.

Jimmie Dale drew back, flattening himself against the wall. Spider Jack entered the room, stumbled across it, in the darkness, fumbled for the door that led into his little shop, opened it, passed through, fumbled around in there again, for matches evidently, then lighted a gas jet in the store, and, going to the street door, opened it.

Jimmie Dale had edged along the wall a little to a position where he had an unobstructed view through the open doorway connecting the shop and the room in which he stood. Spider Jack, in trousers and shirt, hastily donned, no doubt, as he had got out of bed, was standing in the street doorway, and beyond him loomed the forms of several men. Spider Jack stepped aside to allow his visitors to enter—and suddenly, a cry barely suppressed upon his lips, Jimmie Dale involuntarily strained forward. Three men had entered, but his eyes were fixed, fascinated, upon only one—the first of the three. Was it an hallucination? Was he mad—dreaming? It was Hilton Travers, *the chauffeur*—the man whom he could have sworn he had last seen dead, lashed in that chair, in that ghastly death chamber of the Crime Club!

"Rather rough on you, Spider, to pull you out of bed at this hour," the chauffeur was saying apologetically.

"Oh, that's all right, seein' it's you, Travers," Spider Jack answered, gruffly amiable. "Only I was kind of lookin' for you last night."

"I know," the chauffeur replied; "but I couldn't connect with my friends here. Shake hands with them, Spider—Bob Marvin—Harry Stead."

"Glad to know you, gents," said Spider Jack, with a handgrip apiece.

The chauffeur lowered his voice a little.

"I suppose we're alone here, eh, Spider? Yes? Well, then, you know what I've come for—that package—Marvin and Stead, here, are the ones that are in on it with me. Get it for me, will you, Spider?"

"Sure—Mr. Johansson!" Spider grinned. "Sure! Come on into the back room and make yourselves comfortable. I'll be mabbe five minutes, or so."

Jimmie Dale's brain was whirling. What did it mean? He could not seem to understand. His mind seemed to refuse its functions. Travers, the chauffeur—*alive*! He drew in his breath sharply. That curtain in the corner! He must see this out now! They were coming! Quick, noiseless, he stole along the side of the wall, reached the corner, and slipped in behind the curtain, as Spider Jack, striking a match, entered the room.

Spider Jack lighted the gas, and, as the others followed behind him, waved them toward the chairs around the table.

"I'll just ask you gents not to leave the room," he said meaningly, over his shoulder, as he stepped toward the rear door. "It's kind of a fad of mine to keep some things even from my wife!"

"All right, Spider—I understand," the chauffeur returned readily.

Jimmie Dale's knife cut a tiny slit in the cretonne on a level with his eyes. The three men had seated themselves at the table, and appeared to be listening intently. Spider Jack's footsteps echoed back as he crossed the rear room, sounded dull and muffled descending the stoop outside, and died away.

"I told you it wasn't in the house!" the man who had been introduced as Stead laughed shortly. "We wasted the hour we had here."

The third man spoke crisply, incisively, to the chauffeur.

"Turn down that gas jet a little! You've got across with it so far—but you can't stand a searchlight, Clarke!"

And at the words, in a flash, the meaning of it, all of it, to the last detail that was spelling death, ruin, and disaster for her, the Tocsin, for himself as well, burst upon Jimmie Dale. That VOICE! He would have known it, recognised it, among a thousand—it was the masked man of the night before, the leader, the head of the Crime Club! And it was not Travers there at all! He remembered now, too well, that second room they had showed him in the Crime Club—its multitude of disguises, though in this case they had the dead man's clothes ready to their hands—the leader's boast that impersonation was but child's play to them! And now he understood why they had covered up the traces of their search in only so curiously inadequate a manner. They had failed to find the package, and, as a last resort, had adopted the ruse of impersonating Hilton Travers, the chauffeur, which made it necessary that when they called Spider Jack from his bed, as they had just done, that Spider Jack, at a casual glance, should notice nothing amiss—but it would be no more than a casual glance, for, who should know better than they, he would not have to go for the package to any place that they had disturbed! And he, Jimmie Dale, could only stand here and watch them, helpless, powerless to move! Three of them! A step out into the room was to invite certain death. It would not matter, his death—if he could gain anything for her, for the Tocsin, by it. But what could he gain—by dying? He clenched his hands until the nails bit into the flesh.

Spider Jack re-entered the room, carrying what looked like a large, bulky, manila envelope, heavily sealed, in his hand. He tossed it on the table.

"There you are, Travers!" he said.

"I wonder," suggested the leader pleasantly, "if, now that we're here, Travers, your friend would mind letting us have this room for a few minutes to ourselves to clean up the business?"

"Sure!" agreed Spider Jack cordially. "You're welcome to it! I'll wait out here in the store until you say the word."

He went out, closing the door after him. The leader picked up the package.

"We'll take no chances with this," he said grimly. "It's been too close a call. After we've had a look at it, we'll put it out of harm's way on the spot, here, while we've got it—before we leave!"

He ripped the package open, and disclosed perhaps a dozen official-looking documents, besides a miscellaneous number of others. He took up the first of the papers, glanced through it hurriedly, then tossed it to the pseudo chauffeur.

"Tear it up, and tear it up—*small*!" he ordered tersely. The next, after examining it as he had the first, he tossed to the other man. "Go ahead!"—curtly. "Work fast! From the looks of these, Travers had us cold! There's proof enough here of LaSalle's murder to send us all to the chair!"

He went on glancing through the documents; and then suddenly, joining the others in their work, began to rip and tear at the papers himself.

A sort of cold horror had settled upon Jimmie Dale, and his forehead was clammy wet. The inhuman irony of it! That he should stand there and watch, impotent to prevent it, the destruction of what he would have given his life to secure! And then slowly, a grim, hard, merciless smile came to his lips. He had recognised the leader's voice—now he would recognise the leader's face. At least, that was left to him—perhaps the master trump of all. It would not be very hard to find the Crime Club now—with that man to lead the way!

The scraps of paper, tiny shreds, mounted into a heap on the table—and with the last of the contents of the package destroyed, the leader stood up.

"Put these pieces in your pockets; we don't want to leave them here," he directed quietly. "And then let's get out."

In scarcely a moment, the last scrap of paper had vanished. The three men walked to the door, passed through it, and joined Spider Jack in the store—and Jimmie Dale, slipping out from behind the curtain, gained the door of the rear room, crept through it, reached the stoop, and then, darting like the wind across the yard, was over the fence in a second, and in another was out of the alleyway and on the street.

He was in time—in plenty of time. They had just left Spider Jack's, and were, perhaps, fifty yards or so ahead of him. He slouched on behind them—the cold, grim smile on his lips once more. It was the Crime Club now, that hell's cradle where their devil's schemes were hatched, that was the one thing left to him; they would lead him to that, and then—and then it would be his turn to *strike*!

They turned the first corner. And suddenly, as the racing engine of an automobile caught his ear, he broke into a run, and dashed around the corner after them—in time to see them jump into a car, and the car speed off along the street! He halted, as though he were suddenly dazed—started involuntarily to run forward again—stopped with a hollow laugh at the futility of it—and stood still and motionless on the sidewalk.

And then he swayed a little, and his face grew gray. Failure, defeat, ruin—in that moment he knew them all to their bitterest dregs. How could he go to her! How could he face her, and tell her that they were beaten, that the last hope was gone, that he had failed!

"God!" he cried aloud, and clenched his hands.

Then deep in his consciousness a thought stirred, and he swept a shaking hand across his eyes. Why had it come again, that thought! Did it mean that *he* must play—the last card! There was a way—there had always been a way. The way the Crime Club took—*murder*. It was their own weapon! If the man who posed as Henry LaSalle were killed! If that man—were killed!

"The Magpie was to be there at three!" he muttered—and started mechanically back along the street.

CHAPTER 13

THE ONLY WAY

It was a horrible thing—and it grew upon him. In a blind, mechanical way, his brain receptive to nothing else, Jimmie Dale walked on along the street. To kill a man! Death he had faced himself a hundred times, witnessed it a hundred times in its most violent forms, had seen murder done before his eyes, had been in straits where, to save his own life, it had seemed the one last desperate chance—and yet his hands were still clean! To kill a man in fair fight, in struggle, when the blood was hot, was terrible enough, a possibility that was always before him, the one thing from which he shrank, the one thing that, as the Gray Seal, he had always feared; but to kill a man deliberately, to creep upon his victim with hideous, cold-blooded premeditation—he shivered a little, and his hand shook as he drew it nervously across his eyes.

But there was no other way! Again and again, insidiously grappling with his revulsion, with the horror that the impulse to murder inspired, came that other thought—there was no other way. If the man who posed as Henry La-Salle were dead! If he were dead! If he were dead! See, now, what would happen if that man were dead! How clear his brain was on that point! The whole plot would tumble like a house of cards about the heads of the Crime Club. The courts would require an auditing of the estate by a trustee of the courts' own appointing, who would continue to administer it until the Tocsin's twenty-fifth birthday, or until there was tangible evidence of her death—but the Tocsin, automatically with her pseudo uncle's death, could publicly appear again. Her death could no longer benefit the Crime Club, since it, the Crime Club, with the supposed uncle dead, could not profit through the false Henry LaSalle inheriting as next of kin! It was the weak link, the vulnerable point in the stupendous scheme of murder and crime with which these hell fiends had played for and won, so far, the stake of eleven millions. Not that they had overlooked or been blind to this, they were too clever, too cunning for that—it was only that they had planned to accomplish the Tocsin's death, as they had her father's and uncle's, and establish the false Henry LaSalle in undisputed possession and ownership of the estate—and had failed in that—up to the present. But the material results remained the same, so long as the Tocsin, to save her life, was forced to remain in hiding, so long as proof that would convict the Crime Club was not forthcoming—*so long as that man lived!*

Time passed to which Jimmie Dale was oblivious. At times he walked slowly, scarcely moving; at times his pace was a nervous, hurried stride, that was almost a run. And as he was oblivious to time, so was he oblivious to his surroundings, to the direction which he took. At times his forehead was damp with moisture that was not there from physical exertion; at times his face, deathly white, was full as of the vision of some shuddering, abhorrent sight; at times his lips were thinned into a straight line, and there was a glitter in the dark eyes that was not good to see, while his hands at his sides clenched until the skin, tight over the knuckles, was an ivory white. To kill a man!

What other way was there? The proof that it had taken Hilton Travers years to obtain, the proof on which the Tocsin's life depended, was destroyed utterly, irreparably. It could never be duplicated—Hilton Travers was dead—*murdered*. Murder! That thought again! It was their own weapon! Murder! Would one kill a venomous reptile in whose fangs was death? What right had this man to life, whose life was forfeit even under the law—for murder? Was she to drag on an intolerable existence among the dregs and the scum of the underworld, she, in her refinement and her purity, to exist among the vile and dissolute, in daily, hourly peril of her life, because the weapons that these inhuman vultures had used to rob her, to destroy those she loved, to make of her life a hideous, joyless thing, should not be used against them?

But to kill a man! To steal upon a man with cold intent in the blackness of the night—and take his life! To be a murderer! To know the horror of blood forever upon one's hands, to rise, cold-sweated, in the night, fearful of the very shadows around one, to live with every detail of that fearsome act sweeping like some dread spectre at unexpected moments upon the consciousness! He put up his hands before his face, as though to blot out the thought from him. Mind and soul recoiled before it—to kill a man!

He walked on and on, until at last, conscious of a sense of fatigue, he stopped. He must have come a long way, been walking a long time. Where was he? He looked about him for a moment in a dazed way—and suddenly, with a low cry, shrank back. As though he had been drawn to it by some ghastly magnet, he found himself standing in front of the LaSalle mansion, on Fifth Avenue. No, no; it was not for that he had come—to kill a man! It was only—only to get that money. Yes—he remembered now—that money from the safe, before the Magpie got it. The Magpie was to be there at three o'clock—and the Tocsin was to be there, too. The Tocsin! That package! He had failed! It had been her one hope, and—and it was gone. What could he say to her? How could he tell her the miserable truth? But—but he had not come there in the dead of night to kill a man, these other things were what had—

"Jimmie!" It was a quick-breathed whisper. A hand was on his arm.

He turned, startled. It was the Tocsin—Silver Mag.

"Jimmie!" in alarm. "Why are you standing here like this? You may be seen!"

Seen! Suppose he *were* seen? He shuddered a little.

"Yes; that's so!" he said hoarsely. He glanced numbly up and down the wide, deserted, but well-lighted, avenue. It was no place, that most aristocratic section of the city, for such as Silver Mag and Larry the Bat to be seen at that hour of night, or, rather, morning. And if anything happened inside that house! "I—I didn't think of that," he said mechanically.

"Come across the street—under the stoop of that house there." She had his arm, and was half dragging him as she spoke, the alarm in her voice intensified. And then, a moment later, safe from observation: "Jimmie, Jimmie, what is the matter? What has happened? What makes you act so strangely?"

"Nothing," he said. "I—"

"Tell me!" she insisted wildly.

And then, with a violent effort, Jimmie Dale forced his mind back to the immediate present. He was only inspiring her with terror—and there was the Magpie—and that money in the safe!

"Where is the Magpie?" he asked, with quick apprehension. "Am I late? Is he in there already?"

"No," she said. "He hasn't come yet."

"What time is it?" he demanded anxiously.

"About half-past two," she replied. "But, Jimmie—"

"Wait!" he broke in. "Where is he now? You were both together! And you were both to be here at three. What are you doing here alone at half-past two?"

A strange little exclamation, one almost of dismay, it seemed, escaped her.

"The Magpie left my place an hour ago—to get his kit, I think. And I came here at once because that was what you and I understood I was to do, wasn't it? Jimmie, you frighten me! You are not yourself. Don't you remember the last words you said, as you nodded to me behind the Magpie's back—that you would be here before us? There was no mistaking your meaning—if I could get away from him, I was to come here and meet you."

Jimmie Dale passed his hand nervously across his eyes. Of course, he remembered now! What a frightful turmoil his brain had been in!

"Yes; of course!" He tried to speak nonchalantly. "I had forgotten for the moment."

She caught his arm in a quick, tight hold, shaking him in a terrified way.

"*You*—forget a thing like that! Jimmie—something terrible has happened. Can't you see that I am nearly mad with anxiety! What is it? What is it? That package, Jimmie—is it the package?"

He did not answer. What could he say? It meant life, hope, joy, everything that the world held for her—and it was gone.

"Yes—it *is* the package!" she whispered frantically. "Quick, Jimmie! Tell me! It—it was not there? You—you could not find it?"

"It was there," he said, as though the words were literally forced from him.

"Then? Then—*what*, Jimmie?" The clutch on his arm was like a vise.

"They got it," he said. It was like a death sentence that he pronounced. "It is destroyed."

She did not speak or move—save that her hands, as though nerveless and without strength, fell away from his arms, and dropped to her sides. It was dark there under the stoop, though not so dark but that he could see her face. It was gray—gray as death. And there was misery and fear and a pitiful helplessness in it—and then she swayed a little, and he caught her in his arms.

"Gone!" she murmured in a dead, colourless way—and suddenly laughed out sharply, hysterically.

"Don't! For God's sake, don't do that!" he pleaded wildly.

She looked at him then for a moment in strange quiet—and lifted her hand and stroked his face in a numbed way.

"It—it would have been better, Jimmie, wouldn't it," she said in the same monotonous voice, "it would have been better if—if I had never found out anything, and they—they had done the same to me that they did to—to father."

"Marie! Marie!" It was the first time he had ever spoken her name, and it was on his lips now in an agony of tenderness and appeal. "Don't! You mustn't speak like that!"

"I'm tired," she said. "I—I can't fight any more."

She did not cry. She lay there in his arms quite still—like a weary child.

The minutes passed. When Jimmie Dale spoke again it was irrelevantly—and his face was very white:

"Marie, describe the upper floor of that house over there for me."

She roused herself with a start.

"The upper floor?" she repeated slowly. "Why—why do you ask that?"

"Have *you* forgotten in turn?" he said, with a steady smile. "That money in the safe—it's yours—we can at least save that out of the wreck. You only drew the basement plan and the first floor for the Magpie—the more I know about the house the better, of course, in case anything goes wrong. Now, see, try and be brave—and tell me quickly, for I must get through before the Magpie comes, and I have barely half an hour."

"No, Jimmie—no!" She slipped out of his arms. "Let it alone! I am afraid. Something—I—I have a feeling that something will happen."

"It is the only way." He said it involuntarily, more to himself than to her.

"Jimmie, let it alone!" she said again.

"No," he said. "I am going—so tell me quickly. Every minute that we wait is one that counts against us."

She hesitated an instant—and then, speaking rapidly, made a verbal sketch of the upper portion of the house for him.

"It's a very large house, isn't it?" he commented innocently—to pave the way for the question, above all others, that he had to ask. "Which is your uncle's, I mean that man's room?"

"The first on the right, at the head of the landing," she answered. "Only, Jimmie, don't—don't go!"

He drew her close to him again.

"Now, listen," he said quietly. "When the Magpie comes and finds I am not here, lead him to think that the money he gave me was too much for me; that I am probably in some den, doped with drug—and hold him as long as you can on the pretext that there is always the possibility I may, after all, show up before he goes in there. You understand? And now about yourself—you must do exactly as I say. On no account allow yourself to be seen by *anyone* except the Magpie. I would tell you to go now, only, unless it is vitally necessary, we cannot afford to arouse the Magpie's suspicions—he'd have every crook in the underworld snarling at our heels. But you are not to wait, even for him, if you detect the slightest disturbance in that house before he comes. And, equally, after he has gone in, whether I have come out or not, at the first indication of anything unusual you are to get away at once. You understand—Marie?"

"Yes," she said. "But—but, Jimmie, you—"

"Just one thing more." He smiled at her reassuringly. "Did the Magpie say anything about how he intended to get in?"

"Yes—by the side away from the corner of the street," she said tremulously. "You see, there's quite a space between the house and the one next door; and, besides, the house next door is closed up, there's nobody there, the family has gone away for the summer. The library window there is low enough to reach from the ground."

For a moment longer he held her close to him, as though he could not let her go—then bent and kissed her passionately. And in that moment all the emotions he had known as he had walked blindly from Spider Jack's that night surged again upon him; and that voice was whispering, whispering, whispering: "It is the only way—it is the only way."

And then, not daring to trust his voice, he released her suddenly, and stepped back out from under the stoop—and the next instant he was across the deserted avenue. Another, and he had slipped through the iron gates that opened on the street driveway—and in yet another he was crouched close up against the front door of the LaSalle mansion.

It was a large house, a very large house, one of the few that, even amid the wealth and luxury of that quarter, boasted its own grounds, and those so restricted as scarcely to deserve the name; but it was set far enough back from the street to escape the radius of the street lamps, and so guarantee in its shadows security from observation. It was not the Magpie's way, the front door—the obvious to the Magpie and his ilk was a thing always to be shunned. Jimmie Dale's lips were set in a grim smile, as his fingers worked with lightning speed, now taking this instrument and now that from the leather pockets in the girdle beneath his shirt—the penitentiaries were full of Magpies who shunned the obvious!

Very slowly, very cautiously the door opened. He listened breathlessly, tensely. The door closed again—behind him. He was inside now. Stillness! Blackness! Not a sound! A minute went by—another. And then, as he stood there, strained, listening, the silence itself began, it seemed, to palpitate, and pound, pound, pound, and be full of strange noises. It was a horrible thing—to kill a man!

CHAPTER 14

OUT OF THE DARKNESS

A moment later, Jimmie Dale stepped forward through the vestibule. He was quite calm now; a sort of cold, merciless precision in every movement succeeding the riot of turbulent emotions that had possessed him as he had entered the house.

The half hour, the maximum length of time before the Magpie would appear, as he had estimated it when out there under the stoop with the Tocsin, had dwindled now to perhaps twenty minutes, twenty-five at the outside. Twenty-five minutes! Twenty-five minutes was so little that for an instant the temptation was strong upon him to sacrifice, rather than any of those precious minutes, the Magpie instead! And then in the darkness, as he stole noiselessly across the hall, he shook his head. It would be a cowardly, brutal thing to do. What chance would a man with a record like the Magpie's stand if caught there? How easy it would be to shift the murder of the supposed Henry LaSalle to the Magpie's shoulders! Jimmie Dale's lips closed firmly. Self-preservation was, perhaps, the first law, but he would save the Magpie if he could—the Magpie should have his chance! The man might be a criminal, might deserve punishment at the hands of the law, his liberty might be a menace to the community—but he was not a murderer, his life forfeit for a crime he had never committed!

If he, Jimmie Dale, could only in some way have arranged with the Tocsin out there to keep the Magpie away altogether! But it could not be done without arousing the Magpie's suspicions; and, as a corollary to that, afterward, with the subsequent events, would come—the deluge! The law of the underworld was clear, concise, and admitting of no appeal on that point; to double cross a pal meant, sooner or later, a knife thrust, a blackjack, or—But what difference did it make what form the execution of the sentence took? And, since, then, that was out of the question, since he could not keep the Magpie away without practically risking his own life, the Magpie at least must have his chance.

Jimmie Dale was at the library door now, that, according to the plan the Tocsin had drawn for the Magpie, and as he remembered her description when she had told him her story earlier in the evening, was just at the foot of the staircase. How dark it was! Though the stairs could be only a few feet away, he could not see them. And how intense the silence was again! Here, where he stood, the slightest stir from above must have reached him—but there was not a sound.

His hand felt out for the doorknob, found it, turned it, and pushed the door open. He stepped inside the room and closed the door behind him. The safe, according to the Tocsin's plan again, was in that sort of alcove at the lower end of the library. Jimmie Dale's flashlight played inquisitively about the room. There was the window, the only one in the room, the window through which the Magpie proposed to enter; there was the archway of the alcove, with its—no, there were no longer any portieres; and there was the safe, he could see it quite plainly from where he stood at the upper end of the room.

The flashlight went out for the space of perhaps thirty seconds—thirty seconds of absolute silence, absolute stillness—then the round, white ray of the light again, but glistening now on the nickel knobs and dial of the safe—and Jimmie Dale was on his knees before it.

A low, scarcely breathed exclamation, that seemed to mingle anxiety and hesitation, escaped him. He, who knew the make of every safe in the country, knew this one for its true worth. Twenty-five minutes! Could he open it in that time, let alone with any time to spare! It was not like the one in Spider Jack's; it was the kind that the Magpie, however clever he might be in his own way, would be forced to negotiate with "soup," and, with the attendant noise, double his chance of discovery and capture—and the responsibility for what might have happened upstairs! No; the Magpie must have his chance! And, besides, the money in the safe apart, why should not he, Jimmie Dale, have his own chance, as well? All this would help. The motive—robbery; the perpetrator, there was grim mockery on his lips now as the light went out and the sensitive fingers closed on the knob of the dial, the perpetrator—the Gray Seal. It would afford excellent food for the violent editorial diatribes under which the police again would writhe in frenzy!

Stillness again! Silence! Only a low, tense breathing; only, so faint that it could not be heard a foot away, a curious scratching, as from time to time the supersensitive fingers fell away from the dial to rub upon the carpet—to increase even their sensitiveness by setting the nerves to throbbing through the skin surface at the tips. And then Jimmie Dale's head, ear pressed close against the safe to catch the tumbler's fall, was lifted—and the flashlight played again on the dial.

"Twenty-eight and a quarter—left."

How fast the time went—and how slowly! Still the black shape crouched there in the darkness against the safe. At times, in strange, ghostly flashes, the nickel dial with the ray upon it seemed to leap out and glisten through the surrounding blackness; at times, the quick intake of breath, as from great exertion; at times, faint, musical little clicks, as, after abortive effort, the dial whirled, preparatory to a fresh attempt. And then, at last—a gasp of relief:

"Ah!"

Came the sound, barely audible, as of steel sliding in well-oiled grooves, the muffled thud of metal meeting metal as the bolts shot back—and the heavy door swung outward.

Jimmie Dale stretched his cramped limbs, and wiped the moisture from his face—then set to work again upon the inner door. This was an easier matter—far easier. Five minutes, perhaps a little more, went by—and then the inner door was open, and the flashlight's ray was flooding the interior of the safe.

A little sound, half of astonishment, half of disappointment, issued from Jimmie Dale's lips. There was money here, a great deal of money, undoubtedly, but there was no such sum as he had, somehow, fantastically imagined from the Magpie's evidently overcoloured story that there would be; there was money, ten packages of banknotes neatly piled in the bottom compartment—but there was no half million of dollars! He picked up one of the packages hurriedly—and drew in his breath. After all, there was a great deal—the notes were of hundred-dollar denomination, and on the bottom were two one-thousand-dollar bills! Calculated roughly, if each of the other nine packages contained a like amount, the total must exceed a hundred thousand.

And now Jimmie Dale began to work with feverish haste. From the leather girdle inside his shirt came the thin metal insignia case—and a gray seal was stuck firmly on the dial knob of the safe. This done, he tucked away the packages of banknotes, some into his pockets and some inside his shirt; and then quickly ransacked the interior of the safe, flauntingly spilling the contents of drawers and pigeonholes out upon the floor.

He stood up, and, leaving the safe door wide open, walked back across the room to the window, unfastened the catch, and opened the window an inch or two. The way was open now for the Magpie! The Magpie would have no need to make any noise in forcing an entrance; he would be able to see almost at a glance that he had been forestalled—by the Gray Seal; and that, as far as he was concerned, the game was up. The Magpie had his chance! If the Magpie did not take the hint and make his escape as noiselessly as he had entered—it was his own fault! He, Jimmie Dale, had given the Magpie his chance.

Jimmie Dale turned from the window, and made his way out of the library to the foot of the stairs, leaving the library door open behind him. How long had he been? Was it more or less than the twenty-five minutes? He did not know—only, as yet, the Magpie had not come, and now perhaps it did not make so much difference.

Where was he going now? His foot was on the first stair—and suddenly he drew it back, the cold sweat bursting out on his forehead. Where was he going now? *"The first room on the right at the head of the landing."* From his inner consciousness, as it were, the answer, in all the bald, naked horror that it implied, flashed upon him. The first room on the right—*that* man's room! God, how the darkness and the stillness began to palpitate again, and suddenly seem to shriek out at him over and over the one single, ghastly word—*murder!*

It had been with him, that thought, all the time he had been working at the safe; but it had been there then only subconsciously, like some heavy, nameless dread, subjugated for the moment by the work he had had to do which had demanded the centred attention of every faculty he possessed. But now the moment had come when there was only that before him, only that, nothing else—only that, the man upstairs in the first room to the right of the landing!

Why did he hesitate? Why did he stand there while the priceless moments before daylight came were passing? The man was a murderer, a blotch on society, and, his life already forfeited, he was living now only because the law had not found him out—the man was a criminal, bloodstained—and his life, because he had taken her father's life and had tried to take the Tocsin's own life, stood between her and every hope of happiness, robbing her even literally, in a material sense, of everything that the world could hold for her! Why did he hesitate? It was that man's life—or hers! It was the only way!

He put his foot upon the bottom step again—paused still another instant—and then began stealthily to mount the stairs. The darkness! There had never been, it seemed, such darkness before! The stillness—he had never known silence so heavy, so full of strange, premonitory pulsings; a silence that seemed so incongruously full of clamouring whispers in his ears! It must be those imagined whispers that were affecting his nerve—for now, as he gained the landing and slipped his automatic from his pocket, his hand was shaking with a twitching motion.

For an instant, fighting for his self-composure, he stood striving to locate his surroundings through the darkness. The staircase was a circular one, making the landing nearly at the front of the house, and rearward from this, the Tocsin had said, a hallway ran down the centre, with rooms on either side. The first room to the right, therefore, should be just at his hand. He reached out, feeling cautiously—there was nothing. He edged to the right—still nothing; edged a little farther, a sense of bewilderment growing upon him, and finally his fingers touched the wall. It was very strange! The hallway must be much wider than he had understood it to be from what she had said!

He moved along now straight ahead of him, his hand on the wall, feeling for the door—and with every step his bewilderment increased. Surely there must be some mistake—perhaps he had misunderstood! He had come fully twice the distance that one would expect—and yet there was no door. Ah, what was that? His fingers closed on soft, heavy velvet hangings. These could hardly be in front of a door, and yet—what else could it be? He drew the hangings warily apart, and felt behind them. It was a window; but it was shuttered in some way evidently, for he could not see out.

Jimmie Dale stood motionless there for fully a minute. It seemed absurd, preposterous, the conviction that was being forced home upon him—that there were no rooms on the right-hand side of the corridor at all! But that was not like the Tocsin, accurate always in the most minute details. The room must be still farther along. He was tempted to use his flashlight—but that, as long as he could feel his way, was an unnecessary risk. A flashlight upstairs, where a sleeping-room door might be ajar, or even wide open, where someone wakeful, that man himself, perhaps, might see it, was quite another matter than a flashlight in the closed and deserted library below!

He went on once more, still guiding himself by a light finger touch upon the wall, passed another portiere similar to the first, and, after that, another—and finally stopped by bringing up abruptly against the end wall of the house. It was certainly very strange! There *were* no rooms on the right-hand side of the corridor. And here, hanging across the end wall, was another of those ubiquitous velvet portieres. He parted it, and, a little to his surprise, found a window that was not shuttered, but that, instead, was heavily barred by an ornamental grille work. He could see out, however, and found that he was looking directly out from the rear of the house. A lamp from the side street threw what was undoubtedly the garage into shadowy outline, and he made out below him a short stretch of yard between the garage and the house. He remembered that now—she had described all that to the Magpie. There was no driveway between the front and the rear. The house being on the corner, the entrance to the garage was directly from the side street. Yes, she had described all that exactly as it was, but—he dropped the portiere and faced around, carrying his hand in a nonplused way to his eyes—but here, upstairs, within the house, it was not as she had said it was at all! What did it mean? She could not have blundered so egregiously as that, unless—he caught his breath suddenly—unless she had done so intentionally! Was that it? Had she surmised, formed a suspicion of what was in his mind, of what he meant to do—and taken this means of defeating it? If so—well, it was too late for that now! There was one way—only one way! Whatever the cost, whatever it might mean for him—there was only one way out for her.

His flashlight was in his hand now, and the round, white ray shot down the corridor—seemed suddenly to falter unsteadily—swept in through an open door that was almost beside him—and then, as though a nerveless hand held it, the ray dropped and played shakily on the toe of his boot before it went out.

A stifled cry rose to his lips. Something cold, like a hand of ice, seemed to clutch at his heart. Those portieres, the wide, richly carpeted corridor! It was the corridor of the night before! That room at his side was the room where he had seen Hilton Travers, the chauffeur, dead, lashed in a chair! He felt the sweat beads burst out anew upon his forehead.

It was the Crime Club!

CHAPTER 15
RETRIBUTION

His brain seemed to whirl, staggered as by some gigantic, ghastly mockery. The Crime Club! Here! He had thought to creep upon that man—and he had run blindly into the very heart and centre of these hell fiends' nest!

Silently he stood there, holding his breath as he listened now, motionless as a statue, forcing his mind to *think*. He remembered that last night his impression of the place had been that it was more like some great private mansion than anything else. Well, he had been right, it seemed! He could have laughed aloud—sardonically, hysterically. It was not so strange now that there were no rooms on the right-hand side of the corridor! And what could have suited their purpose better, what, by its very location, its unimpeachable character, could be a more ideal lair for them than this house! And how grimly simple it was now, the explanation! In the five years that the false Henry LaSalle had been in possession, they had cunningly remodelled the upper floor—that was all! It was quite clear now why the man never entertained—why he had never been caught or found or known to be in communication with his fellow conspirators! It was no longer curious that one might watch the door of the house for months at a stretch and go unrewarded for one's pains, as the Tocsin had done, when access to the house by those who frequented it was so easy through the garage on the side street—and from the garage, if their work there was in keeping with their clever contrivances within the house, by an underground connection into, say, the cellar or basement!

Again Jimmie Dale checked that nervous, unnatural inclination to laugh aloud. Was there anything, any single incident, any single detail of all that had transpired, that was not explained, borne out, as it could be explained and borne out in no other way save that the Crime Club should be no other than this very house itself? It was the exposition of that favourite theory of his—it was so obvious that therein lay its security. He had mocked at the Magpie not many moments before on that score—and now it was the beam in his own eye! It was so obvious now, so glaringly obvious, that the Crime Club could have been nowhere else; so obvious, with every word of the Tocsin's story pointing it out like a signpost—and he had not seen it!

And then suddenly every muscle grew strained and rigid. *Was there someone in the corridor?* Was it someone moving—or was it only fancy? He listened—while he strained his eyes through the darkness. There was no sound; only that abnormal, heavy silence that—yes, he remembered that, too, now—that had clung about him last night like a pall. He could see nothing, hear nothing—but intuitively, bringing a cold dismay, the greater because it was something unknown, intangible, he *felt* as though eyes were upon him, that even in the darkness he was being watched!

And as he stood there, then, slowly there crept upon Jimmie Dale the sense of peril and disaster. It was not intuition now—it was certainty. He was trapped! It was the part of a fool to imagine that with their devil's cunning, their cleverness, their ingenuity, he, or anyone else, could enter that house unknown to its occupants! Had he made electric contact when he had opened the front door, and rung a signal here, perhaps, upstairs—had he set some system of alarm at work when he had touched that window? What did it matter—the details that had heralded his entrance? He was certain now that his presence in the house was known. Only, why had they left him so long without attack? He shook his head with a quick, impatient movement. That, too, was obvious! He was under observation. Who was he? Why had he come? Was he simply a paltry safe-tapper—or was he one whom they had a real need to fear? And then, too, there might well be another reason. It was far from likely, in fact unreasonable, to imagine that all the men he had seen here the night before were in the house now. Not many of them, if any, would live *here*, for *constant*, daily coming and going, even through the garage, could not escape notice; and, of the servants, probably a lesser breed of criminal, some of them, at least, no doubt, were engaged at that moment in watching his own house on Riverside Drive! There was even the possibility that the man posing as Henry LaSalle was, for the time being, here alone.

He shook his head again. He could hardly hope for that—he had no right to hope for anything more now than a struggle, with an inevitably fatal ending to himself, but one in which at least he could sell his life as dearly as possible, one in which, perhaps, he might pay the Tocsin's score with the man he had come to find! If he could do that—well, after all, the price was not too great!

There were no tremours of the muscles now. It was Jimmie Dale, the Gray Seal, every faculty alert, tense, keyed up to its highest efficiency; the brain cool, keen, and active—fighting for his life. The front door through which he had entered was an impossibility; but there was the window in the library that he had opened—if they would let him get that far! That was as good a chance as any. If he made an effort to find, say, a way to the flat above and chanced some means of escape there, it would in no wise obviate an attack upon him, and he would only be under the added disadvantage of unfamiliar surroundings.

Feeling out with his left hand, his automatic thrown a little forward in his right, he began to retrace his way along the blank wall of the corridor, pausing between each step to listen, moving silently, his tread on the heavy carpet as noiseless as though it were some shadow creeping there.

Stillness—utter, absolute! Always that stillness. Always that sense of danger around him—the tense, bated expectancy of momentary attack—a revolver flash through the darkness—a sudden rush upon him. But still there was nothing—only the darkness, only the silence.

He gained the head of the stairs and began to descend—and now the strain began to tell upon his nerves again. Again he was possessed of the mad impulse to cry out, to do anything that would force the issue, that would end the horrible, unbearable suspense. Why did that revolver shot not come? Why had they not yet rushed upon him? Why were they playing with him as a cat with a mouse? Or was it all wild, fanciful imagination? *No!* What was that again! He could have sworn this time that he had heard a sound, but he could neither define its character, nor locate the direction from which it had come.

He was at the foot of the stairs now; and, guiding himself by the wall, moving now barely an inch at a time, he reached the library door that he had left open, and stole in over the threshold. Halfway down the room and diagonally across from where he stood was the window. In a moment now he could gain that, but they would never let him go so easily—and so it must come now, in that next moment, their attack! Where were they? Where were they now? The table—he must remember not to bump into the table! A pause between each step, he was crossing the room. He was halfway to the window. Had it been all fancy, was he to—And then Jimmie Dale stood motionless. *Someone had closed the library door softly!*

Stillness again! A sort of deadly calm upon him, Jimmie Dale felt out behind his back for the big library table that he had been circuiting—if the window were wide open it might be done, but to jump for it and stand silhouetted there during the pause necessary to fling the window up was little less than suicidal. He edged back noiselessly until his fingers touched the table; then, lowering himself to his knees, he backed in underneath it, and lay flat upon the floor. It was not much protection, but it had one advantage: if they switched on the lights it would show an *empty* room for the first instant, and that instant meant—the first shot!

Where were they now? By the library door? How many of them were there? Well, it was their move! Two could play at cat and mouse until—until *daylight*! That wasn't very far off, now, and when that came he might still have the first shot, but after that—he turned his head quickly toward the window. There was a faint scratching noise as of finger nails gripping the sill; then the window, very slowly, almost silently, was pushed steadily upward, and a dark form loomed up outside; and then, crawling through, a man dropped, as though his feet were padded like a cat's on the floor inside the room. The Magpie!

A flashlight's ray shot out—and, with a twisted smile propped now on his left elbow to give free play to his revolver arm, Jimmie Dale followed the white spot eagerly with his eyes. But it did not circle around; instead, the light was turned almost instantly toward the lower end of the room—and, a second later, was holding steadily on the open door of the safe, and the litter of papers on the floor.

Came a savage growl of amazed fury from the Magpie: then his step down the room; and, as he reached the safe, a torrent of unbridled blasphemy—and then, in a sort of staggered gasp, as he leaned suddenly forward examining the knob of the dial:

"The Gray Seal!"

A moment the Magpie stood there; and then, cursing again in abandon, turned, and started back for the window, his flashlight dancing before him—and stopped, a snarl of fury on his lips. The flashlight was playing full on Jimmie Dale under the table!

"Larry the Bat! The Gray Seal! By God!" choked the Magpie. "You—you—" The Magpie's flashlight, as he shifted it from his right hand to his left and wrenched out his revolver, had fallen upon two men crouched close against the wall by the library door—and he screamed out in an access of fury. "De double cross! A plant! De bulls! You damned snitch, Larry!" screamed out the Magpie—and fired.

The bullet tore into the carpet beside Jimmie Dale. Came answering shots from the men by the door; and then the Magpie, emptying his automatic at the two men as he ran, the flame tongues cutting vicious lanes of fire through the darkness, dashed for the window. There was a cry, the crash of a heavy body pitching to the floor—and the Magpie had flung himself out through the window, and in the momentary ensuing silence within the room came the sound of his footsteps running on the gravel below.

There was a low moan, the movement as of someone staggering and lurching around—and then the lights went on. But for an instant Jimmie Dale did not move. He was staring at the form of a man still and motionless on the floor in front of him—the man who had posed as Henry LaSalle. Dead! The man was dead! His mind ran riot for a moment. Where were the others—were there only these two? Only these two in the house! Only these two—and one was dead! And then Jimmie Dale was on his feet. One was dead—but there was still the other, the man who was reeling there, back turned to him, by the electric-light switch. But even as Jimmie Dale sprang forward, this second man, clawing at the wall for support, slipped to his knees and fell upon the carpet.

Jimmie Dale reached him, snatched the revolver from his hand, and bent over him. It was the man whose name he did not know, but whose face he had reason enough to know too well—it was the leader of the Crime Club.

The man, though evidently badly wounded, smiled defiantly in spite of his pain.

"So you're the Gray Seal!" he flung out contemptuously. "A clever enough safe-cracker—but only a lowbrow, like the rest of them. Another illusion dispelled! Well, you've got the money—better run, hadn't you?"

Jimmie Dale made no answer. Satisfied that the man was too badly hurt to move, he went and bent over the silent form in the centre of the room. A moment's examination was enough. "Henry LaSalle" was dead.

He stood there looking down at the man. It was what he had come for—though it was the Magpie, not himself, who had accomplished it! The man was dead! The words began to run through his mind in a strage reiteration. The man was dead—the man was dead! He checked himself sharply. He must think now—think fast, and think *right*.

The Magpie knew that Larry the Bat was the Gray Seal—and as fast as the Magpie could get there, the news would spread like wildfire through the underworld. "Death to the Gray Seal! Death to the Gray Seal!" He could hear that slogan ringing again in his ears, but as he had never heard it before—with a snarl of triumph now as of wolves who at last had pulled their quarry down. He had not a second to spare—and yet—that man wounded there on the floor! What of him—guilty of murder, the brains of this inhuman, monstrous organisation, the one to whom, more even than to that dead man, the Tocsin owed the horror and the misery and the grief and despair that had come into her life! What of him? What of the Crime Club here? What of this nest of vipers? Were they to escape? Were they to—

With a sudden, low exclamation, Jimmie Dale jumped for the table, and, snatching up the telephone, rattled the hook violently.

"Give me"—his voice came in well-simulated gasps, each like a man fighting for every word—"give me—police—headquarters! Quick! *Quick!* I've—been—shot!"

The wounded man on the floor raised himself on his elbow.

"What are you doing?" he demanded in a startled way. "Are you mad! Thank your stars you were lucky enough to get out of this alive—and get out now, while you have the chance!"

Jimmie Dale pressed his hand firmly over the mouthpiece of the telephone.

"I'll go," he said, with a cold smile, "when I've settled with you—for the murder of Henry LaSalle."

"That man!" ejaculated the man scornfully, pointing to the form on the floor. "So that's your game! Going to try and cover your tracks! Why, you fool, I *live* here! Do you think the police would imagine for an instant that I killed him?"

"I said—*Henry LaSalle*," said Jimmie Dale evenly.

The man came farther up on his elbow, a sudden look of fear in his face.

"What—what do you mean?" he cried hoarsely.

But Jimmie Dale was talking again into the telephone—gasping, choking out his words as before:

"Police headquarters? I'm Henry LaSalle. Fifth Avenue. I—I've been shot. Take down this statement. I'll—I'll be dead before you get here—I'm not the real Henry LaSalle at all. We murdered Henry LaSalle—in Australia, and murdered Peter LaSalle here. We—we tried to kill the daughter, but she ran away. This house has been our headquarters for the last five years. The man who shot me tonight is the leader of the gang. We quarrelled over the division of a haul. He's here on the floor now, wounded. Get them all, get them all, damn them!—do you hear?—get them all! They're out of the house now, but lay a trap for them. They always come in through the garage on the side street. Oh, God, I'm done for! Break down the west walls of the rooms upstairs—if—you—want proof of what—the gang's been doing. Hurry! Hurry! I'm—I'm—done for—I—"

Jimmie Dale permitted the telephone to drop with a clash from his hand to the table.

The face of the man on the floor was livid.

"Who are you? In God's name, who are you?" he cried out wildly.

"Does it matter?" inquired Jimmie Dale grimly. "Your game is up. You'll go to the chair for the murder of 'Henry LaSalle'—if it is by proxy! Those rooms upstairs alone are enough to damn you, to prove every word of that dying 'confession'—but tomorrow, added to it, will come the story of Marie LaSalle herself."

For a moment the man hung there swaying on his elbow, his face working in ghastly fashion—and then suddenly, with a strange laugh, he carried one hand swiftly to his mouth—and laughed again—and before Jimmie Dale could reach him was lifeless on the floor.

A tiny vial rolled away upon the carpet. Jimmie Dale picked it up. A drop or two of liquid still remained in it—colourless, clear, like that liquid this same man had dropped into the rabbit's mouth the night before, like the liquid in the glasses they had carried into that third room, like the liquid that his man had said was from a formula of their own, that was instantaneous in its action, that defied detection by autopsy!

The set, stern features of Jimmie Dale relaxed. It was justice—but it was also death. In a surge of emotion, the events of scarcely more than twenty-four hours, began to crowd upon him—and then, ominously dominant, above all else, that slogan of the underworld, "Death to the Gray Seal!" came ringing once more in his ears. It brought him, with a startled movement of his hand across his eyes, to a realisation of his own desperate position. Yes, yes, he must go! The way was clear now for the Tocsin—clear now for her!

He dropped the vial into his pocket, and, running to the safe, quickly scraped the gray seal from the dial's knob; then he drew the packages of money from his shirt and pockets and tossed them on the floor among the litter of papers already there—she would get it back again when it had served its purpose, it would be self-evident that it was the proceeds of that day's sale of the estate's securities over which the "quarrel" had occurred!

And now the window! He ran to it, closed it, and *locked* it; then, laying the revolver he had taken from the leader down beside the man, he stepped across the room again and drew the body of "Henry LaSalle" closer to the table—as though the man had fallen there when the telephone had dropped from his hand.

It was done now! On the floor beside him lay each man's weapon—and both of the revolvers had been discharged several times. Jimmie Dale paused on the library threshold for a final survey of the room. It was done! The way was clear—for her. And now if he could only save himself! There was no chance for Larry the Bat! Could he save—*Jimmie Dale!*

He crossed the hall, a half-grim, half-wistful smile on his lips, unlocked the front door, stepped out, locked it behind him—and in another moment, doubling around the corner, was running along like a hare along the side street.

CHAPTER 16

"DEATH TO THE GRAY SEAL!"

On Jimmie Dale ran. Across on Fourth Avenue he swung on a car that took him to Astor Place. Then striking east once more, making a detour to avoid the Bowery, he ran on at top speed again. To reach the Sanctuary, not before the Magpie should have spread the alarm, that was impossible, but to reach it before the underworld should have had time to recover its breath, as it were, before the underworld should have had time to act—that was his only chance! The Magpie had, at the outside, a start of fifteen minutes; but he, Jimmie Dale, had probably retrieved five minutes of that in the time he had made in getting downtown. That left the Magpie ten to the good. How long would it take the Magpie to bring the underworld swarming like hornets around the Sanctuary?

On Larry the Bat ran. At the Sanctuary were the clothes, the belongings of Jimmie Dale. Could he save Jimmie Dale! If he could get there, change, and get out again, the way was clear for him—as clear as for the Tocsin now. In a few hours the police would have every member of the Crime Club in the trap; there would be no watch any more around his house on Riverside Drive; and he would be free to return there and resume his normal life as Jimmie Dale again if he could make the Sanctuary in time! But let the Magpie get there first, let the underworld tear the place to pieces in its fury as it would do, let them discover that hiding place under the flooring, for instance, and the Gray Seal would not be merely Larry the Bat, but Jimmie Dale as well, and—a cry escaped him even as he ran—it meant ruin, the disgrace of an honoured name, death, crimes without number at his door. Crimes! The Gray Seal had never committed a crime! But the crimes attributed to the Gray Seal he could not disprove, not one of them! He had meant them to appear as crimes—and he had succeeded so well that the Gray Seal's name, execrated, was a synonym for the most callous, dangerous, and unscrupulous criminal of the age!

He was gasping for breath as finally, making for the side door, he darted into the alleyway that flanked the Sanctuary. What story would the Magpie tell? Not the truth, of course—that would let the Magpie in for what had happened that night, for the Magpie must be well aware that he had shot at least one of the two men in that room. But the truth wasn't necessary; it was foreign, and had no bearing on the one outstanding fact—the Gray Seal was Larry the Bat. At the present moment the Magpie had a double incentive for "getting" the Gray Seal—the Gray Seal was the only one who could prove murder against him that night in the LaSalle mansion. And afterwards, when the police version of the affair was made public, the Magpie, to save himself, would be careful enough to do or say nothing to contradict "Henry LaSalle's" confession!

Larry the Bat slipped in through the door, halted there, listened; and then began to mount the rickety stairs, with his silent tread. At the top he paused again. Nothing—no sound! They were not here yet—so far he was in time! He stepped to the Sanctuary door, unlocked it, passed into the squalid, miserable room that had harboured him for so long as Larry the Bat, locked the door behind him, crossed quickly to the window to make sure that the shutters were closed—and then, for the first time, as the gray light streaked in through the interstices, he was conscious that it was already dawn. So much the more need for haste then!

He whipped out his revolver and laid it at his hand on the dilapidated table; then the flooring in the corner was up in an instant, and he began to strip off the rags of Larry the Bat. Boots, mismated socks, the torn, patched trousers, the greasy flannel shirt, the threadbare coat, the nondescript slouch hat were thrown in a pile on the floor; and with them, from their hiding-place, the grease paints and heterogeneous collection of make-up accessories. This done, he began to slip on the clothes of Jimmie Dale; and, when half dressed, turned to the table again to remove the characteristic grime, stain, and paint of Larry the Bat from face, hands, wrists, throat, and neck. This was a longer, more arduous task. He reached for the cracked pitcher to pour more water into the basin—and, snatching up his revolver instead, whirled to face the door.

Someone was outside! He had caught the creak of a footstep upon the stairs. In a flash he was across the room and crouched by the door. Yes, the step was nearer now—at the head of the stairs—on the landing. His revolver lifted, holding a steady bead on the door panel. And then there came a low voice:

"Jimmie! Jimmie! Are you there? Quick, Jimmie! Are you there?"

The Tocsin! What was she doing here! Why had he not warned her up there on the avenue, fool that he was, that of all places she was to keep away from here!

She slipped into the room as he unlocked the door.

"They're coming, Jimmie!" she panted breathlessly. "There's not an instant to lose! Listen! When the Magpie ran from the house, I ran with him—but it"—she tried to smile—"it wasn't to obey you, to run away—I had made up my mind I wouldn't do that—it was to find out from him what had happened. He told me you were the Gray Seal. He did not suspect me. He thinks you were no more than just Larry the Bat to me, as you were to everybody else. He went straight to Chicago Ike's gambling rooms and found the Skeeter's gang there—you know them, Red Mose, the Midget, Harve Thoms, and the Skeeter—you remember your fight with them over old Luddy's diamonds! Well, they have not forgotten, either! They are on their way here, now! The news that you are the Gray Seal is travelling like lightning all through the underworld—there will be a mob here on the Skeeter's heels. So, Jimmie—quick! Run!"

Run! Half Larry the Bat, half Jimmie Dale—and run! In another five minutes, perhaps—yes. But there probably would not be five minutes—and she—if she were found here!

"Yes," he said quietly. "I'll get away in a moment. You go at once. I'll"—he was smiling at her reassuringly—"I'll meet you at—"

She looked at him then for an instant—interrupting him quickly, as she shook her head.

"I didn't notice, Jimmie. You cannot go like that—can you? It would be even worse than being caught as Larry the Bat. Hurry then—I am not going without you."

"No!" he said. "Go now! Go at once, Marie—while you can. You have risked your life as it is to come here and tell me this. For God's sake, go now!"

The great, brown eyes were smiling bravely through a sudden mist. She shook her head again.

"Not without you, Jimmie."

It brought a fierce, wild throb of joy upon him—and then a cold, sickening fear.

"Listen!" he cried out desperately. "You must go now! You cannot take any chances now, Marie. Everything is right for you. That man who posed as your uncle is dead—the leader of the Crime Club is dead. Don't you understand what that means! You have only to be Marie LaSalle again and claim your own. I cannot tell you all now—there's no time. That house was the Crime Club itself. The police will get them all. Don't you see! Don't you see! Everything is clear for you now—and now go! Go—you must go!"

She was staring at him, a strange wonder in her face.

"Clear! All clear—for me! I—I can go back to—to my own life again!" It was as though she were whispering some amazing thing of unbelievable joy to herself.

"Yes!" he cried out again. "Yes! But go—go, Marie!"

But now, for answer, suddenly she reached out and took the key from the door and put it in the pocket of her dress.

"We will go together, Jimmie—or not at all," she said simply. "We are wasting precious moments. Hurry and dress!"

He hesitated miserably. What could he do—if she *would* not go! And it was true—the moments were flying. Better, rather than futile argument, to use them as she said. There was still a chance! Why not! Five minutes! He could do better than that! He *must* do better than that!

Without a word, he ran back across the room. In frantic haste, from face, hands, wrists, and neck came the stain. There was still time. She was standing there by the door, listening. She, the Tocsin, she whom he loved, she who, all through the years that had gone, had been so strangely elusive and yet so intimately a part of his life, *she* was standing there now, here with him—in peril with every second that passed!

He had only to slip on his coat and vest now—and make a bundle of Larry the Bat's things on the floor, so that he could carry them away to destroy them. He stooped to gather up the clothes—and straightened suddenly—and jumped toward the door again.

"They are coming, Jimmie!" she called, in a low voice. But he had already heard them—the stairs were creaking loudly under the tread of many feet. He pushed the Tocsin hurriedly back against the wall at the side of the door.

"Stand there!" he said, under his breath. "Out of the line of fire! Don't move!"

There was a rush against the door—and then a voice growled:

"Aw, cut dat out! Wot do youse want to do—scare him away by bustin' it! Pick de lock, an' we'll lay for him inside till he shows up."

It was the Skeeter's voice. The Skeeter and his gang—the worst apaches in the city of New York! Professional assassins, death contractors, he had called them—and the lowest bidders! A man's life any time for twenty-five dollars! No, they were not likely to forget the affair of the pushcart man, to forget old Luddy and his diamonds, to forget—the Gray Seal! And they were only the vanguard of what was to come!

Someone was working at the lock now. There was one way to stop that. It would not take them long to find out that he *was* there once the door was opened! Better know it with the door *shut*! Jimmie Dale lifted his revolver coolly and fired through the panel.

A burst of yells answered the shot; and among them, high above the others, the Magpie's scream:

"We got him! We got him! He's dere now!"

And then it seemed that pandemonium broke loose—there was a volley of shots, the bullets splintering through the door panels as from a machine gun, so fast they came—and then another rush against the door.

Flat on the floor, but well back and to one side, Jimmie Dale fired steadily—again and again.

Came screams of pain, yells, and oaths—and they fell back from the door.

And now from above, from overhead, came tumult—windows thrown up, the stamp of feet, cries of fright. And from the street, a low, sullen roar. The underworld was gathering fast!

Once more the rush upon the door—and Jimmie Dale, a grim, twisted smile upon his lips, emptied his revolver into the panels. Once more they fell back—and then there came the Skeeter's voice, snarling like an infuriated beast:

"He'll get de lot of us like dis! Cut it out! Besides, we'll have de bulls down here in a minute—an' he's *our* meat, not theirs. Dey'd be too damned soft wid him—dey'd only send him to de chair. Youse chase upstairs, Mose, an' pass de word to beat it—an' beat it quick. We'll *burn* de skunk out—dat's wot. An' de bulls can stand alongside an' watch, if dey likes—but he's our meat."

Jimmie Dale did not dare to look at the Tocsin's face. Mechanically he refilled the magazine of his automatic—and lay there, waiting. The roar from the street grew louder. They seemed to be fighting out there, as though an inadequate number of police were trying to disperse a mob—and not succeeding! Pretty soon, with the riot call in, there would probably be a battle—for the Gray Seal! Sublime irony! It was death at the hands of either one!

Children whimpered on the stairs outside, men swore, women cried, feet shuffled hurriedly by as the tenement emptied. Occasionally, a pertinent invitation to him to remain where he was, there was a vicious rip through the panel, and the drumming whir of a bullet flying through the room. And then a curious, ominous crackling sound—and then the smell of smoke.

Jimmie Dale stood up, his face drawn and haggard. The tenement would go like matchwood, burn like a bonfire, with any kind of a start—and there was no doubt about the start! The Skeeter, the Magpie, and the rest would have seen that it had headway enough to serve their purpose before either firemen or police could thwart them. He, Jimmie Dale, could take his choice: walk out into a bullet, or stay there and—he smiled miserably as his eyes fell upon the pile of Larry the Bat's clothing on the floor. There was no longer need to worry about *its* destruction—the fire would take care of that only too well! And then a low, bitter cry came to his lips, and he clenched his hands. If it were only himself—only himself! He crossed to the Tocsin and caught her in his arms.

"Oh, my God—Marie!" he faltered.

The cape and hood had fallen from her, and with the hood had fallen the gray-streaked hair of Silver Mag—and now as she smiled at him it was from a face that was very beautiful and very brave and very full of tenderness.

And he held her there—and neither spoke.

It seeped in under the threshold of the door, it came from everywhere, filling the room—the black, strangling smoke. Outside in the hall all was silence now—save for that crackle of flame that grew in volume, that came now in quick, sharp reports, like revolver shots. From out in the street swelled a cry: "Death to the Gray Seal!" Then the clang of bells, the roar and rattle of fire apparatus, strident voices bellowing orders, and the crowd again, blood hungry: "Death to the Gray Seal!"

There was a chance, just one—if the fire had no headway along the upper end of the landing—and if they had not thought to set a watch for him *above*! They—the Magpie, the Skeeter, and his gang—must have been driven even out of the house now by the smoke and flame.

"Give me the key, I am going to open the door, Marie," he said quietly. "Cover your face with a handkerchief, anything, and run to the *left* to the next flight of stairs. There are two flats above this—we'll make the roof if we can. Now—are you ready?"

It was an instant before she answered, an instant in which she lifted her face to his, and held his face between her two hands—and then:

"I am ready, Jimmie."

He flung open the door, his arm around her to help her forward—and instinctively, with a cry, fell back for a moment. With the inrush of the draft poured the smoke, and through it, lurid, yellow, showed the flames leaping from the stair well.

And then all was blind madness. Together they ran. At the foot of the stairs she fell, recovered herself, staggered up another—and fell again. He caught her up in his arms and, staggering now as she had staggered, went on. His lungs seemed to be bursting. His limbs grew weak and trembled under him. He could not see or breathe. The nauseating fumes suffocated him, bringing an intolerable agony. He gained the first landing above. There was one more—one more! If he could only rest here for a moment! Yes, that was it—rest. It wasn't so bad here now. She stirred in his arms, struggled to her feet—and he was helping her on again, and up the next flight of stairs.

And suddenly he found himself laughing in hysteria—for they were climbing a half stair, half ladderway at the end of the upper landing, and the open skylight was above them, and they were drinking in the pure, fresh air—and now they were out upon the roof, and the roar from the street was in their ears, like the roar of great waters from some canyon far below. Jimmie Dale tried to speak, and found his lips were cracked and dry. He wet them with his tongue.

"Don't stand up—we'd be seen—*crawl*," he mumbled hoarsely.

It took a long time—over one roof, and then another, and yet another—and then through the skylight of a tenement whose occupants were either craning from the front windows, or were on the street below. It was, perhaps, half an hour—and then they, too, were standing in the street, and all about them the crowd was shouting in wild excitement.

Up the block, inside the fire lines, the Sanctuary was blazing furiously—and now suddenly the wall seemed to bulge outward. It brought a yell from the crowd:

"Death to the Gray Seal!"

She pulled at his arm.

"Let us get away! Let us get away, Jimmie!" she whispered frantically.

A strange smile was on Jimmie Dale's lips.

"We're safe now—for always," he whispered back. "Look!"

The Sanctuary wall bulged farther outward, seemed to hang an instant hesitant in mid-air—and fell with a mighty crash.

The Gray Seal was dead!

THE FURTHER ADVENTURES
OF JIMMIE DALE

CHAPTER 1

SMARLINGHUE

A diminutive gas-jet's sickly, yellow flame illuminated the room with poverty-stricken inadequacy; high up on the wall, bordering the ceiling, the moonlight, as though contemptuous of its artificial competitor, streamed in through a small, square window, and laid a white, flickering path to the door across a filthy and disreputable rag of carpet; also, through a rent in the roller shade, which was drawn over a sort of antiquated French window that opened on a level with the floor and in line with the top-light, the moonlight disclosed a narrow and squalid courtyard without.

In one corner of the room stood a battered easel, while against the wall near it, and upon the floor, were a number of canvases of different sizes. A cot bed, unmade, its covers dirty and in disorder, occupied the wall space opposite the door. In the centre of the mean and uninviting apartment stood a table, its top littered with odds and ends, amongst which the remains of a meal, dishes and food, fraternised gregariously with a painter's palette, brushes and paint tubes. A chair or two, long since disabled, and a rickety washstand completed the appointments.

The moonlight's path across the floor wavered suddenly, the door opened, was locked again, and with a quick, catlike step a man moved along the side of the wall where the shadows lay thickest near the door, dropped on his knees, and began to fumble hurriedly with the base-board of the wall, pausing at every alternate second to listen intently.

A minute passed. A section of the base-board was lifted out, the man's hand was thrust inside—and emerged again with a large roll of banknotes. He turned his head for a quick glance around the room, his eyes, burning out of a gaunt, hollow-cheeked, pallid face, held on the torn window shade—and then, in almost frantic haste, he thrust the banknotes back inside the wall, and began to replace the base-board. But it was not the window shade, nor yet the courtyard without with which he was concerned—it was the sound of a heavy footstep outside the door.

And now the door was tried. The man on the floor, working with desperate energy to replace the base-board, coughed in an asthmatic, wheezing way, as there came the imperative smashing of a fist upon the door panels, coupled with a gruff, curt demand for admittance. Again the man coughed—to drown perhaps the slight rasping sound as the base-board slid back into place—and, rising to his feet, shuffled hastily to the door and unlocked it.

The door was flung violently open from without, a heavy-built, clean-shaven, sharp-featured man stepped into the room, slammed the door shut behind him, re-locked it, and swept a shrewd, inquisitive, suspicious glance about the place.

"It took you a damned long time to open that door, *Mister* Smarlinghue!" he said sharply.

The man addressed touched his lips with the tip of his tongue nervously, shrank back, and made no reply.

The lapel of the visitor's coat thrown carelessly back displayed a police shield on the vest beneath; and now, completing a preliminary survey of the surroundings, the man's eyes narrowed on Smarlinghue.

"I guess you know who I am, don't you? Heard of me perhaps, too—eh? Clancy of headquarters is my name!" He laughed menacingly, unpleasantly.

Smarlinghue's clothes were threadbare and ill-fitting; his coat was a size too small for him, and from the short sleeves protruded blatantly the frayed and soiled wristbands of his shirt. He twined his hands together anxiously, and retreated further back into the room.

"I haven't done anything, honest to God, I haven't!" he whined.

"Ain't, eh?" The other laughed again. "No, of course not! Nobody ever did! But now I'm here—just dropped in socially, you know—I'll have a look around."

He began to move about the room. Smarlinghue, still twining his hands in a helpless, frightened way, still circling his lips nervously with the tip of his tongue, followed the other's movements in miserable apprehension with his eyes.

Clancy, as he had introduced himself, shot up the roller shade, peered out into the courtyard, yanked the shade down again with a callous jerk that almost tore it from its fastenings, and strode over toward the easel, contemptuously kicking a chair that happened to be in his way over onto the floor. Reaching the easel he picked up the canvas that rested upon it, stared at it for a moment—and with a grunt of disdain flung it away from him to the ground.

There was a crash as it struck the floor, a ripping sound as the canvas split, and with a pitiful cry Smarlinghue rushed forward and snatched it up.

"It—it was sold," he choked. "I—I was to get the money tomorrow. I have had bad luck for a month—nothing sold but this—and now—and now—" He drew himself up suddenly, and, with the ruined painting clutched to his breast, shook his other fist wildly. "You have no right here!" he screamed in fury. "Do you hear! I have not done anything! I tell you, I have not done anything! You have no right here! I will make you pay for this! I will! I will!" His voice was rising in a shrill falsetto. "I will make you—"

"You hold your tongue," growled Clancy savagely, "or I'll give you something more than an old chromo to make a row about! I don't want any mass meeting of your kind of citizens. Get that?" He caught Smarlinghue roughly by the shoulder, and pushed him into a chair near the table. "Sit down there, and close your jaw!"

Cowed, Smarlinghue's voice dropped to a mumble, and he let the torn canvas slip from his fingers to the floor.

Clancy laughed gruffly, pulled another chair to the opposite side of the table, sat down himself, and eyed Smarlinghue coldly for a moment.

"Sold it, eh?" he observed grimly. "How much were you going to get for it?"

A cunning gleam flashed in Smarlinghue's eyes—and vanished instantly. He wet his lips with his tongue again.

"Ten dollars," he said hoarsely.

Clancy brushed aside the litter on the table, and nonchalantly laid down a ten-dollar bill.

With a sharp little cry that brought on a fit of coughing, Smarlinghue stretched out his hand for the money eagerly.

Clancy drew the money back out of reach.

"Oh, no, nothing like that!" he drawled unpleasantly. "Don't make the mistake of taking me for a fool. I'm not buying any ten-cent art treasures at ten dollars a throw!"

Smarlinghue's eyes remained greedily riveted on the ten-dollar note. He began to twine his hands together once more.

"I don't know what you mean," he muttered tremulously.

"Don't you!" retorted the other shortly. "Well, I mean exactly what I say. I'm not buying any pictures, I'm buying—*you*. I have been keeping an eye on you for the last three or four months. You're just the guy I've been looking for. As far as I can make out, there ain't a dive or a roost in the Bad Lands where you don't get the glad hand—eh?"

"I—I haven't done anything! Not a thing! I—I swear I haven't!" Smarlinghue burst out frantically.

"Aw, forget it!" Clancy permitted a thin smile to flicker contemptuously across his lips. "You've got a whole lot of friends that I'm interested in. Get the idea? There ain't a crook in New York that's shy of you. You got a 'stand-in' everywhere." He held up the ten-dollar bill. "There's more of these—plenty of 'em."

Smarlinghue pushed back his chair now in a frightened sort of way.

"You—you mean you want me for—for a stool pigeon?" he faltered.

"You got it!" said Clancy bluntly.

Smarlinghue's eyes roved about the room in a furtive, terror-stricken glance, his hand passed aimlessly over his eyes, and he crouched low down in his chair.

"No, no!" he whispered. "No, no—for God's sake, Mr. Clancy, don't ask me to do that! I can't—I can't! I—I wouldn't be any good, I—I can't! I—I won't!"

Clancy thrust head and shoulders aggressively across the table.

"You will—if you know what's good for you!" he said evenly. "And, what's more, there's a little job you're going to break your hand in on to-night."

"No! No, no! I can't! I can't!" Smarlinghue flung out his arms imploringly.

Clancy lowered his voice.

"Cut that out!" he snapped viciously. "What's the matter with you! You'll be well paid for it—*and have police protection*. You ought to know what that'll mean to you—eh? You live like a gutter-snipe here—half starved most of the time, for all you can get out of those ungodly daubs!"

A curious dignity came to Smarlinghue. He sat upright.

"It is my art," he said. "I have starved for it many years. Some day I will get recognition. Some day I—"

"Art—hell!" sneered Clancy; and then he laughed coarsely, as, his fingers prodding under the miscellany of articles on the table, he suddenly held up a hypodermic syringe. "This is *your* art, my bucko! Why, you poor boob, don't you think I know you! Cocaine's the one thing on earth you live for. You're stewed to the eyes with it now. Here, just watch me! Suppose"— he caught the syringe in a quick grip between the fingers of both hands— "suppose I just put this little toy out of commission now, and—"

With a shrill screech, Smarlinghue sprang from his chair, and clawed like a demented man at the other's hands for possession of the hypodermic.

Clancy surrendered the syringe with a mocking grin, and shoved Smarlinghue backward into his chair again.

"Oh, yes; you're an artist all right—a coke artist!" he remarked coolly. "But that's what makes you solid in every den in New York, and that's how you come in useful—to me. Well, what do you say?"

There was a hunted look in Smarlinghue's eyes.

"They'd—they'd kill me," he said huskily.

"Sure, they would!" agreed Clancy easily. "If they found you out it would be good-night, all right—that's what you're getting paid for. But"—his voice hardened—"if you don't come across, I'll tell you what *I'll* do to you. I'll—"

"You can't do anything! Not a thing!" Smarlinghue cried wildly. "You haven't anything on me at all. I've never done a thing, not a single—"

"Oh, I guess there's enough to make you sweat," Clancy cut in brutally. "You give me the icy paw, and I'll see that the tip leaks out from the right quarters that you *are* a stool pigeon. That'll take care of your finish, too, won't it—good and plenty!"

Smarlinghue stared miserably. Again and again his tongue circled his lips. Twice he tried to speak—and only succeeded in mumbling inarticulately.

Clancy got up from the table, walked around it, and, standing over the crouched figure in the chair, tapped with his finger on the hypodermic in Smarlinghue's hands.

"And that ain't all," he announced with a malicious grin. "You come in and play the game with me, or I'll fix it so that you'll never get another squirt of dope if you had a million bucks to buy it with—ah, I thought that would get you!"

Smarlinghue was on his feet. The terror of the damned was in his face.

"No! No! My God—no—not that! You—you wouldn't do that!" He reached out his arms to the other.

"You know—I've gone too far to do without it. If I didn't have it, I—"

"I've seen a few of them in that sort of jim-jams," said Clancy malevolently. "You can't tell me anything about it. If you appreciate it, that's enough—it's up to you. You heard what I said. If you're looking for that particular kind of hell, go to it. Only don't kid yourself. When I pass the word to put the screws on, the lid's down for keeps. Well, what's the answer? Coming across? Quick now! I haven't got all night to spend here!"

Smarlinghue's hands were trembling violently; he sat down in his chair in a pitiful, uncertain way.

"Yes, yes!" he whispered. "*Yes!* I got to do it. I'll do it, Mr. Clancy, I'll do it! I'll—I'll do anything!"

A half leer, half scowl was on Clancy's face, as he stood regarding the other.

"I thought you would!" he grunted roughly. "Well then, we'll get down to business—and tonight's *busi*ness. You know the back entrance to Malay John's hang-out?"

Smarlinghue's eyes widened a little in a startled way. He nodded his head.

"Very good," said Clancy gruffly. "*You'll* have no trouble in getting in there. And once in there you'll have no trouble in getting up to Malay's private den. I've been wised up that Malay and a few of his pals are getting ready to pull off a little game uptown. I want the dope on it—*all* of it. They've been meeting in Malay's den for the last few nights—understand? They drift in between half past eleven and twelve—you get there a little *before* halfpast eleven. You haven't anything to be afraid of, so don't lose your nerve. Malay himself is away this evening and won't be back before midnight; and the door won't be locked, as otherwise the others couldn't get in. Everything's clear for you. Savvy? Once you're in the room, there's plenty of places to hide—and that's all you've got to do, except keep your ears and eyes open. Get the lay?"

Again Smarlinghue nodded—unhappily this time.

"All right!" said Clancy crisply. "I'm not coming around here any more—*unless I have to*. It might put you in bad. You can make your reports and get your orders through Whitie Karn at his dance hall."

"Whitie Karn!" The exclamation seemed to come involuntarily, in a quick, frightened way from Smarlinghue.

Clancy's lips twisted in a smile.

"Kind of a jolt—eh—Smarlinghue? You didn't suspect he was one of *us*, did you?—and there's more than Whitie Karn. Well, it will teach you to be careful. Suppose Whitie, for instance, passed the word that you were a snitch—eh? It won't do you any harm to keep that in mind once in a while." He moved over to the door. "Well, good-night, Smarlinghue! I guess you understand, don't you? You ought to be a pretty valuable man, and I expect a lot from you. If I don't get it—" He shrugged his shoulders, held Smarlinghue for an instant with half-closed, threatening eyes—and then the door closed behind him.

Smarlinghue did not move. The steps receded from the door, and died away along the passage. A minute, two minutes went by. Suddenly Smarlinghue pushed back the wristband of his shirt, and pricked the skin with the needle of the hypodermic. The door, without a sound, swung wide open. Clancy stood in the doorway.

"Good-night again, Smarlinghue," he said coolly.

The hypodermic fell clattering to the floor; Smarlinghue jumped nervously in his chair.

Clancy laughed—significantly; and, without closing the door this time, strode away again. His steps echoed back from the passageway, the front door opened and shut, his boot heel rang on the pavement without—and all was silence.

Smarlinghue rose from his chair, shuffled across the room, closed the door and locked it, then shuffled back again to the roller shade over the little French window, and, taking a pin from the lapel of his coat, fastened the rent together.

A passing cloud for a moment obscured the moonrays from the top-light; the gas-jet choked with air, spluttered, burning with a tiny, blue, hissing flame; then the white path lay across the floor again, and the yellow flare of gas spurted up into its pitiful fulness—and in Smarlinghue's stead stood another man. Gone were the stooping shoulders, gone the hollow cheeks, the thin, extended lips, the widened nostrils, as the little distorting pieces of wax were removed; and out of the metamorphosis, hard and grim, set like chiselled marble, was revealed the face of—Jimmie Dale.

CHAPTER 2

THE WARNING

For a moment Jimmie Dale stood there hesitant, the long, slim, tapering fingers curled into the palms of his hands, his fists clenched tightly, a dull red suffusing his cheeks and burning through the masterly created pallor of his make-up; and then slowly as though his mind were in dismay, he walked across the room, turned off the gas, and going to the cot flung himself down upon it.

What was he to do? What ghastly irony had prompted Clancy to sort *him* out for a police spy? If he refused, if he attempted to stall on Clancy, Clancy's threat to stamp him in the eyes of the underworld as a snitch meant ruin and disaster, absolute and final, for "Smarlinghue" would then have to disappear; on the other hand, to be allied with the police increased his present risks a thousandfold—and they were already hazardous enough! It meant constant surveillance by the police that would hamper him, rob him of his freedom of movement, adding difficulties and perils innumerable to the enacting of this new dual personality of his.

Jimmie Dale's hands clenched more fiercely. It was an impossible situation—it was untenable. That he could play his role in the underworld with only the underworld to reckon with—*yes*; but with the police as well, watching him in his character of a poor, drug-wrecked artist, constantly in touch with him, likely at any moment to make the discovery that Smarlinghue and Jimmie Dale, the millionaire clubman, a leader in New York's most exclusive set, were one and the same—*no*! And yet what was he to do? With the Gray Seal it had been different. Then, police and underworld alike were openly allied as common enemies against him—but none had known who the Gray Seal was until that night when the Magpie had roused the Bad Lands like a hive of swarming hornets with the news that the Gray Seal was Larry the Bat; none had known until that night when it was accepted as a fact that Larry the Bat, and therefore the Gray Seal, had perished miserably in the tenement fire.

Around the squalid room, lighted now only by the moonrays, Jimmie Dale's eyes travelled slowly, abstractedly. Yes, in that one particular it was different; but here was the New Sanctuary, and again he was living the old life in close, intimate companionship with the underworld—the old life that only six months ago he had thought to have done with forever!

He turned his face suddenly to the wall, and lay very still—only his hands still remained tightly clenched, and the hard, set look on his face grew harder still.

Six months ago, like some mocking illusion, like some phantom of unreality that jeered at him, it seemed now, he had lived for a few short weeks in a dreamland of wondrous happiness, a happiness that all his own great wealth had never been able to bring him, a happiness that no wealth could ever buy—the joy of her—the glad promise that for always their lives would be lived together—and then, as though she had vanished utterly from the face of the earth, she was gone.

The Tocsin! Marie LaSalle to the world, she was always, and always would be, the Tocsin to him. *Gone*! A hand unclenched and passed heavily across his eyes and flirted the hair back from his forehead. She had taken her place in her own world again; her fortune had been restored to her, its management placed in the hands of a trust company; the interior of the mansion on Fifth Avenue, with its sliding walls and secret passages, that had served as headquarters for the Crime Club, was in the process of reconstruction—and she had disappeared.

It had come suddenly, and yet—as he understood now, though then he had only attributed it to an exaggerated prudence on her part—not without warning. In the three weeks that had intervened between the night of the fire in the old Sanctuary and her disappearance, she had permitted him to see her only at such times and at such intervals as would be consistent with the most casual of acquaintanceships. He remembered well enough now her answer to his constant protests, an answer that was always the same. "Jimmie," she had said, "a sudden intimacy between us would undo all that you have done—you know that. It would not only renew, but would be almost proof positive to those who are left of the Crime Club that their suspicions of Jimmie Dale were justified, and from that as a starting point it would not take a very clever brain to identify Jimmie Dale as Larry the Bat—and the Gray Seal. Don't you see! You never knew me before all the misery and trouble came—there was nothing between us then. To see too much of each other now, to have too much in common now would only be to court disaster. Our intimacy must appear to come gradually, to come naturally. We must wait—a year at least—Jimmie."

A year! And within a few hours following the last occasion on which she had said that, Jason, his butler, had laid the morning mail upon the breakfast table, and he had found her note.

It seemed as though he were living that moment over again now, as he lay here on the cot in the darkness—his eagerness as he had recognised the well-known hand amongst the pile of correspondence, the thrill akin to tenderness with which he had opened the note; and then the utter misery of it all, the room swirling about him, the blind agony in which he had risen from his chair, and, as he had groped his way from the room, the sudden, pitiful anxiety on the faithful old Jason's face, which, even in his own distress, he had not failed to note and understand and be grateful for.

There had been only a few words in the note, and those few carefully chosen, guarded, like the notes of old, lest they should fall into a stranger's hand; but he had read only too clearly between the lines. She had had only far too much more reason for fear than she had admitted to him; and those fears had crystallised into realities. One sentence in the note stood out above all others, a sentence that had lived with him since that morning months ago, the words seeming to visualise her, high in her courage, brave in the unselfishness of her love: "Jimmie, I must not, I cannot, I will not bring you into the shadows again; I must fight this out alone."

He recalled the feverish haste in which he had acted that morning—the one thought that had possessed him being to reach her if possible before she could put her designs into execution. Benson, his chauffeur, reckless of speed laws, had rushed him to the hotel where, pending the remodelling of the Fifth Avenue mansion, she had taken rooms. Here, he learned that she had given up her apartments on the previous afternoon, and that it was understood she had left for an extended travel tour, and that her baggage had been taken to the Pennsylvania Station. From the hotel he had gone to the trust company in whose hands she had placed the management of her estate. With a few additional details, disquieting rather than otherwise, it was the story of the hotel over again. They did not know where she was, except that she had told them she was going away for a long trip, had given them the fullest powers to handle her affairs, and, on the previous afternoon, had drawn a very large sum of money before leaving the institution.

He had returned then, like a man dazed, to his home on Riverside Drive, and had locked himself in his den to think it out. She had covered her tracks well—and had done it in a masterly way because she had done it simply. It was possible that she had actually gone away for a trip; but it was more probable that she had not. He had had, of course, no means of knowing; but the sort of peril that threatened her, his intuition told him, was not such as to be diverted by the mere expedient of absenting herself from New York temporarily; and, besides, she had said that she would *fight* it out. She could hardly do that in the *person* of Marie LaSalle, or away from New York. She was clever, resourceful, resolute and fearless—and those very traits opened a vista of possibilities that left his mind staggering blindly as in a maze. She was gone—and alone in the face of deadly menace. He remembered then the curious, unnatural calmness underlying the mad whirling of his brain at the thought that that was not literally true, that she was not, nor would she ever be alone—while he lived. It was only a question of *how* he could help her. It had seemed almost certain that the danger threatening her came from one of two sources—either from those who were left of the Crime Club, relentless, savage for vengeance on account of the ruin and disaster that had overtaken them; or else from the Magpie, and behind the Magpie, massed like some Satanic phalanx, every denizen of the underworld, for Silver Mag had disappeared coincidently with Larry the Bat, coincidently with the Magpie's attempted robbery of the supposed Henry LaSalle's safe, to which plot she was held by the underworld to be a party, coincidently with the dispersion of the Crime Club, *and coincidently with the reappearance of the heiress Marie LaSalle*—and, further, Silver Mag stood condemned to death in the Bad Lands as the accomplice of the Gray Seal. But Silver Mag had disappeared. Had the underworld, prompted by the Magpie, solved the riddle—did it know, or guess, or suspect that Silver Mag was Marie LaSalle?

Which was it? The Crime Club, or the Magpie? Here again he could not know, though he inclined to the belief that it was the latter; but here, in either case, the means of knowing, of helping her, the way, the road, was clearly defined—and the road was the road to the underworld. But Larry the Bat was dead and the road was barred. And then a half finished painting standing on an easel at the rear of his den had brought him inspiration. It was one of his hobbies—and it swung wide again for him the door of the underworld. None, in a broken-down, disappointed, drug-shattered artist, would recognise Larry the Bat! The only similarity between the two—the one thing that must of necessity be the same in order to explain plausibly his intimacy with the dens and lairs of Crimeland, the one thing that would, if nothing more, assure an unsuspicious, tolerant acceptance of his presence there, was that, like Larry the Bat, he would assume the rôle of a confirmed dope fiend; but as there were many dope fiends, thousands of them in the Bad Lands, that point of similarity, even if Larry the Bat were not believed to be dead, held little, if any, risk. For the rest, it was easy enough; and so there had come into being these wretched quarters here, the New Sanctuary—and Smarlinghue.

But the mere assumption of a new rôle was not all—it was not there that the difficulty lay; it was in gaining for Smarlinghue the *confidence* of the underworld that Larry the Bat had once held. And that had taken time—was not even yet an accomplished fact. The intimate, personal acquaintance of Larry the Bat with every crook and dive in Gangland had aided him, as Smarlinghue, to gain an initial foothold, but his complete establishment there had necessarily had to be of Smarlinghue's own making. And it had taken time. Six months had gone now, six months that, as far as the Tocsin was concerned, had been barren of results mainly, he encouraged himself to believe, because his efforts had been always limited and held in check; six months of anxious, careful building, and now, just as he was regaining the old-time confidence that Larry the Bat had enjoyed, just as he was reaching that point where the whispered secrets of the underworld once more reached his ears and there was a promise of success if, indeed, she were still alive, had come this thing tonight that spelt ruin to his hopes and ultimate disaster to himself.

If she were still alive! The thought came flashing back; and with a low, involuntary moan, mingling anguish of mind with a bitter, merciless fury, he turned restlessly upon the cot. If she were still alive! No sign, no word had come from her; he had found no clue, no trace of her as yet through the channels of the underworld; his surveillance of the Magpie, whose friendship he had begun to cultivate, had, so far, proved fruitless.

It came upon him now again, the fear, the dread, which he had known so often in the past few months, that seemed to try to undermine his resolution to go forward, that whispered speciously that it was useless—that she was dead. And misery came. And he lay there staring unseeingly into the moonrays as they streamed in through the top-light.

Time passed. Then a smile played over Jimmie Dale's lips, half grim, half wistful; and the strong, square jaw was suddenly out-flung. If she was alive, he would find her; if she was dead—his clenched hand lifted above his head as though to register a vow—the man or men, her murderer or murderers, whether tomorrow or in the years to come, would know a day of reckoning when they should pay the debt!

But that was for the future. Tonight there was this vital, imminent danger that he had to face, this decision to make whose pros and cons seemed each to hold an equal measure of dismay. What was he to do?

He laughed shortly, ironically after a moment. It was as though some malignant ingenuity had conspired to trap him. He was caught either way. What was he to do? The question kept pounding at his brain, growing more sinister with each repetition. What was he to do? Defy the police—and be branded as a stool-pigeon, a snitch, an informer in every nook and cranny of the underworld! He could not do that. Everything, all that meant anything in life to him now would be swept from his reach at even the first breath of suspicion. Nor was it an idle threat that his unwelcome visitor had made. He was not fool enough to blind himself on that score—it could be only too easily accomplished. And on the other hand—but what was the use of torturing his brain with a never-ending rehearsal of details? Was there a middle course? That was his only chance. Was there a way to safeguard Smarlinghue and, yes, this miserable hovel of a place, priceless now as his new Sanctuary.

He followed the moonpath's slant with his eyes to where it touched the floor and disclosed the greasy, threadbare, pitiful carpet. A grim whimsicality fell upon him. It would be too bad to lose it! It was luxury to what Larry the Bat had known! There had not even been a carpet in the old Sanctuary, and—he sat suddenly bolt upright on the cot, his eyes, that had mechanically travelled on along the moonpath, strained now upon where the light fell upon the threshold of the door. There was a little white patch there, a most curious little white patch—that had not been there when he had thrown himself on the cot. Came a sudden, incredulous thought that sent the blood whipping fiercely through his veins; and with a low cry, in mad, feverish haste now, he leaped from the cot and across the room.

It was an envelope that had been thrust in under the door. In an instant he had snatched it up from the floor, and in another, acting instinctively, even while he realised the futility of what he did, he wrenched the door open, stared out into a dark and empty passageway—and, with a strange, almost hysterical laugh, closed and locked the door again.

There was no writing on the envelope; there was not light enough to have deciphered it if there had been—but he had need for neither writing nor light. Those long, slim, tapering fingers, those wonderful fingers of Jimmie Dale, that seemed to combine all human faculties in their sensitive tips, had already telegraphed their message to his brain—it was the same texture of paper that she always used—it was from *her*—it was from the Tocsin.

Joy, gladness, a relief so terrific as it surged upon him as to leave him for the moment physically weak, held him in thrall, and he stumbled back across the room, and slipped down into a chair before the table, and dropped his head forward into his arms, the note tightly clasped in his hand. She was *alive*. The Tocsin was alive—and well—and here in New York—and free—and they had not caught her. It meant all those things, the coming and the manner of the coming of this note. A deep thankfulness filled his heart; it seemed that it was only now he realised the full measure of the fear and anxiety, the strain under which he had been labouring for so many months. She was alive—the Tocsin was alive. It was like some wonderful song that filled his soul, excluding all else. How little the contents of the note itself mattered—the one great, glorious fact for the moment was that she was alive!

It was a long time before Jimmie Dale raised his head, and then he got up suddenly from his chair, and lit the gas. But even then he hesitated as he turned the note over, speculatively now, in his fingers. So she knew him as Smarlinghue! In some way she had found that out! His brows gathered abstractedly, then cleared again. Well, at any rate, it was added proof that so far her cleverness had completely outwitted those who had pitted themselves against her—so much so that even her freedom of action, in whatever role she had assumed, was still left open to her.

He tore the envelope open. There was no preface to the note, no "Dear Philanthropic Crook" as there had always been in the old days—instead, the single, closely-written sheet began abruptly, the writing itself indicating that it had been composed in desperate haste. He glanced quickly over the first few lines.

"You should not have done this. You should never have come into the underworld again. I begged, I implored you not to do so. And now you are in danger tonight. I can only hope and pray that this will reach you in time, and—" He read on, in a startled way now, to the end; then read the note over again more slowly, this time muttering snatches of it aloud: "...Chicago...

Slimmy Jack and Malay… Birdie Lee…released from Sing Sing today… triangular scar on forehead over right eye…."

And then, for a little while, Jimmie Dale stood there staring about the room, motionless, rigid as stone, save that his fingers moved in an automatic, mechanical way as they began to tear the note into little shreds. But presently into his face there crept a menacing look, and an angry red began to tinge his cheeks, and his jaws clamped ominously.

So that was the game at Malay John's, was it? Birdie Lee was out again! She had not needed to mention any scar to enable him to identify Birdie Lee. He knew the man of old. The slickest of them all, the cleverest of them all, before he had been caught and sent to Sing Sing for a five-years' term, was Birdie Lee—the one man of them all that he, Jimmie Dale, might regard as a rival, so to speak, where the mastery of the intricate mechanism of a vaunted and much advertised "guaranteed burglar-proof safe" was concerned! And Birdie Lee was out again!

There was danger if he went to Malay John's, she had said—and it was true. But what if he did *not* go! What, for instance, if Birdie Lee went through with this night's work!

Jimmie Dale walked slowly across the room, halted before the wall near the door, stood for an instant hesitant there—and then, as though in a sudden, final decision, dropped down on his knees, and, working swiftly, removed the section of the base-board from the wall for the second time that night.

Out came the neatly folded clothes of Jimmie Dale; and with them, serving him so well in the days gone by, the leather girdle, or undervest, with its stout-sewn, upright pockets in which nestled, in an array of fine, blue-steel, highly tempered instruments, a compact powerful burglar's kit. It was the one thing that he had saved from the fire in the old Sanctuary—and that more by accident than design. He had been wearing the girdle that night when he had stolen into the Crime Club, and afterwards had returned to the Sanctuary with the intention of destroying forever all traces of Larry the Bat; and then, only half dressed, as he was changing into the clothes of Jimmie Dale, the alarm had come before he had taken off the girdle, and, without thought of it again at the time, he had still been wearing it when he had made his escape. He looked at it now for a moment grimly—and smiled in a mirthless way. He had not used it since that night, and that night he had never meant or thought to use it again—only to destroy it!

He reached into the aperture in the wall once more, drew out a pocket flashlight and an automatic pistol, and laid them down beside the clothes and the leather girdle; then, pulling off his coat and shirt, he ran noiselessly across the room to the washstand. A few drops from a tiny phial poured into the water, and the pallor, the sickly hue from his face was gone. It was to be Jimmie Dale—not Smarlinghue—who would keep the rendezvous at Malay John's!

And now he was back across the room once more, turning out the light as he passed the gas-jet. The leather girdle, that went on much after the fashion of a life-preserver, was fastened over his shoulders and secured around his waist. The remainder of his clothes were stripped off with lightning speed, and in their place were donned the fashionably tailored, immaculate tweeds of Jimmie Dale. It was like some quick-moving, shadowy pantomime in the moonlight. He gathered up the discarded garments, tucked them into the opening in the wall, replaced the baseboard, slipped the automatic and flashlight into the side pockets of his coat—and stood up, his fingers feeling swiftly over his vest and under the back of his coat to guard against the possibility of any tell-tale bulge from the leather girdle underneath.

An instant he stood glancing critically about him; then the roller shade over the window was lifted aside, the window itself, on carefully oiled hinges, was opened noiselessly, closed again—and, hugged close against the wall of the building, hidden in the black shadows, Jimmie Dale, so silent as to be almost uncanny in his movements, crept along the few intervening feet to the fence that enclosed the courtyard. Here, next to the wall, a loosened plank swung outward at a touch, and he was standing in a narrow, black areaway beyond. There was only the depth of the house between himself and the street, and he paused now, crouched motionless against the wall, listening. He heard no footfalls from the pavement—only, like a distant murmur, the night sounds from the Bowery, a block away—only the muffled roar of an elevated train. The way was presumably clear, and he moved forward again—cautiously. He reached the front of the building, which, like the old Sanctuary, was a tenement of the poorer class, paused once more, this time to peer quickly up and down the dark, ill-lighted cross street—and, satisfied that he was safe from observation, stepped out on the sidewalk, and began to walk nonchalantly along to the Bowery.

And here, at the corner, under a street lamp he consulted his watch. It was ten o'clock! He smiled a little ironically. Certainly, they would hardly expect him as early as that! Well, he would be a little ahead of time, that was all!

CHAPTER 3

THE MAN WITH THE SCAR

Jimmie Dale walked on again, rapidly now, heading down the Bowery. At the expiration of perhaps ten minutes, he turned east; and still a few minutes later, in the neighbourhood of Chatham Square, plunged suddenly into a dark alleyway—there was, of course, as there was to all such places, an unobtrusive entrance to Malay John's.

His lips tightened a little as he moved quietly forward. To venture here in an unknown character was not far from being tantamount, if he were discovered, to taking his life in his hands. Malay John was a queer customer and a bad enemy, though counted "straight" by the underworld, and trusted by the crooks and near-crooks as few other men were in the Bad Lands. And, if Malay John was queer, the place he ran was queerer still. Ostensibly he conducted a dance hall, and a profitable one at that; but below the dance hall, known only to the initiated, deep down in a sub-cellar, was perhaps the most remunerative gambling joint and pipe lay-out in Crimeland.

Jimmie Dale halted before a doorway in the alley. The rear of a low building rose black and unlighted above him. A confused jangle from a tinny piano, accompanying a blatant cornet and a squeaky violin, mingled with the dull scrape of many feet, laughter, voices, singing—the dance hall at the front of the building was in full swing. He glanced sharply up and down the dark alleyway, then, leaning forward, placed his ear to the panel of the door—and the next instant opened the door softly and stepped inside.

It was pitch black here, but it was familiar ground to Larry the Bat in the old days, and therefore to Smarlinghue in the new. The short passageway in which he was standing terminated, he knew, in a rear entrance to the dance hall, which was always kept locked and used only by Malay John himself, and which was just at the foot of the stairs that led upward to Malay John's combination of private den, office, and sleeping apartment; while at the side of the passage, half way along, was that other door, always guarded on the inside, that required an "open sesame" to gain admittance to the dive below.

And now he crept stealthily past this latter door, reached the staircase, and went swiftly up to the landing above. Here another door barred his way, and here again he placed his ear to the panel—but this time to listen, it seemed, interminably. Every faculty was strained and alert now. He could take no chances here, and the uproar from the dance hall below, while it had safeguarded his ascent of the stairs, was confusing now and by no means an unmixed blessing.

Still he crouched there, his ear to the panel—and then, satisfied at last, he tried the door. It was locked.

"The penalty of being early!" murmured Jimmie Dale softly to himself.

His hand reached in under his vest to one of the pockets in the leather girdle, and a tiny steel instrument was inserted in the lock. There was a curious snipping sound, the doorknob turned slowly under his hand; then cautiously, inch by inch, he pushed the door open, slipped through—and stood motionless on the other side of the threshold. Save only from the dance hall below, there was not a sound. The door closed again; again that snipping sound as it was relocked—and then the round, white ray of Jimmie Dale's flashlight circled his surroundings.

There was a sort of barbaric splendour to the place. Malay John was something of a sybarite! It was a single room, whose floor was covered with rich Turkish rugs, whose walls were covered with Oriental hangings, and in one corner was a great, wide divan, canopied, also with Oriental hangings at head and foot, serving presumably for a bed; but, striking a somewhat incongruous note, others of the appointments were modern enough—the flat-topped desk in the centre of the room with its revolving chair, for instance, and a large, ponderous safe that stood back against the rear wall.

Jimmie Dale crossed the room for a closer inspection of the safe, and, as his flashlight played over the single dial, he shook his head whimsically. No, it would be hardly true to call *that* modern; it was only an ancient monstrosity, a helpless thing at the mercy of any cracksman who—

The flashlight in his hand went out. Like lightning, Jimmie Dale, his tread silent on the heavy rugs, leaped back across the room, and in an instant slipped in behind the end hangings of the divan and stood, pressed closely, against the wall.

A key turned stealthily in the lock, the door opened as stealthily—then silence—then a flashlight swept suddenly around the room—darkness again—and then a hoarse whisper:

"All clear, Birdie. Lock the door."

The door closed. The flashlight played down the room again—and upon Jimmie Dale's lips came a twisted smile, as, his fingers edging the hanging slightly to one side, he peered out.

The light ray moving before them, two dark forms stole across the room to the safe.

"There you are, Birdie!" said one of them. "Ain't she a beaut! Say, a kid could open it! Didn't I tell you I was handing you one on a gold platter!"

The light ray now flooded the front of the safe, and outlined the forms of the two men. One of them, holding the flashlight, dropped on his knees, and began to twirl the dial tentatively; the other leaned negligently against the corner of the safe.

"I ain't so sure it's easy, Slimmy," replied the man on his knees, after a moment. He stopped twirling the dial, and looked up. "Mabbe it'll take longer than we figured on. Are you sure there ain't no chance of Malay gettin' back? I'd rather stack up against every bull in New York than him."

The twisted smile on Jimmie Dale's lips still lingered. So that was Slimmy Jack there, leaning against the safe! Slimmy Jack—and Birdie Lee! His fingers drew the hangings a little further apart. The room was in complete darkness except for the circle of light around the safe, and it was as though what was being enacted before him were some strange, realistic film thrown upon a screen—just two forms in the white light, their faces masked, against the background of the safe, with its glittering nickel dial. And now Slimmy

Jack, from his negligent pose, straightened sharply and leaned toward Birdie Lee.

"Say, what's the matter with you, Birdie!" he exclaimed roughly. "You didn't let 'em get your nerve up the river, did you? You've been acting kind of queer all day. I told you before, Malay wouldn't be back in time to monkey with *us*. We don't have to stand for this—I told you that, too. You don't think I'm a fool, do you, to steer you into a lay that's got a come-back on myself unless the thing was planted right? Why, damn it, Malay knows I saw the coin put in there. D'ye think I'd give him a chance of suspecting *me*! It's all fixed—you know that. Now, go to it—there's a nice little piece of money in there that'll keep us going till we pull that Chicago deal."

"All right!" Birdie Lee answered tersely. "Keep quiet, then, and I'll see what I can do."

He laid his ear against the safe, listening for the tumblers' fall, as, holding the flashlight in his left hand, its rays upon the dial, the fingers of his right began to work swiftly again with the glistening knob.

From below, the confused, dull medley of sound from the dance hall seemed only to intensify the silence in the room. Slimmy Jack stood motionless at the side of the safe, his elbow resting against the old-fashioned, protruding upper hinge. A minute, two, another, and still another dragged by. Came then a short ejaculation from Birdie Lee.

Slimmy Jack bent forward instantly.

"Got it?" he demanded eagerly.

"No—curse it!" gritted Birdie Lee. "My fingers seem to have lost their touch—I ain't had much practice for the last five years up there in Sing Sing!"

"Well, then, 'soup' it!" grunted Slimmy Jack. "You could blow the roof off, and no one would be the wiser with that racket downstairs. We can't waste all night over it."

"What are you going to 'soup' it with?" Birdie Lee flung back gruffly. "We didn't bring nothing. You said—"

"I know I did!" A sullen menace had crept suddenly into Slimmy Jack's voice. "I said you could open an old tin can like that with your hands tied—and so you can. Try it again!"

Jimmie Dale's fingers stole inside his shirt, and into a pocket of the leather girdle, and brought forth a black silk mask. He slipped it quickly over his face. Birdie Lee was at work once more. It was about time to play his own hand in the game. The Tocsin had made no mistake, he was sure of that now, and—

Birdie Lee spoke again.

"It's no use, Slimmy!" he muttered. "I guess I ain't any good any more. I can't open the damned thing!"

"Try it again!" ordered Slimmy Jack shortly.

"But it's no use, I tell you!" retorted Birdie Lee. "I ain't got the feel in my fingers."

"You—try—it—again!" There was a cold, ominous ring in Slimmy Jack's voice.

Birdie Lee drew back a little on his knees, glancing quickly up at the other.

"What—what d'ye mean by that, Slimmy!" he exclaimed in a startled way.

"I'll show you what I mean, and I'll show you blamed quick if you don't open that safe!" Slimmy Jack threatened hoarsely. "Blast you, you're stalling on me—that's what you're doing! I've seen you work before. You could open that thing with your finger nails, if you wanted to! Now, open it!"

"But, I can't!" protested Birdie Lee. "I wouldn't hand you anything like that, Slimmy—you know that, Slimmy. I—"

"*Open it!* And open it—*quick!*" Slimmy Jack's hand was wrenching at his side pocket.

"But, I tell you, I can't, Slimmy!" cried Birdie Lee, almost piteously. "It's queered me up there in the pen. I"—he was rising to his feet—"Slimmy—for God's, sake—what are you doing—you—"

There was a flash, the roar of the report, a swaying form, a revolver clattering to the floor—and with a crash Slimmy Jack pitched forward and lay motionless.

Then silence.

It had come without warning, in the winking of an eye, and for a moment it seemed to Jimmie Dale that he could not grasp the full significance of what had happened—that Slimmy Jack, his sleeve catching on the hinge of the safe as he had finally succeeded in jerking his revolver from his pocket, had, a grim, ironical trick of fate, accidentally shot himself! Mechanically, automatically, Jimmie Dale's hands went to his pockets and produced his own flashlight and revolver—but he did not move. His eyes now were on Birdie Lee, who, like a man dazed and terror-stricken, had lurched back against the safe, the flashlight that dangled in his hand sweeping patches of light about the floor.

Still silence—only the uproar from the dance hall that would have drowned out to those below the sound of the revolver shot. Then Birdie Lee staggered forward, and knelt beside the prostrate form on the floor. He stood up again presently, swaying unsteadily on his feet, turning his head wildly about, now this way, now that. And then his whisper, broken, hoarse, quavered through the room:

"He's dead. My God—he's—he's dead."

"Drop that flashlight!" Jimmie Dale's voice rang cold, imperative. "*Drop it!*" And, sweeping the hangings aside, the ray of his own light suddenly full upon Birdie Lee, he leaped forward.

With a low, terrified cry, the other let the flashlight fall as though from nerveless fingers, and shrank back against the safe.

"Now put your hands above your head!" directed Jimmie Dale curtly.

The man obeyed.

Dark, frightened eyes stared out at Jimmie Dale from behind the mask that covered Birdie Lee's face. Swiftly, deftly, Jimmie Dale felt over the other's clothing for a weapon. There was none. Then, himself in darkness, the blinding light in Birdie Lee's face, he pulled off the other's mask, and with a grim, quick touch of his revolver muzzle traced out the white, pulsing, triangular scar on the man's forehead.

"So you're up to your old tricks again, are you, Birdie?" he inquired coldly. "Five years up the river wasn't enough for you—eh?"

The man drew himself up suddenly, and, squaring his shoulders, made as though to speak—and then, with a swift, hopeless gesture, turned his back, and, leaning over the top of the safe, buried his head in his arms.

A strange smile touched Jimmie Dale's lips. He stooped down, picked up the revolver from the floor, slipped it into his pocket, bent over Slimmy Jack for an instant to assure himself that the man was dead—then stepping back to the safe, he laid his hand on the ex-convict's shoulder.

"Birdie," he said quietly, "could you open this safe if you wanted to?"

The man swung sharply around, the prison pallor of his face a pitiful, deathlike colour in the flashlight's rays.

"Who are you?" he asked thickly.

"A friend perhaps—if you can open that safe," Jimmie Dale answered.

A puzzled look crept into Birdie's eyes.

"W-what do you mean?" he stammered.

"I mean that I want the *proof* that you are straight," Jimmie Dale said softly. "I've been here in the room all the time. I want to know whether you were stalling on Slimmy Jack, or not. And I want to know, if you *were* stalling, how you came to be here with him."

"That's a queer spiel," said Birdie Lee, in a troubled way. "I thought at first you were a bull—but you don't talk like one. Mabbe you're playin' with me; but, whether you are or not, I guess it won't make much difference what I say. You couldn't help me if you wanted to now—with him dead there"—he jerked his head toward the form on the floor.

"Tell me, anyhow," insisted Jimmie Dale quietly.

Birdie's hand lifted and swept across his eyes.

"Well, all right," he said, after a moment; "I'll tell you. Me and Slimmy used to work together all the time in Chicago and out West after I left New York, and until I came back here one day and pulled one alone and got sent up for it. Well, today, when they let me out of Sing Sing, Slimmy had come on from Chicago and was waitin' for me. He had a deal all fixed in Chicago that we was to pull together, a big one, and this little one here was to keep us goin' until the big one came off. He was with Malay John in this room today when a gambler from up the State somewhere blew in with a roll of about three thousand dollars, and handed it over to Malay to keep while he knocked around town for a day or two. Malay put the money in this safe here, and that's what Slimmy was after for a starter. I told Slimmy I was all through—that I was goin' straight. He wouldn't believe me. I guess you don't. I guess nobody will. I got a record that's mabbe too black to live down, and—oh, well, what's the use! I meant to live decent, but I guess any chance I had is gone now." His voice choked. "That's the way I had doped it out up there in the pen—that I was goin' straight. That's all, isn't it? I told Slimmy I was through—but Slimmy held something over me that was good for twenty years. What could I do? I said I'd come in on this, figurin' that I could queer the game by stallin'. I—I tried it. If you were here, you saw me. I pretended that I couldn't open the safe, and—"

"*Can* you?" inquired Jimmie Dale gently.

"That thing!" Birdie Lee smiled mirthlessly. "Why it's only a double combin—"

"Open it, then," prompted Jimmie Dale.

Birdie Lee stooped impulsively to the dial of the safe; hesitated, then straightened up again, and shook his head.

"No," he said. "I guess I'll take my medicine. I don't know who you are. I might just as well have opened it for Slimmy as for you. It looks as though you were after the same thing he was."

Jimmie Dale smiled.

"Stand a little away from the safe, Birdie—there," he instructed. And, as the other obeyed wonderingly, Jimmie Dale knelt to the dial. "You see, I trust you not to move," he said. The dial was whirling under the sensitive fingers, and, like Birdie before him, his ear was pressed against the face of the safe.

The moments went by. Birdie Lee was watching in an eager, fascinated, startled way. Came at last a sharp, metallic click, as Jimmie Dale flung the handle over—and the door swung wide. He shut it again instantly—and locked it.

"It's your turn, Birdie," he said calmly. "You see that, as far as I or my intentions are concerned, it doesn't matter whether you open it or not."

"Who are you?" There was awed admiration in Birdie's voice. "You're slicker than ever I was, even in the old days. For God's sake, who are you?"

"Never mind," said Jimmie Dale. "Open the safe, if you can."

"I can open it all right," said Birdie, moving slowly forward; "and quicker than you did, because I got the combination when I was workin' on it with Slimmy watchin'. Throw the light on the knob, will you?"

It was barely an instant before Birdie Lee swung back the door.

"Now lock it again," directed Jimmie Dale. And then, as the other obeyed, he held out his hand to Birdie Lee. "You're clear, Birdie."

A tremor came to the other's face.

"Clear?" repeated Birdie unsteadily.

"Yes—you get your chance. That's one reason why I came here to-night—to spoil Slimmy Jack's play, to see that you got your chance if you really wanted it, as"—he added whimsically—"I was informed you did. Go ahead, Birdie—make your get-away—you're free."

But Birdie Lee shook his head.

"No," he said, and his voice caught again. "It's no good." He pointed to the still form on the floor. "I guess I go up for more than safe-crackin' this time. I—I guess it'll be the *chair*. When they find him here—dead—shot—they'll call it murder—and they'll put it onto me. The police know we have been together for years. They know he came here today when I got out. We've been seen together today. We—we were seen *quarrelling* this afternoon in a saloon over on the Bowery. That was when I was refusin' to start the old play again. They'd have what looked like an open and shut game against me. I wouldn't have a hope."

It was a moment before Jimmie Dale answered. What the man said was true—he would not have a hope—for an honest life—after five years in the penitentiary. He lifted his flashlight again and played it over Birdie Lee. They showed, those years, in the pallor, the drawn lines, the wan misery in the other's face.

And then Jimmie Dale's lips set firmly under his mask. There was a way to save the man. It was something he had never intended to do again—but it was worth the price—to save this man. It would be like a bombshell exploded in the underworld; it would arouse the police to infuriated activity; it would stir New York to its depths—but, after all, it could not touch Smarlinghue. It would only instill the belief that somehow Larry the Bat had escaped from the tenement fire; it would only mean a hunt for Larry the Bat day and night—but Larry the Bat no longer existed—and it would save this man.

He clamped the flashlight between his knees, leaving his hands free, and from the leather girdle drew the old-time metal case, thin, like a cigarette case, and from the case, with a pair of little tweezers that precluded the possibility of telltale finger prints, lifted out a small, diamond-shaped, gray-coloured paper seal, adhesive on one side, which he moistened now with his tongue—and, stooping quickly, attached it to the dead man's sleeve.

There was a sharp, startled cry from Birdie Lee.

"*The Gray Seal*! You're—you're Larry the Bat! They passed the word around in Sing Sing that you were dead, and—"

"And it will be the Gray Seal who is wanted for this—not you," said Jimmie Dale quietly. Then, almost sharply: "Now make your get-away, Birdie. Hurry! You and I part here. And the greater distance you put between yourself and this place tonight the better."

But the man seemed as though robbed of the power of movement—and then his lips quivered, and his eyes filled.

"But you," he faltered, "you—you're doing this for me, and I—I—"

Jimmie Dale caught the other's arm in a kindly grip.

"Good-night, Birdie," he said significantly. "I'm the last man now that you could afford to be seen with. You understand that. And I guess you can understand that I've reasons for not wanting to be seen myself. You've got your chance; give me mine to get away—alone." He pushed the man abruptly toward the door.

Still Birdie Lee hesitated; then catching Jimmie Dale's hand, he wrung it hard—and, with a half choked sob, turned and made his way from the room.

For an instant Jimmie Dale stood looking after the other through the darkness, listening as the stealthy steps descended the stairs—then suddenly he knelt again beside the dead man on the floor.

"You were clever, Slimmy!" he murmured. "Smarlinghue wouldn't have had a chance of getting out from under this break—if your plans had worked out! And I didn't know you, of course, because you were a Chicago crook."

He took off the dead man's mask, and played his flashlight for a moment over the cold, set features.

A slight smile twisted Jimmie Dale's lips.

It was "Clancy of Headquarters"!

CHAPTER 4

THE DIAMOND PENDANT

The "murder" of Slimmy Jack had evidently been discovered too late for the make-up of the early morning papers; but from the noon editions onward it had been flung across the front pages in glaring type—even the most stately journals, for the nonce aroused out of their dignified calm, indulging in "display" headlines that, quite apart from the mere text, could not but have startled their equally stately and dignified readers. The Gray Seal, the leech that fed upon society, the murderer, the thief, the menace to the lives and property of law-abiding citizens, the scourge that for years New York had combated in the no more effective fashion than that of gnashing its teeth in impotent fury, had suddenly reappeared with a fresh murder to his credit. And New York had thought him dead!

Jimmie Dale, leaning back on the seat of his limousine as the car, now halting at a corner, now racing with a hundred others to snatch a block or two of distance before the next monarchial traffic officer of Fifth Avenue should hold it up again a victim to the evening rush, turned from first one to another of the pile of papers beside him. His strong, clean-shaven face was grave; and there was a sober light in the dark, steady eyes. In the St. James Club, which he had just left, perhaps the most sedate, certainly the most exclusive club in New York, it had been the one topic of conversation. Elderly gentlemen, not usually given to excitability, had joined with the younger members in a hectic denunciation of the police as criminally inefficient, and had made dire and absurdly vain threats as to what they, electing themselves for the moment a supreme court of last resort, proposed to do under the circumstances. The irony was exquisite, if they had but known! Also there was the element of humour, only there was a grim tinge to the humour that robbed it of its mirth—some day they *might* know!

He glanced out of the window, as the car was held up again. Everybody in the crowd, that waited on the corners for the stream of traffic to pass, seemed to have their eyes glued to their newspapers—even Benson, his chauffeur, during the moment of inaction, was surreptitiously reading a paper which he had flattened out on the seat beside him!

Jimmie Dale's eyes reverted to the newspaper in his hand, one of the most conservative. There was no mistaking the tenor of the leading article on the editorial page:

"It is not so much that a thug and criminal known as Slimmy Jack should have been murdered by another wretch of his own breed; indeed, that such should prey upon one another is far from being a matter of regret, for we might hope in time for the extermination of them all by the simple process of mutual attrition and at correspondingly little expense to ourselves—but that this so-called Gray Seal should still prove to be alive and at large is a matter that concerns every citizen personally. He does not confine his attentions to the Slimmy Jacks. The criminal records of the past few years reek with his acts, that run the gamut of every crime in the decalogue, crimes for the most part actuated apparently by no other motive than a monstrously innate thirst for notoriety—and the victims, for the most part, too, have been the innocent and the defenceless. What is the end of this to be? If the police cannot cope with this blood-mad ruffian, is New York to sit idly by and submit to another reign of terror instituted and carried on under the nose of authority by this inhuman jackal? If so, we are committing a crime against ourselves, we are insulting our intelligence, and—"

The man who had written that was a personal friend! Jimmie Dale threw the paper down, and picked up another, and after that another. They were pretty well all alike. They rehearsed the discovery of Larry the Bat as the Gray Seal; they rehearsed the story of the fire in the tenement of six months ago in which it was supposed that Larry the Bat had perished—they differed only in the virulence, a mere choice of words, with which they now demanded that this Larry the Bat, alias the Gray Seal, should be dug out like a rat from his hole, and the city be freed once and for all, and with no loophole for misadventure this time, of this "ogre of hell," as one paper put it, that was gorging itself upon New York.

The furrows gathered on Jimmie Dale's forehead, as he folded up the papers, and stared at his chauffeur's back through the plate-glass front of the car. He had known that the reappearance of the Gray Seal would arouse the community to a wild pitch of excitement, but he had far underestimated the effect. He could gauge it better now, though—he had only to look out of the windows at the passers-by. And this was only the respectable element of the city whose head and front was the police, and dangerous enough for all the bitter taunts, gibes and recriminations with which the police was maligned! There was still the far more dangerous element of the underworld! He had not been in that quarter since he had left Malay John's the night before, but he could picture it now well enough. God help him if he ever fell into those hands! In dens and dives, in the dark corners of that sordid world, they would be whispering blasphemous vows of vengeance against him one to another— and, relative to the hate and fear that welded them into a single unit, the police sank into insignificance. More than one of their élite had gone to the electric chair through the instrumentality of the Gray Seal; more than one was serving at that moment a long term behind penitentiary walls. Whose turn was it to be next? They needed no editorial prod in the underworld to run Larry the Bat to earth—there was the deeper spur of self-preservation! They knew who the Gray Seal was now, and the first blow that he had aimed upon his reappearance had apparently been at one of themselves. Their search for Larry the Bat would not be an indifferent one!

It was true that Larry the Bat no longer existed, that in that respect he was encompassed by a certain security he had not enjoyed before, but how long would that last? One slip, one moment off his guard, would wreck all that in the twinkling of an eye. Between the police and the underworld New York would be scoured from end to end for Larry the Bat; and, failing to find trace or sign of their quarry, how long would it be before they would put more faith in the evidence of the tenement fire than in the evidence of the Magpie, upon whose testimony alone Larry the Bat had been accepted as the Gray Seal, and believe again that Larry the Bat was dead, and that therefore they had not yet solved the identity of the Gray Seal!

He had never intended that the Gray Seal should ever have been heard of again. He shrugged his shoulders philosophically. One's intentions in this world did not always count for much! His hand had been forced, and he had paid the price to save Birdie Lee. He could not regret that! Whatever the consequences, the price had not been too high, and yet—his eyes roved again over the crowded thoroughfare. A car edged by his own. Two men were in the tonneau. One held a newspaper which he thumped with a menacing fist as he talked. The door windows of Jimmie Dale's limousine were down, and he caught two bitter, angry words:

"...*Gray Seal*—"

The sober expression on Jimmie Dale's face deepened. Only a fool would attempt to minimise or underestimate the meaning of what he saw around him. A hint, for instance, that he, Jimmie Dale, millionaire clubman, riding here in his limousine, was the Gray Seal, and this great, teeming, though orderly, Fifth Avenue would be transformed like magic into a seething, screaming whirl of madmen, and—he did not care to follow that trend of thought. He was quite well aware what would happen!

The car, close up against the curb, stopped once more in a traffic blockade. Smarlinghue was the most vital factor to be considered now, for—he caught his breath quickly. Through the open window of the limousine a white envelope fluttered and fell at his feet. The car was moving forward again. For the fraction of a second Jimmie Dale did not move, save to straighten rigidly as though from some sharply administered galvanic shock; and then, with a low cry—"the Tocsin!"—he was at the door, his head thrust out through the window, his fingers mechanically wrenching at the door handle. A mass of people were surging across the street toward the opposite corner. Eagerly his eyes swept over them; he pushed the door open a little as though to step out—and shut it again quickly, as, with a yell of warning, another car, jockeying for position as his own moved out into the stream of traffic, swept by from behind.

It had been quite useless—he knew that, he had known it subconsciously even at the moment when he had sprung to his feet. Apart entirely from the crowd, she would undoubtedly be in some clever disguise, and he could not have recognised her in any event.

He stooped, picked up the envelope, and sat down again quietly, his eyes travelling swiftly in the direction of his chauffeur. Benson's back was still imperturbably turned toward him. In the roar of dozens of motors all starting forward at once, Benson evidently had not heard the yell of warning, or, if he had, had been too much occupied with his own immediate duties to pay any attention to it.

Jimmie Dale tore the envelope open; and, in a sort of grim, feverish haste, unfolded the sheets which it had contained.

"Dear Philanthropic Crook—since you *will* be called that," he read. A quick, eager flush came to his cheeks. She knew how, since she had shown last night that she knew him as Smarlinghue, that, despite all her own brave, resolute protests, he was determined to fight this thing out to the end—separately, if she would not let him join forces with her—but, in any case, to the end. It was the old name again—Dear Philanthropic Crook! Did it mean that she had surrendered, then, at last, that she had finally accepted the situation, and that he was to enter this shadowland of hers beside her! The flush died away. It was only his own wish that had been father to the thought. This was another "call to arms" of quite a different nature, and born, not out of her own peril, but born, as in the old days again, out of the maze of her strange environment. "You have set New York ablaze, you have made me far more afraid for you than I am for myself; but I cannot see where there is any danger here, or else I would not have written this. You—" He was reading impetuously now, his brain, alert and keen, sorting and sifting out, as it were, the salient, vital points, "… old Colonel Milford and his wife…Louisiana… letter…family heirloom…French descent…old setting, three large diamonds pendant from necklet of smaller ones…ten to twelve thousand dollars…steel bond box…lower right-hand drawer of desk…plan of second floor…West 88th Street…"

He turned the page, studied for a moment the carefully drawn plan that covered the next sheet, then turned to the third and last page—and suddenly his face hardened. He had been called a jackal by the papers—but here were two who bore a clearer title to the name! He knew them both—Jake Kisnieff, better known as Old Attic in the underworld, as crooked as his own bent and twisted form, a miserly, cunning "fence," crafty enough, if report were true, to have garnered a huge, ill-gotten harvest under the nose of the police; and the other, one self-styled Henry Thorold, alias whatever occasion might require, smooth, polished, educated, the most dangerous of all types of crook, was the brains of a certain clique whose versatile operations were restricted only between the limits of porch-climbing and the callous removal, via the murder route, of anyone when deemed expedient for either personal or financial reasons!

Jimmie Dale read on to the end of the page. His jaws were clamped together now, the square, determined chin out-thrust; and while one hand held the letter, the other curled into a clenched fist. It was dirty work—vile, miserable work—a coward's work! And then Jimmie Dale smiled grimly, as his eyes fell upon the glaring headline of the paper on the top of the pile beside him. Perhaps the *morning* papers would carry other headlines that would be still more startling!

He began to study the several sheets again, critically, carefully this time. There should be no danger here, she said. He knew what she meant—that she counted on his being able to nip the whole scheme in the bud. He shook his head thoughtfully. That might be true; he might be able to do that, probably would, for it was still very early; but if not—what then? He glanced out of the window—they were just turning into Riverside Drive. He looked at his watch. It wanted but a few minutes of seven—progress up the Avenue had been unusually slow. He tore the letter into small fragments, and reaching out through the window, let the pieces flutter away in the wind. It was none too early at that, and it was unfortunate that he must first of all go home—there were certain things there indispensable to the night's work. On the other hand, it was fortunate that he did not have to lose even more time by being obliged instead to go to the new Sanctuary for what he needed, fortunate that he had been "Jimmie Dale" last night when he had left Malay John's, and that he had gone directly home from there.

The car stopped. Benson sprang from his seat, and opened the door.

"Don't put up the car yet, Benson; I am going a little further uptown," said Jimmie Dale, with a pleasant nod—and ran up the steps of his house.

Jason, his butler, opened the door for him.

"I shall not be dining at home tonight, Jason." Jimmie Dale handed over his hat—not a suitable one for the evening's special requirements.

The old man's face wrinkled up in disappointment.

"That's too bad, sir, Master Jim." Jason took liberties; but they were the genuine heart liberties of a lifetime's service—and why not, since, as he was fond of saying, he had dandled his Master Jim as a baby on his knee! "There was to be just what you are especially fond of tonight, Master Jim; the cook made a particular point of—"

"Yes; I know." Jimmie Dale's hand squeezed the old man's shoulder in friendly fashion. It was not the cook, but Jason, who would have originated the menu with the painstaking care and thoughtfulness of one dealing with a life-and-death matter. "But it can't be helped. I didn't know until just a little while ago, or I would have telephoned. I am going right out again."

"Very good, sir," Jason bowed. "Your clothes, Master Jim, are—"

"I shan't dress, Jason," said Jimmie Dale—and, crossing the reception hall, with its rich, oriental rugs, he ran up the wide staircase, opened the door of his "den," locked it behind him, and, switching on the lights, began to strip off his coat and vest, as he hurried toward the further end of the great, spacious, luxuriously appointed room that ran the entire depth of the house.

He threw coat and vest on a nearby chair; and, sweeping the portières away from in front of a little alcove, knelt down before the barrel-shaped safe with its multitudinous glistening knobs, that, in the days gone by when he had been with his father in the business of manufacturing safes, the business that had amassed the fortune he had inherited, he had designed himself. His fingers flew over the dials. He swung the outer and the inner doors open, reached inside, took out the leather girdle with its burglar kit, and fastened it around his waist. Then, slipping an automatic and a flashlight into his pocket, he closed the safe, drew the portières together, and put on his coat and vest again.

An instant later he was downstairs, and, selecting a soft slouch hat—Jason for the moment not being in evidence—went down the steps to his waiting limousine.

"The Marleton, Benson," he directed, as he stepped into the car. "And hurry, please."

The car started forward. It was not far to 88th Street, but the car would save time—and time was counting now, every minute of it priceless, if, as the Tocsin had intimated, he was to forestall the game that was in hand. The

Marleton was for Benson's benefit—but the Marleton, unless he had miscalculated the numbers, was barely more than a block away from the house he sought.

And then, besides, there was another reason for haste—Colonel Milford and his wife would probably be at dinner now, and that left the upstairs part of the house at his disposal, since, apart from the elderly couple, the household consisted, according to the Tocsin, of only a single maid. He went over in his mind again the plan the Tocsin had drawn. Yes, she was quite right, there should be no danger, the whole matter as far as he was concerned was almost childishly simple and easy—if he were only in time! He shook his head a little impatiently at that; and, as he saw that they were approaching his destination, consulted his watch. It was exactly twenty minutes after seven.

The car rolled up to the curb in front of the fashionable family hotel. Jimmie Dale alighted.

"I shall not need you any more tonight, Benson," he said.

He walked quietly into the hotel, through the lobby, down a corridor, and out of the entrance that gave on the cross street—then his pace quickened. He traversed the block, crossed the road, turned the corner, and a minute later was approaching the house she had designated. It was one of a row. His pace slowed to a nonchalant stroll again. It was still quite light, and he was by no means the only pedestrian on the street; a moment's preliminary, even if cursory, examination of the exterior would not be amiss! Counting the numbers ahead of him, he had already located the house. He frowned a little. A light burned in the upstairs front room. There was a light in the lower hallway as well, but that was to be expected. Why the one upstairs? Had the Colonel and Mrs. Milford already finished their dinner?

Jimmie Dale reached the house—and casually, without hesitation, mounted the steps—and quite as casually, making a pretence of ringing the electric bell, opened the unlocked outer door, stepped into the vestibule, and, without a sound now, closed the door behind him.

He tried the inner door tentatively. It was locked, of course—but it was locked only for an instant. From the girdle under his vest came a little steel instrument; there was a faint, almost inaudible, protesting *snip* from the interior of the lock; and, his fingers turning the knob with a steady, silent pressure, he opened the door slightly.

Crouched there, he listened. And then, a smile of relief flickering on his lips, he pushed the door open, and slipped into the hallway. The explanation of the light upstairs was that it had probably been left burning inadvertently. They were still at dinner, for he could hear voices from the dining room at the rear of the hall.

As silent as a shadow now, Jimmie Dale, closing the inside door, moved across the hall, and went up the stairs. On the landing he paused; and then advanced cautiously. The light streamed out from the open door of the front room, and there was always the possibility that—no, a glance from where he stood close against the wall at the edge of the door jamb, showed him that the room was unoccupied.

He entered the room quickly, crossed quickly to a quaint old escritoire against the opposite wall, and stooped beside it. The lower right-hand drawer, she had said. The little steel instrument with which he had opened the vestibule door was still in his hand, but he did not use it now! Instead, with a low, dismayed ejaculation, as his fingers ran along the drawer edge, he dropped on his knees for a closer examination—and his lips closed tightly together.

He was too late! The first finger touch had told him that, and now his eyes corroborated it. The drawer had been forced by a jimmy of some sort, judging from the indentations in the wood. The lock was broken, and he pulled the drawer open. Inside lay the steel bond-box, its lid bent back, and wrenched and twisted out of shape. The box was empty.

Without disturbing the box, Jimmie Dale mechanically closed the drawer again and stood up, looking around him. In a subconscious way, when he had entered the room, he had been cognisant of a certain strangeness in its appointments, but then his mind had been centred only on the work in hand; now there seemed a sort of pitiful congruity in the surroundings themselves and in the old heirloom that had been stolen. It seemed as though the room spoke to him of past glories. The furniture was out-of-date, and, too, a little in disrepair. It seemed as though there clung about it the pride and station of other days, a station that it was finding it hard to maintain in these. And he thought he understood. It was a fine old family, that of the Milfords of Louisiana, a very proud old family in the way that it was fine to be proud—proud of its name, proud that its sons were gentlemen, proud of its loyalty to its own traditions and standards, a pride that neither condition nor adversity could mar. And now the diamond pendant was gone! He could well understand how they had clung to that, and—

He started suddenly. Was he a fool, that he had wasted even a moment in giving play to his thoughts! Voices were reaching him now from below, footsteps were sounding from the lower hall, there was a creak upon the stairs. They were coming!

He had hardly any need for the quick, searching glance he flung around him—the plan that the Tocsin, had drawn was mapped out vividly in his mind. He stepped backward softly through half-opened folding doors into the room in the rear. From this room a door, he knew, opened into the hall-way. His escape, after all, need give him little concern. He had only to step out into the hall after they passed, and make his way downstairs. A woman's voice from the stairway came to him:

"My dear, you must have left the light burning."

"Unless, it was you," a man's voice answered in good-humoured banter. "You were the last one in the room."

"But I am sure I didn't!" the feminine tones asserted positively.

The steps passed along the hall, and from behind the folding doors Jimmie Dale saw an elderly couple enter the front room. Both were in evening dress—and somehow, suddenly, at sight of them Jimmie Dale swallowed hard. The old gentleman, kindly, blue-eyed, white-haired, was very erect, very straight in spite of the fact that he must have been close to seventy years of age, and with the sweet-faced, old-fashioned little lady, with the gray hair, who stood beside him, they made a stately pair—for all that their clothes, past glories like the furniture, were grown a little shabby, a little threadbare. But with what a courtly air they wore them! And with what a courtly air now he led her to a chair, and bent over her, and lifted up her face, and held it tenderly between both his hands!

"How well you look tonight in your dress," he said, and his blue eyes shone. "I am very proud of you."

She stroked the hand against her cheek.

"Do you remember the first time I ever wore it?" She was smiling up at him.

"Oh, yes!" he nodded his head slowly. "It is strange, isn't it? That was a long time ago when our friends were married back there in the old State, and tonight again, way up here in New York, they have not forgotten us on this their anniversary."

Silence fell for a moment between them.

Then he spoke again, a little sadly:

"Would you wish those days back again, if you could?"

She hesitated thoughtfully.

"I do not know," she said at last. "Sometimes I think so. We had John then."

"Yes," he said, and turned away his head.

Her hand, as Jimmie Dale watched, seemed to tighten over her husband's; and now, though her lips quivered, there came a little smile.

"But we have his memory now, dear," she whispered.

Agitated, the old gentleman moved abruptly away from the chair, and Jimmie Dale could see that the blue eyes were moist.

"That is true—we have his memory." The old colonel's voice trembled. And then his shoulders squared like a soldier on parade. "Tut, tut!" he chided. "Why, we are to be gay tonight! And it is almost time for us to be going. We, too, shall celebrate. You shall wear the pendant, just as you did that other night."

"Oh, colonel!" There was mingled delight and hesitation in her ejaculation. "Do you really think I ought to—that it wouldn't be out of keeping with our present circumstances?"

"Of course, I think you ought to!" he declared. "And see"—he started across the room—"I will get it for you, and fasten it around your throat myself."

He reached the escritoire, opened a little drawer at the top, took out a key, stooped to the lower drawer, inserted the key, turned it once or twice in a puzzled way, then tried the drawer, pulled it open—and with a sharp, sudden cry, reached inside for the steel bond-box.

The little old lady rose hurriedly, in a startled way, from her chair.

"What is it? What is the matter?" she cried anxiously.

The box clattered from the colonel's hands to the floor.

"It is gone!" he said hoarsely. "It has been stolen!"

"*Gone!*" She ran wildly forward. "Stolen! No, no—it cannot be gone!"

They stared for a moment into each other's faces, and from each other's faces stared at the rifled box upon the floor—and then a look of wan misery crept gray upon the little old lady, and she swayed backward.

With a cry, that to Jimmie Dale seemed one of more poignant anguish than he had ever heard before, the old gentleman caught her in his arms and supported her to a chair; then running quickly to the hall, called loudly for the maid below.

There was a merciless smile on Jimmie Dale's lips. He was retreating now further back into the room toward the door that gave on the hall.

"I wonder," said Jimmie Dale to himself through set teeth, "I wonder if a man wouldn't be justified in putting an end *for keeps* to that devil Thorold for this!"

He heard the maid come rushing up the stairs. He could no longer see into the other room now, but a confused mingling of voices reached him:

"...The police...next door and telephone...the light...while we were at dinner...."

Jimmie Dale opened the door, slipped across the hall, made his way silently and swiftly down the stairs, and with the single precaution of pulling his slouch hat far down over his eyes, stepped boldly out of the front door, walked quietly down the steps, walked briskly, but without apparent haste, along the street—and turned the first corner.

CHAPTER 5

"DEATH TO THE GRAY SEAL!"

Jimmie Dale hurried now, making his way to the nearest subway station, and took a downtown train. "There should be no danger," the Tocsin had written. His eyes darkened with a flash of passion. Danger! Danger was a small, pitiful factor now! He had been too late through no fault either of his or the Tocsin's—but he still knew where the pendant was, or would be! Time was counting again; he was afraid now only that he might be too late a second time. Old Attic would not let any grass grow under his feet in disposing of the diamonds through one of the many channels at his command, and once they had passed out of that scoundrel's hands they were as good as hopelessly lost. Also there was Thorold to reckon with. Thorold would naturally get the pendant first, then turn it over to Jake Kisnieff. Had Thorold already done so? It depended, of course, on when the theft had been committed. That snatch of conversation—"the light…when we were at dinner"—came back to him. His brows gathered. He crouched a little in his seat, staring abstractedly at the black tunnel walls without. Station after station was passed. Jimmie Dale's hand, resting on the window sill, was so tightly clenched that it seemed the skin must crack across the knuckles.

But he was smiling when he left the subway—only it was that same merciless smile once more. It was not alone the mere act of robbery that fanned his anger to a white heat. Again and again, he was picturing in his mind that fine old gray-haired couple; again and again he saw the old colonel bend and lift that sweet face to his, and saw them look into each other's eyes. There was something holy, something reverent in that love which the years had ripened and mellowed with tenderness; something that was profound, that made of this night's work a sacrilege in touching them—and that poor jewel, clung to all too obviously through adversity for its past associations, was probably the last real thing of intrinsic value they possessed!

"I am not sure," muttered Jimmie Dale—he was fingering the automatic in his pocket, "I am not sure that I can trust myself tonight!"

Ten minutes' walk from the subway brought him before a dingy and dilapidated three-story tenement on the East Side. The Nest, they called it in the underworld; and worthily so, for its roof sheltered more of the cheaper and petty class of criminals probably than any other single dwelling in New York—the steerers, the hangers-on, the stalls, those of the lesser breed of vultures, and the more vicious therefore, who at best made but a precarious livelihood from their iniquitous pursuits.

One of Jimmie Dale's shoulders was hunched forward, giving a crude and ill-fitting set to his fashionably tailored, Fifth Avenue coat; he staggered slightly, and the flap of his collar protruded, while his tie, pulled out, sprawled over his vest; also his slouch hat, badly crushed and looking as though it had rolled in the mire of the street, was tilted forward at an unhappy angle until it was balanced on the bridge of his nose. Men, women, and children passed him by—for the street was crowded—paying him not the slightest attention. He lurched in through the front door of the tenement, swayed up against the hallway inside—and stood there, still swaying a little.

It was dark here, and the atmosphere was musty and fetid; a murmur pervaded the place as of voices behind many closed doors, but apart from that the tenement might have been empty and deserted for all the signs of life it evidenced. And then the spot where Jimmie Dale had stood was vacant, and he was along the narrow hallway without a sound, and, opening a door at the rear, stood peering out. After a moment, he closed the door again without fastening it; and, back once more toward the front of the hallway, began to creep silently up the stairs.

He reached the top landing. Old Attic had two miserable rooms here, where he conducted his even more miserable business! Jimmie Dale dropped on his knees before the door that faced the head of the stairs, and placed his ear to the panel. Noiselessly he tried the door. It was locked. He was smiling that merciless smile again in the darkness, as his deft, slim fingers worked at the keyhole. He was not too late this time! Old Jake was there, and—yes, Thorold, too. They were even now haggling over the pendant—he could hear them quite distinctly now with the door open a crack.

He pushed the door open a little wider, but very slowly, scarcely an inch at a time. He was in luck again! They were in the inner room. He opened the door still a little wider, stepped softly over the threshold, and closed the door behind him.

Save for a dim light that filtered out through the half open door of the inner room, it was dark here. Slowly, with that almost uncanny, silent tread that he had acquired on the creaky, rickety stairs of the old Sanctuary, Jimmie Dale began to move forward, the weight of his body wholly and firmly on one foot before the other was lifted from the floor; and, as he advanced, the black silk mask, from a pocket in the leather girdle, was drawn over his face.

He could see them now quite plainly—the twisted, crunched-up form of old Jake, with his tawny-bearded face, and narrow, shifting little black eyes; the smooth-shaven, suave, oily, cunning countenance of Thorold, the super-crook. Both were sitting at a table in the miserly appointed room, whose only other articles of furniture were a cheap iron bed and a few chairs. Old Jake was whining; Thorold's voice held an angry rasp.

"Four thousand, you cursed miser, and not a cent less," Thorold was saying.

"Three," whined the other. "You ain't splitting fair. I got to take the stones out of their setting, and sell 'em for what I can get. Stolen stuff's got to go cheap. You know that."

"It's worth ten or twelve, and you'll get at least eight for it," growled Thorold. "That's four apiece—and I've got to split mine again with the guy that pinched it. Hurry up, d'yer hear—I've got a date with him in half an hour over in my office."

"Ha, ha!" cackled old Jake. "Are you trying to be funny? All the thief gets out of it from you won't make much of a hole in your share!"

"That's my business!" snapped Thorold. "You come across!"

"Three!" whined old Jake again.

"Four!" Thorold flung back angrily.

"Well, let's have a look at it then; I ain't seen it for years," grumbled old Jake. "I ain't trying to do you. We went into this thing so's we'd each get the same out of it; but I tell you it ain't easy to shove big stones when there'll be a police description out against them, and there ain't no big prices for 'em. either."

Thorold reached into his pocket—and even in the dull light of the single gas-jet that alone illuminated the room, Jimmie Dale caught the fire and flash of the magnificent stones in the pendant that swung to and fro now, as the man held it up.

Old Jake, his hand trembling with eagerness, snatched at it, and, as Thorold laughed shortly, dove his fingers into a greasy vest pocket, and produced a jeweller's magnifying glass, which he screwed into his eye.

"One of these has got a flaw, and it's cloudy," he mumbled.

"Never mind about the flaw! Flash your wad!" invited Thorold, with a thin smile.

Jimmie Dale's hand slipped under his vest to a pocket in the leather girdle, and from the thin metal case, with the aid of the tiny tweezers, lifted out a gray seal, and laid it lightly on the inside edge of his left-hand sleeve. He replaced the metal case with his right hand, and with his right hand drew his automatic from his pocket. He crept forward again, inch by inch toward the door of the inner room.

Old Jake laid the pendant on the table, and from some mysterious recess in his clothing pulled out a huge roll of banknotes.

"I'll make it three and a half until I see what I can get for it. That's all I've got here, anyway." He began to count the money, laying it bill by bill on the table. "If I get more than seven, I'll split the difference even. That's fair. That's the way it's been ever since we started this. I don't know exactly what I can get for this, and—"

And then Jimmie Dale was in the room, his automatic covering the two men.

"Don't move please, gentlemen!" he said quietly, as he stepped to the table. His eyes behind the mask travelled from the diamond pendant to the pile of banknotes, and from the banknotes to the two men, whose faces had gone suddenly white, and who now sat rigidly in their chairs, as though turned to stone. "I appear to be in luck tonight!" His lips, just showing beneath the mask, parted in a hard smile. "I was passing by, and—" His left hand reached out, swept up the money and the diamond pendant—and in their place, fluttering from his sleeve, a gray seal fell upon the table.

There was a sharp, quick cry from Thorold—and the muzzle of Jimmie Dale's automatic swung like a flash to a level with the man's eyes. Old Jake had crumpled up now in his chair, and was glaring wildly at the little diamond-shaped piece of paper; he licked his lips with his tongue, there was fear in his eyes.

"The Gray Seal! The Gray Seal!" he muttered hoarsely.

"I appear to be in luck tonight!" said Jimmie Dale again. "And"—he put the money and the diamond pendant coolly in his pocket—"it would be too bad if I didn't play it up, wouldn't it? It doesn't often come as easy as this. Amazing carelessness to leave that outside door unlocked! But, as I was saying, with such a lavish display of opulence on the table, one is almost led to hope that there might be more where that came from. Now—"

"I haven't got any more—not another cent! Honest, I haven't!" old Jake cried hysterically. "I swear to God, I haven't, and—"

"You hold your tongue!" There was a sudden snarl in Jimmie Dale's low tones. The man's voice was rising dangerously loud. "I'll attend to you in a moment!" He swung on Thorold again; and, with his pistol pressed close against the man, felt deftly and swiftly over the other in search of weapons. He laughed tersely, finding none. "Empty your pockets out on the table!" he ordered curtly.

The man hesitated.

Jimmie Dale smiled—unpleasantly.

Thorold swept a bead of sweat from his forehead. His lips were working nervously. All suavity and polish were gone now; there were only viciousness and fear, each struggling with the other for the mastery in the man's smug face.

"Damn you, you blasted snitch!" he burst out furiously. "We'll get you down here some day, and—"

"Some day, perhaps," said Jimmie Dale softly. "But tonight—did I explain that I was in a hurry—*Thorold!* Every pocket inside out, please!"

Thorold's hand went reluctantly to his pockets. He began with the inside pocket of his coat, laying a pile of letters and papers on the table.

"Anything there you want?" he sneered.

"Go on!" prompted Jimmie Dale.

From vest pockets came a varied assortment of articles—watch, cigars, a cigar-cutter, a silver-mounted pencil, and a fountain pen. The man's hands travelled to his outside coat pockets.

"The *inside* pocket of the vest, Thorold," suggested Jimmie Dale coldly.

With a malicious snort, Thorold unbuttoned his vest, and turned the pocket out. There was nothing in it.

Jimmie Dale nodded complacently.

"My mistake, Thorold," he murmured apologetically. "Go on!"

The man continued to denude himself of his effects, but with increasing savagery and reluctance. There was silence in the room—and then suddenly, so faint as to be almost inaudible, there was a soft *pat* upon the floor. Jimmie Dale did not turn his head.

"I think you dropped something, Jake," he observed pleasantly. "Now take your foot off it, and put it on the table!"

A miserable smile twisting his lips, old Jake stooped, picked up a roll of bills, and, mumbling and crooning to himself, laid it on the table. Jimmie Dale immediately transferred it to his pocket.

"Yes," he said, "I certainly seem to be in luck tonight! That all you got, Thorold?" He reached forward, and possessed himself of a well-filled wallet that Thorold had added to the heterogeneous collection in front of him.

Thorold's face was black with fury.

"There's the watch, you cheap poke-getter!" he choked. "Don't forget to frisk that while you're at it!"

Jimmie Dale examined the collection with a sort of imperturbable appraisement.

"No," he said judicially. "You can keep your watch, Thorold; I haven't got the same lay as our friend Jake here, and that sort of thing is too hard to get rid of to make it worth while. I'll take these, and that's all." He whipped the pile of letters and papers into his pocket. "You see, with a man of your profession, there is always the chance of there being something valuable amongst—"

Jimmie Dale never finished the sentence. With a sudden, low, tigerish cry, Thorold heaved the end of the table upward between himself and Jimmie Dale—and, quick as a cat, as Jimmie Dale staggered backward, leaped from behind it.

"Get him, Jake! Get him, Jake!" he cried. "He won't *dare* to fire in here for the noise. Get him, you fool, he—"

But Jimmie Dale was the quicker of the two. A vicious left full on the point of Thorold's jaw stopped the man's rush—but only for the fraction of a second. Thorold, recovering instantly, flung his body forward, and his arms wrapped themselves around Jimmie Dale's neck. And now, old Jake, screeching like a madman, was circling around them, snatching, clawing, striking at Jimmie Dale's face and head.

Thorold was a powerful man; and at the first tight-locked grip, as they swayed together, trained athlete though he was himself, Jimmie Dale realised that he had met his match. Again and again, with all his strength he tried to throw the other from him. Around and around the room they staggered and lurched—and around and around them followed the wizened, twisted form of old Jake, like a hovering hawk, darting in at every opportunity for a blow, shrieking, yelling, cursing with infuriated abandon. And then from below, a greater peril still, came the opening and shutting of doors, voices calling—the tenement, at the racket, like a hive of hornets disturbed, was beginning to stir into life. If they caught him there! If they caught the Gray Seal there! It brought a desperate strength to Jimmie Dale. He had heard too often that slogan of the underworld—*death to the Gray Seal*!

He tore one of Thorold's arms free from his neck—they were cheek to cheek—Thorold was snarling out a torrent of blasphemy with gasping breath—he wrenched himself free still—and then, their two hands out-stretched and clasped together as though in some grim devil's waltz, they reeled toward the bed at the far end of the room, and smashed into a chair. And, as they lost their balance, Jimmie Dale, gathering all his strength for the one supreme effort, hurled the other from him. There was a crash that shook the floor, as Thorold, hurtling backwards, struck his head with terrific force against the iron bedstead, and dropped like a log.

Jimmie Dale was on his feet again in an instant—but not before old Jake had run, yelling madly, from the room. A glance Jimmie Dale gave at Thorold, who lay limp and motionless, a crimson stream beginning to trickle over temple and cheek; then, with a bound, he reached the gas-jet, and turned out the light.

Old Jake's voice screamed from the hallway without:

"Help! The Gray Seal! The Gray Seal! Help! Help! Quick! The Gray Seal!"

The staircase creaked under the rush of feet; yells began to well up from below. Jimmie Dale darted into the outer room, and crouched down beside the doorway.

"Death to the Gray Seal!" The whole building, in a pandemonium of hellish glee, seemed to echo and reecho the shout.

Jimmie Dale was deadly calm now, as his fingers closed around his automatic—and, deadly cool, the keen, alert, active brain was at work. It was black about him, pitch black, there were no lights in the hallway—yes, a dull glimmer now—a door farther along had opened—but dark enough in here where he waited. There was a chance—with the odds heavily against him—but it was the only way.

They were on the landing outside now; and now, old Jake shouting excitedly amongst them, a dozen forms swept through the doorway, and scuffing, stamping, yelling, made for the inner room—and Jimmie Dale slipped out into the hall. His lips pressed tightly together. That had been as he had expected, but the danger still lay before him—in the three flights of stairs. Someone was coming up now, more than one, the stragglers—but there would be stragglers until the last occupant of the tenement was aroused. He dared not wait. In a minute more, in less than a minute, they would have lighted the gas again in there and found him gone.

He jumped for the head of the stairs—a dark form loomed up before him. Jimmie Dale launched himself full at the other. There was a cry of surprise, an oath, the man pitched sideways, and Jimmie Dale sprang by. A yell went up from the man behind him; it was echoed by a wild chorus from above, as of wolves robbed of their prey; it was re-echoed by shouts from the stairways and halls below—and with his left hand on the banisters to guide him, taking the stairs four and five at a time, Jimmie Dale went down—and now, aiming at the ground, his revolver spat and barked a vicious warning, cutting lurid flashes through the murk ahead of him.

Doors that were open along the hallways shut with a hurried bang; dark forms, like rats running for their holes, scuttled to safety; women screamed and shrieked; children whimpered. On Jimmie Dale ran. For the second time he crashed into a form, and won by. They were firing at him from above now—but by guesswork—firing down the stair well. The pound of feet racing down the stairs came from behind him—two flights behind him—he calculated he had that much start. He gained the entrance hallway where all was dark, leaped for the front door, opened it, pulled it shut with a violent slam—and, whirling instantly, running swiftly and silently back along the hall, he reached the rear door that he had left unfastened, darted out, and a moment later, swinging himself over a high, backyard fence, dropped down into the lane beyond. Whipping off his mask, he ran on like a hare until he approached the lane's intersection with a cross street. And here, well back from the street, he paused to regain his breath and rearrange his dishevelled attire; then, edging forward, he peered cautiously up and down—and smiled grimly—and stepped out on the street. He was a good block away from the tenement.

From the direction of the Nest came sounds of disorder and riot. A patrolman's whistle rang out shrilly. It had been as close a call perhaps as the Gray Seal had ever known—but, at that, the night's work was not ended! There was still the actual thief. Thorold had said he was to meet the man in his, Thorold's, office in half an hour to split their ill-gotten gains. Jimmie Dale's jaw squared. The thief! His hand at his side clenched suddenly. Would it be *only* the thief, or would he have to reckon with Thorold again as well? Could Thorold keep the appointment? It was a question of how badly Thorold was hurt, and that he did not know.

Jimmie Dale walked on another block, still another, then turned so as to bring him into, but well up, the street on which the tenement was situated. From here, far down the ill-lighted street, he could see a mob gathered outside the Nest. And then, as he stood hesitant, there came the strident clang of a bell, the beat of hoofs, and he caught the name of the hospital on the side of an ambulance as it tore by—and, at that, he swung suddenly about, and, making his way across to Broadway, boarded an uptown car.

Twenty minutes later, he closed the door of a telephone booth in a saloon on lower Sixth Avenue behind him, and consulting the directory for the number, called the hospital.

"This is police headquarters speaking," said Jimmie Dale coolly. "What's the condition of that tenement case with the broken head?"

"Hold the wire a minute," came the answer; and then, presently: "Not serious; but still unconscious."

"Thank you," said Jimmie Dale.

He hung up the receiver, and made his way out to the street. The coast was clear then, as far as Thorold was concerned. Jimmie Dale walked on halfway up the block, and turned into the lighted hallway of a small building whose second floor, above a millinery establishment, was rented out for offices. It was here that Thorold maintained what he called his "office." Mounting the stairs and emerging upon a narrow corridor, that was lighted at one end by a single incandescent, Jimmie Dale halted before a door that bore the legend: HENRY THOROLD—AGENT. Jimmie Dale's lips twisted into grim lines. Agent—of what? He glanced quickly up and down the corridor, slipped his little steel instrument into the lock, and opened the door.

He stepped inside, closing the door without re-locking it; and, using his flashlight now, moved forward, and entered a sort of inner office that was partitioned off from the rest of the room. There was a flat-topped desk here, a swivel chair, an armchair, a rather good drawing or two on the walls, and a soft yielding carpet underfoot. Thorold was far too clever to overdo anything—it was simply businesslike, with an air of modest success about it.

Jimmie Dale appropriated the swivel chair behind the desk. Half an hour from the time he had left the tenement! He should not have long to wait, for he had used up nearly, if not quite, all of that time already, and the thief would certainly have every incentive to be punctual. He laid his flashlight, turned on, upon the desk, and, taking his automatic from his pocket, examined it. There were still two cartridges remaining in the magazine. He slipped the weapon into the side pocket of his coat, and began to sort over the papers and letters he had taken from Thorold. He opened one—a letter—glanced at its contents—and nodded. It was the one to which the Tocsin had referred. He returned the others to his pocket, began to read the one in his hand and suddenly, leaning forward, snapped out his light. *Was that a step coming up the stairs?*

He listened now intently. Yes, it was coming nearer. He laid down the letter on the desk, and put on his mask. Still nearer came the step. It had halted now before the door. And now the hall door opened and closed. Jimmie Dale sat motionless, except that his hand crept to his coat pocket, and from his coat pocket to the desk again. The door closed softly—a man had entered the outer room—and certainly a man who was no stranger to the place, for he was moving unerringly in the darkness toward the partition door. The man was in the inner office now, passing the desk, so close that Jimmie Dale could have reached out and touched him. There was a soft, rubbing sound as the man's hand felt along the wall for the electric light switch, a click, the room was suddenly flooded with light; and, with a low cry, blinking there in the glare, staring at Jimmie Dale's masked face—stood Colonel Milford.

And then the old gentleman swayed, and caught at the back of the armchair for support—upon the desk lay the diamond pendant, glittering under the light.

"My God!" he whispered. "What does this mean?"

"It means, colonel," said Jimmie Dale softly, "that Thorold couldn't come, that old Jake found one of the diamonds cloudy and with a flaw, and that the deal fell through—and it means, colonel, that you will never be called upon to steal Mrs. Milford's diamonds again; there is a letter here that—"

"The letter!" The old gentleman was staggering toward the desk. He reached out his hand for the letter, hesitated as though he were afraid that Jimmie Dale was only tantalising him, would never let him have it—and then with a little cry of wondrous gladness, he snatched it to him.

"I'd destroy that if I were you," suggested Jimmie Dale quietly. "I don't imagine that Thorold or old Jake will ever bother you again, but there are lots of 'Thorolds' in New York." He motioned toward the pendant. "That is yours, too, colonel."

The old gentleman was fingering the letter over and over, as though to assure himself that it was actually in his possession; and into his blue eyes, as they travelled back and forth from the pendant to Jimmie Dale, there crept a half wondering, half wistful light.

"I do not know why you have done this for me, or who you are, sir," he said brokenly. "But at least I understand that in some strange way you have stepped in between me and—and those men. You—you know the story, then?"

"Only partially," said Jimmie Dale with a smile, as he shook his head. "But you need not—"

"I would wish to thank you, sir." The old Southerner was stately now in his emotion. "I can never do so adequately. You are at least entitled to my confidence." His face grew a little whiter; he drew himself up as though to meet a blow. "My boy, my son, sir, stole a large sum of money from the bank where he was employed in New Orleans. He was not suspected; and indeed, as far as the bank is concerned, the matter remains a mystery to this day. Shortly afterwards the Spanish war broke out. My son was an officer in a local regiment. He obtained an appointment for the front." The old gentleman paused; then he stood erect, head back, at salute, like the gallant old soldier that he was. "My son, sir, was a thief; but he redeemed himself, and he redeemed his name—he fell at the head of his company, leading his men."

Jimmie Dale's eyes had grown suddenly moist.

"I understand," he said simply.

"He wrote this letter to me, making a full confession of his guilt; and gave it to me, telling me not to open it unless he should not come back." The colonel's voice broke; then, with an effort, steadied again. "It would have killed his mother, sir. It strained our resources most severely to pay back the money to the bank, and I lied to her, sir—I told her that our investments were proving unfortunate. Two years ago I completed the final payment without the bank ever having found out where the money came from; and then we moved up here to New York. You see, sir, it was a little difficult to maintain our former position in Louisiana, and amongst strangers less would be expected of us. And then, sir, shortly after that, I do not know how, this letter was stolen, and for two years Thorold has held it over my head, threatening to make it public if I refused his demands; I gave him all the money I could get. I have thought sometimes, sir, that I should put a revolver in my pocket and come down here and shoot him like a dog—but then, sir, the story, I was afraid, would come out. Yesterday he made a final demand for five thousand dollars. I did not have the money. He suggested Mrs. Milford's pendant there. He promised to return the letter, and any sum above the five thousand that he could get for the diamonds. I knew he was lying about the money; but I believed he would return the letter, knowing that I now had nothing left. That is why I am here tonight."

Again the old gentleman paused. It was very still in the room. Jimmie Dale had taken the thin metal case from his leather girdle and was fingering it abstractedly. And then the colonel spoke again:

"And so," he said slowly, "I stole the pendant this afternoon, and pretended tonight that it was done at dinner-time, and—and pretended, too, to make the discovery of the theft myself. You see, sir, it was not only the old name that would be smirched—there was the boy to think of, and he had redeemed himself. And Mrs. Milford would have wanted me to do that, to take a thousand of her jewels, if she had had them, if she had known—but, you see, sir, she could not know without it breaking her heart—I think the dearest thing in life to her is the boy's memory."

Outside on Sixth Avenue an elevated train roared and thundered by—it seemed strangely extraneous and incongruous.

"And now, sir"—the old gentleman's voice seemed tired, a little weary—"though you give me back the pendant, I do not see how I can return it to my wife. It was part of the agreement that I should notify the police—it made it impossible for me to inform against Thorold, for—for I was the thief."

Jimmie Dale nodded. "I was thinking of that," he said.

He opened the metal case; and, while the old gentleman watched in amazement and growing consternation, he lifted out a gray paper seal with his tweezers, moistened the adhesive side with the tip of his tongue, and pressed the seal firmly with his coat sleeve over the central cluster of the pendant.

The old gentleman tried twice to speak before a word would come.

"You! You—the Gray Seal!" he stammered at last. "But only tonight I was reading in the papers, and they said you were a murderer, an ogre of hell, and—"

"And now, possibly," interrupted Jimmie Dale whimsically, "though circumstances will force you to keep your opinion to yourself, you may have an idea that, as between you and the papers, you are the better informed. Well, at least, the Gray Seal's shoulders are broad! You need not worry about Thorold or old Jake; I took pains to make them aware that the Gray Seal—quite inadvertently, of course—had taken a passing fancy to the pendant. You have only to wrap it up, and send it by mail to *yourself*; and when it arrives"—he laughed softly, as he stood up—"notify the police again. Let them do the theorising—it is one of their cherished amusements! And, oh, by the way, colonel, have you any idea how much Thorold and his precious friend Kisnieff have blackmailed you out of in the last two years?"

"I did not have very much left when I came to New York," said the colonel, in a stunned way, still staring at the gray paper seal. "Between four and five thousand dollars."

"That's too bad," murmured Jimmie Dale. He took the banknotes from his pocket, and laid them on the desk. "I am afraid it is not quite all here—but I can assure you it is all they had."

He held out his hand.

"But you're not going! You're not going that way!" cried the colonel, and his eyes filled suddenly. "How am I to repay you, how am I to—"

"Very easily," smiled Jimmie Dale; "and, to use your own expression, very adequately—by remaining here, say, three minutes after I have left." He caught the colonel's hand in his and wrung it hard—and then, with a "Goodnight!" flung over his shoulder, Jimmie Dale was gone.

CHAPTER 4

THE REHABILITATION OF LARRY THE BAT

The small French window of the new Sanctuary, that gave on the dirty little courtyard which, in turn, paralleled a black and narrow lane, with its high, board fence, opened cautiously, noiselessly. A dark form slipped silently into the room. The window was closed again. The dilapidated roller shade was drawn down, and, guided by the sense of touch, the rent that gaped across it was carefully pinned together. There was no moon to shine in through the top-light and uncharitably disclose the greasy, ragged carpet, or the squalor of the room.

The dark form, like a shadow, moved across the room to the door, tried the lock, slipped an inner bolt into place, then returned halfway back to the windows, and paused by the wall. A match flame spurted through the blackness; and then, hissing as though in protest, the miserable, clogged gas-jet, blue with air, still leaving the corners of the room dim and murky, grudgingly lighted up its immediate surroundings—and Jimmie Dale, immaculate in evening clothes, stood looking sharply about him.

Here and there about the room, upon this article and that, as though fixing its exact and precise location, his glance fell critically; then he stepped back quickly to the door, and knelt by the threshold. The tiny, unobtrusive piece of thread, that must break if the door were opened by but that fraction of an inch, was still intact. No one, then, had been here since last, as Smarlinghue, the seedy, drug-wrecked artist, he had left the place the day before; for, on entering, he had already satisfied himself that the French window had not been tampered with.

A hard smile flickered across his lips. It was a grim transition, this, from the luxury, the wealth and refinement of New York's most exclusive club, which he had left but half an hour ago! The smile faded, and he passed his hand a little wearily across his eyes. The strain seemed to grow heavier every day—the underworld more prone to suspicion; the police more vigilant; that ominous slogan, in which Crime and the Law for once were one, "Death to the Gray Seal!" to ring more constantly in his ears. It was becoming more fraught with peril, danger and difficulty than ever before, this dual life he led. And he had thought it all ended—once. That was only a few months ago, when the way had seemed clear for them both, for the Tocsin and himself. Well, he was here tonight to end it again if he could—by playing perhaps the most desperate game he had ever attempted.

He shook his head. It was more than the hazard, the danger and the peril of his dual life that brought the strain—it was the Tocsin, his love for her, *her* peril and *her* danger, the unbearable anxiety and suspense on her account that was never absent from him. And it was that that kept him in the underworld, that had forced him to create again a rôle in gangland, the rôle of Smarlinghue, in the hope that he might track her enemies down. She would not help him. If she knew, and she must know, the authors of this new danger that had driven her once more into hiding, she would not tell him. She was afraid—for *him*. She had said that. She had said that she would fight this out alone, that she would not, could not, whatever the end might be, bring him again into the shadows, throw his life again into the balance. It was her love, pure, unselfish, a wondrous love, that had prompted her to this course, he knew that—and yet—But why all this again! His brain was numbed with its incessant dwelling upon it day after day.

Jimmie Dale's hands clenched suddenly. That night, a week ago, when he had been so nearly caught in the Nest, had brought very forcibly upon him the realisation that he could not risk any longer a haphazard course of action, if he was to be of help to her, for next time his own luck might go out. And so the idea had come—the one, single, definite mode of attack that lay within his power—and he had used the week to advantage, and he was ready now. From the first it had seemed almost certain that the danger which threatened her must come from one of two sources—and there was a way to probe one of these to the bottom. He did not know who they were, those who remained of the Crime Club, or where they were; but he knew the Magpie, and he knew where the Magpie was to be found—and tonight he would know, settling the question once for all, *all* that the Magpie knew!

He turned, walked back across the room, and, a few feet along from the door, knelt down close to the wall. An instant later, with the loose section of the base-board removed, he reached inside, and took out a curious assortment of garments, which he laid on the floor beside him. They were not Smarlinghue's clothes—they were even more shoddy and disreputable. His brows gathered critically as he surveyed the wretched boots, the mismated socks, the frayed, patched trousers, the greasy flannel shirt, the ragged coat, and the battered, shapeless slouch hat. Matched closely enough to the originals to pass without question, gathered from here and there, painstakingly, with infinite trouble during the week that had passed, were the clothes of— Larry the Bat.

It was a dangerous, almost desperate chance; but he, too, was desperate now. To be caught, even to be seen as Larry the Bat meant flinging every stake he had in life into the game. More rabid than ever was the cry of the populace for vengeance upon the Gray Seal; more active than ever, combing den and dive, their dragnet spreading from end to end of the city, were the efforts of the police to effect the Gray Seal's capture; more like snarling wolves than ever, the blood lust upon them, mad to sink their fangs into the Gray Seal, were the denizens of the underworld—and populace and police and underworld alike knew Larry the Bat as the Gray Seal! If he were seen— if he were caught! They had thought that Larry the Bat had perished in the Sanctuary fire that night, and that in Larry the Bat had perished the Gray Seal. But the Gray Seal had been at work again since then; and, logically enough, there had followed the deduction that, after all, Larry the Bat had in some way escaped.

Jimmie Dale began to remove his expensively tailored dress suit. It had made it much easier for him, easier to play the role of Smarlinghue, easier for the Gray Seal to work, that they, the populace, police and underworld, had of late searched only for a *character*, a character that, in truth, until tonight had literally vanished from the face of the earth—a character known as Larry the Bat. But now Larry the Bat was to assume tangible form again, to accept the risk of recognition, to go out amongst those whose one ambition was his destruction, to court his own death, his ruin, the disclosure that Larry the Bat was Jimmie Dale, that Jimmie Dale, the millionaire clubman, a leader in New York's society, was therefore the Gray Seal, and with this disclosure drag an honoured name in the mire, be execrated as a felon. It seemed almost the act of a fool—worse than that, indeed! Even a fool would not invite the blow of a blackjack, the thrust of a knife, or a revolver bullet from the first crook in gangland who recognised him; even a fool would not voluntarily take the chance of thrusting his head through the door of one of Sing Sing's death cells!

And for an instant, fought out with himself times without number though this had been since he had first conceived the plan, Jimmie Dale hesitated. It was very still in the room. In his hands now he held a bundle of neatly folded clothing ready to be tucked away in the aperture in the wall. He looked around him unseeingly. Then suddenly the square jaw clamped hard, and he stooped, thrust the bundle into the opening, and began rapidly to dress again—as Larry the Bat.

If it was the act of a fool, it was even more the act of a *coward* to shrink from it! It was the one way to force the Magpie to lay his cards face up upon the table. It was the Magpie who had discovered that Larry the Bat was the Gray Seal; it was the Magpie who had led gangland to batter down the Sanctuary doors; it was the Magpie who had clamoured the loudest of them all for the Gray Seal's death—and it was the Magpie, therefore, who had reason to fear Larry the Bat as he would fear no other living thing on earth. And it was upon that which he, Jimmie Dale, counted—the psychological effect upon the Magpie on finding himself suddenly face to face and in the power of Larry the Bat, with the unhallowed reputation of the Gray Seal, that did not stop at murder, to discount any thought in the Magpie's mind that the choice between a full confession and death was an idle threat which would not be put into instant execution.

Yes; it was simple enough, and *sure* enough—that part of it. The Magpie would tell what he knew under those circumstances—and tell eagerly. But if, after all, the Magpie knew nothing! Jimmie Dale snarled contemptuously at himself. Childish! That, of course, was possible—but in that case he would at least have run a false lead to earth, and have eliminated the Magpie from any further consideration.

Jimmie Dale took out a make-up box from the opening in the wall, and, carrying it with him to the table, propped up a small mirror against a collection of Smarlinghue's paint tubes. His fingers were working swiftly now with sure, deft touches, supplying to his face, his neck, his hands and wrists, not the unhealthy pallor of Smarlinghue, but the grimy, unwashed, dirty appearance of Larry the Bat. It was the toss of a coin, heads or tails, whether the Magpie was at the bottom of this or not. The Magpie knew that Silver Mag had been in the affair that night when Larry the Bat was discovered to be the Gray Seal; the Magpie knew that Silver Mag was a pal of Larry the Bat, and, therefore, equally with the Gray Seal, the underworld had passed sentence of death upon her—but did the Magpie know that Silver Mag was Marie LaSalle, any more than he knew that Larry the Bat was Jimmie Dale? That was the question—and its answer would be wrung from the Magpie's lips tonight!

A piece of wax was inserted in each nostril, and behind the lobes of his ears, and under his lip. Jimmie Dale stared into the mirror—the vicious, dissolute face of Larry the Bat leered back at him. And then, returning abruptly to the loosened section of the base-board, he restored the make-up box to its hiding place. He reached inside again, and procured a pistol and flashlight, which he stowed away in his pockets; there would be no need tonight for that belt with its compact little kit of burglar's tools; no need for that thin metal box with the gray-coloured, adhesive paper seals, the insignia of the Gray Seal, for tonight the Gray Seal would appear in *person*. No—wait! That collection of little steel picklocks—and a jimmy! He would need those. He felt for them in one of the pockets of the leather girdle, transferred them to the pocket of his ragged trousers, and slipped the base-board back into place.

And now he stepped to the gas-jet, and turned out the light. Then the roller shade was raised, the French window silently opened, silently closed—and Larry the Bat, hugging close against the wall of the building, crept to the fence, and, lifting aside a loose board, passed out into the lane, and from the lane to an empty and drearily-lighted cross street.

There was no "sanctuary" now. Who in the underworld would fail to recognise Larry the Bat! He was out in the open, on the fringes of the Bad Lands, where recognition was to be feared from every passer-by, and where, if caught, he would do well and wisely to use his own automatic upon himself! And he must go deeper still, into the heart of gangland, to reach that room in the basement beneath Poker Joe's gambling hell where the Magpie lived—or, rather, burrowed himself away in those hours that were miserly devoted to sleep.

But Jimmie Dale knew his East Side as no other man in New York knew it; knew it as a man whose life again and again had depended solely upon that knowledge. By lane and alley, by unfrequented streets, now running, now crouched motionless in some dark corner waiting for footsteps to die away along the pavement before he darted across the street in front of him, Jimmie Dale threaded his way through the East Side, as through the twistings and turning of some maze, puzzling, grotesque and intricate, but with whose secrets notwithstanding he was intimately familiar.

When he paused at last, it was in a backyard, which he had entered by the simple expedient of climbing the fence from the lane behind. A low building loomed up before him, whose windows at first glance were dark, but through whose carefully closed blinds and tightly drawn shutters might still be remarked, if one were sufficiently inquisitive, the faint, suffused glow of lights from within.

Jimmie Dale scarcely glanced at the windows. Poker Joe's at this hour—it must be close to eleven o'clock, he calculated—would be just about settling into its night's swing. He was quite well aware both that the place was lighted and that there were by now perhaps a score of gangland's élite already at the tables; and that the blinds and shades were closed and drawn interested him only in that it safeguarded him *without* from being seen by anyone from *within*!

But there was another window upon which Jimmie Dale now centred his entire attention—a narrow, oblong window, cellar-like, just on a level with the ground—and here there was neither a light nor a drawn shade. He stole across the yard, and, five yards from the wall of the house, dropped down on his hands and knees, and crawled silently forward. Keeping a little to one side, he reached the window, and lay there listening intently. There was no sound, save a low, almost inaudible murmur of voices from the windows above him—nothing from the direction of that dark, oblong window that he could reach out and touch now. The Magpie was presumably not at home!

The long, slim, tapering fingers, whose nerves, tingling sensitively at the tips, were as eyes to Jimmie Dale, those fingers that, to the Gray Seal, were like some magical "open sesame" to the most intricate safes and vaults, felt along the window sill, and, from the sill, made a circuit of the sash. The window, he found, was hinged at one side and opened inward; and now, under the pressure of his steel jimmy, inserted between the ledge and the lower portion of the frame, it began to yield.

Lying there on the ground, Jimmie Dale, his head close to the opening, listened with strained attention again. He had not made much noise, scarcely any—not enough even to have aroused the Magpie if, say, by any chance, the Magpie were within asleep. The sounds from the floor above seemed to be louder now, to reach him more distinctly, but from the basement room itself there was nothing, no sound even of breathing.

Satisfied that the room was unoccupied, Jimmie Dale pushed the window wide open, and peered in. It was like looking into some dark cavernous hole, and he could not distinguish a single object. Then his hand slipped into his pocket for his flashlight, and the round, white ray shot downward and around the place. The floor of the room was perhaps five feet below the level of the window sill; to the left, against the wall, was a bed; there was a chair, a table sadly in need of repair, a few garments hanging from nails driven haphazardly into the plaster, and, save for a dirty piece of carpet on the floor, nothing else. The flashlight played slowly around the room. Opposite the window was the door, and suspended from the centre of the ceiling was a single incandescent lamp.

With a sort of grim nod of approval, Jimmie Dale snapped off his flashlight, and, turning around, worked himself in through the window feet first, and dropped silently to the floor. He had only to wait now until the Magpie returned—whether it was a question of hours or minutes.

Jimmie Dale made his way to the chair, and sat down—and again he nodded his head grimly. It was very simple; he had only to wait, and this place, this burrow of the Magpie's, could not have been improved upon for his purpose. It was eminently suitable, so suitable that there seemed something ironical in the fact that it should have been the Magpie who had chosen it. One could commit *murder* here, and none would be the wiser—and none would be more keenly alive to that than the Magpie himself! A threat from the Gray Seal in these surroundings left nothing to be desired. They were making too much noise above to hear anything in this room below the ground, and the little window afforded an instant means of escape without the slightest danger of discovery. Yes; the Magpie, not being a fool, would very thoroughly appreciate all this.

Time passed. It was a nerve racking vigil that Jimmie Dale kept, sitting there in the chair—waiting. It was so dark he could not have seen his hand before his face. And it was silent, in spite of that composite sound of voices, and shuffling feet, and the occasional squeak of chair legs from above—a silence that seemed to belong to this miserable hole alone, that seemed immune from all extraneous noises. And after a time, in a curious way, the silence seemed to palpitate, to beat upon the ear-drums, to grow almost uncanny.

His lips tightened a little, and he smiled commiseratingly at himself. His nerves were getting a little too tautly strung, that was all; he was listening too intently for that expected step upon the stair, for the opening of that door he faced. And it was not like him to have an attack of nerves—and especially in view of the fact that his plan, in the simplicity of its execution did not even warrant anxiety for its success. He had only to remain quiet until the Magpie entered and turned on the light, then clap his automatic to the Magpie's head—the psychology of fear would do the rest. And yet—what was it? As the minutes dragged along, fight it as he would, a distinct depression, a panicky sort of uneasiness, was settling down upon him. The darkness, in a most unpleasant and disconcerting way, seemed to be full of eeriness, of warnings.

For perhaps ten minutes he sat there in the chair, silent and motionless, angry, struggling with himself—but his disquietude would not down; rather, it but grew the stronger, until it took the form of imagining that he was not *alone* in the room. He scowled contemptuously at himself. There was another psychology than that of fear—the psychology of suggestion. That silence, palpitating in his ear-drums, began to whisper: "You are not alone here—you are not alone—you are not alone."

Was that a sound there outside the door? A step cautiously approaching? He leaned forward tensely. No—his laugh was low, short, furious—*no!* It was only from above, that sound.

Jimmie Dale's face hardened. It was childish, this sensation of *presence* in the room; but it was also unnerving. Why should so unusual a thing happen to him tonight? Was it purely over-wrought nerves, due to the strain of the peril he ran as Larry the Bat—or was it intuition? Intuition had never failed him yet. Well, whatever it was, he would put a stop to it. He was here tonight to get the Magpie, and nothing should interfere with that. Nothing! He and the Magpie would square accounts tonight—and square them once for all!

Not alone here in the Magpie's den—eh? His flashlight streamed out, and began slowly and deliberately to circle the room. If his brain was so restless and active that it must indulge in fantasies, it could at least be diverted into another channel than—Jimmie Dale strained forward suddenly in his chair. That was a pair of boots there at the foot of the bed. There was nothing strange in a pair of boots, but these boots were poised most curiously on their heels, with the toes pointing upward. They just barely protruded from the foot of the bed, which accounted for his not having been able to see them from the window when he had flashed his light around—he could not see the upper portions of them even now. And then, under his breath, Jimmie Dale jeered at himself again. True, the boots were in a most peculiar position, but had his nerves reached the state where a pair of boots would throw him into a panic! How logical for someone to be hiding there under the bed—with his feet in plain view! And yet what held the boots upright like that? The foot of the bed itself? Jammed there, perhaps? Or—

"Damn it!" gritted Jimmie Dale. "I'm worse than a child tonight!"

He rose from his chair, stepped across the room to the foot of the bed—and like a man dazed, his flashlight playing on the boots, his automatic flung forward in his hand, he stood staring downward, following his flashlight's ray with his eyes. Was he mad! Was his brain now playing him some hideous trick! The boots were not empty, he could see a man's ankles, the bottoms of a town's trousers; but the ankles and the trousers seemed utterly insignificant—*on the sole of the right boot was a diamond-shaped, gray-coloured, paper seal!* His own insignia—the insignia of the Gray Seal!

For an instant it might have been, he stood there rigidly, realising in a sort of ghastly, subconscious way that the man under the bed made no movement, made no attempt to evade discovery, made no sound; and then Jimmie Dale stooped quickly, and raised one of the other's feet a few inches from the floor. It fell back—a dead weight.

Jimmie Dale's jaws were hard clamped. There was devil's work here—some of the Magpie's, possibly. Every faculty alert now, Jimmie Dale was quietly lifting aside the small iron bed. The Magpie was no fool! By underworld and police alike it would be accepted without questions that the Gray Seal had held a day of reckoning in store for the Magpie. Had the Magpie traded on that—to get rid of someone who was in his way, this out-stretched, inert thing on the floor, and lay it to the door of the Gray Seal? It was clever, hellish in its cunning. And it would appear plausible enough. The Gray Seal had come here, say, searching for the Magpie, and in the darkness had struck another down! Yes, the Magpie could get away with that. It would stand to reason that the Magpie would not lure a victim to his own den, and—

A low cry was on Jimmie Dale's lips. The bed was moved out now, and he was stooping over a man whose head was gruesomely battered above the right temple and back across the skull. The flashlight wavered in his hand, as he held it focussed on the other's face. It was the Magpie—dead.

CHAPTER 7

THE BOND ROBBERY

It seemed to Jimmie Dale that, in the darkness, the room was full of unseen devils laughing and jeering derisively at him. It seemed that reality did not exist; that only unreality prevailed. The Magpie—dead! It seemed for the moment that he had utterly lost his grip upon himself; that mentally he was being tossed helplessly about, the sport of fate. The Magpie—*dead*! It meant—what did it mean? He must think now, and think quickly. It meant, first of all, that any hope for the Tocsin which he had built upon the Magpie was shattered, gone forever. And it meant, that gray seal on the sole of the dead man's boot, that the murder had been committed with even greater cunning and finesse, and an even greater security for the murderer, than he had attributed to the Magpie a moment since, when he had thought the Magpie the instigator, and not the victim, of the crime.

He was examining the wound, searching for the weapon—it must have been a blunt instrument of some sort—with which the blow, or blows, had been struck. There was nothing. The Magpie lay there—dead. That was all.

Mechanically Jimmie Dale replaced the bed in its original position over the murdered man, and stood staring down again at the gray seal on the Magpie's boot. It was not *why* the Magpie had been murdered, it was *who* had murdered him! Once, long, long ago, almost at the outset of the Gray Seal's career, a spurious gray seal had been used before. But this was a vastly different, and far more significant matter. Then it had been an attempt to foist the identity of the Gray Seal upon a poor, miserable devil in order to secure a reward—here it was a crime, *murder*, coolly, callously laid to the Gray Seal, that the guilty man might escape without a breath of suspicion. Just another crime credited to the Gray Seal! No one would dispute it; no one would question it; no one would dream that it had been done by anyone other than the Gray Seal. There was a brutal possibility about the ingenuity of the man who had struck the blow. It was the Magpie who had put his finger upon Larry the Bat as the Gray Seal; it was the Magpie who had tried to accomplish the Gray Seal's death. Would it, then, occasion even surprise that the Magpie should be found murdered in his own den at the hands of the Gray Seal? It was even his own argument, the very reason that had led him to assume the role of Larry the Bat, and had brought him here to the Magpie's tonight!

Jimmie Dale bent down for a closer inspection of the diamond-shaped gray seal on the boot's sole. It was not one of his own; but it was so similar that it would unquestionably pass muster. The red crept to Jimmie Dale's cheeks and burned there, as a sudden, merciless anger swept upon him. *Who* was the man who had done this, who sheltered himself from murder behind the Gray Seal!

He laughed low and bitterly. Only another crime attributed to the Gray Seal! It would not smirch the Gray Seal any—the Gray Seal had been accused of worse than this! But the man who had dared to place that gray seal there would answer for it!

He was still laughing in that low, bitter way, as he knelt now, and took out his pocketknife. The gray seal, at least, would not be found—he was lucky there—he had only to scrape it off, and—No—wait! Would it not be better to leave it there? It would throw the murderer off his guard if he believed that his plan had worked; and it could make little difference to the Gray Seal's record to be held guilty of another murder—temporarily. Temporarily! Yes, that was it! Here was one crime of which the Gray Seal would be vindicated, and the guilty man be—

"*Jimmie!*"

It seemed to quiver, low-breathed, through the darkness—his name. His name! Was he bereft of all his senses! His name! Here in this horrible murder hole! Was he indeed mad with his imaginings, with these voices that had been whispering, and laughing, and jeering at him out of the blackness! And, absurdly, it had seemed this time that it was the Tocsin's voice!

"Jimmie—quick! On the floor under the window!"

He whirled like a flash. Mistake! Imaginings! No! It *was* the Tocsin! It was her voice! The gleam of his flashlight cut the black, and, leaping across the room, played upon the small, narrow, oblong window—it was from there the voice had come. But it was only black and empty there. And around the room his flashlight swept, and it was black and empty there, too—except for a square, white object upon the floor below the window. She was gone.

And it was like a half sob that came from Jimmie Dale's lips.

"Gone!" he whispered miserably. "Gone!"

Why had she gone like that? Why had she not waited—just for a moment, just for the single instant, if he could have had no more, that he would have given his life to have? And the answer was in his soul. He knew, and he, knew that she, too, knew, that it would not have been moment or an instant—that he would never have let her go again. And to follow her? He shook his head. By the time he had climbed out of the window, what trace, any more than there was now, would there of her! She was gone—a sort of finality in her act, as there always was, that left nothing to be done, or said.

But the note! That white thing there upon the floor! He crossed the room, picked it up, tore it open, and, with his flashlight upon it, began to read.

"Jimmie—Jimmie—" It was scrawled in haste, only a few lines. His eyes travelled rapidly over the words, and suddenly his breath came fast.

"My God!" he cried out sharply.

As though he could not have read aright, he read again; disjointed words and phrases muttered audibly: "...Afraid not in time...hurry...this afternoon...the Magpie and Virat...Kenleigh, insurance broker...safe in Kenleigh's house...ground floor—left...one hundred thousand dollars...bonds...will try it...Meighan of headquarters...half-past one at Virat's...Gray Seal...Larry the Bat...if dangerous, keep away..."

One glance around the room Jimmie Dale gave instinctively; and then he was crawling through the window, and, outside, regaining his feet, he darted across the yard, and out into the lane. Kenleigh, the insurance broker—he repeated the address she had given in the note over to himself. It was an apartment house on Avenue near Washington Square.

He ran on, as he had come, through lane and alley, working his way out of the Bad Lands. It was dangerous, of coarse, in any case, but once clear of that section of the city which houses the underworld, his risk of discovery was greatly minimised, since, though familiar to every denizen of gangland, Larry the Bat was naturally not the same intimate figure in the more law-abiding and respectable districts; and he should, except for an extraordinary piece of bad luck, pass in the quarters he was now heading for as no more than exactly what his appearance proclaimed him to be—a disreputable and seedy vagrant.

It was slow work, hurry as he would, doubling and zigzagging his way up through the East Side; discouraging, when time was so great a factor, to cover three and four times the actual distance in order to keep to the lanes and alleys whose shelter he dared not leave; but he was spurred on now by a sort of grim, unholy joy. He knew now who had murdered the Magpie, and why; he knew now who was making a tool, a cat's-paw of the Gray Seal; he knew now who had so cynically elected him, if caught, as a substitute for the other to the electric chair. It was Virat! Frenchy Virat, the suave, sleek gambler, confidence man and crook! Well, the game was of Virat's choosing—and they would play it out now to the end, Virat and the Gray Seal, if it was the last act of his, Jimmie Dale's, life! It was only a question now of whether or not Virat had completed all his work, of whether there was yet time to get to Kenleigh's.

It was close to midnight, as Jimmie Dale came out on Washington Square. He crossed to Waverly Place, and, on the point of starting along Fifth Avenue, drew suddenly back around the corner. A man, walking rapidly, was just turning into Fifth Avenue from the opposite corner. Jimmie Dale drew in his breath sharply. He had got out of sight just in time. He recognised the quick, springy walk of the other. It was Meighan, of Headquarters. And then Jimmie Dale smiled a little whimsically. They were both bound for the same place, he and Meighan, of Headquarters—Kenleigh's apartment, that was a little way further on there along the Avenue.

A short distance behind the other, but on the opposite side of the street, Jimmie Dale followed the detective. There was hardly any use now in going to Kenleigh's, for, if the detective was really bound for there, it made his, Jimmie Dale's, errand useless—the summoning of the Headquarters' man was *prima facie* evidence that the robbery had already been committed. And yet a certain grim curiosity remained. Just how had it been done? And besides, she had said, "half-past one at Virat's," so there was time to spare. The distorted lips of Larry the Bat thinned ominously. No; it was not useless even now. He had a very strong personal interest in all that had taken place—Virat would be the less likely to slip through his fingers, or through the fingers of the law, for the information that the scene of the robbery might supply!

Meighan disappeared suddenly inside an apartment house, which Jimmie Dale recognised as a rather fashionable one, devoted exclusively to bachelors' quarters, Jimmie Dale quickened his step, walked on to the next corner, crossed the street, and came back along the block. As he approached the apartment-house entrance, voices reached him from the vestibule, and then he heard the closing of a door.

"Ground floor—left," murmured Larry the Bat to himself. He smiled facetiously. "Saves an interview with the janitor!"

He glanced sharply around him in all directions—and the next instant was inside the vestibule—and in another, without a sound, was crouched close against the apartment door. A delicate little steel picklock was working now, the deft fingers manipulating it silently, and then stealthily he pushed the door open a crack. A man's voice, agitated, came to him from within: "... Perhaps twenty minutes, I don't know—the length of time it took you to get here. I was dining out. I phoned Headquarters the instant I came in."

Jimmie Dale pushed the door further open, slipped through, and left the door just ajar behind him. He was in the hallway of a very small apartment, of not more than two or three rooms, he judged. Diagonally ahead of him a light streamed out from an open door. He stole toward this, and, pressed close against the jamb of the door, peered in.

It was a sort of sitting-room, or den, cosily furnished with deep, comfortable lounging chairs. There was a flat-topped desk in the centre, a telephone on the desk; and at the rear of the room a connecting door, leading presumably to the bedroom, was open. A clean-shaven, dark-eyed man of perhaps thirty-five, Kenleigh obviously, was pacing nervously up and down. His face was pale, his hair ruffled; and, in his distraction, apparently, he had forgotten to remove the cloak which he was wearing over his evening clothes. In the far corner of the room, Meighan, the detective, knelt upon the floor amidst a scene of grotesque disorder. The door of a very small safe had been "souped," and now sagged open. Books and papers littered the floor, and were strewn over a mattress that, evidently dragged from the inner room, had been swaddled around the safe to deaden the sound of the explosion.

"You don't understand!" Kenleigh burst out, with a groan. "This means absolute ruin to me! A hundred thousand dollars in bonds—payable to bearer—and—and, God help me, they weren't mine!"

"Say"—Meighan, still busily occupied with the fractured safe, spoke gruffly, though not unkindly, over his shoulder—"I understand all right, but don't lose your nerve, Mr. Kenleigh. It won't get you anywhere, and it doesn't follow because the swag is gone that we can't get it back. I know the guy that pulled this job."

"You—*what!*" Kenleigh, his face lighting up as though with a sudden hope, stepped quickly toward the detective. "What did you say? You know who did it!"

"Don't get excited!" advised Meighan coolly. "Sure, I know! That is, it's a toss-up between one of two, and that's easy. We'll round 'em both up before morning, and then I guess it won't be much of a trick to pick the winner. They won't be looking for trouble as quick as this. We'll get 'em. all right. It's a toss-up between Mug Garretty and the Magpie."

Kenleigh was staring incredulously at the detective.

"How do you know?" he gasped out. "I—I don't—"

"I daresay you don't." Meighan was chuckling now. "It's like this, Mr. Kenleigh. A crook's like anyone else, like an artist, say—you get to know 'em. get to spot 'em. especially safe workers, from certain peculiarities about their work. They can't any more help it than stop breathing. Here, for instance, the way he—" Meighan stopped suddenly. He had been pulling the mattress away from the front of the safe, and now, with a sharp, exultant exclamation, he stooped quickly and picked up a small object from the floor. He held it out, twirling It between thumb and forefinger, for Kenleigh's inspection—a flashy scarf pin, horseshoe-shaped, of blatantly imitation diamonds.

Kenleigh shook his head bewilderingly.

"I suppose you mean that you recognise it?" he ventured.

"Recognize it!" Meighan laughed low, and, stepping past Kenleigh to the desk, picked up the telephone, and called Headquarters. "Recognise it!" With the receiver to his ear, waiting for his connection, he turned toward Kenleigh. "Why, say, walk over to the Bowery and show it to the first person you meet, and he'd call the turn. Pretty, isn't it? When he's dolled up, he's some—hello!" He swung around to the telephone. "Headquarters?…Meighan speaking from Kenleigh's apartment…Get a drag out for the Magpie on the jump…. Eh?…Yes!…Left his visiting card…. What?…Yes, wound a mattress around the box and souped it; his scarf pin must have caught in the ticking and pulled out…. Sure, that's the one—the horseshoe—found it on the floor…. What?…Yes, the chances are ten to one he will, it's his only play…. All right, I'll get Mr. Kenleigh's story meanwhile…. I'll be here till you phone…. Yes…. All right!"

Meighan hung up the receiver, sat down in a chair, and motioned toward another that was close alongside the desk.

"Turn out the light, Mr. Kenleigh," he said abruptly; "and sit down here."

Kenleigh looked his amazement.

"Turn out the light?" he repeated perplexedly.

"Yes," Meighan nodded. "And at once, please."

Obeying mechanically, Kenleigh moved toward the electric-light switch. There was a faint click, and the apartment was in darkness. Came then the sound of Kenleigh making his way back across the room, and settling himself in the chair beside the detective.

"I—I don't quite see," said Kenleigh, a little nervously. "I—"

"You will in a minute," interrupted Meighan, in a low voice. "Don't make any noise now, and don't speak much above a whisper. That little glass stick pin is worth twenty years to the Magpie. See? When he finds that he has lost it, he'll take any risk to make sure that he didn't lose it *here*. Get the idea? It would plant him for keeps, and nobody knows it any better than he does."

"You mean he'll come back here?" whispered Kenleigh eagerly.

Meighan chuckled.

"Sure, he'll come back here—if he isn't nabbed beforehand! It's the only chance he's got. Don't you worry, Mr. Kenleigh. He's a shy bird, is the Magpie, or he'd have been up the river long before now, but we've got him coming and going this deal. Now then, I haven't got the details from you yet. What time this evening did you get back here before you went out to dine?"

It was quite dark now, and Jimmie Dale leaned forward a little to catch the words. Both men were speaking in guarded undertones.

"About six o'clock," Kenleigh answered. "I came straight from the office. I put the bonds in that safe there, and I should say it was a quarter to seven by the time I had dressed and gone out again."

"And, say, halfpast eleven when you got back. So some time between seven o'clock and halfpast eleven, Mr. Magpie got into the courtyard, put a jimmy at work on the bathroom window beyond the bedroom there, got busy—more likely to be nearer eleven than seven—he would have been back before now, otherwise, eh?" Meighan seemed to be communing with himself, rather than talking to Kenleigh. "Wouldn't make such an awful noise—didn't need much juice on that safe—pretty slick with the smother game—didn't raise an item, anyway."

There was silence for a moment. Then Meighan spoke again:

"Let's have your story, Mr. Kenleigh. How did you come to bring a hundred thousand dollars' worth of bonds home with you? And how did the Magpie get onto the lay?"

"I don't know, unless he stood in with the bond firm's messenger; that's the only way in which I could account for it," said Kenleigh huskily. "And

I've no right to say that God knows I've no wish to get an innocent man into trouble. I've no proof—but I can't see any other solution." Kenleigh's voice broke. He seemed to steady himself with an effort. "I'm an insurance broker with an office on Wall Street, as I daresay you know. A client of mine, a well-known millionaire here in the city, wanted a hundred thousand dollars' worth of the Canadian War Loan bonds, but for business reasons, he has a large German connection, he did not want his name to appear in the transaction." Kenleigh hesitated.

"Sure!" said Meighan. "I see. Wise guy! Go on!"

"He commissioned me to get them for him." Kenleigh's voice was agitated as he continued. "I telephoned Thorpe, LeLand and Company, the brokers, where I was personally known, explained the circumstances, and placed the order. My client was to give me a check for the amount on the delivery of the bonds to him. I was to place this to my own credit in the bank, and check against it in favour of Thorpe, LeLand and Company. They sent the bonds over to my office by a messenger about five o'clock this afternoon. It was too late to put them in a safe-deposit vault. I locked them first in my office safe, and then I grew nervous about them, and took them out again."

"Anybody see you do that?" queried Meighan quickly.

"No; I don't see how they could. I've only a small one-room office, and there was nobody there but myself."

"And so they kind of got your goat, and you figured the safest thing to do was to bring them home with you?" suggested Meighan.

"Yes." There was a miserable note of dejection in Kenleigh's voice. "Yes; that's what I did. And I put them in that safe. You know the rest, and—and, oh, my God, what am I to do! My client, naturally, won't pay for what he does not receive, and I owe Thorpe, LeLand and Company a hundred thousand dollars." He laughed out a little hysterically. "A hundred thousand dollars! It sounds like a joke, doesn't it? I've got a little money, all I've been able to save in ten years' work, a few thousand. I'm ruined."

"Don't talk so loud!" cautioned Meighan. He whistled low under his breath. "You're certainly up against it, Mr. Kenleigh, but you buck up! We'll get 'em. And, anyway, bonds can be traced."

"These are payable to bearer," said Kenleigh numbly. "There were three classes of bonds in this issue—those payable to bearer; those registered as to principal; and those fully registered, that is where the interest is paid by government check instead of the bonds having coupons. Naturally, under the circumstances, it was the 'payable-to-bearer' bonds that my client wanted."

"Well, they're numbered, aren't they?" Meighan returned encouragingly.

"That's poor consolation for me," said Kenleigh bitterly. "Suppose some of them, or even all of them, were recovered that way in time—where do I stand tomorrow morning?"

"I guess that's right—if the Magpie ever got a chance to hand them over to some fence," admitted Meighan. "The fence could dispose of them by the underground route all over the country where the numbers weren't staring everybody in the face. Yes, I guess they could cash in, all right. Or it wouldn't be much of a trick for a good plate-worker to alter a number or two, either—the game's big enough. But"—Meighan chuckled again—"he hasn't got away with it yet!"

Kenleigh made no answer.

It was still again in the apartment. Through the darkness only a few feet away from Jimmie Dale, the two men sat there silently, waiting, as he had waited, in the darkness, and the silence—for the Magpie. There seemed an abhorrent, gruesome analogy in the situation—this waiting for a *murdered* man to come!

The minutes dragged by, ten, fifteen of them. And now Jimmie Dale, cramped though he was, dared not shift his position; the movement of a foot, the slightest stir would be heard. It would have been better if he had gone before they had ceased talking. He had heard enough long before then, and yet—

Suddenly, startling, like the clash of an alarm bell through the silence, the telephone rang. Jimmie Dale heard Meighan fumble for the receiver; and then, as the other spoke, seizing the opportunity, he began to retreat stealthily back across the hallway toward the vestibule door.

"Hello!" Meighan's voice was still guarded. "Yes—yes… What!" His voice rose suddenly in a rasping cry. "What's that! Dead! *Murdered*! Wait a minute! Kenleigh, they've found the Magpie murdered in his room!"

"Murdered!" cried Kenleigh; then, frantically: "But the bonds, the bonds! Did they find the bonds? Ask them! Tell them to look! The bonds! Are the bonds there?"

"Hello!" Meighan was evidently speaking into the phone again. "Any trace of the bonds?… What?… Yes, yes; go on, I'm listening!… *Who*?… *What*?…Good Lord!" The receiver clicked back on its hook.

"What is it? What do they say?" demanded Kenleigh feverishly.

"Mr. Kenleigh," said Meighan soberly, "there's been a little feud on in the underworld for the last few months. It came to a showdown tonight, and the man that won played in luck—he's killed two birds with one stone, I guess. It looks damned black for your bonds, I'm afraid."

"They're—they're gone?" faltered Kenleigh.

"Yes—and for keeps, I guess," said Meighan gruffly. He laughed shortly, mirthlessly. "You can turn the light on now; we'd wait a long time here—for the Gray Seal!"

CHAPTER 8

AT HALFPAST ONE

Larry the Bat closed the outer door noiselessly behind him, slipped through the vestibule—and, an instant later, was slouching along Fifth Avenue, heading back toward Washington Square. His hands in his ragged pockets clenched. It had been well worked out—with a devil's ingenuity. The police had swallowed the bait, jumped to the inevitable conclusion desired, and credited the Gray Seal with the double crime of theft and murder without an instant's hesitation. Well, why shouldn't they! It had been well planned; it was natural enough! Larry the Bat, in his turn, laughed, mirthlessly. But the game was not yet played out!

Through the by-ways, lanes and alleys of the underworld, Jimmie Dale once more threaded his way, and finally, mounting the dark stairway leading upward from the side entrance of a small house just off Chatham Square, he let himself stealthily into a room on the first landing. It was Virat now, and this was where Virat lived—a locality where a stranger took his life in his hand any time! Below stairs was a pseudo tea-merchant's store—kept by a Chinese "hatchet" man. But Lang Chang had not been in evidence when he, Jimmie Dale, had crept up the stairs, for there had been no light in the store windows.

And now Jimmie Dale's flashlight was playing around the room. Half-past one, she had said. It could not be more than one o'clock as yet There was ample time to search for the bonds.

He began to move noiselessly around the room—a rather ornately furnished combination sitting and bedroom. "Keep away, if dangerous," had been the Tocsin's caution. He smiled grimly. What danger could there be? He had only to face one at a time; the Tocsin could absolutely be depended upon to see to that, and the advantage of surprise was with him. He was pulling out the drawer of a bureau now—and now his hands were searching swiftly under the mattress of the bed. It was necessary to secure the bonds. Barring that little matter of the numbers, they were as good as cash—and the matter of numbers would not trouble Virat. He knew Virat, and he had known Virat very well—but not so well by far as he knew him now! Virat was as suave and polished a gentleman crook as the country possessed. Viral was the sort of man who, after the uproar had died down, would have the nerve and address to take up his residence in some little out-of-the-way place, and either dispose of as many of the bonds at a time as he dared to those he would cultivate as friends, or even have the audacity to secure a loan on a modest number of them from the local bank itself, whose conversance with the missing numbers might be expected to be of the haziest description. Also Virat would be careful to see that his offerings were not made at such dates as to have the interest coupons cause him any inconvenience by falling due within twenty-four hours! It would be quite simple—for Virate! In six months, in as many places, with the length and breadth of the country to choose from, Virat could quite readily dispose of the lot; not quite at the issue price perhaps if he secured loans, but still at a figure that would be very profitable—for Virat! Or, as Meighan had suggested, with the aid of a confederate of the right sort, the change of a figure—ah! Jimmie Dale; flat upon the floor, his hand stretched in under the washstand, drew out a short, round, heavy object. He examined this attentively for a second; and then, his face hardening, he slipped it into his coat pocket.

He resumed his musings, and resumed his search through the room. Virat was clever enough to find means of disposing of the bonds in some fashion or other, and too clever to have ever committed murder for them otherwise—there was no doubt of that. And, after all, what difference did it make whatever Virat's method might be! It was extraneous, immaterial. Jimmie Dale shrugged his shoulders. The vital question was—where were the bonds?

It was a strange search there in the murderer's room, the flashlight winking and flinging its little gleams of light through the blackness; a strange search, thorough as only Jimmie Dale could make it—and still leave no telltale sign behind to witness that a single object in the room had been disturbed. But the search was futile; and at the end Jimmie Dale smiled whimsically.

"The process of elimination again!" he muttered. "I seem to be obsessed with that tonight. Well, not being here, there's only one place the bonds *can* be. The process of elimination has its advantages." The flashlight circled around the room, and held for a moment on the electric-light switch near the door. "It must be after halfpast one," said Jimmie Dale—and suddenly snapped off his light.

There came a faint creaking noise—someone was cautiously mounting the stairs. Jimmie Dale snatched his automatic from his pocket, and without a sound stole forward across the room to a position by the door. The footsteps were on the landing now. The doorknob was tried; the door began to open slowly, inch by inch, wider; a dark form slipped through into the room; the floor was closed again—and Jimmie Dale, reaching forward, clapped the muzzle of his automatic against the other's head. But it was Larry the Bat who spoke—in a hoarse, guttural whisper.

"Youse let a peep outer youse, an' youse goes bye-bye for keeps! See? Put yer hands over yer head, an' do it—*quick*!"

Jimmie Dale's left hand reached out and switched on the light. It was Meighan, hands elevated, startled, angry, who stood blinking in the glare—and then a low cry came from the man.

"Larry the Bat—the Gray Seal! So it's a plant, is it! That damned she-pal of yours handed it to me good over the phone!" Meighan's lips tightened. "And where's Virat—did you kill him, too?"

Jimmie Dale's hand was searching swiftly through the detective's clothes. He transferred a revolver and a pair of handcuffs to his own pockets.

"I had ter take a chance on de light," said Larry the Bat plaintively; "'cause I had ter frisk youse." He turned off the light again. "Sure, she's a slick one!" Larry the Bat, his left hand free again, turned his flashlight upon the detective. "Youse can put yer flippers down now. Mabbe she staked youse ter de tip dat de bonds was here, eh?"

"Yes, blast you—both of you!" growled Meighan.

"Well, dey ain't," said Larry the Bat coolly; "but mabbe, after all, she wasn't handin' youse no steer."

Meighan, savage at his own helplessness, snarled his words.

"What do you mean?" he demanded.

"Mabbe nothin'—mabbe a whole lot." Larry the Bat dropped his voice mysteriously. "I was thinkin' of pullin' off a little show here, an' youse have de luck ter get an invite, dat's all. Mabbe I'll hand youse somethin' on a gold platter, an' mabbe I'll hand youse—*this*!" The automatic was shoved significantly an inch closer to Meighan's face. "Youse know me! Youse know what'll happen if youse play any funny tricks! No guy gets de Gray Seal alive—I guess youse are wise ter dat, ain't youse? Now den, over youse go behind dat big chair on de other side of de table!"

Meighan, a puzzled look replacing the angry expression on his face, blinked.

"What's the lay?" he queried.

"I'm expectin' company," grinned Larry the Bat. "Youse keeps yer yap closed till youse gets de cue—savvy? Dat's all! If youse play fair, mabbe youse'll get a look-in on de rake-off; if youse throws me down, the first shot I fires won't miss *youse*. Go on now, get down behind dat chair—quick!"

Hesitantly, following the flashlight's directing ray, covered by Jimmie Dale's automatic, Meighan, muttering, made his way across the room, and crouched down behind the back of a large lounging chair. Jimmie Dale leaned nonchalantly against the jamb of the door, the flashlight holding a bead upon the chair.

"Youse'll pardon me if I keeps de spot-light on youse," drawled Larry the Bat, "Some of youse dicks ain't trustworthy."

"Look here!" Meighan burst out. "This is a hell of a note! What—"

"Youse shut yer face!" Jimmie Dale's voice had grown suddenly cold and menacing—the stairs were creaking again, this time under a quick tread. "Listen! Say, youse don't have ter wait long fer de curtain, ter go up on de act. Don't youse make a sound!"

The doorknob turned. Jimmie Dale whipped his flashlight into his pocket—and in a flash, as a man entered, switched on the light, and slammed shut the door. A dapper individual, wearing tortoise-rimmed glasses, with black moustache and goatee, was staring into the muzzle of Jimmie Dale's automatic.

"Hello, Frenchy!" observed Larry the Bat suavely. "Feelin' faint?"

The man's face had gone a chalky white. He looked wildly around him, as though seeking some avenue of escape.

"*Mon Dieu!*" he whispered. "Larree ze Bat! It is ze Gray Seal! It is—"

"Aw, cut out dat parlay-voo dope!" Larry the Bat broke in curtly. "Youse don't need ter pull dat stuff wid me, Virat. Talk New York, see?"

Virat moistened his lips with the tip of his tongue.

"What do you want here?" he asked huskily.

"Oh, nothin' much," said Larry the Bat airily. "I thought mabbe youse might figure dere was some of dem bonds comin' ter me."

"Bonds! I don't know anything about any bonds," said Virat, in a low voice. "I don't know what you are talking about."

"You don't—eh?" inquired Larry the Bat ominously. "Well den, I'll help ter put youse wise. But mabbe I'd better get yer gun first, eh?" As he had done to Meighan, he removed a revolver from Virat's pocket. "T'anks!" he said. He pushed Virat with his revolver muzzle toward the table, and forced the other into a chair. He sat down opposite Virat, and smiled unpleasantly. "Now den, come across! Youse croaked de Magpie ter-night!"

"You're dippy!" sneered Virat. "I haven't seen the Magpie in a month."

"An' dat's what youse did it wid." Larry the Bat, as though he had not heard the other's denial, reached into his pocket, and shoved a small, murderous, bloodstained blackjack, the leather-covered piece of lead pipe that he had found beneath the washstand, suddenly across the table under Virat's eyes.

With a sharp cry, staring, Virat shrank back.

"Sure! Now youse're talkin'!" approved Larry the Bat complacently. "But dat ain't all. Say, youse have got a gall! Youse thought youse'd plant me, did youse, wid dat gray seal on de Magpie's boot!" Jimmie Dale's voice was deadly cold again. "Well, what about dat?"

"What do you want?" mumbled Virat.

Jimmie Dale's smile was not inviting.

"I told youse once, didn't I? What do youse suppose I want! If I got ter fall fer it, I want some of dem bonds—dat's what I want!"

A look of relief spread over Virat's face.

"All right," he said hurriedly. "I—that's—that's fair. I—I'll get them for you." He started up from his chair, his eyes travelling instinctively toward the door.

"Youse sit down!" invited Larry the Bat coldly.

"But—but you said—I—I was going to get them," faltered Virat.

"Sure!" said Larry the Bat. "Dat's de idea! An', say, I'm in a hurry. Dey ain't over dere, Frenchy—try nearer home!"

Virat's hands trembled as he unbuttoned his vest. He reached around under the back of his vest, drew out a flat package, and laid it on the table. He began to untie the cord.

"Wait a minute!" said Larry the Bat pleasantly. "I ain't in so much of a hurry now dat I got me lamps on 'em. Youse can count 'em out after—half for youse, an' half fer me. Tell us how youse fixed de lay."

And then, for the first time, Virat laughed, though still a little nervously.

"Yes, that's square," he agreed eagerly. "I—I was afraid you were going to pinch them all. I'll tell you. It was easy. I piped the Magpie off to a chap named Kenleigh having the bonds up there in his rooms in an apartment house. I couldn't crack Kenleigh's safe myself, but it was nuts for the Magpie—see? He cracked the safe. I was with him, and I copped that near-diamond pin of his, and left it there so there wouldn't be any guessing as to who pulled off the job, and then we beat it back to his place to divide—and I beaned him. I wasn't looking into any gun then, and handing over fifty thousand—and besides, with the Magpie out of the way, I had *some* alibi." Virat laughed shortly. "That's where you come in. Everybody knew you had it in for him. All I had to do was—well, what you said I did. If you hadn't tumbled to it, and I'm damned if I can see how you did, there wasn't anything to it at all. It was open and shut that the Magpie pinched the swag, and that you croaked him and beat it with the bonds."

"Say," said Larry the Bat admiringly, "youse're some slick gazabo, youse are! But how did youse know dat guy Kenleigh had de goods?"

"That's none of your business, is it?" replied Virat, a little defiantly. "You're getting yours now."

Larry the Bat appeared to ponder the other's words, a curious smile on his lips.

"Well, mabbe it ain't," he admitted. "Let it go anyway, an' split the swag. Count 'em out!"

Virat picked up the package again, and began to untie it—and again Jimmie Dale's hand slipped into his pocket. And then, quick as the winking of an eye, as Virat's hands came together over a knot, Jimmie Dale leaned across the table, there was a click, and the steel were locked on the other's wrists.

There was a scream of fury, an oath from Virat.

"Dat's yer cue, Meighan," called Larry the Bat calmly. "Come out an' take a look at him!"

A ghastly pallor spreading over his face, staring like a demented man, as Meighan, rising from behind the lounging chair, advanced toward the table, Virat huddled back in his seat.

"Know him?" inquired Larry the Bat.

The detective bent sharply forward.

"My god!" he exclaimed. "It's—no, it can't—"

"Mabbe," murmured Larry the Bat, "youse'd know him better when he ain't dolled up." He swept the glasses from Virat's nose, and wrenched away the black moustache and goatee.

"Kenleigh!" gasped Meighan.

"Mabbe," said Larry the Bat, with a twisted grin, "dere's somethin' he may have fergotten ter wise youse up on, but he didn't mean ter hide nothin' in his confession—did youse, Frenchy? An' mabbe dere's one or two other things in de years he's been playin' Kenleigh dat he'll tell youse about, if youse ask him—nice and pleasant-like!"

Larry the Bat edged around the table, and, covering Meighan with his revolver, backed to the door.

"Well, so long, Meighan!" he said softly, from the threshold. "T'ink of me when dey pins de medal on yer breast fer dis!"

And then Jimmie Dale laid Meighan's revolver down on the floor of the room, and locked the door on the outside with a pick-lock, and went down the stairs.

CHAPTER 9

'WARE THE WOLF

Jimmie Dale's fingers, in the darkness, were deftly tying around his body the leather girdle with its finely-tempered, compact kit of burglar's tools. It was strange, this note of hers tonight—strange, even, where all the notes that she had ever written had been strange! It had been left half an hour ago at the door of the St. James Club—and he had hastened here to the Sanctuary. It was curiously strange! Three nights ago, he had seen Frenchy Virat safely in the hands of the police, and Frenchy Virat was still safely in police custody—but he, Jimmie Dale, was not yet done with Frenchy Virat, it seemed! The note had made that quite clear. There was still the Wolf; and it was the Wolf that filled this anxious, hurried word from her tonight.

The Wolf! He knew the Wolf well—as Larry the Bat in the old days he had even known the other personally as Smarlinghue of today he had progressed that far into the inner ring of the underworld again as to be on nodding terms with the Wolf. The man was a power in the underworld—and a devil in human guise. In a career extending back over many years, a career in which no single crime in the decalogue had been slighted, the Wolf had successfully managed to evade the clutches of the law until his name had become a synonym for craft and cunning in the Bad Lands, and the man himself the object of the vicious hero-worship of that sordid world where murder cradled and foul things lived. The police had marked the man, marked him a score of times; in their records a hundred unsolved crimes pointed to the Wolf—but they had never "got" him—always the thread of evidence that seemed to lead to that queer house near Chatham Square was broken on the way—and the Wolf, with steadily increasing prestige and authority in gangland, laughed in the faces of the police, and here and there a plain-clothes man, over-zealous perhaps, *died*.

That was the Wolf—but that was not all! Jimmie Dale's face hardened into grim lines, as he lifted out from under the baseboard "Smarlinghue's" frayed and seedy coat, and put it on. Between the Wolf and the Gray Seal there was now a personal feud. Above the reek of those whisperings in the underworld, above that muttered slogan, *"death to the Gray Seal,"* that men flung at each other from the twisted corners of their mouths, the Wolf had snarled, and the underworld had listened, and the underworld was waiting now—the Wolf had pledged himself to rid the Bad Lands of the terror that had crept upon it. He had sworn, and staked his reputation on his pledge, to "get" Larry the Bat, *alias* the Gray Seal—and in the eyes of the underworld, as the underworld sighed with relief, it was already accomplished, for the Wolf had never failed.

Jimmie Dale stooped down, felt in under the baseboard again, and took out a little make-up box. The Wolf's incentive was not one of philanthropy toward his fellow denizens of crimeland, whose ranks had been thinned by those who, thanks to the Gray Seal, had gone "up the river," some of them, many of them, to that room in Sing Sing's death-house from which none ever returned alive; nor was it, to give the Wolf his due, through a personal fear that his own career might end, as those others' had, at the hands of the Gray Seal; nor, again, was it through any tardy, eleventh-hour conversion, any belated edging toward the way of grace that found expression in a desire to array himself on the side of those representing the forces of law and order. It was none of these things that actuated the Wolf—it was Frenchy Virat, *alias* one Kenleigh, who was awaiting trial in the Tombs. Frenchy Virat was the Wolf's bosom friend!

The wheezy, air-choked gas-jet spluttered into a blue flame, as Jimmie Dale lighted it. It disclosed, in shadow, the battered easel, the dirty canvases, some finished, some but tentative daubs, that banked the wall in disorder opposite the small French window, whose shade was closely drawn; it crept dimly into the far corner of the room and disclosed the cheap cot, unmade, the blanket upon it rumpled in negligent untidiness; it fell full, such as its fulness was, upon the rickety table that was littered with unwashed dishes and sticky paint tubes, and, at one end of the table, on an evening newspaper, and, beside the newspaper, the Tocsin's note and a newspaper clipping.

Jimmie Dale sat down at the table, brushed the dishes and paint tubes together into a heap, and propped up against them a cracked and streaked mirror. He opened his make-up box, and as, swiftly, with masterly touch, the grey, sickly pallor that was Smarlinghue's transformed his face, and as, from little distorting pieces of wax, there came into being the hollow cheeks, the thin, extended lips, the widened nostrils, he kept glancing at the newspaper, reading again an article that was set, on the front page, under heavy type captions—the article which was identical with the clipping, and which latter the Tocsin had enclosed with her note, lest he should not have seen the original himself.

UNIDENTIFIED BODY FOUND
UNDER PIER IN NORTH RIVER

VICTIM OF FOUL PLAY
FACE IS MUTILATED BEYOND RECOGNITION

The details as set forth in the "story" were gruesomely interesting enough from a morbid point of view; but from the point of view of the police they were both meagre and unsatisfactory. It was murder unquestionably—and murder of a most brutal character. The headline had epitomised it—the face was mutilated beyond recognition. Every belonging, obviously with the design to prevent, or at least retard, identification, had been stripped from the body. One point alone appeared to be established, and that, if anything, but added to the mystery which surrounded the crime. According to medical opinion, the murder had been committed but a very short time before the body was discovered; and, since the victim had been found at three o'clock that afternoon, the body must have been thrown into the water in broad daylight.

Jimmie Dale worked on—his fingers seeming to fly with ever-increasing speed. There was no time to lose; every minute, every second, counted against him. If he could only have acted on the instant, as Jimmie Dale, when he had received the note at the club! But he had not had that leather girdle at the club—no blue-steel tools that would be needed, no mask, and he had not been armed—everything had been here in the Sanctuary. And, once here, since he had been forced to lose that much time, he had risked a little more, precious as the moments were, for the advantages, the safety, the freedom of movement, afforded by the character of Smarlinghue. However, it was still but barely eleven o'clock, and the chances were that the Wolf would hardly have deemed it late enough as yet to set to work. On the other hand—well, on the other hand, if the Wolf had proved the early bird, then, perhaps, he and the Wolf would have, in another place and time tonight, a more personal reckoning than was anticipated in the Tocsin's plan!

His eyes picked up snatches of her note, as they skimmed it swiftly again.

"...The Wolf... old storehouse on river front... through trap into the water... old Webb... Spider Webb... ten thousand dollar Moorcliffe jewel robbery... cash box... safe behind panelling in bedroom directly opposite the door... false bottom... afraid of the Wolf... last few days... unfinished...

Wolf does not know... man and wife upstairs... old couple... keep house for the Spider... no suspicion that anything has happened..." And then, at the end, a more personal, intimate touch: "Jimmie, it is not to save someone else that I have written this tonight, for that is now too late—it is to save *you*. The Wolf is dangerous and I am afraid. You know that he has sworn to trap you. He is cunning, Jimmie—do not underestimate him. That is why I have written this—if you succeed tonight..."

Jimmie Dale's fingers were tearing the note now into infinitesimal shreds, and, with it, the newspaper clipping. The newspaper itself he crumpled up and tossed into the corner. He crossed the room, replaced the make-up box in its hiding place, put back the movable section of the base-board, turned out the light—and a minute later, Smarlinghue, unkempt, stoop-shouldered, let himself out, not by the French window through which he had entered stealthily in the evening clothes of Jimmie Dale, but unconcernedly, as was the right of any tenant, by the door that opened on the ground-floor passage of the tenement, and shuffled down the street.

The Wolf—and Spider Webb—and Larry the Bat! It was a curious trio! Smarlinghue's lips, perhaps because the wax beneath was not yet moulded comfortably into place, twitched oddly. One of them was dead—the Spider. There remained—the Wolf and Larry the Bat! No, he did not underestimate the Wolf—only a fool, and a blinded fool, would do that. The Wolf had shown his fangs in deadly enough fashion that morning—with a brutal murder, craftily planned, and hellishly executed! And yet the Wolf was quite hopelessly illogical! It was no secret in the underworld that the Wolf and Spider Webb had long worked together, and that the Spider was a close friend of the Wolf. Yet the Wolf had murdered the Spider, and at the same time had found a basis for his oath to end Larry the Bat, because Larry the Bat had been instrumental in handing over to the police a *friend* of the Wolf!

Smarlinghue slouched on along the street, but the "slouch" covered the ground at an amazing rate of speed. He had not far to go—but neither had he a moment that he dared lose. Spider Webb's old antique shop, but a few blocks away, nestled in a squalid little courtyard just west of the Bowery, and on the same side of the Bowery as the Sanctuary.

Someone, out of the shadows of the street, flung him a good-night. Smarlinghue mumbled his acknowledgment from the corner of his mouth, and hurried along.

His thoughts were still on the Wolf. He had not exhausted the sum of the Wolf's digressions from the realms of the logical! In the old days there had been an intimacy even between the Wolf and Larry the Bat. That underground passage from the shed into that house near Chatham Square, for instance—which was known only to the *most* intimate! But perhaps the Wolf had forgotten, or perhaps even the Wolf had never known he had been on quite such intimate terms with—Larry the Bat.

Jimmie Dale glanced behind him. There was no one in sight for the moment. He was at the corner of a lane now—and he chose the lane. It was a shorter, and a safer route. It bordered on the rear of the courtyard which was his objective, and obviated the necessity of attempting to steal down past the side of "The Yellow Eastern" unnoticed. No, he did not underestimate the Wolf, but if he had luck tonight—! He shrugged his shoulders in a sort of grim whimsicality.

His mind reverted to the Spider now—Spider Webb. Facetious, in a way, the name was! Webb—Spider Webb! And yet the man had come by it honestly, or dishonestly, enough! The old antique shop for years covered dealings that were shabbier than the shabbiest of its antiques! It was probable that more stolen had found Spider Webb's a clearing house than any other Mecca of the crooks in New York. It was probable, too, that it had known more police raids than any of its competitors—but, unlike many of its competitors, nothing but what indubitably belonged there had ever been found. But then again, the Spider was a specialist—he specialised in small articles, particularly jewelry—no one in the Bad Lands who knew his way about would ever have dreamed of going to the Spider with anything else! Nor was the Spider without justification in thus restricting his operations. The Spider had always managed to hide his questionable wares, until he was able to dispose of them and they passed again out of his possession, with an ingenuity that had baffled, enraged, and mortified the police—and commanded the enthusiastic confidence and admiration of the underworld! But this was, for the most part, past history, and of the days gone by, for the Spider now had grown old—had grown to be an old man—for it had begun of late to be whispered that he talked more than he had been wont to talk in the days of his prime, that he was not as *safe* as he had been, and in consequence his trade of late had begun to drift away from him.

And herein lay the secret of the old man's murder at the hands of the Wolf. The Tocsin's note had not failed to lay stress on this. No one probably, through a career of half a score of years, knew more about the Wolf and the Wolf's doings than did the Spider. Rightly or wrongly, the word was out that the old man, in his garrulity, was not safe—and the Wolf was inviting no chances where the electric chair was concerned, that was all! The old man would henceforth be perfectly safe, as far as any *talking* went! It was brutal, hideous—but it was the Wolf! Also, the Wolf, tritely expressed, had proposed to kill two birds with one stone. The old man's trade was not entirely gone. Yesterday, an old-time lag, who had dealt with the Spider for many years, and who had "pulled" the Moorcliffe job—the robbery of a summer mansion a few miles up the Hudson—had "fenced" the proceeds at the antique shop. Ten thousand dollars' worth of first-water sparklers! Everybody that was anybody in gangland knew this. The Wolf had seen the psychological

and profitable moment to strike—again that was all! And again it was diabolical—but again it was the Wolf!

Jimmie Dale's face was set like flint. And this was the man who had
sworn that he would "get" the Gray Seal! A sort of unholy, passionate joy
surged upon him. Well, they would see, he and the Wolf—and perhaps tonight! It was certain that the Wolf would act *alone*. The man's devilish cunning showed itself in having inveigled the old man to that storehouse on the
river bank, rather than to have killer the Spider in the Spider's own home. It
might be days perhaps before the Spider's absence—for the Spider's peculiar
life had demanded mysterious absences before—was even commented upon,
and the Wolf had taken pains to see that the body was not, immediately at
least, identified. It was very simple—from the Wolf's standpoint! The Wolf
was counting it none too easy a task evidently to find the Spider's ingenious
and storied hiding place, and this would give him a night, two nights, or
more, in which, undisturbed, he might prosecute his search. And, as he had
committed alone, so he would continue to work alone, there were those even
in gangland, and in spite of the acknowledged leadership, who would not
look with friendly eyes upon the Wolf for this!

It was black here in the lane, and now, possibly a distance of a hundred
yards up from the street, Jimmie Dale's fingers, feeling along the left-hand
fence, came upon the latch of a small, narrow door—the courtyard's access
to the lane. He passed through, and stood still—listening—looking sharply
about him. He knew the place well. It was the heart and centre, the core of its
own particular and vicious section of the underworld. Ahead of him, flanking the two-story, tumble-down building that was the Spider's home, was a
narrow alleyway, then a small and filthy courtyard, and, its rear upon this and
fronting the street, the alleyway again at the side, the "The Yellow Lantern"
that he had been careful to avoid a dance hall of the lowest type. The Spider
had not unshrewdly chosen his location; nor the proprietor of "The Yellow
Lantern" his—their clientele was a common one, and their interests did not
clash!

From the direction of "The Yellow Lantern" came a hilarious uproar,
subdued somewhat by the distance, out of which arose the strident notes of
a tinny piano beating blatantly the measure of a turkey trot. There was no
other sound. There were lights from the rear of the dance hall, enough, Jimmie Dale knew, to throw a murky illumination over the front windows of the
antique shop; but there were no lights showing from the Spider's dwelling
itself, that loomed black on the side of the alleyway at his right hand—the old
couple that kept the Spider's house were doubtless long since in bed in their
own particular apartments upstairs.

Jimmie Dale moved softly forward now, gained the back entrance of the
Spider's house, and tried the door cautiously. It was locked. From one of the
little pockets in the girdle under his shirt came a black silk mask, which he

slipped over his face; from another of the pockets came a little steel picklock. He was pressed close against the door now, his body merged with the black shadows of the wall. A minute passed—and then the door swung open, and closed without a sound. Another minute passed, and still another. From upstairs came the sound of stertorous breathing, nothing else, only quiet, and a silence that was heavy in itself—and then the round, white ray of Jimmie Dale's flashlight winked through the blackness. As between himself and the Wolf, he was first, at least, on the ground!

He was in the kitchen of the house. On the opposite side of the room from him were two doors, one of them, the one to the left, open—and the flashlight, playing through, disclosed a passageway leading, obviously, to the shop at the front, and continuing to the stairway. He crossed to the right-hand door noiselessly, opened it, and, with a low ejaculation of satisfaction, stepped in over the threshold. It was the room he sought—the Spider's bed-room, or, better perhaps, the Spider's den that served the man for all purposes. The Spider, it was very plain, was not fastidious! The room was dingy beyond description; the furnishings poor and poverty-stricken in appearance. It was here the Spider met his clients of a sort—and drove his bargains. There was no hint of affluence—the room was miserly.

The flashlight swept in a circle around the room. There was a bed in one corner, a table and two chairs in another, and a miserable washstand in still another. The centre of the room, save for an old carpet on the floor, was quite bare of furnishings. Jimmie Dale's survey of the appointments, however, was most cursory—they concerned him little. The flashlight's ray was even lifted above them, as it moved about. There was only one door—the door by which he had entered; and only one window—which, with a sudden frown, he mentally noted did not open on the alleyway, for the very sufficient reason that the alleyway was on the other side of the house. He stepped quickly to the window, and looked out. It was a moment before he could see; and then, with a quick nod of his head, he began, with extreme caution to loosen the window catches on the sill. There was a narrow space between the house and what was the blank brick wall of the building next to it, and this space extended to the rear, and therefore, indirectly, by circling the house at the back, led to the house and the door in the fence again.

Jimmie Dale smiled grimly, as he swung the old-fashioned windows back on either side. So far he was in luck tonight, and, with luck, in a very few minutes now be out and away from the house by the same way he had entered it—but luck sometimes was a fickle thing, and a goddess most to be trusted by those who looked after themselves!

He walked back to the doorway, and levelled his flashlight across the room directly in front of him. The ray fell upon the wooden panelling, and, holding the light steadily on the same spot, he moved forward across the floor to the opposite wall, dropped on his hands and knees, and began to examine the woodwork critically. It was beautiful work, this panelling that went all around the room, very old, but very beautiful work, and of very beautifully matched wood—it was entirely out of place with the rest of the room, or would have been, were it not that the panelling itself bore witness to the fact that it had been built in there when the house itself had been built, and bore witness, too, to the fact that in those days, long gone by, a relic perhaps even of Dutch handiwork, the house had not been unpretentious amongst its fellows of that generation.

"Behind panelling in bedroom directly opposite the door," she had written. Inch by inch, over an area a yard square, those sensitive finger tips of Jimmie Dale felt their way, lingering here over a knot in the wood, and there over a joint or crevice. Five minutes went by—and the five became ten. An exclamation of annoyance, low, guarded, escaped him. There was nothing—he could find nothing. The Spider's ingenuity had not been over-rated! Somewhere there must be the secret spring which operated the panel, but there was no sign of it; neither was there the slightest sign or indication that any portion of the panelling was even movable.

He drew back for an instant, frowning. Perhaps—and then he shook his head—no, the Tocsin did not make mistakes of that kind. The safe was unquestionably behind the panelling in front of him. Well, there was a way—it was distasteful to him because it was crude and bungling, but he could afford no more time in a search, that he had already convinced himself was hopeless.

From the girdle came a half dozen little blue-steel tools. A jimmy found and nosed its way into the joint between two panels. There was a low, faint creak of rending wood. A wedge followed the jimmy. A faint creak again—and now one a little louder—and Jimmie Dale, half turned, listened intently—the narrow board was in his hand. There was nothing—no sound—save that interrupted, stertorous breathing from above, and the tinny jangle of the piano from the direction of "The Yellow Lantern."

And now Jimmie Dale smiled again—that curious flicker on his lips that mingled whimsicality and a deadly earnestness. The Tocsin had made no mistake. Showing through the aperture, gleaming under the flashlight's ray, was the nickel dial of a safe. He worked rapidly now. The first panel out, the remainder came much more readily—and finally the entire face of the safe was disclosed. Jimmie Dale stared at it—and pursed his lips. It was an ugly safe, extremely ugly—from a cracksman's point of view! Also, there seemed a hint of irony, a jeer almost, in the impassive wall of steel that confronted him. It was one of his own make—one that had helped, in the old days, to amass the millions that his father had left to him—and it was one of the *best*!

In an abstracted, deliberate way, his eyes pondering the safe, the blue-steel tools were replaced in the pockets of the leather girdle; and then the long, slim, tapering fingers closed upon the dial's knob and twirled it tentatively, and his head bent forward until his ear was pressed hard against the face of the safe.

It was very still now—only the breathing from above that seemed in cadence with those strange and paradoxical palpitations that are known only in a great silence—the piano for the moment had ceased its jangle. Jimmie Dale's fingers, from the dial, sought the floor, and frictioned briskly over the rough, threadbare carpet, until the nerves tingled under the delicate skin—and then they shot to the dial again.

Strained, every faculty keyed up to its highest tension, he crouched there against the safe. Again and again his fingers rubbed over the rough carpet, and again the sweat beads oozed out upon his forehead with the strain—and then there came through the stillness a long-drawn intake of his breath. The handle swung the bolt with a low metallic thud—the safe was open.

There was the inner door now. Again those slim fingers, almost raw, quivering now at the tips, rubbed along the carpet, and the lips, just showing beneath the edge of the mask, grew tight with pain. Then he leaned forward, crouched once more, his head and shoulders inside the outer door, like some strange animal burrowing for its prey. Faint, musical, like some far distant tinkle, came the twirling of the dial—and then, suddenly, he drew back sharply, his hand shot to his pocket, whipped out his automatic, and, motionless there on his knees, every muscle rigid, he listened. There was the piano again, the breathing, the weird pound and thump of the silence—nothing else. He shook his head in half angry, half tolerant self-remonstrance. He was under strain, that was all—he had thought he had heard a footstep out there in the alleyway. He laid his automatic on the floor within instant reach, and turned again to the safe—acute and sensitive as his hearing was, it would haw taken good ears indeed to have distinguished a step at that distance on the other side of the house!

But now he worked, seemingly at least, with even greater rapidity than before. Imagination had had one effect, if it had had no other—it was a spur, a reminder that at any moment there might well be a footstep, and one that was born only of the imagination! His jaws clamped. He had not counted on this—an old-fashioned iron monstrosity that was dismaying only in its appearance, perhaps—but not this! He had been here far longer now than he—

"Ah"—tense, low, that deep intake of the breath again.

The inner door swung wide; the flashlight's ray leaped, dazzling white, into the interior, and, on the lower shelf, upon a flat, narrow, black tin box—the cash-box.

In an instant, Jimmie Dale had picked it up. It was not locked, and he lifted the cover. From within there scintillated back the gleam of diamonds—a handful of pendants, brooches, ear-rings lay there disclosed, and, too, a string of pearls. Ten thousand dollars! It was a modest figure! He reached his hand inside the box—and on the instant snatched it back, and thrust the box swiftly into his pocket. The flashlight was out. The room was in darkness.

This time it was not imagination—nor, he knew now, had it been imagination before. There was a faint creak of the flooring in the kitchen, a single incautious step that he placed as having come from near the doorway of the passage—and now someone had halted on the threshold of the room itself. Jimmie Dale's brain was working with lightning speed. There had been no time to reach the window—time only to snatch up his automatic and retreat a little from the immediate vicinity of the safe. Had the other heard the slight sound—it was only the brushing of his coat against the wall! Much less had there been time to close the safe—nor would it have done any good—he could not have replaced the broken panelling! And now—*what*? The man, with a stealth that he, Jimmie Dale, except for that one incautious footfall, could not have excelled, must have entered through a window from the alleyway into the passage. It was dark, utterly dark—save that the window showed dimly like a faint transparent square set in the blackness.

He could not see, but he could *sense* the other standing there in the doorway, motionless, silent, as though listening. Perhaps a minute passed. There was something nerve-racking now in the silence, something sinister, something pregnant with menace. And then, suddenly, there came a low, scratching sound, and a match flame spurted through the darkness, and lighted up a face—a face that was thrust forward through the doorway with a sort of pent-up and malicious eagerness; a vicious face, with sharp, restive black eyes under great, hairy eyebrows; a face with a huge jaw, outflung now, that was like the jaw of a beast. It was the Wolf!

CHAPTER 10

THE CHASE

It held for the fraction of a second, that light—no more. It travelled upward past the face, as though the Wolf were holding it above his head to get his bearings; and then, with a sharp and furious oath, the match was hurled to the floor, there was a scuffling sound—and then silence again.

Jimmie Dale's automatic was thrust a little forward in his hand, as he crouched against the wall. He could have shot the man, as the other stood in the doorway. The Wolf had offered a target that it would have been hard to miss—and it would, one day, have saved the law the same task! He was a fool, perhaps, that he had not taken what was, perhaps again, the one chance he had for his life, for he was at a decided disadvantage now, since he knew intuitively that the Wolf, scuttling back, had now craftily protected himself behind the jamb of the door, and yet at the same time still commanded the interior of the room. But he could not have fired in cold blood like that—

even upon the Wolf, devil though the man was, murderer a dozen times over though he the man to be! He, Jimmie Dale, had never shot to *kill* not yet—but in a fight, cornered, if there was no other way...!

He moved a little, a bare few inches, then a few more—without a sound. In the light of the match, the Wolf must have seen the dismantled panelling and the open safe, and a masked figure crouched against the wall—and the Wolf would have marked the position of that crouched figure against the wall!

Silence—a minute of it—still another!

Again Jimmie Dale moved inch by inch—toward the window. And yet to attempt the window was to invite a shot and expose himself, for, dark as it was, his body would show plainly enough against the background of that lesser gloom of window square.

Jimmie Dale's eyes strained through the blackness across the room. He could just make out the configuration of the doorway. The Wolf was just on the other side of it, just inside the kitchen, he was sure of that. Almost a smile was flickering over Jimmie Dale's tight-pressed lips. There was a way— there was a way now, if the Wolf did not get him with a chance shot. He moved again, and reached the window, crouched low beneath the sill—and passed by the window.

And then the Wolf spoke from the doorway in a hoarse whisper, and in the whisper there was a low, taunting laugh.

"I been waitin' for you to try the window, but you're too foxy—eh? All right, my bucko—then I'll get you another way—with just one shot, see? And then—*good-night*! And say, whoever t'hell you are, thanks for crackin' the box for me!"

The man's voice came from the *right* of the doorway—and the door opened *inward*—and he, Jimmie Dale, remembered that he had opened it *wide*. It was slow, very slow, this creeping inch by inch through the darkness. It seemed as though his breath were as stertorous as that breathing from above, and that the Wolf must hear.

And then the Wolf laughed low again.

There was a curious crackling noise, as of paper being torn—and then, quick, in the doorway, came a yellow flame, and the Wolf's hand showed from around the edge of the jamb, and, making momentary daylight of the room, a flaming piece of paper, tossed in, fell upon the floor.

There was a flash, the roar of the report—and another—as the Wolf fired! There was the sullen *spat* of a bullet upon the panelling an inch from Jimmie Dale's head—and a sharp and sudden pain, as though a hot iron had seared his leg.

And now Jimmie Dale's automatic, too, cut flashes with its vicious flame-tongues through the black. Coolly, steadily, he was firing at the doorway—to hold the Wolf there—to keep the Wolf now in the position of the Wolf's own choosing. The paper was but a dull cinder in the centre of the room; twisted too tightly, it had gone out almost immediately.

There came screams, loud, terrified, in a woman's voice from the floor above—and the hoarser tones of a man shouting. A window was flung open. Snarling blasphemous, furious oaths, the Wolf was firing at the flashes of Jimmie Dale's revolver—but each time as Jimmie Dale fired, the sound drowned in the roar of the report, he moved a good yard forward.

Came the trampling of feet from overhead now; and now, as the woman still screamed, answering shouts and yells came from the dance hall. Jimmie Dale had the foot of the bed now near the corner. He again, and instantly flung himself flat upon the floor—and, in the answering flash of the Wolf's shot, placed the exact location of the *door* itself. There was tumult enough now to deaden the slight sound he made. He crept swiftly past the bed to the wall, against which the door, wide open, was swung back, felt out with his hand, the edge of the door, and, leaping suddenly to his feet, hurled the door shut upon the Wolf. There was a scream of pain—the door as it slammed perhaps had caught the Wolf's arm or wrist—but before it was opened again Jimmie Dale was across the room, and, flinging himself through the window, dropped to the ground.

The door crashing back against the wall again, the Wolf's baffled yell of rage, and an abortive shot, told him that his ruse had been solved. He was running now, as rapidly as he could in the darkness and in the narrow space between the Spider's house and the wall of the brick building. Yells in increasing volume sounded from the direction of "The Yellow Lantern"; and now he could hear the pound of feet racing across the courtyard toward the antique shop. The woman, from the open window above, was still screaming with terror.

If he could gain the door in the fence—and the lane! But there was still the Wolf to reckon with! The Wolf had only to run through the kitchen and out by the back entrance—the shorter distance of the two. But the Wolf had already lost a few seconds so that now the race was a gamble. Could he, Jimmie Dale, get there *first*! He could not run in the other direction—that would take him into the courtyard, and the courtyard now, as evidenced by the yells and shouting, was filled with an excited crowd emptying from the dance hall.

He reached the rear end of the house, and darted across the wider space here, racing for the opening in the fence—and suddenly changed his tactics, and began to zigzag a little. A revolver flash cut the night. Came the Wolf's howl from the back stoop, and, over his shoulder, Jimmie Dale saw the other, dark-shadowed, leap forward in pursuit—and heard the Wolf fire again.

He flung himself against the fence door, and it gave with a crash. Pandemonium reigned behind him. In a blur he saw the courtyard, that was dimly lighted now by the open doors and open windows of the dance hall, swaying with shapes, and, like ghostly figures, a mob tearing toward him down the alleyway.

The Wolf's voice, punctuated with a torrent of blasphemy and vile invective, shrilled out over the tumult:

"Come on! Here he is! Out in the lane!"

"Who is it?" shrilled another voice.

"I don't know!" yelled the Wolf. "Catch him, and we'll damn soon find out!"

Jimmie Dale was running like a hare now down the lane. The Wolf leading, still firing, the crowd poured out into the lane in pursuit. Jimmie Dale zigzagged no longer, there was greater risk in that than in risking the shots— it was black enough in the lane to risk the shots; but his lead, barely twenty-five yards, was too short to risk their gaining upon him through his running from side to side.

His brain, cool in peril, worked swiftly. The Sanctuary! That was the one chance for his life! He had been no more than a masked figure huddled against the wall of the room in there. The Wolf had not recognised him. He would be safe if he could reach the Sanctuary! There were two blocks to go along the street ahead, then the next lane, and from that into the intersecting lane, the loose board in the fence that swung at a touch, the French window—and the Sanctuary. But to accomplish this he must *gain* upon his pursuers, not merely hold his own, but increase the distance between them by at least another fifteen or twenty yards; he must, in other words, be out of range of vision as he disappeared through the fence. Well, he should be able to do that! It was the trained athlete against an ill-conditioned, dissolute mob!

He swerved from the lane into the street. There was grim and hellish humour in the thought that a *wolf* should be leading the snarling, howling pack, blood mad now, at his heels! The Wolf had ceased firing—obviously because the Wolf's revolver was empty. The others, a lesser breed, and previously intent on a peaceful orgy at the dance hall, were evidently not armed.

Jimmie Dale gained five yards, another five, and another ten. He had no fear of being recognised as Smarlinghue even here, where, poorly illuminated as the street was, it was like bright sunlight compared with the darkness of the lane. There was no stooped, bent figure, no slouching gait—there was, instead, a tall, broad-shouldered man, whose face was masked, and who ran with the speed of a greyhound, and whose automatic, spitting ahead of him as he ran, invited none of the few pedestrians, or those rushing to their doorways, to block his path.

He swerved again, into a lane again, the lane he had been making for; and, as he swerved, he flung a sidelong glance down the street. Yes, his twenty-five yards were fifty now, except for the Wolf, who ran perhaps ten yards in advance of any of the others. The howls, yells, shouts and execrations welled into a louder outburst as he dashed into the lane. Ten from fifty left forty. Forty yards clear! It was a very narrow margin, even allowing for the blackness of the lane—but it was enough—it was slightly more than the distance along the intersecting lane to the rear of the Sanctuary—he would have pushed aside that loose board before the Wolf turned the corner from one lane into the other!

Forty yards! Perhaps he could make it forty-five! Forty-five would be *safer*; and—he reeled suddenly, and staggered, and, with a low cry, his hands reached upward to his temples. His head was swimming—a dizziness, a nausea was upon him—his strength seemed as it were being sapped from his limbs. What was it? He—yes—the wound in his leg! Yes—he remembered now—that burning like the searing of a hot iron. He had forgotten it in the excitement. But it could not amount to anything—or he would not have been able to have come this far. It was only a passing giddiness—he was better now—see, he was still running—he had only slowed his pace for an instant—that was all.

They swept into the lane behind him. He looked back—and his lips grew tight, and bitter hard. It was no longer forty yards—he was *not* running so fast now—and it was the Wolf, and the Wolf's pack, who were gaining.

He swerved for the third time—into the stretch of intersecting lane. The Sanctuary was just ahead, but he must reach that loose board in the fence and have disappeared before the Wolf swung around the corner behind him—or else—or else, since that led to nowhere to the French window of Smarlinghue's room, the game was as good as up if he attempted it!

He strained forward, striving to mass his strength and fling it into one supreme effort. He was close now—only another five yards to go. Yes—he was weak. His teeth set. Four yards—three! If only there were not that glimmer of light, faint as it was, seeping down the lane from the street lamp across the road from the Sanctuary! Two yards—now! No! The Wolf's yell, as the man tore around the corner of the two lanes, rang out like a knell of doom.

Drawn, white-faced, Jimmie Dale, stumbling now, lurched past that loose board he had counted upon for what was literally his life—lurched past, and stumbled on. He could not run much farther. There was one chance left—just one—that there should be no one to see him enter the *front* door of the Sanctuary, no one lounging about, no one in the tenement doorway. If that chance failed—well, then it was the end—*the* end of Smarlinghue, the end of Jimmie Dale, the end of Larry the Bat, the end of the Gray Seal—and the Wolf would have kept his pledge to gangland. But it would be an end that gangland would long remember, and an end that the Wolf would share!

The street was just before him now. He turned into it—and there came a little cry, a moan almost, of relief. The doorway of the tenement was *clear*. He sprang for it, entered, and, suddenly silent now in his tread, reached the door of his own room, slipped through and closed it softly behind him.

And now Jimmie Dale worked with frantic speed. He could hear them racing, yelling, shouting along the lane. A match crackled in his hand, and the gas-jet spluttered into flame—the light in the room could not be seen from the lane. He ran across the room, tearing off his mask as he went, and, wrenching the cash-box from his pocket, tucked mask and cash-box behind the disordered array of dirty canvases on the floor—he dared not take the risk or the time that loosening the base board would entail. He flung his hat into a corner, and, ripping off his coat, tossed it upon the cot; then, snatching up a paint tube, he smeared a daub of paint upon the palette that lay on the table, and laid a wet brush hurriedly several times across the canvas on the easel.

From the corner of the lane and street outside came the scuffling to and fro of many feet, as though in uncertainty, in indecision, in hesitancy. A dozen voices spoke at once, high-pitched, wild, frenzied.

"Where is he?… Which way did he go?… Where—"

And then the Wolf's voice, above the rest, in a sudden, excited yell:

"What's that across there! It's him! There he is! He's kept on up the lane! He's—"

The voice was lost in a chorus of shouts, in the pound and stampede of racing feet again, of the pack in cry. The sounds receded and died in the distance. Jimmie Dale drew his hand across his forehead and brought it away damp with sweat. He staggered now to the wash-stand, and from the drawer took out a bottle of brandy, and, heedless of glass, uncorked it, and lifted it to his lips. He would never know a closer call! He had been weaker than he had thought! Thank God for the brandy! The fiery stimulant was whipping the blood in his veins into life again, and—the bottle was still held to his lips, but he was no longer drinking. His eyes were on the washstand's mirror. He heard no sound, but in the mirror he saw the door of his room open, close again, and, leaning with his back against it—*the Wolf!*

Not a muscle of Jimmie Dale's face moved. He allowed another gulp of brandy to gurgle noisily down his throat. The cool, alert, keen brain was at work. It was certain that the Wolf had at no time that night recognised him as Smarlinghue. The Wolf, therefore, at worst, could be no more than *gambling* on the chance that the object of the chase had taken refuge here in the tenement, and, naturally enough then, was beginning his investigation with the ground floor room. And yet, why then had the Wolf, deliberately in that case, sent his pack off on a false scent? In the mirror he could see that huge jaw outthrust, the black eyes narrowed, an ugly leer on the working face—and a revolver in the Wolf's hand that held a bead on his, Jimmie Dale's, head.

It was "Smarlinghue," the wretched, nervous, drug-wrecked creature that turned around—and, as though startled at the sight of the other, almost let the bottle fall from his hand.

"So it was you—eh—Smarlinghue! Curse you!" snarled the Wolf. "Come out here, and stand in the centre of the room!"

Smarlinghue cringed. He put down the bottle with a trembling hand, and slouched forward.

"I ain't done nothing!" he whined.

"No, you ain't done a thing—except crack a box and pinch about ten thousand dollars' worth of sparklers!" The Wolf's face, if possible, was more ugly in its threat than before.

Smarlinghue, in a sort of stupefied amazement, stared around the room—as though he expected to see a gleaming heap of diamonds leap into sight somewhere before him. He shook his head helplessly.

"I don't know what you're talking about," he mumbled. "I—I heard a row outside there a little while ago. Maybe that's it."

"Yes—*mabbe* it is!" sneered the Wolf viciously. "So you don't know anything about it—eh? You've got a hell of a good memory, haven't you! You don't know anything about the Spider's safe, or about a little fight in the Spider's room, or about jumping out of the window, and beating it for here with the gang after you—no, you don't! You never heard of it before—of course, you didn't!"

Smarlinghue began to wring his hands nervously one over the other. He shook his head helplessly again.

"It wasn't me!" He licked his lips. "Honest, it wasn't me! I—I don't know what you're talking about. I ain't been out of this room. Honest! Somebody's trying to put me in wrong. I tell you, I ain't been out of here all night. I—look!" With sudden, feverish eagerness, as though from an inspiration, he pointed to the paint brush, the palette, and the canvas on the easel. "Look! Look for yourself! You can see for yourself! I've been painting."

And then the Wolf laughed—and it was not a pleasant laugh.

"Yes, you've been painting!" he jeered. "Sure, you have! I know that! Only you've been *painting* a damned sight more than you thought you were!"

The revolver muzzle covered Jimmie Dale steadily, unswervingly; in the Wolf's face was malicious and sardonic mockery—but the Wolf's eyes were no longer on Jimmie Dale's face, they seemed curiously intent upon the floor at Jimmie Dale's feet. Mechanically Jimmie Dale followed their direction—and his eyes, too, held on the floor. For a moment neither spoke. *The game was up!* His boot top was soaked with blood, and, trickling down the side of the boot, a little crimson stream was collecting in a pool upon the floor.

"You *painted* some of that on the doorstep!" The Wolf's taunting laugh held a deadly menace. "And you painted a drop or two of it along the street as you ran. I thought when you bust away from the Spider's and that cursed gang nosed in that I was going to lose out; but I figured that I had hit you, and I was keeping my eyes skinned to see. And then you commenced to do the drip act—savvy? I was still looking for it when I came out of the lane—you remember, Smarlinghue, don't you?—you got your memory back, ain't you?—that I was a bit ahead of the rest of 'em. It didn't take a second to spot that on the doorstep, and there's some more of it in the hall. Damned strange, ain't it—that it led right to Smarlinghue's room!" The laugh was gone. The Wolf began to come forward across the room. The snarl was in his voice again. "You come across with those sparklers, and you come across—*quick*!"

But now Smarlinghue was like a crazed and demented creature, and he shook his fists at the Wolf.

"I won't! I won't!" he screamed. "You went there to do the same thing! I had as much right as you! And I *got* them—I *got* them! They said he had them there, they were all talking about them today, and I *got* them! I won! They're mine now! I won't give them to you! I won't! I tell you, I won't!"

"Won't you?" The Wolf had reached Jimmie Dale, and one of the Wolf's hands found and shook Jimmie Dale's throat, while the revolver muzzle pressed hard against Jimmie Dale's breast. "Oh, I guess you will! D'ye hear about a man being murdered today with his face cut up? Oh, you did—eh? Well, I happen to know that man was the Spider, and one of these days, mab-be, the police'll tumble to who it was, too. Get me? Suppose I call some of that gang back, and show 'em the *painting* you've done along the hall—eh? And then, by and by, when the bulls get wise, it'll be yours for the juice route, not just a space or two for cracking a box! Get me again?"

Smarlinghue, struggling weakly, pulled the other's hand from his throat.

"You—you were there, too, at—at the Spider's," he choked craftily. "You're—you're in it as—as bad as I am."

"Sure, I was there!" mocked the Wolf, and snatched at Jimmie Dale's throat again. "Sure, I was there—everybody saw me! The Spider was a *friend* of mine, and everybody knows that, too. I was just going there to pay a pal a little visit—see? And that's how I found you there—see? Anything wrong with that spiel? It's a cinch, aint it?" The fingers closed tighter and tighter on Jimmie Dale's throat. "And that's enough talk—give me them sparklers!" He flung Jimmie Dale savagely away. "Get 'em."

Smarlinghue reeled backward in the direction of the disordered canvases on the floor. It was quite true! If the Wolf carried out his threat—which he most certainly would do if he did not get the diamonds for himself—Smarlinghue, and not the Wolf, would be held for the Spider's murder. Jimmie Dale stooped, fumbled amongst the canvases, and produced the cash-box. Well, the diamonds would have to go, that was all—he had no choice left to him. But he was still "Smarlinghue," still the half cowed, yet half defiant, pale-faced creature that shook with mingled rage and fear, as he turned again. He clutched the cash-box to him, as though loath to let it go; but, too, as though fascinated by the Wolf's revolver, he moved reluctantly toward the Wolf, who now stood by the table.

Smarlinghue's hands twined and twined over the box, caressing it in hideous greed and avarice; and he mumbled, and his lips worked.

"Half—give me half?" he whispered feverishly.

"I'll give you—*nothing*!" snarled the Wolf.

"Half—give me a quarter then?" whimpered Smarlinghue.

"*Drop it*!" The Wolf's revolver jerked forward into Jimmie Dale's face.

And then Smarlinghue screamed out in impotent rage, and, wrenching the cover of the cash-box open, flung the jewels in a glittering heap upon the table—and, dancing in demented fashion upon his toes, like a man gone mad, he hurled the cash-box in fury from him. It went through the canvas on the easel, and clattered to the floor.

The Wolf laughed.

But Smarlinghue had retreated now, and, crouched upon the cot, was mumbling through twisted lips.

And again the Wolf laughed, and, gathering up the jewels, dropped them into his pocket, and backed to the door. He stood there an instant, his eyes narrowed on Jimmie Dale.

"I got the stuff now"—he was snarling low, viciously—"and mabbe that puts it a little more up to me. But if you ever open your mug about this, I'll do to you what I did to the Spider today—and if you want to know what that is, go and ask the police to let you have a look! D'ye understand?"

Came the brutal, taunting laugh again, and the door closed behind the Wolf, and his step died away along the passage, and rang an instant later on the pavement without.

It was a moment before Jimmie Dale moved—but into Smarlinghue's distorted features there came a strange smile. He reeled a little from weakness, as he walked to the door, locked it, and, returning, stooped and picked up the cash-box from the floor. In the false bottom, the Tocsin had said. From the leather girdle came a sharp-pointed tool. He pried with it for an instant inside and around the bottom edges, and loosening a sheet of metal that fitted exactly to the edges of the box, lifted out from beneath it several folded sheets of paper. He glanced at the typewritten sheets, a curious, menacing gleam creeping into the dark eyes, then thrust the papers inside his shirt; and, dropping into a chair, unlaced and kicked off his blood-soaked boot.

He was very weak; he had lost, he must have lost, a great deal of blood—but there was something to do yet—still something to do. There was still—the Wolf!

He tore the sheet on the cot into strips, and washed and dressed his wound—a flesh wound, but bad enough, he saw, just above the knee. And then, this done, he took a damp piece of cloth, went to the door again, opened it, and looked out. There was neither anyone in sight, nor any sound. The passage was murky; one gas-jet alone lighted it, and that was turned down. There were little spots, dark spots on the floor—but the Wolf had told him that. He passed his hand over his head—he was a little dizzy. Then slowly, laboriously, he removed the spots from the hallway—and one from the door-step.

Back in his room once more, he locked the door again. A sense of utter exhaustion was stealing upon him—but there was still something yet to be done. Another gulp of brandy steadied him, steadied his head. He took the papers from his pocket and read them now. Here were the details, minute, exact, with the names of those involved, names of those who would squeal quickly enough to save themselves once they were in the clutches of the law, of two of the most famous murder mysteries that New York had known; the details of two, and, unfinished, the partial details of another. It was the evidence the police had long sought. It was the death sentence upon the Wolf—for murder.

Jimmie Dale's face, very white now, was set and hard. The Spider had been too late—to save himself. Beginning to fear the Wolf, as the Tocsin had explained, he had begun to make a record of those days gone by, meaning to hold it over the Wolf's head in self-protection, deposit it somewhere where it would come to light if any attack were made upon him—only the Wolf had struck before the Spider had finished all he had meant to write, before he had told anyone or had warned the Wolf that the papers were in existence. Too late to save himself—and yet, if the Wolf still paid the penalty for murder, did it matter if he were *convicted* for the taking of another life than that of Spider Webb! It was like some grim, retributive proxy! The Spider, at least, had not been too late—for that!

For a moment longer, Jimmie Dale sat there, staring at the papers in his hand. They were unsigned, the Spider's name nowhere appeared—the Spider had been crafty enough to deal only with crimes in which he had had no personal share. There was nothing, not even handwriting, as the papers now stood, to intimate that they had emanated from the Spider; and therefore, in their disclosure, there could be no suspicion in the Wolf's mind that they bore any relation to this night's work. Nor would the Wolf, tried for another crime, ever mention this night's work. It would be the last thing the Wolf would do. The Wolf had double-crossed the underworld, and the underworld, if it found it out, would not easily forgive—and even in a death cell, clinging to the hope of commutation of sentence, the Wolf would never run the risk of his additional guilt of the Spider's murder leaking out. The rôle of "Smarlinghue" in the underworld was safe.

And now Jimmie Dale's lips twitched. The papers were unsigned. He took from the leather girdle the thin metal box, the tweezers, and a diamond-shaped, adhesive, gray paper seal—and, holding the seal with the tweezers, he moistened it with his tongue, and pressed it down upon the lower sheet. It was signed now! Signed with a signature that the police—*and the Wolf*—knew well!

He rose unsteadily, and, taking the empty cash-box, loosened the base-board from the wall near the door, hid the cash-box away, and felt through the pockets of his evening clothes—there was a blank envelope there, he remembered, in which he had placed some memoranda—an envelope, and the little gold pencil in his dress waistcoat pocket. He found them, and, kneeling on the floor, printing the letters, he addressed the envelope to police headquarters, folded and placed the documents inside, and sealed the envelope.

He replaced the base-board, and stood up—but his hand caught at the wall to support himself.

"Tomorrow," said Jimmie Dale weakly—he was groping his way back across the room to the cot "I—I guess I'm all—all in—tonight."

CHAPTER 11

THE VOICES OF THE UNDERWORLD

Futility! And on top of futility, a week of inaction, thanks to that flesh wound in his leg. Futility seemed to haunt, yes, and torture him! Even his rehabilitation of Larry the Bat, with all its attendant risk and danger, had been futile as far as *she* was concerned. And he had counted so much on that! And that had failed, and nothing was left to him but to pursue again the one possible chance of success, the hope that somewhere in the innermost depths of the Bad Lands he might pick up the clue he sought. And so, tonight, he was listening again to the voices of the underworld—and so far he had heard nothing but ominous mutterings, proof that the sordid denizens of crimeland were more than usually disturbed. The Wolf had gone to join his *friend* Frenchy Virat in the Tombs! The twisted lips of the underworld whispered the name of the Gray Seal!

Jimmie Dale's fingers, twitching, simulating even in that little detail the drug-wrecked role of Smarlinghue that he played, clutched with a sort of hideous eagerness at the hypodermic syringe which he held in his hands. How many times, here in Foo Sen's, or in other lairs that were but the counterpart of Foo Sen's, had he lain, stretched out, a pretended victim to a vice that robbed his face of colour, that shook his miserably clad body, that clouded his eyes and stole from them the light of reason—*while he listened*! How many times—and how many times in the days to come would he do it again! Would it never be his, the secret that he sought—the clue that would divulge the identity of those who threatened the Tocsin's life; those who, like human wolves, like a hell-pack snarling for its prey, had driven her again into hiding and made of her a hunted thing!

The fingers closed convulsively over the hypodermic. Wolves! A hell-pack! A tinge of red dyed the grey-white, hollowed cheeks, as a surge of fury swept upon him. No, it was not futility; no, it was not wasted effort—this haunting of the dens of the underworld! In his soul he knew that some day he would pick up the trail of that hell-pack and those human wolves—and when that some day came it would be a day of reckoning, and the price that he would exact would not be small!

He lay back on the bunk that Foo Sen had ingratiatingly allotted him. The air was close, heavy with the sweet, sickish smell of opium, and full of low, strange sounds and noises. And these sounds, in their composite sense, emanating from unseen sources, were as the ominous and sinister evidence of some foul and grotesque presence; analysed, they resolved themselves into the swish of hangings, the swish of slippered, shuffling feet, the stertorous breathing of a sleeper, the clink of coin as of men at play, the tinkle of glass, the murmur of voices, the restive stir of reclining bodies, whisperings.

And now he looked about him through half closed eyes. He was in a little compartment, whose doorway was a faded and stained hanging of flowered cretonne, and whose walls were but flimsy-boarded affairs that partitioned him off from like compartments on either side. It was very near to the pulse of the underworld. Above ground, opening on a street just off Chatham Square, Foo Sen's, to the uninitiated, was but one of the multitudinous Chinese laundries in New York; below, below even the innocent cellar of the house, a half dozen sub-cellars were merged into one, and here Foo Sen plied his trade. And Foo Sen was cosmopolitan in his wares! Here, one, hard pressed, might find refuge from the law; here a pipe and pill were at one's command; here one might hide his stolen goods, or hatch his projected crime, or gamble, or debauch at will—it was the entree only that was hard to obtain at Foo Sen's!

Jimmie Dale's lips twisted in a grim smile. The old days of Larry the Bat had supplied Smarlinghue with the means which, in the last six months, had been turned to such good account that the Smarlinghue of today was almost as fully in the confidence of the underworld as had been the Larry the Bat of yesterday. And yet there had been nothing! No clue! He had wormed himself again into the inner circle of crimeland; he lay here in Foo Sen's tonight, as he had once lain in one of Foo Sen's competitor's dives as Larry the Bat, months ago, on the night the place had been raided—but there was still nothing—still no clue—only the shuffle of slippered feet, the stertorous breathings, a subdued curse, a blasphemous laugh, a coin ringing upon a table top, the murmur of voices, whisperings!

One might hear many things here if one listened, and he *had* heard many things in his frequent visits to these hidden dens of this lower world that shunned the daylight—many things, but never the *one* thing that he risked his life to hear—many things, from these *friends* of his who, if in Smarlinghue they but suspected for an instant the presence of Larry the Bat, would literally have torn him limb from limb—many things, but never the one thing, never a word of *her*—many things, the hatching of crime, as now, for instance, those muttering voices were hatching it from the other side of the partition next to his bunk. Subconsciously he had caught a word here and there, and now, without a sound, he edged his shoulders nearer to the partition until his ear was pressed close against a crack. It did not concern *her*, but he listened now intently.

"Aw, ferget it!" a voice rasped in a hoarse undertone. "Sure, I saw it! Ain't I just told youse I saw Curley hand de dough over dis afternoon! Fifteen thousand dollars all in big new bills, five-hundred-dollar bills I t'ink dey was—dat's wot!"

"How d'youse know it was fifteen thousand?" demanded another voice.

There was a short, vicious laugh; then the voice of the first speaker again:

"'Cause I heard him say so, an' de old guy counted it, an' sealed it up in an envelope, an' gave Curley a receipt, an' tucked de green boys into de safe. Aw, say, dere's nothin' to it, I can open dat old tin box wid a toothpick!"

"Mabbe youse can, but mabbe de stuff ain't dere now—mabbe it's in de bank," demurred the second voice.

"Don't youse worry! It's dere! Where else would it be! Ain't I told youse it was near five o'clock when I went dere—an' dat's after de banks are closed, ain't it? Well, wot d'youse say?"

"I don't like pinchin' any of Curley's money." The second speaker's voice was still further lowered. "It ain't healthy ter hand Curley anything."

"Who's handin' Curley anything!" retorted the other. "It ain't got nothin' to do wid Curley. It ain't Curley's money any more. He paid it over for whatever he's blowin' himself on, an' he's got his receipt for it. It's none of his funeral after dat! How's he goin' to lose anything if we lift de cash? An' if he ain't goin' to lose nothin', wot's he goin' to care! Ferget it! Wot's de matter wid youse!"

There was a moment's apparent hesitancy; then, hoarsely:

"Youse are sure, eh, dat nobody saw youse dere?"

"Say, youse have got de chilly feet fer fair ter-night, ain't youse! Well, can it! No, dey didn't pipe me, youse can bet yer life on dat. I was goin' inter de office w'en I hears some spielin' goin' on inside, an' I opens de door a crack, an' I keeps it open like dat—savvy? An' w'en de old guy shoots de ready inter de box, an' I makes me fade-away, I didn't shut de door hard enough ter bust de glass panels, neither—see? Dat's de story, an' it's on de level. I beats it den, an' I been huntin' fer youse ever since. Now, wot d'youse say—are youse on?"

"Sure!" The second speaker's voice had lost its hesitancy now; it was gruff, assured, even eager. "Sure! I guess youse have pulled a winner, all right! Wot's de lay? Have youse doped it out?"

"Ask me!" responded the other, with a complacent chuckle. "Youse look after de old guy, dat's all youse have ter do. Hook up wid him, an' keep him busy at his house. Get me? De old nut has a crazy notion of goin' down ter de office in de middle of de night sometimes, an' dere's no use takin' any chances. Youse can put up some hard luck story on him, throw in a weep, an' youse got his goat fer as long as youse can talk. Leave de rest ter me. Only, say, youse keep away from me fer de rest of de night—get me? Dey might smell a plant after youse bein' wid him. Youse go somewhere to an all-night joint so's youse have an alibi all de way through, an'—"

The voice ceased abruptly. In a flash the left sleeve of Jimmie Dale's ragged, threadbare coat was pushed up, leaving the forearm exposed. The hypodermic needle pricked the flesh. There was no sound of any step; but the cretonne hanging wavered almost imperceptibly, as though someone, or perhaps but a current of air from the passage without, had swayed it slightly. Jimmie Dale was mumbling incoherently to himself now; his lips, like his fingers, working in nervous twitches. A few seconds passed—a half minute. Still mumbling, Jimmie Dale, with a caress like that of a miser for his gold, was fondling the shining little instrument in his hand—and then the hanging was suddenly thrust aside.

Jimmie Dale neither looked up, nor appeared to be conscious of anyone's presence—but he had already recognised the voices of the two men from the adjoining compartment, who, he was quite well aware, were staring in at him now. The smaller, with sharp, cunning, beady, black eyes, the prime mover in the scheme that had just been outlined, was a clever and dangerous "box-worker," known as the Rat; the other, a heavy, vicious-faced man, with eyes quite as beady and unpleasant as those of his companion, was Muggy Ladd, who made his living as a "stagehand" for those, such as the Rat, who were more gifted than himself.

"Satisfied?" inquired the Rat "He's full up to de eyes wid it now. Foo said he'd been hittin' it up hard fer de last hour." The Rat addressed Jimmie Dale. "Hello, Smarly!" he called out.

Jimmie Dale lifted his head, and blinked at the cretonne hanging.

"Lemme alone!" he complained thickly. "Go 'way, an' lemme alone!"

"Sure!" said the Rat genially. "Sure, we will! Sweet dreams, Smarly!"

The hanging fell back into place. Jimmie Dale continued to blink at it, and mumble to himself. The Rat's pleasant little plan of robbing somebody's safe of fifteen thousand dollars had nothing to do with *her*—but it involved a moral obligation on his part that he had neither the right nor the intention to ignore. And the fulfilment, or the attempt at fulfilment, of that obligation had suddenly assumed unexpected difficulties. Even while he had listened, and before the Rat was halfway through his story, he, Jimmie Dale, was conscious that he had made up his mind the Rat would rob no safe of fifteen thousand dollars that night if he could prevent it, and he had intended following the Rat from Foo Sen's. He dared not do that now. Muggy Ladd's cautiousness, that had evidently induced the Rat to inspect his, Jimmie Dale's, compartment, had made that impossible. The Rat had seen him there; and, forced to the deception in order to avert any suspicion that he had overheard the others' conversation, the Rat had seen him in the condition of one who was apparently already far gone under the influence of drug. To risk the attempt to follow the

Rat now, to risk discovery by the Rat, was to risk, not only the admission that he had been playing a part, but to risk what he had fought for and staked his life for months now to establish—the role, the character of "Smarlinghue" in the underworld. Nor, for the same reason, would he dare move from the place for some little time—there was Foo Sen and the attendants.

Jimmie Dale dropped his head down on the bunk, turned heavily over, facing the partition, and flung his arm across his face. His lips had ceased their nervous working; they were drawn together, thin and hard now. It was bad enough to be forced to remain temporarily inactive, though that in itself was not so serious, for it was still early, not much more than nine o'clock, and it was only fair to presume that the Rat would make no move for some hours to come; but what was much more serious was the fact that, unable to follow the Rat, he would be obliged to solve for himself the problem of whose was the safe, and whose the fifteen thousand dollars that was the Rat's objective. The Rat had referred to "the old guy"—that meant nothing. "Curley," however, was a little better—Curley, who had paid over the money to the "old guy."

Jimmie Dale's forehead, hidden by his arm, furrowed deeply. From Muggy Ladd's initial objection to touching anything that concerned Curley, it could mean only one Curley. He, Jimmie Dale, knew this Curley by sight, and, slightly, by reputation. Curley and his partner, Haines, kept a small wholesale liquor store in one of the most populous, where all were populous, quarters of the East Side; also Curley had a pull as a ward politician, which might very readily account for Muggy Ladd's diffidence; and Curley was credited with doing a thriving business—both ways—as ward heeler and liquor purveyor. Certainly, at least, he was known always to have money; and had even been known at times to lend it freely to those in want—for a consideration. Yes, it was undoubtedly and unquestionably Curley, of Haines & Curley, familiarly known on the East Side as Reddy Curley from his flaming red hair—but to whom had Curley paid over the sum of fifteen thousand dollars?

For a moment the frown on Jimmie Dale's forehead deepened, then he nodded his head quickly. If he could find Curley, or Haines, or even Patsy Marles, the clerk who worked in the liquor store—which might possibly still be open for another hour or so yet—it should not, after all, and without even any undue inquisitiveness on the part of Smarlinghue, prove very difficult to obtain the necessary information, for, if Curley had been in a deal involving fifteen thousand dollars, he was much more likely to be boastful than reticent about it. It resolved itself then after all, into simply a matter of time.

Whisperings, a raucous laugh, a curse, the clink of coin, the rattle of dice, the scuffle of slippered feet, the low swish of the loose-garbed Chinese attendants went on interminably. Jimmie Dale began to toss uneasily from side to side of his bunk, and began to mumble audibly again. Perhaps half an hour passed, during which, from time to time, the curtain of the compartment was drawn quietly aside and the impassive face of one or other of the Chinese attendants was thrust through the opening—and then suddenly Jimmie Dale raised himself up on his elbow, and pointed a shaking finger at one of these apparitions.

"Foo Sen"—he licked his lips as he spoke—"you tell Foo Sen come here!"

The face disappeared, and a moment later another—the wizened, yellow face of a little old Chinaman—took its place.

"You wantee me, Smarly'oo?" inquired the proprietor suavely.

"Tell 'em to help me out of this." Jimmie Dale essayed vainly to rise, and fell back on the bunk. "D'ye hear, Foo Sen—tell'em! Goin' home!"

"Alee same bletter stay sleep him off," advised Foo Sen.

Jimmie Dale succeeded in sitting upright on the edge of the bunk—and snarled at the other.

"You mind your own business, Foo Sen!" he flung out gutturally. "Goin' home! Tell 'em to help me out—sleep where I like! Makes me sick here—rotten smell—rotten punk sticks!"

"You allee same fool," commented Foo Sen imperturbably, as he clapped his hands. "Mabbe you no get home; mabbe you get run in police cell sleep him off, instead. That your business, you likee that—all right!"

Foo Sen smiled placidly, and was gone.

An instant later, Jimmie Dale, his arms twined around the necks of two Chinamen, and leaning heavily upon them, and stumbling as he walked, was being conducted through a maze of dark and narrow passages that gradually trended upward to a higher level—and presently a door closed behind him, and he was in the open air.

It was dark about him, not even the glimmer of a window light showed from anywhere—but in Foo Sen's there were eyes that saw through the darkness, and his progress, alone now, was both unsteady and slow. He was in a very narrow alleyway between two houses—one of the several hidden entrances to Foo Sen's. The alley opened in one direction on a lane, in the other direction on the street. Jimmie Dale chose the direction of the lane, reached the lane, and, still stumbling and lurching, made his way along for a distance of possibly fifty yards; then, well clear of the neighbourhood of Foo Sen's, he began to quicken his pace—and twenty minutes later, frowning in disappointment, he was standing in front of Reddy Curley's liquor store, only to find that the place was already closed for the night.

CHAPTER 12

IN THE SANCTUARY

It was ten o'clock now, an hour since the Rat and Muggy Ladd had left Foo Sen's. Again Jimmie Dale told himself that it was still early, that the Rat would wait for a much later hour—but at the same time he acknowledged to himself a sense of growing and premonitory uneasiness. Certainly, in any case, he had no time to lose. He turned quickly and hurried along the block that separated him from the Bowery—he had a fair idea of the haunts usually frequented in the evening by the men he sought, and, even failing to find the men themselves, there was always the chance, and a very good one, that, where Curley was known, Curley's fifteen thousand dollar deal might be the subject of gossip which would answer his, Jimmie Dale's, purpose quite as well.

But an hour went by—and yet another. Midnight came—and midnight had brought him nothing. It seemed as though he had combed the East Side from end to end, and he had found neither Curley, nor Haines, nor Patsy Marles—nor had he heard anything—nor had such guarded questions as he had dared to ask without involving possible disastrous consequences to "Smarlinghue," should the Rat, after all, succeed and hear of his activities, had any result. And then, still maintaining his efforts with dogged determination, though conscious now that with the hour so late he might perhaps better return to the Sanctuary, change, say, into the clothes of Jimmie Dale, and, crediting the Rat with already having made a successful inroad on the safe, devote his energies to running down the Rat, and, if possible, to salvaging the plunder, he was in the act of entering again one of the dance halls he had already visited earlier in the evening, when one of the men he was searching for lurched out through the doorway. It was Patsy Marles, garrulous, drunk, exceedingly unsteady on his feet, and accompanied by three or four companions. They crowded out past Jimmie Dale, and gathered aimlessly on the pavement. Marles' voice rose in earnest insobriety for what was very probably by no means the first time.

"Betcher life! Spot cash—fifteen thousand—spot cash! Sure, I saw it! Only—hic!—got one boss now. Little ol' Reddy got the—hic!—papers from lawyer 'safternoon. Know ol' Grenville, don't you—that's him—ol' Grenville. Come on, whatsh's use standin' round here doin' nothin'!"

Jimmie Dale did not enter the dance hall—instead, scuffling hurriedly along to the next corner, he turned off the Bowery, and, choosing the darker and more dimly lighted streets and, at times, a lane or alleyway, broke a run. In the space of a little more than a second he had at last obtained the information that he had searched for vainly for over two hours. There seemed something mockingly ironical in the fact that he had been obliged to search for those two hours! What had happened in that time? Two hours! It was three hours now since the Rat had left Foo Sen's!

He shook his head with sudden impatience at himself. He would gain nothing by speculating on possibilities! He *had* the information now. The one thing to do was to act upon it. So it was old Grenville's safe! Old Grenville, the lawyer; honest old Grenville, the East Side called him, the one man, perhaps, whose word was accepted at its face value, and who was both liked and trusted everywhere in the Bad Lands—because he was honest! Jimmie Dale's lips tightened as he ran. It was more than ordinarily dirty work, then, on the Rat's part. Grenville was an old man, close to seventy, at a guess; and if anyone had earned immunity from the depredations of the underworld it was this curious and lovable old character—honest Grenville. The man was not a criminal lawyer, he had made no enemies even in that way; he was more a paternal family solicitor, as it were, to the dregs of humanity that had crowded his dingy office now, so report had it, for over forty years. He was credited with having amassed a little money, not a fortune, perhaps, for there were many fees never collected and never asked for amongst the needy, but enough to live comfortably on in the simple and unpretentious way in which old Grenville lived.

Yes, it was dirty work—miserable, dirty work, the work of a hound and a cur! And the Rat's logic was unassailable. From Patsy Marles' maudlin babbling it was evident that Reddy Curley had bought Haines, his partner, out; that the price was fifteen thousand dollars; and that Grenville, acting for Haines obviously, had received the purchase money from Curley, and in return had handed over what the Rat had taken to be a receipt, but what was probably in reality much more likely to have been a Bill of Sale. But in either case, it was neither Curley nor Haines who would suffer—it was old Grenville, who, if the funds were stolen and not recovered, would have to make the amount good out of his own pocket, and who, as all who knew old Grenville knew well, would unhesitatingly do so at once if it took the last cent that pocket held.

Jimmie Dale had halted before a small building on one of the cross streets near the upper end of the Bowery. There were some half dozen signs on the doorway, for the most part time worn and shabby, amongst them that of Henry Grenville, Attorney-at-Law.

There were no lights in any of the windows, but Jimmie Dale, as he tried the door, found it unlocked, and, opening it noiselessly, stepped inside. Here, a single incandescent suspended over the stair well gave a murky illumination to the surroundings. A narrow corridor, dotted with office doors, was on his left; the stairway—there was no elevator—was directly in front of him. He stood motionless for an instant, listening. There was no sound. He moved forward then, as silent as the silence around him, and began to mount the stairs. Old Grenville's office, he knew, was at the rear of the corridor on the first landing.

It was after midnight now, quite a little after midnight. Jimmie Dale's fingers, in the right-hand pocket of his tattered coat, closed over the stock of his automatic. Still no sound! Was he too late to forestall the Rat; or, by no means an unlikely possibility, was the Rat there now; or was—a low, muttered exclamation, that mingled surprise and bewilderment, came suddenly from Jimmie Dale's lips. He had reached the landing, and here, from the head of the stairs, he could see a dull yellow glow thrown out into the corridor through the glass panel of the lawyer's door.

An instant's pause, and then, chagrined, the sense of defeat upon him, he moved forward again as silently as before. He reached the door and crouched beside it. A murmur of voices came to him from within. Jimmie Dale's lips parted in grim irony. The game was up, of course, but he was occupying precisely the same coign of vantage that, according to the Rat, the Rat had occupied that afternoon, and if the Rat had been able, undiscovered, to see and hear, then he, Jimmie Dale, could do the same. The slim, tapering, sensitive fingers closed on the doorknob—a thin ray of light began to steal through between the door-edge and the jamb—and grew wider—and the voices, from a confused murmur, became distinct. And now, through the narrow crack of the slightly opened door, he could see inside; and he could see that, as he had already realised, he was too late, very much too late, in time only, as it were, for the post-mortem of the affair—even the police were already on the spot!

It was a curious scene! A rickety old railing across the middle of the musty, bare-floored room served to indicate that the space beyond was the old lawyer's "private" office. And here, inside the railing, a desk, or, rather, a great, flat, deal table, spread with a red, ink-stained cloth, was littered with books and papers; while behind the table, again, stood a huge, old-fashioned safe, its door swung wide open, its erstwhile contents scattered in disorder about the floor.

Jimmie Dale's eyes swept the interior of the room with a single, quick, comprehensive glance—and then, narrowed, travelled from one to another of the faces of the four men who were gathered around the table. He knew them all. The stocky, grizzle-haired man in the centre was a plain-clothes man from headquarters, named Barlow; at the lower end of the table Reddy Curley and Haines, his partner, faced each other, Curley drumming indifferently with his fingers on the table-top, Haines scowling and chewing his lower lip, a certain coarse brutality in both their faces that was neither pleasant nor inviting; but it was the white-haired old man, bent of form, standing at the head of the table, upon whom Jimmie Dale's eyes lingered. Old Grenville! The man's hand, as he raised it to pass it across his eyes, was shaking palpably; his face, kindly still in spite of its worn and haggard expression, was pale with anxiety and strain. Barlow was speaking:

"You say there's nothing else missing, Mr. Grenville, except the sealed envelope that contained the fifteen thousand dollars given you by Mr. Curley this afternoon?"

The old lawyer shook his head.

"I can't say," he answered. "As I told you, I often come here at night to work. Tonight a client kept me very late at my house, so it was only, I should say, a quarter of an hour ago when I reached here. I telephoned you at once, and, awaiting your arrival, I did not disturb anything, so I have not examined any of the papers yet."

"I don't think it's a question of papers," observed the Headquarters man dryly.

"There was nothing else taken then," decided Grenville slowly; "for there was no other money in the safe at the time—in fact, I rarely keep any there."

"Well then," said Barlow crisply, "it's pretty near open and shut that someone was wise to that fifteen thousand being there tonight, and it wasn't just a lucky haul out of any old safe just because the safe looked easy." He turned toward Curley and Haines. "Were either of you talking with anyone around the East Side tonight who would be likely to make a tip of it, or pass the tip along?"

"We weren't there at all tonight," Curley replied. "Haines and I were out in my car, and we'd just got back when you picked us up at the store on the way up here. But, at that, I guess you're right. We didn't make any secret about it, and I daresay after I'd got the business tacked away safe in my inside pocket this afternoon"—he grinned maliciously at Haines—"I may have mentioned it to one or two."

"Got it tucked away safe, have you? Own it, do you?" Haines caught him up truculently.

"Sure!" Curley had wicked, little greenish-grey eyes, and their stare was uninviting as he fixed them on his quondam partner. "If you want to grouch, go ahead and grouch! We've been pretty good friends for a pretty good number of years, but I ain't a fool. Sure, it's mine now! I didn't ask you to employ Grenville, did I? I was satisfied to take any old piece of paper with your fist on it, saying you'd sold out to me; but no, you were for having the thing done with frills on it Well, I'm still satisfied! I came here at five o'clock this afternoon, and paid the coin over to your attorney, and I got a perfectly good little Bill of Sale for it—and that lets me out. It's up to you and your Mister Attorney. Why don't you ask him what *he's* going to do about it, instead of trying to take it out on me the way you've been doing ever since Barlow told us what had happened, and—"

"Mr. Curley is perfectly right, Mr. Haines"—the old lawyer's voice was quiet, though it trembled a little. "The title to the business is now vested in Mr. Curley, and you are entitled to look to me for compensation. I"—he hesitated an instant—"I—I hope the money may be recovered, otherwise—"

"Eh?" inquired Mr. Haines sharply.

"Otherwise," the old lawyer went on with an effort, "I am afraid I shall have a great deal of difficulty in raising so large a sum."

"The hell you are!" said Mr. Haines uncharitably, and leaned forward over the table. "Don't try to come that dodge! Everybody says you're well fixed. Everybody says you've got a neat little pile salted away."

The lawyer's face was ashen, and his lips were quivering; but there was a fine dignity in the poise of the old man's head, and in the squared shoulders.

"Nevertheless, I am, unfortunately, telling you the truth, in spite of any rumours, or public belief to the contrary," he said steadily. "A few thousands, a very few, is all I have ever been able to lay aside. Those are at your disposal, Mr. Haines, and the balance I promise to procure as speedily as possible; but in plain words, if this money is not recovered, and I do not say this to invite either sympathy or leniency, but because you have questioned my word, I shall have lost everything I own."

Mr. Haines scowled.

"Well, I'm glad to know you've at least got enough!" he said roughly. "It sure will surprise a whole lot of people that fifteen thousand wipes Mr. Henry Grenville out!"

A flush dyed the old lawyer's cheeks. He made as though to speak—and, instead, turned silently away from the table, his back to the others. There was silence in the room now for a moment. Again Jimmie Dale's eyes travelled swiftly from one to another of the group—to Curley, grinning maliciously at his ex-partner again—to Haines, gnawing at his lower lip, and scowling blackly—to Barlow, obviously uncomfortable, who was uneasily tracing patterns with his forefinger on the top of the table—and back to the old lawyer, whose shoulders now, as though carrying a load too heavy for their strength, had drooped pathetically, and into whose face, in spite of a brave effort at self-control, had crept a wan and miserable despair.

"Look here!" said Barlow gruffly. "It strikes me you can settle all this some other time. It's got nothing to do with the guy that pulled this break, and I'm losing time. Headquarters is waiting for my report. You two had better beat it; Mr. Grenville won't mind, I guess—I've got your end of the story, and—"

Jimmie Dale was retreating back along the corridor—and a minute later he was in the street, and scuffling along in a downtown direction. His hands, in the pockets of his tattered coat, were clenched, and through the pallor of Smarlinghue's make-up a dull red burned his cheeks. Old Grenville—and the Rat! The smile that found lodgment on Smarlinghue's contorted lips was mirthless. The old man had taken it like the gentleman he was. He had not perhaps hidden the quiver of the lip—who would at seventy! It was not easy to begin life again at seventy! Old Grenville—and the Rat! Well, the game was not played out yet! There would be an accounting of that fifteen thousand dollars before the morning came, and, as between old Grenville and the Rat, it might not perhaps be old Grenville who paid!

Hurrying now, running through lanes and alleyways as he had come, Jimmie Dale headed for the Sanctuary. It was very simple now. The Rat, his work completed, would lay very low—asleep probably, in the *innocent* surroundings of his own room! The Rat would not be hard to find. It was necessary only that, in the little interview he proposed to have with the Rat, "Smarlinghue" should have disappeared!

He reached the tenement where, for months now, that ground floor room, opening on the small and dirty courtyard in the rear, had been his refuge, Smarlinghue's home in the underworld, glanced quickly up and down the street to assure himself that he was not observed, then, darting into the dark hallway, he crossed it silently, unlocked the Sanctuary door, stepped through, and closed and locked the door behind him. Nor, even now, did he make the slightest sound. From the top-light, high up near the ceiling and far above the little French window whose shade was drawn, there came a faint and timid streak of moonlight. It did not illuminate the room; it but lessened the degree of blackness, as it were, giving a dim and shadowy outline to objects scattered here and there about the room—and to a darker shadow amongst those other shadows, a shadow that moved swiftly and in utter silence, a shadow that was Jimmie Dale at work.

No one had seen him enter—not that there should be anything strange in the fact that Smarlinghue should enter Smarlinghue's own room, but it would not be Smarlinghue who went away! No one had seen him enter—it was vital now that he should not be heard moving around the room, and so invite the chance of some aimless caller in the person of a fellow-tenant, for it was no longer Smarlinghue who would be found there!

The ragged outer garments he had been wearing lay discarded in a heap on the floor, close to that section of the wall near the door where the baseboard, ingeniously movable, would, in another moment or so, afford them safe hiding until such time as "Smarlinghue" should reappear in person again; from the nostrils, from beneath the lips, from behind the ears, the tiny, cleverly-inserted pieces of wax, distorting the features, had vanished; and now, over the cracked basin on the rickety washstand, the masterly-created pallor was washed rapidly away—and the thin, hollow-cheeked, emaciated face of Smarlinghue, the drug fiend, was gone, and in its place, clean-cut, clear-eyed, was the face of Jimmie Dale, clubman and millionaire.

He smiled a little whimsically, a little wanly, as he stole back across the room. It was a strange life, a *dangerous* life! He wondered often enough, as he was wondering now, what the end of it would be—would he find the Tocsin—or would he find death at the hands of the underworld—or judicial murder at the hands of the law for a hundred crimes attributed to the Gray Seal! Crimes! The smile grew serious and wistful, as he knelt on the floor and began to loosen the section of the baseboard in front of him. There had never been a crime committed by the Gray Seal! Yes, it was strange, bizarre, incredulous even to himself sometimes, this life of his—the strange partnership formed so long ago now with *her*, the Tocsin, who had prompted those "crimes" that righted a wrong, that brought sunlight into some life where there had been gloom before, and hope where there had been misery—and the love that had come—and then disaster again, and her disappearance—and his resumption once more of a dual life and a role in the underworld—and, yes, in spite of her own danger, those "calls to arms" to the Gray Seal again for the sake of others, while she refused, through love for him, through fear of the peril that it would bring him, help for herself.

He shook his head, as, the base-board removed now, he reached into the hollow beyond for the neatly-folded, expensively-tailored tweeds of Jimmie Dale. She was wrong in that. Could anything add to the peril in which he lived, as it was! If only in some way he might reach her, see her, talk to her, if only for a moment, he could make her see that, and understand, and—

A low, startled cry burst suddenly from his lips; he felt the blood ebb from his cheeks—and surge back again in a burning, mighty tide. It was dark, he could not see; but those wonderfully sensitive finger tips, that were ears and eyes to Jimmie Dale, were telegraphing a wild, mad, amazing message to his brain. The Tocsin had been here—here in the *Sanctuary*! She had been here—here in this room—and within the last few hours—sometime since seven o'clock that evening, when, as Jimmie Dale, he had come here to assume the role of Smarlinghue preparatory to his vigil in Foo Sen's!

His hand, thrust in through the opening to reach for his clothes, had found an envelope where it lay on the top of the folded garments—and his hand was still thrust inside—there was no need to look—the texture of the paper was hers—*hers*—the Tocsin's! The blood was racing wildly through his veins. There was a mad joy upon him—and a sense of keen and bitter emptiness. Wild thoughts, in lightning flashes, swept his brain. She must have been here, then, many times before... she knew the Sanctuary as well as he did... she knew the secret hiding place behind the base-board... she had come, of course, knowing he was absent... she might come some day *thinking* he was absent... yes, why not—why not... perhaps—perhaps that was the way... some day she might come again....

He laughed a little in a shaken way, and drew out the letter. With a mental wrench, he forced his mind into a calmer state. It was very singular that she should have placed the letter in that hiding place! It could evidence but one thing—that the contents of the letter, unlike any she had ever written before, were not of a pressing nature, for she would know very well that it might have been many hours, days even, before he might go there for the clothes of Jimmie Dale again! What, then, did it mean? Had she decided at last to tell him all, to let him take his place beside her, share her danger, fight with her! Was that it?

He reached hurriedly into the opening again, drew out the little leather girdle, and from one of its pockets took out a flashlight. He had not dared to light the gas before; dressed, or, rather, undressed, as he was at present, and no longer Smarlinghue, he dared much less to light it now.

He tore the envelope open, and, still kneeling on the floor, the flashlight upon the pages, began to read:

"Dear Philanthropic Crook: You will be surprised to find this letter in such a place, won't you? Yes, you are quite right, for once, as you will already have told yourself, there is no hurry—for it is too late to hurry. Listen, then! Henry Grenville's safe—the old East Side lawyer, you know—"

He had read eagerly so far. He stared at the letter now, and the words only danced in an unmeaning jumble before him. It was not for herself, it was not that she had thrown the barriers down and was bidding him come to her; it was again another "call to arms" to the Gray Seal—and for another's sake. And there came to Jimmie Dale a miserable disappointment, for his hope, shattered now, had been greater than he had admitted even to himself. And then he was aware that, subconsciously, it had seemed to him a most curious coincidence that the letter should be dealing with the robbery of Henry Grenville's safe that night. Yes, certainly, it was a most curious coincidence, when he was even then on his way—to the Rat! He shrugged his shoulders in his whimsical way. Well, for once, he had forestalled the Tocsin! There could be little here that he did not already know. He began to read again, but skimming over the words and sentences hurriedly now.

"...Curley... liquor business... buying out partner, Haines... this afternoon... fifteen thousand dollars... large bills, one-hundred, five-hundred and thousand-dollar denominations... sealed in envelope by Grenville... placed by Grenville in his safe... head of one of the most successful and desperate gangs in the country... years under cover through position occupied... take your time, Jimmie, and be careful before you act... rest of gang is 'working' Boston and New England this week... backyard from lane, high board fence... in cellar... cleverly concealed door at right of coal bin... knot in wood seventh board from wall on level with your shoulders... short passage beyond leading to door of den... sound-proof room... exit through other side... sliding panel to room above... opened by hanging weight inside..."

In a stunned way now, Jimmie Dale stared for a long minute at the letter in his hand—then he read it again—and yet again. And then, the flashlight out, as he tore the letter into fragments, he stared again, for a long minute—into the blackness.

It was damnable, it was monstrous, this thing that he had read; it plumbed the dregs of human deviltry—but for once the Tocsin was at fault. Of the plot that had been hatched, of those details that she described, there could be no doubt, there was no question there, and there the Tocsin, he knew, had made no mistake; but the Tocsin, yes, and those who had hatched the crime themselves, had taken no account of the possible intervention of an outsider in the person of—the Rat! There was even a sort of grim irony in it all—that the Rat should quite unconsciously have feathered his nest at the expense of a far more elaborately arranged crime than his own, and at the expense of those who were of even a more abandoned, dangerous and unscrupulous type of criminal than himself!

Jimmie Dale's face hardened suddenly—and suddenly he stooped and pulled his clothes from their hiding place, and began to dress. For once, his inside information outreached hers. It was still—the Rat. Her letter changed nothing, save that afterwards, perhaps—well, that afterwards, perhaps, there was another, others beside the Rat, with whom an accounting would be made!

CHAPTER 13

THE SECRET ROOM

Jimmie Dale dressed quickly now. From the pockets of the little leather girdle to the pockets of his tweeds he transferred a steel picklock, a pair of light steel handcuffs, a piece of fine but exceedingly strong cord, a black silk mask, and that small metal case, within which, between sheets of oiled paper, lay those gray-coloured, diamond-shaped, adhesive paper seals that were known in every den in the underworld, known in every police bureau of two continents, as the insignia of the Gray Seal. He slipped the flashlight into his pocket, took his automatic from the discarded garments of Smarlinghue—and, thrusting the ragged clothing into the opening, put the removable section of the base-board back into place.

And now, twin to that streak of lesser gloom that came from the top-light, another filtered into the room. The small French window opened and closed without sound—the room was empty. A shadow in the courtyard, close against the wall of the tenement, moved forward a foot, a yard—a loose board in the fence bordering the lane swung silently aside—and in a moment more, striding nonchalantly up the block, Jimmie Dale turned into the Bowery.

He had some distance to go, almost back as far as the liquor store at the lower end of the Bowery, for the Rat lived, if he, Jimmie Dale, was not mistaken, just one block this side, in a small one-story frame building on the corner of a cross street; and—it seemed incongruous, out of place somehow—the Rat lived with his mother. Home ties, or home relationships, hardly seemed in harmony with the Rat! Still, in this case, it was perhaps very debatable ground as to which was the more pernicious, the old woman or the son! Ostensibly, she kept a little variety store; but her business, if report were true, was the edifying occupation of school mistress—the children graduating under her tuition being ranked by common consent as the most accomplished pickpockets in gangland!

Jimmie Dale shrugged his shoulders, as he swung at last from the Bowery into a narrow, poorly lighted street. Well, at least, if the Rat's criminal career ended tonight, the Rat's punishment need excite no sympathy for the old woman, as far as he, Jimmie Dale, was concerned—it was a pity only that she had not been behind the bars herself long ago! Yes, this was the place—the small frame building diagonally across from the corner on which he had halted. He crossed over for a closer inspection. The front of the house was dark, the little store windows shuttered. He hesitated an instant, then walked around the corner to survey the building from the side and rear. Here, from a window that gave on the intersecting street, there showed a light. The window was low, scarcely above the level of his head, but held no promise on that score as a source of information, for the shade within was tightly drawn. Jimmie Dale scowled at it for a moment, noted its proximity to the backyard and the front of the building. The Rat, then, or the Rat's mother, was still up, and he would need to exercise more than ordinary caution—or else wait—indefinitely, perhaps.

He shook his head at that alternative, as he looked sharply up and down the street. He would gain little by waiting, and—ah! He was crouched in the doorway now, the deft fingers working swiftly with the picklock. There was a faint metallic click, barely audible above his low-breathed exclamation—and the door opened and closed behind him.

The flashlight in his hand winked once—and went out. Small, glass-topped counters were on either side of the somewhat restricted aisle in which he stood; directly in front of him, at the rear of the store, was a door, leading, obviously, to the living rooms beyond.

The old days of Larry the Bat, the rickety, creaky stairs of the old Sanctuary had trained Jimmie Dale's step to a silence that was almost uncanny. It might have been a shadow moving there across the floor of the store, a shadow flitting through that doorway beyond. There was no sound.

And now, at the end of a short, dark passage, he stopped before the door of what was, from its location, the lighted room he had seen from the street; and, slipping his mask over his face, he placed his ear against the door panel to listen. He was rewarded only by absolute silence. His lips, under the mask, twisted as, softly, cautiously, he tried the door. It gave under the steady pressure that he exerted upon it—gave without sound for the measure of a fraction of an inch—it was unlocked. And now Jimmie Dale could see into the room—and suddenly he stepped noiselessly forward, his automatic holding a bead on the crouched figure of the Rat, asleep apparently in his chair, whose head, flung forward, was buried in his crossed arms upon the table in the centre of the room.

"Good evening!" said Jimmie Dale, in a velvet voice.

There was no answer—the man neither turned his head, nor looked up.

And for a moment Jimmie Dale did not stir—only into the dark eyes shining through the mask there came a startled gleam, and through the heavy, palpitating silence the quick, sudden intake of his breath sounded clamourously loud. He saw now—the *gray* of the cheek just showing above the arm that pillowed it, the stiff, hunched, unnatural position of the body, the crimson pool on the floor by the chair leg. *The man was dead*!

Tight-lipped, the strong jaw outthrust a little, his face hard and set, Jimmie Dale moved to the Rat's side, and bent over the man. Yes, it was—*mur-*

der! The Rat had been stabbed in the back just below the left armpit. He glanced sharply around the room. There was no sign of struggle, except— yes—there were bruises on the man's neck, as though a hand had grasped it fiercely, and—he bent over—yes, faintly, but nevertheless distinctly enough, two blood-stained finger prints were discernible on the Rat's collar. He lifted the Rat's hands and examined them critically—it might perhaps have been the man himself clutching his own throat, as he choked and struggled for breath—no, the Rat's fingers showed not the slightest trace of blood.

And then, instinctively, Jimmie Dale reached out toward the other's pocket; but, with a hard smile, dropped his hand to his side, instead. The sealed envelope, the fifteen thousand dollars, was not there—*it was where the Tocsin had said it was*! The Tocsin, not he, had been right! And yet, too, in a way, he had not been entirely wrong. It *was* the Rat who had stolen the sealed envelope from the safe—or else the Rat would not now be dead!

His mind, alert and keen now, was dovetailing together the pieces of the puzzle. Those who had originally planned the crime had in some way discovered that the Rat, in the actual theft, had forestalled them. Possibly, for instance, bent on the same errand, they had seen the Rat leaving the building; then, finding the safe already looted, they had put two and two together, and had trapped the Rat here—and the Rat had paid the price! It might have been that way, but that in itself was a detail, immaterial—they *had* discovered that it was the Rat. The Rat's murder proved it. It was not enough that they should recover the envelope—there would have been no way to avoid exposure or cover their own crime except by murdering the Rat.

He looked down at the silent form sprawled over the table, and his face relaxed, softened a little. The Rat was only the Rat, it was true, and the man was a thief, an outcast, a pariah, a prey upon society; but life to the Rat, too, had been sweet, and his murder was a hideous thing—and even such as the Rat might ask justice. Justice! It had been dirty work—miserable, dirty work, he had called it when he had thought the Rat alone involved—but now, thanks to the Tocsin, he knew it for what it really was, knew it for its damnable, hellish ingenuity, and its abominable, brutal callousness! Justice! Yes—but how?

He began to move about the room, his mind for the moment diverted in an endeavour to reconstruct the scene as it must have been enacted here around him. The Rat had broken into the safe *before* eleven o'clock—that was obvious now. In fact, it was quite likely to have been much nearer ten! He had returned here and had been sitting there at the table, counting over his ill-gotten gains, perhaps, his back to the door, just as he sat now, and they had stolen in upon him. But where was the old woman? True, perhaps little, if any, noise had been made, and yet—Jimmie Dale, pausing on the threshold of the door, listened intently. One of the two rooms, whose doors he saw between this end room and the door opening into the store, must be hers, and if she were there, asleep, for instance, his ear was surely acute enough to catch, in the stillness that lay upon the house, the sound of breathing. But there was nothing. Under the mask, his brows drew together in a perplexed frown. And then suddenly he stood rigid, tense. Yes, there was a sound at last—and an ominous one! The front door leading into the store was being opened, came the scuffling of footsteps—and then a woman's voice, shrill, wailing:

"W'en I come in not twenty minutes ago dere he was—dead. My Gawd— knifed he was! An' den I runs fer youse at de station. I gotta right ter cry, ain't I! He's my son, he is—ain't he! I gotta right—"

"Keep quiet!" snapped a man's voice gruffly. "We've heard all that a dozen times now. It's a pity you didn't think more about being his mother twenty years ago! Mike, you'd better lock that front door!"

Jimmie Dale drew back, and closed the door softly. If he were caught here now! The old woman had brought the police back with her—two of them, it appeared. He smiled in a hard way. Well, he did not propose to be caught. His hand reached up to the electric light switch, there was a click, and the room was in darkness. In the fraction of a second more he was at the window. Shade and window were swiftly, silently raised, and he looked out cautiously. The street was deserted, empty; there was no one in sight. It was very simple, a drop of a few feet to the sidewalk, a dash around the corner—and that was all. They were coming now. He swung one leg over the sill—and sat there motionless, his mind balancing with lightning speed the pros against the cons of a sudden inspiration that had come to him. Justice…justice on those guilty of this wretched murder here, and guilty of many another crime almost as grave…he had asked himself how…here was a way…a daredevil, foolhardy way?… no, the possibility of being winged by a chance shot, perhaps, but otherwise a safe way… escape through that panel door operated by weights… and it was not far to that den the Tocsin had described… nor would he be running into a trap himself… the gang was not there… perhaps no one… but perhaps, with luck, those he might wish would be there… it would be a gracious little act on the part of the Gray Seal, would it not, to invite the police, this Mike and his companion, to that den—they would be deeply interested! He laughed low—they were almost at the door now. Well? The doorknob rattled. Yes, he would do it! Yes—*now*! He stretched out suddenly, and with the toe of his boot kicked over a chair that was within reach. The crash, as the chair fell, was answered by a rush through the door, a hoarse, surprised and quick-flung oath—and, as Jimmie Dale swung out through the window and dropped to the street, the flash and roar of a revolver shot.

Like a cat on his feet, he whirled as he touched the pavement, and darted along past the backyard fence, heading for the lane; and, as he ran, over his shoulder, he saw first one and then the other of the two men, both in police uniform, drop from the window and take up the pursuit. Another shot, and another, a fusillade of them rang out. A bullet struck the pavement at his feet with a venomous *spat*. He heard the humming of another that was like the humming of an angry wasp. And he laughed again to himself—but short and grimly now. Just a few yards more—five of them—to the corner of the lane. It was the chance he had invited—three yards—two—his breath was coming in hard, short panting gasps—*safe*! Yes! He had won now—they would not get another shot at him, at least not another that he would have any need to fear!

He swerved into the lane, still running at top speed. A high board fence, she had said—yes, there it was! And it corresponded in location with where he knew it should be—about three lots in from the street. He sprang for it, and swung lithely to the top—and hung there, as though still scrambling and struggling for his balance. The officers had not turned into the lane yet, and he had no intention of affording them any excuse for losing sight of their quarry!

Ah! There they were! A yell and a revolver shot rang out simultaneously as they caught sight of him—and Jimmie Dale dropped down to the ground on the inside of the fence. In the moonlight he could see quite distinctly. He darted across the yard, heading for the basement door of the building that loomed up in front of him.

The little steel picklock was in his hand as he reached the door. A second—two—three went by. He straightened up—and again he waited—stepping back a few feet to stand sharply outlined in the moonlight.

Again a shout in signal that he was seen, as one of the officers' heads appeared over the top of the fence—and Jimmie Dale, as though in mad haste, plunged through the door.

And now suddenly his tactics changed. He needed every second he could gain, and the police now certainly could no longer lose their way. He swung the door shut behind him, locked it to delay them, and snatched his flashlight from his pocket. He was at the top of a few ladder-like steps that led down into the cellar of the building, and halfway along the length of the cellar the ray of his flashlight swept across a huge coal bin, its sides, it seemed, built almost up to the ceiling.

Jimmie Dale was muttering to himself now, as he took the steps at a single leap, and raced toward the side of the bin that flanked the wall—"seventh board from the wall—knot on a level with shoulders"—and now he was counting rapidly—and now the round, white ray played on the seventh board. They were smashing at the cellar door now. The knot! Ah—there it was! He pressed it. Two of the boards in front of him, the width of a man's body, swung back. He left this open—a blazed trail for his pursuers, battering now at the cellar door—and stepped forward into a little opening, too short to be called a passage, and, silent now, halted before another door.

Brain and eyes and hands were working now with incredible speed. That it was a sound-proof room was not, perhaps, altogether an unmixed blessing! Was the place deserted? Was there anyone within? He could hear nothing. Well, after all, did it make any ultimate difference? The room itself would condemn them!

The picklock was at work again—working silently—working swiftly. And now, in its place, his automatic was in his hand.

He crouched a little—and with a spring, flinging wide the door, was in the room. There was a smothered cry, an oath, the crash of an overturned chair, as two men, from a table heaped with little piles of crisp, new banknotes, sprang wildly to their feet: And Jimmie Dale's lips twisted in a smile not good to see. Standing there before him were Curley and Haines.

"Keep your seats, gentlemen—please!" said Jimmie Dale, with grim irony. "I shall only stay a moment. It is Mr. Curley and Mr. Haines, I believe—in their *private* office! Permit me!"—he reached out with his left hand, and closed the door. "Ah, I see there is a good serviceable bolt on it. I have your permission?"—he slipped the bolt into place. "As I said, I shall only stay a moment; but it would be unfortunate, most unfortunate, if we were by any chance interrupted—prematurely!"

Haines, ashen white, was gripping at the table edge. Curley, a deadly glitter in his wicked little eyes, moistened his lips with the tip of his tongue.

"How'd you get here, and what the hell d'you want?" he burst out fiercely.

"As to the first question, I haven't time to answer it," said Jimmie Dale evenly. "What I want is the sealed envelope stolen from Henry Grenville's safe—and I'm in a *hurry*, Mr. Curley."

"You're a fool!" said Curley, with a sneer. "It's—"

"Yes, I know," said Jimmie Dale, with ominous patience, "it's counterfeit, you miserable pair of curs! Counterfeit like the rest of that stuff there on the table! Nice place you've got here—everything, I see—press, plates, engraver's tools—nothing missing but the rest of the gang! Perhaps, though, they can be found! Now then, that envelope—quick!" Jimmie Dale's automatic swung forward significantly.

"It's in the drawer of the table," snarled Curley. "Curse you, who—"

"Thank you!" Jimmie Dale's lips were a thin line. "Now, you two, stand out there in the middle of the floor—and if either of you make a move other than you are told to make, I'll drop you as I would drop a mad dog!" He jerked the two chairs out from the table, and, still covering Curley and Haines, placed the chairs back to back. "Sit down there, stretch out your arms full length on either side, the palms of your hands against each other's!" he ordered curtly; and, as they obeyed—Haines, cowed, all pretence at nerve gone, Curley cursing in abandon—he slipped the handcuffs over their wrists on one side, and, taking the piece of cord from his pocket that he had intended for the Rat's ankles, he deftly noosed their wrists on the other side with a slip knot, which he fastened securely.

He stepped over to the table.

"Counterfeiting five-hundred and thousand-dollar bills is rather out of the ordinary run, isn't it—I see these on the table here are the regular small variety!" he observed coolly, as he pulled the drawer open. "The big ones make a quick turn-over, though, if you have the plant to turn them out, and can swing a scheme to cash them—after banking hours—and steal them back! Hello, what's this!"—the sealed envelope, torn open at one end, evidently by the Rat in his examination, but still full of the counterfeit notes, was blood-smeared, and on the upper left-hand corner there showed the distinct impression of a finger print.

There was a sudden crash against the door.

Both men, in their chairs, strained around—and now Curley, too, had lost his colour.

"My God, what's that!" he whispered.

The thin metal case was in Jimmie Dale's hand. With the tweezers, he lifted one of the little gray seals to his lips, moistened it, and, using his elbow, pressed it firmly down upon the envelope.

Came another furious thud upon the door—and another.

"What's that!" Curley's voice was a frantic scream now. "For God's sake, do you hear, what's that!"

Jimmie Dale, under a pencilled arrow mark indicating the finger print, was scrawling a few words in printed characters.

"It's the police," said Jimmie Dale calmly. "Somebody murdered the Rat tonight!" He surveyed the envelope in his hand critically. Between the arrow mark and the gray seal were the words: "Look on the Rat's collar—and these gentlemen's fingers." He laid the envelope down on the table—and, as the door suddenly splintered and sagged under a terrific blow from some heavy object, he retreated hurriedly to the farther end of the room. Here a half dozen steps led upward, and hanging from the ceiling beside them was a cord to which was attached a leaden weight. He jerked the cord quickly. A panel above him slid noiselessly back. He leaped to the top of the stairs, and paused for a moment.

"They've been looking for this place for several years, I guess," said Jimmie Dale softly. "And I guess it will change hands tonight for the last time—and without the need of any Bill of Sale from old Henry Grenville! But we were speaking of the Rat—and why the Rat was murdered. If the Rat had had a chance to spread the news that the money paid by Mr. Curley this afternoon was counterfeit, it—"

Jimmie Dale did not finish his sentence. In a bound, as the door from the cellar crashed inward, he was through the panel opening and in the room above. There was light from the open panel behind him—enough to show him that he was in a small room which was fitted up as an office—the office of Haines & Curley, wholesale liquor dealers!

In an instant he was out of the office, and running silently down the length of the store. He snatched off his mask, reached the front door, opened it, stepped out on the quiet, deserted street—and a moment later Jimmie Dale was but one of the many that still, even at that hour, drifted their way along the Bowery.

CHAPTER 14

THE LAST CARD

Two weeks had gone by—or was it three? How long was it since he had found the Tocsin's letter in the secret hiding place of the new Sanctuary! It had seemed to him then that he had been given a new lead, a new hope; for, once he had recovered from his startled amazement at the realisation that she was as conversant with the secrets of the new Sanctuary as she had been with the old, there had come the thought of turning that very fact to his own account—that if he were unable to reach or find her by any other means, he might succeed, instead, by letting her unwittingly come to him. She had come there once to the Sanctuary when he had been absent; she was almost certain to come there again—when she *thought* he was absent! He had put his plan into execution. For days at a stretch he had remained hidden in the Sanctuary—and nothing had come of it—and then the inaction, coupled with the knowledge that the peril which faced her, even though his previous efforts to avert it had all been abortive, had made it unbearable to remain longer passive, and he had given it up, and gone out again, combing and searching through the dens and dives of the underworld.

That had been two weeks ago—or three. And the net result had been nothing!

Jimmie Dale allowed the evening newspaper to slip from his fingers. It dropped to the arm of his lounging chair, and from there to the floor. It was no use. He had been reading mechanically ever since he had returned from the club half an hour ago, and he was conscious in only the haziest sort of way of what he had been reading. The market, the general news items, the editorials, had all blended one into the other to form a meaningless jumble of words; even the leading article on the front page, that proclaimed as imminent the final and complete exposé of what had come to be known as "The Private Club Ring"—an investigation that, from its inception, he had hitherto followed closely, promising as it did to involve and link in partnership with the lowest of the underworld names that heretofore had stood high up in the social circles of New York—seemed uninteresting and unable to hold his attention tonight.

He rose impulsively from his chair, and, walking down the length of the richly furnished room, his tread soundless on the thick, heavy rug, drew the portières aside, and stood looking out of the rear window; It was dark outside, but presently the shadows formed into concrete shapes, and, across the black space of driveway and yard, the wall of the garage assumed a solid background against the night. He passed his hand over his forehead heavily, and a wanness came into his face and eyes. Once before he had stood here at this window of his den, the room that ran the entire depth of his magnificent Riverside Drive residence, and old Jason had stood at the front window—and they had watched, Jason and he—watched the shadows, that were not shadows of walls and buildings, close in around the house. That was the night before he had escaped from the trap set by the Crime Club; the night before the old Sanctuary had burned down, and police and underworld alike had believed the Gray Seal buried beneath the charred and fallen walls; the night before she, the Tocsin, had come for a little while into her own, and for a little while—into his arms.

His lips twisted in pain. A little while! Days of glad and glorious wonder! They were gone now; and in their place was emptiness and loneliness—and a great, overmastering fear and terror that would clutch at times, as it clutched now, cold at his heart.

It was not so very long ago that night, only a few months ago, but it seemed as though the years had come and rolled away since then. She was gone again, driven by a peril that menaced her life into hiding again—a peril that she would not let him share—because she *loved* him.

The pain that showed on his twisted lips was voiced in a low, involuntary cry. Because she loved him! His hands clenched hard. Where was she? Who was it that dogged and haunted her, that was wrecking and ruining her life? God knew! And God knew, employing every resource he possessed, he had done everything he could to reach her. And all that he had accomplished had been the creation of a new character in the underworld! That was all—and yet, strangely enough, in that way there had come to him the one single gleam of relief that he had known, for out of the creation of that character had sprung again the activities of the Gray Seal, and with the resumption of those activities, since, as in the old days, those "calls to arms" of hers had come again he knew that, at least, she was so far alive and safe.

Jimmie Dale swung from the window, and began to pace rapidly up and down the room. Safe—yes! But for how long? She had outwitted those against her up to now, but for how long would—

He had halted abruptly beside the table. Someone was knocking at the door.

"Come!" he called.

And old Jason entered—and it seemed to Jimmie Dale that he must laugh out like one suddenly over-wrought and in hysteria. In the old butler's hand was a silver card tray, and on the tray was—but there was no need to look on the tray, old Jason's face, curiously mingling excitement and disquiet, the imperturbability of the butler gone for the nonce, was alone quite eloquent enough. But Jimmie Dale, master of many things, was most of all master of himself.

"Well, Jason?" His voice was quiet and contained as he spoke. He reached out and took from the tray a white, unaddressed envelope. It was from her, of course—even Jason knew that it was another of those mysterious epistles, one of the many that had passed through the old butler's hands, that had in the last few years so completely revolutionised, as it were, his, Jimmie Dale's, mode of life. "Well, Jason?" He was toying with the envelope in his hand. "How did it come this time?"

"It was in another envelope, Master Jim, sir—addressed to me, sir," explained the old butler nervously. "A messenger boy brought it, sir. I opened the outside envelope, Master Jim, and—and I knew at once, sir, that—that it was one of those letters."

"I see." Jimmie Dale smiled a little mirthlessly. What, after all, did the "how" of it matter? It was a foregone conclusion that, as it had been a hundred times before, it would avail him nothing so far as furnishing a clue to her whereabouts was concerned! "Very well, Jason." His tones were a dismissal.

But Jason did not go; and there was something more in the act than that of a well-trained servant as the old man stooped, picked up the newspaper from the floor, and folded it neatly. He laid the paper hesitantly on the table, and began to fumble awkwardly with the silver tray.

"What is it, Jason?" prompted Jimmie Dale.

"Well, Master Jim, sir," said Jason, and the old face grew suddenly strained, "there *is* something that, begging your pardon for the liberty, sir, I would like to say. I don't know what all these strange letters are about, and it's not for me, sir, it's not my place, to ask. But once, Master Jim, you honoured me with your confidence to the extent of saying they meant life and death; and once, sir, the night this house was watched, I could see for myself that you were in some great danger. I—Master Jim, sir—I—I am an old man now, sir, but I dandled you on my knee when you were only a wee tot, sir, and—and you'll forgive me, sir, if I presume beyond my station, only— only—" His voice broke suddenly; his eyes were full of tears.

Jimmie Dale's hand went out, both of them, and were laid affectionately on the old man's shoulders.

"I put my life in your hands that night, Jason," he said simply. "Go on. What is it?"

"Yes, sir. Thank you, Master Jim, sir." Jason swallowed hard; his voice choked a little. "It isn't much, sir, I—I don't know that it's anything at all; but nights, sir, when I'm sitting up for you, Master Jim, and you don't come home, I—"

"But I've told you again and again that you are not to sit up for me, Jason," Jimmie Dale remonstrated kindly.

"Yes, I know, sir." Jason shook his head. "But I couldn't sleep, sir, anyway—thinking about it, Master Jim, sir. I—well, sir—sometimes I get terribly anxious and afraid, Master Jim, that something will happen to you, and it seems as though you were all alone in this, and I thought, sir, that perhaps if—if someone—someone you could trust, Master Jim, could do something—*anything*, sir, it might make it all right. I—I'm an old man, Master Jim, it—it wouldn't matter about me, and—"

Jimmie Dale turned abruptly to the table. His own eyes were wet. These were not idle words that Jason used, or words spoken without a full realisation of their meaning. Jason was offering, and calling it presumption to do so, his life in place of his, Jimmie Dale's, if by so doing he could shield the master whom he loved.

"Thank you, Jason." Jimmie Dale turned again from the table. "There is nothing you can do now, but if the time ever comes—" He looked for a long minute into Jason's face; then his hands were laid again on the other's shoulders, and he swung the old man gently around. "There's the door, Jason—and God bless you!"

Jason went slowly from the room. The door closed. For the first time that he had ever held a letter of hers in his hand Jimmie Dale was for a moment heedless of it. If the time ever came! He smiled strangely. The love and affection that had come with the years of Jason's service were not all on one side. Not for anything in the world would he put a hair of that gray head in jeopardy! It was not lack of faith or trust that held him back from taking Jason into his full confidence—it was the possibility, always present, that some day the house of cards might totter, the Gray Seal be discovered to be Jimmie Dale, and in the ruin, the disaster, the debacle that must follow, the less old Jason knew, for old Jason's own sake, the better! It was the one thing that would save Jason. The charge of complicity would fall to the ground before the old man's very ingenuousness!

And then Jimmie Dale shrugged his shoulders, a sort of whimsical fatalistic philosophy upon him, and, as he tore the envelope open, he sat down in the lounging chair close to the table. Another "call to arms"! An appeal for someone else—never for herself! He shook his head. How often had he hoped that the summons, instead, would prove to be the one thing he asked and lived for—to take his place beside her, to aid *her*! Not one of these letters had he ever opened without the hope that, in spite of the intuition which told him his hope was futile, it would prove at last to be the call to him for herself! Perhaps this one—he was eagerly unfolding the pages he had taken from the envelope—perhaps this one—no!—a glance was enough—it was far remote from any personal relation to her.

"Dear Philanthropic Crook"—he leaned back in his chair, as his eyes travelled hurriedly over the opening paragraphs, a keen sense of disappointment upon him, despite the intuition that had bade him expect nothing else—and then suddenly, startled, tense, he sat upright, strained forward in his seat. He could not read fast enough. His eyes leaped over words and sentences.

"...They are playing their last card tonight... David Archman... it is murder, Jimmie... letter signed J. Barca... Sixth Avenue stationer... Martin Moore... Gentleman Laroque, the gangster... Niccolo Sonnino... end house to left of courtyard entrance... safe in rear room... lives alone... tonight..."

For a moment Jimmie Dale did not move as he finished reading the letter, save that his fingers began to tear the pages into strips, and the strips over and over again into tiny fragments—then, mechanically, he dropped the pieces into the pocket of his dinner jacket and mechanically reached for the newspaper that Jason had picked up and laid on the table. And now a dull red burned in his cheeks, and the square jaw was clamped and hard. Strange coincidence! Yes, it was strange—but perhaps it was more than mere coincidence! He had an interest, a very personal, vital interest in that article on the front page now, in this combine of those who were frankly of the dregs of the criminal world and those of a blacker breed who hid behind the veneer of respectability and station.

He read the article slowly. It was but the résumé of the case that had been under investigation for the past few weeks, the sensation it had created the greater since the publicity so far given to it had but hinted darkly at the scope of the exposure to come, while as yet no names had been mentioned. "The Private Club Ring," as set forth in the paper, operated a chain of what purported to be small, select and very exclusive clubs, but which in reality were gambling traps of the most vicious description—and the field of their operations was very wide and exceedingly lucrative. Men known to have money, whether New Yorkers or from out of town, were "introduced" there by "members" whose standing and presumed respectability were beyond reproach—and they were bled white; while, to add variety to the crooked games, orgies, revels and carousals of the most depraved character likewise furnished the lever for blackmail—the "member" *ostensibly* being in as bad a hole, and in as desperate a predicament as the "guest" he had introduced!

The article told Jimmie Dale nothing new, nothing that he did not already know, save the statement that the evidence now in the possession of the authorities was practically complete, and that the arrest and disclosure of those involved might be expected at any moment.

He put down the paper, and stood up—and for the second time that night began to pace the room. If the article had told him nothing new, it at least explained that sentence in the Tocsin's letter—*they are playing their last card tonight. They* must strike now, or never—the exposure could be but a matter of a few hours off!

A face crowned with its gray hair rose before him, a kindly face, grave and strong and fine, the face of a man of sterling honesty and unimpeachable integrity—the face of David Archman, the assistant district attorney, who had both instituted and was in charge of the investigation that now threatened New York with an upheaval that promised to shake many a social structure to its foundations. Yes, they would play their last card, a vile, despicable and hellish card—but how little they knew David Archman! They would break his life; it would, indeed, as the Tocsin had said, be murder—but they would never break David Archman's unswerving loyalty to principle and duty! They had tried that—by threats of personal violence, by the offer of bribes in sums large enough to have tempted many!

His face hard, his forehead gathered in puzzled furrows, Jimmie Dale stepped to the door, and locked it; then, drawing aside the portière that hung before the little alcove at the lower end of the room, knelt down before the squat, barrel-shaped safe, and his fingers began to play over the knobs and dials.

Yes, it was a vitally personal matter now; there was an added incentive tonight spurring the Gray Seal on to act. David Archman had been his father's closest friend; and he, Jimmie Dale, himself had always looked on David Archman, and with reason, as little less than a second father. His frown grew deeper—he did not understand. But Tocsin did *not* make mistakes. He had had evidence of that on too many occasions when he had thought otherwise to question it now—but David Archman's son in *this*! It seemed incredible! The boy, he was little more than a boy, scarcely twenty, was and always had been, perhaps, a little wild, but a thief, an associate and accomplice of the city's worst crooks and criminals was something of which he, Jimmie Dale, had never dreamed until this instant, and now, while it staggered him, it brought, too, a sense of merciless fury—a fury against those who would stab like inhuman cowards, pitilessly, at the father through the son. Their last card! The safe swung open. Their last card was—Clarie Archman, the son!

He reached into the safe, took out an automatic, and placed it in his pocket. There was no necessity to go to the Sanctuary—what he would need was here in duplicate, and it would be Jimmie Dale, not Smarlinghue, who played the rôle of the Gray Seal tonight. A dozen small steel picklocks in graded sizes followed the revolver, and after these a black silk mask and a pocket flashlight—the thin, metal insignia case containing the little diamond-shaped, gray-coloured paper seals, never absent from his person since the night he had lost and recovered it again, was already reposing in an inner pocket of his clothes.

His face was still hard, as he stood up and closed the safe. The way out, the way to save David Archman was plain, of course. It was even simple—if it was not too late! And the way out was another "crime" committed by the Gray Seal! Instead of Clarie Archman and J. Barca, alias Gentleman Laroque, robbing the safe of one Niccolo Sonnino, dealer in precious stones, it would be the Gray Seal—if it was not already too late to forestall the others!

If it was not too late! He looked at his watch. It was twenty minutes after eleven. Yes, there should be time; but, if not—what then? And what of that letter? His teeth clamped. Well, he would try it; and he would make every second count now! He was lifting the telephone receiver of the private house installation now, calling the garage. Benson, his chauffeur, answered him almost on the instant.

"The light touring car, Benson, please, and as quickly as possible," said Jimmie Dale pleasantly.

"Yes, sir—at once," Benson answered.

Jimmie Dale replaced the receiver on the hook, and, running now across the floor, unlocked the door, crossed the hall, and entered his dressing room. Here, he changed his dinner clothes for a dark tweed suit—the location of Niccolo Sonnino's place of business was in a neighbourhood where one in evening dress, to say the least of it, would not go unobserved—transferred the metal case and the articles he had taken from the safe to the pockets of the tweed suit, and descended the stairs.

Standing in the hallway, Jason, that model of efficiency, with an appraising glance at his master's changed attire, handed Jimmie Dale a soft hat—and opened the door.

"Benson is outside, Master Jim," said Jason; but the look in the old man's eyes was eloquent far beyond the respectful and studied quiet of his words. The old face was pale and grave with anxiety.

"It's all right, Jason—all right *this* time," Jimmie Dale smiled reassuringly.

"Thank you, sir," said Jason, in a low voice. "I hope so, sir. And, begging your pardon, Master Jim, sir, I pray God it is."

And for answer Jimmie Dale smiled again, and passed down the steps, and entered the car. But the smile was gone as he leaned back in his seat after giving Benson his directions—speed, and a corner a few blocks away from Chatham Square—he was not so sure that it was all right. It was entirely a question of time. Given the time and the opportunity—Niccolo Sonnino out of the road, for instance—given twenty minutes ahead of Clarie Archman and Gentleman Laroque, it would be simple enough. But otherwise—his lips thinned—otherwise, he did not know. Otherwise, there was promise of strange, grim work before daylight came, work that might lead him out of necessity to the role of Smarlinghue, and as Smarlinghue—anywhere! He did not know; he knew only one thing—that, at any cost, if it lay within any power of his to prevent it, David Archman should not live a broken man.

The car speeded its way rapidly along in a downtown direction, Benson keeping, wherever possible, to the unfrequented streets. Jimmie Dale, busy with his problem, his mind sifting and turning this way and that the curious, and in some cases apparently conflicting details of the Tocsin's letter, paid little attention to his surroundings, save to note approvingly from time to time that a request to Benson to hurry was equivalent to something perilously near to a contempt of speed laws. It still seemed incredible that Clarie Archman was a thief, a safe-tapper, even if but an amateur one. The boy must have travelled a pace of late that was fast and furious. How had he ever become intimate enough with Gentleman Laroque to be associated with the other in such a crime as this? How had Laroque come to play a part in the miserable scheme of trickery that was the Private Club Ring's last card.

Jimmie Dale shook his head helplessly at the first question—and shook it again at the second. He knew Laroque—he knew him for one of the most degraded, as well as one of the most dreaded, gang leaders in crimeland. Laroque, in unvarnished language, was a devil, and, worse still, a most callous devil. Laroque stood first and all the time for Laroque. If murder would either further or safeguard Laroque's personal interests, Laroque was the sort of man who would stop only to consider, not whether the murder should be committed, but the method that might best be employed in order to implicate as little as possible one Laroque! Also, to those in the secrets of the underworld, Gentleman Laroque added to his accomplishments, or had done so before he rose to the eminence of gang leader, the profession of "box-worker"—not a very clever exponent of the art, crude perhaps in his methods, but at the same time efficacious, as a dozen breaks and looted safes in the years gone by bore ample witness.

Grimly whimsical came Jimmie Dale's smile. Gentleman Laroque would have made a very much better "confidence" man than safe-worker. The man was suave, polished when he wanted to be, educated; he possessed all the requisites, and, in abundance, the prime requisite of all—a cunning that was the cunning of a fox. This might even have explained his acquaintanceship with Clarie Archman, except for the fact that it did not explain Clarie Archman's co-operation in a premeditated robbery with anyone!

Again Jimmie Dale shook his head—and there came another question, one for which no answer, even of a suggestive nature, had been supplied in the Tocsin's letter. Why had Niccolo Sonnino's safe been selected as the one especial and desirable nut to crack? He knew Niccolo Sonnino, too, in a general way, as all who resided near or had any dealings in the neighbourhood where Sonnino lived, knew the man. True, combined with a small trade in jewelry and precious stones, the former cheap and the latter of an inferior grade to fit the purses of his customers, the man was a money-lender—but in an equally small way. Loans of minor amounts, a very few dollars as a maximum, was probably the extent of Sonnino's ventures along this line. Sonnino himself was a crafty little man, but craftiness, if it did not transgress the law, was not a crime; he was undoubtedly a usurer in his petty way, and he was both feared and disliked, but beyond that no one pretended to know anything about him. Ordinarily, Sonnino's safe, then, might be expected to be rather a barren affair, hardly a lure for a Gentleman Laroque brand of crook! Why, then, Sonnino's safe tonight? What was in that letter signed "J. Barca" that Clarie Archman had received? J. Barca was Gentleman Laroque; that would have been evident in any case, even if the Tocsin had not expressly said so— but the letter! Did the letter, apart from its incriminating ingenuity, supply the answer to his question? Had Sonnino, for instance, by some lucky turn, disposed of his stock in bulk, and was thus for the moment in possession of an unusually large amount of cash; or, inversely, had Sonnino received an unusual stock of stones? Either of these theories, and equally neither one of them, might furnish the answer! Jimmie Dale shrugged his shoulders grimly. He would find the answer—in Sonnino's safe! One thing, however, one thing that might have had some bearing on Laroque's choice, one thing for which he, Jimmie Dale, was grateful to Laroque for making such a choice, was that Sonnino's place lent itself admirably to attack—from the standpoint of the attacker! A black courtyard, screened completely from the street; a house that—

Jimmie Dale looked up suddenly, and, as suddenly, leaning forward, he touched Benson's shoulder. They were just approaching a restaurant and music hall known as "The Sphinx," that was popular for the moment with the slumming parties from uptown.

"This will do. You may let me out here at The Sphinx, Benson," he said quietly; and then, as the car stopped: "I shall not be long, Benson—perhaps half an hour—wait for me."

Benson touched his cap. Jimmie Dale ran up the steps of the restaurant, entered, threaded his way through several crowded rooms where the midnight revelry was in full swing—and passed out of the place by a convenient rear exit that gave on the adjoining cross street. The car standing in front of The Sphinx would attract no notice; and he was now on the same street as Sonnino's place, and only two short blocks away.

He started forward from the restaurant door—and paused, struggling with a refractory match in an effort to light a cigarette. A man brushed by him, making for the restaurant door, a tall, wiry-built, swarthy, sharp-featured man—and Jimmie Dale flipped the stub of his match away from him, and went on. Sonnino himself! There was luck then at the start—the coast was clear!

CHAPTER 15

CAUGHT IN THE ACT

It was one of those countless streets on the East Side each so identical with another—dark, not over clean, flanked on both sides with small shops, basement stores and tenement dwellings that crowded one upon the other in a sort of helpless confusion. Jimmie Dale moved quickly along. The whimsical smile was back on his lips. Sonnino, whose business, the money-lending end of it, would naturally have kept him late at work, was now evidently intent on a belated meal; Sonnino, therefore, could be counted upon as a factor eliminated for at feast the next half hour—and half an hour was enough, a little more than enough!

Jimmie Dale glanced back over his shoulder. There was no one in sight. A yard ahead of him, one of those relics of barbaric architecture, tunnelled as it were through the centre of a building that the space overhead might not be wasted, was the black driveway that gave entrance to the courtyard behind, where Sonnino lived alone in one of a half dozen small, tottering-from-age frame houses. Jimmie Dale drew closer to the wall, came opposite the driveway—and disappeared from the street.

It was the Gray Seal now, the professional Jimmie Dale, as silent in his movements as the shadows about him. He traversed the driveway, and emerged on the courtyard. Here, it was scarcely less dark. There was no moon, and no lights in any of the houses that made the rear of the courtyard. He could just discern the houses as looming shapes against the sky line, that was all.

He crossed the courtyard, and, reaching the line of door-stepless, poverty-stricken hovels—they appeared to be little more than that—crept stealthily along to the end house at the left, halted an instant to press his face against a black window pane, then tried the door cautiously. It was locked, of course. Again there came the whimsical smile, but it was almost hidden now by the black silk mask that he slipped quickly over his face. His finger tips, that were like a magical sixth sense to Jimmie Dale, embodying all the other five, felt tentatively over the lock, then slipped into his pocket, selected unerringly one of his picklocks, and inserted the little steel instrument in the keyhole. An instant more and the door was opening without a sound under Jimmie Dale's hand. And then, the door open, he stepped over the threshold, and, in the act of closing the door behind him, stood suddenly rigid—and where the whimsical smile had been before, his lips were now compressed into a thin, straight line.

"What's that?" came a hoarse, shaken whisper out of the blackness beyond.

"What's *what*?" demanded another voice—the whisper this time sharp and caustic. "I didn't hear anything!"

"Neither did I," admitted the first speaker. "It wasn't that—it was like a draft of air—as though the door or a window had been opened."

"Forget it!" observed the second voice contemptuously. "Cut out the jumps—we've got to get through here before Sonnino gets back. You'd make a wooden Indian nervous!"

There was silence for an instant, then a curious gnawing sound punctuated with quick, low, metallic rasps as of a ratchet at work—and upon Jimmie Dale for a moment came stunned dismay. Time, the one factor upon which he had depended, was lost to him; Clarie Archman and Gentleman Laroque were already at work in there in that room beyond. He stood motionless, his brain whirling; and then slowly, without a sound, an inch at a time, he began to close the door behind him. He could see nothing; but the door connecting the two rooms was obviously open—the distinctness with which the whispering voices had reached him was proof of that. They were working, too, without light, or he would have got a warning gleam when he had looked through the window. And now—what now? The picklock was shifted to his left hand, as he drew his automatic from his pocket. There was only one answer to the question—to play the game out to the end, whatever that end might be!

Beneath the mask his face drew into chiselled lines, as the picklock silently locked the door. There was one exit from that inner room, and only *one*—through the room in which he stood. The Tocsin had drawn an accurate word-plan of the crude, shack-like place, and now in his mind he reconstructed it here in the darkness. The doorway into a small hall that led to the stairs adjoined the doorway of that inner room where the two were now at work—and in that room were no windows, it was a sort of blind cubby-hole where Niccolo Sonnino transacted his most private business.

Jimmie Dale crept forward up the room. There was no answering creak of board or flooring, no sound save that gnawing sound, and the rasping click of the ratchet. His place of vantage was against the wall between the two doors—there, he could both command the exit from, and see into, the inner room, while the doorway into the hall provided him with a means of retreat should the necessity arise. And then, suddenly, halfway up the room, he dropped down behind what was evidently a jeweller's workbench. A whisper, obviously Laroque's this time, came once more from the inner room.

"Shoot the flash again!" And then, savagely: "Curse it, not on the *ceiling*! Can't you hold it steady! What the devil is the matter with you!"

There was no answer. A dull glimmer of light filtered through the doorway, but from the position in which he lay Jimmie Dale could distinguish nothing in the inner room itself.

"All right! That'll do!" Laroque growled presently.

The light went out. Jimmie Dale crept forward again. And now he gained the rear wall of the room, and crouched down close against it between the two doorways.

Came the sound of breathing now, heavy, as from sustained exertion, making almost an undertone of the steady *click-click-click* of the ratchet, and the sullen gnaw of the bit. The minutes passed. The flashlight went on again—and Jimmie Dale strained forward. Two dark forms, backs to him, were outlined against the face of the safe which was at the far side of the room, a nickel dial glistened in the white ray—he could make out nothing else.

Then darkness again. And again, after a time, the flashlight. Ten, fifteen, perhaps twenty minutes dragged by. Jimmie Dale might have been a shadow moving against the wall for all the sound he made as he changed his cramped position; but, just below the mask, his lips were pressed fiercely together. Would Gentleman Laroque never get through! Sonnino was not only likely to return in a very few minutes now, but was almost certain to do so. Under his breath Jimmie Dale cursed the gangster's bungling methods—and not for their crudity alone. His first impulse had been to surprise the two, hold them up at the revolver point, but the result of such an act would have been abortive, for the disfigured safe would stand a mute, incontrovertible witness to the fact that an *attempt* to force it had been made—and, whether it was actual robbery or attempted robbery that was proved against the son, it in no way deflected the blow aimed at David Archman. And, besides, there was the letter! If he, Jimmie Dale, had been in time even to have prevented Gentleman Laroque from sinking a bit into the safe, the letter would have counted not at all—but now it counted to the extent that it literally meant life and death. Who had it? Not Clarie Archman—that was certain. And the Tocsin had not said—obviously because she, too, had been in the dark in that respect. Therefore he could only wait, watch and follow every move of the game throughout the rest of the night, if necessary! It was the only course open to him; the letter, not the robbery, was paramount now.

A curious, muffled, metallic thump, mingled with a quick, low-breathed, triumphant oath, came suddenly from the inner room—and then Laroque's voice, eager, the words clipped off as though in feverish elation:

"There she is! One nice little job—eh? Well, come on—shoot your light into her, and let's take a look at the Christmas tree!"

The flashlight's ray flooded the interior of the open safe. Laroque, on his knees, laughed suddenly, and thrust his hand inside.

"What did I tell you, eh?" he chuckled. "I got the straight tip, eh? Four thousand, if there's a cent!"

Laroque began to remove what were evidently packages of banknotes from the safe—but Jimmie Dale was no longer watching the scene. He had edged suddenly back into the doorway of the hall, and was listening now intently. A footstep—he could have sworn he had caught the sound of a footstep—seemed to have come from just outside the front window. But all was still again. Perhaps he had been mistaken. No! Slight as was the sound, he heard, unmistakably now, a key grate in the lock—and then, stealthily, the front door began to open.

A bewildered look came into Jimmie Dale's face, as he retreated further back into the hallway itself now. It was probably Sonnino; but why did

Sonnino come stealing into his own house like—well, like any one of the three predatory guests already there before him? And then Jimmie Dale's face cleared. Of course! From the window the glow of the flashlight in the inner room could be seen. Sonnino was forewarned, and undoubtedly—fore-armed!

The front door closed softly, so softly that had Jimmie Dale, supersensitive as his hearing was, not been intent upon it, it would have escaped him. The glow from the inner room, faint as it was, threw into shadowy relief a man's form tiptoeing forward—and then a board creaked.

"*What's that!*" came in a wild whisper from Clarie Archman.

"Got 'em again!" Laroque snapped back. "You make me tired!"

"Let's get out of here! Let's get out of here—quick!" Clarie Archman's voice, not so low now, held a tone of frantic appeal.

"Nix!" said Laroque, in a vicious sneer. "Not till the job's done! D'ye think I'm going to spend half an hour cracking a safe and take a chance of missing any bets? We've got the coin all right, but there ought to be one or two of Sonnino's sparklers lying around in some of these drawers, and—"

There was a click of an electric-light switch, a cry from Clarie Archman, the inner room was ablaze with light, and—Jimmie Dale had edged forward again out of the hallway—Sonnino, revolver in hand, was standing just over the threshold facing Gentleman Laroque and the assistant district attorney's son.

Then silence—a silence of seconds that were as minutes. And then Gentleman Laroque laughed gratingly.

"Hello, Sonnino!" he said coolly. "A little late, aren't you? You've kept me stalling for the last five minutes. Know my friend—Mr. Martin Moore, alias Mr. Clarie Archman? Clarie, this is Signor Niccolo Sonnino, the proprietor of this joint."

And then to Jimmie Dale, where before his mind had groped in darkness to reconcile apparently incongruous details, in a flash there came the light. The "plant" was a little more intricate, a little more cunning, a little more hellish—that was all!

The boy, white to the lips, was swaying on his feet, grasping at the table in the centre of the room. He looked from one to the other, a miserable, dawning understanding in his eyes.

"You—you know my name?" His voice was scarcely audible.

"Sure!" said Laroque—and yawned insolently.

"So!" purred Sonnino, in excellent English. "Is it so! A thief! The son of the so-honest Mister Attorney—a thief!"

"It's a lie!" The boy's hands, clenched, were raised above his head, and then shaken almost maniacally in Gentleman Laroque's face. "It's a lie! I—I don't understand, but—but you two, you devils, are together in this!"

"Sure!" retorted Laroque, as insolently as before—and flung the other's hands away. "Sure, we are!"

"It's a lie!" said the boy again. "I was in a hole. I needed money. You told me you knew a man who would lend it to me. That's why I came here with you, and then—and then you held me here with your revolver, and began to open that safe."

"Sure!" returned Laroque, for the third time. "Sure—that's right! Well, what's the answer?"

"This!" cried the boy wildly. "I don't know what your game is, but this is my answer! Do you think I would have touched that money, or have let you—once I got out of here where I could have got help! I'm not a thief—whatever else I may be. That's my answer!"

Niccolo Sonnino's smile was oily.

"It is a little late, is it not?" he leered. "Listen, my little young friend; I will tell you a story. You work for a bank, eh? The bank does not like its young men to speculate—yes? But why should you not speculate a little, a very little, if you like—if you get the very private and good tips, eh? It is not wrong—no, certainly, it is not wrong. But at the same time the bank must not know. Very well! They shall not know—no one shall know. You are not the young Mr. Archman any more, you are—what is the name?—Martin Moore. But Martin Moore must have an address, eh? Very well! On Sixth Avenue there is a little store where one rents boxes for private mail, and where questions are never asked—is it not so, my very dear young friend?"

The boy was staring in a demented way into Sonnino's face, but he did not speak.

"Aw, hand it to him straight!" Gentleman Laroque broke in roughly. "I don't want to hang around here all night. Here, Archman, you listen to me! We piped you off on that lay about two weeks ago—and it looked good to us, and we played it for a winner, see? You got introduced to me, and found me a pretty good sort, and we got thick together—you know all about that. Also, you get introduced to some new brokers, who said they'd take good care of your margins—maybe they only ran a bucket-shop, but you didn't know it! All right! You got snarled up good and plenty. Yesterday you were wiped out, and three thousand dollars to the bad besides, and they were yelling for their money and threatening to expose you. They gave you until tomorrow morning to make good. You told me about it. I told you this morning I thought I knew a man who would lend you the coin, and"—he laughed mockingly, and jerked his hand toward the safe—"well, I led you to it, didn't I?"

"I—I don't understand," the boy mumbled helplessly.

"Don't you!" jeered Laroque. "Well, it looks big enough for a blind man to see! We've got this robbery wished on you to a fare-thee-well! A young man who speculates, who uses an assumed name, and runs a private letter box on Sixth Avenue, and has forty-eight hours in which to square up his debts or face exposure, has a hell of a chance with a jury—*not*!"

The boy circled his lips with the tip of his tongue.

"But why—why?" he whispered. "I—I never did anything to you."

"Sure, you didn't!" Laroque's tones were brutally amiable now. "It's your father. We've an idea that maybe he won't be so keen about going ahead with that little investigation of the private clubs after we've put a certain little proposition about his son up to him."

"No, no! No—you won't!" Clarie Archman's voice rose suddenly shrill, beyond control. "You won't! You can't! You're in it yourselves"—he pointed his finger wildly at one and then the other of the two men—"you—you!"

"Think so?" drawled Laroque. "All right, you tell 'em so—tell the jury about it, tell your father, who is such a shark on evidence, about it. Sure, I'm in on it with you—but you don't know who I am. They'll have a hot time finding J. Barca, Esquire! I'm thinking of taking a little trip to Florida for my health, and my valet's got my grip all packed! Savvy? And now listen to Sonnino. Sonnino's a wonder in the witness box. Niccolo, tell the jury what you know about this unfortunate young man."

Sonnino, a wicked grin on his face, made a dramatic flourish with the hand that held the revolver.

"Well, I was asleep upstairs. I wakened. I thought I heard a noise downstairs. I listened. Then I got up, and went down the stairs quiet like a mouse. I turned on the light quick—like this"—he snapped his fingers. "Two men have broken open my safe, and they have my money, a lot of money, for I keep all my money there; I do not bank—no. They rush at me, they knock me down, they make their escape, but I recognise one of them—it is Mister the young Archman, who I have many times seen at The Sphinx Café—yes. Well, and then on the floor I find a letter." He grinned wickedly again. "Have you the letter that I find—Mister Barca?"

"Sure," said Gentleman Laroque—and reached into his pocket. "It was addressed to Martin Moore on Sixth Avenue, wasn't it?"

"My God!" It came in a sudden, pitiful cry from the boy, and his hand involuntarily went to his own pocket. "You—you've got that letter!"

"Do you think you're up against a piker game!" exclaimed Laroque maliciously. "Well then, forget it! You didn't have this in your pocket half an hour before it was lifted by one of the slickest poke-getters in the whole of little old New York." He was taking a letter from its envelope and opening out the sheet. "That's the kind of a crowd that's in on this, my bucko! Listen, and I'll read the letter. It looked innocent enough when you got it, in view of what I told you about knowing a man who would lend you the money. But pipe how it sounds with Sonnino's safe bored full of holes. Are you listening? 'It's all right. Niccolo Sonnino has got his safe crammed full tonight. Meet me at Bristol Bob's at eleven. J. Barca.'"

There was silence in the room. Clarie Archman had dropped into a chair, and had buried his face in his arms that were out-flung across the table.

Then Laroque spoke again:

"Do you see where you stand—Clarie? Tell your story—and it's the *story* that sounds like a neat 'plant' of your lawyer's to get you off. You only get in deeper with the jury for trying to *trick* them, see? Here's the evidence—and it's got you cold. Sonnino recognises you. The letter is identified at the Sixth Avenue place, and *you* are identified as the guy that's been travelling under the name of Martin Moore. J. Barca has flown the coop and can't be found, and—well, I guess you get it, don't you?"

"What—what do you want?" The boy did not lift his head.

"We want your father to let up, and let up damned quick," said Laroque evenly. "But we'll give *you* a chance to get out from under, and you can take it or leave it—it doesn't matter to us. Your father's got the papers and the affidavits in the 'Private Club' case in his safe at home tonight, and a lot of those affidavits he can never replace—we've seen to that! All right! You've got the combination of the safe. Go home and get that stuff and bring it here. If it's here by four o'clock—that gives you about three hours—you're out of it. If it isn't, then your father gets inside information that the gang is wise to the fact that his son pulled a break tonight, but that they can keep Sonnino's mouth shut if he throws up the sponge, and that if he doesn't call it off with the 'Private Club Ring,' if he's so blamed fond of prosecuting, he'll get a chance to prosecute his own son—as a thief!"

The boy did not move.

"And just one last word," added Laroque sharply. "Don't make the mistake of thinking that if you refuse to get the affidavits it puts a crimp in us. It's only because we're playing white with you, and to give you a chance, that you're getting any choice at all. We didn't intend to give you one, but we don't want to be too rough on you, so if you want to get out that way, and will agree to keep on queering your father's game if he starts it over again, all right. But you want to understand that we hold just as big a club over your father's head the other way."

"*White!* Playing white! Oh, my God!" Clarie Archman had lurched up from the chair to his feet. His face, haggard and drawn, was the face of one damned.

"Good-night!" said Laroque callously. "You know the way out! You've got till four o'clock. If you're not back here then—" He shrugged his shoulders significantly. "You see, I'm not even asking you what you are going to do. We don't care. It's up to you. Either way suits us. And now—beat it!"

Jimmie Dale drew back for a second time that night into the hallway. A step, slow, faltering, unsteady, like that of a man blinded, passed out from the inner room, and passed on down the length of the front room—and the door opened and closed. Clarie Archman, with God alone knew what purpose in his heart, was gone.

From the thin metal case, by means of the tiny tweezers, Jimmie Dale took out a gray seal, laid the seal on his handkerchief, folded the handkerchief carefully, placed it in his pocket—and crept forward toward the inner door again. The two men were bending over the table, over the money on the table, dividing it. Jimmie Dale's lips were mercilessly thin; a fury, not the white, impetuous heat of passion, but a fury that was cold, deadly, implacable, possessed his soul. He crept nearer—still nearer.

"The crowd that put this up says we keep it between us for our work," said Laroque shortly. "A third for you, the rest for me. You sure you put *all* they gave you in the safe—Niccolo?" He screwed up his eyes suspiciously. "You sure you ain't trying to hold anything out on me? If you are, I'll make you—"

The words died short on his lips—his jaw sagged helplessly.

Jimmie Dale was standing in the doorway.

"Niccolo, drop that revolver!" said Jimmie Dale softly. His automatic held a bead on the two men.

The revolver clattered to the table top. Neither of the men spoke—only their faces worked in a convulsive sort of way as they gazed in startled fascination at Jimmie Dale.

"Thank you!" said Jimmie Dale politely. He stepped briskly into the room, shoved Sonnino unceremoniously to one side, shoved his revolver muzzle none too gently into Laroque's ribs, and went through the latter's clothes. "Yes," he said, "I thought quite possibly you might have one." He pocketed Laroque's revolver, and also Sonnino's from the table. "And now that letter—thank you!" He whipped the letter from Laroque's inside coat pocket and transferred it to his own, then stepped back, and smiled—but the smile was not inviting. "I've only about five minutes to spare," murmured Jimmie Dale. "I'm in a *hurry*, Niccolo. I see some wrapping paper and string over there on top of the safe. Get it!"

The man obeyed mechanically, in a stupefied sort of way, and placed several of the sheets and a quantity of string upon the table. Laroque, silent, sullen, under the spell of Jimmie Dale's automatic, watched the proceedings without a word.

"Now," said Jimmie Dale, and an icy note began to creep into the velvet tones, "you two are going to make the first charitable contribution you ever made in your lives—say, to one of the city hospitals. Make as neat and as small a parcel of that money as you can, Niccolo."

"Not by a damned sight!" Laroque roared out suddenly. "Who the blazes are you! Curse you, I—" He shrank hastily back before the ominous outthrust of Jimmie Dale's automatic.

"Wrap it up, Niccolo, and tie a string around it!" snapped Jimmie Dale.

And again, but snarling, cursing now, the man obeyed.

Jimmie Dale's hand went into his pocket, and came out with his handkerchief. He carried the handkerchief to his mouth, moistened the adhesive side of the gray paper seal, and pressed the handkerchief down upon the top of the parcel.

"It would hardly do for anyone to know where the money really came from—would it?" observed Jimmie Dale, and smiled uninvitingly again.

The two men were leaning, straining forward, their eyes on the diamond-shaped gray seal—and into their faces there crept a sickly fear.

"The Gray Seal!" Sonnino stumbled the words.

"Put an outside wrapper around that package!" instructed Jimmie Dale coldly. He watched Sonnino perform the task with trembling fingers; and then, placing the package under his arm, Jimmie Dale backed to the door. There was a key in the lock on the inner side. He transferred it coolly to the outer side—and his voice rasped suddenly with the fury that found vent at last.

"You are a pair of hell hounds," he said between his teeth; "but you are angels compared with the gang that hired you for this. Well, the game is up! David Archman will settle with *them* when they face the investigation—and I will settle with *you*! One night, a year ago, in last January, a certain Fourth Avenue bank was looted of eighteen thousand dollars—*do you remember, Laroque?* Ah, I see you do! The police are still looking for the man who pulled that job. What would you say, Laroque, would be the sentence handed out for that little affair to a man with, say, *your* past record?"

Laroque's lips were twitching; his face had gone gray.

"Fourteen years would be a light sentence, wouldn't it?" resumed Jimmie Dale, an even colder menace in his voice. "And you remember Stangeist, and the Mope, and Australian Ike, don't you, Laroque—you remember they went to the death house in Sing Sing—and you remember that the Gray Seal sent them there? Yes, I see you do; I see your memory is good tonight! Listen, then! I have heard it said that Gentleman Laroque, with his gangsters behind him, would stop at nothing where Gentleman Laroque's own skin was concerned. I have heard it said that where Gentleman Laroque was known he was *feared*. Very well, Laroque, it is your turn to choose. You can choose between yourself and this 'Private Club Ring' who have purchased your services in this game tonight. I fancy you can find a means of inducing Sonnino here to keep his mouth shut; and I fancy that of the two evils—holding young Archman as a club over his father, or of your employers facing their trial and conviction—you can convince the 'Private Club Ring' that the lesser, the lesser as regards *your* risk, say, is to face that trial and conviction. Do I make myself plain—Laroque? It is simply a question of not a word being said of what has happened tonight—or fourteen years in Sing Sing for you! I do not think you will find the task difficult when you add, to whatever arguments of your own you may see fit to employ, the fact that the Gray Seal, if your principals make a move, will expose them for this night's work on top of what they will already have to answer for. Well—Laroque?"

There was silence for a minute. Sonnino, cringing, the suavity, the oiliness of manner gone, a man afraid, kept his eyes on the table, and kept passing his hands one over the other. Laroque was the gambler—a twisted smile was forced to his lips.

"You win," he said hoarsely. "You can take it from me, I'll go up the river for fourteen years for no one—I'll take blasted good care of that! But you"—a rage, ungovernable and elemental, found voice in a sudden torrent of blasphemous invective—"you—we'll get you yet! Some day we'll get you, you cursed snitch, you—"

"Good-night!" said Jimmie Dale grimly, and, stepping swiftly back over the threshold, shut and locked the door.

He gained the street, gained his car in front of The Sphinx—and, twenty minutes later, after a break-neck run in which Benson for the second time that night defied all speed laws, Jimmie Dale alighted from his car at a street corner well uptown, dismissed Benson for the night, retraced his way half the distance back along the block, disappeared into a lane, and presently, taking a high fence with the agility of a cat in spite of, his encumbering package, dropped noiselessly down into a backyard.

It was well known ground to Jimmie Dale—as a boy he had played here in the Archman's backyard, played here with Clarie Archman. His face masked again, he moved swiftly toward the rear of the house. There was still Clarie Archman. What would the boy do? Jimmie Dale's hand, a picklock in it again, clenched fiercely. It was a hell's choice they had given the boy—to rob his father, or go down himself, and drag his father with him, in ruin and disgrace! What would the boy do? Jimmie Dale was working silently at the back door now. It opened, and he stepped inside. He was here well ahead of the other, there was no possibility, granting even the start the boy had had, that Clarie Archman could have made the trip uptown in the same time. It was more likely that the boy might even linger a long while in misery and indecision before he came home. That was why he, Jimmie Dale, had dismissed Benson and the car for the night, and—

With a mental jerk, Jimmie Dale focused his mind on his immediate surroundings. It was dark; there were no lights in any part of the house, but he needed none, not even his flashlight—he knew the house as well and as intimately as his own. He was in the rear hall now, and now he opened a door, paused cautiously as the dull yellow glow from a dying grate fire illuminated the room faintly, then stepped inside. It was the Archman library, the room where David Archman did a great deal of his work at night A desk stood at the lower end of the room; and in the corner near the portière windows was the lawyer's safe.

Jimmie Dale closed the door, moved toward the window, drew the portieres aside, released the window catch, silently raised the window itself—it was only a drop a few feet to the yard! And then Jimmie Dale sat down at the desk.

A clock somewhere in the house struck a single note—that would be halfpast one. Time passed slowly, interminably. The clock struck again—two o'clock. And then suddenly Jimmie Dale rose from his chair, and slipped into the window recess behind the portières. The front door closed, a step came along the hall, the library opened, closed again—and Clarie Archman, his face as the flickering firelight played upon it, like a face of death, came forward into the room.

For a moment the boy held motionless beside the desk, his eyes fixed in a sort of horrible fascination upon the safe—and then, slowly, he moved toward it, and dropped on his knees before it, and his fingers began to twirl the knob of the dial. His fingers shook, and he was a long time at his task—and then the handle turned, and the safe was unlocked, but Clarie Archman did not open the door. Instead, he drew back suddenly, and rose swaying to his feet, and covered his face with his hands.

"I can't! Oh, my God, I—I can't!" he moaned. He lowered his hands after a moment and gazed around him unseeingly, and a ghastly look came into his face. "I—I guess—I guess there's only one—one way to—to beat them," he whispered. "One way to beat them, and—"

The package in Jimmie Dale's hand dropped suddenly to the floor, he wrenched the portières aside, and, with a low, sharp cry, sprang forward. The boy had taken a revolver from his pocket, and was lifting it to his head. Jimmie Dale struck up the other's hand—but in time only to deflect the shot; too late to prevent it being fired. There was a flash in mid-air, the roar of the report went racketing through the silent house, and the revolver, spinning from the other's hands, struck against the wall across the room.

And then Jimmie Dale had the boy by the shoulders, and was shaking him violently. Clarie Archman was like one stunned, numbed, and bereft of his senses.

"It's all right—you're clear! Do you hear—try and understand—you're clear!" Jimmie Dale whispered fiercely. "Here's your letter!" He thrust it into the other's hand. "Destroy it! Those men—Sonnino—Barca—will say nothing. You don't owe anybody any money—that bucket-shop was in the game with the rest, and—" Cries, voices, were coming from above now; and Jimmie Dale, like a flash, turned from the boy, leaped for the safe, wrenched the door open, reached in with both hands, and, snatching up an armful of the contents, spilled books and papers on the floor. He was back beside the boy in an instant. "Listen! You heard someone in here as you entered the house— you came into the room—*you caught me in the act*—you fired—you missed. And now—*fight*! Fight—pull yourself together—fight. They are coming!"

He caught the boy around the waist, and the two, locked together, reeled this way and that about the room. A chair, deliberately kicked over by Jimmie Dale, crashed to the floor. The cries drew nearer. Footsteps came racing madly down the stairs—and then the door of the library burst open, and David Archman, in pajamas, dashed through the doorway, and without a second's hesitation, made for the two struggling forms—and Jimmie Dale, releasing his hold upon the boy, suddenly sent the other staggering backwards full into David Archman, checking David Archman's rush—and, turning, sprang for the window, snatched up his package, hurled himself over the sill, dropped to the ground, and, racing for the fence, climbed it, and made the lane, just as a shot, from David Archman, no doubt, was fired from the window.

A moment more, and Jimmie Dale, his mask in his pocket, had emerged from the lane, and was walking nonchalantly along to the street corner; another, and he had boarded a street car—but under Jimmie Dale's coat was a most suspicious bulge. Conscious of this, he left the street car a few blocks farther along, when he was far enough away to be certain that he would have eluded all pursuit—and walked the rest of the distance to Riverside Drive. If he had escaped unscathed, the package of banknotes had not—it was his coat that shielded them from view, not the wrappers, for the wrappers had been torn almost entirely away in his hasty exit over the fence.

He reached his home, and mounted the steps cautiously. There was Jason to consider—Jason with his lovable pernicious habit of sitting up for his master. Jason must not see those banknotes, that was obvious, and if Jason— yes!—Jimmie Dale was peering now through the monogrammed lace that covered the plate glass doors in the vestibule—yes, Jason was still sitting up. And then Jimmie Dale smiled that strange whimsical smile of his. Jason was still sitting up—asleep in the hall chair.

Softly, without a sound, Jimmie Dale opened the front door, entered, passed the old man, and went up the stairs. In his dressing room, he hid away the package that tomorrow, or at the first opportunity, would enrich some deserving charity, and, as silently as he had come up the stairs, he descended them again, passed by the old man again, and went out to the street once more. There was just one reason why Jason, tired out and asleep, sat there— only one—because Jason, old Jason, faithful, big-hearted Jason, loved his Master Jim.

Into Jimmie Dale's eyes there came a mist. Perhaps that was why, because he could not see clearly, that he stumbled on his way up the steps again; perhaps that was why he made so much noise that it was Jason who opened the door and held out his hands for Jimmie Dale's coat and hat.

"What!" said Jimmie Dale severely. "Sitting up again, Jason? Jason, go to bed at once!"

"Yes, sir," said Jason. "Thank you, sir. Thank you, Master Jim, sir—I will."

CHAPTER 16

ONE CHANCE IN TEN

It was three nights later. Old Jason had placed a tray with after-dinner coffee and a liqueur set on the table at Jimmie Dale's elbow—that was fully an hour ago, and both coffee and liqueur were untouched. Things were not going well. Apart entirely from all lack of success where the Tocsin was concerned, things were not going well. The fate of Frenchy Virat, the fate of the Wolf, and, added to this, the Gray Seal's intervention in the plans and purposes of one Gentleman Laroque and certain gentlemen still higher up than Laroque, had not passed unmarked or unnoticed in the underworld. And now in the underworld a strange, ominous and far-reaching disquiet reigned. It was an underworld rampant with suspicion, mad with fury, more dangerous than it had ever been before.

Jimmie Dale's hand reached abstractedly into the pocket of his dinner jacket for his cigarette case. He lighted a cigarette, leaned back once more in the big, leather-upholstered lounging chair, and his eyes, half closed, strayed introspectively around the luxuriously appointed room, his own particular den in his Riverside Drive residence. Once, a very long while ago, years ago, so long ago now that it seemed as though it must have been in some strange previous incarnation, back in those days when the Tocsin had first come into his life, and when he had known her only as the author of those mysterious letters, those "calls to arms" to the Gray Seal, she had written: "Things are a little too warm, aren't they, Jimmie? Let's let them cool for a year."

A blue thread curled lazily upward from the tip of the cigarette. Jimmie Dale's eyes fastened mechanically on the twisting, wavering spiral, followed it mechanically as it rose and spread out into filmy, undulating, fantastic shapes—and the strong, square jaw set suddenly hard. It was not so very strange that those words should have come back to him tonight! Things were "warm" now—and he could not let them "cool" for a year!

"Warm!" He smiled a little mirthlessly. The comparison was very slight! Then, at the beginning, at the outset of the Gray Seal's career, the police, it was true, had shown a certain unpleasant anxiety for a closer acquaintance-ship, but that was about all. Today, lashed on and mocked by a virulent press, goaded to madness by their own past failures to "get" the Gray Seal, to whose door they laid a hundred crimes and for whom the bars of a death cell in Sing Sing was the goal if they could but catch their prey, the police, to a man, were waging a ceaseless and relentless war against him; and today, joining hands with the police, the underworld in all its thousand ramifications, prompted by fear, by suspicion of one another, reached out to trap him, and to deal out to him a much more speedy, but none the less certain, fate than that prescribed by the statutes of the law!

He shook his head. It could not go on—indefinitely. The role was too hard to play; the dual life, in a sort of grim, ironical self-mockery, brought even in its own successful interpretation added dangers and perils with each succeeding day. As it had been with Larry the Bat, the more he now lived Smarlinghue the more it became difficult to slough off Smarlinghue and live as Jimmie Dale; the more Smarlinghue became trusted and accepted in the inner circles of the underworld, the more he became a figure in those sordid surroundings, and the more dangerous it became to "disappear" at will without exciting suspicion, where suspicion, as it was, was already spread into every nook and corner of the Bad Lands, where each rubbed shoulders with his fellow in the lurking dread that the other was—the Gray Seal!

The police were no mean antagonists, he made no mistake on that score; but the peril that was the graver menace of the two, and the greater to be feared, was—the underworld. And here in the underworld in the last few days, here where on every twisted, vicious lip was the whisper, "Death to the Gray Seal," there had come even another menace. He could not define it, it was intuition perhaps—but intuition had never failed him yet. It was an undercurrent of which he had gradually become conscious, the sense of some unseen, guiding power, that moved and swayed and controlled, and was present, dominant, in every den and dive in crimeland. There had been many gang leaders and heads of little coteries of crime, cunning, crafty in their way, and all of them unscrupulous, like the Wolf, for instance, who had sworn openly and boastingly through the Bad Lands, and had been believed for a season, that they would bring the Gray Seal to a last accounting—but it was more than this now. There was a craftier brain and a stronger hand at work than the Wolf's had ever been! Who was it? He shook his head. He did not know. He had gone far into the innermost circles of the underworld— and he did not know. He sensed a power there; and in a dozen different, intangible ways, still an intuition more than anything else, he had sensed this "someone," this power, creeping, fumbling, feeling its implacable way through the dark, as it were, toward *him*.

Yes, it was getting "warm"—perilously warm! And inevitably there must come an end—some day. The warning stared him in the face. But he could not stop, could not heed the warning, could not let things "cool" now for a year, and stand aside until the storm should have subsided! Where was the Tocsin? If his peril was great—what was hers!

He surged suddenly upward from his chair, his hands clenched until the knuckles stood out like ivory knobs. The Tocsin! The woman he loved— where was she? Was she safe tonight? *Where* was she? He could not stop until that question had been answered, be the consequences what they might! Warnings, the realisation of peril—he laughed shortly, in grim bitterness—counted little in the balance after all, did they not! Where was the Tocsin?

The telephone rang. Jimmie Dale stared at the instrument for a moment, as though it were some singular and uninvited intruder who had broken in without warrant upon his train of thought; and then, leaning forward over the table, he lifted the receiver from the hook.

"Yes? Hello! Yes?" inquired Jimmie Dale. "What is it?"

A man's voice, hurried, and seemingly somewhat agitated, answered him.

"I would like to speak to Mr. Dale—to Mr. Dale in person."

"This is Mr. Dale speaking," said Jimmie Dale a little brusquely. "What is it?"

"Oh, is that you, Mr. Dale?" The voice had quickened perceptibly. "I didn't recognise your voice—but then I haven't heard it for a long while, have I? This is Forrester. Are—are you very busy tonight, Mr. Dale?"

"Oh, hello, Forrester!" Jimmie Dale's voice had grown more affable. "Busy? Well, I don't know. It depends on what you mean by busy."

"An hour or two," the other suggested—the tinge of anxiety in his tones growing more pronounced. "The time to run out here in your car. I haven't any right to ask it, I know, but the truth is I—I want to talk to someone pretty badly, and I need some financial help, and—and I thought of you. I—I'm afraid there's a mess here. The bank examiners landed in suddenly late this afternoon."

"The—*what*?" demanded Jimmie Dale sharply.

"The bank examiners—I—I can't talk over the phone. Only, for God's sake, come—will you? I'll be in my rooms—you know where they are, don't you—on the cottier over—"

"Yes, I know," Jimmie Dale broke in tersely; then, quietly: "All right, Forrester, I'll come."

"Thank God!" came Forrester's voice—and disconnected abruptly.

Jimmie Dale replaced the receiver on the hook, stared at the instrument again in a perplexed way; then, called the garage on the private house wire. There was no answer. He walked quickly then across the room and pushed an electric button.

"Jason," he said a moment later, as the old butler appeared on the threshold in answer to the summons, "Benson doesn't answer in the garage. I presume he is downstairs. I wish you would ask him to bring the touring car around at once. And you might have a light overcoat ready for me—Jason."

"Yes, sir," said the old man. "Yes, Master Jim, sir, at once." His eyes sought Jimmie Dale's, and dropped—but into them had come, not the questioning of familiarity, but the quick, anxious questioning inspired by the affection that had grown up between them from the days when, as the old man was so fond of saying, he had dandled his Master Jim upon his knee. "Yes, sir, Master Jim, at once, sir," Jason repeated—but he still hesitated upon the threshold.

And then Jimmie Dale shook his head whimsically—and smiled.

"No—not tonight, Jason," he said reassuringly. "It's quite all right, Jason—there's no letter tonight."

The old man's face cleared instantly.

"Yes, sir; quite so, sir. Thank you, Master Jim," he said. "Shall I tell Benson that he is to drive you, sir, or—"

"No; I'll drive myself, Jason," decided Jimmie Dale.

"Yes, sir—very good, sir"—the door closed on Jason.

Jimmie Dale turned back into the room, began to pace up and down its length, and for a moment the reverie that the telephone had interrupted was again dominant in his mind. Jason was afraid. Jason—even though he knew so little of the truth—was afraid. Well, what then? He, Jimmie Dale, was not blind himself! It had come almost to the point where his back was against the wall at last; to the point where, unless he found the Tocsin before many more days went by, it would be, as far as he was concerned—too late!

And then he shrugged his shoulders suddenly—and his forehead knitted into perplexed furrows. Forrester—and the telephone message! What did it mean? There was an ugly sound to it, that reference to the bank examiners and the need of financial assistance. And it was a little odd, too, that Forrester should have telephoned him, Jimmie Dale, unless it were accounted for by the fact that Forrester knew of no one else to whom he might apply for perhaps a large sum, of ready money. True, he knew Forrester quite well—not as an intimate friend—but only in a sort of casual, off-hand kind of a way, as it were, and he had known him for a good many years; but their acquaintanceship would not warrant the other's action unless the man were in desperate straits. Forrester had been a clerk in the city bank where his, Jimmie Dale's, father had transacted his business, and it was there he had first met Forrester. He had continued to meet Forrester there after his father had died; and then Forrester had been offered and had accepted the cashiership of a small local bank out near Bayside on Long Island. He had run into Forrester there again once or twice on motor trips—and once, held up by an accident to his car, he had dined with Forrester, and had spent an hour or two in the other's rooms. That was about all.

Jimmie Dale's frown grew deeper. He liked Forrester The man was a bachelor and of about his, Jimmie Dale's, own age, and had always appeared to be a decent, clean-lived fellow, a man who worked hard, and was apparently pushing his way, if not meteorically, at least steadily up to the top, a man who was respected and well-thought of by everybody—and yet just what did it mean? The more he thought of it, the uglier it seemed to become.

He stepped suddenly toward the telephone—and as abruptly turned away again. He remembered that Forrester did not have a telephone in his rooms, for, on the night of the break-down, he, Jimmie Dale, had wanted to telephone, and had been obliged to go outside to do so. Forrester, obviously then, had done likewise tonight. Well, he should have insisted on a fuller explanation in the first place if he had intended to make that a contingent condition; as it was, it was too late now, and he had promised to go.

The sound of a motor car on the driveway leading from the private garage in the rear reached him. Benson was bringing out the car now. Jimmie Dale, as he prepared to leave the room, glanced about him from force of habit, and his eyes held for an instant on the portières behind which, in the little alcove, stood the squat, barrel-shaped safe. Was there anything he would need tonight—that leather girdle, for instance, with its circle of pockets containing its compact little burglar's kit? He shook his head impatiently. He had already told Jason—if in other words—that there was no "call to arms" to the Gray Seal tonight, hadn't he? It was habit again that had brought the thought, that was all! For the rest, in the last few days, since this new intuitive danger from the underworld had come to him, an automatic had always reposed in his pocket by day and under his pillow by night; and by way of defence, too, though they might appear to be curious weapons of defence if one did not stop to consider that the means of making a hurried exit through a locked door might easily make the difference between life and death, his pockets held a small, but very carefully selected collection of little steel picklocks. He smiled somewhat amusedly at himself, as he passed out of the room and descended the stairs to the hall below. The contents of the safe could hardly have added anything that would be of any service even in an emergency! His mental inventory of his pockets had been incomplete—there was still the thin, metal insignia case, and the black silk mask, both of which, like the automatic, were never now out of his immediate possession.

He slipped into his coat as Jason held it out for him, accepted the soft felt hat which Jason extended, and, with a nod to the old butler, ran down the steps, dismissed Benson, who stood waiting, and entered his car.

It was three-quarters of an hour later when Jimmie Dale drew up at the curb on the main street of the little Long Island town that was his destination.

"Pretty good run!" said Jimmie Dale to himself, as he glanced at the car's clock under its little electric bulb. "Halfpast nine."

He descended from the car, and nodded as he surveyed his surroundings. He had stopped neither in front of the bank, nor in front of Forrester's rooms—it was habit again, perhaps, the caution prompted by Forrester's statement relative to the bank examiners. If there was trouble, and the obvious deduction indicated that there was, he, Jimmie Dale, had no desire to figure in it in a public way. Again he nodded his head. Yes, he quite had his bearings now. It was the usual main street of a small town—fairly well lighted, stores and shops flanking the pavements on either side, and of perhaps a distance equivalent to some seven or eight city blocks in length. Two blocks further up, on the same side of the street as that on which he was standing, was the bank—not a very pretentious establishment, he remembered; its staff consisting of but one or two apart from Forrester, as was not unusual with small local banks, though this in no way indicated that the business done was not profitable, or, comparatively, large. Jimmie Dale started forward along the street. On the corner just ahead of him was a two-story building, the second floor of which had been divided into rooms originally designed to be used as offices, as, indeed, most of them were, but two of these Forrester had fitted up as bachelor quarters.

Jimmie Dale turned the corner, walked down the side street to the office entrance that led to the floor above, opened the door, and ran lightly up the stairs. At the head of the stairs he paused to get his bearings once more. Forrester's rooms were here directly at the head of the stairs, but he had forgotten for the moment whether they were on the right or left of the corridor; and the corridor being unlighted now and without any sign of life left him still more undecided. It seemed, though, if his recollection served him correctly, that the rooms had been on the right. He moved in that direction, found the door, and knocked; but, receiving no answer, crossed the hall again, and knocked on the door on the left-hand side. There was no answer here, either. He frowned a little impatiently, and returned once more to the right-hand door. Forrester probably was up at the bank, and had not expected him to make the run out from the city so quickly. He tried the door tentatively, found it unlocked, opened it a little way, saw that the room within was lighted—and suddenly, with a low, startled exclamation, stepped swiftly forward over the threshold, and closed the door behind him.

It was Forrester's room, this one here at the right of the corridor—his recollection had not been at fault. It was Forrester's room, and Forrester himself was there—on the floor—dead.

For a moment Jimmie Dale stood rigid and without movement, save that as his eyes swept around the apartment his face grew hard and set, his lips drooping in sharp, grim lines at the corners of his mouth.

"My God!" Jimmie Dale whispered.

There was a faint, almost imperceptible odour in the room, like the smell of peach blossom—he noticed it now for the first time, as his eyes fastened on a small, empty bottle that lay on the floor a few feet away from the dead man's outstretched arm. Jimmie Dale stepped forward abruptly now, and knelt down beside the man for a hurried; examination. It was unnecessary— he knew that even before he performed the act. Yes—the man was dead He reached out and picked up the bottle. The odour was tell-tale evidence enough. The bottle had contained prussic, or hydrocyanic acid, probably the moist deadly poison in existence, and the swiftest in its action. He replaced the bottle on the spot where he had found it, and stood up.

Again, Jimmie Dale's eyes swept his surroundings. The room in which he stood was a sort of living room or den. There was a desk over by the far wall, a couch near the door, and several comfortable lounging chairs. Forrester lay with his head against the sharp edge of one of the legs of the couch, as though he had rolled off and struck against it.

Opposite the desk, across the room, was the door leading into the second room of the little apartment. Jimmie Dale moved toward this now, and stepped across the threshold. The room itself was unlighted, but there was light enough from the connecting doorway to enable him to see fairly well. It was Forrester's bedroom, and in no way appeared to have been disturbed. He remembered it quite well. There was a door here, too, that gave on the hall. He circled around the bed and reached the door. It was locked.

Jimmie Dale returned to the living room—and stood there in a sort of grim immobility, looking down at the form on the floor. He was not callous. Death, as often as he had seen it, and in its most tragic phases, had not made him callous, and he had liked Forrester—but suicide was not a man's way out, it was the way a coward took, and if it brought pity, it was the pity that was blunted with the sterner, almost contemptuous note of disapproval. What had happened since Forrester had phoned, that had driven the man to this extremity? When Forrester had phoned he had appeared to be agitated enough, but, at least, he had seemed to have had hopes that the appeal he was then making might see him through, and, as proof of that, there had been unmistakable relief in the man's voice when he, Jimmie Dale, had agreed to the other's request. And what had been the meaning of that "financial help"? Had, for instance—for it was pitifully obvious that if the bank had been looted an *innocent* man would not commit suicide on that account—a greater measure of the depredation been uncovered than had been counted on, so much indeed that, say, the financial assistance Forrester had intended to ask for had now increased to such proportions that he had realised the futility of even a request; or, again, had it for some reason, since he had telephoned, now become impossible to restore the funds even if they were in his possession?

A sheet of note paper lying on the desk caught Jimmie Dale's eyes. He stepped forward, picked it up—and his lips drew tight together, as he read the two or three miserable lines that were scrawled upon it:

What's left is in the middle drawer of the desk. There's only one way out now—I don't see any other way. I thought that I could get—but what does that matter! God help me! I'm sorry.

FLEMING P. FORRESTER.

I'm sorry! It was a pitiful epitaph for a man's life! I'm sorry! Jimmie Dale's face softened a little—the man was dead now. "I'm sorry…. Fleming P. Forrester"—he had seen that signature on bank paper a hundred times in the old days; he had little thought ever to see it on a document such as this!

He stared at the paper for a long time, and then, from the paper, his eyes travelled over the desk, then shifted again to Forrester—and then, for the second time, he knelt beside the other on the floor. For the moment, what was referred to as "being all that was left" in the middle drawer of the desk could wait. There was another matter now. He felt hurriedly through Forrester's vest and coat pockets—and from one of the pockets drew out a folded piece of paper. It was not what he was looking for, but it was all that rewarded his search. He unfolded the paper. It was dirty and crumpled, and the few lines written upon it were badly penned and illiterate:

The ante's gone up—get me? Six thousand bucks. You come across with that tomorrow morning by ten o'clock—or I'll spill the beans. And I ain't got any more paper to write any more letters on either—savvy? This is the last.

There was no signature. Jimmie Dale read it again—and abruptly put it in his own pocket. Yes, he had liked Forrester—well enough for this anyway! The man might have a mother perhaps—it would be bad enough in any case. And those other things, the empty bottle, the sheet of note paper with its scrawled confession—what about them? He returned with a sort of hesitant indecision to the desk. He had no right of course to touch them unless—

He shook his head sharply, as he pulled open the middle drawer of the desk.

"Newspapers—publicity—rotten!" he muttered savagely. "One chance in ten, and—ah!"

From the back of the drawer where it had been tucked in under a mass of papers, he had extracted a little bundle of documents that were held together by an elastic band. He snapped off the band, and ran through the papers rapidly. For the most part they were bonds and stock certificates indorsed by their owners, and evidently had been held by the bank as collateral for loans.

And then suddenly Jimmie Dale straightened up, tense and alert. He had no desire, very far from any desire to be caught here, or to figure publicly in any way in the case. The street door had opened and closed again. Footsteps, those of three men, his acute, trained hearing told him, sounded on the stairs. Again there came that hesitant indecision as he stood there, while his eyes travelled in swift succession from the bank's securities in his hand to the note on the desk, to the empty bottle on the floor, to the white, upturned face of the silent form huddled against the couch.

"One chance in ten," muttered Jimmie Dale through his set lips. "One chance in ten—and I guess I'll take it!"

The footsteps came nearer—they were almost at the head of the stairs now. But now Jimmie Dale was in action—swift as a flash and silent as a shadow in every movement. The bundle of securities was thrust into his pocket, the sheet of note paper followed, and, as a knock sounded on the door, he stooped, picked up the bottle from the floor, and darted into the adjoining room—and in another instant he had reached the locked door and was working at it silently and swiftly with a picklock.

CHAPTER 17

THE DEFAULTER

At the other door the knocking still continued—and then it was opened—and there came a chorus of low, horrified, startled cries, and the quick rush of feet into the room.

The picklock went back into Jimmie Dale's pocket, and crouched, now, his hand on the knob, turning it gradually without a sound, drawing the door ajar inch by inch, he kept his eyes on the doorway connecting with the other room. He could see the three men bending over Forrester. Their voices came in confused, broken, snatches:

"...Dead!...Good God!...Are you sure?...Perhaps he's only fainted.... No, he's dead, poor devil!..."

And then one of the men, the youngest of the three, a slight-built, clean-shaven, dark-eyed man of perhaps twenty-eight or thirty, rose abruptly, and glanced sharply around the room.

"Yes, he's dead!" he said bitterly. "Anyone could tell that! But he wouldn't be dead, and this would never have happened if you'd done what I wanted you to do when you first came to the bank this afternoon. I wanted you to have him arrested then, didn't I?"

One of the others—and it was obvious that the others were the two bank examiners—a man of middle age, answered soberly.

"You're upset, Dryden," he said. "You know we couldn't do that—"

"On a teller's word against the cashier's—of course not!" the young man broke in caustically. "Well, you see now, don't you?"

"We couldn't do it then without proof," amended the bank examiner quietly.

"Proof!" Dryden exclaimed. "My God—*proof!* Who tipped your people off to have you drop in there this afternoon? I did, didn't I? Do you think I'd do that without knowing what I was about! Didn't I tell you that there was nothing but the office fixtures left! Didn't I! There were only the two of us on the staff, and didn't I tell you that I had discovered that the books were cooked from cover to cover? Yes, I did! And you had to get your pencils out and start in on a thumb-rule examination, as though nothing were the matter! Well, what did you find? The securities in a mess, what there was left of them—and what was supposed to be twenty thousand dollars that came out from the city yesterday nothing but a package of blank paper!"

"You didn't know that yourself until half an hour ago when we started to check up the cash," returned the other a little sharply.

"Well, perhaps, I didn't," admitted Dryden; "but I knew about the books."

"Besides that," continued the bank examiner, "Mr. Forrester was in town this afternoon when we got to the bank and this is the first time we have seen him, so we could not very well have done anything other than we have done in any case. I mention this because you are talking wildly, and that sort of talk, if it gets out, won't do any of us any good. You don't want to blame Mr. Marner here and myself for Mr. Forrester's death, do you?"

"No—of course, I don't!" said Dryden, in a more subdued voice. "I don't mean that at all. I guess you're right—I'm excited. I—well"—he motioned jerkily toward the form on the floor—"I'm not used to walking into a room and finding *that*."

It was Marner, the other bank examiner, who broke a moment's silence.

"We none of us are," he said, and brushed his hand across his forehead. "A doctor can't do any good, of course, but I suppose we should call one at once, and notify the police, too. I—"

Jimmie Dale had slipped through the door and out into the hall. A moment more and he had descended the stairs and gained the street, still another and he had stepped nonchalantly into his car. The car started forward, passed out of the lighted zone of the town's main street—and in the darkness, headed toward New York, Jimmie Dale, his nonchalance gone now, leaned forward over the wheel, and the big sixty horse-power car leaped into its stride like a thoroughbred at the touch of the spur, and tore onward at dare-devil speed through the night.

His lips twisted in a smile that held little of humour. Back there in that room they would call a doctor, and they would call the police. And the doctor would establish the fact that Forrester had died from the effects of a dose of prussic acid; and the police would establish—what? Prussic acid was swift in its effect. If Forrester had died from that cause, how had he taken it himself, and out of what had he taken it? What the police would see would be quite a different thing from what he, Jimmie Dale, had seen when he opened the door of that room! Instead of the evidence of suicide, there was now every evidence of *murder*. The bank examiners on entering the room, started at what they saw, obsessed with the wreckage of the bank, might still for the moment have jumped to the conclusion, natural enough under the circumstances, of suicide; but the police, after ten minutes of unemotional investigation, would father a very different theory.

Jimmie Dale's jaws clamped, as his eyes narrowed on the flying thread of gray road under the dancing headlights. Well, the die was cast now! For good or bad, his response to Forrester's telephone appeal had become the vital factor in the case. For good or bad! He laughed out sharply into the night. He would see soon enough—old Kronische, the wizened, crafty, little chemist, who burrowed like a fox in its hole deep in the heart of the Bad Lands, would answer that question. Old Kronische had a record that was known to police and underworld alike—and was trusted by neither one, and feared by both. But he was clever—clever with a devilish cleverness. God alone knew what he was up to in the long hours of day and night amongst his retorts and test tubes in his abominable smelling little hole; but every one knew that from old Kronische *anything* of a chemical nature could be obtained if the price, not a small one, was forthcoming, and if old Kronische was satisfied with the credentials of his prospective client.

Yes—old Kronische! Old Kronische was the man, the one than; there was no possible hesitancy or question there—the question was how to reach old Kronische. Jimmie Dale shook his head in a quick, impatient gesture, as though in irritation because his brain would not instantly respond to his demand to formulate a plan. It seemed simple enough, old Kronische was perfectly accessible—but it was, nevertheless, far from simple. He could not go to old Kronische as Jimmie Dale, there was an ugly turn that had been taken in that room of Forrester's now. If, as Jimmie Dale, he had had reason to keep out of the affair before, it was imperative that he should do so now— or he might find himself in a very awkward situation, so awkward, in fact, that the consequences might lead anywhere, and "anywhere" to Jimmie Dale, to the Gray Seal, to Smarlinghue, might mean ruin, wreckage and disaster. Nor, much less, could he risk going to old Kronische as Smarlinghue. He could not trust old Kronische. How, if old Kronische chose to "talk," could Smarlinghue account for any connection with what had transpired in Forrester's room? How long would it be, even if Smarlinghue were no more than put under surveillance, before the discovery would be made that Smarlinghue was but a role that covered—Jimmie Dale!

And then Jimmie Dale's strained, set face relaxed a little. His brain had repented of its stubbornness, it seemed, and was at work again. There was a way, a very sure way as far as old Kronische being "talkative" was concerned, but a very dangerous way from every other point of view. Suppose he went to old Kronische—as Larry the Bat!

The car tore on through the night; towns and villages flashed by; the long, deserted stretches of road began to give way to the city's outskirts—and Jimmie Dale began to drive more cautiously. Larry the Bat! Yes, it was perfectly feasible, as far as feasibility went. The clothes that he had duplicated at such infinite trouble were still hidden there in the Sanctuary. But to be caught as Larry the Bat meant—the end. That was the one thing the underworld knew, the one thing the police knew—that Larry the Bat was, or had been, the Gray Seal. Still, he had done it once before, and it could be done again. He could reach old Kronische's without much fear of discovery after all, he would take good care to secure the few minutes necessary to make a "getaway" from the old chemist's, and *afterwards* old Kronische could talk as much as he liked about—Larry the Bat! Yes, that was the way! Old Kronische—and Larry the Bat. He, Jimmie Dale, would drive, say, to Marlianne's restaurant, and telephone Jason to send Benson for the car—Marlianne's, besides being a very natural stopping place, possessed the added advantage of being quite close to the Sanctuary.

His decision made, Jimmie Dale gave his undivided attention to his car, and ten minutes later, stopping in the shabby street that harboured Marlianne's, he entered the restaurant, threaded his way through the small crowded rooms—for Marlianne's, despite its spotted linen, was crowded at all hours—to a sort of hallway at the rear of the place, and entered the telephone booth.

He called his residence, and, as he waited for the connection, glanced at his watch. He smiled grimly. He could congratulate himself for the second time that night on having made a record run. It was not yet quite half-past ten, and he must have been at least a good twenty minutes in Forrester's rooms. He rattled the hook impatiently. They were a long time in getting the connection! Halfpast ten! He could be at the Sanctuary in another few minutes, ten minutes at the outside; then, say, another twenty to rehabilitate Larry the Bat, and by eleven he—

"Yes—hello!"—he was speaking quickly into the phone, as Jason's voice reached him. "Jason, I am down here at Marlianne's. Tell Benson to come for the car, and—" He stopped abruptly. Jason was talking excitedly, almost incoherently at the other end.

"Master Jim, sir! Is that you, sir, Master Jim! It—it came, sir, not ten minutes after you left tonight, and—"

"Jason," said Jimmie Dale sharply, "what's the matter with you? What are you talking about? What came?"

"Why—why, sir—I beg your pardon, sir, but I've been a bit uneasy ever since, sir. It's—it's one of those letters, Master Jim, sir."

A sudden whiteness came into Jimmie Dale's face, as he stared into the mouthpiece of the telephone. A "call to arms" from the Tocsin—*now*—tonight! What was he to do! It was not a trivial thing which that letter would contain—it never had been, and it never would be, and no matter under what circumstances it found him, he—

Jason's voice faltered over the wire:

"Are you there, sir, Master Jim?"

"Yes," said Jimmie Dale quietly. "Bring the letter with you, Jason, and come down with Benson. I will wait for you here—in the car outside Marlianne's. And hurry, Jason—take a taxi down."

"Yes, sir," said Jason, his voice trembling a little. "At once, Master Jim."

Jimmie Dale hung up the receiver, returned to the street, and seated himself in his car. How long would it take them to get here? Half an hour? Well then, for half an hour his hands were tied, and he could do nothing but wait. He glanced around him. It was curious! It was here in this very place that he had once found a letter from her in his car; it was even here that, without knowing it at the moment, he had really seen her for the first time. And now—what did it hold, this letter, this "call to arms" that he sat here waiting for, while out there in that little town a man lay dead on the floor of his room, and around whom, where there had once been the evidence of a coward's guilt, crowned with the sorriest epitaph that ever man had written, there was now the evidence of a still blacker crime—the crime of murder.

He lighted a cigarette and smoked it through. Could it be *that*—in her letter! Intuition again? Well, why not—if old Kronische should answer the question as the chances were one in ten that old Kronische might answer it! Yes—why not! It would not be strange. Intuition—because somehow the feeling that it *was* so grew stronger with each moment that passed—well, once before tonight he had said that intuition had never failed him yet!

The minutes dragged by interminably. He smoked another cigarette, and after that another. The clock under the hood showed five minutes past eleven; the minute hand crept around to eight, nine, ten minutes past the hour—and then a taxi swerved on little better than two wheels around the corner—and Jimmie Dale, springing from his seat, jumped to the pavement as the taxi drew up at the curb.

Jason, palpably agitated, and followed by Benson, descended from the taxi. Jimmie Dale dismissed the cab, and motioned Benson to the car.

"Well, Jason?" he said quickly.

"It's here, sir, Master Jim"—the old butler fumbled in an inner pocket, and produced an envelope—"I—"

"Thank you! That's all—Jason." Jimmie Dale's quick smile robbed his curt dismissal of any sting. "Benson, of course, will drive you home."

"Yes, sir." The old man went slowly to the car, and climbed in beside the chauffeur. "Good-night, sir!" Jason ventured wistfully. "Good-night, Master Jim!"

"Good-night, Jason—good-night, Benson!" Jimmie Dale answered—and, turning, started briskly along the street. Jason's "good-night" had been eloquent of the old man's anxiety. He would have liked to reassure Jason—but he had neither the time, nor, for that matter, the ability to do so. The old man would be reassured when he saw his Master Jim enter the house again—and not until then!

Jimmie Dale glanced about him up and down the street. The car had gone, and he was well away from the entrance to Marlianne's. The street itself was practically deserted. He nodded quickly, and stepped forward toward a street lamp that was close at hand. As well here as anywhere! There was nothing remarkable in the fact that a man should stand under a street lamp and read a letter—even if he were observed.

He tore the envelope open, and, standing there, leaned in apparent nonchalance against the post—but into the dark eyes had leaped a sudden flash. One word seemed to stand out from all the rest on the written page he held in his hand—"Forrester." He laughed a little in a low, grim way. His intuition had been right again then, and that meant—*what*? If she, the Tocsin, knew, then—his mind was working subconsciously, leaping from premise to a dimly seen, half formed conclusion, while his eyes travelled rapidly over the written lines.

Dear Philanthropic Crook:
    You will have to hurry, Jimmie…. I do not know what may happen…. Forrester… bank cashier at"—yes, he knew all that! But this—what was this? "Money lender…. Abe Suviney…bled him… early days in city bank… fellow clerk's defalcation…. Forrester borrowed the money to cover it and save the other…. Suviney used it as a club for blackmail…. Forrester was trapped… could not extricate himself without inculpating his friend… friend died… Suviney put on the screws… to say anything then was to have it look like a dishonourable method of covering a theft of his own… would ruin his career… original amount four thousand… Forrester has been paying blackmail in the shape of exorbitant interest ever since… Suviney finally demanded six thousand today to be paid at once… this has nothing to do with the bank robbery, but would look black… added evidence…." He read on, his mind seeming to absorb the contents of the letter faster than his eyes could decipher the words. "English Dick… confession forged… organisation widespread… enormously powerful… leadership a mystery… rendezvous that English Dick visits is at Marlopp's… Reddy Mull's room… rear room… leaves cash and securities there under loose board, right-hand corner from door… twenty thousand cash tonight….

Jimmie Dale was walking on down the street, his fingers picking and tearing the sheets of paper in his hand into minute fragments. There was a sort of cold, unemotional, unnatural calm upon him. It was all here, all, the Tocsin had—no, not all! She had not known of the last act in the brutal drama, for her letter had been written prior to that. She had not known that there was—*murder*. But apart from that, to the last detail, in all its hideous, relentless craft, the whole plot was clear. There was no need to go to old Kronische now, no need to assume the role of Larry the Bat. The question was answered—the confession *was* a forgery—the evidence, not of suicide, but of murder, that he, Jimmie Dale, had left behind him in that room, was the evidence of fact.

He walked on—rapidly now—heading over in the direction of the Bowery. There had been neither ink nor pen upon the desk where he had found the confession, nor had there been a fountain pen in Forrester's pocket when he had searched the other! He laughed out a little harshly. A strange oversight on someone's part if there had been foul play—so strange that he had hesitated to believe it possible! And so it had been—one chance in ten, for there was nothing to have prevented Forrester from having written the note elsewhere than in his own room. But if Forrester had written it, he must of necessity have written it very recently, certainly *after* he had telephoned, that is, within an hour; whereas, if it had been written by someone else and brought there, if it was forged, if it was murder and not suicide, the note must have taken long and painstaking effort to prepare beforehand. That was the question that old Kronische, the chemist, was to have answered, a question that was very much in the cunning old fox's line—did the condition of the ink show that the note had been written within the hour? It was a very simple question for old Kronische, the man would have answered it instantly, for even to him, Jimmie Dale, the writing had not looked *fresh*. But there was no need of old Kronische now! And he, Jimmie Dale, understood now, too, the reason for Forrester's appeal over the telephone. In some way Forrester, without going to the bank itself, had learned that the bank examiners had suddenly put in an appearance, had either discovered or deduced that something was wrong, and had realised that should Suviney's demand for money, or Suviney's blackmailing story become known, it would appear as damning evidence of a past record looming up to point suspicion toward him now. That was what he had meant by saying he needed financial help.

Jimmie Dale slipped suddenly into a lane, edged along the wall of the tenement that made the corner, pushed aside a loose board in the fence, passed into the little courtyard beyond, and, still hugging the shadows of the building, opened a narrow French window, and stepped through into a room. He was in the Sanctuary.

CHAPTER 18

ALIAS ENGLISH DICK

But Jimmie Dale lost no time in the Sanctuary. In the darkness he crossed the room, and from behind the movable section of the baseboard possessed himself of a pocket flashlight, and a small, but extremely serviceable, steel jimmy—and in a moment more was back in the lane, and from the lane again was heading still deeper into the heart of the East Side.

English Dick! A twisted smile crossed his lips. Well as he knew the underworld and its sordid citizenship, he might be forgiven for not knowing English Dick. The man's reputation had reached into every corner of the Bad Lands, it was true; but it had not been known that the man himself was on this side of the water. And that the secret had been kept spoke with grim and deadly significance for the power and cunning of the master brain to which the Tocsin had referred, for English Dick was known as the most famous forger in Europe, the best in his line, and as such, from afar, was worshipped as a demi-god by the underworld of New York.

Block after block of dark, ill-lighted streets Jimmie Dale traversed, until, perhaps fifteen minutes after he had left the Sanctuary, he swerved suddenly for the second time that night into a lane. He might not have known English Dick, but he knew Reddy Mull, and he knew Marloff's! Reddy Mull was a gangster, a gunman pure and simple, whose services were at the call of the highest bidder; and Marlopp's was a pool and billiard hall—to the uninitiated. Marlopp's, however, if one had ears well trained enough to hear, resounded to the click of ivory that was not the click of pool and billiard balls! Upstairs, if one could get upstairs, a gambling hell supplanted the billiard hall below. It was an unsavoury place, the resort of crooks, some of whom lived there—amongst them, Reddy Mull.

Jimmie Dale, close against the fence, and halfway down the lane now, paused and looked about him, straining his eyes through the blackness—then with a lithe spring he caught the top of the fence, swung himself over, and dropped to the ground on the other side. The rear of a row of low buildings now loomed up before him across a narrow yard. Window lights showed here and there from the houses on either side; and from the upper windows of the house directly in front of him faint threads of light filtered out into the darkness through the cracks of closed shutters, but the lower part of the house was in blackness.

He crept forward silently across the yard. There was a back entrance, but it led to the basement—Jimmie Dale's immediate attention was directed to the rear window, the window of one Reddy Mull's room. And here, crouched beneath it, Jimmie Dale listened. From the front of the establishment came muffled sounds from the pool and billiard hall; there was nothing else.

The window was above the level of his head, but still easily within reach. He tested it, found it locked—and the steel jimmy crept in under the sash. A moment passed, there was a faint, almost indistinguishable creak; and then Jimmie Dale, drawing himself up with the agility of a cat, had slipped through, and was standing, listening again, inside the room.

The sounds from the pool room were louder, more distinct now, even rising once into a shout of boisterous hilarity; but there was no other sound. The round, white ray of Jimmie Dale's flashlight circled the room suddenly, inquisitively—and went out. It was a bare, squalid place, dirty, filthy, disreputable. There was a bed, unmade, a table, a few chairs, a greasy, thread-bare carpet on the floor—nothing else, save that his eyes had noted that the electric-light switch was on the wall beside the jamb of the door.

The flashlight winked again—and again went out. Jimmie Dale slipped his mask over his face, and moved forward toward the wall.

"Under loose board, right-hand corner from door," murmured Jimmie Dale. He was kneeling on the floor now. "Yes, here it was!" His flashlight was boring down into a little excavation beneath the piece of flooring he had removed. He stared into this for a moment, his lips twitching grimly; then, with a whimsical shrug of his shoulders, he replaced the board, and stood up. He had found the hiding place without any trouble—but he had found it *empty*. "I guess," said Jimmie Dale, with a mirthless smile, "that there's a good deal of the bank's property at large—temporarily!"

There was a chair by the wall close to the door, he had noticed. He moved over, and sat down—but, instead of his flashlight, his automatic was in his hand now. There was the chance, of course, that English Dick had already been here with that twenty thousand from the bank, and in that case, as wit-ness the empty hiding place, Reddy Mull had already passed it on; but it was much more likely that neither one of the two had yet arrived. Which one would come first then—English Dick, or Reddy Mull? If it were Reddy Mull it would be unfortunate—for Reddy Mull. His, Jimmie Dale's, immediate business was with English Dick, and he was quite content to leave Reddy Mull to the later ministrations of the police.

Jimmie Dale's fingers tested the mechanism of his automatic in the dark-ness. Whose was the master brain behind all this? This crime tonight bore glaring evidence to the work of some far-flung, intricate and powerful organ-isation—the Tocsin was indubitably right in that. Was this the first concrete expression he had had of that undercurrent he had sensed of late as permeat-ing the underworld, that he had sensed was reaching out as one of its objects for *him* and that—

He came suddenly without a sound to his feet, and pressed back close against the wall, his body rigid and thrown forward like one poised to spring. There was a footstep outside the door, the rasp of a key in the lock, then a faint, murky path of light as the door opened, and a man stepped forward over the threshold. The key was inserted with another rasping sound in the inner side of the lock, the door closed, the key turned and was withdrawn, thrust evidently into its possessor's pocket—and then Jimmie Dale, silently, in a lightning flash, was upon the other, his hand at the man's throat, the cold, round muzzle of his automatic against the other's face. There was a choked cry, the thud as of something dropping on the floor—and then Jimmie Dale spoke.

"Put your hands up over your head!" he breathed grimly—and, as the other obeyed, his own hand fell away from the man's throat, and in a quick, deft sweep over the other's clothing located the bulge of a revolver, and whipped it from the man's pocket. He pushed the man with his automatic's muzzle back against the wall, closer to the electric-light switch. Was it Reddy Mull—or English Dick? And then Jimmie Dale laughed low, unpleasantly, as he switched on the light. He was staring into a face that was white and colourless—the face of a man with a heavy black moustache, and whose slouch hat was jammed far down over his eyes. The process of elimination made it very simple—it was English Dick.

The man blinked, and wet his lips with his tongue, and at sight of Jimmie Dale's mask, perhaps because it suggested a community of interest, tried to force a smirk.

"What's—what's the game?" he stammered.

"This—to begin with!" said Jimmie Dale grimly—and, stooping, picked up from the floor a small black satchel, the object that English Dick had dropped on entering the room. "Go over to that table!" ordered Jimmie Dale curtly.

The man obeyed.

"Sit down!" Jimmie Dale was clipping off his words in cold menace.

Again the man obeyed.

Jimmie Dale, his back to the door as he faced the other across the table, snapped open the bag. It was full to the top with banknotes and securities. Under his mask his lips curled in a hard, forbidding smile. He took from his pocket the package of the bank's securities he had found in the drawer of Forrester's desk, and laid it in silence on the table beside the satchel; beside this again, still in silence, he placed the bottle that had contained the hydrocyanic acid, and—after an instant's pause—spread out the sheet of note paper bearing Forrester's forged signature.

The man's face, white before, had gone a livid gray.

"W-what do you want?" he whispered.

"I want you to write another confession." There was a deadly monotony in Jimmie Dale's voice, as he tapped the paper with the muzzle of his automatic. "This one is out of date."

"I don't know what you mean," faltered English Dick. "So help me, honest to God, I don't!"

"Don't you!" There was a curious drawl in Jimmie Dale's voice—and then in a flash his free hand swept across the table, jerked away the other's moustache, and pushed the slouch hat up from the man's eyes. "I mean that the game is up—*Dryden*."

There was a low cry; and the man, with working lips, shrank back in his chair.

"You cur!" The words were coming fast and hot from Jimmie Dale's lips now. "English Dick, alias Dryden, the bank teller! So, you don't know what I mean! Listen, then, and I'll tell you! Six months ago you got a position in the bank. Since then you've forged names right and left on securities, falsified the books, and stolen cash and securities. Day by day, working in with your gang, you've brought the loot here, coming in disguise of course, as you've come tonight, for it wouldn't do for 'Dryden' to be seen in this neighbourhood! And you turned the loot over to Reddy Mull—by leaving it, if he didn't happen to be around, under that loose board there in the corner."

"My God!" The man's face was ghastly. "Who—who are you?"

"Today," went on Jimmie Dale, as though he had not heard the other, "you came to the climax of the plan you had been working on for those six months—the bank was wrecked—and what little there was left you took"—he jerked his hand toward the open satchel—"replacing it at the last moment with previously prepared dummy packages. And you took it, you cur"—Jimmie Dale's voice choked suddenly—"not only at the expense of a man's life, but of his good name and reputation. You might have known, I do not know whether you did or not, that Forrester had some private trouble with a money lender, but I do not imagine that had anything to do with your having selected Forrester's bank. Your object was to exploit a small bank where, with only one man from whom to hide your work, you could loot it thoroughly; and a forged confession clever enough to deceive anyone in its handwriting and signature, and the man found dead from a dose of prussic acid, the empty bottle on the floor beside him, needed no other evidence to stamp him as the guilty man."

English Dick was struggling to his feet; his eyes, in a sort of horrible fascination, on Jimmie Dale.

Jimmie Dale, pushed him savagely back into his seat. "Yes—you cur!" he said again. "You got your first fright when you found those evidences of suicide were gone—you even lost your nerve a little in your bluff with the bank examiners—and you hurried here the moment you could get away from the preliminary police investigation that followed—I was even afraid you might get here a little sooner than you did. Shall I give you the details of this afternoon and tonight? The plant was ready. You had sent for the bank examiners. You had already prepared the forged confession, and had a small package of securities ready. Forrester had gone to New York. You turned over the confession and the package of securities to your accomplice, or accomplices, to be left in Forrester's room. I imagine that you telephoned, or sent a message, to New York to Forrester telling him that the bank examiners were in the bank, that there was something the matter, and for him to go to his rooms, and, say, meet you there before going to the bank. Your accomplice, for you established an alibi by remaining with the bank examiners, stole in after him, or even in the dark hallway stunned him with a black-jack, then forced the poison down his throat, laid him on the floor, placed the empty bottle beside him, and left the confession on the desk. The plan was very cunningly worked out. The bruise on Forrester's head was most obviously accounted for—his head had struck, of course, against the leg of the couch—he was found lying in that position! It is strange, though, isn't it, how sometimes the most cunning of plans go astray in the simplest and yet the most perverse of ways? Who, under the circumstances, would have thought of it! Your accomplice had simply to place a document already prepared upon the desk. Even you did not think to warn him yourself. It did not enter his head to see if there were pen and ink there with which it might have been written, or, failing that, a fountain pen in Forrester's pocket—and there was neither the one nor the other. That's all—except the name of the man who killed Forrester." Jimmie Dale leaned forward sharply. "Who was it?"

English Dick wet his lips again.

"I—they—they'd kill me like—like a dog if I told," he mumbled.

"*They?*" The monosyllable came curt and hard.

"I don't know," said English Dick. "That's God's truth—I never knew—there's a big gang—none of us know.".

"But you know who worked with you in this." Jimmie Dale was speaking through clenched teeth. "You know who killed Forrester."

"Yes." The man's whisper was scarcely audible.

"Who?"

"Reddy—Reddy Mull."

"Yes," said Jimmie Dale in his grim monotone, "I thought so."

He reached into the satchel where a small package of securities were wrapped up in a sheet of the bank's stationery, removed the sheet of paper, and spread it out before English Dick. "Write it down!" he commanded—and the muzzle of his automatic jerked forward to touch the fountain pen in the other's vest pocket. "Write it—all of it—your own share—Reddy Mull's—the whole story!"

The man's lips seemed to have gone dry again, and again and again his tongue circled them.

"I can't!" he said hoarsely. "I daren't—they'd kill me. And—and if they didn't, it would send me up, and perhaps—perhaps to the chair."

"You take your chances on that"—Jimmie Dale's voice was low and even—"but you take no chances here—for there are none." The automatic in Jimmie Dale's hand edged ominously forward. "It's Forrester's exoneration—or you. Do you understand? And you make your choice—*now*."

For an instant the man's eyes met Jimmie Dale's, then shifted, as though drawn in spite of himself, to the muzzle of Jimmie Dale's automatic; and then his hand reached into his pocket for his pen.

From the pool room in front came an outburst of hand-clapping and applause—there was evidently a match of some kind going on. Jimmie Dale, his eyes on English Dick, as the latter began to write with a sort of feverish haste as though fear and a miserable desire to have done with it spurred him on, picked up the articles from the table, and placed them in the satchel. He waited silently then—and then English Dick pushed the paper toward him.

Jimmie Dale picked it up, and read it. It was all there, all of it—and the signature this time was not forged! He placed the paper in the satchel, and closed the satchel.

English Dick passed his hand across a forehead that beaded with perspiration.

"What are you going to do?" he asked under his breath.

"I'm going to see that this—and you—reaches the hands of the police," said Jimmie Dale tersely. "We'll leave here in a moment—by the window. There's a patrolman who passes the end of the lane once in a while, and I expect, with the aid of a piece of cord and a pocket handkerchief as a gag, that he'll find you there. My method may be a little crude, but I have reasons of my own for not walking into a police station with you. but before we go, there's still that matter of—the men higher up. They needed a clever penman for this job and one who wouldn't be recognised—and they got the best! Who brought you over from England?"

"A friend over there, one of the 'swell ones,' put it up to me," English Dick answered heavily.

"Yes—and here?" prodded Jimmie Dale. "Who got you into the bank here?"

"I don't know." English Dick shook his head. "I reported to a man called Chester. He doped out the story I was to tell, and told me to go to the bank and apply for the job, and that it was already fixed."

"I'd like to meet 'Chester,'" said Jimmie Dale grimly. "Where does he live?"

"I don't know," said English Dick again. "I tell you, I don't know! They're big—my God, they'll get me for this, if the law doesn't! I don't know where he lives—he always came to me. The only one I know is Reddy Mull, and—"

His voice was drowned out in a louder and more prolonged burst of applause from the pool room, which mingled shouts, cries and the thunderous banging of cue butts on the floor.

"A good shot!" said Jimmie Dale, with a grim smile.

"Yes," said English Dick, "a good shot"—but into his voice had crept a new note, a note like one of malicious triumph.

Jimmie Dale's lips set suddenly hard and tight. Yes, he *heard* now—perhaps too late—what the other *saw*. The uproar that had drowned out all other sounds had subsided—*the door behind him had been unlocked and was now opening slowly*.

And then Jimmie Dale, quick as thought is quick, his fingers closed on the satchel, hurled himself around the table and to the floor. There was the roar of a report, a flash of flame, as Reddy Mull, hand thrust in through the partially open doorway, fired—a wild scream, as the shot, meant for him, Jimmie Dale, found another mark directly behind where he had been standing—and English Dick, reeling to his feet, pitched forward over the table, carrying the table with him to the floor. It had taken the time that a watch takes to tick. Came the roar of a report again, as Jimmie Dale fired in turn—at the electric-light bulb a few feet away from him on the wall. There was the tinkle of shattering glass—and darkness. Came shouts, cries, a yell from the door from Reddy Mull, a fusillade of shots from Reddy Mull's revolver, the rush of many feet from the pool room—and Jimmie Dale, in the blackness, dropped silently from the window to the ground.

He gained the street; and, five minutes later, blocks away, he entered the private stall of a Bowery saloon. Here, Jimmie Dale added another paper to the contents of the satchel. The characters printed, and badly formed, spelled out: "With the compliments of…" followed by his seal.

"And I guess," said Jimmie Dale grimly to himself, "that if I slip this to the police, the police will get—Reddy Mull."

CHAPTER 19

THE BEGINNING OF THE END

How far away last night, with Forrester's murder and the sordid denouement in Reddy Mull's room, seemed! How far away even half an hour ago this very night seemed! Just half an hour ago! Then, with no thought but one of dogged perseverance to keep up his quest, with neither hint nor sign that his quest was any nearer the end than it had ever been, he had entered Bristol Bob's, here, in the role of Smarlinghue; and now, as a rift that had opened in the clouds, there had come sudden and amazing joy. It held him now in thrall. It threatened even to make him *forget* that he was for the moment Smarlinghue—forget what, as Smarlinghue, Smarlinghue dare not forget—the role he played.

He leaned forward suddenly and caught up his whisky glass—whose contents had previously and surreptitiously been spilled into the cuspidor on the floor beside his chair. He lifted the glass to his mouth, his head thrown back as though to drain a final, lingering drop, then he thumped the glass down on the table, licked his lips—thin and distorted by "Smarlinghue's" makeup—and wiped them with the sleeve of his threadbare coat.

A man at the next table, well known as the Pippin, young, flashily dressed, his almost effeminate features giving an added touch of viciousness, through incongruity, to his general appearance, twisted his head around and grinned with malicious derision.

Jimmie Dale's fingers searched hungrily now through first one and then another of his ragged pockets, and finally extricated a dime and a nickel.

With these he tapped insistently on the table, until an attendant answered the summons and supplied him with another drink.

He sat back then for a time; now eyeing the liquor, as though greedy for its taste, yet greedy, too, to prolong the anticipation, since from his actions there was apparently no means of further replenishing the supply; now glancing around the smoke-laden room where, on the polished section of the floor in the centre, a score of laughing, shrieking couples whirled and pranced in the unrestrained throes of the underworld's latest dance; now permitting his eyes to rest with a sudden scowl on the man at the next table. He had no concern with the Pippin—nor had the Pippin any concern with him. The man, as he imbibed a number of drinks, simply seemed to find a certain: malevolent amusement in a contemptuous appraisal of his, Jimmie Dale's, person; but the other, in spite of the new, glad exhilaration Jimmie Dale was experiencing, annoyed Jimmie Dale—the blatant expanse of pink shirt cuff, for instance, in order to display the Pippin's diamond-snake links, famous from One end of the underworld to the other, was eminently typical of the man. The cuff links were undoubtedly an object of envy to the society in which the Pippin moved; they were even beautiful cuff links, it was true, oriental in design, never to be mistaken by anyone who had ever seen them, and the stones with which they were set were credited generally in the underworld as being genuine, but—Jimmie Dale was hesitantly lifting his glass again in a miserly sort of way. The Pippin had jerked a cigarette box from his pocket, stuck what was evidently the single cigarette it had contained between his lips; and now, tossing away the box, he pushed back his chair and stood up—but on the floor beneath the table, where it had fluttered unobserved when the cigarette box had been jerked from the pocket, lay a small folded piece of paper.

"If you hang around long enough, Smarly," gibed the Pippin, as he passed by on his way toward the door, "maybe some of the rubber-necks off the gape-wagon will take pity on you and buy you another—the slumming parties are just crazy about broken-down artists!"

"You go chase yourself!" said Smarlinghue politely, through one corner of his twisted mouth.

Jimmie Dale's eyes followed the other. The Pippin, threading his way amongst the tables, gained the door, and passed out into the street. And then Jimmie Dale's eyes reverted to the piece of paper under the adjacent table. It was not at all likely that it was of the slightest importance or significance, and yet—Jimmie Dale stretched out his foot, drew the paper toward him, and, stooping over, picked it up. He unfolded it, and found it to contain several typewritten lines. He frowned in a puzzled way as he read them; then read them over again, and his frown deepened.

Melinoff has the goods. Go the limit if he squeals. Not later than ten-thirty tonight.

Jimmie Dale's eyes lifted and strayed around the noisy, riotous dance hall. Just what exactly did the message mean? The Pippin was a bad actor—literally, as well as metaphorically. The Pippin, if asked, would probably still have styled himself an actor; but, though still young, his career on the stage had ended several years ago rather abruptly—with a year's imprisonment! Jimmie Dale did not recall the details of the particular offence of which the Pippin had been found guilty, save that it had been for theft. It did not, however, matter very much. The Pippin of today as he was known to the underworld, to which strata of society he had immediately gravitated on his release from prison, was all that was of immediate interest. He had associated himself with a gang run by one Steve Barlow, commonly known as the Mole, and under this august patronage and protection had already more than one "job" of the first magnitude to his credit. The Pippin, in a word, was both an ugly and an unpleasant customer.

Jimmie Dale's eyes continued to circuit the seedy dance hall. What was it that the Pippin was to procure from Melinoff, and for which, if necessary, the Pippin was to go "the limit"? Melinoff himself was not without reproach, either! What was the game? Melinoff was an old-clothes and junk dealer, and, as a side line, at times a very profitable side line, had been known to act as a "fence" for stolen goods. He had skirted for years on the ragged edge with the police, and then, caught red-handed at last, had changed his occupation for a more useful one during a somewhat prolonged sojourn in Sing Sing. Affairs after that had not prospered with Melinoff. His wife, honest if her husband was not, and already an old woman, had been hard put to it with the shabby shop and the meagre business she was able to transact; so hard put to it, indeed, that the wonder had been that she had managed to keep the roof over her head. She had died a few months after her husband's release. Melinoff, if he had had no other virtue, had at least loved his wife, and the Melinoff of old, then a sprightly enough man for his years, was no more, and it was a decrepit, stoop-shouldered, dirty and grey-bearded figure that shuffled now around the old-clothes shop, apathetic of "bargains," where before it had been a man whose keenness was matched only by the sort of eager craft and low cunning with which he had conducted his business.

A smile, half grim, half whimsical, flickered across Jimmie Dale's lips. There were strange lives, strange undercurrents, always, ceaselessly, at work here in the underworld, here where the grist from the human mill found its place. Melinoff, the Pippin, each of those whirling figures out there on the floor, each of those men and women whose laughter rose raucously from the tables, or whose whisperings, as heads were lowered and held close together, seemed an unsavoury, vicious thing, had known a strange and tortuous path; yet strangest, most tortuous of them all, was—his own!

His fingers, as he thrust the Pippin's note into the side pocket of his coat, touched the torn fragments of another note, tiny little particles of paper, torn over and over again into fine and minute shreds—the Tocsin's note—the note that seemed suddenly to have changed all his life. It had come as her communications had always come—without bridging the way that lay between them, without furnishing him with a clue through the method employed for their transmission that would avail him anything, or supply him with any means of reaching her. It had been thrust into his hand by a street urchin, as he had entered the door of Bristol Bob's that half an hour before. He had not even questioned the urchin—it would have been useless, futile, barren of results. A hundred previous experiences had at least taught him that! He could surmise about it, though, if he would; and, in view of the contents of the note itself, surmise, in all probability, with fair accuracy. The Tocsin had satisfied herself that he was neither at home nor at the club, and had, therefore, chosen an inconspicuous messenger to search for "Smarlinghue" through the underworld. And there would have been no risk. For the first time in all the years that her letters had been the motive force, the underlying basis of the Gray Seal's acts, it would not, as far as dangerous consequences were concerned, have mattered if the note had gone astray, or had even been read by others. He need not even have torn it up, as he had done through force of habit, for there was no "plan" tonight, no coup to carry through. The note, for the first time, was not a "call to arms;" it was what he had been longing for, always hoping for, yet never permitting himself to build too strongly upon lest he should lay up for himself a store of disappointment too bitter for endurance—it was a note of *hope*. There were just a few lines, a few sentences; and it had contained neither form of address nor signature. To anyone save himself it meant nothing, it had no significance. Snatches of it ran through his mind again:

"...It is the beginning of the end.... The way is clearing... I am very happy tonight, and I wanted to tell you so...."

The end at last! The end of the years of peril; the end of that fear gnawing always at his heart that she might never live to come out into the sunlight again; the end of this dual life he led; the return to a normal existence where surroundings like the present, where the dens and dives of the underworld, the secret rookeries nursing their hell-hatched crimes, the taint and smell of evil, and the reek of soul-filth would be hereafter no more than a memory! To be through with it all, through with it all, and to know her love instead—because she was safe!

He stared about him, and stared with incredulity at his own miserable clothing. Was it true, was it reality—this figure that the underworld knew as Smarlinghue, who sat here, and with dirty fingers played with a whisky glass on the cheap, liquor-spotted table, and out of half-closed, well-simulated drug-laden eyes gazed on those dancing figures out there on the floor to whom the law from cradlehood had been a natural enemy, and to the door of hardly one of whom but lay crimes that ranged from the paltry to the hideous!

Reality! Yes, it was real! God knew the abysmal depths of its reality. Months piled on months there had been of it! Those voices out there that rose in a jangle of ribald mirth were the same voices that, hushed in deadlier menace, had whispered that grim slogan, "Death to the Gray Seal!" through every hidden cranny in the underworld; these men and women here around him were of the same breed as those who only last night had struck down and brutally murdered Forrester, and not content with murder had plotted to rob their victim of his good name as well!

Jimmie Dale's hand clenched suddenly—his mind was off at a tangent, away for the moment from her. Well, they had failed last night in all save murder! Failed—and one of them had already paid the price, and another, in the Tombs awaiting trial, faced the certainty of the death chair in Sing Sing! But those two, Reddy Mull, and English Dick, had been little more than tools. Whose was the hidden master brain behind them, controlling this evil power that struck in the dark; that lately, though unseen, was permeating the underworld with its presence; that intuitively he had felt was reaching out, feeling its way, to grapple with and, if it could, to strangle him the Gray Seal! He had felt the menace, known that it existed, and the slogan ringing always in his ears, the Whispered "Death to the Gray Seal" had taken on a deeper significance, had brought him a more acute and imminent sense of peril than ever before; but it was only last night, for the first time, that he had equally *felt* that he had had any concrete knowledge of, or contact with this new antagonist. And last night, if there had been a challenge he had accepted it, and if there had been no challenge he had at least thrown down the gauntlet himself! If this was actually the criminal organisation that was arrayed against him, the master brain at the head of it would now have a greater incentive than ever to trap and exterminate the Gray Seal, for English Dick lay dead, and Reddy Mull was behind the bars, and twenty thousand dollars in cash that they had schemed for was in the hands of the police—thanks to the Gray Seal! Added incentive! They would move heaven and earth to reach him now! All the trickery, all the hell-born ingenuity that they possessed would be launched against him now, and—Jimmie Dale's face, that had been set and hard, relaxed suddenly. Well, granted all that! What did it matter now? They would but hunt a myth! Between them and himself now there stood the Tocsin's note. "The way is clearing.... I am very happy tonight." She would not have written that unless she were very sure. Tomorrow, perhaps, and Smarlinghue, and the Gray Seal, and Larry the Bat would have passed forever out of existence, and there would be only Jimmie Dale, and *she,* and love—and a phantom left behind in the underworld against whom the underworld and this evil genius of crime might pit their wits to their hearts' content!

There was an uplift upon him, a sense of freedom so great that it seemed actually physical as well as mental. Peril, danger, the strain of the dual life until the nerves were worn raw, the constant anxiety for her safety—all were gone now. "It is the beginning of the end... the way is clearing"—she had written that tonight. And it meant that, refusing, as she had said, to let him come into the shadows again, she had won through—alone. It brought a little, curious pang of disappointment to him that he should share now only in the reward; but the pang was swallowed up in that it brought him a deeper knowledge of her unselfish love, her splendid courage, and—he could find no other word—her wonderfulness.

Jimmie Dale's fingers stole into the side pocket of his coat to play again in a curiously caressing way with the little torn fragments of her note—and touched again the piece of paper that the Pippin had dropped. He took it out mechanically, and read it over once more. One sentence seemed suddenly to have become particularly ominous—"if he squeals go the limit." He knew nothing as to the authorship of those words, but from what he knew of the Pippin there was a certain ugliness to the word "limit" that he did not like. The "limit" with the Pippin might mean—*anything*.

He thrust the paper back into his pocket, and sat for a moment staring musingly at his whisky glass. Well, why not? Before half past ten, the message said; and it was scarcely ten o'clock yet. In view of the Tocsin's note, he had intended returning to the Sanctuary, resuming his own proper character, and, either at the St. James Club, or at his home, wait for further word from her. There was, indeed, nothing else that he could do—and Melinoff's, for that matter, was on the way from Bristol Bob's to the Sanctuary. Yes, why not? If the Pippin was up to any dirty work, or even if the two of them, Melinoff and the Pippin, were in it together, and the word "squeal" implied that Melinoff was to be held strictly up to his full share of some mutual villainy should he show any inclination to waver, it might not be an altogether unfitting exit from the stage if the Gray Seal should make his final bow to the underworld by playing a role in the Pippin's little drama, whatever that drama might prove to be!

Yes, why not! He passed Melinoff's place in any event, and there was no reason why he should remain any longer here in Bristol Bob's. The second glass of whisky followed the first—into the cuspidor. Again the threadbare sleeve was drawn across the thin, distorted lips, and, pushing back his chair, Jimmie Dale rose from the table and made his way out into the street.

CHAPTER 20

THE OLD-CLOTHES SHOP

Ten minutes later, still in the heart of the East Side, Jimmie Dale reached his destination, and paused on the edge of the sidewalk, ostensibly to light a cigarette while he looked tentatively around him, before the entrance to a courtyard that ran in behind a row of cheap and shabby tenements. He shook his head, as he tossed the match away. It was still early; there were too many people about, to say nothing of the group of half-naked children playing in the gutter under the street lamp in front of the courtyard entrance, and "Smarlinghue" was far too well known a character in that section of the Bad Lands to warrant him in taking any chances. If anything was wrong in Melinoff's dingy little place behind there, if anything had transpired, or was about to transpire that would ultimately, say, invite the attention of the police, it might prove extremely awkward—for Smarlinghue—should it be remembered that he had entered there! There was a better way—a much better way, and one that was exceedingly simple. It would hardly occasion any comment, even if he were noticed, if he entered one of the *tenements*, where, with probably a dozen families living in as many rooms, one could come and go at all hours without question or hindrance.

He moved slowly along, and, out of the radius of the street lamp now and away from the children, paused again, this time before the last tenement in the row that the front of the courtyard in the rear. For the moment there were no pedestrians in the immediate neighbourhood, and Jimmie Dale, stepping through the tenement doorway, gained the narrow, unlighted hall within. He stopped here, hugged close against the wall, to listen, and, hearing or seeing nothing to disturb him, moved forward again, silently, without a sound, along the hall. There must be, he knew, a rear exit to the courtyard behind. Yes—here it was! He had halted again, this time before a door. He tried it, found it unlocked, opened it, stepped outside, and closed the door behind him.

It was dark out here in the courtyard, and objects were only faintly discernible; but there were few localities in that neighbourhood with which Jimmie Dale, either as Smarlinghue, or in the old days as Larry the Bat, was not intimately acquainted. To call it a courtyard hardly described the place. It was more an open backyard common to the row of tenements, and rather narrow and confined in space at that. It was dirty, cluttered with rubbish, and across it, facing the rear of the tenements, was a small building that many years ago had been, possibly, a stable or an outhouse belonging to some private and no doubt pretentious dwelling, which long since now, with the progress northward of the city, had been supplanted by the crowded, poverty-stricken, and anything but pretentious tenements. This outhouse had been to a certain extent remodelled, and to a certain extent made habitable, and as long as anyone could remember Melinoff with his old-clothes shop had been its tenant.

Jimmie Dale began to make his way cautiously across the yard, wary of the tin cans and general rubbish which an inadvertent step might metamorphose most effectively into a decidedly undesirable advertisement of his presence. There was no light that he could see in Melinoff's at all; and he frowned now in a puzzled way. Had the Pippin been and gone; or was he,

Jimmie Dale, ahead of the Pippin? The Pippin would have had ample time, of course, to get here, for he, Jimmie Dale, had probably remained in Bristol Bob's a good half hour after the Pippin had left. In that case, then, Melinoff must have gone away with the Pippin again—that would account for there being no light. But, on the other hand, if the Pippin had not yet arrived, and Melinoff *expected* the visit, it was most curious that the place was in darkness!

And then Jimmie Dale smiled a little mockingly at himself. His deductions would perhaps have been of infinitely more value if he had first waited to make sure of the premise on which they were based! As a matter of fact, there *was* a light! He had reached the front of the little place, and peering cautiously through the window could make out, across the black interior, a thread of light that came through the crack of a closed door, and from what was, evidently, another room in the rear.

Jimmie Dale's fingers closed on the heavy, cumbersome, old-fashioned door latch, pressed it down noiselessly, and exerted a little tentative pressure on the door itself. It was locked. A minute passed in absolute silence, as a little steel instrument was inserted in the lock—and then the door swung inward and was dosed again, and Jimmie Dale, rigid and motionless, stood inside.

He was listening now for some sound, the sound of voices, or the sound of movement from that lighted room. There was nothing. Jimmie Dale's lips tightened suddenly. It was very curious! There was an "upstairs" to the place, such as it was, but if Melinoff was up there alone, or with the Pippin, they were up there in the dark unless they were in the rear upstairs room; in which case they could not, in view of the ramshackle nature of the building, have made the slightest movement without making themselves heard from where he stood.

From his pocket Jimmie Dale produced a flashlight. The ray played once, as though with diffident curiosity, about him, swept once more in a circuit around the room, swiftly, in an almost startled way this time—and there was darkness again. And, instead of the flashlight, Jimmie Dale's automatic was in his hand now, and he was moving quickly and silently forward toward that thread of light and the closed door leading into the rear room.

Around him everything was in disorder; not the disorder habitual to such a place where odds and ends of the heterogeneous accumulation of Melinoff's stock in trade might be expected to be deposited wherever convenience and not system dictated, but a disorder that seemed to hold within itself something of ominous promise. Old clothes, for instance, that might at least have been expected, even with the most profound carelessness and indifference, to have received better treatment, were strewn and scattered about the floor in all directions.

And now Jimmie Dale stood still again. There was a sound at last; but a sound that he could not immediately define. It came from the room beyond—like a dull, muffled thud mingling with a low, long-drawn gasp. It was repeated—and then, unmistakably, there came a moan.

In a flash now, Jimmie Dale, his automatic thrust forward, was at the door. He stooped with his eye to the keyhole; and the next instant, his face hard and tense, he flung the door open, and jumped forward into the room.

Those words of the Pippin's note seemed to be searing through his brain in letters of fire—"go the limit—go the limit." There was no need to speculate longer on their meaning; they meant—*murder*. On the floor, a dark ugly, crimson pool beside him, lay Melinoff, the old-clothes dealer. And as Jimmie Dale sprang to the other's side, there came again that curious muffled thud—as the old man weakly lifted his head a few inches from the floor only to have it fall limply back again. The man was nearly gone—it needed no experienced eye to tell that. Melinoff's face was grayish in its pallor, and his eyes, open, seemed to have lost their lustre; but as Jimmie Dale knelt and lifted the man's shoulders and supported the other's head upon his knee, the light in the old-clothes dealer's black eyes seemed suddenly to return and to glow with a strange, passionate, eager fire, as they fixed on Jimmie Dale's face. Melinoff's lips moved. Jimmie Dale bent his head to Catch the words that were almost inaudible.

"The—the Pippin. Here"—the old man's hand struggled toward his side where a dark crimson blotch had soaked his shirt—"here—he—he stabbed me—because—because—" The voice failed and died away, and the man's head fell back on Jimmie Dale's arm.

Jimmie Dale raised the other's head gently again.

"Yes!" he said quickly, striving to rouse the other. "Yes; go on! I understand. The Pippin stabbed you. Because—what? Go on, Melinoff! Go on! I am listening."

The eyes opened once more—but the light was dying out of them, and they were filming now. And then suddenly the man forced himself forward into a sitting posture, and his voice rang wildly through the room:

"It is a lie! A lie! I played square—do you hear! Old Melinoff played square! I did not understand at first—but I did not forget. I remembered. Old Melinoff would never forget—never forget—never for—"

A tremor ran through the old man's form, the voice was stilled—it was the end.

For a moment, his lips tight and set, Jimmie Dale held the other there in his arms, as he stared at a little object on the floor where Melinoff had been lying, and that previously had been hidden beneath the other's body—an object that glittered and sparkled now as the light caught it. There had even been then, it seemed, no need for Melinoff's dying accusation—the evidence of the Pippin's guilt would have been plain enough to the first person who found old Melinoff and moved the old man's body. For himself, Jimmie Dale, the Pippin's note, since it had actuated him in coming here, would have been enough to have fixed the guilt in his mind where it belonged; but the police, for instance, would not have been so well informed! The police, however, would now have all, and more than all the evidence they required. That little thing that glittered there was one of the Pippin's notorious diamond-snake cuff links.

Jimmie Dale did not disturb it. He laid old Melinoff back on the floor, and the old man's body covered the cuff link again as it had done before. He stood up then, and looked around him. The room seemed to have been used for no one particular purpose. It was partitioned off from the shop proper, it was true; but, equally, it appeared to have been used as a sort of overflow for the shop's stock in trade. Here, as in front, clothing of all descriptions littered the floor; and also there were signs that a violent struggle had taken place. The room, which had obviously served, apart from being a store-room, as kitchen, dining room, and, in fact, for everything save a bedroom, was in a state of chaos—chairs were upset, a table stood up-ended against the wall, aid broken crockery was strewn everywhere.

At the rear of the room was another door. Jimmie Dale reached up, turned off the gas-jet, crossed to the door, found it unlocked, opened it a few inches, and looked out. It gave on the rear of the courtyard, and in the darkness he could just make out a high fence that bordered the adjoining property. It was presumably the way by which the Pippin had made his escape, since he, Jimmie Dale, had found the front door locked.

He closed the door again, relighted the gas, and, moving swiftly now, passed through into the shop and locked the front door. Then, returning to the upper end of the shop close to the connecting door, which he closed until it was just ajar, Jimmie Dale slipped a black silk mask over his face, seated himself on a box of some sort that he found at hand, and, save that his fingers mechanically tested the automatic in his hand, remained motionless, his eyes fixed on the rear door across the lighted room in which old Melinoff lay.

It was dark here and silent, except that from out across the courtyard came faintly now and then the voices of the children at play in the gutters, and except that a faint glow stole timidly out from the slightly opened door only to merge almost immediately with the surrounding blackness. The tight lips had curved downward at the corners of his mouth into a grim, merciless droop; and into the dark, steady eyes there had come a smouldering fire. It was a brutal, cowardly thing that had been done there in that room, and the Pippin had finished his work and gone—but it was not at all unlikely that the Pippin would be back!

The sharp lines at the corners of Jimmie Dale's mouth grew a little more pronounced. Nor should the Pippin be long in returning! A man could not very well lose a cuff link and be unaware of that fact for any extended length of time. And that cuff link was damning, irrefutable, incontrovertible evidence, exactly the evidence the police required to convict the guilty man! Yes, undoubtedly, the Pippin would be back—and at any moment now. Figuring that the Pippin had left Bristol Bob's half an hour before he, Jimmie Dale, had started out, and allowing, say, twenty minutes for the struggle and subsequent murder here, the Pippin could only have been gone a matter of some ten minutes. In the excitement, and probably a run through lanes and alleyways, it was quite possible that the Pippin would not have noticed his loss in that length of time; but he could not, with a loose cuff, and especially when it was usually fastened by so highly prized a link, have remained much longer than that in ignorance of his loss.

Jimmie Dale smiled grimly now in the darkness. It was almost analogous to Meighan's waiting for the return of the Magpie, except that he, Jimmie Dale, had neither the desire nor the intention of usurping the functions of the police. "Smarlinghue," for very obvious reasons, could neither appear nor bear witness in the case; he could take no chances of the discovery being made that "Smarlinghue" was but a *character* that cloaked Jimmie Dale and the Gray Seal—and, above all, he could take no chances tonight when at last he was on the threshold of the return to his old normal life again! But he had, nevertheless, no intention of permitting the Pippin to elude the law, or to escape the consequences of the act to which that mute form lying in there on the crimsoned floor bore hideous testimony. The cuff link, obviously loosened and dropped unnoticed on the floor during the struggle, would not only connect the Pippin with the crime, but would convict him of it as well; he, Jimmie Dale, therefore, did not propose to allow the Pippin to return and remove that evidence—that was all. It should not be very difficult to prevent it; nor should it even necessitate his showing himself to the Pippin. A shot, for instance, fired at the floor, as the Pippin stole in through that rear door again should be enough to send the man flying back for shelter to the recesses of the underworld. The Pippin's nerves, as he crept back to the scene of his crime, would be badly frayed and unstrung, unless he was a man lacking wholly in imagination, which the Pippin, once having been an actor, inherently could not be; and, coupled with this, prompting the Pippin to run at once for cover, would be the fact that he could not by any means be certain that the link had been lost there in the room itself, since it might equally have, been forced loose during his escape, say, for instance, while climbing the series of backyard fences that would have confronted him from the moment he left Melinoff's rear door—providing always, of course, that the Pippin, as it seemed logical and as the evidence seemed to indicate, *had* made his escape in that manner.

The minutes passed; at first quickly enough, and then they began to drag heavily. Jimmie Dale's mind was back now on old Melinoff. What had the man meant by his feverish, eager, pitiful insistence that he had not forgotten, that he had remembered, that he could never forget, and that he had not understood at first? The answer to that question would supply the motive for the Pippin's crime, and for half an hour, sitting there in the darkness, Jimmie Dale pondered the question, but the answer would not come. There were theories without number that he could formulate; but theories at best were indefinite. What had Melinoff meant by saying he had played square? Was it some previous criminal undertaking between himself and the Pippin, in which the Pippin believed himself to have been betrayed by Melinoff, while Melinoff, on the other hand, protested that—and then Jimmie Dale shrugged his shoulders impatiently. What was the use of speculation? The vital matter of the moment was the Pippin's delay in returning for that cuff link!

Another fifteen minutes passed, and still another—and then Jimmie Dale restored his mask to his pocket, rose from his seat, and made his way to the front door of the shop. He had waited there a full hour and over now, his only purpose had been to prevent the removal of the evidence of the Pippin's guilt by the Pippin, and logic told him it was useless to wait longer. It was only fair to assume that the Pippin would have discovered his loss within a reasonably short time after leaving Melinoff's; and, granting that, it was absolutely certain that the Pippin, if he were coming back at all, would have come without an instant's delay if he believed that his life hung on the recovery of his property. He had not come, and therefore, conversely, the Pippin must have weighed the chances and concluded that the risk attendant on his return to the scene of his crime was greater than the risk he ran of the cuff link having been lost in that exact spot. Nor was the Pippin's presumed reasoning entirely faulty—from the Pippin's standpoint. It was obvious that he did not know *where* he had lost the link; it was only a *chance* that he had lost it on the actual scene of the crime; and even if he had lost it there, and even if he returned, it was only a *chance* that he would be able to find it again—and against this was the very grave risk and danger of returning to Melinoff's after having once got safely away. But whatever the Pippin's reasoning might have been, the one morally certain fact remained—every minute of delay increased the risk that the cuff link would be found by someone else, and if the Pippin were coming back at all he would have been back long before this.

Jimmie Dale closed the door of the old-clothes shop behind him, crossed the yard, and using the back door of the tenement again; gained the street. Well, he was quite satisfied! The hour he had spent there mattered little. He had desired only one thing—that the evidence of the Pippin's guilt should not be disturbed. And for the rest—he smiled whimsically as he started briskly along the street—there was Carruthers, of the *Morning News-Argus,* who, if, in the old days, he had been one of the most dogged and relentless in his efforts to run the Gray Seal to earth, was at the same time, though without knowing it—Jimmie Dale's smile broadened—the Gray Seal's most intimate friend and old college pal! If the Pippin was just as surely brought to book that way, why do old Carruthers and his sheet out of a "scoop"!

Jimmie Dale made his way rapidly now over to the Bowery, and here headed in an uptown direction. Two blocks further along, however, on the corner occupied by the Crescent saloon, he turned into the cross street, and passed in through the saloon's side entrance. The Crescent saloon, as he had previously more than once had occasion to remark, was nothing if not thoughtful of the peculiar needs of its somewhat questionable class of patrons. Around the corner of the little passageway, just as it turned into a small lounging room before the barroom proper was reached, was a telephone booth whose privacy could scarcely be improved upon. He opened the door of the booth, stepped inside, and closed the door carefully and tightly behind him. The *Argus* being a morning paper, Carruthers, except on very rare occasions, was always to be found at his office until late into the night; but Jimmie Dale, having deposited his coin in the slot, was rewarded with the information that he had met with one of those "rare occasions." Carruthers was at his home on Long Island, and had not been at the office at all that day. Jimmie Dale shrugged his shoulders, as he found and gave the Long Island number. It did not matter very much; it was simply the difference in time, amounting to, say, the half hour or so that it would take Carruthers to get back to the city and act.

The phone was answered.

"Mr. Carruthers, if you please...yes, personally," said Jimmie Dale pleasantly.

There was a moment's wait, then Jimmie Dale spoke again—his voice still pleasant, but changed in pitch and register to a bass that was far from Jimmie Dale's, though one that Carruthers might possibly remember!

"Mr. Carruthers?.... Good evening, Mr. Carruthers—this is the Gray Seal speaking, and I—" A receptive smile stole suddenly across Jimmie Dale's lips—Carruthers, to put it mildly, was impulsive. "The Gray Seal—yes. I can hear *you* perfectly.... What?... No, it is not a hoax!"—Jimmie Dale's voice had sharpened perceptibly—"I called you once before, you will perhaps remember though it is a very long time ago, in reference to a certain diamond necklace and a—you will pardon the term—gentleman by the name of Markel.... Ah, you recognise the Gray Seal's voice now, do you!... No, don't apologise.... I thought perhaps you might be interested in the possibility of another scoop.... Yes, quite so!... I would suggest then that you get the police to accompany you to the back room of Melinoff's, the old-clothes dealer's shop.... Yes, I thought you might know the place. Perhaps, too, you know of a man who is commonly called the Pippin?... No? Well, no matter. The police do! You'll find the evidence under Melinoff's body.... I beg your pardon?... Yes—murder.... What?... It is a cuff link, the Pippin's cuff link, that was dropped in the struggle.... What?... No, I do not know why; I have told you all I know. There is nothing more, Mr. Carruthers—except that I should advise you to work as quickly as possible, as otherwise someone may stumble on the crime before you do. Good-night, Mr. Carruthers."

Carruthers was still talking, wildly, excitedly. Jimmie Dale calmly hung up the receiver, left the telephone booth, and went out to the street again—by the side entrance. If Carruthers made inquiry of central as to where the call had come from, the reply that it was from the Crescent saloon would in no way serve Carruthers, or anyone else. No one, even in the Crescent saloon, would be able to furnish any information as to who had telephoned. It was, therefore, in a word, up to Carruthers now; the Pippin would be brought to account; and as far as he, Jimmie Dale, was concerned, his connection with the affair was at an end.

Jimmie Dale walked quickly along, turning from one street into another. Here and there, in front of various resorts, and on the corners, he passed little groups of men engaged in bated, low-toned conversation. Ordinarily this would have interested Jimmie Dale, for the groups were composed, not of ordinary citizens, but of the dregs and scum of the underworld, and it was evident that something quite out of the usual run of things had suddenly seized upon the Bad Lands as a subject for gossip. But it was already long after eleven o'clock, and tonight, with Melinoff's murder disposed of now, he was through, he hoped, with the underworld forever. He was anxious only to reach the Sanctuary without any further delay, and, thereafter, equally without further loss of time, to get to his home or to the club, where at any moment he might expect to hear from the Tocsin, and where, most important of all, she would bare no difficulty in communicating instantly with him.

He turned the corner of the street on which the Sanctuary was situated—and halted abruptly. A man coming rapidly from the other direction had grabbed his arm.

"'Ello, Smarly!" greeted the other. "Heard de news?"

Jimmie Dale, with the top of his tongue, shifted the half burnt section of the cigarette that was hanging from his upper lip to the opposite corner of his mouth, as he looked at the other. It was the Wowzer, dip and pick-pocket, the erstwhile pal of one Dago Jim, who, on a certain night, also of the very long ago, that Jimmie Dale had very good cause to remember, had killed Dago Jim in a certain infamous dive. Well, if he, Jimmie Dale, was, after all, to learn the cause of the excitement that seemed suddenly to have possessed the underworld, he could at least have asked for no better or more thoroughly posted informant than the Wowzer. And now his curiosity was aroused. For an instant the idea that it might be Melinoff's murder flashed across his mind; but he dismissed that idea at once. Murder was too trite a thing in the underworld to cause any widespread commotion!

"Hello, Wowzer!" he returned, as he shook his head. "No, I ain't heard anything."

"Youse can take it from me den," said the Wowzer, "dat dere's something doin'! Dey got her!"

"Got who?" enquired Jimmie Dale in a puzzled way.

The Wowzer leaned forward secretively.

"Silver Mag!" he said.

It seemed to Jimmie Dale as though the clutch of an icy hand was suddenly at his heart, as though the ground beneath his feet had grown suddenly unstable and that the Wowzer's face, close to his own, was swirling around and around in swift and endless gyrations—but he was conscious, too, that he was master of himself. The muscles of his face twitched—but it was to express incredulity. His tongue carried the cigarette butt languidly back to the other corner of his mouth.

"Aw, go on!" said Jimmie Dale. "Try it on somebody else! Silver Mag croaked out the night they had that fire down there in the old tenement."

"Yes, she did—nix!" scoffed the Wowzer, with a short laugh. "De same way dat blasted snitch of a Gray Seal did—eh? Say, Smarly, I'm handin' it to youse straight. Dey caught her snoopin' around one of de en-trays into Foo Sen's half an hour ago. Say, de whole mob all de way up de line's been tipped off. I'm givin' youse de real thing. Youse must have been asleep somewhere, or youse'd have been wise before."

"Sure—I believe you!" said Jimmie Dale earnestly. "Who caught her, Wowzer?"

"De Mole," replied the Wowzer. "An' he's got her now over in his layout."

It was a moment before Jimmie Dale spoke. There seemed to be a horrible, ghastly dryness in his mouth; there seemed to well up from his soul and overwhelm him a world of mocking and sardonic irony. The Mole! The Mole was the leader of the gang with which the Pippin was allied; it was at the Mole's place that the Pippin usually lived; it was at the Mole's place that the police would first institute their search for the Pippin—and five minutes ago, through Carruthers, he had unleashed the police! The Wowzer's face seemed to be swirling around and around in front of him again. To get away—and *think*! He could have groaned, cried out aloud!

"Say, thanks, Wowzer, for piping me off!" said Jimmie Dale effusively.

"Oh, dat's all right," responded the Wowzer graciously. "Only keep it under yer hat except wid de crowd. De bulls ain't on, an' de Mole saw her first—see? Dere ain't goin' to be no buttin' in till she gets hers! An' de word's out not to do any pushin' an' crowdin' around de Mole's fer front seats, 'cause den de bulls 'd get wise—savvy? Just leave it to de Mole—get me?"

"Sure—I get you," said Jimmie Dale. "Well, so long, Wowzer—and thanks again."

"S'long, Smarly," replied the Wowzer.

CHAPTER 21
SILVER MAG

It was not far to the Sanctuary, only halfway down the short block to the corner of the lane; but it seemed a distance interminable to Jimmie Dale. His brain was whirling in a chaotic turmoil; and the turmoil seemed barbed with a horrible fear that robbed him for the moment of his mental poise. It was as a man dazed, unconscious of the physical process by which he had arrived there, that he found himself standing in the Sanctuary, leaning like a man spent with effort against the door which, mechanically, he had closed behind him.

In hideous, baleful, jeering reiteration those words which she had written were racing through his brain. "I am very happy tonight, and I wanted to tell you so... happy tonight... happy tonight... happy tonight." Happy tonight—what depth of irony! Happy tonight—and they had caught her—as the "way was clearing"—with the end of peril, with the end of the miserable, hunted existence she had been forced to lead just in sight! Silver Mag—the Tocsin! And he—he, who, too, had been happy tonight, he, who had known that mighty uplift upon him, he, who had dreamed that the morrow might bring life and love and sunshine—he was facing now a blackness of despair that he had never known before. Unwittingly, if such danger as she was in *could* be made the greater, he had made it so. If the underworld was the implacable enemy of Silver Mag, because Silver Mag was known as the ally in the old days of Larry the Bat, and known, therefore, as the ally of the Gray Seal; so, for the same reason exactly, the police were her implacable enemy! And, whether she fell into the hands of one or the other, the end ultimately differed only in the method by which her death would be accomplished; it was murder at the hands of the Mole and his gang; it was the death chair in Sing Sing as an accomplice of the Gray Seal at the hands of the police. "Death to the Gray Seal!"—that was the slogan of the underworld. "The Gray Seal dead or alive—but the Gray Seal"—that was the fiat of the police. And both held good for Silver Mag! With the Mole alone there might have been a chance—but now, he had launched the police as well against her, had sent them to the Mole's, for that was the first place they would raid in their hunt for the Pippin.

The sweat beads started out on Jimmie Dale's forehead. She had discarded the character of "Silver Mag" that night in the tenement fire when he had discarded the character of "Larry the Bat"—and "Silver Mag" had never been seen again until tonight. But he, Jimmie Dale, *had* appeared since then as Larry the Bat—and for some reason tonight she must have found it necessary, in working out her plans to their consummation no doubt, to have assumed again the character of Silver Mag—and she had been caught! But the Mole, it was absolutely certain, if left alone, would first exhaust every means within his power of forcing from Silver Mag the information that he would naturally believe she had concerning the whereabouts of the Gray Seal, before wreaking the vengeance of the underworld upon her; but equally the Mole, if interrupted by the police, would, in a sort of barbarous rivalry, if he, Jimmie Dale, knew the underworld at all, never surrender Silver Mag—alive. It would be the old cry, hideously worded, as he had heard it that night of the long ago in the attack on the old Sanctuary—the Gray Seal and Silver Mag were their *"meat!"* Something like a moan was wrung from Jimmie Dale's lips. With the police out of it there would have been time; with the police a factor, granted even that the Mole gave her up, her death was certain.

The mind works swiftly. An eternity seemed bridged as he stood there against the door, his hands pressed to his temples—in reality scarcely a second had passed. Time! It was like a clarion call, that word, clearing his brain, lashing him into instant action. There *was* time, a small, pitifully inadequate margin, but yet a margin—the few minutes left before Carruthers would have the police hammering at the Mole's door. There was a chance, still a chance to save her life. And if he succeeded in getting her away from the Mole's— what then! It would be touch and go! What of the afterwards—a means of retreat—a temporary sanctuary? Yes, yes—he must think of everything!

He was working with mad speed now, stripping off his clothes, delving into that secret hiding place behind the movable section of the base-board near the door. And now the gas, with its poverty-stricken, meagre, yellow flame, illuminated the place dimly—and Jimmie Dale, with his make-up box and a cracked mirror, worked against the flying minutes. There was only one way to go—as Larry the Bat. It would give the Mole and the underworld nothing to work on afterwards if Larry the Bat went to the rescue of Silver Mag; and if he won through there would then still be "Smarlinghue's" sanctuary, this place here, as a temporary refuge. The transformation to Larry the Bat stole an extra minute or two from the priceless store, but it was the only way—to risk it as Smarlinghue or Jimmie Dale, to risk recognition, would be the act of a fool, for it would render abortive the initial success, if, by any means, he could succeed even to that extent. Thank God for the circumstances that, prior to this, had led him to duplicate Larry the Bat's disreputable apparel; thank God for one chance of life—*for her*—that this afforded now.

The gas was out again, the room was in darkness. Through the little French window, and hugged close against the wall of the tenement, and through the loose Aboard in the fence that gave egress to the lane, Jimmie Dale, as Larry the Bat now, slunk along. And then, in the lane, he broke into a run. And now, an added peril came—a glimpse of Larry the Bat by any of gangland's fraternity, man or woman, and it would be the end! His position now was analogous to hers as Silver Mag before she had been caught! There would be no parley—it would be the end! But that was the chance he took, the only chance there was—for her.

But Jimmie Dale knew the East Side. By alleys and lanes, through yards and over fences, Jimmie Dale made his way along; and when forced into the open to cross a street, it was a dark, ill-lighted section that was chosen, and where for a short distance here and there he must needs keep to the street he held deep in the shadows of the buildings, crouching in doorways to avoid passers-by. It took time—he dared not calculate how long. Carruthers was not the man to let the grass grow under his feet! Carruthers would probably, before leaving home, have telephoned some Headquarters' man to meet him—the detective would have telephoned Headquarters from Melinoff's— and after that it would not take the police long to reach the Mole's!

It took time, this tortuous threading of the East Side—he did not know how long it had taken—but at last, as he swung into a long, black, and very narrow alleyway, he drew a quick breath of relief. So far, at least, he was ahead of the police. It was still and silent, there was no sound of any disturbance, and the Mole's now was only a little way ahead. He stole forward noiselessly. It was very quiet—much more quiet even than usual in that far from savoury neighbourhood. He remembered, with a grim smile of satisfaction, that the Wowzer had explained there was to be no crowding for front seats for fear of attracting the attention of the police. It had been very thoughtful of the Mole to pass that word around—very! With the underworld, prompted by curiosity and seething with hate, swarming here, the single chance he, Jimmie Dale, had of reaching her would have been swept away. He paused now, his lips set hard, crouched by the fence that separated the Mole's backyard from the alleyway. His plan was simple; but it depended for its ultimate success almost entirely on his ability to secure an instant means of disappearance for the Tocsin the moment she was outside the Mole's walls. That he could find her, that he could get her out of the house was another matter—he could only trust to his wits and nerve in that respect. But if he succeeded in that, then—he moved silently a little further up the lane, crossed to the other side and halted again, this time before the back door of a shed. In an instant his picklock was at work; in another he had opened the door a bare fraction of an inch. His lips grew tighter, as he retraced his steps to the Mole's fence. If that shed were ever needed at all, there would not be time to fumble in the dark for knob or latch—and there would be no necessity for that fumbling now! From the shed there was a very sure means of escape across a small interven-ing yard, and out through an areaway into the street, for the shed was one of the many entrances to Foo Sen's, a place with which he was very intimately acquainted—all this, of course, provided that, if the Tocsin were seen to enter the shed, *someone* held the pursuers back long enough to afford her time to reach the street.

Jimmie Dale shrugged his shoulders, as he opened a low gate in the fence silently and stepped through, into the yard beyond, leaving the gate open behind him. He was not a fool, blinded to what probably lay ahead! He could not hope to reach the Tocsin, much less effect her rescue, without warning the inmates of this house that loomed up before him now, without a fight with the Mole and the Mole's gangsters. It was not likely that *he* could reach the shelter of that shed, but the Tocsin could, and, once inside, throwing away her cloak and wig, "Silver Mag" would disappear, and after that there was the Sanctuary, and then her own brave wits. There came a twist to Jimmie Dale's lips, and then a shrug of his shoulders again. It was not likely to be the ending to the night that he had thought it might be when sitting there in Bristol Bob's only a few short hours ago!

Faint streaks of light through the interstices of a shuttered window showed just in front of him, as he stole forward across the yard. Window or back door, it mattered little to Jimmie Dale now, so that he could gain an entry into the house unobserved. It was very quiet—even ominously quiet—that impression came to him suddenly again. The quarter here was full of dives and gambling hells and resorts frequented by the worst in crimeland—but it seemed that the Mole's injunction had been obeyed to the letter! It boded little good—for her! Jimmie Dale's face, under the grime of Larry the Bat's make-up, grew white and set, as he approached the window. God in Heaven, was he already too late! The Mole, with his little tobacco shop in front as a blind, and his rooms above rented to "lodgers," thus housing the gang of Apaches that worked under his leadership, had had every opportunity, once the Tocsin was in his power in there, of doing as he would. And then another thought came flashing quick upon him. If they had gone that far, if she were dead, they must have discovered that under the cloak and the gray, straggling hair of Silver Mag—was Marie LaSalle. He forced a grip of iron upon himself, fighting mentally like a madman with himself for his self-control. The night with every passing moment seemed yawning wider and wider before him in a chasm that threatened ruin, and disaster, and the wreckage of everything that in life was worth the living, and—no,' Not yet! The luck had turned! She was there! Silver Mag was there! There! And safe so far!

The window was shoulder high. He was peering in through the blind. There was no light in the room itself, but a faint glow came in through the open doorway of a lighted room beyond—enough to enable him to make out a woman's form, the grizzled hair streaming over the threadbare cloak, as she lay on a cheap cot across the room, her face to the wall, her hands bound together behind her back.

It was Jimmie Dale working with all the art he knew; now; and those slim, sensitive, wonderful fingers were swift and silent as they had never been before. A steel jimmy loosened the shutters, and they swung apart without a sound. He could see better now—see, at least, that she was alone in the room. He tapped softly on the window pane. It was too dark to see her face, but he saw her raise her head quickly, and then, evidently, quick to meet an emergency as she always was, rise from the cot and steal to the edge of the open door. He was working at the window now. A fever of anxiety was him—it seemed that his fingers stumbled, that they lost their cunning, that an eternity passed as she stood there apparently on guard by the door, her bound hands behind her back like some piteous appeal to him to hurry—to hurry—and, in the name of all that life meant to both of them, to make haste.

And now cautiously, inch by inch, he was raising the window; and in another moment, in obedience to his whisper, the bound wrists were thrust within his reach, and he was severing the cords with his knife.

"Thank God!" breathed Jimmie Dale fervently. "Now jump—across the yard—the door of Foo Sen's shed—it's open—*quick*—"

There came a sudden crash from the front of the house, a sudden turmoil from within, a burst of shouts, a chorus of yells. The police! And now another shout, another burst of yells—from the rear—from the lane! Jimmie Dale's lips were like a thin, straight line. She was free from the house now, standing beside him here in the darkness. He reached swiftly up and closed the shutters—left open they invited immediate attention. His mind was working in lightning flashes. The police were at the front and rear, of course—they would not raid the front and leave the rear unguarded! But why the shouts out there in the lane—why had they not rushed in at once—and why now that *shot*! It was followed by another, and still another—and then a fusillade of them, as though the shots were returned.

"Quick!" he whispered again, and led the way toward the gate in the fence. The police would be pouring out of the house from the back door in a minute—the only chance was a dash for it. His mind was groping now, bewildered. What did it mean? The police who had obviously been detailed to the lane at the rear of the Mole's were fighting now—with whom—why? But the fight was working further on down the lane in the opposite direction from that shed door. "Quick!" he said again. "The shed door—on the other side—quick!"

Together they darted into the lane. From behind, the back door of the Mole's house was flung open, and there came the rush of feet. From down the lane the short, vicious tongue-flames of revolvers stabbed through the black. But in the darkness, save for those quick, myriad flashes like gigantic fireflies winking in the night, he could see nothing. They were racing, racing like mad, he and this form beside him for whose safety he prayed so wildly, so passionately in his soul now. It was only a step further—just another one—and the police, coming out of the Mole's, had not reached the gate yet. Just another step—and then a bullet, straying from the fight down there along the lane, drummed past his ear in an angry buzz—and the form beside him lurched heavily, stumbled, and pitched forward. And, with a low, broken cry, Jimmie Dale swung out a supporting arm, and pushing the shed door open with his elbow, gained the interior, and lowered his burden gently, a dead weight now, to the floor.

And then Jimmie Dale sprang to the door, and swung a heavy bolt that was there into place; then, running across the shed, he locked the other door as well. It was, perhaps, needless precaution. No one had seen them enter here, and there was little chance of the police developing any interest in the shed; while from the other side—Foo Sen's—the fact that there was a police battle in the lane would only cause the inmates of the dive to give the shed and lane the widest possible berth!

It had taken scarcely a second to lock the doors, and now he knelt beside a form that was ominously still upon the floor, and called her name over and over again.

"Marie! Marie! Marie!" he whispered frantically.

There was no answer—no movement. The strong, steady hands shook, those marvellous fingers, usually so deft and sure, faltered now as they loosened the cloak and threw the hood back over the wig of tangled, matted hair. It was not the darkness alone that would not let him see—there was a mist and a blur before his eyes. And now he loosened the heavy wig itself to give her relief—she would have no further need of that, for it would not be as Silver Mag that she left here—if she left here at all—no, no!—his mind seemed breaking—she would leave here, she *must*—yes, yes, she was breathing now—she was not dead—not dead!

He wrenched his flashlight from his pocket. To find the wound and stop the flow of blood! The ray shot out—there was a cry from Jimmie Dale—and like a man distraught he reeled to his feet—and like a man distraught stared at the upturned face, ghastly white under the flashlight's glare.

It was the Pippin.

The wig of grizzled hair that he had unconsciously been holding dropped from Jimmie Dale's hand, and his hand went upward to his temple. Was he mad! Was this joy, relief, rage or fury that, surging upon him, was robbing him of his senses! The Pippin! How could it be the Pippin! The cloak with its hood, and the long, gray matted wig were very like Silver Mag's—very like Silver Mag's! The Pippin! The Pippin!—one-time actor who had murdered old Melinoff, *the old-clothes dealer!* No—he was not mad! Dimly, his mind groping in the darkness, he began to see.

The Pippin's eyes opened.

"Who's there?" he demanded weakly.

Jimmie Dale, without a word, leaned forward, and threw the ray of light upon his own face.

An odd smile flickered across the Pippin's lips; his voice, weak as it was, was debonair and careless.

"Well, we nearly got you, Larry—at that! You fell for it, all right. Only—only someone"—his voice weakened still farther—"must have spilled the beans—to the—police."

Jimmie Dale made no answer. His lips were thinned and tight together. It was plain enough now. It had been a plant to get *him*—to get Larry the Bat, who was known to the underworld to be the Gray Seal—to get the Gray Seal through an appeal to the Gray Seal's loyalty toward his pal, Silver Mag! A plant, devilish enough in its ingenuity—Silver Mag impersonated—the "news" of her capture spread broadcast through the underworld on the chance that it would reach the ears of Larry the Bat, and tempt Larry the Bat into the open—as it had done! He knew now why the Pippin had gone to Melinoff's—old Melinoff's stock, more than any other dealer's, would be the most likely to supply the Pippin with the garments that, if not too closely inspected, would pass muster for Silver Mag's. He knew now why the underworld, believing what it had been told, had been warned to keep away from the Mole's—he knew now that it was because he was to have no inkling that he was walking into a baited trap.

He had torn the Pippin's clothing loose, found the bullet hole in the left side, perilously near the heart, and was striving now to staunch the other's wound. The man had little call for mercy, but at least—

The Pippin pushed his hand away.

"It's no use," said the Pippin. "I'm—I'm done for. But—but I don't understand. When you came to the window, I went to the door and tipped them off that you were there, and the gang that was waiting started around into the lane so that you wouldn't get any chance to make a break that way. I—I don't understand. Where—where did the police come from?"

"I sent them—from Melinoff's," said Jimmie Dale grimly.

The Pippin came up on his elbow.

"You!" he gasped. "You—you know what happened there—you were wise to everything all the time?"

"No," said Jimmie Dale. "I only knew you had murdered Melinoff. You left one of your cuff links there."

"Did I?" said the Pippin. He sank back on the floor again. "I didn't know it. It—it must have fallen out of my shirt when I undressed. I came away wearing women's things, and carrying my own clothes in a bundle." He laughed shortly, huskily. "That's what was the matter with Melinoff. It was the old fool's own fault! I didn't want to hurt him! He didn't understand at first when I was pawing all his stuff over, but when he saw me try the things on, and tumbled that I was—was going to play Silver Mag, he said he wouldn't stand for it. Ha, ha! Silver Mag!" The Pippin's voice had taken on a mumbling note, and his mind seemed to be functioning suddenly in a half-wandering way. "Some role, Silver Mag! I was the star tonight! You remember Silver Mag—how she used to go around in the old days and hand out the silver coins, never a bill, just coins, to the families whose men were doing spaces up the river in Sing Sing? She kept old Melinoff's wife going while he was in limbo—that's what he said. I didn't want to hurt the old fool, but he wouldn't keep his mouth shut. Ha, ha! Silver Mag! It was some play on the boards tonight! Clever brain, the Big Fellow's got! It wasn't any good if Silver Mag and Larry the Bat were together, but Silver Mag was seen buying a ticket and getting on a train for Chicago last night—and last night, later than that, the Gray Seal sent the Forrester stuff to the police—so they couldn't have been together this evening unless he went afterwards to Chicago, too—and he didn't do that because all the trains were watched. It was the biggest chance that ever came across of getting the Gray Seal in a trap. Some stage setting—some play—clever brain that—"

The voice trailed off. Outside there was quiet now, save for the crunch of an occasional footstep. The police who, as Jimmie Dale understood quite clearly now, had run into the Mole's gang as the two converged at the rear of the Mole's house, had evidently now got the better of the gangsters. And that convergence, too, explained why the Pippin had accompanied him so meekly toward the shed—the Pippin's one aim and object at that moment had been to avoid the police! He leaned suddenly forward over the man—the Pippin was going fast now. There was one thing yet, a thing that was vital, paramount, above all others.

"Pippin," he said quietly, "you're going out. Who put up this plant? It wasn't the Mole, he's not big enough, he's only a tool like yourself. Who was it?"

"No—not the Mole," murmured the Pippin. "He—he isn't big enough. Clever brain—clever brain—clever—"

"Who was it? Answer me, Pippin!"

"Yes," said the Pippin, and the odd smile came again, "I—I'll tell you. It—it was someone"—Jimmie Dale could scarcely hear the words—"someone—who will—get you yet!"

The smile was still on the Pippin's lips—but the man was dead. Jimmie Dale stood up again, and then Jimmie Dale, too, smiled; but it was a grim smile, hard and ominous. In his mind he had answered his own question.

It was that unseen hand of last night—only tonight the challenge had been *direct*. Well, he would pick up the gauntlet again—and at the same time, perhaps, add a little "atmosphere" to Carruthers' scoop! From his pocket came the thin, metal insignia case; and, lifting it with the tiny tweezers, moistening the adhesive side with his tongue, Jimmie Dale stooped down and fastened a gray seal on the floor by the Pippin's side.

And then Jimmie Dale crept out of the shed toward Foo Sen's, and crept into the dark areaway, and, as he had come, by alleyways and lanes, and through yards, and by ill-lighted, unfrequented streets, returned again to the Sanctuary—alone.

CHAPTER 22
THE TOCSIN'S STORY

It was a whimsical movement, a whimsical trick of Jimmie Dale's—that outward thrust of his hand that he might study it in a curiously impersonal, yet mercilessly critical way. He laughed a little harshly, as he allowed his hand to drop again to the arm of his chair. No, there was no tremor there—mentally he might be near the breaking point, his nerves raw and on edge; but physically, outwardly, he gave no sign of the strain that, cumulative in its anxiety, had increased hourly, it seemed, in the three days that had passed since the night he had so narrowly escaped the trap laid by that unknown master criminal, whose cunning, power and malignant genius was dominating and making itself felt in every den and dive of the underworld, and for whom the Pippin and the Mole that night had been but blind tools, pawns moved at the will of this unseen, evil strategist upon a chessboard of inhuman deviltry.

An evening newspaper lay open on the table. Jimmie Dale's eyes fixed for an instant on a glaring headline, then travelled slowly around the little room—one of the St. James' Club's private writing rooms—and came back to the paper again. The failure of that night, the Pippin's death, the stir and publicity, the stimulus given to police activity, had, it seemed, in no way acted as a deterrent upon the sinister ingenuity which, he made no doubt, was likewise the author of the mysterious crime that tonight was upon every tongue in the city—the murder of one of New York's most prominent bankers under almost incredible circumstances, and the coincident disappearance of a number of documents which were vaguely hinted at as being of international importance and of priceless worth. The crime had been committed in broad daylight, in mid-afternoon, in the banker's private office, and within call of the entire staff of the bank. No one had been seen either to enter or leave the office during an interval of some fifteen to twenty minutes, previous to which time it had been established by one of the staff that the banker was engaged in his usual occupation at his desk, and at the expiration of which he had been discovered by the cashier lying dead upon the floor, his skull fractured by a blow that had evidently been dealt him from behind, the desk in disorder as though it had been hurriedly searched, and the papers, known to have been in the banker's possession at that time, gone.

Jimmie Dale brushed his hand across his eyes in a dazed way. No, of course, he did not know, he could not actually know that it was the same guiding evil genius at work here that had murdered both Forrester and old

Melinoff, but something beyond actual proof, a sense of intuition, made of it a certainty in his own mind, at least, which left no room for argument. There had been viciously clever work here, as daring and crafty as it was remorseless in its brutality, and—he laughed suddenly, harshly as before, and, rising abruptly from his chair, stepped to the window, pushed aside the portières, and stood staring down on Fifth Avenue, whose great, wide, lighted thoroughfare seemed a curiously and incongruously lonely spot now in its evening quiet and emptiness.

Suppose it was so! Granted that his intuition was in no way astray! What did it matter? It was a thing extraneous, of no personal significance to him! It was even strange that it had succeeded in intruding itself upon his thoughts at all, when mind and soul in these last few days had fought and groped and stumbled against the sickness of a fear that, growing upon him, had blotted out all other things from his consciousness. The Tocsin! Where was she? What had happened? Had she—no, he dared not let himself believe what a brutal logic told him now he should believe. He would not! He could not! And yet since that night when her note had come, the note that had been so full of a glad spontaneity, so full of *victory*—"It is the beginning of the end… The way is clearing… I am very happy tonight, and I wanted to tell you so"—since that night there had been no word from her.

No, that was not literally true. There *had* been word from her; but, rather than having brought hope and reassurance to him, it had only increased his fear and anxiety. That night, after a return to the Sanctuary, where, in lieu of the character of Larry the Bat, he had resumed his own personality again, he had hurried to his home to await the expected word from her that would tell him her success, which her note had indicated was to be looked for at any moment, had been achieved. The night, however, had brought forth nothing; but in the morning, amongst the mail which old Jason, his butler, had handed him, had been a letter from her. It had been written evidently in leisure, and evidently prior to the hurried little note that happiness, a surge of joy, a gladness and a hope whose share she could not hold back from him, had undoubtedly prompted her to write; it had been born out of impulse, that note, an impulse due, apparently, to a sudden turn in the brave fight she was waging which seemed to place the final victory almost within her grasp. The letter was not at all like that; it struck a far sterner note—the possibility of defeat— not in despair, not in a tone of failing courage, but as one who, weighing the chances, was not blind to an opponent's strength, but who, even in one's own defeat, still sought to snatch final victory even after death.

Jimmie Dale turned from the window, sat down again in his chair, and drew the letter from his pocket—and, sitting there, the strong jaws clamped and locked, his face drawn in rigid lines, the dark, steady eyes cold and hard, read it again, as he had read it many times before since Jason had handed it to him that morning several days ago:

Dear Philanthropic Crook:

I wonder if I am writing those words for the last time? I believe I am. I do not mean I am in such danger that I will never have the opportunity again; but, rather, that I will never have the *need* to do so. But tonight should tell. It is very near the end—one way or the other—and I believe it is *my* way. Oh, Jimmie, I pray God it is, and that tomorrow—but I did not start this letter to you to talk of *that*.

Long ago—do you remember, Jimmie?—I wrote you that I would not, could not bring you into the shadows again for me, and that I must fight this out alone. It must be that way, Jimmie; there is no other way, and what I am about to say must not lead you to think that I am hesitating now, or have changed my mind. It is only this—that the game is not won until the last card is played, and, while I am almost certain that I see the way now, there *is* still that last card to play. Do not let us mince matters, Jimmie. If I fail, you know what it means. But, in the bigger way, Jimmie, I can only count for but very little in the balance. There is the afterwards that is of far more moment—that justice, swift and sure, should put an end to the depredations and the menace to society that exists today in the person of one of the cleverest and most conscienceless fiends that ever plotted crime. Nor, in case you should have to take up the work where I leave off, would you be even then obliged to come into those shadows again. It is very strange, Jimmie. It is almost like some grim, terribly grim, ironical joke. Everything, all the power, all the resources that this man possesses have been used against me in the last few months, because he knows that unless he accomplishes my death he must remain in hiding just as he has forced me into hiding; and yet at the same time—and this he does not know, because he does not know that he is known to you, and that you, as Jimmie Dale, a man whose position and prominence would carry conviction with every word you might say, are in a position to testify against him— with my death he automatically accomplishes his own destruction. And so you see, Jimmie, in one sense at least, I cannot fail! No, I do not mean to speak lightly—I—I have as much as you, Jimmie—to live for.

Listen, then! We knew, you and I, that while both my supposed uncle and the head of the Crime Club were killed that night of the old Sanctuary fire, and that the greater number, almost all in fact, of the members of the band were caught by the police, that a few of them still evaded the trap and escaped. But we believed these were so few in number and were so thoroughly disorganised that nothing more was to be feared from them. And this in a very great measure is true; but it is not altogether true. No, I am not going to tell you that the

Crime Club rose from its ashes and is in operation again; but one of the men who escaped that night, one of the Club's leaders, possessed evidently of the secret as to where the Club's surplus funds were hidden, is the man who, through a lavish use of those funds, is operating now through the underworld, who is responsible for Forrester's murder, and is the man who through all these months has sought to reach me. I referred to him as 'one of the leaders'—I believe him now to have been the most dangerous of them all. You know him as—Clarke. Do you remember, Jimmie? He was the man who so cleverly impersonated Travers as the chauffeur, after they had killed Travers. He was the man who was at the house that night when Travers first learned that my father and my uncle had been murdered, and that the same fate was in store for me. I told you that from where he sat in the room that night I could not see his face, that Travers told me who he was—but, apart from not being able to recognise him on that particular occasion, I knew him well, for he had been a frequent visitor to the house even prior to my father's death, and subsequently in company with Travers as one who appeared to have struck up an intimacy with my supposed uncle.

The day after the Crime Club was raided by the police, you will remember that Clarke not being amongst those caught, I gave the authorities what particulars I could in reference to the man. But nothing came of it. A description and the name of 'Clarke' was little enough to work on. The man had disappeared. Time passed, and I supposed, as no doubt you, as well, supposed, that Clarke had made good his escape, that he was probably well content with such good fortune, and that nothing more, if he could help it, would ever be heard of him. Jimmie, I was wrong. Within a month a series of narrow escapes from accidents, any one of which might easily have accomplished my death, seemed to follow me persistently. I will not take the time now to enumerate them all—they were so commonplace, so liable to happen to anyone, such for instance as escaping by a hair's-breadth from being run down by a speeding car swerving, around the corner as I started to cross the street, or again by an iron tackle falling from a scaffolding where work was in progress on the building in which, pending the remodelling of my own house, as you know, I had taken an apartment, that at first I attached no ulterior significance to them. But finally, as they persisted, I became convinced that they were deliberate and premeditated attempts upon my life. I said nothing to you, as I did not wish to alarm you. And then one night Clarke showed himself.

Do you remember the colourless liquid, the poison instantaneous in its action and defying detection by autopsy, which was so favourite a method of murder with the Crime Club? I had expected to be out for the evening, and had given the maids permission to go out together. It was about halfpast eight when I left the apartment. I had only gone a few blocks when I returned for something I had forgotten. I was in my bedroom when I heard the hall door open stealthily. I switched off the bedroom light instantly, and slipped into the clothes closet, leaving the door just ajar. I knew, of course, that if it were another attack directed against me, it was one that was prearranged and that was being made on the presumption that I was out and that the apartment was empty. There was silence for a moment or two, then a step crossed the threshold of the bedroom, and the light went on. It was Clarke. There was a little night table beside the bed on which my maid, before she had gone out, had placed as usual a carafe of ice water and a small tray of biscuits. Clarke was evidently very well acquainted with this fact. He stepped at once to the table, took a vial from his pocket, poured the contents into the carafe—and the next instant the room was in darkness again, and Clarke was gone. I acted as quickly as I could. I dared not move or give any sign of my presence until he was out of the apartment, for I would have accomplished nothing except my death. But the minute the outer door closed I picked up the telephone to communicate with the vestibule. It was a ground-floor apartment, as you know. The one chance was to have the hall porter intercept Clarke in the vestibule. As a matter of fact, the telephone was not answered for fully a minute or so—too late, of course! Clarke had vanished. The boy at the telephone desk said he had been busy with another call. That is all, Jimmie. I saw clearly that night that there was only one thing left for me to do if I hoped to save my life, and that was to fight Clarke with his own weapons. And so I wrote you; and you know now why Marie LaSalle 'left the city for an extended trip,' as her bankers informed you, and why during all these months I have 'disappeared.'

I come now to the last thing I have to say—the reason for writing this letter. My death was essential to Clarke, because he believed that I was the *only* one who could positively identify him *as* 'Clarke,' and that, therefore, as long as I lived he could not resume his own identity and personal freedom of action for fear that I might, even if only through inadvertence, recognise him. He could take no chances. But I believe I have beaten Clarke. I have discovered that 'Clarke' is in reality Peter Marre, the shyster lawyer, better known among his clientele as Wizard Marre. But Marre, too, has disappeared—you understand, Jimmie? And now, hidden, under cover, never showing himself personally, 'Clarke' is working, not only to reach me, but to further all his other schemes, through some agency without appearing himself either as Marre or as 'Clarke.' I believe it is only a matter of a few hours now before I shall either have got to the bottom of who and what this agency is, or else—again do not let us mince matters, Jimmie—'Clarke' will have been too much for me. And in that latter case is found the whole object of this letter. Once I am removed from his path, and believing that no one else could, or would, link 'Clarke' and Peter Marre together, he will naturally resume the freedom of his former life, and Peter Marre will appear again in his old-time surroundings, a Peter Marre unhampered by fear of discovery, and therefore a Peter Marre a hundredfold more dangerous than ever before. And so, Jimmie, if that should happen, you have simply to get this information into the hands of the police without appearing yourself, say, through the agency of the Gray Sealand I shall not have brought you into the shadows again.

The letter was signed simply—"Marie." But there was a postscript:

"You will hear from me the moment that I can tell you I am free at last."

Jimmie Dale sat staring at the postscript. He made no movement; and there was no sound in the room, save that the sheets of paper crackled slightly in his hand. He was afraid tonight, afraid as he had never been in his life before; and the fear that was gnawing at his heart was mirrored in a gray, rigid face, and in the misery that had crept into the dark, half-closed eyes. It was three days ago since he had received that letter, and the awaited, promised word had not come—three days, and the letter stated that it would be but a matter of a few hours before the decision that meant life or death was reached. And the hurried little note, so obviously written subsequent to the letter, though it had been received prior to it, but bore out in its very optimism the fact that the final card was then almost in the very act of being played. And since then—there had been nothing.

He put little faith in the Pippin's belief that she had gone to Chicago. He found no relief in that possibility at all. That they had seen her buy a ticket and board a train—yes. That for her own ends she had let them see her do that—yes. But whether she had ever gone or not was quite a different matter! Her letter would certainly indicate that she had not. But even if she had! She could have communicated with him from Chicago just as easily as she could have communicated with him from any place here in New York!

Jimmie Dale's hand lifted and pressed hard against his temple, as though to still the dull, constant throbbing that brought to his mental agony the added torment of physical pain. For these three days now he had fought with mind and body and soul against the one conclusion that was tenable—the conclusion which tonight, robbing him of every hope in life, bringing a grief and anguish greater than he could bear, cold logic was finally forcing him to accept. She would have known the torment of anxiety in which he lived, and if her plans had only been delayed or checked, if it had been no more than that, she would surely have communicated with him and allayed his fears.

A low sound, a moan of bitter pain, came from Jimmie Dale's lips. Logic had won at last, and was triumphant in the blackest hour that had ever come into his life. The one glimmer of hope to which, as time went on and one by one other hopes had vanished, he had still clung tenaciously, had surrendered, too, and gone down before the face of that brutal logic that weighed neither human agony nor suffering in its remorseless conclusions. Clarke, it was true, had not yet resumed his former life as Peter Marre—but he, Jimmie Dale, was forced to admit now that that meant little or nothing. A thousand and one reasons might account for Clarke postponing his re-entry into his old life—that the man had allowed three days to pass proved nothing.

Marre! Peter Marre! Wizard Marre! A smile that held no mirth hovered for an instant over Jimmie Dale's lips. Yes, he knew Marre, Marre of the underworld, well! The man was brilliant, clever—and possessed of a devil's soul! Also Marre, as certainly no other man had ever held it, held the confidence of crimeland—and crime-land had supplied the tricky lawyer with his clientele. And so Marre was "Clarke," one of the leaders of the old Crime Club! Jimmie Dale's smile disappeared, and his lips drew straight and tight together. It was quite easily understood now. The returns in a financial sense from such a clientele, large even as they perhaps might be, were meagre and pitiful in comparison with the huge sums which, in one way and another, the Crime Club would have acquired; but the returns in another sense had been vast and of incalculable value, not only to Clarke, but to the Crime Club as well. Clarke's power in the underworld as Marre had reached the height where the underworld itself eulogised that power by bestowing on the man the "moniker" of Wizard, investing him, as it were, with a title and a peerage in that inglorious realm. And this power, supplying a foreknowledge of events through intimacy with those whispered secrets in the innermost circles of the citizenry of crimeland, must have been of immeasurable worth. And now Clarke, hidden away somewhere, acting, it appeared, through some unknown agency and go-between, was utilising that power with deadly cunning and effect—not only against the Tocsin, but against society at large, as witness the murder of Forrester of a few days ago, and presumably the murder of Jathan Lane, the banker, not longer ago than this afternoon.

Jimmie Dale shook his head suddenly. Acting through some *unknown* agency? The Tocsin had not said that. Indeed, if she had been as near to the final move in this battle of wits which she had been playing for months, as her letter indicated, she must have known by now who and what and where that agency was. And he could see plainly enough why she had kept her own counsel in that respect. It was through her great, unselfish love for him that she had intentionally refrained from giving him any clue that would enable him to find his way into the danger zone which she reserved for herself alone. Yes, he understood that—but it only made what he feared now the harder to bear. She had been right, of course, in her conclusion as to what he would have done had she given him the opportunity! It was the one thing he had been fighting for, struggling for, battling for all these months, that clue—and she had told him only that "Clarke" was behind it all, and that "Clarke" was Peter Marre. And it had served him little! As though the earth had opened and swallowed the man and his alias up, there was neither trace nor sign of Peter Marre.

He knew that well! He had not been idle since that letter came! He had instantly seized upon what he had hoped would prove the clue that he could follow to the heart of the web—and the clue had led him nowhere. Marre, like the Tocsin, was somewhere "on a trip." Marre's office was not closed. A year ago Marre had taken in with him as partner a young lawyer by the name of Cleaver, who lacked only, through experience, the same degree of dishonest finesse and cunning possessed by Marre himself—a defect which Marre had doubtless counted on speedily rectifying under his own unholy tutelage! Cleaver was carrying on the business. To all inquiries Cleaver's replies had been the same—Mr. Marre, through overwork, had been obliged to take a rest; he did not know where Mr. Marre was other than that Mr. Marre was making an extended tour through the Orient, nor did he know when Mr. Marre might be expected to return; Mr. Marre, purposely, in order that he might escape all thought and care of business, and to preclude the possibility of anything of that nature reaching him, had refrained from giving the office any specific address. But he, Jimmie Dale, had not been content with inquiries alone in those last few days—though the result here again had been nothing. He was satisfied only that, in so far as the main issue was concerned, Cleaver was not in Marre's confidence, and that Cleaver not only did not know Marre's exact whereabouts, but believed, as he had said, that Marre was travelling somewhere in the Orient.

Jimmie Dale drew his hand heavily again across his forehead. It seemed as though the very act of sitting here was a traitorous act to her, that even in this momentary inaction he had cause for bitter self-reproach and even for contempt—and yet he could see no way now to take. In the last three days, as Smarlinghue, as Jimmie Dale, yes, even as Larry the Bat again, working with feverish intensity, with almost sleepless continuity, he had exhausted every means and effort within his power of running Marre, *alias* Clarke, to earth. There seemed nothing now left to do but to wait until Marre should resume his own identity; nothing left but the promise of a vengeance that—again Jimmie Dale laughed harshly, and, as the laugh died away, a smile took its place on the thinned lips that was not good to see. Yes, she was right in that; he knew Marre—he knew Marre, with his thin, cruel face, his black, sleepy eyes; his suave, ingratiating manner that hid under its veneer a devil's treachery! Nor, well as he knew the man, was it strange that he had not known Clarke as Peter Marre, for he had seen Clarke only once—that night in the long ago, in Spider Jack's when the man, with consummate art, a master of disguise, had impersonated Travers, the dead chauffeur, and had succeeded in fooling even Spider Jack himself. But he, Jimmie Dale, knew *now*. Yes, she had been right—a whiteness came and gathered on his lips—in that sense she could not fail, Marre at least would pay! But perhaps not quite as she suggested, perhaps not quite by the simple act of a denunciation to the police, perhaps not quite in so simple a way as that, for, after all—his hand clenched over the sheets of her letter—though it would be easy enough to establish Marre's alias now that the alias was known, there might be another way in which Marre would answer, a more *intimate* way, a more personal way! Not murder—the skin was ivory white across his knuckles—not murder, but—

Jimmie Dale was quietly folding the sheets of paper in his hand. Someone was knocking at the door.

"Come in!" said Jimmie Dale—and slipped the letter back into his pocket, as the door opened.

It was one of the club's attendants.

"I beg pardon, Mr. Dale, sir," said the man; "but there is a phone call for you." He glanced toward the telephone on the table. "I was not sure just where you were, sir. Shall I ask them to connect you here?"

"Thank you!" said Jimmie pleasantly. "Very good, Masters. No—I'll attend to it myself."

The man withdrew, and closed the door again. Jimmie Dale rose from his chair, and, stepping to the table, picked up the instrument.

"There is a call for me, I believe," he said. "This is Mr. Dale."

There was a moment's silence, then Jimmie Dale spoke again.

"Yes—hello!" he said. "Yes, this is Mr. Dale. What—"

The room seemed suddenly to swirl about him—the hand so steady a few moments ago was trembling palpably now as it held the instrument. *Her voice?* No—he was mad! It was his brain, overwrought, strained, not to the breaking point, but beyond, that had broken at last, and was mocking at him now in some cruel phantasy. Her voice? No, it could not be, for she—for she was—

"Jimmie! Jimmie!"—the voice came hurriedly again, almost frantically this time. "Jimmie—are you there?"

"You!" His lips were dry, he moistened them with his tongue. "You!" he whispered hoarsely. "You, Marie—and I thought—I thought that you were—"

"Jimmie," she broke in, a quick, wistful catch in her voice, "I cannot stay here a moment—you understand, don't you? There is not an instant to lose—on the floor by the Sanctuary window—a note—will you hurry, Jimmie—good-bye."

She was gone. Mechanically he replaced the receiver on the hook. She was gone—but it *was* her voice he had heard—hers—and she was alive. The play of emotion upon him robbed him for the moment of coherent thought, and came and swept over him in a mighty surge and engulfed him; and now in the sudden revulsion from despair and the bitterest of agony his mind was dazed and numbed. It seemed as though he were obeying some subconscious power, as he turned and left the room; as though some influence outside of, and extraneous to, himself gave him a spurious self-mastery, a self-command, a mask of nonchalance, as he walked calmly through the club lobby and out to the street.

Benson, his chauffeur, held the door of his car open for him.

"Where to, sir?" Benson asked.

"The Palace—Bowery," Jimmie Dale answered. "And hurry, Benson!"

CHAPTER XXIII. HUNCHBACK JOE

Jimmy Dale flung himself back on the seat of the big touring car. It was an address, the Palace Saloon on the Bowery, that he had often given Benson before—the nearest point to which Benson, trusted as Benson was, had ever been permitted to approach the Sanctuary itself. The night air, the sweep of the wind was grateful, as the machine sped forward. He did not reason, he could not reason—his mind was in turmoil still. Only two things were clear, distinct, rising dominant out of that turmoil—that he had heard her voice, her voice that he had never thought to hear again; and that there was need, a desperate need for haste now, because he must reach the Sanctuary without an instant's loss of time.

And then gradually his brain began to clear, to adjust itself, to function normally; and when finally the car drew up at a corner on the Bowery, it was a Jimmie Dale, keen, self-possessed and alert, who sprang briskly to the pavement.

"Will you need me any further, sir?" Benson asked.

Jimmie Dale was lighting a cigarette deliberately—it was the same question that he was pondering in his own mind, but the answer was dependent upon the contents of that note which was waiting for him in the Sanctuary.

"I am not quite sure, Benson," he replied. "In any case, you had better wait here for twenty, minutes. If I am not back in that time, you may go home. Don't wait any longer."

"Very good, sir," Benson answered.

It was only a short distance to the Sanctuary—down the cross street, a turn into another only to emerge again on one that paralleled the first, and then Jimmie Dale, walking slowly now, was sauntering along an ill-lighted thoroughfare flanked on either side with a miscellany of small shops and tenements of the cheaper class. There were but few pedestrians in sight; but, as he neared the tenement that made the corner of the lane ahead, Jimmie Dale's pace became still more leisurely. A man and a woman were strolling up the street toward him. They passed. Jimmie Dale, at the corner of the lane now, glanced behind him. The two were self-absorbed. And then, like a shadow merging with the darkness of the lane, Jimmie Dale had disappeared.

In an instant, he had gained the loose board in the high fence; and in another, pressing close to the rear wall of the tenement, he had reached the little French window that gave on the dingy courtyard. There was an almost inaudible sound, a faint metallic *snip*, as, kneeling, his fingers loosened the hidden catch beneath the sill—and the window on well-oiled hinges swung silently inward, and closed as silently again behind Jimmie Dale as he entered.

The top-light, high up near the ceiling, threw a misty ray of moonlight along the greasy, threadbare carpet, and threw into relief a folded piece of dark-coloured paper at Jimmie Dale's feet. He stooped and picked it up—and then moving close to the window again, his fingers, in the darkness, felt over the dilapidated roller shade to assure himself that the rents were securely pinned together against the possibility of prying eyes. He stepped quickly then across the room, tested the door lock; and then the single gas-jet, air-choked, hissing spitefully, illuminated the room with a wavering meagre yellow flame.

Under the light, Jimmie Dale unfolded the paper, his face hardening suddenly. It was not like any note she had ever written him before—there was no white envelope here, no paper of fine and delicate texture, no ink-written message carefully penned; instead, evidence enough of her desperate haste, the desperate circumstances probably under which she had written it, the message was on a torn piece of brown wrapping paper, and the words, in pencil, were scrawled in hurried, broken sentences. And standing there, fighting for a grip upon himself, Jimmie Dale read the message—almost illegible! in places—and then, as though a strange incredulity, a strange inability to grasp and understand its import fully, were prompting him, he read it again, murmuring snatches of it aloud.

"…I did not mean to bring you into the shadows…but there is another life, not mine, at stake… I have no right to do anything else… if I intervened, or gave warning, the evidence that will convict Clarke's agent, and will convict Clarke through the agent, is lost…that is why, in spite of all, I am writing this… do you understand?… for three nights he disappeared, and somehow, I do not yet know how, evaded me in the daytime… no trace, just as I believed I had the man through whom Clarke is working trapped… dared not take the chance of giving up watch for an instant… did not know about this afternoon until an hour ago… too late… Jathan Lane's murder at the bank… Klanner, the janitor of the bank… very fair hair, scar on left cheek bone… worked at night… under passage from private office… blackjack with which murder was done, document and money in Klanner's room... unmarried... lives in rear room, first floor of tenement at... you must get the evidence... unto Caesar!... ship chandler's store, junk shop... Larens, Joe Larens, the hunchback... Clarke's agent... another murder to cover up their tracks... must get Clarke through Hunchback Joe... will squeal if he sees no way of escape... Klanner's room at once... Klanner with Kid Greer will be at Baldy Jack's at ten o'clock... will stop at nothing... innocent bystander... document of international importance,... gold and details... Federal authorities, not the police... will see that Secret Service men get tip where to raid at midnight... under the sail cloth in left corner..."

Jimmie Dale was tearing the paper into little shreds. His brain, eagerly now, was leaping from premise to conclusion, fitting the strange, complex parts of her story, seemingly so utterly at variance one with another, into a single, concrete whole. Yes, he understood why, in spite of herself, she had been forced to bring him within those shadows at the last—to save another's life, which she could not do alone without forfeiting the opportunity of securing the evidence that would condemn those actually guilty, and reach, through the lesser lights, the man higher up—Marre, alias Clarke. Yes, he understood, too, that this was the end—if all went well! A grim smile came and flickered across Jimmie Dale's lips. She believed that Hunchback Joe, if caught and trapped, would squeal to the police. The grim smile deepened. Hunchback Joe might, or might not, squeal to the police—*but in any case Hunchback Joe would tell his story*! He, Jimmie Dale, would see to that—whatever the cost, whatever the consequences, if he had to choke and wring it from the man's lips. It was a surer way than trusting to the police—it was the only sure way of reaching the end. The cost! The risk! What did it matter? What was cost, or risk! Her life was in the balance!

He glanced quickly around him. Would it be as Smarlinghue tonight? He shook his head. No, if it were really the end, if he won through tonight, this would be the last time he would ever stand here in the Sanctuary, and to leave the clothes of Jimmie Dale here, even in so secure a hiding place as behind that movable section of the base-board, would impose upon him the *necessity* of returning—was but to hamper himself, and, indeed, as likely as not, if hard pressed, to court disaster.

His glance, strangely whimsical, strangely wistful now, travelled again over the room. If it was the end tonight, this was his good-bye to Smarlinghue, to Larry the Bat—and the Gray Seal. This was his exit from the sordid stage of the underworld—forever. Yes, in time, suspicious of Smarlinghue's continued absence, they would investigate and search the Sanctuary here; they might even discover that hiding place in the wall—but what did it matter? They would find only the trappings of a *character* that had passed out of existence; and out of that fact the police and the underworld would be privileged to make what capital they could! No, it would not be as Smarlinghue that he would work tonight—he was well enough as he was. He had not worn evening clothes since that letter came, for the nights had been spent in constant toil, and the dark suit of tweeds he wore now was not conspicuous. Nor need he even have recourse to that hiding place again—what he required was already in his pockets—for days now, in whatever role he had played, he had been prepared for any emergency.

Jimmie Dale looked at his watch—it was ten minutes after nine—and, reaching up, turned out the light. A minute more and the French window was silently opened and closed again, and Jimmie Dale was once more on the street. Here, walking quickly, but keeping to the less frequented streets, he headed deeper into the East Side. He would have no need of Benson, and Benson without further ado at the expiration of the allotted twenty minutes would obey orders literally and go home. No, he would have no further need of Benson and the car—Jimmie Dale smiled curiously, his mind absorbed now in the immediate problem that confronted him—they worked on a carefully prepared and methodical schedule, these minions of Clarke or Marre, allowing ample time in each successive step in their plans that there might be neither confusion nor mistake in what they did. Well, what was ample time for them, was ample time for him! It was not far from the tenement where the Tocsin had said Klanner lived to Baldy Jack's—and Klanner was not due at Baldy Jack's until ten o'clock.

Under the slouch hat, pulled far down over his eyes, Jimmie Dale's brows knitted into a frown. It was true then, and his intuition had not been at fault! It was Clarke who had planned the murder and robbery at the bank that afternoon—and Hunchback Joe, Clarke's familiar, and his accomplices who had carried it out. Yes, it had been clever enough—but difficult enough too! Yet of two alternatives they had chosen the easiest. The document, containing the secret international arrangements for gold shipments into the United States, embracing European commitments, and including transportation details, was always, except when in the banker's personal possession, carefully locked away in the bank's vaults. In the daytime then, it was impossible for a stranger to reach those vaults; and at night time to attempt to force the strongest vaults in the City of New York, with their intricate electric-alarm system, was a task from which even Clarke might shrink!

The Tocsin had made it very clear. The document, or documents, never left the bank's premises; it never left the bank's vaults except when in the possession of the bank's president in the latter's private office. Clarke had therefore chosen the line of least resistance—the bank president's office! And that accounted, he, Jimmie Dale, understood now, for the sudden failure of the Tocsin's plans three nights ago, since it accounted evidently for the sudden disappearance of Hunchback Joe, which had checkmated her on that night and on subsequent nights—for it had taken those three nights to perfect their plans in the bank, and the work there had evidently been done under the personal supervision of Hunchback Joe.

The plan's cleverness and cunning lay in its devilish simplicity—it required only long, painstaking and laborious preparation. There were, according to the newspapers, two entrances to the banker's private office; the customers' entrance from the main rotunda of the bank, and a rear entrance leading in behind the cages to the working quarters of the staff, which was separated from the general offices by a short, narrow, enclosed passage with a second door at the extreme end. The president's office, as befitted his position, was richly furnished, and the passage, being in reality but an adjunct to the office itself, had not been overlooked—it was carpeted with a long Persian rug. That portion of the basement directly beneath the president's office and the passage had been partitioned off into a storeroom for old files and books, and was consequently rarely visited. For the rest, the method was fairly obvious. The storeroom was ceiled in with wood, which, when carefully cut away, could be replaced during the daytime, and so hide all traces of what was going on should anyone enter the place. It required, then, simply a certain number of nights' work—and it had taken three. An opening had been cut through the flooring into the passage, and the surface flooring of the passage over the aperture refitted into place, so that, covered by the rug, there was no indication that anything was wrong.

The minor details the Tocsin had passed over—but to supply them required but little effort of the imagination. The president customarily devoted a certain amount of time each afternoon to the matter in question, and immediately on his return from lunch always took the papers from the vault and carried them to his private office. It became, then, simply necessary that the man, or men, hiding in the basement should know when the president was *alone*; but this would hardly be a very difficult matter, for, with nothing but the upper skin of the flooring left, one had only to post himself in the opening and he could hear as well, almost, as though he were in the private office itself. The entrance could then be effected in the security of the little passage; the rear door of the passage would be silently locked against interruption; the door leading into the president's office, where the president sat with his back to the door, would be silently opened—then a quick leap, soundless on the heavy carpet—the blow of a blackjack—the limp body caught and lowered to the floor—the documents secured—the escape.

The escape! Jimmie Dale had turned suddenly into a pitch-black areaway, and, cautiously now, was making his way to the rear of a three-story tenement of the poorer class. The escape had naturally been accomplished in exactly the same way—the rear door unlocked again to obviate any immediate attention being paid to the passage—the murderer lowering himself through the aperture, and, as he replaced the flooring, manipulating the rug so that it would drop innocently back into place—and the exit from the basement would of course already have been provided for. Jimmie Dale's face was hard. The newspapers, going to press almost at the moment the murder was discovered, though giving a general description of the bank's premises, had had no opportunity to furnish details of the ensuing police investigation; but that the police would eventually discover the hole in the flooring was obvious; that they would also discover it without much delay was equally obvious—*and it had been intended that they should*. Clarke's object, acting through Hunchback Joe, had been to provide only for the *immediate* escape—and after that, with callous deviltry, he proposed to utilise this very means of escape to cover up the tracks of the tools who were doing his work, and, backed with another murder, to put the crime upon another's shoulders!

Jimmie Dale had halted now to survey his surroundings, and, his eyes grown accustomed to the darkness, he could make out a door opening on the small yard in which he stood, and to the right of the door an unlighted and closed window. That was Klanner's window. He did not know Klanner, the bank's janitor—except that he knew him as an *innocent* man, as the proposed victim of as foul and black and pitiless a conspiracy as had ever been hatched in a human brain! Nor did he know Hunchback Joe—save by reputation. The man was a comparative newcomer in the underworld. He had bought out a small ship-chandler's business, a rickety, out-at-the-heels place on an equally rickety old wharf on the East River; and it was generally understood that he was a "fence" of a sort, making a speciality of, and catering to, a certain extensive and vicious class of thieves, the wharf rats, who infested the city's shipping—his ostensible business of a ship-chandler enabling him to handle and dispose of that class of stolen property with comparative immunity.

Jimmie Dale was crouching at the door, a little steel picklock in his fingers. It was fairly evident now that the underworld in general had but an extremely superficial acquaintance with Hunchback Joe; that Hunchback Joe's minor depredations against the law were but a cloak to—the mental soliloquy ended abruptly. Jimmie Dale drew suddenly back from the door, and, retreating along the wall of the building, crouched down in the darkness beneath the window. *What was that?* It came again—a step, stealthy, cautious, from the areaway—and now another step—there were two men there.

The picklock was back in his pocket, and, in its place, his fingers closed around the stock of his automatic. A shadow showed around the corner of the building, a twisted, misshapen shadow—it was followed by another. Jimmie Dale drew in his breath softly. Hunchback Joe! He had rather expected that the man would already have come and gone, that this initial act of the brutal drama staged for the night's work would already have been performed. Well, it did not matter! There was still time—time to wait while Hunchback Joe did his work here, time in turn to do his own and still reach Baldy Jack's before ten o'clock.

From somewhere in the distance came the roar and rattle of an elevated train; from a neighbouring tenement came the strains of a wheezy phonograph. The figures were at the rear door of the tenement now. A minute passed; the door opened, closed, the two figures had disappeared—and then, in a flash, Jimmie Dale had straightened up, and a steel jimmy was working with deft, silent speed at the window sash. He had the time it would take Hunchback Joe to reach and open Klanner's door from the hall inside—no more. And if he could watch Hunchback Joe at work it would simplify to a very large extent his own task when Hunchback Joe was through; there would be no necessity for a *search*, and—ah! The window gave. He raised it noiselessly, reached inside and pulled down the roller shade to within an inch of the sill, and pulled the window down again to a little below the level of the shade. The opening left was unnoticeable—but he could now both see and hear.

There came a faint sound from within—the creak of a slowly opening door, a step across the floor, then the flare of a match, and the light in the room went on.

Jimmie Dale was drawn back now against the wall at one corner of the window, his eyes on a level with the sill. He had made no mistake about that misshapen, twisted shadow—it was Hunchback Joe. Jimmie Dale's eyes travelled to the hunchback's companion—and narrowed as he recognised the other. The man was well enough known in the underworld, a hanger-on for the most part, a confirmed hop-fighter, though when not under the influence of the drug he was counted one of the cleverest second-story workers and lock-pickers in the Bad Lands—Hoppy Meggs, they called him. Again Jimmie Dale's eyes shifted—to Hunchback Joe once more. Like some abnormal and repulsive toad the man looked. His shoulders were thrust upward until they seemed to merge with the head itself, the body was crooked and bent forward, due to the ugly deformity of the man's back, while the face was carried at an upward tilt, as though tardily to rectify the curvature of the spine, and out of the sinister, bearded face, the beard tawny and ill-kempt, little black eyes from under protruding brows blinked ceaselessly.

A sudden fury, an anger hot and passionate seized upon Jimmie Dale; and there came an impulse almost overpowering to play another role, a deadlier, grimmer role than that of spectator! A toad, he had called the man. He was wrong—the man was a devil in human guise. He crushed back the impulse, a cold smile on his lips. He could afford to wait! It was not time yet. There was still the game to play out. He would have an opportunity to give full sway to impulse before the night was out, *before* the Tocsin should have set the Secret Service men upon the other's trail—before midnight came.

Hunchback Joe was speaking now.

"Go on, Hoppy; get busy!" he ordered sharply, jerking his hand toward a trunk that stood at the foot of the cheap iron bedstead. "Get that opened.

Hurry up! And see that you don't leave any scratches on it, or—you understand!" He leaned forward, leering with sudden savagery at his companion.

Hoppy Meggs moved forward, dropped on his knees in front of the trunk, examined the lock for an instant—and grunted in contempt.

"Aw, it's a cinch! Say, I could do it wid a hairpin!" he grinned—and a moment later threw back the lid.

Hunchback Joe drew a short, ugly blackjack, a packet of papers, and a large roll of bills from his pocket, and tossed the articles into the trunk.

"Lock it again!" he instructed tersely.

Hoppy Meggs hesitated—he was staring into the trunk.

"Say, youse don't mean dat—do youse?" he demanded heavily. "Not dem papers dat—"

Hunchback Joe's smile was not pleasant.

"Lock the trunk!" he said curtly. And then, as Hoppy Meggs closed down the lid: "I didn't bring you here to offer any advice; but as I don't want you to labour under the impression that, not having any brains of your own, there aren't, therefore, any brains at all to stand between you and the police, I'll tell you. If they recover the original document, besides fixing the crime on Klanner, they'll figure they've got it back before any harm has been done, and before it has been passed on to whoever had paid down the little cash advance to Klanner for the job in the shape of that roll there—eh? And figuring that way they won't change any of the plans or details as they stand now in those papers—eh? And meanwhile a *copy* is just as good to the man who is coughing up to you and me and the rest of us for this, isn't it?"

"My Gawd!" said Hoppy Meggs in fervent admiration, as he locked the trunk.

"Yes," said Hunchback Joe—and the snarl was back in his voice. "And now you see to it that you've got the rest of what *you've* got to do straight. It won't pay you to make any mistakes! Let the Mole's crowd start something before you pull the lights—it's got to look like a drunken row where the bystander, with nobody but himself to blame for being in such a place as that, *accidentally* gets his! And you tip the Kid off again to leave Klanner by his lonesome at the table before the trouble starts, or he'll get in bad himself. The Kid can pull a fake play to make up with some moll across the room. Klanner's no friend of his, he never saw the man before—you understand?—just ran into him outside the dance hall, if any questions are asked. But I don't want any questions, and there won't be any if he plays his hand right. Tell him I said his job's over once he has Klanner inside—and to stand from under. Get me?"

"Sure!" said Hoppy Meggs.

"Well, we'll beat it, then," snapped Hunchback Joe.

The room was in darkness again. Jimmie Dale crouched further back along the wall. The rear door opened, two shadows emerged, passed around the corner of the tenement—and disappeared.

The minutes passed, five of them, and then Jimmie Dale, too, was making his way softly along the areaway to the street—but in Jimmie Dale's pockets were the short leaden blackjack, ugly for the stain on its leathern covering, the packet of papers, and the roll of banknotes that had been in Klanner's trunk. He gained the street, paused under the nearest street lamp to consult his watch, and swung briskly along again. It was a matter of only two blocks to Baldy Jack's, one of the most infamous dance halls in the Bad Lands, but it was already ten minutes to ten.

And now a curious metamorphosis came to Jimmie Dale's appearance. The neat, well-fitting Fifth Avenue tweeds did not fit quite so perfectly—the coat bunched a little at the shoulders, the trousers were drawn a little higher until they lost their "set." His hat was pulled still farther over his eyes, but at a more rakish angle, and his tie, tucked into his shirt bosom just below the collar, exposed blatantly a diamond shirt stud. But on Jimmie Dale's lips there was an ominous smile not wholly in keeping with the somewhat jaunty swagger he had assumed, and the lines at the corners of his mouth were drawn down hard and sharp. It was miserable work, the work of a hound and cur! Who, better than the *janitor* of the bank, would have had the opportunity to carry on that work there! And so they had selected Klanner as their victim. But Klanner, if allowed to talk, might be able to defend himself—therefore Klanner would not be allowed to talk. There was only one way to prevent that effectively—by killing Klanner. But, again, Klanner's death must not appear in any way to be consequent to the murder at the bank—therefore it was to bear every evidence of having been purely inadvertent, and, in a way, an accident. Yes, it was crafty enough, hideous enough to be fully worthy even of the fiendish brain that had planned it! Kid Greer, having probably struck up an acquaintance with Klanner during the past few days, had inveigled Klanner tonight into Baldy Jack's, ostensibly, no doubt, for an innocent and casual glass of beer, and in a general row and melee in the dance hall—not an uncommon occurrence in a place like Baldy Jack's—Klanner would be shot and killed. The rest was obvious. The man's effects would naturally be examined, and the evidence of his "guilt" found in his trunk. It was an open and shut game against a dead man! Even his previous good record would smash on the rock of a presumed double life. The fact that Klanner had voluntarily been in a place like Baldy Jack's was damning in itself!

Jimmie Dale, approaching the garishly lighted exterior of the dance hall now, lit a cigarette. The plan, if successful, placed the guilt without question or cavil upon Klanner, but that was not all—strong as that motive might be, Clarke had had still another in view, and one that perhaps took precedence over the first. Hunchback Joe had defined it clearly enough. The documents would have been valueless to Clarke, either to sell, or to put to any use himself, if the plans and arrangements they contained were subsequently altered or changed. But it was obvious that a man in Klanner's station could have no *personal* interest in them; it was obvious, as evidenced by the money, that he was working for someone else, and therefore the documents appearing in his trunk would logically appear to have been recovered *before* he had been able to hand them over to his principal, and *before* any vital harm had been done that would necessitate any change in the details they contained.

Jimmie Dale pushed the door of the dance hall open, and stepped nonchalantly inside. It was the usual scene, there was the usual hilarious uproar, the usual close, almost fetid atmosphere that mingled the odours of stale beer and tobacco. Baldy Jack's was always popular, and the place, even for that early hour, was already doing a thriving business. Jimmie Dale's eyes, from a dozen couples swirling in the throes of the bunny-hug on the polished section of the floor in the centre of the hall, strayed over the little tables that were ranged three and four deep around the walls. At the upper end of the room a man, fair-haired and neatly dressed, though his clothes were evidently not those of one in over-affluent circumstances, sat alone at one of the tables. It might, or might not, be Klanner. Jimmie Dale strolled forward up the hall, and, as though deliberating over his selection of a seat, paused by the table. The man looked up. There was a long, jagged scar on the other's right cheek bone. It was Klanner. Jimmie Dale pulled out a chair at a vacant table directly behind the other, and sat down. A waiter, in beer-spotted apron and balancing a dripping tray, came for his order.

"Suds!" said Jimmie Dale laconically.

Again Jimmie Dale's eyes made a circuit of the place, failed to identify the person of one Kid Greer, and, giving up the attempt, rested speculatively instead on Klanner's back. Yes, he could quite fully understand why the Tocsin could not have warned Klanner to beware, for instance, of Kid Greer. Such a warning, apart from keeping Hunchback Joe from planting the evidence, would even have defeated its own end—for, even to save Klanner, the game had to be played out as Hunchback Joe had planned it. They meant to "get" Klanner, and if not here at Baldy Jack's, then somewhere else. She *knew* what they meant to do here—she *might not* know when, or how, or where they would make the attempt if they had been forced to change their plans.

Jimmie Dale tossed a coin on the table, as the waiter set down a glass of beer in front of him—and then, over the top of the glass, Jimmie Dale resumed his scrutiny of the hall. Directly behind him was a back entrance that opened on a lane at the rear of the building; and between himself and the entrance was only one table, which was unoccupied. Jimmie Dale, playing with his match box, as he lighted another cigarette, dropped the box, stooped to pick it up—and drew his chair unostentatiously nearer to Klanner.

It was ten o'clock now, time that—yes, the game was on—*now!* A man, that he recognised as one of the Mole's gunmen, had dropped into a seat a couple of tables away from Klanner, where there was a clear space between the two men. There was a sudden jostling among the dancers on the floor— then an oath, rising high above the riot of talk and laughter—a swirl of fig- ures—a medley of shouts and women's screams, drowning out the squeak of the musicians' violins and the thump of the tinny piano.

Jimmie Dale's jaws locked hard together. There was a struggling, Furi- ous mob at the lower end of the hall—but his eyes now never left the gun- man two tables away. Klanner, in dazed amazement, had half risen from his seat, as though uncertain what to do. The screams, shouts, oaths and yells grew louder—came the roar of a revolver shot—another—pandemonium was reigning now. It seemed an hour, a great period of time since the first shout had rung through the hall—it had been but a matter of seconds. Jimmie Dale was crouched a little forward in his chair now, tense, motionless. What was holding Hoppy Meggs! This was Hoppy Meggs' cue, wasn't it?—those shots there, aimed at the floor, had only been to create the panic—there was to be *another* shot that—

The hall was in sudden darkness. With a spring, quick on the instant, Jimmie Dale was upon Klanner's back, hurling the man to the floor. The tongue-flame of a revolver split the black over his head; there was the deaf- ening roar of a revolver shot almost in his ears that blotted out for an instant all other sounds—and then came the shouts and cries again in an access of terror and now the rush of feet—a blind stampede in the darkness for the exits. Another shot from the gunman, as though to make his work doubly sure, followed the first—but now some of the fear-stricken crowd had come between them, plunging, falling, tripping over tables and chairs, seeking the rear exit.

"Quick!" Jimmie Dale breathed in Klanner's ear. He was half lifting, half dragging the man along. "Quick—get your feet, man!"

There was a surging mob around them now, pushing, fighting madly to reach the door; and, as Klanner regained his feet, they were both swept forward, and, lunging through the door, were precipitated out into the lane. And here, wary of a riot call that had probably already been rung in by the patrolman on the beat, the crowd was taking to its heels and dispersing in both directions along the lane.

"Quick!" said Jimmie Dale again—and, with his hand on Klanner's arm, broke into a run.

Those running in the same direction turned off from the lane at the first cross street; but Jimmie Dale held to the lane, and it was three blocks away from Baldy Jack's before he stopped.

Klanner was panting from his exertions.

"My God—what's it mean!" he gasped. "I—I thought I saw a revolver in that man's hand, the fellow next to me, just as the lights went out."

"You probably did," said Jimmie Dale grimly.

"Well—what's it mean?" repeated Klanner heavily.

It was a moment before Jimmie Dale answered. For the man's own sake, the less that Klanner knew the better, probably—and yet the man must be kept out of harm's way for the rest of the night. Having failed at Baldy Jack's, it was certain, since Clarke's whole plan hinged on Klanner's death, that they would try again. After tonight—if all went well—it did not matter, for Klanner then would be no longer a factor to Clarke or Hunchback Joe!

"It means," said Jimmie Dale gravely, "that there's been some sort of a gangster's fight pulled off, and that probably there's been dirty work— murder—in there. The police will go the limit to round up everybody they can find who was in Baldy Jack's. There's only one thing to do—keep your mouth shut and lie low tonight. You can't take any chances of getting into this—you look like a man who's got a decent job he doesn't want to lose, and you don't look like a man who is entitled to be saddled with a reputation for hanging around that sort of place. Do you live near here?"

"Yes," said Klanner, a little dully.

"Well then," said Jimmie Dale quietly, "get out of this neighbourhood for the night. Don't risk recognition while the chase is hot. Go uptown some- where to any hotel you like, and *stay* there in your room. You can go to work just as well from there in the morning. Got any money?"

"Yes," said Klanner slowly. "Yes, I got some money—and I guess you're right. Say, who are you anyway? You seem to have a line on this sort of thing, and I guess I owe you a whole skin. If you hadn't—"

"I'm a man in a hurry," said Jimmie Dale whimsically—and then the grim note crept back into his voice. "I am giving you a straight tip. Take it—and take that street car that's coming along there." He held out his hand.

"Sure!" said Klanner. "And I—"

"Good-night," said Jimmie Dale, and started abruptly across the street, entering the lane on the other side again—but here, in the shadows, he paused for a moment, watching until Klanner boarded the uptown car.

CHAPTER 24

AT FIVE MINUTES OF TWELVE

Twenty minutes later, well along the East River front, in an unsavoury and deserted neighbourhood, Jimmie Dale was crouched before the door of a small building that seemed built half on the shore edge, and half on an old and run-down pier that extended out into the water. The building itself was little more than a storage shed, and originally had probably laid claims to nothing more pretentious—today it served as warehouse and office for Hunchback Joe's "business," and, above, for Hunchback Joe's living quarters. Jimmie Dale glanced around him sharply—not for the first time. There were no other buildings in his immediate vicinity, and such as could be seen loomed up only as black, shadowy, distant shapes—warehouses and small factories, for the most part, and empty and deserted now at night. It was intensely black—only a twinkling light here and there from a passing craft on the river, and the glow from thousands of street lamps that, like some strange aerial illumination, hovered over the opposite shore. The shed itself, windowless at least in front, was as silent, as deserted, and as black as all around it.

Jimmie Dale's hand stole into his pocket, produced a black silk mask, adjusted the mask over his face—and then the deft, slim fingers were at work with a little steel instrument on the door lock. A moment more, and the door swung silently inward, slowly, inch by inch. He listened intently. There was no sound. He stepped inside, and silently closed and locked the door behind If Hunchback Joe had not returned yet, it was necessary that Hunchback Joe should find the door as he had left it—locked! Again Jimmie Dale listened—and then the ray of his flashlight circled the place. A miscellany of ship's junk was piled without any attempt at order all over the place; a board partition with two small windows, one on each side of the door, ran from side to side of the shed about a third of the way up its length; and in the sides of the shed itself were also two small, narrow windows—too small and too narrow, Jimmie Dale noted grimly, for the passage of a man's body.

He moved forward cautiously, though he was almost certain that he was ahead of Hunchback Joe. He, Jimmie Dale, had come without an instant's loss of time from Baldy Jack's, and it was more than an even chance that Hunchback Joe would have remained somewhere in the neighbourhood until the affair was over. It would take some little time—not until after the police had restored order—to discover that the attempt upon Klanner had been abortive, that Klanner's body was *not* lying there dead on the floor. But after that—Jimmie Dale opened the door of the partition stealthily, slipped through, and, as his flashlight swept around again, nodded his head sharply—yes, he had thought so!—there was a means of communication here—a telephone. Well then, after that, Hunchback Joe would set every crook and tool over whom he had any control at work to find Klanner. But that meant different men at work in many different directions, and there must therefore be some central spot where Hunchback Joe could be instantly reached and reports made to him should Klanner be found—and what better place, what more likely place than here in the security of his own lair! Yes, Hunchback Joe, since he, Jimmie Dale, was now satisfied that the other had not yet returned, would be back here, and, in all probability, long before midnight. Midnight! Why had the Tocsin set midnight, waited for midnight as the hour for the Secret Service raid? Did she have a hidden purpose in that? Was it possible she knew that someone beside Hunchback Joe would also be here at that hour—that Clarke might be here, too! Well, why not! There might well be need for a conference between Clarke and his unholy chief of staff! There might—Jimmie Dale frowned savagely. His mind was running riot! He had not come here to speculate on possibilities; for, whatever might happen, there was definite and instant work to do.

The white ray of the flashlight played steadily now around him. The place evidently served as the office; it was partitioned off again in exactly the same manner from the rear of the shed, making an oblong enclosure the width of the shed one way, and a good fifteen feet the other. It was electric-lighted, and contained a battered table in lieu of desk, upon which stood the telephone; there were several chairs, and a safe, whose scratched, marred, and apparently ramshackle exterior did not disguise from Jimmie Dale the fact that it was of the finest and most modern make.

A rough, wooden stairway led above. Jimmie Dale mounted this, found that it gave on a crudely furnished, attic-like bedroom, and then descending again, he opened the rear door of the partition, and flashed his light around the back of the shed. There were a few packing cases here—that was all. The shed was evidently built out to the extreme end of the pier, judging from its depth; and there had been side doors, but these were boarded up and bore evidence of having been long out of use—and there were no windows.

Jimmie Dale returned now to the front of the shed.

"Under the sail-cloth in left corner," she had written. Yes, here it was! He stooped down, a twisted smile on his lips, and, taking from his pocket the packet of papers and the blackjack, tucked them under several folds of the cloth. "Unto Caesar!" she had said. Well, he had rendered back to "Caesar" the things that were "Caesar's." He straightened up. The Secret Service men would know where to look—she would have seen to that! "Unto Caesar!" The smile died away, and an angry red tinged Jimmie Dale's cheeks—he was picturing again that scene in Klanner's room, the bestial deviltry of that deformed and hideous creature who, to cover up his own guilt, was railroad-ing an innocent man to death. "Unto Caesar!"—yes, there was grim justice here—but that was not enough! Justice might and *would* have its turn, but before then there was another sort of justice, too!

He went back into the office, and sat down in a chair beside the table where he could command the door. He laid his flashlight, the ray on, upon the table, took from his pocket the metal insignia case, lifted out a seal, dropped it by means of the tweezers on his handkerchief, folded the handkerchief carefully, and replaced the insignia case and handkerchief in his pocket; then, switching off the flashlight, he restored that, too, to his pocket.

It was dark now again—and silent. There was no sound, save the gentle lap of water against the pier, and the distant, muffled murmur of traffic from one of the great bridges that spanned the river. Jimmie Dale's automatic was in his hand. There was one man who stood between the woman whom he loved and her happiness, one man, who had driven her from her home and by every foul art and craft had sought to take her life, one man, one man only—Marre, alias Clarke. And once Clarke were run to earth, she was free forever—no one else had any incentive in hounding her to her death.

Well, there was one man who knew where Marre was—Hunchback Joe. And, come what might, Hunchback Joe would tell him, Jimmie Dale, tonight where Marre was! He was not so sure as the Tocsin that Hunchback Joe would talk to the police; he was sure that Hunchback Joe would talk—*to the Gray Seal.* That was all. That was what he was waiting for here now in the darkness before the police came—for Hunchback Joe.

Time passed—a half hour—an hour. It was getting perilously close to the time when the Secret Service men would be pounding at the door out there, and the margin of time left for that grim interview with Hunchback Joe was narrowing rapidly; but there was a strange, calm, cold patience possessing Jimmie Dale—the man would come, and come in time—he knew that, knew it as he knew that he sat there and lived and breathed.

The silence was oppressive, heavy; it seemed to palpitate in rhythm with the lap of the water against the pier. The minutes dragged by, another five of them—and then suddenly Jimmie Dale sat rigidly forward in his chair. The front door had not been unlocked or opened, but there was the sound of a footstep now—from the rear section of the shed, where there had appeared to be no entrance! The footstep came nearer—the door of the partition opened—there was the click of the electric-light switch—the light came on—and then a low, savage, startled oath came from the doorway.

Jimmie Dale did not move—his automatic was covering the misshapen, toad-like figure of Hunchback Joe, as the other stood just inside the room. For a moment neither spoke—then Hunchback Joe laughed suddenly in cool contempt.

"What's the game?" he demanded. "You don't need any mask on here—I deal with your kind every day. What do you want?"

Jimmie Dale rose to his feet.

"This—to begin with!" he said—and, crossing the room, felt through the other's pockets, and possessed himself of the man's revolver. "Now go over there, and sit down at that table!"

Hunchback Joe laughed contemptuously again, as he obeyed; but there was a hint of deadly menace in his voice as he spoke.

"Go to it—while you can!" he snarled. "You've got the drop on me. Well, what do you want?"

Jimmie Dale followed, and faced the other across the table. Hunchback Joe's eyes, with that curious, unpleasant trick of which the man seemed possessed, were blinking ceaselessly.

"I want to give this back to you," said Jimmie Dale quietly—and flung the roll of bills that he had taken from Klanner's trunk down upon the table.

Hunchback Joe's eyes ceased to blink.

"Why, thanks!" grinned Hunchback Joe. "You're a sort of a night marauder, you are! Sure this is for me, and that you aren't making a mistake?"

"Quite sure," said Jimmie Dale, still quietly. "It's yours. It's the money you planted in Klanner's trunk a couple of hours ago."

"I never heard of Klanner," said Hunchback Joe.

"It's simply the evidence that that isn't all I found in the trunk," said Jimmie Dale. "There was a packet of papers, and the blood-stained blackjack with which Jathan Lane was murdered in the bank this afternoon."

"My God, the man's mad!" muttered Hunchback Joe under his breath. "I'm up against a maniac!"

Jimmie Dale had taken his handkerchief from his pocket, and, carrying it to his mouth, had moistened the adhesive side of the little seal. His voice rasped, as his hand went down upon the table.

"You blot on God's earth!" he said hoarsely. "That's enough of that! The buttons are off the foils tonight, Hunchback Joe!"

For the second time, Hunchback Joe's eyes had ceased to blink. He was staring at the gray seal on the table top in front of him, and now in spite of his effort to maintain nonchalance, a whiteness had come into his face.

"You!" he shrank back a little in his chair. "The Gray Seal!"

Jimmie Dale's lips were thin and drawn tight together. He made no answer.

It was Hunchback Joe who broke the silence.

"What's your price?" he asked thickly. "I suppose you've got those—those other things, or at least you know where they are."

"Yes," said Jimmie Dale grimly, "I know where they are."

"Well"—Hunchback Joe hesitated, fumbling for his words—"we're both tarred with the same brush, only you're worse than I am. I've got to pay your price, of course. Make it reasonable. I haven't got all the money in the world. Tell me where those things are, and name your figures."

"My figure"—Jimmie Dale was clipping off his words—"is a little information. A trade, Hunchback Joe—mine for yours. I want to know where Peter Marre, alias Clarke, is?"

Hunchback Joe drew back from the table with a jerk. The whiteness in his face had changed to an unhealthy, leaden gray. He shook his head.

"I don't know," he said. "That's straight—I've heard of Marre, of course, everybody has, he's a lawyer; but I never heard of Clarke, and that's—"

"A lie!" Jimmie Dale cut in, an ugly calm in his voice "You—"

But Jimmie Dale, too, was interrupted. The telephone on the table was ringing. His automatic covering Hunchback Joe, he pulled the instrument toward him, and lifted the receiver from the hook.

"Hello!" he said gruffly. "What's wanted?"

A voice responded in feverish excitement:

"Say, dat youse, Joe? Dis is Hoppy Meggs. Say, de fly cops has got tipped off; dey're on de way down to yer place now. Youse want to beat it on de jump!"

"Wait a minute!" said Jimmie Dale. He passed the instrument over to Hunchback Joe. "It's for you," he said, with a slight smile.

Hunchback Joe put the receiver to his ear—and a moment later, without a word in reply, returned it to the hook. But he had risen from his seat, and, swaying on his feet, was gripping at the table edge for support.

"I could have told you that," said Jimmie Dale evenly; "but you've got it now from a source that you won't question. I told you the buttons were off the foils tonight, but you don't seem to realise it yet. Three nights ago you laid a trap for me—*and the Pippin died*. Do you understand what I mean now by naked foils? You've one chance for life—and that's to answer my question. But I'll play fair with you, and tell you that I'm going to see that the police get you even if you do answer. Those documents and that blackjack are here in this place, and the Secret Service men know where to find them." Jimmie Dale's watch was in his hand. "It's five minutes to twelve. They'll be here at midnight. I've got to make my getaway before they come. I need two minutes for that, including locking you in so that *you* can't get away. That leaves you three minutes to make up your mind. If you answer, you can have whatever chance your lawyers can get you; if you refuse, you and I settle our score before I leave. It's three minutes against a possible commutation of sentence to life imprisonment. *Where is Marre?*"

The misshapen, shrunken thing was rocking on its feet. There was no answer.

"There are two minutes left," said Jimmie Dale in a monotone.

The man's eyes, coal black, hunted, the pupils gone, swept the room. His lips were working; his hands, clenching and unclenching, clawed at the table.

"*One!*" said Jimmie Dale.

There was a scream of ungovernable fury, the crash of the toppling table, and, reaching out with both hands for Jimmie Dale's weapon, Hunchback Joe hurled himself forward—but quick as the other was, Jimmie Dale was quicker, and with his left hand, palm open, pushed full into the man's face, he flung the other back.

And then there came a cry—a cry in a woman's voice;

"*Marre!*"

It was the Tocsin's voice from the rear doorway of the office. It was her voice; Jimmie Dale could never mistake it even in its startled cry—but he did not look. His eyes were on the man who was standing on the other side of the overturned table, whose beard where he, Jimmie Dale, had grasped the other's face had been wrenched away, and whose shrunken figure seemed to tower up now in height, and whose deformity was a padded coat, awry now because of the erect and upright posture in which the man stood. It was Clarke, the master of disguise, who once had impersonated Travers, the chauffeur; it was Marre—Wizard Marre.

There was a ghastly smile on the man's face.

"Marre," he said. "Yes—Marre. But you never knew it, did you, Miss LaSalle—until now! Well, now is time enough for you, and far too soon for me!" He flung out his hand in an impotent gesture, as he threw back his shoulders. "But I would like to be thought a good loser. I congratulate you, Miss LaSalle!" Again his hand was raised in gesture—and with lightning swiftness, before Jimmie Dale could intervene, swept to his vest pocket and was carried to his mouth. "And so I drink to your success, and—"

A glass vial rolled away upon the floor—and Jimmie Dale, with a bound, had caught the swaying figure in his arms. There was a tremor through the man's form—then inertness. He lowered the other to the ground. Wizard Marre was dead. It was the colourless liquid of the old Crime Club, instantaneous in its action that—

Jimmie Dale swept his hand over his masked face, and pulled the mask away, and looked up. She, the Tocsin; yes, it was the Tocsin; yes, it was Marie—only the beautiful face was deadly pale—it was the Tocsin who was standing over him, shaking him frantically by the shoulder.

"Jimmie! Quick! Quick!" she cried. "The Secret Service men! Don't you hear them? Quick! This way!"

There was a crash, a pound upon the street door. She had caught his hand, and was pulling him forward now out into the rear of the shed. There was a light from the office doorway—enough to see. One of the packing cases was tipped over, and, on hinges, made a trap door. A short ladder led downward to where, a few feet below, two boats were moored.

"I came this way. I followed him," she said. "Quick—Jimmie!"

It took an instant, no more, to swing her through the opening, but as he lowered her down and her hair brushed his cheek, there came a quick half sob to Jimmie Dale's lips.

"Mark!" he whispered. "Marie—at last!"

Came the rip and tear and rend of wood, the thud of a falling door from the front of the shed, the rush of feet—but Jimmie Dale was in the boat now, and the packing case above was swung back into place.

"Right ahead, Jimmie!" she breathed. "The planks at the end of the pier swing aside—yes, there—no, a little to the right—yes!"

The boat shot out into the river—farther out—and the pier and shed merged into the shadows of the shore line and were lost.

And then Jimmie Dale let the oars swing loose. She was crouched in the bottom of the boat close beside him. He bent his head until his lips touched her hair, and lower still until his lips touched hers. And a long time passed.

And the boat drifted on. And he drew her closer into his arms, and held her there. She was safe now, safe for always—and the road of fear lay behind. And into the night there seemed to come a great quiet, and a great joy, and a great thankfulness, and a wondrous peace.

And the boat drifted on.

And neither spoke—for they were going *home*.

JIMMIE DALE AND THE PHANTOM CLUE

CHAPTER 1

THE TOCSIN

The boat drifted on. In the distance a ferry churned its way across the river. From the farther shore the myriad lights of Brooklyn flung a soft glow into the sky, like a canopy between the city and the night.

And in the boat two figures merged as one in the darkness.

"Marie!" Jimmie Dale whispered. His arms tightened about her. "Marie!"

She made answer by a little pressure of her hand.

He looked behind him—in toward the nearer shore. Somewhere back there, somewhere amongst those irregular outlines that thrust out points of deeper darkness into the black, mirror-like surface of the water, was the old pier from beneath which they had escaped, and, above the pier, the shed where but a little while ago—or was it hours, or a lifetime ago?—Clarke, alias Wizard Marre, alias Hunchback Joe, had played his last card, and lost.

A grim smile touched Jimmie Dale's lips. Inside that shed the secret service men had found their quarry—dead. They were there now. In their hands lay the evidence that solved the murder of Jathan Lane; and in their hands, too, was the murderer himself—only Wizard Marre had taken the easier way, and was dead.

Jimmie Dale's smile softened. Inside that shed at the present moment there was commotion enough and light enough; but he could hear nothing, and he could see no light. The Tocsin here and himself were too far away. Too far away! Yes, that was it—at last! Too far away from the old life—forever. The road of fear lay behind them, and she was free, free to come out into the sunlight again. She had said so herself in that letter he had read at the club only a few hours ago. Free! Life lay before them now—and love. With the death of Wizard Marre there could now be an end of his, Jimmie Dale's, own rôles of the Gray Seal, and Larry the Bat, and Smarlinghue, and—no, not hers as the Tocsin, that could never change or terminate, for she would always be the Tocsin to him.

The Tocsin! Memory came surging upon him. That night in the long ago, before he had ever seen her, when he had known her only as the woman who addressed him as "Dear Philanthropic Crook" in those mysterious notes of hers that, supplying the data on which he had acted, the data for those "crimes," where no crime save that of rendering abortive the crimes of others had ever been, had made the name of the Gray Seal anathema to police and underworld alike; that night when, besides a note, he had also found a gold seal ring of hers, a dainty thing that bore a crest, a bell surmounted by a bishop's mitre, and underneath, in the scroll, a motto in French: *Sonnez le Tocsin!* It had seemed so apt! Ring the Tocsin! Sound the alarm! Always her notes had done that—calling the Gray Seal to arms that someone else might be the better or the happier for what she bade him do. The Tocsin! The word had seemed to visualise her then, and, knowing her by no other name, he had called her—the Tocsin.

She stirred a little in his arms.

"What time is it, Jimmie?" she asked.

He shook his head. Time! What did time matter now? To Marie LaSalle, who once had lived in hourly peril of her life as Silver Mag in the days of the old Crime Club, and later, yes even until tonight, had again been forced to live under cover of some rôle which she had never divulged to him and which he had never penetrated; and to him, Jimmie Dale, in whose ears need never sound again that slogan of the underworld, "Death to the Gray Seal!" that reached to every nook and corner of the Bad Lands—to her and to him what did time count for now, save as a great, illimitable mine of happiness, a wealth beyond all telling that they were to spend *together*!

She spoke again:

"What time is it, Jimmie?"

And now he answered her.

"I don't know," he said happily. "It was just midnight when the shed back there was raided. Since then there hasn't been any such thing as time, Marie."

"Listen!" she said.

From somewhere across the water, faintly, a tower clock struck the hour.

"One o'clock!" she exclaimed, as though in dismay. "We must be getting ashore. I—I did not think it was so late. And please, Jimmie, I'd like to row the boat. I—I feel quite—quite cold."

He felt her shiver a little in his arms.

"Cold!" he echoed anxiously; and then, as he released her: "All right, if you really want to. It isn't very far. And I guess it's safe now. Pull in and skirt along the shore until we can find some good place to land."

She nodded as she picked up the oars, then turned the boat's head in toward the shore and began to row.

Jimmie Dale moved back into the stern of the boat and settled himself in his seat. He watched her, drinking in the lithe, graceful swing of her body, the rhythmic stroke of the heavy oars. He could not see her face for the night shadows hid it, but he could see the poise of her head and the contour of the full, perfect throat. And he clasped his hand behind his head, and a great happiness and a great peace fell upon him.

It seemed somehow as though the voyage of this little boat in which they had fled out here into the night for safety epitomised a voyage of great immensity that had begun in the very long ago, a voyage of interminable night through which his eyes had been straining and his soul had been yearning for a glimpse of the beacon light that should signal the approach to a wondrous Port of Dawn. And now the voyage was almost at an end. Marie there at the oars, and the peace and quiet around them, was the beacon light at last; and they could no more lose their way because the way was charted now to that Port of Dawn where there was no more any strife and peril and sordid crime, and where only love was.

He smiled at his fancy, and suddenly laughed out into the night.

"Keep in a little to the right, Marie," he called. "There's something that looks like a low wharf ahead that ought to do."

"Yes; I see it," she answered.

Jimmie Dale sat abruptly upright in his seat. Perhaps it was only the rasp and creak of the oars in the rowlocks, but it had sounded so *human*—like a short, quick, suppressed sob. He leaned forward.

"Was that you, Marie?" he asked quickly. "What is it?"

He could not see her face. Her voice came back to him steady and untroubled:

"Nothing, Jimmie."

Across the night, far up above them and in the distance, a great bridge stretched from shore to shore, its arc of sparkling lights like a tiara crowning the brow of the heavens. Faintly there came the roar of traffic, ever restless, ever sleepless. A trolley clanged its way unseen somewhere near the shore which the boat was now rapidly approaching; and here, where the lights showed but sparsely, many buildings, small and large, loomed out in grotesque and fanciful shapes.

Jimmie Dale's dark eyes lighted. All this was as it always was and always had been—only it was *changed*. It held a promise now that it had never held before. He felt his pulse beat quicken.

The Port of Dawn!

"Here we are, Marie!" he cried.

The bow of the boat touched the edge of a low wharf—and then Jimmie Dale, like a man stunned, bewildered, his mind and brain in turmoil and riot, was standing up in the stern of the boat. Quick, like a flash, the Tocsin had

lifted the oars from the rowlocks, flung them away in the water, and, springing to the string-piece of the wharf, had pushed the boat out again.

"Jimmie! Oh, Jimmie!" Her voice reached him in a low, broken sob.
"There was no other way. It's in your pocket, Jimmie. I put it there when—
when you were—were holding me."

"Marie!" he cried out wildly. "In God's name, what are you doing, Marie!" He flung himself upon his knees and began to paddle furiously with his
hands. "Marie!" he cried again.

A shadow flitted swiftly along the wharf shorewards; it grew filmy and
mingled with a thousand other shadows—and was lost.

She was gone! The Tocsin was gone—as she had gone so many times before. He paddled on with his hands, but the act was purely mechanical. Gone!
A cold chill was at his heart; an agony of fear seized upon him. Gone—when
life in all its fulness....Gone! Why? An abyss seemed to yawn before him.

After a time the boat bumped against the wharf. He sprang out and ran
madly to the shore. He found himself groping like a blind man amongst
buildings, in alleys, along dimly lighted streets. And then suddenly he stood
still with the consciousness of stark futility upon him. Had he learned no lesson from the past? It was useless to search for her. He might have known that
from the first! He *had* known it, only—only things had seemed so *changed*
tonight.

Fear took its toll of him again. It brought the sweat beads out upon his
forehead. *Fear for her.* Subconsciously he realised now that something,
somewhere, had, after all, gone wrong tonight; that she was still in danger,
a danger that she still meant he should not share. No other reason save that
brave, unselfish love of hers would have prompted her to this.

"It's in your pocket, Jimmie." Her words came back to him.

He searched quickly, and with a sharp little cry of pain drew out a sealed
envelope. Under a street lamp in a deserted street, he tore it open. Words that
he had never thought to see again danced unsteadily before his eyes. He read:

Dear Philanthropic Crook—

Since you *must* be that again, I do not know under what circumstances you will receive this. I only know that before the night is
over I shall be with you, and we will be together—for a little while.
And, Jimmie, I am writing this instead of telling you what I must
say, because I am afraid of myself and our love, afraid that I would
not be strong enough to hold out against the plea of our hearts that
at all costs we should remain together, and against your arguments,
and perhaps against your physical restraint—for you *are* masterful,
Jimmie. I cannot bring you any more into the shadows in which I
know now I must live again. I must not, Jimmie; for it might only too
well mean your certain destruction, the certain revelation to both the

police and the underworld that the Gray Seal and Larry the Bat and Smarlinghue are none other than Jimmie Dale, the Riverside Drive millionaire and clubman. You see, I am writing without reserve, putting upon paper what has never been put upon paper before, because I know that in some way I shall personally place this letter in your possession, and that no other hands shall touch it and no other eyes shall see it save yours and mine.

I am writing this half an hour before midnight, while I am waiting for midnight to come with its disclosure at the old junk-shop on the East River that Hunchback Joe is Wizard Marre—and Clarke. And only a day or so ago, Jimmie, I wrote you another letter telling you that once Clarke was in the hands of the police I would be safe for always. And Clarke *will* be caught tonight, and you will believe that a new world stretches before us, and that all our hopes and aspirations are to come true at last, and you will be happier perhaps in that moment than you have ever been before. Oh, Jimmie, it is so hard even to *write* this, for I love you so; but it is because I do love you with all my heart and soul and life that I will not, shall not, must not let a breath of suspicion exist that there is anything between Marie LaSalle and Jimmie Dale. God keep and guard you! I shall pray always and always for that. And some day, some time perhaps—no, not perhaps, but surely, surely....

Jimmie, I did not mean to write like this. Listen! You know, through the letter to which I referred above, why during all these past months I have 'disappeared.' You know that I was the *only* one who could identify Clarke as one of the leaders of the old Crime Club, and that it was a question of my life or his. You know that he went into hiding, and that there followed attempt after attempt upon my life. And then I 'left the city for an extended trip,' as my bankers informed you. And while you sought to find me, which, for the same reasons that still exist tonight, I could not let you do, I fought Clarke under cover with his own weapons. A few days ago I believed I had won; it seemed only a question of hours. I had placed Clarke in his true person as Marre, the shyster lawyer, and in his other alias as Hunchback Joe. And then suddenly, as though he had never existed, I lost him.

You now know why. He and some of his band were at work under the bank making that opening into the president's private office that resulted this afternoon in the murder of Jathan Lane. I was too late to prevent that, but almost immediately afterwards I picked up Clarke's trail again. I found out that in some way, to cover their own tracks, to end all investigation, false evidence was somehow to be planted, and that to bear this out another murder was to be added to that of the bank president. Jimmie, what could I do? I could not stand passively aside, even when by so doing my own victory was assured. I had to go on. It was to save a man's life. There was a way to get the information necessary to forestall them, though it involved a risk that I would otherwise never have taken. In a measure I succeeded; I learned how the papers and money, and the black-jack with which the murder was committed, were to be placed in Klanner's, the bank janitor's, trunk in his boarding house, and that the man was to be lured into Baldy Jack's dance hall, where, in a riot staged for the occasion, their victim, apparently an innocent bystander, but with his reputation further blasted by being found in that unsavory resort, was to be shot. A dead man could refute no false evidence! I managed to get word to you, and, thank God, in time. But *I* was caught—and in my own character of Marie LaSalle. I was carried to one of Clarke's lairs, and left there a prisoner. They meant to finish me when the rest of the night's work was over.

But I must hurry on, Jimmie. It is getting late.

As I shall have been with you for a little while before you will have read this, you will know of course that I escaped. I have no time now to tell you how. The details do not matter. What matters is this: That while, before, Clarke was the only one who had any concern in putting me out of the way, and that for his own personal safety, that enmity is now transferred to an even more formidable enemy—those, and particularly one, who during the last year have been associated with Clarke. They will be actuated by two motives. First, revenge for the trap that will place Clarke in the hands of the police for the murder of Jathan Lane, and revenge for my interference in their attempt upon Klanner; and, second, the fear—a much more potent motive—that I know far more about them and who they are than I really do, the fear that I am in possession of all the knowledge needed to place them too behind the bars of the death house in Sing Sing. I do not know them, Jimmie—except one man, and that man I am not sure of at all. He is a bigger, brainier, far more crafty man than ever Clarke was, and far more powerful. There are times when I think I know him, and times when I am equally sure that I do not. I have come to call him the Phantom. If I am right, he has a score of aliases, a score of domiciles, and possesses the facility of appearing convincingly in each one of a bewildering number of different characters. I said that they had caught me in my own person. I do not need to tell you now, Jimmie, that if I were to go back to New York and resume my life as Marie LaSalle it would but be going to certain death.

Just one thing more. I do not believe that the bank's papers, valuable as they were, that they took from Jathan Lane in his office, were the sole motive for his murder; indeed, I am not sure that they were the *real* motive. I do not know, of course. But I overheard snatches of something about a safe at Jathan Lane's house tonight at two o'clock, something that was to have its fulfilment later in a rendezvous at half-past three with an old acquaintance of yours, one Gentleman Laroque. I may be quite wrong; it may be that, even if I am right, my escape and Clarke's capture would effectually put a stop to anything further they might have schemed to do; but if there *is* anything in it, and if they go on, there will be others at Gentleman Laroque's who are not expected—the police. I will see to that. And so, perhaps, Jimmie, even tonight, after all, something may happen that will point the way to this Phantom and those with him—and to happiness for us.

And now you must not be too anxious, Jimmie. In a measure I am safe. They have never penetrated the rôle which I have been playing, and I do not think they ever will. And you are going to help me, too, Jimmie, whenever—oh, Jimmie, those old days!—whenever I can 'sound the Tocsin' without allying you with me in the eyes of those upon whom Clarke's mantle has fallen.

Jimmie Dale raised haggard eyes. The signature seemed somehow blurred. "Marie...Marie...!"

CHAPTER 2
THE GRAY SEAL

For a time Jimmie Dale stood motionless under the light, then he started automatically on along the street. He tore the letter into small fragments and the fragments into tiny shreds as he went along. The world seemed a void. No, not that! It was more as though fate jeered at him ironically. He was exactly, in respect of the Tocsin and in respect of the fulfilment of his hopes and plans, where he had been yesterday and a thousand yesterdays ago.

He walked on. The tiny shreds of paper, a few at a time, fluttered from his fingers and were lost. Mechanically he found himself boarding a street car. Thereafter he sat, his strong jaw clamped and hard, staring out through the window.

Who was the Phantom?

Twice, at long intervals, he changed cars. Finally, far uptown, he alighted, and, traversing several blocks, paused in front of a large corner house in a most select and exclusive neighbourhood. Ostensibly, had anyone been observing his movements, he had paused in order that, under the street lamp, he might consult his watch. It was a quarter of two. A smile, half grim, half whimsical, as though he were suddenly aroused from some deep reverie to actual physical reality, flickered across his lips. The house on the corner was the residence of Jathan Lane, the bank president, who had been murdered that afternoon.

Jimmie Dale replaced his watch, and nonchalantly turned the corner; but the dark, steady eyes were alight now, sweeping the side street in every direction. His glance detected and held for a bare instant on the black mouth of a lane that showed at the rear of Jathan Lane's house. Jimmie Dale edged toward the inner side of the pavement, still walking nonchalantly. And then, gradually merging more and more with the shadow of the house itself, he came abreast of the lane—and the street was empty. A moment more, and lithe, active, silent as a cat in his movements, he had swung himself over a fence; still another moment, and lost utterly in the shadows of the porch, he was crouching at the basement door of the house.

It was Jimmie Dale, the Gray Seal again, in action now. From under his vest, from one of the multitudinous little upright pockets of that leather girdle where nestled an array of vicious blued-steel implements, a compact burglar's kit, he selected a pick-lock. From another pocket came a black silk mask. Jimmie Dale slipped the mask over his face, and leaned closer to the door. For perhaps five seconds the slim, sensitive fingers were at work, then the door opened noiselessly, and closed again, and was locked behind him.

He stood silent, motionless—listening. There was no sound. Apart from the staff, there should be no one in the house. The papers had overlooked few details in their account of the murder that afternoon. Mrs. Lane was away in Europe, and they had taken the body of Jathan Lane to the house of his married daughter. Under the mask there came again that grim flicker to Jimmie Dale's lips. There were only the servants then—since it was not yet *two o'clock*!

The round, white ray of a flashlight stabbed through the blackness, vanished, and blackness fell again.

"Stairs ahead and to the right," Jimmie Dale confided to himself. "Servants' quarters on top floor probably; only the cellar and storage here."

The flashlight played steadily, impudently now, pointing the way upstairs; and, as silent as the ray itself, Jimmie Dale followed. As he reached the head of the stairs he found a closed door before him. The light went out. He listened again; then, in the darkness, he opened the door and stepped through. Again he listened. Still there was no sound. The flashlight winked once inquisitively—then darkness again. He was standing at the rear of the hall. The basement stairs came up under what was evidently the main staircase.

And now a shadow flitted with incredible swiftness here and there; and doors opened, and some were closed again, and some were left open—and there was no sound. And presently Jimmie Dale stood again at the rear of the hall. He could command the open door that led to the basement stairs; and along the hall, where a slight rift in the blackness made by the plate glass panels was distinguishable, he could command the front doors.

He nodded in quiet satisfaction to himself. Jathan Lane's safe was in a sort of private den or office that opened off the rear of the library, and portières hung between the two rooms; each room had a door opening off the hall, and both doors stood open now. A clock struck somewhere in the house. His lips tightened. It was two o'clock.

Alert, tense, he listened—listened until the silence itself throbbed and beat at the ear drums, and palpitated, and made noises of its own.

There wasn't much chance. He knew that. After what had happened that night, unless under extraordinary conditions, Jathan Lane's safe should be the most inviolate piece of property to be found anywhere in New York. And even if anyone came, the corollary of whatever held its premise in that safe was to be found at Gentleman Laroque's, and the Tocsin had said that the police would be warned in time. Yes, he understood. She had obviously made no effort to render anything abortive here at the source, for the very reason that she hoped it would but lead to the trap she would have prepared at Gentleman Laroque's. Her attitude had been quite logical, quite plausible. So why was *he* here?

Jimmie Dale's hands clenched at his sides. The answer was simple enough, and yet, too, in its very self seemed to hold a world of mockery and, yes, even futility. He was here to pick up the threads of yesterday and of those thousand yesterdays gone—anything—the grasping at any straw that might bring him into that arena where she was battling for her life, and from which, striving to shield him, she sought to bar him out.

He could not very well pick up those threads at Gentleman Laroque's, if indeed there were any threads *to* pick up, for the simple reason that the police would be there! And so he was *here*.

Gentleman Laroque! His brow furrowed. Yes, he remembered Gentleman Laroque—and Niccolo Sonnino—and a certain night that had so nearly cost young Clarie Archman his life. So Gentleman Laroque was in this new combine! Gentleman Laroque had played the rôle of safe-breaker that other night—but Gentleman Laroque had missed his calling, whether as a safe-breaker or as the gang leader that he was. He would have made an infinitely better confidence man, for he was educated, suave, and, when it suited him, polished to a degree; he possessed all the requisites, and, in abundance, the prime requisite of all—a cunning that was the cunning of a fox. Also he, Jimmie Dale, remembered something else about Gentleman Laroque; he remembered Gentleman Laroque's last words to the Gray Seal on that night in question, and now here in the darkness, waiting for he knew not what, with Laroque emerging so unexpectedly from the past, those words, hoarse in their rage and elemental fury, seemed to ring again with strange significance in his ears: "You win tonight, but we'll get you yet! Some day we'll get you, you cursed snitch, you—"

What was that?

The sound came neither from below through the open door of the basement staircase, nor yet from the front doors along the hall. The sound persisted. It was like the gnawing of a rat. And then Jimmie Dale placed its general location. It seemed to come from outside the house, and in direction from the little den or office at his right that contained the safe. He moved stealthily to the doorway, and, still in the hall, protected by the door jamb, peered into the darkness of the room. He could see nothing.

But now the sound was still more clearly defined, and he placed it exactly. Rather than a gnawing, it was a scratching at the wall outside and below the window; and as it continued it seemed at times to grow almost human with impatience and irritability as it quickened its tempo.

And then suddenly Jimmie Dale turned his head. Imagination? No, there was another sound—and it, too, now repeated itself, low, cautious, stealthy. Someone was creeping down the third story stairs from the top of the house.

For an instant Jimmie Dale stood without movement, then a hard, quick smile compressed his lips. That scratching sound outside the window, which still persisted, had not been loud enough to *awaken* anybody. It was rather curious, rather singular! His ears, acute, trained to the slightest sound, caught the footfalls coming now along the upper hall, still low, still cautious and stealthy—and Jimmie Dale slipped across the threshold, and in an instant had passed into the library and was crouched behind the portières that hung between the two rooms.

A minute passed. A tread creaked softly on the main staircase; then a form bulked in irregular outline in the doorway of the little den, paused for the fraction of a second, came into the room, closed the door, and glided swiftly to the window. The window was cautiously opened. There was the soft *pad* of feet as a man crawled through and dropped to the floor. A hoarse whisper vibrated through the room.

"Damn it, why didn't you keep me there all night?" a voice demanded angrily. "You didn't go to *sleep*, did you, or *forget* to leave the window of your room open so's you could *hear*?"

Another voice answered. The words came in a choked, broken way, as though with great effort:

"No; I—I didn't go to sleep. Not likely! I heard you the minute you came, but—but I couldn't help it. I had a—a bit of a turn. I came as soon as I could. I—I was sick."

A ray of a flashlight lanced through the blackness. It played on the tall, gaunt figure of an old, gray-haired man arrayed in a dressing gown, and on a face that was drawn and pallor-like in colour.

Then darkness again.

Behind the portière, Jimmie Dale's face suddenly hardened. There were little gray "mutton-chop" side whiskers, that was the only change. He recognised the man in an instant. It was the "Minister," alias Patrick Denton, one of the cleverest "inside" crooks that had ever infested New York. The man, pronounced an incurable heart case, and even then supposed to be in a dying condition, had been pardoned two years ago while serving a sentence in Sing Sing. Since then he had dropped out of sight; and indeed, generally, was supposed to be dead.

There was a callous grunt from the man at the window.

"Well, you look it!" said the man. "And that's no lie!" He laughed shortly. "And maybe it's a good thing. You could get away with the faithful-butler-mourning-for-his-dead-master stuff without batting an eyelid, if you had to."

There was no answer.

Jimmie Dale's hand slipped into his pocket and came out again with his automatic. So that was it! He began to understand. The Minister was back at his old inside game again—this time in the rôle of Jathan Lane's butler!

The man who had crawled in through the window spoke again—sharply now:

"Well, let's get busy! We've lost too much time as it is. If a light's safe, shoot her on; we can work quicker that way."

"Yes," said the Minister. "It's—it's safe enough." He stifled a cough. "The rest are all asleep; and on account of what happened this afternoon, I had every shade in the house drawn. I—" He broke off with a quick gasp, as coincident with the faint click of an electric-light switch, a single, shaded incandescent on the desk in front of the safe went on. "You!" he exclaimed. "I—I thought it was to be Hunchback Joe."

The fold of the portière in Jimmie Dale's hand drew closer in against the edge of the wall projection until there was left but the veriest crack. A pucker came and nested in little wrinkles at the corners of his eyes. He was not so sure, after all, that he had begun to understand. In view of the Tocsin's letter, he did not understand at all. The man who stood there in the room beside the Minister, the man with the cool, contemptuous black eyes, the thin, cunning lips parted in a grim smile, was Gentleman Laroque.

"So it was," said Laroque coolly. "You've got it straight. Hunchback Joe was to come here for the sparklers, smear the trail by bringing them back to me, and then I was going to slip them to old Isaac Shiftel. But Hunchback Joe couldn't come, and as it's a rather fussy job I didn't dare trust anyone else, so I came myself. I'll take them direct from here to Shiftel's."

The pucker cleared from Jimmie Dale's eyes. Shiftel—old Isaac Shiftel—the fence! The man was an outstanding figure in the underworld! Yes, he *did* begin to understand. But for once, for the first time since those days in the years gone by when the Tocsin had begun to sound those "calls to arms," the Tocsin was astray. It was not her fault. It was nothing that she could by any possibility have foreseen. Only as matters now stood the police trap at Laroque's would be abortive—it should have been at Isaac Shiftel's! Jimmie Dale's lips pressed together. Well, he knew where Isaac Shiftel lived, and instead of the police, it would perhaps be—

Jimmie Dale's mental soliloquy ended abruptly. The Minister was walking with weak, unsteady steps across the room, groping at the desk for support, and speaking as he went.

"There isn't anything the matter, is there?" he asked anxiously. "I mean nothing's gone wrong with that other thing to keep Hunchback Joe away? He's safe, isn't he?"

An oath fell softly from Gentleman Laroque's lips. He still smiled; but the cool contempt had gone from his eyes, and in its place was a smouldering passion.

"Wrong?" he echoed. "No; nothing's gone wrong, except that the whole plant is blown, the papers pinched by the police, and Hunchback Joe is dead."

"What's that, you say?" The old man swayed on his feet, his face a ghastly white. "Dead! You said—dead? I—"

Jimmie Dale straightened up involuntarily. The old man was undeniably ill, desperately ill. He had reeled and would have fallen had not Laroque caught him and placed him in a chair.

"Brandy!" the old man gasped. "Over there—on—on that cabinet."

Laroque procured the stimulant. The Minister gulped it down eagerly. It seemed to revive him. He stared anxiously at Laroque.

"How—what—what happened?" he whispered hoarsely.

"The police were tipped off by someone you don't know, and by someone you do," said Laroque between his teeth. "The someone you know was—the Gray Seal."

"My God!" The white face was set with fear. "The police—and—Hunchback Joe dead! We—we can't go on with this—we'd—"

"We couldn't if Joe *weren't* either trapped or dead," Laroque broke in sharply. "Pull yourself together! We've no time to waste. Don't you understand? It's *safer* than ever it was! If Klanner, the bank janitor, had got his, and the fake evidence had been found the way we planted it, this little deal here tonight was all tucked away neat enough. But Klanner's skin was saved, by luck as we thought then, though we know better now, and that put everything up in the air as far as *this* was concerned—until the police copped Joe with the goods, and Joe snuffed out. That gave them the motive again for the murder this afternoon, and gave them the man who did it. The case is closed now tighter than we figured it could be sewed up even in the first place. Get me?"

The old man shook his head. He looked furtively around him.

"I'm afraid," he said huskily. "If the Gray Seal's in this, it—it ain't safe."

"But I tell you the Gray Seal isn't in this," snapped Laroque impatiently. "That's what I'm trying to get through your thick head! He and every one else will think the curtain rolled down on the *last* act when they got Hunchback Joe. It's safe enough! It's so safe there isn't anything to it, if *your* end is safe. And you ought to know about that—you've been a year getting the dope."

"I—I ain't afraid of that," said the old man. "There's no one in the world knows how many he had. The family knew he had a lot, of course, and knew it was his hobby, and that he kept 'em here where he could look at 'em instead of in a safety deposit vault—though I guess he figured no safety deposit vault had anything on his—but they just knew he had a lot, they didn't know how many."

A strange light came dawning suddenly in Jimmie Dale's eyes. Had the Tocsin been right in this respect? Was this the *real* motive for the murder—not the bank's papers? Jathan Lane's hobby! It was no secret. Jathan Lane was a fellow member of that most exclusive organization, the St. James Club. Dimly there came back to memory a conversation one afternoon when four or five members, Jathan Lane and himself amongst them, were gathered around one of the smoking room tables, and—

"Sure!" said Gentleman Laroque brusquely. "Well, then, what's the matter with you? There's no sign of any robbery; no sign of any entry into the house, not so much as an unlocked door or a scratch on a window sill; and Jathan Lane, the only man who could know that anything had been taken—is dead. And his death"—Laroque grinned—"occurred in such a way as to make what's done here secure from even suspicion. The bank game's a blind. This is what we've been after, and now it's open and shut. And your share is the biggest haul you ever made in your life."

The old man stared around him. Colour crept into his cheeks and glowed in hectic spots. His eyes, deep in their sockets, began to burn with a feverish light. He pulled himself up to his feet.

"Yes, yes!" he mumbled fiercely. "Rich—ha, ha!—rich! It cannot fail; I am a fool"—he caught his breath, and swayed again on his feet. "Come on! Come on! Hurry!" he choked out.

Jimmie Dale watched them, his lips suddenly tight. They had *passed by* the safe, and were coming directly toward where he stood. Another yard and they would reach the portières. His automatic swung silently upward in his hand. And then the old man halted in front of an oil painting that hung from the wall a little less than shoulder high.

For an instant the man stood there breathing heavily, as though even the exertion of crossing the room had taxed him beyond his strength; and then with a quick movement he jerked at the edge of the frame, and the painting itself, as though it were the grooved cover of a box, slid to one side, exposing the wall, which was as bare and as innocent in appearance behind, or, rather, through the frame, as anywhere else in the room.

"Jathan Lane's safe deposit vault," coughed the Minister. He laughed. His cheeks were burning; his eyes were brighter. He leaned suddenly down toward the floor. "This knot in the wainscoting—see?"

Behind the empty frame, a door in the wall swung open—and the light from the room fell upon the nickel dial of a safe.

"That's the boy!" applauded Gentleman Laroque.

"Yes, yes!" whispered the old man. "I'll open it! Wait! A—a long time it took to get the combination, but—but I got it"—his fingers were working at the dial—"there—there it is!"

"Just a second!" said Laroque coolly, as the door of the little wall safe swung open. He glanced around him, then darted across the room to a small, square table on which stood a heavy bronze vase. "Here, this will do!" he said, and laying the vase on the floor, came back with the table. "Shoot the stuff out on this!"

It took a minute, perhaps two; and then upon the table there lay a number of jewellers' cases in both plush and leather, and a dozen or more little chamois bags. Laroque was rapidly opening and shutting the cases, and as he did so the contents of each in its turn, pendants, brooches, ornaments of many designs, all of them set with diamonds, seemed to leap thirstily at the light and hail it with eager scintillating flashes before the covers could be shut down upon them again.

"That all that's in there?" demanded Laroque.

"Yes," breathed the old man. "Yes"—he rubbed his hands rapaciously together—"all except the tray he uses to paw 'em over on."

"That's thoughtful of him!" grunted Gentleman Laroque. "Let's have it."

From the bottom of the safe the Minister pulled out and laid upon the table an oblong, plush-covered tray with raised edges.

"Now!" grunted Laroque again. "Open the bags, and dump the whities into the tray."

Jimmie Dale drew in his breath. It seemed as though little rivers of fire had begun to stream from the mouths of the bags. The men were working fast now; Laroque with almost cynical composure; the old man, wrought up, clumsy in his greed, his hands trembling, mumbling, crooning to himself.

Diamonds, unset stones, of all sizes, poured into the tray; they filled it, heaped it to its edges. An inch deep they lay. It was a fortune whose value Jimmie Dale did not dare attempt to compute—a pool of immortal beauty, restless with vitality, flashing, limpid, shifting, iridescent. Here the facet of a stone struck back at the light, fiery, passionate in its challenge; there another lay, soft in its radiance, glowing, pulsing, breathing, alive.

Laroque drew a cloth bag from his pocket and unfolded it. He ran his finger through the stones, separating them into two almost equal portions; the portion nearer him he began to put into his little sack.

"Slip the rest of them into the chamois bags again, and put 'em back in the safe," he directed tersely. "Divide 'em amongst the bags as equally as you can. And those gew-gaws in the cases, too, of course—put them back. We can't afford to monkey with anything but the unset stones; any one of those ornaments might happen to be just the one that somebody in the family would remember—and miss."

But now the Minister hesitated. The hectic colour had fled from his cheeks, only to enhance, it seemed, the fever fire in his eyes; the muscles of his face twitched; his hands, trembling before, shook now as with the ague.

"*All!*" he whispered fiercely, and touched his lips with the tip of his tongue. "Look at 'em. My God, look at 'em. We've got 'em all here! Take 'em. Take 'em. Let's take 'em all—all the unset stones anyhow! I'll make my get-away with you. Can't we take 'em all?"

Gentleman Laroque continued his work without looking up.

"*I've* never been in Sing Sing," he said, with a thin smile. "That's why I came here myself tonight. I couldn't trust you or anybody else, except Hunchback Joe, to stand up against the temptation of making the bum play that would land us there. All! That's what Sing Sing is full of! You poor fool, aren't you satisfied with a *sure* thing when the sure thing is a fortune? That's what the half we're taking is—a fortune. And nobody to know that any job has been pulled; and Shiftel with a free hand to dispose of the stones at market value! Would you rather pinch them all, make it next to impossible to sell them for anything like what they're worth, and on top of that dodge the police for the rest of your life? You'd have a rosy chance making your get-away—Mr. Jathan Lane's vanishing butler, alias the Minister, alias Patrick Denton, late of Sing Sing!" His voice hardened suddenly. "As I said, *I've* never been in Sing Sing. Hurry up, now! Put the rest of those stones and all the ornaments back in the safe."

The old man swept his hand across his eyes.

"Sure," he said thickly; "you're right, and I—" A spasm of pain contorted his features, and he clutched at his side and staggered; but as Laroque, with a sharp exclamation, reached out a steadying hand, the Minister shook his head. "I'm all right," he said—and began to return the diamonds Laroque had left on the tray to the little chamois bags.

A strange smile crossed Jimmie Dale's lips. Laroque was right—quite right. And from Laroque's standpoint—safe. The scene of the two men at work there beyond the portière seemed suddenly to shift, and he, Jimmie Dale, was again one of that afternoon group gathered around the table in the smoking room of the St. James Club. Jathan Lane, one of the richest men in America, and his hobby! It had been pure pleasantry, the twitting to which they had subjected the multimillionaire. But the banker had answered seriously.

"How many stones have I? What are they worth?" he had said in reply to a question. "I am sure I do not know myself, but I am equally sure there are no finer unset diamonds, in mass you understand, in America. I have been buying them, one, two, half a dozen at a time, for years. I love them; I take a pure delight in them; and I indulge myself without stint, since, after all, my hobby is by no means a bad one even in a business sense. At least, and what can hardly be said of most hobbies, the value is always there."

"But your family?" the questioner had persisted. "I should think Mrs. Lane and your daughter would be raiding you all the time!"

And then Jathan Lane had laughed. "Familiarity and contempt, you know," he had said. "A boy and his bag of marbles. They haven't looked at them for years."

Gentleman Laroque was speaking again.

"That's the idea!" he said more pleasantly. "They may be a little *disappointed*, perhaps even a little surprised that there aren't more, but that's where it ends so far as the family is concerned. No suspicion that everything isn't just as old man Lane left it; no suspicion that anything has been *taken*. And, speaking professionally, therein lies the difference between an artist and a hog!" He tucked the small cloth bag under his coat. The table was clear. "Close her up nice and tidy," he smiled, "and I'll beat it for Shiftel's."

The old man closed the wall safe, and slid the painting back in its grooved frame.

"Fine!" approved Gentleman Laroque. "I'll leave you to put the table back. Come on now, and lock the window behind me."

Jimmie Dale did not move; only his face set a little more grimly as he watched Gentleman Laroque climb through the window and disappear. It would be a pity to let Shiftel get out of this scot-free! His mind, alert, incisive, was sifting, weighing, formulating the details of a plan whose germ had taken root there, it seemed, almost from the moment he had begun to watch the men at work. Neither Gentleman Laroque nor the Minister would eventually escape, for they could be found anytime.... Shiftel was another member of the gang, an oily, craven little rat, and Shiftel in a corner with his own skin in danger was far more likely to *talk* than either of the other two... the Tocsin's letter and the Phantom...what Shiftel knew he could be made to tell...the *evidence* of this robbery here must be taken care of as soon as the Minister there had gone upstairs again to—

There came a low, dull thud; a broken cry:

"Brandy—I—"

With a sudden sweep of his arm Jimmie Dale brushed aside the portière and leaped forward—too late. The heavy bronze vase, fallen from nerveless fingers that had striven to lift it back on the table, was still rolling across the floor, as the old man, with arms outflung, pitched forward beside it, and lay still.

In an instant Jimmie Dale had reached the cabinet and procured the stimulant, and in another was kneeling beside the prostrate figure—and then, after a moment, in a strangely quiet and deliberate way Jimmie Dale laid the brandy aside.

It was very still in the house, still as the form stretched out there on the rug before him, still as the old, white, upturned face. The man was dead.

The grim, sharp lines that drooped the corners of Jimmie Dale's lips faded away, and something seemed to soften the hard, set immobility of his face as he rose finally to his feet. It was just a crook, just the Minister, alias Patrick Denton, just the end of a vicious, miserable career of crime—but it was also the end of a human life. And life even to this warped soul was as sweet, wasn't it, as to another?—more so perhaps for the very fact that death must have stood with beckoning finger for so long now at the other's elbow! Jimmie Dale turned slowly away and walked across the room. Mechanically he slid the painting out along its grooves; mechanically he stooped and found the knot in the wainscoting. Perhaps it was as well, perhaps infinitely better this way, better that the end should come here than behind the steel bars and the gray stone walls where once it had so nearly come. They would not have pardoned the Minister *twice*.

The little door in the wall had swung open, the nickel dial of the safe glittered in the light—and suddenly Jimmie Dale's shoulders straightened, and for an instant his dark eyes studied the closed steel door. Then he leaned forward, his ear pressed against the face of the safe for the tumblers' fall, and the slim, sensitive fingers, the nerves throbbing at the tips, those magical masters of bolts and locks, were at work.

The minutes passed. There was no sound, save at times the faint, musical whir of the dial; then, abruptly, a deep breathed exclamation:

"All thumbs tonight!"

Again the minutes passed; again the dial moved, now with its musical whir, now slowly, with infinite care; and then a sound, so low as to be scarcely audible—the soft thud, muffled within the steel walls, of metal meeting metal, the bolts sliding in their sockets.

The door of the safe stood open.

Jimmie Dale swung around and stared about the room. He was provided with no little cloth sack such as Gentleman Laroque had had; true he had, instead, those little chamois bags, and his pockets might hold them all, but—
With a quick stride he crossed the room to the desk, and picked up a black leather portfolio. It was quite large enough, and, used for carrying docu-

ments, its flap was fitted with a clasp. He opened it, dumped the papers it contained out on the desk, and returned to the wall safe.

Jimmie Dale was working with lightning speed now. The little chamois bags were tucked into the bottom of the portfolio; the small plush and leather jewellers' cases were opened in quick succession, their contents following the chamois bags, the cases themselves being tossed helter-skelter upon the floor.

The safe was empty.

Jimmie Dale closed the portfolio, and cast a sharp, critical glance around the room. He nodded grimly to himself. There was ample evidence now that there had been a robbery, quite ample—everybody knew that there had been *something* in the now empty safe—and it would not therefore be, as Gentleman Laroque expected, so blind a trail now that led to the source of the diamonds with which Isaac Shiftel was to be endowed! Also, for good measure in this respect, some of the ornaments, that were certainly the property of Mrs. Lane, and which Gentleman Laroque had been wise enough to leave alone, would not lack for a speedy identification! And, again, there was the yawning door of the wall safe, and the painting that still protruded so eloquently from its frame!

His eyes softened in their expression as they held now for an instant again on the form that lay upon the floor. Then he shook his head in quick decision. He needed time now before an alarm was sounded that might by any chance reach the ears of Gentleman Laroque, or, more particularly, one Isaac Shiftel!

Jimmie Dale consulted his watch. It was five minutes of three. The electric-light switch clicked under his fingers. The room was in darkness.

Then silence through the house.

And presently a figure crouched again in the shadows of the basement porch, and crossed the yard, and swung itself silently over the fence into the lane—and from here, slipping the black silk mask from his face, Jimmie Dale emerged on the street.

But now Jimmie Dale seemed to be no longer in haste. It was a long way from Jathan Lane's mansion to Mr. Isaac Shiftel's unsavory abode, which was now Jimmie Dale's destination, and the subway would be the quicker, but, instead, Jimmie Dale hailed a belated taxi as it passed him. He was interested in reaching Isaac Shiftel's only *after* Gentleman Laroque had been there and gone. He gave the chauffeur an address on the Bowery that would bring him within a block of the tenement that Isaac Shiftel had chosen as his lair, and stepped into the taxi.

CHAPTER 3

ONE ISAAC SHIFTEL

The taxi rolled and swayed its way along. Jimmie Dale sat staring at the portfolio that bumped with the motion of the car upon his knees. In some thirty-odd minutes, at half-past three to be exact, the police would be paying a visit to Laroque's quarters, and even if the man were not back there by then, the police were patient and would wait! They would get Laroque—but not the evidence. They might even let the man go again—temporarily. It would not matter. Laroque's freedom, if obtained at all, would be of very short duration. The evidence lacking at Gentleman Laroque's would be found within the hour and in abundant measure, together with Mr. Isaac Shiftel himself, at—Isaac Shiftel's!

But that was not all; nor, indeed, that which most vitally interested him. Despite the Tocsin's efforts to keep him out of those shadows, as she had termed it, that seemed to have closed down upon her blacker and more ominous even than before, the night's work had already brought him greater returns than he had ever dared to hope for or expect. He knew three of the pawns who moved at the criminal will of the unknown leader whom she had styled the Phantom. One of the three was dead, but there remained two; and of the two, one was Laroque, and the other was a miserable little rat-like creature, who, under *persuasion*, was not likely to prove over-secretive. And Shiftel's tongue, once made to wag, held promise of almost anything, even the "Open Sesame" to what was now his, Jimmie Dale's, ultimate goal—the Phantom.

Jimmie Dale's eyes travelled to the window, held there for a few minutes noting the taxi's progress, and then fixed introspectively again on the portfolio.

Shiftel! He knew Shiftel as only the *initiated* knew him, as only those knew him whose ears were attune to the whispered confidences of the underworld's exchanges in the dens and dives hidden away from the light of day, where he, Jimmie Dale, once as Larry the Bat, and now in the present day as Smarlinghue, the broken-down artist and hop-fighter, was welcomed as one of the élite of that inglorious realm. He had even seen Shiftel on one or two occasions—an unkempt, bearded, spectacled foreigner of uncertain age, a cringing little beast, hideously cunning, a master in his own peculiar line of deviltry. Shiftel ostensibly, for the benefit of the police should they ever prove inquisitive, made his living in his two-room, dirty, bachelor apartment, by working on garments which he brought from various sweat shops. If he were rarely at home and too lazy to work much, that was his misfortune, his loss, and his sole personal affair! But the underworld held him in quite other regard—as a "fence," a "shover of stolen goods," who was safe, and in cleverness without an equal. There were few crooks in the Bad Lands but were hungry for Isaac Shiftel's services, but Shiftel was not approachable to all; it was understood, and perforce had regretfully come to be accepted as a fact, that he dealt only with a small and select clientele of his own choosing, whose personnel was more guessed at than known; and that to break into the charmed circle was a feat attempted by many but accomplished by few. And as far back as Jimmie Dale could remember, as far back as he could remember even Gentleman Laroque, Shiftel had lived in the same miserable rooms in the same miserable tenement.

The taxi rattled on. At intervals Jimmie Dale kept glancing out of the window. And then, as the taxi turned at last into the Bowery, he smiled suddenly, laid his handkerchief on the portfolio, and reached into one of the pockets of the leather girdle under his vest. Shiftel! He took out a thin metal case, like a cigarette case, and from the case, with a pair of tiny tweezers that mocked at finger-prints, he lifted out a diamond-shaped gray paper seal that was adhesive on one side, and dropped it on the handkerchief. He returned the metal case to its hiding place, folded the handkerchief carefully, and replaced it in his pocket.

A moment later the taxi stopped. Jimmie Dale alighted, paid and dismissed the chauffeur, and as he swung around the corner, walking east from the Bowery, he looked at his watch. It was twenty minutes past three. It became now simply a question whether Laroque was still with Shiftel, or had gone home.

The street, one of the most shabby of East Side streets, was dark, poorly lighted, and free of pedestrians. Jimmie Dale passed by a tenement whose shabbiness was quite in keeping with its surroundings, passed by a narrow areaway which separated the tenement from another which might have been a duplicate of the first—and halted before the entrance of the second tenement.

The outer door was unlocked. In a moment he was inside the hallway, and in utter blackness now stood motionless, listening. Then again the black silk mask was slipped over his face, and again it was as though a shadow moved. Shiftel's apartment was the middle one on the ground floor facing the other tenement across the areaway.

Jimmie Dale passed down the length of the hall, counting the doors on his right by the sense of touch, and, returning, crouched with his ear against the panel of the door he had selected. From within, so faintly as to be indefinable in any concrete way, there came the sound of movement. Still Jimmie Dale listened, even while his fingers worked silently at doorknob and lock.

He nodded his head as he completed his work. There had been no sound of voices. Gentleman Laroque had evidently been and gone. Isaac Shiftel was alone.

And then suddenly Jimmie Dale was on his feet, and in a flash was in the room, the door closed and locked behind him. Through the doorway of a connecting room ahead of him he could see the unkempt, bearded figure of Shiftel as the man, with a cry, sprang wildly to his feet from the chair in which he had been seated, clawing, even as he sprang, at the white, glittering array of diamonds strewn upon the table-top before him.

"Who's that? Who's there?" the man called out hoarsely.

Jimmie Dale's automatic covered the other as he moved swiftly forward to Shiftel's side.

"Quite an elaborate collection you've got here, Isaac," he said softly. "First water stones of course, or *you* wouldn't be handling them. And please don't wriggle, Isaac, until I—ah, thanks!" He had laid the portfolio down on the table, and his fingers passing deftly over Shiftel's clothing had whipped out a revolver from the other's pocket and transferred it to his own.

But now Shiftel seemed to have got a sudden grip upon himself. He leaned forward, peering sharply from behind his spectacles at Jimmie Dale's masked face.

"No," he said with a snarl, "I don't know you, because I don't know *your* kind. But you evidently don't know Isaac Shiftel. Those stones, eh? That's it, is it? Well, you may get out of here with them, but afterwards—eh?—do you think Isaac Shiftel's arm is so short as that?"

Jimmie Dale made no answer. He retreated a step, and with his free hand began to unfasten the portfolio.

Shiftel shook his fist virulently now. The first shock once over, he was, through familiarity, apparently quite at his ease again in dealing with—a crook.

"How'd you get wise to this, eh?" he demanded fiercely. "How'd you—" His glance had travelled to the window that opened on the areaway. "Ah!" he exclaimed. "That's it, eh? The shade's down, but like a fool I left the window open. You had the luck to sneak into that areaway." He peered again into Jimmie Dale's face, and abruptly his tone and manner changed. He rubbed his hands together ingratiatingly. "I said you didn't know Isaac Shiftel," he said smoothly; "but you do—everybody in your line of business knows Isaac Shiftel. I'll make a deal with you—a fair share—eh? You don't want Isaac Shiftel as an enemy. I'll give you—"

"You're getting in ahead of me, Isaac," interrupted Jimmie Dale plaintively. He coughed slightly—and politely pressed his handkerchief to his moistened lips. "*I* meant to be the first to offer something." With a quick jerk of his revolver hand, he plucked a diamond necklace from the top of the portfolio, and tossed it upon the table. "That, for instance—Isaac."

The ornament seemed to fascinate Shiftel. As if drawn to it against his will, he leaned forward staring at it; and then, as though actuated by a sort of frightened incredulity, he reached out a hand toward it—but Jimmie Dale's hand that still held the handkerchief was the quicker. It fell and gripped like a vise upon the back of Shiftel's hand.

"Just a moment, Isaac," said Jimmie Dale coolly. "There is something else that I want you to have—as a little memento of the occasion."

There came a startled cry from Shiftel. Jimmie Dale had withdrawn his hand, and Shiftel was staring now, not at the diamond necklace, but at a diamond-shaped gray paper seal that was pasted on the back of his hand.

"I'll say it for you!" Jimmie Dale's smile was not inviting. "The Gray Seal! I apologise for the melodrama, but I think it will aid you, Isaac, to see things in a clearer light. You've got a little information that I want, and I imagine it will help to quicken your memory and loosen your tongue to know *who* wants it."

There was no answer. The man, his lips twitching, was still staring at the back of his hand.

With a sudden movement, Jimmie Dale emptied the contents of the portfolio upon the table. He brushed them into a heap with the diamonds already there.

"They belong together," said Jimmie Dale, in a curious monotone, "and I couldn't bear to see them left behind. They'll be *found* together too, Isaac, for I am afraid it will be impossible to make anyone believe now that Jathan Lane's safe has never been disturbed." His voice hardened suddenly. "You're going up for this, Isaac. I make no bargain with you. The police are going to be tipped off over the phone, and they are going to find you here trussed up in that chair with the diamonds in front of you. But before the police get you, you are going to deal with me. I want to know who the man is you, and those with you, take your orders from. And before we are *through* you are going to tell me, Isaac—all you know."

Shiftel's tongue was circling his lips. He shook his head. He was cringing now, supplicating with his hands.

"I don't know anything," he protested wildly. "You're all wrong. You're all wrong about everything. I don't know anything about Jathan Lane. I don't know where the diamonds came from. I never ask questions in my business. They were brought in here for me to shove, and—"

"That's enough, Isaac!" snapped Jimmie Dale. "The game is up! Your friend, Patrick Denton, alias the Minister, is dead up there on the floor of Jathan Lane's private library, where he—"

"Dead!" Shiftel's hands had ceased their movements. The man stood rigid. Something stronger than himself seemed to have stripped him of further power to dissimulate. "Dead! You—you killed him?"

"Never mind about that!" Jimmie Dale bit off his words. "It's enough for you to know for the present that he is dead. You're not quite so innocent as you were—are you, Isaac? And as for the man who brought those stones here, a friend of mine has kindly arranged to have the police pay a little visit at Gentleman Laroque's at just about this time; to be precise"—he drew his watch from his pocket—"at—"

Jimmie Dale's words ended abruptly. He, too, was suddenly standing tense and rigid. A footstep, guarded, cautious, was coming along the areaway out there. It was coming nearer to the open window—the drawn shade did not *hide* the sound. Instinctively his eyes sought the dial of his watch.

It was half past three.

"At Laroque's!" Shiftel, his ears strained toward the window, was whispering the words. "The police—at Laroque's!" And then he raised both fists in fury and shook them above his head. "You snitch, you cursed snitch"—the low, whispered words seemed but to accentuate the man's sudden flood of passion—"we'll get you yet for this!"

For an instant Jimmie Dale's brain seemed to reel in turmoil and chaos. That voice was no longer Shiftel's. Those words! Once he had heard those exact words before, and—with a quick step forward, his hand reached out, tearing beard and spectacles from the other's face.

"Gentleman Laroque!"

"Yes, you fool!" said Laroque, still whispering. "So you've tripped at last, eh? You didn't know, and you've brought the police *here*. Well, take the consequences! It's you who's trapped!" He was backing slowly away from both table and window toward the inner wall of the room. "Perhaps *you'll* explain the possession of those stones! You fool, you and that woman with you, you don't know what you're up against, but—"

"Don't move!" ordered Jimmie Dale grimly.

"Just this far," smiled Laroque. "I hear them coming along the hall inside now. Don't forget there's one of your police on guard outside the window, and—"

The room was in instant darkness. The bare fraction of a second passed, not more; there was a faint scraping sound from the direction where Laroque had been standing—and Jimmie Dale's flashlight, whipped from his pocket, was sweeping around him.

The room was empty!

Jimmie Dale's face was set like chiselled marble. Empty! Gone! The man was gone! But that was not all! Voices were ringing that slogan of the old days in his ears again: "Death to the Gray Seal!" He did not need to be told what it meant to be caught by either police or underworld. He, too, heard those guarded footsteps inside the tenement and coming now along the hall. His mind, alert, virile, was working with lightning speed. The doorway was behind him, and Laroque could not have gone that way—nor by the window guarded by the police. There must be some secret exit from the room. If so, given but a second, while he, Jimmie Dale, was attempting an escape, Laroque could get back again and secure the diamonds that lay upon the table. And he, Jimmie Dale, was *responsible* for them now!

And now Jimmie Dale in action was swift as his racing thoughts. Whether he could save himself or not, there was at least a way to save the stones. With the flashlight switched on, he propped it on the end of the table, its ray streaming over the gems and playing in the opposite direction from the connecting door.

"If you can hear me, Laroque," he whispered, "I warn you—don't try it! All you'll get off that table will be a bullet, whether I'm caught or not!"

It was utter blackness behind him. He backed swiftly, silently through the connecting door, and across the outer room to the door that led into the hall. His automatic held a line on the table top. He crouched at the far side of the door casing. They were here now. He heard a whispered consultation outside, as his fingers, closing on the key, silently unlocked the door. Queer! His brain was racing again. A weird sight! All blackness back here—and, through the connecting doorway, a light, apparently coming from nowhere, streamed over a shimmering, scintillating mass of diamonds, and ended by imposing itself in a white, luminous circle on a dirty, greasy wall behind! His eyes never left the table; his automatic never wavered in its line. Queer! The Phantom! Gentleman Laroque—Isaac Shiftel! Could it be? Was that a partial answer to the Tocsin's "score of aliases and score of domiciles"? Was Gentleman Laroque the Phantom? Yet how had she taken this for Laroque's home if she hadn't known the two men were one? And she hadn't known. She had said so. But—yes, it was not unexplainable. It might easily have been—just as it had been with him, Jimmie Dale, as Larry the Bat, or as Smarlinghue. She might have seen Laroque come here some evening—and Shiftel might have come out—while she thought Laroque remained *at home*. It might easily be that she did not know Shiftel, and so—

"Bust it in!" The words came sharp, incisive, from the hall; then a quick exclamation: "Blamed if the door ain't unlocked! Come on!"

The door was flung violently open. A man swung forward into the room—and halted abruptly, staring toward the connecting doorway.

"For Heaven's sake, sergeant, look at that!" he burst out.

A man behind pushed eagerly forward. And Jimmie Dale, crouching low by the baseboard in the blackness, slipped through the doorway behind the other without a sound, and in a moment was outside the tenement and walking quietly along the street—in a direction that ignored the areaway.

Half an hour later Jimmie Dale mounted the steps of a palatial residence on Riverside Drive. He smiled softly as he stumbled and shuffled so noisily that before he had gained the topmost step the door was opened for him by the white-haired old butler, who had been butler to Jimmie Dale's father before him, and whose proudest boast was that he had dandled his Master Jim upon his knee. It would have been so easy to have slipped in, and passed the old man, and gone upstairs to bed—and broken the old man's heart to have been found out *asleep* at his self-appointed post.

"What!" said Jimmie Dale severely—and used identically the same words he had used on a hundred similar occasions: "Sitting up again for me, Jason? How many times am I to tell you that I won't have it? Jason, go to bed at once!"

"Yes, sir," said Jason. "Thank you, sir. Thank you, Master Jim, sir—I will."

CHAPTER 4

THREADS

Two weeks had passed.

It was evening; and Jimmie Dale, as Smarlinghue now, the seedy, down-at-the-heels artist, better known as Smarly in the Bad Lands, and still better known again in the ultra-exclusive dens and dives, where the first citizens of New York's crimeland foregathered, as a dope fiend shattered beyond repair, a character shady enough from any angle to entitle him to homage even in that unhallowed circle of the élite, slouched along an East Side street—but the slouching gait was strangely and incredibly swift. He skulked in the night shadows of the buildings like some evil thing that sought darkness as kindred to itself. But at intervals, as he moved along with that strange illusive swiftness, the rays of a street lamp, as though in ironic mockery at his inability to evade them, brought out into sharp relief the disreputable figure whose coat was a size too small for him, and from the short sleeves of which protruded blatantly the frayed and soiled wristbands of his shirt, whose shoulders were stooped, and whose face, what could be seen of it under a battered felt hat, was hollow cheeked, and gaunt with a half starved look.

And now he entered a house that made the corner of a lane, a house that was as disreputable as himself, a dwelling of some old-time pretentions, but with the city's onward march a derelict now, metamorphosed into a mean and squalid tenement. He passed along the dark, musty hallway to the rear room on the ground floor, and, opening the door, stepped inside. He closed the door, locked it behind him, and for an instant stood still, his glance seeming to search into the very shadows themselves where they lay heaviest in the far corners of the room.

It was the Sanctuary that for a year now—or was it two?—had housed the character of Smarlinghue, as, in the days gone by, the old Sanctuary, before the fire had destroyed it, had housed the character of Larry the Bat. Through a top-light high up near the ceiling above the French window, which latter, a relic of past glory, opened on a level with the floor, the moonlight flickered in. It disclosed in nebulous outline a battered easel in one corner of the room, and near it, against the wall and strewn upon the floor, a number of canvases of different sizes. A cot bed, its covers in disorder, occupied the wall space opposite the door. For the rest, there were a filthy, threadbare rag of carpet upon the floor, a battered table, a rickety washstand, and two disabled chairs.

Satisfied that the moonlight was the sole intruder, Jimmie Dale nodded shortly to himself, and stepping abruptly forward examined the drawn roller shade on the French window, and particularly a rent therein that was fastened together with a pin. Again he nodded. Then a diminutive gas-jet, choked with air, hissed and spluttered under his match, and supplanting the moonlight, threw a sickly yellow glow about the room. He crossed then to the corner near the door, knelt down on the floor, and after an instant's work removed an ingeniously fitted section of the baseboard. From the aperture he took out the carefully folded dinner suit which he had been wearing on the evening when he had last left his residence on Riverside Drive.

He began to cast off the shabby, disreputable garments of Smarlinghue. He worked swiftly. With the clothes discarded, there came another change. The hollow cheeks, the thin, extended lips, the widened nostrils disappeared as little distorting pieces of wax were removed. Before a cracked mirror propped up on the rickety washstand, he washed away the stain that previously had given a jaundiced, unhealthy hue to his face and hands—and with minutest care took stock of the result in the mirror.

And then the light went out. The rest could be completed in the darkness. Smarlinghue was no longer at home.

It was like a shadow now flitting soundlessly here and there in the streak of moonlight. A minute, perhaps two, passed; and then the pin that held together the rent in the window shade was removed, and Jimmie Dale peered cautiously out into the narrow, squalid, moonlit courtyard beyond. Another instant, and the French window opened noiselessly on its carefully oiled hinges, and closed again. A figure, close hugged against the wall of the building, stole along the few intervening feet to the fence that divided the courtyard from the lane. Here, next to the wall, a loosened plank swung outward. The figure slipped through into the lane—and Jimmie Dale, immaculate and faultlessly attired, emerged upon the street from which, but a few minutes before, Smarlinghue, the dope fiend, had vanished.

He walked rapidly now, heading over toward the Bowery, and crossing that thoroughfare, innocuous now in the early evening hours, continued on deeper into the East Side. A half grim, half whimsical smile was on his lips. His objective was a little two-story, tumble-down house where an old widow by the name of Mrs. Kinsey still kept, as she had kept for more years than the East Side could remember, a small and woefully unpretentious confectionery store. It did not further the one interest he had in life now, this objective of his tonight; it would bring him no nearer to his goal, so far as he could see, though it held a logical and even intimate connection therewith. It was no "call to arms" from the Tocsin that he—

His pace slackened involuntarily, and there was a sudden droop to the broad shoulders that were usually so straight. The Tocsin! Where was she—while he, seeking to reach her, groped and groped in pitiful failure, a blind man, a child in strength, a fool in intellect! He clenched his hands. One of those black moments again! One more added to the thousand through which he had lived in the past two weeks. Was she still *alive*?

He choked back a cry of bitter agony, and quickened his pace again; but though his shoulders were once more thrown back, a whiteness had been born into his face.

It was two weeks since she had left him that night in the little boat on the East River, two weeks since the night Gentleman Laroque, alias Isaac Shiftel, had so mysteriously disappeared from that tenement room, and she had begun again to battle alone for her existence, pitting her wits against that unknown super-fiend of the underworld whom she had styled the Phantom. And since that night Gentleman Laroque, both in that character and in the character of Isaac Shiftel, had vanished as effectually as though he had never existed; and there had been no word or sign from her, save a short note that he had found, as once before in the old days he had found one, hidden behind the movable section of the baseboard in the Sanctuary—and that was now a week ago. He had destroyed it, torn it for safety's sake into the same minute fragments that he always tore her notes; but it still remained intact, for it had seared itself word for word indelibly upon his brain.

She had written:

Dear Philanthropic Crook,

Oh, why *will* you do it! You do not know your own danger. Apart from the police, there is only one man who could be interested in the secret of Shiftel's room. That's you, Jimmie. They know that. Keep away from the place. They expect you sooner or later. Oh, I beg of you to keep away! It is a trap. Mother Margot, the new tenant, is one of them. She is only there to throw dust in your eyes, and in the eyes of the police.

As for myself, I am safe so far, Jimmie; but I do not know how much progress I have made. Sometimes I think I have already come far along the road—and sometimes I seem lost again. Yesterday I was sure of the Phantom's identity; today I am sure I was wrong; tomorrow I shall be sure again—but it will be of a totally differ-ent personality. You think, no doubt, that it is Shiftel, alias Laroque. Well, perhaps, it is; but unless you and I are both swept out of the road, neither in the one character nor the other will that man probably ever be heard of again. And so, oh, Jimmie, be careful—*and remember the trap.*

Marie.

The last phrase was heavily underscored. The trap! It brought a grim twist to his lips. He had already been in and out of the trap—and, from what she had said in her note, at perhaps the only time when it had been safe so far as he was concerned, paradoxical though that seemed, for he had visited Shiftel's rooms again the night after the murder, and while the police had, so fortunately it now appeared, obligingly done unconscious picket duty for him without. The diamonds found in Shiftel's room had, thanks to the set pieces, been almost immediately identified; and these, coupled with their owner's murder, and the dead butler's identification as an ex-Sing Sing convict, had aroused a veritable furor in the papers. The police had wanted, and still wanted, Shiftel very badly indeed, and so plain-clothesmen for a week had unostentatiously watched the tenement day and night on the chance that Shiftel would return. But he, Jimmie Dale, had been even more interested in Shiftel's erstwhile domicile than had the police; therefore he had examined it, not entirely to his ultimate satisfaction, but certainly unknown to the headquarters men, whom, not being Shiftel, he had had little difficulty in eluding. The result had been—nothing.

Then, again unknown to the police, he had joined forces with them, and he, too, had watched the tenement. On the first of the month, a week after Shiftel's disappearance, the agent had re-rented the two miserable rooms to an old hag-like creature known as Mother Margot. He had been aware of that before the Tocsin's note had reached him. But prior to that again Mother Margot had passed muster with the police, who had thereupon withdrawn their forces, considering further surveillance of the premises unnecessary and their hopes from that quarter at an end. But Mother Margot had not passed muster with him, in spite of the fact that his own investigation of the woman had resulted in the discovery that she was, and had been for a year, a licensed pushcart vendor, a sort of travelling dry goods emporium, who hawked her wares in that ultra-foreign quarter on Thompson Street, just off West Broadway, where she with a hundred others of her ilk cluttered the narrow street until it was well nigh impassable. He knew what the police did not know. He knew that Shiftel's rooms held a secret that the man whom he, as well as the Tocsin, had now come to call the Phantom would strive his utmost to protect by one means or another. And so he had watched Mother Margot because logic would not down. The Tocsin's note had but confirmed his suspicions; and though her warning had not gone utterly unheeded, and he had thereafter evaded the "trap," he had kept even a still closer watch upon Mother Margot herself. For days at a stretch now he had lived as Smarlinghue—and that had brought him here to his errand tonight.

Jimmie Dale's face hardened suddenly. His errand! It was dirty, miserable, pitiful work that he had partially uncovered. Sooner or later, he had made sure that Mother Margot would bring him into touch with others of the same breed who owned allegiance to the Phantom. And she had at last, tonight—for it was neither probable nor tenable to imagine that, serving the Phantom, she was allied with any other band, or permitted a divided interest. An hour ago he had followed her to the Wistaria Café, one of the lowest type of dance halls in the Bad Lands, where she had joined two men; one named Little Sweeney, a smooth-tongued, oily little rat, fastidious in his dress, and whom he, Jimmie Dale, already knew in the same sense as he knew by sight and name a hundred other crooks of greater or less degree; the other, whom they had addressed not inaptly as Limpy Mack, a stoop-shouldered, bent-over figure in peaked cap, with unkempt gray hair and moustache, who walked with a distinct limp and by the aid of a cane whose tip was heavily rubber-capped like a crutch, he did not know at all. From the dance hall proper the three had adjourned to a private room in the rear; and anticipating their arrival there by the matter of a few seconds, he, Jimmie Dale, as Smarlinghue then, had adjourned to the alleyway without, and the window raised an imperceptible crack, the roller shade raised an equally imperceptible space above the sill, had afforded both sight and hearing—that is, within limitations, in so far as hearing went. He had seen Little Sweeney hand the man who limped a paper which the latter had carefully tucked away in his pocket; and then, as a waiter came in and left a tray of glasses, the three had got their heads together around a table.

Jimmie Dale's brows furrowed now as he hurried along. Again and again the blare of the jazz band had drowned out their low tones. In the ten minutes during which he had crouched there outside the window, he had caught no more than snatches of their conversation; but those snatches had been viciously significant. His mind mulled them over again now; a half completed sentence from one, an interjection from another. It had begun with Mother Margot.

"Mabbe dis Mrs. Kinsey person wid her tin-horn shop ain't got so much!" she had cackled. "Mabbe youse'll lose yer hundred!"

After that a jumble of words from one or other of the three:

"...Forget it!... Never banked a cent in her life.... Up in the thousands, that's what; else where's the insurance alone that was a couple of thousand when the old man bumped off two years ago?... The Chief never pulls a bone.... The old girl's as deaf as a church congregation.... She'll lead us to it.... Cop the sale tonight.... Sure, about bedtime.... No night-hawk, though.... You watch downstairs, I'll watch up...."

In actual detail he had learned little; but in general he had learned enough to know that old Mrs. Kinsey was supposed to possess a hidden store of savings, whose hiding place they in some way expected to trick her into disclosing. The thought of the police had come to him; that he might in some way with safety and without involving his own personality warn the police, instead of playing a lone hand in this himself. He smiled a little wanly. There was one very good reason why he should not communicate with the police. This Little Sweeney and the man who limped offered new fields for investigation, widened his range of action, and were, indeed, a reward for the days and nights that he had hung upon Mother Margot's trail. They might, or they might not, lead to something tangible; but certainly, for the moment, he could not afford to see them in the toils of the police. The alternative was stark enough. He could not stand by inactive and see this miserable, sordid tragedy played out.

And so he had left the three in the back room of the Wistaria Café, and had hurried to the Sanctuary—and Smarlinghue had become Jimmie Dale. That was all. That was why he was here now, why he was approaching that little store on the corner ahead, which, early as the evening was, not more than nine o'clock, had its modest show window already darkened for the night—he had not dared risk "Smarlinghue" here; Smarlinghue, whose position in the underworld, that had literally come to mean life and death to him again, would crumble to dust before the slightest breath of suspicion.

But his visit to the Sanctuary, imperative though it had been, had nevertheless taken time. Against this, however, was the fact that the Sanctuary was not hopelessly out of the direct road between the dance hall and Mrs. Kinsey's little shop; and, besides, he had hurried. He smiled a little grimly. They might, or they might not, have arrived before him; but, in any case, there would not have been time enough for them to have reached here, played out their game, and made their get-away. In that latter respect, at least, it was quite certain—the grim smile deepened—that he could not possibly be too late.

He had halted now on the edge of the curb, the intersecting side street between himself and the small, two-story frame house, where Mrs. Kinsey both lived and transacted her daily business. The house was in darkness, save for a lighted window in a lower, rear room that opened on the cross street. And for a moment he stood here, then suddenly he moved forward again—but this time along and across the side street itself until he stood directly beneath the lighted window. His question had been answered. Even from across the street, and muffled though it necessarily had been, his ear had caught the sound of a voice raised to an abnormal degree from the interior of the house; and now through the curtains of what was a small, plainly-furnished sitting room, he caught a glimpse of a faded little old white-haired woman, in a faded little old black dress, whose wrinkled face was strained in earnest attention as she strove to hear through a huge ear-trumpet. Little Sweeney was standing in front of her, his lips to the mouth of the trumpet.

"I said you were never looking better, Mrs. Kinsey!" bawled Little Sweeney.

And then Jimmie Dale was gone.

A moment more, and he was standing nonchalantly at the door of the little shop. There was apparently no other entrance to the house, and if Mrs. Kinsey had admitted Little Sweeney as a caller, as appeared obvious, it must have been through the shop, and the door therefore, in spite of the shop itself being in darkness, should logically be unlocked. And being unlocked it would also have given entrance to one Limpy Mack and Mother Margot, who were both at the present moment undoubtedly hidden in the house.

"I'll watch upstairs, you watch down," repeated Jimmie Dale softly to himself.

It was possible, though scarcely probable in view of the fact that Mrs. Kinsey's deafness practically offered the freedom of the house, that he might run into that *downstairs* watcher skulking here just inside the shop itself. Well, in that case—he glanced sharply up and down the street that for the moment held no near-by pedestrians—the play would come to a very sudden and abrupt end!

His back was turned to the street now. From a pocket in that curious leather girdle around his waist and under his outer garments he took out a black silk mask and adjusted it over his face. And now the slim, sensitive fingers pressed down the door latch without a sound. His logic had not been at fault. The door was unlocked. It began to open. Still there was no sound. And then Jimmie Dale, his hand snuggled over his automatic in the side pocket of his dinner coat, stood inside the shop with the door closed behind him.

CHAPTER 5

MOTHER MARGOT

No challenge questioned Jimmie Dale's entry—there was only the strident voice of Little Sweeney from the rear room. The shop itself, as he had expected, was not the vantage point chosen by either of Little Sweeney's two confederates.

Jimmie Dale stole forward to the rear of the shop, where through an open door there showed a glimmer of light, which, though it seemed to be strangely obstructed, evidently came from some sort of passage that connected the living quarters of the house with the shop; and here, slipping in behind the single counter that the shop boasted, he listened. Little Sweeney was still bawling at the top of his voice.

"I've been thinking it over for the last few days," said Little Sweeney.

"Please speak a little louder." Mrs. Kinsey's voice came plaintively through the darkness.

"Damn it!" said Little Sweeney in low and fervent tones; and then in a veritable yell: "I said I'd been thinking it over! *Thinking it over!* Our little talk, you know, of a few days ago, about buying out your confectionery business. I promised to come back and let you know what I was going to do about it."

"Yes," said Mrs. Kinsey.

"Well," shouted Little Sweeney, "I've decided to take a chance and buy it, and I've brought you a hundred dollars to bind the bargain."

"But I couldn't think of selling it for a hundred dollars," protested Mrs. Kinsey feebly.

"Not *selling* it, just to bind the bargain!" screamed Little Sweeney. "I'll give you the rest of the thousand when we sign the papers!"

"Would you please speak a little louder," said Mrs. Kinsey anxiously. "Sometimes my hearing ain't quite so good as it used to be."

"I'll keep your secret!" gritted Little Sweeney in a hoarse whisper; then full-lunged again: "Here's a hundred-dollar bill. You don't even need to give me any receipt for it. I'll come across with the rest before the week's out. It's just to show that I'm in earnest, and to keep anybody else from buying the business."

"I don't think anybody else would buy it," said the old lady ingenuously.

"You've said a mouthful!" was Little Sweeney's *sotto voce* retort.

"But I'm so glad," said Mrs. Kinsey wistfully. "I'll be so glad, because I can't move around as spry as once I could. And I was afraid I'd—I wouldn't be able to go on with it much longer."

"That's all right, Mrs. Kinsey," bellowed Little Sweeney cordially. "I guess we're both satisfied with our bargain. Here's the money. And I guess I'll be moving along. I'll see you again in a day or so with the papers."

"Thank you very much indeed," said Mrs. Kinsey earnestly. "And I do so hope that you'll do well with it, and that you won't lose anything."

A chair scraped. Footsteps came from the back passageway, which, as Jimmie Dale crouched lower behind the counter, suddenly grew light. A moment more and Little Sweeney stepped into the shop, making for the front door; behind him followed Mrs. Kinsey, carrying in one hand a lamp, and clutched in the other her ear-trumpet and a hundred-dollar bill.

Jimmie Dale's lips set grimly. Back in the corridor that was now darkened again he thought he saw a shadow move; he distinctly caught the sound of a footstep. The downstairs watcher—and Mrs. Kinsey's hundred-dollar bill! It was quite clear now, the whole mean, sordid, contemptible business. The bait was cunning enough in a low, vicious way; amply cunning enough to succeed with a trusting, simple old woman already on the verge of her dotage. Where Mrs. Kinsey, who distrusted banks, had secreted her savings of years, she would secret a *hundred-dollar* bill.

Little Sweeney—in lieu, no doubt, of shouting on the street—bowed himself out politely.

"Good-night," said Mrs. Kinsey. "And thank you again."

She closed and locked the door, and came back through the shop, passing again into the rear hallway.

As the light receded, Jimmie Dale rose cautiously. Mrs. Kinsey's lamp, as she had passed, disclosed the fact that just beyond the rear door of the shop, the passageway made a jut at right angles. He nodded tersely to himself as he gained this with the trained step, so silent as to be almost uncanny, that had mocked at even the creaky boards of the old Sanctuary, and, in the shadows himself now, he peered along the hallway proper.

Steep, narrow stairs, to the left and a little way down the hall, led to the upper story. Mrs. Kinsey, still carrying her lamp, still clutching at her ear-trumpet and the hundred-dollar bill, was already near the top. The lower portion of the stairs and the hall itself, since her body shaded the lamp, were in almost complete darkness.

And then from somewhere above there came a sharp, whispered interrogation:

"Well?"

From along the lower hall, her figure shrouded in the blackness, a woman's voice answered:

"She's still got it. Watch her."

Mother Margot! Limpy Mack, then, was the upstairs watcher. There seemed something incongruous in this passage of words between the two, like a stage aside that was not supposed to be heard by the intervening figure of the old woman who was climbing the stairs; but it was not the incongruity in itself, it was the callous brutality, the vulture-like preying upon helpless infirmity, that hardened Jimmie Dale's face now in a sort of merciless intentness.

Mrs. Kinsey's light disappeared around the landing at the head of the stairs, and then, contemptuous of any exaggerated attempt at silence, another footstep sounded on the stair treads. Jimmie Dale could not see, it was pitch black in the lower hall now, but it was not necessary to *see* the obvious. Mother Margot was following Mrs. Kinsey upstairs.

And now there came the sound as of someone walking about in a room overhead for a moment or so, and then silence.

Jimmie Dale moved toward the stairs, and without a sound began to make his way upward. Halfway up he paused, and stood tight-pressed against the wall. He could just detect a glow of light filtering into the upper hallway, as though the door of a lighted room, almost directly above his head, stood open into the hall. Then a footstep and still another, starting from a position further back along the hall, moved toward the lighted doorway. Came then the sound as of a piece of furniture being moved on squeaky casters; and then a low-breathed, exultant oath in a man's voice, followed by a woman's vicious chuckle. He could almost discern the outlines of two figures there—Mother Margot and Limpy Mack.

"Pipe de lay!" chuckled Mother Margot. "Dere goes Little Sweeney's century buck. Look at her saltin' it!"

"Close your trap!" ordered Limpy Mack sharply. "Maybe she can't hear, but that's no reason for taking a chance of spilling the beans now we know where they are."

"Aw, forget it! Youse gives me a pain!" retorted Mother Margot acidly, but in a nevertheless more subdued tone. "Youse'd have to write her a letter to tell her youse was makin' a noise before she'd be wise to it, an' mabbe den she wouldn't believe youse!"

"Shut your face!" said Limpy Mack tersely.

The sound of what had seemed to Jimmie Dale like squeaky casters came again, then a footstep traversed the lighted room, a door—obviously one connecting with an adjoining room—opened and closed again, and the light was gone.

"Come on!" prompted Mother Margot's voice. "Dat's her bedroom she's gone into. It's all clear now. Wot're youse waitin' for?"

"I'm waiting till the old bird's tucked away in bed," Limpy Mack's voice answered out of the darkness. "I'm waiting till there isn't any chance of her moseying out for anything just as we're tapping the crib. I haven't noticed that there was anything the matter with her *eyes*; and she's not so *dumb* but that she might start something in the neighbourhood. I don't play the fool when I can play safe."

"Safe!" echoed Mother Margot sarcastically. "Wot's safer dan dis de way it is now? I wanter get home. Youse ought to go down to an antique dump an' buy yerself a suit of armour, an' walk around in dat. Youse'd look fine—an' youse'd always be safe. De pip, dat's wot I'm contractin' from youse!"

There was no answer.

Mother Margot grunted contemptuously, and relapsed into silence.

The minutes passed. There was utter silence now in the house, save for an occasional uneasy movement of one or other of the two watchers in the hall above Jimmie Dale's head.

Jimmie Dale stood in grim patience, close against the wall, still on the stairs, an integral part of the shadows around him. The time dragged interminably, the minutes seeming to expand into endless hours. And then suddenly Limpy Mack's voice broke the silence in a tense undertone:

"All right! Her light's out. Come on!"

There came then the sound of footsteps receding from the hall; and Jimmie Dale in an instant silently gained the head of the stairs, and lay there crouched, half on the landing and half on the topmost treads. From his position, slightly diagonal though it was from where he had placed the door, he had calculated he would be able to see clearly enough into the room that Mother Margot and her companion had obviously just entered. He nodded now in quick self-corroboration. Out of the darkness of the room, lancing it in a little white shaft of light, there came the ray of an electric torch, and two figures were outlined as they bent over a piece of furniture that stood against the far wall, and that looked like an old chest of drawers. But there was no squeak of casters now. Jimmie Dale smiled uninvitingly. They were becoming unduly cautious! The piece of furniture was being lifted, not rolled, until it stood out from the wall, the back of it exposed.

For a moment the two figures leaned over it, the flashlight playing on the back of the dresser; and then from its extreme edge, what looked like a very narrow drawer, its depth almost half of the dresser itself, was pulled out.

"S'help me!" Mother Margot's voice quivered in curious, sibilant excitement. "Say, de old skirt's rich!"

"*Was*," corrected Limpy Mack's voice curtly. "Keep your paws off! We'll make the split tomorrow. In the meantime I'll take care of it. See? Hold the flashlight."

"Sure!" sniffed Mother Margot. "Youse're de only honest one in de bunch. I know 'cause Little Sweeney told me!"

A man's hand dipped into the projecting drawer, disappeared nearly up to the elbow, and came out again with a fistful of banknotes which he stuffed into his pocket. Again the man plunged in his hand. Jimmie Dale rose to his feet, took a step forward—and halted abruptly, as Mother Margot's voice suddenly shrilled out tensely through the silence:

"My Gawd! Listen! Wot's dat? Over by de door!"

Jimmie Dale's jaws clamped together, as his automatic swung up into line. Strange! He could have sworn he had not made the slightest sound. He saw Limpy Mack step forward a pace and stand facing the doorway, listening intently. And then Jimmie Dale's face relaxed. Behind Limpy Mack's back Mother Margot's hand shot stealthily into the drawer, and a wad of bills disappeared stealthily inside her blouse. Once more she helped herself.

With a grim droop to the corners of his mouth, Jimmie Dale retreated suddenly back along the hall, and a little beyond the head of the stairs. Mother Margot! The gods were good! There would be more in the night after all than the mere salvaging of old Mrs. Kinsey's savings. He had no intention now of interrupting the two at their work! Mother Margot had wrought a very drastic change in his plans!

"I don't hear anything!" Limpy Mack's voice growled after a moment. "What's the matter with you?"

"I guess I'm gettin' de creeps," Mother Margot's voice replied. "I t'ought I heard somethin' creak, but I guess it was de wind. Hurry up, Limpy! I wanter get out of dis. I'm gettin' de creeps, dat's wot's de matter wid me."

Perhaps another two minutes passed, and then Jimmie Dale, far back along the hall now, heard the footsteps of the two coming from the room. At the head of the stairs they paused, and Limpy Mack spoke gruffly:

"We don't want to take the chance of being seen leaving here together. You're safe enough, because if anyone saw you, they'd think you were just a friend of the old dame. You wait here, give me five minutes, then beat it yourself. And you go straight home! You'll get what's coming to you tomorrow after the Chief's made the split. We don't meet again tonight unless something breaks, and in that case you know where to find me. Understand?"

Jimmie Dale smiled quietly in the darkness. He owed Limpy Mack thanks for that, at least—it would save him from following Mother Margot.

"Sure!" mocked Mother Margot. "Cookin' a pill in yer dump under Sen Yat's! Why don't youse come across wid de price of a bunk, an' give de Chink a chance once in a while?"

Limpy Mack, without answer, descended the stairs. From the lower hall, faintly, there came the soft *tap-tap* of his rubber-tipped cane. Presently the shop door opened and closed gently.

Jimmie Dale moved silently forward. He could just distinguish Mother Margot's figure as a dark blur at the head of the stairs. She, too, now began to descend.

And then Jimmie Dale spoke.

"I'll keep you company downstairs, Mother Margot," he said softly—and the flashlight in his hand, stabbing suddenly through the darkness, played its ray upon her.

She whirled with a low, terrified cry, and put her hands before her blinking eyes as though to ward off a blow.

"Who's dat? Who're youse?" she cried out.

"Go on, Mother Margot—downstairs," Jimmie Dale prompted more brusquely.

She obeyed in a stumbling, uncertain way.

"My Gawd! My Gawd!" she mumbled wildly. "Who're youse? A dick? I ain't done nothin'! I swear to Gawd, I ain't! I swear—"

"Quite so!" interrupted Jimmie Dale coolly, as they reached the lower hall. "But perhaps you will come across just the same."

She stared at the hand which he had extended significantly in the flashlight's glow, and from under a bedraggled hat whose brim flapped over her straggling gray hair and fell into her eyes, she blinked again; she drew the old threadbare black shawl she wore closer around her shoulders, and clutched at it where it met at her neck.

"I dunno wot youse mean," she croaked hoarsely. "Come across wid wot?"

"With what Limpy Mack *didn't get*." Jimmie Dale was biting off his words now. "There *was* somebody at the door, even if you didn't hear him.

I can use that money myself that you put inside your blouse. And I'm waiting—also I'm in a hurry!"

"Youse ain't a dick, den!" She seemed relieved in the sense that rage and fury now supplanted fear. She snarled at him. "Why didn't youse touch Limpy? I only got a dollar or two."

"I haven't forgotten Limpy," Jimmie Dale answered evenly. His hand was still extended. "Quick!" he snapped suddenly.

For an instant she hesitated, then snarling again, she felt inside her blouse and brought out a few crumpled banknotes.

Jimmie Dale thrust the money into his pocket—and extended his hand again.

"Dat's all!" she announced tartly. "Wot d'youse expect? I didn't have no chance!"

Jimmie Dale smiled thinly.

"Loosen the waistband of your blouse!" he ordered sharply.

She glared at him fiercely.

"I won't," she shrilled out. "Youse can go to blazes! I told youse dat was all. I won't!"

"Oh, yes; I think you will," returned Jimmie Dale grimly. "When I leave you I am going to call on your friend Limpy Mack, and if I explain the double cross you put over on him, I imagine—"

She changed front instantly. Fear seemed to have her in its grip again.

"Youse won't do dat!" She was whimpering suddenly. "My Gawd, youse won't do dat!"

"It depends," said Jimmie Dale.

"Den take it!" she mumbled in a frenzied way—and from the loosened blouse a small shower of banknotes fluttered to the floor.

Jimmie Dale stooped and gathered them up.

"That's better!" he observed coolly. "And now we'll go a little further, Mother Margot. I want quite a lot of information. First, this Limpy Mack's dump, as you called it on the stairs. Does he live there alone?"

"Oh, my Gawd!" She was wringing her hands together in terror. "Youse ain't still goin' dere, are youse? Youse ain't goin' to tell him, are youse? He'd pass de word along, an' if de Chief got wise dey'd bump me off for dis. I—dey'd clean me up before de mornin'!"

"So I imagined," said Jimmie Dale calmly. "That's why I refrained from any interference upstairs. You see, Mother Margot, I rather think we have become indispensable to each other."

"I dunno wot youse mean," she faltered.

"I mean this," said Jimmie Dale coldly, "that if you play straight with me, you are safe in so far as what you put over on your precious pals is concerned. Otherwise—" He shrugged his shoulders. "Is it quite plain?"

Mother Margot licked her lips feverishly.

"Dey'd cut me t'roat!" she whispered. "Dat's wot dey'd do. Wot do youse want? I—I ain't got no chance, have I?"

"We started with Limpy Mack, and we'll finish with him first," said Jimmie Dale tersely; "though you've just mentioned something much more important. Well, does he live alone?"

"Sure, he lives alone," Mother Margot answered. "He's got de basement—"

"Under Sen Yat's," completed Jimmie Dale smoothly. "All right! Now, the really important matter. This Chief you mentioned—who is he?"

Mother Margot shook her head.

"I dunno," she said.

"You don't know!" Jimmie Dale's voice hardened. "That won't do, Mother Margot! I wouldn't advise you to try another trick tonight."

"I ain't!" she protested wildly. "Honest to Gawd, I ain't! I dunno!" She was wringing her hands together again. "He ain't nobody, he's"—she glanced furtively around her, the act seemingly almost subconscious—"he's—he's just a voice."

Jimmie Dale studied her for a moment. The woman was evidently too frightened to be anything but truthful.

"Well, go on!" he prodded.

"Dat's all I knows about him," said Mother Margot fearfully. "Just a voice over de telephone dat youse're always wise to 'cause it's a kind of a queer, thick voice."

"Is that the way you get your orders, then?"

Mother Margot nodded assent.

"But there isn't any telephone in your room," said Jimmie Dale sharply. "I happen to know that you've just moved in where another pal of yours, Mr. Isaac Shiftel, used to live."

Mother Margot swallowed hard. She drew back a little.

"How'd youse know?" she stammered.

"Never mind! How about that telephone?"

"It ain't done in de room," she said tremulously. "I didn't know anythin' about tonight at all. Den dis afternoon w'en I was wid my pushcart down on Thompson Street I'm called into a store to de telephone, an'—"

"What store? Where is this telephone?" Jimmie Dale interrupted tersely. She hesitated.

"Aw, it's in a booth in de back room of Mezzo's second-hand store, if youse've got to know," she blurted out.

"All right," said Jimmie Dale. "Go on!"

"Well, I was called to de telephone," she said, "an' told to go to de Wistaria Café tonight an' meet Limpy Mack."

"And Little Sweeney," added Jimmie Dale quietly; then abruptly: "Who else is in this gang?"

Again Mother Margot shook her head.

"I dunno dem all," she said. "I guess we don't all know each other neither. I only know Limpy Mack an' Shiftel, an' a man named Laroque; but I ain't seen neither of dem last two for weeks, an' I dunno where dey've gone. Little Sweeney was a new one on me tonight."

"H'm!" observed Jimmie Dale curtly. "Then who fixed it for you to move into Shiftel's rooms?"

"The Voice," she replied readily. "I was told to go an' hand de agent de rent in advance."

"Good!" said Jimmie Dale pleasantly. "We're getting on, Mother Margot; and since you and I have become such friends, I'm going to take the liberty of calling on you in a day or so—unless perhaps you can tell me how, well, say, a man like Shiftel can get in or out of those rooms without bothering himself with either doors or windows?"

She drew still farther back, a startled look and a new terror in her face.

"I know who youse are now," she gasped. "Little Sweeney an' Limpy was talkin' about youse. Youse are de Gray Seal! My Gawd!" She wrung her hands. "Don't youse come dere! I'm playin' straight wid youse. I don't know why, an' I don't know nothin' phoney about de rooms, but I knows dat's wot dey wants youse to do."

Again Jimmie Dale studied the dishevelled and distraught creature.

"Yes," he said quietly, "so I believe, and I believe you are playing straight. Well, we'll leave the rooms in abeyance for the time being. I shall always know where to find you—on Thompson Street. You may be called to the phone by *another* voice. Now, one thing more, Mother Margot—I don't want to keep Limpy Mack waiting! What was that paper Little Sweeney gave Limpy Mack in the back room of the Wistaria tonight?"

"Youse—youse know about dat, too?" She stared at him in terrified amazement.

"What was it?" repeated Jimmie Dale.

"Dey didn't let me see it," she said. "Some sort of dope about de gang, I guess, 'cause Little Sweeney was a new man. Little Sweeney just says, 'I got it pat,' he says, w'en he hands it over. I dunno wot was in it; dey didn't let me see it."

"Perhaps Limpy will be more considerate with me," observed Jimmie Dale dryly. He motioned along the hall, switched off the flashlight, and taking Mother Margot's arm, led her into the shop. "You go home now," he ordered.

She hesitated. His hand still on her arm, he felt her shiver.

"If youse—youse're goin' to Limpy Mack's," she quavered, "youse—youse won't split on me? Swear youse won't! Dey—dey'd kill me before de mornin'!"

"You needn't worry," said Jimmie Dale gruffly. "As long as you play straight with me, it's as much to my interest as yours to see that no harm comes to you. You're out of this. The only person I know is Limpy Mack, whom I saw come out of here alone—understand?—and I followed him because I thought perhaps he had made a little haul that—since you've saved me introducing myself—the Gray Seal could use himself."

"My Gawd!" She was whimpering again. "I—I'm afraid. Youse swear it?"

Jimmie Dale opened the door, and with a precautionary glance up and down the street, pushed her not ungently out into the night.

"I swear it," he said. "Good-night, Mother Margot."

CHAPTER 6

THE MAN WITH THE RUBBER-TIPPED CANE

The black silk mask gone from his face, Jimmie Dale too stepped out of Mrs. Kinsey's little shop, and hurried away—but in an opposite direction to that taken by Mother Margot. And now he smiled as he went along. Tomorrow, if he had luck, Mrs. Kinsey would get her money back, all of it, say by registered mail, and accompanied by a suggestion that she would be better advised to use a bank hereafter; a suggestion which fright at the discovery of her loss would probably have the salutary effect of causing her to act upon without loss of time!

He hurried on—and ten minutes later, deep in the Chinese quarter, in the neighbourhood of Chatham Square, in a narrow, crooked, evil-smelling, little street, in fact more an alleyway than a thoroughfare, he was strolling past the entrance of a shuttered tea store that bore the sign: SEN YAT. Again he smiled a little to himself—but now from a different cause. It was quite true that Sen Yat dealt in tea; but it was equally true that upstairs behind the shutters Sen Yat also specialised in another commodity of the East, and to those who had the price and were "safe" the sorry solace of the poppy was always at instant command.

An old and unkempt woman, mumbling to herself, shuffled by. A Chinaman, like a rat taking to its hole, disappeared down a basement entrance from the sidewalk a few yards away. Jimmie Dale turned suddenly. The street for the moment was clear. He retraced his steps to another basement entrance, the one below Sen Yat's, and out of the darkness of which, as he had previously passed by, a crack of light seeping from under the door sill had already informed him that Limpy Mack had returned home.

And then Jimmie Dale was gone from the street—and down the half dozen steps was crouching in the blackness below the sidewalk at Limpy Mack's door. Again the silk mask was slipped over his face; again his fingers sought a pocket in the little leather girdle—and the next instant were silently and deftly at work with a pick-lock.

Perhaps a minute passed. Then Jimmie Dale straightened up, swung the door open, and like a flash was inside the room with the door closed behind him.

A startled oath greeted his entrance. Limpy Mack, peaked cap drawn over his eyes, was seated at a table on which burned an oil lamp. His heavy, rubber-tipped cane also lay across the table. He snatched at this now in lieu of a sheaf of banknotes which he let fall from his hands, and which he had evidently been engaged in counting—and rose, half threateningly, half defensively, to his feet.

"Good evening!" said Jimmie Dale pleasantly. "I seem to be in luck tonight."

His automatic indicated the sheaf of notes, and then held on Limpy Mack. Jimmie Dale's glance swept swiftly, critically around the place. Its furnishings were few and of the crudest; a bed in one corner, near a second door that conveniently opened on the back yard no doubt; a washstand minus one leg, and therefore askew, that boasted a streaked and badly blistered mirror; the table and chair in front of the washstand; a dirty, unswept floor, bare of carpet—and that was all. The place reeked with filth.

"Nice quiet little resort you've got here," smiled Jimmie Dale. His eyes were apparently roving again about the cellar-like room, apparently everywhere save on Limpy Mack. "I'm sure you—*drop that*!"

A revolver, almost free from Limpy Mack's pocket, fell with a clatter to the floor. The man screamed out in rage.

"Why, Limpy, that's raw," said Jimmie Dale in a pained way. "I didn't think you'd fall for it. All I wanted was your gun." He advanced to the table, and kicked the weapon across the floor under the bed.

There was a sudden *swish* through the air, as, quick without warning, Limpy Mack aimed a blow with his cane at Jimmie Dale's wrist and automatic. It missed. Again the man screamed out in fury.

Jimmie Dale's face set.

"Don't raise your voice again like that," he said in flat tones. "Sit down!" His automatic swung to the level of the other's eyes.

With a snarl, Limpy Mack subsided into the chair. He scowled at Jimmie Dale.

"Who are you, anyway, you damned thug?" he demanded thickly.

"I'll tell you," said Jimmie Dale. He was smiling whimsically now—not at Limpy Mack, but at the somewhat exacting demands of the situation in which he found himself. Mother Margot must in no way appear in this; and, besides that money on the table, there was the paper that Little Sweeney had given to Limpy Mack in Mother Margot's presence—a paper, in reference to the contents of which, he, Jimmie Dale, had acquired an intense curiosity.

Ostensibly, therefore, he must appear—in order that no thought of Mother Margot might by any chance enter the other's mind—to be ignorant of even the existence of the paper, and yet, at the same time, get hold of it. "I'll tell you," said Jimmie Dale. "I was walking down a certain street tonight, and I saw you sneak out of a little confectionery store that looked as though it had all been closed up for the night, and I said to myself: 'That's funny, because Limpy Mack never plays for chicken feed.' And then I went and read the sign on the window, and I remembered that everybody said Mrs. Kinsey had a well-filled stocking hidden away somewhere. So I just took a chance, Limpy, thinking that maybe you'd found it, and I followed you. And as I said before, I seem to have played in luck."

"It's a lie!" growled Limpy Mack. "That ain't Mrs. Kinsey's, or anybody else's money. It's mine."

"I'm delighted to know it," murmured Jimmie Dale. "But even so, I still insist that I am in luck tonight. There must be quite a few thousand here." He began to thrust the bills into his pockets.

Limpy Mack sat crouched down in his chair, the posture seeming to accentuate almost to deformity his stooped shoulders.

"Damn you!" he shrieked out. He gnawed at his unkempt gray moustache, and flung another oath at Jimmie Dale.

Jimmie Dale swept the table clean. It was obviously all that Limpy Mack had stolen from Mrs. Kinsey, for he would obviously have had it *all* out to count it—but there was still a certain paper in Limpy Mack's pocket.

"I wonder—since you say it was yours—if you haven't got some more," suggested Jimmie Dale invitingly. "I'm afraid I'll have to trouble you to turn your pockets out, Limpy. Stand up!"

"I—I ain't got any more." The man seemed suddenly cowed. He crouched still lower in his chair.

"Stand up!" repeated Jimmie Dale sternly. "Now I'm quite sure you have!"

"No!" Limpy Mack was whining now. "I—I'll tell you the truth. I got it where you said. But that's all—all of it was on the table. Say, you believe me, don't you? I'd come across if I had any more, wouldn't I? I couldn't help myself."

The man was blatantly stalling now. The paper was—*no, it wasn't on account of the paper*. Behind Limpy Mack's back something showed in the blistered mirror—the head and shoulders of Little Sweeney protruding through the rear doorway, and in Little Sweeney's hand a levelled revolver. Limpy Mack's voice had drowned out any sound made by the opening of the door, if, indeed, there had been any sound at all.

Jimmie Dale's brain was working in lightning flashes now, but not a muscle of his face moved. His automatic dangling in his hand was useless.

To swing it on the door with only a chance aim would be but the signal for Little Sweeney to fire.

"All right, Limpy," said Jimmie Dale, and leaned slightly toward the end of the table. "I'll take your word for it that—"

And then Jimmie Dale was in action. With a sweep of his hand he sent the lamp crashing from the table to the floor, and ducked instantly to one side.

There was a yell from Limpy Mack; and, in the sudden darkness as the lamp went out, from the doorway came the tongue-flame of Little Sweeney's revolver and the roar of the report. Then a rush of feet, the flash and roar of the revolver again, and the next instant Jimmie Dale was locked in a hand to hand struggle with Little Sweeney. Here and there they swayed, the breath of one, panting, hard, on the other's cheek; the table toppled to the floor, carrying the chair with it; their feet crunched on the splintered glass from the lamp and chimney—and then suddenly Jimmie Dale reeled from a terrific blow across the head.

"I got him!" screamed Limpy Mack's voice exultantly. "I got him, Sweeney! I beaned him with the loaded handle of my cane."

But though dazed, lurching, scarcely able to keep his feet, Jimmie Dale was still fighting like a wildcat. Twice since Little Sweeney had grappled with him, he had managed to strike the other with the butt of his automatic. He had only one chance now—to end it quickly—he was too nearly gone himself. He wrenched himself suddenly free, and swung again with all his strength. A gurgling voice—Little Sweeney's—answered the blow:

"Look out—Limpy—beat it—you know why—that paper—beat it—I—"

Again and again Jimmie Dale brushed his hand across his eyes. He fought desperately to clear his brain. His head was sick and dizzy. What was that sound, that strange sound? *Tap, tap, tap!* Little Sweeney—that black outline on the floor was Little Sweeney—Little Sweeney wouldn't trouble anyone for an hour or so—but that *tap, tap, tap*—it sounded from the direction of the rear door. And now it was gone, and there was silence—just silence. But the silence, as nothing else had done, seemed now to penetrate Jimmie Dale's swimming head, and seemed to bring with it a sudden, swift significance.

Fool! He stumbled madly toward the rear door. Limpy Mack was gone—gone with the *tap, tap, tapping* of his cane. That paper! A clue to that super-crook perhaps, that the Tocsin called the Phantom, and Mother Margot called the Voice!

He was outside now. No, not too late! That was Limpy Mack there, wasn't it? That figure running, running! God, how his brain swam! His knees seemed weak under him, as though they were going to double up like the blades of a knife—but he was running too. His surroundings seemed mechanically, subconsciously, to be absorbed—just a back yard that ended in the black, irregular outline of the rear of what was evidently a three or four-story tenement.

On Jimmie Dale stumbled. He could not be more than ten or fifteen yards behind that figure ahead, which, to his whirling brain, seemed to take on the aspect of some grotesque jumping-jack, bobbing up and down in the darkness, until suddenly it disappeared through the back door of the tenement.

Jimmie Dale prodded himself into a spurt, reached the tenement door, found it open, and reeled inside. His faculties seemed miserably unreliable. Couldn't he *think* any more! He stood stock still, and again his hand swept fiercely across his eyes. The man couldn't have gone out of the front door, nor have gained the landing above, because he, Jimmie Dale, had been too close at the other's heels, and would have heard him, would be hearing him now. And there was not a sound—nothing but pitch, inky blackness. Therefore Limpy Mack must be somewhere here in the blackness.

That was better! At least his brain was striving to fight its way back to normal. But his eyes ached brutally. He bit his lips to keep back a groan of pain, and leaned against the wall for support. One of them, he or Limpy Mack, must sooner or later make a move. He forced a twisted smile. If the blow from the loaded cane had not proved too much for him after all, it would not be he who made that move!

And now, after a time, where he had heard no sound before, he became conscious of many sounds—the low indistinct sound of muffled things, the night sounds of a tenanted building filtering vaguely out from behind closed doors only to integrate themselves in a throbbing way into the very silence itself. How long had he been standing here? Once he clutched frantically, but noiselessly, at the wall to keep himself erect. Perhaps it would not be Limpy Mack who moved first! His brain was swimming in that sick, nauseating way again. Perhaps it would be—

A door began to open cautiously a few yards along the hall. And then a man's head and shoulders, a man with a clean shaven face and slouch hat showing quite distinctly in the lighted doorway, was thrust out. The man peered around; then from the threshold he whispered back into the room:

"It's a cinch he thought you beat it straight out through the front door, and went out after you. I'll take a look, and if he's still hanging around outside I'll spot him. You keep under cover, Limpy. You're safe here anyway. I'll be back in ten minutes. Savvy?"

The man, a broad-shouldered, well set-up fellow, stepped out into the hall, and closed the door behind him. His footsteps echoed back as he walked rapidly toward the front of the tenement; then the front door opened and closed again; the footsteps rang faintly from the pavement without, died away—and Jimmie Dale was standing before the door of the room.

He had not heard the door being locked. He was sure of that, in spite of the fact that his head was whirling like a top. His fingers closed silently on the doorknob—and with a swift movement, standing in the hall, his automatic thrown forward, he flung the door wide open.

And then for a moment he stood there like a man stunned. The room was empty. No, not empty! Dangling from the gas-jet hung Limpy Mack's rubber-tipped cane; and stuck upon the cane, flaunting itself in grim, ironical, mocking challenge—*was a diamond-shaped gray paper seal.*

A smile of understanding, bitter in its chagrin, flickered across Jimmie Dale's lips. He had stuck a gray seal on the back of Shiftel's hand that night two weeks ago. This one, he was sure, could have come from nowhere else; and, if that were so, then Shiftel, and Gentleman Laroque, and Limpy Mack, and Limpy Mack in still another guise, in the guise of the man who had just tricked him so neatly, were all one. And from that encounter in Shiftel's rooms, and one other encounter long before that at Niccolo Sonnino's place, Gentleman Laroque, alias Isaac Shiftel, in the character of Limpy Mack to-night, had known that he was dealing with the Gray Seal from the moment his room under Sen Yat's had been entered—could not help but have known it. And at the last here, the man, being then disarmed, had had no choice but to resort to his wits as the only means of escape. Yes, he, Jimmie Dale, quite understood!

He had sought, and found, and lost again—the Phantom.

CHAPTER 7
THE MESSAGE

Days of searching! Days of futility! Days that had brought no reward! Since the night of Limpy Mack's disappearance there had been only failure. Nowhere had he been able to pick up again a thread or clue that would set him once more upon the Phantom's trail—until tonight. And tonight? Jimmie Dale shook his head. He was at sea, troubled—about tonight.

Threadbare, gaunt-cheeked, dissolute in appearance, his battered old felt hat pulled down over his eyes, he was slouching now, as Smarlinghue, with apparent aimlessness along the street. Past him, going to and fro, other figures shuffled by—for the most part Chinamen, their crossed hands tucked in the sleeves of their blouses. A slumming party from a "gape-wagon" disembarked its load of candidates for initiation into those most dark, drear, shivery and hidden things of Chinatown, whose storied mysteries in this more enlightened generation were now within the reach of all—for the insignificant sum of one dollar a ticket!

A twisted smile flickered across Jimmie Dale's lips. This jostling little crowd that was being herded into line now by the stentorian voiced barker would see many things, for the stage was always set. They would see most fearsome opium dens that reeked with the sickly sweetish smell of poppy, where no poppy was; they would see the worshippers at the Shrine of the Thousandth Ancestor; they would see the council chambers where the Tong wars were declared, and most ghastly murders hatched; they would see the Chinamen at their fan-tan; and—Jimmie Dale shrugged his shoulders—they would undeniably get their money's worth. It was quite innocent, and everybody would be satisfied; but into Hip Foo's, for instance, where he was going now, from whose tortuous, bunk-lined, connecting sub-cellars there were two exits separated one from the other by almost a block, and again from the entrance by an entirely different street, their tickets would not take them. Hip Foo made no money from the gape-wagons!

The scene, though it was still before him, was gone from his consciousness as quickly as the train of thought that had obtruded itself upon him, and his mind was instantly back again now on the note that had been laid beside his plate by one of the attendants at the St. James Club, where he had been dining but little more than half an hour ago. The note had contained a single sentence—in the Tocsin's writing:

"Watch Mother Margot—at Hip Foo's tonight."

His lips closed tightly. Was there anything beneath the surface of that one sentence, anything more than its actual wording, anything of a *personal* nature? He had been turning it over and over in his mind from the moment he had received it, even while he had hurried to the Sanctuary and from a millionaire clubman had become the drug-wrecked Smarlinghue, even now again as he walked here along this none too well lighted and unsavory street in the heart of New York's Chinatown. The note was like none he had ever received from her before. Here there was no detailed plan laid out, no evident foreknowledge of what was afoot. It seemed almost a call for help where she herself was helpless, and so—it brought the blood pounding in quicker tempo through his veins—it might well be she had realised and was prepared at last to accept as inevitable the fact that, whether she would or no, he meant to force his way if it were humanly within his power into those shadows, as she termed them, with which the Phantom had surrounded her. Well, why not? She must know that he had already been in perhaps closer, more intimate touch than even herself with this master criminal of a score of aliases and a score of domiciles, first as Gentleman Laroque, then as Isaac Shiftel, and again as Limpy Mack. And besides there was her promise that—no! He shook his head a little bitterly. Why should he try to blind his own eyes? Her promise to call upon him for aid had contained the proviso that it would not identify him as an ally of hers in the Phantom's eyes.

It was a foolish hope fathered only by desire! A hope that out of this watching of Mother Margot tonight at Hip Foo's he and the woman that he loved would come together again, that he would see her, hear her voice, and after that— Yes, she knew that, too! She had said so in the letter she had slipped into the pocket of his coat when she had left him that night on the old East River wharf. She knew that once he found her again no legion of Phantoms, no pleading on her part, could keep him from her side until the end, whatever that end might be. He might shake his head if he chose, he might argue speciously with himself as his love prompted him to do, but in his heart he knew that her note tonight would not bring her and himself together unless—yes, that was it!—tonight saw the end of the Phantom's career.

The end! That brought still another angle into the Tocsin's message, an angle that was represented by this Mother Margot. His eyes grew grimly thoughtful as he walked along. How far was the old hag to be trusted? How much to be depended upon was the hold he had on her through having caught her in the act of purloining an extra share of the loot from one of her own confederates, who though she evidently did not know it herself, had been the Phantom in the guise of Limpy Mack that night at old Mrs. Kinsey's? His hands had been tied in a measure in respect of Mother Margot. True, since that night he had never lost track of her, but his means of communication had been restricted to the same means that the "Voice," as she called the Phantom, had employed—of calling her from her pushcart in Thompson Street to that telephone booth she had spoken of in Mezzo's second-hand store, and questioning her. This he had done each day, sometimes more than once; but the result had always been the same. Each time she had sworn that she had heard nothing further from the Voice. And yet tonight she was to be watched at Hip Foo's!

Was she playing fast and loose? He had not been in personal touch with her—that was where the weakness of his position lay. She knew him to be the Gray Seal, but she knew him only as a man with a mask on his face. He could not stand beside her pushcart on Thompson Street, and, wearing a mask, talk to her. He could not go to her as Smarlinghue and risk even the suspicion that Smarlinghue had any connection with the Gray Seal, let alone being the Gray Seal himself! A word from her, if that thought ever entered her mind, or anybody else's for that matter, and underworld and police would join hands in the one cause that could ever be common to both, and fight as only two packs of wolves might fight for the prey that only one could have.

It was not a pleasant thought!

He withdrew his hands suddenly from his ragged pockets, and, stooping down, picked up a crumpled newspaper from the gutter, as the flaring red type of a headline caught his eye. He glanced at it, and pitched it away again almost immediately. He had been interested to know if it were a special edition announcing some new development in the case of one Connie Pfeffer, alias the Mole. It did not. It was just re-hash.

He smiled wryly. The Gray Seal, "that depraved and degenerate glutton who feasted and lived like some ghoul upon his foul notoriety, and who, with inhuman boastfulness, left his diamond-shaped gray seal upon the scene of every one of his fiendish crimes," the usual stand-by of the sensational headliners, had of late been relegated to obscurity by the newspapers. It was a relief! For the time being the crime that held the public attention was that in which this Connie Pfeffer was involved, but this was more, as a matter of fact, because of the opportunity it afforded for a jeer at the police rather than on account of the actual crime itself. For two days the journals had been full of the Levenson Bank robbery, a private bank in the Wall Street district, where a customer, having just drawn out ten thousand dollars in twenty five-hundred-dollar bills, had been held up almost in front of the teller's wicket at the point of a revolver and relieved of his cash. Connie Pfeffer, alias the Mole, who had answered to the description of the robber, had been apprehended within an hour of the crime by the police, released again for lack of evidence against him—and then had promptly disappeared. New evidence establishing the fact that Connie Pfeffer was the man who had entered the bank had almost immediately come to light, but Connie Pfeffer was no longer to be found, and the police—

Jimmie Dale swung sharply around. Someone was plucking at his sleeve—a tattered and stoop-shouldered old man, who had a tray slung around his neck upon which was displayed a pitiful array of cheap collar buttons.

"Hello, Smarly!" The man spoke low, out of the corner of his mouth. "Say, Smarly, I wanter ask youse somethin'."

For an instant Jimmie Dale surveyed the other. It was Pedler Joe, and Pedler Joe lived just around the corner from the Sanctuary and was therefore in the category of an old acquaintance and neighbour; but his, Jimmie Dale's, business tonight was at Hip Foo's, and he had no time to waste.

"Hello, Joe!" he returned a little ungraciously. "Didn't know you went in for night work. There's a gape-bus back there, and the bunch have gone into Charlie Wong's lay-out. If you stick around when they come you may get away with something."

"I ain't out for business—not dat kind," the man whispered—and still holding Jimmie Dale's coat sleeve, edged out to the curb and halted. "I'm lookin' for someone. Everybody says youse're on de level, Smarly. Youse bats around a lot in places dey won't let me into, so hand it to me straight. Have youse seen Connie anywhere, youse knows who I mean, de Mole?"

Jimmie Dale stared. It was rather curious, rather much of a coincidence! He had been thinking of Connie Pfeffer, alias the Mole, at the moment Pedler Joe had accosted him. And coincidences in the Bad Lands were not always—coincidences!

It was Smarlinghue of the underworld, not Jimmie Dale the millionaire clubman, who spoke.

"What's the lay?" His tones pointed the inquiry with almost exaggerated suspicion.

"Aw, it's straight!" the old man answered. "I'm askin' youse just dat. Have youse seen him, or heard anythin' about him?"

Jimmie Dale still parried the question.

"Sounds like you'd shoved your stake in with the bulls," he scowled. "Did they give you a badge to pin inside your vest? What have you got to do with Connie?"

The old man's face was haggard; he evidently had not shaved for several days, and the short white bristles seemed to accentuate a general woe-begone aspect and feebleness that age and the thin, stooped shoulders already proclaimed loudly enough.

"I got a lot to do wid him," the old man said hoarsely. "He's like my own kid, dat's wot he is. I ain't done much for him mabbe, but I done wot I could to keep him straight, an'—"

"You!" Jimmie Dale laughed outright. Pedler Joe's life history was written on the police blotters! The man had served at least a half dozen sentences in prison. True, Pedler Joe in his declining years—he must be verging on the seventies now—had, outwardly at least, reformed to the extent of earning his living as a legalised mendicant, as witness the collar buttons. But as a guardian and sponsor for young morals—Jimmie Dale, as Smarlinghue, grinned viciously. "Say, it's no wonder he pulled that bank job! He comes by it honestly! Say, what's the—"

Jimmie Dale's grin had died away. Something was wrong here; there was something deeper than appeared on the surface, something that he did not understand. The tears had come suddenly into the faded old eyes, and were trickling now down the wrinkled cheeks.

"Forget it, Joe!" Jimmie Dale laid his hand in quick sympathy on the other's shoulder. "I didn't mean to hand you nothing. Spill the story, Joe—only hurry, 'cause I got a date."

"I picked him outer de gutter w'en he could hardly walk," said Pedler Joe. "An' w'en I wasn't doin' spaces up de river, I kept my eye on him. Sounds like hell from an old lag, don't it? But it's true, Smarly, so help me Gawd, it's true! I wasn't runnin' straight myself, but wot chance I got I tried to show de kid my line wasn't any good. Only I was away a lot, an' I let him down, so it ain't all his fault. Dere wasn't no one to keep him from goin' wild w'en I was doin' time—see? He ain't lived wid me for years, but dat didn't keep him from comin' frequent to see me, I'll say dat for him. An' den dis bank job happened. If youse read de papers youse know he was pinched in my place dat afternoon. He blew in to get a little stake from me, an'—"

"From you!" Jimmie Dale interrupted. "I didn't know you had loose change to—"

"Some days," said the old man simply, "I pick up more'n youse'd t'ink. But dat ain't nothin' to do wid it. Dere was always a few dollars for Connie w'en he was on his uppers. Well, youse know dey didn't have anythin' on him to hold him for de job, an' dey let him go.'"

"And he beat it, and he ain't been seen since," commented Jimmie Dale judicially in his rôle of Smarlinghue. "And now someone else comes along and swears too it was him at the bank. It's open and shut now that he pulled the job all right, and ducked with the cash. That's why they're laughing at the police. You're wasting your time looking for him. He's gone."

"Yes," said Pedler Joe; "he's gone—dat's wot's de matter." He glanced furtively about him. "But he ain't gone de way youse t'ink. I don't say now he didn't pull de job, though I didn't t'ink so until last night; an' I was handin' de police straight goods w'en dey was puttin' me through down at de Chief's de afternoon dey put de nippers on Connie at my place. He's gone—but he ain't gone de way youse t'ink. Dere's somethin' else bein' pulled besides dat. Take a look at dis!"

Jimmie Dale leaned forward. Pedler Joe had loosened his collar. The man's neck and throat were a mass of ugly bruises, discolored, swollen, finger-printed in angry, purplish blotches.

"Good God!" muttered Jimmie Dale. "How'd you get that?"

"It was last night"—Pedler Joe again glanced furtively around him, as he rearranged his collar—"dey nearly bumped me off before dey was satisfied dat I didn't know any more'n wot I'd told de police. Dey wanted to know where de cash was, de ten t'ousand bucks dat Connie stole. Dat's wot dey did to *me*, an' dat's why I'm askin' youse if youse have seen or heard anythin' of Connie."

Jimmie Dale's lips had tightened.

"You think," he said slowly, "they had tried the same game with Connie, and that's why he's—*disappeared*? You mean you've doped it out that they hadn't been able to make him talk up to last night, and that they tried you then on a chance?"

The old man nodded.

"Sure, dey got him," he said miserably. "Dey got him cold. Dat's wot makes me t'ink now dat Connie pulled de job all right, 'cause dey're wise to him."

"Yes," said Jimmie Dale; "but who was it that laid you out?"

"I ain't dead sure," said Pedler Joe. "I woke up last night in bed wid a pair of hands around my t'roat, chokin' me. It was pretty dark in the room. Dere was two of 'em. an' I wasn't sure, an' I ain't sure now, but I thought one of 'em. the little fellow, was Bunty Myers, who used to travel wid Gentleman Laroque's gang."

Gentleman Laroque! *The Phantom!* Jimmie Dale was fumbling aimlessly with the brim of his battered old felt hat. Mother Margot, Hip Foo's, the Phantom—and Connie Pfeffer, alias the Mole! Was this what was at the bottom of the Tocsin's note? Intuitively he was instantly sure of it. It dovetailed perfectly. The Phantom was not likely to be playing *two* games tonight, therefore—

Pedler Joe was whispering hoarsely again:

"Youse're on de level, Smarly, an' on de inside everywhere. I—I thought mabbe youse'd help me. An' if youse heard anythin' or saw anythin' youse'd tip me off."

Jimmie Dale held out his hand.

"Sure, I will, Joe!" he said. He leaned closer to the other. "You keep your map closed about having spoken to me—see? I know Bunty Myers. I'll do my best for you."

"T'anks, Smarly," said the old man gratefully. "I knew youse would."

"Sure!" said Jimmie Dale again. "Well, that goes—and so-long, Joe."

He turned and slouched on again down the street. His face was impassive, but his hands in his pockets were clenched now. So the Phantom's hand was in this, too, was it? And the old broken figure with the tray of collar buttons slung around his neck was one of the victims! It brought the hot anger surging upon him. There was something that struck deep to the root of his sympathy, something pathetic in the strange loyalty, the curious love that old Pedler Joe, himself a thief by profession in the days gone by, held for the gutter snipe that he had tried—and failed—to bring up in the paths of virtue! The Phantom! Well, perhaps, tonight, if at Hip Foo's there was—

Jimmie Dale turned the corner, and halted suddenly in a dazed, stunned way. As at the door of Charlie Wong's back there on the other street, a wagon was drawn up here at the curb in front of Hip Foo's, and a little crowd was disembarking from the wagon and was being marshalled into line, but it was not a gape-wagon that stood at Hip Foo's front door; it was a wagon of quite a very different sort—a police van. And then in an instant, his wits at work again after the first shock of surprise, Jimmie Dale slouched back out of sight around the corner again. Here he broke into a run. A raid! Hip Foo's was being raided.

Jimmie Dale ran on at top speed. His chances were just even—that was all. There were *two* exits a block apart. He could not watch both at once. Which one would Mother Margot use? The police would not get her, nor any of those with her. The police would gather in a few Chinese attendants who would be as phlegmatic and informative as so many cows; the police would collect a little opium-smoking paraphernalia, and Hip Foo would be fined— but that would be all. Before the first blue-coat crossed the threshold of the entrance, the exodus through the sub-cellars would have begun.

And now Jimmie Dale drew into the shadows at the mouth of a dark and narrow lane. It was the toss of a coin. This one or the other! Yes—here they came now, like rats running from a sinking ship. He crouched against the wall unnoticed, or if noticed accepted as one of their own ilk, and watched them. Man after man, woman after woman, passed out into the street. The procession dwindled to a few belated stragglers—and ceased. He waited a minute longer. There was no one else.

Tight-lipped then, Jimmie Dale turned away. Mother Margot had not been amongst them. He had lost the toss, that was all. She had gone out the other way.

He walked rapidly now. There was only one thing left to do, one way left open to him. It would not be very difficult to find Mother Margot—at her home—in those rooms from which, on that first night, the Phantom had so mysteriously disappeared. He had even promised her a visit!

He smiled a little grimly. His promise so far had been unfulfilled. Not because the Tocsin had warned him that the place was a trap, and even Mother Margot, evidently terror-stricken that night at Mrs. Kinsey's, had done likewise; but because, prior to that warning and prior to Mother Margot's occupancy of the rooms, he had already searched the premises and found nothing; and because, until now, it had not seemed that there was anything to be gained by a move which might result in warning the Phantom that he, Jimmie Dale, had been in communication with Mother Margot.

But tonight there was no choice but to go there—unless perhaps she had gone back to her pushcart in Thompson Street. He would try that first, and if she were there call her to the phone as he always did, and arrange a meeting somewhere under conditions such that she would discover no more of his actual identity than that of the man in the mask whom she already knew as the Gray Seal.

He was hurrying now. Time, as measured in minutes, might or might not be precious. He did not know. What had taken place at Hip Foo's, whether for instance the rendezvous that Mother Margot had presumably had there had been prematurely interrupted by the raid, or what were the details of the scheme the Phantom was hatching, he did not know. But in any case, one thing was vital, not only to himself but to the Tocsin, vital to all he hoped for—that the *character* of Smarlinghue should not be endangered. And this, not only because it was in itself the key that opened for him the innermost portals of the underworld, that again and again had alone stood between him and recognition as the Gray Seal, but because tonight he must meet Mother Margot, not as Smarlinghue, but in the only character that she would recognise, and, yes—the grim smile came again—*obey*. And so, first of all, must come the Sanctuary; after that—his shoulders under the ragged coat lifted in an almost fatalistic little shrug—who knew!

CHAPTER 8

JIMMIE DALE PAYS A VISIT

It was Smarlinghue, the drug-wrecked artist, who, ten minutes later, by the street entrance, inviting even the nods of recognition from some of the loungers round about, entered the dingy tenement and scuffled along the musty, dark, unlighted hallway to the squalid rear room on the ground floor—the Sanctuary; it was Jimmie Dale, in dinner jacket, the millionaire clubman, who stealthily gained the street again by way of the old French window, the refuse-strewn courtyard, the board in the high fence that swung aside at a touch, and finally the lane.

Another ten minutes, and he was sauntering nonchalantly along a narrow crowded street, whose curbs were lined with pushcarts, whose sidewalks were thronged with shawled women and coatless, swarthy men, whose gutters were the playground for almost naked children. Thompson Street was in the heart of New York, just off West Broadway, not far from the homes of the old-time aristocracy of Washington Square, but it was also in a foreign land!

But Mother Margot with her pushcart was not here tonight. He had hardly expected she would be. His face was set as he made his way back now to the Bowery, and from there headed still deeper into the East Side. There was nothing for it now but Mother Margot's rooms.

A few blocks farther brought him within sight of the tenement that was his destination, and his pace slowed as he passed the narrow alleyway over which the police had kept abortive guard on the night they had pounded at Isaac Shiftel's door inside. There was a light in the window, the same window through which he and the Phantom, alias Isaac Shiftel, or perhaps better on that occasion, alias Gentleman Laroque, had first had warning that the police were without. Mother Margot, then, had presumably returned home.

He was opposite the tenement door now. He halted abruptly, ostensibly to watch the efforts of a man across the road who was attempting to start an old car that was back-firing viciously, in reality to allow some near-by pedestrians to pass by—and then suddenly Jimmie Dale had disappeared from the street, and in another instant, in the dark, murky hall, was standing before Mother Margot's door.

From one of the pockets in the leather girdle beneath his outer garments, that harboured too its little blued-steel burglar's kit, he took out his black silk mask and slipped it over his face. His lips tightened a little, as his right hand closed over the automatic in the side pocket of his dinner jacket. Who knew!

There was a light in there, it was true; but he was not necessarily *sure* that it was Mother Margot—or that Mother Margot was alone.

He knocked upon the door. There was no answer. He knocked again. This time there came the sound of a shuffling footstep crossing the floor within, and then the door was cautiously opened, and Mother Margot, holding a candle above her head, peered out into the hallway.

"My Gawd—youse!" she whispered hoarsely. "Wot're youse doin' here?"

Jimmie Dale smiled beneath his mask.

"Have you forgotten, Mother Margot?" he said softly. "I promised you a visit, you know."

He stepped forward, but she blocked his way at the threshold.

"Go away! Go away from here!" she breathed wildly.

"I don't see why I should—just yet," said Jimmie Dale quietly. "And wouldn't it be better if we had our interview *inside* instead of out here? It wouldn't be quite so public."

"No!" she said frantically. She kept glancing behind her, over her shoulder in a terrified way. "Aw, go away! For the love of Gawd, go away before we'se gets caught!"

"Who's in there, then?" demanded Jimmie Dale sharply.

"No one!" she answered. "Dere ain't no one dere—at least I don't know whether dere is or not."

Jimmie Dale stared at the old hag for a moment speculatively.

"You don't know!" He injected a caustic note into his voice. "What do you mean by that?"

"Didn't I tell youse de other night!" She was still whispering hoarsely. "Didn't I tell youse wot dey said—dat dey was figurin' on youse comin' here sometime. Dat's wot I means. I ain't never seen no one in here but me, but sometimes I'm scared. Sometimes I'm sure someone is watchin' me—an'—an' I can't *see* no one. Don't youse see I'm playin' straight wid youse. If I wasn't, I'd let youse in, an'—aw, my Gawd, get away from here! If I'm caught tippin' youse off dey'd put a knife into me, dat's wot dey'd do!"

"We'll be less likely to be seen or caught without that light, then," said Jimmie Dale coolly. He leaned forward suddenly, caught her arm, and blew the candle out. "Now, don't move!" He was past her in an instant, and with quick, silent tread, his step as noiseless as though he possessed the padded paws of a cat, he made the circuit of the two rooms. And then he was back again beside her at the threshold. The rooms, so far as any outward and visible evidence of human presence was concerned, were empty. Nevertheless, he drew Mother Margot out into the dark hallway now, and closed the door silently behind them.

"Wot is it?" she faltered. "Wot is it youse wants?"

"A little information—perhaps a little more than information," said Jimmie Dale evenly. "You said something a minute ago about playing straight with me. I'm not so sure about you, Mother Margot. That's why I'm here. I telephoned you this morning, and you swore you had not heard from the Voice since that night at Mrs. Kinsey's."

"It was de truth," she said quickly.

"I'm so glad you always tell the truth," he said tersely, "because then, of course, you'll tell me now all about Hip Foo's tonight."

She drew in her breath sharply.

"My Gawd!" she stammered. "Youse—youse knows about dat?"

"Go on, Mother Margot!" Jimmie Dale prompted curtly.

"Dere—dere ain't nothin' to tell." She was obviously groping for inspiration. "De bulls raided de place almost as soon as I got dere, an' I beat it on de jump for home."

"Don't lie!" snapped Jimmie Dale sternly. "There is a good deal to tell! Shall I help your memory?" He was quite sure of his ground. Pedler Joe's story made the Phantom's and Bunty Myers' connection with the night's work a practical certainty. "Don't you think Bunty Myers, and Connie Pfeffer's ten thousand is worth telling about—Mother Margot?"

The shot went home. The old hag shrank back against the wall. He heard her mumbling incoherently.

"I'm waiting!" said Jimmie Dale coldly.

"I—I can't!" she burst out. "I—I daresn't!"

"I think you can," Jimmie Dale answered sharply. "And I am sure that it will be much the *safer* thing for you to do. As a last resort, for instance, if you forced my hand, the police might be very much interested to learn that Mother Margot knew something about the Levenson Bank robbery, and—"

"I—I'll tell youse!" she broke in. "My Gawd, wot can I do? Wot else can I do? I—I'll come across. Wen youse telephoned me today I hadn't heard nothin'. It was only about six o'clock dat de Voice told me to take de message over to Hip Foo's, an' be dere by half past eight. See? Dere wasn't no way I could tell youse, was dere? I ain't de only one dat don't know where de Gray Seal lives, am I?"

"No," said Jimmie Dale evenly; "and we'll dispense with any discussion as to what you would have done if you had known. Go on!"

"It was to meet Bunty Myers an' another of Gentleman Laroque's gang named Muller." Mother Margot's whisper was scarcely audible. "An'—an' it was about Connie Pfeffer, all right. I was to tell 'em dat Connie had seen de error of his ways an' opened up, an' dat de coin was in de house wid de broken stairs, an' shoved in under one of dem."

She paused, and in the semi-darkness Jimmie Dale could see her jerking her head in a birdlike way furtively about her.

"What's its other name?" demanded Jimmie Dale shortly.

She looked at him puzzled.

"De other name of wot?"

"The house with the broken stairs." Jimmie Dale's tones were uncompromising.

"Why, it's Pedler Joe's, of course!" she answered. "Youse knows where dat is. Everybody does."

Pedler Joe! For a moment Jimmie Dale stared at her. Was Pedler Joe, too, playing a game? The figure of the old man, full of misery from what seemed genuine distress and fear, rose before him. But against this was Pedler Joe's record. Was this the way he had brought up his young protégé—to play in with him hand and glove? And yet those bruises on the man's neck and throat—*they* were genuine enough.

Again Jimmie Dale lunged in the dark, and won.

"Pedler Joe had nothing to do with it!" he snapped. "Don't try any holding out on me, Mother Margot!"

"I ain't holdin' out nothin' on youse," she protested. "I didn't say Pedler Joe was in it. Connie beat it for Joe's after pullin' de robbery at de bank dat day, so's to work up an alibi—see? But de bulls pinched him quicker'n he figured. He hears dem comin' while he's dere—see?—an' w'en Pedler Joe ain't lookin' he shoves de envelope wid de cash in under one of de broken stairs, an' w'en de bulls bust in dey don't find nothin', an' dey ain't got nothin' on Connie, an' after puttin' him through for a few hours down at headquarters dey has to let him go."

Jimmie Dale nodded.

"Exactly!" he said tersely. "And the reason he didn't go back for the money was because he never got a chance. Your gang got him, and started in to apply less humane but evidently more effective measures to make him talk than the police did."

Mother Margot drew in her breath.

"I guess youse knows de whole lay. My Gawd, youse ain't human, are youse?"

"There's Hip Foo's," suggested Jimmie Dale grimly.

"Yes," she mumbled. "But dere ain't nothin' much to dat: now youse knows de rest. I had just give 'em de message w'en de bulls started de raid, an' we beat it. Dey're to go down dere after Pedler Joe gets to sleep, an' pinch de dough—dat's all."

"Not quite!" said Jimmie Dale. "There's Connie Pfeffer. Did they go the limit with him? Is he dead?"

Mother Margot shook her head.

"No, he ain't—not quite. He'll be all right after a while, but I guess he just come through wid de dope in time. Him an' one of Laroque's men, dat's supposed to be a man-nurse in charge of an invalid—see?—is on deir way west for somewhere now. Dat gets Connie outer here so's he don't get a chance to butt in an' spill anythin' to Pedler Joe or some other pal dat'd help him out, an' besides it's a kind of a stake dey're givin' him so's de bulls won't bother him no more."

Again Jimmie Dale was silent for a moment. It was clear-cut, wasn't it, the work that was ahead now? There was no choice, was there? There was only one thing to do. He could not go to a telephone, say, and tip the police off to the hiding place of the money; for the fact that it would be found in Pedler Joe's would convict Pedler Joe as an accomplice. The man, innocent though he was, would not have a chance. His known intimacy with the Mole, and the fact that Connie Pfeffer had been found there shortly after the robbery, both of which reasons had already resulted in a grilling for the old man from the authorities, and above all Pedler Joe's own record would—

"All right!" said Jimmie Dale abruptly. "Let's go!"

"Go!" Mother Margot crouched back against the wall. "Go where?"

"To Pedler Joe's," said Jimmie Dale curtly.

"Me!" She flung out her arms wildly. "Me—go dere! Aw, my Gawd, not dat! If dey caught me dey'd—dey'd croak me. I don't dare! My Gawd, I don't dare! Dey'd kill me. I've told youse all I knows. Youse ain't got no use for me dere."

"Oh, yes, I think I have," said Jimmie Dale coolly. "I'd feel a little more comfortable if I knew where Mother Margot was and what she was doing during the next half hour."

"But—but youse can trust me," she faltered.

"Possibly!" admitted Jimmie Dale evenly. "But not to the extent of staking my life on it. It would be rather awkward for me if you communicated with the Voice, say, while I was—"

"No, no; I swear I won't!" she whispered frantically. "Aw, for Gawd's sake, don't make me do dat! If dey sees me, if dey catches me dey'll know I snitched, an' dey'll twist me t'roat or put a knife into me."

It was quite true. If caught under any such circumstances Mother Margot's life would not be worth a moment's purchase. But then Mother Margot would not be caught. Bunty Myers and whoever was to accompany him were not to go there until late tonight, not until they would expect Pedler Joe to be in bed and asleep; and at the present moment Pedler Joe was out roaming miserably about the streets in his hopeless search. The place would be empty. There would be no risk for Mother Margot—and he, Jimmie Dale, was certainly by no means sure enough of her to leave her free to communicate with her confederates and trap him like a rat if she chose to do so.

"They won't catch you." His tones were peremptory now. "You go ahead. I'll follow—where I can keep my eye on you. I can't very well walk through the streets with a mask on my face, and I would a little rather prefer, Mother Margot, that all *you* saw was—a mask. And, besides, it might be just as well for your sake that you should not be seen in company with anyone. You say you know Pedler Joe's place. Well, so do I. When you turn into the wagon drive I'll join you. Now then!"

Again she shrank back.

"No, no!" she pleaded. "I—I'm scared. Youse don't know wot youse're doin'. Youse're goin' to get me killed, dat's wot it means."

"I don't want to make any noise that might be heard back there in your room by the unseen watcher that you appear to be so much afraid of," he said coldly; "but you are either going with me, or it is going to be a showdown right here, Mother Margot. You understand?" He caught her by the arm, and pushed her toward the front door. "Now go!"

She moved forward along the hall. He could see her wringing her hands.

"My Gawd!" she whispered; and again: "My Gawd!"

CHAPTER 9

THE HOUSE WITH THE BROKEN STAIRS

Mother Margot passed out through the door. Jimmie Dale, a few paces behind, removed his mask as he stepped out to the sidewalk. He crossed instantly to the other side of the road, and, keeping pace with her, followed her as she shuffled down the street.

He was smiling grimly now. The Phantom apparently was becoming cautious—in a personal sense. As Gentleman Laroque, as Isaac Shiftel, as Limpy Mack, the man had but narrowly escaped; tonight, it seemed fairly obvious, he was playing a safer game by delegating the actual work to the members of his old gang over whom he evidently still preserved his authority. Jimmie Dale's smile gave place to tight, set lips. It was a compliment in a way, and a very genuine compliment, to him, Jimmie Dale; but if there was no Phantom tonight, no chance at the man in that personal way, then, equally, there would be no Tocsin tonight either at the end of the quest!

He went on down the street, following the shawled figure of the old hag. Why dwell on that? What good would it do? What would it bring him? Some night, some time, it would be the last night and the last time, and there would be—the end. Meanwhile tonight, at least, he could check-mate the Phantom's game.

His thoughts swept back to the immediate present. Something struck him for the moment as incongruous, out of keeping, a little illogical, in view of the open brutality they had dealt out to Pedler Joe last night when they had not hesitated to break into the old man's house, that tonight the Phantom had switched his tactics to those of almost exaggerated stealth. And then he shook his head. No—it was far from illogical. He saw it now. He owed the Phantom a compliment in return. Mentally he paid it. The man had a sort of super cunning and cleverness cradled in his devil's brain! Pedler Joe knew nothing; Pedler Joe would continue to know nothing. Connie Pfeffer's lips were sealed unless to confess his own guilt. And so the disappearance of the money would remain a mystery—that was all!

The shawled figure on the opposite side shuffled on. It was not far now to Pedler Joe's. He followed her across the Bowery, down a side street again, past the Sanctuary, and around the next corner. Here he closed the gap between them, crossing to her side of the street—and as she disappeared into the blackness of a sort of arched driveway, he joined her.

He slipped the mask over his face again, and took her arm.

"Come on!" he whispered.

The driveway was a wretched, dirty place, once used no doubt for a delivery wagon when the store in front had been in its prime; now it was Pedler Joe's entrance to his domain, which, in turn, had once been an outhouse of some kind, perhaps even the stable, or wagon shed, a miserable little wooden shack, neglected now and in hopeless disrepair.

Jimmie Dale, still holding Mother Margot's arm, emerged from the driveway, crossed the small yard beyond, and halted at the door of the hovel.

It was dark here; nothing showed but the looming shadows of the surrounding buildings. Mother Margot was whimpering again:

"Pedler Joe! Pedler Joe'll see me, an' den—"

"Pedler Joe is out," said Jimmie Dale crisply. "There's no one inside. You won't get into any trouble, Mother Margot, unless you make it yourself. I'll see to that!"

The door was locked. From the leather girdle Jimmie Dale selected a pick-lock. A moment, two, passed. The slim, sensitive fingers of Jimmie Dale, that mocked at even the intricate locks and bolts devised by modern ingenuity, were working quickly, almost contemptuously now, at Pedler Joe's cheap, flimsy fastening. The door swung open. Jimmie Dale motioned Mother Margot to enter, and, following, closed and locked the door again behind them.

For an instant he stood motionless, then his flashlight swept the interior, lancing the blackness with its round, white ray. The place was one of utter, poverty-stricken desolation. There was but a single room, with no furniture in it save an old table and chair; the floor sagged and had rotted away in places; even a window was lacking, for where one once had been, it was now, in lieu of broken panes no doubt, nailed up with boards.

And now the flashlight focussed and held on a flight of stairs obliquely across from the door and on the far side of the room. Mother Margot had called the place "the house with the broken stairs," and it was well named! Half a dozen of the treads at least were broken away and were little more now than so many gaping holes; and for the rest, the whole staircase leaned drunkenly to one side as though scarcely able any longer to sustain its own weight, let alone the added burden of anyone desirous of reaching the floor above.

"Whereabouts in the stairs is it?" Jimmie Dale demanded abruptly.

Mother Margot was crouched close against the door in a frightened attitude. She shook her head.

"I dunno," she answered. "I wish to Gawd I did, so's we could get outer here quick. It's in one of dem holes in de stairs. Connie said he didn't remember which one 'cause he had to act on de jump. He heard de bulls comin', an' Pedler Joe was upstairs, an' he said he hadn't time to figure anythin' except to get de cash outer sight."

"All right!" said Jimmie Dale quietly. "It doesn't much matter. We'll begin at the beginning."

He moved across the room, and with his flashlight began his search under the broken stair treads. But it was not until the fourth attempt that his hand, in under a tread up to the elbow, encountered a sealed envelope. He drew it out quickly, and tore the end open. Yes, here it was! He took out the money and counted it rapidly—twenty five-hundred-dollar banknotes. It was all here—ten thousand dollars. He thrust the money into his pocket, and laid the empty envelope on the stair beside him.

"It's all right, Mother Margot!" he called softly. "We'll go in a minute."

From another pocket in the leather girdle he drew out now the thin metallic case that contained its store of diamond-shaped, gray-paper seals, and with the tiny tweezers—that there might be no tell-tale finger prints—lifted out one of the seals and moistened the adhesive side with his lips. There was Pedler Joe to be considered. Pedler Joe must not be held accountable by the Phantom, any more than by the police. He picked up the empty envelope and pressed the gray seal firmly down upon it. When Bunty Myers and his fellow thugs arrived and found the money gone, Pedler Joe would naturally be the first one they would think of, and their former suspicions that the old man knew more than he pretended would be aroused again with disastrous results for Pedler Joe. But the gray seal here on the envelope would square Pedler Joe and settle all doubts on that score. The Phantom, for instance, was fully—

Mother Margot's whisper cut tensely, suddenly through the room:

"Dey're comin'! Dey're comin'! Aw, for Gawd's sake, dey're comin', an' dere ain't no way to get out!"

In an instant Jimmie Dale was across the room beside her. He caught her wrist fiercely.

"I told youse so!" She was crooning. "Dey'll kill me for dis!"

"Keep quiet!" breathed Jimmie Dale.

Cool, possessed, motionless, he stood there. Mother Margot was right. He could hear the footsteps of three or four men close to the door outside. There was no way out. They were trapped, and Mother Margot—

The door rattled as it was tried. A voice in a low callous laugh reached him through the panels:

"It's a good thing youse piped old Pedler down de line, Bunty; it's saved us wastin' de night hangin' round waitin' for him to hit de hay!"

And then another voice, impatiently:

"Aw, get de door open! Wot's de use playin' wid de lock? Bust it in, an' strike a light! Youse don't have to be careful of de noise when Pedler ain't dere."

Mother Margot! There was a chance. Just one. Not for both of them perhaps, but for Mother Margot. He owed it to her. He had brought her here—to her death—if the chance failed.

He leaned toward her, his lips close against her ear.

"Flatten back here against the wall. The door opens away from you. Don't move till they make a rush, then slip through the door behind them, and get to the street. I'll guarantee at least that no one will *follow* you, and with a little luck you won't be seen at all."

"But youse"—a strange note had come suddenly into her voice—"but youse—youse mean dat—"

"Never mind what I mean," said Jimmie Dale between set teeth. "Do as I tell you, or *neither* of us'll get out!"

The door lock yielded with a little snap—but Jimmie Dale was no longer there. Silent as a shadow in his movements, he was already halfway up the stairs.

He halted here. He was still holding the envelope with its gray seal, but instead of his flashlight his automatic now was in his other hand.

And then for the first time Jimmie Dale made a sound—at the moment that the door swung open. It was as though, suddenly alarmed, he had tripped and fallen upon the rickety stairs. There was a chorus of startled oaths, a rush of feet across the floor in his direction, the white gleam of a flashlight thrown upon him, the chorused shouts again—and he turned, dropping the envelope from his hand, and as it fluttered downward to the floor, he dashed madly up the stairs.

Came the crash and roar of a revolver shot, the spurt of flame, the ugly *spat* of a bullet as it embedded itself in the woodwork somewhere above his head, another, and still another—but Jimmie Dale did not fire in return. There was Mother Margot. They had not noticed her and she should be gone by now, but he could not see. He dared not take the chance of any of them running back for cover in the direction of the door. Just a few seconds more, and then—he flung himself over the topmost stair—yes, it was safe now surely to check their rush if he could. He fired—his shot directed high over their heads. Snarls and curses answered him. The flashlights, more than one of them now, made almost daylight of the place. And suddenly a new shout went up. Someone had picked up the envelope!

"*The Gray Seal!*"

A hail of lead came up the staircase—and a concerted rush of dark, swarming figures. He could not tell how many—three or four—but it seemed as though there were a dozen.

The window! There must be a window here. He remembered that Pedler Joe had spoken of a window. Yes, there it was just across from the stairhead. He hurled himself toward it, flung it open, and swung out over the sill. It could not be very high. In any case it was the only chance. A flashlight's ray caught him now from the head of the stairs, and was accompanied almost simultaneously by an oath and the tongue flame of a revolver.

He let go his hold and dropped. Something, a heap of rubbish, an uneven surface, threw him violently upon his face as he landed, but in an instant he was on his feet again. There was no way out of the place except across the yard and through the archway, and he raced in that direction. He heard a shout signalling his whereabouts from the window. It was echoed by shouts from within.

If he could but gain the street before they poured out of the shack in pursuit! No—here they came now! Over his shoulder he caught a glimpse of shadowy forms behind him.

He had a start of ten yards, perhaps fifteen at the outside. He swerved out into the street. Strange the commotion back there had not aroused the neighbourhood! But it would not take long to do so now if the chase remained in the open!

"The Gray Seal! Get him! Stop him!"

The shouts, the pound of feet rang from behind him. But now a half choked, panting laugh came grimly from Jimmie Dale as a dark shawled figure peered suddenly out from a doorway and drew back again as he dashed by. Mother Margot! Well, at least, he had kept his promise to Mother Margot.

And now windows began to open; people to emerge from the houses. The pound of feet, the shouts seemed to grow even nearer. Jimmie Dale was straining every muscle now, running like a deer. Another few minutes of this in the open and it would be the end. Thank God, the Sanctuary was just around the corner! If he had ever needed it in his life, he needed it now. They might see him enter the tenement; but by the time they had been able to search the place even cursorily the Gray Seal would have vanished, and only Smarlinghue of the underworld, the drug-wrecked peer of that inglorious realm to which they themselves belonged, would be found.

He turned the corner, ran on the few yards up the block to the Sanctuary, and as he flung himself inside the tenement door he saw them swing into the street behind him, and heard them like a pack of bloodhounds give tongue again at sight of their quarry. But in a second now he was along the dark hallway and inside the Sanctuary itself, the door locked behind him.

And now he worked with lightning speed. He could have run on out through the French window, and by the lane perhaps might have had a fair chance of getting away—but almost as important as his life was the vital necessity of protecting the character of Smarlinghue from suspicion, and the Gray Seal making straight for Smarlinghue's room and disappearing thereby, marked an intimacy in time of stress with Smarlinghue's habitation too significant to go unchallenged. He tore off his evening clothes, wrenched open the movable section of the baseboard, brought out the seedy, tattered garments of Smarlinghue, and put them on.

He needed no light—only a few more precious seconds. They were stumbling around outside in the hall now; and now he could hear them break into one of the other rooms. Just a few more seconds—that was all he needed. There were still the little pieces of wax that distorted lips and nostrils, that gave a peculiar set to cheeks and ears; still the facial solution to give the gaunt, pallor-like effect that Smarlinghue—Cold beads of sweat stood out suddenly on Jimmie Dale's forehead. His mask as he pulled it off was sticky; his hand as he put it to his face came away *wet*. No, there was no need for light. He knew! It was blood. His face had been bruised and cut when he had fallen from the window. No make-up, no clothes, no "Smarlinghue" would explain that!

They were coming to his door now, weren't they? His wits—if he had ever possessed any! A chance for his life—and Smarlinghue's! The wax went into the nostrils, under the lips, behind the ears, inside the cheeks—there was no need for pallor on blood-stained skin—and the mask was over his face again.

A footstep was almost at the door.

And then, not Jimmie Dale, but Smarlinghue spoke.

"Help! Help!" he cried in a strange, gurgling, strangled voice. "Help! Let me alone! Help!"

He loosened the catch on the inside of the French window, but without opening the window itself; then, seizing a chair, he hurled it over his head in the direction of the easels and canvases that stood against the far wall. There was an answering crash. He scuffled with his feet, as he flung the evening clothes he had just taken off—saving out only his hat, which he put on—into the hiding place, and put back the movable section of the baseboard again. Another instant, and he had sent the table in the centre of the room hurtling to the floor, and had sprung—silently now—to the door.

They were pounding upon it, flinging themselves against it in an effort to break it in. In the darkness of the hall they would not be able to distinguish clothes. If they followed him, then, with luck, he might still save both himself and Smarlinghue; if they didn't, then—well, it was the end.

He turned the key with a sudden twist of his fingers, and swept the door open. Dark forms loomed before him. He struck right and left with all his body weight behind his blows, cleaving a passage for himself as he plunged forward.

A volley of furious oaths greeted the unexpected attack. Hands snatched at him. He broke from their clutches as they tried to grasp him, and sped down the hall. Yes, they were following! Thank God, they were following!

It was only a step from the street door to the lane, and in barely the fraction of a second he had gained the latter, leaving his hat behind him on the sidewalk as though it had been swept from his head in his flight; in another second he was through the board in the fence that swung aside at a touch of his hand, and was creeping along the rear of the tenement to the French window of the Sanctuary. An instant here he listened as he slipped the mask from his face, then the French window opened and closed silently again—and Smarlinghue, with battered, blood-stained face lay prone and motionless upon the floor amidst the débris and ruin of his squalid room.

A minute passed—two. Fellow tenants began to gather at the doorway, and finally to crowd into the room. The poverty-stricken gas-jet hissed as someone lighted it, and threw a pale, yellow, inadequate light over the surroundings. Jimmie Dale felt someone grasp him by the shoulders and lift him to a sitting posture. He rubbed his hand across his eyes, and stared dazedly around him. Then suddenly he seemed to rouse himself. He shook his fist wildly.

"Get the police!" he croaked hoarsely, as he recognised as Bunty Myers a man who was elbowing his way forward. "Get the police! I want the police! Someone bust in here and said if I made a peep he'd lay me out. I—I was scared for a minute, mabbe two, and then I—I started something."

"Sure! You look it!" snapped Bunty Myers. He swung fiercely on the little crowd and brushed them back to the doorway. "Get outer here!" he snarled. "Dis ain't yer hunt!" He turned again to Jimmie Dale. "Blast youse, Smarly!" he swore. "I ain't blamin' youse, but if youse'd kept quiet we'd have had him cornered cold. He's got away now down the lane." He lowered his voice. "Wot I come back for was to find out if youse'd got a better look at him dan some of de boys wid me on account of his mask, an' if youse'd know him again if youse saw him?"

Jimmie Dale shook his head.

"No, I didn't get no look at him," he said viciously. "But I'll have the police on him, and—"

"De police!" Bunty Myers' laugh was forced, unmirthful. "De police'll be a long time findin' dat bird, youse can take it from me! Say, youse give me de pip, Smarly! Dat was de Gray Seal!"

Jimmie Dale's jaw dropped. He stared helplessly.

"My God!" gasped Jimmie Dale. "The Gray Seal! Him!"

And he was still staring in a dazed and helpless way about him as Bunty Myers swung hurriedly from the room again, presumably to join his companions in their search along the lane.

CHAPTER 10

BEGGAR PETE

The street lights showed mistily, like vague, filmy patches in the darkness. It was raining in torrents, pitilessly. The water dripped from the brim of Smarlinghue's old felt hat, and beating into his face soaked the bandage around his cheek, threatening to displace it. He smiled grimly in reminiscence, as he raised his hand and tightened the dressing a little in its place.

It was four nights ago now since his accident when he had made his escape from Pedler Joe's window, and subsequently had saved himself by playing the dual rôle in the imaginary fight he had staged between Smarlinghue and the Gray Seal in the Sanctuary; and since then the character of Smarlinghue had virtually been a little Old Man of the Sea that had clung with almost sinister tenacity to him, and that he had not been able to shake off and discard as before at will. It was strange! A trick of fate, perhaps; and not an over-kindly one, for it had tied his hands, and for the moment had left him seriously crippled in his efforts to pick up the clues, already found and lost so many times, that must eventually, if there were ever to be life and freedom for the Tocsin, happiness for himself and the woman that he loved, lead to—the Phantom.

Jimmie Dale's face grew hard, anxious, perturbed. Things had not gone well in those four days. Smarlinghue, if such a thing were possible when his life itself had been the stake, had played his part too well that night in the Sanctuary! Already one of the acknowledged aristocracy of the underworld, he had been suddenly elevated to the status of little less than demigod. Smarlinghue had been in actual, physical combat with the Gray Seal! Smarlinghue had become the idol of a morbid awe and curiosity! It was subsiding now, but while it lasted it had made the "disappearance" of Smarlinghue, even for a few hours, far too dangerous a move to consider; he had been too much the attraction, too much on exhibition, as it were. But even if this had not been so, there was still another and perhaps even stronger reason that had temporarily chained him to the rôle of the drug-wrecked artist and to the environment of the Sanctuary. The underworld had eyes and ears, and so too had the police; while, still more to be feared as one who seemed to reach out with cunning versatility into so many different spheres, as one who, of all others, would have his suspicions the most quickly aroused, there was the Phantom. Jimmie Dale, if he had returned to his ordinary life, would have had to do so with a bandaged face curiously like Smarlinghue's! It invited far too much! And so he had telephoned to Jason, that peer of butlers, that he had been called out of town for a few days; and whatever personal fears the old man might have entertained for the safety of his young master, whom, as he was wont to say, he had dandled on his knee as a child, Jason could be trusted to account, both ingeniously and to the entire satisfaction of anyone interested, for the temporary absence of Jimmie Dale from his usual haunts.

In a personal sense, therefore, there had been no serious cause for anxiety; but in those four days it seemed, somehow, as though a wall, impenetrable, thick, had been reared across his path, halting him, and shutting out from both sight and hearing those things that concerned him far more than the consideration of his own security. There had been no word from the Tocsin, no note, no sign, no straw of evidence out of the whispered confidences in the hidden places of the underworld that he could grasp at as indicative of even her continued existence. The old question gnawed at his heart. Was she still alive tonight? What move had the Phantom made in those four days, and if any, had the man with his hell-born cunning been at last successful?

The days had been as a blank. Even Mother Margot had been denied him, for no mask could have hidden the bandages from her eyes. But yet, after all, he had not been idle. He had done what he could. The wave of notoriety that for the moment had swept him to a pinnacle high above his fellows of the underlands had seemed to present the only opportunity for activity left open to him, and he had seized upon it to cultivate the very men who were unconsciously responsible for the ruse to which he had been forced to resort that night in the Sanctuary to save his life, the men who had hammered at his door, voicing for the moment the one rallying cry that alone could unite the myriad, vicious interests of gangland in one common bond, "Death to the Gray Seal!" And in a measure he had been successful, though, as far as results had gone, he might, it seemed, have saved himself the effort. Bunty Myers, Muller and the rest—Gentleman Laroque's, alias the Phantom's, gang—had admitted him, rather pleased to bask in his reflected glory, to their hang-out in the upstairs rear room of Wally Kerrigan's ill-favoured "club," which was half restaurant, half gambling den, and the resort of the worst in the Bad Lands, but he had learned nothing. They had loafed and smoked and played cards and drunk an amazing quantity of liquor, but that was all. There had always been Bunty Myers and Muller, and at times as many as three or four more, but had he, Jimmie Dale, not known that back of it all Gentleman Laroque, unseen, held these men in allegiance, he never would have discovered it there!

He had learned nothing; but though tonight, for perhaps the first time, he could have dispensed with the bandages to the extent of at least being able to use the black silk mask without the risk of Mother Margot suspecting the tell-tale hurt that lay beneath, he was on his way now to Kerrigan's again as the first part of his night's work. Afterwards—He shrugged his shoulders.

Afterwards he would see! Certainly there was always a chance at Kerrigan's. He felt that he had already worked himself into an intimacy that was not far from breeding confidences. Their apparent inaction was also not without its measure of satisfaction, and this in itself alone was worth knowing. It might very well, and probably did, augur that the Phantom too was for the moment inactive, that there was a momentary stagnation, as it were, in that master crook's field of endeavour, and—

Jimmie Dale stopped short. He was opposite the swinging doors of a saloon, run by one Gypsy Dan, from which there emanated a stentorian-lunged voice high-pitched in song, accompanied by the thumping of many fists evidently upon the bar, and the stamping of many feet obviously upon the floor. Subconsciously, he was now aware, he had heard the row half a block away. It was not by any means a select and exclusive neighbourhood; it was one more of squalor than anything else and accustomed to disturbances more strenuous and decidedly more vicious than this, but it was at least within the purlieus of the city and supposedly under the domination of law and order. And now from the opposite corner ahead he caught the ray of a street lamp glinting on the rubber-cloaked shoulders of an officer, as the man crossed the street and headed for the saloon.

Jimmie Dale, as Smarlinghue, smiled thinly. Whoever they were in there, they were friends of Smarlinghue, the riff-raff, the rank and file of the citizenry of that sordid fatherland of the underworld in which he held so high a station! The character of Gypsy Dan's saloon guaranteed that. He turned quickly, pushed the swinging doors open, and stepped to the side of the ragged, unkempt figure at the bar who was yelling at the top of his voice.

"Forget it!" said Smarlinghue roughly. "There's a harness bull on the move out there."

The man, too immersed in his vocal efforts and the liquor he had imbibed, paid no attention; but the barkeeper was alert in an instant.

"T'anks, Smarly!" he grunted. He leaned across the bar and clapped his hand over the singer's mouth, effectually shutting off the flow of song. "Close yer face!" he ordered peremptorily. "Dat'll be Riley out dere, an' he's all to de good if youse'll give him half a chance. D'ye hear? Dat goes for de whole of youse!"

The half dozen loungers around the bar subsided. Comparative silence reigned for a moment, then a slow, measured step sounded outside, a nightstick rattled softly on the swinging doors, as though both in warning and in acknowledgment that the amenities had been observed, and the step died away.

"T'anks, Smarly!" said the barkeeper again, as he once more leaned back against the far side of the bar.

The erstwhile singer blinked.

"Have a drink," he invited cordially; and digging into his pocket, he produced a fistful of bills which he waved with a lordly, inebriated air about him.

Jimmie Dale stared. A moniker in the Bad Lands was always apt and incisive, and it had been particularly so in this instance. He knew the ragged, down-at-the-heels vagrant, as everybody else in the East Side knew the man. *Beggar* Pete! The man was known at times to do odd jobs perhaps if pushed to extremity for food and particularly for drink, but otherwise he lived a miserable, poverty-stricken existence—not criminal, perhaps, just a drifter, lost to all sense of responsibility and self-respect.

"Hello!" said Jimmie Dale, half seriously, half facetiously. "Who stuck you in his will, Pete?"

Someone at the bar guffawed.

"A nice old geezer wid gold spectacles dat Pete croaked wid a blackjack," said the man. "Dere wasn't no one else to inherit wot was in de stiff's pocket!"

Beggar Pete swung suddenly upon the speaker.

"Dat's a damn lie!" he shouted furiously. "Youse t'inks youse're funny, don't youse? Well, mabbe youse won't laugh so loud wid a bust face—see?"

Jimmie Dale edged in between the two men. Beggar Pete was huge-framed and, in spite of dissipation, muscular, and his face, working with rage, was indicative of a row that would bring more than Riley rapping softly in admonition with his night-stick on the swinging doors.

"Sure, I'll have a drink," said Jimmie Dale, diplomatically. He nodded to the barkeeper. "Suds for mine!" Then to Beggar Pete: "Here's how, Pete!"

Beggar Pete's scowl gradually subsided.

"Youse're all right, Smarly!" he said. He grew suddenly confidential. "Say, it came my way all right, an' 'twasn't more'n half an hour ago, neither. I'll tell youse. I was walkin' along an' broke for fair, an' an old gent goes brushin' by in a hurry in de rain. De Mouser t'inks he's funny, but de old geezer did have gold spectacles 'cause just after he gets by me he stops an' reaches into his pocket for a box of matches, an' I sees his face under de umbrella as he lights his cigar. Den he goes on again, an' as he puts de box of matches back in his pocket I sees somet'ing drop out on de sidewalk. I slips along an' grabs it up." Beggar Pete licked his lips, and scowled again at the little crowd. "It's his purse, dat's wot it is, an' a fat one. I ain't no saint, an' jest den I t'ought me luck was out, 'cause I t'ought he looked 'round an' saw me pickin' it up, so I runs after him an' hands it back. Say, he slips me wot I t'ought was one buck, an' wot I guess he t'ought was only one too, but w'en I gets into Kelly's place dat was near dere an' had a snifter it took all de money in de cash register to make change—see? Fifty, dat's wot it was—a fifty-dollar bill."

"Well, den," suggested one of the crowd to whom the story had evidently been retailed before, "set 'em up again, Pete—youse must be dry talkin' about it."

Jimmie Dale, included in the invitation which Beggar Pete promptly accorded, shook his head and left the place.

He smiled a little curiously to himself as he went on again through the rain. It was an incident, that was all; an incident that could have no bearing on him in a personal way, that could carry with it no significance so far as he was concerned, save that it was one of the many little cross-sections of life, bizarre, a scratch under the surface of things, here in the Bad Lands. Yet, naturally enough, it remained uppermost in his thoughts for a few moments as he walked along.

He knew Beggar Pete, and he was not at all convinced by Beggar Pete's story. Benevolent, gold-spectacled gentlemen were not in the habit of handing out fifty-dollar bills—even on a dark and rainy night! There would always be a street lamp within a few paces under whose light the award could be made without any mistake on the donor's part. A five-dollar bill for the service Beggar Pete had rendered—yes; a fifty-dollar bill—no. He found himself growing more and more skeptical. Indeed, he was not sure, for instance, that the gibe the lounger at the bar had flung at Beggar Pete had not more nearly hit the truth, to the extent at least that Beggar Pete had come by the money by methods that would not stand any very close scrutiny.

Jimmie Dale shrugged his shoulders. One thing at least seemed certain. Beggar Pete would sooner or later come to grief, and perhaps the sooner the better. There were too many Beggar Petes who had drifted on the reefs to become broken hulks, worthless to themselves and a menace to others!

He drew his coat collar closer around his throat. What a beastly night! Head down against the storm, he ploughed along. Thank Heaven, he was not far from Kerrigan's now—just around the next corner. For all its evil-smelling, reeking atmosphere, where about the only air there was stole in like a sneak thief through the broken window pane that was covered with cardboard, there would be even *physical* comfort tonight in the company of Bunty Myers and his fellow gangsters in that upstairs back room! There would even be a sort of compensation in the fact that he was under cover and in shelter should the real object of his visit, as it probably would, prove as futile tonight as it had in the past. His face hardened suddenly. What was the matter with him? Was he growing childish, his thoughts feeble-minded and astray? Shelter! A bit of a rain storm! Where was the Tocsin tonight? Where was she? What was *sheltering* her from a storm, not of pattering rain drops, but from one where every moment her life itself stood in peril, where her—

He raised his head. Along the street, through the murk, he noticed a shadowy form, the only other pedestrian in sight. It was too far off in the storm to distinguish even whether it was a woman, or a man wearing what might be a long raincoat, but strangely enough, unaccountably enough, yet neverthe-less existent in his mind was the consciousness of something familiar about the figure. And then, almost the next moment, his impression was verified in a measure that brought every faculty, alert and tense now, into instant ac-tion. The figure was turning the corner, passing under the street lamp. It was Mother Margot!

He did not quicken his pace. He was Smarlinghue! His lips tightened grimly. Mother Margot owed the man she knew as the Gray Seal her life, but how far her gratitude extended he did not know—perhaps not at all in view of the fact that her life would not have been in jeopardy if the Gray Seal had not literally forced her into the situation that had so nearly proved fatal to her that night at Pedler Joe's! In any case, it would be trusting her very far, too far, farther than he would ever dream of doing, if he risked the consequences of handing himself over utterly to her mercy in allowing even a suspicion to arise in her mind that the Gray Seal and Smarlinghue were one! A word of that, a hint, and Smarlinghue, the idol now of the underworld, would know instead a hatred and a vengeance that would not only bring exposure and disgrace to the name of Jimmie Dale, not only play into the Phantom's hands and leave the Tocsin to stand alone, as prompted by that brave, unselfish love of hers she sought to do, but would cost him his life as well. And so, as Smarlinghue, though that was Mother Margot there, he could make no move to intercept her.

But in a moment more he reached the corner. Mother Margot had disap-peared. He nodded his head. She had gone in through Wally Kerrigan's side entrance, her objective beyond question of doubt that upstairs room at the back.

Jimmie Dale moved swiftly now. At last, then, there was something afoot again. Mother Margot was the mouthpiece of the "Voice," as she called the Phantom. For a moment he experienced a sense of chagrin that he should have lost those few minutes in Gypsy Dan's saloon, for otherwise he would have been upstairs with Bunty Myers and the rest on Mother Margot's arriv-al, and Smarlinghue would have been introduced to Mother Margot, and— He shook his head again. No! He had lost nothing. His intimacy had not *quite* reached the point where they would talk before him. They would more likely have kicked him out. It was much better as it was; better that Smarlinghue should not have been in evidence at all if the aftermath of this visit of Mother Margot meant anything that would bring him into any game that might be played tonight.

And now he smiled with grim whimsicality as his thought of *shelter* came back to him. Instead of the back room upstairs, if he was to have any part in the proceedings whatever, he was much more likely to be a silent and unobtrusive occupant of the fire escape outside the window, than which he could imagine no place less sheltered or more uncomfortable in New York that night!

The door of Wally Kerrigan's side entrance closed silently behind Jimmie Dale. It was utterly dark here. The clientele that favored Kerrigan with its patronage, in so far as this portion of his premises was concerned, made no demand for any such extravagance as light! A footstep sounded from above, a woman's footstep; it died away, and a door closed. Mother Margot had run true to form!

Jimmie Dale moved forward as a shadow moves, and began to mount the narrow stairway with which he was already so well acquainted. There was no sound. It was the silence learned in the days of the old Sanctuary on the creaky, rickety stairs there, where an untrained step would have sounded the alarm from top to bottom of the tenement.

He gained the landing. There were three or four rooms here, he knew, but save for a tiny thread of light that seeped out under the threshold of the rear room, which was the rendezvous of Laroque's gang, everything was in darkness. It was early yet, which might be one reason, and the stormy night another, why the other rooms were as yet evidently unoccupied.

And now he was crouching against the door itself, his ear pressed against the panel. It was a possibility, that was all—a possible alternative to the uninviting fire escape. Again he shook his head, then turned swiftly to the window almost at his elbow that gave on the rear of the little hall. He had caught the sound of movement through the panels, even the sound of voices, but the words had been hopelessly indistinguishable.

Cautiously he opened the window, slipped out on the fire escape, and, against the possibility of any of the occupants of the room stepping out into the hall to notice an opened window, he closed it again behind him. Another moment, and, flat on his face, he had crept along the iron platform until he lay beneath the window of the rear room. He would be able to hear now. He had taken no chances on that score. Open or closed, the window above him with its square of cardboard tacked over the broken pane could hardly be improved upon for his purpose. And now, keeping a little back from the wall, he raised himself up and peered in. Mother Margot was talking excitedly, gesticulating with her hands, while gathered around her at the table were Muller, Bunty Myers, and two men he had met there before, who, leaving aside a score of aliases, were known as the Kitten and Spud MacGuire.

A pretty quartette! Jimmie Dale's lips thinned, as, the sense of sight gratified, he shifted his position, placing his ear as close to the edge of the window casing as he dared without exposing himself to the risk of being seen. Yes, he could hear now, but—a dismayed frown furrowed his forehead— Mother Margot appeared already to have imparted whatever information had brought her there.

"…Youse understand, don't youse?" she was saying. "'Cause if youse have got it straight, I'm goin' to beat it outer dis, an' get home an' get dry."

"It kinder took de wind outer us, dat's all!" Bunty Myers' voice responded in a puzzled growl. "I t'ought de whole works was blown up an' we was done!"

"I told youse once," snapped Mother Margot. "It's de panel in de wall."

"Sure!" said Bunty Myers. "We ain't deef, an' we got dat, all right—de middle one at de back of de room. But, den, wot's de use of waitin'?" He broke into a coarse, unpleasant laugh. "I guess old Miser Scroff ain't at home to queer anythin'!"

"De use of waitin'," returned Mother Margot tartly, "is 'cause de Chief says so, an' 'cause some of youse pulled a bum play dat he's got to make good, an' I wouldn't like to be de one dat done it 'cause de Chief is seein' red. Anyway, don't youse make no mistakes again. Youse ain't to make a move until as near ten as'll give youse time to get away wid it, but youse're to be through by den, 'cause at ten de bulls get tipped off."

"All right," agreed Bunty Myers. And then abruptly, as Mother Margot evidently started to leave the room: "Say, wait a minute, mother! Mabbe youse have got de answer to somethin' we'se can't figure out. Wot's de big idea behind de Chief's keepin' under cover? We ain't seen him for weeks—nothin' but telephones an' messages. Where is he?"

"Why don't youse ask him?" suggested Mother Margot acidly.

"Ask him!" echoed Bunty Myers helplessly. "How de hell can I, w'en I don't know where—"

"Dat's de answer!" Mother Margot's interruption was a cackling laugh. "Youse knows all I knows. Do youse t'ink me an' de Chief goes to a picture show every evenin', an' den spends de rest of de night together eatin' hot frankfurters an' stewed ice cream? Say, youse give me a pain! Good-night!"

The door in the hall closed.

For an instant Jimmie Dale stood motionless, then he turned, and, in lieu of an exit via the hall window, began to make his way down the fire escape. And now what? Go to Mother Margot as the Gray Seal and force a detailed explanation from her as he had the other night? He shook his head. It wasn't necessary tonight, was it? He had learned enough, hadn't he?

His mind was working swiftly, in a precise, virile way, as he descended the wet, dripping iron treads. The middle panel at the back of old Miser Scroff's room—and old Miser Scroff was not at home. That was clear enough. And there was no question but that Miser Scroff had money hidden away somewhere. It was only a wonder that it had not been taken from him before. The old man was almost senile. It was common property on the East Side that he had been caught fondling and crooning over packages of banknotes in his room on more than one occasion. For more years than anyone could remember the man, already old, had just kept on growing older in a solitary life in his sordid surroundings. He was supposed to have a small income from some source, but however small it might have been it was certain he saved on it for he never spent a cent save to keep absolute famine from his door. Undoubtedly he had money. Robbery, therefore, as the motive, was equally clear. And at ten o'clock, for some reason, the police were to be notified of the crime by the actual perpetrators themselves. Ten o'clock. It could not be much after nine yet. There should be at least half an hour then before Bunty Myers need be considered as a factor. Meanwhile the Phantom was at work in an effort to rectify some misplay made by his underlings. Was it at Miser Scroff's that the Phantom in person would be employed prior to the arrival of Bunty Myers and his confederates? Was it luck like that? Luck at last! If so, then—

Jimmie Dale dropped from the bottom of the fire escape to the ground. And then, in the shelter of the lane where the fire escape had landed him, he broke instantly into a run.

"Not as Smarlinghue," confided Jimmie Dale grimly to himself as he ran. "I can't risk Smarlinghue—it's got to be the other way in spite of a patched face."

CHAPTER 11
THE PANELLED WALL

Jimmie Dale, a long coat, sodden with rain, covering his evening clothes, crept up the narrow tenement stairs, crept along a bare and dirty hallway, and halted before a closed door. Softly, cautiously, he tried the door. It was locked. His fingers reached in under his outer garments, and then shot swiftly to the door again. There was a moment of utter silence, then a faint *snip*, and the door began to open guardedly, the fraction of an inch at a time. Another instant and Jimmie Dale stood inside the room.

The door closed behind him. A minute he listened, then the round, white ray from his flashlight lanced through the blackness, swept its surroundings in a swift, comprehensive circle—and a low, startled exclamation, involuntary, before it could be checked, came from Jimmie Dale's lips. This was old Miser Scroff's squalid, hovel-like abode, niggardly alike in its furnishings and its cleanliness, since even cleanliness cost money—but—but—it was strange! He did not understand! He had not been very long on his trip to the Sanctuary and back. It had not taken him long. Certainly it could not even yet be half-past nine. And yet it seemed as though, in spite of that, he was already too late.

The flashlight circled again, but more slowly this time, as though puzzled and nonplussed itself. The small room was in dire confusion. The bedding from the cheap cot was flung here and there on the floor; the drawers of an old desk had been pulled out and their contents strewn about, and the desk itself had been hacked to pieces as though on the chance that it might have possessed a hidden receptacle; while even the ragged strip of oilcloth, that was the sole floor covering, had been ripped up and flung into a corner. Where a hiding place might have existed before, there existed now nothing but a pitiful state of wreckage!

Jimmie Dale's mind seemed to echo the confusion. It did not seem possible that Bunty Myers and his companions could already have been here. And besides—the flashlight's ray shot suddenly to the rear of the room—what had all this to do with the panelled wall?

An ironic smile tinged his lips now. Yes, it might by a stretch of imagination be called panelled, but it was simply an extra height of boarding that ran up to meet the plaster all around the room some three or four feet from the flooring. He stepped quickly across the room, and knelt, as nearly as he could judge his position by the flashlight, in front of the middle boards. He nodded grimly. These were at least intact if nothing else in the room was! From a pocket in the leather girdle around his waist he drew out now a small, but incredibly strong and powerful "jimmy." It would have been a useless waste of time to seek for any secret spring that, while it probably existed, was also certainly well and cleverly hidden.

He was working rapidly now, the point of the "jimmy" prying tentatively into, and up and down, the joints of the boards. A low-breathed exclamation of satisfaction came almost instantly from his lips. The "jimmy" had slipped through one of the cracks into an open space behind. It was here, then, the hiding place of old Miser Scroff's hoard that Bunty Myers—

Jimmie Dale stood suddenly erect, tense, every muscle rigid, listening. A footstep, low and stealthy though it was, had caught his ear from the hall outside. It was not another lodger, it was too cautious for that, too guarded; and for the same reason it could not be Miser Scroff. It was not Bunty Myers and his confederates, because there was only one footstep. The Phantom, then! The Phantom had required time for something somewhere. And he, Jimmie Dale, had dared to hope that it might be here. Luck! If he was in luck at last, he would play it to the full. He was crossing the room swiftly, without a sound. There would be a settlement this time from which there would be no escape! It was almost at the door now, that footstep; but he, too, was at the door—on the inside, crouched against the wall.

A grim smile twisted his lips as he stood there, his automatic flung forward, his flashlight ready in his left hand. Here was a good place for that settlement, here in old Miser Scroff's room, here on the scene of one of the Phantom's hell-hatched crimes—there could be no better place for that *final* reckoning!

The doorknob turned, the door began to open slowly. A form, shadowy, a little blacker than the surrounding blackness, bulked in the opening, then stole across the threshold, and the door closed.

And then Jimmie Dale spoke in a cold, merciless whisper, as the stream of his flashlight cut through the black, and his automatic lifted to a level with the line of light:

"Put up your—"

The sentence died on his lips. It seemed to Jimmie Dale that the room was whirling around him, that he was robbed of all power of movement, that his brain had lost the faculty of reason. The light was boring into a pair of brown eyes, startled, it was true, but brave, calm, self-reliant brown eyes that looked out from a wondrously glorious face, the only face in all the world. And then his pulses leaped, and the blood in a furious tide went whipping through his veins. The Tocsin! The Tocsin! Was he mad? Could it be true? The Tocsin!

"Marie!" he cried out hoarsely.

"Jimmie! Is it you? I could not see with the light in my eyes. Oh, Jimmie!" Her voice faltered. Relief was there, but relief was not the note he caught; it was love, yearning, the woman's soul that was in her tones.

The flashlight, the automatic, were thrust into his pockets. She was in his arms. He held her close. Years had gone since he had held her there before! He had fought for this, risked all and everything for this, hoped for it when hope itself seemed dead, and now she was here, close to him, clinging to him—and it was not just for the moment, not just a stolen, pitiful instant out of all eternity, but for always, for all time. He had her now. She would never go again. There was no power on earth would keep him from her side now!

Half laughing, half crying, she struggled to free herself a little.

"Jimmie," she breathed, "don't you know that you are terribly *strong*, dear?"

He released her a little, grudgingly, but still he held her close. His lips found hers, her eyes, her hair—the dark silken strands that, playing truant from under her hat, swept his face.

Her hand had crept up and found his mask, slipped under it, and was resting gently against the strips of plaster on his cheek.

"I—I know of course about the night when—when you got this," she said brokenly. "All the underworld has been talking about Smarlinghue. They very nearly caught you, Jimmie. Oh, Jimmie, why will you do it? I have begged you so, done all I could to keep you out of this. And now tonight again! What are you doing here? What brought you here?"

His arms tightened about her again.

"To find you," he said.

She drew away in amazement, her hands on his shoulders now, holding him at arms'-length.

"To find me!" she echoed helplessly. "But how could you have expected to find me here? You did not know. I sent you no note, no word, for after I heard about that night at Pedler Joe's and what happened later in the Sanctuary, I made up my mind not to——"

He laid his hand softly across her lips.

"I have not been anywhere, done anything, since that night on the East River, Marie," he said quietly, "except with the one end in view of finding you. And had I not found you again now I should still have kept on in the same way. I'm quite sure you know every move that Smarlinghue has made, and you therefore ought to know that I have already gone too far, that I've already been too close to the Phantom more than once to have let anything you did keep me out of this, Marie. The fewer the notes, the more I should have worried, and the harder I should have worked. But that's all at an end now, thank God! There'll be no more separation. We'll work together from now on until we've found the Phantom."

For a moment she did not answer, then she turned her head away.

"No, Jimmie!" she said firmly. "I cannot! I will not! Nothing has been changed since that night on the East River. I cannot prevent you from doing as you have been doing, but there is a great difference between your actions as the Gray Seal and as one who is known to be working hand in glove with Marie LaSalle. It—it would make it almost impossible for me to go on, for I—I could not do anything then without the fear of putting your life in danger. Oh, Jimmie, you do not know, you do not understand, and—and I cannot tell you!" She turned quickly toward him again. "Go, Jimmie, please—at once. There is something that I must do here."

Jimmie Dale reached out for the door.

"We'll go together, Marie—now," he said calmly. "I heard Mother Margot talking about Scroff's panel here. I was on the fire escape outside Kerrigan's place. That's what you mean, isn't it? But *you* are what *I* came for, so we'll go, for there is nothing else that counts here now against the risk of you being caught by Bunty Myers and his crowd, to say nothing of old Miser Scroff himself turning up any minute to——"

"Miser Scroff is dead," she interrupted dully.

"Dead!" he repeated in a startled way.

"Murdered," she said. And then her voice broke again. "Oh, Jimmie, I have failed miserably tonight. I—I have cost a man his life, I am afraid. The least I can do now is to keep them from getting the money—it's in an old leather bag behind the panel—but that I must do. You—you must let me work this out, Jimmie. I have no choice. If you force me out of here, or if you insist on staying to help me, then in an hour, two hours, somehow, Jimmie, I warn you frankly that I will get away from you again."

"I don't think you will—not this time, Marie!" said Jimmie Dale grimly. "I've got you now, and I'm going to keep you no matter what happens."

She smiled at him wanly.

"Very well, Jimmie, if you think so," she said quietly. "Only remember what I have said. Meanwhile there is the panel. *I* can't go until I have got the money."

She started across the room, only to stumble over the broken desk. And then Jimmie Dale's flashlight was in play again, and he followed her.

"Murdered, you said!" He spoke quickly. "Why? I don't understand. And I don't understand what has happened here. The place has been turned inside out."

"The panel, Jimmie!" she answered. "It's near the middle. Get it open! I'll tell you while you work."

"I had already found it before you came in," said Jimmie Dale coolly. He was kneeling by the wall, the "jimmy" in his hand again. "Go on, Marie!"

A joint in the wood gave with a low, rending, creaking sound. She stood at his shoulder, whispering swiftly:

"Some of the gang under the Phantom's orders inveigled Miser Scroff down somewhere in the neighbourhood of that old junk yard near Kelly's saloon, with the intention of keeping him out of the way for an hour or two while the rest of them came here and searched for his money. But Scroff was an old man, and the blow he was hit by the black-jack killed him; and the search here resulted in nothing."

The "jimmy" pried away a narrow board from top to bottom. Jimmie Dale reached in his hand. Yes, there was something in here, a bag of some kind.

"How do you know all this?" he demanded. "And if you know it, where was the Phantom all this time?"

"Under cover," she answered. "I told you long ago that he was a man with a score of domiciles and a score of aliases. Lately he has been driven from one to another—and robbed of some of them by the Gray Seal."

"I thought so!" said Jimmie Dale swiftly. "Well, you've lost your case, now, Marie. It would appear, then, that the Gray Seal has been of service, so why should you attempt to keep him at a distance?"

Her hand found and touched his shoulder.

"It's no good, Jimmie," she said softly. "Shall we call it a woman's inconsistency? I cannot give you any other answer."

Another board came loose. Jimmie Dale frowned. What was the matter? He was not working with his usual deftness and silence. It seemed as though the creaking of the board could be heard throughout the building.

"You said you had failed miserably tonight, and that you were afraid you had cost a man his life," he said. "You mean Miser Scroff?"

"No," she said heavily. "I did not know anything about tonight until after Miser Scroff was killed. That brought the Phantom into it in a personal way. There had been no murder intended, and failure to find anything here would otherwise have ended the matter; but in old Miser Scroff's pocket they found, besides some stock certificates made out in his name, a dirty old piece of paper with a tracing of his room upon it, and a position on the rear wall marked with an arrow, so they knew then where the money was. But this was after the first search had been made and the room torn to pieces as you see it, and though they knew then where the money was, there was a *murder* that had to be covered up."

Jimmie Dale drew out a worn yellow leather bag from the aperture. He opened it, and uttered a sharp exclamation. It was crammed full of loose banknotes.

"How do you know all this?" he asked for the second time, as he shut the bag.

The Tocsin shook her head.

"It is useless to ask me, Jimmie," she said steadily. "If I told you, I might as well enter into the partnership with you that you are so insistent upon—it would amount to the same thing. I cannot tell you. I can only tell you that I know the Phantom means to plant the crime on some outsider's shoulders, someone he has picked out as *suitable*, a seedy character who—it's horrible, Jimmie!—will not have a chance for his life. The securities with Scroff's name on them are to be placed under the innocent victim's mattress; then, with the panel rifled here, the police are to be tipped off about the murder, and where to find the 'murderer' and the evidence. I did my best; I did all I could, but—but I lost the trail, and so I came here to save at least the money, and as a sort of last hope that somehow I might pick up the clue again. The only thing I am sure of is that the Phantom was playing the part of an old gentleman with gold spectacles tonight, and—"

Jimmie Dale had taken the Tocsin's arm, and, carrying the bag, had started back for the door; but now he halted suddenly as though rooted to the spot, and stared at her.

"An old gentleman with gold spectacles!" he ejaculated sharply.

She caught at his sleeve.

"Jimmie!" she whispered tensely. "You—you know something about it! You—you've seen him! You know who it is they mean to railroad to his death for this?"

The room, his surroundings, even the Tocsin, had fled from Jimmie Dale's consciousness for the moment; instead, there came again the scene in Gypsy Dan's saloon, when Beggar Pete had told his story, which he, Jimmie Dale, had but so short a time ago dismissed almost summarily from his mind as having no personal significance for him. Beggar Pete and the gentleman with the gold spectacles! Beggar Pete and his sudden affluence! He had not believed Beggar Pete then, but he believed him now. There was no shadow of doubt but that Beggar Pete was the Phantom's intended cat's-paw, and that the snare was the low, viciously-cunning handiwork of the Phantom. Beggar

Pete's story, once those securities were found beneath his mattress, would, out of its own improbability, only *assure* the man's conviction. Nobody knew how much or how little cash Miser Scroff had had! So this was what the Phantom wanted that extra time for—to plant those securities. God, if he could *catch* the Phantom at Beggar Pete's! No! There was the Tocsin here—he had her now—he would never leave her again. And besides it was too late now. He knew where Beggar Pete lived because of late it had been almost a source of gossip on the East Side, for the simple reason that, for perhaps the first time in his life, Beggar Pete now had a *permanent* address—the cellar of a somewhat questionable lodging house run by a yegg named Harry the Dip—and this in return for the more than questionable agreement on Beggar Pete's part to make himself generally useful when called upon to do so! It was a long way to Beggar Pete's—almost across the whole of the East Side. The Phantom would have completed his work by now, or at least long before he, Jimmie Dale, could reach Beggar Pete's lodging, and that would—

"You *know*! Oh, thank God!" she cried tremulously. "And I—I was so afraid!"

"It is Beggar Pete," he answered mechanically.

"Then quick, Jimmie!" she pleaded. "There is not an instant to lose. You must get those securities before the police do!"

He did not move.

She shook frantically at his sleeve.

"You see that, don't you, Jimmie?" she cried again. "Oh, there's not an instant, not a second to spare—and besides, the rest of them will be here any minute."

He looked at her.

"And you?" he said.

"I'll take the bag of money and see that it reaches the authorities," she replied quickly. "You can't be hampered with that. It will be all you can do to win the race against the police."

"No!" he said fiercely. "Let you get away out of my life again? Not for a dozen Beggar Petes!"

A strange smile, wistful, drooped her lips; and suddenly her eyes were wet; and as suddenly she reached up and drew his face to hers and kissed him.

"You are too big a man for that, Jimmie," she whispered. "And there is no other way, and—and, besides, you know what I have told you. You are too big a man for that, Jimmie, and that—that is why I love you."

He held her close.

"It's no use!" he said hoarsely. "There's been more planted on him than you know anything about; enough so that the robbery here would almost cast suspicion on Beggar Pete without the securities being found at all. He has been spending more money in the saloons tonight than he ever had in all his life before; and he is accounting for its possession in a manner that no one would believe."

"But there's a way out of that," she answered quickly. "A way that the Gray Seal has taken before. Take it again now, Jimmie—because it's a man's way, *my* man's way."

He knew what she meant, but he did not answer. She was gathered in his arms. He could not let her go. He had given his all to find her—he could not let her go.

"Jimmie," she said, steadying her voice with an effort, "every second that we stand here may mean that it has cost a man his life."

With a low cry that seemed wrenched from him in agony, Jimmie Dale's hands dropped to his sides. Through the darkness, that was now a strange mist before his eyes, he saw her pick up the leather bag. And then her whisper came to him:

"Thank God for you, Jimmie! I'll stand guard at the door until you're through."

He found himself at the rear of the room again, working with frantic speed in front of the broken panelling. He knew what she meant; it must be his mind, of course, that was functioning, governing him, and yet his actions seemed purely mechanical. From the leather girdle he drew out the thin metallic case; and from the case, with the tiny tweezers, he lifted out a diamond-shaped, gray-paper seal. If he succeeded in getting the securities before the police did, and if the police found here on the scene of the robbery the insignia of the Gray Seal that they knew so well, then Beggar Pete, a worthless, broken hulk, would go free, and—

Her whisper, from the door now, reached him again:

"Quick, Jimmie! They're coming now. I hear them downstairs. Quick, Jimmie, and—and—good-bye!"

It took an instant, no more, to moisten the adhesive side of the paper seal, and stick it into place on the edge of the broken panelling; and then Jimmie Dale was across the room, and, the door closed behind him, was standing in the blackness of the hallway.

She was gone! His face was set and rigid. Perhaps she was still somewhere here in the hall; but he could not see, and he did not dare call out. The stealthy tread of two or three men was distinctly audible coming up the stairs. He drew farther back along the hall and crouched there in the darkness. Low whisperings reached him; indistinct forms clustered around the door of Miser Scroff's room—and then the door opened and closed again, and the hall was empty. Empty! Where was she? Still here—still within touch perhaps? A bitter smile curved his lips. He was beaten—beaten by a worthless, broken hulk that had drifted on the reefs—a human wreck!

He was crouched outside the door again, and now silently, quickly, with the little steel pick-lock, he locked the men inside. If she were still in the hall here, she too would have her chance, enough time to get away before they discovered that gray seal in there and came pouring out of the room again!

And then he went down the stairs, and in another instant, the mask removed from his face, was outside the tenement, and racing madly through the night. And as he went he looked about him. He had hoped for a passing taxi or a vehicle of some sort, but there was only the torrential rain. And so he could but run. Time! It would take him all of twenty minutes, and it must be later than twenty minutes of ten now, and—he paused for a second under a street lamp to consult his watch—yes, it was a quarter to ten. At ten the Phantom would notify the police—in some anonymous way, of course. But there was still a little leeway. Perhaps ten minutes. The time it would take the police to get to Beggar Pete's *after* ten o'clock.

He ran on and on. Still no taxis, no vehicles—only deserted streets. It seemed as though he had run for hours. He did not stop to look at his watch again. He heard a clock from somewhere boom out the hour.

Was he in time? He glanced up and down the street now, as he halted finally before a small, tumble-down, shabby dwelling house. He did not know. At least there was no one in sight.

Harry the Dip's door was never locked! His lodgers kept hours too uncertain and varied! Jimmie Dale smiled grimly, as slipping suddenly into the shadows of the doorway, he stepped silently inside the place. Another item, this choice of lodging, even if it were the choice of necessity, that would not help Beggar Pete's reputation in a jury's eyes!

The cellar entrance! Where was it? It was dark in here—but not silent. From upstairs he could hear talking and the sound of movement. And then his ear caught another sound—the sound of loud, heavy, stertorous breathing that seemed to come from a direction ahead of him. He risked his flashlight. He was in a short and narrow hall. And now he advanced cautiously. Yes, here it was; and here, too, was the explanation of those laboured, stertorous sounds. Under the stairs at the back of the hall, a door stood half open.

The flashlight's ray played down a flight of bare, ladder-like steps—and coincidentally Jimmie Dale's face set in hard, bitter lines. At the bottom of the steps, a little to one side, in a filthy cellar, sprawled on a torn and filthy mattress from which wisps of mildewed straw protruded blatantly, Beggar Pete lay in a drunken stupor. The man had already been pretty well along at Gypsy Dan's, and in the hour since then it was obvious that he had lost no time!

Jimmie Dale's hand clenched. The sight seemed to fan a latent fury, a merciless passion into flame. It was for this, to save *this*, a vagrant, a bum, a drunken sot, a beast, that he had lost all that was most dear to him in life tonight; it was for this that he had done what he had never thought to do under any circumstances, under any pressure, while life remained to him—lose the Tocsin again if once he ever found her! It seemed to plumb the depths of irony; it seemed as though he could *wish* for nothing better than that this besotted beast should experience exactly what the Phantom had prepared for him!

And yet, mechanically, Jimmie Dale went down the cellar stairs. He stooped over the man. There was no danger of *disturbing* Beggar Pete! He pulled the man aside, and overturned the mattress. A little bundle of stock certificates, held together by a rubber band, lay there. He picked them up. They were made out in the name of Heinrich Scroff.

For an instant he stood staring from the certificates in his hand to the sprawled form upon the floor—and slowly, gradually, the hard, embittered look on Jimmie Dale's face softened. Was he so sure after all that he had paid too much? In his hand he held the death warrant of an *innocent* man, a fellow creature, sunken, low, it was true, but a human being with hopes and fears like his own perhaps, though one, unlike himself, who had had only the rougher road to travel, where plenty was unknown and life's sunshine meagre.

He stooped again, and replaced the mattress, and laid Beggar Pete upon it. He was smiling now softly, as sometimes a woman smiles when her lips mirror her heart. And somehow he was glad.

And then Jimmie Dale turned away and went out into the storm again. Tomorrow the city would awake to find that the Gray Seal had committed another crime!

CHAPTER 12

LITTLE SWEENEY

The air was heavy with drifting layers of smoke, as it always was in this back, upstairs room of Wally Kerrigan's "club," that was the hang-out of Gentleman Laroque's, alias the Phantom's, gang. Four men sat at the table playing stud, and Jimmie Dale, as Smarlinghue, seated a little apart, watched them now as he fumbled with the dirty, frayed sleeves and wristbands of his coat and shirt, and, fumbling then in his pocket, drew out a hypodermic syringe, its nickel-plating worn and brassy, its general appearance as disreputable as himself.

How many nights had he come to this room, as he had come tonight, playing a game, that was not a game of cards, with Bunty Myers here, and the Kitten, and Muller, and Spud MacGuire! How many nights? He had almost lost track of time. The wound in his cheek had healed. He had even resumed, in so far as an occasional appearance at the St. James Club, and here and there a social function went, his normal life as Jimmie Dale. He must have been coming here for many nights!

Through half closed, apparently drug-drowsed eyes, he watched the players at the table. Yes, it must have been for many nights. It was over a week since—his fingers tightened involuntarily in a fierce, spasmodic grip upon the hypodermic—since that night when he had held the Tocsin once again in his arms in old Miser Scroff's room, and had lost her again. Since then he had continued to cultivate these men. They were only pawns, they moved only at the will of that unseen yet ever present spirit of evil, the Phantom; but to be one of them opened the Avenue of a Thousand Chances that might lead to the Phantom himself. He had had no other clue to follow.

But so far nothing had come of it. They did not distrust him—who in the underworld would distrust Smarlinghue, who had the entrée everywhere!—but they had made no advances toward offering him full membership in that unhallowed fraternity to which he knew they belonged. At times he had believed they had been on the verge of doing so, and that applied especially to Bunty Myers, who was the Phantom's apparent chief of staff; but there had been nothing definite, nothing concrete, nothing tangible.

And yet, even in a negative sense, the nights he had spent here of late had not been futile. He was in possession of the fact that there had been *inactivity*. And that meant that the Phantom, whatever might be germinating in that master mind of crime, had for the time being been quiescent; and, as a corollary to that, the almost certain deduction that no further blow had been struck at the Tocsin—that she was still safe. And this had been borne out by Mother Margot, who, so far, had always been the Phantom's mouthpiece. As the Gray Seal, and through the hold that, as the Gray Seal, he had upon her, he had continued to call her daily from her pushcart to the telephone and question her. But she had still protested vehemently each time that she had had no further word of any move, and he was satisfied that she was telling the truth for the simple reason that he did not believe she would dare do anything else. But, even so, unknown to her, he had still maintained, in so far as he could, a personal surveillance over her movements, and there had been nothing to disprove her statements. She still tended her pushcart in Thompson Street; she still lived in those rooms from which the Phantom, in the dual guise of Shiftel, the fence, and Gentleman Laroque, who once had openly led this very gang here, had so mysteriously disappeared.

Smarlinghue's face was vapid, but into the dark eyes behind the creeping eyelids there came a troubled gleam. Those rooms where the Voice, as Mother Margot called the Phantom, had installed the old hag! What was the secret that they held? He was certain that Mother Margot did not know. And twice again, of late, in Mother Margot's absence, and despite the Tocsin's warning that they were a trap for himself, he had explored them, searched them—and found nothing.

And now the men around the table, the room itself, his immediate surroundings, existed only in a subconscious way in Jimmie Dale's mind. That was the negative side of the week just past. There was equally the positive side.

Shiftel had returned to the underworld.

Not openly. Not to his old quarters. At first the rumour had flown from mouth to mouth through the underground exchanges of the Bad Lands that Shiftel was back; that he had been seen a dozen times in the hidden places, the lairs, the hang-outs, the breeding dens of vice: that crooks of his old, exclusive clientele had talked with him, done business with him. And at first, he, Jimmie Dale, had not believed it; and then he had seen the man himself. He was sure of it. Shiftel! Isaac Shiftel, alias Gentleman Laroque, alias Limpy Mack, alias the Gentleman with the Gold Spectacles—the Phantom! The man that the Tocsin had so truly said possessed a score of domiciles and, yes—entities—there was no better word, for in each of his disguises the man seemed to have established himself as a known and breathing entity in the life and surroundings of the particular character which for the moment he might have assumed. As witness Shiftel, the fence, known far and wide in the underworld: as witness Gentleman Laroque, long the leader of this band here, long the most notorious gangster in the Bad Lands.

He had seen Shiftel three nights ago in the Green Dragon, a dance hall of unsavoury repute. And Shiftel, the man who was the cause of his, Jimmie Dale's, return to the life of Smarlinghue and the squalor of the Sanctuary, the man who sought the Tocsin's life, the one man that he, Jimmie Dale, would gladly have sacrificed his all to bring to a final reckoning and account, had escaped him that night in the Green Dragon.

He shook his head, mumbling to himself, almost mechanically continuing to play his part in the presence of these underlings around the table even while his mind was far away. It was not his fault that Shiftel, once seen, had got away. He could not in any fairness hold himself to blame. He had caught but a glimpse of the man far across the hall, as in the swirl of the bunny-hug the dancers on the polished centre of the floor had opened for a moment and closed again. When he had reached the other end of the room Shiftel had disappeared. That was all.

It was strange! What was the game? What was the meaning of this reappearance? The man was running a tremendous risk, and the motive must certainly be commensurate with the danger. What was that motive? Shiftel was wanted, and wanted badly, by the police for his connection with the diamonds stolen from Jathan Lane, the murdered banker. There was no such person, of course, as Shiftel—it was the Phantom. Shiftel was only one of the Phantom's disguises to be put on or off at will. But it was the known character of Shiftel that the police sought. Why had the man shown himself in that character, lived it again? He need only have discarded it utterly, never returned to it, and as far as "Shiftel" was concerned he could have laughed at the police until the day he died.

What was it? What was at the back of that crafty brain whose evil genius had prompted this move? No little thing! Had the Tocsin's note that he, Jimmie Dale, had found amongst the mail Jason had handed him when he had appeared at home for his lunch yesterday, any bearing on the Phantom's motive? He did not think so; rather, out of the ruck of explanations that had suggested themselves, and which were for the most part hopelessly untenable, there had finally comeone that he was almost ready to accept.

Smarlinghue's lips twisted in a grin—apparently one inspired by Spud MacGuire as the man scooped a pot on a bare-faced bluff. Well, why not? Even if it was a back-handed compliment to himself! The Phantom was shy of funds. Time after time of late he, Jimmie Dale, as the Gray Seal, had forestalled the other, and snatched away the fruits of the man's criminal schemes. Where, in the past few weeks, the Phantom had counted upon thousands, many of them, and had even spent lavishly to pave the way to the expected profits, he had received instead not a single penny. The Phantom, therefore, unless he possessed the reserve wealth of a Crœsus, was certainly shy of funds. Yes, that was it. It *must* be it. And as almost irrefutable evidence of this was the fact that the Phantom, as Shiftel, was said to be in communication again with some of those who composed that carefully selected circle of crooks who had been tried and successful business associates in the past; and that was why, too, it was as *Shiftel*, and not as Limpy Mack, not as Gentleman Laroque, or any one of his other aliases, that the Phantom had ventured, cautiously it was true, but nevertheless had ventured out into the underworld again.

The Tocsin's note! It came uppermost into his mind now. It was the first sign of existence she had given since that night at old Miser Scroff's.

His lips were still twisted in a smile, but there was something cold, forbidding, far removed from smiles, that seemed suddenly now to weigh upon his spirits. She had written; but it had only been to accentuate, as it were, her decision, what she had said that night when he had been so sure of taking his place again beside her. Alone! That was it—alone! It was her love, of course, her great unselfish love, that prompted her to try to keep him out of the "shadows," out of *her* dangers. The note reiterated it; he knew it word for word:

"Dear Philanthropic Crook:—I see that you are incorrigible. If I thought that it would do any good I would implore you again—oh, Jimmie, I *do* implore you to leave all this to me, and to go back at once to your own life. I am half mad with fear for you. There is something, some trap being laid, and I cannot find out what it is. I only know that the Phantom has become suspicious that behind the Gray Seal's repeated blows there is more than a mere desire to reap where the Phantom has sown. I only know that the Phantom is convinced that he himself is the Gray Seal's one and only object; and, in turn, the Phantom means to move heaven and earth now to get the Gray Seal—first. Oh, I know you won't do as I ask you! I know you too well. I know that, if anything, this hint of danger will perhaps even urge you on. But I had to write. I had to warn you because I am afraid, and because I know that in some way, with all his hideous cunning behind it, the Phantom is laying a trap for you that—"

Bunty Myers swung around in his chair, and made a grimace at the hypodermic syringe with whose needle Jimmie Dale was now pricking the skin of his forearm.

"Say, can dat, Smarly!" he complained. "Youse give me nerves. Youse've been monkeyin' wid dat squirt gun for de last half hour. If it won't work, for Gawd's sake go down to de Chink's, or somewhere else, and hit a pipe."

The door opened.

Mechanically Jimmie Dale restored the hypodermic to his pocket. He was staring at the doorway. It was not the sudden appearance of that hag-like, black-shawled figure that set his brains at work in swift, lightning flashes, and brought every faculty he possessed into play to preserve the indifference, even apathy, that became the supposedly drug-dulled Smarlinghue, for Mother Margot, he knew, was a frequent visitor here. It was not Mother Margot who caused his pulse to stir now; it was the man who had stepped into the room behind her—Little Sweeney.

It seemed somehow to dovetail and fit most curiously into his thoughts of Shiftel of a few moments gone. His hand, inside his pocket, as it released the hypodermic closed instead upon his automatic. He kept staring at the door—behind Little Sweeney. Was there still *someone* else? The last time these two had been together there had been another with them. That night at Mrs. Kinsey's, when they had tried to rob the old deaf woman of her savings! There had been another with them then—Limpy Mack. But Limpy Mack was also Shiftel, also Gentleman Laroque; in a word, the Phantom. Was Shiftel, or the Phantom in whatever guise he chose to assume, there behind these two tonight? Little Sweeney had not been heard of or seen since that night. This was Little Sweeney's first appearance, and—

The door closed.

Little Sweeney, with a nod that embraced everybody, leaned nonchalantly back against the door and lighted a cigarette. Mother Margot stared around the room, and then her eyes fixed on Jimmie Dale. He saw her glance swiftly then, interrogatively, at Bunty Myers.

Bunty Myers waved his hand.

"Smarly, meet Mother Margot," he said off-handedly. "Mabbe youse knows Little Sweeney."

Meet Mother Margot! There was something exquisitely ironical in this, wasn't there? If Mother Margot but knew how many times and under what circumstances they had met before!

Mother Margot loosened her shawl, and slumped down in a chair.

"Everybody knows Smarlinghue," she grunted.

"Sure," said Little Sweeney from the door.

"Glad to meet you both," said Smarlinghue cordially.

There was silence for a moment. Mother Margot folded her hands patiently in her lap. The silence, prolonged, grew embarrassed. Bunty Myers broke it.

"Beat it!" he suggested uncompromisingly to Jimmie Dale.

Jimmie Dale, as Smarlinghue, vacant eyed as he looked around the room, rose from his chair. It was a little awkward—a little awkward to carry it off as though it were quite a matter of course. He grinned around the circle.

"See you all again," said Smarlinghue pleasantly.

Little Sweeney opened the door.

"Damned thick in here, this smoke," said Little Sweeney, as Smarlinghue shuffled through. "I'll leave it open till the room clears out a bit. 'Night, Smarly!"

"Good-night!" said Jimmie Dale still pleasantly; but out in the hall, and as he turned and went down the stairs, his lips tightened into a straight line.

Little Sweeney was no fool! The fire escape, just within reach, just outside the window of the room where the broken pane mended with cardboard had once before supplied him, Jimmie Dale, with a vantage point from which he could both see and hear all that went on within, was barred to him now by the open door; also the open door, with Little Sweeney standing there, offered no alternative to a prompt and unhesitating exit via the stairs from even the building itself!

Jimmie Dale's lips drew still tighter together as he went on down the stairs. In spite of Smarlinghue's high station in the underworld, he had been treated with scant ceremony! But it was not the hurt of pride in that, as one of the élite of gangland, the honour and deference that was his due had been withheld from him, that brought the grim, set expression to his face now; it was the consciousness of defeat where he had foreseen victory. He had counted too much on the intimacy that he had first cultivated and then believed he had established with Bunty Myers and his fellow gangsters. He had believed and hoped that he was not far from being upon the verge of initiation into their unholy fold, of being invited, in plain words, to becomeone of them.

He shrugged his shoulders as he stepped out on the street. Well, he had lost on that score for the time being, at least. He was wrong, that was all. But he had burned no bridges behind him. Tomorrow night Smarlinghue could still go back there, and be welcome. And as for tonight—well, he was not yet through with tonight! There was something undoubtedly afoot again. What was it? He crossed to the other side of the street, and just opposite the side door of Wally Kerrigan's "club," where he could watch that door unseen, he slipped, unnoticed, into the shadows of a high flight of dwelling house steps.

What was it? He could not, as Smarlinghue, accost Mother Margot when she came out; and by the time he had gone to the Sanctuary and become the man in the evening clothes that she knew as the Gray Seal, she would as likely as not have left Kerrigan's and have disappeared. Queer! Somehow, he was not interested in *what* was afoot tonight in so far as its specific nature was an essential feature. He was more interested in this sudden appearance of Little Sweeney in conjunction with the fact that Shiftel, too, had broken cover. It was the Phantom that interested him—and Shiftel was the Phantom. Was there any connection between this return of both Little Sweeney and Isaac Shiftel to activity? He meant to see! The two had been very closely allied that night at Mrs. Kinsey's, and particularly later on that same night in Limpy Mack's hang-out under Sen Yat's "tea shop."

And so, somehow—he smiled grimly—he was more concerned with Little Sweeney than with Mother Margot tonight. Little Sweeney *might* lead him to Shiftel; Mother Margot he had already tried too often to have any hopeful expectations raised on that score. To reach the Phantom, in the guise of Shiftel, or any other, was the one thing in life that he sought; to meet the man once again face to face was why he was here now, why night after night, and day after day, he still risked his life playing this precarious rôle of Smarlinghue in the underworld. Even a *chance* was worth while. It was rather curious that Little Sweeney and Shiftel, both of whom had dropped completely out of sight for so long a time, should both now have made their appearance again! And so, at the present moment, he was exceedingly interested in Little Sweeney!

Jimmie Dale crouched there in the shadows. Pedestrians passed up and down. Perhaps a quarter of an hour went by. Then the side door of Kerrigan's opened, and a shawled figure stepped out and scurried away. Mother Margot! And then presently the door opened again, and Little Sweeney and Bunty Myers came out together.

Jimmie Dale slipped out on the street, and, on the opposite side, followed the two men as they went down the block. At the corner they separated, and Jimmie Dale took up Little Sweeney's trail.

Block after block the man traversed. Jimmie Dale, hugging the shadows of the buildings, kept a position as nearly opposite the man across the street as he dared, wary always of a corner around which the man might turn, and, with too great a distance separating them, disappear into some place—should that be his objective—before he, Jimmie Dale, could round the corner and pick up the trail again.

Little Sweeney walked fast, obviously unconscious of pursuit, and obviously with some set and fixed destination in view. The chase headed down toward the water front. The quarter now was one of small stores and dwellings, dark for the most part, save for the saloons. Jimmie Dale's face set grimly. It was not an over-inviting neighbourhood.

And then suddenly Little Sweeney swung around a corner.

Jimmie Dale quickened his step, and reached the corner himself in time to see the other, after skirting a fence that enclosed either a vacant lot or a store yard of some sort, turn abruptly at the end of the fence and disappear. In an instant, Jimmie Dale, silent in his movements, though he was running now, crossed the street, and in turn was skirting the fence. There was a lane beyond, of course—that was it! Little Sweeney had not entered any house; he had just turned around the far corner of the fence, and—Jimmie Dale stood suddenly stock still. Out from the corner of the fence, flooding the sidewalk, came streaming a powerful ray of light.

And then Little Sweeney's voice, rasping:

"Of course, it's me! Shut off them damned lights!"

The light disappeared as quickly as it had come. Footsteps crunched faintly in the lane, receding. Jimmie Dale edged quickly forward to the corner of the fence, and peered cautiously around it.

It was quite clear now; there was nothing mysterious about the light that had flung its beams across the sidewalk; it was even commonplace. From a rickety-looking metal garage, which was perhaps twenty-five yards back from the street and in which there stood an automobile, someone had sent the headlights playing along the lane.

For a moment Jimmie Dale stood there watching. There was a single incandescent light burning in the garage which illuminated the place dimly, and, aside from Little Sweeney who was just stepping inside, he could make out the forms of two men standing beside the car. He dared not enter the lane, of course. It would be the act of a fool! A chance sound, those headlights switched upon him, and—

The slouching, bent, almost decrepit figure of Smarlinghue drew back; and the next instant, after a swift glance around him to make sure that he was unobserved, with a spring, lithe and agile as a cat, he swung himself over the fence from the sidewalk, and dropped without a sound to the yard on the other side. He began to move noiselessly along the section of the fence which flanked the lane. It ran straight to the edge of the garage, he had observed from the street, and—yes, it ended there! He was in luck! He was crouched now against the wall of the garage itself, which obviously, though it was too dark to see, served to complete the enclosure, in lieu of fence, at this corner of the yard.

He could hear them talking now as plainly as though he were inside, for he was separated from them only by the thin metal sheeting of the garage; and, furthermore, just above his head, shoulder high, where a faint light seeped out, the window was open.

"This is a sweet, juicy place for a meeting!" Little Sweeney's voice grumbled.

"Wot's de matter wid it?" another voice demanded, with a hint of truculency. "It's as good as anywhere else, I guess, an' a blamed sight better'n most. I told youse I had to make a trip first with some swag for a friend of mine."

"Oh, all right, Goldie!" said Little Sweeney placatingly. "All right! I know you did. Forget it!"

Jimmie Dale raised himself cautiously, and, back at an angle from the window sash that precluded the possibility of being seen, looked inside. His lips tightened suddenly. The other two were no strangers, either to anyone in the underworld or to the police. Goldie Kline and the Weasel! Goldie Kline was one of the cleverest box-workers in the business; the Weasel, a shrivelled little runt, was without a peer as a second-story man.

It was the Weasel now who spoke.

"Me," he said, "I tell youse straight I wouldn't touch dem stones on a bet if anyone but old Shiftel was goin' to fence 'em. 'cause dere ain't no one else could get away wid 'em. De Melville-Dane emerald necklace! Swipe me! Dere ain't a stone in de bunch dat ain't known all over de lot, an' it'll take *some* shovin', even by Shiftel, to cash in on 'em. De lady wid de name parted in de middle'll be—"

"Close your face!" said Little Sweeney politely. "You've seen Shiftel, haven't you, and he's settled that to your satisfaction? All you fellows have to do is get the stones tonight, and leave the rest to him."

"Sure!" said the Weasel blithely. "I ain't kickin'! I'm only sayin' dat I wouldn't go in on de deal wid nobody else but Shiftel. Well, spill de rest of it! We're to slip him de stones as soon as we pinches 'em. Dat's understood. An' youse have come down here to tell us where he's layin' low tonight, an' where we're goin' to find him; so let's have it."

Jimmie Dale leaned forward a little in strained attention. Shiftel! The one man he would risk, that he *had* risked, limb and life and liberty to reach! He had made no mistake in following Little Sweeney!

And then a blank look, that changed swiftly to one of bitter dismay, settled on Jimmie Dale's face. The roar of the engine starting up had suddenly drowned out all other sound. No—it was subsiding a little now. He caught Goldie Kline's voice:

"Aw, we can talk in de car. I gotta get dat job I was tellin' youse about done before ten o'clock. Dat's de only t'ing dere's any hurry about. De necklace job don't come off till de early mornin' when de dame's gone bye-bye. Jump in, Sweeney; we'll drop youse anywhere youse like."

They were gone—the car, Little Sweeney, the Weasel, Goldie Kline! Jimmie Dale stood there alone in the blackness of the yard. He could not follow them. They were gone. It had seemed that success at last had been actually within his grasp. It numbed him now somehow that it had been so swiftly and unexpectedly snatched away. He had little or no chance of finding Little Sweeney again tonight; he *might*, with luck, pick up the trail of Goldie Kline or the Weasel somewhere in the underworld, but—He had turned away from the garage, making his way back toward the street, and now he halted abruptly, staring into the darkness.

Had he lost his wits? What was this that his subconscious mind had kept whispering over and over to him as the key-note of everything from the moment the name had been mentioned? Melville-Dane! Melville-Dane! That was in his *own* world, wasn't it? They were his own friends. Strange! Curious! Yes, he remembered now. Soon after he had ventured home again following his "absence" from the city, due to that night at Pedler Joe's, he had found an invitation to some affair, a reception, if he were not mistaken, at the Melville-Danes' for tonight. He had sent his regrets, it was true; but he was on too intimate a footing with them to have that make any difference.

And now Jimmie Dale moved on again, reached the fence, and gained the sidewalk on the other side. He was also well acquainted with that emerald necklace—a priceless thing that seldom left the shelter of its safe deposit vault. Mrs. Melville-Dane was evidently wearing it tonight at the reception!

He started on along the street. A word of warning, then, to the Melville-Danes—or the police? He shook his head. By the time Goldie Kline and the Weasel attempted the proposed robbery in the Melville-Dane home, they would be in possession of something far more valuable to him, Jimmie Dale, than all the emeralds in existence—*they would know where Shiftel could be found* tonight.

"*And* I think," said Jimmie Dale softly to himself, as he quickened his pace, "I think, Smarlinghue, that we'll leave you at the Sanctuary for the rest of the night!"

CHAPTER 13

THE LESSER BREED

From somewhere in the darkness there came a faint musical purr as of metal whirring swiftly upon metal. It stopped; began again; and stopped again. Then utter silence reigned; then there came a low, deep-breathed exclamation, and simultaneously the ray of a flashlight cut through the black, flooded the interior of a small safe, and reflected back upon a masked figure in evening dress.

"One of the X—38 type," murmured Jimmie Dale to himself; "and, as per catalogue, especially adapted for private residences. Tough little nuts to crack! I haven't seen one since the old days at the plant when dad used to turn them out by the gross!"

He reached inside the safe, lifted out a morocco-leather jewel case, and opened it. For an instant he held it under the light, staring at a magnificent emerald necklace of flawless, matched stones. The Weasel had been quite right! Stones such as these must have been garnered and selected from the markets of more than one continent. They would be, through the usual under-world channels, extremely hard to "fence"; for a small and ordinary emerald was not of any great value, and to "cut" one of these and so disguise it, would instantly rob it of the great part of its worth. It was certainly a job for Shiftel! It quite accounted for Shiftel's reappearance!

Jimmie Dale laid the jewel case, still open, on the top of the safe, and from the leather girdle hidden beneath his vest drew out the thin metal box that was stocked with its little gray, adhesive, diamond-shaped seals. He moistened one of these, lifting it with the tweezers, and stuck it on the inside of the jewel case; then he replaced the metal box in his girdle, and slipped the morocco-leather jewel case into his pocket.

And now the light bored into the safe again. There was nothing else there of value from a thief's standpoint. It contained what were evidently some of Mr. Melville-Dane's private papers; it had only been a temporary refuge for the emerald necklace, in lieu of the safe deposit vault from which it had been removed to grace the evening's reception. Satisfied on this point, Jimmie Dale closed and locked the safe again.

He drew back now across the room, and, smiling curiously, arranged two low-backed chairs side by side before the library table. Then his flashlight played for a moment on the wall, locating precisely the electric-light switch just beside a little alcove that was hung with heavy portières; and then the room was in darkness, and Jimmie Dale sat stretched at ease in a lounging chair in the alcove behind the hangings.

His lips twitched grimly now. It was quite a transition from Smarlinghue and the back room of Wally Kerrigan's "club!" It was somewhat different, too, in another way. At Wally Kerrigan's, night after night, he had waited and watched for something, anything, that would open the road to the goal he had set himself—the Phantom; tonight he waited and watched here, quite sure in his own mind as to the exact nature of what would happen, and with no misgivings any longer but that his goal was in sight! In an hour, two hours, at any rate some time before dawn, he would have run Shiftel, alias the Phantom, to earth. It was the end in sight at last; life, happiness, for the Tocsin and himself.

It was very dark, very still in the library of the Melville-Dane mansion here. Again the twisted smile crossed his lips. Here too was quite a transition from the brilliant assembly of but an hour before when he had been one of the guests at a social function that had been, from a society point of view, one of the events of the season. His smile became a little whimsical. Mrs. Melville-Dane had been superb in that emerald necklace. He had paid her almost marked attention throughout the entire evening! Not once had she been out of his sight, even up to the time when she had taken off the necklace and had handed it to her husband to be placed in the safe here in the library. It had been quite simple. He had bidden his host and hostess good-night—and in the confusion of the departing guests, instead of departing himself, had secreted himself in the house.

He shrugged his shoulders. His attentions had been quite wholly unnecessary perhaps. He had not expected the Weasel and Goldie Kline to make any attempt upon the necklace until, say—*now*. It was highly improbable that they would have attempted to stage anything with the house full of people; and yet, if the Phantom's brain was behind the scheme, such an attempt had always remained a possibility. And since he, Jimmie Dale, for his own ends, to pick up the final clue that would bring him face to face with the Phantom, had elected to give no warning either to the Melville-Danes or to the police, then, of necessity, the moral responsibility for the safety of the necklace was his alone—and so he had taken no chances.

The minutes, the quarter hours dragged by. A clock struck through the silence with a clashing, resonant sound. That would be half past two. It was time now surely for the Weasel and Goldie Kline, for they had already allowed ample leeway for the household to retire and settle down for the night.

He stared into the dark. His brain seemed strangely, abnormally active tonight. It was due, wasn't it, to a sort of exhilaration, an uplift, that was upon him? The promise of the end! The Tocsin might be quite right, and probably was, in her belief that the Phantom was planning a trap for him, Jimmie Dale, for the Gray Seal. But her fears now were groundless. It was a plot that, however cunning, however clever it might be, would never come to maturity. It would not be the Phantom now who struck the *first* blow. After tonight she need never fear the Phantom again.

A faint sound, the sound of a cautious, guarded footstep, caught his ear. He stood up silently, his automatic in his hand. The door at the far end of the library creaked slightly; and then, through the parting of the hangings in front of him, Jimmie Dale saw the white gleam of an electric torch flash around the room.

Low whisperings reached him now. He parted the hangings another half inch. The flashlight was playing on the safe; two dark forms were moving quickly toward it; and now one of the two knelt before the safe and began to manipulate the dial, while the other held the light over the kneeling man's shoulder.

Jimmie Dale stepped noiselessly from behind the portières. His hand reached upward, there was a faint *click* as his fingers closed on the electric-light switch, and the room was ablaze with light. A smothered oath came from the kneeling man as he sprang to his feet; the other, startled, dropped his electric torch to the floor. And then silence, an absence of all movement, save that, in obedience to an eloquent gesture from the muzzle of Jimmie Dale's automatic into which they stared, the two men slowly raised their hands above their heads.

"Hello, Goldie! Hello, Weasel!" said Jimmie Dale softly from behind his mask. "I was almost beginning to think you weren't coming." He waved his hand toward the two chairs by the table. "I've been waiting for you, you see. Sit down, won't you?"

The Weasel, licking at his lips, his shrivelled little face working, swore under his breath.

"Who—who are youse?" he demanded shakily.

"We'll talk about that presently, Weasel," Jimmie Dale answered coolly. "In the meantime"—his voice hardened suddenly, rasping, cold—"go over there and sit down!"

Truculently, hesitatingly, their hands still above their heads, the two men moved forward and sat down in the chairs.

"Now"—Jimmie Dale was biting off his words, as he stepped swiftly behind them—"one at a time. You first, Goldie. Put your hands around the back of the chair, palms together." And then as the man obeyed, Jimmie Dale thrust his left hand into the tail pocket of his evening coat, produced a small coil of stout cord, and shook it out to its full length. It had two loops near the centre in the form of slip knots. He slipped one of the loops over Goldie Kline's wrists, and tightened it. "Now you, Weasel!"

The other loop closed upon the Weasel's wrists. A moment more, and the respective ends of the cord were lashed to the respective chairs, and Jimmie Dale stepped around to the other side of the table to face the two men.

He smiled at them for a moment speculatively.

Goldie Kline burst suddenly into a torrent of blasphemy.

Jimmie Dale's smile became plaintive.

"That's rather foolish of you, Goldie," he said. "You are making quite a little noise, and from your standpoint I should say that was the one thing to avoid."

The Weasel squirmed in his chair.

"Who are youse?" he demanded hoarsely again. "Wot's de lay? Youse're no dick wid dat mask on yer map."

"You are quite right," said Jimmie Dale calmly. "As a matter of fact, I am afraid I am in the same category as yourselves tonight. Shall we say—fellow thieves? The only difference being that I have got what I came for, and you haven't."

The Weasel's rat-like little eyes narrowed. He leaned forward.

"Wot do youse mean?" he snarled.

Jimmie Dale took the morocco-leather jewel case from his pocket, opened it, and laid it down on the table in front of the two men.

"This!" he said tersely.

The men bent forward, staring. It was a minute before either spoke. Goldie Kline raised his eyes and cast a furtive, fear-startled glance at Jimmie Dale. The Weasel licked his lips again.

"My Gawd!" whispered the Weasel thickly. "It's de Gray Seal!"

Jimmie Dale made no answer.

It was Goldie Kline who spoke now. The man seemed to have pulled himself together, and in his tones was a sort of blustering bravado.

"So youse're de Gray Seal, are youse? Well, den, I don't get youse! Youse've beat us to it an' pinched de goods, damn youse! I can see dat! But wot's de big idea in hangin' around after youse've got de swag, an' stickin' up de Weasel an' me?"

Jimmie Dale closed the jewel case, and returned it to his pocket.

"That's a fair question, Goldie," he said pleasantly; "and I'll answer it. It's no cinch to shove that necklace. There's only one man who would have much chance—and that's old Isaac Shiftel." He smiled at them engagingly. "I'm sure you'll agree with me, because—the source of my information is really of no consequence at the moment—I happen to know that it was mainly, if not wholly, because Shiftel agreed to dispose of the stones that you figured the job of getting them would pay. Well, I am in exactly the same position." Jimmie Dale's smile broadened a little. "Without Shiftel the stones wouldn't pay me. I think this answers your question. I have the necklace, and you haven't; but you know where Shiftel, who seems to be extremely difficult of late to locate, can be found tonight, and I don't. And so I waited for you, because I was sure you would be kind enough to give me his address."

Goldie Kline's jaw had dropped. He shut it now with a snap.

"Well, by Gawd!" he burst out furiously. "Can youse beat dat! Say, youse've got yer nerve! Youse grabs de stuff from under our noses, an' den youse has de gall to ask us to wise youse up so's youse can get rid of it! Say, we'll see youse in hell first, won't we, Weasel?"

"Youse have said somethin', Goldie!" agreed the Weasel earnestly. "We sure will!"

"I'm so sorry," said Jimmie Dale patiently. "I really thought you would help me out. In fact, I actually counted on it."

"Youse don't say!" The Weasel was quite at his ease now, sneering broadly.

And then Jimmie Dale leaned suddenly across the table. All trace of facetiousness was gone from both voice and manner now. He drew his watch from his pocket.

"Listen, you two—and listen *hard!*" he said evenly. "I'm going to give you two minutes to come across. It might be compounding a felony to let you get away from here, but you didn't steal anything—though that's not your fault—and I'm thinking of the long terms you would get, even for 'breaking and entering,' with your records behind you. Am I making myself clear? A little noise down here will bring the family and servants about your ears in short order—while I go out the way you came in. If they find you here, even trussed up as you are, I imagine you will find it rather difficult to explain to the police how you came to visit Mr. Melville-Dane at half past two o'clock in the morning. On the other hand, an earnest half-hour's work—the time I should like to feel I was guaranteed against any interference on your part—will free you from that cord, and once free you can walk out of here. I still hope I am making myself clear." He glanced at his watch. "One minute has already gone. Where were you to meet Shiftel?"

A whitish tinge had crept into Goldie Kline's face.

"Damn youse!" he whispered fervently.

The Weasel squirmed again in his chair. He looked at Goldie Kline.

"I ain't for goin' up for nothin'!" There was a sudden nerveless whine in his voice. "He's got de goods anyhow. We ain't goin' to *lose* nothin' by tellin'. Wot—wot d'youse say, Goldie?"

Goldie Kline gnawed at his lips.

"All right," he muttered after a moment. "Spill it. I guess dere ain't nothing else to do."

"Just a minute," said Jimmie Dale coolly. He replaced his watch in his pocket. "It would be unfortunate if there were a *mistake* in the address. I am sure your memories are good enough to recall certain instances in the underworld that will reassure on the point that the Gray Seal always pays his *debts*. I mention this simply in passing. And now—where is Shiftel waiting for you?"

It was the Weasel who answered.

"He's in de room off de back yard, down at Morley's dope joint," he said sullenly.

"Thank you!" said Jimmie Dale grimly. "I know where that is." He moved away from the table and toward the door. Here he paused for a moment. The two men were already tugging and struggling with their bonds. "I forgot to say," he said quietly, "that there is nothing of any value left in the safe! Good-night!"

And then Jimmie Dale was gone.

CHAPTER 14

THE CAT'S-PAW

Five minutes later, Jimmie Dale climbed into the light runabout that, prior to the reception, he had unobtrusively parked in an alleyway a block from the Melville-Dane residence. He replaced his silk hat with a peaked cap which he drew out from under the seat—and the car shot forward into the street.

He drove fast now. He had no thought of speed laws. Shiftel—the Phantom—the end in sight! He had no thought for anything but that; he asked for nothing more than just this, which was at last to be granted him, of playing out the final hand with this inhuman fiend to whom murder was a trade, and crime of the basest sort a pastime. There was room now for only one of them—the Phantom or himself—in this world. The debt that lay between them was too abysmal to be plumbed or spanned in any other way.

And yet the man should have his chance; a chance to fight for his life. He was not entitled to it; he, the Phantom, under the same conditions would have struck as quickly and murderously as he could. In fact, if the Tocsin was right, as no doubt she was, the Phantom even now was preparing a trap which, tomorrow, the next day, or the day after, was intended to be sprung in the hope of snaring him, Jimmie Dale, the Gray Seal; and that trap once sprung successfully he, Jimmie Dale, would go out with no more chance for life than the flame of a candle flung to the storm! But there would be no tomorrow, or the next day, or the day after, for the Phantom and his trap; tonight, now, within the next few minutes, there would be no longer need for the Phantom to cudgel his brain for tricks and devices to lure the Gray Seal into his web!

The streets were deserted. A strange silence seemed to reign over the city. Somehow it seemed sinister, premonitive—aptly so. Still Jimmie Dale drove fast. And then finally, far over on the East Side, deep in a neighbourhood as vicious and abandoned as New York had to offer, he parked his car again in a lane, sprang out, and started at a brisk walk along the block.

There was a grim, set look on his face now, as his hand, slipping into his pocket for his automatic, encountered the morocco-leather jewel case. Shiftel was waiting for the necklace! Well, Shiftel should have it—for a moment. But, at that, its safety was nowhere nearly so greatly imperilled as if it had been left as a temptation for Goldie Kline and the Weasel! Tomorrow, in some way, it would be back in the Melville-Danes' possession again.

Jimmie Dale swerved sharply into a cross street, and from there into an alleyway. His pace slackened, became guarded, cautious. He knew Morley's opium den by more than hearsay. As Smarlinghue, he had been a supposed client more than once. Yes, here it was—the back of it, anyway, over this fence here, and across the yard. Well, it was the back of it he sought, wasn't it? That was what the Weasel had said—the room off the back yard.

He drew himself up to the top of the fence, dropped silently to the other side, and suddenly his pulse beat fast. Across the yard was an open, lighted window, almost on a level with the ground. Unbridled now, almost overwhelming, that sense of exhilaration was upon him again. The end of the chase! What did it not mean—for the Tocsin—for himself!

Jimmie Dale moved forward quietly, noiselessly—ten yards—another ten. He was not far from the window now, not more than another five yards. And now he could see inside. Shiftel! And now he knew another emotion—something cold, merciless, primitive in its naked thirst for retribution. The Weasel had made no "mistake!" Shiftel was there! He could see the bent form in its greasy black coat; he could see the bearded face of the old "fence" bending over a table, as he had seen it once before on a night when he had thought he had run the man to earth in the rooms old Mother Margot lived in now.

A yard more! Yes, the window was not more than a couple of feet above the ground. His automatic was in his hand now, his face masked again. Another yard—and then Jimmie Dale whirled sharply around, his face drawn suddenly in hard, tense lines. Out of the darkness, out of the nowhere, came a voice, ugly in its menace, a voice he recognised—Bunty Myers':

"There he is! Get him! The Gray Seal!"

Out of the darkness, out of the nowhere, a circle of flying shadows seemed to arise and converge upon him.

The trap!

Like lightning his brain worked; like lightning he moved now. The trap! In a flash, out of a strange bewilderment, he grasped the fact that somehow the trap of which the Tocsin had so earnestly warned him, the trap that he had so self-confidently thought he would nip in the making, was even now being sprung upon him; that his own confident plan of reaching Shiftel was in fact the very trap that had been laid for him.

The trap! And the jaws of it were that open window! And there was no other way to turn. Those on-rushing shadows, that were snarling, cursing men now, were almost upon him, blocking his retreat.

Retreat! He had no mind to retreat. It would be the end without a doubt tonight now; he had at least been right in that. But it would not be his end alone. Inside there, in through the jaws of the trap—was Shiftel!

The brain works fast. In the winking of an eye Jimmie Dale had leaped forward, and had sprung for the window sill. It was intuition perhaps that prompted him. The figure at the table, at a slight angle away from the direct line of the window, had risen, revolver levelled. Jimmie Dale plunged forward, as a man plunges in a long, low dive, over the sill and to the floor. And as he plunged, like a machine gun in action behind him, came the roar and flash of what seemed a myriad revolver shots.

It happened quick—quicker almost than the brain could grasp. The bearded, greasy old figure, intent evidently upon his victim alone, had overstepped the zone of safety, stepped a little forward into the line of the window; and now, with a wild cry, with suddenly upflung arms, as the hail of lead swept in, had pitched face forward to the floor.

And something in Jimmie Dale's soul, amidst the turmoil that was raging physically about him, gave quiet, fervent thanks. Not for a man's death—but that the burden and guilt, if it should be termed guilt to destroy such a one as this, one that, to save the life of the woman he loved, he *must* have destroyed if he could before his own end came, had been lifted from his shoulders. Shiftel was dead!

Jimmie Dale had wriggled around on the floor. He was facing the window now, firing in turn with his automatic. The low sill afforded a measure of protection. He fired from the floor over it. Shouts, yells, curses answered him; but the rush was checked, though the shots still poured in from without.

And now pandemonium seemed loosed! He glanced around him quickly. The door of the room was locked. That was obvious because they were pounding upon it now, trying to burst it in; and it had been locked, quite obviously and quite logically, in preparation for his entry into the trap, and against the possibility of any escape through what was the only means of exit he could see—except the window with its hail of bullets!

It was the end! He slipped a fresh clip of cartridges into his automatic. But now he fired with more restraint. True, it was the end, but he must be careful of his ammunition now; he would need it even more when that door gave!

It was an even break. Himself for Shiftel! It was worth it; it had been worth it—for her sake. Shiftel, the Phantom, was—

Was he mad? Had this scene from the pit of the inferno, that bursting door, these shots that hummed with hell's venom above his head, this smoke-filled, acrid-stinking room, turned his brain? Shiftel! That was not Shiftel there! Nor Gentleman Laroque! He was staring now for the first time at the still, motionless figure on the floor. The beard on the upturned face hung awry. He reached for it, and snatched it off. A thousand noises, a thousand sounds pounded at his eardrums and made mockery of the crashing blows upon the door, the vicious *spat* of bullets, the hideous yowling of those human wolves who had the Gray Seal trapped at last. This man on the floor here dead was not Shiftel, nor the Phantom in the guise of Shiftel, nor the Phantom in any other guise. *It was Little Sweeney!*

The door was yielding now. And somehow—he did not understand why or how for his brain seemed stunned—the noise and the shouts without seemed to increase in intensity. He wriggled back a little way across the room where he could best command both window and door. He had still one clip of cartridges left. He had only one hope now—that he could use them to the last one. In another minute the door would give, and—

"*Jimmie!*"

Yes, he was mad! Reason at the last had fled from him. That was her voice, the Tocsin's voice. As those shadows outside the window had suddenly closed in upon him out of the nowhere, so this voice, the voice he loved, came suddenly to him now out of the nowhere.

"*Jimmie!*"

His eyes strained over in the direction of the desk. He could see nothing. There was nothing there, unless—yes, yes, the floor seemed to have risen up a few inches above the surrounding level. A trap door!

"You!" he cried.

"Yes! Quick! Quick, Jimmie, quick!" her voice answered from below.

He flung himself forward, and wrenched the trap door wide open. It was pitch black below; he could see nothing.

"Drop, Jimmie; it's only a few feet," she called up to him. "Bolt the trap door behind you. And, oh, hurry, Jimmie, hurry!"

He swung himself through the opening, and dropped; then reached upward behind him and closed the trap door. His fingers searched for the bolt, found it, and shot it home. He could not stand upright; he had to stoop, the opening was so low. And it was so dark he could not see his hand before his face.

"Where are you?" he cried out. "Marie, thank God for you! Marie, where are you?"

"Here," her voice replied. "Follow me; come this way."

"I can't see you—I can't see anything," he said; then quickly: "Wait! I've got a flashlight."

"No!" Her voice came back instantly. "You mustn't show a light here under any circumstances. Keep your head down, and feel your way. You can touch the walls on each side of you."

"All right!" he answered.

He could hear her moving ahead of him. Half bent over, he followed. Soft earth was under foot. It was a low, narrow tunnel of some sort, that was evident. An underground passage, of course. Morley's drug-den was well equipped!

His brain was in chaos. Shiftel, Bunty Myers, the emerald necklace, Little Sweeney! And the Tocsin here!

"Marie, I don't understand!" he burst out.

"It was the trap I warned you about," she answered back.

"Yes; I know that now," he said. "But Shiftel! That wasn't Shiftel up there. It was Little Sweeney."

"He was the cat's-paw," she said.

He stumbled on. Where did this passage lead to? Was there no end to it?

"Hold on a minute, Marie! Stop!" he pleaded suddenly. "You—"

"There is no time; there is not an instant to lose," she broke in swiftly "I—I—but never mind that. I can tell you in a few words what you do not understand as we go on. Are you listening, Jimmie?"

Listening! Listening to *her*, to her voice!

"Yes," he said; "since you will not wait."

"Well, then," she said rapidly, "the Phantom was not fool enough to close his eyes to what looked as though there were a leak somewhere on the inside. The Gray Seal had put in an appearance with too great *regularity*. He thought, too, at last, as I wrote you, that you were after him in a personal way. Therefore he meant to strike first. And so for tonight's work he sent out his orders and his plans through the *usual* channels. Is that clear?"

"Yes," said Jimmie Dale, as he groped his way along.

"If, then, there was a leak," she went on, "the plan for the night's work would reach the Gray Seal also as usual. But though the Phantom inclined strongly to the belief that *he* was the one you were after, and that the spoils of the various affairs in which you had intervened were a secondary matter, he was still not absolutely sure of it—and therefore, whether he was right or wrong, and while he hoped to get you by offering what you would believe to be himself as a bait, it was not his intention to take any chances with that emerald necklace tonight, and—" She broke off suddenly. "I don't see how you found that out!"

Jimmie Dale brought up abruptly against a sharp turning in the tunnel. He bit his lips in chagrin. In the utter darkness, in spite of the cramped posture he was forced to assume, he had tried to catch up with her, reach her.

"I followed Little Sweeney from Kerrigan's," he said. "He met Goldie Kline and the Weasel, and I overheard enough to know what was going on before I lost Little Sweeney again. They got away in an automobile."

"I see." Her voice floated back. "Well, that part of the plan was *not* passed out through the usual channels. All that was given out to the gang was that Shiftel would be here at Morley's tonight to receive some swag; but it was not until the last minute, not until an hour ago that the gang themselves were ordered to be on hand to get you if you came. After that they were kept *together* so that a leak *then*, when a leak would no longer be a lure but a warning, was impossible. If you were only after spoils, you would know nothing about the necklace, and so would not get it; but if you were after *him* you would come here, and he would get *you*! Do you still understand, Jimmie?"

"Yes," he answered; "all but Little Sweeney's part."

"It was risky business playing the part of Shiftel—something might go wrong," she said bitterly. "And the Phantom takes no risks—when he can let someone else assume them! That is why he had someone play the part of Shiftel. Little Sweeney received his orders through Limpy Mack with whom, as you know, he had worked before, not knowing that Limpy Mack and Shiftel and the unknown 'Chief' were one; and Little Sweeney of course thought it was a clever way to induce two crooks to steal the jewels, for Little Sweeney was made to believe that Shiftel had left the country for good. Limpy Mack supplied the disguise, which was actually of course the one worn by himself when he masqueraded as Shiftel."

"Good God!" gasped Jimmie Dale. "I see now!"

"Yes!" she said. "There is not much more. Little Sweeney was chosen because he had been away during your later appearances, and was therefore free from suspicion that any leak had come through him; and Goldie Kline and the Weasel were chosen for the same reason—they were wholly *outsiders*. That's all—except my share. *I* had sent you no word, no note. I didn't think you could possibly know anything about tonight; and so I didn't expect you would come here, and in that respect I thought the Phantom would fail. But I knew that Shiftel was to be here at this hour—for I believed then that it was actually Shiftel himself—and so I notified the police. If they got Shiftel, then that was the end of our troubles. They—they are there now. They came just as I reached the trap door—but"—her voice seemed to dull a little—"they haven't got the Phantom."

Jimmie Dale made no answer. His lips were tight and grimly set. The Phantom was still alive, still at liberty, still free to carry on his fiendish machinations! But—Jimmie Dale's face relaxed a little the next instant—it was not all utter failure and defeat. *She* was here! The Tocsin was here with him. And he, Jimmie Dale, was alive, where but a few minutes before he had seen no chance of life. They were together—Marie and himself. In a moment more now the tunnel must end, and she—

Her voice, suddenly low and guarded, reached him.

"Wait!" she whispered. "Stay where you are. I'll see if the way is clear."

He stood still.

A minute passed, and then she called again:

"It's all right. Come on!"

His hands still groped out before him as he moved forward again, and, groping, discovered that the tunnel here took an abrupt right-angled bend. And then as he turned the corner, and a cool, fresh current of air fanned his face, he found himself on a flight of steps, and he could straighten up and there was head room as he mounted them.

And then he was standing outside a doorway on a dark and deserted street. He could hear the sound of shouts, of revolver shots, but the sounds came faintly from the distance. They were safe now, quite safe, the Tocsin and himself. He looked quickly, eagerly around him. He called her softly.

But there was no answer—and of the Tocsin there was no sign.

CHAPTER 15

BEHIND THE DOORS OF THE UNDERWORLD

Jimmie Dale turned softly, without sound, upon the bunk, easing his position. Around him were whisperings, murmurings, the stir of humans in troubled sleep, a hundred conglomerate, sinister sounds; and everywhere the sickly sweetish smell of opium.

His face was haggard, worn, drawn, in sharp, pinched lines, and there was a dull, weary look about the eyes that no "make-up" could have supplied, as a smile, grim, unbidden, settled now upon his lips. Was this reality? Perhaps it was all a dream—a dream such as the poppy brought to these dregs and lees of the underworld who stole in here, where no daylight had ever shone, to burn their suicidal incense to the God of Gray Things!

Reality! Could even his existence in itself be reality? Was it any more reality than he, as Smarlinghue, as one known far and wide throughout the underworld as a hopelessly confirmed dope fiend, represented reality? He was not Smarlinghue. There was no such person as Smarlinghue. And yet in that very character which he had created, unkempt and ragged, he lay here now in one of Hip Foo's "private" rooms, hidden deep down in the chain of sub-cellars that housed perhaps the most infamous opium joint in all New York! He was not a dope fiend. Neither taste nor drop of the drug had he ever known. And yet he had burned a thousand "pills," he had toyed with a hypodermic syringe a thousand times, and before him even now lay the pipe that the Chinese attendant had brought him but a few moments since! Was it then reality, or but a dream, ceaseless, unending, whose vividness was so acute that it aped reality? Was it a dream that somewhere, always elusive, always just beyond his reach, always just evading him, a *phantom*, evil as no other human being was evil, cunning as only one from the fiend's pit itself was cunning, diced with him out of the shadows for his life—and hers, the Tocsin's?

Jimmie Dale's eyes closed. He was conscious of great fatigue; not physical—mental. Days of striving, days of utter failure, of futility, nights of unceasing, sleepless effort lay behind him. Reality! The question answered itself. He had but to listen for an instant through these thin, flimsy partitions to know that it was not only reality, but a reality stripped of all glamour, ugly in its nakedness and its menace. It was only his brain voicing its plea for rest, giving warning that it was nearing the breaking point and that the lash could be applied too often to the slave, that had prompted the groping question.

He listened now for a moment almost involuntarily. Here was one of those underground exchanges where the secrets of the underworld passed from mouth to mouth; where the gossip of the Bad Lands circulated; where crimes were born; where he had even heard his own death, the death of the Gray Seal, decreed a score of times.

Whispers reached him. Two yeggs of the lesser breed, whose names he did not know, were in there. Their conversation was snatchy, desultory, due presumably to the fact that the opium was beginning to get in its work. There was a reference to an uptown "job" of a week ago; a dance hall fracas that had ended in a murder; the approval of the sentence passed upon one English Steve by the fellow members of his gang, and the speculation as to how many of the gang English Steve would succeed in "bumping off" before in turn English Steve finally received his own quietus.

Again Jimmie Dale turned noiselessly on his bunk. He was not interested. Ten minutes before he had made a tour of the sub-cellar here; and then, playing his part as Smarlinghue, he had flung himself down on this bunk and given his order. Neither Bunty Myers nor any other of the Phantom's underlings were in evidence. He had not actually expected to find them already here, he did not even expect them later on; but in half an hour, or an hour, luck might change, and they *might* come. He had simply made Hip Foo's his first stopping place night after night of late because it had once been the rendezvous of the men he wanted, because it was here that some of them had met on the night the place had been raided, and because, since the night that the Phantom had laid the trap for him at Morley's, Bunty Myers and the Kitten and Spud MacGuire and Muller no longer met in the back, upstairs room of Wally Kerrigan's "club." Perhaps they would again in the future—some of them—perhaps not!

Jimmie Dale's lips tightened. It had gone very badly with the Phantom's plans that night. Apart from Little Sweeney, Spud MacGuire and Muller, in the subsequent fight with the police, had both been killed. Also, it had apparently forced Bunty Myers and the Kitten into hiding. Certainly, since that night, he, Jimmie Dale, had not been able to pick up the slightest trace of either of them.

He swept his hand heavily across his eyes. He was not so sure that he could wholly glory in the outcome of that night. If the Phantom had received a blow, he, Jimmie Dale, had perhaps received one that was even more disastrous. The Phantom was still at large, still free to pursue his heinous activities, but with the abandonment of Wally Kerrigan's back room, even if only temporarily, by Bunty Myers and the rest of his associates who hung on the Phantom's orders, he, Jimmie Dale, had lost touch with everything and every one connected with the Phantom—except Mother Margot!

Mother Margot! His lips twisted in a weary smile. She had been of little service to him! So far as any information he had been able to obtain from her was concerned, she might as well have been non-existent. Not that she had attempted to mislead or lie to him; he was satisfied on that score because, being the sole connecting link with the Phantom that was left to him, he had naturally watched her more carefully than ever before. As the man in the black silk mask, the man she knew as the Gray Seal, he had held her closely to account; but he was convinced that of the Phantom's plans and movements since that night at Morley's, she was as ignorant as he was himself. Where before she had been the mouthpiece of the "Voice," as she called the Phantom, her office now had apparently become a sinecure. It was as though the Phantom, failing in the supreme effort he had made to find the "leak" among his trusted subordinates, and afraid perhaps to place further trust anywhere, had withdrawn himself completely from every one of those that formerly he had moved as pawns upon his miserable chess-board of crime.

But that did not mean the Tocsin's safety. The Phantom, as she had so well named him, master of impersonation, the Phantom alias Gentleman Laroque, alias Shiftel, alias Limpy Mack, alias heaven alone knew what else, the Phantom with his score of domiciles, if he meant now to play a lone hand, was a far more dangerous antagonist than ever before; one far harder to come at, more elusive, more safely and deeply entrenched behind—

Jimmie Dale's hand reached swiftly out for the opium pipe that lay on the stand beside the bunk. A footstep, one accompanied by a low, soft swish, was coming along the boarded corridor outside. It was probably one of the Chinese attendants, and the swish was the usual swish of the slippered feet; but if there was any one den or dive in the Bad Lands more than another where it meant literally life and death to preserve the character of Smarlinghue from all suspicion, it was here in Hip Foo's where a whisper was alone sufficient to bring down upon him, darting from its every corner and crevice, the drug crazed rat-horde of the underworld that infested the place.

The step came nearer. Jimmie Dale, the pipe apparently at his lips, lay back again upon the bunk. If the Phantom were playing a lone hand now, if he had sloughed off, as dangerous and unfit, the tools he had formerly employed, then he, Jimmie Dale, since the Tocsin was obviously steadfast in her determination to afford him no opportunity of picking up any further clue, was facing a blank wall. If, however, the veil that had shrouded the movements of the Phantom and all those who had been connected with him since that night at Morley's was simply the natural caution inspired by what had so nearly been complete disaster, then certainly, sooner or later, he, Jimmie Dale, would pick up the trail again of those, such as were left of them, who once had congregated at Wally Kerrigan's. That was why he was here in Hip Foo's tonight—on the chance that, either through their appearance in person, or through the mumbled gossip which was the freer in dens like this where the incense burned to the God of Poppy loosened men's and women's tongues, he might find the lost threads again.

He asked no more than that—only to go on to the end while there was yet time. And he was afraid tonight, afraid with a great fear. How did he even know that it was not already too late? How did he know that in her battle of wits with the Phantom which she insisted in waging alone, unaided, with her life at stake, the Tocsin, brave, resourceful, clever though she was, had not already—

Through half-closed eyes Jimmie Dale watched the curtain that hung across the doorway. Yes, undoubtedly, the footstep was no longer in evidence, and undoubtedly the curtain was being drawn stealthily aside. He made no movement. The opening widened, widened still further—and suddenly the blood went whipping through Jimmie Dale's veins in a mad, elated tide, and weariness was gone.

Reward! The light was dim, low, flickering, but he could see well enough. It was not one of the Chinese attendants. It was the shawled head of an old hag that was peering in there. Mother Margot!

Still Jimmie Dale gave no sign that he was aware of the other's presence. It was a reward at last for the days and nights that were gone! Once before she had come here to meet Bunty Myers, once before this had been the rendezvous—what else would she be here for tonight? He had evidently been right then in hoping more from Hip Foo's than from any other place. And it did not mean that she had lied to him as the Gray Seal either. It might very well be, and probably was, that, since last he had communicated with her, the Phantom had suddenly broken silence and through her was issuing his orders again.

She stood there on the threshold now, peering toward the bunk, shading her eyes with her hand as though, even in the dim light, it helped her the better to distinguish objects. And for a moment she hesitated, then she came slowly through the doorway and let the curtain fall behind her.

"Dat's youse, ain't it, Smarly?" she whispered.

Jimmie Dale sat up on the bunk, and blinked at her. There was something of grim, sardonic humour in the situation. They had been formally "introduced" that night at Wally Kerrigan's, and she knew Smarlinghue—as *Smarlinghue*. But between Smarlinghue and the man she knew, yes, and *obeyed*, as the Gray Seal, there was a gulf that she had never crossed. The trumps were very much in his hands!

Jimmie Dale blinked again, rubbed his eyes, and stared at her.

"Oh, hello!" he said, a little ungraciously. "It's Mother Margot, eh?"

She nodded without speaking.

"Well?" It was Smarlinghue who spoke. "What's the idea? I ain't standing any free rides to dreamland—the price has gone up."

Mother Margot shook her head.

"Nobody's askin' youse to," she replied a little tartly. "I ain't never been on dat kind of stuff, t'ank Gawd! I'm lookin' for someone, dat's wot I'm here for."

Jimmie Dale permitted a slightly malicious grin to flicker across his lips.

"You didn't seem to fall in love with me the night I got shown out at Wally's," he observed, "so I guess it ain't me. Try next door!"

She came a little closer, and lowered her voice.

"No, it ain't for youse," she said; "but mabbe youse'll do, if youse ain't too stewed on coke."

Jimmie Dale did not answer for a moment. Was the entrée into the Phantom's circle here at last, an entrée in the sense that, if only in a minor way, he was to be offered the opportunity of participating in the activities of Gentleman Laroque's, alias the Phantom's, gang? She was looking for someone. Who? She was, he knew, the one through whom the Phantom, always invisible himself, issued all his orders. Who, then, would she be searching for tonight save the very men that he himself would willingly pay any price to find—Bunty Myers for one, the Kitten for another!

"I ain't been here long enough, without being butted in on, to get stewed," said Jimmie Dale caustically.

She came still closer, peering at him through her spectacles, drawing her shawl with quick nervous little clutches tighter around her shoulders and throat. And then suddenly her whole manner changed; she seemed frightened, almost in despair.

"Yes, youse're all right, I can see dat now," she burst out in a hoarse, shaken whisper. "Dat was de only thing I was scared of w'en I sees youse in here—dat youse'd be stewed. Listen, Smarly, I got to get some help. An' I want youse to help me. Dere ain't no one on de whole East Side could do it de way youse could, if youse only will."

Jimmie Dale lounged back on the bunk. Mother Margot would at least not find him *eager*.

"Thanks for the bouquet!" he grinned. "The last time all you handed me was a frozen mitt."

"Aw, forget it!" she whispered passionately. "For Gawd's sake forget dat, Smarly. I ain't handin' youse no jolly. Everybody knows Smarlinghue; an' everybody knows dere ain't a dump in de Bad Lands dat he ain't wise to, an' where he don't get de glad hand. An'—an' everybody knows dey can trust Smarlinghue. *I'm* trustin' youse now. Say, give me yer word youse'll keep yer trap closed about me whether youse sits in de game or not, an' I'll come across."

"Sure!" said Jimmie Dale. "That don't cost nothing. I've never seen you tonight, if that suits you. Go ahead! Spill it!"

Mother Margot glanced furtively around her. She listened for a moment to the voices, grown thicker now and almost inaudible, coming through the partition, then she leaned close to Jimmie Dale. Her lips scarcely moved.

"I'll get mine if I'm heard, or youse snitches on me," she breathed in a frightened, jerky way. "But I got to do it. I got to do it. I've been lookin' for hours, ever since early in de afternoon, an' it ain't no good. I've looked everywhere, an' I can't find him, an'—an' I didn't darst get too nosey wid questions. Youse understand, Smarly? It's English Steve. I got to get a message to English Steve, an' if I don't he goes out. My Gawd, Smarly, youse gets dat, don't youse? He goes out."

Jimmie Dale stared at her. He experienced a sudden loss of the elation, the uplift, that he had known but a moment before in such full measure. English Steve! All the underworld knew about English Steve! It was no secret. Even those two hop-fighters in the next room, who ranked little higher than stalls and steerers in the citizenry of the Bad Lands, knew all about English Steve and his gang troubles. He, Jimmie Dale, knew all about it. As Larry the Bat he had even been personally acquainted with English Steve in the olden days. Therefore he also knew—which was the one thing that concerned him now—that English Steve had nothing to do with Bunty Myers. And it was of Bunty Myers, as the first step toward picking up again the Phantom's trail, that he had expected Mother Margot to unburden herself.

His eyes shifted to the ragged sleeve of his coat, to the dirty, frayed, protruding wristband of his shirt. He had hoped for too much evidently. Perhaps he should have known better, but that did not lessen the disappointment. True, he had called this woman from her pushcart on Thompson Street only that morning, and had talked to her as the Gray Seal over the telephone, and he had been thoroughly satisfied then that she was as ignorant as he was of either Bunty Myers' or the Phantom's movements; but until a moment ago, in view of her appearance here, he had thought that in the meantime the Phantom had communicated with her. Well, he had been wrong, it seemed, and tonight was to be only another night of hollow results added to the nights that had gone before. He had lost track of how many! It didn't matter. He had hoped for too much, that was all.

She clutched at his sleeve frantically, in pitiful pleading.

"Youse ain't afraid, are youse, Smarly?" she quavered. "Youse don't have to get in between. All I'm askin' youse is to help me find him, an' if youse finds him first to slip him a message. Youse don't have to do nothin' else."

"What's the message?" inquired Jimmie Dale, a little gruffly.

"Just tell him to duck his nut out of New York tonight, dat's all. Just tell him dat."

Jimmie Dale as Smarlinghue shook his head critically.

"He ain't that kind," he said. "I suppose you're talking about him and his gang, but everybody that ain't deaf knows he swore he'd get every last one of the outfit he used to work with before they got him, if they tried any funny business. What's the use of handing him any steer like that?"

"Never youse mind about dat," said Mother Margot quickly. "He'll go if youse tells him it was me sent de word. He ain't for runnin' into a trap, is he? Nobody but a fool 'ud do dat."

Jimmie Dale appeared to ponder the matter.

"What's the trap?" he demanded after a moment.

"I don't know," she answered miserably.

"Well then," prodded Jimmie Dale, "if you don't know that, how do you know it's tonight they're laying for him, and where do you come in? He ain't a long lost son you've discovered, is he?"

She wrung her hands suddenly.

"Oh, my Gawd, Smarly," she whispered wildly, "we're losin' time, an'—an' I'm afraid. Mabbe it's too late even now. Dere ain't no use askin' me questions dat I can't answer. I don't know how, an' I don't know where, but I knows English Steve gets his tonight if he ain't tipped off in time. For Gawd's sake don't ask me nothin' more. I owe it to English Steve to wise him up. I got to do it if I can, an' I'm askin' youse to help me. Youse will, won't youse, Smarly? Aw, for Gawd's sake, say youse will! Youse won't be sorry. I—I'll make it up to youse. Mother Margot don't never forget."

Jimmie Dale swung his leg slowly over the edge of the bunk. Well, why not? Mother Margot's advent had brought him anything but what he had hoped for, but he was certainly no worse off than he had been before her arrival. English Steve and his gang affairs were too well known, too public, to warrant any suspicion that there was any ulterior object in Mother Margot's actions. He had not the slightest doubt but that the gang had laid their plans for the removal of English Steve tonight. It was quite on the cards. In some way Mother Margot had got an inkling of this. She probably owed English Steve a debt of some kind, due, as probably, to some crooked work in the past in which they had been engaged together. That, too, was quite on the cards. Well, why not? He had no particular interest in English Steve, but certainly he had no desire to stand by and allow a murder, even the murder of a crook, to be committed if he could prevent it. And then, too, there was another angle to the affair. Mother Margot as a *friend* of Smarlinghue might well mean far more than Mother Margot constrained by fear to be the unwilling ally of the Gray Seal. And, besides, from now until dawn his own search would be continued through the underworld anyhow; and where he looked for Bunty Myers or the Kitten, he would, as naturally as though that were his sole quest, look for English Steve.

"All right," said Jimmie Dale abruptly, as he stood up. "I'll help you if I can. I guess I know a few dumps you don't, but you keep on going yourself.

We'll cover more ground that way, and get on quicker. And it wouldn't do either of us any good to be seen hunting together, neither. Beat it!"

Mother Margot caught his hand impulsively.

"I knew youse would, Smarly! I knew youse would!" she whispered in a choked voice. "Gawd bless youse, Smarly, youse're—"

It was Smarlinghue who grinned a little sheepishly, and Smarlinghue who spoke.

"Aw, forget it!" he said. "I thought you said we was losing time." He brushed past her toward the doorway. "I'll go out by the lane, you go out the other way. See?"

"Yes," she answered; "but—"

"So long!" said Smarlinghue, alias Jimmie Dale—and vanished through the doorway.

CHAPTER 16

ENGLISH STEVE

It was growing late, near midnight. Through the murk of an uninviting, almost ominous-looking basement entrance, whose light, such as it was, seeped upward to the sidewalk, Jimmie Dale emerged, and stood for a moment staring up and down the dirty, shabby street.

A grim smile was playing on his lips. Behind him, down those few dark, rickety steps up which he had just come, and thence through an ill-lighted little cobbler's shop, where a cobbler, who was a cobbler in but little more than name, held an inner door against the invasion of undesirables and the law, was a thug's den than which New York knew no worse. Debauchery and crime, unbridled and unlicensed, held sway there. None entered save the initiated—or those the initiated lured there to fleece and work their will upon. Likewise, it was a refuge from the law, and, as a refuge, was without its peer. Mickey the Cobbler might not be a very good cobbler or a past master of his art, but he was a cheery sort and always paid his bills, and never overcharged the poverty-stricken neighbourhood that innocently believed it supported him with its patronage! So why should it not be safe? Mickey the Cobbler stood high in the estimation of the community, and therefore brought no suspicion upon himself from the police.

Jimmie Dale shrugged his shoulders. What did it matter? There were dozens of places like that—and he had been in and out of dozens of them since he had left Mother Margot at Hip Foo's a few hours ago. What did it matter the degree of pest hole from which he had just come? In so far as he was concerned it had yielded him nothing, and in that respect it was like all the rest. His search tonight had been doubly fruitless because he had had a double errand. He had found no trace of Bunty Myers on his own account, or of English Steve on Mother Margot's.

Again he shrugged his shoulders. He had about given the latter up. As a matter of fact, it had only been secondary in any case. And yet he had kept faith with Mother Margot. He had visited English Steve's lodging house, and he had visited the known haunts of the gang that now held English Steve's life forfeit—and all this before even he had widened his search to embrace the secret pest holes of Crimeland such as the one he had just left. And he had been rewarded only by failure everywhere.

He could go on, of course, and he would go on until dawn broke, prompted by the prime urge to find Bunty Myers; but now, for the moment, the weariness of it all seemed to be creeping back upon him again, and this time not without its physical as well as its mental demands for at least a measure of consideration. His eyes roved down the street. At the corner, drawn up to the curb, there was a lunch wagon. He was tired and hungry. A whimsical little smile touched his lips. What could be better? A lunch wagon and Smarlinghue, unkempt, ragged, dissolute in appearance, went well and in perfect harmony one with the other!

Jimmie Dale turned abruptly, and walked to the corner. Here he climbed the three wooden, abbreviated steps that permitted entrance to the antiquated vehicle, and sidled up to the counter.

The lunch wagon for the moment was without customers. The proprietor, rousing himself from a doze, laid a mug of hot coffee and a sandwich on the counter at Jimmie Dale's mumbled request, slid a pot of mustard in the general direction of the sandwich, and subsided again into semi-unconsciousness upon some amazingly existent resting place in the crowded space behind the counter.

Jimmie Dale stared around him, and, as he ate, a sort of ironic facetiousness settled upon him. A picture of the St. James Club, with its polished silver and its snowy napery, rose before his mind's eye. Here he was Smarlinghue; there he was Jimmie Dale, the millionaire. He was almost beginning to wonder which of the two was his real, actual entity. Jimmie Dale; Smarlinghue—the Gray Seal! If it were ever known! His eyes fastened on the ungraceful proprietor, whose white coat was long overdue at the washtub, and whose white cook's hat was limp and grease spotted. It seemed a far cry to the white-haired, immaculate, perfectly trained Jason, his own butler, who, too, sometimes served him with coffee and sandwiches!

His mind mulled on. He kept staring about him. It was strange! The place somehow seemed familiar. Well, why shouldn't it? He had been in a lunch wagon before. Not this one probably, but there wasn't much difference in the genus lunch wagon, was there? No, that wasn't it! It seemed rather to be striving to revive a memory that somehow had to do with—

Yes, he had it now! English Steve! But that was years ago—back in the days when he, Jimmie Dale, was Larry the Bat in the underworld instead of the Smarlinghue of today. It was in a lunch wagon just like this. English Steve had been there, and two or three others of like ilk. They had adjourned to English Steve's room for a game of cards, and he, Jimmie Dale, as Larry the Bat, had accepted the invitation to join them. Well, what of it? That wasn't where English Steve lived now. English Steve had gone up in his profession since he had lived in what was little better than a shed behind old Michael's ship-chandler's shop. And he, Jimmie Dale, had already been to English Steve's more pretentious, if still seedy, quarters of today.

Strange, the stirring of that memory! What was it trying to suggest? That English Steve still—It was absurd, of course! That was years ago. It was the last place in all New York that anyone would look for English Steve today. The last place that anyone would—

Jimmie Dale's fingers fumbled in his pockets, and extracted a coin. He laid it on the counter, mumbled again at the proprietor—this time, a good-night—and shuffled his way out to the street.

The *last* place! The phrase battered at his mind now. If that were so, it was the *one* place to look! And why was it so absurd? There was more than one man in New York who maintained two establishments, and on a far more extensive scale, without publishing the fact broadcast! English Steve was a crook of no mean order, and such an arrangement might well have stood him in good stead more than once in respect of the police, and, for that matter, with his erstwhile associates—as it perhaps was serving him now at this minute. With his increasing prominence, his rise in the sordid realm of crime, English Steve had publicly moved into a more "exclusive" neighbourhood among the élite of Crimeland; but it might well be that he had continued to pay rent for his former lodging—without anyone being the wiser for it save old Michael, his landlord, whose shop was stocked with merchandise which consisted mainly of ships' stores and fittings purloined by the wharf rats along the river front! Birds of a feather!

It was worth putting to the test, at least. Certainly it was a tangible, definite objective—something he had not had before all night. He hurried now, twisting and turning through alleyways and narrow, darkened streets, until finally he had worked his way into a neighbourhood down near the East River shore.

The buildings were fewer here, more scattered; there was a generous sprinkling of vacant lots; few lights, and no pedestrians. He halted at last in front of a low, squat, dingy building, with large double doors and a grimy, unwashed show window, through which latter, from the rays of a distant street lamp, was just discernible a display of miscellaneous second-hand ships' fittings—a heap of tarpaulin, ropes, blocks, tackles and other articles of like nature. This was old Michael's. If the man had another name, he, Jimmie

Dale, did not know what it was. There was only one old Michael on the East Side, and that was enough.

The place was in darkness. It stood detached, unprotected by either fence or enclosure, and Jimmie Dale now made his way rapidly around to the rear. Here a sort of extension, in the shape of an exaggerated lean-to, projected out from the back of the building. It was here that in the days gone by, a miserable, barely weather-proof hole, English Steve had made his home. And here, too, as in front, the place was in utter darkness.

Jimmie Dale stepped to the door, and knocked softly upon it. There was no answer. He knocked louder, insistently. There was still no response. And then he smiled a little ironically at himself. He had come quite a long way—and quite probably on a fool's errand. Certainly English Steve did not appear either to be at home or in hiding here!

He stood at the door for a moment frowning. He had begun to doubt very much now that English Steve had ever cast eyes on the place again from the day he had taken up his quarters nearer the Bowery; but mere doubt did not in any way disprove the theory that, somehow, back there in the lunch wagon, had suddenly taken possession of him. English Steve might very well be absent at this precise moment—and might very well at the same time still be old Michael's tenant.

Jimmie Dale's jaws snapped suddenly together. He had come quite far enough to make it worth while to find out that much anyhow! He tried the door. It was locked, of course.

From one of the upright pockets in the leather girdle beneath his threadbare vest, Jimmie Dale drew out a little blued-steel pick-lock, and from another a diminutive, though none the less powerful, flashlight. For a moment the trained fingers worked swiftly at the lock, then the door swung open, and Jimmie Dale stepped inside.

He closed the door quietly behind him, and for an instant stood still, listening; then the white ray of the flashlight lanced suddenly through the blackness, darting here and there over walls and floor.

A smile crept grimly to Jimmie Dale's lips. English Steve for the moment might not be at home; but he, Jimmie Dale, or his intuition, or what had seemed perhaps a far-fetched deduction from a memory of years gone by, or whatever else one might call it, had after all not been at fault. English Steve still lived here—when it suited English Steve to do so!

The room was in no way changed since the night he had played cards here with English Steve. Even the man's clothes were strewn about, here across a chair, there even on the floor. An empty beer bottle, and beside it a slab of cheese and a portion of a loaf of bread, stood upon the table. But it was not these proofs of occupancy that caused Jimmie Dale's smile to tighten now. *They* might belong to anybody. The flashlight was holding steadily on a large, half-page photograph, cut from a Sunday supplement, that was tacked on the wall. He remembered it very well because English Steve while still sober that night had pointed it out with pride, and thereafter when not so sober had pointed it out another dozen times. It was a treasured possession of English Steve, and whatever else English Steve might have left behind him had he vacated the place for good, he most certainly would not have left that. It did not amount to much; it was utterly valueless; but to English Steve it had been, and still was obviously, a source of intense, if somewhat childish, gratification. It was a photograph intended to demonstrate the extent of a record crowd at a race course somewhere, and in the foreground, perhaps the most prominent figure of all, the photographer by chance had snapped the heavy black-moustached, rather rakish-looking figure of English Steve.

Jimmie Dale leaned back against the table in the centre of the room. Well, that was settled, and for such satisfaction as the establishment of his theory afforded him his trip had had its reward. But what was he to do now? Wait here for English Steve's return? English Steve might return in an hour, or in two days from now—or *never*, if Mother Margot was right, and English Steve fell into whatever trap was set for him tonight! On the other hand, to resume a blind search through the underworld again seemed to offer no greater likelihood of finding the man than was presented by the possibility of English Steve returning here. Indeed if the man were keeping under cover, as seemed more than probable, since, after hours of search, he, Jimmie Dale, had been able to find not a single trace of the other, then the chance that right here was where English Steve might be met with sooner than anywhere else was not without its logical argument. And yet—

The flashlight was still circling inquisitively about the room. Jimmie Dale's eyes followed the ray abstractedly. It passed across the open doorway of an inner room. There had been a cot in there, he remembered—English Steve's bedroom.

Mechanically he moved forward in that direction from the table; and then suddenly, with a low, sharp cry, as the flashlight shot forward into the inner room, he halted, hard-faced, staring ahead of him across the threshold. He had been right in his theory, doubly right, for the search ended here; and Mother Margot had been right, and her fears had been only too well justified! Sprawled across the floor, his head in a dark, crimson pool, lay the body of English Steve.

For the fraction of a second, no more, Jimmie Dale remained motionless, and then he was across the threshold and on his knees beside the other. Yes, the man was dead. Jimmie Dale turned a little then, and the flashlight circled swiftly in all directions about him. There was no weapon—only the bullet hole in English Steve's right temple. The end of the search, the warning that Mother Margot had tried to give, had come too late. English Steve had been murdered.

So the gang had had their way, had they? It was dirty, miserable work, crook though English Steve might be! Jimmie Dale's jaws were clamped now, as he leaned forward again and drew a paper, already protruding as though it had half dropped out when the man had fallen, from the inside pocket of English Steve's coat. It was a folded sheet of foolscap size. He opened it out, his flashlight playing upon it. In the folds was a small newspaper clipping; while the paper itself was covered with a rough design, or plan, as of some interior.

He stared in a perplexed way at the clipping for a moment. It had been cut from the middle of a paragraph, and contained only one complete sentence; but from the sentence itself, and the fragments of context that preceded and followed, it was obviously the report of some jewellery auction. He read it once—and again:

> unusually good value. The pendant was finally knocked down to Mr. Max Linesthal after spirited bidding for four thousand, three hundred and eighty-five dollars. A cluster ring set with the

From the clipping Jimmie Dale looked again at the roughly drawn sketch, then his eyes reverted to the still form on the floor. A minute, two, passed as he stood there. Something seemed to tighten in Jimmie Dale's throat.

"Poor devil!" he whispered—and thrust the clipping and paper abruptly into his own pocket.

He turned away then, and began a rapid search of the two rooms.

Still another ten minutes passed, and then Jimmie Dale stepped out into the night again, locked the door behind him, and, hurrying now, headed back into the East Side.

CHAPTER 17
A DEVIL'S ALIBI

Jimmie Dale's face was drawn in sharp, set lines, as he went swiftly along. In a sense the brutal, sordid affair was clear enough. The clipping spoke for itself; there had been an auction sale of jewellery, and Max Linesthal had brought in a pendant worth roughly four thousand dollars. The drawing was probably a sketch of old man Linesthal's place. Jimmie Dale nodded his head sharply. Everybody knew Linesthal. Max Linesthal was a prominent, if somewhat eccentric figure on the East Side, who lived alone in a combined office and dwelling that consisted of the ground floor of a small, two-story house on a cross street within a block of the Bowery. The old man, sometimes on his own account, sometimes acting for private interests on commission, or even for the bigger jewellers who for very justifiable business reasons did not wish to appear at the auctions, was a large and well-known buyer of second-hand jewellery of the better sort.

This was quite plain, and the inference from it seemed equally so. English Steve had seen the account of the auction, knew that a valuable pendant was in Linesthal's possession, and had in some way managed to obtain the information that had enabled him to make a rough, working sketch of the old jeweller's flat. Following out the inference to its logical conclusion, therefore, English Steve either had already robbed Max Linesthal of the pendant, or had proposed to do so before the night was out.

A puzzled light for an instant crept into Jimmie Dale's dark eyes. What was the *date* of the clipping? It might be a week old; the auction might have been held days ago! He shook his head impatiently, as though irritated at his own momentary stupidity. It was nothing of the sort; or, if it was, then what he had found in English Steve's pocket meant nothing at all. No robbery of any such nature as that could be committed without its being known everywhere in the underworld at least within a short time after the police were on the scene. Therefore, unless the robbery had been committed yesterday, or the day before, or a week ago, which it most certainly had not, since nothing was known of it in the underworld, the clipping, to have any present significance, must almost certainly have been cut from a paper of very recent date, for English Steve would realise that there was no guarantee, rather the opposite in fact, that Max Linesthal would keep the pendant in his possession for any length of time before he disposed of it again.

The whole thing narrowed down then to two suppositions: English Steve had not yet carried out his plans when he was shot down, presumably, by the gang; or he had already committed the robbery just previous to his murder and the pendant was then, at that time, either in his immediate possession or hidden somewhere, probably in his rooms. But he, Jimmie Dale, had searched and had found nothing. It might still be there, still craftily hidden, of course; but if not, and the robbery *had* been committed, then the alternative seemed blatantly obvious. The gang, sworn to English Steve's destruction, had found the pendant in their victim's possession, and taken it—that was all.

Jimmie Dale went on, traversing block after block. And now a whimsical smile brought a softer expression to his face. Those papers were damning evidence, and he had appropriated them without right or reason! He shrugged his shoulders. Perhaps! It had been impulse. He admitted that; but it was not an impulse that he regretted, or would undo now if he could. If it had been only an *intended* robbery, one that had not known fruition, there was sorrow and shame enough for someone—perhaps a mother; perhaps an old father; certainly someone who loved even English Steve—without needlessly adding to a measure already so miserably full. There would be time enough for those papers to come into the hands of the police if they were needed to point the way to a more thorough search of English Steve's rooms than he, Jimmie Dale, had made; or failing that, to English Steve's erstwhile gang and present murderers in whose possession the pendant then must be.

The softer expression vanished, and there came again a troubled look into Jimmie Dale's face. There was still another angle to the affair, one he did not like. If the robbery *had* been committed, it must have taken place, say, quite a little while before midnight in order to have allowed English Steve time enough for its actual accomplishment, the time to get back from Max Linesthal's to old Michael's, and, on top of that, the time to account for what had then occurred in his own rooms. That, then, would be long before he, Jimmie Dale, had started out from the lunch wagon, and had anything come to the ears of the police up to that time, it would as certainly have been known in the resorts. And there had been not even a whisper of it. Why then had not Max Linesthal sent out an alarm, or, rather—*what had happened to Max Linesthal?* Jimmie Dale shook his head again. No; that was putting it in its worst phase. English Steve would not have hesitated at anything in the nature of violence perhaps, if, for instance, he had been caught in the act; but it was far more likely that his work would have been done so secretly and successfully that it had not even now been discovered. And yet, at a fairly early hour of night, before possibly the old jeweller had even gone to bed, to break in, blow a safe, and—

Jimmie Dale shrugged his shoulders. The answer lay at Max Linesthal's. He was going there now—he smiled grimly to himself—via the lane and the back door, secretively, like a thief himself. It would hardly do for Smarlinghue to present himself at the front door, and, if Max Linesthal responded to the summons, inquire if a robbery had been perpetrated! It would be even worse, if a robbery and perhaps violence to Max Linesthal had taken place, should Smarlinghue have been seen in or near the house. And that was the vital question. He could not morally side-step it. The old jeweller lived alone. Had Max Linesthal come to any harm?

Jimmie Dale's pace slowed now suddenly to one of almost hesitancy. He was very near the place now; it was just around the corner. Perhaps it would be safer if, even by the back door, instead of Smarlinghue, it was Jimmie Dale who went! But it was quite a little distance from here to the Sanctuary where through one door Smarlinghue could enter, and through the French window on the squalid courtyard, and thence to the lane, Jimmie Dale could emerge. No! It would take too much time to go to the Sanctuary; and, besides, it could serve no real purpose. He did not propose to be seen—or heard. If nothing had happened in Max Linesthal's place yet, nothing would happen now since English Steve was dead, and he, Jimmie Dale, would leave as unostentatiously as he entered; if, on the other hand, the break had been made, he would leave with equal unostentatiousness and the police in some way, anonymously, could be notified. Even as Smarlinghue then, well known as Smarlinghue was in that neighbourhood, he was quite safe.

He slipped suddenly into the mouth of a lane that opened beside him. The slouching gait was gone now. He was running swiftly, silently, in the darkness. There was no question of locating Max Linesthal's back yard. His years of Larry the Bat in the old Sanctuary, of Smarlinghue in the new, where his life had literally depended upon it, had taught him every inch of the network of lanes and alleyways in this section of the East Side.

And now, with a lithe spring Jimmie Dale was over a fence, and in another instant, running across the yard, was crouched before a door that opened almost on a level with the ground. There was no light anywhere. He could hear no sound—save the distant rumble of the elevated from the direction of the Bowery. And then the slim, sensitive fingers of Jimmie Dale, no less deft or agile for the grime and uncared-for appearance that was theirs as an integral part of Smarlinghue, were at work again with the little pick-lock.

The door opened, closed—without a sound. Jimmie Dale stood inside. It was as though a shadow of but a moment ago outside in the darkness and silence had moved—and vanished.

But it was not dark here in the narrow hallway. A little ahead, a faint light showed through from a partially open doorway. Nor was it silent. Voices reached him, though the words themselves were not distinguishable.

Jimmie Dale stood for an instant motionless. What did it mean? A mare's nest? A late visitor? Something equally commonplace? The sketch in his pocket reproduced itself in a mental picture before his eyes. The four rooms from front to rear each had a door opening into the one next to it, and each had a door opening on this narrow passage here. The room ahead from which the light came was the second one from the front, the room that showed the safe marked on the plan. There had been no light showing as he had come along the lane, of course, because the rooms were on the opposite side of the house, and there were apparently no windows in the hallway here.

What did it mean? If nothing had happened, nothing would happen since English Steve was dead. His mind insisted on reiterating that statement. What was it, then? An ordinary, perhaps business, visitor; or the aftermath of the robbery in the shape of the presence of the police?

He stole forward cautiously, without sound, hugging the wall. The voices grew more distinct. And then, back against the wall, himself unseen, protected both by the angle at which he stood and the angle of the partially opened door, he stood staring into the lighted room.

Reality! Strange how that thought had obsessed him all night. Well, at least, this wasn't reality—or else his reason was in collapse, his sanity a gibing mockery. The room was evidently used by Max Linesthal as a bedroom, even though he kept his safe there, for the bed was there too, and Max Linesthal in his nightclothes sat lashed, a prisoner in a chair. He could understand that; but after that he was either mad or it was all a myth. A man was kneeling at the safe. He knew the man; he knew him quite well. He had even been with him that evening, had even left him not more than half an hour ago—only he had left the man lying dead upon the floor of a miserable shack with a bullet hole through his right temple, and it was the dead man who was kneeling there now at the safe. The man at the safe was English Steve.

Brain and vision now both seemed blurred. Jimmie Dale hung there. He was trying to fight his way out of some mental morass, wasn't he? The man was dead, and he was lying in a pool of blood miles away, and yet he was here, moving, yes, and speaking, just as though he were alive.

"Come on, now! Come across!" the man snapped at the bound figure in the chair. "You know what'll happen if you don't! You know me, don't you? You've seen me often enough around these parts."

"Yes, I—I know you." Max Linesthal was an old man; and it was perhaps only the cords that held him from collapsing in his chair, for his face was deathlike in its fear. "You—you're English Steve."

"Bull's-eye!" snapped the man at the safe again. "Well, that ought to be enough to teach you what's good for your health. You get just one minute. Take your choice. If I have to blow the safe, I might as well set you up against it for the pad! Get me? Now then, what's the combination? Quick!" He reached out and gave a sudden, vicious wrench at the leg of the chair.

"I—I'll tell you," the old man cried out hoarsely. "Wait! I—I'll tell you. It's twenty-eight and a half left, nineteen—"

Jimmie Dale was not listening. Was he *really* mad? Yes, perhaps; but whether the man was dead or not, he was robbing the safe. And he, Jimmie Dale, could do nothing! He was Smarlinghue. To interfere with any crook's work was to bring the enmity of the underworld down upon the offender. It was the law of the underworld. It would destroy Smarlinghue. Better that Linesthal should lose his jewels—a thousand times better. Smarlinghue was the one chance he, Jimmie Dale, had to find the Phantom, the one chance he had to stand between the woman that he loved and the death that threatened her. With the doors of the underworld once closed against Smarlinghue, there was no—

Slowly, as though the act were almost subconscious, his hand crept now toward his pocket, crept into it, snuggled around the butt of his automatic, and, snuggling, tightened suddenly in a fierce, convulsive grip. The safe was open now, and the man kneeling there had his back to Linesthal in the chair, his side face to the door. He was ransacking the interior of the safe. Books and papers were being flung on the floor. A diamond pendant glistened in the light. It was laid on the table beside the safe. There were other jewels. They began to make a glittering little heap. But it was curious, strangely curious that the heavy black moustache should suddenly have seemed to sag down at one side; strange that the man should be taking the time now to pause in his work to twirl at it like some sophisticated dandy! No—it was off! And now the man was carefully readjusting it.

Through Jimmie Dale's veins, as though some floodgates were suddenly rent asunder, his blood was racing now in a wild, mad, surging tide. Laroque! It was Gentleman Laroque, alias *the Phantom!* The master of impersonation! Yes, he understood now! There was no madness in his brain. He understood! It was hellish in its cunning—a devil's alibi. The Phantom, if he were not entirely playing a lone hand through lack of trust in his erstwhile tools and pawns, was at least playing the major rôle. A safe rôle! *His alibi was a dead man!*

Swift as lightning flashes Jimmie Dale's mind worked now. Yes, he understood. It was the Phantom, not the gang, who had murdered English Steve. It was the Phantom, not English Steve, who had taken that clipping from the paper, made that sketch, and placed them in the dead man's pocket. Max Linesthal would be robbed, and would swear that it was English Steve—the Phantom had but a moment gone taken care to make doubly sure of that point—then English Steve would be found murdered; the police would attribute the murder without an instant's hesitation to the gang who had boasted everywhere that they would take English Steve's life; and to the gang, too, having failed to find the jewels elsewhere, would be attributed, even as he, Jimmie Dale, had thought might be the case, the possession of the proceeds of the robbery from Max Linesthal's safe. That was why the robbery was being pulled here now in so open and bare-faced a manner, intentionally so, as part of the plan, an integral, vital part of the plan—to establish the alibi that English Steve could never now refute!

The room seemed to swim before Jimmie Dale's eyes—*red*. Smarlinghue! What did it matter now if Smarlinghue were seen, if Smarlinghue lived or died, so that this inhuman fiend found his end too at the same time! That was what Smarlinghue existed for—the final reckoning—the end. And it was here now. There was the man he had sought through days and nights of ceaseless, torturing effort. The Phantom! Primal, elemental, his soul itself seemed stripped of all else but a blind, savage—

What was that? The doorbell, wasn't it? The doorbell in two quick, short rings! Jimmie Dale, about to step forward into the other room, his automatic already flung forward, instinctively held motionless for an instant—and in that instant he saw the Phantom leap to his feet, and whirl to the electric-light switch just beside the safe. There was a *click*. The house was in utter blackness.

But Jimmie Dale was in action now. A signal, of course, those two rings! Why? From whom? But it didn't matter now. Nothing mattered save to come to grips with the Phantom in there. It was pitch black, but he knew what the other's next move would be as well as though the room were still alight.

With a bound, Jimmie Dale was through the doorway and into the room. The table—those jewels! They were what the Phantom had come here for—and signal or no signal, be its meaning what it might, the Phantom would not leave without them if he could help it.

Jimmie Dale brought up against the table with a crash. His hand swept swiftly across its top, and as he brushed the jewels to the floor, to safety, a hand, groping it seemed, touched his—and was instantly drawn away before he could grasp it.

A snarl came out of the darkness on the other side of the table. A cry of terror rang out from the old man lashed in the chair. And then a blinding flash, the roar of a revolver shot, as the Phantom fired—and missed.

And Jimmie Dale laughed now, laughed with the tongue flame of the shot still hot upon his cheek, and, hurling the table out of the way, he flung himself forward again. He could not see. He could only spring straight for the spot where the shot had come from. He could not fire in return—he might hit the old man in the chair.

His fingers closed, gripped at a sleeve, tightened, and his other hand, with clubbed automatic, swung upward in a fierce, short-arm jab. And his soul cried out in joy as he felt the blow go home.

There was a sharp cry of pain; then a sudden, furious wrench that tore the sleeve from Jimmie Dale's grasp—and then the sound, deadened now, almost lost in Max Linesthal's terrified cries, of a step racing across the floor.

Jimmie Dale's jaws clamped hard together. To use his flashlight was to offer himself as a target that would not be missed a second time. But the man was making for the door, of course. Jimmie Dale leaped back in the darkness across the room—too late! The door slammed. He heard it locked. He heard the footsteps racing down the little hallway toward the back entrance.

But if there was no time to unlock this one, there was still another door—the connecting door from this room into the next, and from there into the hall. His flashlight now! It gleamed as he wrenched it from his pocket and ran to the connecting door. Was this, too, locked! Strange, those scattered jewels on the floor; that uncouth creature in a nightgown lashed in a chair and screaming in fright! He wrenched again at the door. No, it was not locked; but it was badly warped, and it stuck. His shoulder, all his body weight, went against it. It gave now, almost bursting from its hinges.

Jimmie Dale lunged through. It had cost him time; time enough, he was afraid, to allow the Phantom to get away across the yard, and— Yes! He had gained the rear door himself now. No one was in sight. But it was dark, damnably dark, and—What was that noise? It seemed to be a commotion of some sort going on in the street out in front of the house. The neighbours must have heard the old jeweller's screams. He was still screaming. Well, it didn't matter what it was! There was still a chance. The Phantom could not yet be very far away, and he must have gone by the lane.

Jimmie Dale was running now. In an instant he had crossed the yard; and then, as he poised to swing himself over the fence, he drew suddenly back instead, and crouched down in the shadows. Someone was climbing over the fence *from* the lane not ten yards away from where he stood. A voice, muffled, gruff, reached him:

"Look out for that damned nail, sergeant!"

The police! A form, silhouetted against the night, showed on the top of the fence for a moment, then dropped to the ground. It was followed by another. Jimmie Dale crouched closer in against the fence in the shadows. He gnawed his lip now in bitter chagrin. He was not afraid of being discovered, it was far too dark for that; but he knew that with this further delay any hope of finding the Phantom again was definitely at an end.

The two men were joined by a third. They crossed the yard, and disappeared inside the house.

Cautiously now, Jimmie Dale moved farther on along the side of the fence away from the house. With the Phantom gone, it became purely a question of self-preservation now. Smarlinghue found here by the police and subjected to a search, held perhaps until the make-up, worn off in a police cell, disclosed Jimmie Dale, was but little more pleasant to contemplate than was the present realisation of the Phantom's escape!

Well, it should be safe enough here. He was at the far end of the yard now; and silently, quickly, he swung himself over the fence into the lane. He broke into a run, swerved into an alleyway that crossed the lane some fifty yards farther on, and, following this, finally emerged on a cross street a block away from the old jeweller's house.

There was a certain strange, abnormally cold composure upon him now; a sort of philosophical acceptance of the fact that the Phantom had got away. But his mind was probing, sifting, searching for the answer that would explain the direct cause of the Phantom's escape, leaving him, Jimmie Dale, victor only to the extent of having saved for the old jeweller the contents of his safe. Who was it who had given that signal, which, so evidently now, had been a warning that the police were at hand? And how did it happen that the police had known anything about what was going on in Max Linesthal's? It wasn't the shot or Max Linesthal's screams—there hadn't been any disturbance up to the time the doorbell had rung!

Jimmie Dale, shuffling along, as Smarlinghue always shuffled, went up the block, turned the corner of the street on which Max Linesthal's house stood—and as though suddenly attracted by the little crowd that had gathered in front of the old jeweller's, made his way forward in that direction. He reached the fringe of the crowd as a man in the uniform of a police lieutenant, jumping from a car, pushed his way unceremoniously through the rather tough-looking aggregation on the sidewalk, and halted before a policeman who stood on duty at the door. Jimmie Dale's eyes narrowed for an instant. That was Klinger, a lieutenant in the precinct. It might be worth while!

Jimmie Dale, as Smarlinghue, was apparently actuated now by no other motive than an ill-mannered, morbid curiosity that prompted him to secure the best vantage point that he could, for, as he wormed and elbowed his way nearer the lieutenant, his mouth was agape, breathless with interest, in a sort of senile way.

He caught the lieutenant's quick flung question to the officer at the door:

"Did you get him, Lynch?"

"No, sir," the man answered.

"You didn't! How's that? That woman, whoever she was, handed us a fake tip over the phone, then?"

Smarlinghue's ragged form edged still closer to the two officers, as though his curiosity were now beyond the bounds of restraint, as though he were not only utterly oblivious to, but quite innocent of the impropriety of standing there with blear, blinking eyes and gaping mouth, greedily drinking in a conversation by no means intended for his ears. The woman, whoever she was! It was the Tocsin, then, who had sent the warning to the police. It couldn't have been anyone else.

"No, sir," the man addressed as Lynch answered. "It was straight enough, only there was an outside worker on the job, I guess. Anyway, just as we got to the corner over there and started to cross the street, a man ran up to Linesthal's door here, and then beat it like blazes down the street, and got away."

"Did you get a look at him? Know who he was?"

"We aren't sure," Lynch replied. "But O'Grady said he thought it looked like the Kitten."

The Kitten! Jimmie Dale was fumbling with his battered hat. The crowd, as it jostled, had suddenly pushed him none too gently against the police lieutenant's elbow.

Lieutenant Klinger swung sharply around.

"Send this damned mob about their business!" he snapped at the policeman. "And maybe it wouldn't be a bad idea to run in one or two of them while you're at it. Some of 'em look as though they were due for it!" He stared suddenly into Jimmie Dale's face. "You, eh, Smarlinghue? Hop-fighting, I suppose! What the hell are you doing around here?"

"Me?" Smarlinghue circled his lips with his tongue. "I—I ain't doing nothing," he mumbled—and shrinking back through the crowd, and casting furtive glances over his shoulder in the direction of the police lieutenant while the crowd laughed, Smarlinghue scurried hurriedly down the street.

CHAPTER 18
THE VOICE

It was like the glow of a firefly. It flitted here and there, lancing its tiny stabs of light indefatigably through the darkness. From somewhere without, in the distance, muffled, there came faintly the rumbling of wheels, the clatter of a horse's hoofs on the pavement. There was no other sound.

Jimmie Dale rose from his hands and knees, and, with the diminutive flashlight switched off now, stood staring around him in the darkness. Under the black silk mask his forehead furrowed. This was one of Mother Margot's rooms—the room from which the Phantom had so mysteriously disappeared on that first night. He had searched here before—more than once—in an effort to discover the secret of the Phantom's disappearance. But he had never found anything. Tonight, because he had never been satisfied with his previous efforts, and because he had now been afforded a better opportunity of searching the place than ever before, he had returned to it again. He had been at it for two hours now. And still he had found nothing.

Both Mother Margot and the Tocsin had warned him to beware of the place—that it was a trap. Both had warned him that the Phantom asked nothing better than to lure him here. He shook his head. That might well have been true of a month ago, when, in the guise of Isaac Shiftel, alias Gentleman Laroque, the Phantom's unaccountable disappearance from this room before his, Jimmie Dale's, eyes, might naturally have been relied upon to bring him back without loss of time in the hope of getting at the bottom of the mystery. But not today. It was too long ago now. If, as a trap, it had not proved effective almost immediately after it was baited, the Phantom, from the standpoint of pure logic, must long since have given over any hope of it ever proving effective as a trap at all.

Jimmie Dale smiled grimly. He had, in spite of warnings, invaded the place almost immediately after that night—and he had not been able to find even a trap, let alone the secret of the Phantom's disappearance! Nor was Mother Margot in the secret. He was convinced of that. True, she had been installed here by the Phantom when the latter had been forced to vacate the premises after the police raid, and she had obviously been installed here for the purpose of keeping any stranger from renting the rooms, and therefore, by her occupancy, of safeguarding that secret for the Phantom, but of its nature he was sure she was ignorant. He doubted, indeed, if the Phantom trusted anyone to that extent!

But, in any case, Mother Margot was away tonight. And so tonight's conditions offered him the opportunity for a search that, prolong it as he chose, was almost guaranteed against any interruption, or, as he felt confident now, any risk of the place proving a trap. Mother Margot was away. He did not know where she was. It did not matter. Presumably there was devil's work afoot again tonight, and she was engaged in her share of it. He only knew that for the first time since she had succeeded the Phantom as the tenant of these rooms, she had absented herself from her usual haunts. As Smarlinghue, who at her request had haunted the dens and dives of the underworld for one English Steve last night, he had been free, without risk of bringing any suspicion upon the character of "Smarlinghue," to seek her out openly at her pushcart—which covered her real activities—on Thompson Street that morning. But she had not been there. She had, however, in view of what had transpired the previous night, obviously expected him, for he had found a message waiting for him with an old Italian who had his cart next to hers.

"You Smarly?" the old Italian had said. "Margot go away one, two day—come back."

Through the darkness Jimmie Dale stared around him, his brows still knitted. The best opportunity he had ever had of searching these rooms had been his tonight, and he had seized it, but was there any use in continuing the search? He had the rest of the night before him, for that matter, if he chose to devote it to that purpose—but was it worth while? He had covered every inch of the floor, every inch of the walls up to a reasonable height, and his search had gone utterly unrewarded. He had been minute, painstaking, exact, thorough to a degree, and he had found nothing. Was there any use in going all over it again?

He half turned away toward the door, but halted again. There was a secret here—even if he had never been able to find it. There was a clue here— even if so far it had proved but a phantom clue. That fact would not down. He hesitated an instant, and then, with a shrug of his shoulders, moved softly halfway across the room. Well, once more, then!

He began to reconstruct again the scene of that first night—here in this room, the inner one of the two that Mother Margot now occupied. It was exactly here he had stood when Isaac Shiftel, stripped of his disguise, had suddenly turned off the light and in the ensuing darkness had vanished, as that trite saying had it, into thin air. The man could not have gone by the door, because there was only one door, and he, Jimmie Dale, had been blocking the doorway; nor could the man have gone by the single window, because at that time the police had been on guard in the alleyway outside. Through the wall or the floor then? Yes. But how? Where? Neither wall nor floor showed any—

Out of the darkness, without warning, there came suddenly a low, ugly laugh.

"The Gray Seal!" said a voice.

In an instant, strained and tense, his automatic whipped from his pocket and outflung before him, Jimmie Dale drew back against the wall. A trap after all! The trap he had so logically proven to have outlived its usefulness! He strained his eyes through the blackness. Nothing! He could see nothing.

Nor was there any further sound. A minute passed. Was it a minute—or some vast, immeasurable æon of time? He stood rigid, motionless—waiting.

"Where?" said a voice abruptly.

Jimmie Dale turned his head; his automatic swung swiftly. The voice seemed to have come almost from his elbow. Then his jaws locked hard together. No; it was not from there! They were playing with him, were they? A cat-and-mouse game! Well then, he—

A voice spoke again:

"Worth anywhere from thirty to fifty thousand. Easy money."

Jimmie Dale pushed back his hat, and above his mask flirted away a bead of sweat from his forehead. He understood now. There wasn't anyone in the room save himself. It wasn't a trap. It was only uncanny. He was simply listening to snatches of a conversation that came from the nowhere, out of the darkness.

He leaned forward a little, striving to the utmost to *place* the direction of the sounds. The voices, he realised now, while quite distinct, had been curiously heavy and uneven. He nodded sharply to himself. A pipe, a hollow space, almost anything might act as a conductor for the sound waves, and bring them here from no little distance at that!

Once more a voice broke through the stillness:

"Easy money, yes; but old Twisty Munn's no fool, and neither is Kid Gregg. The stuff will be pinched by now, but we've plenty of time left—enough to see that there are no mistakes made."

Again there came the low, ugly laugh.

"There won't be any! One o'clock at Twisty's—"

The voice ended as abruptly as though, if speaking over a telephone, the wire had been suddenly cut. There seemed to Jimmie Dale no other way to describe it. He stared around him in a helpless way. Now the voices had seemed to come from here, now from there. His lips twisted in grim self-mockery. The longer he had listened the more confusing it had become. The voices simply came from *everywhere* in the room.

Had they ended now?

The tiny glow of the flashlight played for an instant on the crystal of his watch. It was fourteen minutes past twelve.

Noiselessly now Jimmie Dale moved across the room to a chair. The sort of finality with which that last sentence had been broken off held out little hope, he felt intuitively, of his hearing anything more. But there was a chance. He sat down quietly. Strange! Where had the voices come from? From below, above—where? He did not know. He knew only that *one* of those voices must be the Phantom's. It did not require proof. It was axiomatic. He could not locate the direction from which the voices had come, but the opening through which the Phantom had once vanished from this room was obviously the medium through which the voices entered. How cleverly deduced! He snapped at himself mentally. The only trouble was that after prolonged and laborious search he had not been able to locate that opening either!

His fingers played softly in a curiously caressing way over his automatic. It hadn't been any trap. The allusion to the Gray Seal that had so startled him had been only a snatch of the conversation which had at first, through some cause or other that he was unable to define, reached him only in broken fragments. Or perhaps, after all, it was a trap—the other way around. A trap for the trapper! If he could not locate the voices here, it might not possibly be so difficult to do so at, say, one Twisty Munn's—at one o'clock!

He sat there in the darkness listening, his mind at work. One of the voices had been the Phantom's, that was beyond question or doubt; but which one of the two it was he did not know. He could, he was certain, have recognised Gentleman Laroque's, alias the Phantom's, voice anywhere under ordinary circumstances, but here, due unquestionably to the mysterious way in which the sound waves had been transmitted, all sense of inflexion had been lost. Nor did the conversation itself, as he went over it again in his mind, help to differentiate in that respect one speaker from the other. Either one of the two, from what had been said, might have been the Phantom.

Twisty Munn's at one o'clock! He smiled grimly. One of the two voices at least, possibly both of them, would be at Twisty Munn's at one o'clock. Well, if nothing further eventuated here, he, too, would be at Twisty Munn's at that hour. His search, the hours he had spent here, had perhaps not been so fruitless after all! It was an even chance at least that, in spite of the continued silence in this room now, he would hear *the* voice again tonight. And if he did—

His face hardened suddenly. Last night he had held the Phantom at his mercy, last night he could have shot to kill before the man had even been aware of his presence; and last night, because he had failed to realise that it was a Thing blood-flecked with murder, a Thing that preyed upon every decency in life, and not a human being, the Phantom had escaped. Last night this had happened. *There would be no second time.* There was another life at stake—hers—the Tocsin's. Last night he had jeopardised that life because he had not fought the Phantom with the Phantom's own weapons, but all that was now at an end.

And as he sat there listening, and there was still no further sound, he found himself strangely, abnormally calm, strangely callous even, as though this decision were but commonplace and one of everyday occurrence. He asked now only for one more meeting with the Phantom. Where, or how, it did not matter. Just once more!

The minutes passed. The tiny flashlight winked again through the darkness and lighted up the dial of Jimmie Dale's watch.

It was twenty-five minutes of one.

Jimmie Dale stood up. There was evidently nothing more to be heard here, or if there was, and he waited any longer, then the chance of hearing anything at Twisty Munn's must go by the board—and as a choice between the two he very much inclined toward Twisty Munn's now. He moved softly through the connecting doorway, and traversed the adjoining room that opened on the hall. Here, the door opened and closed silently behind him, and Jimmie Dale, lost in the darkness of the unlighted hallway, reached the rear door of the tenement, and stepped out into a small back yard. A moment more, and he was over the fence, and, slipping his mask from his face, was running noiselessly along a lane.

Two blocks away he emerged upon a dingy, ill-lighted and uninviting street. He smiled a little whimsically, as he pulled his soft felt hat somewhat rakishly to one side and well down over his eyes, and, hunching the perfectly fitting dinner coat at one of the shoulders, turned up the collar around his neck. True, the costume was hardly *de rigueur* in the East Side, but he was Jimmie Dale, not Smarlinghue, tonight. He shrugged his shoulders. Well, did it matter? He was not on his way to attend any *public* function, and as for the streets there were always the shadows of the buildings to hug a little closer, always a loose, slouching gait to assume.

Twisty Munn! Kid Gregg! What was the game these two were playing tonight? He shook his head impatiently. That did not matter either. It mattered only that the Phantom was concerned in their movements. It was common knowledge in the underworld that Twisty Munn was a "buyer" for a certain class of apparently honest establishments, where, if the alibi were good enough, stolen goods, disguised of course, were offered over the counters to the public at prices well in excess of what could be obtained through the underground channels employed by the regular "fences." It was profitable for all concerned, even taking into account the commission charged by the crafty Twisty Munn, who lived apparently—for the benefit of the police—in a condition approaching almost abject poverty in a squalid, ill-furnished room at the top of a seedy and somewhat questionable tenement over in the direction of the East River. Kid Gregg, less known save by the inner circle of the underworld, which latter had already marked him for preferment, was a young and budding crook, still outside the ken of the police, who showed exceeding promise in the profession he had chosen. In a word, neither of them had ever had any dealings or were in any way connected with Gentleman Laroque's, alias the Phantom's gang.

Jimmie Dale's dark eyes narrowed grimly as he went along. The conclusion was somewhat obvious. The Phantom was by no means averse to plucking the plums ripened by someone else, and it was fairly evident that in some way or another he had got wind of one that had been ripened by Twisty Munn and Kid Gregg. It looked very much therefore as though the night were likely to develop into a three-cornered game, counting in himself, Jimmie Dale, with the added possibility that the trumps perhaps might be in the hand that neither Twisty Munn nor Kid Gregg in the first place, nor the Phantom in the second, suspected!

Jimmie Dale covered block after block at a swinging stride. His mind reverted to Mother Margot's rooms. It was strange where those voices had come from! He could not tear the building down to find out. He had already known there was a secret exit from that room. The voices in that respect had not proved anything further. His mind mulled on. A search of the rooms adjacent to Mother Margot's offered no prospect of help in the solution of the problem. If the room itself, where he *knew* the secret exit to be, was so apparently search proof, what better chance would any other room offer? Or why, as a matter of fact, should the secret exit even lead into any other room? Well, the cellar then, for the Phantom could not have gone up through the roof! There was no cellar! The ground floor was a sort of basement in itself! Those voices—

Cycles! He was beginning all over again. He shook his head in self-exasperation, and with a mental effort dismissed these thoughts from his mind. He had almost reached his destination, and the immediate present demanded his full attention.

Under a street lamp he looked at his watch. Twelve minutes to one. He nodded. He was well on time. Just ahead of him was the three-story tenement where Twisty Munn made his home.

CHAPTER 19
JACKALS

The street was deserted. The tenement itself was dark. Not a light showed from any window. But Twisty Munn lived in an upstairs room at the rear, therefore the fact that no light could be seen from the street had no bearing whatever on Twisty Munn.

Jimmie Dale stepped suddenly into the doorway. The door itself, the entrance common to heaven alone knew how many who hived in wretchedness and squalor within, and to whom a latchkey would have been not far removed from mockery, was unlocked as he had expected. He moved noiselessly into the hall. The place was close and dank to the nostrils; also it reeked with the odour of garlic. It was dark, too; but through the murk he could just make out the stairs ahead of him and to the left.

There was a curious tightening of Jimmie Dale's lips as he moved forward and tested the tread of the first stair cautiously. Yes, he knew the breed! Old and in disrepair, the stairs would certainly shriek their protest to high heaven if any liberty were taken with them. But it was Jimmie Dale of the old days, Jimmie Dale of the days of Larry the Bat and the rickety stairs of the old Sanctuary, worse even than these stairs were, where his life had literally depended upon his silence a score of times, as he went upward now.

He gained the first landing. There were doors around him here, and, because they were flimsy doors and flimsy partitions, from behind them the night sounds reached him—the restless movement of a sleeper, the sick, querulous cry of a child, a stertorous snore.

Twelve minutes of one! Ten now, wasn't it?

There were three flights. At the third landing Jimmie Dale paused for an instant to adjust the black silk mask over his face again, then stole forward, feeling out with his hand along the wall, toward a thin, irregular thread of light that seeped out from under the ill-fitting threshold of a door at the rear end of the hall. Twisty Munn, at least, was evidently keeping the rendezvous!

Faintly, no more than a murmur, voices reached Jimmie Dale from the other side of the door now as he stood before it. And now a pick-lock in his hand was silently at work. Perhaps half a minute passed. Then, by the barest fraction of an inch at a time, the doorknob turned without sound under the slim, trained, sensitive fingers, and the door opened by a crack. The murmur from within became distinct, disintegrated itself into words and sentences.

"...Sure, de goods is all right, but wot about de rest of it? De guys I have to slip dese over to ain't takin' chances, not if youse handed 'em de stuff for nothin' an' paid 'em for takin' it."

The door opened another crack. Twisty Munn and Kid Gregg! Yes, that was what the voice in Mother Margot's room had said. Jimmie Dale could just see the two. They were at a table in the upper corner of the room. His eyes narrowed. There was what looked like a small fortune in the shape of jewellery on the table between them. Twisty Munn! The stoop-shouldered, almost hunch-backed form of the shabby old man was bent forward over the table, while his thin, hooked fingers clawed at the jewels, picking up one after the other to hold it close to short-sighted, squinting eyes. And opposite him Kid Gregg, young, in an over-loud checked suit, a peaked cap pulled so low over his forehead as almost to hide the small, roving black eyes, scowled in evident impatience.

"Aw, it's sewed up—tight!" the latter snapped. "Ain't I told youse dat?"

"Sure, youse told me dat," agreed the old man sharply. "Two days ago youse told me youse had it all fixed for tonight, an' dat everythin' was safe, an' dat youse'd bring me de sparklers. Well, dat's all right, youse've brought 'em. an' dey're all right; but I ain't heard yet how safe dey are, an' dat's wot puts de deal across wid de crowd I works for. See?"

A cigarette dangled from Kid Gregg's upper lip. With the tip of his tongue he deftly transferred it to the corner of his mouth.

"Well, den, listen!" he grinned complacently. "Some job, Twisty; an' all me own—see? I used to know a guy dat worked for old Froomes up on de Avenue, an' he was forever shootin' off his face about de sparklers de family wore. Well, a month ago I gets a job dere myself—taken on regular. Get me? Polishin' de hardwood floors, an' keepin' de windows of de mansion washed. Ah, say, it was soft! I hadn't been dere a week before I knew where de combination of de safe was kept in a drawer in de library right alongside de safe itself—so's Mrs. Froomes wouldn't have to walk far to get it!"

Kid Gregg chuckled, and sucking at his cigarette only to find it out, began to search through his pockets for a match.

Jimmie Dale stared. Froomes! It was Martin K. Froomes, of course, the retired broker. He knew Froomes very well indeed, and on several "stag" occasions had been in Froomes' house; and Froomes knew him—as Jimmie Dale, a fellow member of the St. James Club. So that was where that haul of jewellery on the table there had come from! What was it the voice in Mother Margot's room had said?—"anywhere from thirty to fifty thousand." He could well believe it. Froomes was an exceedingly wealthy man, and, besides a wife, had two daughters who moved constantly in society.

"Go on!" prompted Twisty Munn impatiently.

"Watch me!" boasted Kid Gregg. "I could have made de pinch anytime, but den I'd have had to make me get-away, an' duck outer little old New York. I wasn't for dat—not some! I've still got me job polishin' de floors, an' tomorrow mornin' I'll be polishin' 'em de same as though nothin' had happened. See? Some day de bulls may write up me autobeeography an' keep me photograph handy to look at w'en dey wants to see somethin' handsome—but not if I sees 'em first! Nix on dat stuff! So far I'm a nice, quiet, hard-working young man. Get me? Well, dere ain't no hurry, an' I sits tight, keepin' me lamps open lookin' for goats. An' I don't have to wait long, neither. One day I was out on a window sill washin' de window, an' I hears de boss in de next room handin' out a Sunday school spiel like he was talkin' to a naughty son. 'From a business standpoint,' says de old man, 'dis has nearly lost youse yer job here, an' no man ever made anythin' out of himself on that basis. An' from a moral standpoint,' he says, 'it's simply de road dat leads from bad to worse.'"

Jimmie Dale, an ominous droop at the corners of his mouth, dared another half inch of door space, as Kid Gregg paused for a moment to drag on his cigarette. Was there a wall switch for that single, dangling incandescent that lighted the room? Yes, there it was—just inside the door. He could almost have reached in and touched it from where he stood.

"Well, dat's all I heard," went on Kid Gregg; "but, take it from me, I watches to see who comes outer dat room. Say, can youse beat it! It's a little red-headed dude named Culver, dat's a typewriter, or secretary, or somethin' like dat to de boss. After dat, dere's nothin' to it. Culver's de bird I'm after, an' I gets his number for fair. Some high-roller wid his dinkey shirts an' his imitation diamond shirt studs! He don't live dere wid de boss, y'understand, but he dresses up every night like he owned a bank, an' hits de high spots on de first speed. Youse knows de kind, don't youse?"

Twisty Munn was twining the long, bony fingers of his hands in and out of the heap of brooches, pins, rings and pendants in front of him, seemingly fascinated by the fiery little gleams of light that he made to flash from their countless facets.

"Up de river," observed Twisty Munn, "dere's a whole cageful of dem birds dat dress up *all* de time—only dey don't sport de shirt studs any more. I get youse! Wot did youse do wid *Mister* Culver?"

Kid Gregg indulged in a fresh cigarette. There was a smirk of unabashed conceit upon his face, as he blew a smoke ring in the air.

"Him? He's down at Hoy Loo's."

Twisty Munn leaned suddenly across the table.

"Wot's dat?" he demanded tensely. "Hoy Loo's?"

"Youse said it!" nodded Kid Gregg complacently. "He's gone bye-bye down at Hoy Loo's wid a nice little pipe of coke laid out beside de bunk."

Twisty Munn squinted blear eyes at the other.

"I don't get youse!" he grunted after a moment. "Dat don't stick nothin' on him. I don't get youse!"

Kid Gregg smiled pityingly.

"Dat's why youse won't never be nothin' more dan youse are today, Twisty," he murmured; "just runnin' around an' doin' de dirty work. It's de bean dat counts."

"Youse close yer face!" snapped Twisty Munn. "Go on, an' spill de rest of it."

"All right," grinned Kid Gregg. "I fixed it up for tonight, after I'd tipped off another guy I knows to make up wid Culver about a week ago. Me pal plays de game. Savvy? He chums up wid Culver, an' promises to show Culver some of de *real* goods around town. Youse gets it now, don't youse? Tonight de two of dem goes to Hoy Loo's, an' dey starts in wid a drink, an' Culver gets a pill slipped into his, an' den he's laid out peaceful on a bunk just as though he'd got stewed on too many pipes. Soft, eh? He'll be dere tomorrow mornin'. He don't know who me pal is because somehow me pal ain't got a good memory even for his own name; an' besides, bein' dolled up for de occasion wid a little waxed moustache an' a cute little beard, youse'd have taken him for a French Count—which he ain't. Well, de bulls get Mister Culver dere in de mornin'—an' Hoy Loo gets a piece of de money youse're goin' to hand out 'cause he's got to stand for a police fine."

Kid Gregg paused and grinned at Twisty Munn, as the latter puckered the leathery skin of his forehead into wrinkles.

"Never mind about de bean stuff dis time," said Twisty Munn gruffly. "I ain't wise yet, but I'll say it begins to listen good. How'd youse hang it onto him?"

"De easiest thing youse know," said the Kid cheerfully. "A letter—dat's wot. Dere's a letter in de mail now dat de police gets in de mornin', just about de same time dat de family on de Avenue wakes up an' t'rows a fit w'en dey finds de safe open an' de sparklers gone. De letter just says dat mabbe de police'd like to know dat a guy blew into Hoy Foo's tonight, an' got stewed to de eyes hittin' de pipe, an' got frisked of a bagful of rings an' jewels an' stuff by some yeggs dat was floatin' around dere. An' it's signed: 'A Friend.' I guess dat's all to de mustard, ain't it? Dat takes care of de missin' goods! De bulls slip over dere, an' dey finds it's me red-headed friend Culver, de typewriter expert for Mr. Froomes dat owns de safe dat's been cracked."

Twisty Munn blinked.

"Dat's all right," he said judicially; "but it don't actually prove he pulled de job. If he was frisked, which he wasn't, den—"

"Sure, he was frisked!" said Kid Gregg with a vicious grin. "All dis happened before I went up to de nabob's house an hour ago. Dat was midnight, y'understand, an' de Froomes bunch was all in bed. I wasn't takin' no chances. He was frisked, all right!" The Kid with studied effect blew another smoke ring in the air. "I frisked him—of one of dose near-diamond shirt studs of his dat youse can buy from de hawkers at three for a nickel!"

Enlightenment was dawning on Twisty Munn's wily countenance.

"Say dat again!" he whispered hoarsely.

"Sure!" said Kid Gregg. "Dat's wot! D'youse know of anythin' dat's easier to lose widout youse bein' wise to it dan a shirt stud dat falls out w'en youse're pawin' over de stuff in a safe youse've cracked? Dat's where it is now—on de floor up dere in de Froomes' library under some papers dat was yanked out of de safe."

For a moment Twisty Munn stared at his companion, then his long, bony hand shot out across the table.

"Youse'll go a long way, Kid! Shake!" he cackled admiringly. "Take it from me, youse will—a long way!"

"Youse bet yer life—an' nothin' but dust behind me!" agreed Kid Gregg boastfully. "Youse said somethin', Twisty!"

"S'help me!" gulped Twisty Munn. His fingers clawed the jewels on the table again. "As sweet a haul as ever I've seen, an' open an' shut—open an' shut!" He pushed the heap suddenly toward Kid Gregg. "Put 'em back in dat little sack," he gloated. "I'll take 'em. Kid—dere's big money in dis all round."

Under his mask a dull red had suffused Jimmie Dale's cheeks; subconsciously almost his hand had crept into his pocket, and his fingers had closed around the stock of his automatic. It was brutal work; miserable, inhuman work. A shirt stud, three for a nickel—and five, ten, fifteen years, the best of a man's life, behind the drear walls and the steel bars of Sing Sing. Was it possible that men like these two lived, festering God's green earth! His automatic came from his pocket. They were stuffing the jewels into a small canvas bag now. Well, the game wasn't finished yet; there was still another hand to play! The little sack would prove a convenient receptacle. It ought not to take but a moment more before *all* the jewels were inside, and—

Jimmie Dale drew suddenly back from the doorway. Had he *forgotten?* In the natural sweep of anger, in the hot-blooded fury that the scene in there had brought him, had he forgotten—those voices in Mother Margot's rooms! What was that now? A creak upon the stairs? Yes, he was sure of it! Another! One o'clock! It must be after one o'clock. Someone was coming!

Every faculty alert, he crouched back now—farther back, away from the door, where he was lost in the darkness of the hall. Yes, there was someone almost at the head of the stairs now, coming stealthily, almost without sound—only once in a while a faint, protesting squeak from a stair tread that would not be audible inside Twisty Munn's room. Those jewels, Twisty Munn, Kid Gregg were the lesser issue now. It was the Phantom who had brought him here, the hope that the Phantom would come himself in person.

Tense, silent, Jimmie Dale crouched there. The Phantom! If it were the Phantom in any one of the characters that he, Jimmie Dale, could recognise, there would be no failure this time such as there had been last night! Whoever passed from the hall into that room would stand out, if only for an instant, clearly defined in the lighted doorway—and an instant would be enough!

A second passed—still another. A dark form bulked at the head of the stairs. It was joined by another. Two of them, then! And now there was no sound—yet the two dark forms there moved. They came on down the hall like wavering, intangible shapes that seemed almost like brain hallucinations in the darkness.

Outflung before him, Jimmie Dale's automatic held a bead on the doorway. They had stopped there now, stopped in that thin crack of light that seeped out through the inch of open door that he himself had left. And the face of one came into the light. Bunty Myers! It was not the Phantom; it was Bunty Myers, the Phantom's unholy chief-of-staff! But *both* of the men could not be the Phantom. The other! Who was the other?

A whisper came. A revolver barrel glinted in the light-thread. Jimmie Dale strained forward. The other! Just a glimpse of the man's face! There could be no disguise that would blind his eyes to Gentleman Laroque, the *real* man, any longer; no disguise however clever that could—

The door crashed inward, a wave of light flooded out into the hall, and the two forms at the door leaped forward into the room. But, for the single instant Jimmie Dale had asked, the light had shone on the second man's face—and upon Jimmie Dale there surged a sense of bitter disappointment that seemed to engulf him, seemed to hold him momentarily stunned. Neither was the second man the Phantom; it was only the Kitten, one of the gang that used to rendezvous in the back upstairs room of Wally Kerrigan's "club."

The Kitten who only last night had—Well, he might have known! It was the Phantom's way. It was the Phantom and Bunty Myers he had heard talking—he knew that now—but the Phantom had left the actual work, as he had done a score of times before, to his tools and pawns.

His mind seemed strangely numbed. He stared into the room. Two men had just leaped through that lighted doorway. It was like some scene flashing upon a cinema screen, wasn't it? Shirt studs, three for a nickel—and the best of a man's life behind the bars of Sing Sing! He shook himself free as from some clogging mental weight. Yes, that was what it meant, whether Bunty Myers or Kid Gregg came off the victor—and there wasn't any other issue now because the Phantom wasn't here.

He crept forward to the door. Old Twisty Munn was cringing in a corner, twining his claw-like fingers in and out of each other, licking at his lips, his face gray with fear. On the table stood the little canvas bag, tied now with a string at the top—and behind the table, Kid Gregg, a cigarette still dangling from his upper lip, had risen from his chair, and was staring with an inane smile into the muzzle of Bunty Myers' revolver a yard or so away.

"Put up your hands!" snarled Bunty Myers.

"Sure!" smiled Kid Gregg; and—the revolver in his hand previously hidden by the edge of the table—whipped up the weapon and fired.

It was answered by almost simultaneous reports as Bunty Myers and the Kitten fired together; it was answered by a scream of terror from Twisty Munn—and then the crash of the overturned table as Kid Gregg spun half around like a spent top and pitched against it.

But Jimmie Dale, too, was in action now. From the edge of the door jamb his hand shot forward, closed upon the electric-light switch, and the room was in darkness. And the next instant he had flung himself forward across the room. The little canvas bag! He had marked the exact spot on the floor where it had fallen from the table. Queer, this scuffling of feet around him; savage oaths; snarls of confusion; doors opening somewhere below in the tenement; the creak of stairs, and— Yes, here it was! His hand closed upon the bag and thrust it into his pocket. He turned and sprang for the doorway again. Something blocked his way, struck at him viciously, clutched at his clothing. He struck back with a short-arm jab, tore himself free, and lunged forward again.

A revolver flash lanced through the blackness behind him—another. Twisty Munn still screamed in terror. And a bedlam seemed loosed now throughout the tenement. But Jimmie Dale had gained the door.

He slammed it shut behind him, and, springing for the stairs, took them three and four at a jump. A man holding a candle, peering upward from the landing below, blocked his way for an instant—and went down before Jimmie Dale's rush.

Two more flights to go! Doors opened. Frightened faces were thrust out. There came the cries of children—and then from above the pound of feet, racing as madly as his own down the upper stairs.

Jimmie Dale laughed strangely to himself. That would be Bunty Myers and the Kitten, but they mattered nothing now. There had been murder above, Kid Gregg was dead, and their one concern would be to hunt cover without loss of time, because if they were known to Twisty Munn they were in desperate case indeed!

He was not concerned with any pursuit from Bunty Myers or the Kitten. It was a question only of what margin he himself had before the uproar here would have brought the police upon the scene. It was the shouts and yells that pursued him from the awakened and terrified occupants of the tenement wherein lay his real source of danger.

A minute! That was all he asked. The margin of a minute! He risked a leap of almost half the length of the lower stairs, stumbled at the bottom, recovered himself, jumped for the front door, wrenched it open and dashed out. The street was still empty. Thank God! He ran like a deer for the corner, gained it, doubled at the next one, and then dropped into an nonchalant walk.

CHAPTER 20

AT A QUARTER TO THREE

He was safe now. He laughed shortly, without mirth. Safe! Yes, for the moment—but the night wasn't ended yet. He laboured under no delusions on that score. The rendezvous at Twisty's, instead of the hoped-for meeting with the Phantom, had left him with the heritage of a little canvas bag whose physical contents became but a handful of miserable, worthless baubles compared with the potentialities it held for a long-term penitentiary sentence for an innocent man. Nothing that had transpired at Twisty Munn's had changed by one iota the vile, low, cunning trap that Kid Gregg had laid for his victim—and had now paid for with his own life. The police would receive the letter; the police would find that shirt stud at the scene of the robbery, find this young fool Culver at Hoy Loo's, and find in Culver's shirt that a stud was missing from amongst its fellows.

Jimmie Dale's face darkened now, as he turned at the next street and headed over in the direction of the Bowery. Young fool! Yes, that was it! Why should he take any further risk? He did not know Culver. He knew nothing about Culver except that he had a red head, and was evidently somewhat of a bounder who probably very richly deserved what—No; he knew more than that. He knew that Culver was *innocent*.

And then a smile came to Jimmie Dale's lips, a half whimsical, half troubled smile. Yes, of course! It was inevitable! He knew that. He had known it all along. Why else had he taken the risk of snatching up that little bag in Twisty Munn's room? Well, then?

Hoy Loo's? He shook his head. He would find nothing there but a limp, red-headed boy, drugged into unconsciousness. He could do nothing with Culver; for, even if he managed to get Culver out of and away from the dope joint, there still remained the one outstanding, damning piece of evidence in the shape of that shirt stud in the library of the Froomes' home. Neither would Culver's removal from Hoy Loo's offset the letter that the police would receive simply because they did not find the boy there, for they would find that Culver *had* been there, had spent most of the night there. Equally, there were no means of intercepting that letter.

There was only one alternative. Jimmie Dale shrugged his shoulders, and again the whimsical smile broke across his lips. It was perhaps a fortunate thing for Culver that he, Jimmie Dale, was not red-headed too!

He hurried on now, breaking at times almost into a run. There was only one way, and—yes—he saw that way clearly enough now. It remained merely a question of whether by any chance the robbery at the Froomes' mansion would be discovered before he could act. It was not likely, since Kid Gregg had said the household had all retired by midnight; but it nevertheless left the matter of time an unknown factor whose latent possibilities were by no means to be ignored. Well, he would lose no time!

Near the Bowery, in an all-night café, he entered the telephone booth. He gave the number of his residence on Riverside Drive, and as he waited for the connection into his dark eyes, strangely, there crept a softer light. Old Jason would answer the phone. Faithful old Jason, butler to the father, more than butler to the son! Despite injunctions, despite the nights, many and many of them, when he, Jimmie Dale, did not return at all, Jason would even now probably be maintaining his self-appointed vigil in the armchair in the vestibule waiting for his Master Jim—and almost certainly asleep! Jason was an old man, and nature was stronger than the flesh. Well, it was Jason's way, a rather splendid way, a way of great devotion. Strange? No—not strange! It was just Jason. Jason knew perhaps too little or too much; enough, in any case, so that the old man lived in constant anxiety anent the safety of his Master Jim, and—

"Yes! Hello! That you, Jason?" said Jimmie Dale quickly.

"Yes, sir—Master Jim, sir," the old man answered.

"Listen, Jason!" said Jimmie Dale. "Rouse up Benson, and send him down here with the light car as fast as he can make it. Tell him the Palace—he knows where that is."

"Yes, sir; at once," Jason replied; and then, a curious hesitancy, a curious yearning, in his voice: "Is there any—anything else, Master Jim, sir?"

"Yes!" said Jimmie Dale sharply. "You've been sitting up again, Jason!" Jimmie Dale's smile belied the severity of his tone. How many times had he used exactly the same words to Jason—and with probably the same effect! "Go to bed, Jason! Good-night!"

"Yes, sir, Master Jim," said Jason. "Good-night, sir."

Jimmie Dale hung up the receiver and went out into the street again, making for the Bowery now, and walking in an uptown direction. It would save time to meet Benson by part of the way. By the time he walked to the Palace Saloon, Benson should have about reached there too.

He began a mental calculation as he went along. Say, twenty-five minutes for Benson to get downtown, then another twenty for himself, Jimmie Dale, to reach his objective on Fifth Avenue, still another twenty for the work there was to do, and, yes, that was pretty close figuring, though it gave Benson, who was far safer away from the car and would have to walk, a leeway of twenty minutes. Allow an extra ten minutes, then, as a factor of safety. That made seventy-five minutes—an hour and a quarter. He looked at his watch. It was exactly half-past one. That would bring it, then, to a quarter to three.

He nodded. A quarter to three! He could depend on Benson literally to the extent of his life, and indeed had done so on more than one occasion; Benson as a chauffeur was almost on the same plane with Jason as a butler. As he had remarked many times before, there was perhaps no man in New York who was served as he was—and it was not a service of money. Rare thing? Yes! But it was true. It *did* exist in the world. Thank God for it!

Jimmie Dale walked briskly. He reached the corner in front of the Palace Saloon that he had given his chauffeur as a rendezvous. Benson had not yet arrived. Consulting his watch, Jimmie Dale waited a minute, and then taking out a little notebook began to write rapidly under the rays of the street lamp. This, too, would save time—or, at least, preserve the schedule. It would save the two or three minutes necessary to give Benson verbal instructions, though he could, of course, taken Benson along with him in the car since their roads would lie in the same direction for part of the way, but he had definitely decided against that. If anything went amiss, it would be infinitely better for Benson that there should be no possibility of the two of them having been seen *together* in the car. He owed that to Benson. It was quite another matter that Benson, obeying orders, should have turned the car over to his employer here where he had been instructed to do so.

He tore the leaf from his notebook and folded it carefully. There was one minute left for Benson to make the rendezvous on the timetable set for— Yes, here he was now!

A car drew up at the curb. Benson's clean-cut, strong young face showed in the light as he touched his cap.

"Good work, Benson!" said Jimmie Dale approvingly. "What time is it?"

Benson leaned forward to consult the car's clock.

"By your *watch*, Benson," said Jimmie Dale. He held his own in his hand.

Benson looked at his wrist watch.

"Five minutes of two, sir," he said.

"Right!" said Jimmie Dale. He motioned Benson from the car. "I'll take the car, Benson." And then, as he swung into the driver's seat, he leaned out and handed Benson the folded note. "Follow these instructions to the letter, Benson," he said quietly. "And *destroy* that note. Good-night."

The car turned and headed uptown. Jimmie Dale drove fast. The streets were deserted. The minutes passed—ten, fifteen, eighteen. He kept glancing at the time—and nodded as he finally parked his car on a side street within half a block of one of the most exclusive residential sections of Fifth Avenue. He had taken nineteen minutes from the Palace Saloon.

The black silk mask covered his face again, as he stole forward now and slipped into an areaway that ran in the rear of the corner house on the Avenue. The rest would be slower work. This was Martin K. Froomes' residence.

It was moonlight; light enough to see. There was a high fence here that flanked both sides of what was evidently a garage. Jimmie Dale swung himself over the fence, and alighted in a small, cement-floored courtyard. He was across this in an instant, and in another was lost in the shadows of a basement entrance.

Again the little steel pick-lock was at work. The door opened and closed—silently. Jimmie Dale stood inside. For a moment he listened; and then, the diminutive flashlight in service again, darting its tiny gleams before him, Jimmie Dale moved forward once more, and, locating the stairs, began to climb them—and a moment later found himself standing in the main hall of the house.

So far, all was well! The library now—no, first, the telephone! He must make sure that his memory had served him right on that score. He had been here once or twice before—under quite different auspices!—as a guest. The flashlight's ray played down the hall. Yes, it was all right! It was there on a little stand in an alcove near the foot of the central staircase. He could hardly have forgotten that rather unique door, shaped in a half circle, which at will could transform the alcove into a booth!

Jimmie Dale turned now. He was not quite so sure of the library, but the impression was strong that it was here at the rear. He tried a door on his right. The dining room. He stepped back then into the hall, and opened a door on the opposite side. The flashlight circled the interior, went out—and Jimmie Dale closed the door softly behind him.

His lips, beneath the mask, tightened now, as the flashlight, playing again through the darkness, focused on an open safe near the window at the rear of the room, and upon what had evidently been a very large proportion of the contents of the safe which were now strewn about on the floor in front of it. He stepped forward quickly, and kneeling on the floor began to search carefully beneath the litter of documents, papers and books. A minute, two, three, went by—and then Jimmie Dale stood up again. Between his fingers he held a cheap and tawdry shirt stud.

He stood looking at it for a moment, balancing it now in his hand. And a softer light crept into his eyes, and a strange smile tempered the grimness of his tightened lips. No, it wasn't worth much, just a rhinestone—just ten years in the penitentiary, that was all!

And then Jimmie Dale shrugged his shoulders. The margin of time was narrowing. He slipped the shirt stud into his pocket, and sent the flashlight's ray playing inquisitively around the room. There was still the letter that the police would receive in the morning, and which must be made to disprove even itself, be made to stand out so glaringly as a plant to saddle a crime on an innocent man's shoulders that none could mistake it for what it was. And there was only one way to accomplish that!

His eyes followed the ray of the flashlight. Yes, that single bracket light over there would do when the time came. He could not afford to be too generous! And now the window. He walked over to it and raised the drawn shade. It looked out on the courtyard. Silently, cautiously, he opened the window wide. Ten feet to the ground. Well, it might be worse!

At a quarter to three! He returned to the centre of the room, and consulted his watch. He had not needed all of that extra ten minutes. He was four minutes to the good.

He stood there in the darkness. It was very silent in the house, and yet it was strange what noises even silence possessed if one listened for them. They began very low and grew louder, but always in a palpitating sort of way, and finally beat with almost thunderous clamour at the ear drums.

The flashlight was on the dial of the watch again. Seventeen minutes to three. Benson would be at work now. It would take a minute or two, of course. He smiled with grim whimsicality. It always did! He had allowed for that.

The flashlight held on the dial of the watch—and suddenly went out.

A quarter to three.

Faintly, from the front of the house, the telephone rang—and Jimmie Dale was in action. The side light went on, filling the room with a soft mellow glow. He stepped silently to the closed door, and with his ear to the panel listened. The telephone rang again—and still again. And then, barely audible on the thickly carpeted stairs, he caught the sound of a footstep descending.

And presently Jimmie Dale's lips twisted again in a grim smile. He could not hear, he did not have the receiver at his ear, but it was Benson speaking from a slot booth in the Grand Central station where, though they might eventually trace the call, they would never trace Benson. It was Benson speaking, but the words were his, Jimmie Dale's:

"I don't want to appear in this, so never mind who I am. I couldn't find a phone any nearer, so it's about ten minutes ago that I saw a man climb over your back fence and steal into your house. I guess if you've got such a thing as a safe there, you'll know where to find him; and if you're quiet enough about it you ought to get him yet."

That was what Benson was saying! It was quite all right. The call *would* be traced—but it would "hold water." The Grand Central was just about within a ten-minute range of the Froomes' residence.

Jimmie Dale's ear was still pressed against the door panel. The footstep was mounting the stairs now—but evidently with extreme caution, for Jimmie Dale could scarcely catch a sound. It was probably the butler. Reinforcements! He would return with Mr. Froomes, perhaps, and an added footman or two!

A minute—two! The cautious tread was coming *down* the stairs again.

Jimmie Dale retreated across the room to the open door of the safe. He crouched there, tense, his muscles rigid. In his hand now he held the little canvas sack of jewels, the string at the top untied. They were almost at the door there. And now—

The door burst open.

With a well simulated startled cry of alarm, Jimmie Dale jumped to the window side of the safe—and as he jumped he allowed his arm apparently to hit sharply against the top of the safe door and knock the canvas bag from his grasp, strewing the floor with a sparkling heap of gems. He was darting for the window now. A voice roared out to him to halt. Froomes! Froomes himself in dressing gown, and behind Froomes two other men. And for a bare instant Jimmie Dale faced them, then he vaulted for the window sill. They had seen him, hadn't they—quite plainly—seen that he wasn't Culver!

"Stop! Stop, or I'll fire!" Froomes yelled out.

But Jimmie Dale was astride the window sill now, and—a vivid flash like a fork of lightning seemed to leap toward him to sting and blister and bring him agony, and the room seemed to swirl and be full of deafening, racketing reports. He dropped to the ground outside, staggered, steadied himself, leaped across the courtyard, and swung the fence, as a fusillade of shots followed him from the window.

He was racing along the areaway now. Another instant, and he had flung himself into his car. It shot forward with a bound. He whipped off his mask, as he bent over the wheel. He was gnawing at his lips now until the blood came.

The car swung the corner and tore uptown. But it wouldn't steer properly. It swayed from side to side. No, it wasn't the car, it was himself. Something in his side tortured him, and something hot, sticky hot, was running down his leg. His head swam. Nausea strove to set its grip upon him. He fought it off. He had been hit, of course, but it wasn't far to go—not far to go—not far to go—and what—what was the matter? Everything was all right, wasn't it? They had seen the man who had tried to rob the safe and had left the jewels on the floor, hadn't they; and they knew it wasn't Culver because—it was extremely funny, wasn't it?—because Culver had a red head.

Giddiness, nausea, hot and cold flashes! Jimmie Dale fought frantically for his senses. He drove clinging to the wheel. It wasn't far. There wasn't any pursuit; they'd never find him—if—if he could hold out just a little longer.

A sort of mental fog settled upon him that blotted out time and distance; and action was purely mechanical—and then he found himself staggering up the steps of his home on Riverside Drive. And at the top of the steps the door opened. He brushed his hand across his eyes. That was Jason, wasn't it? Jason had been sitting up again!

"Go to bed, Jason!" said Jimmie Dale severely.

The old man's face was ashen.

"My God, Master Jim, sir, what's the matter?" he cried out wildly.

Jimmie Dale lunged through the doorway.

"Nothing," said Jimmie Dale. "I—I was just looking for a shirt stud. You know the kind, Jason, three for a nickel and—"

Jimmie Dale pitched f

CHAPTER 21

THE CALL OF THE NIGHT

A night light on the stand beside the bed glowed dimly, throwing curious little shadowy patterns on walls and ceilings. Jimmie Dale turned restlessly in the bed. His hand stole beneath his pajamas and mechanically, in a sort of tentative way, felt over his tightly bandaged side. There was a nervous disquiet upon him, growing with the minutes, obsessing him. He reached out to the bed table for his watch. Half past nine.

For a moment he lay still, tracing with his eyes the shadows' fanciful shapes on the ceiling; and then suddenly he flung the covers from him, got out of bed, snatched up a dressing gown, and crossed the room to an easy chair by the window. He sat down and stared out into the night.

Rest! Quiet! He could no longer rest, because his mind would no longer remain quiet but ground on and on like the turning of a mill wheel that never ceased. The first night—when he had been wounded and the loss of blood had weakened him—yes. But not now! Thank God, he had regained consciousness in time that night to prevent Jason telephoning for a doctor! With the papers full of the burglar in evening clothes who was believed to have been hit by a shot as he had leaped through the library window of the Froomes' mansion on Fifth Avenue, it would have been perhaps a little awkward for Jimmie Dale to explain a bullet wound in his side even to a trusted physician! It had been only a flesh wound. Jason and Benson between them had done famously with him here at home. It was healing now. That was three nights ago. It was still sore and stiff—he gritted his teeth as a twinge of pain caught him suddenly—but it was healing nicely.

He had not stayed in bed any more than he could help after the first day—when he could elude Jason's watchfulness. He had been afraid of that, more afraid of doing that than of the wound itself. One got weak staying in bed. One's legs needed exercise—and there had been the combined lengths of the dressing room and bedroom for surreptitious constitutionals!

Well, he had been well repaid for the wound; not merely in the sense that young Culver was probably walking the streets tonight a free man, but in the sense that there had come into his hands another clue, another instrument through which his chances of running the Phantom to earth became at once now definite, tangible and concrete. Bunty Myers, the rat-faced underling, the chief tool of the Phantom! It was Bunty Myers who had been talking to the Phantom that night when he, Jimmie Dale, had heard those voices which had seemed to come out of the nowhere in Mother Margot's room. Therefore Bunty Myers knew *where* that conversation had taken place; and therefore, whether the man himself realised the full significance of it or not, Bunty Myers held the secret of the phantom clue to the lair where his master hatched his devil's work.

Jimmie Dale nodded to himself. It was a decided, even drastic change from the Phantom's accustomed line of action. From the time the Phantom had physically disappeared as Gentleman Laroque, the man had drawn a veil of secrecy and seclusion about himself that had rarely been broken—certainly never to the extent of admitting anyone into the secret of his actual retreat before. True, he had many domiciles, many aliases. That was why the Tocsin had first called him the Phantom. But this was the *centre of the web*, the one place that he, Jimmie Dale, had sought and struggled vainly with every resource at his command to find. And now Bunty Myers had been admitted, if not into the secret itself, at least into the precincts of the hidden refuge. Why? Did it evidence weakness? The first cracking of the line of defence? It was certain that the Phantom's ranks had become sadly thinned. Little Sweeney, perhaps the most versatile and cunning of the Phantom satellites, was dead; and two out of the four trusted pawns who had had their rendezvous in the back upstairs room at Wally Kerrigan's "club," Spud MacGuire and Muller, were dead. The percentage was very heavy! There remained only Bunty Myers, the Kitten, and Mother Margot. The circle was narrowing. Was that why, where previously Mother Margot had always been called from the pushcart on Thompson Street to the telephone in the rear of that malodorous little second-hand store to act as the mouthpiece of the "Voice," where previously all communications had passed through her, the Phantom had now changed his tactics and admitted his tools to personal interviews?

A frown, half of perplexity, half of annoyance, gathered on Jimmie Dale's forehead. This might or might not be the reason. Very much more likely not! He had forgotten for the moment that Mother Margot had been away that night.

He brushed his hand across his eyes, as he winced suddenly again with pain. He wondered if Mother Margot were back yet. That was a curious telephone booth at the back of the second-hand store where she received her messages! A side door that opened on the lane—and the booth in a sort of back storeroom! He had, of course, investigated the place almost immediately after that night at Mrs. Kinsey's when Mother Margot had imparted her unwilling information about it, and the result of that investigation had been to make it plain that the telephone itself was purely a part, just as Mother Margot's rooms were, of the Phantom's equipment, and that Mezzo himself, who was a doddering, almost senile old man, was not even a pawn—merely a convenience. The old Italian, whose hearing was probably just good enough and no more to distinguish the ringing of the bell, whose trade was among a clientele far removed from such luxuries, could have no possible use for a telephone, let alone one in a booth, and less possible excuse for the expense that one involved. He was simply paid to keep it there. That was obvious. Well, it had served still another purpose—since he, Jimmie Dale, had not infrequently used it himself! The Phantom was not the only one who called Mother Margot to the phone, or the only one to whom the old hag paid allegiance! He smiled grimly. Perhaps he counted too much on that! Because he, Jimmie Dale, as the Gray Seal, had once caught Mother Margot in the act of double-crossing her own pals, it was no guarantee that, though he might hold her in a sort of allegiance therefrom, she would be above double-crossing him too!

He shook his head. No! He had watched her too closely. He was not prepared to say what she might do if she got the chance, but so far he was satisfied that she had played straight with him—only, so far, the little information she had had to give had not brought him much nearer to his goal.

His mind reverted to Bunty Myers. Bunty Myers had come out of the affair that night at Twisty Munn's when he had shot Kid Gregg without a breath of suspicion attaching to him. Again Jimmie Dale smiled grimly. He remembered that, as he had run down the stairs with the awakened tenement howling about his ears, the thought had flashed through his mind that if Twisty Munn had recognised Bunty Myers the latter would have the police drag-net sweeping the city, yes, and the country, for him, and he would be hard put to it to find cover. But, as it had turned out, whether Twisty Munn had really recognised Bunty Myers or not, Twisty Munn had remained silent on the subject. Yesterday's papers had been full of the affair. Twisty Munn was by nature an ingenious and versatile liar, and he had run true to form. Himself in the very act of receiving the stolen contents of Martin K. Froomes' safe when the shooting occurred, Twisty Munn had, of course, as an incentive for remaining silent the undesirability of implicating himself in a criminal transaction; and again, he might not actually have known who Bunty Myers was, or, if he had, the fear of reprisals if he snitched might also very logically account for his reticence. Twisty Munn, so Twisty Munn swore, knew absolutely nothing about the matter, except that he and Kid Gregg had been sitting in his room talking when the door had burst open and a couple of men he had never seen before had entered. Kid Gregg had jumped to his feet and pulled his gun, and just as he fired one of the others had dropped him. He, Twisty Munn, didn't know what it was all about, s'help him God! But he had a hunch it was a personal row between Kid Gregg and one of the other men over some moll or other.

Quite so! Into Jimmie Dale's dark eyes there came an ironical gleam. There was nothing to disprove it. Twisty Munn's story fitted into the balance of the night as perfectly as though it were the truth! Well, that left Bunty Myers free! That was what counted. It would be easier to find Bunty Myers now than if he had taken to cover from the police. And it was Bunty Myers that he, Jimmie Dale, wanted now!

And then Jimmie Dale shook his head again—in sudden irritation now. Had he forgotten too that since the night Little Sweeney had masqueraded as Isaac Shiftel and paid for it with his life, Bunty Myers had already sought cover, perhaps more as a precautionary measure than because he was actually "wanted" for that affair, but nevertheless had completely forsaken his usual haunts; and had he also forgotten a night not long ago when, as Smarlinghue, he had searched vainly through the length and breadth and in the most hidden places of the underworld for the man? He had wanted Bunty Myers then, hadn't he? And he had not found him.

The strong, square jaws locked with a snap. Yes! That was true! But he wanted the man *more* now, wanted him vitally. He would find him, that was all!

And then, what?

Jimmie Dale's laugh, short, hard, mirthless, rang low through the room. And then, what? The answer to that was simple. The buttons were off the foils. What Bunty Myers knew he would be *made* to tell. Bunty Myers wasn't tired of life, and if he found himself cornered by, say, the Gray Seal, and given the choice of telling where he had had that conversation with the Phantom or of paying the price of silence with his life, there was very little question as to what the man would do, for out of his own experience Bunty Myers would not credit the Gray Seal with trifling! Nor would there be any trifling. The knowledge Bunty Myers now possessed meant that the Phantom at last could be trapped; it meant that at last *her* life, the Tocsin's, could be made safe; that the nightmare of horror which must even now be turning her soul sick within her could be brought to an end; that sunshine could come, and love and the joy of living could be hers once more, and—

With a low cry, Jimmie Dale leaned suddenly with his elbows on the window sill, staring out into the blackness of the night. It seemed to be beckoning, calling to him.

She was out there somewhere.

Was she? Was he even certain that she was still alive? Something cold, an icy grip, seemed to clutch at his heart. Since the night at Miser Scroff's, true to her stated determination to keep him out of the shadows, as she called them, that enveloped her, that held her life in peril, he had had no word from her.

Jimmie Dale was gnawing at his lips now; his arms fell from the window sill, and his hands clenched at his sides. She had simply kept her word. That was what she had said she would do. Why then this sudden access that verged on panic? He laughed out shortly again. It wasn't sudden. It wasn't a new phase. It hadn't just at this moment germinated in his brain. It was what had been growing there ever since he had lain wounded in bed. It was the seat of that constant disquiet and restlessness that was culminating now in—What?

He was on his feet; and now he began to pace the room. To protect her life she had arrayed herself against the merciless cunning of the Phantom— not a man; a monster. There was no middle course between them. There was but one end. One of the two must fall. And the Phantom was still safe, still secure, still at his hell-born deviltries.

And she?

A bead of moisture oozed out on Jimmie Dale's forehead. He flirted it away with a sweep of his hand. It meant little that her silence was exactly in accordance with what she herself had stated was her proposed line of action. There was something that meant infinitely more. She might propose, but immeasurably true was the trite old saying applied to her that she could not always dispose! He, as Smarlinghue, as the Gray Seal, excluded from working in conjunction with her, had worked nevertheless in the days and weeks that were gone with identically the same end in view as she, working independently, had had—the unearthing of the Phantom. Why had their paths then, in spite of herself, not crossed since that night in Miser Scroff's room, save perhaps on the one occasion when he had *presumed* that the tip to the police in reference to the jewel robbery at Linesthal's had come from her? *He* had been in touch with the Phantom, with the Phantom's criminal efforts since then. And if she were still free, still alive, and making progress in her fight, how was it that she and he had not inevitably been brought into contact with each other?

His hands clenched tighter. And there was more even than that; one outstanding brutal thing, ugly in its promise, that brought him a deadly fear. She *had* made progress while she had been mistress of her actions; she had said so in her notes up to the time when those notes had ceased; her appearance at Miser Scroff's that night had proved that she had penetrated the Phantom's outer defences, and had had a certain foreknowledge of the man's proposed coups. Therefore the presumption was that, had all still been well with her, she would have had knowledge of what had happened three nights ago, and she would have known that he, Jimmie Dale, had been shot.

His brain seemed to whirl; the blood to pound in hammer beats at his temples. Not a sign had come from her, not a word over the telephone, not a message of any kind, direct or indirect. His mind, his soul, seemed to falter now before the ugly deduction that flung itself pitilessly at him. She loved him, as he loved her. He knew that. She loved him with a love so great and unselfish that daily, hourly she had faced alone the peril that menaced her so that he might not also be in danger, so that he might be sheltered from it. Would she then, if she knew he had been shot, and if she were able even with her last effort to communicate with him, have remained silent, made no attempt to discover how serious was his condition, or whether indeed he were alive or dead?

Alive or dead! The phrase battered at his brain. It applied to her. White-faced he stood at the window again, and stared out into the darkness. It was black! How black it was! And she was out there in the night somewhere—somewhere—alive or dead.

Inactive! His wound as an excuse! He swore savagely now in his emotion. What was he—a weakling! Too long he had stayed here now inactive when she—she was out there somewhere—perhaps dead. Something caught in his throat. His hands raised above his head and clenched until under the tightened skin the knuckles showed like knobs, bloodless, white.

If she were dead! He laughed! It was a merciless sound. He swung from the window and went into the dressing room. He began to dress. How should he dress? Tweeds or dinner clothes? That sounded as though his brain were unhinged. He wasn't going to a party! Foolish word that—party!

He began to get into his dinner clothes. He knew what he was doing now. There had been what Jason would have called a rush of blood to the head for an instant, blurring him a bit, as it were. His side wasn't so bad—a twinge or two—nothing to speak of. There was something else out there in the night—a clue to pick up somewhere. He didn't know how—or where. It might be as Smarlinghue, somewhere in one of the hidden sink-holes of the underworld, that he would pick up the trail of Bunty Myers, or Bunty Myers' pal, the Kitten; or, if Mother Margot were back—Well, it was as a man in a dinner coat and mask that Mother Margot knew the Gray Seal. He was dressing for Mother Margot. Quite the thing, wasn't it—to dress for the ladies?

Damn it! He must hold himself in! He stepped to the liqueur stand and poured himself out a little brandy, and drank it. He responded instantly to the stimulant. It steadied him. Over his underclothes he strapped on the leather girdle with its kit of blued-steel implements nestling in the little up-right pockets, and where nestled, too, the thin metal case that contained the diamond-shaped, gray-paper, adhesive seals, the insignia of the Gray Seal. He put on his shirt, his waistcoat and jacket, and into the side pocket of his jacket he slipped his automatic. He was dressed now.

He stared at himself in the glass. Jason would have to be told. It wasn't fair to the faithful old man to slip out without a word. Jason would be mad with anxiety if he found him gone. Jimmie Dale rang the bell.

The reflection in the mirror returned him a twisted contortion of the lips. The damned thing was trying to ape a smile, wasn't it? It looked like a death's-head, gaunt and pasty-white, with lines like an old man's. Well, what of it? He felt all right, except that the bandage was infernally tight.

A knock sounded at the door.

"Come in," said Jimmie Dale.

Jason's white head appeared in the doorway—and then the door was shut with nervous haste, and the old butler came hurriedly forward across the room.

"Master Jim, sir!" he gasped. "Master Jim, what—what are you doing, sir?"

Jimmie Dale smiled.

"I'm going out, Jason," he said.

The old man cast an anxiously suspicious glance at his master.

"Yes, of course, Master Jim, sir," he said soothingly. "But the exertion of dressing, sir—if you'll just sit down for a little while now, Master Jim, then by and by—"

"Jason," said Jimmie Dale, whimsically, "you couldn't be a fraud even in a minor degree—you're too transparent. I'm quite myself. I'm not in de-lirium. I'm simply going out."

The old man's face grew a little white.

"You can't mean it, Master Jim," he faltered. "In the state you're in, sir, it's likely to cost you your life to go out."

"It's likely to cost me more than that to stay in," said Jimmie Dale, qui-etly.

The old man twisted his hands together; he coughed in a sort of helpless way.

"I'm an old man, Master Jim, sir"—the tears were welling into Jason's eyes—"and you'll pardon me, Master Jim, for taking liberties, but when you were a baby I dandled you, Master Jim, on my knee, and—and I know there's something strange and—and danger—that's come into your life—and it isn't my place to ask what it is, but—but for God's sake, Master Jim, sir, don't you go out until you're well enough."

Jimmie Dale stepped toward the old man, and laid both hands on the other's shoulders—gently.

"Jason," he said, steadily, "get me an overcoat, light weight, dark color—and a slouch hat. Tell Benson I'm waiting for him—and to pamper my infirmities we'll take the limousine tonight." He turned Jason around, and pushed the old man quietly toward the door. "Look sharp, please, Jason," he said.

The door closed behind the old butler. For an instant Jimmie Dale stood staring at the door, his face softened, almost a mistiness in the dark, steady eyes; then he turned abruptly to the liqueur stand again.

"I guess perhaps I'll need it," he muttered.

He took out a small silver flask, filled it with brandy, and slipped it into his pocket. He went out then, closing the door behind him. As he descended the stairs he caught the sound of the car on the driveway coming from the garage at the rear of the house. That was Benson—another Jason! He felt suddenly humbled. Benson young, Jason old—at the extremes of life—and each without an instant's hesitation would give their all for him. It was a strange, strange thing, the love of men one for another—the love of these two for him. He had accepted it all too matter-of-factly perhaps in the past, not stopping to appraise it always for its immeasurable worth, or, when he thought of it, perhaps priding himself on it only as a possession that other men did not have, like a suit of clothes perhaps made by an exclusive tailor where the same pattern was not supplied to anyone else. He did not know how he had won it.

He took his coat and hat from Jason in the hallway. The old man's lips were twitching.

"God bless you, Jason!" said Jimmie Dale suddenly, and swung through the door.

At the curb Benson, the chauffeur, touched his cap, as he reached out to open the door of the big closed car—then hesitated.

"You'll excuse me, Mr. Dale," he stammered, "but—but I—"

Jimmie Dale smiled.

"It's a wonderful night, isn't it, Benson—for a drive?" he said. "West Broadway, Benson—and, oh, yes, stop anywhere within a block of Thompson Street."

"Yes, sir," said Benson mechanically—and opened the door.

Jimmie Dale stepped into the car. The door closed. He saw Benson, in the act of swinging into his seat, turn and face for an instant the open doorway of the lighted vestibule where Jason stood. Benson's shoulders lifted in a helpless gesture.

"What the hell can I do?" said Benson's shoulders eloquently.

CHAPTER 22

A TAPPED WIRE

Jimmie Dale settled back in his seat. The car moved swiftly, smoothly downtown. It wasn't so bad; not so very much worse than being in bed. He was quite all right.

He stared out of the windows. He had no plans—no definite plans. How could he have? Somewhere, somehow, he must pick up the trail of the Phantom's associates. That was all. And Mother Margot offered by far the best and surest way—if she were back. Obviously, therefore, the first move was to find out if Mother Margot had returned, and he would know that in a few minutes now.

And if she were still away?

His lips tightened grimly. The Sanctuary—Smarlinghue—a spectre haunting the Bad Lands through the night! Perhaps hopelessly! He had done that on so many nights before. What other way was there—to find Bunty Myers?

He lighted a cigarette. Occasionally he shifted his position. He told himself that it was only because the bandage was so tight that he was beginning to experience a little discomfort.

The car circled around Washington Square, and made its way into West Broadway. Presently it stopped. Jimmie Dale got out.

"Wait half an hour for me, Benson," he said quietly. "No more. If I'm not here by then take the car back home."

He did not wait for a reply. Half a block ahead was Thompson Street. He started toward it. His coat was tightly buttoned around his throat, his collar turned up, his slouch hat pulled toughly down over his eyes.

He swung around the corner, walking with his hands in his pockets. The narrow street seethed with its usual night life. Half naked children tumbled in the gutters, and played beneath the wheels of the pushcarts that flanked the sidewalks on both sides of the road. Banjo torches spluttered and flung out fantastic flares; shawled women, dark, swarthy, elbowed about the carts; men who wore earrings and chattered in strange tongues lounged on the sidewalk or jostled their way along in a sort of aimless fashion. The place was a din, a hubbub. The hawkers cried their wares.

Jimmie Dale made his way along with studied carelessness, and suddenly, nodding sharply to himself in satisfaction, he edged out to the curb. Mother Margot was back! True, the old hag herself was nowhere in sight, but this was her pushcart here laden with its miscellany of small articles like the notion counter of a department store. He picked up a cheap, gaudy, colored kerchief and pretended to examine it. At the next cart was the old Italian whom he, Jimmie Dale, as Smarlinghue then, had accosted three days before when, as now, he had been in search of Mother Margot.

"How much?" he demanded, holding up the kerchief.

The Italian shrugged his shoulders.

"Wait-a da minute," he said. "She just gone-a da telephone. She come-a right back."

Jimmie Dale put down the kerchief.

"I don't want it bad enough to wait," he said indifferently—and drew back into the throng on the sidewalk. But the next instant he had sidled out of the crowd again into a dark, narrow and dirty little alleyway that made the side of an equally dirty and uninviting second-hand shop, on whose unwashed window painted letters, that had once been white, announced that its proprietor was one Antonio Mezzo.

The telephone! Luck! He felt his pulses quicken. There were only two persons who ever called Mother Margot to this telephone here, himself and—the Phantom. His fingers had crept to a pocket in the leather girdle. They came out with his mask. He slipped it quickly over his face. Mother Margot would have news tonight, then! He was at the side door now. It was slightly ajar; and, yes, he could just catch the old hag's miserable jargon, the shrill, complaining voice, muffled, of course, by the telephone booth itself that stood just within beside the door:

"I can't hear youse. De buzzin's got me feazed."

Jimmie Dale's lips straightened suddenly. It wasn't Mother Margot he wanted to hear. Why trust her? He had never caught her at the phone before! He could make her talk, but he had no guarantee that it would be the whole truth. He pushed the door open softly and stepped inside. There was a dim light coming from a blackened, nearly burned-out incandescent that dangled from the ceiling. The back room here, littered with old junk and broken furniture, was cut off from the front by a closed door. Being inside the booth, she had not seen him. She was still reiterating the fact that she could not hear distinctly.

Jimmie Dale crept a step forward, another—then with a swift movement he jerked the door of the booth open, and leaning forward clapped his hand firmly over the mouthpiece of the telephone.

There was a startled cry from the old hag, as she shrank back. The side of the booth creaked with her weight.

"My Gawd!" she whispered wildly. "De—de Gray Seal!"

"Yes!" said Jimmie Dale grimly. "Give me that receiver. Quick! You answer as I tell you."

He put the receiver to his ear.

"What's the matter?" demanded a voice imperatively. "What's that noise?"

"Tell him it's Mezzo moving some furniture about," ordered Jimmie Dale swiftly.

He took his hand from the transmitter.

"It's de old dago shovin' some of his junk around," said Mother Margot into the phone.

Again Jimmie Dale's hand closed over the transmitter.

"All right!" snapped the voice. "Can you hear now?"

"Tell him you can hear now," breathed Jimmie Dale.

"Sure," obeyed Mother Margot. "Sure—I gets youse now."

"Go to the Crescent as I told you, then," said the voice, "and give Curley this message: *The black box, Sadie Foy's at eleven o'clock.* Understand?"

Jimmie Dale nudged Mother Margot significantly as he nodded his head affirmatively, and again removed his hand from the phone.

"Sure!" said Mother Margot.

"Hurry!" said the voice, curtly.

The receiver at the other end of the wire was hung up.

"Let's get out of here," said Jimmie Dale, coolly.

Mother Margot stumbled out of the booth. She was twisting her hands together, casting frightened, hurried glances toward the closed door that led into the second-hand shop in front, glancing furtively, too, at Jimmie Dale from under her hooded shawl.

"My Gawd!" she mumbled thickly. "My Gawd!"

Outside in the lane, the side door closed, Jimmie Dale drew the old woman against the wall of the building, and for a moment stood staring at her speculatively in the darkness.

Suddenly she reached out, and clawed at his sleeve.

"Wot youse goin' to do?" she whispered wildly. "My Gawd! De Gray Seal! Wot youse goin' to do?"

Jimmie Dale ignored her question. He spoke sharply.

"So Curley down at the Crescent Saloon is one of the gang too, is he?" he demanded.

"No; he ain't!" She shook her head vehemently. "Not de way youse means, he ain't."

"I suppose that is why a message is sent to him, then," observed Jimmie Dale caustically.

"He gets lot of 'em." she said quickly; "but he don't know wot any of 'em means, an' he don't know where any of 'em goes to. I watched him once. Someone calls him up on de phone, an' he just says de message over, dat's all."

"Quite so!" said Jimmie Dale softly. "But in that case, did it ever strike you that the Voice, as you call him, would save quite a little time, to say nothing of making you trudge around town, by phoning Curley direct?"

Mother Margot was twisting her hands again.

"Youse don't believe me!" she cried out hoarsely. "Youse t'ink I'm stringin' youse. I ain't! Honest to Gawd, I ain't! I'm handin' youse de straight goods. Dat's why no one gets next to de Voice unless he wants 'em to. De trail's gummed up. See? He don't trust no one. He was gettin' leery of me. Dat's why he sent me away. See? Dere's been a lot of leaks. He sent me away for three days on a fake lay. An' w'en I was away one of his games gets a hole all bust in it again, an' I guess it was youse did it. So he's sure it ain't me dat's spillin' any of de beans. Youse see, don't youse? Say, for God's sake, youse see, don't youse, dat I ain't stringin' youse?"

The old hag's voice was full of nervous anxiety. She kept wringing her hands together. Jimmie Dale nodded. She was undoubtedly telling the truth. He could quite understand now why she had been away—and could understand, perhaps better than she could, the Phantom's dire need of looking to his fences.

"But the phone?" he suggested.

"Well, dat's de answer, ain't it?" she said. "It ain't so much of a trick to trace a telephone call, is it? Not if de dicks want to do it. Dat's why he don't telephone dat sort of stuff nowhere except here, an' not to nobody except me. An'—an' if he was wise to wot happened in dere just now he'd—he'd—my Gawd, youse know wot he'd do! Say, youse ain't goin' to stop me, are youse? Youse're goin' to tell me wot dat message is, ain't youse, an' let me put it acrost?" She was clawing pitifully, frantically at Jimmie Dale's sleeve again. "If youse don't, an' I don't give Curley dat message, dey'll kill me. Mabbe youse got away wid it bein' de dago bumpin' furniture dat made de row in de booth, but if de message don't go, dat don't go neither, an'—an' dey'll slit me troat. Aw, for Gawd's sake! Youse knows dat! Dat's wot dey'll do!"

It was literally true. The failure of Mother Margot to deliver the message was exactly equivalent to her death sentence. Jimmie Dale's lips were a straight line. There was no quibbling on that point. The Phantom's trade was murder. He would strike without an instant's hesitation at the slightest indication that the old hag had played him false. On the other hand if he, Jimmie Dale, allowed Mother Margot to deliver the message he delivered himself without reservation into her hands—either that, or go back home to bed and leave Sadie Foy's alone. But again, if the message were delivered it promised almost to a certainty that at Sadie Foy's he would pick up the trail he had come out tonight to find. The Crescent Saloon and Curley did not interest him. That was only a relaying station. The rendezvous was at Sadie Foy's. Suppose he refused to give Mother Margot the message? Would it stop the projected devilry that was obviously afoot? And on that basis alone ought he to refuse? If he did, it would cost the woman her life. There was no supposition about that. That was fact. He couldn't do that, could he? And yet, since he must then assume the moral responsibility, and if for no other reason than that play a hand at Sadie Foy's, his own life very probably hung on whether Mother Margot would keep faith with him or not.

"Dey'll kill me!" Mother Margot whispered hoarsely. She pulled at his sleeve, clung to it; she was rocking on her feet.

"Yes," said Jimmie Dale calmly, "they'd kill you; and they would equally kill me if, once out of my sight, you added to the message the information that I was in this game again tonight. And so you see it's a case of you being killed to a certainty, or the *chance*, depending on you, of the same thing happening to me." He smiled suddenly, whimsically. "I haven't very much choice, have I? I can't send you to your death. The message? Oh, yes! It's this: The black box. Sadie Foy's at eleven o'clock. That's all."

She drew in her breath suddenly.

"My Gawd, youse're *white*!" she said in a low, catchy way. "I gets youse. Youse're goin' to be at Sadie Foy's, an' youse're takin' de chance of me splittin' on youse. Well, youse needn't worry, an' I'll tell youse why. I ain't forgot de night at Pedler Joe's. Youse made me go dere, I knows; but youse risked yer life to get me out of it, an' I ain't forgot."

"I've wondered about that," said Jimmie Dale, half to himself; then, briskly: "Do you know anything about this black box or what the message means?"

She shook her head.

"Do you know where Bunty Myers is?"

Again she shook her head.

"I ain't heard anythin' for three days until in dere tonight," she said earnestly. "I only just got back."

"All right," said Jimmie Dale quietly. "You'd better go now. And hurry—in case there's a check on the time when you should be at Curley's."

She hesitated an instant. Then she brushed a hand quickly across her eyes.

"My Gawd, youse're white," she said again, huskily—and turned, and shuffled hurriedly down the alleyway toward the street.

Jimmie Dale watched her until she had disappeared.

"Perhaps!" said Jimmie Dale grimly. "And perhaps I am—a fool!"

CHAPTER 23

THE PIECES OF A PUZZLE

Five minutes later Jimmie Dale was staring at Benson's back through the plate glass, as the big limousine, continuing its progress in a downtown direction, rolled rapidly along.

He was frowning heavily. He did not like this! He did not like having Benson along like this. Not because Benson could not be trusted to the uttermost, but for Benson's own sake. There wasn't much risk for Benson, of course; in fact there wasn't any, as far as he could see, but he would have felt easier in his mind had he been alone. They were going ostensibly now to the Silver Dragon, a famous resort of slumming parties in Chinatown, and Benson would park outside where other cars were parked, and simply wait. But for all that, there was—

He shrugged his shoulders. What else could he do? His side was behaving very nicely so far, better than he had hoped for, in fact, but that condition was dependent, he knew very well, on saving himself all he could. That was why, for example, he had not gone to the Sanctuary, and, as Smarlinghue then, gone alone to Sadie Foy's. There would have been time—ample time. But he wasn't fit to play the rôle of Smarlinghue tonight.

He dismissed the subject from his mind. He had done what had seemed the wisest and best thing. The rest was in the lap of the gods. He began a little mental calculation as he took out his watch. It was twenty minutes to eleven now. It was roughly about ten minutes ago when Mother Margot had started on her errand. She should be at Curley's by now. That left a leeway of twenty minutes for somebody to telephone Curley and, presumably, make the rendezvous at Sadie Foy's at eleven o'clock.

Jimmie Dale replaced the watch in his pocket—and stared again at the back of Benson's head. The black box! Sadie Foy's! He shook his head. The combination meant nothing to him, of course. But Sadie Foy herself was quite a different matter. In Chinatown Sadie Foy was a celebrity—a very shady and notorious celebrity. She was seldom sober. She was a white woman, old now, who had married a Chinaman. But Charley Foy, her husband, had perished in a Tong feud. That was many years ago. Since then she had lived in a little rat-hole of a place as dissolute as herself, a few blocks from Chatham Square, supported, according to the police, by a pension from the Tong for which her lamented Charlie Foy had given up his life.

A smile flickered across Jimmie Dale's lips. As Larry the Bat in the days of old, as Smarlinghue of today, he was in this particular very much better informed than the police. There was no question whatever about the pension; but the pension was not based on purely philanthropic motives, or due to a deep-seated sorrow for Charlie Foy's untimely and violent decease. It satisfied the police. Actually, Sadie Foy drove a lively trade in bulk opium, or in anything else of an illicit character that promised her a profit. The bulk opium accounted for the pension; an innate evilness and cunning accounted for her general depravity. It was a choice place for a rendezvous of any questionable sort, or for any purpose!

The minutes passed as the car sped along. Jimmie Dale half closed his eyes. Sadie Foy, or for that matter her iniquities, meant nothing—it was the trail now that so obviously led to Sadie Foy's door. The Phantom was interested in something at Sadie Foy's at eleven o'clock. Would the trail broaden—or break? What did the night hold? A final reckoning with the Phantom? Freedom for *her*—if she still lived? Success, partial or whole? Failure? What?

The car slowed, and stopped. Jimmie Dale stepped to the sidewalk.

"We'll raise the limit a little this time, Benson," he said. "Wait an hour."

Jimmie Dale mounted the steps of the garishly lighted restaurant before which the car had stopped, and passed inside. The place was a riot of noise; the clatter of dishes, laughter, song, the never ceasing hum of numberless voices from numberless tables where the diners sat. He walked leisurely from room to room, making for the rear of the establishment—and here nonchalantly walked out into the cross street behind. The Silver Dragon was blest with two entrances.

And now Jimmie Dale quickened his step. He was in a narrow, twisting, ill-lighted little street in the heart of Chinatown. Shuttered windows threw out stealthy gleams of light from their interstices; scuffling figures sidled by him. He passed a small frame house, mouldy and in decay, weather-streaked, which paint had not touched in years. It was in complete darkness; not a light showed from it anywhere. And then in another minute he had slipped into the adjacent lane, and in still another was creeping cautiously across a filthy back yard—with the rear of the small house that was mouldy and in decay looming up before him. This was Sadie Foy's.

His eyes narrowed now a little grimly. It was black here all around him, but the house itself was not quite so dark at the rear as it had been in front! From a lower window just ahead of him little undulating threads of light seeped out from behind the edges of a drawn shade. It was the air did that, of course—made the shade sway slightly. Therefore the window must be open.

Voices, in what seemed like low, guttural undertones, began to reach him. He stole cautiously forward. There was refuse in the yard, and it was pitch black. It was not easy to assure silence even from step to step. A tin can became an object of dire menace. A minute, two, passed—and then Jimmie Dale, from a stooping position, stood upright. His head was just on a level with the window sill. He could hear now distinctly.

"Well, we're gettin' fed up waitin'!" said a silky voice. "It's eleven o'clock, and we've been patient for about a couple of hours. If youse ain't comin' across nice an' pleasant, mabbe we can help yer memory a little more de other way. Sadie's got everything locked up nice for de night in front, an' nobody'll disturb us. Ain't youse, Sadie?"

Jimmie Dale's dark eyes lighted with a sudden gleam. He could see little, scarcely more than a group of shadows on the shade, but he had recognised the purring voice. The trail was here! It was the Kitten's voice—and with the Kitten at work, hand in glove with him somewhere should be the Phantom and Bunty Myers. If the light breeze would only stir that shade a little more—just half an inch!

A woman cackled hoarsely.

"Sure! I'll take care of dat! Don't youse worry!"

"D'ye hear?" It was the Kitten's voice again. "We've let youse off easy so far, but we're gettin' fed up. I ask youse for de last time before youse gets hurt some more, where's de black box? Yer brother didn't take it up de river wid him; an' de mob of boobs youse played for suckers ain't got it, 'cause dey're mostly on de street now wid de kids pickin' up deir free lunches in de gutters; an' it wasn't left around loose in de crib w'en yer sweet little Banco Santos was pinched; an' youse've been hidin' all de time—so where is it?"

There was no answer. In the silence Jimmie Dale, almost involuntarily, startled, had drawn back a little. The Banco Santos! He did not need to see in there. He knew what the black box was now! The trial was scarcely a week old. The papers had been full of it. Two brothers, two Portuguese, Georges and Manuel Santos, had run a private bank, garnering in the savings of, for the most part, the poorer element among the foreign class, the tenement dwellers. They had played the game craftily, with vicious patience, for nearly two years, piling up the savings of the poor—only the final coup had been disrupted a little by a sudden suspicion that had arisen in the minds of the authorities. And one evening, as the latter had descended on the place, the two brothers had decamped by the back window, one of them carrying under his arm a black, oblong security box. One of the brothers, as likewise the black box, had not been seen or heard of since. The other brother, Georges, had been caught, and only a few days ago had started to serve a fifteen-years' sentence in Sing Sing. The missing funds were estimated at between twenty-five and thirty thousand dollars.

The Kitten purred again:

"Ain't it too bad he's lost his voice as well as his memory! An' we ain't done hardly anythin' but be civil to him since we runs into him back dere in Mickey de Cobbler's dump. Mabbe he's sore 'cause we didn't go right up an' shake hands wid him den! But youse see we was just sittin' around havin' a drink, an' thought mabbe we'd had one too many an' was seein' things w'en de cellar door opens, an' one of dese guys here says he'll bet a million bucks dat it was Manuel Santos, an' by de time we gets our breaths back he's slipped out. We hadn't never travelled together none of us before, but dis looked like we all had tickets for de same place. So we follows him. An' over he sneaks to Sadie's here to buy some coke, an' we trails in, an' sure enough w'en we gets a real good look at him Steenie's right an' it's Manuel Santos. Only he ain't got de black box dat dey talked about in de papers wid him." He laughed a little, low, viciously. "I'm sick of askin' him. Youse ask him, Steenie, same as youse did before—only a little harder."

There was a sudden blurred movement of the figures on the shade—a sudden low, throttled cry of pain and fear.

Jimmie Dale's fingers touched the lower edge of the shade. They were not occupied in there with the window now! And it might even have been but the stirring of the night breeze. The shade swayed gently inward an inch, two—and floated almost imperceptibly back into place again.

Jimmie Dale's face was hard and strained. It was not difficult to pick out Manuel Santos from the group! The man's hands were tied, and he drooped over the table as though in a half swoon; his face was battered ferociously, and blood trickled in two or three little streams from his cheeks. Behind him stood the Kitten. In a corner Sadie Foy cackled applause, and rubbed skinny hands together joyously. There were four other men—dregs, rats, jacks-of-all-trades in the underworld. He knew three of them by name: Steenie Klotz; Red Jack; the Bummer. Nice names! But in the underworld the monikers were apt!

There came the sound of a blow, another, and another—and then a cry again. A voice gasped out weakly:

"Stop! For God's sake, stop! I—I'll tell."

"Blamed if youse ain't a great memory worker, Steenie!" purred the Kitten's voice. "He's goin' to tell. Well, Manuel, where is it?"

"It—it's at the camp." The man's words came painfully.

"Where's dat?" demanded the Kitten.

"It's on the Sound. It—it's just this side of the Martin-Holmes place."

Jimmie Dale's brows contracted suddenly. The Martin-Holmes had nothing to do with this, of course; but he remembered now—

"Youse mean dat summer shack youse an' yer brother had?" inquired the Kitten softly.

"Yes," the man answered.

"Nix on dat!" The Kitten jeered suddenly. "De bulls lived dere for about two weeks pawin' it over. Don't youse try any of dat stuff, my bucko! If it'd been in de house dey'd have found it. I heard dey even pulled de floors up. Say, Steenie, youse'd better try again!"

"No, no!" Manuel Santos' voice rose shrilly. "It's true! I'm telling you the truth. The police could never find it, but it's there."

"All right," said the Kitten evenly. "Tell us about it, den."

"It ain't really in the house, it—it's outside the attic window." The words came slowly in a mumbling sort of way. "It looks as though the eaves were all boarded in around the house, but you can move one of them above the window. There—there's only one window. It—it's there."

There was a low, muttered chorus of exultant oaths; and then the Kitten's voice:

"Dat sounds good enough to be true." He was purring again. "I'll get a closed car, an' we'll hike along out dere, an' youse'll come too, Manuel, so's dere won't be no tricks. Youse ain't such a fool after all, Manuel! A little trip to South America where youse'll be out of everybody's road, an' a lot safer yourself dan youse have been for de last six weeks tryin' to hide yerself away, is better'n takin' a last ride in a wooden box where youse can't look at de scenery! Youse're among friends, Manuel, if youse only knew it. Dere's some—"

Jimmie Dale was retreating from the window. A moment more, and he had gained the street; and, hurrying now, returning by the same way he had come, he reached his car in front of the Silver Dragon.

"Benson," he said quietly, "we seem fated to make quite a night of it. Off and on, you've driven me a number of times to Mr. Martin-Holmes' summer residence out on the Sound. I know it's closed now for the season, but do you remember just exactly where it is?"

"Perfectly, sir," said Benson.

"Good!" nodded Jimmie Dale. "Drive there now—that is to within, say, half a mile this side of the place. If I remember correctly, it's quite thickly wooded there. I leave it entirely to you to find a convenient spot in about that neighbourhood to run the car off the road and park it where it will not be seen."

Benson stared, a hesitant, anxious expression creeping into his face. Jimmie Dale smiled.

"I'm still quite all right, Benson," he said.

"Yes, sir," said Benson mechanically.

"And, by the way"—Jimmie Dale paused in the act of stepping into the car—"I might say that I am in a very great hurry, Benson."

"Yes, sir," said Benson heavily.

For a moment, as he settled back on the cushions and the car started forward, the smile held on Jimmie Dale's lips. Benson, like Jason, was comparable to a hen with her chick. Benson at this precise instant probably—to mix metaphors—was inwardly wriggling like an eel. He was probably debating with himself whether he should not drive directly home, and there, by brute force if necessary, with the assistance of Jason, put him, Jimmie Dale, back to bed again—even if he got fired for it! Benson, however, in the last analysis wouldn't do anything of the kind—he would play the game.

The smile faded now from Jimmie Dale's lips, and a puzzled, anxious look settled on his face as he dismissed Benson from his mind. He had acted quickly back there at Sadie Foy's because he had realised that there was no time to lose; and though, even then, he had realised too that the pieces of the puzzle seemed somehow strangely mismated, he had also realised that the final act in any case would be played out where he was going now—at the Santos' camp. Further, there was the moral responsibility to save that money, and nothing would have induced him to shift that responsibility to, say, the police, when instinctively he sensed, as he did, that the Phantom had still a card to play, a card that also must be played out at the same place. But what was that card? If it were only the Kitten who was involved, he could pick up the Kitten's trail again at the Santos camp; but it was more than the Kitten that he wanted, more than the Kitten that he still hoped for, and in which hope intuition told him he was justified. He wanted the Phantom—or Bunty Myers.

He had time now to solve the puzzle—if he could. But the pieces on closer examination only seemed the more mismated. They contradicted even the sense of intuition that was so strong upon him. Where was the Phantom's hand in this? The Kitten? Well, then, why that message?—"Sadie Foy's at eleven o'clock." The Kitten had said himself he had been there long *before* eleven. The Kitten was therefore *already* at Sadie Foy's when the message was delivered to Curley at the Crescent Saloon. And then, again, the four men who were with the Kitten, he was absolutely certain, had no intimate connection with the Phantom; they were not the kind the Phantom gathered around him; they were simply apaches, buzzards of the underworld, mentally the lowest type of criminal, whose only knowledge of finesse was embodied in the use of a black-jack, a knife, or a revolver. They did not belong! Suppose then they had been hired for this special occasion? In that case the Kitten was already fully equipped to carry through the night's work. Why, then, the message?

The miles flew by; the minutes passed into quarter hours. They had long since been out on a country road.

What did it mean?

Jimmie Dale, save that at long intervals he subconsciously eased his position, sat motionless, staring introspectively at the window.

What did it mean?

And then suddenly Jimmie Dale sat erect. He had it! It had come like a flash. It dovetailed; it fitted in its minutest part. It postulated only that the Kitten had a means of ready communication with his unhallowed master, the Phantom, which in itself was axiomatic. The Kitten had haphazardly been in the company of the four apaches when one of the four, this Steenie, had recognised the fugitive, Manuel Santos. It was a "find" worth thirty thousand dollars—which the Kitten did not propose the other four should share. It was very simple! The Kitten had taken the leadership, and in the early stages at Sadie Foy's had undoubtedly gone out on some excuse and sent the Phantom word of what was afoot, stating probably that he was sure they could make Manuel Santos talk, and if so he would somehow stall on any move being made until the Phantom had time to act, setting that time at eleven o'clock. Obviously, then, someone would be on hand at that time to receive from the Kitten the information as to where the black box was hidden, if that information had been obtained, and the "someone" would then arrive first at the hiding place, while the Kitten and the four thugs would arrive later only to find a rifled nest! And the Kitten would be secure from any complicity in the eyes of the four thugs—wherein the Kitten was very wise!

Jimmie Dale stooped suddenly forward and picked up the speaking tube. He wasn't racing any more then against the Kitten on whom he had a known start. He was racing against "someone" else, someone who would race like mad so as to keep the Kitten in countenance and not force his stalling to become apparent through lingering on the road when his hungry dupes would be urging speed.

"Faster, Benson!" he said sharply. "All you've got the rest of the way!"

He leaned back in his seat again. It was clear enough now. But who was this "someone?" It wasn't the Phantom himself, for the Phantom had sent the message. Who, then, was the Phantom's delegate? Jimmie Dale's lips drooped curiously until grim little lines formed at the corners of his mouth. It was more likely than anyone else to be the man he had started out to find— Bunty Myers. He frowned quickly. Had he made a mistake? Should he have remained at Sadie Foy's? This delegate must have been there somewhere at eleven—when the Kitten was going out again with the excuse of getting a closed car. And then he shook his head impatiently. Perhaps! If he had known what he was so sure of now, he might have acted differently—perhaps not. This, after all, was the surer way, both of finding that delegate, and securing possession of the black box.

The car was eating up the miles now, keeping check almost with the minutes as they passed.

He ran his hand through his hair. Dog eat dog! It was dirty, miserable work all the way through, beginning with Manuel Santos, who was perhaps the most despicable of the lot. His hands clenched suddenly. If nothing else came of it, getting that money back to those to whom it meant their all was worth whatever it might cost him tonight. Thirty thousand dollars! There was something fiendish, damnable, in the vicious premeditation, the vicious patience with which the two Portuguese had worked! He remembered in the account of the trial it had come out in evidence that the authorities had not been lax. Always on demand securities in the shape of bonds had been produced to make the balances. Of course! And of a sudden those bonds had been transferred into cash, and—presto!—the squalid little bank was no more! He smiled grimly. It was probably the steady demand for so many bills of large denominations during the two or three days prior to the end that had first aroused the suspicions of the authorities, and—

The car was slowing down. And now it jolted over rough ground. A branch slapped smartly against the window pane. The headlights, streaming out, threw tree trunks into spectral relief against a background of utter blackness. And then the headlights went off, and the car stopped.

Jimmie Dale stepped out.

"You're sure of the place, Benson, and that you're hidden from the road?" he asked crisply.

"Yes, sir," Benson answered. "Quite sure, sir."

"Very well!" said Jimmie Dale. "Keep your lights off, wait for me, and don't leave the car under any circumstances." He sensed a protest anent himself rising to Benson's lips, and he turned quickly away. "I'll be back in a few minutes, Benson," he said.

CHAPTER 24

THE BLACK BOX

Jimmie Dale moved forward through the trees. It could not be far, not more than three or four hundred yards, for the Santos house lay between himself and the Martin-Holmes estate. That was why he had told Benson to stop half a mile this side of the latter place. The general direction, he knew, was a diagonal one—toward the Martin-Holmes' residence, and toward the shore, away from the road. He smiled a little to himself as he went along. He remembered that during a weekend visit to Holmes a year or so ago, the latter had expressed his annoyance at what he had called an unsightly shack that two Portuguese had put up on the beach close to his place. He, Jimmie Dale, had not been very much interested then; he was vitally interested in that so-called shack now!

He frowned suddenly. He had been making fair progress, and should have reached his destination by now; but, instead, he was still in the woods and the ground was growing wet and soggy underfoot. He edged off in the direction of the shore—the house was at the water's edge, Holmes had said—and went on for another hundred yards. It grew worse. He could hear now the lapping of the waves. The trees grew fewer, and began to be replaced by a reedy growth—and then of a sudden Jimmie Dale halted. A glimmer of moonlight flickered on water and waving marsh grass. It was impassable—it reached out into the Sound itself.

It was disaster! He felt his face whiten. He must already have been ten minutes on the way—and ten minutes was the utmost limit of margin he had any right to count upon. Ten minutes! It was far worse than that! It would take that much more to retrace his steps and circle around the other way before he could get started again.

He gnawed at his lips now as he turned and began to run. It was almost certain disaster; disaster to the moral responsibility he had assumed, disaster to the hope he had cherished that tonight—He stumbled. He could not be careful of his footing now. Defeat, yes, perhaps—but he would not accept it. He ran doggedly. Again he stumbled, and again. And now he winced with pain. This hurt his side brutally. It wasn't like riding on the cushions of a luxurious limousine, or even of walking when no unusual effort was required.

He went on. His breath came hard. He swept beads of moisture away from his forehead—and then once he reeled. It was hours, wasn't it, since he had started over again? There wasn't much chance—one perhaps in a thousand—not that much! His jaws clamped hard together. He was making a mess of it with that cursed side, and—

Jimmie Dale came suddenly out of the edge of the woods. Well, at least, this was better! Fifty yards away across a clearing a house loomed shadowy out of the darkness. He listened intently. There was no sound. He darted silently across the clearing and gained the house. It was a small place so close to the shore that, as he crept now noiselessly up the steps of a verandah that apparently ran all around the house, he could make out a little wharf and what looked like an old, neglected boat drawn up on the beach. Certainly, there was no mistaking the house for there was no other of this description, he knew, in the neighbourhood.

A pick-lock came from a pocket in the leather girdle, and with it again the black silk mask. A moment more, and Jimmie Dale stood inside the house. And now he listened again, straining his ears for the slightest sound. Nothing! His face was white and haggard. There was only one answer of course—the Phantom's delegate had been and gone. There had been time enough—so much and to spare that even the Kitten was due now.

He took out a flashlight and circled it around him. The place was crude, to a certain extent unfinished; exactly what Manuel Santos himself had called it—a camp. It seemed to be divided into several rooms by thin, unpainted partitions. Here at his right, steps led upward. Well, he had come this far, and even if the chances now were all against him, he was still going up there, but he had to think of the Kitten now—the possibility of being trapped himself by the Kitten and his thugs. There was time enough now to take the precaution of arming himself with a knowledge of the general plan of the place. He stepped hurriedly through the several rooms that made the depth of the house. He nodded in quick understanding. The "camp" was of uniform design. One took his choice as to which was the rear and which was the front.

Here, where he stood now, a door opened on the verandah; and here, too, a rough staircase led to the upper story, or attic, as Manuel Santos had called it.

Well, the attic now! That window! He went quickly up the stairs. At the top, his flashlight disclosed a broad landing and a closed door. The door was unlocked, and he stepped forward over the threshold. The flashlight circled the interior. Again he nodded. It was an attic, nothing more or less, without partitions, that reached from one end of the house to the other. There was a single window, halfway down one side—the right-hand side from where he stood now facing the Sound.

He was at the window now. He opened it, and stood up on the sill—and suddenly, poised there, he remained motionless. From the direction of the road he thought he had caught the sound of a motor. It was gone now. Perhaps he had been mistaken. The road was, as nearly as he could calculate it, a good hundred and fifty yards back from the water.

He felt swiftly up above his head outside the window. He did not dare use the flashlight now. Whether he was mistaken about the motor or not, the Kitten was already due, and a light would show a long way through the darkness. And, besides, there was partial moonlight, and he could see a little. His fingers were feeling, searching, prying over the rough boarding. It was very ingenious, this—the eaves boarded in to meet the wall of the house—only he could not find any section of it that seemed at all loose or movable. It would be craftily done, of course; he would hardly expect anything else, but— It was strange! Very strange! The Kitten had been able to pass on no more detailed information about this than he, Jimmie Dale, had overheard; and if he, Jimmie Dale, could not open it, how could the Kitten's confederate have done so? Just luck? A stumbling on the trick of it? It was rather strange!

Jimmie Dale became motionless again, intent, alert. There could be no question about it now. There was the unmistakable crunch of *several* footsteps approaching the house from the direction of the road. The Kitten was coming!

In a flash Jimmie Dale reached into the leather girdle, and a powerful little blued-steel jimmy was in his hand. It was very strange! So strange that he meant to see inside there, Kitten or no Kitten! The jimmy ripped into a board above his head, and pried one end of it loose. He felt quickly inside. It was naturally hollow here, and he reached in as far as he could, feeling in both directions. Nothing! He tore the board completely away now, and moving a little along the sill, reached in from the other end. *It was here!* He was wrenching out an oblong shaped, black metal box of the style generally used in the safe deposit vaults. It was here! His brain seemed stunned for a moment. He did not understand. He could not understand—except that he had been wrong—wrong in his deduction from that scene at Sadie Foy's, wrong in his theory of the meaning of that message. And yet it had been so logical, so surely the truth! And yet, just as logically now, he was forced to the conclusion that he had been wrong. There had seemed, still seemed, to be no other possible explanation of that message, and yet—and yet he must have been wrong. Nobody—no Phantom's delegate—had been here. And the Kitten himself was coming now—because those were the footsteps of four or five men. Perhaps the—He pried the box itself hurriedly open. No; the contents had not been taken and the box left! The faint light disclosed package after package of banknotes.

The crunch of footsteps came again, still nearer to the house. Jimmie Dale lowered himself from the sill, and, carrying the box, retreated quickly across the attic to the door opposite to that by which he had entered—the door that faced the Sound. He opened it silently, stepped out on the landing—and the next instant crouched quickly back in the angle between the door jamb and the wall, on the side of the jamb away from the stairs. Too late! He had not thought they were so *near*. There was a footstep below. One of them was coming up this way—was even on the stairs now. He could not see, he could only *hear*. His automatic swung forward. Someone was close to him now. His jaws clamped. No, he had not been seen, either. The footstep passed the threshold of the door, entered the attic, and was crossing it now in the direction of the window. And now through the open door Jimmie Dale could make out a figure, little more than a shadowy outline, in the faint ray of moonlight from the window.

And then Jimmie Dale hung there riveted to the spot. It was quick—quick as the winking of an eye. The figure, at the window now, halted abruptly, and swung sharply around to face the opposite doorway. And, coincidently, it seemed, the door opened, and as a flashlight streamed in and fell full upon the figure, and Jimmie Dale saw the man's face, there was a chorus of savage oaths, and almost simultaneously the flash and roar of a revolver shot. And the figure turned and ran toward the doorway near which Jimmie Dale stood.

It was Bunty Myers.

A voice screamed out in rage:

"Blast youse, Kitten, if youse hadn't bumped against my arm I'd have got him, an' got him good!"

Jimmie Dale's face was set, drawn, rigid, a tightness about the corner of his lips. He had been right, a thousand times right! It was not he who had been wrong, nor his intuition, nor his logic at fault. It was Bunty Myers who had been wrong—something had gone wrong with the man's plans, something had—

A fusillade of shots poured into the room after the flying figure. Bunty Myers stumbled, recovered himself, came on again, staggered through the doorway, and stumbled again—this time dropping to the floor.

And then Jimmie Dale was at work. He slammed the door shut, and snatching out his pick-lock, locked it. Bunty Myers! *He* wanted Bunty Myers! This was the man he had set out to find tonight, and—No, it wasn't only that! Thank God, he wasn't quite so raw as that! Those thugs in there, those apaches, would kill the man like a dog, as they had already tried to do, for interfering with their meat. And the more so now that they would find that meat gone! The Kitten couldn't stop them without giving himself away. It wasn't Bunty Myers, it was a man's life now—if the man were not already too far gone.

He held the box under his left arm, as he bent forward to the huddled form on the floor.

"Quick!" he whispered. "Put your arm around my neck. Do you hear? Make an effort! It's your only chance."

The man, with Jimmie Dale's assistance, lurched to his feet. They staggered, half fell down the stairs together. Bunty Myers was mumbling almost incoherently:

"I—I had a breakdown on the way—out—Kitten. Damn fool, Kitten, why couldn't youse hold—back—eh?—only a—a little late—youse—"

A sweat of agony was standing out on Jimmie Dale's forehead. He was half carrying the man. His side was torturing him.

"My God!" whispered Jimmie Dale between drawn lips.

Behind, upstairs, they were smashing at the locked door. They would either have to break it down or come around the other way through the house. It was worth a couple of minutes' start—and there was the boat there now on the shore just a few yards away.

He plunged on, staggering. Bunty Myers had become almost a dead weight. Well, he couldn't leave the man to be *killed*, could he? The man kept muttering now, muttering, muttering:

"…Up an' down—see?—'ell of a note—up an' down—up an' down—"

Bunty Myers collapsed a limp heap in the bottom of the boat. Jimmie Dale shoved it off, and jumped in. There were no oars, save a broken one. He seized it, and began to paddle. Footsteps pounded on the verandah, racing around the house. A yell went up:

"Dere he is! Dere he is—in de boat!"

There was the crash and flame spurt of shots, the spat of lead on the water. Jimmie Dale threw himself flat in the boat beside Bunty Myers. With the initial push, and the few strokes he had managed, the boat was quite a little distance from the shore, and what breeze there was was carrying it still farther out and also in the direction of the marshy tract through which he had first tried to reach the house. They could not, therefore, follow him along the shore.

A medley of voices from the shore, punctuated by oaths, reached him:

"Get a boat…. Dere'll be one up at dat swell ranch even if it is closed for de summer…. Sure! Bust de boathouse in…. Beat it quick…. He's good an' hurt, an' he won't get far…. He was winged upstairs in de attic w'en he fell—"

Jimmie Dale wrenched his flask from his pocket. They had only seen *one* man. Of course! His head was swimming crazily. He gulped down some brandy, and then felt for Bunty Myers' lips.

"Drink this!" he said hoarsely.

The liquor gurgled. He felt it run down the man's chin—but Bunty Myers must have swallowed some of it, for he began to mutter again, obviously in delirium now.

"Up an' down, I tell youse!" mumbled Bunty Myers. "It's honest to Gawd's truth. She don't know it, 'cause it's in de next house. It goes up an' down, I tell youse. I saw it. Up an'—" His voice trailed off.

What did the man mean? Jimmie Dale swept his hand across his eyes. It encountered his mask. He pulled it off and put it in his pocket. They were both delirious, weren't they—he and Bunty Myers? This was the man he had come to find, and from whose lips he had sworn he would tear the Phantom's secret, and all the man did was to croak, "Up and down, up and down!" Why didn't he say, "See-saw, Marjorie Daw!"

He gulped down another mouthful of brandy. Yes, that was better now. He raised his head. The shore was indistinct; not so much through distance, but because what little moonlight there had been was gone now—under a cloud. They would have a boat after him pretty soon. He must paddle now—risk a shot—he wouldn't be very distinct, either.

He dipped in the broken oar. It brought a moan of agony from his lips. The shots he had invited from the shore came—and missed. He *must* paddle—if it tore his side to pieces.

Only *one* man in the boat. That's what they thought. Well, then, why not? He could easily save himself. Drop overboard and swim ashore somewhere in the marshy tract. He had strength enough for that. They'd find the boat—and find a man in it! But there was some reason why he couldn't do that. He shook his head fiercely as though to clear his brain. Yes, of course! He couldn't leave that huddled figure there at his feet to be killed, could he? So it would have to be a fight, unless he could evade them in the darkness. And—and there wasn't much chance of that. He listened. That sounded like a boat coming from somewhere far behind now. But there weren't any more shots from the shore. Naturally! He must be opposite the marsh now, and they couldn't follow him any more on the land.

He couldn't leave the man to be killed—and that's what they'd do, kill the man. The Kitten couldn't prevent it without the others understanding the whole game and turning on the Kitten too. The Kitten had done all he could when he had bumped against the arm of the man who had fired that first shot. Funny, that Bunty Myers should be here! No, it was clear, quite clear! Bunty Myers had started out all right for the box, but a breakdown had made him late, so late that he—

A shout came from the shore behind. It was answered from the water. There was no further question but that they had secured a boat, though it was still a good way off. His broken oar suddenly touched bottom as he made a stroke. It wasn't the shore—it was just shallow water here fronting the marshland. Well, it didn't matter! He couldn't paddle much more, and not fast enough anyway to escape them, nor run fast enough with a wounded man even if he were ashore to get away from them. He laughed a little harshly. It was a case of fight for it, then. Perhaps Bunty Myers might be roused, propped up against a seat to help. It would be ironical if Bunty Myers hit the Kitten!

He stopped paddling, and leaned forward with his flask once more.

"Here! Quick! Take some more of this!" he said.

There was no answer. The head he lifted slid from his grasp, and thudded with a dull, ugly sound against the side of the boat. And for an instant Jimmie Dale stared at the limp, huddled form. And then, with a low, quick cry, he reached for the other's wrist, searching for the pulse—and then for the man's heart beat. There was none. He drew his breath in sharply. The man was dead.

The splash of oars mingled with the growl and snarl of voices came distinctly now across the water. *Bunty Myers was dead.* It was strange! It seemed to carry with it some significance beyond the mere fact of death. What was it? He had started out to find Bunty Myers for something or other. His head was swimming miserably again. It had nothing to do with that black box there on the floor of the boat. Nothing to do with—

He spurred himself to action. One man in the boat. There need be only *one* man in the boat now! He looked behind him, straining his eyes through the darkness. He could not see the other boat. Therefore they could not see him. He picked up the black box, and slipped over the side. The water could not be very deep since his oar had touched the bottom—no—it was less than waist high. He began to wade as quickly as he could, and still avoid making any splash, toward the shore.

The sounds from the oncoming boat grew louder, the voices more distinct. And then Jimmie Dale, reeling a little, stepped from the water's edge, and began to make his way silently through the woods. He knew the way. There was no danger of losing it. He was on the same side of the marshy tract that Benson was. He had only to keep straight ahead toward the road. And it wasn't far.

Curious, how heavy the black box was! He smiled grimly. Back there they would think Bunty Myers must have let it drop overboard. What else could they think? But tomorrow the police would get it—with the compliments of the Gray Seal. And the Phantom—no, Bunty Myers! His head was swirling again, but his brain seemed to be fighting desperately to tell him that what Bunty Myers had said about "up and down" and a "next house" somewhere was something he should understand, because he was to make Bunty Myers tell him something if Bunty Myers died for it, and he knew very well that Bunty Myers had died.

He gnawed at his lips. His head was very bad—very bad. He couldn't think any more. Not now! Not tonight! But he had no need to think any more now, had he? There was Benson and the car looming up just ahead of him. The rest was for tomorrow, and the tomorrows.

The tomorrows....

CHAPTER 25

IN THE SANCTUARY

A door opened and closed softly. A shadow moved in the darkness. Came then the crackle of a match, and a gas jet, air-choked, wheezing in protest, emitted a thin blue flame, grew yellow, and cast a meagre glow over its immediate surroundings. Unkempt, disreputable in his ragged, threadbare attire as Smarlinghue, Jimmie Dale stood for an instant staring around him at the squalid appointments of the place, and then moving abruptly to the far end of the room, flung himself down upon the already crumpled coverings of the dilapidated cot bed against the wall.

This was the Sanctuary. He half closed his eyes, staring at the asthmatic, stuttering gas jet. Well, it would be in every verity a sanctuary for another hour or so; a retreat where he could strive quietly to bring mental order out of chaos, and, yes, physically rest for a little while until it was time to carry out the plan that he proposed to put into execution before another morning came.

Since last night, all through the day, those mumbled words of Bunty Myers, the dying gangster, had been ringing in his ears. They had become an obsession. He could not rid his mind of them—or of the insistently growing intuition that they were the key to the Phantom's lair if he could only make head or tail of them. "Up an' down, I tell youse.... She don't know it, 'cause it's in de next house.... It goes up an' down, I tell youse...."

Who was "she"? He could not actually deduce it logically, but he was nevertheless sure that "she" was Mother Margot. The voices he had heard in her room but could not locate, the certainty that the clue, the phantom clue as he came to call it, was to be found in Mother Margot's rooms, was of course the basis for this interpretation; but it was the "next house" that bothered him. What did that mean? If he were right, and it was Mother Margot who did not know "'cause it's in de next house," where was this "next house"? There was nothing there but another tenement across the narrow areaway.

He frowned suddenly, impatiently. His mind was simply beginning to go over again, vainly, ineffectually, what it had already gone over a thousand times, it seemed, since last night. He had already made a decision—hours ago. He would know tonight whether he was right or not; he would know before he slept whether Bunty Myers' dying words linked up the Phantom's secret with Mother Margot's rooms or not. Tonight, finally, the phantom clue that *was* in any case connected with the old hag's rooms would be a mystery no longer if he literally had to wreck the place to unearth it.

Jimmie Dale nodded grimly to himself. Tonight! *In a* little while—it was too early yet. Just ten o'clock.

His lips tightened. Yes; wreck it! His was a single purpose now—that tonight he would strike with all his might; strike without counting the personal cost; and, above all, strike while for once he possessed the certainty that it would not be too late in the sense that even success in the unearthing of the Phantom and in a final reckoning with the man might only hold a bitter emptiness because she, the Tocsin, the woman he loved, would already have been beyond all aid.

There would be no thought of that. He was lighter of heart on that score than he had been for many days. She was alive; yes, and well, and safe. He knew that tonight. The torment, the fear for her safety that, finding no trace of her, he had known yesterday, and for so many yesterdays before, was gone now. She was alive; and, so far, she was safe. His lips moved silently. Thank God for that! And now he asked only that, whatever the outcome to himself in what he was about to do, she might after tonight be safe for always.

He shook his head a little grimly. Suppose, instead of success, he failed? Too often the Phantom had slipped from his grasp; and he was only too well aware that tonight he was almost literally going up against a stacked hand held by the other. Mother Margot had warned him that her rooms were a trap for the Gray Seal; the Tocsin had warned him. He had never doubted this simply because more than once he had ventured into those rooms and emerged unscathed. And, though it might well be, as he had argued with himself on his last visit there, that it was now so long ago since the trap had been baited that the Phantom no longer built any hopes upon it as a means of snaring his prey, that argument, however well founded, did not apply tonight. He could not very well expect to attack the trap itself and proceed to demolish it without *inviting* the attention of the trapper, which was, indeed, his prime intention.

A fool? Perhaps! But there was no other way of getting to grips with the Phantom. And tonight she was alive and safe; and there might be no tomorrow night. And, besides, if the worst happened, he would not go out *alone*— the Phantom would go with him. He was somehow sure of that; it was like a deep-seated consciousness, a strange reassuring certainty. And if that were so, he had no quarrel with the price, whatever it might be!

His fingers, fumbling in the pocket of his ragged jacket, found and drew out an envelope. He stared at it for a long time. Hers! The Tocsin's! The first word he had had from her for so many days! His eyes softened. Alive! And he had known so great a fear—a fear that had grown day after day into an almost hopeless agony of dread. She who loved him, and had made no effort to communicate with him after he had been wounded that other night—no effort when he knew that under ordinary conditions she would have moved heaven and earth to do so. That was why, last night, in spite of Jason, in spite of his wound, he had tried to pick up the Phantom's trail again through Bunty Myers—and in a measure had succeeded. He had found Bunty Myers, but Bunty Myers was dead now.

A strange, grim light crept into Jimmie Dale's half-closed eyes. The circle had indeed narrowed. Of the Phantom's satellites, of all those who once had gathered in that back, upstairs room of Wally Kerrigan's "club," there were left now only two—the Kitten and Mother Margot. Those two—and somewhere in his hidden lair the Phantom. Well, tonight then—

He nodded quickly to himself. He was only waiting until it was a little later. He turned impatiently on the cot. Time seemed to drag interminably. The stage was already set. He had warned Mother Margot to keep away from her rooms tonight; to find an alibi for herself. It was a little quixotic, perhaps, a little of added danger to himself; but again, as it had been last night, her life, if things went wrong, might very well pay part of the forfeit, and even Mother Margot was entitled to her life. What else could he have done? It was true that, at best, he could consider her but an unwilling sort of ally; but nevertheless, even though it might have been but through fear, she had, he was sure, always played straight with him. And so tonight he could have done no less than to have given her her chance again.

Jimmie Dale rose abruptly from the cot, and, with the envelope in his hand, stepped back across the room again to a position under the gas jet. He had found the note here in the usual place behind the movable section of the baseboard when, late that afternoon, after having previously called Mother Margot from her pushcart on Thompson Street to that rather singularly-placed telephone in the rear of Antonio Mezzo's shop and had given her her warning, he had come to the Sanctuary for the purpose of assuming the rôle of Smarlinghue, and of spending at least a portion of the waiting hours in the underworld's inner circles which were always pregnant with the possibility of affording an additional thread or clue that might lend strength to his intended stroke against the Phantom. He read the note again. It was dated that afternoon:

Dear Philanthropic Crook:—What have you been thinking? With you wounded, and believing I would be in a position to know of it, and no word from me, it could only have been one of two things. Either I was heartless, or—or what you had feared so greatly had happened. It could not be the former, and so I know that in your love you must have been, as I would have been, mad with anxiety.

I said I would not write to you or communicate with you until the shadows had all gone out of our lives again, but this afternoon I would indeed be heartless if I did not send you this word. I am well; and I am safe. Through circumstances that I shall not enter into, I did not know that you were wounded until last night, and then, almost coincidently, I also knew that from last night's activities your wound could not have been serious, and so *my* anxiety was relieved.

Just one word more. Once before, long, long ago, so long ago that it seems now it were in some other age, I wrote you that it was near the end, that I had all but won, that victory was in sight, and—and, Jimmie, only disaster came. And so now I hesitate to say anything but just this: Things are going very well, and it may be, Jimmie—oh, I can not help but say it—only *hours* before the shadows will have gone forever.

Marie.

Jimmie Dale replaced the note in his pocket. Somehow, he could not bring himself to destroy it, as he had always done before. It had been so long since he had heard from her; it was physical, tangible evidence that she was *alive*. He swept his hand across his eyes. Those fears of last night—that had driven him, wounded, from his bed! It was as though she had almost read his mind, read the argument he had followed and from which he had deduced the worst. It was strange, though, that she had not known—if things were going so very well! Circumstances! What circumstances?

He began to pace up and down the squalid room; and then, as abruptly as he had left it, he went and flung himself down on the cot again. He was restless. It was not his wound. His wound was all right, and was none the worse for last night's experiences. His side was sore and stiff, of course, and in that sense caused him a certain discomfort, but otherwise he was quite normal.

It was not his wound that caused his restlessness; it was this dragging of time, this waiting for the moment to arrive when he could supplant inaction with activity. Perhaps he would have done better to have remained longer in those various hidden places of the inner circles of the underworld that he had visited after he had received the Tocsin's note? He shrugged his shoulders. No; he was better here. He had learned all that he could have hoped to learn—yes, and more! No; that was not quite true. He had, rather, only substantiated beyond question what he had already decided in his own mind could be the only logical conclusion to the affair of last night when the Kitten and Bunty Myers, playing Steenie Klotz and his companion apaches for dupes, had attempted to secure the stolen funds of the defunct Banco Santos.

His jaws closed with a snap. Whisperings! How many times before had he listened to the voice of the underworld breathing its secrets through the underground exchanges where none save those of the aristocracy might find entrance, and where the peers of that abandoned realm of Crimeland kept their fingers on the pulse of a seething, disturbed and moiling citizenry! And tonight the underworld was in a sort of tense ferment, watching in unholy anticipation a game of life and death that was being played out behind its guarded doors that were so effectually closed to the outer world.

Jimmie Dale smiled suddenly, grimly now. He had found the underworld viciously agog, intent with gluttonous eagerness upon a drama whose dénouement promised to be blood-thirsty and murderous enough to satisfy even its unbridled lusts! Steenie Klotz, Red Jack and their companions had been played for dupes by Bunty Myers and the Kitten, but the dupes were not altogether fools, nor their intellects fallen to so low an estate that they had failed to absorb the fact that one plus one made two! The Kitten, and very certainly indeed Bunty Myers, had not expected that the night would end with the dupes finding Bunty Myers dead at their hands in that boat on the shore of the Sound! And of the two now Bunty Myers was perhaps in the better case! The Kitten, it transpired, had had sense enough not to stand on the order of his going, and had incontinently fled for his life. He had not been heard of since last night.

Again Jimmie Dale smiled grimly. It was the logical conclusion—and it was very simple. Bunty Myers and the Kitten for years had been well known characters in the underworld; and for years they had been known to work *together* in Gentleman Laroque's gang. And one and one made two, that was all!

Whisperings! Whisperings, as ghouls might whisper in hideous enthusiasm at the promise of some abominable feast to come, whisperings everywhere through the underground exchanges of Gangland! Of the passing of Bunty Myers the police as yet were apparently in ignorance; but Steenie Klotz and his outraged apaches had not hesitated in "safe" quarters to spread the story and make known the sentence they had passed upon their betrayer. And the underworld in its blood lust waited. It was the law. The Kitten was being hunted mercilessly to his death. But so far they had not found the Kitten.

Jimmie Dale nodded at the gas jet. That was what he had learned in the underworld's inner circles; and then he had returned here to the Sanctuary, for it was not as Smarlinghue but as the Gray Seal that he meant to play out the night. And now time dragged. He could not even begin to strip off these rags and discard the character of the drug-broken, dissolute artist until the moment arrived when he was ready to leave. It was too dangerous, for in the meantime someone, anyone, a lodger even in the same tenement here, might come, and—

He sat up suddenly erect on the cot. Someone *was* coming. He listened. A footstep shuffled along in the hall outside and reached the door; and then someone knocked guardedly upon the panel.

It was Smarlinghue, not Jimmie Dale, who spoke.

"Who's there?" he demanded ungraciously.

"It's me," a voice croaked hurriedly. "Let me in, Smarly. It's Mother Margot."

Mother Margot! A smile flickered across Jimmie Dale's lips, as he rose from the cot and started across the room toward the door. Mother Margot who *obeyed* him as the Gray Seal, when she couldn't help it perhaps; Mother Margot who accepted Smarlinghue as one of her own ilk, and, on one occasion at least, as a source of assistance and an ally in her turbulent life! What did Mother Margot want with Smarlinghue tonight? He opened the door, and, as the old hag, her shawl drawn closely around her head, entered, he closed it again behind her.

"Hello, Mother!" said Jimmie Dale facetiously. "Ain't business good down on Thompson Street tonight?"

She glanced around her furtively.

"Dere ain't no one here, is dere?" she asked anxiously.

Jimmie Dale shook his head.

"Spill it!" he invited. "What's the matter?"

Again she glanced around her, and it was almost a minute before she spoke. She twisted her hands nervously together.

"Youse helped me once before, Smarly," she whispered finally. "I—I ain't got no one else to ask, an'—an' tonight I'm in bad. Youse—youse'll help me again, won't youse, Smarly?"

Jimmie Dale pushed one of the two rickety chairs the Sanctuary possessed toward her.

"How do I know?" he countered cautiously. "I ain't making promises on the blind. Help yourself to the chair, and I'll listen."

Mother Margot shook her head quickly.

"I ain't got no time to sit down. An' I ain't got no chance for anythin' only mabbe to get croaked tonight if youse won't help me. I ran all de way over here, an'—an' I was scared youse wouldn't be here." She was wringing her hands together again in evident terror and nervousness. "Oh, my Gawd, if youse hadn't been here, Smarly, I—" Her voice broke and ended in a choked sob.

Jimmie Dale's eyes, from the crouching, dishevelled shawled and spectacled old creature, sought the shadows cast by the flickering gas jet that played along the edge of the threadbare strip of carpet at his feet. He did not question the genuineness of her distress. He had very good reason to believe in it most thoroughly. He was even vitally, personally, intimately concerned in it; for, back of it, where Mother Margot was involved, must be the Phantom's hand. He smiled to himself. What it was that had brought her here he, as Jimmie Dale, *must* know; but that knowledge could only be obtained through Smarlinghue, and Smarlinghue was—well, Smarlinghue was Smarlinghue.

"Well, don't lose your nerve," said Smarlinghue a little sharply, "or maybe you'll get me scared too, and the deal'll be off before it's started. The time before you got me to go hunting for English Steve, and I found him—murdered. What is it this time?"

"I—I've got to try an' get a message to someone," she said anxiously.

"That's what you said when it was English Steve," observed Smarlinghue judicially. "Well, shoot! Who is it tonight?"

Again she did not answer immediately; again she glanced furtively around her. And then she spoke, her voice scarcely audible:

"De Gray Seal."

"The Gray Seal!" Involuntarily Jimmie Dale gasped. He stared at her. He could quite understand that she might seek the Gray Seal; but this was irony in its sublimest form, wasn't it? And then suddenly he remembered. The night he had saved himself here by playing his dual rôle! The new heights to which Smarlinghue had risen in the underworld through that supposed encounter! It had almost secured him initiation into the confidences of Bunty Myers, and the rest of the Phantom's followers, of which Mother Margot here was one. That was it! Because he had *once* been known to have been in actual, physical touch with the Gray Seal, and would therefore perhaps be able to recognise him again! And she had come to the Gray Seal himself! It was exquisite!

He felt her eyes boring into him from behind her heavy-lensed spectacles. He smiled with exaggerated derision. But mentally now he knew no mirth. That was only one side of it, the strange irony of it. There must be something of no ordinary importance that could have prompted her to act like this. What was it? She who, again and again, had been compelled to act under the Gray Seal's orders, under *his* orders; who, only that afternoon, had received her instructions, or, perhaps better, warning from him over the telephone!

"It's too easy!" scoffed Smarlinghue, and grinned broadly. "All anybody's got to do that wants the Gray Seal is to go out on the corner and whistle for him."

"My Gawd!" The exclamation came piteously. She wrung her hands the harder together.

"Well," said Jimmie Dale, still facetiously, "what's the idea, then? Do you think just because he rough-housed me here one night that he left his calling card, and wrote his address on it before he went away? Or maybe you think he took his mask off, and says: 'Smarly, drop around any afternoon for a cup of tea; I'll always be at home—to you!' Well, he didn't! There ain't a bull or a lag that ain't been hunting him for years—and they're still hunting! How'd you expect me to find him?"

She seemed hardly to be paying any attention. Her fingers were working nervously with her shawl, now loosening it, now tightening it around her throat; and she still kept on glancing in all directions furtively around her.

"Smarly, for Gawd's sake, listen!" she burst out wildly. "I ain't askin' youse to find him. I'm askin' youse to help me. I got to have someone I can trust. Mabbe youse won't have to do nothin' at all. Youse won't see him; it'll only be on de telephone. I—I've been workin' wid him for weeks now."

It was exquisite! There was humour here for Jimmie Dale—but Smarlinghue's jaw dropped helplessly.

"The Gray Seal—and *you*!" He gulped, swallowing hard.

She nodded her head in a sort of helpless way.

"Yes," she said. "My Gawd, I'm handin' it to youse straight, an'—an' I'm in bad tonight. Youse helped me once, an' dere ain't no one else I dares go to. An' youse *will* help me, won't youse, Smarly, if I swear to youse dat dere ain't no risk or nothin' like dat for youse, an' dat dere ain't no one goin' to know youse was in it at all?"

Jimmie Dale, as Smarlinghue, examined meditatively the ragged, frayed sleeve of his coat.

"All right," said Jimmie Dale cautiously. "If I'm as safe as that, I won't see you stuck. But you've got to show me first. What do you want me to do?"

She reached out and caught his hand impulsively, and wrung it hard.

"Gawd bless youse, Smarly!" There was a world of relief in her voice, husky and broken though it was. "I knew youse would, Smarly; I knew youse would. Listen! Youse knows where my pushcart is on Thompson Street. Well, just near it is Mezzo's second-hand shop, an' dere's a side door to dat—up de lane. Dat door ain't locked, an' old Mezzo's away tonight, an' de shop is shut up. Dere's a telephone in dere in de back storeroom. It's kept dere on de quiet—see? All youse've got to do, Smarly, is go in dere an' wait, an' answer de telephone if it rings. Dere ain't nobody goin' to see youse, an' dere ain't nobody goin' to know youse're dere. If it rings it'll be de Gray Seal, an' youse'll give him a message from me."

Jimmie Dale, as Smarlinghue, whistled a little dubiously under his breath.

"And they said he always worked alone!" he observed plaintively. "Say, you'd get bumped off for this if any of the fleets knew about it! You're pretty thick, ain't you? He puts in a telephone for you, and—"

"No, he didn't!" She shook her head vigorously. "He had nothin' to do wid it. It's—it's another crowd. He got wise to it, dat's all, an' one night he caught me cold in—oh, my Gawd, Smarly, never mind about dat! I—I'm in wrong wid de whole works. I—I got to get a message to him tonight if I can."

"Well, why don't you go and find him then, and can the telephone stuff?" inquired Jimmie Dale, in his rôle of Smarlinghue.

"'Cause I don't know where he is, an' no more about him dan youse does," she said almost hysterically. "Don't youse understand, Smarly? He calls me to de phone when he wants me, an' de times he's shown himself was when he was wearin' a mask like he had de night he bust in on youse here."

"Well, then," prodded Jimmie Dale, "why don't you stick around and listen for the telephone yourself tonight?"

Mother Margot was wringing her hands again.

"D'youse t'ink I'd have come here an' put youse wise to wot I have, if I could've done dat?" she cried wildly. "Dat's wot's de matter. It—it's de other crowd dat's pullin' somethin' tonight, an'—an' I got to go an' do somethin' dey's told me to do. I got to go. I don't dare not to go. Dey—dey'd cut me t'roat if I didn't—an'—an' it's somethin' de Gray Seal's got to know about, or else he—oh, my Gawd, Smarly, can't youse understand?—he'd put me in wrong, an' I'd get finished anyway. He's pullin' somethin' himself tonight, but it's no good now, 'cause somethin' else is goin' to happen, an' he'd know afterwards dat I knew, an' if I didn't wise him up dat's my finish too."

Smarlinghue circled his lips with the tip of his tongue, and scowled unhappily.

"Say," he said heavily, "you're in nice, ain't you? How do you know it won't be the other crowd you're talking about, the bunch that you said put the phone in there, that rings up—and then I'd get stung too?"

"'Cause dey knows I ain't goin' to be dere. Ain't I tellin' youse dat?" Mother Margot answered miserably. "If de phone rings, it'll be de Gray Seal. Dere's no one else'd ask for Mother Margot."

"And suppose he don't ring up at all?" inquired Smarlinghue.

"I dunno!" Mother Margot's face seemed to whiten a little. "My Gawd, Smarly, I dunno—dat's wot's got me so scared. I ain't even sayin' he will; I—I'm only hopin'. It's de only chance I got. I know mabbe where I could find him a couple of hours from now, but it'll be too late den. I—I can't do nothin' more, Smarly, can I? I can't do nothin' more. If he don't telephone, de only chance I got is to try an' make him believe I did me best—dat's all! An' if he don't believe me, I—I guess I goes out for keeps."

Jimmie Dale for a moment appeared to consider the matter.

"I ain't quite sure I get you," he said slowly at last, "except that it looks to me like, between the two of them, it don't make much difference whether you're coming or going. And this telephone stunt looks like a long shot to me. But I don't see where I get hurt any, and if it's going to ease your mind I'll stand in. So what's the message I'm to give if he telephones?"

Mother Margot's face brightened.

"T'ank God for youse, Smarly!" she faltered. "Youse're as white as dey makes 'em. Youse just say dat de message is from me, an' dat de Voice is goin' to pull de big bump tonight, an' to watch French Jeff down at de White Rat. Y'understand, Smarly?"

Jimmie Dale shook his head.

"No; I don't," he said. "But if he does, it's all right, I suppose. I'm satis-fied. I'm not for mixing in and getting my hair singed. But if he asks me what the bump is, and what time it's going to bust loose, what do I say?"

"Nothin'," said Mother Margot. "Dere ain't nothin' more to tell him, 'cause dat's all I knows myself; but I knows it's de big showdown all right, an' de dope is straight. He won't need nothin' more, I guess, if he wants to butt in."

Jimmie Dale nodded indifferently. It was precisely what he wanted to know—the exact extent of the old hag's information.

Mother Margot shuffled her feet nervously.

"I got to go, Smarly," she said anxiously. "De Dago's runnin' me push-cart for me for de rest of de night, but he don't know nothin' about dis, so don't youse give him de high sign. Youse understand about de side door in de lane?"

"Sure!" said Smarlinghue. "And while we're standing here talking may-be he's telephoned already and pulled a bone."

Mother Margot shook her head.

"Dat don't matter," she said. "He knows Mezzo don't always hear, an' sometimes it's hard to get an answer. If he was tryin' to get me, he'll try again until he does." She hesitated, drew her shawl tightly about her head again, took a step toward the door, and once more hesitated. "Gawd bless youse, Smarly!" she said brokenly. "Mabbe youse t'inks youse does, but youse don't know wot youse're doin' for me tonight. Mabbe I'll pull out of dis alive, an' mabbe I won't, but don't youse ever forget, Smarly, if youse never sees me again, dat dere ain't no one in dis world means anythin' to Mother Margot like youse does, Smarly. An'—an'—" Her voice broke.

She was crying. Jimmie Dale started forward impulsively as he saw the old shoulders shake, and a tear, followed by another, trickle unchecked down her cheek. But she turned her head quickly away, and scuffled hurriedly to-ward the door before he had reached her.

But at the door she turned again.

"Gawd bless youse, Smarly!" she called again—and closed the door be-hind her.

CHAPTER 26

AT "THE WHITE RAT"

Mother Margot's footsteps, shuffling, receded along the hall, and died away with the opening and closing of the street door.

Jimmie Dale stood staring across the empty room. He had not fully re-alised before how secure was the hold that he, as the Gray Seal, had upon the old hag! She was afraid of the Phantom, or the Voice, as she called the man;

but she was equally afraid of the Gray Seal, it now appeared—and between the two, unable to steer any middle course tonight, she was in mortal terror.

He frowned. He might have eased her mind a little in some way, perhaps. No! He shook his head decisively. Her coming, the story she had told, changed materially, and of necessity, his own plans for tonight—at least for the next few hours. Mother Margot's rooms had interested him only because of the probability that they were the outer portal to the Phantom's sanctum; but if the Phantom's movements tonight centred around French Jeff and "The White Rat," it was French Jeff and The White Rat that automatically and at once became the centre of attraction for him as well. And particularly so since, deprived of the Kitten's assistance, practically the one remaining satellite, any play that the Phantom made must, leaving Mother Margot out, be made in *person*. It was the Phantom that he sought!

Jimmie Dale stepped swiftly across the room and locked the door, then kneeling on the floor near by lifted aside the movable section of the baseboard. He could no more have afforded to risk the character of Smarlinghue by some well-meaning but ill-advised word in an effort to calm her fears, than he could afford, after what she had said, to go to The White Rat *as* Smarlinghue. She was as likely to be there as not. If she saw Smarlinghue there it would be—Well, she would never again after that have need to fear the Gray Seal! A hint that Smarlinghue was not what he seemed would be the end, swift and inevitable, of the Gray Seal and Jimmie Dale!

He nodded sharply to himself as he stripped off his ragged attire, and, quickly now, removing the little pieces of wax from nostrils and from beneath the lips, that distorted the contour of his face, and removing, too, the stain of make-up, began to dress again as Jimmie Dale in the carefully folded suit which he took from the hiding place behind the baseboard. Again he nodded to himself. Tweeds tonight. It was fortunate! He had naturally been wearing tweeds that afternoon when he had left his house. The White Rat was not usually frequented by gentlemen in evening dress!

A minute, two, three passed. The gas jet, spitting like an angry cat, became suddenly silent. The room was in darkness, save for a nebulous shaft of night light that came in through the top-light high up over the French doors that opened on the small, ill-kept courtyard without. And now a shadow moved and bulked itself against the French doors, and one of the French doors opened without sound and closed again, and the shadow crept along the wall of the building, and strangely, like an apparition, disappeared through the fence that bordered the lane.

A moment more, and Jimmie Dale, as though Smarlinghue had never existed, was walking quietly along the street. His mind was working now with cool, judicial precision, sifting, weighing, appraising the factors of the problem before him. Mother Margot would not be near Thompson Street again tonight. If the Gray Seal's hand appeared tonight, it would be no more than she expected. Whether it was as the Gray Seal or as Smarlinghue that first he next saw Mother Margot, the statement that the Gray Seal had phoned and received his information was wholly in accord with the old hag's own suggestion. He, Jimmie Dale, was free to go at once to The White Rat. He was not even abusing the trust that she had reposed in Smarlinghue! There was something ironical in that!

Her distress had been genuine enough, and her story was beyond doubt or question. Who should know better than himself? She had said that later on she might have known where to find the Gray Seal, but that it would be too late then. She had meant, of course, her own rooms that he had, that afternoon, warned her to keep away from. That statement alone stamped her story with the ring of truth. But why bring distrust of Mother Margot even into question! She had never yet played him false; and tonight it was glaringly obvious that, voluntarily, in the only way she could, though that way depended purely on chance, she had done her utmost to keep her pact with him.

He shrugged his shoulders. Mother Margot, as a factor in the problem tonight, could from now on be eliminated. French Jeff and The White Rat, then! What was the game that the Phantom was playing, the key to which, which was all the information that Mother Margot had possessed, was French Jeff and The White Rat?

Jimmie Dale was walking more quickly now, threading his way through the more unfrequented streets, as he worked deeper into the lower East Side. French Jeff and The White Rat were equally notorious; the one as a sort of plenipotentiary of crookdom from the other side of the water, and the other as the favourite hostelry of foreign visitors whose credentials were properly viséd. This was the understanding that the New York underworld had of French Jeff and The White Rat; ostensibly, however, to the police, and to the public at large, the man was but the quiet, law-abiding proprietor of a small establishment that, while it could not be dignified by the name of hotel, yet, nevertheless, embodied in itself a bar, a restaurant, and a few rooms for guests—which latter, to the public, were always "engaged."

Quite so! In the enormously fat little Frenchman and his White Rat lay potentialities for evil that were limitless. Suave, cunning in his international affiliations, the man was credited with playing big games for big stakes. That he was successful was evidenced by the fact that for years now he had carried on business without coming under the ban of the police.

Jimmie Dale frowned. He, like the rest of the underworld, for his eyes were Smarlinghue's now, could only view the man in the large; there were no details to the picture. And this was so, naturally enough, because French Jeff confined himself strictly to his own foreign connections, and stood wholly aloof from local entanglements no matter how alluring the promise of their reward might be. What then was the Phantom's interest in this man tonight? Had French Jeff at last broken his rule and gone in on some deal, working hand in glove with the Phantom; or was the Phantom preparing, as he so often did, to pick the ripened plums from another's tree? Or was it—

Jimmie Dale had halted before an uninviting three-story frame building on the corner of an equally uninviting street. A sign, somewhat battered and aping the Continental style, swung in the breeze over the front door. It bore the design of an animal, its species none too easily recognisable, done in white on a green background; the lettering, however, below this inartistic effort was informative: *The White Rat.*

Within, as could be seen from the street, the ground floor was a sort of combination restaurant and bar. A few customers occupied tables; a few more were at the bar. Jimmie Dale's slouch hat was pulled rakishly down over his eyes, his cravat flashily tucked into the bosom of his shirt, as he stepped now inside, and, walking up to the bar, ordered a drink. He glanced around him nonchalantly. He had never been in the place before, but in common with everybody else in the underworld he knew the fat proprietor by sight. French Jeff was not in evidence.

"Ain't the boss around?" inquired Jimmie Dale casually out of the corner of his mouth, as the barkeeper slid a glass toward him across the bar.

"Sure! He's upstairs on de office," replied the man, evidently, too, a Frenchman, in broken English. "You want to see him?"

Jimmie Dale shook his head.

"Nope!" he said indifferently. "Not hard enough to bring him down. I'd have said hello to him if he'd been handy, that's all."

Jimmie Dale set his now empty glass back on the bar, and with a wave of his hand to the barkeeper, went out again to the street. French Jeff was "upstairs on de office." He went on around the corner. The White Rat, if it were efficient along the lines upon which it was supposed to run, would certainly possess a side entrance for the benefit of those who, with the necessary credentials, were privileged to occupy rooms there. Yes, here it was.

Jimmie Dale opened the door quietly and stepped inside. Even if seen, it meant only that he must then find some other means of getting into proximity with French Jeff. The glib excuse that he thought this was but another entrance to the restaurant, as indeed it might well be also, would be quite sufficient to guarantee an orderly retreat on his part. And then he flung a mental gibe at himself. He was borrowing trouble, whereas, as a matter of fact, he appeared to be playing in wholesale luck.

He found himself standing in a dimly lighted hall, rather seedily furnished, and quite deserted. The only sounds were those that sifted through from the restaurant in the front of the establishment, the clatter of dishes, the muffled voices of those at the tables and at the bar. No; he was wrong! From above him, up the stairs that were directly in front of him, his ear caught now a curious, irregular rasping sound. He could not at once definite it as he began quickly and silently to mount the stairs, but halfway up the sound took on a concrete meaning, and a smile broadened his lips. The sound had resolved itself into nothing more than a series of well defined snores!

And now at the top of the landing, he placed the direction of the sound. Doors here opened off on each side of the hall, and at the far end the light streamed out through one that was open, and disclosed, facing it, the door on the opposite side of the hall to be ajar. It was from the lighted room that the snores emanated.

Jimmie Dale moved softly along the hall, keeping close against the wall on the opposite side from the lighted door, and finally paused. From where he stood now, he could just see at an angle into the lighted room. For an instant he stood listening, then he slipped through the already partially opened door beside him that faced the lighted doorway. He was playing in luck, in unbounded luck! Here was a vacant room, and across the hall, the door wide open, French Jeff and his "office" were in plain view. Perhaps it was almost too much luck! This room here might be occupied after all, the "guest" out only temporarily, and likely to return at any minute.

He glanced critically around him. There was light enough from across the hall to see. No; it was quite all right. There was no sign of occupancy, no clothing, no belongings of any kind in evidence. And if by any chance a new arrival should be allotted the room, it would certainly not be until French Jeff in there had been advised and had passed upon the applicant's desirability, and there would be time enough then to consider a means of retreat.

Jimmie Dale, leaving the door no more ajar than would enable him to see readily into the opposite room, drew up a chair and coolly seated himself for his vigil. The fat little French crook was sprawled back in his desk chair, his hands folded over an ample and undulating paunch, his feet up and resting on a black handbag that in turn occupied the seat of a second chair. The man was fast asleep.

What was it? What was the game? Had that black handbag, guarded by the other's feet, anything to do with it? "Watch French Jeff at The White Rat." That was all Mother Margot had known.

The minutes passed, became quarter hours, a half hour—more. Occasionally French Jeff stirred uneasily, awakened, settled himself drowsily, and went to sleep again; occasionally Jimmie Dale silently changed his own position.

What time was it? It had been well after ten o'clock when Mother Margot had come to the Sanctuary; it must be long after eleven now. He began to know not so much a sense of impatience as one of disquiet. It was still early yet, of course, and the hours, most likely of all the twenty-four for criminal activities, were still to come, but somehow the pig-like serenity of the fat Frenchman disturbed him.

Still the minutes dragged by. Another quarter of an hour passed. And then Jimmie Dale suddenly straightened up alertly. There was a footstep now on the stairs; and now it came along the hall. Jimmie Dale retreated a little from the door, his automatic in his hand.

It was one of the waiters from downstairs. The man passed into the other room.

"It's time to go, monsieur," he heard the waiter say in French.

French Jeff, with a grunt, roused himself.

"All right, Emile," he said shortly.

The waiter left the room and went downstairs again.

French Jeff spent a moment at his desk, then closed it down, picked up the black handbag from the chair, extinguished the light, and left the room.

Jimmie Dale stole out into the darkened corridor. French Jeff descended the stairs, and went out through the side door. Another minute and Jimmie Dale, too, had gained the street, and crossing to the opposite side took up the fat proprietor's trail.

It led to the nearest subway station, and an uptown train. French Jeff got off at the Grand Central Station, and Jimmie Dale followed. At a ticket window, French Jeff bought a ticket and berth on the midnight train for Boston. Jimmie Dale, for the first time in evidence, and now at the other's elbow, made exactly the same purchase—but on Jimmie Dale's lips now there was a smile of almost self-pity.

"If I'm going where I think I am," confided Jimmie Dale softly to himself, as he followed the other through the gates and to the Pullman, "it'll be a rather expensive ride for the mileage—but the gatemen are inviolable and the porter might not have stood for a bribe."

The berths in the car were all made up. The fat little Frenchman swished down the aisle, waddling after the porter. Jimmie Dale, finding his berth to be opposite that of French Jeff, sat down on the edge of it, and drew the curtains together in front of him. A few minutes passed. The train pulled out. A wry smile began to settle on Jimmie Dale's lips—and at 125th Street it had hardened into lines of grim, unmirthful chagrin.

French Jeff had undressed and gone to bed, and the car was already reverberating to the fat man's snores.

Jimmie Dale got off the train.

CHAPTER 27

THE LAIR

Tight-lipped, Jimmie Dale stared out at the black, flying walls as the subway train roared its way back to lower New York. He had been properly done! There could be no question about that. But by whom? And why? What did it mean? Intuition, even back there in The White Rat, had warned him that something was wrong, but he would in no way have been justified in being swayed wholly by intuition. He could not in justice blame himself for that. What was it? What was the meaning of it? Something *had* happened some-where—but not at The White Rat. And he had been very neatly side-tracked. All that was obvious.

Was it Mother Margot? He shook his head. She had never yet double-crossed him, and he did not believe that she would dare to do so. Even her visit to the Sanctuary tonight, and her very evident wholesome respect for the Gray Seal, not to say fear, was almost proof in itself, it would seem, that she had not deliberately tried to mislead him.

What, then? There seemed to be only one logical explanation left. The Phantom. It would not have been altogether a new move on the Phantom's part, for, while not wholly analogous, the man had in a way tried the same game before. The Phantom knew only too well, and to his cost, that there had been a leak somewhere in his entourage, a leak that had brought the Gray Seal very inopportunely on his heels more than once. But tonight that entou-rage, in view of the fact that the rest were dead and that the Kitten was being hunted mercilessly by his own fellow crooks of the underworld, was reduced now to Mother Margot alone. Therefore, if the leak still existed, it must exist in the person of Mother Margot, and therefore, as a precautionary measure if nothing more, should the Phantom be up to some play tonight in which he particularly wanted to guard against any interference, he would logically turn the possibility that the leak still existed to his own advantage, and at the same time, perhaps, test out, and even trap, Mother Margot.

"Yes," said Jimmie Dale grimly to himself. "I guess that's it."

He nodded sharply. He had been side-tracked from his original plan to-night, but the night was not yet ended, and if he had the Phantom to thank for the bubble he had been chasing, the Phantom might yet have reason to remember tonight from another cause very different indeed! The phantom clue at Mother Margot's rooms was again his goal. The delay had mattered little. What he had meant to do as he had lain there on the cot in the Sanctu-ary, he meant to do now.

Jimmie Dale looked at his watch, as he left the subway at Astor Place and headed into the Bowery. It was ten minutes to one. He walked quickly now. It was not far to those two tenements with the narrow areaway between, in one of which Mother Margot had lived since Gentleman Laroque, alias Isaac Shiftel, alias the Phantom, had so mysteriously made his escape from the room which the old hag now occupied; just a little lower down, a little off the Bowery, in one of the East Side's most unenviable neighbourhoods.

Five minutes brought him to his destination. It was quiet here, save for the distant sounds of night life from the Bowery, dark, deserted. A light showed sparsely here and there from a window—that was all. He passed the areaway between the two tenements, smiled grimly at the recollection of the officer who had stood guard therein beneath the window on the night the

Phantom had escaped and he, Jimmie Dale, had been so nearly trapped, and slipped unobtrusively into the dark hallway of the further tenement.

A moment more and, masked, he stood listening, at the door of Mother Margot's rooms. There was no sound from within. Why should there be? Even if Mother Margot, according to her own story, had not been ordered somewhere else by the Phantom, she would not be here since he, Jimmie Dale, had warned her to keep away. There was no sound, but—the slim, sensitive fingers were working tentatively at the doorknob—this was a little strange. The door was unlocked!

It swung open now silently, an inch at a time, under his hand. He stepped inside and, as silently, closed the door behind him. It was black in here. He could not see a yard in front of him. But he was familiar, a little more than familiar, with his surroundings! He stole forward to the doorway connecting with the inner room, moving without sound, as Larry the Bat in the days of old in the old Sanctuary had moved, and paused on the threshold. It was from here those voices that other night had come; here was the *mise en scène* of the phantom clue.

Again he listened. There was still no sound. Jimmie Dale's automatic was already in his hand, and now from his pocket he took out a flashlight. Still he waited another instant, listening; and then, the round, white ray stabbing through the blackness, Jimmie Dale, his face set hard and grim, his lips a straight line, stood staring at the wall opposite him.

The phantom clue was a phantom clue no longer. It lay there clothed in tangible, yes, even mocking, form, so blatantly did it flaunt now the disclosal of its own existence! The flashlight was boring into a great oblong-shaped opening through the wall.

Still Jimmie Dale stood motionless. Through his mind in swift, lightning flashes swept the oft-repeated admonition of both the Tocsin and Mother Margot. A trap. He had been told the place was a trap for him. Was the door of the trap open now—a little *too* invitingly open—the door he had never been able to find before, patiently and thoroughly though he had searched? Had this anything to do with what had gone before tonight, with the fool's errand upon which he had run to French Jeff and The White Rat? How could it have? And yet—

His eyes swept the opening, and the wall adjacent to it, above and on both sides. He understood now, of course. And it brought no sense of self-reproof that, though knowing it had existed somewhere here, he had not, in the times he had searched before, been able to find it. It was clever, ingenious, a replica almost of the old Crime Club with its false, movable walls, though here not nearly so elaborate—but perhaps even built by the same men, at that, as one of their outposts, since Clarke, alias Wizard Marre, who had been the Phantom's confederate in the murder of Jason Lane, had been a member of that original organisation. A dado of cheap, painted burlap at the height of some five feet ran around the room; this was surmounted by a wide moulding, and the whole divided into oblong panels by vertical, though narrower, strips of moulding again. It was one of these oblong sections that now had disappeared into the floor, disclosing an inner wall, that was obviously the real wall of the room, set back perhaps slightly more than two feet from the false wall with the dado. This made a little passageway within, so that while he, Jimmie Dale, might have tapped the entire length of the wall in an effort to discover the opening by the sense of sound, in no place would it have sounded *more* hollow than in any other; and, again, the mouldings covered the joints, and the section slid up and down behind them, so that unless they had been ripped off bodily it would have been impossible to—

His face grew harder. That was what he had meant to do tonight, *wreck* the room if necessary, throw the caution that before had actuated him to the winds; but tonight all lay there *open* before him, starkly, vauntingly open. It was obvious enough now. The section slid up and down through the floor and—*Up and down!* That was what Bunty Myers had said. But Bunty Myers had said too that *she* didn't know because it was in the next house. That passage there! Invitingly open now! It could only lead to one place then—the next house—and there was only one next house on this side. The other tenement! A trap! Well, he had come for this, hadn't he?—to find the trap, no matter what the consequences, no matter what the cost, if it would but bring him into touch with the Phantom.

He stepped forward now silently across the room, and, with his flashlight switched off, knelt down at the opening. The passage in there was very narrow, certainly quite long, and certainly inky black. One could therefore fairly expect that somewhere in the passage between here and the other tenement there would be a light; and if so, and if it were lighted now, it would disclose for the benefit of the "quarry" any "trapper" who might be lurking there. Also if there were a light it would naturally be readily accessible from the entrance here.

Half crouched, he leaned forward into the opening, and felt inside, up and down along the edges of the wall. His fingers encountered a switch button. He pressed it now—but instead of a light showing anywhere, the movable section of the wall under him began to rise. He jabbed at the switch quickly again, even as he flung himself clear of the opening, and then found that the section had receded once more to its original position below the level of the baseboard.

Jimmie Dale drew in his breath sharply. So that was it! The thing was electrically controlled. That was plain enough, and from the *inside* there was no concealment of how it was set in motion; but how was it operated from within the room? He might not have been able in his several previous searches to have located the position of the opening, but he was quite certain that had there been a concealed switch, say, anywhere along the wall under the dado, or at the edges of the mouldings, he would have found it, for his fingers had felt over every inch of that space.

He shrugged his shoulders. Well, it didn't matter now, did it, since some-one else had supplied the "open sesame!" And since there was no other light—

His body well back from the opening, he reached his hand inside, and, pointing his flashlight parallel with the passage in the direction of the other tenement, flung a beam of light along it. It brought no response; no answering shot, for example, that he had half expected. He risked more now. Flat on the floor, with head and shoulders this time inside the opening, the flashlight's ray shot out again. But this time he could see. What was at the other end he could not tell, but immediately in front of him the way was clear. A series of steps led downward, then seemed to reach a level, until, in perspective, from where he lay, the roof and the base of the passage merged together.

The passage, then, beyond surmise, led down under the narrow alleyway to the "next house"—the tenement which was the counterpart of this one here. He rose to his feet, and cautiously, without sound, moved forward, descending the steps. The passage was extremely narrow, his shoulders kept brushing the walls on either side.

At every few steps he stopped to listen. His flashlight was out now. When he moved it was the sense of touch alone that guided him. He reached a level. This would be the section of the tunnel directly under the areaway, of course. And now, as the series of steps began again, this time leading upward, a faint glow of light showed through the darkness, and for the first time his ear caught a sound—it was like a low, strange moaning.

Jimmie Dale went down on his hands and knees now as he crawled up-ward. He would be less a target in that position, for it was obvious that the other end of the secret passage was open, and that the room or the space into which it opened was lighted—*and occupied.* Also, it was no longer a mystery where the voices had come from that had been heard in Mother Margot's rooms!

Noiselessly he reached the top step. Here the arrangement was the ex-act duplicate of the other end of the passage. A wall section was open, a lighted room beyond. The moaning, naturally more distinct now, continued unabated.

Cautiously Jimmie Dale edged forward until he could see into the room—and then, in an instant, he was on his feet and through the opening, and running toward a man's form that was stretched out on the floor.

The Kitten!

The man's face was gray with the pallor of approaching death, and there was a great crimson blotch over the left side of his shirt where the vest had been torn open, but he roused himself now with almost superhuman energy, staring in most strange eagerness and excitement at Jimmie Dale.

"Who are youse?" he cried out. "Who in 'ell are youse wid dat mask on?"

"It doesn't matter," said Jimmie Dale gently. The man was dying; it needed no professional eye to discern that fact. The Kitten! Well, even the Kitten was a fellow-human. "It doesn't matter," he said again; "let me try and make you more comfortable, and—"

"It does matter!" There was fierce insistence, so fierce that it was almost bizarre, in the man's gasping words. "It matters more'n anythin' else whether a guy dat wears a mask is a friend of Laroque's or ain't. Youse can't do any-thin' for me. I—I ain't got but a few minutes left. If youse're a friend of La-roque's beat it out of here an' leave me alone; if youse ain't, I got somethin' to tell youse. Quick! Who are youse?"

Gentleman Laroque, alias the Phantom! The Kitten the last remaining satellite! What did this mean? The man's mind was wandering, perhaps—and yet he seemed coherent enough.

"I think you'd know me best," said Jimmie Dale simply, "as the Gray Seal."

The Kitten struggled to his elbow.

"De Gray Seal! Prove it! Prove it for de love of Gawd!" he cried out wildly. "Mabbe dey've got him, but if dey ain't, youse will—if youse *are* de Gray Seal. Prove it!"

There was something of vital, paramount moment here. The man seemed possessed of a hatred and fury that had given him, in his dying condition, an unnatural strength. From the leather girdle Jimmie Dale took out the thin, metallic case that was the receptacle of those diamond-shaped, gray-paper seals that had given him his name, and, lifting one out, held it up before the Kitten's eyes.

The man laughed. It seemed to carry a shudder in its depths. It echoed around the room in a strangled, horrible way.

"Dat's enough!" screamed the Kitten. "Youse're de guy dat's been after him for weeks. Youse're de guy he's afraid of. Mabbe dey've got him, but I ain't takin' no chances, for if dey ain't, youse will. Damn him! It was La-roque dat give me dis—in dere—in de passage. It was Laroque dat plugged me cold, an—" He caught at his throat, choking, struggling for breath.

"Laroque!" exclaimed Jimmie Dale tensely. "Do you know what you are saying—that it was Gentleman Laroque who shot you?"

The Kitten clutched at Jimmie Dale's arm, dragging himself up again.

"Yes, I know wot I'm sayin'." He was whispering hoarsely now. "Listen! Mabbe youse heard I was up against it wid a gang dat was after me, mabbe youse didn't—it doesn't matter. I hid since yesterday. Tonight dey nosed me out, an'—an' I had to beat it for me life. I didn't have much start. I pinched a car, but dey got another—see? I didn't have nowheres to go but here, den—I thought Laroque'd hide me—it was de only chance I had."

He fought for his breath, paused, and struggled on again, his words coming more thickly and with greater effort.

"I left de car around de corner, an' came in here. Laroque an' Mother Margot was here. I—I was tellin' 'em about it. I thought I'd given de gang de slip. But I hadn't. Dey came smashin' at de door. Laroque didn't say nothin', only he looked wicked when he jumped for de electric wall bracket an' gave dat brass fittin' against de wall a twist. Dat opened de door in de wall—see? 'Come on!' he says den to Mother Margot an' me. 'De two of youse! Quick!'

"De gang was bustin' in de door of de room by now, an' dey saw us. We followed Laroque through de wall, an' he pushes de switch inside an' de wall closes up. It—it was black in dere. My Gawd, it was black! An' Laroque kind of laughs. 'Dat was a close squeak, an' mabbe we ain't safe yet,' he says. 'Mother, youse an' me'll go down to Blind Peter's, since de Kitten's been thoughtful enough to bring us a car; an' youse, Kitten, youse'll go where youse deserves to go for takin' any chance on givin' me away.' Just like dat he said it, an' he was laughin'. My Gawd, he was *laughin'* all de time. 'Youse overrated de value of yer life, Kitten,' he says, an'—an' shot me—cold."

The man with a nervous grip that locked like a vise around Jimmie Dale's arm and shoulder, had heaved himself up into a sitting posture. His lips and face were working.

"D'ye understand?" he choked.

"Yes," said Jimmie Dale through tight lips.

"Quick!" gasped the Kitten. "Listen! I—I ain't got much more time. He thought he'd finished me. I—I guess I lost consciousness. Den I heard de gang in here poundin' at de wall. Dey couldn't do me no more harm. I knew Laroque had put me out for keeps, an'—an' he was goin' to pay for it—see?—pay for it—pay for it. I crawled to de switch an' opened de wall. Dey made a rush for me, but I gets a chance to speak. Dey thought I'd got away wid some money last night—a—a black box—Banco Santos—but I hadn't—I don't know no more'n youse where it is—see?"

The Kitten's voice was growing weaker; his grip was loosening, the strength ebbing from his fingers.

"I told 'em it was Laroque an' de woman put up de whole plant, an'—an' dat dey had de money, an' dat I'd only done wot Laroque told me—an' de proof Laroque an' Margot was in de game was dis hole in de wall an' de passage—an' dat dey was runnin' for Blind Peter's." He caught at his throat. "De gang went through de hole dere after Laroque—ten minutes ago—Blind Peter's—understand? Double chance—de Gray Seal'll get 'em if Steenie don't—de Gray—"

Jimmie Dale stood up. The Kitten was dead. For an instant he looked around him. He seemed most curiously to be possessed of two entities—one that rejoiced fiercely over what now seemed a certainty that the Phantom, either at the hands of the apaches that the Kitten in his dying vengeance had set upon the other, or, failing that, through himself, Jimmie Dale, would be finally and irrevocably trapped tonight; the other that looked out as through a strange veil of unreality upon his immediate surroundings. This was the Phantom's lair at the end of the phantom trail.

CHAPTER 28

BLIND PETER'S

Jimmie Dale stepped swiftly across the room, and with a small steel jimmy which he took from his leather girdle, ripped aside, from where it fitted close against the wall, the round brass plaque or fitting, technically called the canopy, of the electric-light fixture. There was no time to lose, but he could spare an instant for this! Yes, it was as the Kitten had said. It concealed an electrical connection quite apart from the electric light itself; and by giving the canopy a half turn the contact could be made.

He nodded, as he turned now in a flash toward the window. He was satisfied. That was how the movable section of the wall was manipulated from within. And the window here, unless his calculations were hopelessly at fault, faced, exactly across the areaway, the window in Mother Margot's room. He raised the shade—and suddenly, with a low, suppressed cry, wrenched it down again, and leaped for the opening in the wall. In an instant he was inside, and, pressing the switch, the movable section had closed behind him.

The police! The window *did* face Mother Margot's, and, as there had been on the first night that he had come here, so too tonight an officer was lurking outside there now in the alleyway. The light streaming out from the window with the lifting shade had disclosed a man in uniform crouched against the wall. And also, even as he had wrenched back the shade, his ear had caught the muffled tread of several men in the hall outside the room. And that, too, was as it had been on the first occasion!

He ran now, his flashlight streaming ahead of him, through the tunnel, gained Mother Margot's room, and, indifferent now as to whether the movable section here was left closed or not, since it could in no way affect his own movements, and since the tunnel was now an open secret through its discovery by the apaches, he made no attempt to close it behind him; and, as he had done before when wary of the police here, he slipped out at the rear of the tenement, sped silently across the backyard in the darkness, and disappeared in the lane behind. And thereafter, keeping always when he could to the lanes and alleyways, grudging the sedate though crisp walk when forced out into the open, he went on at top speed.

But swiftly as he went, his mind ran the swifter. The police—not at Mother Margot's, but at that *other* tenement! His own escape had been a sinecure, thanks to the Phantom's secret passage. It would take the police some time to find that movable section in the room where the Kitten lay! But he did not understand. Why were the police there at all? They had not followed on the heels of the Kitten and the apaches, for in that case they would have been there much *sooner*. It was not the sound of the shot that the Phantom had fired, for that had been deadened inside the walls of the passage; nor did it seem possible that any other disturbance made there had been reported to them, say, by the inmates of the tenement, for in that case there would have been commotion amongst the tenants themselves, who would have been swarming about like bees. It was strange! The whole night was strange! He did not understand.

He ran on. The point was not vital. It was vital only that he should reach Blind Peter's without delay. Thank God, it wasn't far! But they had had ten minutes' start, and it was almost certain that neither the Phantom nor the apaches had gone on foot. Blind Peter's! He was not so sure after all that men like Steenie Klotz and Red Jack would be able to trap the Phantom there. It was the *safest* place in the underworld if one knew its secrets, and on that score the Phantom had made no mistake. But Steenie Klotz and his followers were of the lesser breed, the hangers-on, the purely thug element, not of the élite, not of the initiated, and Blind Peter's might well be to them but a name, a place whose mysteries were reserved for the upper strata of the criminal realm from which they themselves were far removed. It might well be—but against this was the fact that the underworld, its aristocracy and its proletariate alike, were behind Steenie Klotz and his companions in their determination to wreak vengeance upon the Kitten, and with the explanation made of why it was Gentleman Laroque now instead of the Kitten who was the object of this vengeance, the Phantom might find far else but sanctuary at Blind Peter's.

He did not know. He knew only that if he were in time the Phantom would not only find no safety there, but, forced to attempt flight again, would find no escape. And he would be in time! He *must* be!

It was the end! The end! The end! The words pounded over and over again at his brain, as he ran on. In either case, it was the end tonight. What Steenie Klotz and his pack might not know of Blind Peter's, he, Jimmie Dale, knew as perhaps few outside Blind Peter himself knew. It was the years of Larry the Bat, the years of Smarlinghue, the knowledge he had thus garnered, the height to which those alter ego characters of his had risen in the inner circles of Crimeland, that were bearing fruit now.

Yes, he knew Blind Peter's! Blind Peter was a very old and wizened little man of dark-skinned, doubtful origin, who wore spectacles with lenses that were coloured and that were of the thickness of heavy plate-glass, and who groped out with hands and stick when he walked—and who was not blind. He ran, supposedly, a small general store in one of a block of four houses in a neighbourhood that, to speak mildly, was unsavory at best. The other three houses were, supposedly again, lodging houses, and in a sense they were lodging houses, just as in a sense they were anything else one wished to call them. But Blind Peter owned them, and they had made Blind Peter rich— or, rather, a maze-like cavern of vice beneath their cellars had. Here, where sound never reached to the outer air, where the cellars above, rubbish-filled, were a benign and protecting mantle, toll from the lusts of the gaming table, toll from the overlords of crime who rented council chambers there, toll from the fear-stricken who had fled from daylight and the law, toll from every human weakness, was paid to Blind Peter. And, discreet beyond any of his ilk in the selection of his clientele, Blind Peter's place was safe. There was but one entrance and one exit—through the back of Blind Peter's store, where none might enter or depart except under the closest scrutiny.

Jimmie Dale had halted. A smile twisted his lips. Was there? Well, in the old days there had been another entrance, guessed at by many, but known only to a few, of which he, as Larry the Bat then, had been one—and it was here. He was crouched in the darkness before a low basement door, that of the house in the block farthest away from Blind Peter's store. Behind him was a small backyard, and behind that again the lane. The door was locked of course. But his pick-lock was at work now; and now the door opened slowly, gradually, wary of a protesting creak.

Jimmie Dale closed the door behind him without locking it, and descending a short flight of steps, stood still to listen. He was in the cellar now. He could hear nothing either from above or *below*. There would be no guard here. This entrance was for emergency only, a reserve margin of safety that Blind Peter held up his sleeve for himself and his intimates; it probably had not been used in months, and naturally anyone using it at all was, in the very fact that the secret was in his possession, beyond the necessity of challenge. Besides, a guard of any kind would but scream out aloud to Blind Peter's entire clientele the fact that this entrance, or exit, existed. Nor would one entering by this means, if he took but ordinary precautions, blazon the existence of the entrance to those already below. Blind Peter was far, very far, from being a fool! Here in this cellar the entrance was craftily hidden; but below it was still more so.

Jimmie Dale's flashlight winked through the blackness. He moved quickly forward to the far corner of the cellar. Rubbish, an untidy heap of kindling wood, the flotsam and jetsam of broken and discarded household effects littered the place. He worked rapidly now, brushing aside a thin, scattered layer of the kindling wood at the edge of the pile—and lifted up a small trap door.

It was black below, intensely black. The flashlight sent its ray streaming down a steep flight of steps—and went out. Jimmie Dale nodded sharply to himself. It was as it had always been. These steps led to the rear wooden wall—of a coal bin. But the coal bin would not be inconveniently full, and the front of it was quite open, and in the back of it a board or two could at a touch be moved aside.

He began to descend the steps cautiously. Across the narrow little chamber that contained the coal bin was a door leading into Blind Peter's unholy nest. And since that door must exist in order to make this exclusive entrance of any practical avail, a door the existence of which must almost of necessity be a matter of common knowledge to all who frequented Blind Peter's, that door itself must excite no suspicion. Therefore when it was opened it exhibited to all but the initiated in Blind Peter's nothing more than an apparently essential adjunct to the establishment—a storeroom that contained boxes of supplies, many of them, and a coal bin!

Almost down the steps now, Jimmie Dale paused suddenly—and as suddenly took the remaining ones at a leap. Dull, muffled, the report of a revolver shot had reached his ears. It was echoed by another—still another. The flashlight was in play again. Those boards! Yes, here they were! He moved them aside—and stepped through into the coal bin, so innocently almost empty.

The coal rattled a little under his feet, but the sound was drowned out now by shouts that added their quota of muffled uproar to the quickened reports of the revolver shots—and the sounds were coming nearer, nearer to that door there that opened into this supposed storeroom. The Phantom and the apaches! It could be nothing else! Steenie Klotz had gained admittance—the law of the underworld was at work. Blind Peter had evidently not dared oppose it. Did the Phantom know of the existence of this exit? A trapped rat, was he fighting for escape this way?

Jimmie Dale's lips were a thin line. Well, the Phantom would *not* escape this way! Whatever the penalty that he, Jimmie Dale, might pay, the Phantom's career ended tonight. That was what he was here for. No matter what happened to himself, the price would be a small and pitiful thing to pay. Tomorrow, no, tonight, the Tocsin, the woman he loved, she who in her great unselfish courage, aye and her love, had chosen to risk death alone, to fight out her fight alone that he too might not be sacrificed, would be free, free from peril, free to live in God's sunshine as—

He was at the door now. The sounds from the other side had risen into almost riot noise. The panel here—it used to move a little so that one intending entrance might first satisfy himself that he was not observed. Yes, it still moved—the space of a few inches.

He could see through—into a small room, garishly appointed, its roof supported by ornamental rafters from which hung several lanterns of curious, antique design, its walls draped with oriental hangings, the whole furnished in a sort of barbaric luxury. It was Blind Peter's private retreat—and naturally again offered a further bulwark and protection against the detection of the hidden entrance.

The door opening out on the other side of this room and directly opposite the one behind which Jimmie Dale stood was closed, but now suddenly it burst open. Shots, yells, curses, rose crescendo in a hideous uproar. A figure reeled in, stumbled, fell upon its knees, and began to drag itself away from the threshold. The old hag! Mother Margot! But Jimmie Dale's eyes rested for but an instant on her. There was another figure, the figure of a man, on the threshold itself now, a man at bay, fighting, pumping his shots from his automatic, cursing as he fought—Gentleman Laroque, alias Isaac Shiftel, alias Limpy Mack, alias the Phantom!

Outside, beyond that door, Jimmie Dale could not see. He could only hear—above the shots—the oaths and yells from, it seemed, a multitude of throats, like the screech of beasts, like animals giving tongue to a blood lust that was upon them.

It was very plain! They had dug the Phantom out of wherever he had been in hiding in Blind Peter's here, and had driven him in a running fight to the end of the chain of underground rooms and passages. It was the end! The Phantom could go no further—*save through the door behind which he, Jimmie Dale, stood*. And through that door the Phantom, for the Tocsin's sake, would never pass while he, Jimmie Dale, lived!

The end! Yes—but it was ending there on the threshold now. The Phantom half spun around, and screamed as a bullet struck him, made a desperate effort to slam shut the door and, instead, crumpled to the floor.

Jimmie Dale's jaws were clamped, his features set like iron. The end! Well, he could go now. Go the way he had come—unseen. It was over! The Tocsin was free. And *he* too was free, free of hurt or harm, free to the years that stretched ahead where only love and happiness should hold sway, and the—

"Kill 'em....Bump 'em both off!...The cursed snitches...."

Shots seemed to be still pouring a leaden hail into the prostrate form of the Phantom on the threshold, as he lay there, sprawled out, a dead thing now. Then a rush! Faces appeared at the doorway—Steenie's! The man levelled his revolver at the old hag on the floor as she crawled for protection toward the end of a sort of divan at the side of the room.

The mind works swiftly, swift beyond all measure of time. She was only an old hag, an abandoned thing steeped in her crimes, the last of the Phantom's satellites—all the rest had gone—it was justice that she should go too. What had he to do with it? The road to life and happiness lay the other way. Suppose she was a woman, suppose it *was* murder that would be done in the next second, what had he to do with it! What had—

Through the opening in the panel Jimmie Dale fired. The revolver in Steenie Klotz's outstretched hand clattered to the floor, and the man with a yell of mingled pain, fury and surprise leaped back from the open doorway—

and with him, from this new attack, the others took hasty cover, leaving the doorway clear again.

"Quick! This way, Mother Margot." Jimmie Dale called out sharply. "Don't stand up! Crawl!"

He fired steadily, coolly, sweeping the opposite doorway with his bullets—working with pick-lock in his other hand at the door behind which he stood. The old hag came crawling, weakly it seemed, across the floor, nearer and nearer to him. The shots were pouring into the room again—but they were coming at an angle. He laughed a little—without mirth. Steenie Klotz and his men were crouched on both sides of the door casing out there beyond, of course, and they could not fire in a direct line now without exposing themselves. But how much could they see? The danger would come when he opened the door for Mother Margot, and when he could not for the moment command the other doorway.

It would be a race for it then—nothing else.

"You fool!" an inner voice snarled at him. "Don't you know the Phantom is dead! You fool, to have risked this now! You poor, feeble, quixotic fool!"

The old hag was close to the door now. He called to her again.

"When I open the door, jump for it!" he said grimly. "Are you ready?"

He caught a faint, affirmative reply. He fired at the opposite doorway again, then closed the panel; and then with a sudden wrench pulled the door before him halfway open; and, as Mother Margot scurried through, he flung it shut again, locked it, and reaching out in the darkness for the old hag, jerked her forward, making for the rear of the coal bin. She staggered weakly, making a strange, half crooning noise. If he could win behind the bin to the stairs, there would be comparative safety, time enough at least to get to the lane above. Blind Peter, if he, Jimmie Dale, knew the man at all, having profound respect for his own skin, would not be taking a *personal* part in the fight, and those apaches back there would certainly never find the opening until they had gone for Blind Peter and had either persuaded or forced him to disclose it.

An age of time seemed to have passed, though he had reached the rear of the bin now. And now the boards swung back—but they were smashing at the door behind, battering at it, raining blows upon it. Just an instant more—if the door would hold for but an instant more, so that when the light poured in they would not *see*!

She was slow—God, how slow she was! He pushed her roughly through the opening, and sprang quickly after her. And as he swung the boards back into place, he heard the door crash open. But he was safe now—safe for a moment anyhow.

"Quick! The stairs! Right ahead of you!" he whispered.

But there was no answer. He stretched out his hand, groping down and around him. Mother Margot lay an inert heap at his feet. His jaws shut with a snap. Where was his margin of safety now? She was either hurt or wounded, or had fainted, and—

"You fool!" snarled that inner voice again, as he picked the old hag up in his arms, and began to climb the stairs.

CHAPTER 29

THE PORT OF DAWN

Muffled voices reached Jimmie Dale's ears from below. He staggered on upward, making what speed he could. It was not easy with this burden in his arms. In the darkness he gained the cellar; and from the cellar emerged on the small backyard, and thence on the lane.

Here, he drew a great, gasping breath of relief. He was safe so far, but he had still to get away from the immediate vicinity of that cellar entranceway. Blind Peter, at any moment, might solve the problem for Steenie Klotz and his pack!

He went on again, running heavily, lurching under his load. Thank God for the darkness! He looked, as he ran, for some place of shelter or hiding. He could not go out into the open street with Mother Margot unconscious in his arms—certainly not anywhere in *this* neighbourhood; nor could he run on indefinitely like this, whether by lane or street.

Fifty yards, a hundred he covered. There were no sounds of pursuit, and now he had no further anxiety on that score, for he was already too far away for them to pick up the trail if he could only find temporary cover somewhere until Mother Margot's condition, which must necessarily govern his future movements, could be—

She was stirring in his arms now uneasily, commencing to mutter incoherent words. He kept straining his eyes to right and left as he ran—and suddenly swerved close up against the left-hand side of the fence. This would do admirably. He could ask for nothing better. There was a shed here, or an outhouse of some kind. He laid Mother Margot down, worked swiftly for a moment with the door lock, then picking her up again carried her inside and laid her upon the floor.

But now, her senses evidently almost fully back, she raised herself quickly to her elbow, and tried to struggle to her feet.

"It's all right!" said Jimmie Dale reassuringly. "We're safe now. Are you badly hurt? Let me see."

He bent down and played his flashlight upon her—and like a man dazed and stunned then stood swaying on his feet. The flashlight trembled in his hand, throwing wavering beams across the floor. And then he was on his knees, and with a great cry he had gathered her into his arms, and was calling out hoarsely, calling her name over and over, a man unhinged, almost, with the mad uplift that had surged upon him.

"Marie—it's you! The Tocsin! Marie! Marie!"

The hooded shawl had fallen from her, the gray, tangled wig was awry. The Tocsin! Marie! And he had not known—he had known only that in some character here in the underworld she had been bravely striving to fight out her battle alone—just as she once had as Silver Mag. Silver Mag! Mother Margot! And he had thought that Smarlinghue was unknown to Mother Margot!

She was crying softly.

"Jimmie," she whispered, "dear Jimmie, I—I was afraid that I was saying good-bye to you for—for always in the Sanctuary tonight."

He held her closely. His face was buried in her hair. His shoulders heaved—as though a strong man sobbed. It was a long while before he answered her.

"I know. I know now," he said at last. "I didn't understand then. How could I? I had investigated Mother Margot and she had been in existence long before you left me that night in the boat on the East River. If it hadn't been for that I might—"

She stroked his face with her hand, very gently, very tenderly.

"Yes," she said; "but I was always Mother Margot—after Silver Mag. I was Mother Margot when they forced me into hiding the time before this. Don't you remember in the boat, Jimmie, that I would not tell you even then, even when Clarke was dead and you thought everything was all right again, how or where I had lived all through that time?"

"Yes, I remember," said Jimmie Dale; and then, with a quick, anxious cry: "And I remember now that you've been hurt, wounded, I am afraid, and need—"

"No," she said, and shook her head. "It is true that I was hit with something, a heavy stool that one of those gangsters threw when the fight first started at the upper end of Blind Peter's cellars, and it made me a little dizzy and giddy perhaps. But I am not hurt. I am afraid I only fainted, Jimmie, just—just like a woman." She laughed a little, bravely, tremulously, as she looked around her. "I know you said we were safe now, and I know that the Phantom is dead, but I'm all right again, and I'm able to go on. We can't be very far away from—"

"We're safer here just now, quite safe," Jimmie Dale answered. "If we went out we might only invite a chase and have to run for it, and you haven't got your strength back yet. And"—he too laughed a little tremulously now—"besides I want you—like this, Marie—like this for a little while."

Her head was on his shoulder now. He brushed back the hair from her forehead, and kissed her, and laid his face against hers.

"Like this." Her voice broke a little. "God is very good, Jimmie. I—I did not dare to hope that it would be like this when I sent you to The White Rat tonight."

"That was a plant!" said Jimmie Dale a little ruefully. "Why did you send me there?"

She drew slightly away from him so that she could lift her hands and clasp and hold his face between them.

"What else could I do, Jimmie?" she said with a catch in her voice. "You—you were so persistent. I had to get rid of you. I knew you were going to those rooms tonight—you had told me so. Well, the Phantom, or the Voice, had ordered me to be in the hallway of the *other* tenement at half past twelve. I knew then that there must be some connection between the two tenements, which would account for the voices that I had heard when I had been alone in the rooms where I was supposed to live. But I didn't know how, or where. It was certain, though, that if the Phantom brought me that far tonight, he would bring me all the way—you see, he was at the end of his rope nearly; there were only the Kitten and myself left. Well, I meant to end it tonight with the help of the police, and—"

"The police!" Jimmie Dale smiled strangely. "It was you, then, who were accountable for the police!"

"Yes," she said. "But I had first to get you out of the road, or you would almost certainly have been trapped in those rooms either by the Phantom or the police. I hadn't the least idea of what French Jeff might be doing tonight, but his reputation made him a likely subject for *anything*, and I felt sure that once set on his trail with the idea that the Phantom was mixed up in it too, you would watch him until something happened—which, since I expected nothing to happen, would mean all night. I don't see why you didn't."

"He went to bed on the midnight train to Boston," said Jimmie Dale grimly.

She laughed a little now, still holding his face captive with her hands; and then abruptly her voice was grave and serious again.

"Just before going to the other tenement at half past twelve," she said, "I notified the police to be there at one o'clock—if they wanted Isaac Shiftel; and that if they came before they would only ruin their one chance of getting their man. I needed that half hour to find out all I could, to get to the bottom of the Phantom's secret, or to make sure at least of where he lived in that other tenement, so that there could be no possible means of escape for him; and I wanted that much time in case he was late in keeping his appointment, and so that I would be sure to be with him and make sure that he did *not* escape. I—I am not sure that I expected to—to live through it myself. If he had any suspicion aroused it—" Her voice broke suddenly. "But—but he hadn't, Jimmie, and—and you must know what happened afterward since you, too, went to Blind Peter's."

"Yes," said Jimmie Dale simply. "I know. And I know a great deal more now. I know now that the night I caught you, as I thought, double-crossing Limpy Mack, you were trying to save what you could of old Mrs. Kinsey's money. And I understand now that the reason you did not know when I was wounded was because it happened at the time when you, as Mother Margot, were away. And that night in the tunnel at Morley's place, when you wouldn't let me show any light or come near you, you were Mother Margot, weren't you?"

"Yes, Jimmie," she whispered.

For a moment he was silent, and then suddenly he cried out, and in his voice was the yearning of the days and weeks when it had seemed this moment could never be:

"Marie!...Marie!...Marie!..."

He was holding her close to him again, his arms around her, her face against his own. And neither spoke now. Here in the shed it was very dark and very silent; but radiant in their souls was the glad sunrise of a new life, and in their hearts was song, like the song of springtime, a song of great joy, and of peace.

For they had come at last to the Port of Dawn.